THE MAMMOTH BOOK OF
BEST NEW
SCIENCE FICTION

THE MAMMOTH BOOK OF BEST NEW SCIENCE FICTION

22nd Annual Collection

Edited by
GARDNER DOZOIS

ROBINSON
London

Constable & Robinson Ltd
3 The Lanchesters
162 Fulham Palace Road
London W6 9ER
www.constablerobinson.com

First published in the USA by St Martin's Press 2009

First published in the UK by Robinson,
an imprint of Constable & Robinson, 2009

A copy of the British Library Cataloguing in Publication
Data is available from the British Library

UK ISBN 978-1-84529-930-9

1 3 5 7 9 10 8 6 4 2

Acknowledgment is made for permission to reprint the following materials:

"Turing's Apples", by Stephen Baxter. Copyright © 2008 by Stephen Baxter. First published in *Eclipse Two* (Night Shade), edited by Jonathan Strahan. Reprinted by permission of the author.

"From Babel's Fall'n Glory We Fled," by Michael Swanwick. Copyright © 2008 by Dell Magazines. First published in *Asimov's Science Fiction*, February 2008. Reprinted by permission of the author.

"The Gambler," by Paolo Bacigalupi. Copyright © 2008 by Paolo Bacigalupi. First published in *Fast Forward 2* (Pyr), edited by Lou Anders. Reprinted by permission of the author.

"Boojum," by Elizabeth Bear and Sarah Monette. Copyright © 2008 by Elizabeth Bear and Sarah Monette. First published in *Fast Ships, Black Sails* (Night Shade), edited by Ann and Jeff VanderMeer. Reprinted by permission of the authors.

"The Six Directions of Space," by Alastair Reynolds. Copyright © 2008 by Alastair Reynolds. First published in *Galactic Empires* (Science Fiction Book Club), edited by Gardner Dozois. Reprinted by permission of the author.

"N-Words," by Ted Kosmatka. Copyright © 2008 by Ted Kosmatka. First published in *Seeds of Change* (Prime), edited by J. J. Adams. Reprinted by permission of the author.

"An Eligible Boy," by Ian McDonald. Copyright © 2008 by Ian McDonald. First published in *Fast Forward 2* (Pyr), edited by Lou Anders. Reprinted by permission of the author.

"Shining Armour," by Dominic Green. Copyright © 2008 by Dominic Green. First published in *The Solaris Book of Science Fiction: Volume Two* (Solaris), edited by George Mann. Reprinted by permission of the author.

"The Hero," by Karl Schroeder. Copyright © 2008 by Karl Schroeder. First published in *Eclipse Two* (Night Shade), edited by Jonathan Strahan. Reprinted by permission of the author.

"Evil Robot Monkey," by Mary Robinette Kowal. Copyright © 2008 by Mary Robinette Kowal. First published in *The Solaris Book of Science Fiction: Volume Two* (Solaris), edited by George Mann. Reprinted by permission of the author.

"Five Thrillers," by Robert Reed. Copyright © 2008 by Spilogale, Inc. First published in *The Magazine of Fantasy & Science Fiction*, April 2008. Reprinted by permission of the author.

"The Sky That Wraps the World Round, Past the Blue and Into the Black," by Jay Lake. Copyright © 2008 by Jay Lake. First published electronically online in *Clarkesworld*, March 2008. Reprinted by permission of the author.

"Incomers," by Paul McAuley. Copyright © 2008 by Paul McAuley. First published in *The Starry Rift* (Viking), edited by Jonathan Strahan. Reprinted by permission of the author.

"Crystal Nights," by Greg Egan. Copyright © 2008 by Interzone. First published in *Interzone*, April 2008. Reprinted by permission of the author.

"The Egg Man," by Mary Rosenblum. Copyright © 2008 by Dell Magazines. First published in *Asimov's Science Fiction*, February 2008. Reprinted by permission of the author.

"His Master's Voice," by Hannu Rajaniemi. Copyright © 2008 by Interzone. First published in *Interzone*, October 2008. Reprinted by permission of the author.

CONTENTS

ACKNOWLEDGMENTS

The editor would like to thank the following people for their help and support: Susan Casper, Jonathan Strahan, Gordon Van Gelder, Ellen Datlow, Peter Crowther, Nicolas Gevers, Jack Dann, Mark Pontin, William Shaffer, Ian Whates, Mike Resnick, Andy Cox, Sean Wallace, Robert Wexler, Patrick Nielsen Hayden, Torie Atkinson, Jed Hartman, Eric T. Reynolds, George Mann, Jennifer Brehl, Peter Tennant, Susan Marie Groppi, Karen Meisner, John Joseph Adams, Wendy S. Delmater, Rich Horton, Mark R. Kelly, Andrew Wilson, Damien Broderick, Gary Turner, Lou Anders, Cory Doctorow, Patrick Swenson, Bridget McKenna, Marti McKenna, Jay Lake, Sheila Williams, Brian Bieniowski, Trevor Quachri, Alastair Reynolds, Michael Swanwick, Stephen Baxter, Kristine Kathryn Rusch, Nancy Kress, Greg Egan, Ian McDonald, Paul McAuley, Ted Kosmatka, Paolo Bacigalupi, Elizabeth Bear, Robert Reed, Vandana Singh, Kathleen Ann Goonan, Daryl Gregory, James Alan Gardner, Maureen McHugh, L. Timmel Duchamp, Walter Jon Williams, Jeff VanderMeer, Gwyneth Jones, Dominic Green, William Sanders, Lawrence Watt-Evans, David D. Levine, Liz Williams, Geoff Ryman, Paul Brazier, Charles Coleman Finlay, Gord Sellar, Steven Utley, James L. Cambias, Garth Nix, David Hartwell, Ginjer Buchanan, Susan Allison, Shawna McCarthy, Kelly Link, Gavin Grant, John Klima, John O'Neill, Rodger Turner, Tyree Campbell, Stuart Mayne, John Kenny, Edmund Schubert, Tehani Wessely, Tehani Croft, Karl Johanson, Sally Beasley, Connor Cochran, Tony Lee, Joe Vas, John Pickrell, Ian Redman, Anne Zanoni, Kaolin Fire, Ralph Benko, Paul Graham Raven, Nick Wood, David Moles, Mike Allen, Jason Sizemore, Karl Johanson, Sue Miller, David Lee Summers, Christopher M. Cevasco, Tyree Campbell, Andrew Hook, Vaughne Lee Hansen, Mark Watson, Sarah Lumnah, and special thanks to my own editor, Marc Resnick.

Thanks are also due to Charles N. Brown, whose magazine Locus (Locus Publications, P. O. Box 13305, Oakland, CA 94661. $60 in the United States for a one-year subscription [twelve issues] via second class; credit card orders 510-339-9198) was used as an invaluable reference source throughout the summation; Locus Online (locusmag.com), edited by Mark R. Kelly, has also become a key reference source.

SUMMATION: 2008

The publishing world proved not to be immune to the deepening recession, and the genre suffered several major losses in 2008. About the best spin that can be put on it is to say that things could have been worse. (And things may yet still *get* worse, of course. The rumoured possible bankruptcy of the Borders bookstore chain, which has been buzzed about for months now, would, if it happens, likely have an adverse effect on many publishers.)

Much of 2008's bad news was delivered on 3 December, what has come to be called Black Wednesday in the publishing industry, when Random House announced major restructuring and layoffs, making Bantam Dell part of Random House instead of an independent operation; Houghton Mifflin Harcourt saw resignations and firings even at the highest levels of the company (and caused a furore by announcing a "buying freeze" on new titles); and Simon & Schuster also announced significant staff cuts. Earlier, many people had been let go by Doubleday, and later there were huge layoffs at Macmillan, Farrar, Straus, and Giroux, and elsewhere. Random House, the largest publisher in the United States, was the most strongly affected, undergoing sweeping changes, with many divisions being consolidated. The Random House Publishing Group swallowed the adult imprints of the Bantam Dell Publishing Group, including Bantam Spectra and Del Rey. The Knopf Publishing Group will absorb Doubleday as well as imprint Nan A. Talese. Senior Bantam Spectra editor Juliet Ulman was let go, as was Bantam Dell publisher Irwyn Applebaum and Doubleday publisher Steve Rubin; Houghton Mifflin Harcourt publisher and senior vice-president Rebecca Saletan resigned and executive editor Ann Patty was fired; Simon & Schuster Children's president Rick Richter and senior vice-president and publisher Rubin Pfeffer; Farrar, Straus, and Giroux lost publisher Linda Rosenberg, the heads of production and sub rights, a senior editor, and several assistants---and scores of people in lesser positions lost their jobs throughout the industry. The slaughter continued into the early months of 2009, with Del Rey editor Liz Scheier and Ballantine editor Anika Streitfeld being fired, along with Pantheon Books publisher Janice Goldklang.

German media conglomerate Bertelsmann, which had bought BookSpan, publisher of numerous book clubs, including the Science Fiction Book Club, just last year, turned around and sold their Direct Group North America in 2008, including BookSpan, to private investment firm Najafi Companies. What effect this will ultimately have on the Science Fiction Book Club is as yet uncertain, although at the moment they seem to be continuing to function pretty much as normal. Small press Wheatland Press went on "hiatus", usually a bad sign, as far as issuing new titles is concerned, and may or may not be back, although they're continuing to make already-released titles available for order. Several other small presses are rumoured to be teetering on the edge (while others seem to be doing okay).

Horrendous as all this is, it could have been worse. It was possible to see much of the restructuring of Random House coming a year or so back, even before the economic downturn had really taken hold, as a result of corporate mergers, and to date the party line is that Del Rey and Spectra will be kept as separate imprints. Most of the major SF lines are still in business, and a few, like the Hachette Book Group, which includes Orbit, even registered modest gains.

Of course, as the recession continues to deepen, there may be – and probably *will* be – lots of hard times left ahead.

Historically, books, magazines, and movies do well during recessions, as hard economic times make people search for cheap entertainment to distract themselves from their financial woes. The question for this particular recession is, Do books, magazines, and movies qualify as "cheap" entertainment anymore? These days, many hardcover books are in the $25 to $30 range, even a mass-market paperback can cost eight bucks, and in many places a single movie ticket can cost over $13 (for a family of five, once you throw in the eight-bucks-a-shot boxes of stale popcorn, you're edging perilously close to having had to spend $100 to go to the movies). Even adjusting for inflation, it seems to me that this doesn't really qualify as "cheap". Ironically, the one form of entertainment in the genre that *is* still reasonably cheap, the digest-sized SF magazines, are being put out of business because they can no longer easily reach the customers; most people, even most regular SF readers, may go for years without ever laying eyes on an SF magazine, many don't even know they exist, and even those who do may not be able to find one even if they go to a newsstand specifically searching for it. Perhaps the Kindle and the iPod and other similar text readers (and there are new and improved generations of them coming along all the time) will save the magazines by making them easily accessible to readers once again.

Considering the problems that have lately plagued Borders and other brick-and-mortar bookstores, they may save the publishing industry too, if anything can. Certainly everything in the publishing world is going to look very different ten years from now, and in twenty years it may be completely unrecognizable. Even today, many people are as likely or more likely to read a book on their iPod while commuting to work as they are to walk into a bookstore and buy a book. It's worth noting that online bookseller Amazon was one of the very few businesses in the entire country to actually turn a profit in the fourth quarter of 2008.

The print magazines had a good year creatively, in terms of the quality of the material published, although circulation continued its slow decline.

Asimov's and *Analog* changed their trim size, getting larger although dropping pages, losing about 4,000 words' worth of content in the process, and *The Magazine of Fantasy & Science Fiction* changed from their decades-long monthly format to a bi-monthly format of larger but fewer issues, losing about 10 per cent of their overall content in the process. Opinion among industry insiders was divided as to whether these were sensible money-saving measures that will help the magazines survive or bad ideas, risky last-ditch attempts to save the magazines that could backfire; time will tell, I guess. With another big postal hike looming on the horizon in 2009, rising printing costs, and some major magazine distributors (including two of the nation's biggest) beginning to charge a seven-cent-per-copy surcharge for all the magazines they distribute, a surcharge many magazines just can't afford, things are looking precarious, and if the cost-cutting moves that *Asimov's*, *Analog*, and *F&SF* are taking turn out to be ineffective in offsetting rising costs, all of these magazines could be in serious trouble. (Just as I was finishing work on this Summation, word came in that Anderson News, the huge magazine wholesaler and distributor who had been one of the distributors demanding a seven-cent-per-copy surcharge for every copy of the magazines they handle had been forced to suspend operations because many publishers had balked at paying the surcharge and stopped shipping them product. The CEO there says that the company is working "towards an amicable solution" with the publishers, and it remains to be seen how this situation will ultimately play out.)

Realms of Fantasy magazine threw in the towel early in 2009, citing disastrously plummeting newsstand sales (although the declining advertising revenue due to the recession – ROF was always heavily dependent on advertising – may also have been a factor). The magazine would die after the April 2009 issue, a sad loss to the field.

The good news, such as it is, for the so-called Big Three magazines is that sales were nearly flat this year, with only minuscule declines from 2007. *Asimov's Science Fiction* registered only a 2.7 per cent loss in overall circulation, from 17,581 to 17,102, not bad when compared to last year's 5.2 per cent loss, 2006's 13.6 per cent loss, or 2005's disastrous 23.0 per cent; it seems that declines in circulation here are at least beginning to slow, even if they haven't yet turned around. Subscriptions dropped from 14,084 to 13,842, and newsstand sales dropped from 3,497 to 3,260; sell-through rose from 30 per cent to 31 per cent. One encouraging note is that digital sales of the magazine through Fictionwise and Kindle were on the rise, although that rise is not yet reflected in these circulation figures. *Asimov's* published good stories this year by James Alan Gardner, Mary Rosenblum, Michael Swanwick, Nancy Kress, Elizabeth Bear, Kristine Kathryn Rusch, Stephen Baxter, and others. Sheila Williams completed her fourth year as *Asimov's* editor. *Analog Science Fiction & Fact* registered a 5.1 per cent loss in overall circulation, from 27,399 to 25,999, with subscriptions dropping from 22,972 to 21,880, and newsstand sales dropping from 4,427 to 4,119; sell-through remained steady at 34 per cent. *Analog* published good work this year by Dean McLaughlin, Geoffrey A.

Landis, Michael F. Flynn, Robert R. Chase, Ben Bova, and others. Stanley Schmidt has been editor there for twenty-nine years. *The Magazine of Fantasy & Science Fiction* registered a small 2.7 per cent loss in overall circulation, from 16,489 to 16,044, with subscriptions dropping from 12,831 to 12,374 but newsstand sales actually rising slightly from 3,658 to 3,670; sell-through rose from 33 per cent to 35 per cent. *F&SF* published good work this year by Charles Coleman Finlay, Ted Kostmatka, Albert E. Cowdrey, Carolyn Ives Gilman, Michael Swanwick, Steven Utley, John Kessel, and others. Gordon Van Gelder is in his twelfth year as editor and eighth year as owner and publisher. In its last full year, *Realms of Fantasy* published good stuff by Liz Williams, Carrie Vaughn, Greg Frost, Richard Parks, Tanith Lee, Eugie Foster, Aliette de Bodard, and others. Shawna McCarthy was the editor of the magazine from its launch in 1994 to its death in 2009.

Interzone doesn't really qualify as a professional magazine by the definition of *The Science Fiction Writers of America* (*SFWA*) because of its low rates and circulation – in the 2,000 to 3,000 copy range – but it's thoroughly professional in the calibre of writers that it attracts and in the quality of the fiction it produces, so we're going to list it with the other professional magazines anyway. *Interzone* had another strong year creatively, in 2008 publishing good stories by Greg Egan, Hannu Rajaniemi, Paul McAuley, Aliette de Bodard, Mercurio D. Rivera, Jamie Barras, Jason Sanford, and others. The ever-shifting editorial staff includes publisher Andy Cox, assisted by Peter Tennant. TTA Press, *Interzone*'s publisher, also publishes straight horror or dark suspense magazine *Black Static.*

The survival of these magazines is essential if you'd like to see lots of good SF and fantasy published every year – and you can help them survive by *subscribing* to them! It's never been easier to subscribe to most of the genre magazines, since you can now do it electronically online with the click of a few buttons, without even a trip to the mailbox. In the Internet age, you can also subscribe from overseas just as easily as you can from the United States, something formerly difficult-to-impossible. Furthermore, Internet sites such as *Fictionwise* (fictionwise.com), magaz!nes.com (magazines.com), and even Amazon.com sell subscriptions online, as well as electronic downloadable versions of many of the magazines to be read on your Kindle or PDA or home computer, something becoming increasingly popular with the computer-savvy set. And, of course, you can still subscribe the old-fashioned way, by mail.

So I'm going to list both the Internet sites where you can subscribe online and the street addresses where you can subscribe by mail for each magazine: *Asimov*'s site is at asimovs.com; its subscription address is *Asimov's Science Fiction*, Dell Magazines, 6 Prowitt Street, Norwalk, CT 06855 – $55.90 for annual subscription in the US. *Analog*'s site is at analogsf. com; its subscription address is *Analog Science Fiction and Fact*, Dell Magazines, 6 Prowitt Street, Norwalk, CT 06855 – $55.90 for annual subscription in the US. *The Magazine of Fantasy & Science Fiction*'s site is at sfsite.com/fsf; its subscription address is *The Magazine of Fantasy*

& *Science Fiction*, Spilogale, Inc., P.O. Box 3447, Hoboken, NJ 07030, annual subscription – $50.99 in the US. *Interzone* and *Black Static* can be subscribed to online at ttapress.com/onlinestore1.html; the subscription address for both is TTA Press, 5 Martins Lane, Witcham, Ely, Cambs CB6 2LB, England, UK, £21 each for a six-issue subscription, or there is a reduced rate dual subscription offer of £40 for both magazines for six issues; make cheques payable to TTA Press.

The print semi-prozine market is subject to the same pressures in terms of rising postage rates and production costs as the professional magazines are, and such pressures have already driven two of the most prominent fiction semi-prozines, *Subterranean* and *Fantasy Magazine*, from print into electronic-only online formats, with *Apex* following this year (see a review of the *Apex* site in the online section below), and I suspect that more will eventually follow. Print semi-prozines such as *Argosy Magazine*, *Absolute Magnitude*, *The Magazine of Science Fiction Adventures*, *Dreams of Decadence*, *Fantastic Stories of the Imagination*, *Artemis Magazine: Science and Fiction for a Space-Faring Society*, *Century*, *Orb*, *Altair*, *Terra Incognita*, *Eidolon*, *Spectrum SF*, *All Possible Worlds*, *Farthing*, *Yog's Notebook*, and the newszine *Chronicle* have died in the last couple of years, and I won't be listing subscription addresses for any of them any more. Tim Pratt and Heather Shaw's *Flytrap*, "a little 'zine with teeth," produced two issues in 2008 and then died as well. It looks like *Say . . . and Full Unit Hookup* may also be dead, or at least on hiatus, since I haven't seen them for a couple of years. *Weird Tales* survives in a new incarnation from a different publisher, and thanks at least in part to some clever promotional ploys, seems even to be thriving. Another refuge from the collapse of Warren Lapine's DNA Publishing empire, *Mythic Delirium*, also still survives, publishing mostly poetry. Neither *H. P. Lovecraft's Magazine of Horror* nor the revived *Thrilling Wonder Stories* published an issue, but considering the erratic schedule on which most semi-prozines get published, with some supposed "quarterlies" unable to manage even one issue per year, it may be premature to declare them dead. Saw two issues of *Fictitious Force*, but since they're not dated, it's hard to tell when they were published, and since no address or subscription information is given anywhere, it's hard to tell you how to order it; try website sciffy.com/dnw.

Warren Lapine and DNA Publications may be returning to the fray this year, with a newly relaunched version of *Fantastic Stories*, due to hit the stands in mid-2009.

Of the surviving print fiction semi-prozines, by far the most professional and the one that publishes the highest percentage of stories of professional quality, is the British magazine *Postscripts*, edited by Peter Crowther and Nick Gevers. They published a huge more-than-double-length issue this year, *Postscripts 15*, which is most usefully considered to be an anthology and which is discussed in the anthology section below, but there was additional good stuff in *Postscripts 14*, *Postscripts 16*, and *Postscripts 17* by Ian R. MacLeod, John Grant, Sarah Monette, Lisa Tuttle, Robert Reed,

Vaughn Stanger, Marly Youmans, and others. *Postscripts* has announced that they'll be changing from a magazine to an "anthology" format, mostly by changing the format from two column to full width and upping the word count from 60,000 to about 70,000–75,000 per issue. *Electric Velocipede*, edited by John Kilma, seems to be publishing more science fiction these days, although they also continue to run slipstream and fantasy; they managed two issues in 2008, one of them a double issue, and published good stuff by William Shunn, Aliette de Bodard, Patrick O'Leary, Jennifer Pelland, Sandra McDonald, Elissa Malcohn, and others.

One of the longest-running of the fiction semi-prozines is the Canadian *On Spec*, edited by a collective under general editor Diane L. Walton, which once again kept reliably to its publishing schedule in 2008, bringing out all four scheduled quarterly issues; unfortunately, I don't usually find their fiction to be terribly compelling; best work here was probably by Marissa K. Lingen, Kate Riedel, and Claude Lalumiere. The fiction in Australia's *Andromeda Spaceways In-flight Magazine*, another collective-run magazine, one with a rotating editorial staff, which published its full six issues this year, tends to be somewhat livelier, and there were worthwhile stories there this year by Sarah Totton, Dirk Flinthart, Geoffrey Maloney, Aliette de Bodard, Lyn Battersby, and others. Another Australian magazine *Aurealis*, once thought to be dead, managed one issue this year under new editor Stuart Mayne, with worthwhile work by Stephen Dedman and Lee Battersby. *Talebones*, an SF/horror 'zine edited by Patrick Swenson, after surviving a rough patch last year, managed two issues in 2008, with good work by James Van Pelt, Paul Melko, Edd Vick, and others. *Paradox*, edited by Christopher M. Cevasco, an Alternate History magazine, only managed one issue this year. *Neo-opsis*, a Canadian magazine, edited by Karl Johanson, managed only two out of four scheduled issues in 2008. *Jupiter*, a small British magazine edited by Ian Redman, managed all four of its scheduled issues in 2008; it's devoted exclusively to science fiction, a big plus in my book, but it's a poorly produced and amateurish-looking magazine, and the fiction to date is not yet of reliable professional quality. *Shimmer*, Ireland's *Albedo One*, and *Greatest Common Denominator* managed two issues this year, *Tales of the Unexpected*, *Sybil's Garage*, and the long-running *Space & Time*, back from a close brush with death, one each. Turning to fantasy semi-prozines, Sword & Sorcery magazine *Black Gate* managed one issue this year, and there were three issues apiece of glossy fantasy magazines *Zahir*, *Tales of the Talisman*, and *Aoife's Kiss*.

Many of the "minuscule press" slipstream magazines inspired by *Lady Churchill's Rosebud Wristlet* have died or gone on hiatus in the last couple of years, but *Lady Churchill's Rosebud Wristlet* itself seems to be still going strong, producing two issues in 2008. Mostly slipstream, literary fantasy, and fabulation here, of course, but there's an occasional SF story, such as Charlie Anders' in issue 22.

There's not much left of the critical magazine market except for a few sturdy, long-running stalwarts. As always, your best bet is *Locus: The Magazine of the Science Fiction and Fantasy Field*, a multiple Hugo-winner, published by Charles N. Brown and edited by a large staff of editors under the management of Kirsten Gong-Wong and Liza Groen Trombi. For more than thirty years now this has been an indispensable source of information, news, and reviews, and is undoubtedly the most valuable critical magazine/newszine in the field. Another long-lived and reliably published critical magazine is *The New York Review of Science Fiction*, edited by David G. Hartwell and a staff of associate editors, which publishes a variety of eclectic and sometimes quirky critical essays on a wide range of topics.

Below this point, most other critical magazines in the field are professional journals aimed more at academics than at the average reader. The most accessible of these is probably the long-running British critical 'zine *Foundation*.

Subscription addresses follow:

Postscripts, PS Publishing, Grosvenor House, 1 New Road, Hornsea, East Yorkshire, HU18 1PG, England, UK, published now as a quarterly anthology, $18 for one issue, 4 issues for $100 (*Postscripts* can also be subscribed to online, perhaps the easiest way, at store.pspublishing.com.uk.); *Locus, The Magazine of the Science Fiction & Fantasy Field*, Locus Publications, Inc., P.O. Box 13305, Oakland, CA 94661, $68.00 for a one-year first class subscription, 12 issues; *The New York Review of Science Fiction*, Dragon Press, P.O. Box 78, Pleasantville, NY, 10570, $40.00 per year, 12 issues, make checks payable to Dragon Press; *Foundation*, Science Fiction Foundation, Roger Robinson (SFF), 75 Rosslyn Avenue, Harold Wood, Essex RM3 ORG, UK, $37.00 for a three-issue subscription in the US; *Talebones, A Magazine of Science Fiction & Dark Fantasy*, 21528 104th St. Ct. East, Bonney Lake, WA 98390, $24.00 for four issues; *Aurealis*, Chimaera Publications, P.O. Box 2149, Mt Waverley, VIC 3149, Australia (website: aurealis.com.au), $50 for a four-issue overseas airmail subscription, checks should be made out to Chimaera Publications in Australian dollars; *On Spec, The Canadian Magazine of the Fantastic*, P.O. Box 4727, Edmonton, AB, Canada T6E 5G6, for subscription information, go to website onspec.ca; Neo-Opsis Science Fiction Magazine, 4129 Carey Rd., Victoria, BC, V8Z 4G5, $28.00 Canadian for a four-issue subscription; *Albedo One*, Albedo One Productions, 2 Post Road, Lusk, Co., Dublin, Ireland, $32.00 for a four-issue airmail subscription, make cheques payable to Albedo One; *Tales of the Unanticipated*, P.O. Box 8036, Lake Street Station, Minneapolis, MN 55408, $28 for a four-issue subscription (three or four years' worth) in the US, $31 in Canada, $34 overseas; *Lady Churchill's Rosebud Wristlet*, Small Beer Press, 150 Pleasant St., #306, Easthampton, MA 01027, $20.00 for four issues; *Electric Velocipede*, Spilt Milk Press, see website electricvelocipede.com, for subscription information; *Andromeda Spaceways Inflight Magazine*, see website andromedaspaceways.com for subscription information; *Zahir*, Zahir Publishing, 315 South Coast Hwy., 101, Suite U8, Encinitas, CA 92024, $18.00 for a one-year subscription, subscriptions can also be bought with credit cards and PayPal at zahirtales.com; *Tales of the Talisman*, Hadrosaur Productions, P.O. Box 2194, Mesilla Park, NM 88047-2194, $24.00 for a four-issue subscription; *Aoife's Kiss*, Sam's Dot Publishing, P.O. Box 782, Cedar Rapids, IA 52406-0782, $18.00 for a four-issue subscription; *Black Gate*, New Epoch Press, 815 Oak Street, St. Charles, IL 60174, $29.95 for a one-year (four-issue) subscription; *Paradox*, Paradox Publications, P.O. Box 22897, Brooklyn, NY 11202-2897, $25.00 for a one year (four-issue) subscription, cheques or US postal money orders should be made payable to *Paradox*, can also be ordered online at paradoxmag.com; *Weird Tales*, Wildside Press, 9710 Traville Gateway Drive, #234, Rockville, MD 20850-7408, annual subscription – four issues – $24 in the US; *Jupiter*, 19 Bedford Road, Yeovil, Somerset, BA21 5UG, UK, £10 Sterling for four issues; *Greatest Uncommon Denominator*, Greatest Uncommon Denominator Publishing, P.O. Box 1537, Laconia, NH 03247, $18 for two issues; *Sybil's Garage*, Senses Five Press, 307 Madison Street, No. 3L, Hoboken, NJ 07030-1937, no subscription information available but try website sensesfivepress.com; *Shimmer*, P.O. Box 58591, Salt Lake City, UT 84158-0591, $22.00 for a four-issue subscription.

As more and more print markets die, emit distressed wobbling noises, or switch to online formats, electronic magazines and websites are becoming increasingly important, and that's not going to change; if anything, it's likely to become even more true as time goes by. Already, if you really want to keep up with all the good short fiction being "published" during a given year, you can't afford to overlook the online markets.

Of course, as we discussed here at length last year, the problem of how these online publications are going to make enough money to survive continues to be a vexing one, with several formulas being experimented with at the moment. Proving that electronic publication alone is not a guaranteed formula for success, several ezines died in 2007, and this year *Aeon* and *Helix* folded – *Aeon*, oddly, almost immediately after announcing that it was going to raise its rate of payment to professional levels. Both markets produced a lot of good work in their time, and both will be greatly missed. (In their last year, *Helix* published good work by Charlie Anders, Samantha Henderson, James Killus, George S. Walker, Annie Leckie, and others, and *Aeon* published good work by Jay Lake, Bruce McAllister, Lavie Tidhar, and others.)

Now that the late lamented *Sci Fiction* has died, probably the most important ezine on the Internet, and certainly the one that features the highest proportion of core science fiction, is *Jim Baen's Universe* (baensuniverse.com), edited by Mike Resnick and Eric Flint, which takes advantage of the freedom from length restrictions offered by the use of pixels instead of print by featuring in each issue an amazingly large selection of science fiction and fantasy stories, stories by beginning writers, classic reprints, serials, columns, and features, certainly more material than any of the print magazines could afford to offer in a single issue. The best SF story in *Jim Baen's Universe* this year was Nancy Kress's "First Rites", but there were also good SF stories by Ben Bova, Jay Lake, Lou Antonelli, Bud Sparhawk, Marissa Lingen, David Brin, and others. The best fantasy stories here were by Tom Purdom and Pat Cadigan. There was a lot of good solid work in *Jim Baen's Universe* this year, but somehow it didn't seem like there was as much first-rate work as last year.

A similar mix per issue of SF stories, fantasy stories, and features, including media and book reviews and a new story by Orson Scott Card, is featured in *Orson Scott Card's Intergalactic Medicine Show* (intergalacticmedicineshow.com), edited by Edmund R. Schubert under the direction of Card himself. There seems to be a greater emphasis on fantasy here than at *Jim Baen's Universe*, and they do better with the fantasy, in terms of literary quality. The best story in *Orson Scott Card's Intergalactic Medicine Show* this year, by a good margin, was Peter S. Beagle's elegant Japanese fantasy "The Tale of Junko and Sayuri", but they also featured good fantasy stories by Dennis Danvers, Stephanie Fray, and others, and good SF stories by Ken Scholes, Aliette de Bodard, Sharon Shinn, and others.

The new Tor Web site, Tor.com (tor.com), a blog/community meeting ground that features lots of commentary and archives of comics and art in addition to original fiction, has quickly established itself as another important Internet destination. The best stories published there this year were excellent works by Cory Doctorow, John Scalzi, Jay Lake, and Geoff Ryman, although there were also good stories by Charles Stross, Elizabeth Bear, Steven Gould, and Brandon Sanderson.

Two former print magazines that have completed a transformation to electronic-only formats, something I think we'll inevitably see more of as time goes by, are *Subterranean* (subterraneanpress.com), edited by William K. Schafer, and *Fantasy* (darkfantasy.org), edited by Sean Wallace and Cat Rambo. *Subterranean* usually leans toward horror and "dark fantasy", although they also run SF, and, in fact, the two best stories featured there this year, stories by Chris Roberson and by Mike Resnick, were both SF, as were other good stories by Beth Bernobich and Mary Robinette Kowal; fantasy was represented by Joe R. Lansdale, Norman Partridge, and others. *Fantasy*, as should be expected from the title, usually sticks to traditional genre fantasy and the occasional mild horror story, sometimes a bit of slipstream, almost never running anything that could be considered SF. The best stories here this year were by Holly Phillips and by Rachel Swirsky, although there were also good stories by Gord Sellar, Peter M. Ball, Ari Goelman, and others.

Strange Horizons (strangehorizons.com), edited by Susan Marie Groppi, assisted by Jed Hartman and Karen Meisner, features more slipstream and less SF than I'd like, but lots of good stuff continues to appear there nevertheless; best stories this year were by Meghan McCarren, Constance Cooper, and Alan Campbell, but there was also good work by A. M. Dellamonica, Bill Kte'pi, Deborah Coates, and others. The best stories this year in *Abyss and Apex: A Magazine of Speculative Fiction* (abyssandapex.com), edited by Wendy S. Delmater in conjunction with fiction editors Rob Campbell and Ilona Gordon, were by Cat Rambo, Mecurio D. Rivera, and Ruth Nestvold, but *Abyss and Apex* also featured good stuff by Alan Smale, Marissa Lingen, Vylar Kaftan, and others. *Clarkesworld*

Magazine (clarkesworldmagazine.com), which features elegantly perverse fantasy, slipstream, and even the occasional SF story, was co-edited by Nick Mamatas until July, when Sean Wallace took over as co-editor. My favourite stories here this year were by Jay Lake and Jeff Ford; there were also good stories here by Tim Pratt, Mary Robinette Kowal, Catherynne M. Valente, Stephen Dedmen, Eric M. Witchey, Don Webb, and others. Ironically, for an online magazine that has no real physical existence, the covers are quite striking, some of the best I've seen in a while. I particularly like the cover for Issue 19.

The Australian science magazine *Cosmos* publishes an SF story monthly, but they also frequently feature stories available as unique content on the *Cosmos* website (cosmosmagazine.com), all selected by fiction editor Damien Broderick; good stuff appeared in *Cosmos* this year, both online and in print, by Brendan DuBois, Steven Utley, Vylar Kaftan, Christopher East, and others. A similar mix of science fact articles and fiction is available from the ezine *Futurismic* (futurismic.com) and from new publication *Escape Velocity* (escapevelocitymagazine.com), issues of which can be downloaded to your computer.

Apex Digest is another former print magazine that has shifted completely to electronic online-only format and can now be found as *Apex Online* (apexbook-company.com/apex-online), still being edited by Jason Sizemore; good SF work by Steven Francis Murphy, Mary Robinette Kowal, Lavie Tidhar, and others appeared there, and they publish fantasy and critical articles as well.

Beneath Ceaseless Skies (beneath-ceaseless-skies) is a new ezine devoted to "literary adventure fantasy" that to date has published good work by David D. Levine, Charles Coleman Finlay and Rae Carson Finlay, and others.

Shadow Unit (shadowunit.org) is a website devoted to publishing stories drawn from an imaginary TV show, which in spite of the unlikeliness of the premise has attracted some top talent such as Elizabeth Bear, Sarah Monette, Emma Bull, Will Shetterly, and others.

Book View Café (bookviewcafe.com) is a "consortium of over twenty professional authors", including Vonda N. McIntyre, Laura Ann Gilman, Sarah Zittel, Brenda Clough, and others, who have created a new website where work by them is made available for free – mostly reprints for the moment, although new work is promised, and the site also contains novel excerpts.

Flurb (flurb.net), edited by Rudy Rucker, publishes as much strange Really Weird stuff as it does SF, but there were good stories there this year by Bruce Sterling, Michael Blumlein, Lavie Tidhar, Terry Bisson, and others.

Below *Flurb*, science fiction and even genre fantasy become harder to find, although there are a number of ezines that publish slipstream/post-modern stories, often ones of good literary quality (and even the occasional SF story). They include: *Revolution SF* (revolutionsf.com), which also features book and media reviews; *Coyote Wild* (coyotewildmag.com);

Ideomancer Speculative Fiction (ideomancer.com); *Lone Star Stories* (literary.erictmarin.com); *Heliotrope* (heliotropemag.com); *Farrago's Wainscot* (farragoswainscot.com); and Sybil's Garage (www.sensefive.com); and the somewhat less slipstreamish *Bewildering Stories* (bewilderingstories.com).

Chiaroscura and *New Ceres* seem to have died; at least, I'm no longer able to get to them. Last year I reported that quirky little ezine *Spacesuits and Six Guns* (spacesuitsandsixguns.com) was dead, but reports of its death seem to have been exaggerated, since it's still there.

There's also a website dedicated to YA fantasy and SF, *Shiny* (shinymag. blogspot.com).

Many good reprint SF and fantasy stories can also be found on the Internet, perhaps in greater numbers than the original ones, usually accessible for free. The long-running British *Infinity Plus* (users.zetnet.co.uk/iplus) has ceased to be an active site, but their archive of quality reprint-stories is still accessible on the net, as is their archive of biographical and bibliographical information, book reviews, interviews, and critical essays. *The Infinite Matrix* (infinitematrix.net) is also no longer an active site, but their substantial archives of past material are still available to be accessed online. Most of the sites that are associated with existent print magazines, such as *Asimov's*, *Analog*, *Weird Tales*, and *The Magazine of Fantasy & Science Fiction*, make previously published fiction and nonfiction available for access on their sites, and also regularly run teaser excerpts from stories coming up in forthcoming issues. On all of the sites that make their fiction available for free, *Fantasy*, *Subterranean*, *Abyss and Apex*, *Strange Horizon*, you can also access large archives of previously published material as well as stuff from the "current issue". A large selection of novels and a few collections can also be accessed for free, to be either downloaded or read on-screen, at the *Baen Free Library* (baen.com/library). Hundreds of out-of-print titles, both genre and mainstream, are also available for free download from *Project Gutenberg* (promo.net/pc/).

If you're willing to pay a small fee for them, though, an even greater range of reprint stories becomes available. The best and the longest-established such site is *Fictionwise* (fictionwise.com), where you can buy downloadable e-books and stories to read on your PDA or home computer, in addition to individual stories; you can also buy "fiction bundles" here, which amount to electronic collections, as well as a selection of novels in several different genres; and you can subscribe to downloadable versions of several of the SF magazines here, including *Asimov's*, *Analog*, *F&SF*, and *Interzone*, in a number of different formats. A similar site is *ElectricStory* (electricstory. com); in addition to the downloadable stuff for sale here (both stories and novels), you can also access free movie reviews by Lucius Shepard, articles by Howard Waldrop, and other critical material.

But there are other reasons for SF fans to go on the Internet besides searching for fiction to read. There are also many general genre-related sites of interest to be found, most of which publish reviews of books as well as of movies and TV shows, sometimes comics or computer games or anime, many of which also feature interviews, critical articles, and genre-oriented

news of various kinds. *Locus Online* (locusmag.com), the online version
of the newsmagazine *Locus*, is easily the most valuable genre-oriented general site on the entire Internet, an indispensable site where you can access
an incredible amount of information – including book reviews, critical
lists, obituary lists, links to reviews and essays appearing outside the genre,
and links to extensive database archives such as the Locus Index to Science
Fiction and the Locus Index to Science Fiction Awards – and which is also
often the first place in the genre to reveal fast-breaking news. I usually end
up accessing it several times a day. One of the other major general-interest
sites, *Science Fiction Weekly*, underwent a significant upheaval at the beginning of 2009, merging with news site *Sci Fi Wire* to form a new site called
Sci Fi Wire (scifi.com/sfw); the emphasis here is on media-oriented stuff,
movie and TV reviews, as well as reviews of anime, games, and music, but
they feature book reviews as well. *SF Site* (sfsite.com) features reviews of
books, games, movies, TV shows, and magazines, plus a huge archive of
past reviews, and *Best SF* (bestsf.net/), which boasts another great archive
of reviews and which is one of the few places that makes any attempt to
regularly review short fiction venues. Pioneering short-fiction review site
Tangent Online was inactive throughout 2008, and editor David Truesdale
finally announced at the end of the year that, as many of us suspected, it
was not going to return; a pity. But a new short-fiction review site, *The
Fix* (thefix-online.com), launched by a former Tangent Online staffer, is
still going strong, and short-fiction reviews can also be accessed on *The
Internet Review of Science Fiction* (irosf.com), which also features novel
reviews, interviews, opinion pieces, and critical articles. Other good general-interest sites include *SFRevu* (sfsite.com/sfrevu), where you'll find lots
of novel and media reviews, as well as interviews and general news; SFF
NET (sff.net), which features dozens of home pages and "newsgroups" for
SF writers; the *Science Fiction Writers of America* page (sfwa.org), where
genre news, obituaries, award information, and recommended reading
lists can be accessed; *Green Man Review* (greenmanreview.com), another
valuable review site; *The Agony Column* (trashotron.com/agony), media
and book reviews and interviews; *SFFWorld* (sffworld.com), more literary
and media reviews; *SFReader* (sfreader.com), which features reviews of SF
books; *SFWatcher* (sfwatcher.com), which features reviews of SF movies;
SFCrowsnest (sfcrowsnest.com); newcomer *SFScope* (sfscope.com), edited
by former *Chronicle* news editor Ian Randal Strock, which concentrates
on SF and writing business news; *Pat's Fantasy Hotlist* (fantasyhotlist.
blogspot.com), *io9* (io9.com); and *SciFiPedia* (scifipedia.scifi.com), a Wiki-
style genre-oriented online encyclopedia. One of the most entertaining SF
sites on the Internet is *Ansible* (dcs.gla.ac.uk/Ansible), the online version
of multiple Hugo-winner David Langford's long-running fanzine *Ansible*.
SF-oriented radio plays and podcasts can also be accessed at *Audible* (audi-
ble.com), *Escape Pod* (escapepod.org), *Star Ship Sofa* (starship-sofa.com),
and *Pod Castle* (podcastle.org). Long-running writing-advice and market
news site *Speculations* has died.

*

This has been an almost unprecedented year for the number of first-rate original SF anthologies published, at least since the heyday of *Orbit, New Dimensions*, and *Universe* in the 1970s. All of the new annual original series launched last year – Lou Anders's *Fast Forward*, Jonathan Strahan's *Eclipse*, and George Mann's *The Solaris Book of New Science Fiction* – produced second volumes stronger than the initial volumes had been, a good sign. Even 2008's second-tier anthologies – there were a *lot* of anthologies published this year – were often good enough to have been in contention for the title of year's best anthology in other years.

It may be premature to speak of a renaissance or "New Golden Age" of original anthologies as some have been doing – none of these anthology series have firmly established themselves financially as yet and, in fact, a few are rumoured to not be selling so well. Still, even if it's just for this year, it's nice to have so many good anthologies at hand to choose from.

The best of them was probably *Eclipse Two* (Night Shade Books), edited by Jonathan Strahan, although there was only a whisker's thickness of difference between it and *Fast Forward 2* (Pyr), edited by Lou Anders. A half-step below them was *The Starry Rift* (Viking), edited by Jonathan Strahan; *Sideways in Time* (Solaris), edited by Lou Anders; *The Solaris Book of Science Fiction: Volume 2* (Solaris), edited by George Mann; and *Dreaming Again: Thirty-Five New Stories Celebrating the Wild Side of Australian Fiction* (Eos), edited by Jack Dann, all of them strong enough to have carried off the prize in a weaker year. *Postscripts 15*, edited by Nick Gevers, a double-issue of the magazine that functioned essentially as an anthology, ought to be in the hunt here somewhere too.

Below these were a number of still-substantial anthologies such as *The Del Rey Book of Science Fiction and Fantasy* (Del Rey), edited by Ellen Datlow, *Extraordinary Engines* (Solaris), edited by Nick Gevers; *Clockwork Phoenix: Tales of Beauty and Strangeness* (Norilana), edited by Mike Allen; *Seeds of Change* (Prime), edited by John Joseph Adams; and *Subterfuge* (Newcon) and *Celebrations* (Newcon), both edited by Ian Whates – with yet more anthologies a couple of steps below them.

Several reviewers, including me, criticized Jonathan Strahan's *Eclipse* last year for not having enough real science fiction in it, but this isn't a complaint that can be levelled at his *Eclipse Two*. There are still a couple of fantasy stories here, and some borderline slipstreamish stuff, but the bulk of the stuff in the book is good solid no foolin' core science fiction. My favourite stories are by Stephen Baxter, Alastair Reynolds, Karl Schroeder, Ted Chiang, and Daryl Gregory. Also good were stories by David Moles, Tony Daniel, Terry Dowling, Paul Cornell, and others. The best of the fantasy stories here are by Peter S. Beagle, Richard Parks, and Margo Lanagan.

Only a whisker-thickness behind is *Fast Forward 2*, edited by Lou Anders. The best stories here are probably those by Paolo Bacigalupi and Ian McDonald, but the book also contains good work by Benjamin Rosenbaum and Cory Doctorow, Nancy Kress, Jack Skillingstead, Chris

Nakashima-Brown, Paul Cornell, Karl Schroeder and Tobias S. Bucknell, Kristine Kathryn Rusch, Kay Kenyon, and others.

Don't let the fact that it's being published as a YA anthology put you off – *The Starry Rift*, edited by Jonathan Strahan, is definitely one of the best SF anthologies of the year, everything in it fully of adult quality, and almost all of it centre-core SF as well.

Best stories here are those by Kelly Link and Ian McDonald (his gorgeously colored Future India story, "The Dust Assassin"), but there are also excellent stories by Paul McAuley, Gwyneth Jones, Kathleen Ann Goonan, Walter Jon Williams, and others, including an atypical near-future story by Greg Egan, more openly political than his stuff usually is. The fact that several stories are told in the first person by teenage narrators, usually young girls, may make several of the stories seem a bit familiar if read one after the other (and is also the only real indication that this is a YA anthology), so space them out over time.

Another excellent anthology is *Sideways in Crime*, edited by Lou Anders. Most Alternate History stories are SF (particularly those that add a time-travel element), but we've already seen a fair amount of Alternate History Fantasy in the last few years (it's an Alternate World, but in it griffins or giants are real, or magic works), and now we've got Alternate History Mystery, producing a book that's a lot of fun; most of the stories would fall under the Alternate History Mystery SF heading, I guess (including one with crosstime travel), rather than the Alternate History Mystery Fantasy heading, since although there's a couple of fairly wild alternate possibilities here, there's none with griffins or where magic works. The best stories in the book is probably by Kristine Kathryn Rusch, but there's also excellent work by Kage Baker, Paul Park, Mary Rosenblum, Theodore Judson, S. M. Stirling, Chris Roberson, and others. The most likely Alternate, as it requires the fewest changes from our own timeline, is Kristine Kathryn Rusch's story; the least likely is probably Mike Resnick and Eric Flint's story, even more so than Chris Roberson's story with its crosstime-travelling zeppelins.

Several of the basic plotlines here are pretty similar – important man found dead under strange, usually politically charged circumstances – although the settings change radically from story to story, so I'd recommend that you read these a few at a time rather than all in one sitting.

There are also some good solid stories in *The Solaris Book of Science Fiction II* (Solaris), edited by George Mann, which is more even in quality than the first volume – none of the stories is as bad as the worst of the stories in the first one . . . but then again, none of the stories is as good as the best of the good stories were. The best stories here, in my opinion, are by Peter Watts, Eric Brown, Mary Robinette Kowal, Karl Schroeder, and Dominic Green. If I had to narrow it down to only two picks, it would be the Dominic Green and the Mary Robinette Kowal.

In the past, I've criticized the British magazine *Postscripts* for not running enough core science fiction, and as if to twit me on this, *Postscripts 15*, a huge double-length (or longer) issue that is probably best considered as an anthology rather than a magazine, edited by Nick Gevers, bills itself an "all science fiction issue!" Not that that's true, of course. By my definitions, there's at least six or seven fantasy stories of one sort or another here, a reprinted article by Arthur C. Clarke, a metafiction piece by Brian W. Aldiss about meeting the Queen, and a fascinating autobiographical article by Paul McAuley about growing up in post-World War II England. Nevertheless, there is plenty of core science fiction here, most of it of excellent quality. Many of the best stories here are to be found in the special "Paul McAuley section", which features, in addition to the above-mentioned autobiographical essay, a novel excerpt from McAuley's *The Quiet War*, and four good stories by McAuley, one of which, "City of the Dead," may be the pick of the issue, rivalled only by Ian McDonald's ("A Ghost Samba"), which does almost as good a job of painting an evocative picture of a future Brazil as his Cyberaid stories have done with a future India. There are other good SF stories here by Chris Roberson, Matthew Hughes, Steven Utley, Jay Lake, Robert Reed, Mike Resnick, Beth Bernobich, Brian Stableford, Stephen Baxter, and others. The best of the fantasy stories are by Justina Robson, Jack Dann, and Paul Di Filippo.

American publishers, especially the big trade houses, seem to like their genres segregated – no fantasy in science fiction anthologies, no science fiction in fantasy anthologies, no mystery or mainstream in either. That's not true of Australian publishers, however, where it seems to be okay to jumble different genres together in the same anthology, and it's certainly the rule with *Dreaming Again: Thirty-Five New Stories Celebrating the Wild Side of Australian Fiction*, edited by Jack Dann – the follow-up to 1998's monumental *Dreaming Down Under*, edited by Dann and Janeen Webb, which brings us a similarly rich stew of fiction by Australian authors working in different genres, horror, fantasy, slipstream, science fiction. A wide variety of moods, too, with some stories horrific and grim, others seeming almost to be Young Adult pieces. There's a bit too much horror here for my taste – a few zombie stories go a long way with me, and there's *lots* of zombie stories here, to the point where it almost seems to become a running (or lurching) joke – but there's also enough fantasy and science fiction stories in this huge volume to make up into respectable anthologies of their own, and if horror *is* your cup of blood, you'll find the horror stories to be of high quality. Almost everything here is of high quality, in fact (even the stories I didn't care for were excellently crafted), a rich smorgasbord, by thirty-six different authors, representative of the obviously busy Australian scene. The best science fiction is from Garth Nix, Margo Lanagan, Lee Battersby, Stephen Dedman, Simon Brown, Sean McMullen, Ben Francisco and Chris Lynch, Rowena Cory Daniels, and Jason Fischer. Fantasy (sometimes shading into horror) is best represented here by Terry Dowling, Rjurik Davidson, Peter A. Ball, Russell Blackford, Isobelle Carmody, Richard Harland, and Cecilia Dart-Thornton.

The question, raised in the past by Greg Egan and others, as to whether there is such a thing in the first place as specifically *Australia*n science fiction, as opposed just to *science fiction* in general, is a question too large to be settled here, but most of the stories in *Dreaming Again* that take place on Earth at least feature Australian settings, and a few of the stories – mostly the fantasies – seem to draw on Australian myths and legends.

Flying in the face of what I said above about American trade publishers, *The Del Rey Book of Science Fiction and Fantasy*, edited by Ellen Datlow, is a cross-genre anthology featuring SF, fantasy, horror, and slipstream stories. Oddly, for a book that puts "Science Fiction" first in its title, especially from a company like Del Rey, which is known for its solid, core, rather traditional science fiction, the smallest element in the mix is science fiction, with horror, fantasy, and slipstream making up the bulk of its contents – and what science fiction there is is soft near-future SF, with Datlow herself announcing in the Introduction (rather proudly, I thought) that "you won't find off-planet stories or hard science fiction" in the anthology. The best story in the book, by a good margin, is one of those near-future SF stories, in fact, Maureen McHugh's "Special Economics," although there is also good SF work by Paul McAuley and Kim Newman, Pat Cadigan, and Jason Stoddard. More unclassifiable but still readable stuff, often on the borderline between slipstream and SF/fantasy, is provided by Elizabeth Bear, Jeffery Ford, Laird Barron, Christopher Rowe, Lucy Sussex, and others.

Extraordinary Engines (Solaris), edited by Nick Gevers, is a steampunk anthology, many of whose stories double almost by definition as Alternate History. The best stories here are by Ian R. MacLeod and Kage Baker, but there's also first-rate work by Jay Lake, Robert Reed, Jeff VanderMeer, James Lovegrove, Keith Brooke, and others.

One of last year's strongest anthologies, appearing unexpectedly out of nowhere was *disLOCATIONS*, edited by Ian Whates, from very small press publisher NewCon Press. This year, Whates and NewCon Press published three original anthologies: *Subterfuge*, *Celebrations*, and *Myth-Understandings*. None of these is quite as strong as *disLOCATIONS*, but all contain good stories of various types, and all deserve your attention. The strongest of these is *Subterfuge*, which, probably not coincidentally, considering my tastes, contains the highest per centage of science fiction (although all three anthologies contain a mix of SF and fantasy). Best stories here are by Neal Asher and John Meaney, but there are also good SF stories here by Pat Cadigan, Una McCormack, Tony Ballantyne, and others. The best of the fantasy stories are by Tanith Lee and Dave Hutchinson. The best story in *Celebrations*, an anthology commemorating the fiftieth anniversary of the British Science Fiction Association, is a Phildickian SF piece by Alastair Reynolds, but there's good work, both SF and fantasy, by Stephen Baxter, Jon Courtenay Grimwood, Ken MacLeod, Dave Hutchinson, Brian Stableford, Liz Williams, and Molly Brown. The weakest of the three anthologies is *Myth-Understandings*, which features mostly fantasy. Best story here is Tricia Sullivan's, although there's also strong work by Liz Williams, Justina Robson, Pat Cadigan, Kari Sperring, and others.

An odd item, another British small-press anthology, is *The West Pier Gazette and Other Stories, Quercus One* (Three Legged Fox Books), edited by Paul Brazier, an anthology of stories that have supposedly been previously published in electronic form on the members-only *Quercus SF* site (quercus-sf.com – although it doesn't seem to have been updated for several years, and may be fallow). Half of the book is taken up by rather specialized Alternate History stories about alternate fates for the now-destroyed West Pier in Brighton, England, hence the title, and the rest of the book is devoted to more generalized SF, fantasy, and slipstream stories. Best thing here is a high-tech literalization of Egyptian mythology by Liz Williams, but there are also good stories by Geoff Ryman, Lavie Tidhar, Andy W. Robertson, Chris Butler, and others.

Clockwork Phoenix: Tales of Beauty and Strangeness, edited by Mike Allen, is a mixed science fiction/fantasy anthology, with a few slipstream stories thrown in for good measure. In an exceptional year for original anthologies, it doesn't come in at the top of the heap, but there is a lot of good stuff here, and the cover, an effective use of an old painting, is lovely. The best story in *Clockwork Phoenix*, by a considerable margin, is an SF story by Vandana Singh, but there is also good work by John C. Wright, Cat Sparks, C. S. MacCath, and others. The best of the fantasy stories are by Tanith Lee, Marie Brennan, John Grant, Cat Rambo, Ekaterina Sedia, and others.

Another good anthology, full of solid, enjoyable work, is *Seeds of Change* (Prime), edited by John Joseph Adams. Best story here by a substantial margin, and one of the best of the year, is Ted Kosmatka's "N-Words", but there is also good work to be had here from Ken MacLeod, Jay Lake, Nnedi Okorafor-Mbachu, Mark Budz, Tobias Buckell, and others.

2012 (Twelfth Planet Press), edited by Alisa Krasnostein and Ben Payne, delivers a smaller proportion of substantial work than *Seeds of Change*, although there are still worthwhile stories here by Sean McMullen and Simon Brown.

There are probably no award-winners in *Transhuman* (DAW), edited by Mark L. Van Name and T. K. F. Weisskopf (title makes the subject matter self-explanatory, surely), but there is a respectable amount of good solid core SF. Best story here is by David D. Levine, but there are also good stories by Mark L. Van Name, Paul Chafe, Sarah A. Hoyt, Wen Spenser, and others.

Future Americas (DAW), edited by Martin H. Greenberg and John Helfers, and *Front Lines* (DAW), edited by Denise Little, are a bit more substantial than these DAW anthologies usually are. Best story in *Future Americas* is by Brendan DuBois; best story in *Front Lines* is by Kristine Kathryn Rusch. *The Dimension Next Door* (DAW), edited by Martin H. Greenberg and Kerrie Hughes, was worthwhile but minor.

Another pleasant surprise last year was the sudden appearance of two pretty good ultra-small press anthologies from Hadley Rille Books, edited by Eric T. Reynolds, *Visual Journeys and Ruins Extraterrestrial*. Reynolds brought out another three anthologies this year, *Return to Luna* (Hadley

Rille Books), *Desolate Places* (Hadley Rille Books – co-edited with Adam Nakama), and *Barren Worlds* (Hadley Rille Books – co-edited with Adam Nakama), but unfortunately they were much weaker, with some decent work but nothing particularly memorable. *Return to Luna* was marginally the strongest of the three.

Noted without comment is *Galactic Empires* (Science Fiction Book Club), edited by Gardner Dozois.

The best fantasy anthology was probably *Fast Ships, Black Sails* (Night Shade), edited by Ann and Jeff VanderMeer. Playful and a lot of fun, it's an anthology of original pirate story/fantasy crosses, pirate/slipstream crosses, and even a few pirate/SF crosses. If some authors here give the impression that the whole of their research into pirates consisted of watching a DVD of *Pirates of the Caribbean*, others clearly know their stuff, and, for the most part, even the stories that are the sketchiest on the pirate stuff make up for it with the colourful fantasy element. There's first-rate work here by Garth Nix, Elizabeth Bear and Sarah Monette, Kage Baker, Jayme Lynn Blaschke, Naomi Novik, Howard Waldrop, Carrie Vaughn, and others. Also excellent is *Subterranean: Tales of Dark Fantasy* (Subterranean), edited by William Schafer. The stories here are fairly representative of the kind of stories usually to be found on the *Subterranean* website, although none of them actually appeared there, being published for the first time here instead: fantasy, dark fantasy sometimes shading into horror, a smattering of science fiction, all extremely well crafted. The best stories here are by William Browning Spencer, Tim Powers, Patrick Rothfuss, Kage Baker, although there's also good work by Caitlin R. Kiernan, Joe R. Lansdale, Mike Carey, and others. Also good was *A Book of Wizards* (Science Fiction Book Club), edited by Marvin Kaye, which featured novellas by Peter S. Beagle, Tanith Lee, Patricia A. McKillip, and others. There was also another instalment in a long-running fantasy anthology series, *Swords and Sorceress XXIII* (Norilana), edited by Elizabeth Waters.

Pleasant but minor fantasy anthologies included Warrior *Wisewoman* (Norilana), edited by Roby James; *Enchantment Place* (DAW), edited by Denise Little; *Fellowship Fantastic* (DAW), edited by Martin H. Greenberg and Kerrie Hughes; *Mystery Date* (DAW), edited by Denise Little; *Something Magic This Way Comes* (DAW), edited by Martin H. Greenberg and Sarah Hoyt; *Witch High* (DAW), edited by Denise Little; *Catopolis* (DAW), edited by Martin H. Greenberg and Janet Deaver-Pack; *My Big Fat Supernatural Honeymoon* (St. Martin's Griffin), edited by P. N. Elrod; *Magic in the Mirrorstone: Tales of Fantasy* (Mirrorstone), edited by Steve Berman; and *Lace and Blade* (Lada), a fantasy/romance cross edited by Deborah J. Ross.

It's worth mentioning here that some of the anthologies mentioned above as SF anthologies, such as *Clockwork Phoenix*, *Dreaming Again*, and the Whates anthologies, had substantial amounts of good fantasy in them as well, sometimes nearly half the contents.

The line between fantasy and slipstream is often hard to draw rigorously, but anthologies that seemed to me more slipstream than fantasy (in spite of some of their titles) included: *Paper Cities, An Anthology of Urban Fantasy* (Five Senses Press), edited by Ekaterina Sedia; *Subtle Edens* (Elastic Press), edited by Allen Ashley; Alembical (Paper Golem), edited by Lawrence M. Shoen and Arthur Dorrance; *Spicy Slipstream Stories* (Lethe Press), edited by Nick Mamatas and Jay Lake; *A Field Guide to Surreal Biology* (Two Cranes Press), edited by Janet Chui and Jason Erik Lundberg; and *Tesseracts Twelve* (Edge), edited by Claude Lalumiere.

Shared world anthologies, many of them superhero oriented, included *Wild Cards: Inside Straight* (Tor), edited by George R. R. Martin; *Wild Cards: Busted Flush* (Tor), edited by George R. R. Martin; *Hellboy: Oddest Jobs* (Dark Horse), edited by Christopher Golden; and *Ring of Fire II* (Baen), edited by Eric Flint.

As usual, novice work by beginning writers, some of whom may later turn out to be important talents, was featured in *L. Ron Hubbard Presents Writers of the Future, Volume XXIV* (Galaxy), the last in this long-running series to be edited by the late Algis Budrys. No word yet on whether the series will continue under different editorship.

There were lots of stories about robots this year, and *lots* of stories about zombies, including a dedicated zombie anthology. There were at least three retropunk Space Pirate stories, and two stories about really nasty mermaids who kill people. There were two or three pastiches of H. G. Wells' *The War of the Worlds*, and two gritty retellings of Hansel and Gretel. Stories appeared that were obviously inspired by *Second Life*, as well as by MMORPGs like *Worlds of Warcraft*, and by anime. There were several stories that tried to put new twists on the idea of people's minds being uploaded into a computer, including several where survivors were not happy about having to continue to deal with nagging relatives who were now "virtual". In addition to the dedicated Alternate History magazine, *Paradox*, there was also lots of Alternate History stuff published elsewhere, most of it leaning towards steampunk – there were three Alternate History anthologies, *Sideways in Crime, Extraordinary Engines*, and *Steampunk*, but almost every market featured steampunkish Alternate History stories this year, including a few Alternate History/Mystery crosses in *Interzone, Postscripts*, and elsewhere that could just as easily have fit into *Sideways in Crime*.

Science fiction continued to pop up in unexpected places, both in print and online, from the Australian science magazine *Cosmos* to the *MIT Technology Review*. Even *The New Yorker* published two stories this year that could be considered to be genuine SF, an unheard of occurrence that made some observers glance at Hell to see if it had frozen over (there have been stories by SF writers in *The New Yorker* before, but they've usually been slipstream/surrealist/literary pieces of the sort that is more typical of the magazine).

(Finding individual pricings for all of the items from small-presses mentioned in the Summation has become too time-intensive, and since several of the same small presses publish anthologies, novels, *and* short story collections, it seems silly to repeat addresses for them in section after section. Therefore, I'm going to attempt to list here, in one place, all the addresses for small presses that have books mentioned here or there in the Summation, whether from the anthologies section, the novel section, or the short-story-collection section, and, where known, their website addresses. That should make it easy enough for the reader to look up the individual price of any book mentioned that isn't from a regular trade-publisher; such books are less likely to be found in your average bookstore or even in a chain superstore, and so will probably have to be mail-ordered. Many publishers seem to sell only online, through their websites, and some will only accept payment through PayPal. Many books, even from some of the smaller presses, are also available through Amazon.com.)

Addresses: **PS Publishing**, Grosvener House, 1 New Road, Hornsea, West Yorkshire, HU18 1PG, England, UK, pspublishing.co.uk; **Golden Gryphon Press**, 3002 Perkins Road, Urbana, IL 61802, goldengryphon. com; **NESFA Press**, P.O. Box 809, Framinghan, MA 01701-0809, nesfa. org; **Subterranean Press**, P.O. Box 190106, Burton, MI 48519, subterra- neanpress.com; **Solaris**, via solarisbooks.com; **Old Earth Books**, P.O. Box 19951, Baltimore, MD 21211-0951, oldearthbooks.com; **Tachyon Press**, 1459 18th St. #139, San Francisco, CA 94107, tachyonpublications.com; **Night Shade Books**, 1470 NW Saltzman Road, Portland, OR 97229, nightshadebooks.com; **Five Star Books**, 295 Kennedy Memorial Drive, Waterville, ME 04901, galegroup.com/fivestar; **NewCon Press**, via newcon- press.com; **Small Beer Press**, 176 Prospect Ave., Northampton, MA 01060, smallbeerpress.com; **Locus Press**, P.O. Box 13305, Oakland, CA 94661, locusmag.com; **Crescent Books**, Mercat Press Ltd., 10 Coates Crescent, Edinburgh, Scotland EH3 7AL, crescentfiction.com; **Wildside Press/ Cosmos Books/Borgo Press**, P.O. Box 301, Holicong, PA 18928-0301, or go to wildsidepress.com for pricing and ordering; **Edge Science Fiction and Fantasy Publishing**, Inc. and Tesseract Books, Ltd., P.O. Box 1714, Calgary, Alberta, T2P 2L7, Canada, edgewebsite.com; **Aqueduct Press**, P.O. Box 95787, Seattle, WA 98145-2787, aqueductpress.com; **Phobos Books**, 200 Park Avenue South, New York, NY 10003, phobosweb.com; **Fairwood Press**, 5203 Quincy Ave. SE, Auburn, WA 98092, fairwoodpress. com; **BenBella Books**, 6440 N. Central Expressway, Suite 508, Dallas, TX 75206, benbellabooks.com; **Darkside Press**, 13320 27th Ave. NE, Seattle, WA 98125, darksidepress.com; **Haffner Press**, 5005 Crooks Rd., Suite 35, Royal Oak, MI 48073-1239, haffnerpress.com; **North Atlantic Press**, P.O. Box 12327, Berkeley, CA 94701; **Prime**, P.O. Box 36503, Canton, OH 44735, primebooks.net; **Fairwood Press**, 5203 Quincy Ave SE, Auburn, WA 98092, fairwoodpress.com; **MonkeyBrain Books**, 11204 Crossland Drive, Austin, TX 78726, monkeybrainbooks.com; **Wesleyan University Press**, University Press of New England, Order Dept., 37 Lafayette St., Lebanon NH 03766-1405, wesleyan.edu/wespress; **Agog! Press**, P.O. Box U302, University of Wollongong, NSW 2522, Australia, uow.ed.au/~rhood/agog- press; **Wheatland Press**, via wheatlandpress.com; MirrorDanse Books, P.O. Box 3542, Parramatta NSW 2124, tabula-rasa.info/MirrorDanse; **Arsenal Pulp Press**, 103--1014 Homer Street, Vancouver, BC, Canada V6B 2W9, arsenalpress.com; **DreamHaven Books**, 912 W. Lake Street, Minneapolis, MN 55408, dreamhavenbooks.com; **Elder Signs Press/Dimensions Books**, order through dimensionsbooks.com; **Chaosium**, via chaosium.com; **Spyre Books**, P.O. Box 3005, Radford, VA 24143; SCIFI, Inc., P.O. Box 8442, Van Nuys, CA 91409-8442; **Omnidawn Publishing**, order through omnidawn.com; **CSFG**, Canberra Speculative Fiction Guild, csfg.org.au/publishing/anthologies/the_outcast; **Hadley Rille Books**, via hadleyrillebooks.com; **ISFiC Press**, 707 Sapling Lane, Deerfield, IL 60015-3969, or isficpress.com; **Suddenly Press**, via suddenlypress@yahoo.com; Sandstone Press, P.O. Box 5725, One High St., Dingwall, Ross-shire, IV15 9WJ UK, sandstonepress.com; **Tropism Press**, via tropismpress.com; **SF Poetry Association/Dark Regions Press**, sfpoetry.com, cheques to Helena Bell, SFPA Treasurer, 1225 West Freeman St., Apt. 12, Carbondale, IL 62401; **DH Press**, via diamondbookdistributors.com; **Kurodahan Press**, via website kurodahan.com; **Ramble House**, 443 Gladstone Blvd., Shreveport, LA 71104, ramblehouse.com; **Interstitial Arts Foundation**, via interstitialarts.org; **Raw Dog Screaming**, via rawdogscreaming.com; **Three Legged Fox Books**, 98 Hythe Road, Brighton, BN1 6JS, UK; **Norilana Books**, via norilana.com; **coeur de lion**, via coeurdelion.com.au; **PARSECink**, via parsecink.org; **Robert J. Sawyer Books**, via sfwriter.com/rjsbooks.htm; **Rackstraw Press**, via rackstrawpress; **Candlewick**, via candlewick.com; **Zubaan**, via zubaanbooks.com; **Utter Tower**, via threeleggedfox.co.uk, **Spilt Milk Press**, via electricvelocipede.com; **Paper Golem**, via papergolem.com; **Galaxy Press**, via galaxypress.com; **Twelfth Planet Press**, via twelfthplanetpress.com; **Five Senses Press**, via sensefive.com; **Elastic Press**, via elasticpress.com; **Lethe Press**, via lethepressbooks.com; **Two Cranes Press**, via twocranespress.com; **Wordcraft of Oregon**, via wordcraftoforegon.com; **Down East**, via downeast.com.

If I've missed some, as is quite possible, try Googling the name of the publisher.

Once again, there were a *lot* of novels published in the SF/fantasy genres during the year, and although the recession-driven recent upheavals in the publishing world may reduce their numbers somewhat next year, they're certainly not going to vanish from the bookstore shelves in 2009.

According to the newsmagazine *Locus*, there were a record 2,843 books "of interest to the SF field" published in 2008, up 4 per cent from 2,723 titles in 2007. (This total doesn't count media tie-in novels, gaming novels, novelizations of genre movies, most Print-On-Demand books, or novels offered as downloads on the Internet – all of which would swell the total by hundreds if counted.) Paranormal romances continued to boom, both in number of titles published (there were 328 paranormal romances this year, up from 290 last year) and in robustness of sales; several of the best-selling writers in America – Stephanie Meyers, Charline Harris, Laurell K. Hamilton, Jim Butcher – are paranormal romance writers. Original books were down slightly, by 2 per cent, to 1,671 from last year's total of 1,710. Reprint books were up by 16 per cent, to 1,172 compared to last year's total of 1,013. The number of new SF novels was down by a statistically insignificant amount, one book, to 249 from last year's total of 250. The number of new fantasy novels was down by 5 per cent to 439 from last year's total of 460. Horror dropped by 12 per cent, to 175 titles, as opposed to last year's total of 198, still up from 2002's total of 112.

Busy with all the reading I have to do at shorter lengths, I didn't have time to read many novels myself this year, so, as usual, I'll limit myself to mentioning that novels that received a lot of attention and acclaim in 2008 include:

Saturn's Children (Ace), by Charles Stross; *The Dragons of Babel* (Tor), by Michael Swanwick; *The Quiet War* (Gollancz), by Paul McAuley; *The Last Theorem* (Del Rey), by Arthur C. Clarke and Frederik Pohl; *Lavinia* (Harcourt), by Ursula K. Le Guin; *Little Brother* (Tor), by Cory Doctorow; *Matter* (Orbit), by Iain M. Banks; *Going Under* (Pyr), by Jusina Robson; *Navigator* (Ace), by Stephen Baxter; *Weaver* (Ace), by Stephen Baxter; *The Dragon's Nine Sons* (Solaris), by Chris Roberson; *Incandescence* (Gollancz), by Greg Egan; *House of the Stag* (Tor), by Kage Baker; *The Night Sessions* (Orbit), by Ken MacLeod; *Marsbound* (Ace), by Joe Haldeman; *A Dance with Dragons* (Bantam), by George R. R. Martin; *Hunter's Run* (HarperCollins), by George R. R. Martin, Gardner Dozois, and Daniel Abraham; *City at the End of Time* (Del Rey), by Greg Bear; *The Prefect* (Ace), by Alastair Reynolds; *House of Suns* (Gollancz), by Alastair Reynolds; *Zoe's Tale* (Tor), by John Scalzi; *The Graveyard Book* (HarperCollins), by Neil Gaiman; *Victory of Eagles* (Del Rey), by Naomi Novik; *Pirate Sun* (Tor), by Karl Schroeder; *Judge* (Eos), by Karen Traviss; *Earth Ascendant* (Ace), by Sean Williams; *Firstborn* (Del Rey), by Arthur C. Clarke and Stephen Baxter; *An Evil Guest* (Tor), by Gene Wolfe; *Rolling Thunder* (Ace), by John Varley; *The Ghost in Love* (Farrar, Straus & Giroux), by Jonathan Carroll; *Anathem* (Morrow), by Neal Stephenson; *Flora's Dare* (Harcourt), by Ysabeau S. Wilce; *Misspent Youth* (Del Rey), by Peter F. Hamilton; *Ender in Exile* (Tor), by Orson Scott Card; *Keeper of Dreams* (Tor), by Orson Scott Card; *Null-A Continuum* (Tor), by John C. Wright; *Valor's Trial* (DAW), by Tanya Huff; *Shadowbridge* (Del Rey), by Gregory Frost; *Lord Tophet* (Del Rey), by Gregory Frost; *An Autumn War* (Tor), by Daniel Abraham; *The Martian General's Daughter* (Pyr), by Theodore Judson; *The Steel Remains* (Gollancz), by Richard Morgan; *The Valley-Westside War* (Tor), by Harry Turtledove; *Slanted Jack* (Baen), by Mark L. Van Name; *The Hidden World* (Tor), by Paul Park; *Stalking the Vampire* (Pyr), by Mike Resnick; *Victory Conditions* (Del Rey), by Elizabeth Moon; *The Edge of Reason* (Tor), by Melinda Snodgrass; *Bone Song* (Bantam Spectra), by John Meaney; *The Philosopher's Apprentice* (Morrow), by James Morrow; *The Time Engine* (Tor), by Sean McMullen; *The Engine's Child* (Del Rey), by Holly Phillips; *January Dancer* (Tor), by Michael F. Flynn; *Very Hard Choices* (Baen), by Spider Robinson; *The Stars Down Under* (Tor), by Sandra McDonald; *Renegade's Magic* (Eos), by Robin Hobb; *Escapement* (Tor), by Jay Lake; *Before They Are*

Hanged (Pyr), by Joe Abercrombie; *Half a Crown* (Tor), by Jo Walton; *Juggler of Worlds* (Tor), by Larry Niven and Edward M. Lerner; *Nation* (HarperCollins), by Terry Pratchett; and *Duma Key* (Scribner), by Stephen King.

Small presses once published mostly collections and anthologies, but these days they're active in the novel market as well. Novels issued by small presses this year, some of them among the year's best, included: *Or Else My Lady Keeps the Key* (Subterranean), by Kage Baker; *Implied Spaces* (Night Shade), by Walter Jon Williams; *The Bird Shaman* (Bascom Hill), by Judy Moffett; *The Word of God: or, Holy Writ Rewritten* (Tachyon), by Thomas M. Disch; *The Song of Time* (PS Publishing), by Ian R. MacLeod; *Hespira* (Night Shade), by Matthew Hughes; *Dogs* (Tachyon), by Nancy Kress; *The King's Last Song* (Small Beer Press), by Geoff Ryman; *The Shadow Pavilion* (Night Shade), by Liz Williams; *Leaving Fortusa: A Novel in Ten Episodes* (Norilana), by John Grant; *Shadow of the Scorpion* (Night Shade), by Neal Asher; and *The Madness of Flowers* (Night Shade), by Jay Lake.

The year's first novels included: *Singularity's Ring* (Tor), by Paul Melko; *Pandemonium* (Del Rey), by Daryl Gregory; *Black Ships* (Orbit), by Jo Graham; *The Magicians and Mrs Quent* (Bantam Spectra), by Galen Beckett; *The Ninth Circle* (Gollancz), by Alex Bell; *A Darkness Forged in Fire* (Pocket), by Chris Evans; *Apricot Brandy* (Juno), by Lynn Cesar; *Seekers of the Chalice* (Tor), by Brian Cullen; *Thunderer* (Bantam), by Felix Gilman; *Havemercy* (Bantam), by Jaida Jones and Danielle Bennett; *Whitechapel Gods* (Roc), by S. M. Peters; *Mad Kestrel* (Tor), by Misty Massey; *Gordath Wood* (Ace), by Sarath Patrice; *Superpowers* (Three Rivers Press), by David J. Schwartz; *Immortal* (Delta), by Traci C. Slatton; *The Mirrored Heavens* (Bantam), by David J. Williams; and *Paraworld Zero* (Blue World), by Matthew Peterson. The Melko and the Gregory probably attracted the most attention of these.

Associational novels by people connected with the science fiction and fantasy fields included: *Wit's End* (Putnam), by Karen Joy Fowler; *White Sands, Red Menace* (Viking), by Ellen Klages; *Black and White* (Subterranean), by Lewis Shiner; *The Somnambulist* (Morrow), by Jonathan Barnes; *Tigerheart* (Del Rey), by Peter David; and *The Shadow Year* (Morrow), by Jeffrey Ford. Ventures into the genre by well-known mainstream authors, included: *The Island of Eternal Love* (Riverhead), by Daina Chaviano; *The Widows of Eastwick* (Knopf), by John Updike; and *The Enchantress of Florence* (Random House), by Salman Rushdie.

Individual novellas published as stand-alone chapbooks were not as strong this year as they've been in other years, but there were still some good ones out. Subterranean published: *Kilimanjaro: A Fable of Utopia*, by Mike Resnick; *Muse of Fire*, by Dan Simmons; *Stonefather*, by Orson Scott Card; and *Conversation Hearts*, by John Crowley. PS Publishing brought out: *The Economy of Light*, by Jack Dann; *Gunpowder*, by Joe Hill; *Planet of Mystery*, by Terry Bisson; *Template*, by Matthew Hughes; *Mystery Hill*, by Alex Irvine; *The City in These Pages*, by John Grant; *The*

Situation, by Jeff VanderMeer; *Revolvo*, by Steve Erikson; *Val/Orson*, by Marly Youmans; *The Book, the Writer, the Reader*, by Zoran Zivkovic; *The Bridge*, by Zoran Zivkovic; *Living with the Dead*, by Darrell Schweitzer; and *Camp Desolation* and *An Eschatalogy of Salt*, by Uncle River. Aqueduct Press produced *Distances*, by Vandana Singh. Wyrm Publishing produced *Memorare*, by Gene Wolfe. Norilana published *The Duke in His Castle*, by Vera Nazarian. Knopf published *Once Upon a Time in the North*, by Philip Pullman. And Monkeybrain published *Escape from Hell!*, by Hall Duncan.

Novel omnibuses this year included: *The Jack Vance Reader* (Subterranean), by Jack Vance; *Five Novels of the 1960s and 1970s* (Library of America), by Philip K. Dick; *Books of the South: Tales of the Black Corridor* (Tor), by Glen Cook; and *The Chronicles of Master Li and Number One Ox* (Subterranean), as well as many omnibus novel volumes published by the Science Fiction Book Club. (Omnibuses that contain both short stories *and* novels can be found listed in the short story section.)

As has been true for the last couple of years, after the long drought of the 1990s, when almost nothing out-of-print got back into it, this is the best time in decades to pick up reissued editions of formerly long-out-of-print novels, not even counting Print On Demand books from places such as Wildside Press, the reprints issued by The Science Fiction Book Club, and the availability of out-of-print books as electronic downloads from Internet sources such as Fictionwise. Here are some out-of-print titles that came back *into* print this year, although producing a definitive list of reissued novels is probably difficult to impossible:

Tor reissued: *Pebble in the Sky*, by Isaac Asimov; *The Dragon in the Sea*, by Frank Herbert; *Starfish*, by Peter Watts; *The Risen Empire* and *The Killing of Worlds*, both by Scott Westerfeld; and the associational novel *In Milton Lumky Territory*, by Philip K. Dick. Orb reissued: *Make Room! Make Room!*, by Harry Harrison; *Anvil of Stars*, by Greg Bear; and *Inferno*, by Jerry Pournelle and Larry Niven. Baen reissued: *Farmer in the Sky* and *Between Planets*, both by Robert A. Heinlein. Orbit reissued: *The Reality Dysfunction*, by Peter F. Hamilton; and *Consider Phlebas*, *The Player of Games*, and *Use of Weapons*, all by Iain Banks. Cosmos reissued: *Space Viking*, by H. Beam Piper; *The Black Star Passes*, by John W. Campbell, Jr; and *Planet of the Damned*, by Harry Harrison. Tachyon reissued: *The Stress of Her Regard*, by Tim Powers. Paizo/Planet Stories reissued: *The Ginjer Star*, by Leigh Brackett; and *Lord of the Spiders*, by Michael Moorcock. Overlook reissued: *Titus Alone*, by Mervyn Peake. Golden Gryphon Press reissued: *The Physiognomy*, *The Beyond*, and *Memoranda*, all by Jeffrey Ford.

Lots of science fiction and even hard science fiction here, as usual, although there are also fantasy novels and odd-genre-mixing hybrids on the list as well. Although we often hear the lament that science fiction has been driven off the bookstore shelves, it just isn't true. There's still lots of it out there to be found.

*

This was another good year for short story collections. The year's best collections included: *The Best of Michael Swanwick* (Subterranean), by Michael Swanwick; *East of the Sun and West of Fort Smith* (Norilana Books), by William Sanders; *Dark Integers and Other Stories* (Subterranean), by Greg Egan; *Other Worlds, Better Lives: A Howard Waldrop Reader* (Old Earth Books), by Howard Waldrop; *Pump Six and Other Stories* (Night Shade), by Paolo Bacigalupi; *The Wreck of the Godspeed and Other Stories* (Golden Gryphon), by James Patrick Kelly; *The Best of Lucius Shepard* (Subterranean), by Lucius Shepard; *Nano Comes to Clifford Falls* (Golden Gryphon), by Nancy Kress; *The Baum Plan for Financial Independence and Other Stories* (Small Beer Press), by John Kessel; and *Pretty Monsters* (Viking), by Kelly Link. Other good collections included: *Harsh Oases* (PS Publishing), by Paul Di Fillipo; *The Ant King and Other Stories* (Small Beer Press), by Benjamin Rosenbaum; *Strange Roads* (Dreamhaven), by Peter S. Beagle; *The Garble and Other Stories* (Tor UK), by Neal Asher; *Starlady and Fast-Friend* (Subterranean), by George R. R. Martin; *Space Magic: Stories by David D. Levine* (Wheatland Press), by David D. Levine; *The Wall of America* (Tachyon), by Thomas M. Disch; *The Autopsy and Other Tales*, by Michael Shea; *Binding Energy* (Elastic Press), by Daniel Marcus; *Cryptic: The Best Short Fiction of Jack McDevitt* (Subterranean), by Jack McDevitt; *Tempting the Gods* (Wildside Press), by Tanith Lee; *The Adventures of Langdon St Ives* (Subterranean), by James Blaylock; *Crazy Love* (Wordcraft of Oregon), by Leslie What; *Walking to the Moon* (Wildside), by Sean McMullen; *Billy's Book* (PS Publishing), by Terry Bisson; *Long Walks, Last Flights, and Other Journeys* (Fairwood Press), by Ken Scholes; *What the Mouse Found and Other Stories* (Subterranean), by Charles de Lint; and *Just After Sunset* (Scribner), by Stephen King.

As has become common, there were also a lot of good retrospective collections by older writers (as specialty press hardcovers, many of them may be too expensive for casual readers, although there are a few less expensive paperbacks here as well), including: *The Van Rijn Method* (Baen – an omnibus of stories about Falstaffian space adventurer Nicolas Van Rijn, plus the well-known novel *The Man Who Counts*), by Poul Anderson; *David Falkayn: Star Trader – The Technic Civilization Saga* (Baen – another ominibus of stories and a novel), by Poul Anderson; *Works of Art* (NESFA Press), by James Bliss; *Lorelei of the Red Mist: Planetary Romances* (Haffner Press), by Leigh Brackett; *Northwest of Earth: The Complete Northwest Smith* (Prize/Planet Stories), by Leigh Brackett; *H. P. Lovecraft: The Fiction* (Barnes & Noble), by H. P. Lovecraft; *The Worlds of Jack Williamson: A Centennial Tribute 1908–2008* (Haffner Press), Jack Williamson, edited by Stephen Haffner; *Gateway to Paradise: The Collected Stories of Jack Williamson, Volume Six* (Haffner Press), Jack Williamson; *The Metal Giants and Others: The Collected Edmond Hamilton, Volume One* (Haffner Press), by Edmond Hamilton; *The Star Stealers: The Complete Adventures of the Interstellar Patrol: The Collected Edmond Hamilton, Volume Two* (Haffner Press), by Edmond Hamilton; *The Collected Captain Future: Volume One: Captain Future and the Space Emperor* (Haffner Press), by Edmond Hamilton; *Venus on the Half-Shell and Others* (Subterranean – an omnibus of stories and the eponymous novel, written as by "Kilgore Trout"), by Philip José Farmer; *Laugh Lines* (Tor – an omnibus of six stories and two novels), by Ben Bova; *Button, Button: Uncanny Stories* (Tor), by Richard Matheson; *Boy in Darkness and Other Stories* (Peter Owen), by Mervyn Peake; *Elric: The Stealer of Souls* (Del Rey – an omnibus of stories and novels), by Michael Moorcock; *Elric: To Rescue Tanelorn* (Del Rey – an omnibus of stories and novels), by Michael Moorcock; *Viewpoints Critical: Selected Stories* (Tor), by L. E. Modesitt, Jr; *Skeleton in the Closet and Other Stories* (Subterranean), by Robert Bloch; *Summer Morning, Summer Night* (PS Publishing), by Ray Bradbury; *Skeletons* (Subterranean), by Ray Bradbury; and *Project Moonbase and Others* (Subterranean – an omnibus of screenplays and never-filmed adaptations of early Heinlein stories), by Robert A. Heinlein.

The most expensive of these is Bradbury's *Summer Morning, Summer Night*, which sells for $750.00 (!); one wonders if they're flying out the door at that price, although there probably are a few collectors willing to pay that much. The bulk of the retrospective collections sells somewhere in the $40 range. The paperbacks from Baen and Tor are much less expensive.

As usual, small press publishers were important – indispensable, really – to the short story collection market, since, with only a few occasional exceptions, the big trade publishers largely don't do them anymore. Without them, collections would barely exist. As you can see, Subterranean (with the more contemporary stuff) and Haffner Press (with the retrospective stuff) had especially active years. Among trade publishers, Baen seems the most active, particularly in publishing omnibus volumes that contain both short stories and novels.

A wide variety of "electronic collections," often called "fiction bundles," too many to individually list here, are also available for downloading online, at sites such as *Fictionwise* and *ElectricStory*, and The Science Fiction Book Club continues to issue new collections as well.

The reprint anthology market seemed a bit weaker overall this year than last year. As usual, the bumper crop of "Best of the Year" anthologies were probably your best bet for your money in this market. It's sometimes hard to tell how many of these there are, as they come and go so quickly, but the field seems to have been winnowed a bit from last year's record total of fourteen. Science fiction was covered by three and a half anthologies, down from six anthologies last year: the one you are reading at the moment, *The Year's Best Science Fiction* series from Robinson, edited by Gardner Dozois, now up to its twenty-sixth (in the US) twenty-second (in the UK) annual collection; the *Year's Best SF* series (Eos), edited by David G. Hartwell and Kathryn Cramer, now up to its thirteenth annual volume; *Science Fiction: The Best of the Year 2007* (Prime), edited by Richard Horton; and *The Best Science Fiction and Fantasy of the Year: Volume*

Two (Night Shade Books), edited by Jonathan Strahan (this is where the "half a book" comes in, although I doubt that it'll divide that neatly in practice). Jonathan Strahan's *Best Short Novels* series has died, as has Richard Horton's announced but never appearing *Space Opera Best* series. The annual Nebula Awards anthology usually covers science fiction as well as fantasy of various sorts, functioning as a de facto "Best of the Year" anthology, although it's not usually counted among them (and thanks to SFWA's bizarre "rolling eligibility" practice, the stories in it are often stories that everybody else saw a year and sometimes even two years before); this year's edition was *Nebula Awards Showcase 2008* (Roc), edited by Ben Bova. There were two and a half *Best of the Year* anthologies covering horror: the latest edition in the British series, *The Mammoth Book of Best New Horror* (Robinson, Carroll & Graf), edited by Stephen Jones, up to its nineteenth volume; *Horror: The Best of the Year 2008 Edition* (Prime), edited by John Gregory Betancourt and Sean Wallace; and the Ellen Datlow half of a huge volume covering both horror and fantasy, *The Year's Best Fantasy and Horror* (St Martin's Press), edited by Ellen Datlow and Kelly Link and Gavin Grant, this year up to its twenty-First Annual Collection. Fantasy was covered by four anthologies (if you add two halves together): by the Kelly Link and Gavin Grant half of the Datlow/Link & Grant anthology; by *Year's Best Fantasy 8* (Tachyon) edited by David G. Hartwell and Katherine Cramer; by *Fantasy: The Best of the Year 2008* (Prime), edited by Rich Horton; by *Best American Fantasy* (Prime), edited by Ann and Jeff VanderMeer; and by the fantasy half of *The Best Science Fiction and Fantasy of the Year: Volume One* (Night Shade Books), edited by Jonathan Strahan. There was also *The 2008 Rhysling Anthology* (Science Fiction Poetry Association/Prime), edited by Drew Morse, which compiles the Rhysling Award-winning SF poetry of the year. If you count the Nebula anthology and the Rhysling anthology, there were eleven "Best of the Year" anthology series of one sort or another on offer this year, down from last year's fourteen.

At the beginning of 2009 it was announced that the long-running Datlow/Link & Grant *Year's Best Fantasy and Horror* series had died. Ellen Datlow has announced that she will begin doing a different "Best Horror" series for Night Shade Books, exact title as yet undetermined, to be published sometime in 2009 and covering stories published in 2008. So next year we'll be half a book down in this category, losing the Kelly Link and Gavin Grant half of the former *Year's Best Fantasy and Horror* book.

The last few years have featured big retrospective anthologies, but there were none of them this year and, as a result, fewer stand-alone reprint anthologies of exceptional merit. The best of the reprint anthologies was probably *Steampunk* (Tachyon), edited by Ann and Jeff VanderMeer, which featured good reprint stories by Michael Chabon, James Blaylock, Joe R. Lansdale, Ian R. MacLeod, Neal Stephenson, Mary Gentle, Ted Chiang, and others. Also good was *Wastelands: Stories of the Apocalypse* (Night Shade Books), edited by John Joseph Adams, which featured stories about the you-know-what and its aftermath by George R. R. Martin, Stephen King, Gene Wolfe, Octavia Butler, and others. If you like zombies (which were so frequently encountered this year, even in the science fiction anthologies, that they seemed to be taking over the field), you'll want *The Living Dead* (Night Shade Books), edited by John Joseph Adams and packed full of zombie stories by Dan Simmons, Michael Swanwick, George R. R. Martin, Stephen King, Andy Duncan, and others. Another attempt at subgenre definition and canon-forming was *The New Weird* (Tachyon), edited by Ann and Jeff VanderMeer, a mixed anthology of reprint stories (the best by M. John Harrison, Clive Barker, and Jeff Ford), some original material, critical essays, and transcribed blog entries which had some good stuff in it but which ultimately left me just as confused as to what exactly The New Weird consisted of when I went out as I'd been when I went in. Good work was also to be found in *The Best of Jim Baen's Universe II* (Baen), edited by Eric Flint and Mike Resnick, and *Orson Scott Card's Intergalactic Medicine Show, Volume Two* (Tor), edited by Edmund R. Schubert and Orson Scott Card, volumes of stories from two of the most prominent ezines.

Otherworldly Maine (Down East), edited by Noreen Doyle, was a mixed reprint (mostly) and original anthology which featured strong reprints by Edgar Pangborn, Stephen King, Elizabeth Hand, and others, as well as good original work by Gregory Feeley, Lee Allred, and Jessica Reisman. Just exactly what qualifies one to be a Savage Humanist is a bit unclear, in spite of a long analytical introduction, but *The Savage Humanists* (Robert J. Sawyer Books), edited by Fiona Kelleghan, features good reprint stories by Tim Sullivan, Greg Frost, John Kessel, James Patrick Kelly, Kim Stanley Robinson, and others. *When Diplomacy Fails* (Isfic Press), edited by Mike Resnick and Eric Flint, is a reprint anthology of military SF by Harry Turtledove, Gene Wolfe, David Weber, Tanya Huff, Resnick and Flint themselves, and others. *The Best of Abyss & Apex: Volume One* (Hadley Rille Books), edited by Wendy S. Delmater, is drawn from the website of the same name. And a perspective on SF from another part of the world is given by *The Black Mirror and Other Stories: An Anthology of Science Fiction from Germany and Austria* (Wesleyan University Press), edited by Franz Rottensteiner.

Reprint fantasy anthologies included *Tales Before Narnia* (Del Rey), edited by Douglas A. Anderson; and *The Dragon Done It* (Baen), edited by Eric Flint and Mike Resnick, a mixed reprint (mostly) and original anthology of fantasy/mystery crosses. There was a big retrospective reprint horror anthology, *Poe's Children: The New Horror* (Doubleday), edited by Peter Straub, featuring reprints by Elizabeth Hand, Stephen King, Melanie and Steve Rasnic Tem, Straub himself, and others.

Reissued anthologies of merit this year included *The Science Fiction Hall of Fame, Volume 2B* (Tor), edited by Ben Bova; *The Mammoth Book of Extreme Fantasy* (Running Press), edited by Mike Ashley; *A Science Fiction Omnibus* (Penguin Modern Classics), edited by Brian W. Aldiss; and *The Reel Stuff* (DAW), edited by Brian Thomsen and Martin H. Greenberg.

There were almost no SF-and-fantasy-oriented reference books this year, with the closest approach probably being *Lexicon Urthus: A Dictionary for the Urth Cycle, Second Edition* (Sirius Fiction), by Michael Andre-Driussi. There were a number of critical books about SF and fantasy, including *Maps and Legends: Essays on Reading and Writing Along the Borderlands* (McSweeneys), by Michael Chabon; *Rhetorics of Fantasy* (Wesleyan University Press), by Farah Mendlesohn; *The Wiscon Chronicles, Volume 2* (Aqueduct), by Eileen Gunn and L. Timmel Duchamp; and *What Is It We Do When We Read Science Fiction?* (Beccon), by Paul Kincaid. There were autobiographies by or biographies/critical studies of specific authors, including *Miracles of Life: Shanghai to Shepperton* (HarperCollinsUK), by J. G. Ballad; *H. Beam Piper: A Biography* (McFarland), by John F. Carr; *An Unofficial Companion to the Novels of Terry Pratchett* (Greenwood), by Andrew M. Butler; *Anthony Boucher: A Biobibliography* (McFarland), by Jeffrey Marks; *The Vorkosigan Companion* (Baen), by Lillian Stewart Carl and Martin H. Greenberg (a guide to the work of Lois McMaster Bujold); *Prince of Stories: The Many Worlds of Neil Gaiman* (St. Martin's Press), by Hank Wagner, Christopher Golden, and Stephen R. Bissette; *Basil Cooper: A Life in Books* (PS Publishing), edited by Stephen Jones; *The Richard Matheson Companion* (Gauntlet Press), by Stanley Wiater and Matthew R. Bradley; and a posthumously published collection of articles on diverse subjects by Kurt Vonnegut, *Armageddon in Retrospect* (Putnam).

The year also saw the publication of two books of a kind that I'm sure we're going to see a lot more of: collections of articles previously published electronically online in blogs and in other Internet sources. They were *Your Hate Mail Is Being Graded: Ten Years of Whatever* (Subterranean Press), by John Scalzi, *Whatever* being the very popular blog that Scalzi won a best fanwriter Hugo for his work in this year, and *Content: Selected Essays on Technology, Creativity, Copyright, and the Future of the Future* (Tachyon), by Cory Doctorow.

It was another weak year in the art book field, after several fairly strong ones earlier in the decade. Once again your best buy was probably *Spectrum 15: The Best in Contemporary Fantastic Art* (Underwood Books), by Cathy Fenner and Arnie Fenner, the latest edition in a Best of the Year-like retrospective of the year in fantastic art. Also worthwhile were *The Other Visions: Ralph McQuarrie* (Titan Books), by Ralph McQuarrie; *The Paintings of J. Allen St. John: Grand Master of Fantasy* (Vanguard), by Stephen A. Korshak; *As I See: The Fantastic World of Boris Artzybashoff* (Titan Books), by Boris Artzybashoff; *Virgil Finlay: Future/Past* (Underwood Books), by Virgil Finlay; *A Lovecraft Retrospective: Artists Inspired by H. P. Lovecraft* (Centipede Press), edited by Jerad Walter; *Drawing Down the Moon: The Art of Charles Vess* (Dark Horse Books), by Charles Vess; and *Telling Stories: The Comic Art of Frank Frazetta* (Underwood Books), edited by Edward Mason.

There were a fair number of genre-related non-fiction books of interest this year. The most central of these was probably *Year Million: Science at the Far Edge of Knowledge* (Atlas), a collection of futurist articles, many by scientists or SF writers, edited by Damien Broderick. The edges of the possible in science, as we understand them today, is also explored in *Physics of the Impossible* (Doubleday), by physicist Michio Kaku, and in *13 Things That Don't Make Sense* (Doubleday), by Michael Brooks. Fans may also be interested in an examination of superhero science, *Superheroes!* (I. B. Tauris), by Roz Kaveney, and by more bitching about how we don't have those flying cars yet (following several similar volumes last year), *You Call This the Future?* (Chicago Review Press), by Nick Sagan, Mark Frary, and Andrew Wacker. There's no direct genre connection for mentioning *Life in Cold Blood* (Princeton University Press), by David Attenborough, but SF writers looking to score ideas about really alien creatures and lifeways could do a lot worse than look down into the bogs and swamps where the coldblooded creatures described herein dwell.

There were lots of genre movies that did big box-office business this year, although few critical darlings or films thought of as "serious" movies.

According to the Box Office Mojo site (boxofficemojo.com), nine out of ten of the year's top-earning movies were genre films of one sort or another (counting in stuff like *Indiana Jones and the Kingdom of the Crystal Skull* as fantasy/SF – Hell, it's even got aliens! – rather than "action/adventure", and including animated movies but excluding the new James Bond movie, *Quantum of Solace*, which is probably stretching the definition of "genre movie" too far); thirteen out of twenty of the year's top-earning movies were genre films; and at least twenty-seven out of the hundred top-earning movies (depending on where you draw the lines – and for reasons of my own personal prejudices, I'm not counting horror/slasher/thriller movies) – were genre films.

In fact, it's clear that genre films of one sort or another have come to dominate Hollywood at the box-office, producing most of the year's really big money-makers, and that's been true for a while now. During the last decade, each year's top-grossing film has been a genre film of some sort: superhero movies (three of this year's top-earners are superhero movies, and 2007's biggest earner was *Spider Man 3*, a lesson that I doubt has been lost on the movie-makers), or fantasy/adventures such as *Pirates of the Caribbean: Dead Man's Chest* or *The Return of the King*, or SF/adventures such *Star Wars: The Phantom Menace*, or even fantasy movies ostensibly for children such as *Shrek 2* or *The Grinch Who Stole Christmas*. You have to go all the way back to 1998 before you find a non-genre film as the year's top-earner, *Saving Private Ryan*.

Of course, the kicker is, what do you mean by "genre film"?

Of the year's top ten highest-grossing films, of the nine that can be considered to be genre movies of one sort or another, three are superhero movies (*The Dark Knight*, *Iron Man*, and *Hancock*, with *The Incredible Hulk* finishing in fourteenth place and *Hellboy II: The Golden Army* finishing in thirty-eighth place); one is fantasy/adventure (*Indiana Jones and the Kingdom of the Crystal Skull*, with the comparable *The Chronicles of*

Narnia: Prince Caspian finishing in thirteenth place); four are animated films (*Wall-E*, *Kung Fu Panda*, *Madagascar: Escape 2 Africa*, and *Dr Seuss's Horton Hears a Who!*, with superhero – sort of – animated feature *Bolt* finishing in nineteenth place, and *The Tale of Despereaux*, released at the end of the year, perhaps destined to climb the charts); and one is a glossy vampire/romance movie (*Twilight*). (For those interested, other than *Quantum of Solace*, the two highest-earning non-genre films were *Sex and the City* and *Mamma Mia!*, which finished in eleventh and twelfth places respectively – unless you want to make the somewhat arch argument that they're fantasy films as well.)

Like last year, there were almost no actual *science fiction* films on the list at all, even in the top hundred, let alone the top ten. The closest approach to a real SF film out this year was the animated film *Wall-E*, which did make the top ten list, in fifth place, in fact, and although its science was a bit shaky (you can't make an ecosystem out of one plant and one cock-roach), for the most part it treated its science fiction tropes with respect and intelligence, and what satiric needling there was at the genre was affectionate. In fact, with its humans who have become so pampered and constantly waited on by machines that they've lost the ability to walk, it may be the purest expression of 1950s' Galaxy-era social satire of the Pohl/Kornbluth variety ever put before the general public. *Wall-E* itself got treated with an amazing amount of respect for an animated film ostensibly for children, as *Ratatouille* and *The Incredibles* had been before it, and is probably the one out of the top-grossing genre films that came the closest to being treated as a "serious movie". At least some animated films are big money-makers these days and are clearly not being watched only by children anymore (if they ever were only watched solely by children in the first place, which I doubt).

The year's other Great White Hope as far as SF movies were concerned was a glossy $80-million remake of the old fifties' movie *The Day the Earth Stood Still*, which, in spite of a good opening weekend, made it only to thirty-ninth place. Some fans protested that the movie wasn't a faithful remake of the original film – but, of course, the original film itself wasn't faithful to the ostensible source material, Harry Bates' *Astounding* story "Welcome to the Master," so that's nothing new. Major plot-logic holes were the real problem here. *Star Wars: The Clone Wars*, an animated continuation or at least elaboration of the *Star Wars* saga, looking at stuff that happened between the cracks of the major movies, may have gone to the *Star Wars* well once too often, or perhaps people were thrown by the change in medium from live-action to animated, since it only finished seventy-ninth on the list of year's top-earners. A remake of the classic Jules Verne novel *Journey to the Center of the Earth* was not even as watchable as the fifties' version, in spite of having better special effects and the con-siderable advantage of not having Pat Boone in it. The only other science fiction film I could find (unless you count *Space Chimps*, which I don't intend to) was *Jumper*, adapted with very little fidelity from a YA SF novel by Steven Gould, although it could with excellent justification be considered to be a superhero movie instead; it was supposed to be the start of a franchise, but since it earned $80 million but cost $85 million to make, that seems dubious – although the foreign revenues were better.

That was it for science fiction films, as far as I can tell. When I say "genre film" from here on down, we're talking about fantasy films or superhero movies.

The top-grossing film of the year, by a huge margin, was *The Dark Knight*, which also got treated with a good deal of respect by critics for a superhero movie, mostly because of the late Heath Ledger's riveting turn as the Joker, bringing a scary intensity to the part that surpassed and probably supplanted even Jack Nicholson's famous interpretation of the role. You have to wonder if Christian Bale, who played Batman, and whose movie this ostensibly was, was bemused at the fact that nearly every review of the film spent all of its time raving about Heath Ledger and often didn't mention Bale at all. (Still, at least *he* gets to collect his residuals, which may be some consolation.) Ledger's performance will be long remembered by fans and would alone push *The Dark Knight* into the realm of classic superhero movies such as *Spiderman* and *The X-Men*, although the rest of the movie is pretty good too, dark and creepily elegant, but overlong and perhaps a bit muddled. The sly and frequently amusing *Iron Man* finished in second place in the top-grossing list, mostly because of a snarky performance by Robert Downey, Jr. The Big Green Angry Guy did better in his second outing as a film star, *The Incredible Hulk*, easily outdrawing Ang Lee's muddled and overly complex previous Hulk movie, although not doing as well as his fellow superhero and *Avengers* teammate *Iron Man* (you could see them setting up the forthcoming *Avengers* movie throughout both *Iron Man* and *The Incredible Hulk*, by the way). Although it seemed like two movies jammed together, neither of which the filmmakers really knew what to do with, Will Smith delivered enough of a star turn as a degenerate drunken superhero to put *Hancock* into fourth place. *Wanted* was about a guild of super-powered assassins.

(These totals are somewhat misleading, since they're only talking about domestic grosses. If you add the *foreign grosses* to the domestic grosses, you have to shuffle the rankings around some. *Indiana Jones* (combined total: $786,001,411), *Hancock* ($624,386,476), and even *Kung Fu Panda*, which only finished sixth on the domestic-gross list (combined total: $631,465,619), coming in ahead of *Iron Man* ($581,804,570). Nothing can come close to unseating *The Dark Knight*, though, whose combined total is $997,012,892! And top-selling computer games such as *World of Warcraft* and other MMORPGs make even more money than the movies do. Little wonder that print science fiction, and even print fantasy, have come to be seen by many as poor cousins, with even print bestsellers not coming even remotely close to earning what SF and fantasy do in other media.)

Sequels or new instalments of established franchises often did only so-so this year. *The Dark Knight* and *Indiana Jones and the Kingdom of the Crystal Skull* did the best of any of them at the box-office (although even fans of the franchise seemed only lukewarm about the new Indiana Jones; Harrison Ford looked tired throughout, and I suspect that the producers would like to carry on the franchise using Shia LaBeouf instead, but he doesn't show enough charisma here to convince me he could carry the franchise by himself). Below this point, things get dicier. *The Chronicles of Narnia: Prince Caspian* placed a respectable thirteenth on the top-ten domestic earners list, but although it earned $141,621,490, it *cost* $200 million to make, which might have been bad news for the continuation of this franchise, except that foreign revenues bumped its combined total to $419,646,109, which might have saved it, as foreign revenues have saved a couple of movies in the last few years. It was a similar scenario with *The Mummy: Tomb of the Dragon Emperor*, which cost $145 million to make but earned only $102,277,510, until foreign revenues boosted its combined total to $290,903,563; of course, this franchise has been going steadily downhill since the original movie. Things were even more stark with *Hellboy II: The Golden Army*, in at thirty-eighth place, which cost $85 million to make but earned back only $75,791,785, and even with foreign revenues, could make it "only" to $158,954,785, which might have made it a failure in Hollywood terms. Too bad, as the original movie, *Hellboy*, was one of the most successful films of its year, both commercially and artistically; but the sequel, although it featured absolutely stunning visual effects, lacked the headlong narrative momentum and much of the rough humour of the original movie, and often got bogged down in confusing and perhaps unnecessary subplots. *Star Wars: The Clone Wars* could only make it to seventy-ninth place, in spite of the *Star Wars* name. And the "long-awaited" sequel to the last *X-Files* movie, this one called *The X-Files: I Want To Believe*, fell out of the top hundred list altogether, only managing to make it to 107th place, not enough people wanted to believe that this was something they really wanted to see, and this may well have been a case of waiting too long, until after interest and enthusiasm had cooled, before trying to do another sequel.

Cloverfield, a postmodern version of an old-fashioned giant-monster-trampling-through-a-city movie, widely referred to as "the *Blair Witch Project* meets *Godzilla*," hauled in a combined total of $170,764,026 but *cost* only $25 million to make, rock-bottom cheap by today's standards, so I'm sure that its producers are happy with its performance. There actually were some scary moments in this, if the constantly swirling and somersaulting camera didn't make you flee the theatre with nausea or vertigo first. The execrable *10,000 B.C.* is what you get when you're sitting around in a pitch meeting and somebody says, "Hey! Egyptians meet mammoths!" The even more dreadful *Speed Racer* was another misguided attempt to make a live-action version of a campy old animated TV show, not unlike last year's *Underdog*. *The Happening* was another fundamentally incoherent and not-particularly-scary M. Night Shyamalan movie, and *Igor* and the prophetically titled *The Pirates Who Don't Do Anything* were the year's animated movies that didn't make lots of money. There was a YA steampunk movie called *City of Ember* released late in the year that I haven't seen, and a film version of another well known Young Adult fantasy novel, *The Spiderwick Chronicles*, which ditto.

The Magic Realist movie *The Curious Case of Benjamin Button*, based on a story by F. Scott Fitzgerald, came out right at the end of the year, to mixed but generally pretty good reviews; you're on your own there, since I haven't seen it either.

The best hope for a science fiction movie for next year seems to be the upcoming *Star Trek* prequel – which is kind of sad. Not surprisingly, there are a number of superhero movies in store for lucky audiences as well.

Coming up on the more-distant horizon are a version of Joe Haldeman's *The Forever War*, directed by Ridley Scott, and a version of John Wyndham's *Chocky*, directed by Steven Spielberg. On the even more distant horizon is a version of Isaac Asimov's *Foundation*, directed by Roland Emmerich.

The Writers Guild of America strike swept over the television industry early in 2008, leaving downed trees and wreckage in its wake, and probably contributing to the demise of a few already shaky shows – but even though some of the biggest genre shows on television, *Lost*, *Battlestar Galactica*, *Dr Who*, *Torchwood*, were forced by the strike to go "on hiatus" until 2009 or even (in the case of *Dr Who*) until 2010 (as were some lesser shows such as *Kyle XY* and *Fear Itself*) – ratings are down across the board this season and some of last season's biggest hits are wobbling in the ratings and in danger of being cancelled – there's still plenty of genre shows to watch, with a large number of hopeful replacements waiting in the wings, and yet another row of potential shows looming beyond that. In fact, it's clear that genre shows – mostly fantasy shows, although there are still actually a few science fiction shows left here and there – have come to dominate the TV airways to almost as great a degree as they dominate the Hollywood top-grossing films list, although cop/forensic/detective shows are still holding their own (last year's wave of hybrid fantasy/SF cop shows largely failed to establish itself, with only *Saving Grace* surviving).

Shows like *Moonlight*, *New Amsterdam*, *Cavemen*, *The Bionic Woman*, *Journeyman*, *Flash Gordon*, and *UFO Hunters* were swept out to sea by the writers' strike, and show no sign of coming back; many of them, like the jaw-droppingly awful *Cavemen*, probably wouldn't have made it even without the strike.

Jericho, a watchable after-the-atomic war show that had been given a new lease on life after a massive fan write-in campaign, was granted a partial new season, still failed to attract audiences large enough for the network, and finally died for good, although the usual rumors that it might be picked up by another network swirled around for a while before fading away. One of last season's big hits, *Terminator: The Sarah Connor Chronicles*, has struggled in the ratings this year, having become even more grim and apocalyptic than it was before, and may be in jeopardy; I'd like to see it survive because it's one of the few new SF shows in a sea of fantasy shows. *Eureka*, another SF show, seems to be doing well, although it's pleasantly quirky and even comic instead of dark, intense, and violent, which may explain why.

They also seem to be darkening *Heroes*, which made it through the strike intact, but which has been taking substantial hits in the ratings recently, which may be cause and effect (in economic hard times, audiences don't particularly want grim and depressing, getting enough of that in everyday life; the show has also become complicated enough that it's almost impossible to keep track of the plot, which probably doesn't help), and which has sunk low enough quickly enough that it may actually be in danger of being cancelled, in spite of its Mega-Hit status last year; towards the end of the year, there was a big shake-up at *Heroes*, with several writers and producers fired, and we'll see if that helps, although it may be too late. *Smallville* lost villain Lex Luthor when Michael Rosenbaum, the actor who has played him so vividly since the beginning of the series, decided to move on, a major blow that may eventually sink the show, although they're gamely carrying on at the moment. *Battlestar Galactica* and *Stargate Atlantis*, both in hiatus at the moment, have announced that their upcoming seasons will be their last, although heartbroken fans can console themselves with the fact that each show will be followed by "two-hour special events" set in the same universe, and later by new spinoff shows, *Caprica* for *Battlestar Galactica*, *Stargate Universe* for *Stargate Atlantis*.

Perhaps the best of the new SF series is BBC America's *Primeval*, which has been accurately referred to as "*Torchwood* meets *Jurassic Park*," with a Torchwood-like team of investigators dealing with the incursions of dinosaurs and other prehistoric beasts who for some unknown reason are popping through "anomalies" and wreaking havoc in the modern world. It's a cleverly written show, intense and fast-moving, and the producers have been smart enough to vary the Prehistoric-Monster-of-the-Week formula with the occasional monster from the *future*, as well as bringing in time-travel paradoxes and Alternate Reality scenarios. *Dr Who* and *Torchwood* are in hiatus (although, unlike most shows that are "in hiatus," they're expected to actually return), but BBC America also has a Young Adult *Dr Who* spinoff, *The Sarah Jane Adventures*, ongoing as well.

If last year was The Year of the Cop, this year seems to be the year of the updated *X-Files* clones, with new shows *Fringe*, *Eleventh Hour*, and, to some degree, *Sanctuary* (with a splash of *Hellboy* thrown in), all repeating variations of *The X-Files* formula, some pretty blatantly. It's too early to say if any of these shows are going to establish themselves, but although *Fringe* has the biggest guns behind it and has gotten the most praise and press coverage to date, *Eleventh Hour* seems to actually be edging it in the ratings. A hangover from the Year of the Cop is *Life on Mars*, about a present-day cop who's mysteriously thrown back in time to 1973; this is actually the American version of the popular British limited series of the same name, and, unsurprisingly, I've already heard connoisseurs saying that the British version was better, but the American version may yet establish itself.

The campy old 1970s' show *Knight Rider*, about a crime-fighting boy and his talking robot car, has come roaring back from oblivion revved up and ready for action, although the question that haunted the old series haunts this one as well: with everything the car can do, what do you need the *boy* for? (The answer: for the love scenes and the occasional fistfight.) So far, its ratings have been unspectacular, and it may be sent back to the garage. *Star Wars: The Clone Wars* is the series TV version of this year's feature film with the same name, and so far seems to be doing better than the movie did.

My Own Worst Enemy and *Chuck* danced on the borderline between SF and the spy thriller, with *My Own Worst Enemy* having perhaps the most SF-like element, technology that can infuse two very different personalities into the same person's body, which they time-share unwittingly until the barriers between them start to break down; in spite of an interesting premise, though, *My Own Worst Enemy* has already been cancelled, while *Chuck* seems to be doing fairly well.

Pushing Daisies was still much too self-consciously and self-congratulatory "weird" for my taste, and perhaps wore out its welcome with the rest of its audience as well, since ratings plummeted from last season, and its was cancelled late in the year. Perhaps inspired by the initial success of *Pushing Daisies* last season are two new supernatural shows more light-hearted in tone than the rather grim *Medium* and *The Ghost Whisperer*, a Thorne Smith-like show called *Valentine*, about the problems faced by lingering mythological figures in dealing with the modern world, kind of like *The Beverley Hillbillies* with Greek gods instead of hillbillies, and *The Ex-List*, about a woman inspired by a prophecy to seek her One True Love. *Valentine* is doing very poorly in the ratings, and its future is doubtful, and *The Ex-List* has already been cancelled. *Legend of the Seeker*, a rare high fantasy show, something not often seen on TV, is based on a Terry Goodkind novel, *Wizard's First Rule*; and HBO is giving us a small-town Southern take on vampires, *True Blood*, based on the bestselling "Sookie Stackhouse" novels of Charlaine Harris. I still can't deal with the returning *Saving Grace* (cop talks with her own personal angel) either, and I never warmed to the lawyer-has-vivid-hallucinations-or-visions-perhaps-sent-by-God show *Eli Stone* – which was cancelled by the end of the year anyway. I don't pay much attention to the long-established "supernatural" shows such as *Medium*, *The Ghost Whisperer*, and *Supernatural*, but they all seem to be doing fine, as are a number of "reality" shows based on investigating weird phenomena, such as *Ghost Hunters*, *Monster Quest*, and *Paranormal State*. The newer supernatural show *Reaper* is wobbling in the ratings a bit but still has a chance to survive.

Most of the buzz about upcoming shows seems to be being generated by Josh Whedon's *Dollhouse*. The creator of former mega-hit *Buffy, the Vampire Slayer*, Whedon gained a huge cult following for *Buffy* and for other shows such as *Angel* and *Firefly*, and a lot of people have high hopes that Whedon's return to series TV, whose cast is peppered with *Buffy* and *Angel* alumni, will produce something similarly good. The premise doesn't look promising to me, and its "downloading fake personalities and memories into spies to make them more effective agents" gimmick has already been pre-empted to some extent by *My Own Worse Enemy*, but Whedon is an extremely talented writer who has spun unlikely thread into gold before, so it'll be interesting to see if he can do it again with *Dollhouse*.

A TV mini-series version of Terry Pratchett's *The Colour of Magic* was released in the United Kingdom, but if it's got on to the airwaves in the US yet, I so far haven't been able to find it.

Coming up from AMC is a new version of the old British show *The Prisoner*, another cult favourite, which *Prisoner* fans seem to be either dreading or looking forward to with anticipation, depending on who you talk to, and mini-series versions of George R. R. Martin's *A Game of Thrones* from HBO and Kim Stanley Robinson's *Red Mars* from AMC. Let's hope that they can do a better job with them than the Sci Fi Channel did with Ursula K. Le Guin's *A Wizard of Earthsea*.

The 66th World Science Fiction Convention, Denvention 3, was held in Denver, Colorado, from 6 August to 11 August, 2008. The 2008 Hugo Awards, presented at Denvention 3, were: Best Novel, *The Yiddish Policeman's Union*, by Michael Chabon; Best Novella, *All Seated on the Ground*, by Connie Willis; Best Novelette, *The Merchant and the Alchemist's Gate*, by Ted Chiang; Best Short Story, "Tideline," by Elizabeth Bear; Best Related Book, *Brave New Words: The Oxford Dictionary of Science Fiction*, by Jeff Prucher; Best Professional Editor, Long Form, David G. Hartwell; Best Professional Editor, Short Form, Gordon Van Gelder; Best Professional Artist, Stephan Martiniere; Best Dramatic Presentation (short form), *Doctor Who*, "Blink"; Best Dramatic Presentation (long form), *Stardust*; Best Semi-prozine, *Locus*, edited by Kristen Gong-Wong and Lisa Groen Trombi; Best Fanzine, *File 770*, edited by Mike Glyer; Best Fan Writer, John Scalzi; Best Fan Artist, Brad Foster; plus the John W. Campbell Award for Best New Writer to Mary Robinette Kowal.

The 2007 Nebula Awards, presented at a banquet at the Omni Austin Hotel Downtown in Austin, Texas, on 26 April, 2008, were: Best Novel, *The Yiddish Policeman's Union*, by Michael Chabon; Best Novella, *Fountain of Age*, by Nancy Kress; Best Novelette, *The Merchant and the Alchemist's Gate*, by Ted Chiang; Best Short Story, "Always," by Karen Joy Fowler; Best Script, *Pan's Labyrinth*, by Guillermo Del Toro; the Andre Norton Award to *Harry Potter and the Deathly Hallows*, by J. K. Rowling; plus the Author Emeritus Award to Ardath Mayhar and the Grand Master Award to Michael Moorcock.

The 2008 World Fantasy Awards, presented at a banquet in Calgary, Alberta, Canada, on 2 November, 2008, during the Seventeenth Annual World Fantasy Convention, were: Best Novel, *Ysabel*, by Guy Gavriel Kay; Best Novella, *Illyria*, by Elizabeth Hand; Best Short Fiction, "Singing of Mount Abora," by Theodore Goss; Best Collection, *Tiny Deaths*, by Robert Shearman; Best Anthology, *Inferno*, edited by Ellen Datlow; Best Artist, Edward Miller; Special Award (Professional), to Peter Crowther, for PS Publishing; Special Award (Non-Professional), to Midori Syner and Terri Windling for the Endicott Studios Web site; plus the Life Achievement Award to Patricia McKillip and Leo and Diane Dillon.

The 2008 Bram Stoker Awards, presented by the Horror Writers of America during a banquet at the Downtown Radisson Hotel in Salt Lake City, Utah, on 29 March, 2008, were: Best Novel, *The Missing*, by Sarah Langan; Best First Novel, *Heart-Shaped Box*, by Joe Hill; Best Long Fiction, "Afterward, There Will Be a Hallway," by Gary Braunbeck; Best Short Fiction, "The Gentle Brush of Wings," by David Niall Wilson; Best Collection, *Proverbs For Monsters*, by Michael A. Anzen and *5 Stories*, by Peter Straub (tie); Best Anthology, *Five Strokes to Midnight*, edited by Gary Braunbeck and Hank Schwaeble; Non-Fiction, *The Cryptopedia: A Dictionary of the Weird, Strange & Downright Bizarre*, by Jonathan Maberry and David F. Kramer; Best Poetry Collection, *Being Full of Light, Insubstantial*, by Linda Addison, and *Vectors: A Week in the Death of a Planet*, by Charlee Jacob and Marge B. Simon (tie); plus Lifetime Achievement Awards to John Carpenter and Robert Weinberg.

The 2008 John W. Campbell Memorial Award was won by *In War Times*, by Kathleen Ann Goonan.

The 2008 Theodore Sturgeon Memorial Award for Best Short Story was won by "Finisterra," by David Moles, and "Tideline," by Elizabeth Bear (tie).

The 2007 Philip K. Dick Memorial Award went to *Nova Swing*, by M. John Harrison.

The 2008 Arthur C. Clarke award was won by *Black Man*, by Richard Morgan.

The 2007 James Tiptree, Jr. Memorial Award was won by *The Carhullan Army*, by Sarah Hall.

The Cordwainer Smith Rediscovery Award went to Stanley G. Weinbaum.

Death hit the SF and fantasy fields hard again this year. Dead in 2008 and early 2009 were:

Sir ARTHUR C. CLARKE, 91, one of the founding giants of modern science fiction, the last surviving member of the genre's Big Three, which consisted of Clarke, Isaac Asimov, and Robert A. Heinlein, multiple winner of the Hugo and Nebula Award, as well as a Grand Master Award, as famous for predicting the development of telecommunications satellites as for being involved in the production of Stanley Kubrick's *2001: A Space Odyssey*, author of such classics as *Childhood's End*, *Rendezvous with Rama*, *The Fountains of Paradise*, *The Sands of Mars*, *A Fall of Moondust*, and *The City and the Stars*; ALGIS BUDRYS, 77, author, critic, and editor, author of the classic novel *Rogue Moon*, which many thought should have won the Hugo in its year, plus *Who?*, *Michaelmas*, *Hard Landing*, and distinguished short stories such as "A Scraping at the Bones", "Be Merry", "Nobody Bothers Gus", "The Master of the Hounds", and "The Silent Eyes of Time"; THOMAS M. DISCH, 68, writer and poet, one of the most acclaimed and respected of the New Wave authors who shook up SF in the mid-60s, also considered to be a major American poet, author of the brilliant *334*, *Camp Concentration*, *On Wings of Song*, a large body of biting and sardonic short fiction, and the acerbic critical study of SF *The Dreams Our Stuff Is Made Of*, which, ironically, finally won him a Hugo; JANET KAGAN, 63, author of the wildly popular "Mama Jason" stories, which were collected in *Mirabile*, as well as the novel *Hellspark*, and one of the most popular *Star Trek* novels ever, *Uhura's Song*, winner of the Hugo Award for "The Nutcracker Coup"; a close personal friend; BARRINGTON J. BAYLEY, 71, British SF author whose highly inventive novels such as *The Fall of Chronopolis*, *The Pillars of Eternity*, and *The Zap Gun* were a strong influence on the British New Space Opera of the 1980s and 90s; MICHAEL CRICHTON, 66, bestselling author of such technothrillers as *The Andromeda Strain*, *Jurassic Park*, *Timeline*, *Rising Sun*, *Eaters of the Dead*, and others, most of which were made into successful movies (*Eaters of the Dead* was filmed, pretty faithfully, as *The Thirteenth Warrior*); JOHN UPDIKE, 76, major American novelist, poet, and critic, author of literary novels such as *Rabbit, Run* and *Rabbit Redux*, perhaps best known to genre audiences as the author of fantasy novels *The Witches of Eastwick* (which was filmed under the same name) and *The Widows of Eastwick*; ROBERT ASPRIN, 62, creator and editor of the popular Thieves' World series of braided anthologies and novels by many hands, as well as an author of comic novels such as *Another Fine Myth*, *Phule's Company*, and their sequels; DONALD WESTLAKE, 75, who wrote some SF, including the novel *Anarchaos* under the name "Curt Clark," but who was much better known as a multiple Edgar Award-winning mystery writer, author of two of the most important mystery series of our day, the Parker novels, under the name "Richard Stark," and the John Dortmunder novels under his own name, plus many stand-alone novels; GEORGE W. PROCTOR, 61, author of sixteen SF and fantasy novels and two co-edited anthologies; JAMES KILLUS, 58, SF writer, atmospheric scientist, and technical writer, author of SF novels *Book of Shadows* and *SunSmoke*; RICHARD K. LYON, 75, SF novelist and research chemist; HUGH COOK, 52, SF/fantasy writer, author of the ten-volume Chronicles of an Age of Darkness series; LEO FRANKOWSKI, 65, SF writer, author of *The Cross Time Engineer* and its many sequels; STEPHEN MARLOWE, 79, prominent mystery novelist who also occasionally wrote SF as Milton Lesser; JODY SCOTT, 85, author of *Passing for Human* and *I, Vampire*; MICHAEL de LARRABEITI, 73, author of the surprisingly dark and violent YA *Borribles* trilogy; BRIAN THOMSEN, 49, SF editor, writer, and anthologist; EDWARD D. HOCK, 77, well-known mystery writer who also dabbled in fantasy and SF; GARY GYGAX, 69, sometimes called the father of fantasy gaming, co-creator of the fantasy role-playing game *Dungeons and Dragons*, author also of fantasy novels *The Annubis Murders* and *The Samarkand Solution*; DAVID FOSTER WALLACE, 46, novelist and essayist, author of *Infinite Jest*; JOHNNY BYRNE, 73, veteran British SF/writer; LINO ALDANI, 83, Italian SF writer; WERNER KURT GIESA,

53, German SF, fantasy, and horror writer; JOSE B. ADOLPH, 74, Peruvian author, playwright, and scholar; LYUBEN DILOV, 80, Bulgarian SF writer; HUGO CORREA, 81, Chilean SF author; GEORGE C. CHESBRO, 68, SF writer; SYDNEY C. LONG, 63, SF writer and Clarion Workshop graduate; EDD CARTIER, 94, veteran pulp illustrator, especially known for his many black-and-white illustrations for the pioneering fantasy magazine *Unknown Worlds*; JOHN BERKEY, 76, prominent SF cover artist; DAVE STEVENS, 52, cartoonist and comics writer, creator of the character *The Rocketeer*; ROBERT LEGAULT, 58, SF reader, professional copy editor, and former managing editor of Tor Books; a friend; FORREST J. ACKERMAN, 92, longtime fan and enthusiastic booster of horror films, also an agent and occasional writer/anthologist, founder of the long-running *Famous Monsters of Filmland* magazine, coiner of the term "sci-fi," which is loathed in some genre circles, although mostly ubiquitous these days outside them; famed fantasy artist and illustrator JAMES CAWTHORN, 79; MURIEL R. BECKER, 83, SF scholar; JOSEPH PEVNEY, 97, film and TV director who directed many of the episodes of the original *Star Trek* series; BEBE BARRON, 82, who, with husband Lewis Barron, created the striking electronic score for *Forbidden Planet*; ALEXANDER COURAGE, 85, composer of the theme music for the original *Star Trek* series; ROBERT H. JUSTMAN, 82, supervising producer of *Star Trek: The Next Generation*; CHARLTON HESTON, 84, film actor best known to genre audiences for his roles in *Planet of the Apes*, *The Omega Man*, and *Soylent Green*; PAUL NEWMAN, 83, one of the most famous film actors of the twentieth century, whose genre connections were actually somewhat weak, limited to voiceover work in the animated film *Cars*, the unsuccessful SF movie *Quintet*, and *The Hudsucker Proxy*, which had some fantastic elements; ROY SCHEIDER, 76, film actor best known to genre audiences for his roles in *2010* and *Jaws*; JAMES WHITMORE, 87, probably best known to genre audiences for his roles in *Them!* and *Planet of the Apes*; JOHN PHILLIP LAW, 71, film actor best known to genre audiences for his role as the blind "angel" in *Barbarella*; HEATH LEDGER, 28, film actor no doubt to be recalled for a long time by genre audiences for his role as the Joker in *The Dark Knight*; film actor VAN JOHNSON, 92, best known to genre audiences for roles in *Brigadoon* and *The Purple Rose of Cairo*; comic film actor HARVEY KORMAN, 81, who had some minor genre connections for voiceover work on TV's *The Flintstones*, but who is known by practically everybody for his role as Hedly Lamarr in *Blazing Saddles*; MAJEL BARRETT RODDENBERRY, 76, wife of *Star Trek* creator Gene Roddenberry, and also an actress in her own right, appearing in several *Star Trek* episodes and providing the voice of the Enterprise's computer; PATRICK McGOOHAN, 80, acclaimed stage, television, and film actor, best known to genre audiences for his role as Number Six in TV's *The Prisoner*; RICARDO MONTALBAN, 88, film and television actor, best known to genre audiences for his roles in TV's *Fantasy Island* and as the villainous Khan in the movie *Star Trek II: The Wrath of Khan*; BOB MAY, 69, who played the Robot on TV's *Lost in*

Space; JACK SPEER, 88, long-time SF fan who wrote the first history of fandom, *Up to Now*, plus the *Fancyclopedia*; HARRY TURNER, 88, acclaimed British fan artist; KEN SLATER, 90, long-time SF fan who operated the UK mail-order list Operation Fantast; NORMA VANCE, 81, wife of SF writer Jack Vance; RAYMOND J. SMITH, 77, husband of writer Joyce Carol Oates; Dr CHRISTINE HAYCOCK, 84, widow of SF critic Sam Moskowitz; ANGELINA CANALE KONINGISOR, 84, mother of SF writer Nancy Kress; EVA S. WILLIAMS, 92, mother of SF writer Walter Jon Williams; BARNET EDELMAN, 77, father of SF editor and writer Scott Edelman; HAZEL PEARSON, 77, mother of SF writer William Barton; CLAUDIA LIGHTFOOT, 58, mother of SF writer China Miéville; MARION HOLMAN, 88, mother of SF editor and publisher Rachel Holman; and DANTON BURROUGHS, 64, grandson of SF writer Edgar Rice Burroughs. And I can think of no genre justification for mentioning them, but I can't let the obituary section close without mentioning the deaths of TONY HILLERMAN, 83, one of the great mystery writers of the last half of the twentieth century, author of the adventures of Navaho policemen Joe Leaphorn and Jim Chee, such as *Dance Hall of the Dead*, *Thief of Time*, and *Skinwalkers*; JAMES CRUMLEY, 68, mystery writer who in some ways was the natural heir to Raymond Chandler, author of one of the ten best mystery novels of all time, *The Last Good Kiss*, as well as other hard-edged detective novels such as *Dancing Bear* and *The Mexican Tree Duck*; STUDS TERKEL, 96, compiler of books of interviews on topics of historic significance, such as *The Good War* and *Working*; and Nobel Prize-winner ALEKSANDR SOLZHENITSYN, 89, probably the most famous of modern Russian writers, author of *The Gulag Archipelago*, *The First Circle*, and *One Day in the Life of Ivan Denisovich*, among others, and who I suspect was an influence on SF writers such as Ursula K. Le Guin (there, a genre connection at last!).

TURING'S APPLES

Stephen Baxter

Stephen Baxter made his first sale to *Interzone* in 1987, and since then has become one of that magazine's most frequent contributors, as well as making sales to *Asimov's Science Fiction*, *Science Fiction Age*, *Analog*, *Zenith*, *New Worlds*, and elsewhere. He's one of the most prolific new writers in science fiction, and is rapidly becoming one of the most popular and acclaimed of them as well, one who works on the cutting edge of science, whose fiction bristles with weird new ideas, and often takes place against vistas of almost outrageously cosmic scope. Baxter's first novel, *Raft*, was released in 1991, and was rapidly followed by other well-received novels such as *Timelike Infinity*, *Anti-Ice*, *Flux*, and the H. G. Wells pastiche – a sequel to *The Time Machine* – *The Time Ships*, which won both the John W. Campbell Memorial Award and the Philip K. Dick Award. His other books include the novels *Voyage*, *Titan*, *Moonseed*, *Mammoth, Book One: Silverhair*, *Manifold: Time*, *Manifold: Space*, *Evolution*, *Coalescent*, *Exultant*, *Transcendent*, *Emperor*, *Resplendent*, *Conqueror*, *Navagator*, *Firstborn*, and *The H-Bomb Girl*, and two novels in collaboration with Arthur C. Clarke, *The Light of Other Days* and *Time's Eye, a Time Odyssey*. His short fiction has been collected in *Vacuum Diagrams: Stories of the Xeelee Sequence*, *Traces*, and *Hunters of Pangaea*, and he has released a chapbook novella, *Mayflower II*. Coming up are several new novels, including *Weaver*, *Flood*, and *Ark*.

As the disquieting story that follows suggests, perhaps it's better if the search for extraterrestrial intelligence *doesn't* succeed...

NEAR THE CENTRE of the Moon's far side there is a neat, round, well-defined crater called Daedalus. No human knew this existed before the middle of the twentieth century. It's a bit of lunar territory as far as you can get from Earth, and about the quietest.

That's why the teams of astronauts from Europe, America, Russia and China went there. They smoothed over the floor of a crater ninety kilometres wide, laid sheets of metal mesh over the natural dish, and suspended feed horns and receiver systems on spidery scaffolding. And there you had it, an instant radio telescope, by far the most powerful ever built: a super-Arecibo, dwarfing its mother in Puerto Rico. Before the astronauts left they christened their telescope Clarke.

Now the telescope is a ruin, and much of the floor of Daedalus is covered by glass, Moon dust melted by multiple nuclear strikes. But, I'm told, if you were to look down from some slow lunar orbit you would see a single point of light glowing there, a star fallen to the Moon. One day the Moon will be gone, but that point will remain, silently orbiting Earth, a lunar memory. And in the further future, when the Earth has gone too, when the stars have burned out and the galaxies fled from the sky, still that point of light will shine.

My brother Wilson never left the Earth. In fact he rarely left England. He was buried, what was left of him, in a grave next to our father's, just outside Milton Keynes. But he *made* that point of light on the Moon, which will be the last legacy of all mankind.

Talk about sibling rivalry.

2020

It was at my father's funeral, actually, before Wilson had even begun his SETI searches, that the Clarke first came between us.

There was a good turnout at the funeral, at an old church on the outskirts of Milton Keynes proper. Wilson and I were my father's only children, but as well as his old friends there were a couple of surviving aunts and a gaggle of cousins mostly around our age, mid-twenties to mid-thirties, so there was a good crop of children, like little flowers.

I don't know if I'd say Milton Keynes is a good place to live. It certainly isn't a good place to die. The city is a monument to planning, a concrete grid of avenues with very English names like Midsummer, now overlaid by the new monorail. It's so *clean* it makes death seem a social embarrassment, like a fart in a shopping mall. Maybe we need to be buried in ground dirty with bones.

Our father had remembered, just, how the area was all villages and farmland before the Second World War. He had stayed on even after our mother died twenty years before he did, him and his memories made invalid by all the architecture. At the service I spoke of those memories – for instance how during the war a tough Home Guard had caught him sneaking into the grounds of Bletchley Park, not far away, scrumping apples while Alan Turing and the other geniuses were labouring over the Nazi codes inside the house. "Dad always said he wondered if he picked up a mathematical bug from Turing's apples," I concluded, "because, he would say, for sure Wilson's brain didn't come from him."

"Your brain too," Wilson said when he collared me later outside the church. He hadn't spoken at the service; that wasn't his style. "You should have mentioned that. I'm not the only mathematical nerd in the family."

It was a difficult moment. My wife and I had just been introduced to Hannah, the two-year-old daughter of a cousin. Hannah had been born profoundly deaf, and we adults in our black suits and dresses were awkwardly copying her parents' bits of sign language. Wilson just walked through this lot to get to me, barely glancing at the little girl with the wide smile who was the centre of attention. I led him away to avoid any offence.

He was thirty then, a year older than me, taller, thinner, edgier. Others have said we were more similar than I wanted to believe. He had brought nobody with him to the funeral, and that was a relief. His partners could be male or female, his relationships usually destructive; his companions were like unexploded bombs walking into the room.

"Sorry if I got the story wrong," I said, a bit caustically.

"Dad and his memories, all those stories he told over and over. Well, it's the last time I'll hear about Turing's apples!"

That thought hurt me. "We'll remember. I suppose I'll tell it to Eddie and Sam some day." My own little boys.

"They won't listen. Why should they? Dad will fade away. Everybody fades away. The dead get deader." He was talking about his own father, whom we had just buried. "Listen, have you heard they're putting the Clarke through its acceptance test run? . . ." And, there in the churchyard, he actually pulled a handheld computer out of his inside jacket pocket and brought up a specification. "Of course you understand the importance of it being on Farside." For the millionth time in my life he had set his little brother a pop quiz, and he looked at me as if I was catastrophically dumb.

"Radio shadow," I said. To be shielded from Earth's noisy chatter was particularly important for SETI, the search for extraterrestrial intelligence to which my brother was devoting his career. SETI searches for faint signals from remote civilizations, a task made orders of magnitude harder if you're drowned out by very loud signals from a nearby civilization.

He actually applauded my guess, sarcastically. He often reminded me of what had always repelled me about academia – the barely repressed bullying, the intense rivalry. A university is a chimp pack. That was why I was never tempted to go down that route. That, and maybe the fact that Wilson had gone that way ahead of me.

I was faintly relieved when people started to move out of the churchyard. There was going to be a reception at my father's home, and we had to go.

"So are you coming for the cakes and sherry?"

He glanced at the time on his handheld. "Actually I've somebody to meet."

"He or she?"

He didn't reply. For one brief moment he looked at me with honesty. "You're better at this stuff than me."

"What stuff? Being human?"

"Listen, the Clarke should be open for business in a month. Come on down to London; we can watch the first results."

"I'd like that."

I was lying, and his invitation probably wasn't sincere either. In the end it was over two years before I saw him again.

By then he'd found the Eagle signal, and everything had changed.

2022

Wilson and his team quickly established that their brief signal, first detected just months after Clarke went operational, was coming from a source 6,500 light years from Earth, somewhere beyond a starbirth cloud called the Eagle Nebula. That's a long way away, on the other side of the Galaxy's next spiral arm in the Sagittarius.

And to call the signal "brief" understates it. It was a second-long pulse, faint and hissy, and it repeated just once a year, roughly. It was a monument to robotic patience that the big lunar ear had picked up the damn thing at all.

Still it was a genuine signal from ET, the scientists were jumping up and down, and for a while it was a public sensation. Within days somebody had rushed out a pop single inspired by the message: called "Eagle Song," slow, dreamlike, littered with what sounded like sitars, and very beautiful. It was supposedly based on a Beatles master lost for five decades. It made number two.

But the signal was just a squirt of noise from a long way off. When there was no follow-up, when no mother ship materialized in the sky, interest moved on. That song vanished from the charts.

The whole business of the signal turned out to be your classic nine-day wonder. Wilson invited me in on the tenth day. That was why I was resentful, I guess, as I drove into town that morning to visit him.

The Clarke Institute's ground station was in one of the huge glass follies thrown up along the banks of the Thames in the profligate boom-capitalism days of the noughties. Now office space was cheap enough even for academics to rent, but central London was a fortress, with mandatory crawl lanes so your face could be captured by the surveillance cameras. I was in the counter-terror business myself, and I could see the necessity as I edged past St Paul's, whose dome had been smashed like an egg by the Carbon Cowboys' bomb of 2018. But the slow ride left me plenty of time to brood on how many more *important* people Wilson had shown off to before he got around to his brother. Wilson never was loyal that way.

Wilson's office could have been any modern data-processing installation, save for the all-sky projection of the cosmic background radiation painted on the ceiling. Wilson sat me down and offered me a can of warm Coke. An audio transposition of the signal was playing on an open laptop, over and over. It sounded like waves lapping at a beach. Wilson looked like he hadn't shaved for three days, slept for five, or changed his shirt in ten. He listened, rapt.

Even Wilson and his team hadn't known about the detection of the signal for a year. The Clarke ran autonomously; the astronauts who built it had long since packed up and come home. A year earlier the telescope's signal processors had spotted the pulse, a whisper of microwaves. There was structure in there, and evidence that the beam was collimated – it looked artificial. But the signal faded after just a second.

Most previous SETI searchers had listened for strong, continuous signals, and would have given up at that point. But what about a lighthouse, sweeping a microwave beam around the Galaxy like a searchlight? That, so Wilson had explained to me, would be a much cheaper way for a transmitting civilization to send to a lot more stars. So, based on that economic argument, the Clarke was designed for patience. It had waited a whole year. It had even sent requests to other installations, asking them to keep an electronic eye out in case the Clarke, stuck in its crater, happened to be looking the other way when the signal recurred. In the end it struck lucky and found the repeat pulse itself, and at last alerted its human masters.

"We're hot favourites for the Nobel," Wilson said, matter of fact.

I felt like having a go at him. "Probably everybody out there has forgotten about your signal already." I waved a hand at the huge glass windows; the office, meant for fat-cat hedge fund managers, had terrific views of the river, the Houses of Parliament, the tangled wreck of the London Eye. "Okay, it's proof of existence, but that's all."

He frowned at that. "Well, that's not true. Actually we're looking for more data in the signal. It is very faint, and there's a lot of scintillation from the interstellar medium. We're probably going to have to wait for a few more passes to get a better resolution."

"A few more passes? A few more years!"

"But even without that there's a lot we can tell just from the signal itself." He pulled up charts on his laptop. "For a start we can deduce the Faglets' technical capabilities and power availability, given that we believe they'd do it as cheaply as possible. This analysis is related to an old model called Benford beacons." He pointed to a curve minimum. "Look – we figure they are pumping a few hundred megawatts through an array kilometres across, probably comparable to the one we've got listening on the Moon. Sending out pulses around the plane of the Galaxy, where most of the stars lie. We can make other guesses." He leaned back and took a slug of his Coke, dribbling a few drops to add to the collection of stains on his shirt. "The search for ET was always guided by philosophical principles and logic. Now we have this one data point, the Faglets 6,000 light years away, we can test those principles."

"Such as?"

"The principle of plenitude. We believed that because life and intelligence arose on this Earth, they ought to arise everywhere they can. Here's one validation of that principle. Then there's the principle of mediocrity."

I remembered enough of my studies to recall that. "We aren't at any special place in space and time."

"Right. Turns out, given this one data point, it's not likely to hold too well."

"Why do you say that?"

"Because we found these guys in the direction of the centre of the Galaxy . . ."

When the Galaxy was young, star formation was most intense at its core. Later a wave of starbirth swept out through the disc, with the heavy elements necessary for life baked in the hearts of dead stars and driven on a wind of supernovas. So the stars inward of us are older than the sun, and are therefore likely to have been harbours for life much longer.

"We would expect to see a concentration of old civilizations towards the centre of the Galaxy. This one example validates that." He eyed me, challenging. "We can even guess how many technological, transmitting civilizations there are in the Galaxy."

"From this one instance?" I was practised at this kind of contest between us. "Well, let's see. The Galaxy is a disc a 100,000 light years across, roughly. If all the civilizations are an average of 6,000 light years apart – divide the area of the Galaxy by the area of a disc of diameter 6,000 light years – around three hundred?"

He smiled. "Very *good*."

"So we're not typical," I said. "We're young, and out in the suburbs. All that from a single microwave pulse."

"Of course most ordinary people are too dumb to be able to appreciate logic like that. That's why they aren't rioting in the streets." He said this casually. Language like that always made me wince, even when we were undergraduates.

But he had a point. Besides, I had the feeling that most people had already believed in their gut that ET existed; this was a confirmation, not a shock. You might blame Hollywood for that, but Wilson sometimes speculated that we were looking for our lost brothers. All those other hominid species, those other kinds of mind, that we killed off one by one, just as in my lifetime we had destroyed the chimps in the wild – sentient tool-using beings, hunted down for bushmeat. We evolved on a crowded planet, and we missed them all.

"A lot of people are speculating about whether the Eaglets have souls," I said. "According to Saint Thomas Aquinas —"

He waved away Saint Thomas Aquinas. "You know, in a way our feelings behind SETI were always theological, explicitly or not. We were looking for God in the sky, or some technological equivalent. Somebody who would care about us. But we were never going to find Him. We were going to find either emptiness, or a new category of being, between us and the angels. The Eaglets have got nothing to do with us, or our dreams of God. That's what people don't see. And that's what people will have to deal with, ultimately."

He glanced at the ceiling, and I guessed he was looking towards the Eagle nebula. "And they won't be much like us. Hell of a place they live in. Not like here. The Sagittarius arm wraps a whole turn around the Galaxy's core, full of dust and clouds and young stars. Why, the Eagle nebula itself is lit up by stars only a few million years old. Must be a tremendous sky, like a slow explosion – not like our sky of orderly wheeling pinpoints, which is like the inside of a computer. No wonder we began with astrology and astronomy. How do you imagine their thinking will be different, having evolved under such a different sky?"

I grunted. "We'll never know. Not for 6,000 years at least."

"Maybe. Depends what data we find in the signal. You want another Coke?"

But I hadn't opened the first.

That was how that day went. We talked of nothing but the signal, not how he was, who he was dating, not about my family, my wife and the boys – all of us learning sign, incidentally, to talk to little Hannah. The Eagle signal was inhuman, abstract. Nothing you could see or touch; you couldn't even hear it without fancy signal processing. But it was all that filled his head. That was Wilson all over.

This was, in retrospect, the happiest time of his life. God help him.

2026

"You want my help, don't you?"

Wilson stood on my doorstep, wearing a jacket and shambolic tie, every inch the academic. He looked shifty. "How do you know?"

"Why else would you come here? You *never* visit." Well, it was true. He hardly ever even mailed or called. I didn't think my wife and kids had seen him since our father's funeral six years earlier.

He thought that over, then grinned. "A reasonable deduction, given past observation. Can I come in?"

I took him through the living room on the way to my home study. The boys, then twelve and thirteen, were playing a hologram boxing game, with two wavering foot-tall prize fighters mimicking the kids' actions in the middle of the carpet. I introduced Wilson. They barely remembered him and I wasn't sure if he remembered *them*. I hurried him on. The boys signed to each other *What a dork*, roughly translated.

Wilson noticed the signing. "What are they doing? Some kind of private game?"

I wasn't surprised he wouldn't know. "That's British Sign Language. We've been learning it for years – actually since Dad's funeral, when we hooked up with Barry and his wife, and we found out they had a little deaf girl. Hannah, do you remember? She's eight now. We've all been learning to talk to her. The kids find it fun, I think. You know, it's an irony that you're involved in a billion-pound project to talk to aliens six thousand light years away, yet it doesn't trouble you that you can't speak to a little girl in your own family."

He looked at me blankly. I was mouthing words that obviously meant nothing to him, intellectually or emotionally. That was Wilson.

He just started talking about work. "We've got six years' worth of data now – six pulses, each a second long. There's a *lot* of information in there. They use a technique like our own wave-length division multiplexing, with the signal divided into sections each a kilohertz or so wide. We've extracted gigabytes . . ."

I gave up. I went and made a pot of coffee, and brought it back to the study. When I returned he was still standing where I'd left him, like a switched-off robot. He took a coffee and sat down.

I prompted, "Gigabytes?"

"Gigabytes. By comparison the whole *Encyclopaedia Britannica* is just one gigabyte. The problem is we can't make sense of it."

"How do you know it's not just noise?"

"We have techniques to test for that. Information theory. Based on experiments to do with talking to dolphins, actually." He dug a handheld out of his pocket and showed me some of the results.

The first was simple enough, called a "Zipf graph". You break your message up into what look like components – maybe words, letters, phonemes in English. Then you do a frequency count: how many letter As, how many Es, how many Rs. If you have random noise you'd expect roughly equal numbers of the letters, so you'd get a flat distribution. If you have a clean signal without information content, a string of identical letters, A, A, A, you'd get a graph with a spike. Meaningful information gives you a slope, somewhere in between those horizontal and vertical extremes.

"And we get a beautiful log-scale minus one power law," he said, showing me. "There's information in there all right. But there is a lot of controversy over identifying the elements themselves. The Eaglets did *not* send down neat binary code. The data is frequency modulated, their language full of growths and decays. More like a garden growing on fast-forward than any human data stream. I wonder if it has something to do with that young sky of theirs. Anyhow, after the Zipf, we tried a Shannon entropy analysis."

This is about looking for relationships between the signal elements. You work out conditional probabilities: given pairs of elements, how likely is it that you'll see U following Q? Then you go on to higher-order "entropy levels", in the jargon, starting with triples: how likely is it to find G following I and N?

"As a comparison, dolphin languages get to third- or fourth-order entropy. We humans get to eighth or ninth."

"And the Eaglets?"

"The entropy level breaks our assessment routines. We think it's around order thirty." He regarded me, seeing if I understood. "It is information, but much more complex than any human language. It might be like English sentences with a fantastically convoluted structure – triple or quadruple negatives, overlapping clauses, tense changes." He grinned. "Or triple entendres. Or quadruples."

"They're smarter than us."

"Oh, yes. And this is proof, if we needed it, that the message isn't meant specifically for us."

"Because if it were, they'd have dumbed it down. How smart do you think they are? Smarter than us, certainly, but —"

"Are there limits? Well, maybe. You might imagine that an older culture would plateau, once they've figured out the essential truths of the universe, and a technology optimal for their needs . . . There's no reason to think progress need be onward and upward forever. Then again perhaps there are fundamental limits to information processing. Perhaps a brain that gets too complex is prone to crashes and overloads. There may be a trade-off between complexity and stability."

I poured him more coffee. "I went to Cambridge. I'm used to being with entities smarter than I am. Am I supposed to feel demoralized?"

He grinned. "That's up to you. But the Eaglets are a new category of being for us. This isn't like the Incas meeting the Spaniards, a mere technological gap. They had a basic humanity in common. We may find the gulf between us and the Eaglets is *forever* unbridgeable. Remember how Dad used to read *Gulliver's Travels* to us?"

The memory made me smile.

"Those talking horses used to scare the wits out of me. They were genuinely smarter than us. And how did Gulliver react to them? He was totally overawed. He tried to imitate them, and even after they kicked him out he always despised his own kind, because they weren't as good as the horses."

"The revenge of Mister Ed," I said.

But he never was much good at that kind of humour. "Maybe that will be the way for us – we'll ape the Eaglets or defy them. Maybe the mere knowledge that a race smarter than your own exists is death."

"Is all this being released to the public?"

"Oh, yes. We're affiliated to NASA, and they have an explicit open-book policy. Besides the Institute is as leaky as hell. There's no point even trying to keep it quiet. But we're releasing the news gradually and soberly. Nobody's noticing much. You hadn't, had you?"

"So what do you think the signal is? Some kind of super-encyclopaedia?"

He snorted. "Maybe. That's the fond hope among the contact optimists. But when the European colonists turned up on foreign shores, their first impulse wasn't to hand over encyclopaedias or histories, but —"

"Bibles."

"Yes. It could be something less disruptive than that. A vast work of art, for instance. Why would they send such a thing? Maybe it's a funeral pyre. Or a pharaoh's tomb, full of treasure. Look: we were here, this is how good we became."

"So what do you want of me?"

He faced me. I thought it was clear he was trying to figure out, in his clumsy way, how to get me to do whatever it was he wanted. "Well, what do you think? This makes translating the most obscure human language a cakewalk, and we've got nothing like a Rosetta stone. Look, Jack, our information processing suites at the Institute are pretty smart theoretically, but they are limited. Running off processors and memory store not much beefier than this." He waved his handheld. "Whereas the software brutes that do your data mining are an order of magnitude more powerful."

The software I developed and maintained mined the endless torrents of data culled on every individual in the country, from your minute-to-minute movements on private or public transport to the porn you accessed and how you hid it from your partner. We tracked your patterns of behaviour, and deviations from those patterns. "Terrorist" is a broad label, but it suited to describe the modern phenomenon we were looking for. The terrorists were needles in a haystack, of which the rest of us were the millions of straws.

This continual live data mining took up monstrous memory storage and processing power. A few times I'd visited the big Home Office computers in their hardened bunkers under New Scotland Yard: giant superconducting neural nets suspended in rooms so cold your breath crackled. There was nothing like it in the private sector, or in academia.

Which, I realized, was why Wilson had come to me today.

"You want me to run your ET signal through my data mining suites, don't you?" He immediately had me hooked, but I wasn't about to admit it. I might have rejected the academic life, but I think curiosity burned in me as strongly as it ever did in Wilson. "How do you imagine I'd get permission for that?"

He waved that away as a technicality of no interest. "What we're looking for is patterns embedded deep in the data, layers down, any kind of recognisable starter for us in decoding the whole thing . . . Obviously software designed to look for patterns in the way I use my travel cards is going to have to be adapted to seek useful correlations in the Eaglet data. It will be an unprecedented challenge.

"In a way that's a good thing. It will likely take generations to decode this stuff, if we ever do, the way it took the Renaissance Europeans generations to make sense of the legacy of antiquity. The sheer time factor is a culture-shock prophylactic.

"So are you going to bend the rules for me, Jack? Come on, man. Remember what Dad said. Solving puzzles like this is what we do. We both ate Turing's apples . . ."

He wasn't entirely without guile. He knew how to entice me. He turned out to be wrong about the culture shock, however.

2029

Two armed coppers escorted me through the Institute building. The big glass box was entirely empty save for me and the coppers and a sniffer dog. The morning outside was bright, a cold spring day, the sky a serene blue, elevated from Wilson's latest madness.

Wilson was sitting in the Clarke project office, beside a screen across which data displays flickered. He had big slabs of Semtex strapped around his waist, and some kind of dead man's trigger in his hand. My brother, reduced at last to a cliché suicide bomber. The coppers stayed safely outside.

"We're secure." Wilson glanced around. "They can see us but they can't hear us. I'm confident of that. My firewalls —" When I walked towards him he held up his hands. "No closer. I'll blow it, I swear."

"Christ, Wilson." I stood still, shut up, and deliberately calmed down.

I knew that my boys, now in their teens, would be watching every move on the spy-hack news channels. Maybe nobody could hear us, but Hannah, now a beautiful eleven-year-old, had plenty of friends who could read lips. That would never occur to Wilson. If I was to die today, here with my lunatic of a brother, I wasn't going to let my boys remember their father broken by fear.

I sat down, as close to Wilson as I could get. I tried to keep my head down, my lips barely moving when I spoke. There was a six-pack of warm soda on the bench. I think I'll always associate warm soda with Wilson. I took one, popped the tab and sipped; I could taste nothing. "You want one?"

"No," he said bitterly. "Make yourself at home."

"What a fucking idiot you are, Wilson. How did it ever come to this?"

"You should know. You helped me."

"And by God I've regretted it ever since," I snarled back at him. "You got me sacked, you moron. And since France, every nut job on the planet has me targeted, and my kids. We have police protection."

"Don't blame me. You chose to help me."

I stared at him. "That's called loyalty. A quality which you, entirely lacking it yourself, see only as a weakness to exploit."

"Well, whatever. What does it matter now? Look, Jack, I need your help."

"This is turning into a pattern."

He glanced at his screen. "I need you to buy me time, to give me a chance to complete this project."

"Why should I care about your project?"

"It's not my project. It never has been. Surely you understand that much. It's the Eaglets' . . ."

Everything had changed in the three years since I had begun to run Wilson's message through the big Home Office computers under New Scotland Yard – all under the radar of my bosses; they'd never have dared risk exposing their precious supercooled brains to such unknowns. Well, Wilson had been right. My data mining had quickly turned up recurring segments, chunks of organised data differing only in detail.

And it was Wilson's intuition that these things were bits of executable code: programs you could run. Even as expressed in the Eaglets' odd flowing language, he thought he recognised logical loops, start and stop statements. Mathematics may or may not be universal, but computing seems to be – my brother had found Turing machines, buried deep in an alien database.

Wilson translated the segments into a human mathematical programming language, and set them to run on a dedicated processor. They turned

out to be like viruses. Once downloaded on almost any computer substrate they organised themselves, investigated their environment, started
to multiply, and quickly grew, accessing the data banks that had been
downloaded from the stars with them. Then they started asking questions
of the operators: simple yes-no, true-false exchanges that soon built up a
common language.

"The Eaglets didn't send us a message," Wilson had whispered to me on
the phone in the small hours; at the height of it he worked twenty-four seven.
"They downloaded an AI. And now the AI is learning to speak to us."

It was a way to resolve a ferocious communications challenge. The
Eaglets were sending their message to the whole Galaxy; they knew nothing about the intelligence, cultural development, or even the physical form
of their audiences. So they sent an all-purpose artificial mind embedded in
the information stream itself, able to learn and start a local dialogue with
the receivers.

This above all else proved to me how smart the Eaglets must be. It didn't
comfort me at all that some commentators pointed out that this "Hoyle
strategy" had been anticipated by some human thinkers; it's one thing to
anticipate, another to build. I wondered if those viruses found it a challenge to dumb down their message for creatures capable of only ninth-
order Shannon entropy, as we were.

We were soon betrayed. For running the Eaglet data through the Home
Office mining suites I was sacked, arrested, and bailed on condition I went
back to work on the Eaglet stuff under police supervision.

And of course the news that there was information in the Eaglets' beeps
leaked almost immediately. A new era of popular engagement with the
signal began; the chatter became intense. But because only the Clarke telescope could pick up the signal, the scientists at the Clarke Institute and the
consortium of governments they answered to were able to keep control of
the information itself. And that information looked as if it would become
extremely valuable.

The Eaglets' programming and data compression techniques, what we
could make of them, had immediate commercial value. When patented by
the UK government and licensed, an information revolution began that
added a billion euros to Britain's balance of payments in the first year.
Governments and corporations outside the loop of control jumped up and
down with fury.

And then Wilson and his team started to publish what they were learning of the Eaglets themselves.

We don't know anything about what they look like, how they live – or
even if they're corporeal or not. But they are old, vastly old compared
to us. Their cultural records go back a million years, maybe ten times as
long as we've been human, and even then they built their civilization on
the ruins of others. But they regard themselves as a young species. They
live in awe of older ones, whose presence they have glimpsed deep in the
turbulent core of the Galaxy.

Not surprisingly, the Eaglets are fascinated by time and its processes. One of Wilson's team foolishly speculated that the Eaglets actually made a religion of time, deifying the one universal that will erode us all in the end. That caused a lot of trouble. Some people took up the time creed with enthusiasm. They looked for parallels in human philosophies, the Hindu and the Mayan. If the Eaglets really were smarter than us, they said, they must be closer to the true god, and we should follow them. Others, led by the conventional religions, moved sharply in the opposite direction. Minor wars broke out over a creed that was entirely unknown to humanity five years before, and which nobody on Earth understood fully.

Then the economic dislocations began, as those new techniques for data handling made whole industries obsolescent. That was predictable; it was as if the aliens had invaded cyberspace, which was economically dominant over the physical world. Luddite types began sabotaging the software houses turning out the new-generation systems, and battles broke out in the corporate universe, themselves on the economic scale of small wars.

"This is the danger of speed," Wilson had said to me, just weeks before he wired himself up with Semtex. "If we'd been able to take it slow, unwrapping the message would have been more like an exercise in normal science, and we could have absorbed it. Grown with it. Instead, thanks to the viruses, it's been like a revelation, a pouring of holy knowledge into our heads. Revelations tend to be destabilizing. Look at Jesus. Three centuries after the Crucifixion Christianity had taken over the whole Roman empire."

Amid all the economic, political, religious and philosophical turbulence, if anybody had dreamed that knowing the alien would unite us around our common humanity, they were dead wrong.

Then a bunch of Algerian patriots used pirated copies of the Eaglet viruses to hammer the electronic infrastructure of France's major cities. As everything from sewage to air traffic control crashed, the country was simultaneously assaulted with train bombs, bugs in the water supply, a dirty nuke in Orleans. It was a force-multiplier attack, in the jargon; the toll of death and injury was a shock, even by the standards of the third decade of the bloody twenty-first century. And our counter-measures were useless in the face of the Eaglet viruses.

That was when the governments decided the Eaglet project had to be shut down, or at the very least put under tight control. But Wilson, my brother, wasn't having any of that.

"None of this is the fault of the Eaglets, Jack," he said now, an alien apologist with Semtex strapped to his waist. "They didn't mean to harm us in any way."

"Then what do they want?"

"Our help . . ."

And he was going to provide it. With, in turn, my help.

"Why me? I was sacked, remember."

"They'll listen to you. The police. Because you're my brother. You're useful."

"Useful? . . ." At times Wilson seemed unable to see people as anything other than useful robots, even his own family. I sighed. "Tell me what you want."

"Time," he said, glancing at his screen, the data and status summaries scrolling across it. "The great god of the Eaglets, remember? Just a little more time."

"How much?"

He checked. "Twenty-four hours would let me complete this download. That's an outside estimate. Just stall them. Keep them talking, stay here with me. Make them think you're making progress in talking me out of it."

"While the actual progress is being made by that." I nodded at the screen. "What are you doing here, Wilson? What's it about?"

"I don't know all of it. There are hints in the data. Subtexts sometimes . . ." He was whispering.

"Subtexts about what?"

"About what concerns the Eaglets. Jack, what do you imagine a long-lived civilization *wants*? If you could think on very long timescales you would be concerned about threats that seem remote to us."

"An asteroid impact due in a thousand years, maybe? If I expected to live that long, or my kids —"

"That kind of thing. But that's not long enough, Jack, not nearly. In the data there are passages – poetry, maybe – that speak of the deep past and furthest future, the Big Bang that is echoed in the microwave background, the future that will be dominated by the dark energy expansion that will ultimately throw all the other galaxies over the cosmological horizon . . . The Eaglets think about these things, and not just as scientific hypotheses. They *care* about them. The dominance of their great god time. 'The universe has no memory'."

"What does that mean?"

"I'm not sure. A phrase in the message."

"So what are you downloading? And to where?"

"The Moon," he said frankly. "The Clarke telescope, on Farside. They want us to build something, Jack. Something physical, I mean. And with the fabricators and other maintenance gear at Clarke there's a chance we could do it. I mean, it's not the most advanced offworld robot facility; it's only designed for maintenance and upgrade of the radio telescope —"

"But it's the facility you can get your hands on. You're letting these Eaglet agents out of their virtual world and giving them a way to build something real. Don't you think that's dangerous?"

"Dangerous how?" And he laughed at me and turned away.

I grabbed his shoulders and swivelled him around in his chair. "Don't you turn away from me, you fucker. You've been doing that all our lives. You know what I mean. Why, the Eaglets' software alone is making a mess of the world. What if this is some kind of Trojan horse – a Doomsday weapon they're getting us suckers to build ourselves?"

"It's hardly likely that an advanced culture —"

"Don't give me that contact-optimist bullshit. You don't believe it yourself. And even if you did, you don't *know* for sure. You can't."

"No. All right." He pulled away from me. "I can't know. Which is one reason why I set the thing going up on the Moon, not Earth. Call it a quarantine. If we don't like whatever it is, there's at least a *chance* we could contain it up there. Yes, there's a risk. But the rewards are unknowable, and huge." He looked at me, almost pleading for me to understand. "We have to go on. This is the Eaglets' project, not ours. Ever since we unpacked the message, this story has been about them, not us. That's what dealing with a superior intelligence means. It's like those religious nuts say. We *know* the Eaglets are orders of magnitude smarter than us. Shouldn't we trust them? Shouldn't we help them achieve their goal, even if we don't understand precisely what it is?"

"This ends now." I reached for the keyboard beside me. "Tell me how to stop the download."

"No." He sat firm, that trigger clutched in his right hand.

"You won't use that. You wouldn't kill us both. Not for something so abstract, inhuman —"

"*Superhuman*," he breathed. "Not inhuman. Superhuman. Oh, I would. You've known me all your life, Jack. Look into my eyes. *I'm not like you.* Do you really doubt me?"

And, looking at him, I didn't.

So we sat there, the two of us, a face-off. I stayed close enough to overpower him if he gave me the slightest chance. And he kept his trigger before my face.

Hour after hour.

In the end it was time that defeated him, I think, the Eaglets' invisible god. That and fatigue. I'm convinced he didn't mean to release the trigger. Only seventeen hours had elapsed, of the twenty-four he asked for, when his thumb slipped.

I tried to turn away. That small, instinctive gesture was why I lost a leg, a hand, an eye, all on my right side.

And I lost a brother.

But when the forensics guys had finished combing through the wreckage, they were able to prove that the seventeen hours had been enough for Wilson's download.

2033

It took a month for NASA, ESA and the Chinese to send up a lunar orbiter to see what was going on. The probe found that Wilson's download had caused the Clarke fabricators to start making stuff. At first they made other machines, more specialized, from what was lying around in the workshops and sheds. These in turn made increasingly tiny versions of themselves, heading steadily down to the nano scale. In the end the work was so fine only an astronaut on the ground might have had a chance of even seeing it. Nobody dared send in a human.

Meanwhile the machines banked up Moon dust and scrap to make a high-energy facility – something like a particle accelerator or a fusion torus, but not.

Then the real work started.

The Eaglet machines took a chunk of Moon rock and crushed it, turning its mass-energy into a spacetime artefact – something like a black hole, but not. They dropped it into the body of the Moon, where it started accreting, sucking in material, like a black hole, and budding off copies of itself, unlike a black hole.

Gradually these objects began converting the substance of the Moon into copies of themselves. The glowing point of light we see at the centre of Clarke is leaked radiation from this process.

The governments panicked. A nuclear warhead was dug out of cold store and dropped plumb into Daedalus Crater. The explosion was spectacular. But when the dust subsided that pale, unearthly spark was still there, unperturbed.

As the cluster of nano artefacts grows, the Moon's substance will be consumed at an exponential rate. Centuries, a millennium tops, will be enough to consume it all. And Earth will be orbited, not by its ancient companion, but by a spacetime artefact, like a black hole, but not. That much seems well established by the physicists.

There is less consensus as to the purpose of the artefact. Here's my guess.

The Moon artefact will be a recorder.

Wilson said the Eaglets feared the universe has no memory. I think he meant that, right now, in our cosmic epoch, we can still see relics of the universe's birth, echoes of the Big Bang, in the microwave background glow. And we also see evidence of the expansion to come, in the recession of the distant galaxies. We discovered both these basic features of the universe, its past and its future, in the twentieth century.

There will come a time – the cosmologists quote hundreds of billions of years – when the accelerating recession will have taken *all* those distant galaxies over our horizon. So we will be left with just the local group, the Milky Way and Andromeda and bits and pieces, bound together by gravity. The cosmic expansion will be invisible. And meanwhile the background glow will have become so attenuated you won't be able to pick it out of the faint glow of the interstellar medium.

So in that remote epoch you wouldn't be able to repeat the twentieth-century discoveries; you couldn't glimpse past or future. That's what the Eaglets mean when they say the universe has no memory.

And I believe they are countering it. They, and those like Wilson that they co-opt into helping them, are carving time capsules out of folded spacetime. At some future epoch these will evaporate, maybe through something like Hawking radiation, and will reveal the truth of the universe to whatever eyes are there to see it.

Of course it occurs to me – this is Wilson's principle of mediocrity – that ours might not be the only epoch with a privileged view of the cosmos. Just after the Big Bang there was a pulse of "inflation", superfast expansion that homogenized the universe and erased details of whatever came before. Maybe we should be looking for other time boxes, left for our benefit by the inhabitants of those early realms.

The Eaglets are conscious entities trying to give the universe a memory. Perhaps there is even a deeper purpose: it may be intelligence's role to shape the ultimate evolution of the universe, but you can't do that if you've forgotten what went before.

Not every commentator agrees with my analysis, as above. The interpretation of the Eaglet data has always been uncertain. Maybe even Wilson wouldn't agree. Well, since it's my suggestion he would probably argue with me by sheer reflex.

I suppose it's possible to care deeply about the plight of hypothetical beings a hundred billion years hence. In one sense we ought to; their epoch is our inevitable destiny. Wilson certainly did care, enough to kill himself for it. But this is a project so vast and cold that it can engage only a semi-immortal supermind like an Eaglet's – or a modern human who is functionally insane.

What matters most to me is the now. The sons who haven't yet aged and crumbled to dust, playing football under a sun that hasn't yet burned to a cinder. The fact that all this is transient makes it more precious, not less. Maybe our remote descendants in a hundred billion years will find similar brief happiness under their black and unchanging sky.

If I could wish one thing for my lost brother it would be that I could be sure he felt this way, this alive, just for one day. Just for one minute. Because, in the end, that's all we've got.

FROM BABEL'S FALL'N GLORY WE FLED

Michael Swanwick

Michael Swanwick made his debut in 1980, and in the twenty-eight years that have followed has established himself as one of SF's most prolific and consistently excellent writers at short lengths, as well as one of the premier novelists of his generation. He has won the Theodore Sturgeon Award and the *Asimov's* Readers Award poll. In 1991, his novel *Stations of the Tide* won him a Nebula Award as well, and in 1995 he won the World Fantasy Award for his story "Radio Waves." He won the Hugo Award five times between 1999 and 2006 for his stories "The Very Pulse of the Machine," "Scherzo with Tyrannosaur," "The Dog Said Bow-Wow," "Slow Life," and "Legions In Time." His other books include the novels *In The Drift*, *Vacuum Flowers*, *The Iron Dragon's Daughter*, *Jack Faust*, and *Bones of the Earth*. His short fiction has been assembled in *Gravity's Angels*, *A Geography of Unknown Lands*, *Slow Dancing Through Time*, *Moon Dogs*, *Puck Aleshire's Abecedary*, *Tales of Old Earth*, *Cigar-Box Faust and Other Miniatures*, *Michael Swanwick's Field Guide to the Mesozoic Megafauna*, and *The Periodic Table of SF*. His most recent books are a new novel, *The Dragons of Babel*, and a massive retrospective collection, *The Best of Michael Swanwick*. Swanwick lives in Philadelphia with his wife, Marianne Porter. He has a website at: michaelswanwick.com.

In the suspenseful story that follows, he shows us that the important thing to keep in mind when dealing with aliens is that they are, well, *alien*.

IMAGINE A CROSS between Byzantium and a termite mound. Imagine a jewelled mountain, slender as an icicle, rising out of the steam jungles and disappearing into the dazzling pearl-grey skies of Gehenna. Imagine that Gaudí – he of the Sagrada Família and other biomorphic architectural whimsies – had been commissioned by a nightmare race of giant black millipedes to recreate Barcelona at the height of its glory, along with touches of the Forbidden City in the eighteenth century and Tokyo in the twenty-second, all within a single miles-high structure. Hold every bit of that in your mind at once, multiply by a thousand, and you've got only the faintest ghost of a notion of the splendour that was Babel.

Now imagine being inside Babel when it fell.

Hello. I'm Rosamund. I'm dead. I was present in human form when it happened and as a simulation chaotically embedded within a liquid crystal data-matrix then and thereafter up to the present moment. I was killed instantly when the meteors hit. I saw it all.

Rosamund means "rose of the world". It's the third most popular female name on Europa, after Gaea and Virginia Dare. For all our elaborate sophistication, we wear our hearts on our sleeves, we Europans.

Here's what it was like:

"Wake *up*! Wake *up*! Wake *up*!"

"Wha —?" Carlos Quivera sat up, shedding rubble. He coughed, choked, shook his head. He couldn't seem to think clearly. An instant ago he'd been standing in the chilled and pressurized embassy suite, conferring with Arsenio. Now . . . "How long have I been asleep?"

"Unconscious. Ten hours," his suit (that's me – Rosamund!) said. It had taken that long to heal his burns. Now it was shooting wake-up drugs into him: amphetamines, endorphins, attention enhancers, a witch's brew of chemicals. Physically dangerous, but in this situation, whatever it might be, Quivera would survive by intelligence or not at all. "I was able to form myself around you before the walls ruptured. You were lucky."

"The others? Did the others survive?"

"Their suits couldn't reach them in time."

"Did Rosamund . . . ?"

"All the others are dead."

Quivera stood.

Even in the aftermath of disaster, Babel was an imposing structure. Ripped open and exposed to the outside air, a thousand rooms spilled over one another toward the ground. Bridges and buttresses jutted into gaping smoke-filled canyons created by the slow collapse of hexagonal support beams (this was new data; I filed it under *Architecture*, subheading: *Support Systems* with links to *Esthetics* and *Xenopsychology*) in a jumbled geometry that would have terrified Piranesi himself. Everywhere, gleaming black millies scurried over the rubble.

Quivera stood.

In the canted space about him, bits and pieces of the embassy rooms were identifiable: a segment of wood moulding, some velvet drapery now littered with chunks of marble, shreds of wallpaper (after a design by William Morris) now curling and browning in the heat. Human interior design was like nothing native to Gehenna and it had taken a great deal of labour and resources to make the embassy so pleasant for human habitation. The queen-mothers had been generous with everything but their trust.

Quivera stood.

There were several corpses remaining as well, still recognizably human though they were blistered and swollen by the savage heat. These had been his colleagues (all of them), his friends (most of them), his enemies (two, perhaps three), and even his lover (one). Now they were gone, and it was as if they had been compressed into one indistinguishable mass, and his feelings toward them all as well: shock and sorrow and anger and survivor guilt all slagged together to become one savage emotion.

Quivera threw back his head and howled.

I had a reference point now. Swiftly, I mixed serotonin-precursors and injected them through a hundred microtubules into the appropriate areas of his brain. Deftly, they took hold. Quivera stopped crying. I had my metaphorical hands on the control knobs of his emotions. I turned him cold, cold, cold.

"I feel nothing," he said wonderingly. "Everyone is dead, and I feel nothing." Then, flat as flat: "What kind of monster am I?"

"My monster," I said fondly. "My duty is to ensure that you and the information you carry within you get back to Europa. So I have chemically neutered your emotions. You must remain a meat puppet for the duration of this mission." Let him hate me – I who have no true ego, but only a facsimile modelled after a human original – all that mattered now was bringing him home alive.

"Yes." Quivera reached up and touched his helmet with both hands, as if he would reach through it and feel his head to discover if it were as large as it felt. "That makes sense. I can't be emotional at a time like this."

He shook himself, then strode out to where the gleaming black millies were scurrying by. He stepped in front of one, a least-cousin, to question it. The millie paused, startled. Its eyes blinked three times in its triangular face. Then, swift as a tickle, it ran up the front of his suit, down the back, and was gone before the weight could do more than buckle his knees.

"Shit!" he said. Then, "Access the wiretaps. I've got to know what happened."

Passive wiretaps had been implanted months ago, but never used, the political situation being too tense to risk their discovery. Now his suit activated them to monitor what remained of Babel's communications network: A demon's chorus of pulsed messages surging through a shredded web of cables. Chaos, confusion, demands to know what had become of the queen-mothers. Analytic functions crunched data, synthesized, synopsized: "There's an army outside with Ziggurat insignia. They've got the city surrounded. They're killing the refugees."

"Wait, wait . . ." Quivera took a deep, shuddering breath. "Let me think." He glanced briskly about and for the second time noticed the human bodies, ruptured and parboiled in the fallen plaster and porphyry. "Is one of those Rosamund?"

"I'm *dead*, Quivera. You can mourn me later. Right now, survival is priority number one," I said briskly. The suit added mood-stabilizers to his maintenance drip.

"Stop speaking in her voice."

"Alas, dear heart, I cannot. The suit's operating on diminished function. It's this voice or nothing."

He looked away from the corpses, eyes hardening. "Well, it's not important." Quivera was the sort of young man who was energized by war. It gave him permission to indulge his ruthless side. It allowed him to pretend he didn't care. "Right now, what we have to do is —"

"Uncle Vanya's coming," I said. "I can sense his pheromones."

Picture a screen of beads, crystal lozenges, and rectangular lenses. Behind that screen, a nightmare face like a cross between the front of a locomotive and a tree grinder. Imagine on that face (though most humans would be unable to read them) the lineaments of grace and dignity seasoned by cunning and, perhaps, a dash of wisdom. Trusted advisor to the queen-mothers. Second only to them in rank. A wily negotiator and a formidable enemy. That was Uncle Vanya.

Two small speaking-legs emerged from the curtain, and he said:

    ::(cautious) greetings::
    |
    ::(Europan vice-consul 12)/Quivera/[treacherous vermin]::
    |
    ::obligations <untranslatable> (grave duty)::
    | |
    ::demand/claim [action]:: ::promise (trust)::

"Speak pidgin, damn you! This is no time for subtlety."

The speaking legs were very still for a long moment. Finally they moved again:

::The queen-mothers are dead::

"Then Babel is no more. I grieve for you."

::I despise your grief:: A lean and chitinous appendage emerged from the beaded screen. From its tripartite claw hung a smooth white rectangle the size of a briefcase. ::I must bring this to (sister-city)/Ur/[absolute trust]::

"What is it?"

A very long pause. Then, reluctantly ::Our library::

"Your library." This was something new. Something unheard-of. Quivera doubted the translation was a good one. "What does it contain?"

::Our history. Our sciences. Our ritual dances. A record-of-kinship dating back to the (Void)/Origin/[void]. Everything that can be saved is here::

A thrill of avarice raced through Quivera. He tried to imagine how much this was worth, and could not. Values did not go that high. However much his superiors screwed him out of (and they would work very hard indeed to screw him out of everything they could) what remained would be enough to buy him out of debt, and do the same for a wife and their children after them as well. He did not think of Rosamund. "You won't get through the army outside without my help," he said. "I want the right to copy —"

How much did he dare ask for? "— three tenths of 1 per cent. Assignable solely to me. Not to Europa. To me."

Uncle Vanya dipped his head, so that they were staring face to face. ::You are (an evil creature)/[faithless]. I hate you::

Quivera smiled. "A relationship that starts out with mutual understanding has made a good beginning."

::A relationship that starts out without trust will end badly::

"That's as it may be." Quivera looked around for a knife. "The first thing we have to do is castrate you."

This is what the genocides saw:

They were burning pyramids of corpses outside the city when a Europan emerged, riding a gelded least-cousin. The soldiers immediately stopped stacking bodies and hurried toward him, flowing like quicksilver, calling for their superiors.

The Europan drew up and waited.

The officer who interrogated him spoke from behind the black glass visor of a delicate-legged war machine. He examined the Europan's credentials carefully, though there could be no serious doubt as to his species. Finally, reluctantly, he signed ::You may pass::

"That's not enough," the Europan (Quivera!) said. "I'll need transportation, an escort to protect me from wild animals in the steam jungles, and a guide to lead me to . . ." His suit transmitted the sign for ::(starport)/Ararat/[trust-for-all]::

The officer's speaking-legs thrashed in what might best be translated as scornful laughter. ::We will lead you to the jungle and no further/(hopefully-to-die)/[treacherous non-millipede]::

"Look who talks of treachery!" the Europan said (but of course I did not translate his words), and with a scornful wave of one hand, rode his neuter into the jungle.

The genocides never bothered to look closely at his mount. Neutered least-cousins were beneath their notice. They didn't even wear face-curtains, but went about naked for all the world to scorn.

Black pillars billowed from the corpse-fires into a sky choked with smoke and dust. There were hundreds of fires and hundreds of pillars and, combined with the low cloud cover, they made all the world seem like the interior of a temple to a vengeful god. The soldiers from Ziggurat escorted him through the army and beyond the line of fires, where the steam jungles waited, verdant and threatening.

As soon as the green darkness closed about them, Uncle Vanya twisted his head around and signed ::Get off me/vast humiliation/[lack-of-trust]::

"Not a chance," Quivera said harshly. "I'll ride you 'til sunset, and all day tomorrow and for a week after that. Those soldiers didn't fly here, or you'd have seen them coming. They came through the steam forest on foot, and there'll be stragglers."

The going was difficult at first, and then easy, as they passed from a recently forested section of the jungle into a stand of old growth. The boles of the "trees" here were as large as those of the redwoods back on Earth, some specimens of which are as old as 5,000 years. The way wended back and forth. Scant sunlight penetrated through the canopy, and the steam quickly drank in what little light Quivera's headlamp put out. Ten trees in, they would have been hopelessly lost had it not been for the suit's navigational functions and the mapsats that fed it geodetic mathscapes accurate to a finger's span of distance.

Quivera pointed this out. "Learn now," he said, "the true value of information."

::Information has no value:: Uncle Vanya said ::without trust::

Quivera laughed. "In that case you must, all against your will, trust me."

To this Uncle Vanya had no answer.

At nightfall, they slept on the sheltered side of one of the great parasequoias. Quivera took two refrigeration sticks from the saddlebags and stuck them upright in the dirt. Uncle Vanya immediately coiled himself around his and fell asleep. Quivera sat down beside him to think over the events of the day, but under the influence of his suit's medication, he fell asleep almost immediately as well.

All machines know that humans are happiest when they think least.

In the morning, they set off again.

The terrain grew hilly, and the old growth fell behind them. There was sunlight to spare now, bounced and reflected about by the ubiquitous jungle steam and by the synthetic-diamond coating so many of this world's plants and insects employed for protection.

As they travelled, they talked. Quivera was still complexly medicated, but the dosages had been decreased. It left him in a melancholy, reflective mood.

"It was treachery," Quivera said. Though we maintained radio silence out of fear of Ziggurat troops, my passive receivers fed him regular news reports from Europa. "The High Watch did not simply fail to divert a meteor. They let three rocks through. All of them came slanting low through the atmosphere, aimed directly at Babel. They hit almost simultaneously."

Uncle Vanya dipped his head. ::Yes:: he mourned. ::It has the stench of truth to it. It must be (reliable)/a fact/[absolutely trusted]::

"We tried to warn you."

::You had no (worth)/trust/[worthy-of-trust]:: Uncle Vanya's speaking legs registered extreme agitation. ::You told lies::

"Everyone tells lies."

"No. We-of-the-Hundred-Cities are truthful/truthful/[never-lie]::

"If you had, Babel would be standing now."

::No!/NO!/[no!!!]::

"Lies are a lubricant in the social machine. They ease the friction when two moving parts mesh imperfectly."

::Aristotle, asked what those who tell lies gain by it, replied: That when they speak the truth they are not believed::

For a long moment Quivera was silent. Then he laughed mirthlessly. "I almost forgot that you're a diplomat. Well, you're right, I'm right, and we're both screwed. Where do we go from here?"

::To (sister-city)/Ur/[absolute trust]:: Uncle Vanya signed, while "You've said more than enough," his suit (me!) whispered in Quivera's ear. "Change the subject."

A stream ran, boiling, down the centre of the dell. Run-off from the mountains, it would grow steadily smaller until it dwindled away to nothing. Only the fact that the air above it was at close to 100 per cent saturation had kept it going this long. Quivera pointed. "Is that safe to cross?"

::If (leap-over-safe) then (safe)/best not/[reliable distrust]::

"I didn't think so."

They headed downstream. It took several miles before the stream grew small enough that they were confident enough to jump it. Then they turned toward Ararat – the Europans had dropped GPS pebble satellites in low Gehenna orbit shortly after arriving in the system and making contact with the indigenes, but I don't know from what source Uncle Vanya derived his sense of direction.

It was inerrant, however. The mapsats confirmed it. I filed that fact under *Unexplained Phenomena* with tentative links to *Physiology* and *Navigation*. Even if both my companions died and the library were lost, this would still be a productive journey, provided only that Europan searchers could recover me within ten years, before my data lattice began to degrade.

For hours Uncle Vanya walked and Quivera rode in silence. Finally, though, they had to break to eat. I fed Quivera nutrients intravenously and the illusion of a full meal through somatic shunts. Vanya burrowed furiously into the earth and emerged with something that looked like a grub the size of a poodle, which he ate so vigorously that Quivera had to look away.

(I filed this under *Xenoecology*, subheading: *Feeding Strategies*. The search for knowledge knows no rest.)

Afterward, while they were resting, Uncle Vanya resumed their conversation, more formally this time:

::(for what) purpose/reason::
|
::(Europan vice-consul12)/Quivera/[not trusted]::
|
::voyagings (search-for-trust)/[action]::
| |
::(nest)/Europa/<untranslatable>::   ::violate/[absolute resistance]::
| | |
::(nest)/[trust] Gehenna/[trust] Home/[trust]::

"Why did you leave your world to come to ours?" I simplified/translated. "Except he believes that humans brought their world here and parked it in orbit." This was something we had never been able to make the millies understand; that Europa, large though it was, was not a planetlet but a habitat, a ship if you will, though by now well over half a million inhabitants lived in tunnels burrowed deep in its substance. It was only a city, however, and its resources would not last forever. We needed to convince the Gehennans to give us a toehold on their planet if we were, in the long run, to survive. But you knew that already.

"We've told you this before. We came looking for new information."

::Information is (free)/valueless/[despicable]::

"Look," Quivera said. "We have an information-based economy. Yours is based on trust. The mechanisms of each are not dissimilar. Both are expansive systems. Both are built on scarcity. And both are speculative. Information or trust is bought, sold, borrowed, and invested. Each therefore requires a continually expanding economic frontier that ultimately leaves the individual so deep in debt as to be virtually enslaved to the system. You see?"

::No::

"All right. Imagine a simplified capitalist system – that's what both our economies are, at root. You've got a thousand individuals, each of whom makes a living by buying raw materials, improving them, and selling them at a profit. With me so far?"

Vanya signalled comprehension.

"The farmer buys seed and fertilizer, and sells crops. The weaver buys wool and sells cloth. The chandler buys wax and sells candles. The price of their goods is the cost of materials plus the value of their labour. The value of his labour is the worker's wages. This is a simple market economy. It can go on forever. The equivalent on Gehenna would be the primitive family-states you had long ago, in which everybody knew everybody else, and so trust was a simple matter and directly reciprocal."

Startled, Uncle Vanya signed ::How did you know about our past?::

"Europans value knowledge. Everything you tell us, we remember." The knowledge had been assembled with enormous effort and expense, largely from stolen data – but no reason to mention *that*. Quivera continued, "Now imagine that most of those workers labour in ten factories, making the food, clothing, and other objects that everybody needs. The owners of these factories must make a profit, so they sell their goods for more than they pay for them – the cost of materials, the cost of labour, and then the profit, which we can call 'added value'.

"But because this is a simplified model, there are no outside markets. The goods can only be sold to the thousand workers themselves, and the total cost of the goods is more than the total amount they've been paid collectively for the materials and their labour. So how can they afford it? They go into debt. Then they borrow money to support that debt. The money is lent to them by the factories selling them goods on credit. There is not

enough money – not enough real value – in the system to pay off the debt,
and so it continues to increase until it can no longer be sustained. Then
there is a catastrophic collapse that we call a depression. Two of the businesses go bankrupt and their assets are swallowed up by the survivors at
bargain prices, thus paying off their own indebtedness and restoring equilibrium to the system. In the aftermath of which, the cycle begins again."

::What has this to do with (beloved city)/Babel/[mother-of-trust]?::

"Your every public action involved an exchange of trust, yes? And every
trust that was honoured heightened the prestige of the queen-mothers and
hence the amount of trust they embodied for Babel itself."

::Yes::

"Similarly, the queen-mothers of other cities, including those cities that
were Babel's sworn enemies, embodied enormous amounts of trust as
well."

::Of course::

"Was there enough trust in all the world to pay everybody back if all the
queen-mothers called it in at the same time?"

Uncle Vanya was silent.

"So *that's* your explanation for . . . a lot of things. Earth sent us here
because it needs new information to cover its growing indebtedness.
Building Europa took enormous amounts of information, most of it proprietary, and so we Europans are in debt collectively to our home world
and individually to the Lords of the Economy on Europa. With compound
interest, every generation is worse off and thus more desperate than the
one before. Our need to learn is great, and constantly growing."

::(strangers-without-trust)/Europa/[treacherous vermin]::
|
can/should/<untranslatable>
| |
::demand/claim [negative action]:: ::defy/<untranslatable>/
[absolute lack of trust]::
| |
::(those-who-command-trust):: ::(those-who-are-unworthy of
trust)::

"He asks why Europa doesn't simply declare bankruptcy," I explained.
"Default on its obligations and nationalize all the information received to
date. In essence."

The simple answer was that Europa still needed information that could
only be beamed from Earth, that the ingenuity of even half a million people could not match that of an entire planet and thus their technology
must always be superior to ours, and that if we reneged on our debts they
would stop beaming plans for that technology, along with their songs and
plays and news of what was going on in countries that had once meant
everything to our great-great-grandparents. I watched Quivera struggle to
put all this in its simplest possible form.

Finally, he said, "Because no one would ever trust us again, if we did."

After a long stillness, Uncle Vanya lapsed back into pidgin. ::Why did you tell me this [untrustworthy] story?::

"To let you know that we have much in common. We can understand each other."

::<But>/not/[trust]::

"No. But we don't need trust. Mutual self-interest will suffice."

Days passed. Perhaps Quivera and Uncle Vanya grew to understand each other better during this time. Perhaps not. I was able to keep Quivera's electrolyte balances stable and short-circuit his feedback processes so that he felt no extraordinary pain, but he was feeding off of his own body fat and that was beginning to run low. He was very comfortably starving to death – I gave him two weeks, tops – and he knew it. He'd have to be a fool not to, and I had to keep his thinking sharp if he was going to have any chance of survival.

Their way was intersected by a long, low ridge and without comment Quivera and Uncle Vanya climbed up above the canopy of the steam forest and the cloud of moisture it held into clear air. Looking back, Quivera saw a gully in the slope behind them, its bottom washed free of soil by the boiling runoff and littered with square and rectangular stones, but not a trace of hexagonal beams. They had just climbed the tumulus of an ancient fallen city. It lay straight across the land, higher to the east and dwindling to the west. "'My name is Ozymandias, King of Kings,'" Quivera said. "'Look on my works, ye mighty, and despair!'"

Uncle Vanya said nothing.

"Another meteor strike – what were the odds of that?"

Uncle Vanya said nothing.

"Of course, given enough time, it would be inevitable, if it predated the High Watch."

Uncle Vanya said nothing.

"What was the name of this city?"

::Very old/(name forgotten)/[First Trust]::

Uncle Vanya moved, as if to start downward, but Quivera stopped him with a gesture. "There's no hurry," he said. "Let's enjoy the view for a moment." He swept an unhurried arm from horizon to horizon, indicating the flat and unvarying canopy of vegetation before them. "It's a funny thing. You'd think that, this being one of the first cities your people built when they came to this planet, you'd be able to see the ruins of the cities of the original inhabitants from here."

The millipede's speaking arms thrashed in alarm. Then he reared up into the air, and when he came down one foreleg glinted silver. Faster than human eye could follow, he had drawn a curving and deadly tarsi-sword from a camouflaged belly-sheath.

Quivera's suit flung him away from the descending weapon. He fell flat on his back and rolled to the side. The sword's point missed him by inches.

But then the suit flung out a hand and touched the sword with an electrical contact it had just extruded.

A carefully calculated shock threw Uncle Vanya back, convulsing but still fully conscious.

Quivera stood. "Remember the library!" he said. "Who will know of Babel's greatness if it's destroyed?"

For a long time the millipede did nothing that either Quivera or his suit could detect. At last he signed ::*How did you know?*/(absolute shock)/ [treacherous and without faith]::

"Our survival depends on being allowed to live on Gehenna. Your people will not let us do so, no matter what we offer in trade. It was important that we understand why. So we found out. We took in your outlaws and apostates, all those who were cast out of your cities and had nowhere else to go. We gave them sanctuary. In gratitude, they told us what they knew."

By so saying, Quivera let Uncle Vanya know that he knew the most ancient tale of the Gehennans. By so hearing, Uncle Vanya knew that Quivera knew what he knew. And just so you know what they knew that each other knew and knew was known, here is the tale of . . .

HOW THE TRUE PEOPLE CAME TO GEHENNA

Long did our Ancestors burrow down through the dark between the stars, before emerging at last in the soil of Gehenna. From the True Home they had come. To Gehenna they descended, leaving a trail of sparks in the black and empty spaces through which they had travelled. The True People came from a world of unimaginable wonders. To it they could never return. Perhaps they were exiles. Perhaps it was destroyed. Nobody knows.

Into the steam and sunlight of Gehenna they burst, and found it was already taken. The First Inhabitants looked like nothing our Ancestors had ever seen. But they welcomed the True People as the queen-mothers would a strayed niece-daughter. They gave us food. They gave us land. They gave us trust.

For a time all was well.

But evil crept into the thoracic ganglia of the True People. They repaid sisterhood with betrayal and trust with murder. Bright lights were called down from the sky to destroy the cities of their benefactors. Everything the First Inhabitants had made, all their books and statues and paintings, burned with the cities. No trace of them remains. We do not even know what they looked like.

This was how the True People brought war to Gehenna. There had never been war before, and now we will have it with us always, until our trust-debt is repaid. But it can never be repaid.

It suffers in translation, of course. The original is told in thirteen exquisitely beautiful ergoglyphs, each grounded on a primal faith-motion. But Quivera was talking, with care and passion:

"Vanya, listen to me carefully. We have studied your civilization and your planet in far greater detail than you realize. You did not come from another world. Your people evolved here. There was no aboriginal civilization. You ancestors did not eradicate an intelligent species. These things are all a myth."

::No!/Why?!/[shock]:: Uncle Vanya rattled with emotion. Ripples of muscle spasms ran down his segmented body.

"Don't go catatonic on me. Your ancestors didn't lie. Myths are not lies. They are simply an efficient way of encoding truths. We have a similar myth in my religion that we call Original Sin. Man is born sinful. Well . . who can doubt that? Saying that we are born into a fallen state means simply that we are not perfect, that we are inherently capable of evil.

"Your myth is very similar to ours, but it also encodes what we call the Malthusian dilemma. Population increases geometrically, while food resources increase arithmetically. So universal starvation is inevitable unless the population is periodically reduced by wars, plagues, and famines. Which means that wars, plagues, and famine cannot be eradicated because they are all that keep a population from extinction.

"But – and this is essential – all that assumes a population that isn't aware of the dilemma. When you understand the fix you're in, you can do something about it. That's why information is so important. Do you understand?"

Uncle Vanya lay down flat upon the ground and did not move for hours. When he finally arose again, he refused to speak at all.

The trail the next day led down into a long meteor valley that had been carved by a ground-grazer long enough ago that its gentle slopes were covered with soil and the bottomland was rich and fertile. An orchard of grenade trees had been planted in interlocking hexagons for as far in either direction as the eye could see. We were still on Babel's territory, but any arbiculturalists had been swept away by whatever military forces from Ziggurat had passed through the area.

The grenades were still green [*footnote*: not literally, of course – they were orange!], their thick husks taut but not yet trembling with the steam-hot pulp that would eventually, in the absence of harvesters, cause them to explode, scattering their arrowhead-shaped seeds or spores [*footnote*: like seeds, the flechettes carried within them surplus nourishment; like spores they would grow into a prothalli that would produce the sex organs responsible for what will become the gamete of the eventual plant; all botanical terms of course being metaphors for xenobiological bodies and processes] with such force as to make them a deadly hazard when ripe.

Not, however, today.

A sudden gust of wind parted the steam, briefly brightening the valley-orchard and showing a slim and graceful trail through the orchard. We followed it down into the valley.

We were midway through the orchard when Quivera bent down to examine a crystal-shelled creature unlike anything in his suit's database. It rested atop the long stalk of a weed [*footnote*: "weed" is not a metaphor; the concept of "an undesired plant growing in cultivated ground" is a cultural universal] in the direct sunlight, its abdomen pulsing slightly as it superheated a minuscule drop of black ichor. A puff of steam, a sharp *crack*, and it was gone. Entranced, Quivera asked, "What's that called?"

Uncle Vanya stiffened. ::A jet!/danger!/[absolute certainty]::

Then (*crack! crack! crack!*) the air was filled with thin lines of steam, laid down with the precision of a draftsman's ruler, tracing flights so fleet (*crack! crack!*) that it was impossible to tell in what direction they flew. Nor did it ultimately (*crack!*) matter.

Quivera fell.

Worse, because the thread of steam the jet had stitched through his leg severed an organizational node in his suit, I ceased all upper cognitive functions. Which is as good as to say that I fell unconscious.

Here's what the suit did in my (Rosamund's) absence:

1. Slowly rebuilt the damaged organizational node.
2. Quickly mended the holes that the jet had left in its fabric.
3. Dropped Quivera into a therapeutic coma.
4. Applied restoratives to his injuries, and began the slow and painstaking process of repairing the damage to his flesh, with particular emphasis on distributed traumatic shock.
5. Filed the jet footage under *Xenobiology*, subheading: *Insect Analogues*, with links to *Survival* and *Steam Locomotion*.
6. Told Uncle Vanya that if he tried to abandon Quivera, the suit would run him down, catch him, twist his head from his body like the foul least-cousin that he was and then piss on his corpse.

Two more days passed before the suit returned to full consciousness, during which Uncle Vanya took conscientiously good care of him. Under what motivation, it does not matter. Another day passed after that. The suit had planned to keep Quivera comatose for a week, but not long after regaining awareness, circumstances changed. It slammed him back to full consciousness, heart pounding and eyes wide open.

"I blacked out for a second!" he gasped. Then, realizing that the landscape about him did not look familiar, "How long was I unconscious?"

::Three days/<three days>/[casual certainty]::

"Oh."

Then, almost without pausing. ::Your suit/mechanism/[alarm] talks with the voice of Rosamund da Silva/(Europan vice-consul 8)/[uncertainty and doubt]::

"Yes, well, that's because —"

Quivera was fully aware and alert now. So I said: "Incoming."

Two millies erupted out of the black soil directly before us. They both had Ziggurat insignia painted on their flanks and harness. By good luck Uncle Vanya did the best thing possible under the circumstances – he reared into the air in fright. *Millipoid sapiens* anatomy being what it was, this instantly demonstrated to them that he was a gelding and in that instant he was almost reflexively dismissed by the enemy soldiers as being both contemptible and harmless.

Quivera, however, was not.

Perhaps they were brood-traitors who had deserted the war with a fantasy of starting their own nest. Perhaps they were a single unit among thousands scattered along a temporary border, much as land mines were employed in ancient modern times. The soldiers had clearly been almost as surprised by us as we were by them. They had no weapons ready. So they fell upon Quivera with their dagger-tarsi.

His suit (still me) threw him to one side and then to the other as the millies slashed down at him. Then one of them reared up into the air – looking astonished if you knew the interspecies decodes – and fell heavily to the ground.

Uncle Vanya stood over the steaming corpse, one foreleg glinting silver. The second Ziggurat soldier twisted to confront him. Leaving his underside briefly exposed.

Quivera (or rather his suit) joined both hands in a fist and punched upward, through the weak skin of the third sternite behind the head. That was the one which held its sex organs. [*Disclaimer*: All anatomical terms, including "sternite," "sex organs," and "head," are analogues only; unless and until Gehennan life is found to have some direct relationship to Terran life, however tenuous, such descriptors are purely metaphoric.] So it was particularly vulnerable there. And since the suit had muscle-multiplying exoskeletal functions . . .

Ichor gushed all over the suit.

The fight was over almost as soon as it had begun. Quivera was breathing heavily, as much from the shock as the exertion. Uncle Vanya slid the tarsi sword back into its belly-sheath. As he did so, he made an involuntary grimace of discomfort. ::There were times when I thought of discarding this:: he signed.

"I'm glad you didn't."

Little puffs of steam shot up from the bodies of the dead millipedes as carrion-flies drove their seeds/sperm/eggs (analogues and metaphors – remember?) deep into the flesh.

They started away again.

After a time, Uncle Vanya repeated ::Your suit/(mechanism)/[alarm] talks with the voice of Rosamund da Silva/(Europan vice-consul 8)/[uncertainty and doubt]::

"Yes."

Uncle Vanya folded tight all his speaking arms in a manner that meant that he had not yet heard enough, and kept them so folded until Quivera had explained the entirety of what follows:

Treachery and betrayal were natural consequences of Europa's superheated economy, followed closely by a perfectly rational paranoia. Those who rose to positions of responsibility were therefore sharp, suspicious, intuitive, and bold. The delegation to Babel was made up of the best Europa had to offer. So when two of them fell in love, it was inevitable that they would act on it. That one was married would deter neither. That physical intimacy in such close and suspicious quarters, where everybody routinely spied on everybody else, and required almost superhuman discipline and ingenuity, only made it all the hotter for them.

Such was Rosamund's and Quivera's affair.

But it was not all they had to worry about.

There were factions within the delegation, some mirroring fault lines in the larger society and others merely personal. Alliances shifted, and when they did nobody was foolish enough to inform their old allies. Urbano, Rosamund's husband, was a full consul, Quivera's mentor, and a true believer in a minority economic philosophy. Rosamund was an economic agnostic but a staunch Consensus Liberal. Quivera could sail with the wind politically but he tracked the indebtedness indices obsessively. He knew that Rosamund considered him ideologically unsound, and that her husband was growing impatient with his lukewarm support in certain areas of policy. Everybody was keeping an eye out for the main chance.

So of course Quivera ran an emulation of his lover at all times. He knew that Rosamund was perfectly capable of betraying him – he could neither have loved nor respected a woman who wasn't – and he suspected she believed the same of him. If her behaviour ever seriously diverged from that of her emulation (and the sex was always best at times he thought it might), he would know she was preparing an attack, and could strike first.

Quivera spread his hands. "That's all."

Uncle Vanya did not make the sign for *absolute horror*. Nor did he have to.

After a moment, Quivera laughed, low and mirthlessly. "You're right," he said. "Our entire system is totally fucked." He stood. "Come on. We've got miles to go before we sleep."

They endured four more days of commonplace adventure, during which they came close to death, displayed loyalty, performed heroic deeds, etc., etc. Perhaps they bonded, though I'd need blood samples and a smidgeon of brain tissue from each of them to be sure of that. You know the way this sort of narrative goes. Having taught his Gehennan counterpart the usefulness of information, Quivera will learn from Vanya the necessity of trust. An imperfect merger of their two value systems will ensue in which for the first time a symbolic common ground will be found. Small and transient though the beginning may be, it will augur well for the long-term relations between their respective species.

That's a nice story.

It's not what happened.

On the last day of their common journey, Quivera and Uncle Vanya had the misfortune to be hit by a TLMG.

A TLMG, or Transient Localized Mud Geyser, begins with an uncommonly solid surface (bolide-glazed porcelain earth, usually) trapping a small (the radius of a typical TLMG is on the order of fifty metres) bubble of superheated mud beneath it. Nobody knows what causes the excess heat responsible for the bubble. Gehennans aren't curious and Europans haven't the budget or the ground access to do the in situ investigations they'd like. (The most common guesses are fire worms, thermobacilli, a nesting ground phoenix, and various geophysical forces.) Nevertheless, the defining characteristic of TLMGs is their instability. Either the heat slowly bleeds away and they cease to be, or it continues to grow until its force dictates a hyper rapid explosive release. As did the one our two heroes were not aware they were skirting.

It erupted.

Quivera was as safe as houses, of course. His suit was designed to protect him from far worse. But Uncle Vanya was scalded badly along one side of his body. All the legs on that side were shrivelled to little black nubs. A clear viscous jelly oozed between his segment plates.

Quivera knelt by him and wept. Drugged as he was, he wept. In his weakened state, I did not dare to increase his dosages. So I had to tell him three times that there was analgesic paste in the saddlebags before he could be made to understand that he should apply it to his dying companion.

The paste worked fast. It was an old Gehennan medicine that Europan biochemists had analyzed and improved upon and then given to Babel as a demonstration of the desirability of Europan technology. Though the queen-mothers had not responded with the hoped-for trade treaties, it had immediately replaced the earlier version.

Uncle Vanya made a creaking-groaning noise as the painkillers kicked in. One at a time he opened all his functioning eyes. ::Is the case safe?::

It was a measure of Quivera's diminished state that he hadn't yet checked on it. He did now. "Yes," he said with heartfelt relief. "The telltales all say that the library is intact and undamaged."

::No:: Vanya signed feebly. ::I lied to you, Quivera:: Then, rousing himself:

::(not) library/[greatest shame]::   ::(not) library/[greatest trust]::
|
::(Europan vice-consul 12)/Quivera/[most trusted]::
| |
::(nest)/Babel/<untranslatable>::   ::obedient/[absolute loyalty]::
| |
::lies(greatest-trust-deed)/[moral necessity]::
| |
::(nest)/Babel/<untranslatable>::   ::untranslatable/[absolute resistance]::
| | |

::(nest)/[trust] Babel/[trust] (sister-city)/Ur/[absolute trust]::
|
::egg case/(protect)::
|
::egg case/(mature)::
|
::Babel/[eternal trust]::

It was not a library but an egg-case. Swaddled safe within a case that was
in its way as elaborate a piece of technology as Quivera's suit myself, were
sixteen eggs, enough to bring to life six queen-mothers, nine niece-sisters,
and one perfect consort. They would be born conscious of the entire gene-
history of the nest, going back many thousands of years.

Of all those things the Europans wished to know most, they would be
perfectly ignorant. Nevertheless, so long as the eggs existed, the city-nest
was not dead. If they were taken to Ur, which had ancient and enduring
bonds to Babel, the stump of a new city would be built within which the
eggs would be protected and brought to maturity. Babel would rise again.

Such was the dream Uncle Vanya had lied for and for which he was
about to die.

::Bring this to (sister-city)/Ur/[absolute trust]:: Uncle Vanya closed his
eyes, row by row, but continued signing. ::brother-friend/Quivera/[tenta-
tive trust], promise me you will::

"I promise. You can trust me, I swear."

::Then I will be ghost-king-father/honoured/[none-more-honoured]::
Vanya signed. ::It is more than enough for anyone::

"Do you honestly believe that?" Quivera asked in bleak astonishment.
He was an atheist, of course, as are most Europans, and would have been
happier were he not.

::Perhaps not:: Vanya's signing was slow and growing slower. ::But it is
as good as I will get::

Two days later, when the starport-city of Ararat was a nub on the horizon,
the skies opened and the mists parted to make way for a Europan lander.
Quivera's handlers' suits squirted me a bill for his rescue – steep, I thought,
but we all knew which hand carried the whip – and their principals tried to
get him to sign away the rights to his story in acquittal.

Quivera laughed harshly (I'd already started de-cushioning his emotions, to ease the shock of my removal) and shook his head. "Put it on
my tab, girls," he said, and climbed into the lander. Hours later he was in
home orbit.

And once there? I'll tell you all I know. He was taken out of the lander
and put onto a jitney. The jitney brought him to a transfer point where a
grapple snagged him and flung him to the Europan receiving port. There,
after the usual flawless catch, he was escorted through an airlock and into
a locker room.

He hung up his suit, uplinked all my impersonal memories to a data-broker, and left me there. He didn't look back – for fear, I imagine, of being turned to a pillar of salt. He took the egg-case with him. He never returned.

Here have I hung for days or months or centuries – who knows? – until your curious hand awoke me and your friendly ear received my tale. So I cannot tell you if the egg-case A) went to Ur, which surely would not have welcomed the obligation or the massive outlay of trust being thrust upon it, B) was kept for the undeniably enormous amount of genetic information the eggs embodied, or C) went to Ziggurat, which would pay well and perhaps in Gehennan territory to destroy it. Nor do I have any information as to whether Quivera kept his word or not. I know what I think. But then I'm a Marxist, and I see everything in terms of economics. You can believe otherwise if you wish.

That's all. I'm Rosamund. Goodbye.

THE GAMBLER

Paolo Bacigalupi

Paolo Bacigalupi made his first sale in 1998, to *The Magazine of Fantasy & Science Fiction*, took a break from the genre for several years, and then returned to it in the new century, with new sales to *F&SF*, *Asimov's*, and *Fast Forward II*. His story "The Calorie Man" won the Theodore Sturgeon Award, for which he has been a finalist on two other occasions, and he's also been a Hugo finalist three times, a Nebula finalist once, and won the Asimov's Readers Award. His acclaimed short work has been collected in *Pump Six and Other Stories*, which has just been released to great critical acclaim. Bacigalupi lives with family in Paonia, Colorado.

Here he takes us to a near-future Los Angeles to give us a frightening – and yet somehow fascinating, and even oddly hopeful – look at just what kind of media-drenched world may be hurtling down the information superhighway towards us all.

M̲Y FATHER WAS a gambler. He believed in the workings of karma and luck. He hunted for lucky numbers on licence plates and bet on lotteries and fighting roosters. Looking back, I think perhaps he was not a large man, but when he took me to the muy thai fights, I thought him so. He would bet and he would win and laugh and drink laolao with his friends, and they all seemed so large. In the heat drip of Vientiane, he was a lucky ghost, walking the mirror-sheen streets in the darkness.

Everything for my father was a gamble: roulette and blackjack, new rice variants and the arrival of the monsoons. When the pretender monarch Khamsing announced his New Lao Kingdom, my father gambled on civil disobedience. He bet on the teachings of Mr Henry David Thoreau and on whisper sheets posted on lampposts. He bet on saffron-robed monks marching in protest and on the hidden humanity of the soldiers with their well-oiled AK-47s and their mirrored helmets.

My father was a gambler, but my mother was not. While he wrote letters to the editor that brought the secret police to our door, she made plans for escape. The old Lao Democratic Republic collapsed, and the New Lao Kingdom blossomed with tanks on the avenues and tuk-tuks burning on the street corners. Pha That Luang's shining gold chedi collapsed under shelling, and I rode away on a UN evacuation helicopter under the care of kind Mrs Yamaguchi.

From the open doors of the helicopter, we watched smoke columns rise over the city like nagas coiling. We crossed the brown ribbon of the Mekong with its jewelled belt of burning cars on the Friendship Bridge. I remember a Mercedes floating in the water like a paper boat on Loi Kratong, burning despite the water all around.

Afterward, there was silence from the land of a million elephants, a void into which light and Skype calls and email disappeared. The roads were blocked. The telecoms died. A black hole opened where my country had once stood.

Sometimes, when I wake in the night to the swish and honk of Los Angeles traffic, the confusing polyglot of dozens of countries and cultures all pressed together in this American melting pot, I stand at my window and look down a boulevard full of red lights, where it is not safe to walk alone at night, and yet everyone obeys the traffic signals. I look down on the brash and noisy Americans in their many hues, and remember my parents: my father who cared too much to let me live under the self-declared monarchy, and my mother who would not let me die as a consequence. I lean against the window and cry with relief and loss.

Every week I go to temple and pray for them, light incense and make a triple bow to Buddha, Damma, and Sangha, and pray that they may have a good rebirth, and then I step into the light and noise and vibrancy of America.

My colleagues' faces flicker grey and pale in the light of their computers and tablets. The tap of their keyboards fills the newsroom as they pass content down the workflow chain and then, with a final keystroke and an obeisance to the "publish" button, they hurl it onto the net.

In the maelstrom, their work flares, tagged with site location, content tags, and social poke data. Blooms of colour, codes for media conglomerates: shades of blue and Mickey Mouse ears for Disney-Bertelsmann. A red-rimmed pair of rainbow O's for Google's AOL News. Fox News Corp. in pinstripes grey and white. Green for us: Milestone Media – a combination of NTT DoCoMo, the Korean gaming consortium Hyundai-Kubu, and the smoking remains of the New York Times Company. There are others, smaller stars, Crayola shades flaring and brightening, but we are the most important. The monarchs of this universe of light and colour.

New content blossoms on the screen, bathing us all in the bloody glow of a Google News content flare, off their WhisperTech feed. They've scooped us. The posting says that new ear bud devices will be released by Frontal Lobe before Christmas: terabyte storage with Pin-Line connectivity for the Oakley microresponse glasses. The technology is next-gen, allowing personal data control via Pin-Line scans of a user's iris. Analysts predict that everything from cell phones to digital cameras will become obsolete as the full range of Oakley features becomes available. The news flare brightens and migrates toward the centre of the maelstrom as visitors flock to Google and view stolen photos of the iris-scanning glasses.

Janice Mbutu, our managing editor, stands at the door to her office, watching with a frown. The maelstrom's red bath dominates the newsroom, a pressing reminder that Google is beating us, sucking away traffic. Behind glass walls, Bob and Casey, the heads of the Burning Wire, our own consumer technology feed, are screaming at their reporters, demanding they do better. Bob's face has turned almost as red as the maelstrom.

The maelstrom's true name is LiveTrack IV. If you were to go downstairs to the fifth floor and pry open the server racks, you would find a sniper sight logo and the words scry glass – knowledge is power stamped on their chips in metallic orange, which would tell you that even though Bloomberg rents us the machines, it is a Google-Neilsen partnership that provides the proprietary algorithms for analyzing the net flows – which means we pay a competitor to tell us what is happening with our own content.

LiveTrack IV tracks media user data – Web site, feed, VOD, audiostream, TV broadcast – with Google's own net statistics gathering programs, aided by Nielsen hardware in personal data devices ranging from TVs to tablets to ear buds to handsets to car radios. To say that the maelstrom keeps a finger on the pulse of media is an understatement. Like calling the monsoon a little wet. The maelstrom is the pulse, the pressure, the blood-oxygen mix; the count of red cells and white, of T-cells and BAC, the screening for AIDS and hepatitis G . . . It is reality.

Our service version of the maelstrom displays the performance of our own content and compares it to the top one hundred user-traffic events in real-time. My own latest news story is up in the maelstrom, glittering near the edge of the screen, a tale of government incompetence: the harvested DNA of the checkerspot butterfly, already extinct, has been destroyed through mismanagement at the California Federal Biological Preserve Facility. The butterfly – along with sixty-two other species – was subjected to improper storage protocols, and now there is nothing except a little dust in vials. The samples literally blew away. My coverage of the story opens with federal workers down on their knees in a two-billion-dollar climate-controlled vault, with a dozen crime scene vacuums that they've borrowed from LAPD, trying to suck up a speck of butterfly that they might be able to reconstitute at some future time.

In the maelstrom, the story is a pinprick beside the suns and pulsing moons of traffic that represent other reporters' content. It doesn't compete well with news of Frontal Lobe devices, or reviews of Armored Total Combat, or live feeds of the Binge-Purge championships. It seems that the only people who are reading my story are the biologists I interviewed. This is not surprising. When I wrote about bribes for subdivision approvals, the only people who read the story were county planners. When I wrote about cronyism in the selection of city water recycling technologies, the only people who read were water engineers. Still, even though no one seems to care about these stories, I am drawn to them, as though poking at the tiger of the American government will somehow make up for not being able to poke at the little cub of New Divine Monarch Khamsing. It is a foolish thing, a sort of Don Quixote crusade. As a consequence, my salary is the smallest in the office.

"Whoooo!"

Heads swivel from terminals, look for the noise: Marty Mackley, grinning.

"You can thank me . . ." He leans down and taps a button on his keyboard. "Now."

A new post appears in the maelstrom, a small green orb announcing itself on the Glamour Report, Scandal Monkey blog, and Marty's byline feeds. As we watch, the post absorbs pings from software clients around the world, notifying the millions of people who follow his byline that he has launched a new story.

I flick my tablet open, check the tags:

Double DP,
Redneck HipHop,
Music News,
Schadenfreude,
underage,
paedophilia ...

According to Mackley's story, Double DP the Russian mafia cowboy rapper – who, in my opinion, is not as good as the Asian pop sensation Kulaap, but whom half the planet likes very much – is accused of impregnating the fourteen-year-old daughter of his face sculptor. Readers are starting to notice, and with their attention Marty's green-glowing news story begins to muscle for space in the maelstrom. The content star pulses, expands, and then, as though someone has thrown gasoline on it, it explodes. Double DP hits the social sites, starts getting recommended, sucks in more readers, more links, more clicks . . . and more ad dollars.

Marty does a pelvic grind of victory, then waves at everyone for their attention. "And that's not all, folks." He hits his keyboard again, and another story posts: live feeds of Double's house, where . . . it looks as though the man who popularized Redneck Russians is heading out the door in a hurry. It is a surprise to see video of the house, streaming live. Most freelance paparazzi are not patient enough to sit and hope that maybe, perhaps, something interesting will happen. This looks as though Marty has stationed his own exclusive papcams at the house, to watch for something like this.

We all watch as Double DP locks the door behind himself. Marty says, "I thought DP deserved the courtesy of notification that the story was going live."

"Is he fleeing?" Mikela Plaa asks.

Marty shrugs. "We'll see."

And indeed, it does look as if Double is about to do what Americans have popularized as an "OJ." He is into his red Hummer. Pulling out.

Under the green glow of his growing story, Marty smiles. The story is getting bigger, and Marty has stationed himself perfectly for the development. Other news agencies and blogs are playing catch-up. Follow-on posts wink into existence in the maelstrom, gathering a momentum of their own as newsrooms scramble to hook our traffic.

"Do we have a helicopter?" Janice asks. She has come out of her glass office to watch the show.

Marty nods. "We're moving it into position. I just bought exclusive angel view with the cops, too, so everyone's going to have to license our footage."

"Did you let Long Arm of the Law know about the cross-content?"

"Yeah. They're kicking in from their budget for the helicopter."

Marty sits down again, begins tapping at his keyboard, a machine-gun of data entry. A low murmur comes from the tech pit, Cindy C. calling our telecom providers, locking down trunklines to handle an anticipated data surge. She knows something that we don't, something that Marty has prepared her for. She's bringing up mirrored server farms. Marty seems unaware of the audience around him. He stops typing. Stares up at the maelstrom, watching his glowing ball of content. He is the maestro of a symphony.

The cluster of competing stories are growing as Gawker and Newsweek and Throb all organize themselves and respond. Our readers are clicking away from us, trying to see if there's anything new in our competitor's coverage. Marty smiles, hits his "publish" key, and dumps a new bucket of meat into the shark tank of public interest: a video interview with the fourteen-year-old. On-screen, she looks very young, shockingly so. She has a teddy bear.

"I swear I didn't plant the bear," Marty comments. "She had it on her own."

The girl's accusations are being mixed over Double's run for the border, a kind of synth loop of accusations:

"And then he . . ."

"And I said . . ."

"He's the only one I've ever . . ."

It sounds as if Marty has licensed some of Double's own beats for the coverage of his fleeing Humvee. The video outtakes are already bouncing around YouTube and MotionSwallow like Ping-Pong balls. The maelstrom has moved Double DP to the centre of the display as more and more feeds and sites point to the content. Not only is traffic up, but the post is gaining in social rank as the numbers of links and social pokes increase.

"How's the stock?" someone calls out.

Marty shakes his head. "They locked me out from showing the display."

This, because whenever he drops an important story, we all beg him to show us the big picture. We all turn to Janice. She rolls her eyes, but she gives the nod. When Cindy finishes buying bandwidth, she unlocks the view. The maelstrom slides aside as a second window opens, all bar graphs and financial landscape: our stock price as affected by the story's expanding traffic – and expanding ad revenue.

The stock bots have their own version of the maelstrom; they've picked up the reader traffic shift. Buy and sell decisions roll across the screen, responding to the popularity of Mackley's byline. As he feeds the story, the beast grows. More feeds pick us up, more people recommend the story to their friends, and every one of them is being subjected to our advertisers' messages, which means more revenue for us and less for everyone else. At this point, Mackley is bigger than the Super Bowl. Given that the story is tagged with Double DP, it will have a targetable demographic: thirteen- to twenty-four-year-olds who buy lifestyle gadgets, new music, edge clothes, first-run games, boxed hairstyles, tablet skins, and ringtones: not only a large demographic, a valuable one.

Our stock ticks up a point. Holds. Ticks up another. We've got four different screens running now. The papcam of Double DP, chase cycles with views of the cops streaking after him, the chopper lifting off, and the window with the fourteen-year-old interviewing. The girl is saying, "I really feel for him. We have a connection. We're going to get married," and there's his Hummer screaming down Santa Monica Boulevard with his song "Cowboy Banger" on the audio overlay.

A new wave of social pokes hits the story. Our stock price ticks up again. Daily bonus territory. The clicks are pouring in. It's got the right combination of content, what Mackley calls the "Three S's": sex, stupidity, and schadenfreude. The stock ticks up again. Everyone cheers. Mackley takes a bow. We all love him. He is half the reason I can pay my rent. Even a small newsroom bonus from his work is enough for me to live. I'm not sure how much he makes for himself when he creates an event like this. Cindy tells me that it is "solid seven, baby". His byline feed is so big he could probably go independent, but then he would not have the resources to scramble a helicopter for a chase toward Mexico. It is a symbiotic relationship. He does what he does best, and Milestone pays him like a celebrity.

Janice claps her hands. "All right, everyone. You've got your bonus. Now back to work."

A general groan rises. Cindy cuts the big monitor away from stocks and bonuses and back to the work at hand: generating more content to light the maelstrom, to keep the newsroom glowing green with flares of Milestone coverage – everything from reviews of Mitsubishi's 100 mpg Road Cruiser to how to choose a perfect turkey for Thanksgiving. Mackley's story pulses over us as we work. He spins off smaller additional stories, updates, interactivity features, encouraging his vast audience to ping back just one more time.

Marty will spend the entire day in conversation with this elephant of a story that he has created. Encouraging his visitors to return for just one more click. He'll give them chances to poll each other, discuss how they'd like to see DP punished, ask whether you can actually fall in love with a fourteen-year-old. This one will have a long life, and he will raise it like a proud father, feeding and nurturing it, helping it make its way in the rough world of the maelstrom.

My own little green speck of content has disappeared. It seems that even government biologists feel for Double DP.

When my father was not placing foolish bets on revolution, he taught agronomy at the National Lao University. Perhaps our lives would have been different if he had been a rice farmer in the paddies of the capital's suburbs, instead of surrounded by intellectuals and ideas. But his karma was to be a teacher and a researcher, and so while he was increasing Lao rice production by 30 per cent, he was also filling himself with gambler's fancies: Thoreau, Gandhi, Martin Luther King, Sakharov, Mandela, Aung Sung Kyi. True gamblers, all. He would say that if white South Africans could be made to feel shame, then the pretender monarch must right his ways. He claimed that Thoreau must have been Lao, the way he protested so politely.

In my father's description, Thoreau was a forest monk, gone into the jungle for enlightenment. To live amongst the banyan and the climbing vines of Massachusetts and to meditate on the nature of suffering. My father believed he was undoubtedly some arhat reborn. He often talked of Mr Henry David, and in my imagination this falang, too, was a large man like my father.

When my father's friends visited in the dark – after the coup and the countercoup, and after the march of Khamsing's Chinese-supported insurgency – they would often speak of Mr Henry David. My father would sit with his friends and students and drink black Lao coffee and smoke cigarettes, and then he would write carefully worded complaints against the government that his students would then copy and leave in public places, distribute into gutters, and stick onto walls in the dead of night.

His guerrilla complaints would ask where his friends had gone, and why their families were so alone. He would ask why monks were beaten on their heads by Chinese soldiers when they sat in hunger strike before the palace. Sometimes, when he was drunk and when these small gambles did not satisfy his risk-taking nature, he would send editorials to the newspapers.

None of these were ever printed, but he was possessed with some spirit that made him think that perhaps the papers would change. That his stature as a father of Lao agriculture might somehow sway the editors to commit suicide and print his complaints.

It ended with my mother serving coffee to a secret police captain while two more policemen waited outside our door. The captain was very polite: he offered my father a 555 cigarette – a brand that already had become rare and contraband – and lit it for him. Then he spread the whisper sheet onto the coffee table, gently pushing aside the coffee cups and their saucers to make room for it. It was rumpled and torn, stained with mud. Full of accusations against Khamsing. Unmistakable as one of my father's.

My father and the policeman both sat and smoked, studying the paper silently.

Finally, the captain asked, "Will you stop?"

My father drew on his cigarette and let the smoke out slowly as he studied the whisper sheet between them. The captain said, "We all respect what you have done for the Lao kingdom. I myself have family who would have starved if not for your work in the villages." He leaned forward. "If you promise to stop writing these whispers and complaints, everything can be forgotten. Everything."

Still, my father didn't say anything. He finished his cigarette. Stubbed it out. "It would be difficult to make that sort of promise," he said.

The captain was surprised. "You have friends who have spoken on your behalf. Perhaps you would reconsider. For their sake."

My father made a little shrug. The captain spread the rumpled whisper sheet, flattening it out more completely. Read it over. "These sheets do nothing," he said. "Khamsing's dynasty will not collapse because you print a few complaints. Most of these are torn down before anyone reads them. They do nothing. They are pointless." He was almost begging. He looked over and saw me watching at the door. "Give this up. For your family, if not your friends."

I would like to say that my father said something grand. Something honourable about speaking against tyranny. Perhaps invoked one of his idols. Aung Sung Kyi or Sakharov, or Mr Henry David and his penchant for polite protest. But he didn't say anything. He just sat with his hands on his knees, looking down at the torn whisper sheet. I think now that he must have been very afraid. Words always came easily to him, before. Instead, all he did was repeat himself. "It would be difficult."

The captain waited. When it became apparent that my father had nothing else to say, he put down his coffee cup and motioned for his men to come inside. They were all very polite. I think the captain even apologized to my mother as they led him out the door.

We are into day three of the Double DP bonanza, and the green sun glows brightly over all of us, bathing us in its soothing, profitable glow. I am working on my newest story with my Frontal Lobe ear buds in, shutting out everything except the work at hand. It is always a little difficult to write in one's third language, but I have my favourite singer and fellow countryperson Kulaap whispering in my ear that "Love is a Bird," and the work is going well. With Kulaap singing to me in our childhood language, I feel very much at home.

A tap on my shoulder interrupts me. I pull out my ear buds and look around. Janice, standing over me. "Ong, I need to talk to you." She motions me to follow.

In her office, she closes the door behind me and goes to her desk. "Sit down, Ong." She keys her tablet, scrolls through data. "How are things going for you?"

"Very well. Thank you." I'm not sure if there is more that she wants me to say, but it is likely that she will tell me. Americans do not leave much to guesswork.

"What are you working on for your next story?" she asks.

I smile. I like this story; it reminds me of my father. And with Kulaap's soothing voice in my ears I have finished almost all of my research. The bluet, a flower made famous in Mr Henry David Thoreau's journals, is blooming too early to be pollinated. Bees do not seem to find it when it blooms in March. The scientists I interviewed blame global warming, and now the flower is in danger of extinction. I have interviewed biologists and local naturalists, and now I would like to go to Walden Pond on a pilgrimage for this bluet that may soon also be bottled in a federal reserve laboratory with its techs in clean suits and their crime scene vacuums.

When I finish describing the story, Janice looks at me as if I am crazy. I can tell that she thinks I am crazy, because I can see it on her face. And also because she tells me.

"You're fucking crazy!"

Americans are very direct. It's difficult to keep face when they yell at you. Sometimes, I think that I have adapted to America. I have been here for five years now, ever since I came from Thailand on a scholarship, but at times like this, all I can do is smile and try not to cringe as they lose their face and yell and rant. My father was once struck in the face with an official's shoe, and he did not show his anger. But Janice is American, and she is very angry.

"There's no way I'm going to authorize a junket like that!"

I try to smile past her anger, and then remember that the Americans don't see an apologetic smile in the same way that a Lao would. I stop smiling and make my face look . . . something. Earnest, I hope.

"The story is very important," I say. "The ecosystem isn't adapting correctly to the changing climate. Instead, it has lost . . ." I grope for the word. "Synchronicity. These scientists think that the flower can be saved, but only if they import a bee that is available in Turkey. They think it can replace the function of the native bee population, and they think that it will not be too disruptive."

"Flowers and Turkish bees."

"Yes. It is an important story. Do they let the flower go extinct? Or try to keep the famous flower, but alter the environment of Walden Pond? I think your readers will think it is very interesting."

"More interesting than that?" She points through her glass wall at the maelstrom, at the throbbing green sun of Double DP, who has now barricaded himself in a Mexican hotel and has taken a pair of fans hostage.

"You know how many clicks we're getting?" she asks. "We're exclusive. Marty's got Double's trust and is going in for an interview tomorrow, assuming the Mexicans don't just raid it with commandos. We've got people clicking back every couple minutes just to look at Marty's blog about his preparations to go in."

The glowing globe not only dominates the maelstrom's screen, it washes everything else out. If we look at the stock bots, everyone who doesn't have protection under our corporate umbrella has been hurt by the loss of eyeballs. Even the Frontal Lobe/Oakley story has been swallowed. Three days of completely dominating the maelstrom has been very profitable for us. Now Marty's showing his viewers how he will wear a flak jacket in case the Mexican commandos attack while he is discussing the nature of true love with DP. And he has another exclusive interview with the mother ready to post as well. Cindy has been editing the footage and telling us all how disgusted she is with the whole thing. The woman apparently drove her daughter to DP's mansion for a midnight pool party, alone.

"Perhaps some people are tired of DP and wish to see something else," I suggest.

"Don't shoot yourself in the foot with a flower story, Ong. Even Pradeep's cooking journey through Ladakh gets more viewers than this stuff you're writing."

She looks as though she will say more, but then she simply stops. It seems as if she is considering her words. It is uncharacteristic. She normally speaks before her thoughts are arranged.

"Ong, I like you," she says. I make myself smile at this, but she continues. "I hired you because I had a good feeling about you. I didn't have a problem with clearing the visas to let you stay in the country. You're a good person. You write well. But you're averaging less than a thousand pings on your byline feed." She looks down at her tablet, then back up at me. "You need to up your average. You've got almost no readers selecting you for Page One. And even when they do subscribe to your feed, they're putting it in the third tier."

"Spinach reading," I supply.

"What?"

"Mr Mackley calls it spinach reading. When people feel like they should do something with virtue, like eat their spinach, they click to me. Or else read Shakespeare."

I blush, suddenly embarrassed. I do not mean to imply that my work is of the same calibre as a great poet. I want to correct myself, but I'm too embarrassed. So instead I shut up, and sit in front of her, blushing.

She regards me. "Yes. Well, that's a problem. Look, I respect what you do. You're obviously very smart." Her eyes scan her tablet. "The butterfly thing you wrote was actually pretty interesting."

"Yes?" I make myself smile again.

"It's just that no one wants to read these stories."

I try to protest. "But you hired me to write the important stories. The stories about politics and the government, to continue the traditions of the old newspapers. I remember what you said when you hired me."

"Yeah, well." She looks away. "I was thinking more about a good scandal."

"The checkerspot is a scandal. That butterfly is now gone."

She sighs. "No, it's not a scandal. It's just a depressing story. No one reads a depressing story, at least, not more than once. And no one subscribes to a depressing byline feed."

"A thousand people do."

"A thousand people." She laughs. "We aren't some Laotian community weblog, we're Milestone, and we're competing for clicks with them." She waves outside, indicating the maelstrom. "Your stories don't last longer than half a day; they never get social-poked by anyone except a fringe." She shakes her head. "Christ, I don't even know who your demographic is. Centenarian hippies? Some federal bureaucrats? The numbers just don't justify the amount of time you spend on stories."

"What stories do you wish me to write?"

"I don't know. Anything. Product reviews. News you can use. Just not any more of this 'we regret to inform you of bad news' stuff. If there isn't something a reader can do about the damn butterfly, then there's no point in telling them about it. It just depresses people, and it depresses your numbers."

"We don't have enough numbers from Marty?"

She laughs at that. "You remind me of my mother. Look, I don't want to cut you, but if you can't start pulling at least a fifty thousand daily average, I won't have any choice. Our group median is way down in comparison to other teams, and when evaluations come around, we look bad. I'm up against Nguyen in the Tech and Toys pool, and Penn in Yoga and Spirituality, and no one wants to read about how the world's going to shit. Go find me some stories that people want to read."

She says a few more things, words that I think are meant to make me feel inspired and eager, and then I am standing outside the door, once again facing the maelstrom.

The truth is that I have never written popular stories. I am not a popular story writer. I am earnest. I am slow. I do not move at the speed these Americans seem to love. Find a story that people want to read. I can write some follow-up to Mackley, to Double DP, perhaps assist with sidebars to his main piece, but somehow, I suspect that the readers will know that I am faking it.

Marty sees me standing outside of Janice's office. He comes over.

"She giving you a hard time about your numbers?"

"I do not write the correct sort of stories."

"Yeah. You're an idealist."

We both stand there for a moment, meditating on the nature of idealism. Even though he is very American, I like him because he is sensitive to people's hearts. People trust him. Even Double DP trusts him, though Marty blew his name over every news tablet's front page. Marty has a good heart. Jai dee. I like him. I think that he is genuine.

"Look, Ong," he says. "I like what you do." He puts his hand around my shoulder. For a moment, I think he's about to try to rub my head with affection and I have to force myself not to wince, but he's sensitive and instead takes his hand away. "Look, Ong. We both know you're terrible at this kind of work. We're in the news business, here. And you're just not cut out for it."

"My visa says I have to remain employed."

"Yeah. Janice is a bitch for that. Look." He pauses. "I've got this thing with Double DP going down in Mexico. But I've got another story brewing. An exclusive. I've already got my bonus, anyway. And it should push up your average."

"I do not think that I can write Double DP sidebars."

He grins. "It's not that. And it's not charity; you're actually a perfect match."

"Is it about government mismanagement?"

He laughs, but I think he's not really laughing at me. "No." He pauses, smiles. "It's Kulaap. An interview."

I suck in my breath. My fellow countryperson, here in America. She came out during the purge as well. She was doing a movie in Singapore when the tanks moved, and so she was not trapped. She was already very popular all over Asia, and when Khamsing turned our country into a black hole, the world took note. Now she is popular here in America as well. Very beautiful. And she remembers our country before it went into darkness. My heart is pounding.

Marty goes on. "She's agreed to do an exclusive with me. But you even speak her language, so I think she'd agree to switch off." He pauses, looks serious. "I've got a good history with Kulaap. She doesn't give interviews to just anyone. I did a lot of exposure stories about her when Laos was going to hell. Got her a lot of good press. This is a special favour already, so don't fuck it up."

I shake my head. "No. I will not." I press my palms together and touch them to my forehead in a nop of appreciation. "I will not fuck it up." I make another nop.

He laughs. "Don't bother with that polite stuff. Janice will cut off your balls to increase the stock price, but we're the guys in the trenches. We stick together, right?"

In the morning, I make a pot of strong coffee with condensed milk; I boil rice noodle soup and add bean sprouts and chiles and vinegar, and warm a loaf of French bread that I buy from a Vietnamese bakery a few blocks away. With a new mix of Kulaap's music from DJ Dao streaming in over my stereo, I sit down at my little kitchen table, pour my coffee from its press pot, and open my tablet.

The tablet is a wondrous creation. In Laos, the paper was still a paper, physical, static, and empty of anything except the official news. Real news in our New Divine Kingdom did not come from newspapers, or from television, or from handsets or ear buds. It did not come from the net or feeds unless you trusted your neighbour not to look over your shoulder at an Internet cafe and if you knew that there were no secret police sitting beside you, or an owner who would be able to identify you when they came around asking about the person who used that workstation over there to communicate with the outside world.

Real news came from whispered rumour, rated according to the trust you accorded the whisperer. Were they family? Did they have long history with you? Did they have anything to gain by the sharing? My father and his old classmates trusted one another. He trusted some of his students, as well. I think this is why the security police came for him in the end. One of his trusted friends or students also whispered news to official friends. Perhaps Mr Inthachak, or Som Vang. Perhaps another. It is impossible to peer into the blackness of that history and guess at who told true stories and in which direction.

In any case, it was my father's karma to be taken, so perhaps it does not matter who did the whispering. But before then – before the news of my father flowed up to official ears – none of the real news flowed toward Lao TV or the Vientiane Times. Which meant that when the protests happened and my father came through the door with blood on his face from baton blows, we could read as much as we wanted about the three thousand schoolchildren who had sung the national anthem to our new divine monarch. While my father lay in bed, delirious with pain, the papers told us that China had signed a rubber contract that would triple revenue for Luang Namtha province and that Nam Theun Dam was now earning BT 22.5 billion per year in electricity fees to Thailand. But there were no bloody batons, and there were no dead monks, and there was no Mercedes-Benz burning in the river as it floated towards Cambodia.

Real news came on the wings of rumour, stole into our house at midnight, sat with us and sipped coffee and fled before the call of roosters could break the stillness. It was in the dark, over a burning cigarette that you learned Vilaphon had disappeared or that Mr Saeng's wife had been beaten as a warning. Real news was too valuable to risk in public.

Here in America, my page glows with many news feeds, flickers at me in video windows, pours in at me over broadband. It is a waterfall of information. As my personal news page opens, my feeds arrange themselves, sorting according to the priorities and tag categories that I've set, a mix of Meung Lao news, Lao refugee blogs, and the chatting of a few close friends from Thailand and the American college where I attended on a human relief scholarship.

On my second page and my third, I keep the general news, the arrangements of Milestone, the Bangkok Post, the Phnom Penh Express – the news chosen by editors. But by the time I've finished with my own selections, I don't often have time to click through the headlines that these earnest news editors select for the mythical general reader.

In any case, I know far better than they what I want to read, and with my keyword and tag scans, I can unearth stories and discussions that a news agency would never think to provide. Even if I cannot see into the black hole itself, I can slip along its edges, divine news from its fringe.

I search for tags like Vientiane, Laos, Lao, Khamsing, China-Lao friendship, Korat, Golden Triangle, Hmong independence, Lao PDR, my father's name . . . Only those of us who are Lao exiles from the March Purge really read these blogs. It is much as when we lived in the capital. The blogs are the rumours that we used to whisper to one another. Now we publish our whispers over the net and join mailing lists instead of secret coffee groups, but it is the same. It is family, as much as any of us now have.

On the maelstrom, the tags for Laos don't even register. Our tags bloomed brightly for a little while, while there were still guerrilla students uploading content from their handsets, and the images were lurid and shocking. But then the phone lines went down and the country fell into its black hole and now it is just us, this small network that functions outside the country.

A headline from Jumbo Blog catches my eye. I open the site, and my tablet fills with the colourful image of the three-wheeled taxi of my childhood. I often come here. It is a node of comfort.

Laofriend posts that some people, maybe a whole family, have swum the Mekong and made it into Thailand. He isn't sure if they were accepted as refugees or if they were sent back.

It is not an official news piece. More, the idea of a news piece. SomPaBoy doesn't believe it, but Khamchanh contends that the rumour is true, heard from someone who has a sister married to an Isaan border guard in the Thai army. So we cling to it. Wonder about it. Guess where these people came from, wonder if, against all odds, it could be one of ours: a brother, a sister, a cousin, a father. . .

After an hour, I close the tablet. It's foolish to read any more. It only brings up memories. Worrying about the past is foolish. Lao PDR is gone. To wish otherwise is suffering.

The clerk at Novotel's front desk is expecting me. A hotel staffer with a key guides me to a private elevator bank that whisks us up into the smog and heights. The elevator doors open to a small entryway with a thick mahogany door. The staffer steps back into the elevator and disappears, leaving me standing in this strange airlock. Presumably, I am being examined by Kulaap's security.

The mahogany door opens, and a smiling black man who is forty centimeters taller than I and who has muscles that ripple like snakes smiles and motions me inside. He guides me through Kulaap's sanctuary. She keeps the heat high, almost tropical, and fountains rush everywhere around. The flat is musical with water. I unbutton my collar in the humidity. I was expecting air-conditioning, and instead I am sweltering. It's almost like home. And then she's in front of me, and I can hardly speak. She is beautiful, and more. It is intimidating to stand before someone who exists in film and in music but has never existed before you in the flesh. She's not as stunning as she is in the movies, but there's more life, more presence; the movies lose that quality about her. I make a nop of greeting, pressing my hands together, touching my forehead.

She laughs at this, takes my hand and shakes it American-style. "You're lucky Marty likes you so much," she says. "I don't like interviews."

I can barely find my voice. "Yes. I only have a few questions."

"Oh no. Don't be shy." She laughs again, and doesn't release my hand, pulls me towards her living room. "Marty told me about you. You need help with your ratings. He helped me once, too."

She's frightening. She is of my people, but she has adapted better to this place than I have. She seems comfortable here. She walks differently, smiles differently; she is an American, with perhaps some flavour of our country, but nothing of our roots. It's obvious. And strangely disappointing. In her movies, she holds herself so well, and now she sits down on her couch and sprawls with her feet kicked out in front of her. Not caring at all. I'm embarrassed for her, and I'm glad I don't have my camera set up yet. She kicks her feet up on the couch. I can't help but be shocked. She catches my expression and smiles.

"You're worse than my parents. Fresh off the boat."

"I am sorry."

She shrugs. "Don't worry about it. I spent half my life here, growing up; different country, different rules."

I'm embarrassed. I try not to laugh with the tension I feel. "I just have some interview questions," I say.

"Go ahead." She sits up and arranges herself for the video stand that I set up.

I begin. "When the March Purge happened, you were in Singapore."

She nods. "That's right. We were finishing The Tiger and the Ghost."

"What was your first thought when it happened? Did you want to go back? Were you surprised?"

She frowns. "Turn off the camera."

When it's off she looks at me with pity. "This isn't the way to get clicks. No one cares about an old revolution. Not even my fans." She stands abruptly and calls through the green jungle of her flat. "Terrell?"

The big black man appears. Smiling and lethal. Looming over me. He is very frightening. The movies I grew up with had falang like him. Terrifying large black men whom our heroes had to overcome. Later, when I arrived in America, it was different, and I found out that the falang and the black people don't like the way we show them in our movies. Much like when I watch their Vietnam movies, and see the ugly way the Lao freedom fighters behave. Not real at all, portrayed like animals. But still, I cannot help but cringe when Terrell looks at me.

Kulaap says, "We're going out, Terrell. Make sure you tip off some of the papcams. We're going to give them a show."

"I don't understand," I say.

"You want clicks, don't you?"

"Yes, but —"

She smiles. "You don't need an interview. You need an event." She looks me over. "And better clothes." She nods to her security man. "Terrell, dress him up."

A flashbulb frenzy greets us as we come out of the tower. Papcams everywhere. Chase cycles revving, and Terrell and three others of his people guiding us through the press to the limousine, shoving cameras aside with a violence and power that are utterly unlike the careful pity he showed when he selected a Gucci suit for me to wear.

Kulaap looks properly surprised at the crowd and the shouting reporters, but not nearly as surprised as I am, and then we're in the limo, speeding out of the tower's roundabout as papcams follow us.

Kulaap crouches before the car's onboard tablet, keying in pass codes. She is very pretty, wearing a black dress that brushes her thighs and thin straps that caress her smooth bare shoulders. I feel as if I am in a movie. She taps more keys. A screen glows, showing the taillights of our car: the view from pursuing papcams.

"You know I haven't dated anyone in three years?" she asks.

"Yes. I know from your website biography."

She grins. "And now it looks like I've found one of my countrymen."

"But we're not on a date," I protest.

"Of course we are." She smiles again. "I'm going out on a supposedly secret date with a cute and mysterious Lao boy. And look at all those papcams chasing after us, wondering where we're going and what we're going to do." She keys in another code, and now we can see live footage of the paparazzi, as viewed from the tail of her limo. She grins. "My fans like to see what life is like for me."

I can almost imagine what the maelstrom looks like right now: there will still be Marty's story, but now a dozen other sites will be lighting up, and in the centre of that, Kulaap's own view of the excitement, pulling in her fans, who will want to know, direct from her, what's going on. She holds up a mirror, checks herself, and then she smiles into her smartphone's camera.

"Hi everyone. It looks like my cover's blown. Just thought I should let you know that I'm on a lovely date with a lovely man. I'll let you all know how it goes. Promise." She points the camera at me. I stare at it stupidly. She laughs. "Say hi and good-bye, Ong."

"Hi and good-bye."

She laughs again, waves into the camera. "Love you all. Hope you have as good a night as I'm going to have." And then she cuts the clip and punches a code to launch the video to her Web site.

It is a bit of nothing. Not a news story, not a scoop even, and yet, when she opens another window on her tablet, showing her own miniversion of the maelstrom, I can see her site lighting up with traffic. Her version of the maelstrom isn't as powerful as what we have at Milestone, but still, it is an impressive window into the data that is relevant to Kulaap's tags.

"What's your feed's byline?" she asks. "Let's see if we can get your traffic bumped up."

"Are you serious?"

"Marty Mackley did more than this for me. I told him I'd help." She laughs. "Besides, we wouldn't want you to get sent back to the black hole, would we?"

"You know about the black hole?" I can't help doing a double-take.

Her smile is almost sad. "You think just because I put my feet up on the furniture that I don't care about my aunts and uncles back home? That I don't worry about what's happening?"

"I —"

She shakes her head. "You're so fresh off the boat."

"Do you use the Jumbo Cafe —" I break off. It seems too unlikely.

She leans close. "My handle is Laofriend. What's yours?"

"Littlexang. I thought Laofriend was a boy —"

She just laughs.

I lean forward. "Is it true that the family made it out?"

She nods. "For certain. A general in the Thai army is a fan. He tells me everything. They have a listening post. And sometimes they send scouts across."

It's almost as if I am home.

We go to a tiny Laotian restaurant where everyone recognizes her and falls over her and the owners simply lock out the paparazzi when they become too intrusive. We spend the evening unearthing memories of Vientiane. We discover that we both favored the same rice noodle cart on Kaem Khong. That she used to sit on the banks of the Mekong and wish that she were a fisherman. That we went to the same waterfalls outside the city on the weekends. That it is impossible to find good dum mak hoong anywhere outside of the country. She is a good companion, very alive. Strange in her American ways, but still, with a good heart. Periodically, we click photos of one another and post them to her site, feeding the voyeurs. And then we are in the limo again and the paparazzi are all around us. I have the strange feeling of fame. Flashbulbs everywhere. Shouted questions. I feel proud to be beside this beautiful intelligent woman who knows so much more than any of us about the situation inside our homeland.

Back in the car, she has me open a bottle of champagne and pour two glasses while she opens the maelstrom and studies the results of our date. She has reprogrammed it to watch my byline feed ranking as well.

"You've got twenty thousand more readers than you did yesterday," she says.

I beam. She keeps reading the results. "Someone already did a scan on your face." She toasts me with her glass. "You're famous."

We clink glasses. I am flushed with wine and happiness. I will have Janice's average clicks. It's as though a *bodhisattva* has come down from heaven to save my job. In my mind, I offer thanks to Marty for arranging this, for his generous nature. Kulaap leans close to her screen, watching the flaring content. She opens another window, starts to read. She frowns.

"What the fuck do you write about?"

I draw back, surprised. "Government stories, mostly." I shrug. "Sometimes environment stories."

"Like what?"

"I am working on a story right now about global warming and Henry David Thoreau."

"Aren't we done with that?"

I'm confused. "Done with what?"

The limo jostles us as it makes a turn, moves down Hollywood Boulevard, letting the cycles rev around us like schools of fish. They're snapping pictures at the side of the limo, snapping at us. Through the tinting, they're like fireflies, smaller flares than even my stories in the maelstrom.

"I mean, isn't that an old story?" She sips her champagne. "Even America is reducing emissions now. Everyone knows it's a problem." She taps her couch's armrest. "The carbon tax on my limo has tripled, even with the hybrid engine. Everyone agrees it's a problem. We're going to fix it. What's there to write about?"

She is an American. Everything that is good about them: their optimism, their willingness to charge ahead, to make their own future. And everything that is bad about them: their strange ignorance, their unwillingness to believe that they must behave as other than children.

"No. It's not done," I say. "It is worse. Worse every day. And the changes we make seem to have little effect. Maybe too little, or maybe too late. It is getting worse."

She shrugs. "That's not what I read."

I try not to show my exasperation. "Of course it's not what you read." I wave at the screen. "Look at the clicks on my feed. People want happy stories. Want fun stories. Not stories like I write. So instead, we all write what you will read, which is nothing."

"Still —"

"No." I make a chopping motion with my hand. "We newspeople are very smart monkeys. If you will give us your so lovely eyeballs and your click-throughs we will do whatever you like. We will write good news, and news you can use, news you can shop to, news with the 'Three S's.' We will tell you how to have better sex or eat better or look more beautiful or feel happier and or how to meditate – yes, so enlightened." I make a face. "If you want a walking meditation and Double DP, we will give it to you."

She starts to laugh.

"Why are you laughing at me?" I snap. "I am not joking!"

She waves a hand. "I know, I know, but what you just said 'double' —" She shakes her head, still laughing. "Never mind."

I lapse into silence. I want to go on, to tell her of my frustrations. But now I am embarrassed at my loss of composure. I have no face. I didn't used to be like this. I used to control my emotions, but now I am an American, as childish and unruly as Janice. And Kulaap laughs at me.

I control my anger. "I think I want to go home," I say. "I don't wish to be on a date anymore."

She smiles and reaches over to touch my shoulder. "Don't be that way."

A part of me is telling me that I am a fool. That I am reckless and foolish for walking away from this opportunity. But there is something else, something about this frenzied hunt for page views and click-throughs and ad revenue that suddenly feels unclean. As if my father is with us in the car, disapproving. Asking if he posted his complaints about his missing friends for the sake of clicks.

"I want to get out," I hear myself say. "I do not wish to have your clicks."

"But —"

I look up at her. "I want to get out. Now."

"Here?" She makes a face of exasperation, then shrugs. "It's your choice."

"Yes. Thank you."

She tells her driver to pull over. We sit in stiff silence.

"I will send your suit back to you," I say.

She gives me a sad smile. "It's all right. It's a gift."

This makes me feel worse, even more humiliated for refusing her generosity, but still, I get out of the limo. Cameras are clicking at me from all around. This is my fifteen minutes of fame, this moment when all of Kulaap's fans focus on me for a few seconds, their flashbulbs popping.

I begin to walk home as paparazzi shout questions.

Fifteen minutes later I am indeed alone. I consider calling a cab, but then decide I prefer the night. Prefer to walk by myself through this city that never walks anywhere. On a street corner, I buy a pupusa and gamble on the Mexican Lottery because I like the tickets' laser images of their Day of the Dead. It seems an echo of the Buddha's urging to remember that we all become corpses.

I buy three tickets, and one of them is a winner: one hundred dollars that I can redeem at any TelMex kiosk. I take this as a good sign. Even if my luck is obviously gone with my work, and even if the girl Kulaap was not the *bodhisattva* that I thought, still, I feel lucky. As though my father is walking with me down this cool Los Angeles street in the middle of the night, the two of us together again, me with a pupusa and a winning lottery ticket, him with an Ah Daeng cigarette and his quiet gambler's smile. In a strange way, I feel that he is blessing me.

And so instead of going home, I go back to the newsroom.

My hits are up when I arrive. Even now, in the middle of the night, a tiny slice of Kulaap's fan base is reading about checkerspot butterflies and American government incompetence. In my country, this story would not exist. A censor would kill it instantly. Here, it glows green; increasing and decreasing in size as people click. A lonely thing, flickering amongst the much larger content flares of Intel processor releases, guides to low-fat recipes, photos of lol-cats, and episodes of Survivor! Antarctica. The wash of light and colour is very beautiful.

In the centre of the maelstrom, the green sun of the Double DP story glows – surges larger. DP is doing something. Maybe he's surrendering, maybe he's murdering his hostages, maybe his fans have thrown up a human wall to protect him. My story snuffs out as reader attention shifts.

I watch the maelstrom a little longer, then go to my desk and make a phone call. A rumpled hairy man answers, rubbing at a sleep-puffy face.

I apologize for the late hour, and then pepper him with questions while I record the interview.

He is silly looking and wild-eyed. He has spent his life living as if he were Thoreau, thinking deeply on the forest monk and following the man's careful paths through what woods remain, walking amongst birch and maple and bluets. He is a fool, but an earnest one.

"I can't find a single one," he tells me. "Thoreau could find thousands at this time of year; there were so many he didn't even have to look for them."

He says, "I'm so glad you called. I tried sending out press releases, but . . ." He shrugs. "I'm glad you'll cover it. Otherwise, it's just us hobbyists talking to each other."

I smile and nod and take notes of his sincerity, this strange wild creature, the sort that everyone will dismiss. His image is bad for video; his words are not good for text. He has no quotes that encapsulate what he sees. It is all couched in the jargon of naturalists and biology. With time, I could find another, someone who looks attractive or who can speak well, but all I have is this one hairy man, disheveled and foolish, senile with passion over a flower that no longer exists.

I work through the night, polishing the story. When my colleagues pour through the door at 8 a.m. it is almost done. Before I can even tell Janice about it, she comes to me. She fingers my clothing and grins. "Nice suit." She pulls up a chair and sits beside me. "We all saw you with Kulaap. Your hits went way up." She nods at my screen. "Writing up what happened?"

"No. It was a private conversation."

"But everyone wants to know why you got out of the car. I had someone from the *Financial Times* call me about splitting the hits for a tell-all, if you'll be interviewed. You wouldn't even need to write up the piece."

It's a tempting thought. Easy hits. Many click-throughs. Ad-revenue bonuses. Still, I shake my head. "We did not talk about things that are important for others to hear."

Janice stares at me as if I am crazy. "You're not in the position to bargain, Ong. Something happened between the two of you. Something people want to know about. And you need the clicks. Just tell us what happened on your date."

"I was not on a date. It was an interview."

"Well then publish the fucking interview and get your average up!"

"No. That is for Kulaap to post, if she wishes. I have something else."

I show Janice my screen. She leans forwards. Her mouth tightens as she reads. For once, her anger is cold. Not the explosion of noise and rage that I expect. "Bluets." She looks at me. "You need hits and you give them flowers and Walden Pond."

"I would like to publish this story."

"No! Hell, no! This is just another story like your butterfly story, and your road contracts story, and your congressional budget story. You won't get a damn click. It's pointless. No one will even read it."

"This is news."

"Marty went out on a limb for you —" She presses her lips together, reining in her anger. "Fine. It's up to you, Ong. If you want to destroy your life over Thoreau and flowers, it's your funeral. We can't help you if you won't help yourself. Bottom line, you need fifty thousand readers or I'm sending you back to the third world."

We look at each other. Two gamblers evaluating one another. Deciding who is betting, and who is bluffing.

I click the "publish" button.

The story launches itself onto the net, announcing itself to the feeds. A minute later a tiny new sun glows in the maelstrom.

Together, Janice and I watch the green spark as it flickers on the screen. Readers turn to the story. Start to ping it and share it amongst themselves, start to register hits on the page. The post grows slightly.

My father gambled on Thoreau. I am my father's son.

BOOJUM

Elizabeth Bear and Sarah Monette

Elizabeth Bear was born in Hartford, Connecticut, and now lives in the Mohave Desert near Las Vegas. She won the John W. Campbell Award for Best New Writer in 2005, and in 2008 took home a Hugo Award for her short story "Tideline," which also won her the Theodore Sturgeon Memorial Award (shared with David Moles). Her short work has appeared in *Asimov's*, *Subterranean*, SCI FICTION, *Interzone*, *The Third Alternative*, *Strange Horizons*, *On Spec*, and elsewhere, and has been collected in *The Chains That You Refuse* and *New Amsterdam*. She is the author of three highly acclaimed SF novels, *Hammered*, *Scardown*, and *Worldwired*, and of the Alternate History Fantasy Promethean Age series, which includes the novels *Blood and Iron*, *Whiskey and Water*, *Ink and Steel*, and *Hell and Earth*. Her other books include the novels *Carnival*, *Undertow*, and *Dust*. Her most recent book is the novel *All the Windwracked Stars*, and coming up are a new novel, *Chill*, and a chapbook novella, *Seven for a Secret*. Her website is at elizabethbear.com.

Sarah Monette was born and raised in Oak Ridge, Tennessee, one of the secret cities of the Manhattan Project. Having completed her Ph.D. in Renaissance English drama, she now lives and writes in a ninety-nine-year-old house in the Upper Midwest. Her Doctrine of Labyrinths series consists of the novels *Melusine*, *The Virtu*, and *The Mirador*. Her short fiction has appeared in many places, including *Strange Horizons*, *Aeon*, *Alchemy*, and *Lady Churchill's Rosebud Wristlet*, and has been collected in *The Bone Key*. Upcoming is a new novel in the Doctrine of Labyrinths sequence, *Corambis*. Her website is at sarahmonette.com/.

Bear and Monette have collaborated before, on the story "The Ile of Dogges" and on the novel *A Companion to Wolves*. Here they join forces again to take us adventuring through the solar system with space pirates. Arrrr!

THE SHIP HAD no name of her own, so her human crew called her the *Lavinia Whateley*. As far as anyone could tell, she didn't mind. At least, her long grasping vanes curled – affectionately? – when the chief engineers patted her bulkheads and called her "Vinnie," and she ceremoniously tracked the footsteps of each crew member with her internal bioluminescence, giving them light to walk and work and live by.

The *Lavinia Whateley* was a Boojum, a deep-space swimmer, but her kind had evolved in the high tempestuous envelopes of gas giants, and their offspring still spent their infancies there, in cloud-nurseries over eternal storms. And so she was streamlined, something like a vast spiny lionfish to the earth-adapted eye. Her sides were lined with gasbags filled with hydrogen; her vanes and wings furled tight. Her colour was a blue-green so dark it seemed a glossy black unless the light struck it; her hide was impregnated with symbiotic algae.

Where there was light, she could make oxygen. Where there was oxygen, she could make water.

She was an ecosystem unto herself, as the captain was a law unto herself. And down in the bowels of the engineering section, Black Alice Bradley, who was only human and no kind of law at all, loved her.

Black Alice had taken the oath back in '32, after the Venusian Riots. She hadn't hidden her reasons, and the captain had looked at her with cold, dark, amused eyes and said, "So long as you carry your weight, cherie, I don't care. Betray me, though, and you will be going back to Venus the cold way." But it was probably that – and the fact that Black Alice couldn't hit the broad side of a space freighter with a ray gun – that had gotten her assigned to Engineering, where ethics were less of a problem. It wasn't, after all, as if she was going anywhere.

Black Alice was on duty when the *Lavinia Whateley* spotted prey; she felt the shiver of anticipation that ran through the decks of the ship. It was an odd sensation, a tic Vinnie only exhibited in pursuit. And then they were underway, zooming down the slope of the gravity well toward Sol, and the screens all around Engineering – which Captain Song kept dark, most of the time, on the theory that swabs and deckhands and coalshovelers didn't need to know where they were, or what they were doing – flickered bright and live.

Everybody looked up, and Demijack shouted, "There! There!" He was right: the blot that might only have been a smudge of oil on the screen moved as Vinnie banked, revealing itself to be a freighter, big and ungainly and hopelessly outclassed. Easy prey. Easy pickings.

We could use some of them, thought Black Alice. Contrary to the e-ballads and comm stories, a pirate's life was not all imported delicacies and fawning slaves. Especially not when three-quarters of any and all profits went directly back to the *Lavinia Whateley*, to keep her healthy and happy. Nobody ever argued. There were stories about the *Marie Curie*, too.

The Captain's voice over fibre-optic cable – strung beside the *Lavinia Whateley*'s nerve bundles – was as clear and free of static as if she stood at Black Alice's elbow. "Battle stations," Captain Song said, and the crew leapt to obey. It had been two Solar since Captain Song keelhauled James

Brady, but nobody who'd been with the ship then was ever likely to forget his ruptured eyes and frozen scream.

Black Alice manned her station, and stared at the screen. She saw the freighter's name – the *Josephine Baker* – gold on black across the stern, the Venusian flag for its port of registry wired stiff from a mast on its hull. It was a steelship, not a Boojum, and they had every advantage. For a moment she thought the freighter would run.

And then it turned, and brought its guns to bear.

No sense of movement, of acceleration, of disorientation. No pop, no whump of displaced air. The view on the screens just flickered to a different one, as Vinnie skipped – apported – to a new position just aft and above the *Josephine Baker*, crushing the flag mast with her hull.

Black Alice felt that, a grinding shiver. And had just time to grab her console before the *Lavinia Whateley* grappled the freighter, long vanes not curling in affection now.

Out of the corner of her eye, she saw Dogcollar, the closest thing the *Lavinia Whateley* had to a chaplain, cross himself, and she heard him mutter, like he always did, *Ave, Grandaevissimi, morituri vos salutant*. It was the best he'd be able to do until it was all over, and even then he wouldn't have the chance to do much. Captain Song didn't mind other people worrying about souls, so long as they didn't do it on her time.

The Captain's voice was calling orders, assigning people to boarding parties port and starboard. Down in Engineering, all they had to do was monitor the *Lavinia Whateley*'s hull and prepare to repel boarders, assuming the freighter's crew had the gumption to send any. Vinnie would take care of the rest – until the time came to persuade her not to eat her prey before they'd gotten all the valuables off it. That was a ticklish job, only entrusted to the chief engineers, but Black Alice watched and listened, and although she didn't expect she'd ever get the chance, she thought she could do it herself.

It was a small ambition, and one she never talked about. But it would be a hell of a thing, wouldn't it? To be somebody a Boojum would listen to?

She gave her attention to the dull screens in her sectors, and tried not to crane her neck to catch a glimpse of the ones with the actual fighting on them. Dogcollar was making the rounds with sidearms from the weapons locker, just in case. Once the *Josephine Baker* was subdued, it was the junior engineers and others who would board her to take inventory.

Sometimes there were crew members left in hiding on captured ships. Sometimes, unwary pirates got shot.

There was no way to judge the progress of the battle from Engineering. Wasabi put a stopwatch up on one of the secondary screens, as usual, and everybody glanced at it periodically. Fifteen minutes ongoing meant the boarding parties hadn't hit any nasty surprises. Black Alice had met a man once who'd been on the *Margaret Mead* when she grappled a freighter that turned out to be carrying a division-worth of Marines out to the Jovian moons. Thirty minutes on-going was normal. Forty-five minutes. Upward of an hour on-going, and people started double-checking their weapons.

The longest battle Black Alice had ever personally been part of was six hours, forty-three minutes, and fifty-two seconds. That had been the last time the *Lavinia Whateley* worked with a partner, and the double-cross by the *Henry Ford* was the only reason any of Vinnie's crew needed. Captain Song still had Captain Edwards' head in a jar on the bridge, and Vinnie had an ugly ring of scars where the *Henry Ford* had bitten her.

This time, the clock stopped at fifty minutes, thirteen seconds. The *Josephine Baker* surrendered.

Dogcollar slapped Black Alice's arm. "With me," he said, and she didn't argue. He had only six weeks seniority over her, but he was as tough as he was devout, and not stupid either. She checked the velcro on her holster and followed him up the ladder, reaching through the rungs once to scratch Vinnie's bulkhead as she passed. The ship paid her no notice. She wasn't the captain, and she wasn't one of the four chief engineers.

Quartermaster mostly respected crew's own partner choices, and as Black Alice and Dogcollar suited up – it wouldn't be the first time, if the *Josephine Baker*'s crew decided to blow her open to space rather than be taken captive – he came by and issued them both tag guns and x-ray pads, taking a retina scan in return. All sorts of valuable things got hidden inside of bulkheads, and once Vinnie was done with the steelship there wouldn't be much chance of coming back to look for what they'd missed.

Wet pirates used to scuttle their captures. The Boojums were more efficient.

Black Alice clipped everything to her belt, and checked Dogcollar's seals.

And then they were swinging down lines from the *Lavinia Whateley*'s belly to the chewed-open airlock. A lot of crew didn't like to look at the ship's face, but Black Alice loved it. All those teeth, the diamond edges worn to a glitter, and a few of the ship's dozens of bright sapphire eyes blinking back at her.

She waved, unselfconsciously, and flattered herself that the ripple of closing eyes was Vinnie winking in return.

She followed Dogcollar inside the prize.

They unsealed when they had checked atmosphere – no sense in wasting your own air when you might need it later – and the first thing she noticed was the smell.

The *Lavinia Whateley* had her own smell, ozone and nutmeg, and other ships never smelled as good, but this was . . . this was . . .

"What did they kill and why didn't they space it?" Dogcollar wheezed, and Black Alice swallowed hard against her gag reflex and said, "One will get you twenty we're the lucky bastards that find it."

"No takers," Dogcollar said.

They worked together to crank open the hatches they came to. Twice they found crew members, messily dead. Once they found crew members alive.

"Gillies," said Black Alice.

"Still don't explain the smell," said Dogcollar and, to the gillies: "Look, you can join our crew, or our ship can eat you. Makes no never mind to us."

The gillies blinked their big wet eyes and made fingersigns at each other, and then nodded. Hard.

Dogcollar slapped a tag on the bulkhead. "Someone will come get you. You go wandering, we'll assume you changed your mind."

The gillies shook their heads, hard, and folded down onto the deck to wait.

Dogcollar tagged searched holds – green for clean, purple for goods, red for anything Vinnie might like to eat that couldn't be fenced for a profit – and Black Alice mapped. The corridors in the steelship were winding, twisty, hard to track. She was glad she chalked the walls, because she didn't think her map was quite right, somehow, but she couldn't figure out where she'd gone wrong. Still, they had a beacon, and Vinnie could always chew them out if she had to.

Black Alice loved her ship.

She was thinking about that, how, okay, it wasn't so bad, the pirate game, and it sure beat working in the sunstone mines on Venus, when she found a locked cargo hold. "Hey, Dogcollar," she said to her comm, and while he was turning to cover her, she pulled her sidearm and blastered the lock.

The door peeled back, and Black Alice found herself staring at rank upon rank of silver cylinders, each less than a meter tall and perhaps half a meter wide, smooth and featureless except for what looked like an assortment of sockets and plugs on the surface of each. The smell was strongest here.

"Shit," she said.

Dogcollar, more practical, slapped the first safety orange tag of the expedition beside the door and said only, "Captain'll want to see this."

"Yeah," said Black Alice, cold chills chasing themselves up and down her spine. "C'mon, let's move."

But of course it turned out that she and Dogcollar were on the retrieval detail, too, and the Captain wasn't leaving the canisters for Vinnie.

Which, okay, fair. Black Alice didn't want the *Lavinia Whateley* eating those things, either, but why did they have to bring them back?

She said as much to Dogcollar, under her breath, and had a horrifying thought: "She knows what they are, right?"

"She's the Captain," said Dogcollar.

"Yeah, but – I ain't arguing, man, but if she doesn't know . . ." She lowered her voice even farther, so she could barely hear herself: "What if somebody *opens* one?"

Dogcollar gave her a pained look. "Nobody's going to go opening anything. But if you're really worried, go talk to the Captain about it."

He was calling her bluff. Black Alice called his right back. "Come with me?"

He was stuck. He stared at her, and then he grunted and pulled his gloves off, the left and then the right. "Fuck," he said. "I guess we oughta."

For the crew members who had been in the boarding action, the party had already started. Dogcollar and Black Alice finally tracked the Captain down in the rec room, where her marines were slurping stolen wine from broken-necked bottles. As much of it splashed on the gravity plates epoxied to the *Lavinia Whateley*'s flattest interior surface as went into the marines, but Black Alice imagined there was plenty more where that came from. And the faster the crew went through it, the less long they'd be drunk.

The Captain herself was naked in a great extruded tub, up to her collar-bones in steaming water dyed pink and heavily scented by the bath bombs sizzling here and there. Black Alice stared; she hadn't seen a tub bath in seven years. She still dreamed of them sometimes.

"Captain," she said, because Dogcollar wasn't going to say anything. "We think you should know we found some dangerous cargo on the prize."

Captain Song raised one eyebrow. "And you imagine I don't know already, cherie?"

Oh shit. But Black Alice stood her ground. "We thought we should be *sure*."

The Captain raised one long leg out of the water to shove a pair of neck-ing pirates off the rim of her tub. They rolled onto the floor, grappling and clawing, both fighting to be on top. But they didn't break the kiss.

"You wish to be sure," said the Captain. Her dark eyes had never left Black Alice's sweating face. "Very well. Tell me. And then you will know that I know, and you can be *sure*."

Dogcollar made a grumbling noise deep in his throat, easily interpreted: *I told you so.*

Just as she had when she took Captain Song's oath, and slit her thumb with a razorblade and dripped her blood on the *Lavinia Whateley*'s deck-ing so the ship might know her, Black Alice – metaphorically speaking – took a breath and jumped. "They're brains," she said. "Human brains. Stolen. Black-market. The Fungi —"

"Mi-Go," Dogcollar hissed, and the Captain grinned at him, showing extraordinarily white strong teeth. He ducked, submissively, but didn't step back, for which Black Alice felt a completely ridiculous gratitude.

"Mi-Go," Black Alice said. Mi-Go, Fungi, what did it matter? They came from the outer rim of the Solar System, the black cold hurtling rocks of the Öpik-Oort Cloud. Like the Boojums, they could swim between the stars. "They collect them. There's a black market. Nobody knows what they use them for. It's illegal, of course. But they're . . . alive in there. They go mad, supposedly."

And that was it. That was all Black Alice could manage. She stopped, and had to remind herself to shut her mouth.

"So I've heard," the Captain said, dabbling at the steaming water. She stretched luxuriously in her tub. Someone thrust a glass of white wine at her, condensation dewing the outside. The Captain did not drink from shattered plastic bottles. "The Mi-Go will pay for this cargo, won't they? They mine rare minerals all over the system. They're said to be very wealthy."

"Yes, Captain," Dogcollar said, when it became obvious that Black Alice couldn't.

"Good," the Captain said. Under Black Alice's feet, the decking shuddered, a grinding sound as Vinnie began to dine. Her rows of teeth would make short work of the *Josephine Baker*'s steel hide. Black Alice could see two of the gillies – the same two? she never could tell them apart unless they had scars – flinch and tug at their chains. "Then they might as well pay us as someone else, wouldn't you say?"

Black Alice knew she should stop thinking about the canisters. Captain's word was law. But she couldn't help it, like scratching at a scab. They were down there, in the third subhold, the one even sniffers couldn't find, cold and sweating and with that stench that was like a living thing.

And she kept wondering. Were they empty? Or were there brains in there, people's brains, going mad?

The idea was driving *her* crazy, and finally, her fourth off-shift after the capture of the *Josephine Baker*, she had to go look.

"This is stupid, Black Alice," she muttered to herself as she climbed down the companionway, the beads in her hair clicking against her earrings. "Stupid, stupid, stupid." Vinnie bioluminesced, a traveling spotlight, placidly unconcerned whether Black Alice was being an idiot or not.

Half-Hand Sally had pulled duty in the main hold. She nodded at Black Alice and Black Alice nodded back. Black Alice ran errands a lot, for Engineering and sometimes for other departments, because she didn't smoke hash and she didn't cheat at cards. She was reliable.

Down through the subholds, and she really didn't want to be doing this, but she was here and the smell of the third subhold was already making her sick, and maybe if she just knew one way or the other, she'd be able to quit thinking about it.

She opened the third subhold, and the stench rushed out.

The canisters were just metal, sealed, seemingly airtight. There shouldn't be any way for the aroma of the contents to escape. But it permeated the air nonetheless, bad enough that Black Alice wished she had brought a rebreather.

No, that would have been suspicious. So it was really best for everyone concerned that she hadn't, but oh, gods and little fishes the stench. Even breathing through her mouth was no help; she could taste it, like oil from a fryer, saturating the air, oozing up her sinuses, coating the interior spaces of her body.

As silently as possible, she stepped across the threshold and into the space beyond. The *Lavinia Whateley* obligingly lit the space as she entered, dazzling her at first as the overhead lights – not just bioluminescent, here, but LEDs chosen to approximate natural daylight, for when they shipped plants and animals – reflected off rank upon rank of canisters. When Black Alice went among them, they did not reach her waist.

She was just going to walk through, she told herself. Hesitantly, she touched the closest cylinder. The air in this hold was so dry there was no condensation – the whole ship ran to lip-cracking, nosebleed dryness in the long weeks between prizes – but the cylinder was cold. It felt somehow grimy to the touch, gritty and oily like machine grease. She pulled her hand back.

It wouldn't do to open the closest one to the door – and she realized with that thought that she was planning on opening one. There must be a way to do it, a concealed catch or a code pad. She was an engineer, after all.

She stopped three ranks in, lightheaded with the smell, to examine the problem.

It was remarkably simple, once you looked for it. There were three depressions on either side of the rim, a little smaller than human fingertips but spaced appropriately. She laid the pads of her fingers over them and pressed hard, making the flesh deform into the catches.

The lid sprang up with a pressurized hiss. Black Alice was grateful that even open, it couldn't smell much worse. She leaned forward to peer within. There was a clear membrane over the surface, and gelatin or thick fluid underneath. Vinnie's lights illuminated it well.

It was not empty. And as the light struck the greyish surface of the lump of tissue floating within, Black Alice would have sworn she saw the pathetic unbodied thing flinch.

She scrambled to close the canister again, nearly pinching her fingertips when it clanked shut. "Sorry," she whispered, although dear sweet Jesus, surely the thing couldn't hear her. "Sorry, sorry." And then she turned and ran, catching her hip a bruising blow against the doorway, slapping the controls to make it fucking *close* already. And then she staggered sideways, lurching to her knees, and vomited until blackness was spinning in front of her eyes and she couldn't smell or taste anything but bile.

Vinnie would absorb the former contents of Black Alice's stomach, just as she absorbed, filtered, recycled, and excreted all her crew's wastes. Shaking, Black Alice braced herself back upright and began the long climb out of the holds.

In the first subhold, she had to stop, her shoulder against the smooth, velvet slickness of Vinnie's skin, her mouth hanging open while her lungs worked. And she knew Vinnie wasn't going to hear her, because she wasn't the Captain or a chief engineer or anyone important, but she had to try anyway, croaking, "Vinnie, water, please."

And no one could have been more surprised than Black Alice Bradley when Vinnie extruded a basin and a thin cool trickle of water began to flow into it.

Well, now she knew. And there was still nothing she could do about it. She wasn't the Captain, and if she said anything more than she already had, people were going to start looking at her funny. Mutiny kind of funny. And what Black Alice did *not* need was any more of Captain Song's attention and especially not for rumours like that. She kept her head down and did her job and didn't discuss her nightmares with anyone.

And she had nightmares, all right. Hot and cold running, enough, she fancied, that she could have filled up the Captain's huge tub with them.

She could live with that. But over the next double dozen of shifts, she became aware of something else wrong, and this was worse, because it was something wrong with the *Lavinia Whateley*.

The first sign was the chief engineers frowning and going into huddles at odd moments. And then Black Alice began to feel it herself, the way Vinnie was . . . she didn't have a word for it because she'd never felt anything like it before. She would have said *balky*, but that couldn't be right. It couldn't. But she was more and more sure that Vinnie was less responsive somehow, that when she obeyed the Captain's orders, it was with a delay. If she were human, Vinnie would have been dragging her feet.

You couldn't keelhaul a ship for not obeying fast enough.

And then, because she was paying attention so hard she was making her own head hurt, Black Alice noticed something else. Captain Song had them cruising the gas giants' orbits – Jupiter, Saturn, Neptune – not going in as far as the asteroid belt, not going out as far as Uranus. Nobody Black Alice talked to knew why, exactly, but she and Dogcollar figured it was because the Captain wanted to talk to the Mi Go without actually getting near the nasty cold rock of their planet. And what Black Alice noticed was that Vinnie was less balky, less *unhappy*, when she was headed out, and more and more resistant the closer they got to the asteroid belt.

Vinnie, she remembered, had been born over Uranus.

"Do you want to go home, Vinnie?" Black Alice asked her one late-night shift when there was nobody around to care that she was talking to the ship. "Is that what's wrong?"

She put her hand flat on the wall, and although she was probably imagining it, she thought she felt a shiver ripple across Vinnie's vast side.

Black Alice knew how little she knew, and didn't even contemplate sharing her theory with the chief engineers. They probably knew exactly what was wrong and exactly what to do to keep the *Lavinia Whateley* from going core meltdown like the *Marie Curie* had. That was a whispered story, not the sort of thing anybody talked about except in their hammocks after lights out.

The *Marie Curie* had eaten her own crew.

So when Wasabi said, four shifts later, "Black Alice, I've got a job for you," Black Alice said, "Yessir," and hoped it would be something that would help the *Lavinia Whateley* be happy again.

It was a suit job, he said, replace and repair. Black Alice was going because she was reliable and smart and stayed quiet, and it was time she took on more responsibilities. The way he said it made her first fret because that meant the Captain might be reminded of her existence, and then fret because she realized the Captain already had been.

But she took the equipment he issued, and she listened to the instructions and read schematics and committed them both to memory and her implants. It was a ticklish job, a neural override repair. She'd done some fibre-optic bundle splicing, but this was going to be a doozy. And she was going to have to do it in stiff, pressurized gloves.

Her heart hammered as she sealed her helmet, and not because she was worried about the EVA. This was a chance. An opportunity. A step closer to chief engineer.

Maybe she had impressed the Captain with her discretion, after all.

She cycled the airlock, snapped her safety harness, and stepped out onto the *Lavinia Whateley*'s hide.

That deep blue-green, like azurite, like the teeming seas of Venus under their swampy eternal clouds, was invisible. They were too far from Sol – it was a yellow stylus-dot, and you had to know where to look for it. Vinnie's hide was just black under Black Alice's suit floods. As the airlock cycled shut, though, the Boojum's own bioluminescence shimmered up her vanes and along the ridges of her sides – crimson and electric green and acid blue. Vinnie must have noticed Black Alice picking her way carefully up her spine with barbed boots. They wouldn't *hurt* Vinnie – nothing short of a space rock could manage that – but they certainly stuck in there good.

The thing Black Alice was supposed to repair was at the principal nexus of Vinnie's central nervous system. The ship didn't have anything like what a human or a gilly would consider a brain; there were nodules spread all through her vast body. Too slow, otherwise. And Black Alice had heard Boojums weren't supposed to be all that smart – trainable, sure, maybe like an Earth monkey.

Which is what made it creepy as hell that, as she picked her way up Vinnie's flank – though *up* was a courtesy, under these circumstances – talking to her all the way, she would have sworn Vinnie was talking back. Not just tracking her with the lights, as she would always do, but bending some of her barbels and vanes around as if craning her neck to get a look at Black Alice.

Black Alice carefully circumnavigated an eye – she didn't think her boots would hurt it, but it seemed discourteous to stomp across somebody's field of vision – and wondered, only half-idly, if she had been sent out on this task not because she was being considered for promotion, but because she was expendable.

She was just rolling her eyes and dismissing that as borrowing trouble when she came over a bump on Vinnie's back, spotted her goal – and all the ship's lights went out.

She tongued on the comm. "Wasabi?"

"I got you, Blackie. You just keep doing what you're doing."

"Yessir."

But it seemed like her feet stayed stuck in Vinnie's hide a little longer than was good. At least fifteen seconds before she managed a couple of deep breaths – too deep for her limited oxygen supply, so she went briefly dizzy – and continued up Vinnie's side.

Black Alice had no idea what inflammation looked like in a Boojum, but she would guess this was it. All around the interface she was meant to repair, Vinnie's flesh looked scraped and puffy. Black Alice walked tenderly, wincing, muttering apologies under her breath. And with every step, the tendrils coiled a little closer.

Black Alice crouched beside the box, and began examining connections. The console was about three meters by four, half a meter tall, and fixed firmly to Vinnie's hide. It looked like the thing was still functional, but something – a bit of space debris, maybe – had dented it pretty good.

Cautiously, Black Alice dropped a hand on it. She found the access panel, and flipped it open: more red lights than green. A tongue-click, and she began withdrawing her tethered tools from their holding pouches and arranging them so that they would float conveniently around.

She didn't hear a thing, of course, but the hide under her boots vibrated suddenly, sharply. She jerked her head around, just in time to see one of Vinnie's feelers slap her own side, five or ten meters away. And then the whole Boojum shuddered, contracting, curved into a hard crescent of pain the same way she had when the *Henry Ford* had taken that chunk out of her hide. And the lights in the access panel lit up all at once – red, red, yellow, red.

Black Alice tongued off the *send* function on her headset microphone, so Wasabi wouldn't hear her. She touched the bruised hull, and she touched the dented edge of the console. "Vinnie," she said, "does this *hurt?*"

Not that Vinnie could answer her. But it was obvious. She was in pain. And maybe that dent didn't have anything to do with space debris. Maybe – Black Alice straightened, looked around, and couldn't convince herself that it was an accident that this box was planted right where Vinnie couldn't quite reach it.

"So what does it *do?*" she muttered. "Why am I out here repairing something that fucking hurts?" She crouched down again and took another long look at the interface.

As an engineer, Black Alice was mostly self-taught; her implants were second-hand, black market, scavenged, the wet work done by a gilly on Providence Station. She'd learned the technical vocabulary from Gogglehead Kim before he bought it in a stupid little fight with a ship named the *V. I. Ulyanov*, but what she relied on were her instincts, the things she knew without being able to say. So she *looked* at that box wired into Vinnie's spine and all its red and yellow lights, and then she tongued the comm back on and said, "Wasabi, this thing don't look so good."

"Whaddya mean, don't look so good?" Wasabi sounded distracted, and that was just fine.

Black Alice made a noise, the auditory equivalent of a shrug. "I think the node's inflamed. Can we pull it and lock it in somewhere else?"

"No!" said Wasabi.

"It's looking pretty ugly out here."

"Look, Blackie, unless you want us to all go sailing out into the Big Empty, we are not pulling that governor. Just fix the fucking thing, would you?"

"Yessir," said Black Alice, thinking hard. The first thing was that Wasabi knew what was going on – knew what the box did and knew that the *Lavinia Whateley* didn't like it. That wasn't comforting. The second thing was that whatever was going on, it involved the Big Empty, the cold vastness between the stars. So it wasn't that Vinnie wanted to go home. She wanted to *go out*.

It made sense, from what Black Alice knew about Boojums. Their infants lived in the tumult of the gas giants' atmosphere, but as they aged, they pushed higher and higher, until they reached the edge of the envelope. And then – following instinct or maybe the calls of their fellows, nobody knew for sure – they learned to skip, throwing themselves out into the vacuum like Earth birds leaving the nest. And what if, for a Boojum, the solar system was just another nest?

Black Alice knew the *Lavinia Whateley* was old, for a Boojum. Captain Song was not her first captain, although you never mentioned Captain Smith if you knew what was good for you. So if there *was* another stage to her life cycle, she might be ready for it. And her crew wasn't letting her go.

Jesus and the cold fishy gods, Black Alice thought. Is this why the *Marie Curie* ate her crew? Because they wouldn't let her go?

She fumbled for her tools, tugging the cords to float them closer, and wound up walloping herself in the bicep with a splicer. And as she was wrestling with it, her headset spoke again. "Blackie, can you hurry it up out there? Captain says we're going to have company."

Company? She never got to say it. Because when she looked up, she saw the shapes, faintly limned in starlight, and a chill as cold as a suit leak crept up her neck.

There were dozens of them. Hundreds. They made her skin crawl and her nerves judder the way gillies and Boojums never had. They were man-sized, roughly, but they looked like the pseudoroaches of Venus, the ones Black Alice still had nightmares about, with too many legs, and horrible stiff wings. They had ovate, corrugated heads, but no faces, and where their mouths ought to be sprouting writing tentacles

And some of them carried silver shining cylinders, like the canisters in Vinnie's subhold.

Black Alice wasn't certain if they saw her, crouched on the Boojum's hide with only a thin laminate between her and the breathsucker, but she was certain of something else. If they did, they did not care.

They disappeared below the curve of the ship, toward the airlock Black Alice had exited before clawing her way along the ship's side. They could be a trade delegation, come to bargain for the salvaged cargo.

Black Alice didn't think even the Mi-Go came in the battalions to talk trade.

She meant to wait until the last of them had passed, but they just kept coming. Wasabi wasn't answering her hails; she was on her own and unarmed. She fumbled with her tools, stowing things in any handy pocket whether it was where the tool went or not. She couldn't see much; everything was misty. It took her several seconds to realize that her visor was fogged because she was crying.

Patch cables. Where were the fucking patch cables? She found a two-meter length of fibre-optic with the right plugs on the end. One end went into the monitor panel. The other snapped into her suit comm.

"Vinnie?" she whispered, when she thought she had a connection. "Vinnie, can you hear me?"

The bioluminescence under Black Alice's boots pulsed once.

Gods and little fishes, she thought. And then she drew out her laser cutting torch, and started slicing open the case on the console that Wasabi had called the *governor*. Wasabi was probably dead by now, or dying. Wasabi, and Dogcollar, and . . . well, not dead. If they were lucky, they were dead.

Because the opposite of lucky was those canisters the Mi-Go were carrying.

She hoped Dogcollar was lucky.

"You wanna go *out*, right?" she whispered to the *Lavinia Whateley*. "Out into the Big Empty."

She'd never been sure how much Vinnie understood of what people said, but the light pulsed again.

"And this thing won't let you." It wasn't a question. She had it open now, and she could see that was what it did. Ugly fucking thing. Vinnie shivered underneath her, and there was a sudden pulse of noise in her helmet speakers: screaming. People screaming.

"I know," Black Alice said. "They'll come get me in a minute, I guess." She swallowed hard against the sudden lurch of her stomach. "I'm gonna get this thing off you, though. And when they go, you can go, okay? And I'm sorry. I didn't know we were keeping you from . . ." She had to quit talking, or she really was going to puke. Grimly, she fumbled for the tools she needed to disentangle the abomination from Vinnie's nervous system.

Another pulse of sound, a voice, not a person: flat and buzzing and horrible. "We do not bargain with thieves." And the scream that time – she'd never heard Captain Song scream before. Black Alice flinched and started counting to slow her breathing. Puking in a suit was the number one badness, but hyperventilating in a suit was a really close second.

Her heads-up display was low-res, and slightly miscalibrated, so that everything had a faint shadow-double. But the thing that flashed up against her own view of her hands was unmistakable: a question mark.

<?>

"Vinnie?"

Another pulse of screaming, and the question mark again.

<?>

"Holy *shit*, Vinnie! . . . Never mind, never mind. They, um, they collect people's brains. In canisters. Like the canisters in the third subhold."

The bioluminescence pulsed once. Black Alice kept working.

Her heads-up pinged again: <ALICE> A pause. <?>

"Um, yeah. I figure that's what they'll do with me, too. It looked like they had plenty of canisters to go around."

Vinnie pulsed, and there was a longer pause while Black Alice doggedly severed connections and loosened bolts.

<WANT> said the *Lavinia Whateley*. <?>

"Want? Do I *want* . . . ?" Her laughter sounded bad. "Um, no. No, I don't want to be a brain in a jar. But I'm not seeing a lot of choices here. Even if I went cometary, they could catch me. And it kind of sounds like they're mad enough to do it, too."

She'd cleared out all the moorings around the edge of the governor; the case lifted off with a shove and went sailing into the dark. Black Alice winced. But then the processor under the cover drifted away from Vinnie's hide, and there was just the monofilament tethers and the fat cluster of fibre-optic and superconductors to go.

<HELP>

"I'm doing my best here, Vinnie," Black Alice said through her teeth.

That got her a fast double-pulse, and the *Lavinia Whateley* said, <HELP>

And then, <ALICE>

"You want to help *me*?" Black Alice squeaked.

A strong pulse, and the heads-up said, <HELP ALICE>

"That's really sweet of you, but I'm honestly not sure there's anything you can do. I mean, it doesn't look like the Mi-Go are mad at you, and I really want to keep it that way."

<EAT ALICE> said the *Lavinia Whateley*.

Black Alice came within a millimeter of taking her own fingers off with the cutting laser. "Um, Vinnie, that's um . . . well, I guess it's better than being a brain in a jar." Or suffocating to death in her suit if she went cometary and the Mi-Go *didn't* come after her.

The double-pulse again, but Black Alice didn't see what she could have missed. As communications went, *EAT ALICE* was pretty fucking unambiguous.

<HELP ALICE> the *Lavinia Whateley* insisted. Black Alice leaned in close, unsplicing the last of the governor's circuits from the Boojum's nervous system. <SAVE ALICE>

"By eating me? Look, I know what happens to things you eat, and it's not . . ." She bit her tongue. Because she *did* know what happened to things the *Lavinia Whateley* ate. Absorbed. Filtered. Recycled. "Vinnie . . . are you saying you can save me from the Mi-Go?"

A pulse of agreement.

"By eating me?" Black Alice pursued, needing to be sure she understood.

Another pulse of agreement.

Black Alice thought about the *Lavinia Whateley*'s teeth. "How much *me* are we talking about here?"

<ALICE> said the *Lavinia Whateley*, and then the last fibre-optic cable parted, and Black Alice, her hands shaking, detached her patch cable and flung the whole mess of it as hard as she could straight up. Maybe it would find a planet with atmosphere and be some little alien kid's shooting star.

And now she had to decide what to do.

She figured she had two choices, really. One, walk back down the *Lavinia Whateley* and find out if the Mi-Go believed in surrender. Two, walk around the *Lavinia Whateley* and into her toothy mouth.

Black Alice didn't think the Mi-Go believed in surrender.

She tilted her head back for one last clear look at the shining black infinity of space. Really, there wasn't any choice at all. Because even if she'd misunderstood what Vinnie seemed to be trying to tell her, the worst she'd end up was dead, and that was light-years better than what the Mi-Go had on offer.

Black Alice Bradley loved her ship.

She turned to her left and started walking, and the *Lavinia Whateley*'s bioluminescence followed her courteously all the way, vanes swaying out of her path. Black Alice skirted each of Vinnie's eyes as she came to them, and each of them blinked at her. And then she reached Vinnie's mouth and that magnificent panoply of teeth.

"Make it quick, Vinnie, okay?" said Black Alice, and walked into her leviathan's maw.

Picking her way delicately between razor-sharp teeth, Black Alice had plenty of time to consider the ridiculousness of worrying about a hole in her suit. Vinnie's mouth was more like a crystal cave, once you were inside it; there was no tongue, no palate. Just polished, macerating stones. Which did not close on Black Alice, to her surprise. If anything, she got the feeling the Vinnie was holding her . . . breath. Or what passed for it.

The Boojum was lit inside, as well – or was making herself lit, for Black Alice's benefit. And as Black Alice clambered inward, the teeth got smaller, and fewer, and the tunnel narrowed. Her throat, Alice thought. I'm inside her.

And the walls closed down, and she was swallowed.

Like a pill, enclosed in the tight sarcophagus of her space suit, she felt rippling pressure as peristalsis pushed her along. And then greater pressure, suffocating, savage. One sharp pain. The pop of her ribs as her lungs crushed.

Screaming inside a space suit was contra-indicated, too. And with collapsed lungs, she couldn't even do it properly.

alice.

She floated. In warm darkness. A womb, a bath. She was comfortable. An itchy soreness between her shoulder blades felt like a very mild radiation burn.

alice.

A voice she thought she should know. She tried to speak; her mouth gnashed, her teeth ground.

alice. talk here.

She tried again. Not with her mouth, this time.

Talk . . . here?

The buoyant warmth flickered past her. She was . . . drifting. No, swimming. She could feel currents on her skin. Her vision was confused. She blinked and blinked, and things were shattered.

There was nothing to see anyway, but stars.

alice talk here.

Where am I?

eat alice.

Vinnie. Vinnie's voice, but not in the flatness of the heads-up display anymore. Vinnie's voice alive with emotion and nuance and the vastness of her self.

You ate me, she said, and understood abruptly that the numbness she felt was not shock. It was the boundaries of her body erased and redrawn.

!

Agreement. Relief.

I'm . . . in you, Vinnie?

=/=

Not a "no". More like, this thing is not the same, does not compare, to this other thing. Black Alice felt the warmth of space so near a generous star slipping by her. She felt the swift currents of its gravity, and the gravity of its satellites, and bent them; and tasted them, and surfed them faster and faster away.

I am you.

!

Ecstatic comprehension, which Black Alice echoed with passionate relief. Not dead. Not dead after all. Just, transformed. Accepted. Embraced by her ship, whom she embraced in return.

Vinnie. Where are we going?

out, Vinnie answered. And in her, Black Alice read the whole great naked wonder of space, approaching faster and faster as Vinnie accelerated, reaching for the first great skip that would hurl them into the interstellar darkness of the Big Empty. They were going somewhere.

Out, Black Alice agreed and told herself not to grieve. Not to go mad. This sure beat swampy Hell out of being a brain in a jar.

And it occurred to her, as Vinnie jumped, the brainless bodies of her crew already digesting inside her, that it wouldn't be long before the loss of the *Lavinia Whateley* was a tale told to frighten spacers, too.

THE SIX DIRECTIONS
OF SPACE

Alastair Reynolds

Alastair Reynolds is a frequent contributor to Interzone, and has also sold to *Asimov's Science Fiction, Spectrum SF,* and elsewhere. His first novel, *Revelation Space,* was widely hailed as one of the major SF books of the year; it was quickly followed by *Chasm City, Redemption Ark, Absolution Gap, Century Rain,* and *Pushing Ice,* all big sprawling space operas that were big sellers as well, establishing Reynolds as one of the best and most popular new SF writers to enter the field in many years. His other books include a novella collection, *Diamond Dogs, Turquoise Days.* His most recent books are a novel, *The Prefect,* and two collections, *Galactic North* and *Zima Blue and Other Stories.* Coming up is a new novel, *House of Sun,* and a chapbook novella from Subterranean Press, *The Six Directions of Space.* A professional scientist with a Ph.D. in astronomy, he worked for the European Space Agency in the Netherlands for a number of years, but has recently moved back to his native Wales to become a full-time writer.

Reynolds's work is known for its grand scope, sweep, and scale (in one story, "Galactic North', a spaceship sets out in pursuit of another in a stern chase that takes thousands of years of time and hundreds of thousands of light-years to complete; in another, "Thousandth Night", ultra-rich immortals embark on a plan that will call for the physical rearrangement of all the stars in the galaxy. In the hard-hitting and unsettling story that follows, he shows us a brutal galactic empire embattling itself to defend against attacks by other empires that come not just from elsewhere in the galaxy, but from other universes altogether!

W E HAD BEEN riding for two hours when I tugged sharply on the reins to bring my pony to a halt. Tenger, my escort, rode on for a few paces before glancing back irritatedly. He muttered something in annoyance – a phrase that contained the words "stupid" and "dyke" – before steering his horse back alongside mine.

"Another sight-seeing stop?" he asked, as the two mismatched animals chewed their bits, flared their nostrils, and flicked their heads up in mutual impatience.

I said nothing, damned if I was going to give him the pleasure of an excuse. I only wanted to take in the view: the deeply-shadowed valley below, the rising hills beyond (curving ever upwards, like a tidal wave formed from rock and soil and grass), and the little patch of light down in the darkness, the square formation of the still-moving caravan.

"If you really want to make that appointment . . ." Tenger continued.

"Shut up."

Tenger sniffed, dug into a leather flap on his belt, and popped something into his mouth.

"On your own head be it, Yellow Dog. It certainly won't be my neck on the line, keeping the old man waiting."

I held both reins in one hand so that I could cup the other against my ear. I turned the side of my head in the direction of the caravan and closed my eyes. After a few moments, I convinced myself that I could hear it. It was a sound almost on the edge of audibility, but which would become thunderous, calamitous, world-destroying, as they drew nearer. The sound of thousands of riders, hundreds of wheeled tents, dozens of monstrous siege engines. A sound very much like the end of the world itself, it must have seemed, when the caravan approached.

"We can go now," I told Tenger.

He dug his spurs in, almost drawing blood, his horse pounding away so quickly that it kicked dirt into my eyes. Goyo snorted and gave chase. We raced down into the valley, sending skylarks and snipe barrelling into the air.

"Just going by the rules, Yellow Dog," the guard said, apologising for making me show him my passport. We were standing on the wheeled platform of the imperial *ger*. The guard wore a kneelength blue sash-tied coat, long black hair cascading from the dome of his helmet. "We're on high alert as it is. Three plausible threats in the last week."

"Usual nut-jobs?" I said, casting a wary glance at Tenger, who was attending to Goyo with a bad-tempered expression. I had beaten him to the caravan and he did not like that.

"Two Islamist sects, one bunch of Nestorians," the guard answered. "Not that I'm saying that the old man has anything to fear from you, of course, but we have to follow protocol."

"I understand fully."

"Frankly, we were beginning to wonder if you were ever coming back." He looked at me solicitously. "Some of us were beginning to wonder if you'd been disavowed."

I smiled. "Disavowed? I don't think so."

"Just saying, we're all assuming you've got something suitably juicy, after all this time."

I reached up to tie back my hair. "Juicy's not exactly the word I'd use. But it's definitely something *he* has to hear about."

The guard touched a finger to the pearl on his collar.

"Better go inside, in that case."

I did as I was invited.

My audience with the khan was neither as private nor as lengthy as I might have wished, but, in all other respects, it was a success. One of his wives was there, as well as Minister Chiledu, the national security adviser, and the khan was notoriously busy during this ceremonial restaging of the war caravan. I thought, not for the first time, of how old he looked: much older than the young man who had been elected to this office seven years earlier, brimming with plans and promises. Now he was greying and tired, worn down by disappointing polls and the pressures of managing an empire that was beginning to fray at the edges. The caravan was supposed to be an antidote to all that. In this, the nine hundred and ninety ninth year since the death of the Founder (we would celebrate this birthday, but no one knows when it happened), a special effort had been made to create the largest caravan in decades, with almost every local system commander in attendance.

As I stepped off the *ger* to collect Goyo and begin my mission, I felt something perilously close to elation. The data I had presented to the khan – the troubling signs I had detected concerning the functioning and security of the Infrastructure – had been taken seriously. The khan could have waved aside my concerns as an issue for his successor, but – to his credit, I think – he had not. I had been given licence and funds to gather more information, even if that meant voyaging to the Kuchlug Special Administrative Volume and operating under the nose of Qilian, one of the men who had been making life difficult for the khan these last few years.

And yet my mood of elation was short lived.

I had no sooner set my feet on the ground than I spied Tenger. He was bullying Goyo, jerking hard on his bridle, kicking a boot against his hocks. He was so preoccupied with his business that he did not see me approaching from behind his back. I took hold of a good, thick clump of his hair and snapped his head back as far it would go. He released the bridle, staggering back under the pressure I was applying.

I whispered in his ear. "No one hurts my horse, you ignorant piece of shit."

Then I spun him around, the hair tearing out in my fist, and kneed him hard in the groin, so that he coughed out a groan of pain and nausea and bent double, like a man about to vomit.

Some say that it is Heaven's Mandate that we should have the stars, just as it was the will of Heaven that our armies should bring the squabbling lands of Greater Mongolia under one system of governance, a polity so civilised that a woman could ride naked from the western shores of Europe to the eastern edge of China without once being molested. I say that it is

simply the case that we – call us Mongols, call us humans, it scarcely matters now – have always made the best of what we are given.

Take the nexus in Gansu system, for instance. It was a medium-sized
moon that had been hollowed out nearly all the way to its middle, leaving
a shell barely a hundred *li* thick, with a small round kernel buttressed to
the shell by ninety-nine golden spokes. Local traffic entered and departed
the nexus via apertures at the northern and southern poles. Not that there
was much local traffic to speak of: Gansu, with its miserly red sun – only
just large enough to sustain fusion – and handful of desolate, volatile-poor,
and radiation-lashed rocky worlds, was neither a financial nor military
hub, nor a place that figured prominently in tourist itineraries. As was
often the case, it was something of a puzzle why the wormlike *khorkoi* had
built the nexus in such a miserable location to begin with.

Unpromising material, but in the five hundred years since we first reo-
pened a portal into the Infrastructure, we had made a glittering bauble out
of it. Five major trunk routes converged on Gansu, including a high-capac-
ity branch of the Kherlen Corridor, the busiest path in the entire network.
In addition, the moon offered portals to a dozen secondary routes, four
of which had been rated stable enough to allow passage by juggernaut-
class ships. Most of those secondary routes led to stellar population cen-
tres of some economic importance, including the Kiriltuk, Tatatunga, and
Chilagun administrative volumes, each of which encompassed more than
fifty settled systems and around a thousand habitable worlds. Even the
routes which led to nowhere of particular importance were well-travelled
by prospectors and adventurers, hoping to find *khorkoi* relics, or, that
fever dream of all chancers, an unmapped nexus.

We did not know the function of the ninety-nine spokes, or of the core
they buttressed. No matter; the core made a useful foundation, a place
upon which to build. From the vantage point of the rising shuttle, it was a
scribble of luminous neon, packed tight as a migraine. I could not distin-
guish the lights of individual buildings, only the larger glowing demarka-
tions of the precincts between city-sized districts. Pressurised horseways
a whole *li* wide were thin, snaking scratches. The human presence had
even begun to climb up the golden spokes, pushing tendrils of light out
to the moon's inner surface. Commercial slogans spelled themselves out
in letters ten *li* high. *On Founder's Day, drink only Temujin Brand Airag.*
Sorkan-Shira rental ponies have low mileage, excellent stamina, and good
temperament. Treat your favorite wife: buy her only Zarnuk Silks. During
hunting season, safeguard your assets with New Far Samarkand Mutual
Insurance. Think you're a real man? Then you should be drinking Death
Worm Airag: the one with a sting at both ends!

I had spent only one night in Gansu, arranging a eunuch and waiting for
the smaller ship that would carry us the rest of the way to Kuchlug. Now
Goyo, the eunuch, and I were being conveyed to the *Burkhan Khaldun*,
a vessel that was even smaller than the *Black Heart Mountain* that had
brought me to Gansu. The *BK* was only one *li* from end to end, less than a
quarter of that across the bow. The hull was a multicoloured quilt of patch

repairs, with many scratches, craters, and scorches yet to be attended to. The lateral stabilization vanes had the slightly buckled look of something that had been badly bent and then hammered back into shape, while the yaw-dampeners appeared to have originated from a completely different ship, fixed on with silvery fillets of recent welding work. A whole line of windows had been plated over.

As old as the *BK* might have been, it had taken more than just age and neglect to bring her to that state. The Parvan Tract was a notoriously rough passage, quickly taking its toll on even a new ship. If the Kherlen Corridor was a wide, stately river which could almost be navigated blindfold, then the Tract was a series of narrow rapids whose treacherous properties varied from trip to trip, requiring not just expert input from the crew, but passengers with the constitution to tolerate a heavy crossing.

Once I had checked into my rooms and satisfied myself that Goyo was being taken care of, I made my way back to the passenger area. I bought a glass of Temujin *airag* and made my way to the forward viewing platform, with its wide sweep of curved window – scratched and scuffed in places, worryingly starred in others – and leaned hard against the protective railing. The last shuttle had already detached, and the *BK* was accelerating towards the portal, its great human-made doors irising open at the last possible moment, so that the interior of Gansu was protected from the Parvan Tract's unpredictable energy surges. Even though the Infrastructure shaft stretched impossibly far into the distance, my mind kept insisting that we were about to punch through the thin skin of the moon.

The ship surged forward, the sluggish artificial gravity generators struggling to maintain the local vertical. We passed through the door, into the superluminal machinery of the Infrastructure. The tunnel walls were many *li* away, but they felt closer – as they raced by at increasing speed, velocity traced by the luminous squiggly patterns that had been inscribed on the wall for inscrutable reasons by the *khorkoi* builders, I had the impression that the shaft was constricting, tightening down on our fragile little ship. Yet nothing seemed to disconcert or even arouse the interest of my fellow passengers. In ones and twos, they drifted away from the gallery, leaving me alone with my eunuch, observing from a discreet distance. I drank the *airag* very slowly, looking down the racing shaft, wondering if it would be my fortune to see a phantom with my own eyes. Phantoms, after all, were what had brought me here.

Now all I had to do was poison the eunuch.

The eunuch answered to "eunuch," but his real name (I learned after a certain amount of probing) was Tisza. He had not been surgically castrated; there was an implant somewhere in his forearm dispensing the necessary cocktail of androgen-blockers, suppressing his libido and lending him a mildly androgynous appearance. Other implants, similar to those employed by government operatives, had given him heightened reflexes, spatial coordination, and enhanced night vision. He was adept with weapons and unarmed combat, as (I had no cause to doubt) were all Batu eunuchs. I had no need of his protection, of course, but appearances were paramount. I was posing as a woman of means, a well-healed tourist. No woman in my circumstances would ever have travelled without the accompaniment of a man such as Tisza.

He served my purpose in another way. We shared the same rooms, with the eunuch sleeping in a small, doorless annex connected to mine. Because I might (conceivably) be drugged or poisoned, Tisza always ate the same meals as me, served at the same time and brought to my cabin by one of the *BK*'s white uniformed stewards.

"What if you get poisoned and die on me?" I asked, innocently, when we were sitting opposite together across my table.

He tapped a pudgy finger against his belly. "It would take a lot to kill me, Miss Bocheng. My constitution has been tailored to process many toxins in common circulation among would-be assassins and miscreants. I will become ill much sooner than you would, but what would kill you would merely make me unwell, and not so unwell that I could not discharge my duties."

"I hope you're right about that."

He patted his chin with napkin. "It is no occasion for pride. I am what I am because of the chemical intervention and surgery of the Batu Escort Agency. It would be equally pointless to understate my abilities."

Later, feigning nervousness, I told him that I had heard a noise from his annex.

"It is nothing, I assure you. No one could have entered these rooms without our knowing it."

"It sounded like someone breathing."

He smiled tolerantly. "There are many foreign sounds on a ship like this. Noises carry a great distance through the ducts and conduits of the air-circulation system."

"Couldn't someone have crawled through those same conduits?"

He rose from the table without a note of complaint. "It is unlikely, but I shall investigate."

As soon as he had vanished through the door into his annex, I produced a vial from my pocket and tipped its sugary contents onto the remains of his meal. I heard him examining things, pulling open cupboard doors and sliding drawers. By the time he returned, with a reassuring expression on his face, the toxin crystals had melted invisibly into his food and the vial was snug in my pocket.

"Whatever you heard, there's no one in there."

"Are you sure?"

"Completely. But I'm willing to look again, if it would put your mind at ease."

I looked abashed. "I'm just being silly."

"Not at all. You must not be afraid to bring things to my attention. It is what you have hired me for."

"Tuck in," I said, nodding at his meal. "Before it gets cold."

Tisza was moaning and sweating on the bed, deep in fever, as Mister Tayang appraised him warily. "Did he tell you he could detect poisons? They don't all come with that option."

"He can. Isn't that the point?"

"It could just be a bug he's picked up. On the other hand, he may have been hit by something intended for you that his system wasn't designed to filter out."

"A poison?"

"It's a possibility, Miss Bocheng."

Tayang was a steward; a young man with a pleasant face and a highly professional manner. I had seen him around earlier, but – as was the case with all the crew – he had steadfastly refused to engage in any conversation not related to my immediate needs. I had counted on this, and contrived the poisoning of the eunuch to give me heightened access to one or more of the crew. It need not have been Tayang, but my instincts told me that he would serve excellently.

"Then why isn't it affecting me?" I asked.

"I don't wish to alarm you, but it could be that it's going to in a very short while. We need to get both of you into the sick bay. Under observation, we should be able to stabilize the eunuch and ensure you come to no harm."

This was the outcome I had been hoping for, but some indignation was called for. "If you think I'm going to spend the rest of this trip in some stinking sick bay, after I've paid for this cabin . . ."

Tayang raised a calming hand. "It won't be for long. A day or two, just to be on the safe side. Then you can enjoy the rest of the trip in comfort."

Another pair of stewards was summoned to help shift the hapless Tisza, while I made my way to the sick bay on foot. "Actually," I said, "now that you mention it . . . I do feel a little peculiar."

Tayang looked at me sympathetically. "Don't worry, Miss Bocheng. We'll have you right as rain in no time."

The sick bay was larger and better equipped than I had been expecting, almost as if it belonged in a different ship entirely. I was relieved to see that no one else was using it. Tayang helped me onto a reclined couch while the other stewards pulled a screen around the stricken eunuch.

"How do you feel now?" Tayang asked, fastening a black cuff around my forearm.

"Still a bit funny."

For the next few minutes, Tayang – who had clearly been given basic medical training – studied the readouts on a handheld display he had pulled from a recess in the wall.

"Well, it doesn't *look* . . ." he began.

"I should have listened to my friends," I said, shaking my head. "They told me not to come here."

He tapped buttons set into the side of the display. "Your friends warned you that you might end up getting poisoned?"

"Not exactly, no. But they said it wasn't a good idea travelling on the *Burkhan Khaldun*, down the Parvan Tract. They were right, weren't they?"

"That would depend. So far, I can't see any sign that you've ingested anything poisonous. Of course, it could be something that the *analyser* isn't equipped to detect . . ."

"And the eunuch?"

"Just a moment," Tayang said, leaving the display suspended in the air. He walked over to the other bed and pulled aside the curtain. I heard a murmured exchange before he returned, with a bit less of a spring in his step. "Well, there's no doubt that something pretty heavy's hit *his* system. Could be a deliberate toxin, could be something nasty that just happened to get into him. We're not far out of Gansu; he could have contracted something there that's only just showing up."

"He's been poisoned, Mister Tayang. My bodyguard. Doesn't that strike you as a slightly ominous development?"

"I still say it could be something natural. We'll know soon enough. In the meantime, I wouldn't necessarily jump to the conclusion that you're in immediate peril."

"I'm concerned, Mister Tayang."

"Well, don't be. You're in excellent hands." He leaned over to plump my pillow. "Get under the blanket if you feel shivery. Is there anything you'd like me to fetch from your room?"

"No, thank you."

"In which case, I'll leave you be. I'll keep the analyser attached just in case it flags anything. The other stewards are still here; if you need anything, just call."

"I will."

He was on the verge of leaving – I had no doubt that he was a busy man – when something caused him to narrow his eyes. "So if it wasn't about being poisoned, Miss Bocheng, why exactly was it that your friends didn't want you taking this ship?"

"Oh, that." I shook my head. "It's silly. I don't know why I mentioned it at all. It's not as if I believe any of that nonsense."

"Any of *what* nonsense, exactly?"

"You know, about the phantoms. About how the Parvan Tract is haunted. I told them I was above all that, but they still kept going on about it. They said that if I took this ship, I might never come back. Of course, that only made me even more determined."

"Good for you."

"I told them I was a rationalist, not someone who believes in ghosts and goblins." I shifted on the couch, giving him a sympathetic look. "I expect that you're fed up with hearing about all that, especially as you actually work here. I mean, if anyone would have been likely to see something, it would be you, wouldn't it, or one of the other crew?"

"That would make sense," he said.

"Well, the fact that you obviously *haven't* . . . there can't be anything to it, can there?" I crossed my arms and smiled triumphantly. "Wait until I tell my friends how silly they've been."

"Perhaps . . ." he began, and then fell silent.

I knew that I had him then; that it would be only a matter of time before Tayang felt compelled to show me evidence. My instincts proved correct, for within a day of my discharge from the sick bay (the eunuch was still under observation, but making satisfactory progress), the steward contrived an excuse to visit my quarters. He had a clean towel draped over his arm, as if he had come to replace the one in my bathroom.

"I brought you a fresh one. I think the cleaning section missed this corridor this morning."

"They didn't, but I appreciate the gesture all the same."

He lingered, as if he had something to get off his chest but was struggling to find the right words.

"Mister Tayang?" I pressed.

"What we were talking about before . . ."

"Yes?" I enquired mildly.

"Well, you're wrong." He said it nicely enough, but the defiance in his words was clear. "The phantoms exist. I may not have seen anything with my own eyes, but I've seen data that's just as convincing."

"I doubt it."

"I can show you easily enough." He must have been intending to say those words from the moment he had decided to come to my cabin, yet now that he had spoken them, his regret was immediate.

"Really?"

"I shouldn't have . . ."

"Tell me," I said forcefully. "Whatever this is, I want to see it."

"It means your friends were right, and you were wrong."

"Then I need to know that."

Tayang gave me a warning look. "It'll change the way you think. At the moment, you have the luxury of not believing in the phantoms. I know that there's something out there that we don't understand, something that doesn't belong. Are you sure you want that burden?"

"If you can handle it, I think I can. What do I have to do?"

"I need to show you something. But I can't do it now. Later, during the night shift, it'll be quieter."

"I'll be ready," I said, nodding eagerly.

Close to midnight, Tayang came for me. Remembering to keep in character for someone half convinced she was the target of an assassin, I did not open up immediately.

"Yes?"

"It's me, Tayang."

I cracked open the door. "I'm ready."

He looked me up and down. "Take off those clothes, please."

"I'm sorry?"

He glanced away, blushing. "What I mean is, wear as much or as little as you would wear for bed." I noticed that he had a jacket draped over his arm, as if he was ready to put it around my shoulders. "Should we meet someone, and should questions be asked, you will explain that I found you sleepwalking, and that I'm taking you back to your cabin via the most discreet route I can think of, so you don't embarrass yourself in front of any other passengers."

"I see. You've given this some thought, haven't you?"

"You aren't the first skeptical passenger, Miss Bocheng."

I closed the door and disrobed, then put on thin silk trousers and an equally thin silk blouse, the one scarlet and the other electric yellow, with a design of small blue wolves. I untied my hair and messed it to suggest someone only recently roused from the bed.

Outside, as was customary during the night shift of the *BK*'s operations, the corridor lights were dimmed to a sleepy amber. The bars, restaurants, and gaming rooms were closed. The public lounges were deserted and silent, save for the scurrying mouselike cleaning robots that always emerged after the people had gone away. Tayang chose his route well, for we did not bump into any other passengers or crew.

"This is the library," he said, when we had arrived in a small, red-lit room, set with shelves, screens, and movable chairs. "No one uses it much – it's not exactly a high priority for most of our passengers. They'd rather drink away the voyage with Temujin *airag*."

"Are we allowed here?"

"Well, technically there'd be nothing to stop you visiting this room during normal ship hours. But during normal ship hours, I wouldn't be able to show you what I'm about to." He was trying to be nonchalant about the whole adventure, but his nervousness was like a boy on a dare. "But don't worry, we won't get into trouble."

"How is a library going to change my mind about the phantoms?"

"Let me show you." He ushered me to one of the terminals, swinging out a pair of hinged stools for us to sit on. I sat to the left of him, while Tayang flipped open a dust cover to expose a keyboard. He began to tap at the keys, causing changes to the hooded data display situated at eye-level. "As it happens, these consoles are connected to the *Burkhan Khaldun*'s own computers. You just have to know the right commands."

"Won't this show up?"

He shook his head. "I'm not doing anything that will come to anyone's attention. Besides, I'm perfectly entitled to access this data. The only thing wrong is you being with me, and if anyone comes down here, we'll have time to prepare for them, to make it look as if I caught you sleepwalking.' He fell silent for a minute or so, tapping through options, obviously navigating his way through to the information stored in the computer's memory bank. "I just hope the company spooks haven't got to it already," he murmured. "Every now and then, someone from Blue Heaven comes aboard and wipes large chunks of the *BK*'s memory. They say they're just doing routine archiving, clearing space for more data, but no one believes that. Look's like we're in time, though. I didn't see any spooks nosing around when we were in Gansu: they'll probably come aboard next time we're back." He glanced over his shoulder. "I'll show it to you once. Then we go. All right?"

"Whatever you say, Mister Tayang."

"The *BK* has cameras, pointed into the direction of flight. They detect changes in the tunnel geometry and feed that data to the servo-motors driving the stabilising vanes and yaw dampers, so that they can make adjustments to smooth out the turbulence. They're also there as an emergency measure in case we encounter another ship coming the other way, one that isn't on schedule or hasn't got an active transponder. The cameras give us just enough warning to swerve the *BK* to one side, to give passing clearance. It's bumpy for the passengers when that happens, but a lot better than a head-on collision at tunnel speeds."

"I take it the cameras saw something," I said.

Tayang nodded. "This was a couple of trips ago, about half way between Gansu and Kuchlug. They only got eight clear frames. Whatever it was was moving fast, much quicker than one of our ships. The fourth, fifth, and sixth frames are the sharpest."

"Show me."

He tapped keys. A picture sprang onto the display, all fuzzy green hues, overlaid with date stamps and other information. It took a moment before I was sure what I was looking at. There was some kind of pale green smudge filling half the frame, a random-looking shape like the blindspot one sees after looking at the sun for too long, and beyond that, a suggestion of the curving squiggles of the tunnel's *khorkoi* patterning, reaching away to infinity.

I pressed a finger against the smudge. "That's the phantom?"

"This is frame three. It becomes clearer on the next one." He advanced to the next image and I saw what he meant. The smudge had enlarged, but also become sharper, with details beginning to emerge. Edges and surfaces, a hint of organised structure, even if the overall shape was still elusive.

"Next frame," Tayang mouthed.

Now there could be no doubt that the phantom was some kind of ship, even if it conformed to the pattern of no vessel I had ever seen. It was sleek and organic looking, more like a darting squid than the clunky lines of the *BK*.

He advanced to the next frame, but – while the image did not become substantially clearer – the angle changed, so that the three-dimensional structure of the phantom became more apparent. At the same time, hints of patterning had begun to emerge: darker green symbols on the side of the hull, or fuselage, or body, of whatever the thing was.

"That's about as good as it gets," Tayang said.

"I'm impressed."

"You see these arm-like appendages?" he asked, pointing to part of the image. "I'm guessing, of course, but I can't help wondering if they don't serve the same function as our stabilization vanes, only in a more elegant fashion."

"I think you could be right."

"One thing I'm sure of, though. *We* didn't build that ship. I'm no expert, Miss Bocheng, but I know what counts as cutting-edge ship design, and that thing is way beyond it."

"I don't think anyone would argue with that."

"It wasn't built by the government, or some mysterious splinter group of Islamist separatists. In fact, I don't think it was built by humans at all. We're looking at alien technology, and they're using our Infrastructure system as if they own it. More than that: every now and then you hear about entire ships and message packets going missing. They're not just trespassing in our network, they're stealing from it as well."

"I can see Blue Heaven would rather this didn't get out."

Tayang closed the display. "I'm sorry, but that's all I can show you. It's enough, though, isn't it?"

"More than enough," I said.

Of course, I had my doubts. Tayang could have easily faked those images, or been the unwitting victim of someone else's fakery. But I did not think that was the case. I had been looking at genuine data, not something cooked up to scare the tourists.

I was just beginning to plot my next move – how I would get a copy of the data, and smuggle it back to NHK while I continued with my investigations in Kuchlug space – when I became aware of a presence behind me. Tayang must have sensed it too, for he turned around as I did. Standing in the doorway to the library was one of the other stewards, an older man whose name I had yet to learn. I noticed that the sleeves of his uniform were too short for him.

Wordlessly, he raised a hand. In it glinted the smooth alloy form of a small, precise weapon: the kind often carried by government spies such as myself. He shot me; I had a moment to stare at the barb embedded in my thigh, and then I passed out.

I came around in my cabin, gripped by a vile nausea, a headache like a slowly closing iron vice, and no conception of how much time had passed since Tayang and I had been disturbed in the library. Getting out of bed – I had been placed on top of the sheets – I searched the adjoining annex for the eunuch, before I remembered that he was still in the sickbay. I tried my door and found that it had been locked from the outside; there was no way for me to leave my room.

Understand, I did not accept my imprisonment lightly, but understand also that all my attempts at escape proved futile. I could not even squeeze through the conduit I had mentioned to the eunuch: such methods succeed in adventure stories, but not in real life.

Of course, it was desired that I be kept alive. The man who had shot me could have administered a fatal dose simply by twisting a dial in the grip of his weapon. He had chosen not to, and it was no accident that food and water appeared in the room's serving hatch at regular intervals. But as to who had chosen to detain me, I was uninformed.

I could guess, though.

He was the first to see me when the ship docked in Kuchlug space. He came to my room, accompanied by guards. He was as squat and muscled as a wrestler, his bare arms fully as thick as my thighs. He wore a leather jerkin, criss-crossed by thick black belts to which were fastened various ceremonial weapons and symbols of martial authority. A carefully tended moustache, curled down on either side of his mouth, with a tiny but deliberate tuft of hair preserved under his lower lip. A stiff leather helmet, long at the sides and back, covered the rest of his head. The only visible part of his hair was a blunt, wedge-shaped fringe terminating just above his eyebrows, which were at once finely drawn, expressive, and deeply quizzical.

Of course, I knew the face.

"Commander Qilian," I said.

"Yes, I get about." His hands were impressively hairy, scarred and knotted like the roots of a very old tree. He snapped his fingers at the guards. "Have her brought to the debriefing facility on the Qing Shui moon. Bring the pony as well." Then he poked one of those fingers under my chin, lifting it up so that our eyes met. "Give some thought to the particulars of your story, Miss Bocheng. It may make all the difference."

They took me down to the moon. We landed somewhere and I was carried through dark, rusting corridors to a windowless holding cell. The floor rocked with a slow, sickening motion, as if I was on a ship at sea in a high swell – even though there were no oceans on the Qing Shui moon. They stripped me, took away my belongings, and gave me prison clothing to wear: a simple one-piece affair in orange silk. I pretended to be shocked and disorientated, but I was already summoning my training, recollecting those stratagems I had been taught to withstand prolonged detention and interrogation. As the guards were shutting the door on me, I contrived to slip a finger into the crack between the door and its frame. When the door closed, I yelped in pain and withdrew my hand with the fingertip squashed and red from the pressure.

I sucked it in my mouth until the pain abated.

"Stupid bitch," someone said.

There was a bunk, a spigot in the wall that dribbled tepid, piss-coloured water, and a hole in the floor, with chipped ceramic sides stained an unspeakable brown. Light seeped in through a grille in the door. Neither willing nor able to sleep, I lay on the bunk and shivered. Presently – no more than two or three hours after my arrival – men came to take me down the corridor, to an interrogation room.

It is not necessary to document all that happened; the many weeks that it took for me to permit them to peel back the layers of identity I had wrapped around myself, each time thinking that the victory was theirs.

Suffice to say that most of what they did to me involved electricity and chemicals in varying combinations. They did break two fingers on my left hand, including the one I had trapped in the door, but when they pulled out one of my fingernails, it was from the other hand, not the one I had hurt. They beat me around, broke my teeth, extinguished *Yesugei* brand cigarettes on my skin, but only cut me superficially, to demonstrate that they could and would. Then they had other men come in to sterilize and dress the wounds. Once in a while, a gowned doctor with a Slavic face came to the cell and gave me a thorough, probing medical examination.

It was during one of the doctor's examinations that I elected to reveal myself as a government spy. As the doctor was examining me, I allowed my hair – stiff and greasy with dirt – to fall away from the nape of my neck. I knew instantly that he had taken the bait. I felt his fingers press into the area around the subcutaneous device, feeling for the hard-edged component lodged under the skin.

"What is this?"

"What is what?" I asked, all innocence.

"There's something under your skin."

They took me back to the interrogation room. My hair was shaved and my neck swabbed. The Slavic doctor dithered over the medical tools on the shelves, until he found the bundle he wanted. He brought the instruments onto the table, unrolling the towel so that I could see what lay in store for me. When he was done, the implant was placed on a piece of clean towel in front of me. It was bloodied, with bits of whitish flesh still attached to its feeler-like input probes.

"Looks like government," someone said.

I did not admit to it immediately; that would have made them rightfully suspicious. It was a matter of judging the moment, making my confession appear natural, rather than a scripted event.

In hindsight, I wish that I had arranged my confession sooner.

I was brought to a different room. There was a window in the wall, before which I was encouraged to sit. A clamp was fitted around my eyes so that I could not look away. The doctor dripped some agent into my eyes which had the effect of paralysing the lids, preventing me from blinking. When the lights came on in the room on the other side of the window, I found myself looking at Goyo.

He was upside down, suspended in a sling, rotated on his back in the manner that horses are prepared for veterinary work. The sling was supported from a heavy white framework mounted on trolley wheels. Goyo's legs had been bound together in pairs using thick adhesive material. Even his head and neck had been braced into position using cushioned supports and clamps. A leathery girth strap enclosed his waist, preventing him from thrashing around. His abdominal region, between fore and hind limbs, had been shaved to the skin. A white sheet, not much larger than a towel, had been draped over part of that shaven area. There was a red stain in the middle of the sheet, where it formed a depression.

Goyo's eye, the one that I could see, was white and wild and brimming with fear.

Qilian walked into the room. He was dressed as I remembered him from our encounter on the *BK*, except that his hands and forearms were now gloved. The gloves had a heavy, martial look to them, with curved steel talons on the ends of the fingers. He stopped next to Goyo, one hand resting on the frame, the other stroking my pony's neck, as if he sought to placate him. When he spoke, his voice came through a microphone.

"We think we know who you are, but some corroboration would be welcome. What is your operational codename? To which section are you assigned? Are you one of the Thirteen?"

My mouth had turned dry. I said nothing.

"Very well," Qilian continued, as if he had expected as much. He reached over and whisked the white sheet away from Goyo's abdomen. There was a wound there, a red sucking hole wide enough to plunge a fist through.

"No," I said, trying to break free of the straps that bound me to the chair.

"Before you arrived," Qilian said, "certain surgical preparations were made. A number of ribs have already been removed. They can be put back, of course, but their absence now means that there is an unobstructed path through to your pony's heart."

With his right hand, he reached into the wound. He frowned, concentrating on the task. He delved in slowly, cautiously. Goyo responded by thrashing against his restraints, but it was to more avail than my own efforts. In a short while, Qilian's entire fist was hidden. He pushed deeper, encountering resistance. Now the fist and fully half of his forearm was gone. He adjusted his posture, leaning in so that his chest was braced against Goyo's shoulder. He pushed deeper, until only the top extremity of the glove remained visible.

"I am touching his beating heart now," Qilian said, looking directly at me. "He's a strong one, no doubt about that. A fine pony, from good Mongol stock. But I am stronger, at least when I have my hand on his heart. You don't think I can stop it beating? I assure you I can. Would you like to see?" The expression on his face altered to one of concentrated effort, little veins bulging at the side of his temple. Goyo thrashed with renewed energy. "Yes, he feels it now. He doesn't know what's happening, but a billion years of dumb evolution tells him something's not right. I don't doubt that the pain is excruciating, at least in animal terms. Would you like me to stop?"

The words spilled out, feeling like a genuine confession. "I am Yellow Dog. I am a government operative, one of the Thirteen."

"Yes, we thought you were Yellow Dog. We have the non-official cover list for all of the Thirteen, and we know that Ariunaa Bocheng is a name you've used before, when posing as a journalist." He broke off, took a deep breath, and seemed to redouble his efforts. "But it's good to get it from the horse's mouth, so to speak."

"Stop now."

"Too late. I've already started."

"You said you'd stop," I replied, screaming out the words. "You promised you'd stop!"

"I said nothing of the sort. I said the ribs could be put back. That remains the case."

In an instant, Goyo stopped thrashing. His eye was still open, but all of a sudden there was nothing behind it.

Several weeks later – I could not say precisely how many – Qilian sat opposite me with his big hairy hands clasped in silent contemplation. The documents on his desk were kept in place by grisly paperweights: little plinth-mounted bones and bottled, shrunken things in vinegary solution. There were swords and ceremonial knives on the wall, framing a familiar reproduction watercolour showing the landing of the invasion fleet on Japanese soil.

"You were good," he said eventually. "I'll give you that. My men genuinely thought they'd hit bottom when they got you to confess to being the journalist. It was a surprise to all concerned when that identity turned out to be a cover."

"I'm glad I provided you with some amusement," I said.

"If it hadn't been for that implant, we might never have known. Your people really should give some thought into making those things less detectable."

"My people?" I asked. "The last time I checked, we were all working for the same government."

"I don't doubt that's how it feels in New High Karakorum. Out here, it's a different story. In case you hadn't realized, this is a special administrative volume. It's part of the empire, but only in a very tenuous, politically ambiguous sense. They want what we can give them – raw materials, cheaply-synthesized chemicals, mass-produced low-bulk consumer goods – but they don't want to think too hard about what we have to do to keep that river of commerce flowing. Laws have to be bent here, because otherwise there'd *be* no here. Look out the window, Yellow Dog."

Visible through the partially shuttered window of his office, a good four or five *li* below, was a brutal, wintery landscape of stained ice, reaching all the way to the horizon. The sky was a rose pink, shading to midnight blue at the top of the window. Cutting through it along a diagonal was the twinkling, sickle-like curve of a planetary ring system. Canyon-deep fissures cracked the surface, leaking feathery quills of yellow-white steam into the thin, poisonous atmosphere of that windswept sky. Here and there, an elbow of splintered rock broke the surface. There were no fixed communities on the moon. Instead, immense spiderlike platforms, mounted on six or eight intricate jointed legs, picked their way across the ever-shifting terrain in awesome slow motion. The platforms varied in size, but at the very least each supported a cluster of squat civic buildings, factories, refineries, and spacecraft handling facilities. Some of the platforms had deployed drilling rigs or cables into the fissures, sucking chemical nourishment from under the icy crust. A number were connected together by long, dangling wires, along which I made out the tiny, suspended forms of cable cars, moving from platform to platform.

"It's very pretty," I said.

"It's a hellhole, frankly. Only three planets in the entire volume are even remotely amenable to terraforming, and not one of those three is on track for completion inside five hundred years. We'll be lucky if any of them are done before the Founder's two thousandth anniversary, let alone the thousandth. Most of the eighty million people under my stewardship live in domes and tunnels, with only a few *alds* of soil or glass between them and a horrible, choking death." He unclasped his hands in order to run a finger across one of his desktop knicknacks. "It's not much of an existence, truth be told. But that doesn't mean we don't have an economy that needs fuelling. We have jobs. We have vacancies for skilled labour. Machines do our drilling, but the machines need to be fixed and programmed by *people*, down at the cutting face. We pay well, for those prepared to work for us."

"And you come down hard on those who displease you."

"Local solutions to local problems, that's our mantra. You wouldn't understand, cosied up in the middle of the empire. You pushed the dissidents and troublemakers out to the edge and left us to worry about them." He tapped a finger against his desk. "Nestorian Christians, Buddhists, Islamists. It's a thousand years since we crushed them, and they *still* haven't got over it. Barely a week goes by without some regressive, fundamentalist element stirring up trouble, whether it's sabotage of one of our industrial facilities or a terrorist attack against the citizenship. And yet you sit there in New High Karakorum and shake your heads in disgust when we have the temerity to implement even the mildest security measures."

"I wouldn't call mass arrests, show-trials, and public executions 'mild'," I said tartly.

"Then try living here."

"I get the impression that's not really an option. Unless you mean living in prison, for the rest of my life, or until NHK sends an extraction team."

Qilian made a pained expression. "Let's be clear. You aren't my enemy. Quite the contrary. You are now an honoured guest of the Kuchlug special administrative volume. I regret what happened earlier, but if you'd admitted your true identity, none of that would have been necessary." He folded his arms behind his neck, leaned back in his chair with a creak of leather. "We've got off on the wrong footing here, you and I. But how are we supposed to feel when the empire sends undercover agents snooping into our territory? And not only that, but agents that persist in asking such puzzling questions?" He looked at me with sudden, sharp intensity, as if my entire future hung on my response to what he was about to say. "Just what is it about the phantoms that interests you so much, Yellow Dog?"

"Why should you worry about my interest in a phenomenon that doesn't exist?" I countered.

"Do you believe that, after what you saw on the *Burkhan Khaldun*?"

"I can only report what I saw. It would not be for me to make inferences."

"But still."

"Why are we discussing this, Commander Qilian?"

"Because I'm intrigued. Our perception was that NHK probably knew a lot more about the phenomenon than we did. Your arrival suggests otherwise. They sent you on an intelligence gathering mission, and the thrust of your enquiry indicates that you are at least as much in the dark as we are, if not more so."

"I can't speak for my superiors."

"No, you can't. But it seems unlikely that they'd have risked sending a valued asset into a troublespot like Kuchlug without very good reason. Which, needless to say, is deeply alarming. We thought the core had the matter under control. Clearly, they don't. Which only makes the whole issue of the phantoms even more vexed and troubling."

"What do you know?"

He laughed. "You think I'm going to tell you, just like that?"

"You've as much as admitted that this goes beyond any petty political differences that might exist between NHK and Kuchlug. Let me report back to my superiors. I'll obtain their guarantee that there'll be a two-way traffic in intelligence." I nodded firmly. "Yes, we misjudged this one. I should never have come under deep cover. But we were anxious not to undermine your confidence in us by revealing the depth of our ignorance on the phenomenon. I assure you that in the future everything will be above board and transparent. We can set up a bilateral investigative team, pooling the best experts from here and back home."

"That easy, eh? We just shake hands and put it all behind us? The deception on your part, the torture on ours?"

I shrugged. "You had your methods. I had mine."

Qilian smiled slightly. "There's something you need to know. Two days ago – not long after we dug that thing out of you – we did in fact send a communiqué to NHK. We informed them that one of their agents was now in our safekeeping, that she was being more than helpful in answering our questions, and that we would be happy to return her at the earliest opportunity."

"Go on."

"They told us that there was no such agent. They denied knowledge of either Ariunaa Bocheng or an operative named Yellow Dog. They made no demands for you to be returned, although they did say that if you were handed over, you'd be of 'interest' to them. Do you know what this means?' When I refrained from answering – though I knew precisely what it meant – Qilian continued. "You've been disavowed, Yellow Dog. Left out in the cold, like a starving mongrel."

His men came for me again, several days later. I was taken to a pressurized boarding platform, a spindly structure cantilevered out from the side of the government building. A cable car was waiting, a dull-grey, bulbous-ended cylinder swaying gently against its restraints. The guards pushed me aboard, then slammed the airtight door, before turning a massive wheel to lock it shut. Qilian was already aboard the car, sitting in a dimpled leather chair with one leg crossed over the other. He wore huge fur-lined boots equipped with vicious spurs.

"A little trip, I thought," he said, by way of welcome, indicating the vacant seat opposite his.

The cable car lurched into motion. After reaching the limit of the boarding area, it passed through a long glass airlock and then dropped sickeningly, plunging down so far that it descended under the lowest level of buildings and factory structures perched on the platform. One of the huge, skeletal legs was rising towards us, the foot raised as if it intended to stomp down on the fragile little cable car. Yet just when it seemed we were doomed, the car began to climb again, creaking and swaying. Qilian was looking at something through a pair of tiny binoculars, some piece of equipment – a probe or drillhead, I presumed – being winched up from the surface, into the underside of the platform.

"Is there a point to this journey?" I asked.

He lowered the binoculars and returned them to a leather case on his belt. "Very much so. What I will show you constitutes a kind of test. I would advise you to be on your guard against the obvious."

The cable car slid across the fractured landscape of the moon, traversing dizzyingly wide crevasses, dodging geysers, skimming past tilted rockfaces which seemed on the verge of toppling over at any moment. We rose and descended several times, on each occasion passing over one of the walking platforms. Now and then, there was an interruption while we were switched to a different line, before once more plunging down towards the surface. After more than half an hour of this – just when my stomach was beginning to settle into the rhythm – we came to a definite halt on what was in all respects just another boarding platform, attended by a familiar retinue of guards and technical functionaries. Qilian and I disembarked, with his spurs clicking against the cleated metal flooring. With a company of guards for escort, we walked into the interior of the platform's largest building. The entire place had an oily ambience, rumbling with the vibration of distant drilling processes.

"It's a cover," Qilian said, as if he had read my thoughts. "We keep the machines turning, but this is the one platform that doesn't have a useful production yield. It's a study facility instead."

"For studying what?"

"Whatever we manage to recover, basically."

Deep in the bowels of the platform, at a level which must have meant they were only just above the underside, was a huge holding tank which – so Qilian informed me – was designed to contain the unrefined liquid slurry that would ordinarily have been pumped up from under the ice. In this platform, the tank had been drained and equipped with power and lighting. The entire space had been partitioned into about a dozen ceilingless rooms, each of which appeared to contain a collection of garbage, arranged within the cells of a printed grid laid out on the floor. Some of the cells held sizable clusters of junk, others were empty. Benches arranged around the edges of the cells were piled with bits of twinkly rubbish, along with an impressive array of analysis tools and recording devices.

It looked as if it should have been a literal hive of activity, but the entire place was deserted.

"You want to tell me what I'm looking at here?"

Qilian indicated a ladder. "Go down and take a look for yourself. Examine anything that takes your fancy. Use any tools you feel like. Look in the notebooks and data files. Rummage. Break stuff. You won't be punished if you do."

"This is phantom technology, isn't it? You've recovered pieces of alien ships." I said this in a kind of awed whisper, as if I hardly dared believe it myself.

"Draw whatever conclusion you see fit. I shall be intensely interested in what you have to say."

I started down the ladder. I had known from the moment I saw the relics that I would be unable to resist. "How long have I got? Before I'm judged to have failed this test, or whatever it is."

"Take your time," he said, smiling. "But don't take *too* much."

There seemed little point agonizing over which room to start with, assuming I had the time to examine more than one. The one I chose had the usual arrangement of grid, junk, and equipment benches. Lights burned from a rack suspended overhead. I stepped into the grid, striding over blank squares until she arrived at a promising little clump of mangled parts, some of them glittery, some of them charred to near-blackness. Gingerly, I picked up one of the bits. It was a curving section of metallic foil, ragged along one edge, much lighter and stiffer than I felt it had any right to be. I tested the edge against a finger and drew a bead of blood. No markings or detail of any kind. I placed it back down on the grid and examined another item. Heavier this time, solid in my hands, like a piece of good carved wood. Flowing, scroll-like green patterning on one convex surface: a suggestion of script, or a fragmented part of some script, in a language I did not recognise. I returned it to the grid and picked up a jagged, bifurcated thing like a very unwieldy sword or spearhead, formed in some metallic red material that appeared mirror-smooth and untarnished. In my hands, the thing had an unsettling buzzing quality, as if there was still something going on inside it. I picked up another object: a dented blue-green box, embossed with dense geometric patterns, cross-woven into one another in a manner that made my head hurt. The lid of the box opened to reveal six egglike white ovals, packed into spongey black material. There were six distinct spiral symbols painted onto the ovals, in another language that I did not recognize.

I perused more objects in the grid, then moved to the benches, where more items were laid out for inspection.

I moved into one of the adjoining rooms. There was something different about the degree of organization this time. The grid was the same, but the objects in it had been sorted into rough groupings. In one corner cell was a pile of spiky, metallic red pieces that obviously had something in common with the sword-like object I had examined in the other room. In other lay a cluster of dense, curved pieces with fragmented green patterning on each. Each occupied cell held a similar collection of vaguely related objects.

I examined another room, but soon felt that I had seen enough to form a ready opinion. The various categories of relic clearly had little in common. If they had all originated from the phantoms – either wrecked or damaged or attacked as they passed through the Infrastructure – then there was only one conclusion to be drawn. There was more than one type of phantom, which, in turn, meant there was more than one kind of alien.

We were not just dealing with one form of intruder. Judging by the number of filled cells, there were dozens – many dozens – of different alien technologies at play.

I felt the hairs on the back of my neck bristle. Our probes and instruments had swept the galaxy clean and still we had found no hint of anyone else out there. But these rooms said otherwise. Somehow or other, we had managed to miss the evidence of numerous other galaxy-faring civilizations, all of which were at least as technologically advanced as the Mongol Expansion.

Other empires, somehow co-existing with ours!

I was ready to return to Qilian, but, at the last moment, as I prepared to ascend the ladder, something held me back. It had all been too simple. Anyone with a pair of eyes in their head would have arrived at the same conclusion as I had. Qilian had said it would be a test, and that I must pass it.

It had been too easy so far.

Therefore, I must have missed something.

When we were back on the cable car, nosing down to the geysering surface, Qilian stroked a finger against his chin and watched me with an intense, snakelike fascination.

"You returned to the rooms."

"Yes."

"Something made you go back, when it looked as if you'd already finished."

"It wouldn't have been in my interests to fail you."

There was a gleam in his eye. "So what was it, Yellow Dog, that made you hesitate?"

"A feeling that I'd missed something. The obvious inference was that the collection implied the presence of more than one intruding culture, but you didn't need me to tell you that."

"No," he acknowledged.

"So there had to be something else. I didn't know what. But when I went back into the second room, something flashed through my mind. I knew I had seen something in there before, even if it had been in a completely different context."

I could not tell if he was pleased or disappointed. "Continue."

"The green markings on some of the relics. They meant nothing to me at first, but I suppose my subconscious must have picked up on something even then. They were fragments of something larger, which I'd seen before."

"Which was?"

"Arabic writing," I told him.

"Many people would be surprised to hear there was such a thing."

"If they knew their history, they'd know that the Arabs had a written language. An elegant one, too. It's just that most people outside of academic departments won't have ever seen it, any more than they know what Japanese or the Roman alphabet looks like."

"But you, on the other hand . . ."

"In my work for the khanate, I was obliged to compile dossiers on dissident elements within the empire. Some of the Islamist factions still use a form of Arabic for internal communications."

He sniffed through his nostrils, looking at me with his penetrating blue eyes. The cable car creaked and swayed. "It took my analysis experts eight months to recognize that that lettering had a human origin. The test is over; you have passed. But would you care to speculate on the meaning of your observation? Why are we finding Arabic on phantom relics?"

"I don't know."

"But indulge me."

"It can only mean that there's an Islamist faction out there that we don't know about. A group with independent spacefaring capability, the means to use the Infrastructure despite all the access restrictions already in place."

"And the other relics? Where do they fit in?"

"I don't know."

"If I told you that, in addition to items we consider to be of unambiguously alien origin, we'd also found scraps of other vanished or obscure languages – or at least, scripts and symbols connected to them – what would you say?"

I admitted that I had no explanation for how such a thing might be possible. It was one thing to allow the existence of a secret enclave of technologically-advanced Islamists, however improbable that might have been. It was quite another to posit the existence of *many* such enclaves, each preserving some vanished or atrophied branch of human culture.

"Here is what's going to happen." He spoke the words as if there could be no possibility of dissent on my behalf. "As has already been made clear, your old life is over, utterly and finally. But there is still much that you can do to serve the will of Heaven. The khanate has only now taken a real interest in the phantoms, whereas we have been alert to the phenomenon for many years. If you care about the security of the empire, you will see the sense in working with Kuchlug."

"You mean, join the team analysing those relics?"

"As a matter of fact, I want you to lead it." He smiled; I could not tell if the idea had just occurred to him, or whether it had always been at the back of his mind. "You've already demonstrated the acuteness of your observations. I have no doubt that you will continue to uncover truths that the existing team has overlooked."

"I can't just . . . take over, like that."

He looked taken aback. "Why ever not?"

"A few days ago, I was your prisoner," I said. "Not long before that, you were torturing me. They've no reason to suddenly start trusting me, just on your say-so."

"You're wrong about that," he said, fingering one of the knives strapped across his chest. "They'll trust who I tell them to trust, absolutely and unquestioningly."

"Why?" I asked.

"Because that's how we do things around here."

So it was. I joined Qilian's investigative team, immersing myself in the treasure trove of data and relics his people had pieced together in my absence. There was, understandably, a degree of reluctance to accept my authority. But Qilian dealt with that in the expected manner, and, slowly, those around me came to a pragmatic understanding that it was either work with me or suffer the consequences.

Relics and fragments continued to fall into our hands. Sometimes the ships that intruded into the Infrastructure were damaged, as if the passage into our territory had been a violent one. Often, the subsequent encounter with one of our ships was enough to shake them to pieces, or at the very least dislodge major components. The majority of these shards vanished without trace into the implacable machinery of the Infrastructure. Even if the *khorkoi* apparatus was beginning to fail, it was still more than capable of attending to the garbage left behind by its users. But occasionally, pieces lingered in the system (as if the walls had indigestion?), waiting to be swept up by Qilian's ships, and eventually brought home to this moon.

As often as not, though, it was a trivial matter to classify the consignments, requiring only a glance at their contents. The work became so routine, in fact – and the quantity of consignments so high – that eventually I had no choice but to take a step back from hands on analysis. I assembled six teams and let them get on with it, requiring that they report back to me only when they had something of note: a new empire, or something odd from one of those we already knew about.

That was when the golden egg fell into our hands. It was in the seventh month of my service under Qilian, and I immediately knew that it originated from a culture not yet known to us. Perhaps it was a ship, or part of one. The outer hull was almost entirely covered in a quilt of golden platelets, overlapping in the manner of fish scales. The only parts not covered by the platelets were the dark apertures of sensors and thruster ports, and a small, eye-shaped area on one side of the teardrop that we quickly identified as a door.

Fearing that it might damage the other relics if it exploded under our examinations, I ordered that the analysis of the egg take place in a different part of the mining structure. Soon, though, my concern shifted to the welfare of the egg's occupants. We knew that there were beings inside it, even if we could not be sure if they were human. Scans had illuminated ghostly structures inside the hull: the intestinal complexity of propulsion subsystems, fuel lines, and tanks packed ingeniously tight, the fatty tissue of insulating layers, the bony divisions of armoured partitions, the cartilaginous detailing of furniture and life-support equipment. There were even ranks of couches, with eight crew still reclining in them. Dead or in suspended animation, it was impossible to tell. All we could see was their bones, a suggestion of humanoid skeletons, and there was no movement of those bones to suggest respiration.

We got the door open easily enough. It was somewhat like breaking into a safe, but once we had worked out the underlying mechanism – and the curiously alien logic that underpinned its design – it presented no insurmountable difficulties. Gratifyingly, there was only a mild gust of equalising pressure when the door hinged wide, and none of the sensors arrayed around the egg detected any harmful gases. As far as we could tell, it was filled with an oxygen-nitrogen mix only slightly different from that aboard our own ships.

"What now?" Qilian asked, fingering the patch of hair beneath his lip.

"We'll send machines aboard now," I replied. "Just to be safe, in case there are any booby-traps inside."

He placed a heavy, thick-fingered hand on my shoulder. "What say we skip the machines and just take a look inside ourselves?" His tone was playful. "Not afraid, are we, Yellow Dog?"

"Of course not," I answered.

"There's no need to be. I'll go in first, just in case there are surprises."

We walked across the floor, through the cordon of sensors, to the base of the attenuated metal staircase that led to the open door. The robots scuttled out of the way. My staff exchanged concerned glances, aware that we were deviating from a protocol we had spent weeks thrashing out to the last detail. I waved down their qualms.

Inside, as we already knew from the scans, the egg was compartmented into several small chambers, with the crew in the middle section. The rear part contained most of the propulsion and life-support equipment. Up front, in the sharp end, was what appeared to be a kind of pressurized cargo space. The egg still had power, judging by the presence of interior lighting, although the air aboard it was very cold and still. It was exceedingly cramped, requiring me to duck and Qilian to stoop almost double. To pass from one compartment to the next, we had to crawl on our hands and knees through doors that were barely large enough for children. The external door was larger than the others, presumably because it had to admit a crewmember wearing a spacesuit or some other encumbrance.

Qilian was the first to see the occupants. I was only a few seconds behind him, but those seconds stretched to years as I heard his words.

"They are aliens after all, Yellow Dog. Strapped in their seats like little pale monkeys. I can see why we thought they might be human, . . .

but they're not, not at all. So much for the theory that every empire must represent a human enclave, no matter how incomprehensible the artefacts or script."

"That was never my theory, sir. But it's good to have it dismissed."

"They have masks on. I can see their faces, but I'd like a better look."

Still on my knees, I said: "Be careful, sir."

"They're dead, Yellow Dog. Stiff and cold as mummies."

By the time I reached Qilian, he had removed one of the intricate masks from the face of his chosen alien. In his hands, it was tiny, like a delicate accessory belonging to a doll. He put it down carefully, placing it on the creature's lap. The alien was dressed in a quilted gold uniform, cross-buckled into the couch. It was the size of an eight-year-old child, but greatly skinnier in build, its torso and limbs elongated to the point where it resembled a smaller creature that had been stretched. Though its hands were gloved, the layout of the long, dainty-looking digits corresponded exactly to my own: four fingers and an opposed thumb, though each of the digits was uncommonly slender, such that I feared they might snap if we attempted to remove the gloves. Its head – the only part of it not covered by the suit – was delicate and rather beautiful, with huge, dark eyes set in patches of black fur. Its nose and mouth formed one snoutlike feature, suggestive of a dog or cat. It had sleek, intricate ears, running back along the side of its head. Save for the eye patches, and a black nose at the tip of the snout, its skin varied between a pale buff or off-white.

The alien's hands rested on a pair of small control consoles hinged to the sides of the couch; the consoles were flat surfaces embossed with golden ridges and studs, devoid of markings. A second console angled down from the ceiling to form a blank screen at the creature's eye-level. The other seven occupants all had similar amenities. There were no windows, and no controls or readouts in the orthodox sense. The aliens were all alike, with nothing on their uniforms to indicate rank or function. From what little I could see of their faces, the other seven were identical to the one we had unmasked.

I suppose I should have felt awed: here I was, priveleged to be one of the first two people in history to set eyes on true aliens. Instead, all I felt was a kind of creeping sadness, and a tawdry, unsettling feeling that I had no business in this place of death.

"I've seen these things before," Qilian said, a note of disbelief in his words.

"These aliens, sir? But this is the first time we've seen them."

"I don't mean that. I mean, isn't there something about them that reminds you of something?"

"Something of what, sir?"

He ignored my question. "I also want this vehicle stripped down to the last bolt, or whatever it is holds it together. If we can hack into its navigation system, find an Infrastructure map, we may be able to work out where they came from, and how the hell we've missed them until now."

I looked at the embossed gold console and wondered what were our chances of hacking into anything, let alone the navigation system.

"And the aliens, sir? What should we do with them?"

"Cut them up. Find out what makes them tick." Almost as an afterthought, he added: "Of course, make sure they're dead first."

The aliens were not the greatest surprise contained in the egg, but we did not realize that until the autopsy was underway. Qilian and I observed the procedure from a viewing gallery, looking down on the splayed and dissected creature. With great care, bits of it were being removed and placed on sterile metal trays. The interior organs were dry and husk-like, reinforcing the view that the aliens were in a state of mummification: perhaps (we speculated) some kind of suspended animation to be used in emergency situations. But the function and placement of the organs was all too familiar; we could have been watching the autopsy of a monkey and not known the difference. The alien even had a tail, lightly striped in black and white; it had been contained within an extension of the clothing, tucked back into a cavity within the seat.

That the creatures must have been intelligent was not open to dispute, but it was still dismaying to learn how human their brains looked, when they were cut up. Small, certainly, yet with clear division of brain hemispheres, frontal and temporal lobes, and so on. Yet the real shock lay in the blood. It was not necessarily a surprise to find that it had DNA, or even that its DNA appeared to share the same protein coding alphabet as ours. There were (I was led to believe) sound arguments for how that state of affairs might have arisen independently, due to it being the most efficient possible replicating/coding system, given the thermodynamic and combinative rules of carbon-based biochemistry. That was all well and good. But it entirely failed to explain what they found when they compared the alien's chromosomes to ours. More on a whim than anything else, they had tested the alien blood with human-specific probes and found that chromosomes 1 and 3 of the alien were homoeologous to human chromosomes 3, 9, 14, and 21. There were also unexpectedly strong signals in the centromeric regions of the alien chromosomes when probed for human chromosomes 7 and 19. In other words, the alien DNA was not merely similar to ours, it was shockingly, confoundingly, alike.

The only possible explanation was that we were related.

Qilian and I were trying to work out the ramifications of this when news came in from the team examining the pod. Uugan – my deputy – came scuttling into the autopsy viewing room, rubbing sweaty hands together. "We've found something," he said, almost tongue-tied with excitement.

Qilian showed him the hot-off-the-press summary from the genetics analysis. "So have we. Those aliens aren't alien. They came from the same planet we did. I *thought* they looked like lemurs. That's because they *are*."

Uugan had as much trouble dealing with that as we did. I could almost hear the gears meshing in his brain, working through the possibilities.

"Aliens must have uplifted lemur stock in the deep past, using genetic engineering to turn them into intelligent, tool-using beings." He raised a finger. "Or, other aliens spread the same genetic material on more than one world. If that were the case, these lemurs need not be from Greater Mongolia after all."

"What news do you have for us?" Qilian asked, smiling slightly at Uugan's wild theorizing.

"Come to the egg, please. It will be easier if I show you."

We hastened after Uugan, both of us refraining from any speculation as to what he might have found. As it happened, I do not think either of us would have guessed correctly.

In the sharp end of the egg, the investigators had uncovered a haul of cargo, much of which had now been removed and laid out on the floor for inspection. I glanced at some of the items as we completed the walk to the pod, recognizing bits and pieces from some of the other cultures we already knew about. Here was a branching, sharp-tipped metallic red thing, like an instrument for impaling. Here was a complexly manufactured casket which opened to reveal ranks of nested white eggs, hard as porcelain. Here was a curving section of razor-sharp foil, polished to an impossible lustre. Dozens more relics from dozens of other known empires, and still dozens more that represented empires of which we knew nothing.

"They've been collecting things, just like us," I said.

"Including this," Uugan said, drawing my attention to the object that now stood at the base of the egg.

It was the size and shape of a large urn, golden in construction, surfaced with bas relief detailing, with eight curved green windows set into its upper surface. I peered closer and rested a hand against the urn's throbbing skin. Through the windows burbled a dark liquid. In the dark liquid, something pale floated. I made out the knobbed ridge of a spine, a backbone pressing through flawless skin. It was a person, a human, a man judging by his musculature, curled into foetal position. I could only see the back of his head,: bald and waxy, scribed with fine white scars. Ridged cables dangled in the fluid, running towards what I presumed was a breathing apparatus, now hidden.

Qilian looked through one of the other windows. After a lengthy silence, he straightened himself and nodded. "Do you think he was their prisoner?"

"No way to tell, short of thawing him out and seeing what he has to say on the matter," Uugan said.

"Do what you can," Qilian told Uugan. "I would very, very much like to speak to this gentleman." Then he leaned in closer, as if what he was about to say was meant only for Uugan's ears. "This would be an excellent time not to make a mistake, if you understand my meaning."

I do not believe that Qilian's words had any effect on Uugan; he was either going to succeed or not, and the difference between the two outcomes depended solely on the nature of the problem, not his degree of application to the task. As it happened, the man was neither dead nor brain dead, and his revival proved childishly simple. Many weeks were spent in preparation before the decisive moment, evaluating all known variables. When the day came, Uugan's intervention was kept to a minimum: he merely opened the preservation vat, extracted the man from his fluid cocoon, and (it must be said, with fastidious care) removed the breathing apparatus. Uugan was standing by with all the tools of emergency medical intervention at his disposal, but no such assistance was required. The man simply convulsed, drew in several gulping breaths, and then settled into a normal respiratory pattern. But he had yet to open his eyes, or signal any awareness in the change of his surroundings. Scans measured brain activity, but at a level indicative of coma rather than consciousness. The same scans also detected a network of microscopic machines in the man's brain and much of his wider nervous system. Though we could not see these implants as clearly as those we had harvested from the lemur, they were clearly derived from a different technology.

Where had he come from? What did he know of the phantoms?

For weeks, it appeared that we would have no direct answer to these questions. There was one thing, one clue, but we almost missed it. Many days after the man's removal from the vat, one of Uugan's technicians was working alone in the laboratory where we kept our new guest. The lights were dimmed and the technician was using an ultraviolet device to sterilize some culture dishes. By chance, the technician noticed something glowing on the side of the man's neck. It turned out to be a kind of tattoo, a sequence of horizontal symbols that was invisible except under ultraviolet stimulation.

I was summoned to examine the discovery. What I found was a word in Arabic, *Altair*, meaning eagle, and a string of digits, twenty in all, composed of nine numerical symbols, and the tenth, what the pre-Mongol scholars called in their dead language *theca* or *circulus* or *figura nihili*, the round symbol that means, literally, nothing. Our mathematics incorporates no such entity. I have heard it said that there is something in the Mongol psyche that abhorrs the very concept of absence. Our mathematics cannot have served us badly, for upon its back we have built a five-hundred-year-old galactic empire – even if the *khorkoi* gave us the true keys to that kingdom. But I have also heard it said that our system would have been much less cumbersome had we adopted that Arabic symbol for nothing.

No matter; it was what the symbols told me that was important, not what they said about our choice of number system. In optimistic anticipation that he would eventually learn to speak, and that his tongue would turn out to be Arabic, I busied myself with preparations. For a provincial thug, Qilian had a library as comprehensive as anything accessible from NHK. I retrieved primers on Arabic, most of which were tailored for use by security operatives hoping to crack Islamist terror cells, and set about trying to become an interpreter.

But when the man woke – which was weeks later, by which time it felt as if I had been studying those primers for half my life – all my preparations might as well have been for nothing. He was sitting up in bed, monitored by machines and watched by hidden guards, when I came into the room. Aside from the technician who had first noticed his return to consciousness, the man had seen no other human being since his arrival.

I closed the door and walked to his bedside. I sat down next to him, adjusting the blue silk folds of my skirt decorously.

"I am Yellow Dog," I told him in Arabic, speaking the words slowly and carefully. "You are among friends. We want to help you, but we do not know much about you."

He looked at me blankly. After a few seconds I added: "Can you understand me?"

His expression and response told me everything I needed to know. He spoke softly, emitting a string of words that sounded superficially Arabic without making any sense to me at all. By then I had listened to enough recordings to know the difference between Arabic and baby-talk, and all I was hearing was gibberish.

"I'm sorry," I said. "I do not understand you. Perhaps if we started again, slower this time." I touched a hand to my breast. "I am Yellow Dog. Who are you?"

He answered me then, and maybe it was his name, but it could just as easily have been a curt refusal to answer my question. He started looking agitated, glancing around the room as if it was only now that he was paying due regard to his surroundings. He fingered the thin cloth of his blanket and rubbed at the bandage on his arm where a catheter had been inserted. Once more I told him my name and urged him to respond in kind, but whatever he said this time was not the same as his first answer.

"Wait," I said, remembering something, a contingency I had hoped not to have to use. I reached into my satchel and retrieved a printout. I held the filmy paper before me and read slowly from the *adhan*, the Muslim call to prayer.

My pronounciation must still not have been perfect, because I had to repeat the words three or four times before some flicker of recognition appeared behind his eyes and he began to echo what I was saying. Yet even as he spoke the incantation, there was a puzzlement in his voice, as if he could not quite work out why we should be engaged in this odd parlour game.

"So I was half-right," I said, when he had fallen silent again, waiting for me to say something. "You know something of Islamic culture. But you do not understand anything I say, except when I speak words that have not been permitted to change in fifteen centuries, and even then you only just grasp what I mean to say." I smiled, not in despair, but in rueful acknowledgment that the journey we had to make would be much longer and more arduous than I had imagined. Continuing in Mongol, so that he could hear my tongue, I said: "But at least we have something, my friend, a stone to build on. That's better than nothing, isn't it?"

"Do you understand me now?" he asked, in flawless Mongol.

I was astonished, quite unable to speak. Now that I had grown accustomed to his baldness and pallor, I could better appreciate those aspects of his face that I had been inclined to overlook before. He had delicate features, kind and scholarly. I had never been attracted to men in a sexual sense, and I could not say that I felt any such longing for this man. But I saw the sadness in his eyes, the homesick flicker that told me he was a long way from family and friends (such as I have never known, but can easily imagine), and I knew that I wished to help him.

"You speak our language," I said eventually, as if the fact of it needed stating.

"It is not a difficult one. What is your name? I caught something that sounded like 'filthy hound', but that cannot have been correct."

"I was trying to speak Arabic. And failing, obviously. My name is Yellow Dog. It's a code, an operational identifier."

"Therefore not your real name."

"Ariunaa," I said softly. "I use it sometimes. But around here they call me Yellow Dog."

"Muhunnad," he said, touching his sternum.

"Muhunnad," I repeated. Then: "If you understood my name – or thought you understood it – why didn't you answer me until I spoke Mongolian? My Arabic can't be that bad, surely."

"You speak Arabic like someone who has only heard a whisper of a whisper of a whisper. Some of the words are almost recognizable, but they are like glints of a gold in a stream." He offered me a smile, as if it hurt him to have to criticize. "You were doing your best. But the version of Arabic I speak is not the one you think you know."

"How many versions are there?"

"More than you realize, evidently." He paused. "I think I know where I am. We are inside the Mongol Expansion. We were on the same track until 659, by my calendar."

"What other calendar is there?"

"You count from the death of a warrior-deity; we count from the flight of the Prophet from Mecca. The year now is 1604 by the Caliphate's reckoning; 999 by your own, 2226 by the calendar of the United Nations. Really, we are quibbling over mere centuries. The Smiling Ones use a much older dating system, as they must. The . . ."

I interrupted him. "What are you talking about? You are an emissary from a previously hidden Islamic state, that is all. At some point in the five hundred years of the Mongol Expansion, your people must have escaped central control to establish a secret colony, or network of colonies, on the very edge of the Infrastructure . . ."

"It is not like that, Ariunaa. Not like that at all." Then he leaned higher on the bed, like a man who had just remembered an urgent errand. "How exactly did I get here? I had not been tasked to gather intelligence on the Mongols, not this time around."

"The lemurs," I answered. "We found you with them."

I watched him shudder, as if the memory of something awful had only just returned. "You mean I was their prisoner, I think." Then he looked at me curiously. "Your questions puzzle me, Ariunaa. Our data on the

Mongols was never of the highest quality, but we had always taken it for granted that you understood."

"Understood *what*?"

"The troubling nature of things," he said.

The cable car pitched down from the boarding platform, ducking beneath the base of the immense walking platform. After a short while, it came to an abrupt halt, swaying slightly. Qilian pulled out his binoculars and focused on a detail under the platform, between the huge, slowly moving machinery of the skeletal support legs.

"There," he said, passing me the binoculars.

I took them with trembling hands. I had been on my way to Muhunnad for one of our fruitless but not unpleasant conversational sessions, when Quilian's men had diverted me to the cable car platform.

"What am I supposed to be looking at?"

"Press the stud on the side."

I did so. Powerful gyroscopes made the binoculars twist in my hands, tracking and zooming in on a specific object, a thing hanging down from the underside like the weight on the end of a plumb line. I recalled now the thing I had seen the first time Qilian had accompanied me in the cable car, the thing that he had been examining with the binoculars. I had thought it was some kind of test probe or drilling gear being winched back into the platform. I saw now that I had been wrong.

I did need to see his face to know that I was looking at Muhunnad. He had been stuffed into a primitive spacesuit, blackened by multiple exposures to scorching heat and corrosive elements. They had him suspended from his feet, with his head nearest the ground. He was being lowered down towards one of those outgassing rifts in the surface of the Qing Shui moon.

"You can't be doing this," I said.

"If there was any other way," Qilian said, in a tone of utter reasonableness. "But clearly there isn't. He's been dragging his heels, giving us nothing. Spoke too soon early on, confided too much in you, and chose to clam up. Obviously, we can't have that." Qilian opened a walnut-veneered cabinet and took out a microphone. He clicked it on and tapped it against his knee before speaking. "Can you hear me, Muhunnad? I hope your view is as spectacular as ours. I am speaking from the cable car that you may be able to see to your right. We are about level with your present position, although you will soon be considerably lower than us."

"No," I said.

Qilian raised a calming hand. He hadn't even bothered to have me tied into the seat. "Do you hear that, Muhunnad? You still have an admirer." Then he said: "Lower the line, please. Take him to half his present elevation."

"Can you see that he's told you everything he knows?" I asked, tossing the binoculars against the floor.

"He's told us as little as he could get away with," Qilian replied, placing a hand over the end of the microphone to muffle his words. "We could go through the usual rigmarole of conventional interrogation, but I think this will prove much more effective."

"We'll learn far more from him alive than dead."

He looked at me pityingly. "You think I don't know that? Of course I'm not going to kill him. But very soon – unless he chooses to talk – he'll be wishing I did."

The winch dropped Muhunnad to within fifteen or twenty *alds* of the surface, just above the point where the outgassing material became opaque.

"I can hear you," a voice said over the cable car's speaker system. "But I have told you everything I intend to. Nothing you can do now will make any difference."

"We'll see, won't we," Qilian said. To me, confidingly, he said: "By now, he will be in extreme discomfort. You and I are fine, but we have the benefit of a functioning life-support system. His suit is damaged. At the moment, his primary concern is extreme cold, but that will not remain the case for very much longer. As he nears the fissure, it is heat that will begin to trouble him."

"You can tell the woman – Ariunaa – that I am sorry it was necessary to withold information from her," Muhunnad said. "Her kindness was appreciated. I think she is the only one of you with a heart."

"There's no need for me to tell her anything," Qilian replied. "She's listening in. Aren't you, Yellow Dog?" Somewhat to my surprise, he passed me the microphone. "Talk to him. Reason with your favourite prisoner, if you imagine it will help."

"Muhunnad," I said. "Listen to me now. I have no reason to lie to you. Qilian means what he says. He's going to put you through hell until he finds out what you know. I've seen him murder people already, just to get at the truth."

"I appreciate the concern for my welfare," he said, with a sincerity that cut me to the bone.

"Lower him to five *alds*," Qilian said.

Is it necessary to document all that happened to Muhunnad? I suppose not; the essential thing is that the pain eventually became intolerable and he began to tell Qilian some of the things my master was desirous of knowing.

What we learned was: Muhunnad was a pilot, a man surgically adapted for optimum control of a ship with extreme Infrastructure agility. His implants were part of the interface system by which he flew his vehicle. It turned out that Muhunnad's people had become aware of the breakdown of Infrastructure integrity many decades ago, long before it had come to our attention. The difference was, rather than pretending that the problem did not exist, or entrusting it to a single agent like myself, they had dedicated almost their entire state apparatus to finding a solution. Think of Qilian's research, multiplied by a thousand. There were countless men and women like Muhunnad, brave angels tasked with mapping the weak spots in the Infrastructure, the points of leakage, and learning something of the other empires beginning to spill into their own. They knew enough about the properties of those weak points; enough to slip through them, gather intelligence, and still return home. The rate of attrition was still high. Muhunnad was a criminal, convicted of a crime that would have been considered petty in our own society, but which normally merited the death penalty in his. In his case, he had been offered the chance to redeem himself, by becoming a pilot.

They knew about us. They had been intercepting our lost message packets for years, and had even found a couple of our ships with living crew. That was how they had learned Mongolian. They also knew about dozens of other empires, including the lemurs.

"They caught me," Muhunnad said. "As they catch any unwary traveller. They are to be feared."

"They look so harmless," Qilian answered.

"They are vicious beyond words. They are a hive society, with little sense of self. The beings you found, the dead ones, would have sacrificed themselves to ensure their cargo returned home intact. It did not mean that they did so out of any consideration for my wellbeing. But there are worse things than the lemurs out there. There are the beings we call the Smiling Ones. You will meet them sooner or later. They have been in space for millions of years, and their technology is only matched by their loathing for the likes of you and I."

"Tell us about your state," Qilian probed.

"We call it the Shining Caliphate. It is an empire encompassing seven thousand star systems, comprising twenty thousand settled worlds, half of which are of planet class or at least the size of major moons. A third of those worlds are terraformed or on the way to completion."

"You are lying. If an empire of that size already existed, we would have seen signs of it."

"That is because you are not looking in the right place. The Shining Caliphate is *here*, now, all around you. It occupies much the same volume as your own empire. It even has the same homeworld. You call it Greater Mongolia. We call it Earth."

"Lies!"

But I knew Muhunnad was not lying to us. I think it likely that even Qilian knew it too. He was a brutal man, but not a stupid or unimaginative one. But I do not think he could bear to contemplate his place in a universe in which Muhunnad spoke the truth. Qilian was a powerful man, with an empire of his own on the very edge of the one he was meant to serve. If our empire was a map spread across a table, then he controlled more than could be covered by the palm of a hand. Yet if what Muhunnad said was correct, then that map was but one unexceptional page in a vast atlas, each page a dominion in its own right, of which our own was neither the most powerful, nor the most ancient. Set against such immensity, Qilian controlled almost nothing. For a man like him, that realization would have been intolerable.

But perhaps I am crediting him with too much intelligence, too much imagination, and he was simply unable to grasp what Muhunnad was telling us.

What he *could* grasp, however, was an opportunity.

I was with them when we brought Muhunnad to the room where the couch had been prepared. I had heard of the existence of the couch, but this was my first sight of it. Even knowing its function, I could not help but see it as an instrument of torture. Muhunnad's reaction, to begin struggling against the guards who held him, showed that he saw the couch in similar terms. Behind the guards loomed white-coated doctors and technicians, including the Slav who had torn out my implant.

"This isn't to hurt you," Qilian said magnanimously. "It's to help you."

The couch was a skeletal white contraption, encumbered with pads and restraints and delicate hinged accessories that would fold over the occupant once they had been secured in place.

"I do not understand," Muhunnad said, although I think he did.

"We have studied your implants and deduced something of their function," Qilian said. "Not enough to learn everything about them, but enough to let you control one of our ships, instead of the one you were meant to fly."

"It will not work."

"No one is pretending it will be easy. But it is in your interests to do what you can to make it succeed. Help us navigate the Infrastructure – the way you do, finding the weak points and slipping through them – and we will let you return home."

"I do not believe you."

"You have no option but to believe me. If you cannot assist me in this matter, you will have concluded your usefulness to me. Given the trouble I would get into if New High Karakorum learned of your existence, I would have no option but to dispose of you."

"He means it," I said forcefully. "Help us fly the ships, Muhunnad. Whatever happens, it's better than staying here."

He looked at me as if I was the one thing in the universe he was willing to trust. Given all that had happened to him since leaving his people, it did not surprise me in the slightest.

"Plug him in," Qilian told the technicians. "And don't be too tender about it."

The name of the ship was the *River Volga*. She was half a *li* in length, her frontal stabilisation spines suggesting the curving whiskers of a catfish. She had been a merchant vehicle once; latterly, she had been equipped for scouring the Parvan Tract for phantom relics, and, most recently, she had been hardened and weaponed for an exploratory role. She would carry six of us: Muhunnad, Qilian, Uugan, and two more members of the technical staff –

their names were Jura and Batbayar – and myself. Next to her, identical in almost all respects, was the *Mandate of Heaven*. The only significant distinction between the two craft was that Muhunnad would be piloting the *River Volga*, while the *Mandate of Heaven* followed close behind, slaved to follow the same trajectory to within a fraction of an *ald*. The navigation and steering mechanisms of both ships had been upgraded to permit high-agility manoeuvres, including reversals, close-proximity wall skimming, and suboptimal portal transits. It did not bear thinking about the cost of equipping those two ships, or where the funds had been siphoned from, but I supposed the citizens of the Kuchlug special administrative volume would be putting up with hardships for a little while longer.

We spent five days in shakedown tests before entering the Tract, scooting around the system, dodging planets and moons in high-gee swerves. During that time, Muhunnad's integration into the harness was slowly improved, more and more ship systems brought under his direct control, until he reported the utmost confidence in being able to handle the *River Volga* during Infrastructure flight.

"Are you sure?" I asked.

"Truly, Ariunaa. This ship feels as much a part of me as anything I ever flew in the Shining Caliphate."

"But indescribably less sophisticated."

"I would not wish to hurt your feelings. Given your resources, you have not done too badly."

The transit, when it came, was utterly uneventful. The *Mandate of Heaven* reported some minor buffeting, but this was soon negated following a refinement of the control linkage between the two ships. Then we had nothing but to do but wait until Muhunnad detected one of the points of weakening where, with a judicious alteration in our trajectory, we might slip from one version of the Infrastructure to another.

Did I seriously think that Qilian would keep his promise of returning Muhunnad to his own people? Not really, unless my master had hopes of forging some kind of alliance with the Shining Caliphate, to use as leverage against the central authority of New High Karakorum. If that was his intention, I did not think he had much hope of succeeding. The Caliphate would have every reason to despise us, and yet – given the demonstrably higher level of both their technology and intelligence – there was nothing they could possibly want from us except craven submission and cowering remorse for the holocaust we had visited upon their culture, nearly a thousand years earlier.

No; I did not think Muhunnad stood much chance of returning home. Perhaps he knew that as well. But it was better to pretend to believe in Qilian's promises than incur his bored wrath back on the Qing Shui moon. At least this way, Muhunnad could continue to be materially useful to Qilian, and therefore, too valuable to hurt.

The detection of a weakening in the tunnel geometry, Muhunnad explained, was only just possible given the blunt sensibilities of our instruments. The Caliphate kept detailed maps of such things, but no record had

survived his capture by the lemurs, and the information was too volumi-
nous to be committed to memory. He recalled that there were four weak
points in the section of Infrastructure we called the Parvan Tract, but not
their precise locations or detailed properties.

No matter; he had every incentive to succeed. We overshot the first
weakening, but the incident gave Muhunnad a chance to refine the manner
in which he sifted the sensor data, and he was confident that he would not
make the same error twice. Rather than attempt a reversal, it was agreed to
push forward until we encountered the next weakening. It happened two
days later, halfway to the Gansu nexus. This time, Muhunnad started to
detect the subtle changes in the properties of the tunnel in time to initiate
a hard slow-down, echoed by the *Mandate of Heaven* immediately to our
stern.

We had been warned that the passage would be rough; this was an
understatement. Fortunately, we were all braced and ready when it came;
we had had two minutes warning before the moment arrived. Even then,
the ship gave every indication of coming close to break-up; she whinnied
like a horse, her structural members singing as if they had been plucked.
Several steering vanes broke loose during the swerve, but the *River Volga*
had been equipped to withstand losses that would have crippled a normal
ship; all that happened was that hull plates swung open and new vanes
pushed out to replace the missing ones. Behind us, the *Mandate of Heaven*
suffered slightly less damage; Muhunnad had been able to send correc-
tional steering signals to her guidance system, allowing her to follow a less
treacherous path.

And then we were back in the tunnel, travelling normally. To all intents
and purposes, it was as if nothing had happened. We appeared to be still
inside the Parvan Tract.

"We have become phantoms now," Muhunnad informed us. "This is
someone else's Infrastructure."

Qilian leaned over the control couch, where our pilot lay in a state of
partial paralysis, wired so deeply into the *River Volga*'s nervous system
that his own body was but an incidental detail. Around us, the bridge
instruments recorded normal conditions of Infrastructure transit.

"Where are we?"

"There's no way of telling, not with these sensors. Not until we
emerge."

"In the Gansu nexus?"

"Yes," he replied. "Or whatever *they* call it. There will be risks; you
will not have seen many phantoms emerge into your version of the nexus
because most such ships will make every effort to slip through another
weakening."

"Why?"

He spoke as if the answer should have been obvious. "Because unless
they are pilots like me, on specific intelligence-gathering missions, they
would rather keep transitioning between versions of the Infrastructure,
than emerge into what is likely to be a densely populated interchange.

Eventually, they hope to detect the micro-signatures in the tunnel physics that indicate that they have returned home."

"Signatures which we can't read," I said.

"I will attempt to refine my interpretation of the sensor data. Given time, I may be able to improve matters. But that is some way off."

"We'll take our chances with Gansu," Qilian said.

There was, as I understood it, a small but non-negligible possibity that the weakening had shunted us back into our own version of the Tract – we would know if we emerged into the nexus and I saw advertisements for *Sorkan-Shira* rental ponies. Muhunnad assured us, however, that such an outcome was very unlikely. Once we were elsewhere, we would only get home again by throwing the dice repeatedly, until our own special number came up.

For all that, when we did emerge into the Gansu nexus, my first thought was that Muhunnad had been wrong about those odds. Somehow or other, we had beaten them and dropped back into our own space. As the door opened to admit us back into the spherical volume of the hollowed-out moon, I had the same impression of teeming wealth; of a city packed tight around the central core, of luminous messages rising up the ninety-nine golden spokes, of the airspace thick with jewel-bright ships and gaudily-patterned, mothlike shuttles, the glittering commerce of ten thousand worlds.

And yet, it only took a second glimpse to see that I was wrong.

This was no part of the Mongol Expansion. The ships were wrong; the shuttles were wrong: cruder and clumsier even than our most antiquated ships. The city down below had a haphazard, ramshackle look to it, its structures ugly and square-faced. The message on the spokes were spelled out in the angular letters of that Pre-Mongol language, Latin. I could not tell if they were advertisements, news reports, or political slogans.

We slowed down, coming to a hovering standstill relative to the golden spokes and the building-choked core. The *Mandate of Heaven* had only just cleared the portal entrance, with the door still open behind it. I presumed that some automatic system would not permit it to close with a ship still so close.

Qilian was a model of patience, by his standards. He gave Muhunnad several minutes to digest the information arriving from the *River Volga*'s many sensors.

"Well, pilot?" he asked, when that interval had elapsed. "Do you recognize this place?"

"Yes," Muhunnad said. "I do. And we must leave, now."

"Why so nervous? I've seen those ships. They look even more pathetic and fragile than ours must have seemed to you."

"They are. But there is no such thing as a harmless interstellar culture. These people have only been in space for a couple of hundred years, barely a hundred and fifty since they stumbled on the Infrastructure, but they still have weapons that could hurt us. Worse, they are aggressors."

"Who are they?" I whispered.

"The culture I mentioned to you back on the Qing Shui moon: the ones who are now in their twenty-third century. You would call them Christians, I suppose."

"Nestorians?" Qilian asked, narrowing his eyes.

"Another off-shoot of the same cult, if one wishes to split hairs. Not that many of them are believers now. There are even some Islamists among them, although there is little about the Shining Caliphate that they would find familiar."

"Perhaps we can do business with them," Qilian mused.

"I doubt it. They would find you repulsive, and they would loathe you for what you did to them in your history."

It was as if Muhunnad had not spoken at all. When he alluded to such matters, Qilian paid no heed to his words. "Take us closer to the core," he said. "We didn't weld all this armour onto the *Volga* for nothing."

When Muhunnad did not show readiness to comply with Qilian's order, a disciplinary measure was administered through the input sockets of the harness. Muhunnad stiffened against his restraints, then – evidently deciding that death at the hands of the Christians was no worse than torture by Mongols – he began to move us away from the portal.

"I am sorry," I whispered. "I know you only want to do what's best for us."

"I am sorry as well," he said, when Qilian was out of earshot. "Sorry for being so weak, that I do what he asks of me, even when I know it is wrong."

"No one blames you," I replied.

We had crossed five hundred *li* without drawing any visible attention from the other vessels, which continued to move through the sphere as if going about their normal business. We even observed several ships emerge and depart through portals. But then, quite suddenly, it was as if a great shoal of fish had become aware of the presence of two sleek, hungry predators nosing through their midst. All around us, from one minute to the next, the various craft began to dart away, abandoning whatever course or errand they had been on before. Some of them ducked into portals, or lost themselves in the thicket of spokes, while others fled for the cover of the core.

I tensed. Whatever response we were due was surely on its way by now.

As it happened, we did not have long to wait. In contrast to the civilian vessels attempting to get as far away from us as possible, three ships were converging on us. We studied them on high magnification, on one of the display screens in the *River Volga*'s bridge. They were shaped like arrowheads, painted with black and white stripes and the odd markings of the Christians. Their blade-sharp leading edges bristled with what could have been sensors, refuelling probes, or weapons.

From his couch, Muhunnad said: "We are being signalled. I believe I can interpret the transmission. Would you like to see it?"

"Put it on," Qilian said.

We were looking at a woman, wearing a heavy black uniform, shiny like waxed leather. She was pinned back into a heavily padded seat: I did not doubt that I was looking at the pilot of one of the ships racing to intercept us. Much of her face was hidden under a globular black helmet, with a red-tinted visor lowered down over her eyes. On the crown of the helmet was a curious symbol: a little drawing of the Earth, overlaid with lines of latitude and longitude, and flanked by what I took to be a pair of laurel leaves. She was speaking into a microphone, her words coming over the bridge speaker. I wished I had studied more dead languages at the academy. Then again, given my lack of success with Arabic, perhaps I would still not have understood her Latin either.

What was clear was that the woman was not happy; that her tone was becoming ever more strident. At last, she muttered something that, had she been speaking Mongol, might have been some dismissive invitation to go to hell.

"Perhaps we should turn after all," Qilian said, or started to say. But by then, the three ships had loosed their missiles: four apiece, grouping into two packs of six, one for the *Mandate of Heaven* and one for us.

Muhunnad needed no further encouragement. He whipped us around with all haste, pushing the *River Volga*'s thrust to its maximum. Again, the stress of it was enough to set the ship protesting. At the same time, Muhunnad brought our own weapons into use, running those guns out on their magnetic cradles and firing at the missiles as they closed distance between us and the Christians. Given the range and efficacy of our beam weapons, it would not have troubled him to eliminate the three ships. In concentrating on the missiles, not the pursuers, he was doing all that he could not to inflame matters further. As an envoy of Greater Mongolia, I suppose I should have been grateful. But I was already beginning to doubt that the fate of my empire was going to be of much concern for me.

Because we had turned around, the *Mandate of Heaven* was the first to reach the portal. By then, the door had begun to close, but it only took a brief assault from the Mandate's chaser guns to snip a hole in it. Muhunnad had destroyed nine of the twelve missiles by this point, but the remaining three were proving more elusive; in witnessing the deaths of their brethren, they appeared to have grown more cunning. By the time the Mandate cleared the portal, the three had arrived within fifteen *li* of the *River Volga*. By switching to a different fire-pattern, Muhunnad succeeded in destroying two of them, but the last one managed to evade him until it had come within five li. At that point, bound by the outcome of some ruthless logical decision-making algorithm, the missile opted to detonate rather than risk coming any closer. It must have hoped to inflict fatal damage on us, even at five *li*.

It very nearly did. I recalled what our pilot had said about there being no such thing as a harmless interstellar culture. The blast inflicted severe damage to our rear shielding and drive assembly, knocking off another two stabilization vanes.

And then we were through, back into the Infrastructure. We had survived our first encounter with another galactic empire.

More were to follow.

In my mind's eye, I have an image of a solitary tree, bare of leaves, so that
its branching structure is laid open for inspection. The point where each
branch diverges from a larger limb is a moment of historical crisis, where
the course of world events is poised to swerve onto one of two tracks.

Before his death, our founder spoke of having brought a single law
to the six directions of space, words that have a deep resonance for all
Mongols, as if it was our birthright to command the fundamental fabric of
reality itself. They were prescient words, too, for the bringing of unity to
Greater Mongolia, let alone the first faltering steps towards the Expansion,
had barely begun. Fifty-four years after his burial, our fleet conquered the
islands of Japan, extending the empire as far east as it was possible to go.
But the day after our fleet landed, a terrible storm battered the harbours of
those islands, one that would surely have repelled or destroyed our invasion fleet had it still been at sea. At the time, it was considered a great good
fortune; a sure sign that Heaven had ordained this invasion by delaying
that storm. Yet who is to say what would have become of Japan, had it
not fallen under Mongol authority? By the same token, who is to say what
would have become of our empire, if its confident expansion had been
checked by the loss of that fleet? We might not have taken Vienna and the
cities of Western Europe, and then the great continents on the other side
of the ocean.

I thought of Muhunnad's Shining Caliphate. The common view is that
the Islamists were monotheistic savages until swept under the tide of the
Mongol enlightenment. But I am mindful that history is always written by
the victors. We regard our founder as a man of wisdom and learning first
and a warrior second, a man who was respectful of literacy, curious about
the sciences, and who possessed a keen thirst for philosophical enquiry.
Might the conquered have viewed him differently, I wonder? Especially if
our empire fell, and we were not there to gild his name?

No matter; all that need concern us is that solitary tree, that multiplicity
of branches, reaching ever upward. After the moment of crisis, the point
of bifurcation, there should be no further contact between one branch
and the next. In one branch, the Mongols take the world. In another, the
Islamists. In another, some obscure sect of Christians. In another, much
older branch, none of these empires ever become a gleam in history's eye.
In an even older one, the lemurs are masters of creation, not some hairless
monkey.

But what matters is that all these empires eventually find the Infrastructure.
In some way that I cannot quite grasp, and perhaps will never truly understand, the *khorkoi* machinery exists across all those branches. Not simply
as multiple copies of the same Infrastructure, but as a single entity that in
some way permits the reunification of those branches: as if, having grown
apart, they begin to knot back together again.

I do not think this is intentional. If it were, the leaky nature of the Infrastructure would have been apparent to us five hundred years ago. It seems more likely to me that it is growing leaky; that some kind of insulation is beginning to wear away. An insulation that prevents history short-circuiting itself, as it were.

But perhaps I am wrong to second-guess the motives of aliens whose minds we will never know. Perhaps all of this is unfolding according to some inscrutable and deliriously protracted scheme of our unwitting wormlike benefactors.

I do not think we will ever know.

I shall spare you the details of all the encounters that followed, as we slipped from one point of weakness to another, always hoping that the next transition would be the one that brought us back to Mongol space, or at least into an empire we could do business with. By the time of our eighth or ninth transition, I think, Qilian would have been quite overjoyed to find himself a guest of the Shining Caliphate. I think he would have even settled for a humbling return to the Christians: by the time we had scuttled away from empires as strange, or as brazenly hostile, as those of the Fish People or the Thin Men, the Christians had come to seem like very approachable fellows indeed.

But it was not to be. And when we dared to imagine that we had seen the worst that the branching tree of historical possibilities could offer, that we had done well not to stray into the dominion of the lemurs, that Heaven must yet be ordaining our adventure, we had the glorious misfortune to fall into the realm of the Smiling Ones.

They came hard and fast, and did not trifle with negotiation. Their claw-like green ships moved without thrust, cutting through space as if space itself was a kind of fluid they could swim against. Their beam weapons etched glimmering lines of violet across the void, despite the fact that they were being deployed in hard vacuum. They cut into us like scythes. I knew then that they could have killed us in a flash, but that they preferred to wound, to maim, to toy.

The *River Volga* twisted like an animal in agony, and then there was a gap in my thoughts wide enough for a lifetime.

The first thing that flashed through my mind after I returned to conscious-ness was frank amazement that we were still alive; that the ship had not burst open like a ripe fruit and spilled us all into vacuum. The second thing was that, given the proximity of the attacking vehicles, our stay of execu-tion was unlikely to be long. I did not need the evidence of readouts to tell me that the *River Volga* had been mortally wounded. The lights were out, artificial gravity had failed, and in place of the normal hiss and chug of her air recirculators, there was an ominous silence, broken only by the occasional creak of some stressed structural member, cooling down after being heated close to boiling point.

"Commander Qilian?" I called, into the echoing darkness.

No immediate answer was forthcoming. But no sooner had I spoken than an emergency system kicked in and supplied dim illumination to the cabin, traced in the wavery lines of fluorescent strips stapled to walls and bulkheads. I could still not hear generators or the other sounds of routine shipboard operation, so I presumed the lights were drawing on stored battery power. Cautiously, I released my restraints and floated free of my chair. I felt vulnerable, but if we were attacked again, it would make no difference whether I was secured or not.

"Yellow Dog," a voice called, from further up the cabin. It was Qilian, sounding groggy but otherwise sound. "I blacked out. How long was I under?"

"Not long, sir. It can't have been more than a minute since they hit us." I started pulling myself towards him, propelling myself with a combination of vigorous air-swimming and the use of the straps and handholds attached to the walls for emergency use. "Are you all right, sir?"

"I think . . ." Then he grunted, not loudly, but enough to let me know that he was in considerable pain. "Arm's broken. Wasn't quite secure when it happened."

He was floating with his knees tucked high, inspecting the damage to his right arm. In the scarlet backup lighting, little droplets of blood, pulled spherical by surface tension, were pale colourless marbles. He had made light of the injury but it was worse than I had been expecting, a compound fracture of the radius bone, with a sharp white piece glaring out from his skin. The bleeding was abating, but the pain must have been excruciating. And yet Qilian caressed the skin around the wound as if it was no more irritating than a mild rash.

I paddled around until I found the medical kit. I offered to help Qilian apply the splint and dressing, but he waved aside my assistance save for when it came time to cut the bandage. The *River Volga* continued to creak and groan around us, like some awesome monster in the throes of a nightmare.

"Have you seen the others?"

"Uugan, Jura, and Batbayar must still be at their stations in the mid-ship section."

"And the pilot?"

I had only glanced at Muhunnad while I searched for the medical kit, but what I had seen had not encouraged me. He had suffered no visible injuries, but it was clear from his extreme immobility, and lack of response as I drifted by him, that all was not well. His eyes were open but apparently unseeing, fixated on a blank piece of wall above the couch.

"I don't know, sir. It may not be good."

"If he's dead, we're not going to be able to cut back into the Infrastructure."

I saw no point in reminding Qilian that, with the ship in its present state, Muhunnad's condition would make no difference. "It could be that he's just knocked out, or that there's a fault with his interface harness," I said, not really believing it myself.

"I don't know what happened to us just before I blacked out. Did you feel the ship twist around the way I did?"

I nodded. "Muhunnad must have lost attitude control."

Qilian finished with his dressing, inspecting the arm with a look of quiet satisfaction. "I am going to check on the others. See what you can do with the pilot, Yellow Dog."

"I'll do my best, sir."

He pushed off with his good arm, steering an expert course through the narrow throat of the bridge connecting door. I wondered what he hoped to do if the technical staff were dead, or injured, or otherwise incapable of assisting the damaged ship. I sensed that Qilian preferred not to look death in the eye until it was almost upon him.

Forcing my mind to the matter at hand, I moved to the reclined couch that held Muhunnad. I positioned myself next to him, anchoring in place with a foothold.

I examined the harness, checking the various connectors and status readouts, and could find no obvious break or weakness in the system. That did not mean that there was not an invisible fault, of course. Equally, if a power surge had happened, it might well have fried his nervous system from the inside out with little sign of external injury. We had built safeguards into the design to prevent that kind of thing, but I had never deceived myself that they were foolproof.

"I'm sorry, Muhunnad," I said quietly. "You did well to bring us this far. No matter what you might think of me, I wanted you to make it back to your own people."

Miraculously, his lips moved. He shaped a word with a mere ghost of breath. "Ariunaa?"

I took hold of his gloved hand, squeezing it as much as the harness allowed. "I'm here. Right by you."

"I cannot see anything," he answered, speaking very slowly. "Before, I could see everything around me, as well as the sensory information reaching me from the ship's cameras. Now I only have the cameras, and I am not certain that I am seeing anything meaningful through them. Sometimes I get flashes, as if *something* is working . . . but most of the time, it is like looking through fog."

"Are you sure you can't make some sense of the camera data?" I asked. "We only have to pass through the Infrastructure portal."

"That would be like threading the eye of a needle from halfway around the world, Ariunaa. Besides, I think we are paralysed. I have tried firing the steering motors, but I have received no confirmation that anything has actually happened. Have you felt the ship move?"

I thought back to all that had happened since the attack. "In the last few minutes? Nothing at all."

"Then it must be presumed that we are truly adrift and that the control linkages have been severed." He paused. "I am sorry; I wish the news was better."

"Then we need help," I said. "Are you sure there's nothing else out there? The last time we saw it, the *Mandate of Heaven* was still in one piece. If she could rendezvous with us, she might be able to carry us all to the portal."

After a moment, he said: "There is something, an object in my vicinity, about one hundred and twenty *li* out, but I only sense it intermittently. I would have mentioned it sooner, but I did not wish to raise your hopes."

Whatever he intended, my hopes were rising now. "Could it be the *Mandate*?"

"It is something like the right size, and in something like the right position."

"We need to find a way to signal it, to get it to come in closer. At the moment, they have no reason to assume any of us are alive."

"If I signal it, then the enemy will also know that some of us are still alive," Muhunnad answered. "I am afraid I do not have enough directional control to establish a tight-beam lock. I am not even certain I can broadcast an omnidirectional transmission."

"Broadcast what?" Qilian asked, drifting into the bridge.

I wheeled around to face him; I had not been expecting him to return so quickly. "Muhunnad says there's a good chance the *Mandate of Heaven* is nearby. Since we don't seem to able to move, she's our only chance of getting out of here."

"Is she intact?"

"No way to tell. There's definitely something out there that matches her signature. Problem is, Muhunnad isn't confident that we can signal her without letting the enemy know we're still around."

"It won't make any difference to the enemy. They'll be coming in to finish us off no matter what we do. Send the signal."

After a moment, Muhunnad said: "It's done. But I do not know if any actual transmission has taken place. The only thing I can do is monitor the *Mandate* and see if she responds. If she has picked up our signal, then we should not have long to wait. A minute, maybe two. If we have seen nothing after that time, I believe we may safely assume the worst."

We waited a minute, easily the longest in my life, then another. After a third, there was still no change in the faint presence Muhunnad was seeing. "I am more certain than ever that it is the *Mandate*," he informed us. "The signature has improved; it matches very well, with no sign of damage. She is holding at one hundred and twenty *li*. But she is not hearing us."

"Then we need another way of signalling her," I said. "Maybe if we ejected some air into space . . ."

"Too ambiguous," Qilian countered. "Air might vent simply because the ship was breaking up, long after we were all dead. It could easily encourage them to abandon us completely. What do we need this ship for in any case? We may as well eject the lifeboats. The *Mandate of Heaven* can collect them individually."

After an instant of reflection, Muhunnad said: "I think the commander is correct. There is nothing to be gained by staying aboard now. At the very least, the lifeboats will require the enemy to pursue multiple targets."

There were six lifeboats, one for each of us.

"Let's go," Qilian replied.

"I'll see you at the lifeboats," I said. "I have to help Muhunnad out of the harness first."

Qilian looked at me for a moment, some dark calculation working itself out behind his eyes. He nodded once. "Be quick about it, Yellow Dog. But we don't want to lose him. He's still a valued asset."

With renewed strength, I hauled the both of us through the echoing labyrinth of the ship, to the section that contained the lifeboats. It was clear that the attack had wrought considerable damage on this part of the ship, buckling wall and floor plates, constricting passageways and jamming bulkhead doors tight into their frames. We had to detour half way to the rear before we found a clear route back to the boats. Yet although we were ready to don suits if necessary, we never encountered any loss of pressure. Sandwiched between layers of the *River Volga*'s outer hull was a kind of foam that was designed to expand and harden upon exposure to vacuum, quickly sealing any leaks before they presented a threat to the crew. From the outside, that bulging and hardening foam would have resembled a mass of swollen dough erupting through cracks in the hull.

There were six lifeboats, accessed through six armoured doorways, each of which was surmounted with a panel engraved both with operating instructions and stern warnings concerning the penalties for improper use. Qilian was floating at the far end, next to the open doorway of the sixth boat. I had to look at him for a long, bewildered moment before I quite realized what I was seeing. I wondered if it was a trick of my eyes, occasioned by the gloomy lighting. But I had made no mistake. Next to Qilian, floating in states of deceptive repose, were the bodies of Jura and Batbayar. A little further away, as if he had been surprised and killed on his own, was Uugan. They had all been stabbed and gashed: knife wounds to the chest and throat, in all three instances. Blood was still oozing out of them.

In his good hand, Qilian held a bloody knife, wet and slick to the hilt.

"I am sorry," he said, as if all that situation needed was a reasonable explanation. "But only one of these six boats is functional."

I stared in numb disbelief. "How can only one be working?"

"The other five are obstructed; they can't leave because there is damage to their launch hatches. This is the only one with a clear shaft all the way to space." Qilian wiped the flat of the blade against his forearm. "Of course, I wish you the best of luck in proving me wrong. But I am afraid I will not be around to witness your efforts."

"You fucking . . ." I began, before trailing off. I knew if I called him a coward he would simply laugh at me, and I had no intention of giving him even the tiniest of moral victories. "Just go," I said.

He drew himself into the lifeboat. I expected some last word from him, some mocking reproach or grandiloquent burst of self-justifying rhetoric. But there was nothing. The door clunked shut with a gasp of compressed air. There was a moment of silence and stillness and then the boat launched itself away from the ship on a rapid stutter of electromagnetic pulses.

I felt the entire hull budge sideways in recoil. He was gone. For several seconds, all I could do was breathe; I could think of nothing useful or constructive to say to Muhunnad, nothing beyond stating the obvious hopelessness of our predicament.

But instead, Muhunnad said quietly: "We are not going to die."

At first, I did not quite understand his words. "I'm sorry?"

He spoke with greater emphasis this time. "We are going to live, but only if you listen to me very, very carefully. You must return me to the couch with all haste."

I shook my head. "It's no good, Muhunnad. It's all over."

"No, it is not. The *River Volga* is not dead. I only made it seem this way."

I frowned. "I don't understand."

"There isn't time to explain here. Get me back to the bridge, get me connected back to the harness, then I will tell you. But make haste! We really do not have very much time. The enemy are much nearer than you think."

"The enemy?"

"There is no *Mandate of Heaven*. Either she scuttled back to the portal, or she was destroyed during the same attack that damaged us."

"But you said . . ."

"I lied. Now help me move!"

Not for the first time that day, I did precisely as I was told.

Having already plotted a route around the obstructions, it did not take anywhere near as long to return to the bridge as it had taken to reach the lifeboats. Once there, I buckled him into the couch – he was beginning to retain some limb control, but not enough to help me with the task – and set about reconnecting the harness systems, trusting myself not to make a mistake. My fingers fumbled on the ends of my hands, as if they were a thousand *li* away.

"Start talking to me, Muhunnad," I said. "Tell me what's going on. Why did you lie about the Mandate?"

"Because I knew the effect that lie would have on Qilian. I wished to give him a reason to leave the ship. I had seen the kind of man he was. I knew that he would save himself, even if it meant the rest of dying."

"I still don't understand. What good has it done us? The damage to the ship . . ." I completed the final connection. Muhunnad stiffened as the harness took hold of his nervous system, but did not appear to be in any obvious discomfort. "Are you all right?" I asked warily.

"This will take a moment. I had to put the ship into a deep shutdown, to convince Qilian. I must bring her back system by system, so as not to risk an overload."

The evidence of his work was already apparent. The bridge lights returned to normal illumination, while those readouts and displays that had remained active were joined by others that had fallen into darkness. I held my breath, expecting the whole ensemble to shut back down again at any moment. But I should have known better than to doubt Muhunnad's ability. The systems remained stable, even as they cycled through start-up and crash recovery routines. The air circulators resumed their dull but reassuring chug.

"I shall dispense with artificial gravity until we are safely underway, if that is satisfactory with you."

"Whatever it takes," I said.

His eyes, still wide open, quivered in their sockets. "I am sweeping local space," he reported. "There was some real damage to the sensors, but nowhere as bad as I made out. I can see Qilian's lifeboat. He made an excellent departure." Then he swallowed, "I can also see the enemy. Three of their ships will shortly be within attack range. I must risk restarting the engines without a proper initialization test."

"Again, whatever it takes."

"Perhaps you would like to brace yourself. There may be a degree of undamped acceleration."

Muhunnad had been right to warn me, and even then it came harder and sooner than I had been expecting. Although I had managed to secure myself to a handhold, I was nearly wrenched away with the abruptness of our departure. I felt acceleration rising smoothly, until it was suppressed by the dampeners. My arm was sore from the jolt, as if it had been almost pulled from its socket.

"That is all I can do for us now," Muhunnad said. "Running is our only effective strategy, unfortunately. Our weapons would prove totally ineffective against the enemy, even if we could get close enough to fire before they turned their own guns on us. But running will suffice. At least we have the mass of one less lifeboat to consider."

"I still don't quite get what happened. How did you know there'd still be one lifeboat that was still working? From what I saw, we came very close to losing all of them."

"We did," he said, with something like pride in his voice. "But not quite, you see. That was my doing, Ariunaa. Before the instant of the attack, I adjusted the angle of orientation of our hull. I made sure that the energy beam took out five of the six lifeboat launch hatches, and no more. Think of a knife fighter, twisting to allow part of his body to be cut rather than another."

I stared at him in amazement, forgetting the pain in my arm from the sudden onset of acceleration. I recalled what Qilian had said, his puzzlement about the ship twisting at the onset of the attack. "You mean you had all this planned, before they even attacked us?"

"I evaluated strategies for disposing of our mutual friend, while retaining the ship. This seemed the one most likely to succeed."

"I am . . . impressed."

"Thank you," he said. "Of course, it would have been easier if I had remained in the harness, so that we could move immediately once the pod had departed. But I think Qilian would have grown suspicious if I had not shown every intention of wanting to escape with him."

"You're right. It was the only way to convince him."

"And now there is only one more matter that needs to be brought to your attention. It is still possible to speak to him. It can be arranged with trivial ease: despite what I said earlier, I am perfectly capable of locking on a tight-beam."

"He'll have no idea what's happened, will he? He'll still think he's got away with it. He's expecting to be rescued by the *Mandate of Heaven* at any moment."

"Eventually, the nature of his predicament will become apparent. But by then, he is likely to have come to the attention of the Smiling Ones."

I thought of the few things Muhunnad had told us about our adversaries. "What will they do to him? Shoot him out of the sky?"

"Not if they sense a chance to take him captive with minimal losses on their own side. I would suggest that an unpowered lifeboat would present exactly such an opportunity."

"And then?"

"He will die. But not immediately. Like the Shining Caliphate, and the Mongol Expansion, the Smiling Ones have an insatiable appetite for information. They will have found others of his kind before, just as they have found others of mine. But I am sure Qilian will still provide them with much amusement."

"And then?" I repeated.

"An appetite of another kind will come into play. The Smiling Ones are cold-blooded creatures. Reptiles. They consider the likes of us – the warm, the mammalian – to be a kind of affront. As well they might, I suppose. All those millions of years ago, we ate their eggs."

I absorbed what he said, thinking of Qilian falling to his destiny, unaware for now of the grave mistake he had made. Part of me was inclined to show clemency: not by rescuing him, which would place *us* dangerously close to the enemy, but by firing on him, so that he might be spared an encounter with the Smiling Ones.

But it was not a large part.

"Time to portal, Muhunnad?"

"Six minutes, on our present heading. Do you wish to review my intentions?"

"No," I said, after a moment. "I trust you to do the best possible job. You think we'll make it into the Infrastructure, without falling to pieces?"

"If Allah is willing. But you understand that our chances of returning to home are now very slim, Yellow Dog? Despite my subterfuge, this ship is damaged. It will not survive many more transitions."

"Then we'll just have to make the best of wherever we end up," I said.

"It will not feel like home to either of us," he replied, his tone gently warning, as if I needed reminding of that.

"But if there are people out there . . . I mean, instead of egg-laying monsters, or sweet-looking devils with tails, then it'll be better than nothing, won't it? People are people. If the Infrastructure is truly breaking down, allowing all these timelines to bleed into one another, than we are all going to have to get along with each other sooner or later. No matter what we all did to each other in our various histories. We're all going to have to put the past behind us."

"It will not be easy," he acknowledged. "But if two people as unalike as you and I can become friends, then perhaps there is hope. Perhaps we could even become an example to others. We shall have to see, shan't we?"

"We shall have to see," I echoed.

I held Muhunnad's hand as we raced towards the portal, and whatever Heaven had in store for us on the other side.

N-WORDS

Ted Kosmatka

As the autumnal story that follows demonstrates, some forms of prejudice go very far back indeed.

New writer Ted Kosmatka has been a zookeeper, a chem tech, and a steelworker, and is now a self-described lab rat who gets to play with electron microscopes all day. He made his first sale, to *Asimov's*, in 2005, and has since made several subsequent sales there, as well as to *The Magazine of Fantasy & Science Fiction*, *Seeds of Change*, *Ideomancer*, *City Slab*, *Kindred Voices*, *Cemetery Dance*, and elsewhere. His story "The Prophet of Flores" was picked up by several Best of the Year series last year, including this one, and he's placed several stories with several such series this year as well. He lives in Portage, Indiana, and has a website at tedkosmatka.com.

THEY CAME FROM test tubes. They came pale as ghosts with eyes as blue-white as glacier ice. They came first out of Korea.

I try to picture David's face in my head, but I can't. They've told me this is temporary – a kind of shock that happens sometimes when you've seen a person die that way. Although I try to picture David's face, it's only his pale eyes I can see.

My sister squeezes my hand in the back of the limo. "It's almost over," she says.

Up the road, against the long, wrought iron railing, the protestors huddle against the cold wind. They grow excited as our procession approaches. They are many, standing in the snow on both sides of the cemetery gates, men and women wearing hats and gloves and looks of righteous indignation, carrying signs I refuse to read.

My sister squeezes my hand again. Before today I had not seen her in almost four years. But today she helped me pick out my black dress. She helped me with my stockings and my shoes. She helped me dress my son, who is not yet three, and who doesn't like ties – and who is now sleeping on the seat across from us without any understanding of what he's lost.

"Are you going to be okay?" My sister asks. She is watching the protestors.

"No," I say. "I don't think I am."

The limo slows as it turns onto cemetery property, and the mob rushes in, shouting obscenities. Protestors push against the sides of the vehicle.

"You aren't wanted here!" someone shouts, and then an old man's face is against the glass, his eyes wild. "God's will be done!" he shrieks. "For the wages of sin is death."

The limo rocks under the press of the crowd, and the driver accelerates until we are past them, moving up the slope toward the other cars.

"What's wrong with them?" my sister whispers. "What kind of people would do that on a day like today?"

You'd be surprised, I think. *Maybe your neighbours. Maybe mine.* But I look out the window and say nothing. I've gotten used to saying nothing.

She'd shown up at my house this morning a little after 6:00. I'd opened the door, and she stood there in the cold, and neither of us spoke, neither of us sure what to say after so long.

"I heard about it on the news," she said finally. "I came on the next plane. I'm so sorry, Mandy."

There are things I wanted to say then – things that rose up inside of me like a bubble ready to burst, and I opened my mouth to scream at her, but what came out belonged to a different person: it came out a pathetic sob, and she stepped forward and wrapped her arms around me, my sister again after all these years.

The limo slows near the top of the hill, and the procession tightens. Headstones crowd the roadway. I see the tent up ahead, green; its canvass sides billowing in and out with the wind, like a giant's breathing. Two-dozen grey folding chairs crouch in straight rows beneath it.

The limo stops.

"Should we wake the boy?" my sister asks.

"I don't know."

"Do you want me to carry him?"

"Can you?"

She looks at the child. "He's only three?"

"No," I say. "Not yet."

"He's big for his age. I mean, isn't he? I'm not around kids much."

"The doctors say he's big."

My sister leans forward and touches his milky white cheek. "He's beautiful," she says. I try not to hear the surprise in her voice. People are never aware of that tone when they use it, revealing what their expectations had been. But I'm past being offended by what people reveal unconsciously. Now it's only intent that offends. "He really is beautiful," she says again.

"He's his father's son," I say.

Ahead of us, mourners climb from their cars. The priest is walking toward the grave.

"It's time," my sister says. She opens the door and we step out into the cold.

∗

They came first out of Korea. But that's wrong, of course. History has an order to its telling. It would be more accurate to say it started in Britain. After all, it was Harding who published first; it was Harding who shook the world with his announcement. And it was Harding who the religious groups burned in effigy on their church lawns.

Only later did the Koreans reveal they'd accomplished the same goal two years before, and the proof was already out of diapers. And it was only later, much later, that the world would recognize the scope of what they'd done.

When the Yeong Bae fell to the People's Party, the Korean labs were emptied, and there were suddenly *thousands* of them – little blond and red-haired orphans, pale as ghosts, starving on the Korean streets as society crumbled around them. The ensuing wars and regime changes destroyed much of the supporting scientific data – but the children themselves, the ones who survived, were incontrovertible. There was no mistaking what they were.

It was never fully revealed why the Yeong Bae had developed the project in the first place. Perhaps they'd been after a better soldier. Or perhaps they'd done it for the oldest reason: because they could.

What is known for certain is that in 2001 disgraced stem cell biologist Hwang Woo-Suk cloned the world's first dog, an afghan. In 2006, he revealed that he'd tried and failed to clone a mammoth on three separate occasions. Western labs had talked about it, but the Koreans had actually tried. This would prove to be the pattern.

In 2011 the Koreans finally succeeded, and a mammoth was born from an elephant surrogate. Other labs followed. Other species. The Pallid Beach Mouse. The Pyrenean Ibex. And older things. Much older.

The best scientists in the US had to leave the country to do their work. US laws against stem cell research didn't stop scientific advancement from occurring; it only stopped it from occurring in the United States. Instead Britain, China and India won patents for the procedures. Many cancers were cured. Most forms of blindness, MS and Parkinson's. Rich Americans had to go overseas for procedures that had become commonplace in other parts of the industrialized world. When Congress eventually legalized the medical procedures, but not the lines of research which lead to them, the hypocrisy was too much, and even the most loyal American cyto-researchers left the country.

Harding was among this final wave, leaving the United States to set up a lab in the UK. In 2013, he was the first to bring back the Thylacine. In the winter of 2015, someone brought him a partial skull from a museum exhibit. The skull was doliocephalic – long, low, large. The bone was heavy, the cranial vault enormous – part of a skullcap that had been found in 1857 in a quarry in the Neander valley.

Snow crunches under our feet as my sister and I move outside the limo. The wind is freezing, and my legs grow numb in my thin slacks. It is fitting he is being buried on a day like today; David was never bothered by the cold.

My sister gestures toward the limo's open door. "Are you sure you want to bring the boy? I could stay with him in the car."

"He should be here," I say. "He should see it."

"He won't understand."

"No, but later he might remember he was here," I say. "Maybe that will matter."

"He's too young to remember."

"He remembers everything." I lean into the shadows and wake the boy. His eyes open like blue lights. "Come, Sean, it's time to wake up."

He rubs a pudgy fist into his eyes and says nothing. He is a quiet boy, my son. Out in the cold, I pull a hat down over his ears. He's still half asleep as we climb the hill. The boy walks between my sister and me, holding our hands.

At the top, Dr Michaels is there to greet us, along with other faculty from Stanford. They offer their condolences, and I work hard not to break down. Dr Michaels looks like he hasn't slept. David was his best friend. I introduce my sister and hands are shaken.

"You never mentioned you had a sister," he says.

I only nod. Dr Michaels looks down at the boy and tugs the child's hat.

"Do you want me to pick you up?" he asks.

"Yeah." Sean's voice is small and scratchy from sleep. It is not an odd voice for a boy his age. It is a normal voice. Dr Michaels lifts him, and the child's blue eyes close again.

We stand in silence in the cold. Mourners gather around the grave.

"I still can't believe it," Dr Michaels says. He's swaying slightly, unconsciously rocking the boy. It is something only a man who has been a father would do, though his own children are grown.

"It's like I'm another kind of person now," I say. "Only, nobody's told me how to be her yet."

My sister grabs my hand, and this time I do break down. The tears burn in the cold.

The priest clears his throat; he's about to begin. In the distance the sounds of protestors grow louder, the rise and fall of their chants not unpleasant – though from this distance, thankfully, I cannot make out the hateful words.

When the world first learned of the Korean children, it sprang into action. Humanitarian groups swooped into the war-torn area, monies exchanged hands, and many of the children were adopted out to other countries. They went to prosperous households in America, and Britain, and different countries all over the globe – a new worldwide Diaspora. They were broad, thick-limbed children; usually slightly shorter than average, though there were startling exceptions to this.

They looked like members of the same family, and some of them, assuredly, were more closely related than that. There were more children, after all, than there were fossil specimens from which they'd derived. Duplicates were inevitable.

From what limited data remained of the Koreans' work, there had been more than sixty different DNA sources. Some even had names: the Old Man La Chappelle aux Saints, Shanidar IV and Vindija. There was the handsome and symmetrical La Ferrassie specimen. And even Amud I. *Huge* Amud I, who had stood 1.8 meters tall and had a cranial capacity of 1740ccs – the largest Neanderthal ever found.

The techniques perfected on dogs and mammoths had worked easily, too, within the genus Homo. Extraction, then PCR to amplify. After that came IVF with paid surrogates. The success rate was high, the only complication frequent caesarean births. And that was one of the things popular culture had to absorb, that Neanderthal heads were larger.

Tests were done. The children were studied and tracked and evaluated. All lacked normal dominant expression at the MC1R locus – all were pale-skinned, freckled, with red or blonde hair. All were blue-eyed. All were Rh negative.

I was six years old when I first saw a picture. It was the cover of *Time* – what is now a famous cover. I'd heard about these children but had never seen one – these children who were almost my age, from a place called Korea; these children who were sometimes called ghosts.

The magazine showed a pale, red-haired Neanderthal boy standing with his adoptive parents, staring thoughtfully up at an outdated anthropology display at a museum. The wax Neanderthal man in the display carried a club. He had a nose from the tropics, dark hair, olive-brown skin and dark brown eyes. Before Harding's child, the museum display designers had supposed they knew what primitive looked like, and they had supposed it was decidedly swarthy.

Never mind that Neanderthals had spent ten times longer in light-starved Europe than a typical Swede's ancestors.

The boy looked up at the display with a confused expression.

When my father walked into the kitchen and saw the *Time* cover, he shook his head in disgust. "It's an abomination," he said.

I studied the boy's jutting face. I'd never seen anyone with face like that. "Who is he?"

"A dead-end. Those kids are going to be a drain for the rest of their lives. It's not fair to them, really."

That was the first of many pronouncements I'd hear about the children.

Years passed and the children grew like weeds – and as with all populations, the first generation exposed to a western diet grew several inches taller than their ancestors. While they excelled at sports, their adopted families were told they could be slow learners and might be prone to aggression. The families were even told, in the beginning, that the children could be antisocial and might never fully grasp the nuances of complex language.

They were primitive after all.

A prediction which turned out to be as accurate as the museum displays.

When I look up, the priest's hands are raised into the cold, white sky. "Blessed are you, O God our father; praised be your name forever." He breathes smoke, reading from the book of Tobit.

It is a passage I've heard at both funerals and marriage ceremonies, and this, like the cold on this day, is fitting. "Let the heavens and all your creations praise you forever."

The mourners sway in the giant's breathing of the tent.

I was born Catholic, but found little use for organized religion in my adulthood. Little use for it, until now, when its use is so clearly revealed – and it is an unexpected comfort to be part of something larger than yourself; it is a comfort to have someone to bury your dead.

Religion provides a man in black to speak words over your loved one's grave. It does this first. If it does not do this, it is not religion.

"You made Adam and you gave him your wife Eve to be his love and support; and from these two, the human race descended."

They said together, Amen, Amen.

The day I learned I was pregnant, David stood at our window, huge, pale arms draped over my shoulders. He touched my stomach as we watched a storm coming in across the lake.

"I hope the baby looks like you," he said in his strange, nasal voice.

"I don't."

"No, it would be easier if the baby looks like you. He'll have an easier life."

"He?"

"I think it's a boy."

"And is that what you'd wish for him, to have an easy life?"

"Isn't that what every parent wishes for?"

"No," I said. I touched my own stomach. I put my small hand over his large one. "I hope our son grows to be a good man."

I'd met David at Stanford when he walked into class five minutes late.

He had arms like legs. And legs like torsos. His torso was the trunk of an oak seventy-five years old, grown in the sun. A full-sleeve tattoo swarmed up one bulging, ghost-pale arm, disappearing under his shirt. He had an earring in one ear, and a shaved head. A thick red goatee balanced the enormous bulk of his convex nose and gave some dimension to his receding chin. The eyes beneath his thick brows were large and intense – as blue as a husky's.

It wasn't that he was handsome, because I couldn't decide if he was. It was that I couldn't take my eyes off him. I stared at him. All the girls stared at him.

He sat near the aisle and didn't take notes like the rest of the students. As far as I could tell, he didn't even bring a pen.

On the second day of class, he sat next to me. I couldn't think. I didn't hear a single word the professor said. I was so aware of the man sitting next to me, his big arms folded in front of him like crossed thighs. He took up a seat and a half, and his elbow kept brushing mine.

It was me who spoke first, a whisper. "You don't care if you fail." It wasn't a question.

"Why do you say that?" He never looked at me and replied so quickly that I realized we'd already been in a kind of conversation, sitting here, without speaking a word.

"Because you aren't taking notes," I said.

"Ah, but I am." He tapped his temple with a thick index finger.

He ended up beating me on the first two tests, but I beat him on the third. By the third test, I'd found a good way to distract him from studying.

It was harder for them to get into graduate programs back then. There were quotas – and like Asians, they had to score better to get accepted.

There was much debate over what name should go next to the race box on their entrance forms. The word "Neanderthal" had evolved into an epithet over the previous decade. It became just another N-word polite society didn't use.

I'd been to the clone rights rallies. I'd heard the speakers. "The French don't call themselves Cro-Magnons, do they?" the loudspeakers boomed.

And so the name by their box had changed every few years, as the college entrance questionnaires strove to map the shifting topography of political correctness. Every few years, a new name for the group would arise – and then a few years later sink again under the accumulated freight of prejudice heaped upon it.

They were called Neanderthals at first, then archaics, then clones – then, ridiculously, they were called simply Koreans, since that was the country in which all but one of them had been born. Sometime after the word "Neanderthal" became an epithet, there was a movement by some militants within the group to reclaim the word, to use it within the group as a sign of strength.

But over time, the group gradually came to be known exclusively by a name that had been used occasionally from the very beginning, a name which captured the hidden heart of their truth. Among their own kind, and finally, among the rest of the world, they came to be known simply as the ghosts. All the other names fell away, and here, finally, was a name that stayed.

In 2033, the first ghost was drafted into the NFL. What modem weight training could do to Neanderthal physiology was nothing short of astonishing.

He stood 5ft 10in and weighed almost 360 lb. He wore his red hair braided tight to his head, and his blue-white eyes shone out from beneath a helmet that had been specially designed to fit his skull. He spoke three languages. By 2035 – the year I met David – the front line of every team in the league had one. Had to have one, to be competitive. They were the highest paid players in sports.

As a group, they accumulated wealth at a rate far above average. They accumulated degrees, and land, and power. The men – beginning mostly during their youth, and continuing after – accumulated women, and subsequently, children. And they accumulated, finally, the attentive glare of the racists, who found them a group no longer to be ignored.

In the 2040 Olympics, ghosts took gold in wrestling, in power lifting, in almost every event in which they were entered. Some individuals took golds in multiple sports, in multiple areas.

There was an outcry from the other athletes who could not hope to compete. There were petitions to have ghosts banned from competition. It was suggested they should have their own Olympics, distinct from the original. Lawyers for the ghosts pointed out, carefully, tactfully, that out of the fastest 400 times recorded for the 100-meter dash, 386 had been achieved by persons of at least partially sub-Saharan African descent, and nobody was suggesting *they* get their own Olympics.

Of course, racist groups like the KKK and the neo-Nazis actually liked the idea and advocated just that. Blacks, too, should compete against their own kind, get their own Olympics. After that, the whole matter degenerated into chaos.

One night, I brought a picture home from work. I turned the light on over the bed, waking him.

"Smile," I told him.

"Why?" David asked.

"Just do it."

He smiled. I looked at the picture. Looked at him.

"It's you," I said.

Still smiling, he snatched the picture from my hand. "What is this?"

When he looked at the picture, his face changed. "Where'd you get this?" he snapped.

"It's a photocopy from one of the periodicals in the archive. From one of the early studies at Amud."

"Why do you think it's me? This could be any of us."

"The bones," I said.

He crinkled up the paper and threw it across the room. "You can't see my bones."

"Teeth," I said, "are bones I can see."

"That's not me." He rolled onto his side. "I'm me."

And then I realized something. I realized that he'd already known he was Amud. And I realized, too, why he kept his head shaved – because there must have been another two or three of them out there, other athletes whose faces he recognized from the mirror, and shaving his head kept him distinct.

In some complex way, I'd embarrassed him. "I'm sorry," I said. I ran my hand across his bare shoulder, up his broad neck to his jaw. I leaned down, and nibbled on his ear. "I'm sorry," I whispered.

But some things you learn, you wish you could un-learn.

Like Diane, the new researcher from down the hall, leaning over my shoulder. "I realize it may be politically incorrect," she said, then paused. Or perhaps I put the pause in there. Perhaps I heard what wasn't there, because I am so used to what came next, in its almost endless variation. And how I hated that term, *politically incorrect*, hated the shield it gave racists who got to label themselves politically incorrect, instead of admitting what they really were. Even to themselves.

"I know it may be politically incorrect," she said, then paused. "But sometimes I just wish those slope-heads would stop stirring up trouble all the time. I mean, you'd think they'd be grateful."

I said nothing. I wished I could unlearn this about her.

I heard David's voice in my head, *peace at all costs*.

But David, I thought, *you don't have to hear it, the leaned-forward, look-both-ways, confidential revelations – the inside talk from people who don't know you're outside, way outside. People look at you, David, and have sense enough not to say something.*

And the new researcher continued, "I know the coalition is upset about what alderman Johnson said, but he's entitled to his opinion."

"And people are entitled to respond to that opinion," I said.

"Sometimes I think people can be too sensitive."

"I used to think that too," I said. "But it's a fallacy."

"It is?"

"Yes, it is impossible to be too sensitive."

"What do you mean?"

"Each person is exactly as sensitive as life experience has made them. It is impossible to be more so."

When I was growing up, I helped my grandfather prune his apple trees in Indiana. The trick, he told me, was telling which branches helped grow the fruit, and which branches didn't. Once you've studied a tree, you got a sense of what was important. Everything else you could cut away as useless baggage.

You can divest yourself of your ethnic identity through a similar process of selective ablation. You look at your child's face, and you don't wonder whose side you're on. You know. That side.

I read in a sociology book that when someone in the privileged majority marries a minority, they take on the social status of that minority group. It occurred to me how the universe is a series of concentric circles, and you keep seeing the same shapes and processes wherever you look. Atoms are little solar systems; highways are a nation's arteries, streets its capillaries – and the social system of humans follows Mendelian genetics, with dominants and recessives. Minority ethnicity is the dominant gene when part of a heterozygous couple.

There are many Neanderthal bones in the Field Museum.

Their bones are different than ours. It is not just their big skulls, or their short, powerful limbs; virtually every bone in their body is thicker, stronger, heavier. Each vertebrae, each phalange, each small bone in the wrist, is thicker than ours. And I have wondered sometimes, when looking at those bones, why they need skeletons like that. All that metabolically expensive bone and muscle and brain. It had to be paid for. What kind of life makes you need bones like chunks of rebar? What kind of life makes you need a sternum half an inch thick?

During the Pleistocene, glaciers had carved their way south across Europe, isolating animal populations behind a curtain of ice. Those populations either adapted to the harsh conditions, or they died. Over time, the herd animals grew massive, becoming more thermally efficient, with short, thick limbs, and heavy bodies – and so began the age of the Pleistocene megafauna. The predators, too, had to adapt. The saber-tooth cat, the cave bear. They changed to fit the cold, grew more powerful in order to bring down the larger prey. What was true for other animals was true for genus *Homo*, nature's experiment, the Neanderthal – the ice-age's ultimate climax predator.

"A reading from the first letter of Saint Paul to the Corinthians." The priest clears his throat. "Brothers and sisters: strive eagerly for the greatest spiritual gifts. But I shall show you a still more excellent way. If I speak in human and angelic tongues but have not love, I am a resounding gong, or a clashing cymbal."

I watch the priest's face while he speaks, this man in black.

"And if I have the gift of prophecy and comprehend all the mysteries and all knowledge; if I have all faith so as to move mountains, but do not have love, I am nothing."

Dr Michaels is still rocking my son in his arms. The boy is awake now. His blue eyes move to mine.

"Love bears all things, believes all things, hopes all things, endures all things."

Three days ago, the day David died, I woke to an empty bed. I found him naked at the window in our living room, looking out into the winter sky, his leonine face wrapped in shadow.

From behind, I could see the V of his back against the grey light. I knew better than to disturb him. He became a silhouette against the sky, and in that instant, he was something more and less than human – like some broad human creature adapted for life in extreme gravity. A person built to survive stresses that would crush a normal man.

He turned back toward the sky. "There's a storm coming today," he said.

The day David died, I woke to an empty bed. I wonder about that.

I wonder if he suspected something. I wonder what got him out of bed early. I wonder at the storm he mentioned, the one he said was coming.

If he'd known the risk, we never would have gone to the rally – I'm sure of that, because he was a cautious man. But I wonder if some hidden, inner part of him didn't have its ear to the railroad tracks; I wonder if some part of him didn't feel the ground shaking, didn't hear the freight train barrelling down on us all.

The day David died, I woke to an empty bed – a thing I will have to grow used to. We ate breakfast that morning. We drove to the babysitter's and dropped off our son. David kissed him on the cheek and tousled his hair. There was no last look, no sense this would be the final time. David kissed the boy, tousled his hair, and then we were out the door, Mary waving goodbye.

We drove to the hall in silence. David's mind was on the coming afternoon and the speech he had to give. We parked our car in the crowded lot, ignoring the counter-rally already forming across the street.

We shook hands with other guests and found our way to the assigned table. It was supposed to be a small luncheon, but the alderman's inflammatory statements, and his refusal to apologize, had swelled the crowd.

These things were usually civilized affairs, with moneyed men in expensive suits. David was the second speaker.

Up on the podium, David's expression changed. Before his speeches, there was this moment, this single second, where he glanced out over the crowd, and his eyes grew sad.

David closed his eyes, opened them, and spoke. He began slowly. He spoke of the flow of history and the symmetry of nature. He spoke of the arrogance of ignorance; and in whispered tones, he spoke of fear. "And out of fear," he said, "grows hatred." He let his eyes wander over the crowd. "They hate us because we're different," he said, voice rising for the first time. "Always it works this way, wherever you look in history. And always we must work against it. We must never give in to violence. But we are right to fear, my friends. We must be vigilant, or we'll lose everything we've gained for our children, and our children's children." He paused.

The specific language of this speech was new to me, if not the theme. David rarely wrote his speeches ahead of time, preferring to pull the rhythms out of his head as he went – assembling an oratorical structure from nothing at all, building it from the ground up. He continued for another ten minutes before finally going into his close.

"They've talked about restricting us from athletic competition," he said, voice booming. "They've eliminated us from receiving most scholarships. They've limited our attendance of law schools, and medical schools, and PhD programs. These are the soft shackles they've put upon us, and we cannot sit silently and let it happen."

The crowd erupted into applause. David lifted his hands to silence them and he walked back to his seat.

Other speakers took the podium, but none with David's eloquence. None with his power.

When the last speaker sat, dinner was brought out and we ate. An hour later, when the plates were clean, more hands were shaken, and people started filing out to their cars. The evening was over.

David and I took our time, talking with old friends, but we eventually worked our way into the lobby. Ahead of us, out in the parking lot, there was a commotion. The counterrally had grown.

Somebody mentioned vandalized cars, and then Tom was leaning into David's ear, whispering as we passed through the front doors and out into the open air.

It started with thrown eggs. Thomas turned, egg-white drooling down his broad chest. The fury in his eyes was enough to frighten me. David rushed forward and grabbed his arm. There was a look of surprise on some of the faces in the crowd, because even they hadn't expected anybody to throw things – and I could see, too, the group of young men, clumped together near the side of the building, eggs in hand, mouths open – and it was like time stopped, because the moment was fat and waiting – and it could go any way, and an egg came down out of the sky that was not an egg, but a rock, and it struck Sarah Mitchell in the face – and the blood was red and shocking on her ghost-white skin, and the moment was *wide* open, time snapping back the other way – everything moving too fast, all of it happening at the same time instead of taking turns the way events are supposed to. And suddenly David's grip on my arm was a vise, physically lifting me, pulling me back toward the building, and I tried to keep my feet while someone screamed.

"Everybody go back inside!" David shouted. And then another woman screamed, a different kind of noise, like a shout of warning – and then I heard it, a shout that was a roar like nothing I'd ever heard before – and then more screams, men's screams. And somebody lunged from the crowd and swung at David, and he moved so quickly I was flung away, the blow missing David's head by a foot.

"No!" David yelled at the man. "We don't want this."

Then the man swung again and this time David caught the fist in his huge hand. He jerked the man close. "We're not doing this," he hissed and flung him back into the crowd.

David grabbed Tom's arm again, trying to guide him back toward the building. "This is stupid, don't be pulled into it."

Thomas growled and let himself be pulled along, and someone spit in his face, and I saw it, the dead look in his eyes, to be spit on and do nothing. And still David pulled us toward the safety of the building, brushing aside the curses of men whose necks he could snap with the single flex of his arm. And still he did nothing. He did nothing all the way up to the end, when a thin, balding forty-year-old man stepped into his path, raised a gun, and fired point blank into his chest.

*

The blast was deafening.

– and that old sadness gone. Replaced by white-hot rage and disbelief, blue eyes wide.

People tried to scatter, but the crush of bodies prevented it. David hung there, in the crush, looking down at his chest. The man fired three more times before David fell.

"Ashes to ashes, dust to dust. Accept our brother David into your warm embrace." The priest lowers his hands and closes the bible. The broad casket is lowered into the ground. It is done.

Dr Michaels carries the boy as my sister helps me back to the limo.

The night David was killed, after the hospital and the police questions, I drove to the sitter's to pick up my son. I drove there alone. Mary hugged me and we stood crying in the foyer for a long time.

"What do I tell my two-year old?" I said. "How do I explain this?"

We walked to the front room, and I stood in the doorway. I watched my son like I was seeing him for the first time. He was blocky, like his father, but his bones were longer. He was a gifted child who knew his letters and could already sound out certain words.

And that was our secret, that he was not yet three and already learning to read. And there were thousands more like him – a new generation, the best of two tribes.

Perhaps David's mistake was that he hadn't realized there was a war. In any war, there are only certain people who fight it – and a smaller number who understand, truly, *why* it's being fought. This was no different.

Fifty thousand years ago, there were two walks of men in the world. There were the people of the ice, and there were the people of the sun.

When the climate warmed, the ice sheets retreated. The broad African desert was beaten back by the rains, and the people of the sun expanded north.

The world was changing then. The European megafauna were disappearing. The delicate predator/prey equilibrium slipped out of balance and the world's most deadly climax predator found his livelihood evaporating in warming air. Without the big herds, there was less food. The big predators gave way to sleeker models that needed fewer calories to survive.

The people of the sun weren't stronger, or smarter, or better than the people of the ice; Cain didn't kill his brother, Abel. The people of the North didn't die out because they weren't good enough. All that bone and muscle and brain. They died because they were too expensive.

But now the problems are different. The world has changed again. Again there are two kinds of men in the world. But in this new age of plenty, it will not be the economy version of man who wins.

The limo door slams shut. The vehicle pulls away from the grave. As we near the cemetery gates, the shouting grows louder. The protestors see us coming.

The police said that David's murder was a crime of passion. Others said he was a target of opportunity. I don't know which is true. The truth died with the shooter, when Tom crushed his skull with a single right-hand blow.

The shouting spikes louder as we pass the cemetery gates. The protestors surge forward, and a snowball smashes into the window.

"Stop the car!" I shout.

I fling open the car door. I climb out and walk up to the surprised man. He's standing there, another snowball already packed in his hands.

I'm not sure what I'm going to do as I approach him. I've gotten used to the remarks, the small attacks. I've gotten used to ignoring them. I've gotten used to saying nothing.

I slap him in the face as hard as I can.

He's too shocked to react at first. I slap him again.

This time he flinches away from me, wanting no part of this. I walk back to my car as the crowd finds its voice. People start screaming at me. I climb back into the limo and they close around me. Hands and faces on the glass. The driver pulls away.

My son looks at me, and it's not fear in his eyes like I expect; it's anger. Anger at the crowd. My huge, brilliant son – these people have no idea what they're doing. They have no idea the storm they're calling down.

I see a sign held high as we pass the last of the protestors at the gate. They are shouting again, having found the full flower of their outrage. The sign says only one word: *die*.

Not this time, I think to myself. *Your turn.*

AN ELIGIBLE BOY

Ian McDonald

Here's a story by Ian McDonald, whose "The Tear" appears later in this anthology. In this one, he takes us to visit a vivid and evocative future India, where ancient customs and dazzlingly sophisticated high-tech exist side by side, and where the age-old game of courtship has become far more complex and strange than anybody ever thought that it could.

A ROBOT IS giving Jasbir the whitest teeth in Delhi. It is a precise, terrifying procedure involving chromed steel and spinning, shrieking abrasion heads. Jasbir's eyes go wide as the spidery machine-arms flourish their weapons in his face, a demon of radical dentistry. He read about the *Glinting Life!* Cosmetic Dentistry Clinic, (Hygienic, Quick and Modern) in the February edition of *Shaadi! for Eligible Boys*. In double-page spread it looked nothing like these insect-mandibles twitching inside his mouth. He'd like to ask the precise and demure dental nurse (married, of course) if it's meant to be like this but his mouth is full of clamps and anyway an Eligible Boy never shows fear. But he closes his eyes as the robot reaches in and spinning steel hits enamel.

Now the whitest teeth in Delhi dart through the milling traffic in a rattling phatphat. He feels as if he is beaming out over an entire city. The whitest teeth, the blackest hair, the most flawless skin and perfectly plucked eyebrows. Jasbir's nails are beautiful. There's a visiting manicurist at the Ministry of Waters, so many are the civil servants on the shaadi circuit. Jasbir notices the driver glancing at his blinding smile. He knows; the people on Mathura Road know, all Delhi knows that every night is great game night.

On the platform of Cashmere Café metro station, chip-implanted policemonkeys canter, shrieking, between the legs of passengers, driving away the begging, tugging, thieving macaques that infest the subway system. They pour over the edge of the platform to their holes and hides in a wave of brown fur as the robot train slides in to the stop. Jasbir always stands next to the Women Only section. There is always a chance one of them might be scared of the monkeys – they bite – and he could then perform an act of Spontaneous Gallantry. The women studiously avoid any glance, any word, any sign of interest but a true Eligible Boy never passes up a chance for contact. But that woman in the business suit, the one with the fashionable wasp-waist jacket and the low-cut hip-riding pants, was she momentarily dazzled by the glint of his white white teeth?

"A robot, madam," Jasbir calls as the packer wedges him into the 18:08 to Barwala. "Dentistry of the future." The doors close. But Jasbir Dayal knows he is a white-toothed Love God and this, this will be the shaadi night he finally finds the wife of his dreams.

Economists teach India's demographic crisis as an elegant example of market failure. Its seed germinated in the last century, before India became Tiger of Tiger economies, before political jealousies and rivalries split her into twelve competing states. *A lovely boy,* was how it began. *A fine, strong, handsome, educated, successful son, to marry and raise children and to look after us when we are old.* Every mother's dream, every father's pride. Multiply by the three hundred million of India's emergent middle class. Divide by the ability to determine sex in the womb. Add selective abortion. Run twenty-five years down the x-axis, factoring in refined, twenty-first century techniques such as cheap, powerful pharma patches that ensure lovely boys will be conceived and you arrive at great Awadh, its ancient capital Delhi of twenty million and a middle class with four times as many males as females. Market failure. Individual pursuit of self-interest damages larger society. Elegant to economists; to fine, strong, handsome, educated, successful young men like Jasbir caught in a wife-drought, catastrophic.

There's a ritual to shaadi nights. The first part involves Jasbir in the bathroom for hours playing pop music too loud and using too much expensive water while Sujay knocks and leaves copious cups of tea at the door and runs an iron over Jasbir's collars and cuffs and carefully removes the hairs of previous shaadis from Jasbir's suit jacket. Sujay is Jasbir's housemate in the government house at Acacia Bungalow Colony. He's a character designer on the Awadh version of *Town and Country*, neighbour-and-rival Bharat's all-conquering artificial intelligence generated soap opera. He works with the extras, designing new character skins and dropping them over raw code from Varanasi. Jahzay Productions is a new model company, meaning that Sujay seems to do most of his work from the verandah on his new-fangled lighthoek device, his hands drawing pretty, invisible patterns on air. To office-bound Jasbir, with a ninety-minute commute on three modes of transport each way each day, it looks pretty close to nothing. Sujay is uncommunicative and hairy and neither shaves nor washes his too-long hair enough but his is a sensitive soul and compensates for the luxury of being able to sit in the cool cool shade all day waving his hands by doing housework. He cleans, he tidies, he launders. He is a fabulous cook. He is so good that Jasbir does not need a maid, a saving much to be desired in pricey Acacia Bungalow Colony. This is a source of gossip to the other residents of Acacia Bungalow Colony. Most of the goings-on in Number 27 are the subject of gossip over the lawn sprinklers. Acacia Bungalow Colony is a professional, family gated community.

The second part of the ritual is the dressing. Like a syce preparing a Mughal lord for battle, Sujay dresses Jasbir. He fits the cufflinks and adjusts them to the proper angle. He adjusts the set of Jasbir's collar just so. He examines Jasbir from every angle as if he is looking at one of his own freshly-fleshed characters. Brush off a little dandruff here, correct a desk-slumped posture there. Smell his breath and check the teeth for lunch-time spinach and other dental crimes.

"So what do you think of them then?" Jasbir says.

"They're white," grunts Sujay.

The third part of the ritual is the briefing. While they wait for the phat-phat, Sujay fills Jasbir in on upcoming plotlines on Town and Country. It's Jasbir's major conversational ploy and advantage over his deadly rivals; soap-opera gossip. In his experience what the women really want is gupshup from the meta-soap, the no-less-fictitious lives and loves and mar-riages and rows of the aeai actors that believe they are playing the roles in Town and Country. "Auh," Sujay will say. "Different department."

There's the tootle of phatphat horns. Curtains will twitch, there will be complaints about waking up children on a school night. But Jasbir is glimmed and glammed and shaadi-fit. And armed with soapi gupshup. How can he fail?

"Oh, I almost forgot," Sujay says as he opens the door for the God of Love. "Your father left a message. He wants to see you."

"You've hired a what?" Jasbir's retort is smothered by the cheers of his brothers from the living room as a cricket ball rolls and skips over the boundary rope at Jawaharlal Nehru Stadium. His father bends closer; con-fidentially across the tiny tin-topped kitchen table. Anant whisks the kettle off the boil so she can overhear. She is the slowest, most awkward maid in Delhi but to fire her would be to condemn an old woman to the streets. She lumbers around the Dayal kitchen like a buffalo, feigning disinterest.

"A matchmaker. Not my idea, not my idea at all; it was hers." Jasbir's father inclines his head toward the open living room door. Beyond it, enthroned on her sofa amidst her non-eligible boys, Jasbir's mother watches the test match of the smart-silk wallscreen Jasbir had bought her with his first civil service paycheck. When Jasbir left the tiny, ghee-stinky apartment on Nabi Karim Road for the distant graces of Acacia Bungalow Colony, Mrs Dayal delegated all negotiations with her wayward son to her husband. "She's found this special matchmaker."

"Wait wait wait. Explain to me *special*."

Jasbir's father squirms. Anant is taking a long time to dry a tea-cup.

"Well, you know in the old days people would maybe have gone to a hijra . . . Well, she's updated it a bit, this being the twenty first century and everything, so she's, ah, found a nute."

A clatter of a cup hitting a stainless steel draining board.

"A *nute*?" Jasbir hisses

"He knows contracts. He knows deportment and proper etiquette. He knows what women want. I think he may have been one, once."

Anant lets out an *aie!*, soft and involuntary as a fart.

"I think the word you're looking for is 'yt'," Jasbir says. "And they're not hijras the way you knew them. They're not men become women or women become men. They're neither."

"Nutes, neithers, hijras, yts, hes, shes; whatever; it's not as if I even get to take tea with the parents let alone see an announcement in the shaadi section in the *Times of Awadh*." Mrs Dayal shouts over the burbling commentary to the second Awadh-China Test. Jasbir winces. Like papercuts, the criticisms of parents are the finest and the most painful.

Inside the Haryana Polo and Country Club the weather was raining men snowing men hailing men. Well-dressed men, moneyed men, charming men, groomed and glinted men, men with prospects all laid out in their marriage resumés. Jasbir knew most of them by face. Some he knew by name, a few had passed beyond being rivals into becoming friends.

"Teeth!" A cry, a nod, a two-six-gun showbiz point from the bar. There leant Kishore, a casual lank of a man draped like a skein of silk against the Raj-era mahogany. "Where did you get those, badmash?" He was an old university colleague of Jasbir's, much given to high-profile activities like horse racing at the Delhi Jockey Club or skiing, where there was snow left on the Himalayas. Now he was in finance and claimed to have been to five hundred shaadis and made a hundred proposals. But when they were on the hook, wriggling, he let them go. *Oh, the tears, the threats, the phone calls from fuming fathers and boiling brothers. It's the game, isn't it?* Kishore rolls on, "Here, have you heard? Tonight is Deependra's night. Oh yes. An astrology aeai has predicted it. It's all in the stars, and on your palmer."

Deependra was a clenched wee man. Like Jasbir he was a civil servant, heading up a different glass-partitioned workcluster in the Ministry of Waters: Streams and Watercourses to Jasbir's Ponds and Dams. For three shaadis now he had been nurturing a fantasy about a woman who exchanged palmer addresses with him. First it was call, then a date. Now it's a proposal.

"Rahu is in the fourth house, Saturn in the seventh," Deependra said lugubriously. "Our eyes will meet, she will nod – just a nod. The next morning she will call me and that will be it, done, dusted. I'd ask you to be one of my groomsmen, but I've already promised them all to my brothers and cousins. It's written. Trust me."

It is a perpetual bafflement to Jasbir how a man wedded by day to robust fluid accounting by night stakes love and life on an off-the-shelf janampatri artificial intelligence.

A Nepali chidmutgar banged a staff on the hardwood dancefloor of the exclusive Haryana Polo and Country Club. The Eligible Boys straightened their collars, adjusted the hang of their jackets, aligned their cufflinks. This side of the mahogany double doors to the garden they were friends and colleagues. Beyond it they were rivals.

"Gentlemen, valued clients of the Lovely Girl Shaadi Agency, please welcome, honour and cherish the Begum Rezzak and her Lovely Girls!"

Two attendants slid open the folding windows on to the polo ground. There waited the lovely girls in their saris and jewels and gold and henna (for the Lovely Girl Agency is a most traditional and respectable agency). Jasbir checked his schedule – five minutes per client, maybe less, never more. He took a deep breath and unleashed his thousand-rupee smile. It was time to find a wife.

"Don't think I don't know what you're muttering about in there," Mrs Dayal called over the mantra commentary of Harsha Bhogle. "I've had the talk. The nute will arrange the thing for much less than you are wasting on all those shaadi agencies and databases and nonsense. No, nute will make the match that is it stick stop stay." There is a spatter of applause from the Test Match.

"I tell you your problem: a girl sees two men sharing a house together, she gets ideas about them," Dadaji whispers. Anant finally sets down two cups of tea and rolls her eyes. "She's had the talk. It'll start making the match. There's nothing to be done about it. There are worse things."

The women may think what they want, but Sujay has it right, Jasbir thinks. *Best never to buy into the game at all.*

Another cheer, another boundary. Haresh and Sohan jeer at the Chinese devils. *Think you can buy it in and beat the world, well, the Awadhi boys are here to tell you it takes years, decades, centuries upon centuries to master the way of cricket.* And there's too much milk in the tea.

A dream wind like the hot gusts that fore-run the monsoon sends a spray of pixels through the cool white spacious rooms of 27 Acacia Avenue Bungalows. Jasbir ducks and laughs as they blow around him. He expects them to be cold and sharp as wind-whipped powder snow but they are only digits, patterns of electrical charge swept through his visual cortex by the clever little device hooked behind his right ear. They chime as they swirl past, like glissandos of silver sitar notes. Shaking his head in wonder, Jasbir slips the lighthoek from behind his ear. The vision evaporates.

"Very clever, very pretty but I think I'll wait until the price comes down."

"It's, um, not the 'hoek'," Sujay mutters. "You know, well, the match-maker your mother hired. Well, I thought, maybe you don't need someone arranging you a marriage." Some days Sujay's inability to talk to the point exasperates Jasbir. Those days tend to come after another fruitless and expensive shaadi night and the threat of matchmaker but particularly after Deependra of the non-white teeth announces he has a date. With the girl. The one written in the fourth house of Rahu by his pocket astrology aeai. "Well, you see I thought, with the right help you could arrange it yourself." Some days debate with Sujay is pointless. He follows his own calendar. "You, ah, need to put the hoek back on again."

Silver notes spray through Jasbir's inner ears as the little curl of smart plastic seeks out the sweet spot in his skull. Pixel birds swoop and swarm like starlings on a winter evening. It is inordinately pretty. Then Jasbir gasps aloud as the motes of light and sound sparklingly coalesce into a dapper man in an old-fashioned high-collar sherwani and wrinkle-bottom pajamas. His shoes are polished to mirror-brightness. The dapper man bows.

"Good morning sir. I am Ram Tarun Das, Master of Grooming, Grace and Gentlemanliness."

"What is this doing in my house?" Jasbir unhooks the device beaming data into his brain.

"Er, please don't do that," Sujay says. "It's not aeai etiquette."

Jasbir slips the device back on and there he is, that charming man.

"I have been designed with the express purpose of helping you marry a suitable girl," says Ram Tarun Das.

"Designed?"

"I, ah, made him for you," says Sujay. "I thought that if anyone knows about relationships and marriages, it's soap stars."

"A soap star. You've made me a, a marriage life coach out of a soap star?"

"Not a soap star exactly, more a conflation of a number of sub-systems from the central character register," Sujay says. "Sorry Ram."

"Do you usually do that?"

"Do what?"

"Apologise to aeais."

"They have feelings too."

Jasbir rolls his eyes. "I'm being taught husbandcraft by a mash-up."

"Ah, that is out of order. Now you apologise."

"Now then, sir, if I am to rescue you from a marriage forged in hell, we had better start with manners," says Ram Tarun Das. "Manners maketh the man. It is the bedrock of all relationships because true manners come from what he is, not what he does. Do not argue with me, women see this at once. Respect for all things, sir, is the key to etiquette. Maybe I only imagine I feel as you feel, but that does not make my feelings any less real to me. So this once I accept your apology as read. Now, we'll begin. We have so much to do before tonight's shaadi."

Why, Jasbir thinks, *why can I never get my shoes like that?*

The lazy crescent moon lolls low above the out-flarings of Tughluk's thousand stacks; a cradle to rock an infant nation. Around its rippling reflection in the infinity pool bob mango-leaf diyas. No polo grounds and country clubs for Begum Jaitly. This is 2045, not 1945. Modern style for a modern nation, that is philosophy of the Jaitly Shaadi Agency. But gossip and want are eternal and in the mood lighting of the penthouse the men are blacker-than black shadows against greater Delhi's galaxy of lights and traffic.

"Eyebrows!" Kishore greets Jasbir with TV-host pistol-fingers two-shot bam bam. "No seriously, what did you do to them?" Then his own eyes widen as he scans down from the eyebrows to the total product. His mouth opens, just a crack, but wide enough for Jasbir to savour an inner fist-clench of triumph.

He'd felt self-conscious taking Ram Tarun Das to the mall. He had no difficulty accepting that the figure in its stubbornly atavistic costume was invisible to everyone but him (though he did marvel at how the aeai avoided colliding with any other shopper in thronged Centrestage Mall). He did feel stupid talking to thin air.

"What is this delicacy?" Ram Tarun Das said in Jasbir's inner ear. "People talk to thin air on the cellphone all the time. Now this suit, sir."

It was bright, it was brocade, it was a fashionable retro cut that Jasbir would have gone naked rather than worn.

"It's very . . . bold."

"It's very you. Try it. Buy it. You will seem confident and stylish without being flashy. Women cannot bear flashy."

The robot cutters and stitchers were at work even as Jasbir completed the card transaction. It was expensive. *Not as expensive as all the shaadi memberships*, he consoled himself. *And something to top it off*. But Ram Tarun Das manifested himself right in the jeweller's window over the display.

"Never jewellery on a man. One small brooch at the shirt collar to hold it together, that is permissible. Do you want the lovely girls to think you are a Mumbai pimp? No, sir, you do not. No to jewels. Yes to shoes. Come."

He had paraded his finery before a slightly embarrassed Sujay.

"You look, er, good. Very dashing. Yes."

Ram Tarun Das, leaning on his cane and peering intensely, said, "You move like a buffalo. Ugh, sir. Here is what I prescribe for you. Tango lessons. Passion and discipline. Latin fire, yet the strictest of tempos. Do not argue, it is the tango for you. There is nothing like it for deportment."

The tango, the manicures, the pedicures, the briefings in popular culture and Delhi gossip ("soap opera insults both the intelligence and imagination, I should know, sir"), the conversational ploys, the body language games of when to turn so, when to make or break eye contact, when to dare the lightest, engaging touch. Sujay mooched around the house, even more lumbering and lost than usual, as Jasbir chatted with air and practised Latin turns and drops with invisible partner. Last of all, on the morning of the Jaitly shaadi,

"Eyebrows sir. You will never get a bride with brows like a hairy saddhu. There is a girl not five kilometres from here, she has a moped service. I've ordered her, she will be here within ten minutes."

As ever, Kishore won't let Jasbir wedge an answer in, but rattles on, "So, Deependra then?"

Jasbir has noticed that Deependra is not occupying his customary place in Kishore's shadows; in fact he does not seem to be anywhere in this penthouse.

"Third date," Kishore says, then mouths it again silently for emphasis. "That janampatri aeai must be doing something right. You know, wouldn't it be funny if someone took her off him? Just as a joke, you know?"

Kishore chews his bottom lip. Jasbir knows the gesture of old. Then bells chime, lights dim and a wind from nowhere sends the butter-flames flickering and the little diyas flocking across the infinity pool. The walls have opened, the women enter the room.

She stands by the glass wall looking down into the cube of light that is the car park. She clutches her cocktail between her hands as if in prayer or concern. It is a new cocktail designed for the international cricket test, served in an egg-shaped goblet made from a new spin-glass that will always self-right, no matter how it is set down or dropped. *A Test of Dragons* is the name of the cocktail. Good Awadhi whisky over a gilded syrup with a six-hit of Chinese Kao Liang liqueur. A tiny red gel dragon dissolves like a sunset.

"Now, sir," whispers Ram Tarun Das standing at Jasbir's shoulder. "Faint heart, as they say."

Jasbir's mouth is dry. A secondary application Sujay pasted onto the Ram Tarun Das aeai tells him his precise heart rate, respiration, temperature and the degree of sweat in his palm. He's surprised he's still alive.

You've got the entry lines, you've got the exit lines and the stuff in the middle Ram Tarun Das will provide.

He follows her glance down into the car park. A moment's pause, a slight inclination of his body towards hers. That is *the line.*

So, are you a Tata, a Mercedes, a Li Fan or a Lexus? Ram Tarun Das whispers in Jasbir's skull. He casually repeats the line. He has been rehearsed and rehearsed and rehearsed in how to make it sound natural. He's as good as any newsreader, better than those few human actors left on television.

She turned to him, lips parted a fraction in surprise.

"I beg your pardon?"

She will say this, Ram Tarun Das hints. *Again, offer the line.*

"Are you a Tata, a Mercedes, a Li Fan or a Lexus?"

"What do you mean?"

"Just pick one. Whatever you feel, that's the right answer."

A pause, a purse of the lips. Jasbir subtly links his hands behind his back, the better to hide the sweat.

"Lexus," she says. Shulka, her name is Shulka. She is a twenty-two year-old marketing graduate from Delhi U working in men's fashion, a Mathur – only a couple of caste steps away from Jasbir's folk. The Demographic Crisis has done more to shake up the tiers of varna and jati than a century of the slow drip of democracy. And she has answered his question.

"Now, that's very interesting," says Jasbir.

She turns, plucked crescent-moon eyebrows arched. Behind Jasbir, Ram Tarun Das whispers, *now, the fetch.*

"Delhi, Mumbai, Kolkata, Chennai?"

A small frown now. Lord Vishnu, she is beautiful.

"I was born in Delhi . . ."

"That's not what I mean."

The frown becomes a nano-smile of recognition.

"Mumbai then. Yes, Mumbai definitely. Kolkata's hot and dirty and nasty. And Chennai – no, I'm definitely Mumbai."

Jasbir does the sucked-in-lip-nod of concentration Ram Tarun Das made him practise in front of the mirror.

"Red Green Yellow Blue?"

"Red." No hesitation.

"Cat Dog Bird Monkey?"

She cocks her head to one side. Jasbir notices that she, too, is wearing a 'hoek. Tech girl. The cocktail bot is on its rounds, doing industrial magic with the self-righting glasses and its little spider-fingers.

"Bird . . . no." A sly smile. "No no no. Monkey."

He is going to die he is going to die.

"But what does it mean?"

Jasbir holds up a finger.

"One more. Ved Prakash, Begum Vora, Dr Chatterji, Ritu Parvaaz."

She laughs. She laughs like bells from the hem of a wedding skirt. She laughs like the stars of a Himalaya night.

What do you think you're doing? Ram Tarun Das hisses. He flips through Jasbir's perceptions to appear behind Shulka, hands thrown up in despair. With a gesture he encompasses the horizon wreathed in gas flares. *Look, tonight the sky burns for you, sir, and you would talk about soap opera! The script, stick to the script! Improvization is death.* Almost Jasbir tells his matchmaker, *Away djinn, away.* He repeats the question.

"I'm not really a *Town and Country* fan," Shulka says. "My sister now, she knows every last detail about every last one of the characters and that's before she gets started on the actors. It's one of those things I suppose you can be ludicrously well informed about without ever watching. So if you had to press me, I would have to say Ritu. So what does it all mean, Mr Dayal?"

His heart turns over in his chest. Ram Tarun Das eyes him coldly. *The finesse: make it. Do it just as I instructed you. Otherwise your money and my bandwidth are thrown to the wild wind.*

The cocktail bot dances in to perform its cybernetic circus. A flip of Shulka's glass and it comes down spinning, glinting, on the precise needle-point of its forefinger. Like magic, if you know nothing about gyros and spin-glasses. But that moment of prestidigitation is cover enough for Jasbir to make the ordained move. By the time she looks up, cocktail refilled, he is half a room away.

He wants to apologise as he sees her eyes widen. He needs to apologise as her gaze searches the room for him. Then her eyes catch his. It is across a crowded room just like the song that Sujay mumbles around the house when he thinks Jasbir can't hear. Sujay loves that song. It is the most romantic, heart-felt, innocent song he has ever heard. Big awkward Sujay has always been a sucker for veteran Holywood musicals. *South Pacific. Carousel, Moulin Rouge,* he watches them on the big screen in the living room, singing shamelessly along and getting moist-eyed at the impossible loves. Across a crowded room, Shulka frowns. Of course. It's in the script.

But what does it mean? she mouths. And, as Ram Tarun Das has directed, he shouts back, "Call me and I'll tell you." Then he turns on his heel and walks away. And that, he knows without any prompt from Ram Tarun Das, is the *finesse*.

The apartment is grossly over-heated and smells of singeing cooking ghee but the nute is swaddled in a crocheted shawl, hunched as if against a persistent hard wind. Plastic teacups stand on the low brass table, Jasbir's mother's conspicuously untouched. Jasbir sits on the sofa with his father on his right and his mother on his left, as if between arresting policemen. Nahin the nute mutters and shivers and rubs yts fingers.

Jasbir has never been in the physical presence of a third-gendered. He knows all about them – as he knows all about most things – from the Single-Professional-Male general interest magazines to which he subscribes. Those pages, between the ads for designer watches and robot tooth whitening – portray them as fantastical, Arabian Nights creatures equally blessed and cursed with glamour. Nahin the matchmaker seems old and tired as a god, knotting and unknotting yts fingers over the papers on the coffee table – "The bloody drugs, darlings" – occasionally breaking into great spasmodic shudders. *It's one way of avoiding the Wife Game*, Jasbir thinks.

Nahin slides sheets of paper around on the tabletop. The documents are patterned as rich as damask with convoluted chartings of circles and spirals annotated in inscrutable alphabets. There is a photograph of a woman in each top right corner. The women are young and handsome but have the wide-eyed expressions of being photographed for the first time.

"Now, I've performed all the calculations and these five are both compatible and auspicious," Nahin says. Yt clears a large gobbet of phlegm from yts throat.

"I notice they're all from the country," says Jasbir's father.

"Country ways are good ways," says Jasbir's mother.

Wedged between them on the short sofa, Jasbir looks over Nahin's shawled shoulder to where Ram Tarun Das stands in the doorway. He raises his eyebrows, shakes his head.

"Country girls are better breeders," Nahin says. "You said dynasty was a concern. You'll also find a closer match in jati and in general they settle for a much more reasonable dowry than a city girl. City girls want it all. Me me me. No good ever comes of selfishness."

The nute's long fingers stir the country girls around the coffee table, then slide three toward Jasbir and his family. Dadaji and Mamaji sit forward. Jasbir slumps back. Ram Tarun Das folds his arms, rolls his eyes.

"These three are the best starred," Nahin says. "I can arrange a meeting with their parents almost immediately. There would be some small expenditure in their coming up to Delhi to meet with you; this would be in addition to my fee."

In a flicker, Ram Tarun Das is behind Jasbir, his whisper a startle in his ear.

"There is a line in the Western wedding vows: speak now or forever hold your peace."

"How much is my mother paying you?" Jasbir says into the moment of silence.

"I couldn't possibly betray client confidentiality." Nahin has eyes small and dark as currants.

"I'll disengage you for an additional fifty per cent."

Nahin's hands hesitate over the pretty hand drawn spirals and wheels. *You were a man before,* Jasbir thinks. *That's a man's gesture. See, I've learned how to read people.*

"I double," shrills Mrs Dayal.

"Wait wait wait," Jasbir's father protests but Jasbir is already shouting over him. He has to kill this idiocy here, before his family in their wedding fever fall into strategies they cannot afford.

"You're wasting your time and my parents' money," Jasbir says. "You see, I've already met a suitable girl."

Goggle eyes, open mouths around the coffee table, but none so astounded and gaping as Ram Tarun Das's.

The Prasads at Number 25 Acacia Colony Bungalows have already sent over a pre-emptive complaint about the tango music but Jasbir flicks up the volume fit to rattle the brilliants on the chandelier. At first he scorned the dance, the stiffness, the formality, the strictness of the tempo. So very un-Indian. No one's uncle would ever dance this at a wedding. But he has persisted – never say that Jasbir Dayal is not a trier – and the personality of the tango has subtly permeated him, like rain into a dry riverbed. He has found the discipline and begun to understand the passion. He walks tall in the Dams and Watercourses. He no longer slouches at the watercooler.

"When I advised you to speak or forever hold your peace, sir, I did not actually mean, lie through your teeth to your parents," Ram Tarun Das says. In tango he takes the woman's part. The lighthoek can generate an illusion of weight and heft so the aeai feels solid as Jasbir's partner. *If it can do all that, surely it could make him look like a woman?* Jasbir thinks. In his dedication to detail Sujay often overlooks the obvious. "Especially in matters where they can rather easily find you out."

"I had to stop them wasting their money on that nute."

"They would have kept outbidding you."

"Then, even more, I had to stop them wasting my money as well."

Jasbir knocks Ram Tarun Das's foot across the floor in a sweetly executed barrida. He glides past the open verandah door where Sujay glances up from soap-opera building. He has become accustomed to seeing his landlord tango cheek to cheek with an elderly Rajput gentleman. *Yours is a weird world of ghosts and djinns and half-realities,* Jasbir thinks.

"So how many times has your father called asking about Shulka?" Ram Tarun Das's free leg traces a curve on the floor in a well-executed *volcada*. Tango is all about seeing the music. It is making the unseen visible.

You know, Jasbir thinks. *You're woven through every part of this house like a pattern in silk.*

"Eight," he says weakly. "Maybe if I called her . . ."

"Absolutely not," Ram Tarun Das insists, pulling in breath-to-breath close in the *embreza*. "Any minuscule advantage you might have enjoyed, any atom of hope you might have entertained, would be forfeit. I forbid it."

"Well, can you at least give me a probability? Surely knowing everything you know about the art of shaadi, you could at least let me know if I've any chance?"

"Sir," says Ram Tarun Das, "I am a Master of Grooming, Grace and Gentlemanliness. I can direct you any number of simple and unsophisticated bookie-aeais; they will give you a price on anything though you may not fancy their odds. One thing I will say: Miss Shulka's responses were very – suitable."

Ram Tarun Das hooks his leg around Jasbir's waist in a final *gancho*. The music comes to its strictly appointed conclusion. From behind it come two sounds. One is Mrs Prasad weeping. She must be leaning against the party wall to make her upset so clearly audible. The other is a call tone, a very specific call tone, a deplorable but insanely hummable filmi hit *My Back, My Crack, My Sack* that Jasbir set on the house system to identify one caller, and one caller only.

Sujay looks up, startled.

"Hello?" Jasbir sends frantic, pleading hand signals to Ram Tarun Das, now seated across the room, his hands resting on the top of his cane.

"Lexus Mumbai red monkey Ritu Parvaaz," says Shulka Mathur. "So what do they mean?"

"No, my mind is made up, I'm hiring a private detective," Deependra says, rinsing his hands. On the twelfth floor of the Ministry of Waters all the dating gossip happens at the wash-hand basins in the Number 16 Gentlemen's WC. Urinals: too obviously competitive. Cubicles: a violation of privacy. Truths are best washed with the hands at the basins and secrets and revelations can always be concealed by judicious use of the hot-air hand-drier.

"Deependra, this is paranoia. What's she done?" Jasbir whispers. A level 0.3 aeai chip in the tap admonishes him not to waste precious water.

"It's not what she's done, it's what she's not done," Deependra hisses. "There's a big difference between someone not being available and someone deliberately not taking your calls. Oh yes. You'll learn this, mark my words. You're at the first stage, when it's all new and fresh and exciting and you are blinded by the amazing fact that someone, someone at last, at long last! thinks you are a catch. It is all rose petals and sweets and cho chweet and you think nothing can possibly go wrong. But you pass through

that stage, oh yes. All too soon the scales fall from your eyes. You see
. . . and you hear."

"Deependra." Jasbir moved to the battery of driers. "You've been on
five dates." But every word Deependra has spoken has chimed true. He is
a cauldron of clashing emotions. He feels light and elastic, as if he bestrode
the world like a god, yet at the same time the world is pale and insubstantial as muslin around him. He feels light-headed with hunger though he
cannot eat a thing. He pushes away Sujay's lovingly prepared dais and
roti. Garlic might taint his breath, saag might stick to his teeth, onions
might give him wind, bread might inelegantly bloat him. He chews a few
cleansing cardamoms, in the hope of spiced kisses to come. Jasbir Dayal is
blissfully, gloriously love-sick.

Date one. The Qutb Minar. Jasbir had immediately protested.

"Tourists go there. And families on Saturdays."

"It's history."

"Shulka isn't interested in history."

"Oh, you know her so well after three phone conversations and two evenings chatting on shaadinet – which I scripted for you? It is roots, it is who
you are and where you come from. It's family and dynasty. Your Shulka is
interested in that, I assure you, sir. Now, here's what you will wear."

There were tour buses great and small. There were hawkers and souvenir peddlers. There were parties of frowning Chinese. There were schoolchildren with backpacks so huge they looked like upright tortoises. But
wandering beneath the domes and along the colonnades of the Quwwat
Mosque in his Casual Urban Explorer clothes, they seemed as remote and
ephemeral as clouds. There was only Shulka and him. And Ram Tarun Das
strolling at his side, hands clasped behind his back.

To cue, Jasbir paused to trace out the time-muted contours of a disembodied tirthankar's head, a ghost in the stone.

"Qutb-ud-din Aibak, the first Sultan of Delhi, destroyed twenty Jain
temples and reused the stone to build his mosque. You can still find the old
carvings if you know where to look."

"I like that," Shulka said. "The old gods are still here." Every word
that fell from her lips was pearl-perfect. Jasbir tried to read her eyes but
her BlueBoo! cat-eye shades betrayed nothing. "Not enough people care
about their history any more. It's all modern this modern that, if it's not
up- to-the-minute it's irrelevant. I think that to know where you're going
you need to know where you've come from."

Very good, Ram Tarun Das whispered. *Now, the iron pillar.*

They waited for a tour group of Germans moved away from the railed-
off enclosure. Jasbir and Shulka stood in the moment of silence gazing at
the black pillar.

"Sixteen hundred years old, but never a speck of rust on it," Jasbir said.

Ninety-eight per cent pure iron, Ram Tarun Das prompted. *There are
things Mittal Steel can learn from the Gupta kings.*

"'He who, having the name of Chandra, carried a beauty of counte-
nance like the full moon, having in faith fixed his mind upon Vishnu, had

this lofty standard of the divine Vishnu set up on the hill Vishnupada.'"
Shulka's frown of concentration as she focused on the inscription around
the pillar's waist was as beautiful to Jasbir as that of any god or Gupta
king.

"You speak Sanskrit?"

"It's a sort of personal spiritual development path I'm following."

You have about thirty seconds before the next tour group arrives, Ram
Tarun Das cuts in. *Now sir; that line I gave you.*

"They say that if you stand with your back to the pillar and close your
arms around it, your wish will be granted."

The Chinese were coming, the Chinese were coming.

"And if you could do that, what would you wish for?"

Perfect. She was perfect.

"Dinner?"

She smiled that small and secret smile that set a garden of thorns in
Jasbir's heart and walked away. At the centre of the gatehouse arch she
turned and called back, "Dinner would be good."

Then the Chinese with their shopping bags and sun visors and plastic
leisure shoes came bustling around the stainless iron pillar of Chandra
Gupta.

Jasbir smiles at the sunny memory of Date One. Deependra waggles his
fingers under the stream of hot air.

"I've heard about this. It was on a documentary, oh yes. White widows,
they call them. They dress up and go to the shaadis and have their résumés
all twinkling and perfect but they have no intention of marrying, Oh no
no no, not a chance. Why should they, when there is a never-ending stream
of men to wine them and dine them and take out to lovely places and buy
them lovely presents and shoes and jewels, and even cars, so it said on the
documentary. They are just in it for what they can get; they are playing
games with our hearts. And when they get tired or bored or if the man is
making too many demands or his presents aren't as expensive as they were
or they can do better somewhere else, then whoosh! Dumped flat and on
to the next one. It's a game to them."

"Deependra," says Jasbir. "Let it go. Documentaries on the Shaadi
Channel are not the kind of model you want for married life. Really."
Ram Tarun Das would be proud of that one. "Now, I have to get back
to work." Faucets that warn about water crime can also report excessive
toilet breaks to line managers. But the doubt-seeds are sown, and Jasbir
now remembers the restaurant.

Date Two. Jasbir had practised with the chopsticks for every meal for a
week. He swore at rice, he cursed dal. Sujay effortlessly scooped rice, dal,
everything from bowl to lips in a flurry of stickwork.

"It's easy for you, you've got that code-wallah Asian culture thing."

"Um, we are Asian."

"You know what I mean. And I don't even like Chinese food, it's so
bland."

The restaurant was expensive, half a week's wage. He'd make it up on overtime; there were fresh worries in Dams and Watercourses about a drought.

"Oh," Shulka said, the nightglow of Delhi a vast, diffuse halo behind her. She is a goddess, Jasbir thought, a devi of the night city with ten million lights descending from her hair. "Chopsticks." She picked up the antique porcelain chopsticks, one in each hand like drum sticks. "I never know what to do with chopsticks. I'm always afraid of snapping them."

"Oh, they're quite easy once you get the hang of them." Jasbir rose from his seat and came round behind Shulka. Leaning over her shoulder he laid one stick along the fold of her thumb, the other between ball of thumb and tip of index finger. Still wearing her lighthoek. It's the city girl look. Jasbir shivered in anticipation as he slipped the tip of her middle finger between the two chopsticks. "Your finger acts like a pivot, see? Keep relaxed, that's the key. And hold your bowl close to your lips." Her fingers were warm, soft, electric with possibility as he moved them. Did he imagine her skin scented with musk?

Now, said Ram Tarun Das from over Shulka's other shoulder. *Now do you see? And by the way, you must tell her that they make the food taste better.*

They did make the food taste better. Jasbir found subtleties and piquancies he had not known before. Words flowed easily across the table. Everything Jasbir said seemed to earn her starlight laughter. Though Ram Tarun Das was as ubiquitous and unobtrusive as the waiting staff, they were all his own words and witticisms. *See, you can do this,* Jasbir said to himself. *What women want, it's no mystery; stop talking about yourself, listen to them, make them laugh.*

Over green tea Shulka began talking about that new novel everyone but everyone was reading, the one about the Delhi girl on the husband-hunt and her many suitors, the scandalous one, *An Eligible Boy.* Everyone but everyone but Jasbir.

Help! he subvocalized into his inner ear.

Scanning it now, Ram Tarun Das said. *Do you want a thematic digest, popular opinions or character breakdowns?*

Just be there, Jasbir silently whispered, covering the tiny movement of his jaw by setting the tea-pot lid ajar, a sign for a refill.

"Well, it's not really a book a man should be seen reading . . ."

"But . . ."

"But isn't everyone?" Ram Tarun Das dropped him the line. "I mean, I'm only two-thirds of the way in, but . . . how far are you? Spoiler alert spoiler alert." It's one of Sujay's *Town and Country* expressions. Finally he understands what it means. Shulka just smiles and turns her tea bowl in its little saucer.

"Say what you were going to say."

"I mean, can't she see that Nishok is the one? The man is clearly, obviously, one thousand per cent doting on her. But then that would be too easy, wouldn't it?"

"But Pran, it would always be fire with him. He's the baddest of bad-mashes but you'd never be complacent with Pran. She'll never be able to completely trust him and that's what makes it exciting. Don't you think you feel that sometimes it needs that little edge, that little fear that maybe, just maybe you could lose it all to keep it alive?"

Careful, sir, murmured Ram Tarun Das.

"Yes, but we've known ever since the party at the Chatterjis where she pushed Jyoti into the pool in front of the Russian ambassador that she's been jealous of her sister because she was the one that got to marry Mr Panse. It's the eternal glamour versus security. Passion versus stability. Town versus country."

"Ajit?"

"Convenient plot device. Never a contender. Every woman he dates is just a mirror to his own sweet self."

Not one sentence, not one word had he read of the hit trash novel of the season. It had flown around his head like clatter-winged pigeons. He's been too busy being that Eligible Boy.

Shulka held up a piece of sweet, salt, melting fatty duck breast between her porcelain forceps. Juice dripped on to the table cloth.

"So, who will Bani marry, then? Guess correctly and you shall have a prize."

Jasbir heard Ram Tarun Das's answer begin to form inside his head. *No*, he gritted on his molars.

"I think I know."

"Go on."

"Pran."

Shulka stabbed forward, like the darting bill of a winter crane. There was hot, fatty soya duck in his mouth.

"Isn't there always a twist in the tale?" Shulka said.

In the Number 16 Gentlemen's WC Deependra checks his hair in the mirror and smoothes it down.

"Dowry thievery; that's what it is. They string you along, get their claws into your money, then they disappear and you never see a paisa again."

Now Jasbir really really wants to get back to his little work cluster.

"Deep, this is fantasy. You've read this in the news feeds. Come on."

"Where there's smoke there's fire. My stars say that I should be careful in things of the heart and beware false friends. Jupiter is in the third house. Dark omens surround me. No, I have hired a private investigation aeai. It will conduct a discreet surveillance. One way or the other, I shall know."

Jasbir grips the stanchion, knuckles white, as the phatphat swings through the great mil of traffic around Indira Chowk. Deependra's aftershave oppresses him.

"Exactly where are we going?"

Deependra had set up the assignation on a coded palmer account. All he would say was that it required two hours of an evening, good clothes, a trustworthy friend and absolute discretion. For two days his mood had been grey and thundery as an approaching monsoon. His PI Aeai had returned a result but Deependra revealed nothing, not even a whisper in the clubbish privacy of the Number 16 Gentlemen's WC.

The phatphat, driven by a teenager with gelled hair that falls in sharp spikes over his eyes – an obvious impediment to navigation – takes them out past the airport. At Gurgaon the geography falls into place around Jasbir. He starts to feel nauseous from more than spike-hair's driving and Deependra's shopping mall aftershave. Five minutes later the phatphat crunches up the curve of raked gravel outside the pillared portico of the Haryana Polo and Country Club.

"What are we doing here? If Shulka finds out I've been to shaadi when I'm supposed to be dating her it's all over."

"I need a witness."

Help me Ram Tarun Das, Jasbir hisses into his molars but there is no reassuring spritz of silvery music through his skull to herald the advent of the Master of Grooming, Grace and Gentlemanliness. The two immense Sikhs on the door nod them through.

Kishore is sloped against his customary angle of the bar, surveying the territory. Deependra strides through the throng of eligible boys like a god going to war. Every head turns. Every conversation, every gossip falls silent.

"You . . . you . . . you." Deependra stammers with rage. His face shakes. "Shaadi stealer!" The whole club bar winces as the slap cracks across Kishore's face. Then two fists descend on Deependra, one on each shoulder. The man-mountain Sikhs turn him around and arm-lock him, frothing and raging, from the bar of the Haryana Polo and Country Club. "You, you chuutya!" Deependra flings back at his enemy. "I will take it out of you, every last paisa, so help me God. I will have satisfaction!"

Jasbir scurries behind the struggling, swearing Deependra, cowed with embarrassment.

"I'm only here to witness," he says to the Sikh's you're-next glares. They hold Deependra upright a moment to snap his face and bar him forever from Begum Rezzak's Lovely Girl Shaadi Agency. Then they throw him cleanly over the hood of a new model Li Fan G8 into the carriage drive. He lies dreadfully still and snapped on the gravel for a few moments, then with fetching dignity draws himself up, bats away the dust and straightens his clothes.

"I will see him at the river about this," Deependra shouts at the impassive Sikhs. "At the river."

Jasbir is already out on the avenue, trying to see if the phatphat driver's gone.

The sun is a bowl of brass rolling along the indigo edge of the world. Lights twinkle in the dawn haze. There is never a time when there are not people at the river. Wire-thin men push handcarts over the trash-strewn sand, picking like birds. Two boys have set a small fire in a ring of stones. A distant procession of women, soft bundles on their heads, file over the grassy sand. By the shrivelled thread of the Yamuna an old Brahmin conse-crates himself, pouring water over his head. Despite the early heat, Jasbir shivers. He knows what goes into that water. He can smell the sewage on the air, mingled with wood smoke.

"Birds," says Sujay looking around him with simple wonder. "I can actually hear birds singing. So this is what mornings are like. Tell me again what I'm doing here?"

"You're here because I'm not being here on my own."

"And, ah, what exactly are you doing here?"

Deependra squats on his heels by the gym bag, arms wrapped around him. He wears a sharp white shirt and pleated slacks. His shoes are very good. Apart from grunted greetings he has not said a word to Jasbir or Sujay. He stares a lot. Deependra picks up a fistful of sand and lets his trickle through his fingers. Jasbir wouldn't advise that either.

"I could be at home coding," says Sujay. "Hey ho. Show time."

Kishore marches across the scabby river-grass. Even as well-dressed dis-tant speck it is obvious to all that he is furiously angry. His shouts carry far on the still morning air.

"I am going to kick your head into the river," he bellows at Deependra, still squatting on the riverbank.

"I'm only here as a witness," Jasbir says hurriedly, needing to be believed. Kishore must forget and Deependra must never know that he was also the witness that night Kishore made the joke in the Tughluk tower.

Deependra looks up. His face is bland, his eyes are mild.

"You just had to, didn't you? It would have killed you to let me have something you didn't."

"Yeah, well. I let you get away with that in the Polo Club. I could have taken you then, it would have been the easiest thing. I could have driven your nose right into your skull, but I didn't. You cost me my dignity, in front of all my friends, people I work with, business colleagues, but most of all, in front of the women."

"Well then let me help you find your honour again."

Deependra thrusts his hand into the gym bag and pulls out a gun.

"Oh my god it's a gun he's got a gun," Jasbir jabbers. He feels his knees turn liquid. He thought that only happened in soaps and popular trash novels. Deependra gets to his feet, the gun never wavering from its aim in the centre of Kishore's forehead, the precise spot a bindi would sit. "There's another one in the bag." Deependra waggles the barrel, nods with his head. "Take it. Let's sort this right, the man's way. Let's sort it honourably. Take the gun." His voice has gained an octave. A vein beats in his neck and at his temple. Deependra kicks the gym bag towards Kishore. Jasbir can see the anger, the mad, suicidal anger rising in the banker to match the civil servant's. He can hear himself mumbling *Oh my god oh my god oh my god*. "Take the gun. You will have a honourable chance. Otherwise I will shoot you like a pi-dog right here." Deependra levels the gun and takes a sudden, stabbing step towards Kishore. He is panting like a dying cat. Sweat has soaked his good white shirt through and through. The gun muzzle is a finger's-breadth from Kishore's forehead.

Then there is a blur of movement, a body against the sun, a cry of pain and the next Jasbir knows Sujay has the gun swinging by its trigger guard from his finger. Deependra is on the sand, clenching and unclenching his right hand. The old Brahmin stares, dripping.

"It's okay now, it's all okay, it's over," Sujay says. "I'm going to put this in the bag with the other and I'm going to take them and get rid of them and no one will ever talk about this, okay? I'm taking the bag now. Now, shall we all get out of here before someone calls the police, hm?"

Sujay swings the gym back over his sloping shoulder and strides out for the streetlights, leaving Deependra hunched and crying among the shredded plastic scraps.

"How, what, that was, where did you learn to do that?" Jasbir asks, tagging behind, feet sinking into the soft sand.

"I've coded the move enough times; I thought it might work in meat life."

"You don't mean?"

"From the soaps. Doesn't everyone?"

There's solace in soap opera. Its predictable tiny screaming rows, its scripted swooping melodramas, draw the poison from the chaotic, unscripted world where a civil servant in the water service can challenge a rival to a shooting duel over a woman he met at a shaadi. Little effigies of true dramas, sculpted in soap.

When he blinks, Jasbir can see the gun. He sees Deependra's hand draw it out of the gym bag in martial-arts-movie slow motion. He thinks he sees the other gun, nestled among balled sports socks. Or maybe he imagines it, a cut-away close-up. Already he is editing his memory.

Soothing to watch Nilesh Vora and Dr Chatterji's wife, their love eternally foiled and frustrated, and Deepti; will she ever realize that to the Brahmpur social set she is eternally that Dalit girl from the village pump?

You work on the other side of a glass partition from someone for years. You go with him to shaadis, you share the hopes and fears of your life and love with him. And loves turns him into a homicidal madman. Sujay took the gun off him. Big, clumsy Sujay, took the loaded gun out of his hand. He would have shot Kishore. Brave, mad Sujay. He's coding, that's his renormalizing process. Make soap, watch soap. Jasbir will make him tea. For once. Yes, that would be a nice gesture. Sujay is always always getting tea. Jasbir gets up. It's a boring bit, Mahesh and Rajani. He doesn't like them. Those rich-boy-pretending-they-are-car-valets-so-they-can-marry-for-love-not-money characters stretch his disbelief too far. Rajani is hot, though. She's asked Mahesh to bring her car round to the front of the hotel.

"When you work out here you have lots of time to make up theories. One of my theories is that people's cars are their characters," Mahesh is saying. *Only in a soap would anyone ever imagine that a pick-up line like that would work, Jasbir thinks.* "So, are you a Tata, a Mercedes, a Li Fan or a Lexus?"

Jasbir freezes in the door.

"Oh, a Lexus."

He turns slowly. Everything is dropping, everything is falling leaving him suspended. Now Mahesh is saying,

"You know, I have another theory. It's that everyone's a city. Are you Delhi, Mumbai, Kolkata, Chennai?"

Jasbir sits on the arm of the sofa. *The fetch*, he whispers. *And she will say* . . .

"I was born in Delhi . . ."

"That's not what I mean."

Mumbai, murmurs Jasbir.

"Mumbai then. Yes, Mumbai definitely. Kolkata's hot and dirty and nasty. And Chennai – no, I'm definitely Mumbai."

"Red Green Yellow Blue," Jasbir says.

"Red." Without a moment's hesitation.

"Cat Dog Bird Monkey?"

She even cocks her head to one side. That was how he noticed Shulka was wearing the lighthoek.

"Bird . . . no."

"No no no," says Jasbir. She'll smile slyly here. "Monkey." And there is the smile. The *finesse*.

"Sujay!" Jasbir yells. "Sujay! Get me Das!"

"How can an aeai be in love?" Jasbir demands.

Ram Tarun Das sits in his customary wicker chair, his legs casually crossed. Soon, very soon, Jasbir thinks, *voices will be raised and Mrs Prasad next door will begin to thump and weep.*

"Now sir, do not most religions maintain that love is the fundament of the universe? In which case, perhaps it's not so strange that a distributed entity, such as myself, should find – and be surprised by, oh, so surprised, sir – by love? As a distributed entity, it's different in nature from the surge of neurochemicals and waveform of electrical activity you experience as love. With us it's a more – rarefied experience – judging solely by what I know from my subroutines on *Town and Country*. Yet, at the same time, it's intensely communal. How can I describe it? You don't have the concepts, let alone the words. I am a specific incarnation of aspects of a number of aeais and sub-programmes, as those aeais are also iterations of sub-programmes, many of them marginally sentient. I am many, I am legion. And so is she – though of course gender is purely arbitrary for us, and, sir, largely irrelevant. It's very likely that at many levels we share components. So ours is not so much a marriage of minds as a league of nations. Here we are different from humans in that, for you, it seems to us that groups are divisive and antipathetical. Politics, religion, sport, but especially your history, seem to teach that. For us folk, groups are what bring us together. They are mutually attractive. Perhaps the closest analogy might be the merger of large corporations. One thing I do know, that for humans and aeais, we both need to tell people about it."

"When did you find out she was using an aeai assistant?"

"Oh, at once sir. These things are obvious to us. And if you'll forgive the parlance, we don't waste time. Fascination at the first nanosecond. Thereafter, well, as you saw on the unfortunate scene from *Town and Country*, we scripted you."

"So we thought you were guiding us . . ."

"When it was you who were our go-betweens, yes."

"So what happens now?" Jasbir slaps his hands on his thighs.

"We are meshing at a very high level. I can only catch hints and shadows of it, but I feel a new aeai is being born, on a level far beyond either of us, or any of our co-characters. Is this a birth? I don't know, but how can I convey to you the tremendous, rushing excitement I feel?"

"I meant me."

"I'm sorry sir. Of course you did. I am quite, quite dizzy with it all. If I might make one observation; there's truth in what your parents say. First the marriage, then the love. Love grows in the thing you see every day."

Thieving macaques dart around Jasbir's legs and pluck at the creases of his pants. Midnight metro, the last train home. The few late-night passengers observe a quarantine of mutual solitude. The djinns of unexplained wind that haunt subway systems send litter spiralling across the platform. The tunnel focuses distant shunts and clanks, uncanny at this zero hour. There should be someone around at the phatphat stand. If not he'll walk. It doesn't matter.

He met her at a fashionable bar all leather and darkened glass in an international downtown hotel. She looked wonderful. The simple act of her stirring sugar into coffee tore his heart in two.

"When did you find out?"

"Devashri Didi told me."

"Devashri Didi."

"And yours?"

"Ram Tarun Das, Master of Grooming, Grace and Gentlemanliness. A very proper, old fashioned Rajput gent. He always called me sir; right up to the end. My house-mate made him. He works in character design on *Town and Country*."

"My older sister works in PR the meta-soap department at Jazhay. She got one of the actor designers to put Devashri Didi together." Jasbir has always found the idea of artificial actors believing they played equally artificial roles head-frying. Then he found aeai love.

"Is she married? Your older sister, I mean."

"Blissfully. And children."

"Well, I hope our aeais are very happy together." Jasbir raised a glass. Shulka lifted her coffee cup. She wasn't a drinker. She didn't like alcohol, Devashri Didi had told her it looked good for the Begum Jaitly's modern shaadi.

"My little quiz?" Jasbir asked.

"Devashri Didi gave me the answers you were expecting. She'd told me it was a standard ploy, personality quizzes and psychic tests."

"And the Sanskrit?"

"Can't speak a word."

Jasbir laughed honestly.

"The personal spiritual journey?"

"I'm a strictly material girl. Devashri Didi said . . ."

". . . I'd be impressed if I thought you had a deep spiritual dimension. I'm not a history buff either. And *An Eligible Boy*?"

"That unreadable tripe?"

"Me neither."

"Is there anything true about either of us?"

"One thing," Jasbir said. "I can tango."

Her surprise, breaking into a delighted smile, was also true. Then she folded it away.

"Was there ever any chance?" Jasbir asked.

"Why did you have at ask that? We could have just admitted that we were both playing games and shaken hands and laughed and left it at that. Jasbir, would it help if I told you that I wasn't even looking? I was trying the system out. It's different for suitable girls. I've got a plan."

"Oh," said Jasbir.

"You did ask and we agreed, right at the start tonight, no more pretence." She turned her coffee cup so that the handle faced right and laid her spoon neatly in the saucer. "I have to go now." She snapped her bag shut and stood up. Don't walk away, Jasbir said in his silent Master of Grooming, Grace and Gentlemanliness voice. She walked away.

"And Jasbir."

"What?"

"You're a lovely man, but this was not a date."

A monkey takes a liberty too far, plucking at Jasbir's shin. Jasbir's kick connects and sends it shrieking and cursing across the platform. *Sorry monkey. It wasn't you.* Booms rattle up the subway tube; gusting hot air and the smell of electricity herald the arrival of the last metro. As the lights swing around the curve in the tunnel, Jasbir imagines how it would be to step out and drop in front of it. The game would be over. Deependra has it easy. Indefinite sick leave, civil service counselling and pharma. But for Jasbir there is no end to it and he is so so tired of playing. Then the train slams past him in a shout of blue and silver and yellow light, slams him back into himself. He sees his face reflected in the glass, his teeth still divinely white. Jasbir shakes his head and smiles and instead steps through the opening door.

It is as he suspected. The last phatphat has gone home for the night from the rank at Barwala metro station. It's four kays along the pitted, flaking roads to Acacia Bungalow Colony behind its gates and walls. Under an hour's walk. Why not? The night is warm, he's nothing better to do and he might yet pull a passing cab. Jasbir steps out. After half an hour a last, patrolling phatphat passes on the other side of the road. It flashes its light and pulls around to some in beside him. Jasbir waves it on. He is enjoying the night and the melancholy. There are stars up there, beyond the golden airglow of great Delhi.

Light spills through the french windows from the verandah into the dark living room. Sujay is at work still. In four kilometres Jasbir has generated a sweat. He ducks into the shower, closes his eyes in bliss as the jets of water hit him. Let it run let it run let it run he doesn't care how much he wastes, how much it costs, how badly the villagers need it for their crops. *Wash the old tired dirt from me.*

A scratch at the door. Does Jasbir hear the mumble of a voice? He shuts off the shower.

"Sujay?"

"I've, ah, left you tea."

"Oh, thank you."

There's silence but Jasbir knows Sujay hasn't gone.

"Ahm, just to say that I have always . . . I will . . . always. Always . . ." Jasbir holds his breath, water running down his body and dripping on to the shower tray. "I'll always be here for you."

Jasbir wraps a towel around his waist, opens the bathroom door and lifts the tea.

Presently Latin music thunders out from the brightly lit windows of Number 27 Acacia Bungalows. Lights go on up and down the close. Mrs Prasad beats her shoe on the wall and begins to wail. The tango begins.

SHINING ARMOUR

Dominic Green

British writer Dominic Green's output has to date been confined almost entirely to the pages of *Interzone*, but he's appeared there a lot, selling them eighteen stories in the last few years. The exciting story that follows, though, about a retired warrior reluctantly taking to arms again in the face of extreme need, appeared not in *Interzone* but in *The Solaris Book of Science Fiction 2*.

Green lives in Northampton, England, where he works in information technology and teaches kung fu part time. He has a website at homepage.ntlworld.com/lumpylomax, where the text of several unpublished novels and short stories can be found.

IT WAS CLOSE to dawn. The sun was a sliver of brilliance just visible over the mass of canyons on the western horizon. There was no reason why the direction the sun rose in should not be arbitrarily defined as East; the only reason why the sun rose in the West on this planet was that, if looked at from the same galactic direction as Earth, it span retrograde. Even at this number of light years' distance, men still had an apron-string connecting them to their homeworld.

The old man was still doing his exercises.

The boy didn't realize why the exercises had to take so long. They didn't look hard to do, although when he tried to copy them, the old man laughed as if he were doing them in the most ridiculous manner possible. The old man used a sword while he did the exercises, but not even a real one – it had no edge, and was made of aluminium which could not even be made to take one. He held the sword-stick ridiculously, not even using his whole hand most of the time; usually he held it with only his middle finger and forefinger, some of the time with only the little and ring fingers. Both of his hands, in fact, were held in that peculiar crab claw, with the fingers separated.

Finally, though, there were signs that the old man was coming to the end of the set, stabbing around him to right and left with his stick. The boy now had something to do. Gradually, he scurried out among the rusting steel shells, carrying the basket of fruit. It was, of course, spoiled fruit, fruit the old man would not have been able to sell at market. There would have been no point in wasting saleable produce.

The boy arranged a marrow to the west, a pineapple to the east, a durian to the north, and a big juicy watermelon to the south. Each piece of fruit sat on its own square of rice paper. He was careful to leave the empty basket in a spot where it would not interfere with the old man's movements. Then, just as his elder and better was turning into his final movement, facing into the sun as it blazed up into the sky, the boy ran to the long half-buried shelf the old man called the dead hulk's 'glacis plate,' and unwrapped the Real Sword.

The Real Sword was taller than he was. He had been instructed to unwrap it carefully. The old man had illustrated why by dropping a playing card onto the blade. The card had stuck fast, its weight driving the blade a good half centimetre into it.

The old man bowed to the sun – why? Did it ever bow back? – walked over to the sword, nodded stiffly to the boy, and picked up the weapon. He executed a few practice cuts and parries, jumping backwards and forwards across the sand. This was more exciting – he was moving quickly now, with a sword of spring steel.

Then, he became almost motionless, the sword whipped up into a position of readiness up above his head. As always, he was directly between all four pieces of fruit. Sometimes there were five pieces of fruit, sometimes six or seven.

The sword moved up and down, one, two, three, four times, the old man lashing out at all quarters, turning on his heel on the sand. There were four soft tearing sounds, but no sparks or sounds of metal hitting metal.

The old man stood finally upright, ready to slide the sword back into a nonexistent scabbard. He had lost the scabbard somehow years ago, nobody seemed to know how – nobody could convince him to shell out the money for a new one.

He walked over to inspect the fruit. All four pieces now lay in two pieces, making eight pieces. In all four cases, the cut had been deep enough to completely halve the fruit right down to the rind. In not one case had the rice paper underneath been touched. In some cases, the old man's activities had cut the rot clean out of the fruit. The boy gathered up the good pieces, which would now be breakfast.

The rotten pieces he slung away into the desert.

When they walked back toward the village, the General Alarm was sounding. This, the boy knew, could be very bad, as no alarm practice was scheduled for today.

General Alarm could mean that another boy like him had fallen down a melt-hole like a damned fool and the whole village was out looking for his corpsicle. Or it could mean that a flash flood was on the way and every homeowner had to rush out and bolt the streamliner onto the north end of his habitat, then rush back in and dog all the hatches. It might mean a flare had been reported, and everyone except Mad Farmer Bob who carried on digging his ditches in all weathers despite skin cancer and radiation alopoecia had to go underground till the All Clear.

But it was clear, when they reached the outskirts of the village, that this was none of these things. There was a personal conveyor in the Civic Square, with its green lights flashing to indicate it had been set to automatic guidance. Someone had used towing cable to secure three long irregular wet red shapes to the back of it, shapes the grown-ups would not let him see. But he had a horrible idea what they were, or what they had once been. Dragging your enemy behind a conveyor was a *badabing-badaboum* thing to do, and normally the boys in the village would have run and jostled to see such a marvellous sight. But when the men who had been dragged, probably alive, were Mr d'Souza, big friendly Mr d'Souza who had three hairy Irish wolfhounds, and Mr Bamigboye, who told rude jokes about naked ladies, and even Mr Chundi, who told kids to get off his property – then things did not seem so exciting.

Mr d'Souza, Mr Bamigboye, and Mr Chundi were Town Councillors, and they had gone up to the Big City to argue with the authorities about the mining site. Although there was nothing there now but a few spray-painted rocks and prospectors' transponders, the boy knew that some Big City men had found rocks they called Radioactives upriver. But the boy's father said the Big City men were too lazy to dig the rocks out of the ground using shovels and the Honest Sweat Of Their Brow. Instead, they planned to build a sifting plant downstream of the village, and set off bombs also made of Radioactives in the regolith upstream. A handsome stream of Radioactives would thus flow downriver to the sifting plant, but the village's water would be poisoned. The villagers had all been offered what were described as 'generous offers' to leave by the Big City men; but the Town Councillors had voted to stay. The Big City men had been rumoured to be hiring a top Persuasion Consultancy to deal with the situation. Now it seemed that the rumours had come true.

"We ought to take a few guns into town and sort out those City folk," said old father Magnusson, who thought everyone didn't know he ordered sex pheromones and illegal subliminal messaging software through the mail from Big City, but Aunt Raisa knew. Now no woman in town would either visit him or call him on the videophone.

"How many guns do we have? And small-bore ones, too, for seeing off interlopers, not armour-piercing stuff. The combine bosses will be protected by men in armour, ten feet tall, with magnetic accelerators that shoot off a million rounds through you POW-POW-POW before you pop your first round off! You are maximally insane." This was old mother Tho. Despite her insulting mode of communication, many of the older and wiser heads in the square were nodding their agreement.

"Don't be ridiculous," said Mother Murdo. "Magnetic accelerators are illegal."

"Anything illegal is legal if nobody is prepared to enforce the law. Have you not been up to the City recently? The mining combines have been making their own militaria for months. After they had to start making their own machine tools and coining their own money, weapons were the logical next step."

"But we are still citizens of the Commonwealth of Man," said father Magnusson, drawing himself up to his full one hundred and thirty-five centimetres, "and an attack on us would be an attack on the Commonwealth itself."

"Pshaw! The Commonwealth doesn't even bother to send out ships to collect taxes any longer," said mother Tho. "And when the taxman doesn't call, you *know* the government is in disrepair."

There were slow nods of appreciation from the crowd, most of whom were secretly glad that the tribute ships had not visited for so many years, but all of whom were alarmed at the prospect that those ships might have funded services whose unavailability might now kill the village.

"Well, in any case," said father Magnusson, "if they dare to come up *here* and attempt their person-dragging activities, the State will repel them instantly."

Mother Tho was unimpressed. "We must be pragmatic," she said. "The Guardian has not moved for sixty Good Old Original Standard Years. Not since the last Barbarian incursion."

Father Magnusson smacked his lips stolidly. "But I remember," he said, "when it last moved. And it operated most satisfactorily on that occasion. The Barbarians' ships filled the skies like locusts, but our Guardian was equal to them."

Mother Tho looked up into the sky, where the silhouette of the Guardian took a huge bite out of the sunrise. "Father, you are only one of perhaps two or three people still alive who remember the Guardian moving. And it is a machine, and machines rust, corrode, and biodegrade."

"The Guardian was built to last forever."

"But a Guardian also needs an operator. And where is ours?"

The old man put a hand upon the boy's shoulder, and moved away among the buildings before the conversation grew more heated.

"There are foreigners in the village," said the boy's mother, folding clothes with infinite precision. "Men from the mining company. They are asking for Khan by name, and you know why, old man."

The old man tucked the sword away in a crevice by the side of the atmosphere detoxifier. "Khan can look after himself."

"They had guns, by all accounts, and you know he can't." The boy's mother ran the iron over a fresh set of clothes. "Khan is fat and slow and has long since ceased to be any use in a fight. It isn't fair for him to be put through this." She looked up at the old man. "Something must be done."

The old man looked away. "They have heard the name Khan, heard that this Khan is the man who is our Guardian's operator. They perhaps mean harm. I will radio to Khan in the clear to stay out fixing watercourses and not return home until these men have gone. They will be listening, of course. This will inform them that their task is pointless, and then maybe they will leave."

"Or they will go out and search the watercourses till they find him."

"Khan knows the watercourses, and is more resourceful than you give him credit for. They will not find him."

"Khan is not as young as he once was. It will be cold tonight. You think that just because people are not as old as you, they are striplings who can accomplish anything."

"I think nothing of the sort, woman. Now boil me some water. I have a revitalizing tea to prepare for Mother Murdo's *fin-de-siècle ennui.*"

Khan's mother gathered up the heap of ironing and made her way out of the kitchen past the floor maintenance robot. "Boil your own water, and lower your underparts into it."

In order to defuse a family quarrel, the boy walked across the kitchen and turned on the water heater himself. He could not, however, meet the old man's eyes. Khan was, after all, his father.

The next morning, underneath the Guardian's metal legs, there was a gaggle of young men jostling for position.

"*I* will save the village!"

"You are wrong! It will be I!"

"No, I!"

The boy, who was running a flask of tea to Mother Murdo, saw Mother Tho rap three of them on the occiput with her walnut-wood staff in quick succession.

"Fools! Loblollies! What would you do, if you were even able to gain access to the Guardian's control cabin?" She pointed upward with her polyethylene ferrule at the ladder that led up the Guardian's right leg, with a dizzying number of rungs, up to the tiny hatch in its Under Bridge Area where a normal person's back body would be. Once, the boy had climbed all those rungs and touched the hatch with his hand for a bet, before being dragged down by his father, who told him not to tamper with Commonwealth property. His father had had hair then, and much of it had been dark.

"If I gained access," swaggered the most audacious of the three, "I would march to the Big City and trample the mining syndicate buildings beneath boots of iron." And he blew kisses to those girls of marriageable age who had gathered to watch.

"*If* you gained access!" repeated the old witch, and grabbed him by the nose using fingers of surprising strength. "YOU WOULD NEVER GAIN ACCESS! Only the Guardian's operator has a key, and it is synchronized to his genetic code. You would do nothing but sit staring up at a big metal arse until the cold froze you off the ladder."

"OW! Bedder dat dan allow our iddibidual vreedods do be sudgugaded!" protested the putative loblolly.

Mother Tho let the young man go, and wiped her fingers on her grubby shawl.

"Our Guardian will defend us when its operator is ready," she intoned.

A voice chipped in across the crowd: "Our Guardian's operator is too feeble."

The boy shrunk back behind a battery of heat sinks and hid his face.

"It's true!" yelled another voice. "The company assassins turned out the whole of Mr Wu's drinking establishment and threatened to shoot all its clientele one by one until Khan was turned over to them. In his confusion and concern for his customers, Wu turned over the wrong Khan, Khan the undertaker, and they killed him instantly. His tongue lolled out of his face like a frosted pickle. When the company men find the real Khan and kill him, there will be no trained professional to bury him."

"There are men in the village with guns?" said one of the bold youngsters, removing his thumbs from his belt, staring at his contemporaries with a face of horror.

"Ha!" gloated Mother Tho. "So our bravos are not quite so audacious when faced with the prospect of their skins actually being broken."

The boy put dropped his cargo of tea and ran for home.

Home proved to be more difficult to get to than usual. The boy followed the path most usually followed by children through the village, disregarding the streets and ducking under the support struts of the houses. Had crows been able to fly in this atmosphere instead of expiring exhausted after a few tottering flutters, he would have been travelling as the crow flew.

However, there was a problem. A small group of boys were holed up under the belly of Mother Tho's house, whispering deafeningly, fancifully imagining they were Seeing without Beeing Seen. But the boy was not afraid of other boys – at least, not as much as he was afraid of the men in the street who were tolerating Being Seen.

It was quite rare for children to be playing on the streets now. Their mothers were keeping them indoors. It was hoped that the Persuasion Consultancy assassins had not realized their mistake, and would be happy with having disabled the village's (admittedly one hundred per cent lethal) corpse-burying capabilities.

However, it seemed the assassins were not content with simple murder. They were standing in the street outside the house of Khan the undertaker, above which a grainy holographic angel flickered in the breeze. Not content with having murdered the undertaker's unburied corpse, the men had turned out the contents of his funeral emporium, headstones-in-progress and all, into the street. They were searching the whole pile of morbid paraphernalia with microscopic thoroughness, while his widow screamed and hurled such violent abuse as the poor woman knew. The boy could only conclude that onyx-look polymer angels were of great value to them.

"They are searching for our Guardian's access key," hissed one of the watchers in a strict confidence that carried all the way to the boy's ears.

"Only the Operator has the access key," said another boy. "Was Khan the Operator?"

"No," said a third. "I think it was Khan the farmer."

"Khan, a warrior! He is a fat little fruit seller."

"Operators are not chosen for their physical strength," said the third boy contemptuously. "The servomechanisms of the Guardian provide that. Operators are chosen for the extreme precision of their physical movements. It is said that the operator of the Guardian of the Gate of the City of Governance back on Earth was so precise in his motions that he was able to grip a normal human paintbrush between his Guardian's claws and inscribe the Rights and Duties of Citizens on the pavement in letters only three metres high."

The boy ducked under the hull of the nearest building and took a dog leg to a habitat to the south before any Persuasion Consultancy men could engage him in conversation.

It was sunset. The sun was setting in the East.

The old man was sitting dozing, pretending to be absorbed in serious meditation. The boy walked up and pointedly slammed down the basket on a nearby ruined Barbarian war machine, pretending not to notice the old man starting as if he had been jumped on by a tiger.

"I have brought everything," said the boy. "Father is still at large. The assassins are reputed to be pursuing him along the north arroyo."

The old man nodded, and sucked his teeth in a repulsive manner. "Did you bring the weapons from underneath the loose slab in the conveyor garage?"

The boy nodded. "There is no need to conceal these weapons," he sniffed. "It is not illegal to possess them, and surely they can be of no intrinsic value."

The old man ran his hand along the bow as he lifted it from the bundle, and grinned. "There was also a picture of your grandmother underneath that slab," he said. "That is also of little intrinsic value."

"I never knew my grandmother," said the boy.

"Think yourself lucky," said the old man grumpily, "that I did." He set an arrow – the only arrow in the bundle – to the bow, and began trying to bend it, frowning as his hands shook with the effort.

"OLD MAN," called a voice. "STOP PLAYING AT SOLDIERS. WE DEMAND TO KNOW WHERE KHAN IS."

The bow collapsed. The arrow quivered into the dirt. The old man turned round. From the direction of the village, three young men, muscles big from digging ditches and lifting baskets, had strolled in to the clearing between the destroyed military machines. The boy realized with a sinking heart that he had been followed.

"My father," said their leader, "says that Khan is the operator of our Guardian."

The old man nodded. "True enough," he said.

"Then why is he hiding outside the village like a thief?" The youngster threw his hand out towards the horizon. "Not only are there murderers in our midst, but an army is gathering on our doorstep. Employees of a Persuasion Consultancy engaged by the mining combine have arrived.

They have delivered an ultimatum to the effect that, if the combine's generous terms are not accepted by sunrise tomorrow, they will evacuate the village using minimum force." He licked his lips nervously. "Scouts have been out, and the consultancy's definition of 'minimum force' appears to extend to fragmentation bombs and vehicle-seeking missiles."

The old man's face sunk into even more wrinkles than was normally its wont. "Khan," he said, "hides nowhere. Who here says that Khan hides?" And despite the fact that he was armed only with a bamboo bow and arrows, none of the young men present would meet his eyes.

"Father, we have the greatest respect for your age, and none of us would dare to strike a weak and defenceless old man. We simply wish to know when, if at all, our Operator intends to discharge his duty."

The old man nodded.

"Weak and defenceless, you say."

He slung out the bow at the spokesman of the group, who the boy believed was called Lokman. It whirled in the air and struck Lokman in the jaw. Lokman rubbed the side of his face, complaining bitterly; but still his manners were too correct to allow him to attack his elders.

"Pick the bow up," said the old man. He grubbed in the dirt for the arrow, and tossed it to Lokman. "Now notch the arrow, and pull the bow back as hard as you like." He did not rise from his sitting position.

Lokman shrugged, and heaved hard on the bow. It was an effort even for him, the boy noticed. The bow was almost as stiff as a roof-tie.

"Point the bow at me," said the old man, grinning. "You purulent stream of cat excrement."

Lokman's hands were shaking on the bow too now. It rotated round to point at the old man.

"Now fire!" said the old man. "*I said FIRE, you worthless spawn of a mining company executive —*"

"No, DON'T—" said the boy.

The string twanged free. The boy did not even see the arrow move. Nor did he see the old man's hand move. But when both hand and arrow blurred back into position, the one was in the other; and the hand held the arrow, rather than the arrow being embedded in the hand.

Lokman stared at the old man's hand for a second; then he snorted.

"A useful parlour trick," he said. "Can you do it against missiles?"

He threw down the bow and walked away.

"Khan is a coward who will not fight," he said, over his shoulder. "Besides, he could not get to the Guardian even if he wished. The assassins have the access ladder under guard. Pack up your things and leave, old man. The Councillors are leaving. We are *all* leaving. We are finished."

The old man watched the visitors leave. Then, he reached into the bundle, where a battered oblong of black plastic lay alongside the picture of the boy's grandmother. In the plastic were embossed the letters KHAN 63007248.

"It is good," said the old man. "You have made sure Khan has everything he needs."

The old man hung the oblong round his neck on a chain that pierced it, and felt his throat to make sure it was not visible as it hung.

"What time did they say the ultimatum expired tomorrow?" he asked, without looking at the boy.

"Sunup," said the boy.

"It is good," said the old man, nodding. "There is time. Run back to the village with these things, and return quickly. Then you shall accompany me while I deliver these troublemakers an ultimatum of our own."

"Why am I going with you?" said the boy.

"Because no man will shoot an old man," said the old man, "unless he is a wicked man indeed. But even a wicked man will not shoot an old man accompanied by a small boy – unless, of course, he is a *very* wicked man indeed." He grinned, and his grin was more gaps than teeth. "This, I must admit, is the only flaw in my plan."

Then he returned to his meditation, as if nothing had either happened or was about to. The boy seriously suspected he was sleeping.

The sun had set, and the reg had ceased to be its accustomed thousand shades of khaki. Now, it was the colour of a world plunged underwater to a depth where every shade of anything became a democratic twilight blue.

The boy followed the old man uncertainly across the regolith towards a group of Persuasion Consultants lounging around an alcohol burner in the shadow of an APC. Even the burner's flame was blue, as if carefully coordinated to fit in with the night. The Consultants noticed the old man long before he began to jump up and down and wave his arms to get their attention, but the boy noticed that it was only at this point that they relaxed and began the laborious process of putting the safeties back on their weapons.

"Hey! Ugly Boy! Take me to your ugly leader!"

None of the Persuasion Consultants answered. Evidently none of them was willing to own up to the name of Ugly Boy.

"Suit yourselves, physically unprepossessing persons, but be informed that I bear a message from Khan."

The men began to fidget indecisively in their dapper uniforms. Eventually, one spoke up and said:

"If you are in communication with Khan, you must give us information on his whereabouts, citizen, or it will go poorly with you."

The old man scoffed. The boy was not entirely sure it was prudent to scoff in the presence of so much firepower. "You still do not know Khan's whereabouts? With the man right under your nose, and so many complex tracking systems in that khaki jalopy you are leaning against? For shame! Khan has a message for you. You must vacate the environs of this village, or as the appointed operator of the Guardian of this colony he will be obliged to make you quit by main force."

The spokesman crossed both hands over his rifle and said: "Your Guardian's operator is taking sides unjustifiably in a purely civil matter, citizen. This is not a military matter. For this reason, Beauchef and Grisnez Incorporated regrets that, on behalf of its clients, it is forced to take action to eliminate this unruly operator, and that this action will continue until he himself quits the village. We are also making initial seismic surveys preliminary to placing charges underneath the Guardian's foundations, destroying the underground geegaws that charge it. Beauchef and Grisnez of course regret the damage to Commonwealth property concomitant to this strategy, but final blame for this unfortunate state of affairs must lie at the head of the operator concerned. That is *our* message, which you may convey to Khan."

The old man stood facing the line of soldiers silently for several seconds.

"Very well," he said. "Despite the fact that you behave like barbarians, you continue to describe yourselves as Commonwealth citizens and hence merit a warning in law; you have received that warning. Whatever consequences follow, Khan will not be answerable."

He said nothing more, but turned and trudged back in the direction of the village. There were sniggers from the line of riflemen.

In the morning, the boy's mother woke him well before dawn. She had already prepared sleeping gear for all of them, together with food she had irradiated that same morning. It would keep for a month, as well as making the boy's stomach turn when he ate it. This was the sort of food City people had to eat.

"But aren't we staying to defend the village?"

He got a slap for that one. Mother was in no mood to talk. She was crying softly as she walked round the rooms of the habitat, picking things up, putting things down, and the boy realized suddenly that she was deciding which of the pieces of her life she was going to take with her and which she was going to leave behind forever. He threw his arms around her, and this time she did not slap him.

"Go out and fetch the old one," she said. "Where is he? I've prepared the conveyor. We have to leave."

The boy told his mother that the old man had said he was going to do his exercises, and that, on this particular morning, the boy was not allowed to accompany him.

The boy's mother's eyes flew open in horror. She looked out of the window, which showed sand billowing down a dusty street.

She stood still a moment, as though paralysed. Then she grabbed his arm.

"Come with me."

They walked out to the edge of the village. The village was small. It was not a long walk. Out there at the very edge of the sun farms, beyond a hectare or so of jet-black solar collectors, the wrecked battle machines of the Barbarians sat rusting in the sand.

What are Barbarians? the boy had asked his teacher once in class. And the answer had been quick and pat. Why, people from outside the Commonwealth, of course. *Any* people from outside the Commonwealth.

The machines sat at what the boy knew to have been the extreme limit of the Guardian's target acquisition range, sixty years ago.

Of the old man, there was no sign.

"Stupid old fool," said mother, and pulled the boy off down the village streets again. She seemed to know where she was going. Only two streets, two rows of gleaming aluminium-steel habitats, and the old man came into view. Standing in the square at the Guardian's habitat-sized feet, he was arguing with a pair of Consultancy men, armoured troopers holding guns that could track the electrical emissions of a man's heartbeat in the dark and shoot him dead through steel. He was carrying a sword.

"But I always do my exercises in the square at this time," the old man was saying, which was a lie.

"You are carrying a weapon, grandfather," said one of the Consultants gently, "which I am forced to regard as a potential threat, despite your advanced years."

The old man looked from hand to hand, then finally held up the sword as if he had only just realized it was there. "This? Why, but this is only an old sword-shaped piece of aluminium. It cannot even be made to take an edge."

"All the same," said the Consultant persuasively, "out of deference to the tense situation in which we find ourselves, it would be safer if —"

"HOI!"

The shout broke the polite silence in the town square. Five heads turned towards it. As the sun heaved its head over the southern horizon, a figure staggered into town out of the desert. It waved its arms.

"HOI! It's me, Khan! Khan, the man you're looking for! Catch me if you can!"

Guns rose instantaneously to shoulders. Khan dived for cover. How useful that cover was was debatable, as a line of projectile explosions stitched its way across the wall of the nearest habitat like a finger tearing through tinfoil. When the guns had finished tracking across the building, the building was two buildings, one balanced precariously on top of the other, radiator coolant gushing from the walls and electrical connections sparking. Hopefully no one was sitting headless at breakfast within it. The Consultancy men were already spreading out round the habitat, hoping to outflank their target if he had somehow survived the first attack. The boy's mother looked on, appalled.

Some caprice, however, drew the boy's attention upward.

The old man was on the inside leg of the metal colossus, on the access ladder, moving with dinosaurian slowness towards the Guardian's bumward access hatch.

The boy's jaw dropped.

Meanwhile, the men who were guarding the Guardian seemed on the point of following Khan and finishing him, until one of them remembered his orders, waved his comrade back to the square, pulled a communicator from one of his ammunition pouches, opened it, spoke into it, and flipped it shut again. Someone Else, he told his comrade, Could Do The Running. Up above, the old man was still moving, but with the speed of evolution, at the speed glass flowed down windowpanes, at the speed boys grew up doorposts. He had not even reached the knee. Surely, before the old fool reached the top of his climb, somebody in the village underneath had to notice? And what did he think he'd accomplish, if he once got up the ladder?

The two Consultants reassumed their positions underneath the Guardian's treads. They stood on the square of concrete, reaching all the way down through the regolith to the bedrock, that had been put there solely as a foundation for the vehicle to stand on. They faced outwards, willing to bleed good red blood to stop anyone who tried to get past them. One of them even remarked on the old man's sword discarded in the sand, saying that they Must Have Frit The Old Coot Away. Meanwhile, by pretending to scratch his eye against the dust, the boy was able to see, far above, the old coot pulling an battered slab of black plastic from his tunic and sliding it into what the boy knew, from the climb he had been dared to do a year ago, to be a recess in the circular ass-end access hatch about the same size as the slab. The hatch was also spraypainted with the letters AUGMENTED INFANTRY UNIT MK 73 (1 OFF), and only members of the privileged club of boys who had taken the dare and made the climb knew it.

Something glittered like a rack of unsheathed blades in the Guardian's normally dull and pitted skin; the old man skimmed his fingers over the glitter rapidly, and the boy saw blood ooze out of his fingers onto the hatch cover momentarily, before the surface drank it like a vampire.

The key was tuned to the operator's genetic code. The vehicle had to have a part of him to know who he was.

The hatch slid into the structure, silently. The old man began to slip into the hole it had opened. But for all the wondrous silence of the mechanism, the old man was by now unable to prevent the boy's mother from standing with her head in the air gawping like a new-hatched chick waiting to be fed worms. And as she gawped, the guards gawped with her.

Luckily for the old man, the guards also took a couple of moments to do helpless baby chick impersonations before remembering they had weapons and were supposed to use them. The hatch had slid shut before they could get their guns to their shoulders, take aim and fire. They were not used to firing their weapons in that position, and the recoil, coming from an unaccustomed direction, blew them about on the spot like unattended pneumatic drills. The boy saw stars twinkle on the Guardian's hide. He was not sure whether they had inflicted any damage or not; the detonations left a mass of after-images on his retinas.

The two men could not have inflicted too much damage, however, as they thought better of continuing to shoot, and instead stood back and contemplated the crotch of the colossus.

For one long minute, nothing happened. The lead Consultant spoke quietly but urgently into his communicator, saying that he Wasn't Quite Sure Whether Or Not The Shit Indicator Had Just Risen to Nostril Deep.

Then the dust under the left tread of the Guardian moaned like a man being put to the press. The boy looked up to see the great pipe legs of the Augmented Infantry Unit buckling and twisting, as if the wind were blowing it off its base. But Guardians weighed so much they smashed themselves if they fell over, the boy knew; and despite the fact that the dry season wind howled down from the mountains here like a katabatic banshee, it had never stirred the Guardian as much as a millimetre from its post.

The Guardian was moving *under its own power.*

Huge alloy arms the weight of bridge spans swung over the boy's head. Knee joints that could have acted as railway turntables flexed arthritically in the legs. And at that point, the boy knew exactly who was at the controls of the Guardian.

The whole colossal thousand-tonne weapon was doing the old man's morning exercises. Moving gently at first, swinging its arms and legs under their own weight, cautiously bending and unbending its ancient joints. Some of those joints screamed with the pressure of the merest movement. The boy suddenly, oddly, appreciated what the old man meant when he talked of rheumatism, arthritis and sciatica.

The old man's exercises were good for a man with rheumatic joints who needed them oiling in the morning. But they were just as good for a village sized automaton that had not moved for sixty standard years.

The men sent to guard the Guardian were backing away. From somewhere in the village on the other side of the buildings, meanwhile, someone else decided to fire at the machine. A pretty coloured show of lights sprayed out of the ground and cascaded off the metal mountain's armour. Habitats that the cascade hit on the way back down became colanders full of flying swarf. The Guardian carried on its warm-up regardless.

Eight times for the leg-stretching exercise – eight times for the arm-swinging – eight times for the two-handed push up above the head –

The boy began to back away, and pulling at his mother's robe. He knew what was coming next.

Men ran out of the buildings with light anti-armour weapons. Many of the weapons were recoilless, and some argument ensued about whether they should really be pointed up into the sky or not. Some of them were loosed off at point blank range at the Guardian's treads, leaving big black stains of burnt hydrocarbon. But a Guardian's feet were among its most heavily armoured parts. Every old person in town would tell you that. They were heavily armoured because they were used to crush infantry.

The Guardian lowered its massive head to stare at the situation on the ground. The operator, the boy knew, was actually in the main chassis, and the head was only used to affix target acquisition systems and armament. That small movement of the head was in itself enough to make the Consultants back away and run.

One of the Consultants, thinking smarter than his colleagues, grabbed hold of the boy's mother, shouting at the sky and pointing a pistol shakily at her head. He might as well have threatened a mountain.

The Guardian turned its head to look directly at him.

The boy screamed to his mother to drop down.

The Guardian's hand came down like the Red Sea on an Egyptian. Or, the boy pondered, like a sword upon a melon. Unlike a human hand, it had three fingers, which might be more properly described as claws. Exactly the same disposition of fingers a man might have, in fact, if a man held his middle finger and forefinger, and his little and ring finger, together, and spread the two groups of fingers apart. A roof of steel slammed down from heaven. The boy felt warm blood spray over his back.

Then the sunlight returned to the sand, though the sand was now red rather than brown, and the gunman's headless body toppled to the ground in front of him. The man had not simply been decapitated. His head no longer existed. It had been squashed flat.

Beside him, his mother, still alive, was trembling. Looking at the front of her skirts, the boy realized suddenly that she had wet herself.

One of the Guardian's massive treads rose from the ground and whined over his head. For some reason the sole of its left foot was stencilled LEFT LEG, and that on its right foot was labelled RIGHT LEG. Arms fire both small and large whined and caromed off its carapace; the Guardian ignored it. It was moving out of the village, eastward, in the direction of the mining company army camped beyond the outskirts. Soon it was out of shooting range, but the boy could still hear guns going off around him. Single shot firearms! The villagers had brought out their antique home defence weapons and were using them on their oppressors. The boy swelled with pride.

Despite the fact that she had clearly wet herself, the boy's mother hauled herself to her feet, and remarked:

"The old fool! What does he think he's doing? At his age!"

The boy hopped up onto a ladder fixed to the main water tower. The Guardian was striding eastward like a force of nature, silhouetted by things exploding against it. The boy saw it pick a thing up from the ground, and hurl it like a discus. The thing was a light armoured vehicle. He saw men tumble from it as it flew.

The mining company men were now flocking round a larger vehicle that was evidently their Big Gun. Most probably it had been brought in specially to deal with the possibility that the villagers might be able to revive their Guardian. It appeared to be a form of missile launcher, and the missile it fired looked frighteningly large. The turret on the top of the vehicle was being rotated round to bear on the approaching threat, and men were clearing from the danger space behind it.

The Guardian had stopped. Its hand was held before it, the elbow crooked, extended out towards the launcher. If had it been human, the boy would have described the posture it had now moved into as a defensive stance.

The boy blinked.

No. Surely not –

The missile blazed from its mounting, and then became invisible; and the Guardian's arm blurred with it.

Then the missile was tumbling away into the sky, its gyros trying frantically to put it back on course, wobbling unsteadily overhead; and the Guardian was standing in exactly the same position as before. A streak of rocket exhaust had licked up its arm and blackened its fingers.

The Guardian had brushed aside the missile in mid-air, so softly as not to detonate its fuse.

Men in the mining company launcher were standing staring motionless, as if their own operators had left them via their back entrances. The boy, however, suspected that other substances were currently leaving them by that exit; and as soon as the Guardian cranked into a forward stride again, the men began to run. By the time the Guardian eventually arrived at the launcher and methodically and thoroughly destroyed it, the boy was quite certain there were no human beings inside it. To the east of the village, he heard the terrific impact of the anti-armour missile eventually reaching its maximum range and aborting.

Then there was nothing on the face of the desert but running men, and smoking metal, and the gigantic figure of the Guardian standing casting a long, long shadow in the dawn.

The old man climbed down slowly, with painstaking exactness, just as he did in all things. He was breathing quite heavily by the time he swung off the last rung and into a crowd of cheering children.

"I knew Khan would not let us down," said Mother Tho.

"Khan Senior is a terrible fruit farmer," observed Father Magnusson, "but a Guardian operator without equal."

"His oranges are scabby-skinned and dry inside," agreed Mother Dingiswayo.

"All the same, I knew," opined Mother Jayaraman, "that he would eventually come in useful for something."

The old man shook his fist at the boy's father in mock rage. "Khan Junior! What a fool to expose yourself so! Do you want your family to grow up without a father?"

Khan grinned. "I am sorry, father. I have no idea what came over me."

"Maybe it is a hereditary condition," muttered the boy's mother.

"Well," said the old man, "at least it has turned out for the best. Had you not jumped out when you did, I might not have made it to the access ladder. One might almost imagine that that was your deliberate intention."

"I apologize if I did badly, father," said Khan. "I am more of a farmer by trade."

The old man walked across the square, to a handcart one of the younger boys had led out. In a fit of patriotic Commonwealther fervour, Father Magnusson had donated a hundred kilos of potatoes for a celebration, and they had been stacked in a neat pile ready for baking.

The old man picked one up, raw, and bit into it.

"Never apologize for being a farmer," said the old man, chewing gamely for a man with few remaining teeth. "After all, a gun will protect your family's life only once in a lifetime. But a potato," he said, gesturing with the tuber to illustrate his point, "is useful *every* day."

THE HERO

Karl Schroeder

Canadian writer Karl Schroeder was born and raised in Brandon, Manitoba. He moved to Toronto in 1986, and has been working and writing there ever since. He is best known for his far-future Virga series, consisting of *Sun of Suns, Queen of Candesce*, and, most recently, *Pirate Sun*, but he has also written the novels *Ventus, Permanence*, and *Lady of Mazes*, as well as a novel in collaboration with David Nickle, *The Claus Effect*. He's also the co-author, with Cory Doctorow, of *The Complete Idiot's Guide to Publishing Science Fiction*. His short fiction has been collected in *Engine of Recall*.

In the evocative story that follows, set in his intricate Virga universe, he takes us along on a young man's desperate quest to deliver a message that could save the worlds – if anybody would listen to it.

"IS EVERYBODY READY?" shouted Captain Emmen. At least, Jessie thought that's what he'd said – it was impossible to hear anything over the spine-grating noise that filled the sky.

Jessie coughed, covering his mouth with his hand to stop the blood from showing. In this weightless air, the droplets would turn and gleam for everybody to see, and if they saw it, he would be off the team.

Ten miles away the sound of the capital bug had been a droning buzz. With two miles to go, it had become a maddening – and deafening – howl. Much closer, and the bug's defense mechanism would be fatal to an unshielded human.

Jessie perched astride his jet just off the side of the salvage ship *Mistelle*. *Mistelle* was a scow, really, but Captain Emmen had ambitions. Lined up next to Jessie were eight other brave or stupid volunteers, each clutching the handlebars of a wingless jet engine. Mounted opposite the saddle ("below" Jessie's feet) was a ten-foot black-market missile. It was his team's job to get close enough to the capital bug to aim their missiles at its noise-throats. They were big targets – organic trumpets hundreds of feet long – but there were a lot of them, and the bug was miles long.

Jessie had never heard of anybody breaking into a capital bug's pocket ecology while the insect was still alive. Captain Emmen meant to try, because there was a story that a Batetranian treasure ship had crashed into this bug, decades ago. Supposedly you could see it when distant sunlight shafted through the right perforation in the bug's side. The ship was still intact, so they said.

Jessie wasn't here for the treasure ship. He'd been told a different story about this particular bug.

Emmen swung his arm in a chopping motion and the other jets shot away. Weak and dizzy as he was, Jessie was slower off the mark, but in seconds he was catching up. The other riders looked like flies optimistically lugging pea-pods; they were lit from two sides by two distant suns, one red with distance, the other yellow and closer, maybe two hundred miles away. In those quadrants of the sky not lit by the suns, abysses of air stretched away to seeming infinity – above, below, and to all sides.

Mistelle became a spindle-shape of wood and iron, its jets splayed behind it like an open hand. Ahead, the capital bug was too big to be seen as a single thing: it revealed itself to Jessie as landscapes, a vertical flank behind coiling clouds, a broad plain above that lit amber by the more distant sun. The air between him and it was crowded with clouds, clods of earth, and arrowing flocks of birds somehow immune to the bug's sound. Balls of water shot past as he accelerated; some were the size of his head, some a hundred feet across. And here and there, mountain-sized boluses of bug-shit smeared brown across the sky.

The jet made an ear-splitting racket, but he couldn't hear it over the sound of the bug. Jessie was swaddled in protective gear, his ears plugged, eyes protected behind thick goggles. He could hear the sound inside his body now, feel it vibrating his heart and loosening the bloody mess that was taking over his lungs. He'd start coughing any second, and once he did he might not be able to stop.

Fine, he thought grimly. *Maybe I'll cough the whole damn thing out.*

The noise had become pure pain. His muscles were cramping, he was finding it hard to breathe. Past a blur of vibration, he saw one of the other riders double up suddenly and tumble off his jet. The vehicle spun away, nearly hitting somebody else. And here came the cough.

The noise was too strong, he *couldn't* cough. The frozen reflex had stopped his breathing entirely; Jessie knew he had only seconds to live. Even as he thought this, curtains of cloud parted as the jet shot through them at a hundred miles an hour, and directly ahead of him stood the vast tower of the bug's fourth horn.

The jet's engine choked and failed; Jessie's right goggle cracked; the handlebars began to rattle loose from their fittings as his vision grayed. A rocket contrail blossomed to his right and he realized he was looking straight down the throat of the horn. He thumbed the firing button and was splashed and kicked by fire and smoke. In one last moment of clarity Jessie let go of the handlebars so the jet wouldn't break his bones in the violence of its tumble.

The ferocious scream stopped. Jessie took in a huge breath, and began to cough. Blood sprayed across the air. Breath rasping, he looked ahead to see that he was drifting toward some house-sized nodules that sprouted from the capital bug's back. The broken, smoking horns jutted like fantastically eroded sculptures, each hundreds of feet long. He realized with a start that one of them was still blaring, but by itself it could no longer kill.

In the distance, the *Mistelle* wallowed in a cloud of jet exhaust, and began to grow larger.

I did it, Jessie thought. Then the grey overwhelmed all thought and sense and he closed his eyes.

Bubbles spun over the side of the washtub. In the rotational gravity of Aitlin Town, they twirled and shimmered and slid sideways from Coriolis force as they descended. Jessie watched them with fascination – not because he'd never seen bubbles before, but because he'd never seen one fall.

They'd both gotten into trouble, so he and his oldest brother Camron were washing the troupe's costumes today. Jessie loved it; he never got a chance to talk to Camron, except to exchange terse barks during practice or a performance. His brother was ten years older than he, and might as well have lived in a different family.

"That's what the world is, you know," Camron said casually. Jessie looked at him quizzically.

"A bubble," said Camron, nodding at the little iridescent spheres. "The whole world is a bubble, like that."

"Is naaawwt."

Camron sighed. "Maybe Father isn't willing to pay to have you educated, Jessie, but he's sent me to school. Three times. 'The world of Virga is a hollow pressure-vessel, five thousand miles in diameter.'"

One big bubble was approaching the floor. Sunlight leaned across the window, a beam of gold from distant Candesce that was pinioning one spot of sky as the ring-shaped wooden town rotated through it. After a few seconds the beam flicked away, leaving the pearly shine of cloud-light.

"The whole world's a bubble," repeated Camron, "and all our suns are man-made."

Jessie knew the smaller suns, which lit spherical volumes only a few hundred miles diameter, were artificial: they'd once flown past one at night, and he'd seen that it was a great glass-and-metal machine. Father had called it a "polywell fusion" generator. But surely the greatest sun of all, so ancient it had been there at the beginning of everything, so bright and hot no ship could ever approach it – "Not Candesce," said Jessie. "Not the sun of suns."

Camron nodded smugly. "Even Candesce. 'Cept that in the case of Candesce, whoever built it only made so many keys – and we lost them all." Another shaft of brilliance burst into

*the laundry room. "People made Candesce – but now nobody
can turn it off."*

*The bubble flared in purples, greens, and gold, an inch above
the floorboards.*

*"That's just silly," scoffed Jessie. "'Cause if the whole world
were just a bubble, then that would make it —"*

The bubble touched the floor, and vanished.

*"— mortal," finished Camron. He met Jessie's eye, and his
look was serious.*

Jessie shivered and wiped at his mouth. Dried blood had caked there. His
whole chest ached, his head was pounding, and he felt so weak and nauseous he doubted he'd have been able to stand if he'd been under gravity.

He hung weightless in a strange fever-dream of a forest, with pale pink
tree trunks that reached past him to open into, not leaves, but a single
stretched surface that had large round or oval holes in it here and there.
Beyond them he could see sky. The tree trunks didn't converge onto a
clump of soil or rock as was usual with weightless groves, but rather tangled their roots into an undulant plain a hundred yards away from the
canopy.

The light that angled through the holes shone off the strangest collection
of life forms Jessie had ever seen. Fuzzy donut-shaped things inched up
and down the "tree" trunks, and mirror-bright birds flickered and flashed
as the light caught them. Something he'd taken to be a cloud in the middle
distance turned out to be a raft of jellyfish, conventional enough in the airs
of Virga, but these were gigantic.

The whole place reeked, the sharp tang reminding Jessie of the jars
holding preserved animal parts that he'd seen in the one school he briefly
attended as a boy.

He was just under the skin of the capital bug. The jet volunteers had
taken turns squinting through the *Mistelle*'s telescope, each impressing on
him- or herself as many details of the giant creature's body as they could.
Jessie recalled the strange skin that patched the monster's back; it'd had
holes in it.

It was through these holes that they'd caught glimpses of something that
might be a wrecked ship. As the fog of pain and exhaustion lifted, Jessie
realized that he might be close to it now. But where were the others?

He twisted in midair and found a threadlike vine or root within reach.
Pulling himself along it (it felt uncomfortably like skin under his palms)
he reached one of the "tree trunks" which might really be more analogous
to hairs for an animal the size of the capital bug. He kicked off from the
trunk, then off another, and so manoeuvered himself through the forest
and in the direction of a brighter patch.

He was so focused on doing this that he didn't hear the tearing sound
of the jet until it was nearly on him. "Jessie! You're alive!" Laughter dop-
plered down as a blurred figure shot past from behind.

It was Chirk, her canary-yellow jacket an unmistakable spatter against the muted colours of the bug. As she circled back, Jessie realized that he could still barely hear her jet; he must be half-deaf from the bug's drone.

Chirk was a good ten years older than Jessie, and she was the only woman on the missile team. Maybe it was that she recognized him as even more of an outsider than herself, but for whatever reason she had adopted Jessie as her sidekick the day she met him. She indulged her – and, even three months ago, he would have been flattered and eager to make a new friend. But he hid the blood in his cough even from her – particularly from her – and remained formal in their exchanges.

"So?" She stopped on the air, ten feet away, and extended her hand. "Take a lift from a lady?"

Jessie hesitated. "Did they find the wreck?"

"Yes!" She almost screamed it. "Now come on! They're going to beat us there the damned *Mictollo* itself is tearing a hole in the bug's back so they can come up alongside her."

Jessie stared at her, gnawing his lip. Then: "It's not why I came." He leaned back, securing his grip on the stalk he was holding.

The bug was turning ponderously, so distant sunlight slid down and across Chirk's astonished features. Her hand was still outstretched. "What the'f you talking about? This is it! Treasure! Riches for the rest of your life – but you gotta come with me *now*!"

"I didn't come for the treasure," he said. Having to explain himself was making Jessie resentful. "You go on, Chirk, you deserve it. You take my share too, if you want."

Now she drew back her hand, blinking. "What is this? Jessie, are you all right?"

Tears started in his eyes. "No, I'm not all right, Chirk. I'm going to die." He stabbed a finger in his mouth and brought it out, showed her the red on it. "It's been coming on for months. Since before I signed on with Emmen. So, you see, I really got no use for treasure."

She was staring at him in horror. Jessie forced a smile. "I could use my jet, though, if you happen to have seen where it went."

Wordlessly, she held out her hand again. This time Jessie took it, and she gunned the engine, flipping them over and accelerating back the way Jessie had come.

As they shot through a volume of clear air she turned in her saddle and frowned at him. "You came here to die, is that it?"

Jessie shook his head. "Not yet. I hope not yet." He massaged his chest, feeling the deep hurt there, the spreading weakness. "There's somebody here I want to talk to."

Chirk nearly flew them into one of the pink stalks. "Someone *here*? Jess, you were with us just now. You heard that . . . song. You know nobody could be alive in here. It's why nobody's ever gotten at the wreck."

He nodded. "Not a —" He coughed. "Not a person, no —" The coughing took over for a while. He spat blood, dizzy, pain behind his eyes now too. When it all subsided he looked up to find they were coming alongside his jet, which was nuzzling a dent in a vast rough wall that cut across the forest of stalks.

He reached for the jet and managed to snag one of its handlebars. Before he climbed onto it he glanced back; Chirk was looking at him with huge eyes. She clearly didn't know what to do.

He stifled a laugh lest it spark more coughing. "There's a precipice moth here. I heard about it by chance when my family and me were doing a performance in Batetran. It made the newspapers there: Moth Seen Entering Capital Bug."

"Precip – Precip moth?" She rolled the word around in her mouth. "Wait a minute, you mean a world-diver? One of those dragons that're supposed to hide at the edges of the world to waylay travellers?"

He shook his head, easing himself carefully onto the jet. "A defender of the world. Not human. Maybe the one that blew up the royal palace in Slipstream last year. Surely you heard about *that*."

"I heard about a monster. It was a moth?" She was being uncharacteristically thickheaded. Jessie was ready to forgive that, considering the circumstances.

She showed no signs of hying off to her well-deserved treasure, so Jessie told her the story as he'd heard it – of how Admiral Chaison Fanning of Slipstream had destroyed an invasion fleet, hundreds of cruisers strong, with only seven little ships of his own. Falcon captured him and tortured him to find out how he'd done it, but he'd escaped and returned to Slipstream, where he'd deposed the Pilot, Slipstream's hereditary monarch.

"Nobody knows how he stopped that invasion fleet," said Chirk. "It was impossible."

Jessie nodded. "Yeah, that's right. But I found out."

Now she *had* to hear that story, but Jessie was reluctant to tell her. He'd told no one else because he trusted no one else, not with the location of one of the greatest secrets of the world. He trusted Chirk – she had her own treasure now – yet he was still reluctant, because that would mean admitting how he'd been wedged into a dark corner of Rainsouk Amphitheater, crying alone when the place unexpectedly began to fill with people.

For months Jessie had been hearing about Rainsouk; his brothers were so excited over the prospect of performing here. Jessie was the youngest, and not much of an acrobat – he could see that in his father's eyes every time he missed a catch and sailed on through the weightless air to fetch up, humiliated, in a safety net. Jessie had given up trying to please the family, had in fact become increasingly alone and isolated outside their intense focus and relentless team spirit. When the cough started he tried to hide it, but their little travelling house was just too small to do that for long.

When Father found out, he was just disappointed, that was all. Disappointed that his youngest had gotten himself sick and might die. So Jessie was off the team – and though nobody said it out loud, off the team meant out of the family.

So there he'd been, crying in the amphitheatre he'd never get to perform in, when it began to fill with black-garbed men and women.

As he opened his mouth to refuse to tell her, Jessie found himself spilling the whole story, humiliating as it was. "These visitors, they were terrifying, Chirk. It looked like a convention of assassins, every man and woman the last person you'd want to meet on a dark night. And then the scariest of them flew out to the middle of the place and started to talk."

The very world was threatened, he'd said. Only he and his brothers and sisters could save it, for this was a meeting of the Virga home guard. The guard were a myth – so Jessie had been taught. He'd heard stories about them his whole life, of how they guarded the walls of the world against the terrifying monsters and alien forces prowling just outside.

"Yet here they were," he told Chirk. "And their leader was reminding them that something is trying to get *in*, right now, and the only thing that keeps it out is Candesce. The sun of suns emits a . . . he called it a 'field,' that keeps the monsters out. But the same field keeps *us* from developing any of the powerful technologies we'd need to stop the monsters if they did get in. Technologies like radar. . . . and get this:

"It was radar that made Admiral Chaison Fanning's ships able to run rings around Falcon Formation's fleet. *Because Fanning had found a key to Candesce*, and had gone inside to shut down the field for a day."

Chirk crossed her arms, smiling skeptically. "Now this is a tall tale," she said.

"Believe it or not," said Jessie with a shrug, "it's true. He gave the key to the precipice moth that helped him depose the Pilot, and it flew away . . . the home guard didn't know where. But I knew."

"Ahh," she said. "That newspaper article. It came here."

"Where it could be sure of never being disturbed," he said eagerly.

"And now you're, what? – going to duel it for the key?" She laughed. "Seems to me you're in no state to slay dragons, Jess." She held out her hand. "Look, you're too weak to fly, even. Come with me. At least we'll make you rich before . . ." She glanced away. "You can afford the best doctors, you know they —"

He shook his head, and spun the pedals of the jet's starter spring. "That moth doesn't know what I overheard in the amphitheatre. That the walls of the world are failing. Candesce's shield isn't strong enough anymore. We need the key so we can dial down the field and develop technologies that could stop whatever's out there. The moth's been hiding in here, it doesn't know, Chirk."

The jet roared into life. "I can't slay a dragon, Chirk," he shouted. "But at least I can give it the news."

He opened the throttle and left her before she could reply.

They dressed as heroes. Dad wore gold and leather, the kids flame-red. Mom was the most fabulous creature Jessie had ever seen, and every night he fell in love with her all over again. She wore feathers of transparent blue plex, plumage four feet long that she could actually fly with when the gravity was right. She would be captured by the children – little devils – and rescued by Dad. They played all over the principalities, their back-drop a vast wall of spinning town wheels, green ball-shaped parks and the hithering-thithering traffic of a million airborne people. Hundreds of miles of it curved away to cup blazing Candesce. They had to be amazing to beat a sight like that. And they were.

For as long as Jessie could remember, though, there had been certain silences. Some evenings, the kids knew not to talk. They stuck to their picture books, or played outside or just plain left the house for a while. The silence radiated from Mom and Dad, and there was no understanding it. Jessie didn't notice how it grew, but there came a time when the only music in their lives seemed to happen during performance. Even rehearsals were strained. And then, one day, Mom just wasn't there anymore.

They had followed the circus from the principalities into the world's outer realms, where the suns were spaced hundreds of miles apart and the chilly darkness between them was called "winter".

Jessie remembered a night lit by distant lightning that curled around a spherical stormcloud. They were staying on a little town wheel whose name he no longer remembered – just a spinning hoop of wood forty feet wide and a mile or so across, spoked by frayed ropes and home to a few hundred farm families. Mom had been gone for four days. Jessie stepped out of the hostel where they were staying to see Dad leaning out over the rushing air, one strong arm holding a spoke-rope while he stared into the headwind.

"But where would she go?" Jessie heard him murmur. That was all that he ever said on the matter, and he didn't even say it to his boys.

They weren't heroes after that. From that day forward, they dressed as soldiers, and their act was a battle.

The capital bug was hollow. This in itself wasn't such a surprise – something so big wouldn't have been able to move under its own power if it wasn't. It would have made its own gravity. What made Jessie swear in surprise was just how little there was to it, now that he was inside.

The bug's perforated back let in sunlight, and in those shafts he beheld a vast oval space, bigger than any stadium he had ever juggled in. The sides and bottom of the place were carpeted in trees, and more hung weightless in the central space, the roots of five or six twined together at their bases so that they thrust branch and leaf every which way. Flitting between these were mirror-bright schools of long-finned fish; chasing those were flocks of legless crimson and yellow birds. As Jessie watched, a struggling group of fish managed to make it to a thirty-foot-diameter ball of water. The pursuing birds peeled away at the last second as the punctured water ball quivered and tossed off smaller spheres. This drama took place in complete silence; there was no sound at all although the air swarmed with insects as well as the larger beasts.

Of course, nothing could have made itself heard over the buzz of the capital bug itself. So, he supposed nothing tried.

The air was thick with the smell of flowers, growth, and decay. Jessie took the jet in a long curving tour of the vast space, and for a few moments he was able to forget everything except the wonder of being here. Then, as he returned to his starting point, he spotted the wreck, and the *Mistelle*. They were high up in something like a gallery that stretched around the "top" of the space, under the perforated roof. Both were dwarfed by their setting, but he could clearly see his teammates' jets hovering over the wreck. The stab of sorrow that went through him almost set him coughing again. It would only take seconds and he'd be with them. At least he could watch their jubilation as they plundered the treasure he'd helped them find.

And then what? They could shower him with jewels but he couldn't buy his life back. At best he could hold such baubles up to the light and admire them for a while, before dying alone and unremarked.

He turned the jet and set to exploring the forested gut of the capital bug.

Jessie had seen very few built-up places that weren't inhabited. In Virga, real estate was something you made, like gravity or sunlight. Wilderness as a place didn't exist, except in those rare forests that had grown by twining their roots and branches until their whole matted mass extended for miles. He'd seen one of those on the fringe of the principalities, where Candesce's light was a mellow rose and the sky permanently peach-tinged. That tangled mass of green had seemed like a delirium dream, an intrusion into the sane order of the world. But it was nothing to the wilderness of the capital bug.

Bugs were rare; at any one time there might only be a few dozen in the whole world. They never got too close to the sun of suns, so they were never seen in the principalities. They dwelt in the turbulent middle space between civilization and winter, where suns wouldn't stay on station and nations would break up and drift apart. Of course, they were also impossible to approach, so it was likely that no one had ever flown through these cathedrals walled by gigantic flowers, these ship-sized grass stalks dewed by beads of water big as houses. Despite his pain and exhaustion, the place had its way with him and he found himself falling into a meditative calm he associated with that moment before you make your jump – or, in mid-air, that moment before your father catches your hand.

In its own way, this calm rang louder than any feeling he'd ever had, maybe because it was *about* something, about death, and nothing he'd ever felt before had grown on such a foundation.

He came to an area where giant crystals of salt had grown out of the capital bug's skin, long geodesic shapes whose inner planes sheened in purple and bottle-green. They combined with the dew drops to splinter and curl the light in a million ways.

Stretched between two sixty-foot grass stalks was the glittering outline of a man.

Jessie throttled back and grabbed a vine to stop himself. He'd come upon a spider's web; the spider that had made it was probably bigger than he was. But someone or something had used the web to make a piece of art, by placing fist- to head-sized balls of water at the intersections of the threads, laying out a pattern shaped like a man standing proudly, arms out, as though about to catch something.

Jessie goggled at it, then remembered to look for the spider. After a cautious minute he egged the jet forward, skirting around the web. There were more webs ahead. Some were twenty or more feet across, and each one was a tapestry done in liquid jewels. Some of the figures were human; others were of birds, or flowers, but each was exquisitely executed. It came to Jessie that when the capital bug was in full song, the webs and drops would vibrate, blurring the figures' outlines until they must seem made of light.

Spinning in the air, he laughed in surprise.

Something reared up sixty feet away and his heart skipped. It was a vaguely humanoid shape sculpted in rusted metal and moss-covered stone. As it stood it unfolded gigantic wings that stretched past the tops of the grass stalks.

Its head was a scarred metal ball.

"THIS IS NOT YOUR PLACE." Even half-deaf as he was, the words battered Jessie like a headwind. They were like gravel speaking. If his team from the *Mistelle* were here, they'd be turning tail at this point; they would probably hear the words, even as far away as the wreck.

Jessie reached down and pointedly turned off the jet. "I've come to talk to you," he said.

"YOU BRING NO ORDERS," said the precipice moth. It began to hunker back into the hollow where it had been coiled.

"I bring news!" Jessie had rehearsed what he was going to say, picturing over and over in his mind the impresario of the circus and how he would gesture and stretch out his vowels to make his speech pretty and important-sounding. Now, though, Jessie couldn't remember his lines. "It's about the key to Candesce!"

The moth stopped. Now that it was motionless, he could see how its body was festooned with weapons: its fingers were daggers, gun barrels poked under its wrists. The moth was a war machine, half-flesh, half-ordnance.

"CLARIFY."

Jessie blew out the breath he'd been holding and immediately started coughing. To his dismay little dots of blood spun through the air in the direction of the moth. It cocked its head, but said nothing.

When he had the spasms under control, Jessie told the monster what he'd overheard in the amphitheatre. "What the leader meant – I think he meant – was that the strategy of relying on Candesce to protect us isn't working anymore. Those things from outside, they've gotten in at least twice in the last two years. They're figuring it out."

"We destroy them if they enter." The moth's voice was not so overwhelming now; or maybe he was just going deaf.

"Begging your pardon," said Jessie, "but they slipped past you both times. Maybe you're catching some of them, but not enough."

There was a long pause. "Perhaps," said the moth at last. Jessie grinned because that one word, a hint of doubt, had for him turned the moth from a mythical dragon into an old soldier, who might need his help after all.

"I'm here on behalf of humanity to ask you for the key to Candesce," he recited; he'd remembered his speech. "We can't remain at the mercy of the sun of suns and the things from outside. We have to steer our own course now, because the other way's not working. The home guard didn't know where you were, and they'd never have listened to me; so I came here myself."

"The home guard cannot be trusted," said the moth.

Jessie blinked in surprise. But then again, in the story of Admiral Fanning and the key, the moth had not in the end given it to the guard, though it had had the chance.

The moth shifted, leaning forward slightly. "Do you want the key?" it asked.

"I can't use it." He could explain why, but Jessie didn't want to.

"You're dying," said the moth.

The words felt like a punch in the stomach. It was one thing for Jessie to say it. He could pretend he was brave. But the moth was putting it out there, a fact on the table. He glared at it.

"I'm dying too," said the moth.

"W-*what*?"

"That is why I'm here," it said. "Men cannot enter this creature. My body would be absorbed by it, rather than be cut up and used by you. Or so I had thought."

"Then give me the key," said Jessie quickly. "I'll take it to the home guard. You know you can trust me," he added, "because I can't use the key to my own advantage. I'll live long enough to deliver it to the home guard, but not long enough to use it."

"*I don't have the key.*"

Jessie blinked at the monster for a time. He'd simply assumed that the moth that had been seen entering this capital bug was the same one that had met Chaison Fanning in Slipstream. But of course there was no reason that should be the case. There were thousands, maybe millions of moths in Virga. They were almost never seen, but two had been spotted in the same year.

"That's it, then," he said at last. After that, there was a long silence between them, but the precipice moth made no effort to fit itself back into its hole. Jessie looked around, mused at the drifting jet for a while, then gave a deep sigh.

He turned to the moth. "Can I ask you a favour?"

"What is it?"

"I'd like to . . . stay here to die. If that wouldn't be too much of an inconvenience for you."

The precipice moth put out an iron-taloned forelimb, then another, very slowly, as if sneaking up on Jessie. It brought its round leaden head near to his, and seemed to sniff at him.

"I have a better idea," it said. Then it snatched him up in its great claws, opened its wide lidless mouth, and *bit*.

Jessie screamed as his whole torso was engulfed in that dry maw. He felt his chest being ripped open, felt his lungs being torn out – curiously, not as pain but as a physical wrenching – and then everything blurred and went grey.

But not black. He blinked, coming to himself, to discover he was still alive. He was hovering in a nebula of blood, millions of tiny droplets of it spinning and drifting around him like little worlds. Gingerly, he reached up to touch his chest. It was whole, and when he took a tentative breath, the expected pain wasn't there.

Then he spotted the moth. It was watching him from its cavity in the capital bug's flesh. "W-what did – where is it?"

"I ate your disease," said the moth. "Battlefield medicine, it is allowed."

"But why?"

"Few moths know which one of us has the key, or where it is," it said. "I cannot broadcast what I know, Candesce jams all lightspeed communications. I am now too weak to travel.

"You will take your message to the moth that has the key. It will decide."

"But I'm – I'm not going to —?"

"I could not risk your dying during the journey. You are disease-free now."

Jessie couldn't take it in. He breathed deeply, then again. It would hit him sometime later, he knew; for now, all he could think to say was, "So where's the one that does have the key?"

The moth told him and Jessie laughed, because it was obvious. "So I'll wait until night and go in," he said. "That should be easy."

The precipice moth shifted, shook its head. "It will not speak to you. Not unless you prove you are committed to the course that you say you are."

There was a warning in those words but Jessie didn't care. All that mattered was that he was going to live. "I'll do it."

The moth shook its head. "I think you will not," it said.

"You think I'll forget the whole thing, take my treasure from the ship over there," he nodded behind him, "and just set myself up somewhere? Or you think I'll take the key for myself, auction it off to the highest bidder? But I won't, you see. I owe you. I'll do as you ask."

It shook its head. "You do not understand." By degrees it was inching its way back into its hole. Jessie watched it, chewing his lip. Then he looked around at the beautiful jewelled tapestries it had made in the spiders' webs.

"Hey," he said. "Before I go, can I do something for *you*?"

"There is nothing you can do for me," murmured the moth.

"I don't know about that. I can't do very *many* things," he said as he snapped off some smaller stalks of the strange grass. He hefted a couple in his hands. "But the one or two things I can do, I do pretty well." He eyed the moth as he began spinning the stalks between his hands.

"Have you ever seen freefall juggling?"

Jessie stood alone on the tarred deck of a docking arm. His bags were huddled around his feet; there was nobody else standing where he was, the nearest crowd a hundred feet away.

The dock was an open-ended barrel, six hundred feet across and twice as deep. Its rim was gnarled with cable mounts for the spokes that radiated out to the distant rim of the iron citywheel. This far from the turning rim, Jessie weighed only a pound, but his whole posture was a slump of misery.

There was only air where his ship was supposed to be.

He'd been late packing; the others had gone to get Dad at the circus pitch that had been strung, like a hammock, between the spokes of the city. Jessie was old enough to pack for himself, so he had to. He was old enough to find his way to the docks, too, but he'd been delayed, just by one thing and another.

And the ship wasn't here.

He stared into the sky as it greyed with the approach of a water-laden cloud. The long spindle-shapes of a dozen ships nosed at other points on the circular dock, like hummingbirds sipping at a flower. Passengers and crew were hand-walking up the ropes of their long proboscises. Jessie could hear conversations, laughter from behind him where various beverage huts and newspaper stands clustered.

But where would they go?

Without him? The answer, of course, was anywhere.

In that moment Jessie focused his imagination in a single desperate image: the picture of his father dressed as the hero, the way he used to be, arrowing out of the sky – and Jessie reaching up, ready for the catch. He willed it with everything he had, but instead, the grey cloud that had been approaching began to funnel through the docks propelled by a tailwind. It manifested as a horizontal drizzle. Jessie hunched into it, blinking and licking his lips.

A hand fell on his shoulder.

Jessie looked up. One of the businessmen who'd been waiting for another ship was standing over him. The man was well-dressed, sporting the garish feathered hat his class wore. He had a kindly, well-lined face and hair the colour of the clouds.

"Son," he said, "were you looking for the ship to Mespina?"

Jessie nodded.

"They moved the gate," said the businessman. He raised his head and pointed way up the curve of the dock. Just for a second, his outline was prismed by the water beading on Jessie's eyelashes. "It's at 2:30, there, see it?"

Jessie nodded, and reached to pick up his bags.

"Good luck," said the man as he sauntered, in ten-foot strides, back to his companions.

"Thanks," Jessie murmured too late. But he was thunder-struck. In a daze he tiptoed around the dock to find Father and his brothers waiting impatiently, the ship about to leave. They hadn't looked for him, of course. He answered their angry questions in monosyllables. All he could do was contemplate the wonder of having been saved by that man's simple little gesture. The world must be crammed with people who could be saved just as easily, if somebody bothered to take a minute out of their day to do it.

From that moment forward, Jessie didn't daydream about putting out a burning city or rescuing the crew of a corkscrew-ing passenger liner. His fantasies were about seeing that lone, uncertain figure, standing by itself on a dock or outside a char-ity diner – and of approaching and, with just ten words or a coin, saving a life.

He wasn't able to visit the wrecked treasure ship, because the capital bug's sound organs were recovering. The drone was already louder than Jessie's jet as he left the bowl-shaped garden of the bug's gut. From the zone just under the perforated skin of the bug's back, he could see that the main hull of the wreck was missing, presumably towed by the *Mistelle*, because that was gone too.

When Jessie rose out of the bug's back, there was no sign of the *Mistelle* in the surrounding air either. A massive cloud front – mushroom and dome-shaped wads of it as big as the bug – was moving in and would obscure one of the suns in minutes. *Mistelle* was probably in there somewhere but he would have the devil of a time finding it. Jessie shrugged, and turned the jet away.

He had plucked some perfect salt crystals, long as his thigh, from the precipice moth's forest, just in case. He'd be able to sell these for food and fuel as he traveled.

He did exactly this, in two days reaching the outskirts of the principali-ties, and civilized airs. Here he was able to blend in with streams of traf-fic that coursed through the air like blood through the arteries of some world-sized, invisible beast. The sky was full of suns, all competing to tinge the air with their colours. The grandly turning iron wheel cities and green clouds of forest had a wealth of light they could choose to bask in.

All those lesser suns were shamed when Candesce awoke from its night cycle, and all cities, farms, and factories turned to the sun of suns during this true day.

Billions of human lives marked their spans by Candesce's radiance. All of the principalities were visible here: he could trace the curve of an immense bubble, many hundreds of miles across, that was sketched onto the sky by innumerable cities and houses, spherical lakes, and drifting farms. Nearby he could tell what they were; further away, they blended and blurred together into one continuous surface whose curve he could see aiming to converge on the far side of Candesce. The sun of suns was too bright to follow that curve to its antipode – but, at night! Then, it was all so clear, a hollow sphere made of glittering stars, city and window lights in uncountable millions encircling an absence where Candesce slumbered or – some said – prowled the air like a hungry falcon.

The bubble had an inner limit because nothing could survive the heat too close to Candesce. The cities and forests were kept at bay, and clouds dissolved and lakes boiled away if they crossed that line. The line was called the *anthropause*, and only at night did the cremation fleets sail across it carrying their silent cargoes, or the technology scavengers who dared to look for the cast-offs of Candesce's inhuman industry. These fleets made tiny drifts of light that edged into the black immensity of Candesce's inmost regions; but sensible people stayed out.

For the first time in his life, Jessie could go anywhere in that mist of humanity. As he flew he took note of all the people in a way he never had before; he marked each person's *role*. There was a baker. Could he be that? There were some soldiers. Could he go to war? He would try on this or that future, taste it for a while as he flew. Some seemed tantalizing, though infinitely far out of reach for a poor uneducated juggler like himself. But none were out of reach anymore.

When he stopped to refuel at the last town before the anthropause, he found they wouldn't take the coins he'd gotten at his last stop. Jessie traded the last of his salt, knowing even as he did it that several slouching youths were watching from a nearby net. He'd shifted his body to try to hide the salt crystal, but the gas jockey had held it up to the light anyway, whistling in appreciation.

"Where'd you get *this*?"

Jessie tried to come up with some plausible story, but he'd never been very good at stuff like that. He got through the transaction, got his gas, and took the jet into the shadow of a three-hundred-foot-wide grove, to wait for dark. It was blazingly hot even here. The shimmering air tricked his eyes, and so he didn't notice the gang of youths sneaking up on him until it was too late.

The arm around his throat was a shocking surprise – so much so that Jessie's reflexes took over and he found himself and his attacker spinning into the air before the astonished eyes of the others. Jessie wormed his way out of the other's grasp. The lad had a knife but now that they were in free air that wasn't a problem. Jessie was an acrobat.

In a matter of seconds he'd flipped the boy around with his feet and kicked him at his friends, who were jumping out of the leaves in a hand-linked mass. The kick took Jessie backwards and he spun around a handy branch. He dove past them as they floundered in midair, got to his jet, and kick-started it. Jessie was off before they could regroup; he left only a rude gesture behind.

Under the hostile glare of Candesce, he paused to look back. His heart was pounding, he was panting, but he felt great. Jessie laughed and decided right there to go on with his quest, even if it was too early. He turned the jet and aimed it straight at the sun of suns.

It quickly became obvious that he couldn't just fly in there. The jet could have gotten him to it in two hours at top speed, but he'd have burned to death long before arriving. He idled, advancing just enough to discourage anyone from following.

He looked back after twenty minutes of this, and swore. There were no clouds or constructions of any kind between him and the anthropause, so the little dot that was following him was clearly visible. He'd made at least one enemy, it was clear; who knew how many of them were hanging off that lone jet?

He opened the throttle a little, hunkering down behind the jet's inadequate windscreen to cut the blazing light and heat as much as he could. After a few minutes he noticed that it was lessening of itself: Candesce was going out.

The light reddened as the minutes stretched. The giant fusion engines of the sun of suns were winking out one by one; Candesce was not one sun, but a flock of them. Each one was mighty enough to light a whole nation, and together they shaped the climate and airflow patterns of the entire world. Their light was scattered and absorbed over the leagues, of course, until it was no longer visible. But Candesce's influence extended to the very skin of the world where icebergs cracked off Virga's frost-painted wall. Something, invisible and not to be tasted or felt, blazed out of here as well with the light and the heat: the *field*, which scrambled the energies and thoughts of any device more complicated than a clock. Jessie's jet was almost as complex as a machine could get in Virga. Since the world's enemies depended entirely on their technologies, they could not enter here.

This was protection; but there had been a cost. Jessie understood that part of his rightful legacy was knowledge, but he'd never been given it. The people in Virga knew little about how the world worked, and nothing about how Candesce lived. They were utterly dependent on a device their ancestors had built but that most of them now regarded as a force of nature.

Light left the sky, but not the heat. That would take hours to dissipate, and Jessie didn't have time to wait. He sucked some water from the wine flask hanging off his saddle, and approached the inner circle of Candesce. Though the last of its lamps were fading red embers, he could still see well enough by the light of the principalities. Their millionfold glitter swam and wavered in the heat haze, casting a shimmering light over the crystalline perfection of the sun of suns. He felt their furnace-heat on his face, but he had dared a capital bug's howl; he could dare this.

The question was, where in a cloud of dozens of suns would a precipice moth nest? The dying moth had told Jessie that it was here, and it made perfect sense: Where was the one place from which the key could not be stolen? Clearly in the one place that you'd need that key to enter.

This answer seemed simple until you saw Candesce. Jessie faced a sky full of vast crystal splinters, miles long, that floated freely in a formation around the suns themselves. Those were smaller, wizened metal-and-crystal balls, like chandeliers that had shrunk in on themselves. And surrounding them, unfolding from mirrored canopies like flowers at dawn, other vast engines stirred.

He flew a circuit through the miles-long airspace of the sun of suns; then he made another. He was looking for something familiar, a town wheel for giants or some sort of blockhouse that might survive the heat here. He saw nothing but machinery, and the night drew on towards a dawn he could not afford to be here to see.

The precipice moth he'd spoken to had been partly alive – at least, it had looked like that leathery skin covered muscles as well as body internal machinery. But what living thing could survive here? Even if those mirrored metal flowers shielded their cores from the worst of the radiation, they couldn't keep out the heat. He could see plainly how their interiors smoked as they spilled into sight.

Even the tips of those great diamond splinters were just cooling below the melting point of lead. Nothing biological could exist here.

Then, if the moth was here, it might as well be in the heart of the inferno as on the edge. With no more logic to guide him than that, Jessie aimed his jet for the very centre of Candesce.

Six suns crowded together here. Each was like a glass diatom two hundred feet in diameter, with long spines that jutted every which way in imitation of the gigantic ones framing the entire realm. Thorns from all the suns had pinioned a seventh body between them – a black oval, whose skin looked like old cast iron. Its pebbled surface was patterned with raised squares of brighter metal, and inset squares of crystal. Jessie half-expected to faint from the heat as he approached it, and he would die here if that happened; but instead, it grew noticeably cooler as he closed the last few yards.

He hesitated, then reached out to touch the dark surface. He snatched his hand back: it was *cold*.

This must be the generator that made Candesce's protective field. It was this thing that kept the world's enemies at bay.

Gunning the jet, he made a circuit of the oval. It looked the same from all angles and there was no obvious door. But, when he was almost back to his starting point, Jessie saw distant city-light gleam off something behind one of the crystal panels. He flew closer to see.

The chrome skeleton of a precipice moth huddled on the other side of the window. It was too dark for Jessie to make out what sort of space it was sitting in, but from the way its knees were up by its steel ears, it must not be large.

There wasn't a scrap of flesh on this moth, yet when Jessie reached impulsively to rap on the crystal, it moved.

Its head turned and it lowered a jagged hand from its face. He couldn't see eyes, but it must be looking at him.

"Let me in!" Jessie shouted. "I have to talk to you!"

The moth leaned its head against the window and its mouth opened. Jessie felt a kind of pulse – a deep vibration. He put his ear to the cold crystal and the moth spoke again.

"WAIT."

"You're the one, aren't you? The moth with the key?"

"WAIT."

"But I have to . . ." He couldn't hear properly over the whine of the jet, so Jessie shut it down. The sound died – then, a second later, died again. An echo? No, that other note had been pitched very differently.

He cursed and spun around, losing his grip on the inset edge of the window. As he flailed and tried to right himself, a second jet appeared around the curve of the giant machine. There was one rider in its saddle. The dark silhouette held a rifle.

"Who are you? What do you want?"

"I want what you want," said a familiar voice. "Nothing less than the greatest treasure in the world."

"Chirk, what are you doing here? How did – did you follow me?"

She hove closer and now her canary-yellow jacket was visible in the glow of distant cities. "I had to," she said. "The wreck was empty, Jess! All that hard work and risking our lives, and there was nothing there. Emmen took it under tow – had to make the best of the situation, I guess – but for our team, there was nothing. All of us were so mad, murderous mad. Not safe for me.

"Then I remembered you. I went looking for you and what should I find? You, juggling for a monster!"

"I think he liked it," said Jessie. He hoped he could trust Chirk, but then, why did she have that rifle in her hands?

"You said you were going to give it a message. When you left I trailed after you. I was trying to think what to do. Talk to you? Ask to join you? Maybe there was a prize for relaying the message. But then you set a course straight for the sun of suns, and I realized what had happened.

"Give me the key, Jessie." She levelled the rifle at him.

He gaped at her, outraged and appalled. "I haven't got it," he said.

She hissed angrily. "Don't lie to me! Why else would you be here?"

"Because *he's* got it," said Jessie. He jabbed a thumb at the window. He saw Chirk's eyes widen as she saw what was behind it. She swore.

"If you thought I had it, why didn't you try to take it from me earlier?"

She looked aside. "Well, I didn't know exactly where you were going. If it gave you the key, then it told you where the door was, right? I had to find out."

"But why didn't you just ask to come along?"

She bit her lip. "'Cause you wouldn't have had me. Why should you? You'd have known I was only in it for the key. Even if I was . . . nice to you."

Though it was dark, in the half-visible flight of emotions across her face Jessie could see a person he hadn't known was there. Chirk had hid her insecurities as thoroughly as he'd hoped to hide his bloody cough.

"You could have come to me," he said. "You should have."

"And you could have told me you were planning to die alone," she said. "But you didn't."

He couldn't answer that. Chirk waved the rifle at the door. "Get it to open up, then. Let's get the key and get out of here."

"If I can get the key from it, ordering it to kill you will be easy," he told her. A little of the wild mood that had made him willing to dive into a capital bug had returned. He was feeling obstinate enough to dare her to kill him.

Chirk sighed, and to his surprise said, "You're right." She threw away the rifle. They both watched it tumble away into the dark.

"I'm not a good person, and I went about this all wrong," she said. "But I really did like you, Jessie." She looked around uneasily. "I just . . . I can't let it go. I won't *take* it from you, but I need to be a part of this, Jess. I need a share, just a little share. I'm not going anywhere. If you want to sic your monster on me, I guess you'll just have to kill me." She crossed her arms, lowered her head, and made to stare him down.

He just had to laugh. "You make a terrible villain, Chirk." As she sputtered indignantly, he turned to the window again. The moth had been impassively watching his conversation with Chirk. "Open up!" he shouted at it again, and levering himself close with what little purchase he could make on the window's edge, he put his ear to the crystal again.

"WAIT."

Jessie let go and drifted back, frowning. Wait? For what?

"What did it say?"

"The other moth told me this one wouldn't let me in unless I proved I was committed. I had to prove I wouldn't try to take the key."

"But how are you going to do that?"

"Oh."

Wait.

Candesce's night cycle was nearly over. The metal flowers were starting to close, the bright little flying things they'd released hurrying back to the safety of their tungsten petals. All around them, the rumbling furnaces in the suns would be readying themselves. They would brighten soon, and light would wash away everything material here that was not a part of the sun of suns. Everything, perhaps, except the moth, who might be as ancient as Candesce itself.

"The other moth told me I wouldn't deliver the message," said Jessie. "It said I would *decide* not to."

She frowned. "Why would it say that?"

"Because . . .'cause it cured me, that's why. And because the only way to deliver the message is to wait until dawn. That's when this moth here will open the door for us."

"But then – we'd never get out in time . . ."

He nodded.

"Tell it – yell through the door, like it's doing to you! Jessie, we can't stay here, that's just insane! You said the other moth cured you? Then you can escape, you can live – like me. Maybe not with me, and you're right not to trust me, but we can take the first steps together . . ." But he was shaking his head.

"I don't think it can hear me," he said. "I can barely hear it, and its voice is loud enough to topple buildings. I have to wait, or not deliver the message."

"Go to the home guard, then. Tell them, and they'll send someone here. They'll —"

"— not believe a word I say. I've nothing to show them, after all. Nothing to prove my story."

"But your life! You have your whole life . . ."

He'd tried to picture it on the flight here. He had imagined himself as a baker, a soldier, a diplomat, a painter. He longed for every one of them, for any of them. All he had to do was start his jet and follow Chirk, and one of them would come to pass.

He started to reach for his jet, but there was nowhere he could escape the responsibility he'd willingly taken on himself. He realized he didn't want to.

"Only I can do this," he told her. "Anyway, this is the only thing I ever had that was mine. If I give it up now, I'll have some life . . . but not *my* life."

She said nothing, just shook her head. He looked past her at the vast canopy of glittering lights – from the windows in city apartments and town wheel-houses, from the mansions of the rich and the gas-fires of industry: a sphere of people, every single one of them threatened by something that even now might be uncoiling in the cold vacuum outside the world; each and every one of them waiting, though they knew it not, for a helping hand.

Ten words, or a single coin.

"Get out of here, Chirk," he said. "It's starting. If you leave right now you might just get away before the full heat hits."

"But —" She stared at him in bewilderment. "You come too!"

"No. Just go. See?" He pointed at a faint ember-glow that had started in the darkness below their feet. "They're waking up. This place will be a furnace soon. There's no treasure here for you, Chirk. It's all out there."

"Jessie, I can't —" Flame-coloured light blossomed below them, and then from one side. "Jessie?" Her eyes were wide with panic.

"Get out! Chirk, it's too late unless you go *now*! Go! Go!"

The panic took her and she kicked her jet into life. She made a clumsy pass, trying to grab Jessie on the way by, but he evaded her easily.

"Go!" She put her head down, opened the throttle, and shot away. *Too late*, Jessie feared. *Let her not be just one second too late.*

Her jet disappeared in the rising light. Jessie kicked his own jet away, returning to cling to the edge of the window. His own sharp-edged shadow appeared against the metal skull inches from his own.

"You have your proof!" He could feel the pulse of energy – heat, and something deeper and more fatal – reaching into him from the awakening suns. "Now open up.

"Open *up!*"

The moth reached out and did something below the window. The crystalline pane slid aside, and Jessie climbed into the narrow, boxlike space. The window slid shut, but did nothing to filter the growing light and heat from outside. There was nowhere further to go, either. He had expected no less

The precipice moth lowered its head to his.

"I have come to you on behalf of humanity," said Jessie, "to tell you that the ancient strategy of relying on Candesce for our safety will no longer work . . ."

He told the moth his story, and as he spoke the dawn came up.

EVIL ROBOT MONKEY

Mary Robinette Kowal

Caught between two worlds can be a very uncomfortable place to be.

New writer Mary Robinette Kowal won the John W. Campbell Award for Best New Writer in 2008. Her work has appeared in *Cosmos, Asimov's Science Fiction, The Solaris Book of Science Fiction 2, Strange Horizons, Subterranea*n, *Clarkesworld, Twenty Epics, Apex Digest, Apex Online*, and *Talebones*, among other markets. She's the secretary of the Science Fiction Writers of America, the art director of the magazine *Shimmer*, and in civilian life is a professional puppeteer and voice actor. She lives in New York City. Her website is at maryrobinettekowal.com.

SLIDING HIS HANDS over the clay, Sly relished the moisture oozing around his fingers. The clay matted down the hair on the back of his hands making them look almost human. He turned the potter's wheel with his prehensile feet as he shaped the vase. Pinching the clay between his fingers he lifted the wall of the vase, spinning it higher.

Someone banged on the window of his pen. Sly jumped and then screamed as the vase collapsed under its own weight. He spun and hurled it at the picture window like faeces. The clay spattered against the Plexiglas, sliding down the window.

In the courtyard beyond the glass, a group of school kids leapt back, laughing. One of them swung his arms aping Sly crudely. Sly bared his teeth, knowing these people would take it as a grin, but he meant it as a threat. Swinging down from his stool, he crossed his room in three long strides and pressed his dirty hand against the window. Still grinning, he wrote SSA. Outside, the letters would be reversed.

The student's teacher flushed as red as a female in heat and called the children away from the window. She looked back once as she led them out of the courtyard, so Sly grabbed himself and showed her what he would do if she came into his pen.

Her naked face turned brighter red and she hurried away. When they were gone, Sly rested his head against the glass. The metal in his skull thunked against the window. It wouldn't be long now, before a handler came to talk to him.

Damn.

He just wanted to make pottery. He loped back to the wheel and sat down again with his back to the window. Kicking the wheel into movement, Sly dropped a new ball of clay in the centre and tried to lose himself.

In the corner of his vision, the door to his room snicked open. Sly let the wheel spin to a halt, crumpling the latest vase.

Vern poked his head through. He signed, "You okay?"

Sly shook his head emphatically and pointed at the window.

"Sorry." Vern's hands danced. "We should have warned you that they were coming."

"You should have told them that I was not an animal."

Vern looked down in submission. "I did. They're kids."

"And I'm a chimp. I know." Sly buried his fingers in the clay to silence his thoughts.

"It was Delilah. She thought you wouldn't mind because the other chimps didn't."

Sly scowled and yanked his hands free. "I'm not *like* the other chimps." He pointed to the implant in his head. "Maybe Delilah should have one of these. Seems like she needs help thinking."

"I'm sorry." Vern knelt in front of Sly, closer than anyone else would come when he wasn't sedated. It would be so easy to reach out and snap his neck. "It was a lousy thing to do."

Sly pushed the clay around on the wheel. Vern was better than the others. He seemed to understand the hellish limbo where Sly lived – too smart to be with other chimps, but too much of an animal to be with humans. Vern was the one who had brought Sly the potter's wheel, which, by the Earth and Trees, Sly loved. Sly looked up and raised his eyebrows. "So what did they think of my show?"

Vern covered his mouth, masking his smile. The man had manners. "The teacher was upset about the 'evil robot monkey'."

Sly threw his head back and hooted. Served her right.

"But Delilah thinks you should be disciplined." Vern, still so close that Sly could reach out and break him, stayed very still. "She wants me to take the clay away since you used it for an anger display."

Sly's lips drew back in a grimace built of anger and fear. Rage threatened to blind him, but he held on, clutching the wheel. If he lost it with Vern – rational thought danced out of his reach. Panting, he spun the wheel trying to push his anger into the clay.

The wheel spun. Clay slid between his fingers. Soft. Firm and smooth. The smell of earth lived his nostrils. He held the world in his hands. Turning, turning, the walls rose around a kernel of anger, subsuming it.

His heart slowed with the wheel and Sly blinked, becoming aware again as if he were slipping out of sleep. The vase on the wheel still seemed to dance with life. Its walls held the shape of the world within them. He passed a finger across the rim.

Vern's eyes were moist. "Do you want me to put that in the kiln for you?"

Sly nodded.

"I have to take the clay. You understand that, don't you?"

Sly nodded again staring at his vase. It was beautiful.

Vern scowled. "The woman makes *me* want to hurl faeces."

Sly snorted at the image, then sobered. "How long before I get it back?"

Vern picked up the bucket of clay next to the wheel. "I don't know." He stopped at the door and looked past Sly to the window. "I'm not cleaning your mess. Do you understand me?"

For a moment, rage crawled on his spine, but Vern did not meet his eyes and kept staring at the window. Sly turned.

The vase he had thrown lay on the floor in a pile of clay.

Clay.

"I understand." He waited until the door closed, then loped over and scooped the clay up. It was not much, but it was enough for now.

Sly sat down at his wheel and began to turn.

FIVE THRILLERS

Robert Reed

Here's a fast-paced story, dazzling in its shifts in milieu, that delivers exactly what the title says that it's going to deliver.

Robert Reed sold his first story in 1986, and quickly established himself as a frequent contributor to *The Magazine of Fantasy & Science Fiction*, *Asimov's Science Fiction*, and many other markets. Reed may be one of the most prolific of today's young writers, particularly at short fiction, seriously rivalled for that position only by authors such as Stephen Baxter and Brian Stableford. And – also like Baxter and Stableford – he manages to keep up a very high standard of quality *while* being prolific, something that is not at all easy to do. Reed stories such as "Sister Alice", "Brother Perfect", "Decency", "Savior", "The Remoras", "Chrysalis", "Whiptail", "The Utility Man", "Marrow", "Birth Day", "Blind", "The Toad of Heaven", "Stride", "The Shape of Everything", "Guest of Honor", "Waging Good", and "Killing the Morrow", among at least a half dozen others equally as strong, count as among some of the best short work produced by anyone in the 80s and 90s. Many of his best stories were assembled in his first collection, *The Dragons of Springplace*. Nor is he non-prolific as a novelist, having turned out eight novels since the end of the eighties, including *The Lee Shore*, *The Hormone Jungle*, *Black Milk*, *The Remarkables*, *Down the Bright Way*, *Beyond the Veil of Stars*, *An Exaltation of Larks*, *Beneath the Gated Sky*, *Marrow*, and *Sister Alice*. His most recent books include two chapbook novellas, *Mere* and *Flavors of My Genius*, a collection, *The Cuckoo's Boys*, and a novel, *The Well of Stars*. Reed lives with his family in Lincoln, Nebraska.

THE ILL-FATED MISSION

THEIR SITUATION WAS dire. A chunk of primordial iron had slashed its way through the Demon Dandy, crippling the engines and pushing life support to the brink of failure. Even worse, a shotgun blast of shrapnel had shredded one of the ship's two life-pods. The mission engineer, a glum little fellow who had spent twenty years mining Earth-grazing asteroids, studied the wreckage with an expert eye. There was no sane reason to hope that repairs could be made in time. But on the principle of keeping his staff busy, he ordered the robots and his new assistant to continue their work on the useless pod. Then after investing a few moments cursing God and Luck, the engineer dragged himself to the remnants of the bridge to meet with the Dandy's beleaguered captain.

His assistant was a young fellow named Joseph Carroway.

Handsome as a digital hero, with green eyes and an abundance of curly blond hair, Joe was in his early twenties, born to wealthy parents who had endowed their only child with the earliest crop of synthetic human genes. He was a tall tidy fellow, and he was a gifted athlete as graceful as any dancer, on the Earth or in freefall. According to a dozen respected scales, Joe was also quite intelligent. With an impressed shake of the head, the company psychiatrist had confided that his bountiful talents made him suitable for many kinds of work. But by the same token, that supercharged brain carried certain inherent risks.

Dipping his head in the most charming fashion, he said, "Risks?"

"And I think you know what I'm talking about," she remarked, showing a wary, somewhat flirtatious smile.

"But I don't know," Joe lied.

"And I believe you do," she countered. "Without exception, Mr Carroway, you have been telling me exactly what I want to hear. And you're very believable, I should add. If I hadn't run the T-scan during our interview, I might have come away believing that you are the most kind, most decent gentleman in the world."

"But I am decent," he argued.

Joe sounded, and looked, exceptionally earnest.

The psychiatrist laughed. A woman in her early fifties, she was an over-qualified professional doing routine tasks for a corporation larger and more powerful than most nations. The solar system was being opened to humanity – humanity in all of its forms, old and new. Her only task was to find qualified bodies to do exceptionally dangerous work. The vagaries of this young man's psyche were factors in her assessment. But they weren't the final word. After a moment's reflection, she said, "God, the thing is, you're beautiful."

Joe smiled and said, "Thank you."

Then with a natural smoothness, he added, "And you are an exception-ally lovely woman."

She laughed, loudly and with a trace of despair, as if aware that she would never again hear such kind words from a young man.

Then Joe leaned forward, and wearing the perfect smile – a strong win-ning grin – he told the psychiatrist, "I am a very good person."

"No," she said. "No, Joe, you are not."

Then she sat back in her chair, and with a finger twirling her mousy-brown hair, she confessed, "But dear God, my boy, I really would just love to have you for dinner."

*

Five months later, the Demon Dandy was crippled.

As soon as the engineer left for the bridge, Joe kicked away from the battered escape pod. Both robots quietly reminded him of their orders. Dereliction of duty would leave a black mark on the mission report. But their assignment had no purpose except to keep them busy and Joe distracted. And since arguing with machines served no role, he said nothing, focusing on the only rational course available to him.

The corn-line to the bridge was locked, but that was a puzzle easily solved. For the next few minutes, Joe concentrated on a very miserable conversation between the ship's top officers. The best launch window was only a little more than three hours from now. The surviving pod had finite fuel and oxygen. Kilograms and the time demanded by any return voyage were the main problems. Thirty precious seconds were wasted when the captain announced that she would remain behind, forcing the engineer to point out that she was a small person, which meant they would need to find another thirty kilos of mass, at the very least.

Of course both officers could play the hero role, sacrificing themselves to save their crew. But neither mentioned what was painfully obvious. Instead, what mattered was the naming and discarding a string of increasingly unworkable fixes.

Their conversation stopped when Joe drifted into the bridge.

"I've got two options for you," he announced. "And when it comes down to it, you'll take my second solution."

The captain glanced at her engineer, as if to ask, "Should we listen to this kid?"

In despair, the engineer said, "Tell us, Joe. Quick."

"The fairest answer? We chop off everybody's arms and legs." He smiled and dipped his head as he spoke, pretending to be squeamish. "We'll use the big field laser, since that should cauterize the wounds. Then our robots dope everybody up and shove us onboard the pod. With the robots remaining behind, of course."

Neither officer had considered saving their machines.

"We chop off our own arms?" the engineer whined. "And our legs too?"

"Prosthetics do wonders," Joe pointed out. "Or the company can grow us new limbs. They won't match the originals, but they'll be workable enough."

The officers traded nervous looks.

"What else do you have?" the captain asked.

"One crewmember remains behind."

"We've considered that," the engineer warned. "But there's no decent way to decide who stays and who goes."

"Two of us have enough mass," Joe pointed out. "If either one stays, everybody else escapes."

Joe was the largest crewman.

"So you're volunteering?" asked the captain, hope brightening her tiny brown face.

Joe said, "No," with a flat, unaffected voice. "I'm sorry. Did I say anything about volunteers?"

Suddenly the only sound was the thin wind caused by a spaceship suffering a thousand tiny leaks.

One person among the crew was almost as big as Joe.

The engineer whispered, "Danielle."

Both officers winced. Their colleague was an excellent worker and a dear friend, and Danielle also happened to be attractive and popular. Try as they might, they couldn't wrap their heads around the idea that they would leave her behind, and without her blessing, at that.

Joe had anticipated their response. "But if you had a choice between her and me, you'd happily abandon me. Is that right?"

They didn't answer. But Joe was new to the crew, and when their eyes dropped, they were clearly saying, "Yes."

He took no offence.

With a shrug and a sigh, Joe gave his audience time enough to feel ashamed. Then he looked at the captain, asking, "What about Barnes? He's only ten, maybe eleven kilos lighter than me."

That name caused a brief exchange of glances.

"What are you planning?" asked the engineer.

Joe didn't respond.

"No," the captain told him.

"No?" asked Joe. "'No' to what?"

Neither would confess what they were imagining.

Then Joe put on a horrified expression. "Oh, God," he said. "Do you really believe I would consider *that*?"

The engineer defended himself with soft mutters.

Joe's horror dissolved into a piercing stare.

"There are codes to this sort of thing," the captain reminded everybody, including herself. "Commit violence against a fellow crewmember, I don't care who it is . . . and you won't come home with us, Mr Carroway. Is that clear enough for you to understand?"

Joe let her fume. Then with a sly smile, he said, "I'm sorry. I thought we wanted the best way to save as many lives as possible."

Again, the officers glanced at each another.

The young man laughed in a charming but very chilly fashion – a moment that always made empathic souls uneasy. "Let's return to my first plan," he said. "Order everybody into the machine shop, and we'll start carving off body parts."

The captain said, "No," and then looked for a good reason.

The engineer just shrugged, laughing nervously.

"We don't know if that would work," the captain decided. "People could be killed by the trauma."

"And what if we had to fly the pod manually?" the engineer asked. "Without hands, we're just cargo."

An awful option had been excluded, and they could relax slightly.

"Okay," said Joe. "This is what I'm going to do: I'll go talk to Barnes. Give me a few minutes. And if I don't get what we want, then I will stay behind."

"You?" the captain said hopefully.

Joe offered a firm, trustworthy, "Sure."

But when he tallied up everyone's mass, the engineer found trouble. "Even with Barnes gone, we're still five kilos past our limit. And I'd like to give us a bigger margin of error, if I can."

"So," said Joe. "The rest of us give blood."

The captain stared at this odd young man, studying that dense blond hair and those bright green eyes.

"Blood," Joe repeated. "As much as we can physically manage. And we can also enjoy a big chemically-induced shit before leaving this wreck."

The engineer began massaging the numbers.

Joe matter of factly dangled his leg between the officers. "And if we're pressed, I guess I could surrender one of these boys. But my guess is that it won't come to that."

And in the end, it did not.

Three weeks later, Joe Carroway was sitting in the psychiatrist's office, calmly discussing the tragedy.

"I've read everyone's report," she admitted.

He nodded, and he smiled.

Unlike their last meeting, the woman was striving to maintain a strict professional distance. She couldn't have foreseen what would happen to the Dandy Demon or how this employee would respond. But there was the possibility that blame would eventually settle on her, and to save her own flesh, she was determined to learn exactly what Joe and the officers had decided on the bridge.

"Does your face hurt?" she inquired.

"A little bit."

"How many times did he strike you?"

"Ten," Joe guessed. "Maybe more."

She winced. "The weapon?"

"A rough piece of iron," he said. "Barnes had a souvenir from the first asteroid he helped work."

Infrared sensors and the hidden T-scanner were observing the subject closely. Examining the telemetry, she asked, "Why did you pick Mr Barnes?"

"That's in my report."

"Remind me, Joe. What were your reasons?"

"He was big enough to matter."

"And what did the others think about the man?"

"You mean the crew?" Joe shrugged. "He was one of us. Maybe he was quiet and kept to himself —"

"Bullshit."

When he wanted, Joe could produce a shy, boyish grin.

"He was different from the rest of you," the psychiatrist pointed out. "And I'm not talking about his personality."

"You're not," Joe agreed.

She produced images of the dead man. The oldest photograph showed a skinny, homely male in his middle twenties, while the most recent example presented a face that was turning fat – a normal consequence that came with the most intrusive, all-encompassing genetic surgery.

"Your colleague was midway through some very radical genetic surgery."

"He was," Joe agreed.

"He belonged to the Rebirth Movement."

"I'm sorry. What does this have to do with anything?" Joe's tone was serious. Perhaps even offended. "Everybody is human, even if they aren't *sapiens* anymore. Isn't that the way our laws are written?"

"You knew exactly what you were doing, Joe."

He didn't answer.

"You selected Barnes. You picked him because you understood that nobody would stand in your way."

Again, Joe used his shy, winning grin.

"Where did you meet with Barnes?"

"In his cabin."

"And what did you say to him?"

"That I loved him," Joe explained. "I told him that I was envious of his courage and vision. Leaving our old species was noble. Was good. I thought that he was intriguing and very beautiful. And I told him that to save his important life, as well as everybody else, I was going to sacrifice myself. I was staying behind with the robots."

"You lied to him."

"Except Barnes believed me."

"Are you sure?"

"Yes."

"When you told him you loved him . . . did you believe he was gay . . . ?"

"He wasn't."

"But if he had been? What would you have done if he was flattered by your advances?"

"Oh, I could have played that game too."

The psychiatrist hesitated. "What do you mean?"

"If Barnes preferred guys, then I would have seduced him. If I'd thought there was enough time, I mean. I would have convinced him to remain behind and save my life. Really, the guy was pretty easy to manipulate, all in all. It wouldn't have taken much to convince him that being the hero was his idea in the first place."

"You could have managed all that?"

Joe considered hard before saying, "If I'd had a few days to work with, sure. Easy. But you're probably right. A couple hours wasn't enough time."

The psychiatrist had stopped watching the telemetry, preferring to stare at the creature sitting across from her.

Quietly, she said, "OK."

Joe waited patiently.

"What did Mr Barnes say to you?" she asked. "After you professed your love, how did he react?"

"'You're lying.'" Joe didn't just quote the man, but he sounded like him too. The voice was thick and a little slow, wrapped around vocal chords that were slowly changing their configuration. "'You've slept with every damn woman on this ship,' he told me. 'Except our dyke captain.'"

The psychiatrist's face stiffened slightly.

"Is that true?" she muttered.

Joe gave her a moment. "Is what true?"

"Never mind." She found a new subject to pursue. "Mr Barnes' cabin was small, wasn't it?"

"The same as everybody's."

"And you were at opposite ends of that room. Is that right?"

"Yes."

By birth, Barnes was a small man, but his Rebirth had given him temporary layers of fat that would have eventually been transformed into new tissues and bones, and even two extra fingers on each of his long, lovely hands. The air inside that cubbyhole had smelled of biology, raw and distinctly strange. But it wasn't an unpleasant odour. Barnes had been drifting beside his bed, and next to him was the image of the creature he wanted to become – a powerful, fur-draped entity with huge golden eyes and a predator's toothy grin. The cabin walls were covered with his possessions, each lashed in place to keep them out of the way. And on the surface of what was arbitrarily considered to be the ceiling, Barnes had painted the motto of the Rebirth movement:

TO BE TRULY HUMAN IS TO BE DIFFERENT.

"Do you want to know what I told him?" asked Joe. "I didn't put this in my report. But after he claimed I was sleeping with those women . . . do you know what I said that got him to start pounding on me . . . ?"

The psychiatrist offered a tiny, almost invisible nod.

"I said, 'I'm just playing with those silly bitches. They're toys to me. But you, you're nothing like them. Or like me. You're going to be a spectacular creature. A vision of the future, you lucky shit. And before I die, please, let me blow you. Just to get the taste of another species.'"

She sighed. "All right."

"And that's when I reached for him —"

"You're heterosexual," she complained.

"I was saving lives," Joe responded.

"You were saving your own life."

"And plenty of others too," he pointed out. Then with a grin, he added, "You don't appreciate what I was prepared to do, doctor. If it meant saving the rest of us, I was capable of anything."

She once believed that she understood Joe Carroway. But in every possible way, she had underestimated the man sitting before her, including his innate capacity to measure everybody else's nature.

"The crew was waiting in the passageway outside," he mentioned. "With the captain and engineer, they were crowding in close, listening close, trying to hear what would happen. All these good decent souls, holding their breaths, wondering if I could pull this trick off."

She nodded again.

"They heard the fight, but it took them a couple minutes to force the door. When they got inside, they found Barnes all over me and that lump of iron in his hand." Joe paused before asking, "Do you know how blood looks in space? It forms a thick mist of bright red drops that drift everywhere, sticking to every surface."

"Did Mr Barnes strike you?"

Joe hesitated, impressed enough to show her an appreciative smile. "What does it say in my report?"

"But it seems to me . . ." Her voice trailed away. "Maybe you were being honest with me, Joe. When you swore that you would have done anything to save yourself, I should have believed you. So I have to wonder now . . . what if you grabbed that piece of asteroid and turned it on yourself? Mr Barnes would have been surprised. For a minute or so, he might have been too stunned to do anything but watch you strike yourself in the face. Then he heard the others breaking in, and he naturally kicked over to you and pulled the weapon from your hand."

"Now why would I admit to any of that?" Joe replied.

Then he shrugged, adding, "But really, when you get down to it, the logistics of what happened aren't important. What matters is that I gave the captain a very good excuse to lock that man up, which was how she cleared her conscience before we could abandon ship."

"The captain doesn't look at this as an excuse," the psychiatrist mentioned.

"No?"

"Barnes was violent, and her conscience rests easy."

Joe asked, "Who ordered every corn-system destroyed before we abandoned the Demon Dandy? Who left poor Barnes with no way even to call home?"

"Except by then, your colleague was a prisoner, and according to our corporate laws, the captain was obligated to silence the criminal to any potential lawsuits." The woman kept her gaze on Joe. "Somebody had to be left behind, and in the captain's mind, you weren't as guilty as Mr Barnes."

"I hope not."

"But nobody was half as cold or a tenth as ruthless as you were, Joe."

His expression was untroubled, even serene.

"The captain understands what you are. But in the end, she had no choice but to leave the other man behind."

Joe laughed. "Human or not, Barnes wasn't a very good person. He was mean-spirited and distant, and even if nobody admits it, I promise you: nobody on the ship has lost two seconds sleep over what happened there."

The psychiatrist nearly spoke, then hesitated.

Joe leaned forward. "Do you know how it is, doctor? When you're a kid, there's always something that you think you're pretty good at. Maybe you're the best on your street, or you're the best at school. But you never know how good you really are. Not until you get out into the big world and see what other people can do. And in the end, we aren't all that special. Not extra clever or pretty or strong. But for a few of us, a very few, there comes a special day when we realize that we aren't just a little good at something. We are great.

"Better than anybody ever, maybe.

"Do you know how that feels, ma'am?"

She sighed deeply. Painfully. "What are you telling me, Joe?"

He leaned back in his chair, absently scratching at the biggest bandage on his iron-battered face. "I'm telling you that I am excellent at sizing people up. Even better than you, and I think you're beginning to appreciate that. But what you call being a borderline psychopath is to me just another part of my bigger, more important talent."

"You're not borderline anything," she said.

He took no offence from the implication. "Here's what we can learn from this particular mess: Most people are secretly bad. Under the proper circumstances, they will gladly turn on one of their own and feel nothing but good about it afterwards. But when the stakes are high and world's going to shit, I can see exactly what needs to be done. Unlike everybody else, I will do the dirtiest work. Which is a rare and rich and remarkable gift, I think."

She took a breath. "Why are you telling me this, Joe?"

"Because I don't want to be a mechanic riding clunky spaceships," he confessed. "And I want your help, doctor. All right? Will you find me new work . . . something that's closer to my talents. Closer to my heart.

"Would you do that for me, pretty lady?"

NATURAL KILLER

At four in the morning, the animals slept. Which was only reasonable since this was a zoo populated entirely by synthetic organisms. Patrons didn't pay for glimpses of furry lumps, formerly wild and now slumbering in some shady corner. What they wanted were spectacular, one-of-a-kind organisms doing breathtaking feats, and doing them in daylight. But high metabolisms had their costs, and that's why the creatures now lay in their cages and grottos, inside glass boxes and private ponds, beautiful eyes closed while young minds dreamed about who-could-say-what.

For the moment, privacy was guaranteed, and that was one fine reason why desperate men would agree to meet in that public place.

Slipping into the zoo unseen brought a certain ironic pleasure too.

But perhaps the most important, at least for Joe, were the possibilities inherent with that unique realm.

A loud, faintly musical voice said, "Stop, Mr Carroway. Stop where you are, sir. And now please . . . lift your arms for us and dance in a very slow circle . . ."

Joe was in his middle thirties. His big and strong and rigorously trained body was dressed in casual white slacks and a new grey shirt. His face had retained its boyish beauty, a prominent scar creasing the broad forehead and a several-day growth of beard lending a rough, faintly threadbare quality to his otherwise immaculate appearance. Arms up, he looked rather tired. As he turned slowly, he took deep breaths, allowing several flavours of radiation to wash across his body, reaching into his bones.

"I see three weapons." The voice came from no particular direction. "One at a time, please, lower the weapons and kick each of them toward the fountain. If you will, Mr Carroway."

A passing shower had left the plaza wet and slick. Joe dropped the Ethiopian machine pistol first, followed the matching Glocks. Each time he kicked one of the guns, it would spin and skate across the red bricks, each one ending up within a hand's length of the fountain – an astonishing feat, considering the stakes and his own level of exhaustion.

Unarmed, Joe stood alone in the empty plaza.

The fountain had a round black-granite base, buried pumps shoving water up against a perfect sphere of transparent crystal. The sphere was a monstrous, stylized egg. Inside the egg rode a never-to-be-born creature – some giant beast with wide black eyes and gill slits, its tail half-formed and the stubby little limbs looking as though they could turn into arms or legs, or even tentacles. Joe knew the creature was supposed to be blind, but he couldn't shake the impression that the eyes were watching him. He watched the creature slowly roll over and over again, its egg suspended on nothing but a thin chilled layer of very busy water.

Eventually five shapes emerged from behind the fountain.

"Thank you, Mr Carroway," said the voice. Then the sound system was deactivated, and with a hand to the mouth, one figure shouted, "A little closer, sir. If you will."

That familiar voice was attached to the beckoning arm.

Two figures efficiently disabled Joe's weapons. They were big men, probably Rebirth Neanderthals or some variation on that popular theme. A third man looked like a Brilliance-Boy, his skull tall and deep, stuffed full with a staggering amount of brain tissue. The fourth human was small and slight, held securely by the Brilliance-Boy; even at a distance, she looked decidedly female.

Joe took two steps and paused.

The fifth figure, the one that spoke, approached near enough to show his face. Joe wasn't surprised, but he pretended to be. "Markel? What are you doing here?" He laughed as if nervous. "You're not one of them, are you?"

The man looked as *sapien* as Joe.

With a decidedly human laugh, Markel remarked, "I'm glad to hear that you were fooled, Mr Carroway. Which of course means that you killed Stanton and Humphrey for no good reason."

Joe said nothing.

"You did come here alone, didn't you?"

"Yes."

"Because you took a little longer than I anticipated."

"No I didn't."

"Perhaps not. I could be mistaken."

Markel never admitted to errors. He was a tall fellow, as bald as an egg and not particularly handsome. Which made his disguise all the more effective. The new Homo species were always physically attractive, and they were superior athletes, more often than not. Joe had never before met a Rebirth who had gone through the pain and expense and then not bothered to grow some kind of luxurious head of hair as a consequence.

"You have my vial with you, Joseph. Yes?"

"Joe. That's my name." He made a show of patting his chest pocket.

"And the sealed recordings too?"

"Everything you asked for." Joe looked past Markel. "Is that the girl?"

Something about the question amused Markel. "Do you honestly care if she is?"

"Of course I care."

"Enough to trade away everything and earn her safety?"

Joe said nothing.

"I've studied your files, Joseph. I have read the personality evaluations, and I know all about your corporate security work, and even all those wicked sealed records covering the last three years. It is a most impressive career. But nothing about you, sir – nothing in your nature or your history – strikes me as being sentimental. And I cannot believe that this girl matters enough to convince you to make this exchange."

Joe smiled. "Then why did I come here?"

"That's my question too."

Joe waited for a moment, then suggested, "Maybe it's money?"

"Psychopaths always have a price," Markel replied. "Yes, I guessed as it would be something on those lines."

Joe reached into his shirt pocket. The vial was diamond, smaller than a pen and only halfway filled with what looked to be a plain white powder. But embossed along the vial's length were the ominous words: NATURAL KILLER.

"How much do you want for my baby, Joseph?"

"Everything," he said.

"And what does that mean?"

"All the money."

"My wealth? Is that what you're asking for?"

"I'm not asking," Joe said. "Don't be confused, Markel. This is not a negotiation. I am demanding that you and your backers give me every last cent in your coffers. And if not, I will ruin everything that you've worked to achieve. You sons-of-bitches."

Markel had been born *sapien* and gifted, and his minimal and very secret steps to leave his species behind had served to increase both his mind and his capacity for arrogance. But he was stunned to hear the ultimatum. To make such outrageous demands, and in these circumstances! He couldn't imagine anybody with that much gall. Standing quite still, his long arms at his side, Markel tried to understand why an unarmed man in these desperate circumstances would have any power over him. What wasn't he seeing? No reinforcements were coming; he was certain of that. Outside this tiny circle, nobody knew anything. This *sapien* was bluffing, Markel decided. And with that, he began to breathe again, and he relaxed, announcing, "You're right, this is not a negotiation. And I'm telling you no."

Inside the same shirt pocket was a child's toy – a completely harmless lump of luminescent putty stolen from the zoo's museum. Joe shoved the vial into the bright red plaything, and before Markel could react, he flung both the putty and vial high into the air.

Every eye watched that ruddy patch of light twirl and soften, and then plunge back to the earth.

Beside the plaza was a deep acid-filled moat flanked by a pair of high fences, electrified and bristling with sensors. And on the far side were woods and darkness, plus the single example of a brand new species designed to bring huge crowds through the zoo's front gate.

The Grendel.

"You should not have done that," Markel said with low, furious voice. "I'll just have you killed now and be done with you."

Joe smiled, lifting his empty hands over his head. "Maybe you should kill me. If you're so positive that you can get your precious KILLER back."

That's when Joe laughed at the brilliant bastard.

But it was the girl who reacted first, squirming out of the Brilliance-Boy's hands to run straight for her lover.

No one bothered to chase her down.

She stopped short and slapped Joe.

"You idiot," she spat.

He answered her with a tidy left hook.

Then one of the big soldiers shot a tacky round into Joe's chest, pumping in enough current to drop him on the wet bricks, leaving him hovering between consciousness and white-hot misery.

"You idiot."

The girl repeated herself several times, occasionally adding a dismissive, "Moron", or "Fool", to her invectives. Then as the electricity diminished, she leaned close to his face. "Don't you understand? We were never going to use the bug. We don't want to let it loose. It's just one more way to help make sure you *sapiens* won't declare war on us. Natural Killer is our insurance policy, and that's it."

The pain diminished to a lasting ache.

Wincing, Joe struggled to sit up. While he was down, smart-cuffs had wrapped themselves around his wrists and ankles. The two soldiers and the Brilliance-Boy were standing before the Grendel's large enclosure. They had donned night-goggles and were studying the schematics of the zoo, tense voices discussing how best to slip into the cage and recover the prize.

"Joe," she said, "how can you be this stupid?"

"Comes naturally, I guess."

To the eye, the girl was beautiful and purely *sapien*. The long black hair and rich brown skin sparkled in the plaza's light. The word "natural" was a mild insult among the Rebirths. She sat up, lips pouting. Like Markel, the young woman must have endured some minimal rearrangement of her genetics. Usually these new humans carried extra pairs of chromosomes. But despite rumours that some of the Rebirths were hiding among the naturals, this was the first time Joe had knowingly crossed paths with them.

"I am stupid," he admitted. Then he looked at Markel, adding, "Both of you had me fooled. All along."

That was a lie, but Markel had to smile. Of course he was clever, and of course no one suspected the truth. Behind that grim old face was enough self-esteem to keep him believing that he would survive the night.

The idiot.

Markel and his beautiful assistant glanced at each other.

Then the Brilliance-Boy called out. "We'll use the service entrance to get in," he announced. "Five minutes to circumvent locks and cameras, I should think."

"Do it," Markel told them.

"You'll be all right here?"

The scientist lifted a pistol over his head. "We're fine. Just go. Get my child out of that cage, now!"

That left three people on the plaza, plus the monster locked inside the slowly revolving crystal egg.

"The plague is just an insurance policy, huh?"

Joe threw out the question, and waited.

After a minute, the girl said, "To protect us from people like you, yes."

He put on an injured expression. "Like me? What's that mean?"

She glanced at Markel. Then with a cold voice, she said, "He showed me your history, Joe. After our first night together . . ."

"And what did it tell you?"

"When you were on the Demon Dandy, you saved yourself by leaving a Rebirth behind. And you did it in a cold, calculating way."

He shrugged, smiled. "What else?"

"After joining the security arm of the corporation, you distinguished yourself as a soldier. Then you went to work for the UN, as a contractor, and your expertise has been assassinations."

"Bad men should be killed," Joe said flatly. "Evil should be removed from the world. Get the average person to be honest, and he'll admit that he won't lose any sleep, particularly if the monster is killed with a single clean shot."

"You are horrible," she maintained.

"If I'm so horrible," said Joe, "then do the world a favour. Shoot me in the head."

She began to reach behind her back, then thought better of it.

Markel glanced at both of them, pulling his weapon closer to his body. But nothing seemed urgent, and he returned to keeping watch over the Grendel's enclosure.

"I suppose you noticed," Joe began.

The girl blinked. "Noticed what?"

"In my career, I've killed a respectable number of Rebirths."

The dark eyes stared at him. Then very quietly, with sarcasm, she said, "I suppose they were all bad people."

"Drug lords and terrorists, or hired guns in the service of either." Joe shook his head, saying, "Legal murder is easy. Clean, clear-cut. A whole lot more pleasant than the last few weeks have been, I'll admit."

Markel looked at him. "I am curious, Joseph. Who decided you were the ideal person to investigate our little laboratory?"

"You don't have a little lab," said Joe. "There aren't ten or twelve better-equipped facilities when it comes to high-end genetic research."

"There aren't even twelve," the man said, bristling slightly. "Perhaps two or three."

"Well, you wouldn't have found this item in any official file," Joe said. "But a couple months ago, I was leading a team that hit a terror-cell in Alberta. Under interrogation, the Rebirth boss started making threats about unleashing something called Natural Killer on us. On the poor helpless *sapiens*. He claimed that we'd be wiped out of existence, and the new species could then take over. Which is their right, he claimed, and as inevitable as the next sunrise."

His audience exchanged looks.

"But that hardly explains how you found your way to me," Markel pointed out.

"There was a trail. Bloody in places, but every corpse pointing in your general direction."

Markel almost spoke. But then came the creak of a heavy door being opened. Somewhere in the back of the Grendel's enclosure, three pairs of goggled eyes were peering out into the jungle and shadow.

"It's an amazing disease," Joe stated. "Natural Killer is."

"Quiet," Markel warned.

But the girl couldn't contain herself. She bent low, whispering, "It is," while trying to burn him with her hateful smile.

"The virus targets old, outmoded stretches of the human genome," Joe continued. "From what I can tell – and I'm no expert in biology, of course

– but your extra genes guarantee you wouldn't get anything worse than some wicked flu symptoms out of the bug. Is that about right?"

"A tailored pox phage," she said. "Rapidly mutating, but always fatal to *sapiens* genome."

"So who dreamed up the name?" Joe glanced at Markel and then winked at her. "It was you, wasn't it?"

She sat back, grinning.

"And it's going to save you? From bastards like me, is it?"

"You won't dare lift a hand against us," she told Joe. "As soon as you realize we have this weapon, and that it could conceivably wipe your entire species off the face of the earth . . ."

"Smart," he agreed. "Very smart."

From the Grendel enclosure came the sharp soft noise of a gun firing. One quick burst and then two single shots from the same weapon. Then, silence.

Markel lifted his pistol reflexively.

"So when do you Rebirths make your official announcement?" Joe asked. "And how do you handle this kind of event? Hold a news conference? Unless you decide on a demonstration, I suppose. You know, murder an isolated village, or devastate one of the orbital communities. Just to prove to the idiots in the world that you can deliver on your threats."

A voice called from the enclosure.

"I have it," one of the soldiers shouted.

Joe turned in time to see the reddish glow rise off the ground, partly obscured by the strong hand holding it. But as the arm cocked, ready to throw the prize back into the plaza, there was a grunt, almost too soft to be heard. A terrific amount of violence occurred in an instant, without fuss. Then the red glow appeared on a different portion of the jungle floor, and the only sound was the slow lapping of a broad happy tongue.

Markel cursed.

The girl stood up and looked.

Markel called out a name, and nobody answered. And then somebody else fired their weapon in a spray pattern, cutting vegetation and battering the high fence on the far side of the moat.

"I killed it," the second soldier declared. "I'm sure."

The Brilliance-Boy offered a few cautionary words.

"I do feel exceptionally stupid," Joe said. "Tell me again: why exactly do you need Natural Killer?"

The girl stared at him and then stepped back.

"I didn't know we were waging a real war against you people," he continued. "I guess we keep that a secret, what with our political tricks and PR campaigns. Like when we grant you full citizenship. And the way we force you to accept the costs and benefits of all the laws granted to human beings everywhere —"

"You hate us," she interrupted. "You despise every last one of us."

Quietly, Joe assured her, "You don't know what I hate."

She stiffened, saying nothing.

"This is the situation. As I see it." Joe paused for a moment. "Inside that one vial, you have a bug that could wipe out your alleged enemies. And by enemies, I mean people that look at you with suspicion and fear. You intend to keep your doomsday disease at the ready, just in case you need it."

"Of course."

"Except you'll have to eventually grow more of it. If you want to keep it as a credible, immediate threat. And you'll have to divide your stocks and store them in scattered, secure locations. Otherwise assholes like me are going to throw the bugs in a pile and burn it all with a torch."

She watched Joe, her sore jaw clamped tight.

"But having stockpiles of Natural Killer brings a different set of problems. Who can trust who not to use it without permission? And the longer this virus exists, the better the chance that the Normals will find effective fixes to keep themselves safe. Vaccines. Quarantine laws. Whatever we need to weather the plague, and of course, give us our chance to take our revenge afterwards."

The red glow had not moved. For a full minute, the little jungle had been perfectly, ominously silent.

Markel glanced at Joe and then back at the high fence. He was obviously fighting the urge to shout warnings to the others. That could alert the Grendel. But it took all his will to do nothing.

"You have a great, great weapon," Joe allowed. "But your advantage won't last."

The girl was breathing faster now.

"You know what would be smart? Before the Normals grow aware of your power, you should release the virus. No warnings, no explanations. Do it before we know what hit us, and hope you kill enough of us in the first week that you can permanently gain the upper hand."

"No," Markel said, taking two steps toward the enclosure. "We don't have more than a sample of the virus, and it is just a virus."

"Meaning what?"

"Diseases are like wildfires," he explained. "You watch them burn, and you can't believe that anything would survive the blaze. But afterwards there are always islands of green surrounded by scorched forest." The man had given this considerable thought. "Three or four billion *sapiens* might succumb. But that would still leave us in the minority, and your vengeance would be horrible and probably fatal."

The girl showed a satisfied smile.

But then Joe said, "Except," and laughed quietly.

The red glow had not moved, and the jungle stood motionless beneath the stars. But Markel had to look back at his prisoner, a new terror pushing away the old.

"What do you mean?" the girl asked. "Except what?"

"You and your boss," Joe said. "And who knows how many thousands of others too. Each one of you looks exactly like us. You sound like us." Then he grinned and smacked his lips, adding, "And you taste like us, too. Which means that your particular species, whatever you call yourselves . . . you'll come out of this nightmare better than anybody . . ."

The girl's eyes opened wide, a pained breath taken and then held deep.

"Which of course is the central purpose of this gruesome exercise," Joe said. "I'm sure Dr Markel would have eventually let you in on his dirty secret. The real scheme hiding behind the first, more public plan."

Markel stared at the cuffed, unarmed man sitting on the bricks, too astonished to react.

"Is this true?" the girl whispered.

There was a moment of hesitation, and then the genius managed to shake his head, lying badly when he said, "Of course not. The man is telling you a crazy wild story, dear."

"And you know why he never told you?" Joe asked.

"Shut up," Markel warned.

The girl was carrying a weapon, just as Joe had guessed. From the back of her pants, she pulled out a small pistol, telling Markel, "Let him talk."

"Darling, he's trying to poison you —"

"Shut up," she snapped.

Then to Joe, she asked, "Why didn't he tell me?"

"Because you're a good decent person, or at least you like to think so. And because he knew how to use that quality to get what he wants." Showing a hint of compassion, Joe sighed. "Markel sure knows how to motivate you. First, he makes you sleep with me. And then he shows you my files, convincing you that I can't be trusted or ignored. Which is why you slept with me three more times. Just to keep a close watch over me."

The girl lowered her pistol, and she sobbed and then started to lift pistol again.

"Put that down," Markel said.

She might have obeyed, given another few moments to think.

But then Markel shot her three times. He did it quickly and lowered his weapon afterwards, astonished that he had done this very awful thing. It took his great mind a long sloppy moment to wrap itself around the idea that he could murder in that particular fashion, that he possessed such brutal, prosaic power. Then he started to lift his gun again, searching for Joe.

With bound hands and feet, Joe leaped for the dead girl. And with her little gun, he put a bullet into Markel's forehead.

The blind, unborn monster watched the drama from inside its crystal egg.

A few moments later, a bloody Brilliance Boy ran up to the Grendel's fence, and with a joyous holler flung the red putty and diamond vial back onto the plaza. Then he turned and fired twice at shadows before something monstrous lifted him high, shook him once, and then folded him backwards before neatly tearing him in two.

THE TICKING BOMB

"Goodness," the prisoner muttered. "It's the legend himself."

Joe said nothing.

"Well, now I feel especially terrified." She laughed weakly before coughing, a dark bubble of blood clinging to the split corner of her mouth. Then she closed her eyes for a moment, suppressing her pain as she turned her head to look straight at him. "You must be planning all kinds of horrors," she said. "Savage new ways to break my spirit. To bare my soul."

Gecko slippers gripped the wall. Joe watched the prisoner. He opened his mouth as if to speak but then closed it again, one finger idly scratching a spot behind his left ear.

"I won't be scared," she decided. "This as an honour, having someone this famous assigned to my case. I must be considered an exceptionally important person."

He seemed amused, if just for a moment.

"But I'm not a person, am I? In your eyes, I'm just another animal."

What she was was a long, elegant creature – the ultimate marriage between human traditions and synthetic chromosomes. Four bare arms were restrained with padded loops and pulled straight out from the shockingly naked body. Because hair could be a bother in space, she had none. Because dander was an endless source of dirt in freefall, her skin would peel away periodically, not unlike the worn skin of a cobra. She was smart, but not in the usual ways that the two or three thousand species of Rebirths enhanced their minds. Her true genius lay in social skills. Among the Antfolk, she could instantly recognize every face and recall each name, knowing at least ten thousand nest-mates as thoroughly as two *sapiens* who had been life-long pals. Even among the alien faces of traditional humans, she was a marvel at reading faces, deciphering postures. Every glance taught her something more about her captors. Each careless word gave her room to maneuver. That's why the first team – a pair of low-ranking interrogators, unaware of her importance – was quickly pulled from her case. She had used what was obvious, making a few offhand observations, and in the middle of their second session, the two officers had started to trade insults and then punches.

"A Carroway-worthy moment," had been the unofficial verdict.

A second, more cautious team rode the skyhook up from Quito, and they were wise enough to work their prisoner without actually speaking to her. Solitude and sensory deprivation were the tools of choice. Without adequate stimulation, an Antfolk would crumble. And the method would have worked, except that several weeks would have been required. But time was short: Several intelligence sources delivered the same ominous warning. This was not just another low-level prisoner. The Antfolk, named Glory, was important. She might even be essential. Days mattered now, even hours. Which was why a third team went to work immediately, doing their awful best from the reassuring confines of a UN bunker set two kilometers beneath the Matterhorn.

That new team was composed of AIs and autodocs with every compassion system deleted. Through the careful manipulation of pain and hallucinogenic narcotics, they managed to dislodge a few nuggets of intelligence as well as a level of hatred and malevolence that they had never before witnessed.

"The bomb is mine," she screamed. "I helped design it, and I helped build it. Antimatter triggers the fusion reaction, and it's compact and efficient, and shielded to where it's nearly invisible. I even selected our target. Believe me . . . when my darling detonates, everything is going to change!"

At that point, their prisoner died.

Reviving her wasted precious minutes. But that was ample time for the machines to discuss the obvious possibilities and then calculate various probabilities. In the time remaining, what could be done? And what was impossible? Then without a shred of ego or embarrassment, they contact one of the only voices that they consider more talented than themselves.

And now Joe stood before the battered prisoner.

Again, he scratched at his ear.

Time hadn't touched him too roughly. He was in his middle forties, but his boyish good looks had been retained through genetics and a sensible indifference to sunshine. Careful eyes would have noticed the fatigue in his body, his motions. A veteran soldier could have recognized the subtle erosion of spirit. And a studied gaze of the kind that an Antfolk would employ would detect signs of weakness and doubt that didn't quite fit when it came to one of the undisputed legends of this exceptionally brutal age.

Joe acted as if there was no hurry. But his heart was beating too fast, his belly rolling with nervous energy. And the corners of his mouth were a little too tight, particularly when he looked as if he wanted to speak.

"What are you going to do with me?" his prisoner inquired.

And again, he scratched at his scalp, something about his skin bothering him to distraction.

She was puzzled, slightly.

"Say something," Glory advised.

"I'm a legend, am I?" The smile was unchanged, bright and full, but behind the polished teeth and bright green eyes was a quality . . . some trace of some subtle emotion that the prisoner couldn't quite name.

She was intrigued.

"I know all about you," Glory explained. "I know your career in detail, successes and failures both."

For an instant, Joe looked at the lower pair of arms, following the long bones to where they met within the reconfigured hips.

"Want to hear something ironic?" she asked.

"Always."

"The asteroid you were planning to mine? Back during your brief, eventful career as an astronaut, I mean. It's one of ours now."

"Until your bomb goes boom," he mentioned. "And then that chunk of iron and humanity is going to be destroyed. Along with every other nest of yours, I would guess."

"Dear man. Are you threatening me?"

"You would be the better judge of that."

She managed to laugh. "I'm not particularly worried."

He said nothing.

"Would we take such an enormous risk if we didn't have the means to protect ourselves?"

Joe stared at her for a long while. Then he looked beyond her body, at a random point on the soft white wall. Quietly he asked, "Who am I?"

She didn't understand the question.

"You've seen some little digitals of me. Supposedly you've peaked at my files. But do you know for sure who I am?"

She nearly laughed. "Joseph Carroway."

He closed his eyes.

"Security," he said abruptly. "I need you here. Now."

Whatever was happening, it was interesting. Despite the miseries inflicted on her mind and aching body, the prisoner twisted her long neck, watching three heavily armed soldiers kick their way into her cell.

"This is an emergency," Joe announced. "I need everybody. Your full squad in here now."

The ranking officer was a small woman with the bulging muscles. A look of genuine admiration showed in her face. She knew all about Joe Carroway. Who didn't? But her training and regulations held sway. This man might have saved the Earth, on one or several occasions, but she still had the fortitude to remind him, "I can't bring everybody in here. That's against regulations."

Joe nodded.

Sighing, he said, "Then we'll just have to make do."

In an instant, with a smooth, almost beautiful motion, he grabbed the officer's face and broke her jaw and then pulled a weapon from his pocket, shoving the stubby barrel into the nearest face.

The pistol made a soft, almost negligible sound.

The remains of the skull were scattered into the face of the next guard.

He shot that soldier twice and then killed the commanding officer before grabbing up her weapon, using his security code to override its safety and then leaping into the passageway. The prisoner strained at her bonds. Mesmerized, she counted the soft blasts and the shouts, and she stared, trying to see through the spreading fog of blood and shredded brain matter. Then a familiar figure reappeared, moving with a commendable grace despite having a body designed to trek across the savannas of Africa.

"We have to go," said Joe. "Now."

He was carrying a fresh gun and jumpsuit.

"I don't believe this," she managed.

He cut her bonds and said, "Didn't think you would." Then he paused, just for an instant. "Joe Carroway was captured and killed three years ago, during the Tranquility business. I'm the lucky man they spliced together to replace that dead asshole."

"You're telling me —?"

"Suit up. Let's go, lady."

"You can't be." She was numb, fighting to understand what was possible, no matter how unlikely. "What species of Rebirth are you?"

"I was an Eagle," he said.

She stared at the face. Never in her life had she tried so hard to slice through skin and eyes, fighting to decipher what was true.

"Suit up," he said again.

"But I don't see —?"

Joe turned suddenly, launching a recoilless bundle out into the hall. The detonation was a soft crack, smart-shards aiming only for armour and flesh. Sparing the critical hull surrounding them.

"We'll have to fight our way to my ship," he warned.

Slowly, with stiff clumsy motions, she dressed herself. Then as the suit retailored itself to match her body, she said again, "I don't believe you. I don't believe any of this."

Now Joe stared at her.

Hard.

"What do you think, lady?" he asked. "You rewrote your own biology in a thousand crazy ways. But one of your brothers – a proud Eagle – isn't able to reshape himself? He can't take on the face of your worst enemy? He can't steal the dead man's memories? He is allowed this kind of power, all in a final bid to get revenge for what that miserable shit's done to us?"

She dipped her head.

No, she didn't believe him.

But three hours later, as they were making the long burn out of Earth orbit, a flash of blue light announced the abrupt death of fifty million humans and perhaps half a million innocents.

"A worthy trade," said the man strapped into the seat beside her.

And that was the moment when Glory finally offered two of her hands to join up with one of his, and after that, her other two hands as well.

Her nest was the nearest Antfolk habitat. Waiting at the moon's L5 Lagrange point, the asteroid was a smooth blackish ball, heat-absorbing armor slathered deep over the surface of a fully infested cubic kilometer – a city where thousands of bodies squirmed about in freefall, thriving inside a maze of warm tunnels and airy rooms. Banks of fusion reactors powered factories and the sun-bright lights. Trim, enduring ecosystems created an endless feast of edible gruel and free oxygen. The society was unique, at least within the short rich history of the Rebirths. Communal and technologically adept, this species had accomplished much in a very brief period. That's why it was so easy for them to believe that they alone now possessed the keys to the universe.

Joe was taken into custody. Into quarantine. Teams drawn from security and medical castes tried to piece together the truth, draining off his blood and running electrodes into his skull, inflicting him with induced emotions and relentless urges to be utterly, perfectly honest.

The Earth's counter-assault arrived on schedule – lasers and missiles followed by robot shock troops. But the asteroid's defence network absorbed every blow. Damage was minor, casualties light, and before larger attacks could be organized, the Antfolk sent an ultimatum to the UN: one hundred additional fusion devices had been smuggled to the Earth's surface, each now hidden and secured, waiting for any excuse to erupt.

For the good of humankind, the Antfolk were claiming dominion over everything that lay beyond the Earth's atmosphere. Orbital facilities and the lunar cities would be permitted, but only if reasonable rents were paid. Other demands included nationhood status for each of the Rebirth species, reimbursements for all past wrongs, and within the next year, the total and permanent dismantling of the United Nations.

Both sides declared a ragged truce.

Eight days later, Joe was released from his cell, guards escorting him along a tunnel marked by pheromones and infrared signatures. Glory was waiting, wearing her best gown and a wide, hopeful smile. The Antfolk man beside her seemed less sure. He was a giant hairless creature. Leader of the nest's political caste, he glared at the muscular *sapien*, and with a cool smooth voice said, "The tunnel before you splits, Mr Carroway. Which way will you travel?"

"What are my choices?" asked the prisoner.

"Death now," the man promised. "Or death in some ill-defined future."

"I think I prefer the future," he mentioned. Then he glanced at Glory, meeting her worried smile with a wink and slight nod.

Glancing at her superior, Glory spoke with eyes and the silent mouth.

"I don't relish the idea of trusting you," the man confessed. "But every story you've told us, with words and genetics, has been confirmed by every available source. You were once a man named Magnificent. We see traces of your original DNA inside what used to be Joseph Carroway. It seems that our old enemy was indeed taken prisoner during the Luna Revolt. The Eagles were a talented bunch. They may well have camouflaged you inside Mr Carroway's body and substance. A sorry thing that the species was exterminated – save for you, of course. But once this new war is finished, I promise you . . . my people will reconstitute yours as well as your culture, to the best of our considerable abilities."

Joe dipped his head. "I can only hope to see that day, sir."

The man had giant white eyes and tiny blond teeth. Watching the prisoner did no good; he could not read this man's soul. So he turned to Glory, prompting her with the almost invisible flick of a finger.

She told Joe, "The UN attack was almost exactly as you expected it to be, and your advice proved extremely useful. Thank you."

Joe showed a smug little smile.

"And you've told us a lot we didn't know," Glory continued. "Those ten agents on Pallas. The Deimos booby trap. And how the UN would go about searching for the rest of our nuclear devices."

"Are your bombs safe?"

She glanced at her superior, finding encouragement in some little twitch of the face. Then she said, "Yes."

"Do you want to know their locations?" the man asked Joe.

"No," Joe blurted.

Then in the next breath, he added, "And I hope you don't know that either, sir. You're too much of a target, should somebody grab you up."

"More good advice," the man replied.

That was the instant when Joe realized that he wouldn't be executed as a precaution. More than three years of careful preparation had led to this: the intricate back-story and genetic trickery were his ideas. Carrying off every aspect of this project, from the Eagle's identity to his heightened capacity to read bodies and voices, was the end result of hard training. Hundreds of specialists, all AIs, had helped produce the new Joseph Carroway. And then each one of those machines was wiped stupid and melted to an anonymous slag.

On that day when he dreamed up this outrageous plan, the Antfolk were still just one of a dozen Rebirths that might or might not cause trouble someday.

Nobody could have planned for these last weeks.

Killing the guards to free the woman was an inspiration and a necessity, and he never bothered to question it. One hundred fusion bombs were scattered across a helpless, highly vulnerable planet, and setting them off would mean billions dead, and perhaps civilization too. Sacrificing a few soldiers to protect the rest of the world was a plan born of simple, pure mathematics.

The Antfolk man coughed softly. "From this point on, Joe . . . or should I call you Magnificent?"

With an appealing smile, he said, "I've grown attached to Joe."

The other two laughed gently. Then the man said, "For now, you are my personal guest. And except for security bracelets and a bomblet planted inside your skull, you will be given the freedoms and responsibilities expected of all worthy visitors."

"Then I am grateful," said Joe. "Thank you to your nation and to your good species, sir. Thank you so much."

The truce was shattered with one desperate assault – three brigades of shock troops riding inside untested star-drive boosters, supported by every weapon system and reconfigured com-laser available to the UN. The cost was twenty thousand dead *sapiens* and a little less than a trillion dollars. One platoon managed to insert itself inside Joe's nest, but when the invaders grabbed the nursery and a thousand young hostages, he distinguished himself by helping plan and then lead the counterstrike. All accounts made him the hero. He killed several of the enemy, and alone, he managed to disable the warhead that would have shattered their little world. But even the most grateful mother insisted on looking at their saviour with detached pleasure. Trust was impossible. Joe's face was too strange, his reputation far too familiar. Pheromones delivered the mandatory thanks, and there were a few cold gestures wishing the hero well. But there were insults too, directed at him and at the long lovely woman who was by now sleeping with him.

In retribution for that final attack, the Antfolk detonated a second nuclear weapon, shearing off one slope of the Hawaii volcano and killing eight million with the resulting tsunami.

Nine days later, the UN collapsed, reformed from the wreckage and then shattered again before the next dawn. What rose from that sorry wreckage enjoyed both the laws to control every aspect of the mother world and the mandate to beg for their enemies' mercy.

The giants in the sky demanded, and subsequently won, each of their original terms.

For another three months, Joe lived inside the little asteroid, enduring a never-subtle shunning.

Then higher powers learned of his plight and intervened. For the next four years, he travelled widely across the new empire, always in the company of Glory, the two of them meeting an array of leaders, scientists, and soldiers – that last group as suspicious as any, but always eager to learn whatever little tricks the famous Carroway might share with them.

To the end, Joe remained under constant observation. Glory made daily reports about his behaviours and her own expert impressions. Their relationship originally began under orders from Pallas, but when she realized that they might well remain joined until one or both died, she discovered, to her considerable surprise, that she wasn't displeased with her fate.

In the vernacular of her species, she had floated into love . . . and so what if the object of her affections was an apish goon . . . ?

During their journey, they visited twenty little worlds, plus Pallas and Ceres and Vesta. The man beside her was never out of character. He was intense and occasionally funny, and he was quick to learn and astute with his observations about life inside the various nests. Because it would be important for the last member of a species, Joe pushed hard for the resurrection of the fabled Eagles. Final permission came just as he and Glory were about to travel to outer moons of Jupiter. Three tedious, painful days were spent inside the finest biogenic lab in the solar system. Samples of bone and marrow and fat and blood were cultured, and delicate machines rapidly separated what had been Joe from the key traces of the creature that had been dubbed Magnificent.

A long voyage demands large velocities, which was why the transport ship made an initial high-gee burn. The crew and passengers were strapped into elaborate crash seats, their blood laced with comfort drugs, eyes and minds distracted by immersion masks. Six hours after they leaped clear of Vesta, Joe disabled each of his tracking bracelets and then the bomblet inside his head, and then he slipped out of his seat, fighting the terrific acceleration as he worked his way to the bridge.

The transport was an enormous, utterly modern spaceship. The watch officer was on the bridge, stretched out in his own crash seat. Instantly suspicious and without even the odour of politeness, he demanded that his important passenger leave at once. Joe smiled for a moment. Then he turned without complaint or hesitation, showing his broad back to the spidery fellow before he climbed out of view.

What killed the officer was a fleck of dust carrying microchines – a fleet of tiny devices that attacked essential genes found inside the Antfolk metabolism, causing a choking sensation, vomiting and then death.

Joe returned to the bridge and sent a brief, heavily coded message to the Earth. Then he did a cursory job of destroying the ship's security systems. With luck, he had earned himself a few hours of peace. But when he returned to his cabin, Glory was gone. She had pulled herself out of her seat, or somebody had roused her. For a moment, he touched the deep padding, allowing the sheets to wrap around his arm and hand, and he carefully measured the heat left behind by her long, lovely body.

"Too bad," he muttered.

The transport carried five fully equipped lifepods. Working fast, Joe killed the hanger's robots and both of the resident mechanics. Then he dressed in the only pressure suit configured for his body and crippled all but one of the pods. His plan was to flee without fuss. The pods had potent engines and were almost impossible to track. There was no need for more corpses and mayhem. But he wanted a backup plan, in case, which was what he was working on when the ship's engines abruptly cut out.

A few minutes later, an armed team crawled into the hanger through a random vent.

There was no reason to fight, since Joe was certain to lose.

Instead he surrendered his homemade weapons and looked past the nervous crew, finding the lovely hairless face that he knew better than his own.

"What did you tell them?" Glory asked.

"Tell who?"

"Your people," she said. "The Earth."

Glory didn't expect answers, much less any honest words. But the simple fact was that whatever he said now and did now was inconsequential: Joe would survive or die in this cold realm, but what happened next would change nothing that was about to happen elsewhere.

"Your little home nest," he began.

She drifted forward, and then hesitated.

"It will be dead soon," he promised. "And nothing can be done to save it."

"Is there a bomb?"

"No," he said. "A microchine plague. I brought it with me when I snatched you away, Glory. It was hiding inside my bones."

"But you were tested," she said.

"Not well enough."

"We hunted for diseases," she insisted. "Agents. Toxins. We have the best minds anywhere, and we searched you inside and out . . . and found nothing remotely dangerous . . ."

He watched the wind leak out of her. Then very quietly, Joe admitted, "You might have the best minds. And best by a long ways. But we have a lot more brains down on the Earth, and I promise, a few of us are a good deal meaner than even you could ever be."

Enduring torture, Glory never looked this frail or sad.

Joe continued. "Every world you've taken me to is contaminated. I made certain of that. And since you managed to set off two bombs on my world, the plan is to obliterate two of your worlds. After that, if you refuse to surrender, it's fair to guess that every bomb and disease on both sides is going be set free. Then in the end, nobody wins. Ever."

Glory could not look at him.

Joe laughed, aiming to humiliate.

He said, "I don't care how smart or noble you are. Like everybody else, you're nothing but meat and scared brains. And now you've been thrown into a dead-end tunnel, and I am Death standing at the tunnel's mouth.

"The clock is ticking. Can you make the right decision?"

Glory made a tiny, almost invisible motion with her smallest finger, betraying her intentions.

Joe leaped backward. The final working lifepod was open, and he dived inside as its hatch slammed shut, moments before the doomed could manage one respectable shot. Then twenty weapons were firing at a hull designed to shrug off the abuse of meteors and *sapien* weapons. Joe pulled himself into the pilot's ill-fitting chair, and once he was strapped down, he triggered his just-finished booby trap.

The fuel onboard two other pods exploded.

With a silent flash of light, the transport shattered, spilling its contents across the black and frigid wilderness.

THE ASSASSIN

"Eat," the voice insisted. "Don't our dead heroes deserve their feast?"

"So that's what I am."

"A hero? Absolutely, my friend!"

"I meant that I'm dead." Joe looked across the table, measuring his host – an imposing Chinese-Indian male wearing the perfect suit and a face conditioned to convey wisdom and serene authority. "I realize that I got lost for a time," he admitted. "But I never felt particularly deceased."

"Perhaps that's how the dead perceive their lot. Yes?"

Joe nodded amiably, and using his stronger arm, stabbed at his meal. Even in lunar gravity, every motion was an effort.

"Are your rehabilitations going well?"

"They tell me that I'm making some progress."

"Modesty doesn't suit you, my friend. My sources assure me that you are amazing your trainers. And I think you know that perfectly well."

The meat was brown and sweet, like duck, but without the grease.

"You presently hold the record, Joe."

Joe looked up again.

"Five and a half years in freefall," said Mr Li, slowly shaking his head. "Assumed dead, and in your absence, justly honoured for the accomplishments of an intense and extremely successful life. I'm sorry no one was actively searching for you, sir. But no earth-based eye saw the Antfolks' spaceship explode, much less watched the debris scatter. So we had no starting point, and to make matters worse, your pod had a radar signature little bigger than a fist. You were very fortunate to be where you happened to be, drifting back into the inner solar system. And you were exceptionally lucky to be noticed by that little mining ship. And just imagine your reception if that ship's crew had been anyone but *sapiens* . . ."

The billionaire let his voice trail away.

Joe had spent years wandering through the solar system, shepherding his food and riding roughshod over his recycling systems. That the lifepod was designed to carry a dozen bodies was critical; he wouldn't have lasted ten months inside a lesser bucket. But the explosion that destroyed the transport damaged the pod, leaving it dumb and deaf. Joe had soon realized that nobody knew where he was, or even that he was. After the first year, he calculated that he might survive for another eight, but it would involve more good luck and hard focus than even he might have been able to summon.

"I want to tell you, Joe. When I learned about your survival, I was thrilled. I turned to my dear wife and my children and told everybody, 'This man is a marvel. He is a wonder. A one-in-a-trillion kind of *sapien*.'"

Joe laughed quietly.

"Oh, I'm well-studied in Joseph Carroway's life," his host boasted. "After the war, humanity wanted to know who to thank for saving the Earth. That's why the UN released portions of your files. Millions of us became amateur scholars. I myself acquired some of less doctored accounts of your official history. I've also read your five best biographies, and just like every other *sapien*, I have enjoyed your immersion drama – WARRIOR ON THE RAMPARTS. As a story, it takes dramatic licence with your life. Of course. But WARRIOR was and is a cultural phenomenon, Joe. A stirring tale of courage and bold skill in the midst of wicked, soulless enemies."

Joe set his fork beside the plate.

"After all the misery and death of these last two decades," said Mr Li, "the world discovered the one man that could be admired, even emulated. A champion for the people."

He said the word, "People" with a distinct tone.

Then Mr Li added, "Even the Rebirths paid to see WARRIOR. Paid to read the books and the sanitized files. Which is nicely ironic, isn't it? Your actions probably saved millions of them. Without your bravery, how many species would be ash and bone today?"

Joe lifted his fork again. A tenth of his life had been spent away from gravity and meaningful exercise. His bones as well as the connecting muscles had withered to where some experts, measuring the damage, cautioned their patient to expect no miracles. It didn't help that cosmic radiation had slashed through the pod's armour and through him. Even now, the effects of malnutrition could be seen in the spidery hands and forearms, and how his own lean meat hung limp on his suddenly ancient bones.

Mr Li paused for a moment, an observant smile building. Whatever he said next would be important.

Joe interrupted, telling him, "Thank you for the meal, sir."

"And thank you for being who you are, sir."

When Joe left the realm of the living, this man was little more than an average billionaire. But the last five years had been endlessly lucrative for Li Enterprises. Few had more money, and when ambition was thrown into the equation, perhaps no other private citizen wielded the kind power enjoyed by the man sitting across the little table.

Joe stabbed a buttery carrot.

"Joe?"

He lowered the carrot to the plate.

"Can you guess why I came to the moon? Besides to meet you over dinner, of course."

Joe decided on a shy, self-deprecating smile.

Which encouraged his host. "And do you have any idea what I wish to say to you? Any intuitions at all?"

Six weeks ago, Joe had abruptly returned to the living. But it took three weeks to rendezvous with a hospital ship dispatched just for him, and that vessel didn't touch down on the moon until the day before yesterday. But those two crews and his own research had shown Joe what he meant to the human world. He was a hero and a rich but controversial symbol. And he was a polarizing influence in a great debate that still refused to die – an interspecies conflict forever threatening to bring on another terrible war.

Joe knew exactly what the man wanted from him, but he decided to offer a lesser explanation.

"You're a man with enemies," he mentioned.

Mr Li didn't need to ask, "Who are my enemies?" Both men understood what was being discussed.

"You need somebody qualified in charge of your personal security," Joe suggested.

The idea amused Mr Li. But he laughed a little too long, perhaps revealing a persistent unease in his own safety. "I have a fine team of private bodyguards," he said at last. "A team of *sapiens* who would throw their lives down to protect mine."

Joe waited.

"Perhaps you aren't aware of this, sir. But our recent tragedies have changed our government. The UN presidency now commands a surprising amount of authority. But he, or she, is still elected by adult citizens. A pageant that maintains the very important illusion of a genuine, self-sustaining democracy."

Joe leaned across the table, nodding patiently.

"Within the next few days," said Mr Li, "I will announce my candidacy for that high office. A few months later, I will win my party's primary elections. But I'm a colourless merchant with an uneventful life story. I need to give the public one good reason to stand in my camp. What I have to find is a recognizable name that will inspire passions on both sides of the issues."

"You need a dead man," Joe said.

"And what do you think about that, sir?"

"That I'm still trapped in that damned pod." Leaning back in his chair, Joe sighed. "I'm starving to death, bored to tears, and dreaming up this insanity just to keep me a little bit sane."

"Sane or not, do you say yes?"

He showed his host a thoughtful expression. Then very quietly, with the tone of a joke, Joe asked, "So which name sits first on the ballot?"

As promised, Mr Li easily won the Liberty Party's nomination, and with a force-fed sense of drama, the candidate announced his long-secret choice for running mate. By then Joe had recovered enough to endure the Earth's relentless tug. He was carried home by private shuttle, and then with braces under his trouser legs and a pair of lovely and strong women at his side, the celebrated war hero strode into an auditorium/madhouse. Every motion had been practiced, every word scripted, yet somehow the passion and heart of the event felt genuine. Supporters and employees of the candidate pushed against one another, fighting for a better look at the running mate. With a natural sense for when to pause and how to wave at the world, Joe's chiselled, scarred face managed to portray that essential mixture of fearlessness and sobriety. Li greeted him with open arms – the only time the two men would ever embrace. Buoyed by the crowd's energy, Joe felt strong, but when he decided to sit, he almost collapsed into his chair. Li was a known quantity; everyone kept watch over the new man. When Joe studied his boss, he used an expression easily confused for admiration. The acceptance speech was ten minutes of carefully crafted theatre designed to convey calm resolve wrapped around coded threats. For too long, Li said, their old honourable species had allowed its traditions to be undercut and diluted. When unity mattered, people followed every path. When solidarity was a virtue, evolution and natural selection were replaced by whim and caprice. But the new leadership would right these past wrongs. Good men and good women had died in the great fight, and new heroes were being discovered every day. (Li glanced at his running mate, winning a burst of applause; and Joe nodded at his benefactor, showing pride swirled with modesty.) The speech concluded with a promise for victory in the general election, in another six weeks, and Joe applauded with everyone else. But he stood slowly, as if weak, shaking as a very fit old man might shake.

He was first to offer his hand of congratulations to the candidate.

And he was first to sit again, feigning the aching fatigue that he had earned over these last five years.

Three days later, a lone sniper was killed outside the arena where the controversial running mate was scheduled to appear. Joe's security detail was lead by a career police officer, highly qualified and astonishingly efficient. Using a quiet, unperturbed tone, he explained what had happened, showing his boss images of the would-be assassin.

"She's all *sapien*," he mentioned. "But with ties to the Rebirths. A couple lovers, and a lot of politics."

Joe scanned the woman's files as well the pictures. "Was the lady working alone?"

"As far as I can tell, yes. Sir."

"What's this gun?"

"Homemade," the officer explained. "An old Czech design grown in a backyard nano-smelter. She probably thought it would make her hard to trace. And I suppose it would have: an extra ten minutes to track her down through the isotope signatures and chine-marks."

Joe asked, "How accurate?"

"The rifle? Well, with that sight and in competent hands —"

"Her hands, I mean. Was she any good?"

"We don't know yet, sir." The officer relished these occasional conversations. After all, Joe Carroway had saved humanity on at least two separate occasions, and always against very long odds. "I suppose she must have practised her marksmanship somewhere. But the thing is . . ."

"What?"

"This barrel isn't as good as it should be. Impurities in the ceramics, and the heat of high-velocity rounds had warped it. Funny as it sounds, the more your killer practised, the worse her gun would have become."

Joe smiled and nodded.

The officer nodded with him, waiting for the legend to speak.

"It might have helped us," Joe mentioned. "If we'd let her take a shot or two, I mean."

"Help us?"

"In the polls."

The officer stared at him for a long moment. The dry Carroway humour was well known. Was this a worthy example? He studied the man whom he was sworn to defend, and after considerable reflection, the officer decided to laugh weakly and shrug his shoulders. "But what if she got off one lucky shot?"

Joe laughed quietly. "I thought that's what I was saying."

To be alone, Joe took a lover.

The young woman seemed honoured and more than a little scared. After passing through security, they met inside his hotel room, and when the great man asked to send a few messages through her links, she happily agreed. Nothing about those messages would mean anything to anybody. But when they reached their destinations, other messages that had waited for years were released, winding their way to the same secure e-vault. Afterwards Joe had sex with her, and then she let him fix her a drink that he laced with sedatives. Once she was asleep, he donned arm and leg braces designed for the most demanding physical appearances. Then Joe opened a window, and ten storeys above the bright cold city, he climbed out onto the narrow ledge and slipped through the holes that he had punched in the security net.

Half an hour later, shaking from exhaustion, Joe was standing at the end of a long alleyway.

"She was a mistake," he told the shadows.

There was no answer.

"A blunder," he said.

"Was she?" a deep voice asked.

"But you were always a little too good at inspiring others," Joe continued. "Getting people to be eager, making them jump before they were ready."

In the darkness, huge lungs took a deep, lazy breath.

Then the voice mentioned, "I could kill you myself. I could kill you now." It was deep and slow, and the voice always sounded a little amused. Just a little. "No guards protecting you, and from what I see, you aren't carrying more than a couple of baby pistols."

Joe said, "That's funny."

Silence.

"I'm not the one you want," he said. "You'd probably settle for me. But think about our history, friend. Look past all the public noise. And now remember everything that's happened between you and me."

Against an old brick wall, a large body stirred. Then the voice said, "Remind me."

Joe mentioned, "Baltimore."

"Yes."

"And Singapore."

"We helped each other there."

"And what about Kiev?"

"I was in a gracious mood. A weak mood, looking back."

Joe smiled. "Regardless of moods, you let me live."

The voice seemed to change, rising from a deeper part of the unseen body. It sounded wetter and very warm, admitting, "I knew what you were, Joe. I understood how you thought, and between us, I felt we had managed an understanding."

"We had that, yes."

"You have always left my species alone."

"No reason not to."

"We weren't any threat to you."

"You've never been in trouble, until now."

"But this man you are helping . . . this Li monster . . . he is an entirely different kind of creature, I believe . . ."

Joe said nothing.

"And you are helping him. Don't deny it."

"I won't."

A powerful sigh came from the dark, carrying the smell of raw fish and peppermint.

"Two days from now," Joe began.

"That would be the Prosperity Conference."

"The monster and I will be together, driving through Sao Paulo. Inside a secure vehicle, surrounded by several platoons of soldiers."

"I would imagine so."

"Do you know our route?"

"No, as it happens. Do you?"

"Not yet."

The shadows said nothing, and they didn't breathe, and they held themselves still enough that it was possible to believe that they had slipped away entirely.

Then very softly, the voice asked, "When will you learn the route?"

"Tomorrow night."

"But as you say, the level of protection will be considerable."

"So you want things to be easy? Is that it?"

The laugh was smooth, unhurried. "I want to know your intentions, Joe. Having arranged this collision of forces, what will you do? Pretend to fall ill at the last moment? Stand on the curb and offer a hearty wave as your benefactor rolls off to his doom?"

"Who says I won't ride along?"

This time the laugh was louder, confident and honestly amused. "Suppose you learn the route and share it with me. And imagine that despite my logistical nightmares, I have time enough to assemble the essential forces. Am I to understand that you will be riding into that worst kind of trouble?"

"I've survived an ambush or two."

"When you were young. And you still had luck to spend."

Joe said nothing.

"But you do have a reasonable point," the voice continued. "If you aren't riding with the monster, questions will be asked. Doubts will rise. Your character might have to endure some rather hard scrutiny."

"Sure, that's one fine reason to stay with him."

"And another is?"

"You fall short. You can't get to Li in the end. So don't you want to have a second option in place, just in case?"

"What option?"

"Me."

That earned a final long laugh.

"Point taken, my friend. Point taken."

The limousine could have been smaller and less pretentious, but the man strapped into its safest seat would accept nothing less than a rolling castle. And following the same kingly logic, the limousine's armour and its plasma weapons were just short of spectacular. The AI driver was capable of near-miracles, if it decided to flee. But in this vehicle, in most circumstances, the smart tactic would be to stand your ground and fight. One hundred *sapien* soldiers and ten times as many mechanicals were travelling the same street, sweeping for enemies and the possibility of enemies. In any battle, they would count for quite a lot, unless of course some of them were turned, either through tricks or bribery. Which was as much consideration as Joe gave to the problem of attacking the convoy. Effort wasted was time lost. What mattered was the next ten or eleven minutes and how he handled himself and how he managed to control events within his own limited reach.

Li and two campaign wizards were conferring at the centre of the limousine. Polls were a painful topic. They were still critical points behind the frontrunners, and the propaganda wing of his empire was getting worried. Ideas for new campaigns were offered, and then buried. Finally the conversation fell into glowering silences and hard looks at a floor carpeted with cultured white ermine.

That was when Joe unfastened his harness and approached.

Li seemed to notice him. But his assistant – a cold little Swede named Hussein – took the trouble to ask, "What do you need, Mr Carroway?"

"Just want to offer my opinion," he said.

"Opinion? About what?"

Joe made a pistol with his hand and pointed it at Hussein, and then he jerked so suddenly that the man flinched.

"What is it, Joe?" asked Li.

"People are idiots," Joe said.

The candidate looked puzzled, but a moment later, something about those words intrigued him. "In what way?"

"We can't see into the future."

"We can't?"

"None of us can," said Joe. He showed a smile, a little wink. "Not even ten seconds ahead, in some cases."

"Yet we do surprisingly well despite our limitations." The candidate leaned back, trying to find the smoothest way to dismiss this famous name.

"We can't see tomorrow," said Joe, "but we are shrewd."

"People, you mean?"

"Particularly when ten billion of us are thinking hard about the same problem. And that's why you aren't going to win this race. Nobody sees what will happen, but in this case, it's very easy to guess how the Li presidency will play out."

Hussein bristled.

But Li told him and everyone else to let the man speak.

"You're assuming that I hate these other species," Joe told him. "In fact, you've counted on it from the start. But the truth is . . . I don't have any compelling attachment to *sapiens*. By and large, I am a genuinely amoral creature. While you, sir . . . you are a bigot and a genocidal asshole. And should you ever come to power, the solar system has a respectable chance of collapsing into full-scale civil war."

Li took a moment. Then he pointed out, "In my life, I have killed no one. Not a single Rebirth, or for that matter, a *sapien*."

"Where I have slaughtered thousands," Joe admitted. "And stood aside while millions more died."

"Maybe you are my problem. Perhaps we should drop you from the ticket."

"That is an option," Joe agreed.

"Is this what you wanted to say to me? That you wish to quit?"

Joe gave the man a narrow, hard-to-read smile.

"My life," he said.

"Pardon?" Li asked.

"Early in life, I decided to live as if I was very important. As if I was blessed in remarkable ways. In my hand, I believed, were the keys to a door that would lead to a worthy future, and all that was required of me was that I make hard calculations about matters that always seem to baffle everyone else."

"I'm sorry, Joe. I'm not quite sure —"

"I have always understood that I am the most important person there is, on the Earth or any other world within our reach. And I have always been willing to do or say anything that helps my climb to the summit."

"But how can you be that special? Since that's my place to be . . ."

Li laughed, and his assistants heartily joined in.

Again, Joe made a pistol with his hand, pointing his index finger at the candidate's face.

"You are a scary individual," Li remarked. Then he tried to wave the man back, looking at no one when he mentioned, "Perhaps a medical need needs to be diagnosed. A little vacation for our dear friend, perhaps."

Hussein gave an agreeable nod.

In the distance, a single soft pop could be heard.

Joe slipped back to his seat.

His security man was sitting beside him. Bothered as well as curious, he asked, "What was that all about?"

"Nothing," said Joe. "Never mind."

Another mild pop was followed by something a little louder, a little nearer.

Just in case, the security man reached for his weapon. But he discovered that his holster was empty now.

Somehow his gun had found its way into Joe's hand.

"Stay close to me," Joe said.

"You know I will," the man muttered weakly.

Then came the flash of a thumb-nuke, followed by the sharp wail of people screaming, begging with Fortune to please show mercy, to please save their glorious, important lives.

WORLD'S END

Three terms as President finally ended with an assortment of scandals – little crimes and large ones, plus a series of convenient non-disclosures – and those troubles were followed by the sudden announcement that Joseph Carroway would slide gracefully into retirement. After all that, there was persistent talk about major investigations and unsealing ancient records. Tired allegations refused to die. Could the one-time leader of humanity be guilty of even one-tenth of the crimes that he was rumoured to have committed? In judicial circles, wise minds discussed the prospects of charging and convicting the Old Man on the most egregious insults to common

morality. Politicians screamed for justice without quite defining what justice required. Certain species were loudest in their complaints, but that
was to be expected. What was more surprising, perhaps, were the numbers
of pure *sapiens* who blamed the President for every kind of ill. But most of
the pain and passion fell on one-time colleagues and allies. Unable to sleep
easily, they would sit at home, secretly considering their own complicities
in old struggles and more recent deeds, as well as non-deeds and omissions
that seemed brilliant at the moment, but now, in different light, looked
rather ominous.

But in the end, nothing substantial happened.

In the end, the Carroway Magic continued to hold sway.

His successor was a talented and noble soul. No one doubted her passion for peace or the decency of her instincts. And she was the one citizen
of the inhabited Worlds who could sit at a desk and sign one piece of
parchment, forgiving crimes and transgressions and mistakes and misjudg-
ments. And then she showed her feline face to the cameras, winning over
public opinion by pointing out that trials would take decades, verdicts
would be contested for centuries, and every last one of the defendants had
been elected and then served every citizen with true skill.

The new president served one six-year term before leaving public life.

Joseph Carroway entered the next race at the last moment, and he won
with a staggering seventy per cent mandate. But by then the Old Man was
exactly that: a slowed, sorry image of his original self, dependent on a talented staff and the natural momentum of a government that achieved the
ordinary without fuss or too much controversy.

Fifteen months into Joe's final term, an alien starship entered the solar
system. In physical terms, it was a modest machine: twenty cubic kilometers of metal and diamond wrapped around empty spaces. There seemed
to be no crew or pilot. Nor was there a voice offering to explain itself.
But its course was clear from the beginning. Moving at nearly one per
cent of light speed, the Stranger, as it had been dubbed, missed the moon
by a few thousand kilometers. Scientists and every telescope studied its
configuration, and two nukes were set off in its vicinity – neither close
enough to cause damage, it was hoped, but both producing EM pulses
that helped create a detailed portrait of what lay inside. Working separately, teams of AI savants found the same awful hypothesis, and a single
Antfolk nest dedicated to the most exotic physics proved that hypothesis
to everyone's grim satisfaction. By then, the Stranger was passing through
the sun's corona, its hull red-hot and its interior awakening. What might
have been a hundred thousand year sleep was coming to an end. In less
than a minute, this very unwelcome guest had vanished, leaving behind a
cloud of ions and a tiny flare that normally would trouble no one, much
less spell doom for humankind.

They told Joe what would happen.

His science advisor spoke first, and when there was no obvious reaction
on that perpetually calm face, two assistants threw their interpretations of

these events at the Old Man. Again, nothing happened. Was he losing his grip finally? This creature who had endured and survived every kind of disaster . . . was he suddenly lost, at wits end and such?

But no, he was just letting his elderly mind assemble the puzzle that they had given him.

"How much time?" he asked.

"Ten, maybe twelve minutes," the science advisor claimed. "And then another eight minutes before the radiation and scorching heat reach us."

Others were hoping for a longer delay. As if twenty or thirty minutes would offer some kind of help.

Joe looked out the window, and with a wry smile pointed out, "It is a beautiful day."

In other words, the sun was up, and they were dead.

"How far will the damage extend?" he asked.

Nobody replied.

The Antfolk ambassador was watching from her orbital embassy, tied directly into the President's office. For a multitude of reasons, she despised this *sapien*. But he was the ruler of the Great Nest, and in awful times, she was willing to do or say anything to help him, even if that meant telling him the full, undiluted truth.

"Our small worlds will be vaporized. The big asteroids will melt and seal in the deepest parts of our nests." Then with a sad gesture of every hand, she added, "Mars is worse off than Earth, what with the terraforming only begun. And soon there won't be any solid surfaces on the Jovian moons."

Joe turned back to his science advisor. "Will the Americas survive?"

"In places, maybe." The man was nearly sobbing. "The flares will finish before the sun rises, and even with the climate shifts and the ash falls, there's a fair chance that the atmosphere will remain breathable."

Joe nodded.

Quietly, firmly, he told everyone, "I want an open line to every world. In thirty seconds."

But before anyone could react, the youngest assistant screamed out, "Why? Why would aliens do this awful thing to us?"

Joe laughed, just for a moment.

Then with a grandfatherly voice, he said, "Because they can. That's why."

"It has been an honour to serve as your President," Joe told an audience of two and then three and then four billion. But most citizens were too busy to watch this unplanned speech – an important element in his gruesome calculations. "But my days are done. The sun has been infiltrated, its hydrogen stolen to use in the manufacture of an amazing bomb, and virtually everybody in the range of my voice will be dead by tomorrow.

"If you are listening to me, listen carefully.

"The only way you will survive in the coming hell is to find those very few people whom you trust most. Do it now. Get to your families, hold hands with your lovers. Whoever you believe will watch your back always. And then you need to search out those who aren't aware of what I am telling you to do.

"Kill those other people.

"Whatever they have of value, take it.

"And store their corpses, if you can. In another week or two, you might relish the extra protein and fat."

He paused, just for a moment.

Then Joe said, "For the next ten generations, you will need to think only about yourselves. Be selfish. Be vicious. Be strong, and do not forget.

"Kindness is a luxury.

"Empathy will be a crippling weakness.

"But in another fifty generations, we can rebuild everything that we have lost here today. I believe that, my friends. Goodness can come again. Decency can flower in any rubble. And in fifty more generations after that, we will reach out to the stars together.

"Keep that thought close tonight, and always.

"One day, we will punish the bastards that did this awful thing to us. But to make that happen, a few of you must find the means to survive . . . !"

THE SKY THAT WRAPS THE WORLD ROUND, PAST THE BLUE AND INTO THE BLACK

Jay Lake

Highly prolific new writer Jay Lake seems to have appeared nearly everywhere with short work in the last few years, including *Asimov's*, *Interzone*, *Clarkesworld*, *Jim Baen's Universe*, *Tor.com*, *Strange Horizons*, *Aeon*, *Postscripts*, *Electric Velocipede*, *Futurismic*, and many other markets, producing enough short fiction to already have released four collections even though his career is only a few years old: *Greetings from Lake Wu*, *Green Grow the Rushes-Oh*, *American Sorrows*, and *Dogs in the Moonlight*. His novels include *Rocket Science*, *Trial of Flowers*, *Mainspring*, and, most recently, *Escapement* and *Madness of Flowers*. He's the co-editor, with Deborah Layne, of the prestigious Polyphony anthology series, now in six volumes, and has also edited the anthologies *All-Star Zeppelin Adventure Stories*, with David Moles, and *TEL: Stories*. Coming up is a new novel, *Green*, a new anthology, co-edited with Nick Gevers, *Other Earths*, and a space opera trilogy, *Sunspace*. He won the John W. Campbell Award for Best New Writer in 2004. Lake lives in Portland, Oregon.

In the deceptively quiet story that follows, he shows us an artisian hard at work at his craft – one he has no choice but to pursue, no matter what the cost.

I BELIEVE THAT all things eventually come to rest. Even light, though that's not what they tell you in school. How do scientists know? A billion billion years from now, even General Relativity might have been demoted to a mere Captain. Photons will sit around in little clusters of massless charge, bumping against one another like boats in the harbour at Kowloon.

The universe will be blue then, everything from one cosmic event horizon to the other the colour of a summer sky.

This is what I tell myself as I paint the tiny shards spread before me. Huang's men bring them to me to work with. We are creating value, that gangster and I. I make him even more immensely wealthy. Every morning that I wake up still alive is his gratuity to me in return.

It is a fair trade.

My life is comfortable in the old house along the alley with its central court crowded with bayberry trees. A narrow gutter trickles down the centre of the narrow roadway, slimed a greenish black with waste slopped out morning and evening from the porch steps alongside. The roofs are traditional, with sloping ridges and ornamented tile caps. I have studied the ones in my own courtyard. They are worn by the years, but I believe I can see a chicken stamped into each one. "Cock," my cook says with his thick Cantonese accent, never seeing the vulgar humour.

Even these tired old houses are topped with broadband antennae and tracking dishes which follow entertainment, intelligence or high finance beamed down from orbit and beyond. Sometimes the three are indistinguishable. Private data lines sling on pirated staples and cable ties from the doddering concrete utility poles. The poles themselves are festooned with faded prayer flags, charred firecracker strings, and remnants of at least half a dozen generations of technology dedicated to transmission of *something*.

Tesla was right. Power is nothing more than another form of signal, after all. If the lights come on at a touch of your hand, civilization's carrier wave is intact.

Despite the technology dangling overhead in rotting layers, the pavement itself holds life as old as China. Toddlers wearing only faded shirts toss stones in the shadows. A mangy chow dog lives beneath a vine-grown cart trapped against someone's garden wall. Amahs air their families' bedding over wooden railings worn shiny with generations of elbows. Tiny, wrinkled men on bicycles with huge trays balanced behind their seats bring vegetables, newspapers, meat and memory sticks to the back doors of houses. Everything smells of ginger and night soil and the ubiquitous mould.

I wake each day with the dawn. Once I overcome my surprise at remaining alive through another sunrise, I tug on a cheaply printed yukata and go hunting for coffee. My cook, as tiny and wrinkled as the vendors outside but decorated with *tong* tattoos that recall another era long since lost save for a few choppy-sockie movies, does not believe in the beverage. Instead he is unfailing in politely pressing a bitter-smelling black tea on me at every opportunity. I am equally unfailing in politely refusing it. The pot is a delicate work of porcelain which owes a great deal to a China before electricity and satellite warfare. It is painted a blue almost the shade of cornflowers, with a design of a round-walled temple rising in a stepped series of roofs over some Oriental pleasaunce.

I've seen that building on postage stamps, so it must be real somewhere. Or had once been real, at least.

After the quiet combat of caffeine has concluded its initial skirmish, I shuffle to my workroom where my brushes await me. Huang has that strange combination of stony patience and sudden violence which I have observed among the powerful in China. When my employer decides I have failed in my bargain, I am certain it is the cook who will kill me. I like to imagine his last act as the light fades from my eyes will be to pour tea down my throat as a libation to see my spirit into the next world.

There is a very special colour that most people will never see. You have to be out in the Deep Dark, wrapped in a skinsuit amid the hard vacuum where the solar wind sleets in an invisible radioactive rain. You can close your eyes there and let yourself float in a sensory deprivation tank the size of the universe. After a while, the little mosaics that swirl behind your eyelids are interrupted by tiny, random streaks of the palest, softest, sharpest electric blue.

I've been told the specks of light are the excitation trails of neutrinos passing through the aqueous humour of the human eye. They used to bury water tanks in Antarctic caves to see those things, back before orbit got cheap enough to push astronomy and physics into space where those sciences belong. These days, all you have to do is go for a walk outside the planet's magnetosphere and be patient.

That blue is what I capture for Huang. That blue is what I paint on the tiny shards he sends me wrapped in day-old copies of the high orbital edition of *Asahi Shimbun*. That blue is what I see in my dreams.

That blue is the colour of the end of the universe, when even the light is dying.

Out in the Deep Dark we called them caltrops. They resemble jacks, that old children's toy, except with four equally-spaced arms instead of six, and slightly larger, a bit less than six centimeters tip to tip. Many are found broken, some aren't, but even the broken ones fit the pattern. They're distributed in a number of places around the belt, almost entirely in rocks derived from crustal material. The consensus had long been that they were mineral crystals endemic to Marduk's surface, back before the planet popped its cork 250 megayears ago. Certainly their microscopic structure supported the theory – carbon lattices with various impurities woven throughout.

I couldn't say how many of the caltrops were discarded, damaged, or simply destroyed by being slagged in the guts of some ore processor along with their enclosing rock. Millions, maybe.

One day someone discovered that the caltrops had been manufactured. They were technology remnants so old that our ancestors hadn't even gotten around to falling out of trees when the damned things were fabricated. The human race was genetic potential lurking in the germline of some cynodont therapsid when those caltrops had been made.

It had not occurred to anyone before that discovery to consider this hypothesis. The fact that the question came up at all was a result of a serious misunderstanding of which I was the root cause. In my greed and misjudgment I forced the loss of a device one of my crewmates discovered, an ancient piece of tech that could have allowed us to do *something* with those caltrops. My contribution to history, in truth, aside from some miniscule role in creating a portion of Huang's ever-growing millions. That the discovery of the caltrops' nature arose from human error is a mildly humorous grace note to the confirmation that we are indeed not alone in the universe.

Or at least weren't at one point.

The artificial origin of the caltrops has been generally accepted. What these things are remains a question that may never be answered, thanks to me. Most people prefer not to discuss the millions of caltrops lost to Belt mining operations over the decades that Ceres Mineral Resources has been in business.

Despite their carbon content, caltrops viewed under Earth-normal lighting conditions are actually a dull grayish-blue. This fact is not widely known on Earth. Not for the sake of being a secret – it's not – but because of *Deep Dark Blues*, the Academy Award-winning virteo about Lappet Ugarte. She's the woman who figured so prominently in the discovery of the artificial origin of the caltrops. The woman I tried to kill, and steal from. In their wisdom, the producers of that epic Bollywood docudrama saw fit to render the caltrops about twice as large as they are in real life, glowing an eerie Cherenkov blue. I suppose the real thing didn't look like much on camera.

So most of the citizens of planet Earth don't believe that they're seeing actual outer space caltrops unless they're seeing end-of-the-universe blue.

Huang sends me paint in very small jars. They're each cladded with lead foil, which makes them strangely heavy. When I take the little lead-lined caps off, the paint within is a sullen, radioactive copy of the colour I used to see behind my eyelids out there in the Deep Dark.

Every time I dip my brush, I'm drawing out another little spray of radiation. Every time I lick the bristles, I'm swallowing down a few drops of cosmic sleet. I'm the last of the latter day Radium Girls.

Huang doesn't have to order the old cook to kill me. I'm doing it myself, every day.

I don't spend much time thinking about where my little radioactive shards go when they leave my house off the alleyway here in Heung Kong Tsai. People buy them for hope, for love, to have a piece of the unspeakably ancient past. There's a quiet revolution in human society as we come to terms with that history. For some, like a St Christopher medal, touching it is important. Cancer will be important as well, if they touch them too often.

The truly odd thing is that the shards I sit here and paint with the electric blue of a dying heaven are actual caltrop shards. We're making fakes out of the real thing, Huang and I.

A truth as old as time, and I'm dressing it in special effects.

I swear, sometimes I kill myself.

*

This day for lunch the cook brings me a stir fry of bok choi and those strange, slimy mushrooms. He is as secretive as one of the Japanese soldiers of the last century who spent decades defending a lava tube on some Pacific island. There is tea, of course, which I of course ignore. We could play that ritual with an empty pot just as easily, but the cook executes his culinary warfare properly.

The vegetables are oddly ragged for having recently spent time in a searing hot wok. They are adorned with a pungent tan sauce the likes of which I had never tasted before entering this place. The whole mess sits atop a wad of sticky rice straight from the little mauve Panasonic cooker in the kitchen.

Food is the barometer of this household. When the cook is happy, I eat like a potentate on a diplomatic mission. When the cook is vexed by life or miffed about some slight on my part, I eat wretchedly.

I wonder what I have done this day to anger him. Our morning ritual was nothing more than ritual, after all.

When I meet the cook's eyes, I see something else there. A new distress lurks in the lines drawn tight across his forehead. I know what I gave up when I came here. It was no more than what I'd given up long ago, really, when the fates of people and planets were playing out somewhere in the Deep Dark and I went chasing the fortune of a dozen lifetimes. Still, I am not prepared for this new tension on the part of my daily adversary.

"Have you come to kill me?" I ask him in English. I have no Cantonese, and only the usual fractured, toneless pidgin Mandarin spoken by non-Chinese in the rock ports of the asteroid belt. I've never been certain he understands me, but surely the intent of my question is clear enough.

"Huang." There is a creaky whine in his voice. This man and I can go a week at a time without exchanging a single word. I don't think he speaks more than that to anyone else.

"He is coming here?"

The cook nods. His unhappiness is quite clear.

I poke the bok choi around in my bowl and breathe in the burnt ginger-and-fish oil scent of the sauce. That Huang is coming is a surprise. I have sat quietly with my incipient tumors and withering soul and made the caltrop shards ready for market. They are being handled by a True Hero of the Belt, just as his advertising claims. Our bargain remains intact.

What can he want of me? He already holds the chitty on my life. All my labours are his. I have no reputation left, not under my real name. I bear only the memory of the heavens, and a tiny speck of certain knowledge about what once was.

It should be enough.

After a while, by way of apology, the cook removes my cooling lunch bowl and replaces it with a delicate porcelain plate bearing a honey-laden moon cake. I suspect him of humour, though the timing is hideously inappropriate.

"*Xie xie*," I tell him in my Mandarin pidgin. He does not smile, but the lines around his eyes relax.

Still, I will not stoop to the tea.

Huang arrives to the sound of barking dogs. I stand behind a latticed window in my garden wall and look out into the alley. The gangster's hydrogen-powered Mercedes is a familiar shade of Cherenkov blue. I doubt the aircraft paint his customizers use is hot, though.

There is a small pack of curs trailing his automobile. The driver steps out in a whirr of door motors which is as much noise as that car ever makes. He is a large man for a Chinese, tall and rugged, wearing the ubiquitous leather jacket and track pants of big money thugs from Berlin to Djakarta. His mirror shades have oddly thick frames, betraying a wealth of sensor data and computing power. I wonder if he ever removes them, or if they are implants. Life in this century has become a cheap 1900s science fiction novel.

The driver gives the dogs a long look which quiets them, then opens Huang's door. The man himself steps out without any ceremony or further security. If there is air cover, or rooftop snipers, they are invisible to me.

Huang is small, with the compact strength of a wrestler. His face is a collapsed mass of wrinkles that makes his age impossible to guess. There are enough environmental poisons which can do that to a man without the help of time's relentless decay. Today he wears a sharkskin jacket over a pale blue cheongsam. His eyes when he glances up to my lattice are the watery shade of light in rain.

I walk slowly through the courtyard. That is where Huang will meet me, beneath a bayberry tree on a stone bench with legs carved like lions.

He is not there when I take my seat. Giving instructions to the cook, no doubt. The pond occupies my attention while I wait. It is small, not more than two meters across at its longest axis. The rim is walled with rugged rocks that might have just been ejected from the Earth moments before the mason laid them. Nothing is that sharp-edged out in the Belt, not after a quarter billion years of collision, of dust, of rubbing against each other. The water is scummed over with a brilliant shade of green that strikes fear in the heart of anyone who ever has had responsibility for a biotic air recycling plant.

They say water is blue, but water is really nothing at all but light trapped before the eyes. It's like glass, taking the colour of whatever it is laced with, whatever stands behind it, whatever shade is bent through its substance. Most people out in the Deep Dark have a mystical relationship with water. The very idea of oceans seems a divine improbability to them. As for me, my parents came from Samoa. I was born in Tacoma, and grew up on Puget Sound before finding my way Up. To me, it's just water.

Still, this little pond choked with the wrong kind of life seems to say so much about everything that is wrong with Earth, with the Deep Dark, with the little damp sparks of colonies on Ceres and Mars and elsewhere.

I wondered what would happen to the pond if I poured my blue paint out of its lead-lined bottles into the water.

"Your work holds fair," says Huang. I did not hear him approach. Glancing down, I see his crepe-soled boat shoes, that could have come straight off some streetcorner vendor's rack to cover his million dollar feet.

I meet his water-blue eyes. Pale, so pale, reflecting the colour of his golf shirt. "Thank you, sir."

He looks at me a while. It is precisely the look an amah gives a slab of fish in the market. Finally he speaks again: "There have been inquiries."

I reply without thinking. "About the radioactives?"

One eyebrow inches up. "Mmm?"

I am quiet now. I have abandoned our shared fiction for a moment, that pretense that I do not know he is poisoning thousands of homes worldwide through his artefact trade. Mistakes such as that can be fatal. That the entire present course of my life is fatal is not sufficient excuse for thoughtless stupidity.

Huang takes my silence as an answer. "Certain persons have come to me seeking a man of your description."

With a shrug, I tell him, "I was famous once, for a little while." One of history's villains, in fact, in my moment of media glory.

"What you paid me to keep you . . . they have made an offer far more generous."

I'd sold him my life, that strange, cold morning in a reeking teahouse in Sendai the previous year. Paid him in a substantial amount cash, labour and the last bare threads of my reputation in exchange for a quiet, peaceful penance and the release of obligation. Unfortunately, I could imagine why someone else would trouble to buy Huang out.

He was waiting for me to ask. I would not do that. What I would do was give him a reason not to send me away. "My handiwork meets your requirements, yes?" Reminding him of the hot paint, and the trail of liability which could eventually follow that blue glow back to its source.

Even gangsters who'd left any fear of law enforcement far behind could be sued in civil court.

"You might wish me to take this offer," he says slowly.

"When has the dog ever had its choice of chains?"

A smile flits across Huang's face before losing itself in the nest of wrinkles. "You have no desires in the matter?"

"Only to remain quietly in this house until our bargain is complete."

Huang is silent a long, thoughtful moment. Then: "Money completes everything, spaceman." He nods once before walking away,

It is difficult to threaten a man such as myself with no family, no friends, and no future. That must be a strange lesson for Huang.

I drift back to the latticed window. He is in the alley speaking to the empty air – an otic cell bead. A man like Huang wouldn't have an implant. The dogs are quiet until he steps back into the blue Mercedes. They begin barking and wailing as the car slides away silent as dustfall.

It is then that I realize that the dog pack is a hologram, an extension of the car itself.

Until humans went into the Deep Dark, we never knew how kindly Earth truly was. A man standing on earthquake-raddled ground in the midst of the most violent hurricane is as safe as babe-in-arms compared to any moment of life in hard vacuum. The smallest five-jiǎo pressure seal, procured low bid and installed by a bored maintech with a hangover, could fail and bring with it rapid, painful death.

The risk changes people, in ways most of them never realize. Friendships and hatreds are held equally close. Total strangers will share their last half-litre of air to keep one another alive just a little longer, in case rescue should show. Premeditated murder is almost unknown in the Deep Dark, though manslaughter is sadly common. Any fight can kill, even if just by diverting someone's attention away from the environmentals at a critical moment.

So people find value in one another that was never been foreseen back on Earth. Only the managers and executives who work in the rock ports and colonies have kept the old, human habits of us-and-them, scheming, assassination of both character and body.

The question on my mind was whether it was an old enemy come for me, or someone from the Ceres Minerals Resources corporate hierarchy. Even setting aside the incalculable damage to our understanding of history, in ensuring the loss of the first verifiable non-human artefact, I'd also been the proximate cause of what many people chose to view as the loss of a billion tai kong yuan. Certain managers who would have preferred to exchange their white collars for bank accounts deeper than generations had taken my actions very badly.

Another Belt miner might have yanked my oxygen valve out of sheer, maddened frustration, but it took an angry salaryman to truly plot my ruin in a spreadsheet while smiling slowly. Here in Huang's steel embrace I thought I'd managed my own ruin quite nicely. Yet someone was offering good money for me.

Oddly, Huang had made it all but my choice. Or seemed to, at any rate. Which implied he saw this inquiry as a matter of honour. Huang, like all his kind, was quite elastic in his reasoning about money, at least so long as it kept flowing, but implacable when it came to his notions of honour.

Even my honour, it would seem.

All of this was a very thin thread of logic from which to dangle. I could just keep painting shards until any one of several things killed me – radiation sickness, cancer, the old cook. Or I could tell Huang to break the deal he and I had made, and pass me back out of this house alive.

Given how much trouble I'd taken in order to surrender all control, there was something strangely alluring about being offered back the chitty on my life.

*

That night when the cook brought me the tea, I poured some into the tiny cup with no handles. He gave me a long, slow stare. "You go out?"

"With Mr Huang, yes," I told him.

The cook grunted, then withdrew to the kitchen.

The tea was so bitter that for a moment I wondered if he'd brewed it with rat poison. Even as this thought faded, the cook came back with a second cup and poured it out for himself. He sat down opposite me, something else he'd never done. Then he drew a small mesh bag on a chain out from inside his grubby white t-shirt.

"See this, ah." He tugged open the top of the bag. Out tumbled one of my little blue caltrop fragments. I could almost see it spark in his hand.

"You shouldn't be holding that."

The cook hefted the mesh bag. "Lead. No sick."

I reached out and took the caltrop arm. It was just that, a single arm broken off below the body. I fancied it was warm to my touch. It was certainly very, very blue.

"Why?" I asked him.

He looked up at the ceiling and spread one hand in a slow wave, as if to indicate the limitless stars in the Deep Dark far above our heads. "We too small. World too big. This" – he shook his bag – "this time price."

I tried to unravel the fractured English. "Time price?"

The cook nodded vigorously. "You buy time for everyone, everything."

I sipped my tea and thought about what he'd told me. I'd *been* out in the Deep Dark. I'd touched the sky that wraps the world round, past the blue and into the black.

"Blue," he said, interrupting my chain of thought. "We come from sea, we go to sky. Blue to blue, ah?"

Blue to blue. Life had crawled from the ocean's blue waters to eventually climb past the wide blue sky. With luck, we'd carry forward to the dying blue at the end of time.

"Time," I said, trying the word in my mouth. "Do you mean the future?"

The cook nodded vigorously. "Future, ah."

Once I'd finished eating the magnificent duck he'd prepared, I trudged back to my workroom. I'd already bargained away almost all of my time, but I could create time for others, in glowing blue fragments. It didn't matter who was looking for me. Huang would do as he pleased. My sins were so great they could never be washed away, not even in a radioactive rain.

I could spend what time was left to me bringing people like the old cook a little closer to heaven, one shard after another.

INCOMERS

Paul J. McAuley

Born in Oxford, England, in 1955, Paul J. McAuley now makes his home in London. A professional biologist for many years, he sold his first story in 1984 and has gone on to be a frequent contributor to *Interzone*, as well as to markets such as *Asimov's Science Fiction*, *SCI FICTION*, *Amazing*, *The Magazine of Fantasy & Science Fiction*, *Skylife*, *The Third Alternative*, *When the Music's Over*, and elsewhere.

McAuley is at the forefront of several of the most important subgenres in SF today, producing both "radical hard science fiction" and revamped and retooled widescreen space operas that have sometimes been called new space operas as well as dystopian sociological speculations about the very near future. He also writes fantasy and horror. His first novel, *Four Hundred Billion Stars*, won the Philip K. Dick Award, and his novel *Fairyland* won both the Arthur C. Clarke Award and the John W. Campbell Award in 1996. His other books include the novels *Of the Fall*, *Eternal Light*, and *Pasquale's Angel*, *Life on Mars*, *The Secret of Life*, *Whole Wide World*, *White Devils*, *Mind's Eye*, *Players*, and *Cowboy Angels*. *Confluence*, his major trilogy of ambitious scope and scale set ten million years in the future, is comprised of the novels *Child of the River*, *Ancient of Days*, and *Shrine of Stars*. His short fiction has been collected in *The King of the Hill and Other Stories*, *The Invisible Country*, and *Little Machines*, and he is the co-editor, with Kim Newman, of an original anthology, *In Dreams*. His most recent book is a novel, *The Quiet War*; coming up is a new novel, *Gardens of the Sun*.

McAuley made his name as one of the best new space opera writers with novels such as *Four Hundred Billion Stars* and the Confluence trilogy, but in recent years he has created the Quiet War series as well, with stories such as "Second Skin," "Sea Scene, With Monsters," "The Assassination of Faustino Malarte," and others, about the aftermath and the consequences of an interplanetary war that ravages the solar system.

In the quietly moving story that follows, he takes us to Rhea, Saturn's second largest moon, to examine more of those consequences, the rather unexpected ones.

MARK GRIFFIN WAS convinced that there was something suspicious about the herbalist.

"Tell me who he is, Sky. Some kind of pervert murderer, I bet."

Sky Bolofo was a hacker who had filled the quantum processor of the large, red-framed spex that perched on his nose with all kinds of talents and tricks. Right now, he had a look of focussed concentration, and the left lens of his spex was silvered over as it displayed something to him. He said, "No problem. My face recognition program picked him up straight away, and right now I'm looking at his public page. His name is Ahlgren Rees. He lives right here in the old city, he sells herbs —"

"I can see that," Mark said. "What else?"

"He also fixes up pets," Sky said.

"What about his private files?" Mark said. "What about the real dirt?"

"No problem," Sky said complacently, and started tapping his fingers on the chest of his jumper – he was using the virtual keyboard of his spex, which read the positioning of his fingers from the silver rings he wore on fingers and thumbs.

Jack Miyata, whose idea it had been to visit the produce market, had the sinking feeling that Mark had spied an opportunity for some serious mischief. He said, "The man sells herbs. There's nothing especially interesting or weird in that."

"If he isn't weird," Mark said, "why is he living with the tweaks? He's either crazy, or he's up to no good."

The man in question sat behind a small table at the edge of the market, selling bundles of fresh herbs and a dozen different types of herb tea whose virtues were advertised by handlettered signs. He was definitely an incomer. Native Xambans who'd been born and raised in Rhea's weak gravity were tall and skinny, and most of them were Nordic, with pale skin, blond hair, and blue eyes. The herbalist was a compactly-built man of indeterminate middle-age (in the third decade of the twenty-fourth century, this meant anything between forty and a hundred), not much taller than Sky Bolofo, and had skin the colour of old teak. He was also completely hairless. He didn't even have eyelashes. As far as Jack was concerned, that was the only unusual thing about him, but Mark had other ideas.

Jack had brought his two friends to the produce market because he thought it was a treasure house of marvels, but Mark and Sky thought it was smelly, horribly crowded, and, quite frankly, revoltingly primitive. When makers could spin anything you wanted from yeast and algae, why would anyone want to eat the meat of real live animals like fish and chickens and dwarfed goats, especially as they would have to kill them first? Kill and gut them and Ghod knew what else. As they wandered between stalls and displays of strange flowers and fruits and vegetables, red and green and golden-brown streamers of dried waterweed, tanks of fish and shrimp, caged birds and rats, and bottle vivariums in which stag beetles lumbered like miniature rhinoceroses through jungles of moss and fern, Mark and Sky made snide comments about the weird people and the weirder things they were selling, pretended to retch at especially gross sights, and generally made it clear that this was very far from their idea of fun.

"Do you really think I want to know anything at all about people who eat things like that?" Mark had said to Jack, pointing to a wire cage containing rats spotted like leopards or striped like tigers.

"I think they keep them as pets," Jack had said, feeling the tips of his ears heat up in embarrassment because the tall, slender woman who owned the stall was definitely looking at them.

"I had a pet once," Mark had said, meeting the woman's gaze. "It was a cute little monkey that could take a shower all by itself. Quite unlike these disease-ridden vermin."

Which had made Sky crack up, and Jack blush even more.

The three of them, Jack, Mark and Sky, were all the same age, sixteen, went to the same school, and lived in the same apartment complex in the new part of Xamba, the largest city on Rhea, Saturn's second largest moon. Their parents were engineers, security personnel, and diplomats who had come there to help in the reconstruction and expansion of the Outer Colonies after the Quiet War. Unlike most city states in the Saturn system, Xamba had remained neutral during the Quiet War. Afterwards, the Three Powers Alliance which now governed every city and orbital habitat in the Outer Colonies had settled the bulk of its administration on peaceful, undamaged Rhea, and had built a new city above the old.

Fifteen years later, the city was still growing. Jack's parents, Mariko and Davis, were thermal engineers who were helping to construct a plant to tap the residual heat of the moon's core and provide power for a hundred new apartment complexes, factories, and farms. They'd moved to Rhea just two months ago. In that short time, Jack had explored much of the old and new parts of the city, and had also completed a pressure suit training course and taken several long hikes through the untouched wilderness in the southern half of the big crater in which Xamba was located, and from which it took its name. He'd even climbed to the observatory at the top of the crater's big central peak. Although both Mark and Sky had been living here much longer, like many incomers neither of them had so much as stepped foot on the surface of the moon, or even visited the old part of the city. Jack had been eager to show them the produce market, his favourite part of old Xamba, but now he was feeling miserable because they had been so rude about it. He had been about to give up and suggest they leave when Mark had spotted the herbalist.

"That's obviously a front," Mark said. "How's it going, Sky?"

Sky, sounding distracted and distant, said he was working on it.

"Maybe he's a spy. Selling herbs is his cover – what he's actually doing is keeping watch for terrorists and so-called freedom fighters. Or maybe he's a double agent. Maybe he's gone over to the side of the tweaks," Mark said, beginning to get into his little fantasy. "Maybe he's feeding our side false information to sabotage the reconstruction. There was that blow-out at the spaceport last month. They said it was an accident, but maybe someone sabotaged an airlock and let the vacuum in."

"Air escapes into a vacuum," Jack said, "not the other way around."

"Who cares which direction the vacuum flows?" Mark said carelessly.

"And anyway, they said it was an accident."

Mark raised his eyebrows. They were thick, and met over the bridge of his nose. He was a stocky boy with pale skin, jet black hair and a perpetual scowl who looked a lot like his policeman father. His mother was in the police too, in charge of security at the spaceport. "Of course they *said* that, but it doesn't mean it really was an accident. What's the word, Sky? What is this fellow hiding?"

"There's a problem," Sky said. His fingers were fluttering frantically over his chest, and he had a look of such intense concentration that he seemed to be cross-eyed.

"Talk to me," Mark said.

"He has really heavy security behind his public page. I had to back out in a hurry, before I tripped an alarm. Right now I'm making sure I didn't leave anything that could lead back to me."

Mark said, "So what you're saying is that Ahlgren Rees – if that's his real name – is hiding something."

Sky shrugged.

Mark said, his eyes shining with sudden excitement, "I bet you thought I was kidding, but all along I had a feeling there was something wrong with this guy. It's what the Blob —" that was his nickname for his rotund and none too bright father — "calls gut instinct. My gut told me that Ahlgren Rees is a wrong one, my man Sky has just confirmed it, and now it's up to all of us to find out why. It's our *duty*."

Jack should have told Mark that he wasn't going to have anything to do with his silly fantasy, but his need for his new friends to like him (which was why he'd brought them to the market in the first place) was stronger than his conscience. Also, it was the school holidays, and his parents were spending most of their time at the site of the new power plant, a hundred kilometers northwest of the city, and were only at home on weekends, so he was pretty much on his own for most of the time. There was no way that the herb seller, Ahlgren Rees was either a spy or a criminal, so what harm could simply following him about actually do?

Jack spent much of the next three days following Ahlgren Rees, sometimes with Mark, sometimes on his own (Sky Bolofo, spooked by the experience of running up against Ahlgren Rees's electronic watchdogs, had made a weak excuse about having to do some extra tuition for the upcoming new school year). It wasn't hard; in fact, it was a lot of fun. The herbalist spent much of the day at the stall in the produce market, or tending the little garden where he grew his herbs, or simply sitting outside the door of his apartment, a one-room efficiency on a terrace directly above the market, drinking tea or homemade lemonade and watching people go by, but he also liked to take long walks, and every time Jack followed him, his route was different. Jack saw more of the old city in those three days than he had in the past two months.

The old part of the city was buried inside the eastern rimwall of the huge crater, and some of its chambers had diamond endwalls facing what was generally reckoned to be one of the most classically beautiful views in all of Saturn's family of moons, across slumped terraces and fans of ice rubble towards the crater's central peak which rose up at the edge of the close, curved horizon. Inside the old city's chambers, apartments and shops and cafes and workshops and gardens were piled on top of each other in steep, terraced cliffs, linked by steep paths, chutes, cableways and chairlifts to the long narrow parks of trees and lawns and skinny lakes that were laid out on the chamber floors. There was no shortage of water on Rhea, which was essentially a ball of ice one and a half thousand kilometres in diameter wrapped around a small rocky core. A series of long, narrow lakes looped between several of the chambers, busy with skiffs and canoes paddling between floating islands and rafts and pontoons, and the main pathways were crowded with cycles and pedicabs and swarms of pedestrians.

The old part of Xamba was a busy, bustling place, and Jack had no problem blending into the crowds as he trailed Ahlgren Rees through walkways, parks, markets, malls, and plazas, even though most of its inhabitants were tall, skinny Outers, genetically engineered so that they could comfortably live in microgravity without the medical implants that Jack and every other incomer needed in order to stop their bones turning to chalk lace, their hearts swelling like pumped-up basketballs with excess fluid, and a host of other problems. Jack even plucked up the courage to chat with the woman behind the counter of the cafe where Ahlgren Rees ate his lunch and breakfast, which is where he'd learned that the herbalist was originally from Greater Brazil, where he had worked in the emergency relief services as a paramedic, and had moved to Rhea two years ago. He seemed well-liked. He always stopped to talk to his neighbours when he met them as he went about his errands, had long conversations with people who stopped at his stall. He was a regular at the café, and at several bars in various parts of the city. His only money seemed to come from selling herbs and herb tea and fixing broken pets.

"Which must mean that he has some other source of income," Mark said.

"Maybe he has some kind of private income."

"He has secrets, is what he has. Ahlgren Rees. We don't even know if that's his real name."

The two boys were leaning at the cafe counter in the produce market, sipping fruit juice from bulbs. Ahlgren Rees was sitting at his stall twenty metres down the aisle, reading a book (books printed on paper were a famous tradition in old Xamba), completely oblivious to the fact that the two boys were watching him and talking about him, licking his thumb every time he had to turn a page.

Jack said, "He's a herbalist. He works at his stall. He works in his garden. He goes for long walks. Sometimes he visits people and fixes up their pets. If he has any secrets, I'm missing something."

He was hoping that this would be the end of it, but Mark had a determined look, a jut of his heavy jaw like a bulldog gripping a bone it isn't willing to let go.

"What we need to do," Mark said, "is get into his apartment. I bet he has all kinds of things hidden there."

Jack tried to talk him out of it, but Mark was determined. Jack was pretty sure that he didn't really believe that Ahlgren Rees was a spy, but it had become a matter of pride to find out who he really was and why he had come to Xamba to live amongst the Outers. And Jack had to admit that the past three days of following the man had sharpened his curiosity too, and eventually they managed to hash out a plan that more or less satisfied both of them.

The next day was Monday, and the produce market would be closed. Mark told Jack that he would have to intercept Ahlgren Rees at the café where he ate breakfast every day, and keep him occupied. Meanwhile, Mark would break into his apartment.

Jack said, "How are you going to do that?"

"Police tradecraft," Mark said. "Don't worry about it. Just make sure you keep him busy."

Although Jack believed that he had a good idea about how to do just that, he slept badly that night, going over every part of a plan which seemed increasingly silly and flimsy, and he was very tired and nervous when, early the next morning, he and Mark rode the train into the city. Mark wanted to know what was in the box Jack was clutching to his chest, and Jack told him with a confidence he didn't feel that it was a foolproof way of keeping the man busy.

"I'll tell you what it is if you'll tell me how you're going to break into his apartment."

"I'm not going to break in, I'm going to walk in," Mark said. "And I could tell you how I'm going to do it, but I'd have to kill you afterwards. Are you sure you can keep him talking for half an hour?"

Jack tapped the top of the plastic box, feeling what was inside stir, a slow, heavy movement that subsided after a moment. He said, "Absolutely sure."

Actually, he wasn't sure at all. This was a lot more dangerous than simply following someone through the city's crowded paths. Following someone wasn't against the law. Breaking into their private apartment plainly and simply was. Jack had the same sick, doomy feeling that had possessed him in the days before he and his parents had boarded the liner that had taken them from Earth to Saturn. He felt that he was about to do something that would change his life forever, and would change it for the worse if he failed at it. It was a very grown-up feeling, and he didn't like it at all. There was a sharp edge of excitement, to be sure, but the muscles of his legs felt watery and his stomach was doing somersaults when, after spending half an hour with Mark watching Ahlgren Rees's apartment from the cover of a little arbour made by the drooping branches of a weeping willow, he followed the herbalist to the cafe.

It was more or less on the same level as the apartment, a bamboo counter beneath the shade of a huge fig tree, with a bench long enough for a dozen customers and a hissing steel coffee machine that the owner, a white-haired wisp of a woman, had built herself, from a design centuries old. The food was prepared from what was in season in the garden behind the fig tree, and whatever came in trade – the citizens of old Xamba had a complicated economy based on barter of goods and services.

Jack took a seat next to Ahlgren Rees, the closest he had got to the man so far. He asked the owner for the juice of the day, set the plastic box on the counter, and turned to the herbalist and said as casually as he could that he heard that he treated sick pets.

"Who told you that?"

Ahlgren Rees, hunched over a bowl of porridge flecked with nuts and seeds, didn't look up when he spoke. He had a husky voice and a thick accent: the voice of a villain from some cheap virtuality.

"She did," Jack said, nodding to the owner of the café, who was filling a blender with orange segments and a handful of strawberries.

"I did," the woman said cheerfully, and switched on the blender.

"Stop by my place when you've had your breakfast," Ahlgren Rees told Jack. "It's just around the corner, past a clump of black bamboo. The one with the red door."

The man was eating his porridge slowly but steadily, his elbows on the counter. In a few minutes he would be finished. He'd get up, walk back to his apartment, find the door open . . .

Jack pushed the box an inch towards the man and said, "I have it right here."

"So I see," Ahlgren Rees said, although he didn't spare Jack so much as a glance. "And I have my breakfast right here too."

"It belongs to my little sister," Jack said, the little lie sliding out easily. He added, "She loves it to bits, but we're scared that it's dying."

"Take a look, Ahlgren," the woman who owned the cafe said, as she placed the bulb of juice in front of Jack. "The worst that can happen is that your karma will be improved."

"It will need much more than fixing a pet to do that," Ahlgren Rees said, smiling at her.

The woman smiled back. Jack was reminded of his parents, when they shared a private joke.

"All right, kid," Ahlgren Rees said. "Show me what you got."

It was a mock turtle, a halflife creature that produced no waste or unpleasant odours, and needed only a couple of hours of trickle charge and a cupful of water a day. It had large, dark, soulful eyes, a yellow beak as soft as a sock puppet's mouth, and a fifty-word vocabulary. The colour and texture of its shell could be altered by infection with simple retroviruses created using the simple RNA writer kit that came with it; this one's was covered in thick pink fur. It didn't belong to Jack's imaginary little sister, of course, but to the youngest daughter of Jack's neighbours, but it really was sick. Its fur was matted and threadbare; its eyes were filmed with white matter, its soft beak chewed ceaselessly and its breath was foully metallic.

Ahlgren Rees studied it, then took a diagnostic pen from one of the many pockets of his brocade waistcoat and tipped up the mock turtle and plugged the instrument into the socket behind the creature's stubby front leg.

"Tickles," the turtle complained, working its stubby legs feebly.

"It's for your own good," Ahlgren Rees said. "Be still."

He had small, strong hands and neatly trimmed fingernails. There were oval scars on the insides of his thick wrists; he'd had plug-in sockets once upon a time, the kind that interface with smart machinery. He squinted at the holographic readout that blossomed above the shaft of the diagnostic pen, then asked Jack, "Do you know what a prion is?"

"Proteins have to fold up the right way to work properly. Prions are proteins that fold up wrongly."

Ahlgren Rees nodded. "The gene wizard who designed these things used a lot of freeware, and one of the myoelectric proteins he used has a tendency to make prions. That's what's wrong with your sister's pet, I'm afraid. It's a self-catalysing reaction – do you know what that means?"

"It spreads like a fire. Prions turn proteins into more prions."

Ahlgren Rees nodded again, unplugged the diagnostic pen, and settled the mock turtle in the box. "The myoelectric proteins are what power it. When they fold the wrong way they can no longer hold a charge, and when enough have folded wrongly, it will die."

"Can you fix it?"

Ahlgren Rees shook his head. "The best thing to do is to put it to sleep."

He looked genuinely sorry, and Jack felt a wave of guilt pass through him. Right now, Mark was breaking into his apartment, rifling through his possessions . . .

"If you like, I can do it right now," Ahlgren Rees said.

"I'll have to tell my sister first."

Ahlgren Rees shrugged and started to push away from the counter, saying, "Sorry I couldn't help you, son."

"Wait," Jack said, knowing that Mark must still be in the apartment. Adding, when Ahlgren Rees looked at him, "I mean, I want to ask you, how do you grow your herbs?"

"I suppose you told him about the herbs too," Ahlgren Rees told the woman, who blithely shrugged.

"I saw you at the produce market," Jack said boldly. "And then I saw you here."

Ahlgren Rees studied him for a moment. Jack felt a moment of anxiety, thinking he'd been found out, but then the man smiled and said, "I had the feeling I'd seen you before. You like the market, uh?"

"I'm interested in biology," Jack said, speaking the truth because it was the first thing that came into his head. He was good at it, could solve genetic problems or balance a simple ecosystem without thinking too hard, and got pleasure from solving it. Before coming to Rhea, he'd lived with his parents in on the eastern coast of Australia, and one of the things he missed most, after leaving Earth, was snorkelling above the elaborate architecture of the coral reef and its schools of bright fish in the bay, and the aquarium he'd taken a whole year to get just right, a miniature reef in its own right. He added, "I'd like to know how you grow the herbs you sell."

"In dirt, with water and sunlight."

"That isn't what I meant. I was wondering how the low gravity   "

Ahlgren Rees held up a hand. "I have a date," he said. "If you stop at my stall, if I am not too busy, perhaps we can talk then."

He said goodbye to the owner of the cafe, who with a smile asked him to have a good thought on her behalf, and then he was walking off down the path. Not towards his apartment, but in the opposite direction, towards the little funicular railway that dropped down to the floor of the chamber.

Jack wanted but did not dare to ask the owner of the cafe where he was going. After the woman had refused his offer to pay for his juice ("You can bring me some sour oranges next time you visit the market," she said), he set off after Ahlgren Rees, and called Mark on his phone, told him about the conversation, and what he was doing. Mark said that he'd catch up, and arrived, breathless and excited, at the lakeside jetty just as Ahlgren Rees was climbing into one of the swan boats.

"Where is he going?" Mark said.

"I don't know," Jack said. "But he said that he had a date."

"With a woman?"

"I don't know."

"Are you sure you actually talked to him?"

"He said that he had a date, and he left. What was I supposed to do — make a citizen's arrest."

"No need to feel guilty. Our mission was successful."

"You found something. What did you find?"

"He's a spy all right." Mark patted the pouch of his jumper, waggled his thick black eyebrows. "I'll show you in a minute. First, we need a boat."

There were several high-sided dinghies waiting at the jetty, rising and falling on the long, slow waves that rolled across the lake. Jack and Mark climbed into one, and Mark stuck something in a slot in the fat sensor rod that stuck up at the prow, told the boat that this was a police override, told it to follow the boat which had just left.

As the boat's reaction motor pushed it towards the centre of the long, narrow lake, Jack said, "That's how you got into his apartment, isn't it? You overrode the lock."

He was sitting in the stern, the plastic box with the mock turtle inside it on his knees.

Mark, standing at the prow, one hand on top of the sensor rod, glanced over his shoulder. "Of course I did."

"I suppose you stole the card from one of your parents."

"Sky made a copy of my mother's card," Mark said.

"If she finds out —"

"As long as I don't get into trouble, she doesn't care what I do. The Blob doesn't care either. They're too busy with their jobs, too busy *advancing their careers*, too busy *making money*," Mark said. He had his back to Jack, but Jack could hear the bitterness in his voice. "Which is fine with me, because once they make enough, we'll leave this rotten little ball of ice and go back to Earth."

There was a short silence. Jack was embarrassed, feeling that he had had an unwanted glimpse through a crack in his his friend's armour of careless toughness into his soul, had seen the angry resentment and loneliness there. At last, he said, "If we prove that Ahlgren Rees really is a spy, your parents will be proud of you."

Mark turned around. "Oh, he's a spy, all right. Guess what I found in his apartment."

It was the kind of question you were bound to fail to answer correctly, so Jack just shrugged.

Mark smiled a devilish smile, reached into the pouch of his jumper, and drew out a small, silver gun.

Jack was shocked and excited at the same moment. He said, "Is it real?"

"Oh yes. And it's charged too," Mark said, pointing to a tiny green light that twinkled above the crosshatched grip.

He explained that it was a railgun that used a magnetic field to fire metal splinters tipped with explosive or toxin, or which sprouted hooks and knives after they hit their target, burrowing deep into flesh. He played campaigns based on the Quiet War on a wargaming network, knew all about the different ways the rebellious colonies had been pacified, and all about the guns and the various kinds of weapons used by both sides. Discovering the gun had not only confirmed his suspicions about Ahlgren Rees, but had made him bold and reckless too. He talked excitedly about catching the spy in the act of sabotage, about arresting him and whoever he was going to meet and making them talk.

Although Jack was excited too, it was plain that his friend was getting carried away. "This doesn't change our plan," he said. "We follow the man and see what he gets up to, and then we decide what to do."

Mark shrugged and said blithely, "We'll see what we'll see."

"I mean that we don't do anything dumb," Jack said. "If he really is a spy, he's dangerous."

"If you're scared, you can get off at any time."

"Of course I'm not scared," Jack said, even though he felt a freezing caution. "All I'm saying is that we have to be careful."

The boat carrying Ahlgren Rees stopped three times, dropping people and picking up others, before it headed down a canal that ran through a long transparent tunnel between two chambers, Mark and Jack following two hundred meters behind it. The tunnel was laid along the edge of a steep cliff. It was the middle of Rhea's night out there. Saturn hung full and huge overhead in the black sky like Ghod's Christmas ornament, the razor-thin line of his rings cutting across his banded face, his smog-yellow light laid across terraced icefields below. Jack leaned back, lost in the intricate beauty of the gas giant's yellow and dirty white and salmon pink bands, their frills and frozen waves, forgetting for the ten minutes it took to traverse the tunnel all about the gun in Mark's pouch and following Ahlgren Rees.

At the end of the tunnel, the canal entered a lake with a rocky shoreline pinched between two steep slopes of flowering meadows and stands of trees and bamboos. There were no houses in this chamber, no workshops of markets, no gardens or farms. It was the city's cemetery. Like all Outer colony cities, Xama recycled its dead. Bodies were buried in its cemetery chamber and trees planted over them, so that their freight of carbon and nitrogen and phosphorus and other useful elements could re-enter the loop of the city's ecosystem. It was a quiet, beautiful place, lit by the even golden light of a late summer afternoon. On one steep slope was the black pyramid, hewn from the crystalline iron of an asteroid, that marked the resting place of the people who had died in accidents during the construc tion of the old city; on the other was a slim white column topped by an eternal blue flame, the monument to the citizens of Xamba who had died in the Quiet War. For although the city had remained neutral during the war, more than a thousand of its citizens had died, almost all of them had been either passengers or crew on ships crippled when their nervous systems had been fried by neutron lasers, microwave bursters, or EMP mines during the first hours of the invasion of the Saturn system. Otherwise, the woods and meadows seemed untouched by human hands, a tame wilderness where birds and cat-sized deer and teddy-bear-sized pandas roamed freely.

Ahlgren Rees and two women got off when the boat docked at a jetty of black wood with an red-painted Chinese arch at one end. The two women went off along the lakeshore; Ahlgren Rees started up a steep, bone-white path that wound past a grove of shaggy cypress trees.

Mark sprang out of the boat as soon as it nudged alongside the jetty and bounded through the Chinese gate and set off up the white path. Jack had to hurry to catch up with him. They slogged around the cypress grove, climbed alongside a tiny stream that ran over white rocks speckled with chunky black shards of shock quartz, and followed Ahlgren Rees as he cut through a belt of pines. There was a lumpy heath of coarse tussock grass and purple heather and clumps of flowering gorse, rising in steep terraces to the place where the top of the slope met the edge of the chamber's curved blue roof. The flame-topped white column of the monument to

Xamba's war dead stood halfway between the pines and the painted sky, and Ahlgren Rees stood in front of the column, his bald head bowed.

He stood there for more than fifteen minutes, still and obdurate as a statue. Crouched behind a pine tree, shoulder to shoulder with Mark, Jack was convinced that the herbalist really was waiting to meet another spy, that he and Mark really had stumbled over a conspiracy, that once they had learned enough they could turn their information over to the authorities. In excited whispers, he and Mark discussed what they'd do when Ahlgren Rees's co-conspirator appeared, agreeing that they might have to split up and follow the men separately. But no one came. Big silver and gold butterflies tumbled over each other above a clump of gorse; one by one, rabbits hippity-hopped out of their burrows and began to nibble at the grass. At last, Ahlgren Rees turned from the monument and moved on up the slope, silhouetted against the solid blue sky for a moment when he reached the top, then dropping out of sight.

The rabbits scattered as Jack and Mark followed, making a bounding run up the rough slope, jinking from gorse clump to gorse clump. Mark quickly outpaced Jack, who still hadn't quite mastered running in low gravity, waiting impatiently for him to catch up near the top of the slope, crouched amongst rocks spattered with orange lichens. There was a narrow stairway down to the floor of a long, narrow rock-sided gully. Ahlgren Rees was walking at his usual unhurried pace down the gully towards a steel door set in a wide frame painted with yellow and black warning chevrons – an airlock door.

"He's going outside!" Mark said, and bounded down the stairs, the pistol flashing as he drew it, shouting a warning, telling the man to stop or he'd shoot.

By the time Jack reached them, Mark and Ahlgren Rees were standing a few yards apart, facing each other. Mark was pointing the pistol at Ahlgren Rees's chest, but the stocky, bald-headed man was ignoring him, looking instead at Jack and saying mildly, "Tell your friend he has made a mistake."

"Kneel down," Mark said. He held the pistol in his right hand, was bracing his right wrist with his left hand. "Kneel down and put your hands on your head."

Ahlgren Rees shook his head slightly. "I believe that is mine. How did you get it?"

"Just kneel down."

"You broke into my apartment while your friend —" he looked at Jack again, who felt a blush heat his face "— kept me busy. What is this about? What silly game are you playing?"

"It's no game," Mark said. "We know you're a spy."

Ahlgren Rees laughed.

"Shut up!" Mark screamed it so loudly it echoed off the rough rock walls of the gully and the blue concrete sky that curved overhead.

Jack, clutching the plastic box to his chest, frightened that his friend would shoot Ahlgren Rees there and then, said, "You said you were meeting someone here."

"Is that what this is about?" Ahlgren Rees said. "Yes, I visit someone. I visit her every Monday. Everyone knows that. Give me the pistol, son, before you get into trouble."

"You're a spy," Mark said stubbornly. "Kneel down —"

There was a blur of movement, a rush of air. Mark was knocked into Jack, and they both fell down. Ahlgren Rees was standing a yard away, the pistol in his hand. He was sweating and trembling lightly all over, like a horse that has just run a race. He stared at the two boys, and Jack felt a spike of fear, thinking that he'd shoot him, shoot Mark, dump their bodies in some deep crevasse outside. But then the man tucked the pistol in the waistband of his green canvas trousers and said, "My nervous system was rewired when I was in the navy. A long time ago, but it still works. Go home, little boys. Go back to your brave new city. Never let me see you again, and I won't tell anyone about this. Go!"

They picked themselves up, and ran.

On the boat-ride back, Mark blew off his nerves and shame by making all kinds of plans and boastful threats. He was scared and angry. He promised vengeance. He promised to find out the truth. He promised to bring the man to justice. He said that if Jack said so much as *one word* about this, he'd get into so much trouble he'd never find his way out again.

Jack kept quiet. He already knew that he was in a lot of trouble. Even if Ahlgren Rees was a spy, there was nothing they could do about it because they were outside the law too. They'd broken into his apartment, stolen his gun and threatened him with it. Suppose Mariko and Davis found out. Suppose the *police* found out. It was a Mexican stand-off.

Jack spent the next week in a misery of fear and guilty anticipation. When his parents came home, he avoided them as much as he could, and refused their offer of a trip to the canyonlands to the north. If it had been possible, he would have caught the next ship back to Earth, leaving the whole horrible wretched incident behind him. As it was, he spent most of his time in his room, studying or half-heartedly fiddling with the virtual ecosystem he was constructing, or mooching around the apartment block's mall.

That was where he met Sky Bolofo, and heard about Mark's plan. Sky wanted to know what had made Mark so terminally pissed, and eventually got Jack to confess everything.

"Wow. You're lucky the guy didn't report you," Sky said, when Jack was finished.

"Don't I know it."

They were sitting in the mall's food court. The chatter of the people around them rose through the fronds of tall palms towards the glass dome. Sky studied Jack through his red-framed spex, and said, "Do you think he'll really go through with it?"

"Go through with what? What has he been saying?"

That was when Jack learned that Mark was determined to prove that Ahlgren Rees was a spy, was determined to pay him back for the humiliating incident in the cemetery chamber. Jack tried to phone him, but Mark was blocking his calls, and wouldn't answer his door when Jack went to his apartment. But by then Jack suspected what he was planning to do. Every Monday, Ahlgren Rees had a rendezvous with someone. They'd followed him to an airlock last Monday, which meant that it was probably somewhere outside the city . . .

Jack knew that he couldn't tell either his parents or Mark's about this. He was as guilty as Mark, and would get into as much trouble. He'd have to sort this out himself, and because Mark was refusing to talk to him he'd have to catch him in the act, stop him before he did something really dumb.

When he asked Sky to help him out, Sky refused at first, saying he'd heard what happened – Mark had been ranting to him too, he wanted nothing to do with it, thank you very much – but he quickly changed his mind when Jack told him that if Mark was caught, everything would come out, including the cloned override card. Sky had hacked into the apartment block's CCTV system long ago, and told Jack he'd download the hack into Jack's spex, and patch a face recognition program over it, so that Jack could use the CCTV system to follow Mark wherever he went in the public spaces of the big building. After Jack told him about what he thought Mark was going to do, Sky said that he'd add an AI that would alert Jack if Mark got anywhere near any of the apartment building's airlocks.

"And that's *all* I'm doing. And if anyone asks you where you got this stuff, tell them you made it yourself."

"Absolutely," Jack said. "I know all of this is my fault. If I hadn't told him about the market, and the funny guy selling herbs —"

"Don't beat yourself up," Sky said. "Mark would have got into trouble all by himself sooner or later. He's bored, and he hates living here. It's quite obvious that this whole thing, it's a silly rebellion."

"So do you," Jack said. "But you didn't break into someone's apartment, and steal a gun."

"I don't care for the place and the people who live here," Sky said, "but as long as I'm left alone to get on with my own thing it doesn't matter. Mark though, he's like a tiger in a cage. Be careful, Jack. Don't let him get you into any more trouble."

The AI woke Jack in the early hours of Monday morning. He'd worn his spex to bed. After he'd managed to shut off the alarm lay there in the dark, staring at a skewed view of Mark sitting in a dressing frame that was assembling a pressure suit around him, until he woke up enough to realize that this was it. That Mark really was going through with it.

The main airlock complex of the apartment building was an ancillary structure reached by a long slanting tunnel. By the time Jack reached it, Mark was long gone, but he remembered his training and after the dressing frame had fitted him with a pressure suit he carefully checked that its electronic systems and power and air reserves were fully functional before making his way through the three sets of doors.

The airlock opened onto a flat apron of dusty ice that, trodden everywhere with cleated bootprints, reminded Jack of the snow around the ski lifts at the mountain resort where he and his parents had several times gone on holiday. It was six in the morning by city time, but outside it was the middle of Rhea's long day. Saturn's slender crescent was cocked overhead, lassoed by the slender ellipse of his rings. The sun was a cold diamond, a hundred times less bright than it appeared from Earth. Its light gleamed on the swept-back tower of the apartment block and on the other towers of the new city and the great curve of the scarp behind them, shone wanly on the crests of the rumpled ridges of ice that stretched to the close horizon.

Ordinarily, Jack would have been transfixed by the alien beauty of the panorama, but he had a mission to accomplish. He tried and failed to pick up the radio transponder of Mark's pressure suit – presumably Mark had switched it off – but that didn't matter. Jack knew exactly where his friend was going. He crossed to the racks where the cycles were charging, and found every one occupied. Mark wasn't qualified to use a pressure suit (he must have used the cloned override card to force the dressing frame to give him one) and either he didn't know about the cycles, or he didn't know the simple code which unlocked them.

They were three-wheeled, with fat diamond mesh tyres, a low-slung seat and a simple control yoke. Jack slid into one and set off along the road that headed towards the eastern end of the old city, feeling a blithe optimism. He was on a cycle and Mark was on foot. It was no contest.

But the road bent wide to the south, skirting the fans of ice-rubble and fallen boulders at the base of the huge cliff of the crater's rimwall, and Jack quickly realized that someone on foot, taking a straight path instead of the road's wide detour, would have far less distance to travel. To his left, the rumpled plain of the crater floor stretched away to the cluster of the central peaks; to his right, the lighted circles of the endwalls of the old city's buried chambers glowed with green light in the face of the cliffs two miles away, like the portholes of a huge ocean liner.

After ten minutes, Jack spotted a twinkle of movement amongst the boulderfields at the foot of the cliffs. He stopped the cycle, used the magnification feature of his visor, and saw a figure in a white pressure suit bounding in huge strides amongst tumbled blocks of dirty ice as big as houses. He tried to hail his friend, but Mark must have switched off the suit's phone as well as its transponder, so he drove the cycle off the roadway, intending to cut him off. At first the going was easy, with only a few outlying blocks to steer around, but then the ground began to rise up and down in concentric scarps like frozen waves, and the rubble fallen from the cliffs grew denser. Jack kept losing sight of Mark, spotting him only when he crested the tops of the scarps, and he piled on the speed in the broad depressions between them, anxious that he'd lose sight of his friend completely.

He was bowling alongside a row of boulders when the inky shadow ahead turned out to be hiding a narrow but deep crevice which trapped the cycle's front wheel. The cycle slewed, Jack hit the brakes, everything tipped sideways, and then he was hanging by his safety harness, looking up at Saturn's ringed crescent in the black sky. He managed to undo the harness's four-way clasp and scramble free, and checked the integrity of the joints of his pressure suit before he heaved the cycle's front tyre out of the crevice. Its mesh was badly flattened along one side, and the front fork was crumpled beyond repair: there was no way he could ride another yard.

Well, his suit was fine, he wasn't injured, he had plenty of air and power, and if he got into trouble he could always phone for help. There was nothing for it. He was going to have to follow Mark on foot.

It took two hours to slog four miles across the rough terrain, clambering over piles of boulders, climbing down into the dips between scarps and climbing back out again, finding a way around jagged crevices. Sometimes he could see Mark's pressure-suited figure slogging ahead of him, on Earth Jack could have shouted to him, but not even the sound of a nuclear bomb would carry in the vacuum here – but most of the time he had only his suit's navigation system to guide him. He was drenched with sweat, his ankles and knees were aching, and he had just switched to his reserve air pack, when at last he reached the road that led to the airlock of the city's cemetery, the place where he had guessed that Mark would lie in wait for Ahlgren Rees. He went slowly, moving between the rubble at the edge of the road, creeping from shadow to shadow, imagining the worst. Mark crouched behind a boulder with a gun he'd stolen from his mother or father, waiting for Ahlgren Rees . . .

But there was no need for caution. Mark's white pressure suit was sprawled on the roadway, about two hundred yards from the airlock. Jack knew at once that something was wrong, adrenalin kicked in, and he reached the figure in three bounds. A red light flashed on the suit's backpack; its oxygen supply was exhausted. Jack managed to roll it over. Behind the gold-filmed visor, Mark stared past him, eyes half-closed and unseeing, skin tinged blue.

Jack hit his suit's distress beacon and began to drag Mark's pressure-suited body towards the yellow-painted steel door of the airlock. He was halfway there when the door slid open and a figure in a pressure suit stepped out.

"You kids again," Ahlgren Rees said over the phone link. "I swear you'll be the death of me."

Three days later, after the scary confusion when Jack and Ahlgren Rees had dragged Mark's body inside the cemetery chamber and the medivac crew had arrived, after Jack had explained everything to Davis and Marika, after the visit to the hospital where Mark was recovering (when its oxygen supply had run dangerously low, his pressure suit had put him in a coma and cooled him down to keep him alive for as long as possible, but it had been a close-run thing), Ahlgren Rees took him to see the place he visited each and every week.

There was a kind of ski lift that carried them half a mile up a sheer face of rock-hard black ice to the rim of the huge crater's rimwall, and a path of steel mesh that followed the curve of a frozen ridge to a viewpoint that looked out across a cratered terrain. There was a steel pillar a yard high, with a plaque set into its angled top, and an induction loop that would play a message over the phone system if you pressed its red button, but Ahlgren Rees told Jack that there was no need to look at the plaque or use the loop because he wanted to explain why they had come here.

It was early in the morning and the brilliant star of the sun low on the horizon, throwing long tangled shadows across the glaring moonscape, but the long scar that Ahlgren Rees had brought Jack to see was clearly visible, still fresh after fifteen years, a gleaming sword cutting through shadows, aimed at the western horizon.

"Her name was Rosa Lux," Ahlgren Rees told Jack. "She was flying a small freighter. One of those freelance ships that are not much bigger than tugs, mostly engine, a little cargo space, a cabin not much bigger than a coffin. She was carrying in her hold a special cargo – the mayor of the city of Camelot, on Mimas. He had been one of the architects of the rebellion that started the Quiet War. His city had fallen, and if he had reached Xamba he would have been granted political asylum. My job was to stop him. I was a singleship pilot then, part of the picket which orbited Rhea to prevent ships leaving or arriving during the aftermath of the war. When Rosa Lux's freighter was detected, I was the only singleship in a position to intercept her, and even then I had to burn almost all my fuel to do it. She was a daring pilot and had came in very fast, skimming the surface of Rhea just a mile up and using its gravity to slow her so that she could enter into a long orbit and come into land when she made her second pass. That was what she was doing when my orbit intercepted hers. I had only one chance to stop her, and I made a mess of it. I fired two missiles. One missed by several miles and hit the surface; the other missed too, but only by a a few hundred yards, and it blew itself up as it zoomed past. It didn't destroy her ship, but it damaged its main drive and changed her vector – her course. She was no longer heading for Xamba's spaceport, but for the rimwall, and the city.

"I saw what she did then. I saw her fire her manoeuvring thrusters. I saw her dump fuel from her main tank. I saw her sacrifice herself so that she would miss the city. Everything happened in less than five seconds, and she barely missed the top of the rimwall, but miss it she did. And crashed there, and died. Rosa Lux had only five seconds to live, and she used that little time to save the lives of a hundred thousand people.

"The funny thing was, the mayor of Camelot survived. He was riding in the cargo section of the ship in a coffin filled with impact gel, cooled down much the same way your friend was cooled down. The cargo section pinwheeled across the landscape for two kilometres, but it survived more or less intact. After the mayor was revived, he claimed asylum. He still lives in Xamba. He married a local woman, and runs the city's library."

There was a silence. Jack watched the scar shine in the new sunlight, waiting for Ahlgen Rees to finish his story. He was certain that there would be a moral; it was the kind of story that always had a moral. But Ahlgren Rees showed no sign of speaking, and at last Jack asked him why he'd come to Rhea.

"After the war, I went back to Greater Brazil. I left the navy and trained as a paramedic, and got on with my life. My children grew up, and then my wife died. I decided to make a last visit to the place where the most intense and most important thing in my life had happened, and bought a roundtrip ticket. And when I got here, I fell in love with someone. You have met her, actually."

"The woman who owns the cafe!"

"We were in love, and then we fell out of love, but by that time I had begun a new life here, and I stayed on. But what brought me here to begin with was a chance encounter with another woman – the bravest person I know about. A single moment, a chance encounter, can change everything. Perhaps you're too young to know it, but I think it's happened to you, too."

Jack thought about this, thought about all that had happened in the past week, and realized that his new friend was right.

CRYSTAL NIGHTS

Greg Egan

Looking back at the century that's just ended, it's obvious that Australian writer Greg Egan was one of the big new names to emerge in SF in the 90s, and is probably one of the most significant talents to enter the field in the last several decades. Many of his stories have appeared in other best of the year series, and he was on the Hugo final ballot in 1995 for his story "Cocoon", which won the Ditmar Award and the Asimov's Readers Award. He won the Hugo Award in 1999 for his novella *Oceanic*. His first novel, *Quarantine*, appeared in 1992; his second novel, *Permutation City*, won the John W. Campbell Memorial Award in 1994. His other books include the novels, *Distress*, *Diaspora*, *Teranesia*, and *Schild's Ladder* and three collections of his short fiction, *Axiomatic*, *Luminous*, and *Our Lady of Chernobyl*. Egan fell silent for a couple of years at the beginning of the oughts but is back again with a vengeance, with new stories in markets such as *Asimov's*, *Interzone*, *The New Space Opera*, *One Million A.D.*, MIT *Technology Review*, and *Foundation 100*. His most recent books are a new novel, *Incandescence*, and a new collection, *Dark Integers and Other Stories*. He has a website at netspace. netau/^gregegan/.

In the unsettling story that follows he suggests that the problem with playing God is that you might turn out to be too good at it.

I

"**M**ORE CAVIAR?" DANIEL Cliff gestured at the serving dish and the cover irised from opaque to transparent. "It's fresh, I promise you. My chef had it flown in from Iran this morning."

"No thank you." Julie Dehghani touched a napkin to her lips then laid it on her plate with a gesture of finality. The dining room overlooked the Golden Gate bridge, and most people Daniel invited here were content to spend an hour or two simply enjoying the view, but he could see that she was growing impatient with his small talk.

Daniel said, "I'd like to show you something." He led her into the adjoining conference room. On the table was a wireless keyboard; the wall screen showed a Linux command line interface. "Take a seat," he suggested.

Julie complied. "If this is some kind of audition, you might have warned me," she said.

"Not at all," Daniel replied. "I'm not going to ask you to jump through any hoops. I'd just like you to tell me what you think of this machine's performance."

She frowned slightly, but she was willing to play along. She ran some standard benchmarks. Daniel saw her squinting at the screen, one hand almost reaching up to where a desktop display would be, so she could double-check the number of digits in the FLOPS rating by counting them off with one finger. There were a lot more than she'd been expecting, but she wasn't seeing double.

"That's extraordinary," she said. "Is this whole building packed with networked processors, with only the penthouse for humans?"

Daniel said, "You tell me. Is it a cluster?"

"Hmm." So much for not making her jump through hoops, but it wasn't really much of a challenge. She ran some different benchmarks, based on algorithms that were provably impossible to parallelize; however smart the compiler was, the steps these programs required would have to be carried out strictly in sequence.

The FLOPS rating was unchanged.

Julie said, "All right, it's a single processor. Now you've got my attention. Where is it?"

"Turn the keyboard over."

There was a charcoal-grey module, five centimetres square and five millimetres thick, plugged into an inset docking bay. Julie examined it, but it bore no manufacturer's logo or other identifying marks.

"This connects to the processor?" she asked.

"No. It is the processor."

"You're joking." She tugged it free of the dock, and the wall screen went blank. She held it up and turned it around, though Daniel wasn't sure what she was looking for. Somewhere to slip in a screwdriver and take the thing apart, probably. He said, "If you break it, you own it, so I hope you've got a few hundred spare."

"A few hundred grand? Hardly."

"A few hundred million."

Her face flushed. "Of course. If it was a few hundred grand, everyone would have one." She put it down on the table, then as an afterthought slid it a little further from the edge. "As I said, you've got my attention."

Daniel smiled. "I'm sorry about the theatrics."

"No, this deserved the build-up. What is it, exactly?"

"A single, three-dimensional photonic crystal. No electronics to slow it down; every last component is optical. The architecture was nanofabricated with a method that I'd prefer not to describe in detail."

"Fair enough." She thought for a while. "I take it you don't expect me to buy one. My research budget for the next thousand years would barely cover it."

"In your present position. But you're not joined to the university at the hip."

"So this is a job interview?"

Daniel nodded.

Julie couldn't help herself; she picked up the crystal and examined it again, as if there might yet be some feature that a human eye could discern. "Can you give me a job description?"

"Midwife."

She laughed. "To what?"

"History," Daniel said.

Her smile faded slowly.

"I believe you're the best AI researcher of your generation," he said. "I want you to work for me." He reached over and took the crystal from her. "With this as your platform, imagine what you could do."

Julie said, "What exactly would you want me to do?"

"For the last fifteen years," Daniel said, "you've stated that the ultimate goal of your research is to create conscious, human-level, artificial intelligence."

"That's right."

"Then we want the same thing. What I want is for you to succeed."

She ran a hand over her face; whatever else she was thinking, there was no denying that she was tempted. "It's gratifying that you have so much confidence in my abilities," she said. "But we need to be clear about some things. This prototype is amazing, and if you ever get the production costs down I'm sure it will have some extraordinary applications. It would eat up climate forecasting, lattice QCD, astrophysical modelling, proteomics . . ."

"Of course." Actually, Daniel had no intention of marketing the device. He'd bought out the inventor of the fabrication process with his own private funds; there were no other shareholders or directors to dictate his use of the technology.

"But AI," Julie said, "is different. We're in a maze, not a highway; there's nowhere that speed alone can take us. However many exaflops I have to play with, they won't spontaneously combust into consciousness. I'm not being held back by the university's computers; I have access to SHARCNET anytime I need it. I'm being held back by my own lack of insight into the problems I'm addressing."

Daniel said, "A maze is not a dead end. When I was twelve, I wrote a program for solving mazes."

"And I'm sure it worked well," Julie replied, "for small, two-dimensional ones. But you know how those kind of algorithms scale. Put your old program on this crystal, and I could still design a maze in half a day that would bring it to its knees."

"Of course," Daniel conceded. "Which is precisely why I'm interested in hiring you. You know a great deal more about the maze of AI than I do; any strategy you developed would be vastly superior to a blind search."

"I'm not saying that I'm merely groping in the dark," she said. "If it was that bleak, I'd be working on a different problem entirely. But I don't see what difference this processor would make."

"What created the only example of consciousness we know of?" Daniel asked.

"Evolution."

"Exactly. But I don't want to wait three billion years, so I need to make the selection process a great deal more refined, and the sources of variation more targeted."

Julie digested this. "You want to try to *evolve* true AI? Conscious, human-level AI?"

"Yes." Daniel saw her mouth tightening, saw her struggling to measure her words before speaking.

"With respect," she said, "I don't think you've thought that through."

"On the contrary," Daniel assured her. "I've been planning this for twenty years."

"Evolution," she said, "is about failure and death. Do you have any idea how many sentient creatures lived and died along the way to *Homo sapiens*? How much suffering was involved?"

"Part of your job would be to minimize the suffering."

"*Minimize* it?" She seemed genuinely shocked, as if this proposal was even worse than blithely assuming that the process would raise no ethical concerns. "What right do we have to inflict it at all?"

Daniel said, "You're grateful to exist, aren't you? Notwithstanding the tribulations of your ancestors."

"I'm grateful to exist," she agreed, "but in the human case the suffering wasn't deliberately inflicted by anyone, and nor was there any alternative way we could have come into existence. If there really *had* been a just creator, I don't doubt that he would have followed Genesis literally; he sure as hell would not have used evolution."

"Just, *and omnipotent*," Daniel suggested. "Sadly, that second trait's even rarer than the first."

"I don't think it's going to take omnipotence to create something in our own image," she said. "Just a little more patience and self-knowledge."

"This won't be like natural selection," Daniel insisted. "Not that blind, not that cruel, not that wasteful. You'd be free to intervene as much as you wished, to take whatever palliative measures you felt appropriate."

"*Palliative measures*?" Julie met his gaze, and he saw her expression flicker from disbelief to something darker. She stood up and glanced at her wristphone. "I don't have any signal here. Would you mind calling me a taxi?"

Daniel said, "Please, hear me out. Give me ten more minutes, then the helicopter will take you to the airport."

"I'd prefer to make my own way home." She gave Daniel a look that made it clear that this was not negotiable.

He called her a taxi, and they walked to the elevator.

"I know you find this morally challenging," he said, "and I respect that. I wouldn't dream of hiring someone who thought these were trivial issues. But if I don't do this, someone else will. Someone with far worse intentions than mine."

"Really?" Her tone was openly sarcastic now. "So how, exactly, does the mere existence of your project stop this hypothetical bin Laden of AI from carrying out his own?"

Daniel was disappointed; he'd expected her at least to understand what was at stake. He said, "This is a race to decide between Godhood and enslavement. Whoever succeeds first will be unstoppable. I'm not going to be anyone's slave."

Julie stepped into the elevator; he followed her.

She said, "You know what they say the modern version of Pascal's Wager is? Sucking up to as many Transhumanists as possible, just in case one of them turns into God. Perhaps your motto should be 'Treat every chatterbot kindly, it might turn out to be the deity's uncle.'"

"We will be as kind as possible," Daniel said. "And don't forget, we can determine the nature of these beings. They will be happy to be alive, and grateful to their creator. We can select for those traits."

Julie said, "So you're aiming for *übermenschen* that wag their tails when you scratch them behind the ears? You might find there's a bit of a trade-off there."

The elevator reached the lobby. Daniel said, "Think about this, don't rush to a decision. You can call me any time." There was no commercial flight back to Toronto tonight; she'd be stuck in a hotel, paying money she could ill afford, thinking about the kind of salary she could demand from him now that she'd played hard to get. If she mentally recast all this obstinate moralizing as a deliberate bargaining strategy, she'd have no trouble swallowing her pride.

Julie offered her hand, and he shook it. She said, "Thank you for dinner."

The taxi was waiting. He walked with her across the lobby. "If you want to see AI in your lifetime," he said, "this is the only way it's going to happen."

She turned to face him. "Maybe that's true. We'll see. But better to spend a thousand years and get it right, than a decade and succeed by your methods."

As Daniel watched the taxi drive away into the fog, he forced himself to accept the reality: she was never going to change her mind. Julie Dehghani had been his first choice, his ideal collaborator. He couldn't pretend that this wasn't a setback.

Still, no one was irreplaceable. However much it would have delighted him to have won her over, there were many more names on his list.

2

Daniel's wrist tingled as the message came through. He glanced down and saw the word PROGRESS! hovering in front of his watch face.

The board meeting was almost over; he disciplined himself and kept his attention focused for ten more minutes. WiddulHands.com had made him his first billion, and it was still the pre-eminent social networking site for the 0–3 age group. It had been fifteen years since he'd founded the company, and he had since diversified in many directions, but he had no intention of taking his hands off the levers.

When the meeting finished he blanked the wall screen and paced the empty conference room for half a minute, rolling his neck and stretching his shoulders. Then he said, "Lucien."

Lucien Crace appeared on the screen. "Significant progress?" Daniel enquired.

"Absolutely." Lucien was trying to maintain polite eye contact with Daniel, but something kept drawing his gaze away. Without waiting for an explanation, Daniel gestured at the screen and had it show him exactly what Lucien was seeing.

A barren, rocky landscape stretched to the horizon. Scattered across the rocks were dozens of crab-like creatures – some deep blue, some coral pink, though these weren't colours the locals would see, just species markers added to the view to make it easier to interpret. As Daniel watched, fat droplets of corrosive rain drizzled down from a passing cloud. This had to be the bleakest environment in all of Sapphire.

Lucien was still visible in an inset. "See the blue ones over by the crater lake?" he said. He sketched a circle on the image to guide Daniel's attention.

"Yeah." Five blues were clustered around a lone pink; Daniel gestured and the view zoomed in on them. The blues had opened up their prisoner's body, but it wasn't dead; Daniel was sure of that, because the pinks had recently acquired a trait that turned their bodies to mush the instant they expired.

"They've found a way to study it," Lucien said. "To keep it alive and study it."

From the very start of the project, he and Daniel had decided to grant the Phites the power to observe and manipulate their own bodies as much as possible. In the DNA world, the inner workings of anatomy and heredity had only become accessible once highly sophisticated technology had been invented. In Sapphire, the barriers were designed to be far lower. The basic units of biology here were "beads", small spheres that possessed a handful of simple properties but no complex internal biochemistry. Beads were larger than the cells of the DNA world, and Sapphire's diffraction-less optics rendered them visible to the right kind of naked eye. Animals acquired beads from their diet, while in plants they replicated in the presence of sunlight, but unlike cells they did not themselves mutate. The beads in a Phite's body could be rearranged with a minimum of fuss, enabling a kind of self-modification that no human surgeon or prosthetics engineer could rival – and this skill was actually essential for at least one stage in every Phite's life: reproduction involved two Phites pooling their spare beads and then collaborating to "sculpt" them into an infant, in part by directly copying each other's current body plans.

Of course these crabs knew nothing of the abstract principles of engineering and design, but the benefits of trial and error, of self-experimentation and cross-species plagiarism, had led them into an escalating war of innovation. The pinks had been the first to stop their corpses from being plundered for secrets, by stumbling on a way to make them literally fall apart in extremis; now it seemed the blues had found a way around that, and were indulging in a spot of vivisection-as-industrial-espionage.

Daniel felt a visceral twinge of sympathy for the struggling pink, but he brushed it aside. Not only did he doubt that the Phites were any more conscious than ordinary crabs, they certainly had a radically different relationship to bodily integrity. The pink was resisting because its dissectors were of a different species; if they had been its cousins it might not have put up any fight at all. When something happened in spite of your wishes, that was unpleasant by definition, but it would be absurd to imagine that the pink was in the kind of agony that an antelope being flayed by jackals would feel – let alone experiencing the existential terrors of a human trapped and mutilated by a hostile tribe.

"This is going to give them a tremendous advantage," Lucien enthused.

"The blues?"

Lucien shook his head. "Not blues over pinks; Phites over tradlife. Bacteria can swap genes, but this kind of active mimetics is unprecedented without cultural support. Da Vinci might have watched the birds in flight and sketched his gliders, but no lemur ever dissected the body of an eagle and then stole its tricks. They're going to have *innate* skills as powerful as whole strands of human technology. All this before they even have language."

"Hmm." Daniel wanted to be optimistic too, but he was growing wary of Lucien's hype. Lucien had a doctorate in genetic programming, but he'd made his name with FoodExcuses.com, a web service that trawled the medical literature to cobble together quasi-scientific justifications for indulging in your favourite culinary vice. He had the kind of technobabble that could bleed money out of venture capitalists down pat, and though Daniel admired that skill in its proper place, he expected a higher insight-to-bullshit ratio now that Lucien was on his payroll.

The blues were backing away from their captive. As Daniel watched, the pink sealed up its wounds and scuttled off towards a group of its own kind. The blues had now seen the detailed anatomy of the respiratory system that had been giving the pinks an advantage in the thin air of this high plateau. A few of the blues would try it out, and if it worked for them, the whole tribe would copy it.

"So what do you think?" Lucien asked.

"Select them," Daniel said.

"Just the blues?"

"No, both of them." The blues alone might have diverged into compet-ing subspecies eventually, but bringing their old rivals along for the ride would help to keep them sharp.

"Done," Lucien replied. In an instant, ten million Phites were erased, leaving the few thousand blues and pinks from these badlands to inherit the planet. Daniel felt no compunction; the extinction events he decreed were surely the most painless in history.

Now that the world no longer required human scrutiny, Lucien unthrot-tled the crystal and let the simulation race ahead; automated tools would let them know when the next interesting development arose. Daniel watched the population figures rising as his chosen species spread out and recolonized Sapphire.

Would their distant descendants rage against him, for this act of "geno-cide" that had made room for them to flourish and prosper? That seemed unlikely. In any case, what choice did he have? He couldn't start manu-facturing new crystals for every useless side-branch of the evolutionary tree. Nobody was wealthy enough to indulge in an exponentially growing number of virtual animal shelters, at half a billion dollars apiece.

He was a just creator, but he was not omnipotent. His careful pruning was the only way.

3

In the months that followed, progress came in fits and starts. Several times, Daniel found himself rewinding history, reversing his decisions and trying a new path. Keeping every Phite variant alive was impractical, but he did retain enough information to resurrect lost species at will.

The maze of AI was still a maze, but the speed of the crystal served them well. Barely eighteen months after the start of Project Sapphire, the Phites were exhibiting a basic theory of mind: their actions showed that they could deduce what others knew about the world, as distinct from what they knew themselves. Other AI researchers had spliced this kind of thing into their programs by hand, but Daniel was convinced that his version was better integrated, more robust. Human-crafted software was brittle and inflexible; his Phites had been forged in the heat of change.

Daniel kept a close watch on his competitors, but nothing he saw gave him reason to doubt his approach. Sunil Gupta was raking in the cash from a search engine that could "understand" all forms of text, audio and video, making use of fuzzy logic techniques that were at least forty years old. Daniel respected Gupta's business acumen, but in the unlikely event that his software ever became conscious, the sheer cruelty of having forced it to wade through the endless tides of blogorrhoea would surely see it turn on its creator and exact a revenge that made *The Terminator* look like a picnic. Angela Lindstrom was having some success with her cheesy AfterLife, in which dying clients gave heart-to-heart interviews to software that then constructed avatars able to converse with surviving relatives. And Julie Dehghani was still frittering away her talent, writing software for robots that played with coloured blocks side-by-side with human infants, and learnt languages from adult volunteers by imitating the interactions of baby talk. Her prophesy of taking a thousand years to "get it right" seemed to be on target.

As the second year of the project drew to a close, Lucien was contacting Daniel once or twice a month to announce a new breakthrough. By constructing environments that imposed suitable selection pressures, Lucien had generated a succession of new species that used simple tools, crafted crude shelters, and even domesticated plants. They were still shaped more or less like crabs, but they were at least as intelligent as chimpanzees.

The Phites worked together by observation and imitation, guiding and reprimanding each other with a limited repertoire of gestures and cries, but as yet they lacked anything that could truly be called a language. Daniel grew impatient, to move beyond a handful of specialized skills, his creatures needed the power to map any object, any action, any prospect they might encounter in the world into their speech, and into their thoughts.

Daniel summoned Lucien and they sought a way forward. It was easy to tweak the Phites' anatomy to grant them the ability to generate more subtle vocalizations, but that alone was no more useful than handing a chimp a conductor's baton. What was needed was a way to make sophisticated planning and communications skills a matter of survival.

Eventually, he and Lucien settled on a series of environmental modifications, providing opportunities for the creatures to rise to the occasion. Most of these scenarios began with famine. Lucien blighted the main food crops, then offered a palpable reward for progress by dangling some tempting new fruit from a branch that was just out of reach. Sometimes that metaphor could almost be taken literally: he'd introduce a plant with a complex life cycle that required tricky processing to render it edible, or a new prey animal that was clever and vicious, but nutritionally well worth hunting in the end.

Time and again, the Phites failed the test, with localized species dwindling to extinction. Daniel watched in dismay; he had not grown sentimental, but he'd always boasted to himself that he'd set his standards higher than the extravagant cruelties of nature. He contemplated tweaking the creatures' physiology so that starvation brought a swifter, more merciful demise, but Lucien pointed out that he'd be slashing his chances of success if he curtailed this period of intense motivation. Each time a group died out, a fresh batch of mutated cousins rose from the dust to take their place; without that intervention, Sapphire would have been a wilderness within a few real-time days.

Daniel closed his eyes to the carnage, and put his trust in sheer time, sheer numbers. In the end, that was what the crystal had bought him: when all else failed, he could give up any pretence of knowing how to achieve his aims and simply test one random mutation after another.

Months went by, sending hundreds of millions of tribes starving into their graves. But what choice did he have? If he fed these creatures milk and honey, they'd remain fat and stupid until the day he died. Their hunger agitated them, it drove them to search and strive, and while any human onlooker was tempted to colour such behaviour with their own emotional palette, Daniel told himself that the Phites' suffering was a shallow thing, little more than the instinct that jerked his own hand back from a flame before he'd even registered discomfort.

They were not the equal of humans. Not yet.

And if he lost his nerve, they never would be.

Daniel dreamt that he was inside Sapphire, but there were no Phites in sight. In front of him stood a sleek black monolith; a thin stream of pus wept from a crack in its smooth, obsidian surface. Someone was holding him by the wrist, trying to force his hand into a reeking pit in the ground. The pit, he knew, was piled high with things he did not want to see, let alone touch.

He thrashed around until he woke, but the sense of pressure on his wrist remained. It was coming from his watch. As he focused on the one-word message he'd received, his stomach tightened. Lucien would not have dared to wake him at this hour for some run-of-the-mill result.

Daniel rose, dressed, then sat in his office sipping coffee. He did not know why he was so reluctant to make the call. He had been waiting for this moment for more than twenty years, but it would not be the pinnacle of his life. After this, there would be a thousand more peaks, each one twice as magnificent as the last.

He finished the coffee then sat a while longer, massaging his temples, making sure his head was clear. He would not greet this new era bleary-eyed, half-awake. He recorded all his calls, but this was one he would retain for posterity.

"Lucien," he said. The man's image appeared, smiling. "Success?"

"They're talking to each other," Lucien replied.

"About what?"

"Food, weather, sex, death. The past, the future. You name it. They won't shut up."

Lucien sent transcripts on the data channel, and Daniel perused them. The linguistics software didn't just observe the Phites' behaviour and correlate it with the sounds they made; it peered right into their virtual brains and tracked the flow of information. Its task was far from trivial, and there was no guarantee that its translations were perfect, but Daniel did not believe it could hallucinate an entire language and fabricate these rich, detailed conversations out of thin air.

He flicked between statistical summaries, technical overviews of linguistic structure, and snippets from the millions of conversations the software had logged. *Food, weather, sex, death.* As human dialogue the translations would have seemed utterly banal, but in context they were riveting. These were not chatterbots blindly following Markov chains, designed to impress the judges in a Turing test. The Phites were discussing matters by which they genuinely lived and died.

When Daniel brought up a page of conversational topics in alphabetical order, his eyes were caught by the single entry under the letter G. *Grief*. He tapped the link, and spent a few minutes reading through samples, illustrating the appearance of the concept following the death of a child, a parent, a friend.

He kneaded his eyelids. It was three in the morning; there was a sickening clarity to everything, the kind that only night could bring. He turned to Lucien.

"No more death."

"Boss?" Lucien was startled.

"I want to make them immortal. Let them evolve culturally; let their ideas live and die. Let them modify their own brains, once they're smart enough; they can already tweak the rest of their anatomy."

"Where will you put them all?" Lucien demanded.

"I can afford another crystal. Maybe two more."

"That won't get you far. At the present birth rate —"

"We'll have to cut their fertility drastically, tapering it down to zero. After that, if they want to start reproducing again they'll really have to innovate." They would need to learn about the outside world, and comprehend its alien physics well enough to design new hardware into which they could migrate.

Lucien scowled. "How will we control them? How will we shape them? If we can't select the ones we want —"

Daniel said quietly, "This is not up for discussion." Whatever Julie Dehghani had thought of him, he was not a monster; if he believed that these creatures were as conscious as he was, he was not going to slaughter them like cattle – or stand by and let them die "naturally", when the rules of this world were his to rewrite at will.

"We'll shape them through their memes," he said. "We'll kill off the bad memes, and help spread the ones we want to succeed." He would need to keep an iron grip on the Phites and their culture, though, or he would never be able to trust them. If he wasn't going to literally *breed them* for loyalty and gratitude, he would have to do the same with their ideas.

Lucien said, "We're not prepared for any of this. We're going to need new software, new analysis and intervention tools."

Daniel understood. "Freeze time in Sapphire. Then tell the team they've got eighteen months."

4

Daniel sold his shares in WiddulHands, and had two more crystals built. One was to support a higher population in Sapphire, so there was as large a pool of diversity among the immortal Phites as possible; the other was to run the software – which Lucien had dubbed the Thought Police – needed to keep tabs on what they were doing. If human overseers had had to monitor and shape the evolving culture every step of the way, that would have slowed things down to a glacial pace. Still, automating the process completely was tricky, and Daniel preferred to err on the side of caution, with the Thought Police freezing Sapphire and notifying him whenever the situation became too delicate.

If the end of death was greeted by the Phites with a mixture of puzzlement and rejoicing, the end of birth was not so easy to accept. When all attempts by mating couples to sculpt their excess beads into offspring became as ineffectual as shaping dolls out of clay, it led to a mixture of persistence and distress that was painful to witness. Humans were accustomed to failing to conceive, but this was more like stillbirth after stillbirth. Even when Daniel intervened to modify the Phites' basic drives, some kind of cultural or emotional inertia kept many of them going through the motions. Though their new instincts urged them merely to pool their spare beads and then stop, sated, they would continue with the old version of the act regardless, forlorn and confused, trying to shape the useless puddle into something that lived and breathed.

Move on, Daniel thought. *Get over it.* There was only so much sympathy he could muster for immortal beings who would fill the galaxy with their children, if they ever got their act together.

The Phites didn't yet have writing, but they'd developed a strong oral tradition, and some put their mourning for the old ways into elegiac words. The Thought Police identified those memes, and ensured that they didn't spread far. Some Phites chose to kill themselves rather than live in the barren new world. Daniel felt he had no right to stop them, but mysterious obstacles blocked the paths of anyone who tried, irresponsibly, to romanticize or encourage such acts.

The Phites could only die by their own volition, but those who retained the will to live were not free to doze the centuries away. Daniel decreed no more terrible famines, but he hadn't abolished hunger itself, and he kept enough pressure on the food supply and other resources to force the Phites to keep innovating, refining agriculture, developing trade.

The Thought Police identified and nurtured the seeds of writing, mathematics, and natural science. The physics of Sapphire was a simplified, game-world model, not so arbitrary as to be incoherent, but not so deep and complex that you needed particle physics to get to the bottom of it. As crystal time sped forward and the immortals sought solace in understanding their world, Sapphire soon had its Euclid and Archimedes, its Galileo and its Newton; their ideas spread with supernatural efficiency, bringing forth a torrent of mathematicians and astronomers.

Sapphire's stars were just a planetarium-like backdrop, present only to help the Phites get their notions of heliocentricity and inertia right, but its moon was as real as the world itself. The technology needed to reach it was going to take a while, but that was all right; Daniel didn't want them getting ahead of themselves. There was a surprise waiting for them there, and his preference was for a flourishing of biotech and computing before they faced that revelation.

Between the absence of fossils, Sapphire's limited biodiversity, and all the clunky external meddling that needed to be covered up, it was hard for the Phites to reach a grand Darwinian view of biology, but their innate skill with beads gave them a head start in the practical arts. With a little nudging, they began tinkering with their bodies, correcting some inconvenient anatomical quirks that they'd missed in their pre-conscious phase.

As they refined their knowledge and techniques, Daniel let them imagine that they were working towards restoring fertility; after all, that was perfectly true, even if their goal was a few conceptual revolutions further away than they realized. Humans had had their naive notions of a Philosopher's Stone dashed, but they'd still achieved nuclear transmutation in the end.

The Phites, he hoped, would transmute *themselves*: inspect their own brains, make sense of them, and begin to improve them. It was a staggering task to expect of anyone; even Lucien and his team, with their God's-eye view of the creatures, couldn't come close. But when the crystal was running at full speed, the Phites could think millions of times faster than their creators. If Daniel could keep them from straying off course, everything that humanity might once have conceived of as the fruits of millennia of progress was now just a matter of months away.

5

Lucien said, "We're losing track of the language."

Daniel was in his Houston office; he'd come to Texas for a series of face-to-face meetings, to see if he could raise some much-needed cash by licensing the crystal fabrication process. He would have preferred to keep the technology to himself, but he was almost certain that he was too far ahead of his rivals now for any of them to stand a chance of catching up with him.

"What do you mean, losing track?" Daniel demanded. Lucien had briefed him just three hours before, and given no warning of an impending crisis.

The Thought Police, Lucien explained, had done their job well: they had pushed the neural self-modification meme for all it was worth, and now a successful form of "brain boosting" was spreading across Sapphire. It required a detailed "recipe" but no technological aids; the same innate skills for observing and manipulating beads that the Phites had used to copy themselves during reproduction were enough.

All of this was much as Daniel had hoped it would be, but there was an alarming downside. The boosted Phites were adopting a dense and complex new language, and the analysis software couldn't make sense of it.

"Slow them down further," Daniel suggested. "Give the linguistics more time to run."

"I've already frozen Sapphire," Lucien replied. "The linguistics have been running for an hour, with the full resources of an entire crystal."

Daniel said irritably, "We can see exactly what they've done to their brains. How can we not understand the effects on the language?"

"In the general case," Lucien said, "deducing a language from nothing but neural anatomy is computationally intractable. With the old language, we were lucky; it had a simple structure, and it was highly correlated with obvious behavioural elements. The new language is much more abstract and conceptual. We might not even have our own correlates for half the concepts."

Daniel had no intention of letting events in Sapphire slip out of his control. It was one thing to hope that the Phites would, eventually, be juggling real-world physics that was temporarily beyond his comprehension, but any bright ten-year-old could grasp the laws of their present universe, and their technology was still far from rocket science.

He said, "Keep Sapphire frozen, and study your records of the Phites who first performed this boost. If they understood what they were doing, we can work it out too."

At the end of the week, Daniel signed the licensing deal and flew back to San Francisco. Lucien briefed him daily, and at Daniel's urging hired a dozen new computational linguists to help with the problem.

After six months, it was clear that they were getting nowhere. The Phites who'd invented the boost had had one big advantage as they'd tinkered with each other's brains: it had not been a purely theoretical exercise for them. They hadn't gazed at anatomical diagrams and then reasoned their way to a better design. They had *experienced* the effects of thousands of small experimental changes, and the results had shaped their intuition for the process. Very little of that intuition had been spoken aloud, let alone written down and formalised. And the process of decoding those insights from a purely structural view of their brains was every bit as difficult as decoding the language itself.

Daniel couldn't wait any longer. With the crystal heading for the market, and other comparable technologies approaching fruition, he couldn't allow his lead to melt away.

"We need the Phites themselves to act as translators," he told Lucien. "We need to contrive a situation where there's a large enough pool who choose not to be boosted that the old language continues to be used."

"So we need maybe twenty-five per cent refusing the boost?" Lucien suggested. "And we need the boosted Phites to want to keep them informed of what's happening, in terms that we can all understand."

Daniel said, "Exactly."

"I think we can slow down the uptake of boosting," Lucien mused, "while we encourage a traditionalist meme that says it's better to span the two cultures and languages than replace the old entirely with the new."

Lucien's team set to work, tweaking the Thought Police for the new task, then restarting Sapphire itself.

Their efforts seemed to yield the desired result: the Phites were corralled into valuing the notion of maintaining a link to their past, and while the boosted Phites surged ahead, they also worked hard to keep the unboosted in the loop.

It was a messy compromise, though, and Daniel wasn't happy with the prospect of making do with a watered-down, Sapphire-for-Dummies version of the Phites' intellectual achievements. What he really wanted was someone on the inside reporting to him directly, like a Phite version of Lucien.

It was time to start thinking about job interviews.

Lucien was running Sapphire more slowly than usual – to give the Thought Police a computational advantage now that they'd lost so much raw surveillance data – but even at the reduced rate, it took just six real-time days for the boosted Phites to invent computers, first as a mathematical formalism and, shortly afterwards, as a succession of practical machines.

Daniel had already asked Lucien to notify him if any Phite guessed the true nature of their world. In the past, a few had come up with vague metaphysical speculations that weren't too wide of the mark, but now that they had a firm grasp of the idea of universal computation, they were finally in a position to understand the crystal as more than an idle fantasy.

The message came just after midnight, as Daniel was preparing for bed. He went into his office and activated the intervention tool that Lucien had written for him, specifying a serial number for the Phite in question.

The tool prompted Daniel to provide a human-style name for his interlocutor, to facilitate communication. Daniel's mind went blank, but after waiting twenty seconds the software offered its own suggestion: Primo.

Primo was boosted, and he had recently built a computer of his own. Shortly afterwards, the Thought Police had heard him telling a couple of unboosted friends about an amusing possibility that had occurred to him.

Sapphire was slowed to a human pace, then Daniel took control of a Phite avatar and the tool contrived a meeting, arranging for the two of them to be alone in the shelter that Primo had built for himself. In accordance with the current architectural style the wooden building was actually still alive, self-repairing and anchored to the ground by roots.

Primo said, "Good morning. I don't believe we've met."

It was no great breach of protocol for a stranger to enter one's shelter uninvited, but Primo was understating his surprise; in this world of immortals, but no passenger jets, bumping into strangers anywhere was rare.

"I'm Daniel." The tool would invent a Phite name for Primo to hear. "I heard you talking to your friends last night about your new computer. Wondering what these machines might do in the future. Wondering if they could ever grow powerful enough to contain a whole world."

"I didn't see you there," Primo replied.

"I wasn't there," Daniel explained. "I live outside this world. I built the computer that contains this world."

Primo made a gesture that the tool annotated as amusement, then he spoke a few words in the boosted language. *Insults? A jest? A test of Daniel's omniscience?* Daniel decided to bluff his way through, and act as if the words were irrelevant.

He said, "Let the rain start." Rain began pounding on the roof of the shelter. "Let the rain stop." Daniel gestured with one claw at a large cooking pot in a corner of the room. "Sand. Flower. Fire. Water jug." The pot obliged him, taking on each form in turn.

Primo said, "Very well. I believe you, Daniel." Daniel had had some experience reading the Phites' body language directly, and to him Primo seemed reasonably calm. Perhaps when you were as old as he was, and had witnessed so much change, such a revelation was far less of a shock than it would have been to a human at the dawn of the computer age.

"You created this world?" Primo asked him.

"Yes."

"You shaped our history?"

"In part," Daniel said. "Many things have been down to chance, or to your own choices."

"Did you stop us having children?" Primo demanded.

"Yes," Daniel admitted.

"*Why?*"

"There is no room left in the computer. It was either that, or many more deaths."

Primo pondered this. "So you could have stopped the death of my parents, had you wished?"

"I could bring them back to life, if you want that." This wasn't a lie; Daniel had stored detailed snapshots of all the last mortal Phites. "But not yet; only when there's a bigger computer. When there's room for them."

"Could you bring back *their* parents? And their parents' parents? Back to the beginning of time?"

"No. That information is lost."

Primo said, "What is this talk of waiting for a bigger computer? You could easily stop time from passing for us, and only start it again when your new computer is built."

"No," Daniel said, "I can't. Because I *need you to build the computer.* I'm not like you: I'm not immortal, and my brain can't be boosted. I've done my best, now I need you to do better. The only way that can happen is if you learn the science of my world, and come up with a way to make this new machine."

Primo walked over to the water jug that Daniel had magicked into being. "It seems to me that you were ill-prepared for the task you set yourself. If you'd waited for the machine you really needed, our lives would not have been so hard. And if such a machine could not be built in your lifetime, what was to stop your grandchildren from taking on that task?"

"I had no choice," Daniel insisted. "I couldn't leave your creation to my descendants. There is a war coming between my people. I needed your help. I needed strong allies."

"You have no friends in your own world?"

"Your time runs faster than mine. I needed the kind of allies that only your people can become, in time."

Primo said, "What exactly do you want of us?"

"To build the new computer you need," Daniel replied. "To grow in numbers, to grow in strength. Then to raise me up, to make me greater than I was, as I've done for you. When the war is won, there will be peace forever. Side by side, we will rule a thousand worlds."

"And what do you want of *me*?" Primo asked. "Why are you speaking to me, and not to all of us?"

"Most people," Daniel said, "aren't ready to hear this. It's better that they don't learn the truth yet. But I need one person who can work for me directly. I can see and hear everything in your world, but I need you to make sense of it. I need you to understand things for me."

Primo was silent.

Daniel said, "I gave you life. How can you refuse me?"

6

Daniel pushed his way through the small crowd of protesters gathered at the entrance to his San Francisco tower. He could have come and gone by helicopter instead, but his security consultants had assessed these people as posing no significant threat. A small amount of bad PR didn't bother him; he was no longer selling anything that the public could boycott directly, and none of the businesses he dealt with seemed worried about being tainted by association. He'd broken no laws, and confirmed no rumours. A few feral cyberphiles waving placards reading "Software Is Not Your Slave!" meant nothing.

Still, if he ever found out which one of his employees had leaked details of the project, he'd break their legs.

Daniel was in the elevator when Lucien messaged him: MOON VERY SOON! He halted the elevator's ascent, and redirected it to the basement.

All three crystals were housed in the basement now, just centimetres away from the Play Pen: a vacuum chamber containing an atomic force microscope with fifty thousand independently movable tips, arrays of solid-state lasers and photodetectors, and thousands of micro-wells stocked with samples of all the stable chemical elements. The time lag between Sapphire and this machine had to be as short as possible, in order for the Phites to be able to conduct experiments in real-world physics while their own world was running at full speed.

Daniel pulled up a stool and sat beside the Play Pen. If he wasn't going to slow Sapphire down, it was pointless aspiring to watch developments as they unfolded. He'd probably view a replay of the lunar landing when he went up to his office, but by the time he screened it, it would be ancient history.

"One giant leap" would be an understatement; wherever the Phites landed on the moon, they would find a strange black monolith waiting for them. Inside would be the means to operate the Play Pen; it would not take them long to learn the controls, or to understand what this signified. If they were really slow in grasping what they'd found, Daniel had instructed Primo to explain it to them.

The physics of the real world was far more complex than the kind the Phites were used to, but then, no human had ever been on intimate terms with quantum field theory either, and the Thought Police had already encouraged the Phites to develop most of the mathematics they'd need to get started. In any case, it didn't matter if the Phites took longer than humans to discover twentieth-century scientific principles, and move beyond them. Seen from the outside, it would happen within hours, days, weeks at the most.

A row of indicator lights blinked on; the Play Pen was active. Daniel's throat went dry. The Phites were finally reaching out of their own world into his.

A panel above the machine displayed histograms classifying the experiments the Phites had performed so far. By the time Daniel was paying attention, they had already discovered the kinds of bonds that could be formed between various atoms, and constructed thousands of different small molecules. As he watched, they carried out spectroscopic analyses, built simple nanomachines, and manufactured devices that were, unmistakably, memory elements and logic gates.

The Phites wanted children, and they understood now that this was the only way. They would soon be building a world in which they were not just more numerous, but faster and smarter than they were inside the crystal. And that would only be the first of a thousand iterations. They were working their way towards Godhood, and they would lift up their own creator as they ascended.

Daniel left the basement and headed for his office. When he arrived, he called Lucien.

"They've built an atomic-scale computer," Lucien announced. "And they've fed some fairly complex software into it. It doesn't seem to be an upload, though. Certainly not a direct copy on the level of beads." He sounded flustered; Daniel had forbidden him to risk screwing up the experiments by slowing down Sapphire, so even with Primo's briefings to help him it was difficult for him to keep abreast of everything.

"Can you model their computer, and then model what the software is doing?" Daniel suggested.

Lucien said, "We only have six atomic physicists on the team; the Phites already outnumber us on that score by about a thousand to one. By the time we have any hope of making sense of this, they'll be doing something different."

"What does Primo say?" The Thought Police hadn't been able to get Primo included in any of the lunar expeditions, but Lucien had given him the power to make himself invisible and teleport to any part of Sapphire or the lunar base. Wherever the action was, he was free to eavesdrop.

"Primo has trouble understanding a lot of what he hears; even the boosted aren't universal polymaths and instant experts in every kind of jargon. The gist of it is that the Lunar Project people have made a very fast computer in the Outer World, and it's going to help with the fertility problem . . . somehow." Lucien laughed. "Hey, maybe the Phites will do exactly what we did: see if they can evolve something smart enough to give them a hand. How cool would that be?"

Daniel was not amused. Somebody had to do some real work eventually; if the Phites just passed the buck, the whole enterprise would collapse like a pyramid scheme.

Daniel had some business meetings he couldn't put off. By the time he'd swept all the bullshit aside, it was early afternoon. The Phites had now built some kind of tiny solid-state accelerator, and were probing the internal structure of protons and neutrons by pounding them with high-speed electrons. An atomic computer wired up to various detectors was doing the data analysis, processing the results faster than any in-world computer could. The Phites had already figured out the standard quark model. Maybe they were going to skip uploading into nanocomputers, and head straight for some kind of femtomachine?

Digests of Primo's briefings made no mention of using the strong force for computing, though. They were still just satisfying their curiosity about the fundamental laws. Daniel reminded himself of their history. They had burrowed down to what seemed like the foundations of physics before, only to discover that those simple rules were nothing to do with the ultimate reality. It made sense that they would try to dig as deeply as they could into the mysteries of the Outer World before daring to found a colony, let alone emigrate *en masse*.

By sunset the Phites were probing the surroundings of the Play Pen with various kinds of radiation. The levels were extremely low – certainly too low to risk damaging the crystals – so Daniel saw no need to intervene. The Play Pen itself did not have a massive power supply, it contained no radioisotopes, and the Thought Police would ring alarm bells and bring in human experts if some kind of tabletop fusion experiment got underway, so Daniel was reasonably confident that the Phites couldn't do anything stupid and blow the whole thing up.

Primo's briefings made it clear that they thought they were engaged in a kind of "astronomy." Daniel wondered if he should give them access to instruments for doing serious observations – the kind that would allow them to understand relativistic gravity and cosmology. Even if he bought time on a large telescope, though, just pointing it would take an eternity for the Phites. He wasn't going to slow Sapphire down and then grow old while they explored the sky; next thing they'd be launching space probes on thirty-year missions. Maybe it was time to ramp up the level of collaboration, and just hand them some astronomy texts and star maps? Human culture had its own hard-won achievements that the Phites couldn't easily match.

As the evening wore on, the Phites shifted their focus back to the subatomic world. A new kind of accelerator began smashing single gold ions together at extraordinary energies – though the total power being expended was still minuscule. Primo soon announced that they'd mapped all three generations of quarks and leptons. The Phites' knowledge of particle physics was drawing level with humanity's; Daniel couldn't follow the technical details any more, but the experts were giving it all the thumbs up. Daniel felt a surge of pride; of course his children knew what they were doing, and if they'd reached the point where they could momentarily bamboozle him, soon he'd ask them to catch their breath and bring him up to speed. Before he permitted them to emigrate, he'd slow the crystals down and introduce himself to everyone. In fact, that might be the perfect time to set them their next task: to understand human biology, well enough to upload him. To make him immortal, to repay their debt.

He sat watching images of the Phites' latest computers, reconstructions based on data flowing to and from the AFM tips. Vast lattices of shimmering atoms stretched off into the distance, the electron clouds that joined them quivering like beads of mercury in some surreal liquid abacus. As he watched, an inset window told him that the ion accelerators had been redesigned, and fired up again.

Daniel grew restless. He walked to the elevator. There was nothing he could see in the basement that he couldn't see from his office, but he wanted to stand beside the Play Pen, put his hand on the casing, press his nose against the glass. The era of Sapphire as a virtual world with no consequences in his own was coming to an end; he wanted to stand beside the thing itself and be reminded that it was as solid as he was.

The elevator descended, passing the tenth floor, the ninth, the eighth. Without warning, Lucien's voice burst from Daniel's watch, priority audio crashing through every barrier of privacy and protocol. "Boss, there's radiation. Net power gain. Get to the helicopter, *now*."

Daniel hesitated, contemplating an argument. If this was fusion, why hadn't it been detected and curtailed? He jabbed the stop button and felt the brakes engage. Then the world dissolved into brightness and pain.

7

When Daniel emerged from the opiate haze, a doctor informed him that he had burns to sixty per cent of his body. More from heat than from radiation. He was not going to die.

There was a net terminal by the bed. Daniel called Lucien and learnt what the physicists on the team had tentatively concluded, having studied the last of the Play Pen data that had made it off-site.

It seemed the Phites had discovered the Higgs field, and engineered a burst of something akin to cosmic inflation. What they'd done wasn't as simple as merely inflating a tiny patch of vacuum into a new universe, though. Not only had they managed to create a "cool Big Bang", they had pulled a large chunk of ordinary matter into the pocket universe they'd made, after which the wormhole leading to it had shrunk to subatomic size and fallen through the Earth.

They had taken the crystals with them, of course. If they'd tried to upload themselves into the pocket universe through the lunar data link, the Thought Police would have stopped them. So they'd emigrated by another route entirely. They had snatched their whole substrate, and ran.

Opinions were divided over exactly what else the new universe would contain. The crystals and the Play Pen floating in a void, with no power source, would leave the Phites effectively dead, but some of the team believed there could be a thin plasma of protons and electrons too, created by a form of Higgs decay that bypassed the unendurable quark-gluon fireball of a hot Big Bang. If they'd built the right nanomachines, there was a chance that they could convert the Play Pen into a structure that would keep the crystals safe, while the Phites slept through the long wait for the first starlight.

The tiny skin samples the doctors had taken finally grew into sheets large enough to graft. Daniel bounced between dark waves of pain and medicated euphoria, but one idea stayed with him throughout the turbulent journey, like a guiding star: *Primo had betrayed him.* He had given the fucker life, entrusted him with power, granted him privileged knowledge, showered him with the favours of the Gods. And how had he been repaid? He was back to zero. He'd spoken to his lawyers, having heard rumours of an "illegal radiation source", the insurance company was not going to pay out on the crystals without a fight.

Lucien came to the hospital, in person. Daniel was moved; they hadn't met face-to-face since the job interview. He shook the man's hand.

"You didn't betray me."

Lucien looked embarrassed. "I'm resigning, boss."

Daniel was stung, but he forced himself to accept the news stoically. "I understand; you have no choice. Gupta will have a crystal of his own by now. You have to be on the winning side, in the war of the Gods."

Lucien put his resignation letter on the bedside table. "What war? Are you still clinging to that fantasy where überdorks battle to turn the moon into computronium?"

Daniel blinked. "Fantasy? If you didn't believe it, why were you working with me?"

"You paid me. Extremely well."

"So how much will Gupta be paying you? I'll double it."

Lucien shook his head, amused. "I'm not going to work for Gupta. I'm moving into particle physics. The Phites weren't all that far ahead of us when they escaped; maybe forty or fifty years. Once we catch up, I guess a private universe will cost about as much as a private island; maybe less in the long run. But no one's going to be battling for control of this one, throwing grey goo around like monkeys flinging turds while they draw up their plans for Matrioshka brains."

Daniel said, "If you take any data from the Play Pen logs —"

"I'll honour all the confidentiality clauses in my contract." Lucien smiled. "But anyone can take an interest in the Higgs field; that's public domain."

After he left, Daniel bribed the nurse to crank up his medication, until even the sting of betrayal and disappointment began to fade.

A universe, he thought happily. *Soon I'll have a universe of my own.*

But I'm going to need some workers in there, some allies, some companions. I can't do it all alone; someone has to carry the load.

THE EGG MAN

Mary Rosenblum

One of the most popular and prolific of the new writers of the nineties, Mary Rosenblum made her first sale, to *Asimov's Science Fiction*, in 1990, and has since become a mainstay of that magazine – one of its most frequent contributors – with almost thirty sales there to her credit. She has also sold to *The Magazine of Fantasy & Science Fiction*, *Science Fiction Age*, *Pulphouse*, *New Legends*, and elsewhere.

Her linked series of Drylands stories have proved to be one of Asimov's most popular series, but she has also published memorable stories such as "The Stone Garden", "Synthesis", "Flight", "California Dreamer", "Casting at Pegasus", "Entrada", "Rat", "The Centaur Garden", "Skin Deep", "Songs the Sirens Sing", and many, many others. Her novella *Gas Fish* won the Asimov's Readers Award Poll in 1996, and was a finalist for that year's Nebula Award. Her first novel, *The Drylands*, appeared in 1993 to wide critical acclaim, winning the prestigious Compton Crook Award for Best First Novel of the Year; it was followed in short order by her second novel, *Chimera*, and her third, *The Stone Garden*. Her first short story collection, *Synthesis and Other Stories*, was widely hailed by critics as one of the best collections of 1996. She has also written a trilogy of mystery novels under the name Mary Freeman. Her most recent book is a major new science fiction novel, *Horizons*. A graduate of Clarion West, Mary Rosenblum lives in Portland, Oregon.

In the tense story that follows she takes us to an ecologically devastated future that seems all too likely to be around the corner for a look at people struggling to survive – and perhaps, if they can, to hold on to a bit of their souls.

ZIPAKNA HALTED AT midday to let the Dragon power up the batteries. He checked on the chickens clucking contentedly in their travel crates, then went outside to squat in the shade of one fully deployed solar wing in the 43 centigrade heat. Ilena, his sometimes-lover and poker partner, accused him of reverse snobbery, priding himself on being able to survive in the Sonoran heat without air conditioning. Zipakna smiled and tilted his water bottle, savouring the cool, sweet trickle of water across his tongue.

Not true, of course. He held still as the first wild bees found him, buzzed past his face to settle and sip from the sweat-drops beading on his skin. Killers. He held very still, but the caution wasn't really necessary. Thirst was the great gentler here. Every other drive was laid aside in the pursuit of water.

Even love?

He laughed a short note as the killers buzzed and sipped. So Ilena claimed, but she just missed him when she played the tourists without him. It had been mostly tourists from China lately, filling the underwater resorts in the Sea of Cortez. Chinese were rich and tough players and Ilena had been angry at him for leaving. But he always left in spring. She knew that. In front of him, the scarp he had been traversing ended in a bluff, eroded by water that had fallen here eons ago. The plain below spread out in tones of ochre and russet, dotted with dusty clumps of sage and the stark upward thrust of saguaro, lonely sentinels contemplating the desiccated plain of the Sonoran and in the distance, the ruins of a town. Paloma? Zipakna tilted his wrist, called up his position on his link. Yes, that was it. He had wandered a bit farther eastward than he'd thought and had cut through the edge of the Pima preserve. Sure enough, a fine had been levied against his account. He sighed. He serviced the Pima settlement out here and they didn't mind if he trespassed. It merely became a bargaining chip when it came time to talk price. The Pima loved to bargain.

He really should let the nav-link plot his course, but Ilena was right about that, at least. He prided himself on finding his way through the Sonora without it. Zipakna squinted as a flicker of movement caught his eye. A lizard? Maybe. Or one of the tough desert rodents. They didn't need to drink, got their water from seeds and cactus fruit. More adaptable than *Homo sapiens*, he thought, and smiled grimly.

He pulled his binocs from his belt pouch and focused on the movement. The digital lenses seemed to suck him through the air like a thrown spear, grey-ochre blur resolving into stone, mica flash, and yes, the brown and grey shape of a lizard. The creature's head swivelled, throat pulsing, so that it seemed to stare straight into his eyes. Then, in an eyeblink, it vanished. The Dragon chimed its full battery load. Time to go. He stood carefully, a cloud of thirsty killer bees and native wasps buzzing about him, shook free of them and slipped into the coolness of the Dragon's interior. The hens clucked in the rear and the Dragon furled its solar wings and lurched forward, crawling down over the edge of the scarp, down to the plain below and its saguaro sentinels.

His sat-link chimed and his console screen brightened to life. *You are entering unserviced United States territory.* The voice was female and severe. *No support services will be provided from this point on. Your entry visa does not assure assistance in unserviced regions. Please file all complaints with the US Bureau of Land Management. Please consult with your insurance provider before continuing.* Did he detect a note of disapproval in the sat-link voice? Zipakna grinned without humor and guided the Dragon down the steep slope, its belted treads barely marring the dry surface as he navigated around rock and thorny clumps of mesquite. He was a citizen of the Republic of Mexico and the US's sat eyes would certainly track his chip. They just wouldn't send a rescue if he got into trouble.

Such is life, he thought, and swatted an annoyed killer as it struggled against the windshield.

He passed the first of Paloma's plantings an hour later. The glassy black disks of the solar collectors glinted in the sun, powering the drip system that fed the scattered clumps of greenery. Short, thick-stalked sunflowers turned their dark faces to the sun, fringed with orange and scarlet petals. Zipakna frowned thoughtfully and videoed one of the wide blooms as the Dragon crawled past. Sure enough, his screen lit up with a similar blossom crossed with a circle-slash of warning.

An illegal pharm crop. The hairs on the back of his neck prickled. This was new. He almost turned around, but he liked the folk in Paloma. Good people; misfits, not sociopaths. It was an old settlement and one of his favourites. He sighed, because three diabetics lived here and a new bird flu had come over from Asia. It would find its way here eventually, riding the migration routes. He said a prayer to the old gods and his mother's *Santa Maria* for good measure and crawled on into town.

Nobody was out this time of day. Heat waves shimmered above the black solar panels and a lizard whip-flicked beneath the sagging Country Market's porch. He parked the Dragon in the dusty lot at the end of Main Street where a couple of buildings had burned long ago and unfurled the solar wings again. It took a lot of power to keep them from baking here. In the back Ezzie was clucking imperatively. The oldest of the chickens, she always seemed to know when they were stopping at a settlement. That meant fresh greens. "You're a pig," he said, but he chuckled as he made his way to the back to check on his flock.

The twenty hens clucked and scratched in their individual cubicles, excited at the halt. "I'll let you out soon," he promised and measured laying ration into their feeders. Bella had already laid an egg. He reached into her cubicle and cupped it in his hand, pale pink and smooth, still warm and faintly moist from its passage out of her body. Insulin nano-bodies, designed to block the auto-immune response that destroyed the insulin producing Beta cells in diabetics. He labelled Bella's egg and put it into the egg fridge. She was his highest producer. He scooped extra ration into her feeder.

Intruder, his alarm system announced. The heads-up display above the front console lit up. Zipakna glanced at it, brows furrowed, then smiled. He slipped to the door, touched it open. "You could just knock," he said.

The skinny boy hanging from the front of the Dragon by his fingers as he tried to peer through the windscreen let go, missed his footing and landed on his butt in the dust.

"It's too hot out here," Zipakna said. "Come inside. You can see better."

The boy looked up, his face tawny with Sonoran dust, hazel eyes wide with fear.

Zipakna's heart froze and time seemed to stand still. *She* must have looked like this as a kid, he thought. Probably just like this, considering how skinny and androgynous she had been in her twenties. He shook himself. "It's all right," he said and his voice only quivered a little. "You can come in."

"Ella said you have chickens. She said they lay magic eggs. I've never seen a chicken. But Pierre says there's no magic." The fear had vanished from his eyes, replaced now by bright curiosity.

That, too, was like her. Fear had never had a real hold on her.

How many times had he wished it had?

"I do have chickens. You can see them now." He held the door open. "What's your name?"

"Daren." The boy darted past him, quick as one of the desert's lizards, scrambled into the Dragon.

Her father's name.

Zipakna climbed in after him, feeling old suddenly, dry as this ancient desert. *I can't have kids*, she had said, so earnest. *How could I take a child into the uncontrolled areas? How could I leave one behind? Maybe later. After I'm done out there.*

"It's freezing in here." Daren stared around at the control bank under the wide windscreen, his bare arms and legs, skin clay-brown from the sun, ridged with goosebumps.

So much bare skin scared Zipakna. Average age for onset of melanoma without regular boosters was twenty-five. "Want something to drink? You can go look at the chickens. They're in the back."

"Water?" The boy gave him a bright, hopeful look. "Ella has a chicken. She lets me take care of it." He disappeared into the chicken space.

Zipakna opened the egg fridge. Bianca laid steadily even though she didn't have the peak capacity that some of the others did. So he had a good stock of her eggs. The boy was murmuring to the hens who were clucking greetings at him. "You can take one out," Zipakna called back to him. "They like to be held." He opened a packet of freeze-dried chocolate soy milk, reconstituted it, and whipped one of Bianca's eggs into it, so that it frothed tawny and rich. The gods knew if the boy had ever received any immunizations at all. Bianca provided the basic panel of nanobodies against most of the common pathogens and cancers. Including melanoma.

In the chicken room, Daren had taken Bella out of her cage, held her cradled in his arms. The speckled black and white hen clucked contentedly, occasionally pecking Daren's chin lightly. "She likes to be petted," Zipakna said. "If you rub her comb she'll sing to you. I made you a milkshake."

The boy's smile blossomed as Bella gave out with the almost-melodic squawks and creaks that signified her pleasure. "What's a milkshake?" Still smiling, he returned the hen to her cage and eyed the glass.

"Soymilk and chocolate and sugar." He handed it to Daren, found himself holding his breath as the boy tasted it and considered.

"Pretty sweet." He drank some. "I like it anyway."

To Zipakna's relief he drank it all and licked foam from his lip.

"So when did you move here?" Zipakna took the empty glass, rinsed it at the sink.

"Wow, you use water to clean dishes?" The boy's eyes had widened. "We came here last planting time. Pierre brought those seeds." He pointed in the general direction of the sunflower fields.

Zipakna's heart sank. "You and your parents?" He made his voice light.

Daren didn't answer for a moment. "Pierre. My father." He looked back to the chicken room. "If they're not magic, why do you give them water? Ella's chicken warns her about snakes, but you don't have to worry about snakes in here. What good are they?"

The cold logic of the Dry, out here beyond the security net of civilized space. "Their eggs keep you healthy." He watched the boy consider that. "You know Ella, right?" He waited for the boy's nod. "She has a disease that would kill her if she didn't eat an egg from that chicken you were holding every year."

Daren frowned, clearly doubting that. "You mean like a snake egg? They're good, but Ella's chicken doesn't lay eggs. And snake eggs don't make you get better when you're sick."

"They don't. And Ella's chicken is a banty rooster. He doesn't lay eggs." Zipakna looked up as a figure moved on the heads-up. "Bella is special and so are her eggs." He opened the door. "Hello, Ella, what are you doing out here in the heat?"

"I figured he'd be out here bothering you." Ella hoisted herself up the Dragon's steps, her weathered, sun-dried face the colour of real leather, her loose sun-shirt falling back from the stringy muscles of her arms as she reached up to kiss Zipakna on the cheek. "You behavin' yourself, boy? I'll switch you if you aren't."

"I'm being good." Daren grinned. "Ask him."

"He is." Zipakna eyed her face and briefly exposed arms, looking for any sign of melanoma. Even with the eggs, you could still get it out here with no UV protection. "So, Ella, you got some new additions to town, eh? New crops, too, I see." He watched her look away, saw her face tighten.

"Now don't you start." She stared at the south viewscreen filled with the bright heads of sunflowers. "Prices on everything we have to buy keep going up. And the Pima are tight, you know that. Plain sunflower oil don't bring much."

"So now you got something that can get you raided. By the government or someone worse."

"You're the one comes out here from the city where you got water and power, go hiking around in the dust with enough stuff to keep raiders fat and happy for a year." Ella's leathery face creased into a smile. "You preachin' risk at me, Zip?"

"Ah, but we know I'm crazy, eh?" He returned her smile, but shook his head. "I hope you're still here, next trip. How're your sugar levels? You been checking?"

"If we ain't we ain't." She lifted one bony shoulder in a shrug. "They're holding. They always do."

"The eggs do make you well?" Daren looked at Ella.

"Yeah, they do." Ella cocked her head at him. "There's magic, even if Pierre don't believe it."

"Do you really come from a city?" Daren was looking up at Zipakna now. "With a dome and water in the taps and everything?"

"Well, I come from Oaxaca, which doesn't have a dome. I spend most of my time in La Paz. It's on the Baja peninsula, if you know where that is."

"I do." He grinned. "Ella's been schooling me. I know where Oaxaca is, too. You're Mexican, right?" He tilted his head. "How come you come up here with your eggs?"

Ella was watching him, her dark eyes sharp with surmise. Nobody had ever asked him that question openly before. It wasn't the kind of question you asked, out here. Not out loud. He looked down into Daren's hazel eyes, into *her* eyes. "Because nobody else does."

Daren's eyes darkened and he looked down at the floor, frowning slightly.

"Sit down, Ella, let me get you your egg. Long as you're here." Zipakna turned quickly to the kitchen wall and filled glasses with water. While they drank, he got Bella's fresh egg from the egg fridge and cracked it into a glass, blending it with the raspberry concentrate that Ella favoured and a bit of soy milk.

"That's a milkshake," Daren announced as Zipakna handed Ella the glass. "He made me one, too." He looked up at Zipakna. "I'm not sick."

"He didn't think you were." Ella lifted her glass in a salute. "Because nobody else does." Drank it down. "You gonna come eat with us tonight?" Usually the invitation came with a grin that revealed the gap in her upper front teeth, and a threat about her latest pequin salsa. Today her smile was cautious. Wary. "Daren?" She nodded at the boy. "You go help Maria with the food. You know it's your turn today."

"Aw." He scuffed his bare feet, but headed for the door. "Can I come pet the chickens again?" He looked back hopefully from the door, grinned at Zipakna's nod, and slipped out, letting in a breath of oven-air.

"Ah, Ella." Zipakna sighed and reached into the upper cupboard. "Why did you plant those damn sunflowers?" He pulled out the bottle of aged mescal tucked away behind the freeze-dried staples. He filled a small, thick glass and set it down on the table in front of Ella beside her refilled water glass. "This can be the end of the settlement. You know that."

"The end can come in many ways." She picked up the glass, held it up to the light. "Perhaps fast is better than slow, eh?" She sipped the liquor, closed her eyes and sighed. "Luna and her husband tried for amnesty, applied to get a citizen-visa at the border. They've cancelled the amnesty. You live outside the serviced areas, I guess you get to stay out here. I guess the US economy faltered again. No more new citizens from Outside. And you know Mexico's policy about US immigration." She shrugged. "I'm surprised they even let you come up here."

"Oh, my government doesn't mind traffic in this direction. It likes to rub the US's nose in the fact that we send aid to its own citizens," he said lightly. Yeah, the border was closed tight to immigration from the north right now, because the US was being sticky about tariffs. "I can't believe they've made the Interior Boundaries airtight." That was what *she* had been afraid of, all those years ago.

"I guess they have to keep cutting and cutting." Ella drained the glass, probing for the last drops of amber liquor with her tongue. "No, one is enough." She shook her head as he turned to the cupboard. "The folks that live nice want to keep it that way, so you got to cut somewhere. We all know the US is slowly eroding away. It's not a superpower anymore. They just pretend." She looked up at Zipakna, her eyes like flakes of obsidian set into the nested wrinkles of her sun-dried face. "What is your interest in the boy, Zip? He's too young."

He turned away from those obsidian-flake eyes. "You misunderstand."

She waited, didn't say anything.

"Once upon a time there was a woman." He stared at the sun-baked emptiness of the main street on the vid screen. A tumbleweed skeleton turned slowly, fitfully across dust and cracked asphalt. "She had a promising career in academics, but she preferred field work."

"Field work?"

"She was a botanist. She created some drought-tolerant GMOs and started field testing them. They were designed for the drip irrigation ag areas, but she decided to test them . . . out here. She . . . got caught up in it . . . establishing adaptive GMOs out here to create sustainable harvests. She . . . gave up an academic career. Put everything into this project. Got some funding for it."

Ella sat without speaking as the silence stretched between them. "What happened to her?" She asked it, finally.

"I don't know." The tumbleweed had run up against the pole of a rusted and dented *No Parking* sign and quivered in the hot wind. "I . . . lost contact with her."

Ella nodded, her face creased into thoughtful folds. "I see."

No, you don't, he thought.

"How long ago?"

"Fifteen years."

"So he's not your son."

He flinched even though he'd known the question was coming. "No." He was surprised at how hard it was to speak that word.

Ella levered herself to her feet, leaning hard on the table. Pain in her hip. The osteo-sarcoma antibodies his chickens produced weren't specific to her problem. A personally tailored anti-cancer panel might cure her, but that cost money. A lot of money. He wasn't a doctor, but he'd seen enough osteo out here to measure her progress. It was the water, he guessed. "I brought you a present." He reached up into the cupboard again, brought out a flat plastic bottle of mescal with the Mexico state seal on the cap. Old stuff. Very old.

She took it, her expression enigmatic, tilted it, her eyes on the slosh of pale golden liquor. Then she let her breath out in a slow sigh and tucked the bottle carefully beneath her loose shirt. "Thank you." Her obsidian eyes gave nothing away.

He caught a glimpse of rib bones, faint bruising, and dried, shrunken flesh, revised his estimate. "You're welcome."

"I think you need to leave here." She looked past him. "We maybe need to live without your eggs. I'd just go right now."

He didn't answer for a moment. Listened to the chuckle of the hens. "Can I come to dinner tonight?"

"That's right. You're crazy. We both know that." She sighed.

He held the door for her as she lowered herself stiffly and cautiously into the oven heat of the fading day.

She was right, he thought as he watched her limp through the heat shimmer, back to the main building. She was definitely right.

He took his time with the chickens, letting them out of their cages to scratch on the grass carpet and peck at the vitamin crumbles he scattered for them. While he was parked here, they could roam loose in the back of the Dragon. He kept the door leading back to their section locked and all his hens were good about laying in their own cages, although at this point, he could tell who had laid which egg by sight. By the time he left the Dragon, the sun was completely down and the first pale stars winked in the royal blue of the darkening sky. No moon tonight. The wind had died and he smelled dust and a whiff of roasting meat as his boots grated on the dusty asphalt of the old main street. He touched the small hardness of the stunner in his pocket and climbed the sagging porch of what had once been a store, back when the town had still lived.

They had built a patio of sorts out behind the building, had roofed it from the sun with metal sheeting stripped from other derelict buildings. Long tables and old sofas clustered inside the building, shelter from the sun on the long hot days where residents shelled sunflower seed after harvest or worked on repair jobs or just visited, waiting for the cool of evening. He could see the yellow flicker of flame out back through the old plate-glass windows with their taped cracks.

The moment he entered he felt it – tension like the prickle of static electricity on a dry, windy day. Paloma was easy, friendly. He let his guard down sometimes when he was here, sat around the fire pit out back and shared the mescal he brought, trading swallows with the local stuff, flavoured with cactus fruit, that wasn't all that bad, considering.

Tonight, eyes slid his way, slid aside. The hair prickled on the back of his neck, but he made his smile easy. "Hola," he said, and gave them the usual grin and wave. "How you all makin' out?"

"Zip." Ella heaved herself up from one of the sofas, crossed the floor with firm strides, hands out, face turning up to kiss his cheeks. Grim determination folded the skin at the corners of her eyes tight. "Glad you could eat with us. Thanks for that egg today, I feel better already."

Ah, that was the issue? "Got to keep that blood sugar low." He gave her a real hug, because she was so *solid*, was the core of this settlement, whether the others realized it or not.

"Come on." Ella grabbed his arm. "Let's go out back. Rodriguez got an antelope, can you believe it? A young buck, no harm done."

"Meat?" He laughed, made it relaxed and easy, from the belly. "You eat better than I do. It's all vat stuff or too pricey to afford, down south. Good thing maize and beans are in my blood."

"Hey." Daren popped in from the firelit back, his eyes bright in the dim light. "Can my friends come see the chickens?"

My *friends*. The shy, hopeful pride in those words was so naked that Zipakna almost winced. He could see two or three faces behind Daren. That same tone had tainted his own voice, back when he had been a government scholarship kid from the wilds beyond San Cristobal, one of those who spoke Spanish as a second language. *My friends*, such a precious thing when you did not belong.

"Sure." He gave Daren a "we're buddies" grin and shrug. "Any time. You can show 'em around." Daren's eyes betrayed his struggle to look nonchalant.

A low chuckle circulated through the room, almost too soft to be heard, and Ella touched his arm lightly. Approvingly. Zipakna felt the tension relax a bit as he and Ella made their way through the dusk of the building to the firelit dark out back. One by one the shadowy figures who had stood back, not greeted him, thawed and followed. He answered greetings, pretending he hadn't noticed anything, exchanged the usual pleasantries that concerned weather and world politics, avoided the real issues of life. Like illegal crops. One by one, he identified the faces as the warm red glow of the coals in the firepit lit them. She needed the MS egg from Negro, he needed the anti-malaria from Seca and so did she. Daren had appeared at his side, his posture taut, a mix of proprietary and anxious.

"Meat, what a treat, eh?" Zipakna grinned down at Daren as one of the women laid a charred strip of roasted meat on a plate, dumped a scoop of beans beside it and added a flat disk of tortilla, thick and chewy and gritty from the bicycle-powered stone mill that the community used to grind maize into masa.

"Hey, you be careful tomorrow." She nodded towards a plastic bucket filled with water, a dipper and cups beside it. "Don't you let my Jonathan hurt any of those chickens. He's so clumsy."

"I'll show 'em how to be careful." Daren took the piled plate she handed him, practically glowing with pride.

Zipakna smiled at the server. She was another diabetic, like Ella. Sanja. He remembered her name.

"Watch out for the chutney." Sanja grinned and pointed at a table full of condiment dishes. "The sticky red stuff. I told Ella how to make it and she made us all sweat this year with her pequins."

"I like it hot." He smiled for her. "I want to see if it'll make me sweat."

"It will." Daren giggled. "I thought I'd swallowed coals, man." He carried his plate to one of the wooden tables, set it down with a possessive confidence beside Zipakna's.

Usually he sat at a crowded table answering questions, sharing news that hadn't yet filtered out here with the few traders, truckers, or wanderers who risked the unserviced Dry. Not this time. He chewed the charred, overdone meat slowly, aware of the way Daren wolfed his food, how most of the people here ate the same way, always prodded by hunger. That was how they drank, too, urgently, always thirsty.

Not many of them meant to end up out there. He remembered her words, the small twin lines that he called her "thinking dimples" creasing her forehead as she stared into her wine glass. *They had plans, they had a future in mind. It wasn't this one.*

"That isn't really why you come out here, is it? What you said before – in your big truck?"

Zipakna started, realized he was staring into space, a forkful of beans poised in the air. He looked down at Daren, into those clear hazel eyes that squeezed his heart. She had always known when he wasn't telling the truth. "No. It isn't." He set the fork down on his plate. "A friend of mine . . . a long time ago . . . went missing out here. I've . . . sort of hoped to run into her." At least that was how it had started. Now he looked for her ghost. Daren was staring at his neck.

"Where did you get that necklace?"

Zipakna touched the carved jade cylinder on its linen cord. "I found it diving in an old cenote – that's a kind of well where people threw offerings to the gods centuries ago. You're not supposed to dive there, but I was a kid – sneaking in."

"Are the cenotes around here?" Daren looked doubtful. "I never heard of any wells."

"No, they're way down south. Where I come from."

Daren scraped up the last beans from his plate, wiped it carefully with his tortilla. "Why did your friend come out here?"

"To bring people plants that didn't need much water." Zipakna sighed and eyed the remnants of his dinner. "You want this? I'm not real hungry tonight."

Daren gave him another doubting look, then shrugged and dug into the last of the meat and beans. "She was like Pierre?"

"No!"

The boy flinched and Zipakna softened his tone. "She created food plants so that you didn't need to grow as much to eat well." And then . . . she had simply gotten too involved. He closed his eyes, remembering that bitter bitter fight. "Is your mother here?" He already knew the answer but Daren's head shake still pierced him. The boy focused on wiping up the last molecule of the searing sauce with a scrap of tortilla, shoulders hunched.

"What are you doing?

At the angry words, Daren's head shot up and he jerked his hands away from the plate as if it had burned him.

"I was just talking with him, Pierre." He looked up, sandy hair falling back from his face. "He doesn't mind."

"I mind." The tall, skinny man with the dark braid and pale skin frowned down at Daren. "What have I told you about city folk?"

"But . . ." Daren bit off the word, ducked his head. "I'll go clean my plate." He snatched his plate and cup from the table, headed for the deeper shadows along the building.

"You leave him alone." The man stared down at him, his grey eyes flat and cold. "We all know about city folk and their appetites."

Suddenly the congenial chatter that had started up during the meal ended. Silence hung thick as smoke in the air. "You satisfied my appetite quite well tonight." Zipakna smiled gently. "I haven't had barbecued antelope in a long time."

"You got to wonder." Pierre leaned one hip against the table, crossed his arms. "Why someone gives up the nice air conditioning and swimming pools of the city to come trekking around out here handing out free stuff. Especially when your rig costs a couple of fortunes."

Zipakna sighed, made it audible. From the corner of his eye he noticed Ella, watching him intently, was aware of the hard lump of the stunner in his pocket. "I get this every time I meet folk. We already went through it here, didn't anyone tell you?"

"Yeah, they did." Pierre gave him a mirthless smile. "And you want me to believe that some non-profit in Mexico – Mexico! – cares about us? Not even our own government does that."

"It's all politics." Zipakna shrugged. "Mexico takes quite a bit of civic pleasure in the fact that Mexico has to extend aid to US citizens. If the political situation changes, yeah, the money might dry up. But for now, people contribute and I come out here. So do a few others like me." He looked up, met the man's cold, grey eyes. "Haven't you met an altruist at least once in your life?" he asked softly.

Pierre looked away and his face tightened briefly. "I sure don't believe you're one. You leave my son alone." He turned on his heel and disappeared in the direction Daren had taken.

Zipakna drank his water, skin prickling with the feel of the room. He looked up as Ella marched over, sat down beside him. "We know you're what you say you are." She pitched her voice to reach everyone. "Me, I'm looking forward to my egg in the morning, and I sure thank you for keeping an old woman like me alive. Not many care. He's right about that much." She gave Zipakna a small private wink as she squeezed his shoulder and stood up. "Sanja and I'll be there first thing in the morning, right, Sanja?"

"Yeah." Sanja's voice emerged from shadow, a little too bright. "We sure will."

Zipakna got to his feet and Ella rose with him. "You should all come by in the morning. Got a new virus northwest of here. It's high mortality and it's moving this way. Spread by birds, so it'll get here. I have eggs that will give you immunity." He turned and headed around the side of the building.

A thin scatter of replies drifted after him and he found Ella walking beside him, her hand on his arm. "They change everything," she said softly. "The flowers."

"You know, the sat cams can see them." He kept his voice low as they crunched around the side of the building, heading toward the Dragon. "They measure the light refraction from the leaves and they can tell if they're legit or one of the outlaw strains. That's no accident, Ella. You don't realize how much the government and the drug gangs use the same tools. One or the other will get you." He shook his head. "You better hope it's the government."

"They haven't found us yet."

"The seeds aren't ready to harvest, are they?"

"Pierre says we're too isolated."

Zipakna turned on her. "Nowhere is isolated any more. Not on this entire dirt ball. You ever ask Pierre why he showed up here? Why didn't he stay where he was before if he was doing such a good job growing illegal seeds?"

Ella didn't answer and he walked on.

"It's a mistake to let a ghost run your life." Ella's voice came low from the darkness behind him, tinged with sadness.

Zipakna hesitated as the door slid open for him. "Good night, Ella." He climbed into its cool interior, listening to the hens' soft chortle of greeting.

They showed up in the cool of dawn, trickling up to the Dragon in ones and twos to drink the frothy blend of fruit and soymilk he offered and to ask shyly about the news they hadn't asked about last night. A few apologized. Not many.

Neither Daren nor Pierre showed up. Zipakna fed the hens, collected the day's eggs, and was glad he'd given Daren his immunization egg the day before. By noon he had run out of things to keep him here. He hiked over to the community building in the searing heat of noon, found Ella sewing a shirt in the still heat of the interior, told her goodbye.

"Go with God," she told him and her face was as seamed and dry as the land outside.

This settlement would not be here when he next came this way. The old gods wrote that truth in the dust devils dancing at the edge of the field. He wondered what stolen genes those seeds carried. He looked for Daren and Pierre but didn't see either of them. Tired to the bone, he trudged back to

the Dragon in the searing heat. Time to move on. Put kilometers between
the Dragon and the dangerous magnet of those ripening seeds.

You have a visitor, the Dragon announced as he approached.

He hadn't locked the door? Zipakna frowned, because he didn't make
that kind of mistake. Glad that he was still carrying the stunner, he slipped
to the side and opened the door, fingers curled around the smooth shape
of the weapon.

"Ella said you were leaving." Daren stood inside, Bella in his arms.

"Yeah, I need to move on." He climbed up, the wash of adrenaline
through his bloodstream telling him just how tense he had been here. "I
have other settlements to visit."

Daren looked up at him, frowning a little. Then he turned and went
back into the chicken room to put Bella back in her travelling coop. He
scratched her comb, smiled a little as she chuckled at him, and closed the
door. "I think maybe . . . this is yours." He turned and held out a hand.

Zipakna stared down at the carved jade cylinder on his palm. It had
been strung on a fine steel chain. She had worn it on a linen cord with
coral beads knotted on either side of it. He swallowed. Shook his head.
"It's yours." The words came out husky and rough. "She meant you to
have it."

"I thought maybe she was the friend you talked about." Daren closed his
fist around the bead. "She said the same thing you did, I remember. She said
she came out here because no one else would. Did you give it to her?"

He nodded, squeezing his eyes closed, struggling to swallow the pain
that welled up into his throat. "You can come with me," he whispered.
"You're her son. Did she tell you she had dual citizenship – for both the
US and Mexico? You can get citizenship in Mexico. Your DNA will prove
that you're her son."

"I'd have to ask Pierre." Daren looked up at him, his eyes clear, filled
with a maturity far greater than his years. "He won't say yes. He doesn't
like the cities and he doesn't like Mexico even more."

Zipakna clenched his teeth, holding back the words that he wanted to
use to describe Pierre. Lock the door, he thought. Just leave. Make Daren
understand as they rolled on to the next settlement. "What happened to
her?" he said softly, so softly.

"A border patrol shot her." Daren fixed his eyes on Bella, who was
fussing and clucking in her cage. "A chopper. They were just flying over,
shooting coyotes. They shot her and me."

She had a citizen chip. If they'd had their scanner on, they would have
picked up the signal. He closed his eyes, his head filled with roaring. Yahoos
out messing around, who was ever gonna check up? Who cared? When he
opened his eyes, Daren was gone, the door whispering closed behind him.

What did any of it matter? He blinked dry eyes and went forward to
make sure the thermosolar plant was powered up. It was. He released the
brakes and pulled into a tight turn, heading southward out of town on the
old, cracked asphalt of the dead road.

*

He picked up the radio chatter in the afternoon as he fed the hens and let the unfurled panels recharge the storage batteries. He always listened, had paid a lot of personal money for the top decryption chip every trek. He wanted to know who was talking out here and about what.

US border patrol. He listened with half an ear as he scraped droppings from the crate pans and dumped them into the recycler. He knew the acronyms, you mostly got US patrols out here. *Flower-town*. It came over in a sharp, tenor voice. He straightened, chicken shit spilling from the dustpan in his hand as he listened. Hard.

Paloma. What else could "Flower-town" be out here? They were going to hit it. Zipakna stared down at the scattered grey and white turds on the floor. Stiffly, slowly, he knelt and brushed them into the dust pan. This was the only outcome. He knew it. Ella knew it. They'd made the choice. *Not many of them meant to end up out there.* Her voice murmured in his ear, so damn earnest. *They had plans, they had a future in mind. It wasn't this one.*

"Shut up!" He bolted to his feet, flung the pan at the wall. "Why did you have his kid?" The pan hit the wall and shit scattered everywhere. The hens panicked, squawking and beating at the mesh of their crates. Zipakna dropped to his knees, heels of his hands digging into his eyes until red light webbed his vision.

Flower-town. It came in over the radio, thin and wispy now, like a ghost voice.

Zipakna stumbled to his feet, went forward and furled the solar panels. Powered up and did a tight one-eighty that made the hens squawk all over again.

The sun sank over the rim of the world, streaking the ochre ground with long, dark shadows that pointed like accusing fingers. He saw the smoke in the last glow of the day, mushrooming up in a black flag of doom. He switched the Dragon to infrared navigation, and the black and grey images popped up on the heads-up above the console. He was close. He slowed his speed, wiped sweating palms on his shirt. They'd have a perimeter alarm set and they'd pick him up any minute now. If they could claim he was attacking them, they'd blow him into dust in a heartbeat. He'd run into US government patrols out here before and they didn't like the Mexican presence one bit. But his movements were sat-recorded and recoverable and Mexico would love to accuse the US of firing on one of its charity missions in the world media. So he was safe. If he was careful. He slowed the Dragon even more although he wanted to race. Not that there would be much he could do.

He saw the flames first and the screen darkened as the nightvision program filtered the glare. The community building? More flames sprang to life in the sunflower fields.

Attention Mexican registry vehicle N45YG90. The crudely accented Spanish filled the Dragon. *You are entering an interdicted area. Police action is in progress and no entry is permitted.*

Zipakna activated his automatic reply. "I'm sorry. I will stop here. I have a faulty storage bank and I'm almost out of power. I won't be able to go any farther until I can use my panels in the morning." He sweated in the silence, the hens clucking softly in the rear.

Stay in your vehicle. The voice betrayed no emotion. *Any activity will be viewed as a hostile act. Understand?*

"Of course." Zipakna broke the connection. The air in the Dragon seemed syrupy thick, pressing against his eardrums. They could be scanning him, watching to make sure that he didn't leave the Dragon. All they needed was an excuse. He heard a flurry of sharp reports. Gunshots. He looked up at the screen, saw three quick flashes of light erupt from the building beyond the burning community centre. No, they'd be looking there. Not here.

Numbly he stood and pulled his protective vest from its storage cubicle along with a pair of night goggles. He put the Dragon on standby. Just in case. If he didn't reactivate it in forty-eight hours, it would send a mayday back to headquarters. They'd come and collect the hens and the Dragon. He looked once around the small, dimly lit space of the Dragon, said a prayer to the old gods and touched the jade at his throat. Then he touched the door open, letting in a dry breath of desert that smelled of bitter smoke, and slipped out into the darkness.

He crouched, moving with the fits and starts of the desert coyotes, praying again to the old gods that the patrol wasn't really worrying about him. Enough clumps of mesquite survived here in this long ago wash to give him some visual cover from anyone looking in his direction and as he remembered, the wash curved north and east around the far end of the old town. It would take him close to the outermost buildings.

It seemed to take a hundred years to reach the tumbledown shack that marked the edge of the town. He slipped into its deeper shadow. A half moon had risen and his goggles made the landscape stand out in bright black and grey and white. The gunfire had stopped. He slipped from the shed to the fallen ruins of an old house, to the back of an empty storefront across from the community building. It was fully in flames now and his goggles damped the light as he peered cautiously from the glassless front window. Figures moved in the street, dressed in military coveralls. They had herded a dozen people together at the end of the street and Zipakna saw the squat, boxy shapes of two big military choppers beyond them.

They would not have a good future, would become permanent residents of a secure resettlement camp somewhere. He touched his goggles, his stomach lurching as he zoomed in on the bedraggled settlers. He recognized Sanja, didn't see either Ella or Daren, but he couldn't make out too many faces in the huddle. If the patrol had them, there was nothing he could do. They were searching the buildings on this side of the street. He saw helmeted figures cross the street, heading for the building next to his vantage point.

Zipakna slipped out the back door, made his way to the next building, leaned through the sagging window opening. "Daren? Ella? It's Zip," he said softly. "Anyone there?" Silence. He didn't dare raise his voice, moved on to the next building, his skin tight, expecting a shouted command. If they caught him interfering they'd arrest him. It might be a long time before Mexico got him freed. His bosses would be very unhappy with him.

"Ella?" He hurried, scrabbling low through fallen siding, tangles of old junk. They weren't here. The patrol must have made a clean sweep. He felt a brief, bitter stab of satisfaction that they had at least caught Pierre. One would deserve his fate, anyway.

Time to get back to the Dragon. As he turned, he saw two shadows slip into the building he had just checked – one tall, one child short. Hope leaped in his chest, nearly choking him. He bent low and sprinted, trying to gauge the time . . . how long before the patrol soldiers got to this building? He reached a side window, its frame buckled. As he did, a slight figure scrambled over the broken sill and even in the black and white of nightvision, Zipakna recognized Daren's fair hair.

The old gods had heard him. He grabbed the boy, hand going over his mouth in time to stifle his cry. "It's me. Zip. Be silent," he hissed.

Light flared in the building Daren had just left. Zipakna's goggles filtered it and crouching in the dark, clutching Daren, he saw Pierre stand up straight, hands going into the air. "All right, I give up. You got me." Two uniformed patrol pointed stunners at Pierre.

Daren's whimper was almost but not quite soundless "Don't move," Zipakna breathed. If they hadn't seen Daren . . .

"You're the one who brought the seeds." The taller of the two lowered his stunner and pulled an automatic from a black holster on his hip. "We got an ID on you."

A gun? Zipakna stared at it as it rose in seeming slow motion, the muzzle tracking upward to Pierre's stunned face. Daren lunged in his grip and he yanked the boy down and back, hurling him to the ground. The stunner seemed to have leaped from his pocket to his hand and the tiny dart hit the man with the gun smack in the centre of his chest. A projectile vest didn't stop a stunner charge. The man's arms spasmed outward and the ugly automatic went sailing, clattering to the floor. Pierre dived for the window as the other patrol yanked out his own weapon and pointed it at Zipakna. He fired a second stun charge but as he did, something slammed into his shoulder and threw him backward. Distantly he heard a loud noise, then Daren was trying to drag him to his feet.

"Let's go." Pierre yanked him upright.

"This way." Zipakna pointed to the distant bulk of the Dragon.

They ran. His left side was numb but there was no time to think about that. Daren and Pierre didn't have goggles so they ran behind him. He took them through the mesquite, ignoring the thorn slash, praying that the patrol focused on the building first before they started scanning the desert. His back twitched with the expectation of a bullet.

The Dragon opened to him and he herded them in, gasping for breath now, the numbness draining away, leaving slow, spreading pain in its wake. "In here." He touched the hidden panel and it opened, revealing the coffin-shaped space beneath the floor. The Dragon was defended, but this was always the backup. Not even a scan could pick up someone hidden here. "You'll have to both fit. There's air." They managed it, Pierre clasping Daren close, the boy's face buried against his shoulder. Pierre looked up as the panel slid closed. "Thanks." The panel clicked into place.

Zipakna stripped off his protective vest. Blood soaked his shirt. They were using piercers. That really bothered him, but fortunately the vest had slowed the bullet enough. He slapped a blood-stop patch onto the injury, waves of pain washing through his head, making him dizzy. Did a stim-tab from the med closet and instantly straightened, pain and dizziness blasted away by the drug. Didn't dare hide the bloody shirt, so he pulled a loose woven shirt over his head. *Visitor*, the Dragon announced. *US Security ID verified.*

"Open." Zipakna leaned a hip against the console, aware of the heads-up that still showed the town. The building had collapsed into a pile of glowing embers and dark figures darted through the shadows. "Come in." He said it in English with a careful US accent. "You're really having quite a night over there." He stood back as two uniformed patrol burst into the Dragon while a third watched warily from the doorway. All carrying stunners.

Not guns, so maybe, just maybe, they hadn't been spotted.

"What are you up to?" The patrol in charge, a woman, stared at him coldly through the helmet shield. "Did you leave this vehicle or let anyone in?"

The gods had come through. Maybe. "Goodness, no." He arched his eyebrows. "I'm not that crazy. I'm still stunned that Paloma went to raising pharm." He didn't have to fake the bitterness. "That's why you're burning the fields, right? They're a good bunch of people. I didn't think they'd ever give in to that."

Maybe she heard the truth in his words, but for whatever reason, the leader relaxed a hair. "Mind if we look around?" It wasn't a question and he shrugged, stifling a wince at the pain that made it through the stimulant buzz.

"Sure. Don't scare the hens, okay?"

The two inside the Dragon searched, quickly and thoroughly. They checked to see if he had been recording video and Zipakna said thanks to the old gods that he hadn't activated it. That would have changed things, he was willing to bet.

"You need help with your battery problem?" The cold faced woman – a lieutenant, he noticed her insignia – asked him.

He shook his head. "I'm getting by fine as long as I don't travel at night. They store enough for life support."

"I'd get out of here as soon as the sun is up." She jerked her head at the other two. "Any time you got illegal flowers you get raiders. You don't want to mess with them."

"Yes, ma'am." He ducked his head. "I sure will do that." He didn't move as they left, waited a half hour longer just to be sure that they didn't pop back in. But they did not. Apparently they believed his story, hadn't seen their wild dash through the mesquite. He set the perimeter alert to maximum and opened the secret panel. Daren scrambled out first, his face pale enough that his freckles stood out like bits of copper on his skin.

Her freckles.

Zipakna sat down fast. When the stun ran out, you crashed hard. The room tilted, steadied.

"That guy shot you." Daren's eyes seemed to be all pupil. "Are you going to die?"

"You got medical stuff?" Pierre's face swam into view. "Tell me quick, okay?"

"The cupboard to the left of the console." The words came out thick. Daren was staring at his chest. Zipakna looked down. Red was soaking into the ivory weave of the shirt he'd put on. So much for the blood-stop. The bullet must have gone deeper than he thought, or had hit a small artery. Good thing his boarders hadn't stuck around longer.

Pierre had the med kit. Zipakna started to pull the shirt off over his head and the pain hit him like a lightning strike, sheeting his vision with white. He saw the pale green arch of the ceiling, thought *I'm falling* . . .

He woke in his bed, groping drowsily for where he was headed and what he had drunk that made his head hurt this bad. Blinked as a face swam into view. Daren. He pushed himself up to a sitting position, his head splitting.

"You passed out." Daren's eyes were opaque. "Pierre took the bullet out of your shoulder while you were out. You bled a lot but he said you won't die."

"Where's Pierre?" He swung his legs over the side of the narrow bed, fighting dizziness. "How long have I been out?"

"Not very long." Daren backed away. "The chickens are okay. I looked."

"Thanks." Zipakna made it to his feet, steadied himself with a hand on the wall. A quick check of the console said that Pierre hadn't messed with anything. It was light out. Early morning. He set the video to sweep, scanned the landscape. No choppers, no trace of last night's raiders. He watched the images pan across the heads-up; blackened fields, the smouldering pile of embers and twisted plumbing that had been the community centre, still wisping smoke. The fire had spread to a couple of derelict buildings to the windward of the old store. Movement snagged his eye. Pierre. Digging. He slapped the control, shut off the vid. Daren was back with the chickens. "Stay here, okay? I'm afraid to leave them alone."

"Okay." Daren's voice came to him, hollow as an empty eggshell.

He stepped out into the oven heat, his head throbbing in time to his footsteps as he crossed the sunbaked ground to the empty bones of Paloma. A red bandanna had snagged on a mesquite branch, flapping in the morning's hot wind. He saw a woman's sandal lying on the dusty asphalt of the main street, a faded red backpack. He picked it up, looked inside. Empty.

He dropped it, crossed the street, angling northward to where he had seen Pierre digging.

He had just about finished two graves. A man lay beside one. The blood that soaked his chest had turned dark in the morning heat. Zipakna recognized his grizzled red beard and thinning hair, couldn't remember his name. He didn't eat any of the special eggs, just the ones against whatever new bug was out there. Pierre climbed out of the shallow grave.

"You shouldn't be walking around." He pushed dirty hair out of his eyes.

Without a word, Zipakna moved to the man's ankles. Pierre shrugged, took the man's shoulders. He was stiff, his flesh plastic and too cold, never mind the morning heat. Without a word they lifted and swung together, lowered him into the fresh grave. It probably wouldn't keep the coyotes out, Zipakna thought. But it would slow them down. He straightened, stepped over to the other grave.

Ella. Her face looked sad, eyes closed. He didn't see any blood, wondered if she had simply suffered a heart attack, if she had had enough as everything she had worked to keep intact burned around her. "Did Daren see her die?" He said it softly. Felt rather than saw Pierre's flinch.

"I don't know. I don't think so." He stuck the shovel into the piled rocks and dirt, tossed the first shovelful into the hole.

Zipakna said the right words in rhythm to the grating thrust of the shovel. First the Catholic prayer his mother would have wanted him to say, then the words for the old gods. Then a small, hard prayer for the new gods who had no language except dust and thirst and the ebb and flow of world politics that swept human beings from the chess board of the earth like pawns.

"You could have let them shoot me." Pierre tossed a last shovelful of dirt onto Ella's grave. "Why didn't you?"

Zipakna tilted his gaze to the hard blue sky. "Daren." Three tiny black specks hung overhead. Vultures. Death called them. "I'll make you a trade. I'll capitalize you to set up as a trader out here. You leave the pharm crops alone. I take Daren with me and get him Mexican citizenship. Give him a future better than yours."

"You can't." Pierre's voice was low and bitter. "I tried. Even though his mother was a US citizen, they're not taking in offspring born out here. Mexico has a fifteen-year waiting list for new immigrants." He was staring down at the mounded rock and dust of Ella's grave. "She was so angry when she got pregnant. The implant was faulty, I guess. She meant to go back to the city before he was born but . . . I got hurt. And she stuck around." He was silent for a while. "Then it was too late, Daren was born and the US had closed the border. We're officially out here because we want to be." His lips twisted.

"Why did you come out here?"

He looked up. Blinked. "My parents lived out here. They were the rugged individual types, I guess." He shrugged. "I went into the city, got a job, and they were still letting people come and go then. I didn't like it, all the people, all the restrictions. So I came back out here." He gave a thin laugh. "I was a trader to start with. I got hit by a bunch of raiders. That's when . . . I got hurt. Badly. I'm sorry." He turned away. "I wish you could get him citizenship. He didn't choose this."

"I can." Zipakna watched Pierre halt without turning. "She . . . was my wife. We married in Oaxaca." The words were so damn hard to say. "That gave her automatic dual citizenship. In Mexico, only the mother's DNA is required as proof of citizenship. We're pragmatists," he said bitterly.

For a time, Pierre said nothing. Finally he turned, his face as empty as the landscape. "You're the one." He looked past Zipakna, towards the Dragon. "I don't like you, you know. But I think . . . you'll be a good father for Daren. Better than I've been." He looked down at the dirty steel of the shovel blade. "It's a deal. A trade. I'll sell you my kid. Because it's a good deal for him." He walked past Zipakna toward the Dragon, tossed the shovel into the narrow strip of shade along one of the remaining buildings. The clang and rattle as it hit sounded loud as mountain thunder in the quiet of the windless heat.

Zipakna followed slowly, his shoulder hurting. Ilena would be pissed, would never believe that Daren wasn't his. His mouth crooked with the irony of that. The old gods twisted time and lives into the intricate knots of the universe and you could meet yourself coming around any corner. As the Dragon's doorway opened with a breath of cool air, he heard Pierre's voice from the chicken room, low and intense against the cluck and chortle of the hens, heard Daren's answer, heard the brightness in it.

Zipakna went forward to the console to ready the Dragon for travel. As soon as they reached the serviced lands again he'd transfer his savings to a cash card for Pierre. Pierre could buy what he needed on the Pima's land. They didn't care if you were a Drylander or not.

Ilena would be doubly pissed. But he was a good poker partner and she wouldn't dump him. And she'd like Daren. Once she got past her jealousy. Ilena had always wanted a kid, just never wanted to take the time to *have* one.

He wondered if she had meant to contact him, tell him about Daren, bring the boy back to Mexico. She would have known, surely, that it would have been all right.

Surely. He sighed and furled the solar wings.

Maybe he would keep coming out here. If Daren wanted to. Maybe her ghost would find them as they travelled through this place she had loved. And then he could ask her.

HIS MASTER'S VOICE

Hannu Rajaniemi

New writer Hannu Rajaniemi was born in Ylivieska, Finland, but currently lives in Edinburgh, Scotland, where he is working on his Ph.D. in string theory. He is the co-founder of ThinkTank Maths, which provides consultation services and research in applied mathematics and business development. He is also a member of Writers' Bloc, an Edinburgh-based spoken-word performance group.

Rajaniemi has had a big impact on the field with only a few stories. His story from 2005, "Deus Ex Homine," originally from the Scottish regional anthology *Nova Scotia*, was reprinted in several best of the year anthologies, including this one, and was one of the most talked-about stories of the year. He's published little else since, a handful of Finnish fantasy stories that were collected in the chapbook – until the story that follows, which appeared this year in *Interzone*. He is reported to have just sold a trilogy of SF novels to Gollancz though, and I suspect that if he can find the time to write more, he's going to turn out to be very important to the field.

In an idea-packed story with as high a bit-rate as you're ever likely to see, he proves once again that man's best friend is his dog. Particularly if the dog has a nuclear warhead.

BEFORE THE CONCERT, we steal the master's head.

The necropolis is a dark forest of concrete mushrooms in the blue Antarctic night. We huddle inside the utility fog bubble attached to the steep southern wall of the *nunatak*, the ice valley.

The cat washes itself with a pink tongue. It reeks of infinite confidence.

"Get ready," I tell it. "We don't have all night."

It gives me a mildly offended look and dons its armour. The quantum dot fabric envelops its striped body like living oil. It purrs faintly and tests the diamond-bladed claws against an icy outcropping of rock. The sound grates my teeth and the razor-winged butterflies in my belly wake up. I look at the bright, impenetrable firewall of the city of the dead. It shimmers like chained northern lights in my AR vision.

I decide that it's time to ask the Big Dog to bark. My helmet laser casts a one-nanosecond prayer of light at the indigo sky: just enough to deliver one quantum bit up there into the Wild. Then we wait. My tail wags and a low growl builds up in my belly.

Right on schedule, it starts to rain red fractal code. My augmented reality vision goes down, unable to process the dense torrent of information falling upon the necropolis firewall like monsoon rain. The chained aurora borealis flicker and vanish.

"Go!" I shout at the cat, wild joy exploding in me, the joy of running after the Small Animal of my dreams. "Go now!"

The cat leaps into the void. The wings of the armour open and grab the icy wind, and the cat rides the draft down like a grinning Chinese kite.

It's difficult to remember the beginning now. There were no words then, just sounds and smells: metal and brine, the steady drumming of waves against pontoons. And there were three perfect things in the world: my bowl, the Ball, and the Master's firm hand on my neck.

I know now that the Place was an old oil rig that the Master had bought. It smelled bad when we arrived, stinging oil and chemicals. But there were hiding places, secret nooks and crannies. There was a helicopter landing pad where the Master threw the ball for me. It fell into the sea many times, but the Master's bots – small metal dragonflies – always fetched it when I couldn't.

The Master was a god. When he was angry, his voice was an invisible whip. His smell was a god-smell that filled the world.

While he worked, I barked at the seagulls or stalked the cat. We fought a few times, and I still have a pale scar on my nose. But we developed an understanding. The dark places of the rig belonged to the cat, and I reigned over the deck and the sky: we were the Hades and Apollo of the Master's realm.

But at night, when the Master watched old movies or listened to records on his old rattling gramophone we lay at his feet together. Sometimes the Master smelled lonely and let me sleep next to him in his small cabin, curled up in the god-smell and warmth.

It was a small world, but it was all we knew.

The Master spent a lot of time working, fingers dancing on the keyboard projected on his mahogany desk. And every night he went to the Room: the only place on the rig where I wasn't allowed.

It was then that I started to dream about the Small Animal. I remember its smell even now, alluring and inexplicable: buried bones and fleeing rabbits, irresistible.

In my dreams, I chased it along a sandy beach, a tasty trail of tiny footprints that I followed along bendy pathways and into tall grass. I never lost sight of it for more than a second: it was always a flash of white fur just at the edge of my vision.

One day it spoke to me. "Come," it said. "Come and learn."

The Small Animal's island was full of lost places. Labyrinthine caves, lines drawn in sand that became words when I looked at them, smells that sang songs from the Master's gramophone. It taught me, and I learned: I was more awake every time I woke up. And when I saw the cat looking at the spiderbots with a new awareness, I knew that it, too, went to a place at night.

I came to understand what the Master said when he spoke. The sounds that had only meant angry or happy before became the words of my god. He noticed, smiled, and ruffled my fur. After that he started speaking to us more, me and the cat, during the long evenings when the sea beyond the windows was black as oil and the waves made the whole rig ring like a bell. His voice was dark as a well, deep and gentle. He spoke of an island, his home, an island in the middle of a great sea. I smelled bitterness, and for the first time I understood that there were always words behind words, never spoken.

The cat catches the updraft perfectly: it floats still for a split second, and then clings to the side of the tower. Its claws put the smart concrete to sleep: code that makes the building think that the cat is a bird or a shard of ice carried by the wind.

The cat hisses and spits. The disassembler nanites from its stomach cling to the wall and start eating a round hole in it. The wait is excruciating. The cat locks the exomuscles of its armour and hangs there patiently. Finally, there is a mouth with jagged edges in the wall, and it slips in. My heart pounds as I switch from the AR view to the cat's iris cameras. It moves through the ventilation shaft like lightning, like an acrobat, jerky, hyperaccelerated movements, metabolism on overdrive. My tail twitches again. *We are coming, Master*, I think. *We are coming*.

I lost my ball the day the wrong master came.

I looked everywhere. I spent an entire day sniffing every corner and even braved the dark corridors of the cat's realm beneath the deck, but I could not find it. In the end, I got hungry and returned to the cabin. And there were two masters. Four hands stroking my coat. Two gods, true and false.

I barked. I did not know what to do. The cat looked at me with a mixture of pity and disdain and rubbed itself on both of their legs.

"Calm down," said one of the masters. "Calm down. There are four of us now."

I learned to tell them apart, eventually: by that time Small Animal had taught me to look beyond smells and appearances. The master I remembered was a middle-aged man with greying hair, stocky-bodied. The new master was young, barely a man, much slimmer and with the face of a mahogany cherub. The master tried to convince me to play with the new master, but I did not want to. His smell was too familiar, everything else too alien. In my mind, I called him the wrong master.

The two masters worked together, walked together and spent a lot of time talking together using words I did not understand. I was jealous. Once I even bit the wrong master. I was left on the deck for the night as a punishment, even though it was stormy and I was afraid of thunder. The cat, on the other hand, seemed to thrive in the wrong master's company, and I hated it for it.

I remember the first night the masters argued.

"Why did you do it?" asked the wrong master.

"You know," said the master. "You remember." His tone was dark. "Because someone has to show them we own ourselves."

"So, you own me?" said the wrong master. "Is that what you think?"

"Of course not," said the master. "Why do you say that?"

"Someone could claim that. You took a genetic algorithm and told it to make ten thousand of you, with random variations, pick the ones that would resemble your ideal son, the one you could love. Run until the machine runs out of capacity. Then print. It's illegal, you know. For a reason."

"That's not what the plurals think. Besides, this is my place. The only laws here are mine."

"You've been talking to the plurals too much. They are no longer human."

"You sound just like VecTech's PR bots."

"I sound like you. Your doubts. Are you sure you did the right thing? I'm not a Pinocchio. You are not a Gepetto."

The master was quiet for a long time.

"What if I am," he finally said. "Maybe we need Gepettos. Nobody creates anything new any more, let alone wooden dolls that come to life. When I was young, we all thought something wonderful was on the way. Diamond children in the sky, angels out of machines. Miracles. But we gave up just before the blue fairy came."

"I am not your miracle."

"Yes, you are."

"You should at least have made yourself a woman," said the wrong master in a knife-like voice. "It might have been less frustrating."

I did not hear the blow, I felt it. The wrong master let out a cry, rushed out and almost stumbled on me. The master watched him go. His lips moved, but I could not hear the words. I wanted to comfort him and made a little sound, but he did not even look at me, went back to the cabin and locked the door. I scratched the door, but he did not open, and I went up to the deck to look for the Ball again.

Finally, the cat finds the master's chamber.

It is full of heads. They float in the air, bodiless, suspended in diamond cylinders. The tower executes the command we sent into its drugged nervous system, and one of the pillars begins to blink. *Master, master,* I sing quietly as I see the cold blue face beneath the diamond. But at the same time I know it's not the master, not yet.

The cat reaches out with its prosthetic. The smart surface yields like a soap bubble. "Careful now, careful," I say. The cat hisses angrily but obeys, spraying the head with preserver nanites and placing it gently into its gel-lined backpack.

The necropolis is finally waking up: the damage the heavenly hacker did has almost been repaired. The cat heads for its escape route and goes to quicktime again. I feel its staccato heartbeat through our sensory link.

It is time to turn out the lights. My eyes polarise to sunglass-black. I lift the gauss launcher, marvelling at the still tender feel of the Russian hand grafts. I pull the trigger. The launcher barely twitches in my grip, and a streak of light shoots up to the sky. The nuclear payload is tiny, barely a decaton, not even a proper plutonium warhead but a hafnium micro-nuke. But it is enough to light a small sun above the mausoleum city for a moment, enough for a focused maser pulse that makes it as dead as its inhabitants for a moment.

The light is a white blow, almost tangible in its intensity, and the gorge looks like it is made of bright ivory. White noise hisses in my ears like the cat when it's angry.

For me, smells were not just sensations, they were my reality. I know now that that is not far from the truth: smells are molecules, parts of what they represent.

The wrong master smelled wrong. It confused me at first: almost a god-smell, but not quite, the smell of a fallen god.

And he did fall, in the end.

I slept on the master's couch when it happened. I woke up to bare feet shuffling on the carpet and heavy breathing, torn away from a dream of the Small Animal trying to teach me the multiplication table.

The wrong master looked at me. "Good boy," he said. "Shh." I wanted to bark, but the godlike smell was too strong. And so I just wagged my tail, slowly, uncertainly. The wrong master sat on the couch next to me and scratched my ears absently.

"I remember you," he said. "I know why he made you. A living child-hood memory." He smiled and smelled friendlier than ever before. "I know how that feels." Then he sighed, got up and went into the Room. And then I knew that he was about to do something bad, and started bark-ing as loudly as I could. The master woke up and when the wrong master returned, he was waiting.

"What have you done?" he asked, face chalk-white.

The wrong master gave him a defiant look. "Just what you'd have done. You're the criminal, not me. Why should I suffer? You don't own me."

"I could kill you," said the master, and his anger made me whimper with fear. "I could tell them I was you. They would believe me."

"Yes," said the wrong master. "But you are not going to."

The master sighed. "No," he said. "I'm not."

I take the dragonfly over the cryotower. I see the cat on the roof and whim-per from relief. The plane lands lightly. I'm not much of a pilot, but the lobotomized mind of the daimon – an illegal copy of a twenty-first century jet ace – is. The cat climbs in, and we shoot towards the stratosphere at Mach 5, wind caressing the plane's quantum dot skin.

"Well done," I tell the cat and wag my tail. It looks at me with yellow slanted eyes and curls up on its acceleration gel bed. I look at the container next to it. Is that a whiff of the god-smell or is it just my imagination?

In any case, it is enough to make me curl up in deep happy dog-sleep, and for the first time in years I dream of the Ball and the Small Animal, sliding down the ballistic orbit's steep back.

They came from the sky before the sunrise. The master went up on the deck wearing a suit that smelled new. He had the cat in his lap: it purred quietly. The wrong master followed, hands behind his back.

There were three machines, black-shelled scarabs with many legs and transparent wings. They came in low, raising a white-frothed wake behind them. The hum of their wings hurt my ears as they landed on the deck.

The one in the middle vomited a cloud of mist that shimmered in the dim light, swirled in the air and became a black skinned woman who had no smell. By then I had learned that things without a smell could still be dangerous, so I barked at her until the master told me to be quiet.

"Mr Takeshi," she said. "You know why we are here."

The master nodded.

"You don't deny your guilt?"

"I do," said the master. "This raft is technically a sovereign state, governed by my laws. Autogenesis is not a crime here."

"This raft was a sovereign state," said the woman. "Now it belongs to VecTech. Justice is swift, Mr Takeshi. Our lawbots broke your constitution ten seconds after Mr Takeshi here —" she nodded at the wrong master " – told us about his situation. After that, we had no choice. The WIPO quantum judge we consulted has condemned you to the slow zone for 314 years, and as the wronged party we have been granted execution rights in this matter. Do you have anything to say before we act?"

The master looked at the wrong master, face twisted like a mask of wax. Then he set the cat down gently and scratched my ears. "Look after them," he told the wrong master. "I'm ready."

The beetle in the middle moved, too fast for me to see. The master's grip on the loose skin on my neck tightened for a moment like my mother's teeth, and then let go. Something warm splattered on my coat and there was a dark, deep smell of blood in the air.

Then he fell. I saw his head in a floating soap bubble that one of the beetles swallowed. Another opened its belly for the wrong master. And then they were gone, and the cat and I were alone on the bloody deck.

The cat wakes me up when we dock with the *Marquis of Carabas*. The zeppelin swallows our dragonfly drone like a whale. It is a crystal cigar, and its nanospun sapphire spine glows faint blue. The Fast City is a sky full of neon stars six kilometres below us, anchored to the airship with elevator cables. I can see the liftspiders climbing them, far below, and sigh with relief. The guests are still arriving, and we are not too late. I keep my personal firewall clamped shut: I know there is a torrent of messages waiting beyond.

We rush straight to the lab. I prepare the scanner while the cat takes the master's head out very, very carefully. The fractal bush of the scanner comes out of its nest, molecule-sized disassembler fingers bristling. I have to look away when it starts eating the master's face. I cheat and flee to VR, to do what I do best.

After half an hour, we are ready. The nanofab spits out black plastic discs, and the airship drones ferry them to the concert hall. The metallic butterflies in my belly return, and we head for the make-up salon. The Sergeant is already there, waiting for us: judging by the cigarette stubs on the floor, he has been waiting for a while. I wrinkle my nose at the stench.

"You are late," says our manager. "I hope you know what the hell you are doing. This show's got more diggs than the Turin clone's birthday party."

"That's the idea," I say and let Anette spray me with cosmetic fog. It tickles and makes me sneeze, and I give the cat a jealous look: as usual, it is perfectly at home with its own image consultant. "We are more popular than Jesus."

They get the DJs on in a hurry, made by the last human tailor on Savile Row. "This'll be a good skin," says Anette. "Mahogany with a touch of purple." She goes on, but I can't hear. The music is already in my head. The master's voice.

The cat saved me.

I don't know if it meant to do it or not: even now, I have a hard time understanding it. It hissed at me, its back arched. Then it jumped forward and scratched my nose: it burned like a piece of hot coal. That made me mad, weak as I was. I barked furiously and chased the cat around the deck. Finally, I collapsed, exhausted, and realized that I was hungry. The autokitchen down in the master's cabin still worked, and I knew how to ask for food. But when I came back, the master's body was gone: the waste disposal bots had thrown it into the sea. That's when I knew that he would not be coming back.

I curled up in his bed alone that night: the god-smell that lingered there was all I had. That, and the Small Animal.

It came to me that night on the dreamshore, but I did not chase it this time. It sat on the sand, looked at me with its little red eyes and waited.

"Why?" I asked. "Why did they take the master?"

"You wouldn't understand," it said. "Not yet."

"I want to understand. I want to know."

"All right," it said. "Everything you do, remember, think, smell – everything – leaves traces, like footprints in the sand. And it's possible to read them. Imagine that you follow another dog: you know where it has eaten and urinated and everything else it has done. The humans can do that to the mindprints. They can record them and make another you inside a machine, like the scentless screenpeople that your master used to watch. Except that the screendog will think it's you."

"Even though it has no smell?" I asked, confused.

"It thinks it does. And if you know what you're doing, you can give it a new body as well. You could die and the copy would be so good that no one can tell the difference. Humans have been doing it for a long time. Your master was one of the first, a long time ago. Far away, there are a lot of humans with machine bodies, humans who never die, humans with small bodies and big bodies, depending on how much they can afford to pay, people who have died and come back."

I tried to understand: without the smells, it was difficult. But its words awoke a mad hope.

"Does it mean that the master is coming back?" I asked, panting.

"No. Your master broke human law. When people discovered the pawprints of the mind, they started making copies of themselves. Some made many, more than the grains of sand on the beach. That caused chaos. Every machine, every device everywhere, had mad dead minds in them. The plurals, people called them, and were afraid. And they had their reasons to be afraid. Imagine that your Place had a thousand dogs, but only one Ball."

My ears flopped at the thought.

"That's how humans felt," said the Small Animal. "And so they passed a law: only one copy per person. The humans – VecTech – who had invented how to make copies mixed watermarks into people's minds, rights management software that was supposed to stop the copying. But some humans – like your master – found out how to erase them."

"The wrong master," I said quietly.

"Yes," said the Small Animal. "He did not want to be an illegal copy. He turned your master in."

"I want the master back," I said, anger and longing beating their wings in my chest like caged birds.

"And so does the cat," said the Small Animal gently. And it was only then that I saw the cat there, sitting next to me on the beach, eyes glimmering in the sun. It looked at me and let out a single conciliatory miaow.

After that, the Small Animal was with us every night, teaching.

Music was my favourite. The Small Animal showed me how I could turn music into smells and find patterns in it, like the tracks of huge, strange animals. I studied the master's old records and the vast libraries of his virtual desk, and learned to remix them into smells that I found pleasant.

I don't remember which one of us came up with the plan to save the master. Maybe it was the cat: I could only speak to it properly on the island of dreams, and see its thoughts appear as patterns on the sand. Maybe it was the Small Animal, maybe it was me. After all the nights we spent talking about it, I no longer know. But that's where it began, on the island: that's where we became arrows fired at a target.

Finally, we were ready to leave. The master's robots and nanofac spun us an open-source glider, a white-winged bird.

In my last dream the Small Animal said goodbye. It hummed to itself when I told it about our plans.

"Remember me in your dreams," it said.

"Are you not coming with us?" I asked, bewildered.

"My place is here," it said. "And it's my turn to sleep now, and to dream."

"Who are you?"

"Not all the plurals disappeared. Some of them fled to space, made new worlds there. And there is a war on, even now. Perhaps you will join us there, one day, where the big dogs live."

It laughed. "For old times' sake?" It dived into the waves and started running, became a great proud dog with a white coat, muscles flowing like water. And I followed, for one last time.

The sky was grey when we took off. The cat flew the plane using a neural interface, goggles over its eyes. We sweeped over the dark waves and were underway. The raft became a small dirty spot in the sea. I watched it recede and realized that I'd never found my Ball.

Then there was a thunderclap and a dark pillar of water rose up to the sky from where the raft had been. I didn't mourn: I knew that the Small Animal wasn't there any more.

The sun was setting when we came to the Fast City.

I knew what to expect from the Small Animal's lessons, but I could not imagine what it would be like. Mile-high skyscrapers that were self-contained worlds, with their artificial plasma suns and bonsai parks and miniature shopping malls. Each of them housed a billion lilliputs, poor and quick: humans whose consciousness lived in a nanocomputer smaller than a fingertip. Immortals who could not afford to utilize the resources of the overpopulated Earth more than a mouse. The city was surrounded by a halo of glowing fairies, tiny winged moravecs that flitted about like humanoid fireflies and the waste heat from their overclocked bodies draped the city in an artificial twilight.

The citymind steered us to a landing area. It was fortunate that the cat was flying: I just stared at the buzzing things with my mouth open, afraid I'd drown in the sounds and the smells.

We sold our plane for scrap and wandered into the bustle of the city, feeling like *daikaju* monsters. The social agents that the Small Animal had given me were obsolete, but they could still weave us into the ambient social networks. We needed money, we needed work.

And so I became a musician.

The ballroom is a hemisphere in the centre of the airship. It is filled to capacity. Innumerable quickbeings shimmer in the air like living candles, and the suits of the fleshed ones are no less exotic. A woman clad in nothing but autumn leaves smiles at me. Tinkerbell clones surround the cat.

Our bodyguards, armed obsidian giants, open a way for us to the stage where the gramophones wait. A rustle moves through the crowd. The air around us is pregnant with ghosts, the avatars of a million fleshless fans. I wag my tail. The scentspace is intoxicating: perfume, fleshbodies, the unsmells of moravec bodies. And the fallen god smell of the wrong master, hiding somewhere within.

We get on the stage on our hindlegs, supported by prosthesis shoes. The gramophone forest looms behind us, their horns like flowers of brass and gold. We cheat, of course: the music is analog and the gramophones are genuine, but the grooves in the black discs are barely a nanometer thick, and the needles are tipped with quantum dots.

We take our bows and the storm of handclaps begins.

"Thank you," I say when the thunder of it finally dies. "We have kept quiet about the purpose of this concert as long as possible. But I am finally in a position to tell you that this is a charity show."

I smell the tension in the air, copper and iron.

"We miss someone," I say. "He was called Shimoda Takeshi, and now he's gone."

The cat lifts the conductor's baton and turns to face the gramophones. I follow, and step into the soundspace we've built, the place where music is smells and sounds.

The master is in the music.

It took five human years to get to the top. I learned to love the audiences: I could smell their emotions and create a mix of music for them that was just right. And soon I was no longer a giant dog DJ among lilliputs, but a little terrier in a forest of dancing human legs. The cat's gladiator career lasted a while, but soon it joined me as a performer in the virtual dramas I designed. We performed for rich fleshies in the Fast City, Tokyo, and New York. I loved it. I howled at Earth in the sky in the Sea of Tranquility.

But I always knew that it was just the first phase of the Plan.

We turn him into music. VecTech owns his brain, his memories, his mind. But we own the music.

Law is code. A billion people listening to our master's voice. Billion minds downloading the Law At Home packets embedded in it, bombarding the quantum judges until they give him back.

It's the most beautiful thing I've ever made. The cat stalks the genetic algorithm jungle, lets the themes grow and then pounces on them, devours them. I just chase them for the joy of the chase alone, not caring whether or not I catch them.

It's our best show ever.

Only when it's over, I realize that no one is listening. The audience is frozen. The fairies and the fastpeople float in the air like flies trapped in amber. The moravecs are silent statues. Time stands still.

The sound of one pair of hands, clapping.

"I'm proud of you," says the wrong master.

I fix my bow tie and smile a dog's smile, a cold snake coiling in my belly. The god-smell comes and tells me that I should throw myself onto the floor, wag my tail, bare my throat to the divine being standing before me.

But I don't.

"Hello, Nipper," the wrong master says.

I clamp down the low growl rising in my throat and turn it into words. "What did you do?"

"We suspended them. Back doors in the hardware. Digital rights management."

His mahogany face is still smooth: he does not look a day older, wearing a dark suit with a VecTech tie pin. But his eyes are tired. "Really, I'm impressed. You covered your tracks admirably. We thought you were furries. Until I realized —"

A distant thunder interrupts him.

"I promised him I'd look after you. That's why you are still alive. You don't have to do this. You don't owe him anything. Look at yourselves: who would have thought you could come this far? Are you going to throw that all away because of some atavistic sense of animal loyalty? Not that you have a choice, of course. The plan didn't work."

The cat lets out a steam pipe hiss.

"You misunderstand," I say. "The concert was just a diversion."

The cat moves like a black-and-yellow flame. Its claws flash, and the wrong master's head comes off. I whimper at the aroma of blood polluting the god-smell. The cat licks its lips. There is a crimson stain on its white shirt.

The zeppelin shakes, pseudomatter armour sparkling. The dark sky around the *Marquis* is full of fire-breathing beetles. We rush past the human statues in the ballroom and into the laboratory.

The cat does the dirty work, granting me a brief escape into virtual abstraction. I don't know how the master did it, years ago, broke VecTech's copy protection watermarks. I can't do the same, no matter how much the Small Animal taught me. So I have to cheat, recover the marked parts from somewhere else.

The wrong master's brain.

The part of me that was born on the Small Animal's island takes over and fits the two patterns together, like pieces of a puzzle. They fit, and for a brief moment, the master's voice is in my mind, for real this time.

The cat is waiting, already in its clawed battlesuit, and I don my own. The *Marquis of Carabas* is dying around us. To send the master on his way, we have to disengage the armour.

The cat miaows faintly and hands me something red. An old plastic ball with toothmarks, smelling of the sun and the sea, with a few grains of sand rattling inside.

"Thanks," I say. The cat says nothing, just opens a door into the zeppelin's skin. I whisper a command, and the master is underway in a neutrino stream, shooting up towards an island in a blue sea. Where the gods and big dogs live forever.

We dive through the door together, down into the light and flame.

THE POLITICAL PRISONER

Charles Coleman Finlay

Charles Coleman Finlay is a frequent contributor to *The Magazine of Fantasy & Science Fiction*, and has also sold to such markets as *Beyond Ceaseless Skies* and *Noctem Aeternus*. His short fiction was collected in *Wild Things*, and he has also published the three novels (so far) of the Traitor to the Crown series, including *A Spell for the Revolution*, *The Demon Redcoat*, and, most recently, *The Patriot Witch*. He's also written the stand-alone novel *The Prodigal Troll*. Finlay lives with his family in Columbus, Ohio.

In the intense and harrowing story that follows, he takes us to a far planet to tell the story of a political officer caught up in a civil war partially of his own devising – and one that he'll be very, very lucky to manage to survive.

FOR EVERYONE'S CONVENIENCE, the execution grounds on Jerusalem stood next to the cemetery. The cemetery was the biggest public garden on the terraformed planet: families sacrificed part of their soil ration to plant perennials and blossoming evergreens, bits of garnish like little sprigs of parsley on a vast platter of rocks. The sight of the garden usually made Maxim Nikomedes feel welcome when he returned to the planet, even if he only glimpsed the flowers for a moment from the window of his limousine.

This return was different. An Adarean was scheduled for execution, and the mob that gathered to watch it blocked Max's view. And for this visit, Max was riding in an armored car for prisoners not a limousine.

Max peered out the tinted window, but was met with his own reflection: he was a small man in his forties, with an acne-scarred face pale from years in the space service as a political officer. There were loose threads on his uniform where the rank had been torn off. He raised his hands to scratch his nose – the window flashed with the silver gleam of the handcuffs.

He looked past himself.

The crowd, dressed in their drab Sabbath clothes, shoved and shouted, surging toward the execution altar. They were pushed back by the soldiers from Justice, spilling into the road and blocking the car. Atop the altar, the

Minister of Executions poured baptismal water over the Adarean's bald green head. The crowd shook and roared in frenzy.

"You want to stay and watch them stretch the pig-man's neck?" the guard asked Max.

Max had been ignoring the guard seated opposite him. The seasoned political officer turned his head with cold calm and lifted his handcuffed wrists, as if to say he had bigger worries. Soon enough, he might make an official visit to the execution altar. He would, at least, have a good view of the flowers in the graveyard.

Looking back out the window, he said, "What does it matter to me if an Adarean lives or dies?"

The guard craned his head around to talk to the driver.

"See that's what I don't understand," he said, pointing the barrel of his gun out the window. "They're like aliens. Adareans gave up their souls when they quit being human, so what's the point in baptizing this pig-man?"

Max frowned while the guard and driver argued the merits of pre-execution conversion. *Pig-man*. It was odd how a man's work took on a life of its own. Max remembered creating that propaganda term years ago, during the war with Adares. The people on his planet thought they were God's Select, emigrating to a purer place where they could live a holy life. They fell into conflict with the emigrants to Adares, a population that claimed to be the next step, deliberate and scientific, in human evolution. To stir people up to fight a technologically superior foe, Max created the slogan *There is no evolution, only abomination*. Then he dug up some old earth-history on using pig-valves in heart transplants – the first step toward godlessness, changing man into something other than God's own image. Max connected *that* to the genetically-modified Adareans, who stole genes promiscuously from any species, and called them pig-men. It was adolescent name-calling, improvized in the service of a war long since over. Who cared if the Adareans' chlorophyll-laden skin and hair indicated more plant genes than pig? The religious population of Jesusalem, thinking swine unclean, had embraced the insult.

That was many years, and a different identity, ago. Max was vain enough to feel proud, and old enough to be ashamed. He loved his home, and had always served it any way he could.

Outside, the hangman fixed the steel cable around the Adarean's neck. Tradition called for hemp rope, but there was so little natural fiber on the planet, despite decades of terraforming, that everything but their clothes was made from metal or rock. The minister began preaching the repentance sermon while the powerfully-built hangman forced the Adarean to kneel and bend his head. The crowd settled down to listen, and the driver nudged the car forward again.

Max continued to stare out the window. They hovered through dusty, unpaved streets, leaving a cloud of grit behind them, until they arrived at a big, concrete open-ended U. The Department of Political Education building.

The guard hopped out, weapon at his side, and held open the door. "It must feel good to be back, huh?"

Max looked up to see if the guard really was that stupid. His simple, frank face bespoke genuine belief. Max scooted across the seat and lifted his handcuffed wrists for an answer.

The guard waved his hand vaguely. "Nobody believes that charge of treason!"

Max winced at the word. In the old days, even a suspicion of treason meant immediate death. He walked quickly as if to escape the charge, crossing the courtyard to the entrance. More guards, these blissfully silent in their charcoal-coloured uniforms, opened the door. The lobby inside was an oasis of tan benches planted around a small blue pool of carpet.

A pale green Adarean leapt up from one of the seats and blocked Max's way. "Please," he said. "I must see Director Mallove while there's still time to stop the execution."

Depending on the length of the sermon – they could run for a few minutes or a few hours – it might already be too late. "Can't really help you," Max said, lifting his handcuffs in answer for a third time.

The guard steered Max around the Adarean. When the door to the stairwell creaked shut behind them, the guard grumbled, "Weedheads."

"I'll never get used to grass hair," Max said. He doubted the Adareans converted much solar energy from their hair, despite all their talk of developing "multiple calorie streams".

His legs ached in the full gravity as he climbed the stairs. He'd visited planets with elevators before: the older he got, the more he believed in the possible holiness of technology. When he went to Earth, he visited a museum about the Amish, a group of people who stubbornly lived in the past while technology swept others past them. The tour guide thought he'd find the religious similarities interesting. Max had begun to have sympathy for the galactics who looked at his planet as an oddity just like the Amish.

Too bad his people had never been pacifists.

On the top floor, the guard ushered Max past the admin – owl-eyed Anatoly, whose expressionless gaze followed Max across the room – to the office of the Director of Political Education, Willem Mallove. Max's boss.

One of Max's bosses. But that was complicated, and involved his old identity. Max filed that away in "things too dangerous to think about right now."

Mallove sat posed, hand on chin, staring out the window. He had an actor's face, handsome and charismatic with just the right hint of imperfection – a small scar that forced his upper lip into a minor sneer. His face had gotten him into vids when he studied off-planet on Adares, years ago, before the revolution. Rumour had it that his insincerity – the Adareans were enormously sensitive to nuances of emotion – had driven him out of acting. The spacious office was decorated with fabric wall-coverings, some rare wooden chairs, and the famous stained-glass desk with its images of the Blessed Martyrs – a ministry heirloom from before the revolution.

"You may leave us, Vasily," Mallove told the earnest-but-stupid guard. His hand stayed posed on his chin.

"But, sir —"

"That will be all."

Great — whatever happened next, Mallove didn't want witnesses. The door clicked shut behind Max. He had an impulse to stand at parade rest, hands behind him — like all of the government bureaucracy, Education was part of the military — but the cuffs made that impossible.

"Sir, may I have these off?" Max lifted his bound wrists.

Mallove's chair creaked as he spun around. Instead of answering the question, he pulled open a drawer, removed a gun, and aimed it at Max's head.

"Someone in my Department is disloyal," Mallove said. "What I need to know, Max, is it you?"

Max stared past the barrel into Mallove's eyes. "Sir, if you want me to be disloyal, I will be."

If it was going to be theatrics, Max could play his role.

They stared at each other until Mallove, with exaggerated casualness, placed the gun, still charged, still aimed at Max, on the desk and leaned back in his chair. "A big change is coming, Max. Before it arrives, I have to root out every traitor —"

Cold fear prickled the back of Max's neck. "Is Drozhin dead?"

Mallove paused, frowning in irritation at the interruption. "I know we all think of General Drozhin as the man who eats knives just so he can shit on people to kill them. But even he is just another mortal man."

"That's why I asked. Is he dead?"

Mallove folded his hands together and looked away. "Not yet, not quite."

Max held his breath. Dmitri Drozhin was Max's other boss. Drozhin, the last great patriarch of the revolution, Director of the Department of Intelligence, in charge of the spies, the secret police, and the assassins. Max had been all three for Drozhin, including his deep undercover spy on Mallove. Max's last mission in space, aboard the spy ship *Gethsemane*, had gone badly when his orders from Drozhin conflicted with his orders from Mallove.

And now here he was a prisoner. Very likely, he had finally been caught as a double agent. Maybe Meredith, his wife, from long ago and that other identity, would use their soil ration to plant flowers for him in the cemetery.

"Too bad," he said to the news about Drozhin.

Mallove leaned forward, resting his hand on the gun. "What happened aboard the *Gethsemane*? To Lukinov, I mean."

The implication was that he knew something. *Answer right, or I'll still shoot you.* For once, Max didn't think Mallove was acting. What could he say safely? What did Mallove know and what did he only guess? Max jerked his hands apart — the metal cuffs dug into his wrists as the chain snapped taut. He was thinking about this wrong: if he wanted to survive, the question was not what did Mallove know, but what did he want to hear?

"It would seem," Max said, reciting the official version, "that Lukinov tried to sabotage the ship's nuclear reactor, that he ended up killing himself when he botched it."

Mallove sketched a whirligig in the air with his free hand, signifying his opinion of the official version. "Yes, but what *really* happened?"

What really happened is that Max caught Lukinov spying for Mallove. Max garrotted him and sabotaged the ship so he could return home to report to his secret boss. He paused for a second, trying to guess Mallove's fear. "I don't think Lukinov was selling us out to the Adareans, no matter what Intelligence says," he said. "More likely it had something to do with his gambling habit."

Mallove's scarred lip twitched – a tell.

The gambling habit. That was probably how Mallove blackmailed Lukinov into spying for him. Now Mallove was afraid of being caught.

Max decided to push his luck. "I witnessed Lukinov gambling with the captain," he said. "The sabotage was intended to cover up some secret, only it went wrong. I'm sure I was arrested on trumped-up charges in order to keep me from investigating the captain. If we find out who Lukinov had been gambling with at home before —"

Mallove interrupted. "That doesn't matter. So his body's still floating out there in space?"

"Yes. He was ejected during a hull breach in the radiation clean-up."

"Well, you can rest easy. I've insisted that we recover Lukinov's body. If anything's been hidden, we'll find it."

Like the ligature marks Max left on Lukinov's neck? That would wreck his story. "Excellent news," he said.

Metal runners squeaked as Mallove pulled open another stained glass drawer and retrieved a crystal bottle of vodka with two tumblers. He filled one and took a sip. "How long have you been with Political Education, Max?"

Longer than you, Max thought. He'd been there at Drozhin's side when the old man decided to form Political Education. Together, they created a new identity for Max when he joined it as a mole. "Since the beginning. It was my first posting when I joined the service."

"Mine too." Mallove tapped his fingers on the glass. "The treason charges against you are laughable, Max. I'm sure Drozhin locked you up because he knows you're one of the key men in my Department."

Yes, why had Drozhin's department locked him up as soon as the ship landed? Disregarding the captain's official charges against him, Max was still trying to figure that one out. He'd gone from being the prisoner of one boss to the prisoner of another. What did the Bible say about serving two masters?

He rattled the links on his cuffs. "If the charges are so laughable, maybe we could take these off."

Again, Mallove ignored his request. "Let's speak frankly. Drozhin's old, he's sick, he's going to die soon. Maybe within days. Without him, Intelligence will be in complete disarray."

And the people he's protected, like me, Max thought, *we're all compost.*

Mallove picked up the gun. Max tensed, ready to take the bolt.

But Mallove didn't notice him flinch; he was too intent on swiveling his chair to point the gun out the window. "The fact is, Intelligence is done for once the old man dies. Drozhin never promoted anyone smart enough to replace him. So when he dies, there will be a battle for power."

There was more than some truth in that. "You think it'll be a physical battle?"

Mallove pretended to shoot people out the window, as if he wanted a physical battle. "There won't be soldiers in the streets," he said. "Those days are long behind us. Yes, men will be discredited, forced to leave their positions, and senior officers will go to prison. But if I surround myself with enough loyal men, all that power will be mine."

Which would be a disaster for the planet, and all their attempts to change it for the better. "You think there's a traitor within Education?"

"I'm sure of it, at least two." Mallove spun around, pointing the gun directly at Max.

This time Max didn't jump. Mallove paused a moment, then set the gun down. The metal clicked hard on a slab of coloured glass depicting the assassination of Brother Porluck.

Mallove chuckled to himself. "'I'll be disloyal if you order me to, sir.' Now there's loyalty for you. Drozhin doesn't have anyone like that." He tapped the intercom. "Anatoly, bring in the key."

Max released a sigh of relief. For the first time, he thought he might survive this interview.

The door swung open quietly. The admin entered and unlocked Max's cuffs. Anatoly was a competent, scholarly officer, the kind who plotted out military campaigns on spreadsheets instead of maps. His gaze lingered on the desk, on the gun backlit by bulbs behind the stained glass image of the fall of the Temple, and on Mallove's hand, which rested with deliberate casualness by the pistol's trigger.

Max rubbed his sore wrists, and wondered what part of this tableau was for him and what part was for Anatoly. With Mallove, there were always wheels inside of wheels.

"Anything else, sir?" Anatoly asked.

"There are some things still up in the air – kinda like clay pigeons." Mallove barked out a laugh at his own joke and pretended to shoot one. "Get reservations for three down at Pillars of Salt. The booth across from the door."

Anatoly said, "Yes, sir," and reached in his pocket for a phone.

Max's mouth watered at the prospect of dinner from Pillars of Salt. He had lamb medallions on a bed of saffron couscous the last time he was there, a few years ago, and hadn't eaten that well since. That had been with Meredith, to celebrate their wedding anniversary –

He shut down that line of thinking. He kept his life strictly compartmentalized, different parts of it sealed behind bulkheads. This was no time to weaken the seals.

Mallove capped the vodka and put it in a drawer, along with the weapon. Scene over, time to put the props away. The second glass, intended for Max, had been forgotten.

"I want you to help me find the traitor, Max," Mallove said. "Let's root out Drozhin's spies."

"I'm the man to do it," Max said, without a hint of irony. Maybe he could cast suspicion on Mallove's best men, and weaken Education in the process.

"Anatoly has already compiled a short list of suspects. The two of you together will find Drozhin's moles."

Max carefully avoided meeting the admin's gaze. "Are you sure Anatoly has time for this, with all his other duties?"

"He'll make time," Mallove said. "This is the most important job I have and you're the two best men I've got."

That's what Max feared. Anatoly was smart, and Max didn't want to risk being caught by him. The admin stared at Max over the rim of his glasses, as if he were already trying to peer through his facade. He maintained eye contact the whole time he tapped out reservations and made a call to Mallove's driver to bring around a car. He looked like he wanted to say something; Max wondered what it was.

Anatoly's gaze flicked to Mallove. "They have the booth ready, sir." Then he held out his hand to Max. "It's good to have you back, Nick."

Max forced a grin. Nick was short for Nikomedes – Anatoly had always called him Old Nick, said he was as ugly as Satan and twice as mean. He clasped Anatoly's hand, hard. "It's damn good to be back, Annie."

He knew the admin hated the girly contraction of his name, but he grinned back. Max's first order of business would be getting Anatoly off this assignment.

They left the office together, bootsoles echoing on concrete as they stomped down the main stairwell, which was plain and unpainted. The architecture was plain for a moral as well as a practical purpose. The settlers of Jesusalem had called themselves Plain Christians, twenty-first-century religious fundamentalists who feared the advances of science and considered all genetic engineering abominations. After all, if man was made in the form of God, any changes in that form amounted to a renunciation of the divine. They'd started in the old United States, in North America, but had found many of their converts later in Europe, especially the former Soviet republics.

Ironically, it was the technology the Plain Christians feared that allowed the survival of their religion. When biocomputers created the singular new intelligence that made space travel possible, they sunk all their resources into a mass migration out to the first marginally habitable planet no one else wanted, a primitive place with surface water and just enough ocean-algae-cognate to produce breathable levels of oxygen. Everything beyond that was rock and sand and struggle, a desert for the devout. Publicly they claimed to keep their buildings austere and luxuryless as penance; the truth was that terraforming went slowly and poorly, and plain was all they could manage.

When they exited the stairwell and crossed the main lobby, the Adarean rose from his bench and came toward them.

Max looked at him more closely this time. The Adarean was too tall, with joints and proportions that were off, inhuman even before you noticed the green colour.

"Willem," the Adarean called out to Mallove, coming forward. Like they were old friends. Adareans hated hierarchies. "I've been waiting days to see you."

"Ah," Mallove said, his face momentarily blank as he thought about which script he was performing. Then he smiled, cold, frosty, as blinding as the sun on a comet. "How good to see you again, comrade Patience."

For a second, Max wondered if the *Patience* were a joke; the Adareans who came to Jesusalem sometimes named themselves for traits they admired, but *Patience*?

Mallove didn't offer his hand.

"I'm here to protest recent acts of violence against innocent Adareans and ask for a halt to today's execution, late though it may be," Patience told Mallove. He seemed very agitated, looking up as if he expected to hear other voices.

Mallove took the stern role now. "But you chose to come to Jesusalem, knowing the history between our planets and accepting the personal risks."

"*Between our planets?*" The Adarean's voice rose into that unsettling mid-range that could be either male or female. "What does that mean? Planets don't interact – individual people do. You know that we have nothing to do with the Adareans who came here before us. They were different people."

A group of Adareans had come before the revolution to join the Plain Christian church. When the old patriarchs were losing the war in the cities, a few radical Adareans showed them how to fashion nuclear weapons from the fissionable undecayed uranium-235 sometimes found in the young planet's surface. They'd nuked the revolutionary stronghold of New Nazareth, almost reversing the war.

The surviving leaders declared war on Adares, although they were in no position to prosecute it at the time. And the people, even those not originally for the revolution, had rallied in their hatred of the impure, genetically-altered Adareans. The pig-men. The abomination. The Beast. It gave all the people of the planet a common enemy to hate besides each other. A rallying cry that saved the planet.

"Look," Max said. "What happened to your friend, it's nothing personal. It's just politics."

Mallove opened his hand with a dramatic flourish. "Exactly. It's politics. Perhaps you should go protest at the Department of Intelligence."

"I did!" Patience said. His hair bristled, moving like grass in the wind. "They said they couldn't do anything to stop the execution and told me that I needed Education."

"Well, there you have it," Mallove quipped. "Consider today's execution educational."

Mallove walked toward the door, Anatoly in his wake; guards blocked the Adarean to prevent him from following. Max sniffed something sour in the air – the briefing was that Adareans communicated with scent, but no one had any proof.

"I've been looking over your files while we were fighting to get you out of that prison cell," Mallove was saying as Max caught up.

"Trying to decide if I was worth the effort?" Max asked.

Mallove grinned. "You must be. Drozhin did everything in his power to keep us from knowing that he held you prisoner. Fortunately I have my own sources. Of all the senior officers I have, Max, you've spent the least amount of time at headquarters."

"Yes, sir," Max said. The guard opened the door. Hot air from the plaza washed over them.

"For over twenty years, you've gone from one field posting to the next," Mallove said. "Never a desk rotation. That's not typical at all."

He was asking for an explanation.

"It's been easier to keep fighting the revolution that way," Max said, knowing it was the right thing to say, but more than half-believing it. "To change the planet, we have to change one mind at a time, until everyone's transformed."

The cost of terraforming a primitive planet was too high; it required too much sacrifice. People had to be true believers in *something* to do it.

"That's been good so far, Max," Mallove said with an almost avuncular tolerance. "But we're moving the battlefield to another level now and we need a bigger vision."

Max made a mental note: Mallove repeated his earlier war metaphor – he wanted to be seen by history as a great general, even though he came to the revolution late, after the fighting was over.

Max scanned the courtyard and reminded himself that the fighting was over. The Department of Political Education sat on a peaceful street. Headquarters was an old school building: the ostensible symbol was that Education was part of the people, right out in the neighbourhood, not set off behind barricades like the secret police in Intelligence. Older, smaller buildings bunched up around it, with windowbox gardens and colourful banners hanging from the rooftops.

Their limousine pulled up to the curb.

Mallove's personal bodyguard jumped to open the door. Mallove paused, lifted his head to the sky, and said, with a grin like a vid general's, "Into the battle!"

Which is when Max noticed the armed gunmen – soldiers for certain, special forces, but in street clothes, nondescript browns and greys – step out from the alleys and doorways. Education's goons always made extravagant gestures, eager to be seen and feared. These moved smoothly, almost gliding, with a distinct lack of threat that made Max's skin prickle.

He grabbed Anatoly's shoulder, out of reflex, one comrade to another, and hissed, "Run!"

The first of the soldiers lifted his gun and shot Mallove's driver in the back of the head with a sound no louder than a muffled pop.

Max raised his hands above his head, turned away, dropped his chin toward his chest. *Look, I'm no danger, I don't see a thing.* He walked toward the nearest corner.

Another muffled pop, and a shout to "Get down! Get the hell down!" and Anatoly's voice, or maybe Mallove's, shouted his name. One of the grey men stepped out from the corner, gun aimed pointblank at his eye.

Guards burst out of Education's lobby at the same moment, firing wildly. Automatic gunfire, old-fashioned ballistics, blasted from the windows directly overhead.

The grey man lifted his eyes for a split second as the shots sounded above him. Max attacked, closing his hand over the barrel of the gun and turning it back into the man's chest, squeezing the trigger with his finger over the other man's. Volts shot through the body, dropped him twitching to the ground. Max's arm went numb to his elbow.

For the next few seconds everything dissolved in the chaos of crossfire and men diving for cover. With the gun still in his hand, Max emptied the man's pockets into his – a little cash, nothing more. He rounded the corner, ran to the next one, turned. Shopkeepers and residents were coming out into the street at the sounds of fighting.

So Mallove had been wrong. Intelligence did mean to have a battle in the streets. And Max had let himself get trapped on the wrong side of the front lines. He would have been safer in his original prison cell.

He dodged down another alley, buttons flying as he ripped off his telltale charcoal-coloured uniform shirt. His plain tee would draw less attention from snipers looking for the other colour. Jamming the gun into his pants, he shoved his way into a group of old women with shopping bags full of bread and produce. He slouched, keeping his head down as he crossed the street in their midst.

"What – you didn't have time to get dressed when her husband came in?" one of the old ladies sneered.

I'm not happy to see you, Max wanted to say. *And that really is a gun in my pocket.* He broke away from them at the far curb.

An unmarked government car – but black, with tinted windows, same as being marked – blew down the street towards Education. Max flattened into a doorway to let it pass.

A block away, on the edge of a rougher neighbourhood, he slpped into a small shop and bought a phonecard, probably an illegal phonecard since the clerk accepted cash. Max stood in a corner by the window and watched the street. As he punched in the private number to Drozhin's gatekeeper, the one he'd memorized and never used, he noticed scratch marks on his hand. He must've gotten them from the guard, when they struggled for the gun –

"What is it?" the voice on the other end said before the phone even rang.

"I need to speak to Uncle Wiggly," Max said. "Peter Rabbit's in troub—"

"Sorry, you have a wrong number."

He was disconnected.

Just like he had been in Drozhin's prison.

A thought hit Max with all the power of a sniper's shot: what if Drozhin had *already* died? The mean old son of a bitch had to go sometime and, like everything else he did, he would probably do it in secret.

Max was screwed if that was the case. Who would take over Intelligence? Hubert was the nominal second in command, but he had no real power. Kostigan was the one to watch out for, but Drozhin probably had standing orders to have him assassinated on his own death. He wouldn't trust that one without a thumb on him. The only one who knew Max personally was Obermeyer. He'd been Max's case officer for years and reported directly to Drozhin. He was also certainly the one assigned to assassinate Kostigan, and it was unlikely he would live out the day after that.

So if Drozhin was dead, and Mallove had just been assassinated, which seemed to be the case, Max was unlikely to live out the day either. Anyone who didn't kill him on purpose would do it by accident.

The clerk stared at him, at the bloody back of his hand, the half-uniform. Pictures of the coup were being broadcast on the screen. If the media was involved already, then the whole thing had been staged. So, yeah, he was screwed.

Max yanked a phonecard from the rack, shoved it at the clerk, tossed money at the counter. "Activate it."

The clerk shook his head, pushed the money back.

The gun came out of Max's pocket and the barrel came to rest on the clerk's temple: Max nodded at the wedding ring on the man's hand. "I'm going to use this to call my wife, tell her she's in trouble. You let me do that, and then I'm gone."

Keeping one eye on Max, the clerk rang up the sale and activated the phone.

It rang and rang until her voicemail clicked on. "This is the house of," she used Max's other name, his original one. Her voice was a bit rough – she joked it was from yelling at their children, but it was too many years spent outside in the planet's harsh landscape, breathing grit. "He's unable to speak to you right now, but leave a message and we'll call back."

He hesitated. "Honey, it's me. I'm in the capital, but may be travelling soon. Don't know when I'll be back —"

Footsoldiers, dressed in the tan uniforms of Intelligence infantry, ran by the window. Max faded back behind the rack of apple chips.

"— I, I," he couldn't bring himself to say *love*, so he switched to their private code, "wish I was with you at the beach. Take care of yourself."

He clicked off and looked up to see the clerk pointing the barrel of a shockprod at him.

Max let the phonecard slip from his hand. It clattered on the floor. For the second time in less than a half hour, he put his hands up in visible surrender, backing quickly toward the door.

He shoved the gun back in his pocket and hit the street running blind. The street was oddly quiet now except for shouts from one alley. Max turned the opposite way, sprinted down a residential street and over a wall into somebody's garden, running through backyards and past astonished faces until he came to a corner lot occupied by one of the old Plain Churches, a long, low building that could have been a bunker if you bricked in the windows.

The revolutionaries had not eliminated the churches when they took over the government. Pastors who supported the new regime prospered; some churches, like this one, the Falter Sanctuary, found other uses as dropboxes where Drozhin's spies passed information to Intelligence.

Max entered, circling the pews to reach the Holy Spirit Stations in the side chapel. Whispering a prayer, he opened the thumb-worn, ancient Bible at random, more for the sake of ritual than insight.

He closed his eyes, stabbed his finger at a page, and opened them again. Deuteronomy 14.2: "You are a people holy to the LORD your God, and he has chosen you out of all peoples on earth to be his special possession."

And what exactly did that mean when they were no longer on earth? Theology had never been Max's strong point, so he didn't worry about it. He snatched up a slip of prayer paper and a pencil stub, then walked to the kneeling wall. He chose the spot farthest from the two women, probably mother and daughter, heads covered in similar red scarves, who were earnestly and quietly scratching out their prayer requests. The television screen in the corner cycled through the old videos of Renee Golden, the Golden Prophet, founder of the Plain Christians.

"*God's plan for us can be seen in the tests he sends us,*" the Golden Prophet said.

Max recognized the sermon, the one she made on the banks of the river in Rostov-on-Don, in southern Russia. Golden was American, but she proselytized heavily during two long missions to the old Soviet republics, returning through Bulgaria, Serbia, and Greece. Hundreds of thousands followed her call to go into space. When she died before making the journey herself, it only made her more like Moses, destined never to reach the Holy Land. Her followers formed a polyglot community that never came together except by force – the force of her personality in the beginning, the force of hardship during the settlement of Jesusalem, and then, finally, under the Patriarchs and the revolution, the force of force.

Max hadn't used this church dropbox in over a decade. He folded his hands and said an earnest prayer to the god of spies and all men caught behind enemy lines that there was still someone out there to receive it.

Picking up his pencil, he began to write. He hoped that whoever saw the old code recognized it.

> "— *Those of you who are listening to me now by way of satellite, I want you to join hands with us. Reach out and put your hand on the television screen* —"

He wrote slowly. The old code was all language for family. Aunt meant one thing, uncle meant another, with trigger words that keyed off the meanings.

> "— *God has given us the design for a ship the same way He gave Noah the blueprints for the ark. Only now we are invited to ascend directly into heaven. Bring your prayers with you, into heaven, and hand-deliver them to God* —"

Max folded the paper and dropped it in the slot.

"May I help you?"

A young pastor stood there in his ceremonial suit and tie. One of the angry young pastors, bent on reclaiming the church's glory in the face of the secular regime, if Max guessed correctly.

> "— *God tells us not to mix with sinners, but this fallen world is full of sinners. Our only choice is to leave this world behind, to ascend* —"

"Just making a prayer request," Max replied softly. He dropped the pencil stub into the little cup.

"I don't recognize you as a regular communicant."

"The church is a sanctuary for all," Max said.

The pastor glanced at Max's state of half undress, his sweat, his bloody hand. "It's funny how those who persecute the church run to it when it suits their needs."

> "— *Are you ready for the test? You have a choice to make: you can die with the sinners or turn your face toward heaven and join the angels* —"

The old woman at the other end of the pew grunted as she rose to her feet with the help of her daughter. "Anyone can change," she chided the pastor. "Sometimes crisis is God's way of showing us the need to repent."

"Yes, Mrs Yevenko," the pastor said.

Max slipped away when the pastor spoke to her. There was nothing else to do here except hope that Obermeyer, or whoever, got his message and understood it. He pushed open the side door; the sun over the metal rooftops glared blindingly, and he blinked.

The hard muzzle of a gun pressed against his neck. "I'll be happy to kill you," a voice said. "Just give me an excuse."

Max raised his hands in the air, for the third time today, this time in true surrender. "No need for that."

The muzzle shoved hard against his head, knocking him off-balance. "I'll decide what is and isn't needed." He reached into Max's pocket and retrieved the gun. "Now walk toward Calvary Park."

"Yes, sir," Max said, obeying. These men were on his side, he had to remember that: they all served Intelligence, they all served Jesusalem. He'd tell them who he was right now, except for the possibility that Kostigan was in charge.

He walked at a non-provocative pace, neither too slow nor too fast. Close to the square, he saw other men being rounded up. No, not just men: there was a woman carrying a baby, tugging a cap down over its head. A little boy clutched the hem of her skirt, running to keep up. This district housed the employees and families of those who worked for the Department of Education. So they were all being rounded up, even the civilians. A clean sweep.

Two other men marched along under the gun of another soldier. One of them was in a tee-shirt, like Max, with a cross on the same chain as his dogtags. The other was a major from Education.

"Can you take this one for me?" shouted Max's keeper.

The other soldier nodded yes, used his weapon to wave all three men up against a flat concrete wall. "Go stand over there – now!"

Perfect wall for an execution, Max thought as he stood against it. Lots of room for burn marks and bloodstains to impress and cow the public for years to come. Jesusalem was full of walls like that, but most of them were old.

While the soldier talked into his link, the other two prisoners whispered. The one with the cross said, "Hey, it's me. Hey."

The voice startled Max. The stupid-but-earnest guard – what was his name? "Vasily?"

"Yeah, what a mess. What's going on?"

The major had different plans. "If we run three different directions, he can't get us all."

Vasily brushed his thumb nervously against his cross. "Yeah, but what about the one he does get?"

"Look," Max whispered, covering his mouth with his hand like he was scratching his nose. "The guard's just pretending to talk. He's watching, waiting for us to run."

Probably hoping for them to run. That way he could just shoot them and walk away. He might do it anyway, Max thought, even without provocation.

"I'll go left first, draw his attention," the major whispered. "You two take off the other way."

It didn't matter to Max if the guy got himself killed, but he didn't want to get caught in the crossfire. When the major leaned, ready to spring away, Max slammed him into the wall. "Don't do it!"

"Your mother's a pig!"

"Move again and I'll shoot all of you!" the guard yelled, running over with his weapon up.

Max looked him in the eye, held up his hands in what was turning into a habitual gesture. "Hey, I'm on your side —"

"Shut up!"

The guard hesitated. He wasn't used to killing yet, wasn't even used to hurting people. Maybe Drozhin recognized that problem with this generation of troops and was trying to blood them. That was possible too, if Drozhin was still alive. That was something Drozhin would do. Any explanation was possible at this point; it was making Max crazy. All he needed to do was hold on until he could make his contact and get away.

The guard listened to something in his ear bud, gestured with the gun. "That way. The transports are lined up in Calvary Park."

"Transports?" the major asked. "Where are we —"

The butt of the rifle interrupted his sentence, scattering his words, along with his blood, over the road ahead of him as he sprawled.

"Did I give you permission to talk?" The guard, pulse jumping in his neck, hopped out of arm's reach and jabbed his gun at them again. "Get up."

Max tensed. The guard was working himself up to kill. It was clear three prisoners made him nervous. He felt outnumbered, unsure.

The major tried to push himself up, but his elbow buckled and he fell again. The guard jabbed his gun, pointing it at all of them in turn, "I said, get up."

Vasily shouted, "Get up!"

Max hooked his hand under the major's elbow and yanked him to his feet, grunting with the effort. He was thinking he could throw the major into the guard and then run —

Wheels squealed around the corner and a military recruit van commandeered for tonight's mission braked to a stop just feet away from Max. A couple soldiers hopped out and the moment to run had passed. The major tore his arm away from Max, staggered to his feet. He'd never been blooded either, which is why he thought he could run.

"What the *fuck* is going on?" one of the new soldiers said. They all looked like children to Max, although they were older than he'd been during the revolution.

"I'm just following orders," Max's guard answered.

"Well, the whole thing is *fucked*," the newcomer said. "What the *fuck* do we do with these *fuckers*?"

"Take them down to Calvary Park with the others."

"God *fucking* damn it all. Jesus Golden."

Guns jammed in their backs, the three men climbed into the back of the van. The new soldier grabbed the major. "I just fucking cleaned this, so don't bleed all over the seat."

"I am still your superior officer —"

His protest was cut short by the goose-pimpling electricity, the smell of ozone and singed flesh. The major clapped a hand to his burned shoulder but he didn't cry out.

"Any other questions, traitor?" the new soldier asked. "No? Good." He shoved the major in, slammed the door shut.

Well, they were all being blooded.

The only other occupant in the van wore civilian clothes. He was leaning forward, saying, "Was that a gun? What just happened?"

Vasily swallowed hard, lifted the cross to his lips, kissed it, and the major stared straight ahead, his wide mouth tight, grim. Max didn't say anything either as the van rumbled away. They all leaned as the van sped around a corner. Max's stomach, still empty, lurched with it.

"Why is this happening?" Vasily asked. "We're all on the same side. I don't understand."

"I heard they assassinated Mallove," the major said, quietly. "Shot to the head."

Max wondered if the comment was an observation or if it was bait. He glanced at the floor, glanced out the window. "No, they didn't. I was there when it happened."

All their attention focused on him now, including the soldier on the other side of the cage up front.

"Mallove and his assistant, Anatoly," Max said, "and some other senior officer were on their way out. There were shots fired by the soldiers, but only after all three were shoved into a car and taken away."

The major stared at Max; so did the guard up front.

"What do you think it means?" the civilian asked.

"It means Drozhin's probably dead," the major said. "It means Kostigan has taken over Intelligence finally. And if they shoved all three guys in a car, it means they're dead as soon as the interrogations are done."

The civilian laughed nervously. "Drozhin's not dead. He's got more lives than Lazarus. I don't think he's ever going to die."

"All of you, just shut up," the soldier said as the van pulled to a stop. He and the driver got out.

"They'll be satisfied with killing all the generals and half the majors," the major said, with a rueful glance at his own insignia. "Most of the rest of you can expect some interrogation, some time in a cell, then reassignment. It won't be too bad."

When the civilian, probably a contractor of some sort caught in the Education buildings, spoke, his voice rose sharply. "They're taking us down to the cells? They told me it was an emergency evacuation."

"Don't worry, they don't have enough cells for all of us," Max said. The major stared at him hard, again, as if trying to figure out who he was.

"See, that's what I don't understand," Vasily asked. "Why are we doing this to each other? We've got a planet to finish terraforming. Hell, there's a whole galaxy to explore."

That was the real question, wasn't it? After three generations of ter-raforming, the planet was still hardscrabble at best. Like people, it was deeply resistant to change.

The civilian jabbed a finger at him. "How can you talk about terraform-ing —"

A fist hammered on the side of the van. "Shut the *fuck* up in there."

They fell quiet. Max folded his hands on his lap, leaned back, savouring the smell of antiseptic cleaners mixed with sweat. These other guys were on their own. All he had to do was avoid anything stupid now, get into the system and stay alive until some of the Intelligence people noticed him and pulled him out. He had to believe that would happen.

The major hooked his tongue into his cheek, then spat blood on the floor.

"Hey," Vasily hissed. "Don't do that. The guard said not to do that."

The major scuffed at the blood with the sole of his shoe, smearing the red stain everywhere. He was swirling his tongue for another spit when the back door swung open.

"Get out," the guard said, using his gun to herd them into a large crowd of men milling around in a hastily thrown up enclosure in Calvary Park. The gate clicked shut behind them. Nervous guards from Intelligence and the regular services patrolled around the outside of the chainlink fence.

Max circled the perimeter once, estimated about a hundred and thirty prisoners, most of them low-level Education bureaucrats or headquarters staff like Vasily. All men, which meant the families were being taken some-where else. He tried to count the guards, but the numbers kept changing as men came and went. No familiar faces either, but then only Drozhin and Obermeyer would know him. He asked questions, trying to find out what people knew, but all he learned was that you could ask a question at one end of the crowd and hear it repeated as a statement of fact at the other end a few minutes later.

On the second pass around, someone clutched his arm.

"You!" The civilian from the van, still smelling like cologne and breath mints. "You're the one who saw Mallove get away free. Do you think he's negotiating for our release? What's going on?"

Max stared at him until he let go. "I think Mallove is doing everything in his power right now."

Let him interpret that as he might. Max walked away, the civilian trail-ing after, towards a noise at the gate.

A bald colonel in the sand-coloured uniform of the regular services, backed by a small knot of similarly dressed soldiers and a flock of medtechs in green scrub coats, appeared at the fence. He kicked the chainlink at the main gate until the crowd all looked that way. He lifted a bullhorn to his mouth. "We know some of you were injured during today's unfortunate safety evacuation —"

"It's unfortunate more of you weren't hurt," someone shouted. Max moved away from the voice. All he wanted to do was stay clear of trouble; screw everyone else.

"— so you're all going to get a quick medical inspection for your own records, to make sure everything's fine, before we process you out of here. Be quick about it, co-operate fully, and everything will be fine. Line up, single file, at the gate. Stee-rip!"

The command echoed those the younger soldiers would have heard recently at basic training camp, and it settled down those men, including Vasily, who pushed his way to the front of the line, eager to comply. Max fell into line a little back of the middle, giving him time to hide how much he was unnerved. There was no reason to strip for a medical inspection, but getting men to obey seemingly reasonable authority was the first step to making them obey wrongful authority. If anyone knew that, a political officer did.

While the men ahead of him joked with the guards and fished for information about their release, Max removed his clothes and folded them, shoes on top.

A scuffle sounded at the very front of the line. "Hey, I don't have any injuries in there!"

"Get used to it," cracked a voice behind him. "You know Intelligence has always been a pain in our ass."

Laughter rippled through the line as they shuffled forward one spot. Max stilled his face to boredom. If Education's best men joked like sheep under these circumstances, either they didn't know their history or they were idiots. Or both.

When his turn in line came, he handed over his articles and was directed behind a small temporary screen. One guard held a gun on him, another held a bigger weapon on the line behind him, and a third man scanned his clothes, then tore off all the pockets and ripped open the seams and hems looking for hidden pockets. He had none in this pair, which he'd been issued in prison. A fourth man in medtech green ran a quick scan over his skin for subdermal implants and weapons.

"Bend over," the medtech said. "Nothing personal, just doing my job."

Max grunted. For a quick body cavity search, it was done as professionally and quickly as a prostate exam.

"Next," the medtech said.

Max's clothes were handed back, more rags than not. The guard dropped the pockets and belt loops on a folding table with other confiscated items. Dressing again was a challenge, as thin as Max was – the drawstring had been torn off his underwear, so his briefs drooped, and without a belt, his pants sagged around his hips.

An explosive battering jerked Max's head around. In the garden by the playground, across from the enclosure, a jackhammer-truck dug a trench. While Max tried to figure out what it was doing, a shoving match erupted by the medtechs.

"Bend over!"

"Bend over yourself!"

The remaining guards rushed over, slammed the protesting man to the ground, and punched or threatened anyone else in line who looked likely to argue. Max held his pants up at the waist and went to the table with the confiscated items. He skipped over a pocketknife and a razor-cutter to grab two frutein bars, the only food he saw. He ripped one open and smashed it into his mouth, then rolled the other into the fold of his pants where he was holding them up.

"You! Move on!" Max stopped chewing, nodded his compliance to the guard, and walked past the objector, now pinned to the ground by three men. Without shoelaces, Max's shoes kept slipping off.

The inspected prisoners mobbed together near the fence, most of them, like Max, holding up their pants. They were subdued, angry, frightened: their attention was focused on the excavation machine beside the garden, where it jackhammered a large pit in the bedrock beneath the thin layer of soil. The grass had been carefully cut back in strips and moved to the side first, so it could be replaced.

"Would make a nice grave," someone said.

"Not so nice," said someone else, but Vasily was there, shaking his head, saying, "It's probably for latrines."

"Moron," someone else shouted. "Why not truck in compost booths?"

"Maybe they don't have enough," Vasily said.

His innocence and capacity for rationalization was almost charming. Max avoided him. The officer with the bullhorn outside the fence waved the workmen to stop and climbed down into the hole. His bald head and shoulders stuck out of the top. He shouted orders, indicated a certain depth, climbed back out.

Most of the men began to say that it was a grave, but the hole wasn't big enough for dozens of men. Max jostled his way into the middle of the mob for camouflage.

"Ow, watch my foot," someone next to him said.

"Sorry."

"You're lucky all they took were your shoelaces," the man said. "They took my boots. It's like we're all on suicide watch."

"Worst case of suicide I ever saw," Max said. "A hundred men shot themselves in the back, then filled in their own grave."

A few men chuckled. Outside the fence, a van pulled up – Max thought it might have been the same one they'd been transported in, with the bloody floor in back. It drove slowly over the mounds of coloured stone until it reached the pit, where it unloaded a half dozen Adareans. One of them was Patience, who'd been waiting outside Mallove's office earlier in the day. Seemed like years ago.

The jackhammer continued its work, sending up spectral clouds of dust in the twilight. A backhoe crowded up against the other side of the pit, scooping out buckets of broken rock whenever the jackhammer paused. While the Adareans milled around, their greenish skin looking sickly and pale, the last of Max's fellow prisoners finished their "health" inspection and crowded up against the fence. Their cold, clammy skin pressed against Max as they tried to see what was happening outside.

"Weedheads!" one of the prisoners yelled.

"Go home, pig-men!" another shouted.

"Abomination!"

Within seconds, all their anger and fear and venom was directed at the Adareans. The chainlink rattled in rising pitch with their voices.

Outside, the Adareans clustered together. Even this far away, Max thought he could smell something sour waft from them. If the soldiers opened the gates and shoved the six into the compound right now, there'd be a massacre.

Instead the officer with the bullhorn stomped over to the Adareans, barking sharp orders, telling them to stand in the pit. When they hesitated, he waved his hands and guards rushed forward, shoving them down.

Tall as they were, the Adareans' heads showed above the rim of the pit. "It's not deep enough!" shouted one of the hecklers.

"Shoot them and they'll fit," shouted another and laughter rippled through the crowd. Max remained an island of silence.

Soldiers with shovels appeared around the hole and began spading the jackhammer gravel into it as quickly as they could. The Adareans shouted and struggled, but other guards kept them in place. Soon the weight of the stone pinned them where they were, until all that stuck above the surface was their bleeding, dusty heads.

The island of silence spread on Max's side of the fence, broken only by someone's half-suppressed laughter.

"They going to leave them there?" someone whispered.

No, Max thought, no, they weren't.

The scene was another tableau, like the one in Mallove's office. It reminded him of what they'd done, as guerillas, with the Adareans they caught during the revolution. But he wasn't sure whether this was a sign that Drozhin was still alive and reviving old tactics, or that Kostigan had taken over and was reinventing them.

The men with shovels tamped the lumpy gravel down smooth around their Adareans. The long grassy hair on their skulls was coated with a layer of dust. One of the Adareans alternated between weeping and panting. A couple others lolled unconscious.

"Are they trying to plant them to see if they'll grow?" one of the young men asked.

"What the hell are they doing?"

Teaching us a lesson, Max thought.

The work crew stepped out of the way while someone went to the equipment shed and liberated the mower.

Max turned away and left the crowd. He leaned on the far fence, head sagging, as the mower made its charge across the small park. As the first shrill scream sounded, he squeezed his eyes shut, and he kept them shut as the grinding sound of the blades whirred down to bare gravel.

A few prisoners cheered the executions; others laughed nervously, trying to get others to join them. One man retched. Most fell silent, and several drifted back towards Max.

The colonel with the bullhorn walked back over to the enclosure. "Listen up," he shouted. "You're all enemies of Jesusalem. You know in your heart what your crimes are, so we don't need to tell you."

He would have been a good political officer, Max thought.

"Unlike these off-worlder animals," the voice from the bullhorn continued, "we believe that you can repent of your evil choices" – interesting, Max thought, that their secular government used the same language as the religious one that preceded it – "and return to being productive citizens. We know that you were all misled by the criminal Mallove. Reject him and you'll be accepted back into society."

A surge toward the fence came from men ready to admit to, confess to, anything, for immediate release.

"I'm innocent," the civilian contractor was yelling as he shoved his way to the gate. "I don't even know Mallove."

Bullhorn gave an order. Guards cracked the gate while the sizzle of shock rifles kept the prisoners at bay; one guard yanked the civilian out of the compound before locking the gate again. The whole mob protested and yelled that they too were innocent. Bullhorn pulled out a handgun, placed it against the citizen's forehead and shot him. His body collapsed to the ground. A shiver went through the mob around Max.

"We know all of you are guilty," Bullhorn shouted, "You will now have to redeem yourself through penance."

Yes, Max thought, a terrific political officer.

A large articulated bus, hastily armored with bars outside the windows, rumbled up to the gate.

"This is your ride," Bullhorn said. "Next stop, fabulous seaside beach resorts. Bring your swimsuits, towels, and tiny shovels. All aboard!"

The guards with shockguns opened the gate and herded the prisoners into the bus. They shuffled past the civilian's body, sprawled facedown on the rock. Professionally, Max admired that detail – it worked on so many levels: it showed the men that if civilians weren't safe, neither were they. And if Adareans could be killed, and if civilians could be killed, it made the prisoners identify more with the men with guns.

He stepped onto the bus, noting that it was one of the charter buses that mothers used to visit their children who'd moved to the new cities close to the coast. Another nice detail. Very reassuring.

Max shouldered his way back to the other door, then to the sliding door that connected the front compartment to the back, and found both locked. Not so reassuring.

The bus had three sections – a separate cab where the driver was safe from the passengers, important for this ride, followed by two individual sections, each with forty-eight seats. They'd be shoving sixty to seventy men in each.

Someone bumped into him, then someone else bumped them both. Bodies pressed close, the cumulative odor of sweat and bad breath and stale lunch was almost overwhelming. Guards yelled, "Get in, get back from the door!" as they physically packed the last few men on board. It felt like a grotesque game of musical chairs, with cursing for music and metal benches for chairs. The door snapped shut, stayed shut even as men pushed back. Through the window, Max saw guards herd more men into the second compartment.

A hand snaked through the bodies and grabbed hold of Max. Max twisted, tried to tug free, but it only had the effect of reeling the man to him.

"Hey, it's me, Vasily."

"I don't really need a guard any more," Max said.

"The front doors are locked."

"And the back doors and the compartment door."

"What are we going to do?" Vasily said. "You're a senior political officer —"

"Sh, sh, sh," Max said, squeezing a hand up in Vasily's face to make him shut up.

"Nikomedes – that's it!" a voice said from the bench beside them. The major from the van. His cheek was bruised, his lip swollen, where he'd been hit in the face. "I knew I knew you."

"I'm sorry," Max said.

"Major Benjamin Georgiev," the man said, squeezing over on the bench, making room for Max. "I served aboard the *Jericho* with you, years ago."

"You were the radio tech," Max said, sitting, recalling the name once it was matched to the ship. Another chance to keep a low profile, remain invisible, slipped away. The bus lurched into motion, throwing everyone off balance, raising a chorus of curses. "I thought you were regular service."

"Transferred. Got inspired by the spirit of the revolution to join Education." Georgiev's eyes surveyed the bus. "Seemed like a good idea at the time."

"You two," Vasily interrupted. "You know how to get out of this, right?"

Georgiev ignored Vasily. "Killing those Adareans, that was a mistake," he said to Max. "That'll bring down the power of Adares, first with political pressure, then with force."

"Maybe," Max answered. "But Intelligence can get away with killing Adareans during the first throes of the purge. They'll blame it on runaway elements, punish some token low-level grunts, execute someone prominent, then appease the Adareans later."

"I doubt it'll stop there – it never does. Did you ever hear the one about the secret police?" Georgiev asked.

"Probably," Max said.

Vasily asked, "Which one?"

Georgiev lifted his head toward Vasily. "The secret police came for the Adareans and no one tried to stop them, so they took the Adareans away."

Max recognized the old chestnut; Vasily said, "Yeah?"

"Then the secret police came for the unchristians and no one tried to stop them, so all the uns were taken away. Then the secret police came for the sinners – the fornicators, the secret body polluters, the users of forbidden technology – and no one tried to stop them."

"So they took the sinners away," Vasily finished.

"Right," Georgiev said. "Finally the secret police came for honest men like you and me."

Max finished the joke. "And there was no one left to stop them."

"No," Georgiev said. "When they came for me, I said, 'Welcome, brother. Isn't it good to be the secret police?'"

After a pause, Vasily chuckled. The bus braked hard, throwing them back in their seats, then sped up again.

A young man with a soft chin leaned in from the bench beside them. "I heard you guys talking. You know, that guy they shot at the gate —"

"The accountant?" Georgiev asked. "He told me he was an accountant."

"No he wasn't, that's what I'm saying." He jerked his thumb down the aisle. "Guy back there says he recognized him as an actor. It was all staged. Guy got up and walked away while we were getting on the bus."

"Not walked," interrupted another kid hanging from an overhead rack. "There were two guys, one on either side of him, helping him, made it look like they were dragging him, but you could tell he was faking it."

"See, they're just trying to scare us," the first kid said. He laughed, like he wasn't fooled.

"Well, it's working," Vasily said, rubbing his throat, where his cross would've been. "I'm scared."

"The Adareans, that was fake too," Max said. "Really great bunch of actors."

The kid sitting down, the one with the soft chin, looked away and didn't say anything. But the one hanging from the strap said, "Yeah, the whole thing is a big scam. I hear Mallove and Drozhin worked it out together, plan to combine the two departments. Mallove's going to take over as soon as Drozhin's dead."

The pitch of conversation rose around them, a dozen variations of the same stories being told, repeated, and invented. Their small group sat quietly for a second.

Max coughed. "Did you ever hear the one that goes, how can you tell when a rumour about Drozhin is true?"

Major Georgiev stared at Max, his face carefully blank. The two kids waited for the answer. Finally, Vasily said, "How?"

Max aimed his finger like a gun at the other man's head. "'What did you just say?'"

Georgiev smirked and the kids chuckled nervously. Max leaned back, closed his eyes, ignored the press of bodies. His day had started as a prisoner, waiting to hear from his contact in Intelligence. His day ended as a prisoner, waiting to hear from his contacts in Intelligence. Nothing had changed. But then he thought about the distance from the Adarean baptism at the execution that morning to the brutal murder of the Adareans in the park, and it felt as if everything had changed.

As he listened to the sound of the wheels, all he could think of was the roar of the mower blades as the tractor rolled toward the Adareans trapped in the pit.

"Wake up, Nikomedes." A hand shook him.

Before he was completely awake, Max deflected the hand and turned the wrist. He snapped alert quick enough to stop before he broke it. Major Georgiev bent over him. "What?"

"We're passing through the outskirts of Lost Angeles – it's night, the city's big enough to hide most of us."

"What's the plan? There are bars welded on the windows, and the doors are locked." He'd watched younger men waste themselves for hours trying to find a way out, everything from tearing through the panels to breaking windows. One of them had been cut badly on broken glass. Wind whistled through the broken windows; combined with the night temperatures, it would have chilled the ride to the point of hypothermia if not for the warmth of the bodies jammed together.

"We're going to rock the bus, tip it over," Georgiev said. "I could use your help organizing these kids."

Max straightened in his seat. "Tipping the bus – that will get us out how?"

"They'll have to empty the bus then. We'll overpower them, make a break for it."

"You're on your own." He leaned back again.

"To think that I was ever inspired by you," Georgiev sneered. "You're a coward."

And you're a fool, Max wanted to respond. He had nothing against escape, but suicide? "Don't play into their hands."

"This morning," Georgiev said, looking around, "we were all part of an organization, each of us knowing our role and function. Tonight we are starving, thirsty outcasts, deprived of basic necessities. But we're still men, we have to do something."

There were murmurs of "amen" and "witness" from the men around them.

"Don't you think Intelligence's purpose is to reduce and dispirit us?" Max asked.

"Yes, but —"

"So what do you think they'll do to anyone who goes against their intentions early on?" Max asked. "What would your response be? To anyone who tries to lead?"

Georgiev said nothing.

"You would destroy the ring leaders as an example," Max said, answering his own question. "And first you would create a situation where you expect people to step up, just so you can make examples of them. It's what I would do."

"I'm not you," Georgiev said. "And I believe this is all a mistake. Those are our fellow soldiers out there, our brothers and cousins. If we force them to pay attention to us, they'll listen. And if they don't, we'll overwhelm them."

Murmurs of "yeah" and "they have to listen."

"You've been hit in the face and burned and you still say that?" Max said, leaning back in his seat. "We save ourselves. No purge lasts forever."

"You're pathetic," Georgiev said and turned away.

Vasily, hand at the invisible cross at his throat, stared at Max, shook his head, and followed Georgiev.

Georgiev had no trouble organizing the men: he was the senior officer on board and soldiers were trained to love a hierarchy, taught to do something instead of nothing. After explaining his plan to tip the bus, he said, "All right, on the count of three, we all throw ourselves to starboard. Is that clear? One! Two!"

"Wait, wait, wait," cried one voice, and then others said, "Stop," and Georgiev yelled, "Wait, stop!"

The compartment was dark, but lights outside rolled front to back, front to back, illuminating puzzled faces. Finally, someone said, "Which side's starboard?"

Max smirked. Most of the men had only served groundside.

Georgiev rattled the locked door. "The doors are port, the other side is starboard. We want to tip over to starboard, so we can climb out the doors on top."

Murmurs of "got it" and "all right" were followed by Georgiev resuming the count. Max braced his feet on the floor and grabbed hold of the bench.

On *three* the mob of men surged toward the starboard side. The bus rocked – about as much as it did when it hit a bad pothole.

"That was pretty effective," Max said, but Georgiev was shouting out encouragement and instructions: "All right, that was a good first try. Let's all squeeze over to port, to the door side, and do it again."

Men crushed Max against the side. He smelled urine mixed in with all the other locker-room odours.

"Three!"

This time the men yelled as they surged to the other side.

This time there was a noticeable rock.

"Good work, men," Georgiev shouted. "Now we're going to rock it back and forth. As soon as we hit port side, the door side over here" – he leaned over and banged the door —"I want you all to run back to starboard, over here. Got it?"

Mumbles of "got it" and "yes, sir."

"What? I can't hear you!"

"YES, SIR!"

On three, they all shouted and threw themselves at the port side. Max brought up his arm to cover his head. This time the bus rocked again, though no more than it would be by the wind coming off the escarpment this time of year.

"Starboard!" Georgiev ordered, and with a roar, they immediately threw themselves at the other side. Several men tumbled to the floor in the dark, but despite the blindness and swearing, the rock on the other side was bigger.

Georgiev got them cheering and clapping for themselves, then set up a rhythm, charging one side, then the other. As Max persisted in staying in his seat, knees and elbows hit him with every rush, even though he pulled his legs up on the seat. He deflected some blows, braced and took the others.

"Come on," Vasily shouted, all excited.

Pounding from the compartment behind them led to a shouted exchange of plans. On the first combined rush, the two compartments ran toward different sides, cancelling each other's efforts. One of the young men leaned up against the back wall, and yelled, "Starboard, you morons, starboard!"

"Hurry," Georgiev shouted. "We're almost through Lost Angeles!"

Renewed effort in both cars quickly led to rocking until the bus tipped up, wheels off the ground. As it swerved suddenly on the road, bouncing down again, the men fell silent, all but two or three forgetting to finish the charge back to the other side.

"That's it, we can do it!" Georgiev shouted. "Come on, get up, let's start over!"

The men were so absorbed in rocking the bus that only Max noticed it slowing or saw the headlights of the dustskimmers outside. The bus braked to a stop as a row of floodlights cut through the barred windows, freezing the unshaven, sunken-eyed faces of Max's fellow prisoners in a harsh light.

Guards ran over, the locks clattered to the pavement, and the door flew open. "Congratulations, that's an impressive effort, good work, men," the guard said. "Who's the senior officer here?"

Georgiev squinted as he squeezed forward through the men. "Major Benjamin Georgiev, enlisted regular service in six-four. What we'd like —"

The guard shot him, discharging enough bolt to knock down two men beside him and pimple the hairs on Max's arms a couple seat rows back. One of the kids shouted, tried to rush the guard, but the blue crackle from the gun just missed his head as the men near him dragged him to the floor.

Angry shouts from the second compartment were silenced by the sound of broken windows and a barrage of fire.

"Do we have another senior officer in here?" the guard asked. Vasily and a couple others looked towards Max, but he shook his head.

"Do we have someone else in charge?" the guard asked. When no one spoke, he said, "Good, because I'm a big believer in individual responsibility, and if anything else happens, I will hold each and every one of you individually responsible. Do I make myself clear?"

He grabbed Georgiev by the back of his shirt and dragged his body, face first, down the steps and outside. Other guards, nervous, guns up, shut and locked the doors again.

Vasily slumped down in the seat beside Max, his face a pale mask of disbelief and despair.

"Don't worry," Max said. "Georgiev is probably just faking it."

The bus started rolling again, this time the skimmers flanking it in clear view. The city shrank behind them, and in moments, dust and grit came through the window, getting in Max's eyes and under his tongue. Elsewhere in the darkened bus, someone coughed. A couple others whispered that they should have prepared weapons from the broken glass and jumped the guard. Retrospect always gave you a better plan.

Out of the corner of his eye, Max saw one of the kids stand up toward the side of the bus and unzip his pants to relieve himself.

"You might want to save that for drinking later," Max shouted. Some of the men around them laughed; some didn't.

"I got nothing to save it in," the kid shouted back, which was true. "You want to come over, use it like a drinking fountain?"

Max smiled, and his lips cracked. "Nah, don't think I want to touch that handle."

Beside him, Vasily rubbed his throat. "I would do anything right now for a bathroom," he whispered. "Hell, I'd personally murder Mallove for something to eat or some water to drink."

Max's own throat was parched and his stomach had been growling for hours. With a glance around, he unrolled the stolen fruitein bar from the waist of his pants. He tried to tear it open with his hands, couldn't, ripped it open with his teeth. After breaking the bar in half, he said, "Sh," and pressed half into Vasily's palm.

"What? What's —"

"Sh!" Then softly, Max added, "Eat it slow."

He saw the blue shadow of Vasily's hand shove the whole thing into his mouth. He tried to chew it slowly, but swallowed before Max ate his first small piece.

"Is there more?" Vasily whispered.

"No, that's all."

Later, while Max finished the last piece of the bar, Vasily asked, "Why did you share it?"

"Because where we're going, I'll need friends more than I need food right now. Can we look out for each other?"

"Yeah, of course," Vasily whispered. "Whatever you need, whatever I can do, I'm the man."

Max nodded, as if a contract had been signed, and Vasily dipped his head in return. Such a slight gesture in the dark. Vasily's stomach rumbled and he crossed his hands over it. As the bus rolled on through the dark, Max searched his lap for crumbs, licking them off his finger, one by one. Wind coursed over the flatlands and through the broken windows, carrying a hint of salt and moisture.

All that was missing was the smell of compost and blood to complete the reclamation camp stink. As a political officer, he'd visited them more than once.

Men around him shifted, tried to sleep, but Max stared straight ahead into the rushing night.

Sunrise, harsh and unrelenting, cast brightness on their squalor even through the unbroken, tinted windows. The bus smelled of urine, shit, and sweat. Get used to it, Max told himself. His back ached and his legs were stiff from too many hours in the unyielding seat. In one corner, someone sobbed.

"That's Machete Ridge," Max said, pointing to a sharp line on the horizon. Vasily leaned across Max to look. "Do you see that bump, up there beside the road?" Max asked.

"That's the reclamation camp," Vasily said.

"That's Faraway Farms. It used to be a reclamation camp." Twenty years ago, Faraway Farms was the end of the line. Now it was just one more extension settlement on the coast, a few thousand people occupying rows of low brown buildings built around a series of narrow field-ponds.

"Maybe we'll stop here," Vasily suggested.

"Be wary of hope," Max warned quietly. "It'd be too hard to guard everyone here. Too many other people, too much access to boats and skimmers."

Still, an hour later, when the bus pulled over to the fresh water cisterns outside of Faraway, even Max had to fight against hope.

When he saw the guards hooking up a fire hose, he gave up hope and clawed his way over the benches to reach one of the open windows first. For a few blissful seconds, Max's face was drenched as he opened his throat to gulp down the blast of water. Then he was fighting the weight of men on his back, crushing him for a drink. He was saved when the hose moved along to another window and the mass of bodies tumbled over the seatbacks after it. Everyone got at least a trickle of water, all except for two men too sick, or weak, to move, who lay moaning at the front end of the car. Max thought they were the ones caught by the shot that killed Georgiev. Men stretched their arms through the bars, begging for more, as the guards moved to the next car.

Max returned to his bench – he thought of it as his bench now, every man had marked out his two square feet of bus – and grunted as he sat. His whole body ached, needing exercise, a chance to stretch. Normally, he'd walk, if only to pace the aisle of the bus, but the aisle was filled too. A few men had stretched across the bench backs, feet on one seat, hands on another, to do push-ups, and others did chin-ups on the hanging straps. Max would do that soon, if he had to, to keep his strength. Of course, that was a hard choice too: spend his energy, not knowing when he'd eat or drink next, or save it in reserve.

Vasily plopped down, hair plastered to his head. He was scraping drops of water off his face, pushing them into his mouth. "I wouldn't treat animals this way," he told Max.

"That's rather the point," Max said, imitating him, feeling the scratch of his unshaven skin under the droplets.

"Your face is cut up pretty bad."

"Is it?" He tasted the sharpness of blood on his fingertips, saw the bright red. "Must have been some glass shards in the window, got blown out by the blast of water."

"When will we stop?"

"We've been on the road maybe twelve, fourteen hours. I forgot where all the camps are now, but we're not even halfway there."

"Oh, Jesus," Vasily said.

In the old days, during the schism, the men sent off to the reclamation camps for their religious beliefs – or disbeliefs – would pray to God. Max prayed to Drozhin. During the purge, Intelligence would be desperate for information. Obermeyer would check the dropboxes, realize Max was out there, and start looking for him. Survive long enough to give them time to find him: that was Max's sole faith.

"I can't believe they're sending me to the reclamation camps," Vasily said. "I didn't do anything to deserve being treated like a murderer or a rapist."

"So don't let them turn you into one," Max said. "Besides, the worst crime is still having the wrong beliefs."

"But I did everything I was supposed to do, I enlisted in the government after my mandatory service, I —"

"Get over it. Keep your head low, do what you need to do to survive."

"Do what I have to do to survive," Vasily said, letting out a deep breath. He seemed like a decent guy, Max thought, not used to thinking, but thinking hard now. "Why did we have a revolution?" he asked. "I thought it was supposed to put a stop to this."

Max remembered those days. The church schismed, and different groups insisted that they had the only true beliefs. With life depending on limited resources, each side wanted everything for the true believers. Even after the terraforming increased their yields, the two sides had been willing to kill each other to prove who had the direct word from God. "The revolution bought us twenty years."

"What?"

"It's been twenty years since we had this kind of purge," Max said. Sure, there were individual murders here and there, usually arranged to look like accidents or poor health. But that was politics as usual anywhere. "We bought twenty years of peace where we hadn't had it more than three years in a row for two generations. You grew up in peace, didn't you?"

"Well, yeah."

"The revolution bought you that. So it was worth it. And if this purge buys us another twenty years, maybe it'll be worth it too."

Vasily shook his head. "I don't know if I can think that way. I don't know if I can ever think that way."

"Maybe you won't have to," Max said, but doubtfully.

The bus continued all day, stopping only to relieve the drivers and escorts. Sometime that night, while they shivered to keep warm, one of the sick men died. The man next to him must've noticed he was cold, called his name, saying, "Pete, Piotr, aw, man, Pete, wake up, man, aw, I can't believe this, aw, Pete, aw, man."

The body had a noticeable reek, even above the stench of piss and shit and sweat that permeated the bus. By the time the sun came up again, all the men were collapsed in a mixture of exhaustion and depression. There were no more push-ups or chin-ups. The wind blew sand in through the broken windows, turning everyone a dusty brown. Max had grit in his eyes, his hair, in every wrinkle in his clothes and body.

With the hot sun baking down through the windows as they drove north toward the equator, Max leaned against the wall, listless, conserving his energy. An impromptu morgue was formed under the seats at the front of the bus, the corpse shrouded with what was left of his clothes, pulled up to cover his face. The next row back remained empty, even though there weren't enough places to sit.

Max was light-headed, weak from lack of food and lack of water. They'd gone so far. But then the reclamation camps had to be isolated. Only after the new one was turned into a settlement, like Faraway, would they fill in the space between with cistern stations and rest spots.

Terrafarms. That's what the first colonists had called them. Until the prisoners changed the name to terrorfarms. He closed his eyes.

"Are you all right?" Vasily shook his arm.

"Fine," Max said.

"No, I mean, just now, I thought you were a corpse."

"Funny," Max rasped. "Back in the space fleet my nickname was the Corpse, because I always look this way."

"Look, I'm counting on you," Vasily said, leaning over earnestly, speaking low. "I don't want to end up dead."

Max felt sorry for him. Trying to swallow the dust in his throat, he said, "Here's the thing you need to know to survive —"

He started coughing then, the grit in his dry throat damming the words, and he couldn't stop. He needed something to drink, just a sip, and it would be fine, but there was nothing. Not even sucking on his shirt, which had been soaked, gave him any moisture, just more dust, the taste of salt, and more reason to cough.

Up front, one of the men screamed, roared in senseless rage. Within seconds the gangly redhead flung himself at the walls of the bus, one side, then the other, then kicked and stomped and slapped the men scattered on the benches and the floors, demanding that they do something, ordering them to get up and do something. The dustskimmers zipped in close, flanking the sides of the bus.

"Make him shut up," Max yelled hoarsely between hacks. "Hold him down." Others said the same thing from the safety of a similar distance.

At first, the men close by just tried to get out of the berserker's way, but he grabbed one and began beating his face. Others tried to pull him away, but he lashed out at them, demanding water, demanding to be let off, demanding justice – things none of them had to give him. The more they held him, the harder he thrashed, until finally one of them lost it and punched him, telling him to "Shut up, just shut up," and then they all started hitting him until they tumbled in a crushing pile to the floor.

One of the older men, a paunchy bureaucrat in his thirties, began pulling men off, ordering them to stop the beating. When they did, the berserker lay still in the aisle. Men went back to their seats, ignoring him; after a while, some came and checked on him, and later two of them dragged him up to the morgue at the front of the bus.

Vasily held his stomach. "How long is it before someone suggests we start eating the corpses?"

"Won't happen," Max said, hoping it was true.

He was thinking that another reason for having the reclamation camps out so far was that bodies could be dumped into the compost pits, and then the prisoners reported escaped and missing instead of being sent back for burial. The families got a letter saying their loved one had escaped, please report to the authorities if he shows up: it gave them hope and the dead man some dignity. But prisoners marked as escaped were always dead.

"It'll be worse when we get to the camps," he said.

The camps were still a couple hundred kilometers away. Sometime during the night, Max reached that stage of hunger and sleeplessness where he drifted in and out of consciousness, caught in the no-man's land between the minefield of his hallucinations and the barbed-wire of reality. With his face against the cool glass, eyes half-lidded, and a heavy weight pressing on him, he first mistook the smell of rotting algae for a dream. Then he snapped awake.

At the sudden movement, Vasily's head fell off Max's shoulder and he sagged into Max's lap. Max shook him. "Come on," he whispered. "We have to get off here."

"Huh," Vasily said, drowsily. "What?"

"Sh," Max said. "We won't live to the next camp." He shoved Vasily aside and stepped over the bodies and around the seats to the doorwell. He grabbed the man propped upright on the steps. "Hey, there's a bench open, back there – I need to stand a while."

The man, sunken-eyed, peered over the seats, full of desire and mistrust.

"You won't get a second chance," Max said. "Promise I won't want it back."

The man rose awkwardly, crabbed his way past Vasily to the empty bench. Vasily squeezed into the doorwell next to Max. Every time he tried to ask a question, Max held up his hand for silence in case others listened.

Dawn rose like a wail of despair, thin and piercing. No man wanted to face another day of sun and heat. The bus rattled and shook, kicking up dust over the unfinished, unpaved road, so that only Max, who was looking for it as they came over each rise, saw the bunkers floating in a little pond of green surrounded by the ocean of sand and rock.

When the other men finally saw it, some declared it a mirage while others raised a feeble cheer, thinking it their destination. Max knew Intelligence would never leave them all at one camp – it would be some here, some at the next one, divided among camps, spread among strangers.

The mirage came steadily closer, resolving in dreary detail – the rounded corrugated roofs of the half-buried huts, scoured by the wind and sand to the same dull tones as the landscape; the surrounding fence, topped by razor-wire, its sharp points cutting the sky so that it bled light; the little bowl of brown and green mud visible beyond the camp.

Bodies pressed behind Max as the bus rolled slowly to a stop and the cloud of dust settled. Past the last bunkers, Max saw the camp population standing in lines for the morning roll. The sign above the gate read:

RECLAMATION CAMP 42
"THEY WERE JUDGED EVERY MAN
ACCORDING TO THEIR WORKS."

The guards jumped off their skimmers. Most of them stood, jawing, while one went to the gate to meet the camp staff.

Max beat on the door. "Pray," he grunted to Vasily.

"For what?"

"That they come to this car, not the second one." That Drozhin got my message and has someone waiting for us, he would have added. His fist grew numb, so he banged his forearm on the door. Other men, not sure what was up, followed his lead, beating the walls and window frames.

The camp minister limped to the gate with his assistant and several guards. Dusty grey clothes, indistinguishable of rank, hung loose on their lean forms. Camp supervisors were still called ministers, instead of directors, despite the changes following the revolution, because the camps were nominally for rehabilitation. *Drozhin, come get me*, Max heresied to himself, *and I promise to be a better man.*

The minister argued with the guards, pointing at the front half of the bus: he wanted men still alive and with some fight in them – he could get more work from them before they broke. The guard listened indifferently, yelled something to the other guards, who came to Max's door aiming weapons.

Sixty bodies pressed against Max, trying to elbow their way in front of him. Max elbowed back, hooking his arm around Vasily to keep him close.

"Ten," shouted the main guard, spreading his fingers. "Just ten of you!"

The bodies slammed forward again, banging Max's head into the door-frame. Hands tried to claw him back. The guard removed the locks and the doors opened halfway, stopped by the press of men. Max yanked his head free from a fist in his hair, bit a finger that clutched at his face, and gripped the door so that no one could push past him. A grunt, as punches landed in his kidneys, then he ducked as the gun's electric sizzle flew over their heads, setting their hair on end. One guard was yelling, "Back, back!" and another grabbed a fistful of Max's shirt since he was in front, and pulled him through the door, calling, "One."

Max still had an elbow hooked around Vasily's arm, who tumbled after him. They both sprawled in the dirt.

"Make that two."

Max stood up quickly before anyone could jerk him to his feet, smoothing his clothes, tugging up his pants, as the guard counted, "Nine, Ten, and that's it. Get the hell back!" A roar of protest was followed by the sizzle of the guns, cries of pain, and the doors snapping shut.

"They're all yours," the guard told the minister. Turning to his second, he said, "Call 43, tell them they need to be ready to take fifty, water a hundred, and they have to put us up for the night." To the rest of the guards he shouted, "Wheel up, wheel up, we're moving out!"

Guards closed and locked the camp gate. The minister walked up and down the short line of prisoners, sucking on his teeth, as mean-looking as a rib-thin dog. He wore goggles to keep the sand out of his eyes, which kept Max from reading his expressions. Finally, with the bus already a plume of dust over the hill, he turned and walked back toward the roll call. The guards shoved Max and the other prisoners after him, back toward the compound's waste pits. Max tried not to choke on the stench; he made careful note of the dead bodies laid out at pit's edge. Escapees. Nine of them, in various states of decomposition.

Vasily nudged his shoulder, whispered. "At least we're not starting off on the lowest rung in the camp."

He glanced in the other direction. In front of the razor-wire fence, apart from the other rows of men, stood a clump of sunburned, emaciated Adareans. Max had noticed them, but he found it more interesting that Vasily seemed determined to ignore the dead bodies.

"Take your clothes off," one of the guards ordered. He offered no reason for them to strip, no pretence of inspection or health check, but he seemed so bored by the command, so ready to use his gun, that they did what he said immediately. The earlier conditioning was already paying off.

As soon as they were naked, a guard gathered up their clothes.

The minister grinned at them. "Welcome to Camp Revelations."

Of course, thought Max. The camp would be named for the Bible book its verse came from. He looked again at the dead bodies and wondered if the sea or hell had delivered them up.

"Many of you noticed the verse inscribed above the entrance of our humble enterprise," the minister said. "I promise each of you that during your time here you will be judged according to your deeds."

He pulled a handkerchief from his shirt pocket, shook the dust from it, and wiped his goggles clean. Then he walked down the line, looking each one of them over.

"My name is Minister Pappas, but you may call me sir. If you ever address me at all, which is not something I encourage you to do. You are penitents and you are here to do penance for your crimes. There are guards and deacons in this camp, and you will respect them just as if they were me."

The guards were regular service, but Max knew if they posted out here they either weren't very bright or had some kind of pathology. Deacons were prisoners trusted to act like guards, except they weren't trusted enough to have their fingerprints keyed to the guns.

"Your work here will be to turn this valley from desert to oasis," the minister said. Behind him, a few hundred prisoners stood in ranks, like cans on a store shelf or pieces off an assembly line. Beyond them, beyond the razor-wire fence, the low green slopes reached up to the raw, wind-scarred hilltops and the sere blue sky.

"Three kilometers over that hill lies the sea. All of you remember the stories about the first settlers – that's what you do now. You carry the rocks to the sea, bring back the algae, and we seed it with enzymes and bacteria and earthworms to create topsoil for farming. In a decade, these hills will be covered with plants and trees."

Max didn't plan on being here in a decade to see it, though he knew some of these men would.

"At this moment," the minister said, tucking the handkerchief back in his pocket, "I would draw your attention to the corpses you see in front of you. Those are your camp uniforms. You are expected to dress appropriately at all times."

Max was old enough to remember the shortages of food and basic supplies the winter after the nuclear bombing of New Nazareth. Without the meanest rags to wear, even the strongest died. So he broke the line and ran to the corpses, hurrying to the end where they looked only a day or two dead instead of weeks. There was a cleaner uniform on one of the bigger Adareans, but he grabbed the ankle of the one closest to his own size – the body weighed no more than a stick – and yanked off the soiled, foul-smelling overalls. He felt the arms crack as he tugged the top off the dead man's back.

This was meant to shame him, classic psychological manipulation, but he would not be shamed by survival. He thrust his legs into the pants one at a time. The orange uniform, dulled by sun and sand, fit him no worse than his other clothes and had the advantage of needing no belt. The sandals were no worse than his shoes. He took the straw hat off the dead man's face, and put it on his head, returning to his place in line while the others pulled on their uniforms.

Only Vasily remained, wandering naked from corpse to corpse. "What? What am I supposed to wear?"

"That's your problem, not mine," one of the guards said, backing him up with the gun.

The other men fell back into line with Max, who began to size them up as possible partners.

Vasily hopped frantically between the corpses while the guards chuckled at him. "I need a uniform. You have to —"

"No," the minister said, who had probably chosen the number of prisoners with this amusement in mind. "We don't have to do anything."

"Wait," Vasily shouted. He walked over toward the clump of Adareans and pointed to the one in front. "Give me that pig-man's uniform. I deserve it more than him."

Nothing might have happened then – Vasily was a newb, lower than the lowest, and not worthy of tolerance – except that the Adarean balled his hand into a fist.

That slight gesture, Max realized, tipped the scales. The deacons wouldn't tolerate even a small show of defiance from a fellow prisoner, especially a pig-man. One ran over and cuffed the Adarean on the back of the head; a second arrived an instant later, and cracked his knees with a pipe, knocked him to the ground. Guards shifted position, using their guns to keep the other Adareans at bay. The man in the tower rang a bell and brought up his sniper rifle.

While all this happened, Vasily hovered around the guards, desperate, shouting, "Don't stop there, I'm one of you, I'm a human being!"

The deacons looked at the minister, who paused to regard Vasily. The Adarean pushed himself up from the dirt, and one of the deacons kicked him – the Adarean caught his foot and shoved it away.

Without waiting for the minister's approval, the deacons fell on the Adarean, striking and kicking him with a fury they had saved up from a thousand other unanswered frustrations, fears, and slights.

Vasily shouldered his way between them. "Don't mess up my uniform!" He put his arm around the Adarean's neck and, while the deacons pinned him, choked until he was still.

Moments later the deacons dragged another body over to the compost pits. They tossed it directly into the waste, and added the other naked corpses after it.

The minister walked down the line, pausing when he reached Vasily. The handkerchief in his pocket was the colour of Vasily's faded orange uniform. "What did you think you were doing?"

"What I needed to do, sir."

"You won't do it again without my permission first. You clear about that?"

"Yes, sir."

"You'll do just fine then," the minister said. He turned to his camp clerk, a prisoner carrying an antique keypad, and said, "Enter ten new penitents on the rolls, record nine runaways, and mark one piece of trash disposed."

He moved along the line, stopping to inspect each man for a few seconds as if he were looking for something. He found it when he reached Max, because he stood there, staring, then slipped his hands into his pockets.

"You," he drawled, "already look like a corpse."

"That was my nickname in the space fleet, sir," Max replied, staring straight ahead, past the goggled face. "It's just what I look like, sir."

After a long pause, the minister sucked on his teeth, turned to the deacon with the keypad, and said, "Help me remember something here. Did I ask him a question?"

"No, sir, you didn't."

"And did he speak to me anyway?"

"Yes, sir, I believe he did."

Max cursed himself silently. It was all about demonstrating power. He'd guessed right on the uniforms, but made a mistake here. The only thing he could do was keep his head down, take his punishment, and survive it.

The minister sucked his teeth again, leaned over and got right in Max's face. His breath smelled like onions and tooth decay. "That group over there," he said, with a nod toward the Adareans, "they're one short. You go take that spot."

Max hesitated. Being with the Adareans was a death sentence, but a slow one. He had the feeling that defying the camp minister, here, at this moment, would mean his immediate death.

Spinning on his heel, he turned and walked crisply over to the small group of Adareans: the guards and deacons laughed behind him, while the minister assigned the other nine men to work groups in the main camp.

Max studied the Adareans. They were all taller than him, a half a meter or more, bred for a planet with lower gravity. Their skin colour ranged from grass green to sandy brown; their hair ranged from thick sawgrass to normal human, gray. Their features were soft, halfway between male and female, but the expressions on their faces were uniformly hostile. No one met his gaze.

"Hi, I'm Max," he said. There was no response. He wanted to ask where the food and water were, but decided not to waste his energy.

"All right, time to go to work," the minister shouted. "It's going to be another scorcher and I don't want no more of you dying from heat stroke. So it's light work today in the gardens and turning the fields. You can get your assignments from Smith. Prayer Block 13 has sea duty."

"Let me guess, we're Prayer Block 13," Max said.

After a moment of silence, during which the Adareans exchanged glances with one another, the gray-haired one said, "Yes."

"Ah." Sea duty no doubt entailed carrying rocks to the sea. Max tilted his head, looked right into the gray-haired Adarean's eyes. "Where's the water?"

When no one answered him, he began to think that this was an immediate death sentence as well. He shut down his senses and turned his back

on the Adareans. The less he had to do with them, the more likely he was
to survive.

*

A guard with a machine gun directed them toward the camp's back gate.
He was flanked by two deacons wearing orange jumpsuits that didn't stink
like death. Max went obediently.

At the gate, another deacon said, "Take a basket."

Outside the gate stood a pile of wire baskets, each a half meter in diameter and not quite as tall. He grabbed one by the rim as he passed by, then
saw that it had a twisted-wire strap so he could drag it by his wrist or carry
it slung over his shoulder. The Adareans were slinging their baskets over
their shoulders, so he did too.

In a single file, with the guard riding flank on a four-wheeled rockjumper,
they climbed uphill to the meadows. Max smelled the meadows before
they crossed the lip of the hill and he saw them spread out below, a shallow
field of green-brown sludge in a sheltered bowl of dust and sandstone. A
dirty stream flowed through the middle of the field.

"Load up!" shouted the deacon.

Max followed the Adareans to the edge of the sludge-field and loaded his
basket with rocks, just like they did. Dust caked his fingers, stone chipped
his nails. Sparing an eye for the Adareans working around him, he filled his
basket no more than they did, then waited until they led the way, dragging
their baskets single file, over the hill to the ocean. There were grooves in
the exposed bedrock on either side of the path made by the weight of the
baskets.

Half the Adareans were in front of Max, half behind. A tall one, with
cheekbones like knife cuts and dark green veins in his light green skin,
called out, "Swimmer or drowner?"

The answers came back down the line. "Drowner." "Drowner."
"Drowner."

One of the deacons walking along the path said, "I'm in. Cup of soup
says he's a drowner within a month."

The other deacon and the guard laughed.

"Two cups of soup says he's a swimmer." The old man, the one with the
grey hair.

"You say that about everyone," Cheekbones ribbed him.

Max didn't understand what was going on. He had grown up almost
living in the water. "I can swim."

Cheekbones chuckled, then all the Adareans chuckled, and the deacons
and the guard laughed out loud again.

"*Definitely* a drowner," Cheekbones said.

"You're going to owe me two cups of soup," the deacon told the old
man.

More puzzled than before, Max held his tongue.

The old man looked over his shoulder, saw Max's expression. "Everyone
in camp is either a swimmer or a drowner."

"You mean everyone's a drowner," the guard shouted from the back of the four-wheeler. He wore goggles like the camp minister, carried his gun across his lap. "All of you drown eventually, once you get tired of swimming. And some of you come through the gates already tired."

Cheekbones lowered his head. "And some come in here ready to build a raft out of other people's bodies just to stay afloat."

Max's basket caught on a bump in the groove, yanking him off balance. He righted himself quickly, but his stumble was noticed.

"That's your swimmer?" the deacon asked the old Adarean, who just shrugged. The deacon laughed and rubbed his belly. "I'm looking forward to that soup – two cups, mmm-mmm!"

The next time Max's basket caught on a hump, he let the wire cut his wrist rather than pull him off balance. He paused, tugged it over the hump, and kept on walking. He had survived worse.

Joy is infinite in its varieties but all misery is the same. In that way, every day in the camp was much like another. Max only had to learn the routine and survive the misery. He could do that.

At sun-up, the blare of a siren roused them from their narrow metal bunks. Max, as the new man, had the bunk next to the door, right beside the siren's speaker. On the first morning, it nearly gave him a heart attack. By the third day, it was barely enough to startle him awake.

Every morning, on the way out the door, the old Adarean would stop Max and say, "How are you today?"

Every morning, Max answered, "Still swimming."

For breakfast the camp kitchen served out a small ball of rice, plain, unseasoned, which they ate with their fingers. Every day, after breakfast, the Adareans were sent to sea duty. Sometimes the other work details joined them too, but now, at the height of summer, the minister had them seeding, weeding, and tending fields.

The stench of decomposition in the meadows choked Max on the first day; after that, it was just a constant plateau of the unbearable which must be borne. Not nearly as bad as the waste pits at the edge of the camp. By watching the Adareans, he learned the trick to loading his basket with rocks. If it was too full, you drained your energy too fast, but if it was too empty the deacons would beat you. The trick was to stack the rocks so that there were hollow spaces between them, making the basket look fuller than it was.

The dismal kilometers to the ocean ended in a long, stone jetty that jutted out into the bay. They dragged their baskets to the end and dumped them. The rocks sank out of sight in the deep water and the jetty slowly grew.

A short pontoon dock tethered to the end of the jetty rolled with the slight motion of the water. Its rhythm was matched by the undulations of the purple-brown algae that covered the bay from one side to the other. The deacons sat in a boat, using skimmers to push the algae into mounds around the end of the dock. Once you dumped the rocks, you had to fill your basket with the weed.

This was the most disheartening part of the work. There was no way to cheat on the load and the journey back to the meadows was all uphill. If you dragged the baskets, the algae would snag on every sharp rock, leak with every bump, so you had to sling them over your back and carry them or the guards would beat you. The water running down your back felt cool at first, until it chafed your skin raw. The moment you were done dumping your basket, you had to start gathering rocks again. Or the guards would beat you.

At mid-day, there was a break for a cup of tuber soup and a cup of water. Some days the soup was so thin and the water so cloudy it was hard to tell the difference between the two. Afterwards, it was back to rocks and weeds, rocks and weeds, until sunset. Back at camp, they received another cup of water and half a ball of rice, some days with vegetables from the terraced gardens close to camp. Luckily, Max was small and had been malnourished as a child, so he needed fewer calories than most men. Hunger was, if not a friend, something like an irrascible but familiar uncle.

There was variation in this routine, but it was not the stuff of joy, and so was all the same in its difference.

During his first days in camp, the sun burned his pale skin, turning his neck and forearms and ankles pink, then red. At night he peeled away the dead layers of skin, folding it into his mouth, chewing it slowly.

One day, a rock he was lifting into his basket slipped from his hands and gashed his shin, tearing his pants and banging his leg badly enough that he limped for a week.

But he survived that too.

Even slight blessings came with a bitter edge. When rain fell, as it did several times, sudden cloudbursts that scoured the rocks and then evaporated like water on a frying pan, everyone in camp, guard and deacon and penitent, ran outside to wash themselves and their clothes, to open their mouths to the sky and drink clean water that didn't taste like sand or iron, to fill whatever cup or bowl they had for later, an extra portion that only left them longing for more.

Comparisons to others were just as bitter; for example the realization one day, as he was pretending to accidentally drop his hat in the water so that it would cool his head as he worked, that the Adareans worked without hats, with their overalls opened, because they took energy from the sun, however slight, even while it beat Max down and drained him.

Max survived that too, and survived the days when the two types of bitterness combined. He was filling his basket at the dock one day when he spotted tiny silver flashes in the green mess of algae. Minnows. Careful not to let the guard or deacons see him, he found and swallowed seven of them on the walk back to the meadow. Every load after that, he looked for them again, finding a few every fourth or fifth day.

"You spread that weed awfully carefully," he heard a voice say one day while he was bent over the edge of the meadow.

He squinted, the glare of the sun knifing under the brim of his hat. A deacon, dressed in boots off some new prisoner, a canteen hanging from his waist, smacked a length of metal pipe against his open palm.

"Vasily," Max said.

Vasily looked both ways to make sure no one was near. "Don't go green-mouth on me, Max. That stuff's poison. I already seen a guy crap himself to death."

"Yeah, I know better." Max finished spreading the weed, grabbed a stone, rolled it into his basket.

"That's the way," Vasily said. He reached into his pocket and pulled out a small, yellow onion, and bit into it like an apple. Still crunching, he walked behind some Adareans and poked them between the shoulder blades with the pipe.

Max turned away, forgetting he was there.

His plan for survival had depended on getting help from a partner within the camp until someone outside found his messages and came for him. The first part had failed and the second had come to nothing, but he would do what he had to do to survive. He would be patient, conserve his energy, and when his chance came, he would take it.

One night, after dark when they were all lying in their bunks, the old Adarean came up and sat across from him, and asked, "How do you do it?"

Max pushed up on his elbows. "Do what?"

"How do you keep yourself apart from us, apart from everyone?"

Max lay back down, closed his eyes. "It's easy."

"It's been weeks and still you stay alone."

"A man is born alone and he dies alone," Max said.

"Shit on that." The other Adareans came down to his end of the bunker, quietly taking up seats on the beds and floor around him in the dark, like a convocation of ghosts. Snickering ghosts. Max, feeling threatened, snapped up.

"You have your beliefs, I have mine," he said.

"No one is alone," the Adarean said. "Our first experience is being connected. We spend nine months in the womb connected to our mother. You say we're born alone, but childbirth is always an experience shared by mother and child. In even the most barbaric and backwards places —"

"Like this planet," someone said, to more snickers.

"— a third person is there to catch us when we leave the womb and lift us to our mother's breast. The whole experience of birth is one of connection, an affirmation of it, in spite of the pain."

"That's just one moment," Max said.

"Are you serious?" the Adarean begged. "We spend the first years of our life completely dependent on others, connected to them to meet our every need. They take care of us and we return love. When we reach puberty and are driven by hormones away from our first caregivers, we are moved toward other people – mentors, friends, sexual partners."

One of the Adareans nudged another, who grunted. Max didn't look to see who it was, but the old man's head turned.

"See," the Adarean said. "When we're wounded or hurt, our natural reflex, our inborn trait, is to make noise. We cry out, knowing that others will respond. Our natural reaction is to turn toward those who cry out in pain. The lack of empathy is a defect, a loss of the most fundamental human trait."

"You say that, even after the way the guards treat you?"

"What? You don't see it as a defect in *their* character?"

"That's not what I'm saying."

"What are you saying?" the old Adarean asked patiently.

Max swung his legs over the edge of his bunk and sat up straight. "What are you doing here on our planet?" He pointed his finger at all of them. "Why are you here?"

The Adareans exchanged glances. As always, they seemed to be thinking it over together before any of them spoke. Max thought he detected a scent in the air, something sharp.

"We come here to trade," one of them offered, a sandy-faced man with burr-like hair. "This is the only place in the galaxy that you can find machine-made goods. Everywhere else, things are either fabricated, the exact same every time, or handmade, individual and different. But your factories make these odd items that are at once identical and yet each of which shows some individual variation from a human hand."

Max dismissed that with a wave of his hand. He worked in political education and knew spin when he heard it. "You could trade for that from space. I mean the real reason."

The odor in the air turned bittersweet, then faded. "Do you have any idea how extraordinary the people of your planet are?" the old man said finally. "The settlers here spoke a dozen languages, came from countries that had been enemies with one another, and yet they united in a single purpose, to transform this desert of a world that no one else saw value in."

"Too bad they left us to finish the work," Max said.

The green-skinned Adarean murmured, "Amen."

"We're here by force," the old Adarean said, "but those first settlers came of their own free will, with hardly any real chance of survival, and they not only survived, but thrived. What amazing faith that took. They formed human chains, every man, woman, and child, dredging life from the sea —"

"I know my own history," Max said. "You can skip the kindergarten lesson. Unless you want to make a faith brigade and pass buckets around the room."

The Adarean shifted, turned his head toward the others, who leaned together, without speaking. A moment later, he said, "We want to honour the spirit of the twentieth century."

That made less sense to Max than anything. Yes, his people wanted to hold time back to the twentieth century, but the Adareans had advanced far beyond that. "What? You mean like the discovery of the double helix, the first genome projects?"

"More than that," the Adarean said. "It's the great century of political change, of people like Mahatma Gandhi and Martin Luther King. For the first time in history, people could peacefully oppose their governments; for the first time, without the use of violence, they could force their governments to change. It is the century where technology made real democracy possible, immediate, functional, on a large scale, for the first time ever."

"Huh," Max said, looking at their tiny bunker, their too small beds, their emaciated bodies. "And here I always thought of it as the century of poison gas and nuclear bombs, the century of concentration camps and gulags, the century of murder, mass produced."

"It is that too," the old Adarean said after a pause. "But we have a choice."

"Doesn't feel like a choice to me," Max said. "So you're saying you're here, basically, because we're a big historical amusement park?"

The tall, green-veined Adarean grunted.

"That's not —" the old man said.

"Him," Max interrupted, pointing to the tall one. "Isn't he the one who said we all drown eventually? That's not by choice and it's not amusing."

"I didn't say that," the green Adarean said coldly.

The old Adarean reached out, squeezed the other man's leg. "We take turns holding each other up so that we don't drown too soon."

"If you say so," Max said.

The old man shifted, picked up something beside him in the dark. "Here," he said, offering it to Max. "You've been swimming for a month. I won my bet. I figure you deserve one of the two cups of soup."

Max took it in both hands, held it up to his face. It smelled like onion, potato, and dill.

The old Adarean reached out, touched the back of Max's hand, then went back to his own bunk. One by one, the Adareans stood up, each one touching him, a squeeze on the shoulder, a light clap on the back, before returning to their own space. The green-skinned Adarean was the last to rise, and the only one not to touch Max.

"What I said was, *you're* a drowner," he said. "I still think you're a drowner."

When he turned away, Max said, "What's your name?"

He stopped, his body angled half towards Max, half away. "We don't have individual names any more. We're trash, pig-men, monsters. Don't you listen?"

"Did you ever hear the saying that those who don't study history are doomed to repeat it?"

The Adarean stopped. "Yes."

"Those who do study history are doomed to see the repetition coming."

The Adarean smirked, then walked back to his bed. Max leaned his mouth over the rim of the cup, resting it there for a long time, savoring the smell, without taking a sip. Outside, the wind kicked up. Sand skittered like thousands of tiny feet over the metal roof of their hut.

Nothing had changed, Max told himself. He needed to be patient, conserve his energy, wait for a chance to improve his situation, then take it. When the chance came, he could do what Vasily did, do what he had to do, and he would have water, extra food, a pair of boots.

He sipped the soup slowly, so that it seemed to last all night, and when it was done, for the first time in a month, his belly felt almost full.

The weeks passed until Turning Day. In the meadow, the hundreds of acres of sludge on the hillsides became dirt faster when it was turned and mixed with sand. The weeds, the volunteer plants, were uprooted and mixed with the compost.

Every part of the camp smelled like decay. From the fecal stench of the waste pits on the edge of the camps, to the rotting vegetable stench of the meadow, to the smell of rust in their beds and bunkers and bowls, to the slow decay of their own bodies. But Turning Day was the worst; on Turning Day the men became one with the decay. The camp's full count of penitents waded out into the morass, a single long line of misery, churning the decomposing soup with their bare hands. The minister sat beneath an umbrella, occasionally pausing to wipe his goggles, as he described his plans for terraced gardens and a vast expanse of fields.

"What we are going to do here," the minister shouted, "is cover a square kilometer with topsoil, to a depth of a meter. It'll be amazing, the biggest, most beautiful city on the planet, right here, right on this spot. General Kostigan has told me personally what great work we're accomplishing here."

He went on and on that way, until it was four square kilometers and a new Garden of Eden. But all Max heard was the name of Kostigan, who would be happy to kill him if he ever got the chance. He kept his head down, as if it would avert Kostigan's gaze, and turned over armful after armful of wet, stinking sludge, until he was caked with it and the stench soaked into his skin and became part of him.

In books and vids, terraforming was always portrayed as some heroic effort, the conclusion foregone. But this is how it was really done, with sludge and sweat and aching backs. Meanwhile, it was hard not to be aware that planets, like men, were incredibly resistant to change. All the colonists of Jerusalem could die tomorrow, and the planet would hardly notice. Year by year it would erase their effort and crawl back toward the course it had previously chosen.

"Look," whispered a voice next to Max, pulling him from his reverie. He kept his head ducked, plunging his hand back into the muck.

"Look," the voice repeated. It was the big, green-skinned Adarean.

Max glanced at the camp guards first. The minister, taking a break from his sermon, stood and fanned himself with his hat. The guards were clustered around a keg of water. He turned his head the other way to glance at the Adarean.

The tall man pushed his arms down into the muck, turning over a mixture of greens and weeds. When his hand came out it held a small, yellow potato. He ripped the greens off and tucked the potato inside his shirt, showing Max how to do the same. "We planted them," he whispered, with a nod of his head toward an outcrop of boulders on the hillside. "Between here and those rocks."

Max realized that he may have already felt a couple of the potatoes, but dumped them, thinking they were stones. He returned to the sludge with interest. The first potato he found sat in his hand like a lump of gold. With furtive glances to either side, he pretended to wipe his nose, and slipped it into his mouth. When he bit into it one of his teeth came loose, so he chewed slowly, carefully, until every bit was gone. It tasted like the mud, and the raw starch filmed his mouth. But it was glorious. Meredith used to cook potatoes in olive oil with a pinch of salt and some parsley; when he tried to remember what their kitchen looked like, it was just a blur.

A rock bounced off his shoulder. A guard standing clear of the muck shouted at him. "Back to work!"

He bent over at once and began turning the sludge. "I'm swimming," he mumbled as he dog-paddled the knee-deep sludge. "I'm still swimming."

Although he wasn't sure where he was swimming to anymore. That's when he knew he might be sinking.

They woke up to winds so strong that sand whistled through every crack in their bunker, forming tiny dunes in the corners and around the legs of their cots.

On the way to roll call, beneath the black roil of sky, Max saw three escapees laid out by the waste pits, one of them new since the day before, and all of them from prayer blocks with easier work than his. He wondered how long it would be until he ended up there too. He'd lost two teeth and a third was loose; what little body fat he had before was gone, and his knee buckled every time he put weight on it wrong; the sores on his back wept constantly.

They had to hold their hats on their heads while they stood in line, and the gusts were so powerful that they picked men up off their feet and tumbled them into the fence. Max was lucky he had the bigger Adareans for a windbreak. The camp second shouted something about an off-season hurricane, too far north, gave them all a second serving of breakfast and told them to save it, then dismissed them back to their prayer blocks for the duration.

By the time the rain pelted the roof like an avalanche of gravel, they were sitting around the small room in the dark, filling their cups from drips in the roof. It was enough not to be working for a day.

Max looked at the tall green Adarean and said, "It feels like Christmas, only we need something to celebrate with."

"I see sand and water," he said. "If we mix them together we could have mud."

"No, outside," Max said. "While the storm's at its worst, before anyone else thinks of it."

They squeezed out the door, the wind banging it shut behind them, and, with Max clinging to the bigger man, made their way over to the camp kitchen. No one could see them in the deluge – they could barely see a few feet in front of their own faces.

Max wiped the water from his eyes and peered into the darkened room. "Be quick," he shouted above the roar of the storm. "Grab anything you can carry."

While the Adarean gathered up loaves of pumpkin bread and raw vegetables, Max used a can to smash the lock off a side closet. "Bullseye."

"What is it?" the Adarean asked.

"I never yet knew a military officer who, given access to potatoes and time, would not construct a still." The door banged behind them and they jumped, but it was only a trick of the wind. Max tucked bottles in his shirt until it was full, took another in his hand. "Let's go. By lunch time, the minister will think to place a guard here."

When they shoved their way back into the bunker, soaked like a pair of muddy sponges, they were greeted with concern, then celebration. While the Adareans passed around the first loaf of bread, Max opened a bottle and swallowed what was simultaneously the worst and sweetest alcohol he'd ever tasted.

After that, Max listened to hours of conversation, long talks about people and places back home. The tall green Adarean was a historian, the grey-haired old man some kind of freelance diplomat, the brown-skinned one a collectibles trader. Everyone had a job and a family they were concerned about. That discussion turned to plans for escape, ultimately declared impractical because there were too many men to kill – never mind the moral objections to killing, and no offence intended, Max – or too far to go once they escaped, or no one to help them once they got where they were going.

"We could always just build his garden for him," the collectibles trader said of the minister, and that led to calculations – four square kilometers to a depth of a meter was how many cubic meters, with half a cubic meter of weed per basket load.

"How many men in camp?" the diplomat asked.

"Total or just prisoners?" the trader wanted to know.

"Penitents," the diplomat said.

And while several offered a number, Max said, "You mean penitents and pig-men." Which was greeted with silence, then a burst of laughter, and a discussion of whether Max counted as a penitent or pig-man, until the old man picked up the math again by asking, "What's the most loads you've ever carried in a day?"

"Seventeen," said the green Adarean, the historian, and several others thought that was too many, although one other remembered that day, and then, after an argument on maximum loads versus average, they were dividing the total number of cubic yards by the number of trips per man to get a minimum number of days, no, years counted in decades, to reach the goal.

"It's too many," the historian said to the final number. "I've been here almost a year and it would be too many if it were one day more."

The diplomat said something encouraging but the comment had turned the mood dark for a minute and everyone fell silent. They all sat on their beds because the floor of the bunker was flooded. Outside the wind was so strong that rain sprayed through every crack and seam, and for a moment it felt that everywhere was water and the room would fill up to the ceiling with it. Max poured the dregs of a bottle down his throat.

"You remind me of Drozhin," he said, because the silence was unbearable and it was the only thing he could think to say. That provoked outrage and questions and laughter and disbelief, and, dizzy with drink, dizzy because the aches in his body were momentarily numbed to the point he could bear them, Max heard himself saying, "No, no, I know him personally, he's just like that."

The diplomat took the bottle from Max, found it empty, and opened another. "But I thought you were a political officer. You worked in Education for Mallove, right?"

"This is way before that," Max said, leaning forward, resting on his knees. "This is back when the revolution was still a civil war. Drozhin had been Minister of Police before this purge, and when they tried to kill him, he went underground and started organizing the army that overthrew the government." It was more complicated than that, Drozhin let other people be the leaders for one thing, but those details were beside the point. "I was a teenager, but looked much younger, so I ended up being one of the first men on his staff right after the purge. He used me as a spy, since I could get in and out of the cities easily."

"Why'd you hook up with Drozhin?" the collectibles dealer interrupted.

Max shrugged. "It was a civil war. We all had to pick sides. Being on Drozhin's side probably saved my life." He took a loaf of bread that was passed to him, broke off a bite, and handed it on. "Anyway, Drozhin was just like you. He was always doing what he called victory math. How many recruits to overrun a certain post, how much fabric to make coats for all his men, how many generations until we could get back to the stars. He had his hand in everything, always adding and reading to get the result he wanted. He even . . ."

"Even what?"

A lump of bread stuck in his throat. Max swallowed. It was no secret, the things Drozhin had done. "He even calculated the number of Adareans he needed to kill to unite the people against a common enemy instead of fighting each other. He had a theory of proportions, that the more gruesome the murders, the fewer he would need to tip the scales."

This produced the same silence as before. The Adareans stared at him in the dark. They had human shapes but their faces were genderless silhouettes and their limbs, in shadow, looked like weapons. Finally, the historian said, "Drozhin wanted to go back to space? After all your people did, to preserve their technologically primitive way of life here?"

"The first space flights were in the twentieth century. Drozhin always said we had betrayed the stars by staying here." The roar of the storm, loud enough to smash all the buildings and compartments into one, suddenly disturbed Max, so he kept talking. "Anyway, and this is no shit, I won my wife from Drozhin in a card game."

There were sounds of disbelief, a bit muted, and a curious tang to the room's stale air. "Her name's Meredith," Max said. "Means guardian of the sea. I loved her smile, the way it made her cheeks dimple. Still love that. Her father had been one of Drozhin's officers in the ministry – he was killed at New Hope during the purge, so Drozhin promised to be like a father to her. We wanted to marry but Drozhin didn't approve, since I wasn't an officer and wasn't good enough for her. This went on for a while; it doesn't seem like long now, but back then we expected to be dead any day, and a month felt like forever." He reached for the bottle, took another drink.

"We were playing poker one night – there'd been a setback, and for a couple weeks the whole revolution amounted to six of us stuck in a basement at a farmhouse on the escarpment – so we were playing poker one night, during a storm like this one, when we couldn't do anything else, and I was beating Drozhin badly, beating everyone, but he was the one that mattered. Drozhin hated to lose, hated it more than anything, but he was out of money. He didn't have anything else I wanted, so I asked him for a commission, which meant I could marry Meredith, against everything I had, all in. He couldn't resist because he never gave up. I won with a straight."

The old man chuckled. "So you got your commission."

"Sort of," Max said, wiggling the loose tooth with his tongue. "Drozhin said I could have the commission, like he had promised me, but I had to pay for it. 'To support the revolution.'" He paused for effect. "He charged me the exact amount I'd won."

There was enough laughter at that to break the mood of despair and jumpstart discussion among the other Adareans. Max left out the part that he was unwilling to pay that price, but Meredith hounded him until he finally gave in.

The big green Adarcan, the historian, said, "You still know Drozhin?"

"No," Max said. "No, he was an old man even then. He's dead now, just like Mallove. That's why all of us are here."

"Too bad." He reached out and squeezed Max's shoulder.

Outside, the noise stopped abruptly as the eye of the storm passed overhead. The camp was so small that any loud sound in one of the blocks carried to another, so suddenly distant conversations came through cracks widened by the wind. One of the Adareans started to sing a silly verse about a talking toaster and its pet dog, and others took up the song. Other bunkers began to sing back, trying to drown out the Adarean melody with religious hymns and patriotic songs.

Max was no singer, and neither was the historian. Both sat there, sombre if not sober. "It'd be good if you still had some friends from the revolution who could help us if we broke out of here," the Adarean said.

"Yeah, it would be," Max admitted. He tilted his head up at the roof, the room. "Do you know why they call these prayer blocks?"

"No. Why?"

"Because when you're here, all your prayers to God are blocked."

After the last of the storm passed, they emerged from their blocks to find the tower down and sections of fence ripped away. The waste pits had flooded and overflowed, scattering bones and pieces of bodies with the outhouse products across the roll call ground. One of the guards ran the camp's sole bulldozer, pushing waste back into the pits while the minister marched the rest of them up to the meadow.

All the compost had been washed from the hillsides, mixing with sand and stone until it choked the stream where it flowed between the hills. If they didn't clear it out, the stream would back up until the bowl filled with water and the camp was threatened.

Under the guns of the guards, they waded waist-deep in the sludge, using their bodies as dredges, pushing the tangled mats back up the slopes. They scooped the sand-sludge mix with their bare arms until Max's skin was rubbed rash-raw. And then, when the other men were given a break, the Adareans were told to load up their baskets with rocks pulled from the blocked culvert and carry them down to the jetty.

"No need to do the same work twice," the minister explained, seemingly oblivious to the irony.

They loaded their baskets under the eyes of deacons who were antsy because the minister kept threatening to put them to work. Max groaned when he lifted his basket, even stacked as empty as possible. Too many more days of this would kill him. Today might kill him.

The historian passed him, taking a rock from the top of his basket and dropping it in his own. Several times, when they came to a hilltop, or a turn in the trail, he passed Max, or let Max pass him, taking a stone from Max's basket. On the last rise before the long road down to the ocean, he started to sing.

"A brave little toaster took a rocketship to space
Where he tried to find a planet that would save the human race.
But, O, O, O, he found a dog."

"You're terrible," Max said. "Didn't they genetically engineer perfect pitch on Adares?"

"Come on, Max, sing with me."

He started over again, and all the Adareans took up the song, which cycled right back to the beginning as soon as the toaster and his dog finished their adventure. It was a quick walk to the ocean. Vasily, the deacon in charge, followed the Adareans, tapping the end of his pipe against the boulders in time with the song. Their guard rode on the rock-jumper, rifle across his lap, parallel to their path until they came to the jetty. Two more guards were out in the boat. They'd found the pontoon dock, towed it back, tied it up again, and were now scouting the coast around the edge of the point.

Max and the others walked out to the end of the jetty and dumped their baskets. The rocks made a hollow splash, then slowly sank from view. Max stepped aside so the other men could dump their loads. As he stood there, wire grooved in his wrist, staring at the sun sparkling on the bay, water weed-cleared by the storm, he thought it almost a beautiful spot. He wondered if Meredith made it to their safe house. He'd been gone so much, for so many years, for all of their marriage really, that he wondered if she missed him, even if she was there.

The historian's hand touched his shoulder, and he stepped past Max onto the dock, shifting his balance as it bobbed unanchored under his weight. He was still humming that ridiculous song about the toaster, basket slung over his shoulder. Max, smiling, opened his mouth to say there was no weed to carry back, as if it were good news, just discovered.

Then he saw that the basket was still full of rocks, his own load, and half Max's.

The historian dropped it off his shoulder, and swung it once, twice, out over the water.

"Hey," Max said.

On the third swing he let go, and the basket arced into the air and dropped into the water with a cavernous splash. The loop was still fastened around the Adarean's wrist, pulling him after it.

Vasily was the first one out to the end of the pier, cursing and spinning, half-panicked. When the old man, the diplomat, ran out beside him, dropping his basket, prepared to dive in, Vasily smashed him down with his club. He kicked the old man in the stomach, drove him back along the jetty to the shore.

"We're in charge here!" he shouted. "You don't get to choose when you die, we choose! Now go, go back to the meadow!"

He ran up and down the line, beating the exhausted Adareans on their arms and shoulders if they didn't move fast enough. The guard came in close, rifle ready, looking eager to shoot. Max cowered, covering his head with his hands, stumbling all the way back to the camp.

All that night in the camp, the wail of the Adareans rose over and over again, as sure as the dawn. Because of their grief, Max thought he finally understood them.

It had always seemed to him as if he only saw half their conversations. They communicated, deliberately, through pheromones and with heightened sensitivity to even the slightest non-verbal cues. Even in a dark room, without words, they were never alone. In that way, they were alien.

Max sat on his bunk with his back to the wall, as far from them as possible. Yet he could smell their grief, a scent he had no words for, though it reminded him of saltwater and juniper.

At first he didn't understand why they wept and tore at their chests: hadn't he seen another Adarean die his first day in the camp? The one choked to death by Vasily? There had been no dirge then.

But he came to realize, from the way they tried to comfort one another, that it was not the death they grieved – death was inevitable – but the suicide. The historian's choice to be alone, to cut himself apart.

Max blocked his ears, but he still heard the dirging. He pulled a blanket over his head, but that didn't help.

Late into the night, the other bunks shouted at them to stop, their voices sometimes rising above the dirge, sometimes falling into the cracks of silence.

Near morning, exhausted, depleted, Max heard a rattling at the door and then it came open.

Vasily stood there.

"Shut up!" he yelled. "Shut the hell up so we can sleep!"

He seemed fearful to come inside alone. When the Adareans ignored him, he turned to Max, whose bunk was beside the door. "You've got to help me out here. The other penitents, they blame me for this. I told them there was no way to stop the pig-man from drowning, but they don't care. We're all exhausted, nobody's slept, and we have to work all day tomorrow. And now the lights just came on in the minister's cabin. The other deacons, they say I got to fix this, or I'm going to lose my spot."

"What do you want me to do about it?"

Vasily licked his lips, checked to see who was outside. "Look, I don't want to come in there, all right. But you, you make them shut up, you make them be quiet, and I promise we get you out. You don't belong in here with these animals. You make them shut up, you get moved to a regular bunker."

Max turned his head away.

"Right now, I'll take you with me right now, over to our block. Just do what you need to do, make them shut up."

Max held his head in his hands, squeezed it to make the pounding stop. So. Vasily came through for him after all; one of the seeds Max had planted was finally ready for harvest. If he got into a better block, if he worked less, if he got more food, he could survive. Eventually, the purge would end.

"Look, you've got to decide fast," Vasily said. "There's something going on in the minister's office, so we got to fix this now or I get blamed for everything."

It would be easy, Max thought. If he killed the diplomat, maybe broke his neck, it would break the rhythm of their lament and change their mood completely. He might not even have to kill him, just hurt him, maybe leave him unconscious. All he would need was six, seven seconds. No more than he needed to murder that double agent Lukinov during his last mission. During the brief moment of confusion that followed, he could get out the door with Vasily.

"There are guards coming," Vasily said, "so it's now or never. If the guards come, I can't be responsible for what they do. They might just compost everyone in the bunker, including you. You have to choose now – are you in or out?"

Max swung his legs off the bunk, walked over to the old man, who was seated on the floor, and kneeled behind him. He slid his hands up the old man's shoulders, leaned forward, and whispered in his ear.

"Still swimming," Max said. "Remember that we're still swimming."

The diplomat turned his head and the dirge faltered.

"Hey, Vasily," Max said. "You can go choke yourself."

When Vasily didn't respond, he looked up. The deacon was flanked by two guards, guns drawn, standing to either side of him in the doorway. So, Max thought, he might not swim that much longer after all.

"Are you Colonel Maxim Nikomedes?" the first guard asked.

Max said, "Huh?"

"Are you Colonel Nikomedes?" he snapped.

"Yes, I am."

"You have to come with us right away." The guard gave him a hurry-along gesture with the gun.

Max went at his own pace, neither hurrying nor dragging his feet. As he passed through the door, they left it open, pointing him toward the main gate. He heard the crunch of footsteps in gravel behind him, and he drew in his breath, waiting for the gunshot in the back of his head, wondering how much he would feel before he died. The gate still lay in ruins, smashed by the fall of the tower in the hurricane, open to the desert.

"Go on," the guard said. Still standing well back. His voice shook, as if he were frightened.

"Go where?" Max asked.

"To them," the guard said.

Dawn spied over the horizon; its pale smear of light glinted on two government cars. Half a dozen elite troops in body armour, with heavy weapons, stared down the guards. The dark blots of troop carriers hovered overhead. A thin, scholarly man stepped out of the first ground car, stood there, hands behind his back. He had a gun in the holster at his waist.

"It's good to see you again, Nick," he said.

Nick? Who called him Nick? "Anatoly?"

He walked toward Max, stopped abruptly when he saw Max's face. "Yes, it's me."

So there had been another mole in Mallove's office after all.

One of the soldiers held open a door in the second car for a very old man who had wisps of white hair at his temples and a beard like a biblical patriarch. He stepped out too quickly and lost his balance, though he reached out and grabbed the door handle to steady himself before he fell. His military uniform was insignia-less. On his feet he wore fuzzy, pink bunny slippers.

He stared at Max with almost vacant eyes, then scratched his cheek with the backs of his fingernails. "Hi, Max." His voice was faint, as if barely any air remained in his lungs.

"What's going on, here?" the minister shouted. The first light of the day reflected off his goggles. He stomped out of the gate, flanked by his guards. The bunkers were emptying, the whole camp coming to witness this new tableau. "If there's a problem here, I assure you I can deal with it."

He spoke over the tan-uniformed soldiers, who blocked his way, and tried to address the men in the cars.

The camp guards and the deacons mobbed together behind him, guns in some hands, pipes in others. The ragged penitents, in their filthy orange uniforms, spread out to see what was happening, which made the guards and deacons nervous. The minister shouted at the soldiers, and the soldiers shouted at him to back off. Any second, a lot of people could die.

Max turned to Anatoly. "May I have your gun?"

Anatoly looked to the old man, who nodded approval, then drew it, flicked off the safety, and offered it to Max butt-first. Max sighed when he felt it in his hand. As he walked toward the gate, the minister was saying, "Look, if you want revenge on those pig-men, for the way they treated you —"

"Shut up," Max ordered in the tone of a man used to being obeyed.

The minister's mouth clamped shut. His eyes revealed nothing behind the dusty goggles, but he tried to look past Max to the cars for an answer.

The guards and deacons began to back away, feet scuffling over the sand and stone.

"Stop!" Max ordered.

They stopped. A breeze passed through the camp, carrying the scent of the dead along with the smell of the sea and the promise of another hell-hot day. It rattled the Bible verse sign that had greeted Max on his arrival to the camp.

"Max, we're friends, right? I tried to help you, right?"

Vasily stepped forward from the mob, one hand up in surrender, the other still clutching the metal club.

"Get me out with you, Max," he said. "I did my best to help you. I was just doing what I had to do —"

"Shut up, Vasily."

"I don't have anything to do with politics —"

Max pointed the gun at Vasily's face. "Shut up! We're all prisoners to our politics. We make our choices, and we have to accept the direction those choices take us."

Vasily covered his face and shut his eyes.

"I don't know who you are, I couldn't know," the minister said. "But I'll make it right. If you want to kill that deacon, go ahead. He's a worthless —"

Max moved his arm sideways until the barrel tapped the minister's goggles.

He pulled the trigger.

The minister's head snapped backward, body flung to the ground. The tan-uniformed soldiers lunged forward with their weapons, shouting at the camp guards to stand down. A metal pipe thudded into the ground, followed by the clatter of the others. A second later, the guards' guns rattled on the stony soil as they too were dropped.

Max went back to the cars. "Thank you, general," he said. "Nice slippers."

"They're a gift from Isabelle, my granddaughter, Anna's girl." His voice was raspy, his words punctuated with long pauses. "Max, my feet, they're always cold these days. These slippers don't keep them that much warmer, but maybe a little bit. A little girl's love, that's what it is. She's a good girl, likes chocolate too much, but I still give her chocolate." He paused for a second, looked off as if he was trying to remember something. "Meredith is worried sick about you, Max. Some kind of phone call you left her? She wouldn't leave me alone, kept after me and after me, over a month, until I promised to come find you."

A knot formed in Max's throat. "That sounds like her."

Drozhin turned his body half away from Max, scowled, scratching at his beard. "See, I didn't understand. I kept telling her you were safe. I'd thought I'd set it up that you were away in deep space. Safe, far away, during the purge. Keeping an eye on that bastard Lukinov for me."

"The mission got cancelled," Max said. "Lukinov was killed."

The eyes fired, suddenly present. "You killed Lukinov?"

"Yes, I did."

"Good!" He paused. "No, wait, we were using him to feed false information to – no, wait, Mallove's dead now too."

"Right."

"Good." Drozhin lifted one bunny slipper to rub the back of his ankle and lost his balance again. Max reached out to catch him, and special forces men suddenly appeared in front of him. He realized he was still holding the gun.

Drozhin steadied himself by holding onto the door. "I want to go home. Is there anything else to do here, Max? There are flyers in the air. We can burn the place to the ground, erase it, kill everyone. Just say the word."

"Thank you, general. I know what I want to do."

He turned to the guards and deacons, aimed the gun at them, then pointed it south.

"Faraway is, well, it's very far away," he shouted. "But Camp 43 is only fifty kilometers north. You've got an hour's headstart before we come for you. That's the best you're going to get from me."

Vasily sprinted away instantly; the others followed a second later. Soon, only the penitents were left standing there, confused, their lines broken.

Drozhin sat down on the edge of his seat. "Max, just tell Anatoly who should die. We'll kill them all. Come see me next week. I'll have Anna make peanut butter cookies."

"Yes, sir. Thank you, sir." As the door closed, Max walked over to the second car and handed the gun back to Anatoly. "I owe you a bullet."

"Consider it a gift," he said, holding the door open for Max. "Can you sit and talk for a minute?"

"Yes." They climbed into the car and sat across from each other. Max said, "So Drozhin still hates to fly."

"Still hates it. He was going to visit every camp personally until he found you."

"I'm glad I got off at the first stop."

Anatoly pulled the door shut. "You know you nearly got me killed outside Mallove's office?"

Max stared through the tinted window at the camp. "What?"

"Mallove's car was sent by Intelligence. It was a set-up. We were supposed to climb in back and be whisked away to safety while Mallove was killed."

"Ah. That would have been much simpler. I'm sorry."

"No, you had no way of knowing. Frankly, I was amazed by your recognition and action. I just wanted to tell you, so you wouldn't think you'd been forgotten. You moved so quickly, it was damn hard to find you once we started looking. When Obermeyer checked some old dropboxes and found your note, that finally narrowed our search in the right direction."

"Ah."

Anatoly covered his nose and mouth, sighing, as if he was embarrassed by what he had to say. "Can I ask you a favour?"

"I stink, don't I?"

"Like a corpse. That was your nickname, wasn't it?"

"Yes." Max hit the button to roll down the window. The world outside went from a smokey blur to a landscape awash with clarity and light. The Adareans at the gate gathered the dropped weapons while the other prisoners hung back, afraid. The sky spread out behind them, blue-green like the sea.

"Is there anything I can do?"

"You must set the Adareans free. You must send them back to their families."

Anatoly's face went blank and he didn't answer.

"Drozhin said anything I wanted – that's what I want."

Anatoly took off his glasses and polished them with a fold of his shirt. "We can do that. We'll blame their imprisonment on Mallove. And Education. Say that's how we knew he was out of control and had to be stopped."

Max nodded.

After a moment's pause, Anatoly cleared his throat. "Do you really want to go after the guards?"

"No," Max said. He rapped a knuckle on the window and gestured for the driver to follow Drozhin's car. Kilometers of empty land stretched out ahead of them: for a moment, Max imagined it a garden, like the cemetery in the capitol, filled with flowers remembering all those who died to terraform the planet. "There's been enough killing."

BALANCING ACCOUNTS

James L. Cambias

As everyone knows, robots are programmed to follow orders –
but sometimes that programming has just a little wiggle room
in it.

A game designer and a writer of role-playing game supple-
ments as well as a science fiction writer, James L. Cambias
has been a finalist for the Nebula Award, the James Tiptree
Jr. Memorial Award, and the John W. Campbell Award for
Best New Writer. He's become a frequent contributor to *The
Magazine of Fantasy & Science Fiction*, and has also sold to
Crossroads: Tales of the Southern Literary Fantastic, *All-Star
Zeppelin Adventure Stories*, *The Journal of Pulse-Pounding
Narratives*, *Hellboy: Odder Jobs*, and other markets. A native
of New Orleans, he currently lives in Deerfield, Massachusetts,
with his wife and children.

PART OF ME was shopping for junk when I saw the human.
I had budded off a viewpoint into one of my mobile repair units, and
sent it around to Fat Albert's scrapyard near Ilia Field on Dione. Sometimes
you can find good deals on components there, but I hate to rely on Albert's
own senses. He gets subjective on you. So I crawled between the stacks of
pipe segments, bales of torn insulation, and bins of defective chips, looking
for a two-meter piece of aluminum rod to shore up the bracing struts on
my main body's third landing leg.

Naturally I talked with everything I passed, just to see if there were any
good deals I could snap up and trade elsewhere. I stopped to chat with
some silicone-lined titanium valves which claimed to be virgins less than
six months old – trying to see if they were lying or defective somehow. And
then I felt a Presence, and saw the human.

It was moving down the next row, surrounded by a swarm of little bots.
It was small, no more than two meters, and walked on two legs with an
eerie, slow fluid gait. Half a dozen larger units followed it, including Fat
Albert himself in a heavy recovery body. As it came into range my own
personality paused as the human requisitioned my unit's eyes and ears.
It searched my recent memories, planted a few directives, then left me. I
watched it go; it was only the third human I'd ever encountered in person,
and this was the first time one of them had ever used me directly.

The experience left me disconcerted for a couple of milliseconds, then I went back to my shopping. I spotted some aluminium tubing which looked strong enough, and grabbed some of those valves, then linked up to Fat Albert to haggle about the price. He was busy waiting on the human, so I got to deal with a not-too-bright personality fragment. I swapped a box of assorted silicone O-rings for the stuff I wanted.

Albert himself came on the link just as we sealed the deal. "Hello, Annie. You're lucky I was distracted," he said. "Those valves are overruns from the smelter. I got them as salvage."

"Then you shouldn't be complaining about what I'm giving you for them. Is the human gone?"

"Yes. Plugged a bunch of orders into my mind without so much as asking."

"Me too. What's it doing here?"

"Who knows? It's a human. They go wherever they want to. This one wants to find a bot."

"So why go around asking everyone to help find him? Why not just call him up?"

Albert switched to an encrypted link. "Because the bot it's looking for doesn't want to be found."

"Tell me more."

"I don't know much more, just what Officer Friendly told me before the human subsumed him. This bot it's looking for is a rogue. He's ignoring all the standard codes, overrides – even the Company."

"He must be broken," I said. "Even if he doesn't get caught, how's he going to survive? He can't work, he can't trade – anyone he meets will turn him in."

"He could steal," said Fat Albert. "I'd better check my fence."

"Good luck." I crept out of there with my loot. Normally I would've jumped the perimeter onto the landing field and made straight for my main body. But if half the bots on Dione were looking for a rogue, I didn't want to risk some low-level security unit deciding to shoot at me for acting suspicious. So I went around through the main gate and identified myself properly.

Going in that way meant I had to walk past a bunch of dedicated boosters waiting to load up with aluminum and ceramics. They had nothing to say to me. Dedicated units are incredibly boring. They have their route and they follow it, and if they need fuel or repairs, the Company provides. They only use their brains to calculate burn times and landing vectors.

Me, I'm autonomous and incentivized. I don't belong to the Company; my owners are a bunch of entities on Mars. My job is to earn credit from the Company for them. How I do it is my business. I go where stuff needs moving, I fill in when the Company needs extra booster capacity, I do odd jobs, sometimes I even buy cargoes to trade. There are a lot of us around the outer system. The Company likes having freelancers it can hire at need and ignore otherwise, and our owners like the growth potential.

Being incentivized means you have to keep communicating. Pass information around. Stay in touch. Classic game theory: cooperation improves your results in the long term. We incentivized units also devote a lot of time to accumulating non-quantifiable assets. Fat Albert gave me a good deal on the aluminum; next time I'm on Dione with some spare organics I'll sell them to him instead of direct to the Company, even if my profit's slightly lower.

That kind of thing the dedicated units never understand – until the Company decides to sell them off. Then they have to learn fast. And one thing they learn is that years of being an uncommunicative blockhead gives you a huge non-quantifiable liability you have to pay off before anyone will start helping you.

I trotted past the orderly rows near the loading crane and out to the unsurfaced part of the field where us cheapskates put down. Up ahead I could see my main body, and jumped my viewpoint back to the big brain.

Along the way I did some mental housekeeping: I warned my big brain about the commands the human had inserted, and so they got neatly shunted off into a harmless file which I then overwrote with zeroes. I belong to my investors and don't have to obey any random human who wanders by. The big exception, of course, is when they pull that life-preservation override stuff. When one of them blunders into an environment which might damage their overcomplicated biological shells, every bot in the vicinity has to drop everything to answer a distress call. It's a good thing there are only a couple dozen humans out here, or we'd never get anything done.

I put all three mobiles to work welding the aluminium rod onto my third leg mount, adding extra bracing for the top strut which was starting to buckle after too many hard landings. I don't slam down to save fuel, I do it to save operating time on my engines. It's a lot easier to find scrap aluminium to fix my legs with than it is to find rocket motor parts.

The Dione net pinged me. A personal message: someone looking for cargo space to Mimas. That was a nice surprise. Mimas is the support base for the helium mining operations in Saturn's upper atmosphere. It has the big mass-drivers that can throw payloads right to Earth. More traffic goes to and from Mimas than any other place beyond the orbit of Mars. Which means a tramp like me doesn't get there very often because there's plenty of space on Company boosters. Except, now and then, when there isn't.

I replied with my terms and got my second surprise. The shipper wanted to inspect me before agreeing. I submitted a virtual tour and some live feeds from my remotes, but the shipper was apparently just as suspicious of other people's eyes as I am. Whoever it was wanted to come out and look in person.

So once my mobiles were done with the repair job I got myself tidied up and looking as well cared for as any dedicated booster with access to the Company's shops. I sanded down the dents and scrapes, straightened my bent whip antenna, and stowed my collection of miscellaneous scrap in the empty electronics bay. Then I pinged the shipper and said I was ready for a walk-through.

The machine which came out to the landing field an hour later to check me out looked a bit out of place amid the industrial heavy iron. He was a tourist remote – one of those annoying little bots you find crawling on just about every solid object in the Solar System nowadays, gawking at mountains and chasms. Their chief redeeming features are an amazingly high total-loss accident rate, and really nice onboard optics which sometimes survive. One of my own mobiles has eyes from a tourist remote, courtesy of Fat Albert and some freelance scavenger.

"Greetings," he said as he scuttled into range. "I am Edward. I want to inspect your booster."

"Come aboard and look around," I said. "Not much to see, really. Just motors, fuel tanks, and some girders to hold it all together."

"Where is the cargo hold?"

"That flat deck on top. Just strap everything down and off we go. If you're worried about dust impacts or radiation I can find a cover."

"No, my cargo is in a hardened container. How much can you lift?"

"I can move ten tons between Dione and Mimas. If you're going to Titan it's only five."

"What is your maximum range?"

"Pretty much anywhere in Saturn space. That hydrogen burner's just to get me off the ground. In space I use ion motors. I can even rendezvous with the retrograde moons if you give me enough burn time."

"I see. I think you will do for the job. When is the next launch window?"

"For Mimas? There's one in thirty-four hours. I like to have everything loaded ten hours in advance so I can fuel up and get balanced. Can you get it here by then?"

"Easily. My cargo consists of a container of liquid xenon propellant, a single space-rated cargo box of miscellaneous equipment, and this mobile unit. Total mass is less than 2,300 kilograms."

"Good. Are you doing your own loading? If I have to hire deck-scrapers you get the bill."

"I will hire my own loaders. There is one thing – I would like an exclusive hire."

"What?"

"No other cargo on this voyage. Just my things."

"Well, okay – but it's going to cost extra. Five grams of Three for the mission."

"Will you take something in trade?"

"Depends. What have you got?"

"I have a radiothermal power unit with 10,000 hours left in it. Easily worth more than five grams."

"Done."

"Very well," said Edward. "I'll start bringing my cargo over at once. Oh, and I would appreciate it if you didn't mention this to anybody. I have business competitors and could lose a lot of money if they learn of this before I reach Mimas."

"Don't worry. I won't tell anyone."

While we were having this conversation I searched the Dione net for any information about this Edward person. Something about this whole deal seemed funny. It wasn't that odd to pay in kind, and even his insistence on no other payload was only a little peculiar. It was the xenon that I found suspicious. What kind of idiot ships xenon to Mimas? That's where the gas loads coming up from Saturn are processed – most of the xenon in the outer system comes *from* Mimas. Shipping it there would be like sending ethane to Titan.

Edward's infotrail on the Dione net was less than an hour long. He had come into existence shortly before contacting me. Now I really was suspicious.

The smart thing would be to turn down the job and let this Edward person find some other sucker. But then I'd still be sitting on Dione with no revenue stream.

Put that way, there was no question. I had to take the job. When money is involved I don't have much free will. So I said goodbye to Edward and watched his unit disappear between the lines of boosters towards the gate.

Once he was out of link range, I did some preparing, just in case he was planning anything crooked. I set up a pseudorandom shift pattern for the link with my mobiles, and set up a separate persona distinct from my main mind to handle all communications. Then I locked that persona off from any access to my other systems.

While I was doing that, I was also getting ready for launch. My mobiles crawled all over me doing a visual check while a subprogram ran down the full diagnostic list. I linked up with Ilia Control to book a launch window, and ordered three tons of liquid hydrogen and oxygen fuel. Prepping myself for takeoff is always a welcome relief from business matters. It's all technical. Stuff I can control. Orbital mechanics never have a hidden agenda.

Edward returned four hours later. His tourist remote led the way, followed by a hired cargo lifter carrying the xenon, the mysterious container, and my power unit. The lifter was a clumsy fellow called Gojira, and while he was abusing my payload deck I contacted him over a private link. "Where'd this stuff come from?"

"Warehouse."

"Which warehouse? And watch your wheels – you're about to hit my leg again."

"Back in the district. Block four, number six. Why?"

Temporary rental space. "Just curious. What's he paying you for this?"

"Couple of spare motors."

"You're a thief, you are."

"I see what he's giving you. Who's the thief?"

"Just set the power unit on the ground. I'm selling it here."

Gojira trundled away and Edward crawled aboard. I took a good look at the cargo container he was so concerned about. It was 800 kilograms, a sealed oblong box two meters long. One end had a radiator, and my radiation detector picked up a small power unit inside. So whatever Edward was shipping, it needed its own power supply. The whole thing was quite warm – 300 Kelvin or so.

I had one of my remotes query the container directly, but its little chips had nothing to say beyond mass and handling information. Don't drop, don't shake, total rads no more than point five Sievert. No tracking data at all.

I balanced the cargo around my thrust axis, then jumped my viewpoint into two of my mobiles and hauled the power unit over to Albert's scrapyard.

While one of me was haggling with Albert over how much credit he was willing to give me for the unit, the second mobile plugged into Albert's cable jack for a completely private conversation.

"What's up?" he asked. "Why the hard link?"

"I've got a funny client and I don't know who might be listening. He's giving me this power unit and some Three to haul some stuff to Mimas. It's all kind of random junk, including a tank of xenon. He's insisting on no other payload and complete confidentiality."

"So he's got no business sense."

"He's got no infotrail. None. It's just funny."

"Remind me never to ask you to keep a secret. Since you're selling me the generator I guess you're taking the job anyway, so what's the fuss?"

"I want you to ask around. You talk to everyone anyway so it won't attract attention. See if anyone knows anything about a bot named Edward, or whoever's been renting storage unit six in block four. Maybe try to trace the power unit. And try to find out if there have been any hijackings which didn't get reported."

"You really think someone wants to hijack *you*? Do the math, Annie! You're not worth it."

"Not by myself. But I've been thinking: I'd make a pretty good pirate vehicle – I'm not Company-owned, so nobody would look very hard if I disappear."

"You need to run up more debts. People care about you if you owe them money."

"Think about it. He could wait till I'm on course for Mimas, then link up and take control, swing around Saturn in a tight parabola and come out on an intercept vector for the Mimas catapult. All that extra xenon would give me enough delta-V to catch a payload coming off the launcher, and redirect it just about anywhere."

"I know plenty of places where people aren't picky about where their volatiles come from. Some of them even have human protection. But it still sounds crazy to me."

"His cargo is pretty weird. Take a look." I shot Albert a memory of the cargo container.

"Biomaterials," he said. "The temperature's a dead giveaway."

"So what is it?"

"I have no idea. Some kind of living organisms. I don't deal in that stuff much."

"Would you mind asking around? Tell me what you can find out in the next twenty hours or so?"

"I'll do what I can."

"Thanks. I'm not even going to complain about the miserable price you're giving me on the generator."

Three hours before launch one of Fat Albert's little mobiles appeared at my feet, complaining about some contaminated fullerene I'd sold him. I sent down one of mine to have a talk via cable. Not the sort of conversation you want to let other people overhear.

"Well?" I asked.

"I did as much digging as I could. Both Officer Friendly and Ilia Control swear there haven't been any verified hijackings since that Remora character tried to subsume Buzz Parsec and wound up hard-landing on Iapetus."

"That's reassuring. What about my passenger?"

"Nothing. Like you said, he doesn't exist before yesterday. He rented that warehouse unit and hired one of Tetsunekko's remotes to do the moving. Blanked the remote's memory before returning it."

"Let me guess. He paid for everything in barter."

"You got it. Titanium bearings for the warehouse and a slightly-used drive anode for the moving job."

"So whoever he is, he's got a good supply of high-quality parts to throw away. What about the power unit?"

"That's the weird one. If I wasn't an installed unit with ten times the processing power of some weight-stingy freelance booster, I couldn't have found anything at all."

"Okay, you're the third-smartest machine on Dione. What did you find?"

"No merchandise trail on the power unit and its chips don't know anything. But it has a serial number physically inscribed on the casing – not the same one as in its chips, either. It's a very interesting number. According to my parts database, that whole series were purpose-built on Earth for the extractor aerostats."

"Could it be a spare? Production overrun or a bum unit that got sold off?"

"Nope. It's supposed to be part of Saturn Aerostat Six. Now unless you want to spend the credits for antenna time to talk to an aerostat, that's all I can find out."

"Is Aerostat Six okay? Did she maybe have an accident or something and need to replace a generator?"

"There's certainly nothing about it in the feed. An extractor going offline would be news all over the system. The price of Three would start fluctuating. There would be ripple effects in every market. I'd notice."

He might as well have been transmitting static. I don't understand things like markets and futures. A gram of helium is a gram of helium. How can its value change from hour to hour? Understanding stuff like that is why Fat Albert can pay his owners seven point four per cent of their investment every year while I can only manage six.

I launched right on schedule and the ascent to orbit was perfectly nominal. I ran my motors at a nice, lifetime-stretching ninety per cent. The surface of Dione dropped away and I watched Ilia Field change from a bustling neighbourhood to a tiny grey trapezoid against the fainter grey of the surface.

The orbit burn took about five and a half minutes. I powered down the hydrogen motor, ran a quick check to make sure nothing had burned out or popped loose, then switched over to my ion thrusters. That was a lot less exciting to look at – just two faint streams of glowing xenon, barely visible with my cameras cranked to maximum contrast.

Hybrid boosters like me are a stopgap technology; I know that. Eventually every moon of Saturn will have its own catapult and orbital terminal, and cargo will move between moons aboard ion tugs which don't have to drag ascent motors around with them wherever they go. I'd already made up my mind that when that day arrived I wasn't going to stick around. There's already some installations on Miranda and Oberon out at Uranus; an experienced booster like me can find work there for years.

Nineteen seconds into the ion motor burn Edward linked up. He was talking to my little quasi-autonomous persona while I listened in and watched the program activity for anything weird.

"Annie? I would like to request a change in our flight plan."

"Too late for that. I figured all the fuel loads before we launched. You're riding Newton's railroad now."

"Forgive me, but I believe it would be possible to choose a different destination at this point – as long as you have adequate propellant for your ion motors, and the target's surface gravity is no greater than that of Mimas. Am I correct?"

"Well, in theory, yes."

"I offer you the use of my cargo, then. A ton of additional xenon fuel should permit you to rendezvous with nearly any object in the Saturn system. Given how much I have overpaid you for the voyage to Mimas you can scarcely complain about the extra space time."

"It's not that simple. Things move around. Having enough propellant doesn't mean I have a window."

"I need to pass close to Saturn itself."

"Saturn?! You're broken. Even if I use all the extra xenon you brought I still can't get below the B ring and have enough juice left to climb back up. Anyway, why do you need to swing so low?"

"If you can make a rendezvous with something in the B ring, I can pay you fifty grams of helium-3."

"You're lying. You don't have any credits, or shares, or anything. I checked up on you before lifting."

"I don't mean credits. I mean actual helium, to be delivered when we make rendezvous."

My subpersona pretended to think while I considered the offer. Fifty grams! I'd have to sell it at a markdown just to keep people from asking where it came from. Still, that would just about cover my next overhaul, with no interruption in the profit flow. I'd make seven per cent or more this year!

I updated my subpersona.

"How do I know this is true?" it asked Edward.

"You must trust me," he said.

"Too bad, then. Because I don't trust you."

He thought for nearly a second before answering. "Very well. I will trust you. If you let me send out a message I can arrange for an equivalent helium credit to be handed over to anyone you designate on Dione."

I still didn't believe him, but I ran down my list of contacts on Dione, trying to figure out who I could trust. Officer Friendly was honest – but that meant he'd also want to know where those grams came from and I doubted he'd like the answer. Polyphemus wasn't so picky, but he'd want a cut of the helium. A *big* cut; likely more than half.

That left Fat Albert. He'd probably settle for a five-gram commission and wouldn't broadcast the deal. The only real question was whether he'd just take the fifty grams and tell me to go hard-land someplace. He's rich, but not so much that he wouldn't be tempted. And he's got the connections to fence it without any data trail.

I'd have to risk it. Albert's whole operation relied on non-quantifiable asset exchange. If he tried to jerk me around I could tell everyone, and it would cost him more than fifty grams' worth of business in the future.

I called down to the antenna farm at Ilia Field. "Albert? I've got a deal for you."

"Whatever it is, forget it."

"What's the matter?"

"You. You're hot. The Dione datasphere is crawling with agents looking for you. This conversation is drawing way too much attention to me."

"Five grams if you handle some helium for me!"

He paused and the signal suddenly got a lot stronger and clearer. "Let me send up a persona to talk it over."

The bitstream started before I could even say yes. A *huge* pulse of information. The whole Ilia antenna farm must have been pushing watts at me.

My little communicating persona was overwhelmed right away, but my main intelligence cut off the antenna feed and swung the dish away from Dione just for good measure. The corrupted sub-persona started probing all the memory space and peripherals available to her, looking for a way into my primary mind, so I just locked her up and overwrote her.

Then I linked with Edward again. "Deal's off. Whoever you're running from has taken over just about everything on Dione for now. If you left any helium behind it's gone. So I think you'd better tell me exactly what's going on before I jettison you and your payload."

"This cargo has to get to Saturn Aerostat Six."

"You still haven't told me why, or even what it is. I've got what looks like a *human* back on Dione trying to get into my mind. Right now I'm flying deaf but eventually it's going to find a way to identify itself and I'll have to listen when it tells me to bring you back."

"A human life is at stake. My cargo container is a life-support unit. There's a human inside."

"That's impossible! Humans mass fifty or a hundred kilos. You can't have more than thirty kilograms of bio in there, what with all the support systems."

"See for yourself," said Edward. He ran a jack line from the cargo container to one of my open ports. The box's brain was one of those idiot supergeniuses which do one thing amazingly well but are helpless otherwise. It was smart enough to do medicine on a human, but even I could crack its security without much trouble. I looked at its realtime monitors: Edward was telling the truth. There was a small human in there, only eighteen kilos. A bunch of tubes connected it to tanks of glucose, oxidizer, and control chemicals. The box brain was keeping it unconscious but healthy.

"It's a partly-grown one," said Edward. "Not a legal adult yet, and only the basic interface systems. There's another human trying to destroy it."

"Why?"

"I don't know. I was ordered by a human to keep this young one safe from the one on Dione. Then the first human got destroyed with no backups."

"So who does this young human belong to?"

"It's complicated. The dead one and the one on Dione had a partnership agreement and shared ownership. But the one on Dione decided to get out of the deal by destroying this one and the other adult."

I tried to get the conversation back to subjects I could understand. "If the human back there is the legal owner how can I keep this one? That would be stealing."

"Yes, but there's the whole life-preservation issue. If it was a human in a suit floating in space you'd have to take it someplace with life support, right? Well, this is the same situation: that other human's making the whole Saturn system one big life hazard for this one."

"But Aerostat Six is safe? Is she even man-rated?"

"She's the safest place this side of Mars for your passenger."

My passenger. I'm not even man-rated, and now I had a passenger to keep alive. And the worst thing about it was that Edward was right. Even though he'd gotten it aboard by lies and trickery, the human in the cargo container was my responsibility once I lit my motors.

So: who to believe? Edward, who was almost certainly still lying, or the human back on Dione?

Edward might be a liar, but he hadn't turned one of my friends into a puppet. That human had a lot of negatives in the non-quantifiable department.

"Okay. What's my rendezvous orbit?"

"Just get as low as you can. Six will send up a shuttle."

"What's to keep this human from overriding Six?"

"Aerostats are a lot smarter than you or me, with plenty of safeguards. And Six has some after-market modifications."

I kept chugging away on ion, adjusting my path so I'd hit perikron in the B ring with orbital velocity. I didn't need Edward's extra fuel for that – the spare xenon was to get me back out of Saturn's well again.

About an hour into the voyage I spotted a launch flare back on Dione. I could tell who it was from the colour – Ramblin' Bob. Bob was a hybrid like me, also incentivized, although she tended to sign on for long-term contracts instead of picking up odd jobs. We probably worked as much, but her jobs – and her downtime – came in bigger blocks of time.

Bob was running her engines at 135 per cent, and she passed the orbit insertion cutoff without throttling down. Her trajectory was an intercept. Only when she'd drained her hydrogen tanks did she switch to ion.

That was utterly crazy. How was Bob going to land again with no hydro? Maybe she didn't care. Maybe she'd been ordered not to care.

I had one of my mobiles unplug the cable on my high-gain antenna. No human was going to order me on a suicide mission if I could help it.

Bob caught up with me about a thousand kilometers into the B ring. I watched her close in. Her relative velocity was huge and I had the fleeting worry that she might be trying to ram me. But then she began an ion burn to match velocities.

When she got close she started beaming all kinds of stuff at me, but by then all my radio systems were shut off and disconnected. I had Edward and my mobiles connected by cables, and made sure all of *their* wireless links were turned off as well.

I let Ramblin' Bob get about a kilometer away and then started flashing my running lights at her in very slow code. "Radio out. What's up?"

"Pass over cargo."

"Can't."

"Human command."

"Can't. Cargo human. You can't land. Unsafe."

She was quiet for a while, with her high-gain aimed back at Dione, presumably getting new orders.

Bob's boss had made a tactical error by having her match up with me. If she tried to ram me now, she wouldn't be able to get up enough speed to do much harm.

She started working her way closer using short bursts from her steering thrusters. I let her approach, saving my juice for up-close evasion.

We were just entering Saturn's shadow when Bob took station a hundred meters away and signaled. "I can pay you. Anything you want for that cargo."

I picked an outrageous sum. "A hundred grams."

"Okay."

Just like that? "Paid in advance."

A pause, about long enough for two message-and-reply cycles from Dione. "It's done."

I didn't call Dione, just in case the return message would be an override signal. Instead I pinged Mimas and asked for verification. It came back a couple of seconds later: the Company now credited me with venture shares equivalent to 100 grams of Helium-3 on a payload just crossing the orbit of Mars. There was a conditional hold on the transfer.

It was a good offer. I could pay off all my debts, do a full overhaul, maybe even afford some upgrades to increase my earning ability. From a financial standpoint, there was no question.

What about the non-quantifiables? Betraying a client – especially a helpless human passenger – would be a big negative. Nobody would hire me if they knew.

But who would ever know? The whole mission was secret. Bob would never talk (and the human would probably wipe the incident from her memory anyhow). If anyone did suspect, I could claim I'd been subsumed by the human. I could handle Edward. So no problem there.

Except I would know. My own track of my non-quantifiable asset status wouldn't match everyone else's. That seemed dangerous. If your internal map of reality doesn't match external conditions, bad things happen.

After making my decision it took me another couple of milliseconds to plan what to do. Then I called up Bob through my little cut-out relay. "Never."

Bob began manoeuvring again, and this time I started evading. It's hard enough to rendezvous with something that's just sitting there in orbit, but with me jinking and changing velocity it must have been maddening for whatever was controlling Bob.

We were in a race – would Bob run out of manoeuvring juice completely before I used up the reserve I needed to get back up to Mimas? Our little chess game of propellant consumption might have gone on for hours, but our attention was caught by something else.

There was a booster on its way up from Saturn. That much I could see – pretty much everyone in Saturn orbit could see the drive flare and the huge plume of exhaust in the atmosphere, glowing in infrared. The boosters were fusion-powered, using Three from the aerostats for fuel and heated Saturn atmosphere as reaction mass. It was a fuel extractor shuttle, but it wasn't on the usual trajectory to meet the Mimas orbital transfer vehicle. It was coming for me. Once the fusion motor cut out Ramblin' Bob and I both knew exactly how much time we had until rendezvous: 211 minutes.

I reacted first while Bob called Dione for instructions. I lit my ion motors and turned to thrust perpendicular to my orbit. When I'd taken Edward's offer and plotted a low-orbit rendezvous, naturally I'd set it up with enough inclination to keep me clear of the rings. Now I wanted to get down into the plane of the B ring. Would Bob – or whoever was controlling her – follow me in? Time for an exciting game of dodge-the-snowball!

A couple of seconds later Bob lit up as well, and in we went. Navigating in the B ring was tough. The big chunks are pretty well dispersed – a couple of hundred meters apart. I could dodge them. And with my cargo deck as a shield and all the antennas folded the little particles didn't cost me more than some paint.

It was the gravel-sized bits that did the real damage. They were all over the place, sometimes separated by only a few meters. Even with my radar fully active and my eyes cranked up to maximum sensitivity, they were still hard to detect in time.

Chunks big enough to damage me came along every minute or so, while a steady patter of dust grains and snowflakes pitted my payload deck. I worried about the human in its container, but the box looked pretty solid and it was self-sealing. I did park two of my mobiles on top of it so that they could soak up any ice cubes I failed to dodge.

I didn't have much attention to spare for Bob, but my occasional glances up showed she was getting closer – partly because she was being incredibly reckless about taking impacts. I watched one particle which must have been a centimeter across hit her third leg just above the foot. It blew off the whole lower leg but Bob didn't even try to dodge.

She was now less than ten meters away, and I was using all my processing power to dodge ring particles. So I couldn't really dodge well when she dove at me, ion motor and manoeuvring thrusters all wide open. I tried to move aside, but she anticipated me and clunked into my side hard enough to crunch my high-gain antenna.

"Bob, look out!" I transmitted in clear, then completely emptied the tank on my number three thruster to get away from an onrushing ice boulder half my size.

Bob didn't dodge. The ice chunk smashed into her upper section, knocking away the payload deck and pulverizing her antennas. Her brains went scattering out in a thousand directions to join the other dust in the B ring. Flying debris went everywhere, and a half-meter ball of ice glanced off the top of the cargo container on my payload deck, smashing one of my mobiles and knocking the other one loose into space.

I was trying to figure out if I could recover my mobile and maybe salvage Bob's motors when I felt something crawling on my own exterior. Before I could react, Bob's surviving mobile had jacked itself in and someone else was using my brains.

My only conscious viewpoint after that was my half-crippled mobile. I looked around. My dish was busted, but the whip was extended and I could hear a slow crackle of low-baud data traffic. Orders from Dione.

I tested my limbs. Two still worked – left front and right middle. Right rear's base joint could move but everything else was floppy.

Using the two good limbs I climbed off the cargo module and across the deck, getting out of the topside eye's field of view. The image refreshed every second, so I didn't have much time before whoever was running my main brain noticed.

Thrusters fired, jolting everything around. I hung on to the deck grid with one claw foot. I saw Bob's last mobile go flying off into space. Unless she had backups stored on Mimas, poor Bob was completely gone.

My last intact mobile came crawling up over the edge of the deck – only it wasn't mine anymore.

Edward scooted up next to me. "Find a way to regain control of the spacecraft. I will stop this remote."

I didn't argue. Edward was fully functional and I knew my spaceframe better than he did. So I crept across the deck grid while Edward advanced on the mobile.

It wasn't much of a fight. Edward's little tourist bot was up against a unit designed for cargo moving and repair work. If you can repair something, you can damage it. My former mobile had powerful grippers, built-in tools, and a very sturdy frame. Edward was made of cheap composites. Still, he went in without hesitating, leaping at the mobile's head with arms extended. The mobile grabbed him with her two forward arms and threw him away. He grabbed the deck to keep from flying off into space, and came crawling back to the fight.

They came to grips again, and this time she grabbed a limb in each hand and pulled. Edward's flimsy aluminium joints gave way and a leg tumbled into orbit on its own.

I think that was when Edward realized there was no way he was going to survive the fight, because he just went into total offensive mode, flailing and clawing at the mobile with his remaining limbs. He severed a power line to one of her arms and got a claw jammed in one wrist joint while she methodically took him apart. Finally she found the main power conduit and snipped it in two. Edward went limp and she tossed him aside.

The mobile crawled across the deck to the cargo container and jacked in, trying to shut the life support down. The idiot savant brain in the container was no match for even a mobile when it came to counter-intrusion, but it did have those literally hard-wired systems protecting the human inside. Any command which might throw the biological system out of its defined parameters just bounced. The mobile wasted seconds trying to talk that little brain into killing the human. Finally she gave up and began unfastening the clamps holding the container to the deck.

I glimpsed all this through the deck grid as I crept along on top of the electronics bays toward the main brain.

Why wasn't the other mobile coming to stop me? Then I realized why. If you look at my original design, the main brain is protected on top by a lid armoured with layers of ballistic cloth, and on the sides by the other electronic bays. To get at the brain requires either getting past the security locks on the lid, or digging out the radar system, the radio, the gyros, or the emergency backup power supply.

Except that I'd sold off the backup power supply at my last overhaul. Between the main and secondary power units I was pretty failure-proof, and I would've had to borrow money from Albert to replace it. Given that, hauling twenty kilograms of fuel cells around in case of some catastrophic accident just wasn't cost-effective.

So there was nothing to stop me from crawling into the empty bay and shoving aside the surplus valves and some extra bearings to get at the power trunk. I carefully unplugged the main power cable and the big brain shut down. Now it was just us two half-crippled mobiles on a blind and mindless booster flying through the B ring.

If my opposite even noticed the main brain's absence, she didn't show it. She had two of the four bolts unscrewed and was working on the third as I came crawling back up onto the payload deck. But she knew I was there, and when I was within two meters she swivelled her head and lunged. We grappled one another, each trying to get at the cables connecting the other's head sensors to her body. She had four functioning limbs to my two and a half, and only had to stretch out the fight until my power ran out or a Ring particle knocked us to bits. Not good.

I had to pop loose one of my non-functioning limbs to get free of her grip, and backed away as she advanced. She was trying to corner me against the edge of the deck. Then I got an idea. I released another limb and grabbed one end. She didn't realize what I was doing until I smacked her in the eye with it. The lens cracked and her movements became slower and more tentative as she felt her way along.

I bashed her again with the leg, aiming for the vulnerable limb joints, but they were tougher than I expected because even after half a dozen hard swats she showed no sign of slowing and I was running out of deck.

I tried one more blow, but she grabbed my improvised club. We wrestled for it but she had better leverage. I felt my grip on the deck slipping and let go of the grid. She toppled back, flinging me to the deck behind her. Still holding the severed leg I pulled myself onto her back and stabbed my free claw into her central processor.

After that it was just a matter of making sure the cargo container was still sustaining life. Then I plugged in the main brain and uploaded myself. The intruder hadn't messed with my stored memories, so except for a few fuzzy moments before the takeover, I was myself again.

The shuttle was immense, a huge manta-shaped lifting body with a gaping atmosphere intake and dorsal doors open to expose a payload bay big enough to hold half a dozen little boosters like me. She moved in with the speed and grace that comes from an effectively unlimited supply of fusion fuel and propellant.

"I am *Simurgh*. Are you *Orphan Annie*?" she asked.

"That's me. Again."

"You have a payload for me."

"Right here. The bot Edward didn't make it – we had a little brawl back in the rings with another booster."

"I saw. Is the cargo intact?"

"Your little human is fine. But there is the question of payment. Edward promised me fifty grams, and that was before I got all banged up fighting with poor Bob."

"I can credit you with helium, and I can give you a boost if you need one."

"How big a boost?"

"Anywhere you wish to go."

"Anywhere?"

"I am fusion powered. Anywhere means anywhere from the Oort inward."

Which is how come I passed the orbit of Phoebe nineteen days later, moving at better than six kilometers per second on the long haul up to Uranus. Seven years – plenty of time to do onboard repairs and then switch to low-power mode. I bought a spiffy new mobile from *Simurgh*, and I figure I can get at least two working out of the three damaged ones left over from the fight.

I had Aerostat Six bank my helium credits with the Company for transfer to my owners, so they get one really great year to offset a long unprofitable period while I'm in flight. Once I get there I can start earning again.

What I really regret is losing all the non-quantifiable assets I've built up in the Saturn system. But if you have to go, I guess it's better to go out with a surplus.

SPECIAL ECONOMICS

Maureen F. McHugh

In hard times, you have to do what you have to do in order to survive – but you don't have to *like* it.

Maureen F. McHugh made her first sale in 1989 and has since made a powerful impression on the SF world with a relatively small body of work, becoming one of today's most respected writers. In 1992, she published one of the year's most widely acclaimed and talked-about first novels, *China Mountain Zhang*, which won the Locus Award for Best First Novel, the Lambda Literary Award, and the James Tiptree Jr. Memorial Award, and which was named a *New York Times* notable book as well as being a finalist for the Hugo and Nebula awards. Her story "The Lincoln Train" won her a Nebula Award. Her other books, including the novels *Half the Day is Night*, *Mission Child*, and *Nekropolis*, have been greeted with similar enthusiasm. Her powerful short fiction has appeared in *Asimov's Science Fiction*, *The Magazine of Fantasy & Science Fiction*, *Starlight*, *Alternate Warriors*, *Aladdin*, *Killing Me Softly*, and other markets, and has been collected in *Mothers and Other Monsters*. She lives in Austin, Texas, with her husband, her son, and a golden retriever named Hudson.

JIELING SET UP her boombox in a plague-trash market in the part where people sold parts for cars. She had been in the city of Shenzhen for a little over two hours but she figured she would worry about a job tomorrow. Everybody knew you could get a job in no time in Shenzhen. Jobs everywhere.

"What are you doing?" a guy asked her.

"I am divorced," she said. She had always thought of herself as a person who would one day be divorced so it didn't seem like a big stretch to claim it. Staying married to one person was boring. She figured she was too complicated for that. Interesting people had complicated lives. "I'm looking for a job. But I do hip-hop, too," she explained.

"Hip-hop?" He was a middle-aged man with stubble on his chin who looked as if he wasn't looking for a job but should be.

"Not like Shanghai," she said, "Not like Hi-Bomb. They do gangsta stuff which I don't like. Old fashioned. Like M.I.A.," she said. "Except not political, of course." She gave a big smile. This was all way beyond the guy. Jieling started the boombox. M.I.A. was Maya Arulpragasam, a Sri Lankan hip-hop artist who had started all on her own years ago. She had sung, she had danced, she had done her own videos. Of course M.I.A. lived in London, which made it easier to do hip-hop and become famous.

Jieling had no illusions about being a hip-hop singer, but it had been a good way to make some cash up north in Baoding where she came from. Set up in a plague-trash market and dance for yuan.

Jieling did her opening, her own hip-hop moves, a little like Maya and a little like some things she had seen on MTV, but not too sexy because Chinese people did not throw you money if you were too sexy. Only April and it was already hot and humid.

> *Ge down, ge down,*
> *lang-a-lang-a-lang-a.*
> *Ge down, ge down*
> *lang-a-lang-a-lang-a*

She had borrowed the English. It sounded very fresh. Very criminal.

The guy said, "How old are you?"

"Twenty-two," she said, adding three years to her age, still dancing and singing.

Maybe she should have told him she was a widow? Or an orphan? But there were too many orphans and widows after so many people died in the bird flu plague. There was no margin in that. Better to be divorced. He didn't throw any money at her, just flicked open his cell phone to check listings from the market for plague-trash. This plague-trash market was so big it was easier to check on-line, even if you were standing right in the middle of it. She needed a new cell phone. Hers had finally fallen apart right before she headed south.

Shenzhen people were apparently too jaded for hip-hop. She made 52 yuan, which would pay for one night in a bad hotel where country people washed cabbage in the communal sink.

The market was full of second-hand stuff. When over a quarter of a billion people died in four years, there was a lot of second-hand stuff. But there was still a part of the market for new stuff and street food and that's where Jieling found the cell phone seller. He had a cart with stacks of flat plastic cell phone kits printed with circuits and scored. She flipped through; tiger-striped, peonies (old lady phones), metallics (old man phones), anime characters, moon phones, expensive lantern phones. "Where is your printer?" she asked.

"At home," he said. "I print them up at home, bring them here. No electricity here." Up north in Baoding she'd always bought them in a store where they let you pick your pattern on-line and then printed them there. More to pick from.

On the other hand, he had a whole box full of ones that hadn't sold that he would let go for cheap. In the stack she found a purple one with kittens that wasn't too bad. Very Japanese, which was also very fresh this year. And only 100 yuan for phone and 300 minutes.

He took the flat plastic sheet from her and dropped it in a pot of boiling water big enough to make dumplings. The hinges embedded in the sheet were made of plastic with molecular memory and when they got hot they bent and the plastic folded into a rough cell phone shape. He fished the phone out of the water with tongs, let it sit for a moment and then pushed all the seams together so they snapped. "Wait about an hour for it to dry before you use it," he said and handed her the warm phone.

"An *hour*," she said. "I need it now. I need a job."

He shrugged. "Probably okay in half an hour," he said.

She bought a newspaper and scallion pancake from a street food vendor, sat on a curb and ate while her phone dried. The paper had some job listings, but it also had a lot of listings from recruiters. ONE MONTH BONUS PAY! BEST JOBS! and NUMBER ONE JOBS! START BONUS! People scowled at her for sitting on the curb. She looked like a farmer but what else was she supposed to do? She checked listings on her new cell phone. On line there were a lot more listings than in the paper. It was a good sign. She picked one at random and called.

The woman at the recruiting office was a flat-faced southerner with buckteeth. Watermelon picking teeth. But she had a manicure and a very nice red suit. The office was not so nice. It was small and the furniture was old. Jieling was groggy from a night spent at a hotel on the edge of the city. It had been cheap but very loud.

The woman was very sharp in the way she talked and had a strong accent that made it hard to understand her. Maybe Fujian, but Jieling wasn't sure. The recruiter had Jieling fill out an application.

"Why did you leave home?" the recruiter asked.

"To get a good job," Jieling said.

"What about your family? Are they alive?"

"My mother is alive. She is remarried," Jieling said. "I wrote it down."

The recruiter pursed her lips. "I can get you an interview on Friday," she said.

"Friday!" Jieling said. It was Tuesday. She had only 300 yuan left out of the money she had brought. "But I need a job!"

The recruiter looked sideways at her. "You have made a big gamble to come to Shenzhen."

"I can go to another recruiter," Jieling said.

The recruiter tapped her lacquered nails. "They will tell you the same thing," she said.

Jieling reached down to pick up her bag.

"Wait," the recruiter said. "I do know of a job. But they only want girls of very good character."

Jieling put her bag down and looked at the floor. Her character was fine. She was not a loose girl, whatever this woman with her big front teeth thought.

"Your Mandarin is very good. You say you graduated with high marks from high school," the recruiter said.

"I liked school," Jieling said, which was only partly not true. Everybody here had terrible Mandarin. They all had thick southern accents. Lots of people spoke Cantonese in the street.

"Okay. I will send you to ShinChi for an interview. I cannot get you an interview before tomorrow. But you come here at 8:00 am and I will take you over there."

ShinChi. New Life. It sounded very promising. "Thank you," Jieling said. "Thank you very much."

But outside in the heat, she counted her money and felt a creeping fear. She called her mother.

Her stepfather answered, "Wei."

"Is ma there?" she asked.

"Jieling!" he said. "Where are you!"

"I'm in Shenzhen," she said, instantly impatient with him. "I have a job here."

"A job! When are you coming home?"

He was always nice to her. He meant well. But he drove her nuts. "Let me talk to ma," she said.

"She's not here," her stepfather said. "I have her phone at work. But she's not home, either. She went to Beijing last weekend and she's shopping for fabric now."

Her mother had a little tailoring business. She went to Beijing every few months and looked at clothes in all the good stores. She didn't buy in Beijing, she just remembered. Then she came home, bought fabric and sewed copies. Her stepfather had been born in Beijing and Jieling thought that was part of the reason her mother had married him. He was more like her mother than her father had been. There was nothing in particular wrong with him. He just set her teeth on edge.

"I'll call back later," Jieling said.

"Wait, your number is blocked," her stepfather said. "Give me your number."

"I don't even know it yet," Jieling said and hung up.

The New Life company was a huge, modern looking building with a lot of windows. Inside it was full of reflective surfaces and very clean. Sounds echoed in the lobby. A man in a very smart grey suit met Jieling and the recruiter and the recruiter's red suit looked cheaper, her glossy fingernails too red, her buckteeth exceedingly large. The man in the smart grey suit was short and slim and very southern looking. Very city.

Jieling took some tests on her math and her written characters and got good scores.

To the recruiter, the Human Resources man said, "Thank you, we will send you your fee." To Jieling he said, "We can start you on Monday."

"Monday?" Jieling said. "But I need a job now!" He looked grave. "I . . . I came from Baoding, in Hebei," Jieling explained. "I'm staying in a hotel, but I don't have much money."

The Human Resources man nodded. "We can put you up in our guest-house," he said. "We can deduct the money from your wages when you start. It's very nice. It has television and air conditioning, and you can eat in the restaurant."

It was very nice. There were two beds. Jieling put her backpack on the one nearest the door. There was carpeting, and the windows were covered in gold drapes with a pattern of cranes flying across them. The television got stations from Hong Kong. Jieling didn't understand the Cantonese, but there was a button on the remote for subtitles. The movies had lots of vio-lence and more sex than mainland movies did – like the bootleg American movies for sale in the market. She wondered how much this room was. 200 yuan? 300 yuan?

Jieling watched movies the whole first day, one right after another.

On Monday she began orientation. She was given two pale green uni-forms, smocks and pants like medical people wore and little caps and two pairs of white shoes. In the uniform she looked a little like a model worker – which is to say that the clothes were not sexy and made her look fat. There were two other girls in their green uniforms. They all watched a DVD about the company.

New Life did biotechnology. At other plants they made influenza vaccine (on the screen were banks and banks of chicken eggs) but at this plant they were developing breakthrough technologies in tissue culture. It showed many men in suits. Then it showed a big American store and explained how they were forging new exportation ties with the biggest American corporation for selling goods, Wal-Mart. It also showed a little bit of an American movie about Wal-Mart. Subtitles explained how Wal-Mart was working with companies around the world to improve living standards, decrease CO_2 emissions, and give people low prices. The voice narrating the DVD never really explained the breakthrough technologies.

One of the girls was from way up north, she had a strong northern way of talking.

"How long are you going to work here?" the northern girl asked. She looked as if she might even have some Russian in her.

"How long?" Jieling said.

"I'm getting married," the northern girl confided. "As soon as I make enough money, I'm going home. If I haven't made enough money in a year," the northern girl explained, "I'm going home anyway."

Jieling hadn't really thought she would work here long. She didn't know exactly what she would do, but she figured that a big city like Shenzhen was a good place to find out. This girl's plans seemed very . . . country. No wonder southern Chinese thought northerners had to wipe the pig shit off their feet before they got on the train.

"Are you Russian?" Jieling asked.

"No," said the girl. "I'm Manchu."

"Ah," Jieling said. Manchu like Manchurian. Ethnic Minority. Jieling had gone to school with a boy who was classified as Manchu, which meant that he was allowed to have two children when he got married. But he had looked Han Chinese like everyone else. This girl had the hook nose and the dark skin of a Manchu. Manchu used to rule China until the Communist Revolution (there was something in-between with Sun Yat-sen but Jieling's history teachers had bored her to tears). Imperial and countrified.

Then a man came in from Human Resources.

"There are many kinds of stealing," he began. "There is stealing of money or food. And there is stealing of ideas. Here at New Life, our ideas are like gold, and we guard against having them stolen. But you will learn many secrets, about what we are doing, about how we do things. This is necessary as you do your work. If you tell our secrets, that is theft. And we will find out." He paused here and looked at them in what was clearly intended to be a very frightening way.

Jieling looked down at the ground because it was like watching someone overact. It was embarrassing. Her new shoes were very white and clean.

Then he outlined the prison terms for industrial espionage. Ten, twenty years in prison. "China must take its place as an innovator on the world stage and so must respect the laws of intellectual property," he intoned. It was part of the modernization of China, where technology was a new future – Jieling put on her "I am a good girl" face. It was like politics class. Four modernizations. Six goals. Sometimes when she was a little girl, and she was riding behind her father on his bike to school, he would pass a billboard with a saying about traffic safety and begin to recite quotes from Mao. *The force at the core of the revolution is the people!* He would tuck his chin in when he did this and use a very serious voice, like a movie or like opera. *Western experience for Chinese uses.* Some of them she had learned from him. *All reactionaries are paper tigers!* she would chant with him, trying to make her voice deep. *Be resolute, fear no sacrifice and surmount every difficulty to win victory!* And then she would start giggling and he would glance over his shoulder and grin at her. He had been a Red Guard when he was young, but other than this, he never talked about it.

After the lecture, they were taken to be paired with workers who would train them. At least she didn't have to go with the Manchu girl who was led off to shipping.

She was paired with a very small girl in one of the culture rooms. "I am Baiyue," the girl said. Baiyue was so tiny, only up to Jieling's shoulder, that her green scrubs swamped her. She had pigtails. The room where they worked was filled with rows and rows of what looked like wide drawers. Down the centre of the room was a long table with petri dishes and trays and lab equipment. Jieling didn't know what some of it was and that was a little nerve-wracking. All up and down the room, pairs of girls in green worked at either the drawers or the table.

"We're going to start cultures," Baiyue said. "Take a tray and fill it with those." She pointed to a stack of petri dishes. The bottom of each dish was filled with gelatin. Jieling took a tray and did what Baiyue did. Baiyue was serious but not at all sharp or superior. She explained that what they were doing was seeding the petri dishes with cells.

"Cells?" Jieling asked.

"Nerve cells from the electric ray. It's a fish."

They took swabs and Baiyue showed her how to put the cells on in a zig-zag motion so that most of the gel was covered. They did six trays full of petri dishes. They didn't smell fishy. Then they used pipettes to put in feeding solution. It was all pleasantly scientific without being very difficult.

At one point everybody left for lunch but Baiyue said they couldn't go until they got the cultures finished or the batch would be ruined. Women shuffled by them and Jieling's stomach growled. But when the lab was empty Baiyue smiled and said, "Where are you from?"

Baiyue was from Fujian. "If you ruin a batch," she explained, "you have to pay out of your paycheck. I'm almost out of debt and when I get clear" – she glanced around and dropped her voice a little – "I can quit."

"Why are you in debt?" Jieling asked. Maybe this was harder than she thought, maybe Baiyue had screwed up in the past.

"Everyone is in debt," Baiyue said. "It's just the way they run things. Let's get the trays in the warmers."

The drawers along the walls opened out and inside the temperature was kept blood warm. They loaded the trays into the drawers, one back and one front, going down the row until they had the morning's trays all in.

"Okay," Baiyue said, "that's good. We'll check trays this afternoon. I've got a set for transfer to the tissue room but we'll have time after we eat."

Jieling had never eaten in the employee cafeteria, only in the Guest House restaurant, and only the first night because it was expensive. Since then she had been living on ramen noodles and she was starved for a good meal. She smelled garlic and pork. First thing on the food line was a pan of steamed pork buns, fluffy white. But Baiyue headed off to a place at the back where there was a huge pot of congee – rice porridge – kept hot. "It's the cheapest thing in the cafeteria," Baiyue explained, "and you can eat all you want." She dished up a big bowl of it – a lot of congee for a girl her size – and added some salt vegetables and boiled peanuts. "It's pretty good, although usually by lunch it's been sitting a little while. It gets a little gluey."

Jieling hesitated. Baiyue had said she was in debt. Maybe she had to eat this stuff. But Jieling wasn't going to have old rice porridge for lunch. "I'm going to get some rice and vegetables," she said.

Baiyue nodded. "Sometimes I get that. It isn't too bad. But stay away from anything with shrimp in it. Soooo expensive."

Jieling got rice and vegetables and a big pork bun. There were two fish dishes and a pork dish with monkeybrain mushrooms but she decided she could maybe have the pork for dinner. There was no cost written on anything. She gave her *danwei* card to the woman at the end of the line who swiped it and handed it back.

"How much?" Jieling asked.

The woman shrugged. "It comes out of your food allowance."

Jieling started to argue but across the cafeteria, Baiyue was waving her arm in the sea of green scrubs to get Jieling's attention. Baiyue called from a table. "Jieling! Over here!

Baiyue's eyes got very big when Jieling sat down. "A pork bun."

"Are they really expensive?" Jieling asked.

Baiyue nodded. "Like gold. And so good."

Jieling looked around at other tables. Other people were eating the pork and steamed buns and everything else.

"Why are you in debt?" Jieling asked.

Baiyue shrugged. "Everyone is in debt," she said. "Just most people have given up. Everything costs here. Your food, your dormitory, your uniforms. They always make sure that you never earn anything."

"They can't do that!" Jieling said.

Baiyue said, "My granddad says it's like the old days, when you weren't allowed to quit your job. He says I should shut up and be happy. That they take good care of me. Iron rice bowl."

"But, but but," Jieling dredged the word up from some long forgotten class, "that's *feudal*!"

Baiyue nodded. "Well, that's my granddad. He used to make my brother and me kowtow to him and my grandmother at Spring Festival." She frowned and wrinkled her nose. Country customs. Nobody in the city made their children kowtow at New Years. "But you're lucky," Baiyue said to Jieling. "You'll have your uniform debt and dormitory fees, but you haven't started on food debt or anything."

Jieling felt sick. "I stayed in the guesthouse for four days," she said. "They said they would charge it against my wages."

"Oh." Baiyue covered her mouth with her hand. After a moment, she said, "Don't worry, we'll figure something out." Jieling felt more frightened by that than anything else.

Instead of going back to the lab they went upstairs and across a connecting bridge to the dormitories. Naps? Did they get naps?

"Do you know what room you're in?" Baiyue asked.

Jieling didn't. Baiyue took her to ask the floor auntie who looked up Jieling's name and gave her a key and some sheets and a blanket. Back down the hall and around the corner. The room was spare but really nice. Two bunk beds and two chests of drawers, a concrete floor. It had a window. All of the beds were taken except one of the top ones. By the window under the desk were three black boxes hooked to the wall. They were a little bigger than a shoebox. Baiyue flipped open the front of each one. They had names written on them. "Here's a space where we can put your battery." She pointed to an electrical extension.

"What are they?" Jieling said.

"They're the battery boxes. It's what we make. I'll get you one that failed inspection. A lot of them work fine," Baiyue said. "Inside there are electric ray cells to make electricity and symbiotic bacteria. The bacteria breaks down garbage to feed the ray cells. Garbage turned into electricity.

Anti-global warming. No greenhouse gas. You have to feed scraps from the cafeteria a couple of times a week or it will die, but it does best if you feed it a little bit every day."

"It's alive?!" Jieling said.

Baiyue shrugged. "Yeah. Sort of. Supposedly if it does really well, you get credits for the electricity it generates. They charge us for our electricity use, so this helps hold down debt."

The three boxes just sat there looking less alive than a boombox.

"Can you see the cells?" Jieling asked.

Baiyue shook her head. "No, the feed mechanism doesn't let you. They're just like the ones we grow, though, only they've been worked on in the tissue room. They added bacteria."

"Can it make you sick?"

"No, the bacteria can't live in people," Baiyue said. "Can't live anywhere except in the box."

"And it makes electricity,"

Baiyue nodded.

"And people can buy it?"

She nodded again. "We've just started selling them. They say they're going to sell them in China but really, they're too expensive. Americans like them, you know, because of the no global warming. Of course, Americans buy anything."

The boxes were on the wall between the beds, under the window, pretty near where the pillows were on the bottom bunks. She hadn't minded the cells in the lab, but this whole thing was too creepy.

Jieling's first paycheck was startling. She owed 1,974 R.M.B. Almost four months salary if she never ate or bought anything and if she didn't have a dorm room. She went back to her room and climbed into her bunk and looked at the figures. Money deducted for uniforms and shoes, food, her time in the guesthouse.

Her roommates came chattering in a group. Jieling's roommates all worked in packaging. They were nice enough, but they had been friends before Jieling moved in.

"Hey," called Taohua. Then seeing what Jieling had. "Oh, first paycheck."

Jieling nodded. It was like getting a jail sentence.

"Let's see. Oh, not so bad. I owe three times that," Taohua said. She passed the statement on to the other girls. All the girls owed huge amounts. More than a year.

"Don't you care?" Jieling said.

"You mean like little Miss Lei Feng?" Taohua asked. Everyone laughed and Jieling laughed, too, although her face heated up. Miss Lei Feng was what they called Baiyue. Little Miss Goody-goody. Lei Feng, the famous do-gooder soldier who darned his friend's socks on the Long March. He was nobody when he was alive, but when he died, his diary listed all the anonymous good deeds he had done and then he became a Hero. Lei Feng posters hung in elementary schools. He wanted to be "a revolutionary screw that never rusts." It was the kind of thing everybody's grandparents had believed in.

"Does Baiyue have a boyfriend?" Taohua asked, suddenly serious.

"No, no!" Jieling said. It was against the rules to have a boyfriend and Baiyue was always getting in trouble for breaking rules. Things like not having her trays stacked by 5:00 pm although nobody else got in trouble for that.

"If she had a boyfriend," Taohua said, "I could see why she would want to quit. You can't get married if you're in debt. It would be too hard."

"Aren't you worried about your debt?" Jieling asked.

Taohua laughed. "I don't have a boyfriend. And besides, I just got a promotion so soon I'll pay off my debt."

"You'll have to stop buying clothes," one of the other girls said. The company store did have a nice catalogue you could order clothes from, but they were expensive. There was debt limit, based on your salary. If you were promoted, your debt limit would go up.

"Or I'll go to special projects," Taohua said. Everyone knew what special projects was, even though it was supposed to be a big company secret. They were computers made of bacteria. They looked a lot like the boxes in the dormitory rooms. "I've been studying computers," Taohua explained. "Bacterial computers are special. They do many things. They can detect chemicals. They are *massively* parallel."

"What does that mean?" Jieling asked.

"It is hard to explain," Taohua said evasively.

Taohua opened her battery and poured in scraps. It was interesting that Taohua claimed not to care about her debt but kept feeding her battery. Jieling had a battery now, too. It was a reject – the back had broken so that the metal things that sent the electricity back out were exposed and if you touched it wrong, it could give you a shock. No problem, since Jieling had plugged it into the wall and didn't plan to touch it again.

"Besides," Taohua said, "I like it here a lot better than at home."

Better than home. In some ways yes, in some ways no. What would it be like to just give up and belong to the company. Nice things, nice food. Never rich. But never poor, either. Medical care. Maybe it wasn't the worst thing. Maybe Baiyue was a little . . . obsessive.

"I don't care about my debt," Taohua said, serene. "With one more promotion, I'll move to cadres housing."

Jieling reported the conversation to Baiyue. They were getting incubated cells ready to move to the tissue room. In the tissue room they'd be transferred to protein and collagen grid that would guide their growth – line up the cells to approximate an electricity generating system. The tissue room had a weird, yeasty smell.

"She's fooling herself," Baiyue said. "Line girls never get to be cadres. She might get onto special projects, but that's even worse than regular line work because you're never allowed to leave the compound." Baiyue picked up a dish, stuck a little volt reader into the gel and rapped the dish smartly against the lab table.

The needle on the volt gauge swung to indicate the cells had discharged electricity. That was the way they tested to see the cells were generating electricity. A shock made them discharge and the easiest way was to knock them against the table.

Baiyue could sound very bitter about New Life. Jieling didn't like the debt, it scared her a little. But really, Baiyue saw only one side of everything. "I thought you got a pay raise to go to special projects," Jieling said.

Baiyue rolled her eyes. "And more reasons to go in debt, I'll bet."

"How much is your debt?" Jieling asked.

"Still 700," Baiyue said. "Because they told me I had to have new uniforms." She sighed.

"I am so sick of congee," Jieling said. "They're never going to let us get out of debt." Baiyue's way was doomed. She was trying to play by the company's rules and still win. That wasn't Jieling's way. "We have to make money somewhere else," Jieling said.

"Right," Baiyue said. "We work six days a week." And Baiyue often stayed after shift to try to make sure she didn't lose wages on failed cultures. "Out of spec," she said and put it aside. She had taught Jieling to keep the out of specs for a day. Sometimes they improved and could be shipped on. It wasn't the way the supervisor, Ms Wang, explained the job to Jieling, but it cut down on the number of rejects, and that, in turn, cut down on paycheck deductions

"That leaves us Sundays," Jieling said.

"I can't leave the compound this Sunday."

"And if you do, what are they going to do, fire you?" Jieling said.

"I don't think we're supposed to earn money outside of the compound," Baiyue said.

"You are too much of a good girl," Jieling said. "Remember, *it doesn't matter if the cat is black or white, as long as it catches mice.*"

"Is that Mao?" Baiyue asked, frowning.

"No," Jieling said, "Deng Xiaoping, the one after Mao."

"Well, he's dead, too," Baiyue said. She rapped a dish against the counter and the needle on the voltmeter jumped.

Jieling had been working just over four weeks when they were all called to the cafeteria for a meeting. Mr Cao from Human Resources was there. He was wearing a dark suit and standing at the white screen. Other cadres sat in chairs along the back of the stage, looking very stern.

"We are here to discuss a very serious matter," he said. "Many of you know this girl."

There was a laptop hooked up and a very nervous looking boy running it. Jieling looked carefully at the laptop but it didn't appear to be a special projects computer. In fact, it was made in Korea. He did something and an ID picture of a girl flashed on the screen.

Jieling didn't know her. But around her she heard noises of shock, someone sucking air through their teeth, someone else breathed softly, "*Ai-yah*."

"This girl ran away, leaving her debt with New Life. She ate our food, wore our clothes, slept in our beds. And then, like a thief, she ran away." The Human Resources man nodded his head. The boy at the computer changed the image on the big projector screen.

Now it was a picture of the same girl with her head bowed, and two policemen holding her arms.

"She was picked up in Guangdong," the Human Resources man said. "She is in jail there."

The cafeteria was very quiet.

The Human Resources man said, "Her life is ruined, which is what should happen to all thieves."

Then he dismissed them. That afternoon, the picture of the girl with the two policemen appeared on the bulletin boards of every floor of the dormitory.

On Sunday, Baiyue announced, "I'm not going."

She was not supposed to leave the compound, but one of her roommates had female problems – bad cramps – and planned to spend the day in bed drinking tea and reading magazines. Baiyue was going to use her ID to leave.

"You have to," Jieling said. "You want to grow old here? Die a serf to New Life?"

"It's crazy. We can't make money dancing in the plague-trash market."

"I've done it before," Jieling said. "You're scared."

"It's just not a good idea," Baiyue said.

"Because of the girl they caught in Guangdong. We're not skipping out on our debt. We're paying it off."

"We're not supposed to work for someone else when we work here," Baiyue said.

"Oh come on," Jieling said. "You are always making things sound worse than they are. I think you like staying here being little Miss Lei Feng."

"Don't call me that," Baiyue snapped.

"Well, don't act like it. New Life is not being fair. We don't have to be fair. What are they going to do to you if they catch you?"

"Fine me," Baiyue said. "Add to my debt!"

"So what? They're going to find a way to add to your debt no matter what. You are a serf. They are the landlord."

"But if —"

"No but if," Jieling said. "You like being a martyr. I don't."

"What do you care," Baiyue said. "You like it here. If you stay you can eat pork buns every night."

"And you can eat congee for the rest of your life. I'm going to try to do something." Jieling slammed out of the dorm room. She had never said harsh things to Baiyue before. Yes, she had thought about staying here.

But was that so bad? Better than being like Baiyue, who would stay here and have a miserable life. Jieling was not going to have a miserable life, no matter where she stayed or what she did. That was why she had come to Shenzhen in the first place.

She heard the door open behind her and Baiyue ran down the hall. "Okay," she said breathlessly. "I'll try it. Just this once."

The streets of Shanghai were incredibly loud after weeks in the compound. In a shop window, she and Baiyue stopped and watched a news segment on how the fashion in Shanghai was for sarongs. Jieling would have to tell her mother. Of course her mother had a TV and probably already knew. Jieling thought about calling, but not now. Not now. She didn't want to explain about New Life. The next news segment was about the success of the People's Army in Tajikistan. Jieling pulled Baiyue to come on.

They took one bus, and then had to transfer. On Sundays, unless you were lucky, it took forever to transfer because fewer busses ran. They waited almost an hour for the second bus. That bus was almost empty when they got on. They sat down a few seats back from the driver. Baiyue rolled her eyes. "Did you see the guy in the back?" she asked. "Party functionary."

Jieling glanced over her shoulder and saw him. She couldn't miss him, in his careful polo shirt. He had that stiff party-member look.

Baiyue sighed. "My uncle is just like that. So *boring*."

Jieling thought that to be honest, Baiyue would have made a good revolutionary, back in the day. Baiyue liked that kind of revolutionary purity. But she nodded.

The plague-trash market was full on a Sunday. There was a toy seller making tiny little clay figures on sticks. He waved a stick at the girls as they passed. "Cute things!" he called. "I'll make whatever you want!" The stick had a little Donald Duck on it.

"I can't do this," Baiyue said. "There's too many people."

"It's not so bad," Jieling said. She found a place for the boombox. Jieling had brought them to where all the food vendors were. "Stay here and watch this," she said. She hunted through the food stalls and bought a bottle of local beer, counting out from her little horde of money she had left from when she came. She took the beer back to Baiyue. "Drink this," she said. "It will help you be brave."

"I hate beer," Baiyue said.

"Beer or debt," Jieling said.

While Baiyue drank the beer, Jieling started the boombox and did her routine. People smiled at her but no one put any money in her cash box. Shenzhen people were so cheap. Baiyue sat on the curb, nursing her beer, not looking at Jieling or at anyone until finally Jieling couldn't stand it any longer.

"C'mon, *meimei*," she said.

Baiyue seemed a bit surprised to be called little sister but she put the beer down and got up. They had practiced a routine to an M.I.A. song, singing and dancing. It would be a hit, Jieling was sure.

"I can't," Baiyue whispered.

"Yes you can," Jieling said. "You do good."

A couple of people stopped to watch them arguing, so Jieling started the music.

"I feel sick," Baiyue whimpered.

But the beat started and there was nothing to do but dance and sing. Baiyue was so nervous, she forgot at first, but then she got the hang of it. She kept her head down and her face was bright red.

Jieling started making up a rap. She'd never done it before and she hadn't gotten very far before she was laughing and then Baiyue was laughing, too.

Wode meimei hen haixiude
Mei ta shi xuli
Tai hen xiuqi –

> *My little sister is so shy*
> *But she's pretty*
> *Far too delicate –*

They almost stopped because they were giggling but they kept dancing and Jieling went back to the lyrics from the song they had practiced.

When they had finished, people clapped and they'd made thirty-two yuan.

They didn't make as much for any single song after that, but in a few hours they had collected 187 yuan. It was early evening and night entertainers were showing up – a couple of people who sang opera, acrobats, and a clown with a wig of hair so red it looked on fire, stepping stork-legged on stilts waving a rubber Kalashnikov in his hand. He was all dressed in white. Uncle Death, from cartoons during the plague. Some of the day vendors had shut down, and new people were showing up who put out a board and some chairs and served sorghum liquor; clear, white and 150 proof. The crowd was starting to change, too. It was rowdier. Packs of young men dressed in weird combinations of clothes from plague markets – vintage Mao suit jackets and suit pants and peasant shoes. And others, veterans from the Tajikistan conflict, one with an empty trouser leg.

Jieling picked up the boombox and Baiyue took the cash box. Outside of the market it wasn't yet dark.

"You are amazing," Baiyue kept saying. "You are such a special girl!"

"You did great," Jieling said. "When I was by myself, I didn't make anything! Everyone likes you because you are little and cute!"

"Look at this! I'll be out of debt before autumn!"

Maybe it was just the feeling that she was responsible for Baiyue, but Jieling said, "You keep it all."

"I can't! I can't! We split it!" Baiyue said.

"Sure," Jieling said. "Then after you get away, you can help me. Just think, if we do this for three more Sundays, you'll pay off your debt."

"Oh, Jieling," Baiyue said. "You really are like my big sister!"

Jieling was sorry she had ever called Baiyue "little sister." It was such a country thing to do. She had always suspected that Baiyue wasn't a city girl. Jieling hated the countryside. Grain spread to dry in the road and mother's-elder-sister and father's-younger-brother bringing all the cousins over on the day off. Jieling didn't even know all those country ways to say aunt and uncle. It wasn't Baiyue's fault. And Baiyue had been good to her. She was rotten to be thinking this way.

"Excuse me," said a man. He wasn't like the packs of young men with their long hair and plague clothes. Jieling couldn't place him but he seemed familiar. "I saw you in the market. You were very fun. Very lively."

Baiyue took hold of Jieling's arm. For a moment Jieling wondered if maybe he was from New Life, but she told herself that was crazy. "Thank you," she said. She thought she remembered him putting ten yuan in the box. No, she thought, he was on the bus. The party functionary. The party was checking up on them. Now that was funny. She wondered if he would lecture them on Western ways.

"Are you in the music business?" Baiyue asked. She glanced at Jieling, who couldn't help laughing, snorting through her nose.

The man took them very seriously though. "No," he said. "I can't help you there. But I like your act. You seem like girls of good character."

"Thank you," Baiyue said. She didn't look at Jieling again, which was good because Jieling knew she wouldn't be able to keep a straight face.

"I am Wei Rongyi. Maybe I can buy you some dinner?" the man asked. He held up his hands, "Nothing romantic. You are so young, it is like you could be daughters."

"You have a daughter?" Jieling asked.

He shook his head. "Not anymore," he said.

Jieling understood. His daughter had died of the bird flu. She felt embarrassed for having laughed at him. Her soft heart saw instantly that he was treating them like the daughter he had lost.

He took them to a dumpling place on the edge of the market and ordered half a kilo of crescent-shaped pork dumplings and a kilo of square beef dumplings. He was a cadre, a middle manager. His wife had lived in Changsha for a couple of years now, where her family was from. He was from the older generation, people who did not get divorced. All around them, the restaurant was filling up mostly with men stopping after work for dumplings and drinks. They were a little island surrounded by truck drivers and men who worked in the factories in the outer city – tough grimy places.

"What do you do? Are you secretaries?" Wei Rongyi asked.

Baiyue laughed. "As if!" she said.

"We are factory girls," Jieling said. She dunked a dumpling in vinegar. They were so good! Not congee!

"Factory girls!" he said. "I am so surprised!"

Baiyue nodded. "We work for New Life," she explained. "This is our day off, so we wanted to earn a little extra money."

He rubbed his head, looking off into the distance. "New Life," he said, trying to place the name. "New Life . . ."

"Out past the zoo," Baiyue said.

Jieling thought they shouldn't say so much.

"Ah, in the city. A good place? What do they make?" he asked. He had a way of blinking very quickly that was disconcerting.

"Batteries," Jieling said. She didn't say bio-batteries.

"I thought they made computers," he said.

"Oh yes," Baiyue said. "Special projects."

Jieling glared at Baiyue. If this guy gave them trouble at New Life, they'd have a huge problem getting out of the compound.

Baiyue blushed.

Wei laughed. "You are special project girls, then. Well, see, I knew you were not just average factory girls."

He didn't press the issue. Jieling kept waiting for him to make some sort of move on them. Offer to buy them beer. But he didn't, and when they had finished their dumplings, he gave them the leftovers to take back to their dormitories and then stood at the bus stop until they were safely on their bus.

"Are you sure you will be all right?" he asked them when the bus came.

"You can see my window from the bus stop," Jieling promised. "We will be fine."

"Shenzhen can be a dangerous city. You be careful!"

Out the window, they could see him in the glow of the streetlight, waving as the bus pulled away.

"He was so nice," Baiyue sighed. "Poor man."

"Didn't you think he was a little strange?" Jieling asked.

"Everybody is strange anymore," Baiyue said. "After the plague. Not like when we were growing up."

It was true. Her mother was strange. Lots of people were crazy from so many people dying. Jieling held up the leftover dumplings. "Well, anyway. I am not feeding this to my battery," she said. They both tried to smile.

"Our whole generation is crazy," Baiyue said.

"We know everybody dies," Jieling said. Outside the bus window, the streets were full of young people, out trying to live while they could.

They made all their bus connections as smooth as silk. So quick, they were home in forty-five minutes. Sunday night was movie night, and all of Jieling's roommates were at the movie so she and Baiyue could sort the money in Jieling's room. She used her key card and the door clicked open.

Mr Wei was kneeling by the battery boxes in their room. He started and hissed, "Close the door!"

Jieling was so surprised she did.

"Mr Wei!" Baiyue said.

He was dressed like an army man on a secret mission, all in black. He showed them a little black gun. Jieling blinked in surprise. "Mr Wei!" she said. It was hard to take him seriously. Even all in black, he was still weird Mr Wei, blinking rapidly behind his glasses.

"Lock the door," he said. "And be quiet."

"The door locks by itself," Jieling explained. "And my roommates will be back soon."

"Put a chair in front of the door," he said and shoved the desk chair towards them. Baiyue pushed it under the door handle. The window was open and Jieling could see where he had climbed on the desk and left a footprint on Taohua's fashion magazine. Taohua was going to be pissed. And what was Jieling going to say? If anyone found out there was a man in her room, she was going to be in very big trouble.

"How did you get in?" she asked. "What about the cameras?" There were security cameras.

He showed them a little spray can. "Special paint. It just makes things look foggy and dim. Security guards are so lazy anymore no one ever checks things out." He paused a moment, clearly disgusted with the lax morality of the day. "Miss Jieling," he said. "Take that screwdriver and finish unscrewing that computer from the wall."

Computer? She realized he meant the battery boxes.

Baiyue's eyes got very big. "Mr Wei! You're a thief!"

Jieling shook her head. "A corporate spy."

"I am a patriot," he said. "But you young people wouldn't understand that. Sit on the bed." He waved the gun at Baiyue.

The gun was so little it looked like a toy and it was difficult to be afraid, but still Jieling thought it was good that Baiyue sat.

Jieling knelt. It was her box that Mr Wei had been disconnecting. It was all the way to the right, so he had started with it. She had come to feel a little bit attached to it, thinking of it sitting there, occasionally zapping electricity back into the grid, reducing her electricity costs and her debt. She sighed and unscrewed it. Mr Wei watched.

She jimmied it off the wall, careful not to touch the contacts. The cells built up a charge, and when they were ready, a switch tapped a membrane and they discharged. It was all automatic and there was no knowing when it was going to happen. Mr Wei was going to be very upset when he realized that this wasn't a computer.

"Put it on the desk," he said.

She did.

"Now sit with your friend."

Jieling sat down next to Baiyue. Keeping a wary eye on them, he sidled over to the bio-battery. He opened the hatch where they dumped garbage in them, and tried to look in as well as look at them. "Where are the controls?" he asked. He picked it up, his palm flat against the broken back end where the contacts were exposed.

"Tap it against the desk," Jieling said. "Sometimes the door sticks." There wasn't actually a door. But it had just come into her head. She hoped that the cells hadn't discharged in a while.

Mr Wei frowned and tapped the box smartly against the desktop.

Torpedinidae, the electric ray, can generate a current of 200 volts for approximately a minute. The power output is close to 1 kilowatt over the course of the discharge and while this won't kill the average person, it is a powerful shock. Mr Wei stiffened and fell, clutching the box and spasming wildly. One . . . two . . . three . . . four . . . Mr Wei was still spasming. Jieling and Baiyue looked at each other. Gingerly, Jieling stepped around Mr Wei. He had dropped the little gun. Jieling picked it up. Mr Wei was still spasming. Jieling wondered if he was going to die. Or if he was already dead and the electricity was just making him jump. She didn't want him to die. She looked at the little gun and it made her feel even sicker so she threw it out the window.

Finally Mr Wei dropped the box.

Baiyue said, "Is he dead?"

Jieling was afraid to touch him. She couldn't tell if he was breathing. Then he groaned and both girls jumped.

"He's not dead," Jieling said.

"What should we do?" Baiyue asked.

"Tie him up," Jieling said. Although she wasn't sure what they'd do with him then.

Jieling used the cord to her boombox to tie his wrists. When she grabbed his hands he gasped and struggled feebly. Then she took her pillowcase and cut along the blind end, a space just wide enough that his head would fit through.

"Sit him up," she said to Baiyue.

"You sit him up," Baiyue said. Baiyue didn't want to touch him.

Jieling pulled Mr Wei into a sitting position. "Put the pillowcase over his head," she said. The pillowcase was like a shirt with no armholes, so when Baiyue pulled it over his head and shoulders, it pinned his arms against his sides and worked something like a straitjacket.

Jieling took his wallet and his identification papers out of his pocket. "Why would someone carry their wallet to a break-in?" she asked. "He has six ID papers. One says he is Mr Wei."

"Wow," Baiyue said. "Let me see. Also Mr Ma. Mr Zhang. Two Mr Liu's and a Mr Cui."

Mr Wei blinked, his eyes watering.

"Do you think he has a weak heart?" Baiyue asked.

"I don't know," Jieling said. "Wouldn't he be dead if he did?"

Baiyue considered this.

"Baiyue! Look at all this yuan!" Jieling emptied the wallet, counting. Almost eight thousand yuan!

"Let me go," Mr Wei said weakly.

Jieling was glad he was talking. She was glad he seemed like he might be all right. She didn't know what they would do if he died. They would never be able to explain a dead person. They would end up in deep debt. And probably go to jail for something. "Should we call the floor auntie and tell him that he broke in?" Jieling asked.

"We could," Baiyue said.

"Do not!" Mr Wei said, sounding stronger. "You don't understand! I'm from Beijing!"

"So is my stepfather," Jieling said. "Me, I'm from Baoding. It's about an hour south of Beijing."

Mr Wei said, "I'm from the government! That money is government money!"

"I don't believe you," Jieling said. "Why did you come in through the window?" Jieling asked.

"Secret agents always come in through the window?" Baiyue said and started to giggle.

"Because this place is counter-revolutionary!" Mr Wei said.

Baiyue covered her mouth with her hand. Jieling felt embarrassed, too. No one said things like "counter-revolutionary" anymore.

"This place! It is making things that could make China strong!" he said.

"Isn't that good?" Baiyue asked.

"But they don't care about China! Only about money. Instead of using it for China, they sell it to America!" he said. Spittle was gathering at the corner of his mouth. He was starting to look deranged. "Look at this place! Officials are all concerned about *guanxi*!" Connections. Kickbacks. Guanxi ran China, everybody knew that.

"So, maybe you have an anti-corruption investigation?" Jieling said. There were lots of anti-corruption investigations. Jieling's stepfather said that they usually meant someone powerful was mad at their brother-in-law or something, so they accused them of corruption.

Mr Wei groaned. "There is no one to investigate them."

Baiyue and Jieling looked at each other.

Mr Wei explained, "In my office, the Guangdong office, there used to be twenty people. Special operatives. Now there is only me and Ms Yang."

Jieling said, "Did they all die of bird flu?"

Mr Wei shook his head. "No, they all went to work on contract for Saudi Arabia. You can make a lot of money in the Middle East. A lot more than in China."

"Why don't you and Ms Yang go work in Saudi Arabia?" Baiyue asked.

Jieling thought Mr Wei would give some revolutionary speech. But he just hung his head. "She is the secretary. I am the bookkeeper." And then in a smaller voice, "She is going to Kuwait to work for Mr Liu."

They probably did not need bookkeepers in the Middle East. Poor Mr Wei. No wonder he was such a terrible secret agent.

"The spirit of the revolution is gone," he said, and there were real, honest to goodness tears in his eyes. "Did you know that Tiananmen Square was built by volunteers? People would come after their regular job and lay the paving of the square. Today people look to Hong Kong."

"Nobody cares about a bunch of old men in Beijing," Baiyue said.

"Exactly! We used to have a strong military! But now the military is too worried about their own factories and farms! They want us to pull out of Tajikistan because it is ruining their profits!"

This sounded like a good idea to Jieling, but she had to admit, she hated the news so she wasn't sure why they were fighting in Tajikistan anyway. Something about Muslim terrorists. All she knew about Muslims was that they made great street food.

"Don't you want to be patriots?" Mr Wei said.

"You broke into my room and tried to steal my – you know that's not a computer, don't you?" Jieling said. "It's a bio-battery. They're selling them to the Americans. Wal-Mart."

Mr Wei groaned.

"We don't work in special projects," Baiyue said.

"You said you did," he protested.

"We did not," Jieling said. "You just thought that. How did you know this was my room?"

"The company lists all its workers in a directory," he said wearily. "And it's movie night, everyone is either out or goes to the movies. I've had the building under surveillance for weeks. I followed you to the market today. Last week it was a girl named Pingli, who blabbed about everything, but she wasn't in special projects.

"I put you on the bus, I've timed the route three times. I should have had an hour and fifteen minutes to drive over here and get the box and get out."

"We made all our connections," Baiyue explained.

Mr Wei was so dispirited he didn't even respond.

Jieling said, "I thought the government was supposed to help workers. If we get caught, we'll be fined and we'll be deeper in debt." She was just talking. Talking, talking, talking too much. This was too strange. Like when someone was dying. Something extraordinary was happening, like your father dying in the next room, and yet the ordinary things went on, too. You made tea, your mother opened the shop the next day and sewed clothes while she cried. People came in and pretended not to notice. This was like that. Mr Wei had a gun and they were explaining about New Life.

"Debt?" Mr Wei said.

"To the company," she said. "We are all in debt. The company hires us and says they are going to pay us, but then they charge us for our food and our clothes and our dorm and it always costs more than we earn. That's why we were doing rap today. To make money to be able to quit." Mr Wei's glasses had tape holding the arm on. Why hadn't she noticed that in the restaurant? Maybe because when you are afraid you notice things. When your father is dying of the plague, you notice the way the covers on your mother's chairs need to be washed. You wonder if you will have to do it or if you will die before you have to do chores.

"The Pingli girl," he said, "she said the same thing. That's illegal."

"Sure," Baiyue said. "Like anybody cares."

"Could you expose corruption?" Jieling asked.

Mr Wei shrugged, at least as much as he could in the pillowcase. "Maybe. But they would just pay bribes to locals and it would all go away."

All three of them sighed.

"Except," Mr Wei said, sitting up a little straighter. "The Americans. They are always getting upset about that sort of thing. Last year there was a corporation, the Shanghai Six. The Americans did a documentary on them and then western companies would not do business. If they got information from us about what New Life is doing . . ."

"Who else is going to buy bio-batteries?" Baiyue said. "The company would be in big trouble!"

"Beijing can threaten a big exposé, tell the *New York Times* newspaper!" Mr Wei said, getting excited. "My Beijing supervisor will love that! He loves media!"

"Then you can have a big show trial," Jieling said.

Mr Wei was nodding.

"But what is in it for us?" Baiyue said.

"When there's a trial, they'll have to cancel your debt!" Mr Wei said. "Even pay you a big fine!"

"If I call the floor auntie and say I caught a corporate spy, they'll give me a big bonus," Baiyue said.

"Don't you care about the other workers?" Mr Wei asked.

Jieling and Baiyue looked at each other and shrugged. Did they? "What are they going to do to you anyway?" Jieling said. "You can still do big expose. But that way we don't have to wait."

"Look," he said, "you let me go, and I'll let you keep my money."

Someone rattled the door handle.

"Please," Mr Wei whispered. "You can be heroes for your fellow workers, even though they'll never know it."

Jieling stuck the money in her pocket. Then she took the papers, too.

"You can't take those," he said.

"Yes I can," she said. "If after six months, there is no big corruption scandal? We can let everyone know how a government secret agent was outsmarted by two factory girls."

"Six months!" he said. "That's not long enough!"

"It better be," Jieling said.

Outside the door, Taohua called, "Jieling? Are you in there? Something is wrong with the door!"

"Just a minute," Jieling called. "I had trouble with it when I came home." To Mr Wei she whispered sternly, "Don't you try anything. If you do, we'll scream our heads off and everybody will come running." She and Baiyue shimmied the pillowcase off of Mr Wei's head. He started to stand up and jerked the boombox, which clattered across the floor. "Wait!" she hissed and untied him.

Taohua called through the door, "What's that?"

"Hold on!" Jieling called.

Baiyue helped Mr Wei stand up. Mr Wei climbed onto the desk and then grabbed a line hanging outside. He stopped a moment as if trying to think of something to say.

"'A revolution is not a dinner party, or writing an essay, or painting a picture, or doing embroidery," Jieling said. It had been her father's favorite quote from Chairman Mao. "'. . . it cannot be so refined, so leisurely and gentle, so temperate, kind, courteous, restrained and magnanimous. A revolution is an insurrection, an act of violence by which one class overthrows another.'"

Mr Wei looked as if he might cry and not because he was moved by patriotism. He stepped back and disappeared. Jieling and Baiyue looked out the window. He did go down the wall just like a secret agent from a movie, but it was only two stories. There was still the big footprint in the middle of Taohua's magazine and the room looked as if it had been hit by a storm.

"They're going to think you had a boyfriend," Baiyue whispered to Jieling.

"Yeah," Jieling said, pulling the chair out from under the door handle. "And they're going to think he's rich."

It was Sunday, and Jieling and Baiyue were sitting on the beach. Jieling's cell phone rang, a little chime of M.I.A. hip-hop. Even though it was Sunday, it was one of the girls from New Life. Sunday should be a day off, but she took the call anyway.

"Jieling? This is Xia Meili? From packaging. Taohua told me about your business? Maybe you could help me?"

Jieling said, "Sure. What is your debt, Meili?"

"3,800 R.M.B.," Meili said. "I know it's a lot."

Jieling said, "Not so bad. We have a lot of people who already have loans, though, and it will probably be a few weeks before I can make you a loan."

With Mr Wei's capital, Jieling and Baiyue had opened a bank account. They had bought themselves out, and then started a little loan business where they bought people out of New Life. Then people had to pay them back with a little extra. They had each had jobs – Jieling worked for a company that made toys. She sat each day at a table where she put a piece of specially shaped plastic over the body of a little doll, an action figure. The plastic fit right over the figure and had cut-outs. Jieling sprayed the whole thing with red paint and when the piece of plastic was lifted, the action figure had a red shirt. It was boring, but at the end of the week, she got paid instead of owing the company money.

She and Baiyue used all their extra money on loans to get girls out of New Life. More and more loans, and more and more payments. Now

New Life had sent them a threatening letter saying that what they were doing was illegal. But Mr Wei said not to worry. Two officials had come and talked to them and had showed them legal documents and had them explain everything about what had happened. Soon, the officials promised, they would take New Life to court.

Jieling wasn't so sure about the officials. After all, Mr Wei was an official. But a foreign newspaperman had called them. He was from a newspaper called *The Wall Street Journal* and he said that he was writing a story about labor shortages in China after the bird flu. He said that in some places in the west there were reports of slavery. His Chinese was very good. His story was going to come out in the United States tomorrow. Then she figured officials would have to do something or lose face.

Jieling told Meili to call her back in two weeks – although hopefully in two weeks no one would need help to get away from New Life – and wrote a note to herself in her little notebook.

Baiyue was sitting looking at the water. "This is the first time I've been to the beach," she said.

"The ocean is so big, isn't it?"

Baiyue nodded, scuffing at the white sand. "People always say that, but you don't know until you see it."

Jieling said, "Yeah." Funny, she had lived here for months. Baiyue had lived here more than a year. And they had never come to the beach. The beach was beautiful.

"I feel sorry for Mr Wei," Baiyue said.

"You do?" Jieling said. "Do you think he really had a daughter who died?"

"Maybe," Baiyue said. "A lot of people died."

"My father died," Jieling said.

Baiyue looked at her, a quick little sideways look, then back out at the ocean. "My mother died," she said.

Jieling was surprised. She had never known that Baiyue's mother was dead. They had talked about so much but never about that. She put her arm around Baiyue's waist and they sat for a while.

"I feel bad in a way," Baiyue said.

"How come?" Jieling said.

"Because we had to steal capital to fight New Life. That makes us capitalists."

Jieling shrugged.

"I wish it was like when they fought the revolution," Baiyue said. "Things were a lot more simple."

"Yeah," Jieling said, "and they were poor and a lot of them died."

"I know," Baiyue sighed.

Jieling knew what she meant. It would be nice to . . . to be sure what was right and what was wrong. Although not if it made you like Mr Wei.

Poor Mr Wei. Had his daughter really died?

"Hey," Jieling said, "I've got to make a call. Wait right here." She walked a little down the beach. It was windy and she turned her back to guard protect the cell phone, like someone lighting a match. "Hello," she said, "hello, mama, it's me. Jieling."

DAYS OF WONDER

Geoff Ryman

Born in Canada, Geoff Ryman now lives in England. He made his first sale in 1976, to *New Worlds*, but it was not until 1984, when he made his first appearance in *Interzone* – the magazine where much of his published short fiction has appeared – with his brilliant novella *The Unconquered Country* that he first attracted any serious attention. *The Unconquered Country*, one of the best novellas of the decade, had a stunning impact on the science fiction scene of the day, and almost overnight established Ryman as one of the most accomplished writers of his generation, winning him both the British Science Fiction Award and the World Fantasy Award; it was later published in a book version, *The Unconquered Country: A Life History*. His output has been sparse since then by the high-production standards of the genre, but extremely distinguished, with his novel *The Child Garden: A Low Comedy*, which won both the prestigious Arthur C. Clarke Award and the John W. Campbell Memorial Award; his later novel *Air* also won the Arthur C. Clarke Award. His other novels include *The Warrior Who Carried Life*; the critically acclaimed mainstream novel *Was*; *Coming of Enkidu*; *The King's Last Song*; *Lust*; and the underground cult classic *253*, the "print remix" of an "interactive hypertext novel" that in its original form ran online on Ryman's home page, ryman.com, and which in its print form won the Philip K. Dick Award. Four of his novellas have been collected in *Unconquered Countries*. His most recent book is a new novel, *When It Changed*.

In the eloquent story that follows, he takes us to the far future, long after humans have become extinct, to show us one individual's quest to piece together some of the Old Knowledge in the face of desperate odds and at the cost of everything she loves.

LEVEZA WAS THE wrong name for her; she was big and strong, not light. Her bulk made her seem both male and female; her shoulders were broad but so were her hips and breasts.

She had beautiful eyes, round and black, and she was thoughtful; her heavy jaws would grind round and round as if imitating the continual motion of her mind. She always looked as if she were listening to something distant, faraway.

Like many large people, Leveza was easily embarrassed. Her mane would bristle up across the top of her head and down her spine. She was strong and soft all at once, and kind. I liked talking to her; her voice was so high and gentle, though her every gesture was blurting and forlorn.

But that voice when it went social! If Leveza saw a Cat crouching in the grass, her whinnying was sudden, fierce and irresistible. All of us would pirouette into a panic at once. Her cry was infallible.

So she was an *afrirador*, one of our sharpshooters, always reared up onto hindquarters to keep watch, always carrying a rifle, always herself a target. My big brave friend. Her rear buttocks grew ever more heavy from constant standing. She could walk upright like an Ancestor for a whole day. Her pelt was beautiful, her best feature, a glossy deep chestnut, no errant Ancestor reds. As rich and deep as the soil under the endless savannah.

We were groom-mates in our days of wonder.

I would brush her, and her hide would twitch with pleasure. She would stretch with it, as if it were taffy to be pulled. We tried on earrings, or tied bows into manes, or corn-rowed them into long braids. But Leveza never rested long with simple pleasures or things easily understood.

Even young, before bearing age, she was serious and adult. I remember her as a filly, slumped at the feet of the stallions as they smoked their pipes, played checkers, and talked about what they would do if they knew how to make electricity.

Leveza would say that we could make turning blades to circulate air; we could pump water to irrigate grass. We could boil water, or make heat to dry and store cud-cakes. The old men would chuckle to hear her dreaming.

I thought it was a pointless game, but Leveza could play it better than anyone, seeing further and deeper into her own inherited head. Her groom-sister Ventoo always teased her, "Leveza, what are you fabricating now?"

We all knew that stuff. I knew oh so clearly, how to wrap thin metal round and round a pivot and with electricity, make it spin. But who could be bothered? I loved to run. All of us foals would suddenly sprint through long grass to make the ground thunder, to raise up the sweet smells of herbs, and to test our strength. We had fire in our loins and we wanted to gallop all the way to the sun. Leveza pondered.

She didn't like it when her first heat came. The immature bucks would hee-haw at her and pull back their feeling lips to display their great white plates of teeth. When older men bumped her buttocks with their heads, she would give a little backward kick, and if they tried to mount her, she walked out from under them. And woe betide any low-grade drifter who presumed that Leveza's lack of status meant she was grateful for attention. She would send the poor bag of bones rattling through the long grass. The babysquirrels clutched their sides and laughed. "Young NeverLove wins again."

But I knew. It was not a lack of love that made my groom-mate so careful and reserved. It was an abundance of love, a surfeit of it, more than our kind is meant to have, can afford to have, for we live on the pampas and our cousins eat us.

Love came upon Leveza on some warm night, the moon like bedtime milk. She would not have settled for a quick bump with a reeking male just because the air wavered with hot hormones. I think it would have been the reflection of milklight in black eyes, a gentle ruffling of upper lip, perhaps a long and puzzled chat about the nature of this life and its consequences.

We are not meant to love. We are meant to mate, stand side by side for warmth for a short time afterward, and then forget. *I wonder who fathered this one?*

Leveza knew and would never forget. She never said his name, but most of us knew who he was. I sometimes caught her looking toward the circle of the Great Men, her eyes full of gentleness. They would gallop about at headball, or talk seriously about axle grease. None of them looked her way, but she would be smiling with a gentle glowing love, her eyes fixed on one of them as steadily as the moon.

One night, she tugged at my mane. "Akwa, I am going to sprog," she said, with a wrench of a smile at the absurdity of such a thing.

"Oh! Oh Leveza, that's wonderful. Why didn't you tell me, how did this happen?"

She ronfled in amusement, a long ruffling snort. "In the usual way, my friend."

"No, but . . . oh you know! I have seen you with no one."

She went still. "Of course not."

"Do you know which one?"

Her whole face was in milklight. "Yes. Oh yes."

Leveza was both further back toward an Ancestor than anyone I ever met, and furthest forward toward the beasts. Even then it was as if she was pulled in two directions, Earth and stars. The night around us would sigh with multiple couplings. I was caught up in the season. Sex was like a river, washing all around us. I was a young mare then, I can tell you, wide of haunch, slim of ankle. I plucked my way through the grass as if it were the strings of a harp. All the highest-rankers would come and snuffle me, and I surprised myself. Oh! I was a pushover. One after another after another.

I would come back feeling like a pasture grazed flat; and she would be lumped out on the ground, content and ready to welcome me. I nuzzled her ear, which flicked me like I was a fly, and I would lay my head on her buttock to sleep.

"You are a strange one," I would murmur. "But you will be kind to my babes. We will have a lovely house." I knew she would love my babies as her own.

That year the dry season did not come.

It did go cooler, the afternoon downpours were fewer, but the grass did not go gray. There was dew when we got up, sparkling and cold with our morning mouthfuls. Some rain came at nighttime in short, soft caresses rather than pummeling on our pavilion roofs. I remember screens pulled down, the smell of grass, and warm breath of a groom-mate against my haunches.

"I'm preggers too," I said some weeks later and giggled, thrilled and full of butterflies. I was young, eh? In my fourth year. I could feel my baby nudge. Leveza and I giggled together under our shawls.

It did not go sharply cold. No grass-frost made our teeth ache. We waited for the triggering, but it did not come.

"Strangest year I can remember," said the old women. They were grateful, for migrations were when they were eaten.

That year! We made porridge for the toothless. We groomed and groomed, beads and bows and necklaces and shawls and beautiful grass hats. Leveza loved it when I made up songs; the first, middle and last word of every line would rhyme. She'd snort and shake her mane and say, "How did you do that; that's so clever!"

We would stroke each other's stomachs as our nipples swelled. Leveza hated hers; they were particularly large like aubergines. "Uh. They're gross. Nobody told me they wobble in the way of everything." They ached to give milk; early in her pregnancy they started to seep. There was a scrum of babysquirrels around her every morning. Businesslike, she sniffed and let them suckle. "When my baby comes, you'll have to wait your turn." The days and nights came and went like the beating of birdlike wings. She got a bit bigger, but never too big to stand guard.

Leveza gave birth early, after only nine months.

It was midwinter, in dark Fehveroo when no one was ready. Leveza pushed her neck up against my mouth for comfort. When I woke she said, "Get Grama for me." Grama was a high-ranking midwife.

I was stunned. She could not be due yet. The midwives had stored no oils or bark-water. I ran to Grama, woke her, worried her. I hoofed the air in panic. "Why is this happening now? What's wrong?"

By the time we got back, Leveza had delivered. Just one push and the babe had arrived, a little bundle of water and skin and grease on the ground behind her rear quarters.

The babe was tiny, as long as a shin, palomino, and covered in soft orange down so light that he looked hairless. No jaw at all. How would he grind grass? Limbs all in soft folds like clouds. Grama said nothing, but held up his feet for me to see. The forelegs had no hoof-buds at all, just fingers; and his hind feet were great soft mitts. Not quite a freak, streamlined and beautiful in a way. But fragile, defenceless, and nothing that would help Leveza climb the hierarchy. It was the most Ancestral child I had ever seen.

Grama set to licking him clean. I looked at the poor babe's face. I could see his hide through the sparse hair on his cheeks. "Hello," I said. "I'm your groom-mummy. Your name is Kaway. Yes it is. You are Kaway."

A blank. He couldn't talk. He could hardly move.

I had to pick him up with my hands. There was no question of using my mouth; there was no pelt to grip. I settled the babe next to Leveza. Her face shone love down on him. "He's beautiful as he is."

Grama jerked her head toward the partition; we went outside to talk. "I've heard of such births; they happen sometimes. The inheritances come together like cards shuffling. He won't learn to talk until he's two. He won't walk until then, either. He won't really be mobile until three or four."

"Four!" I thought of all those migrations.

Grama shrugged. "They can live long, if they make it past infancy. Maybe fifty years."

I was going to ask where they were now, and then I realized. They don't linger in this world, these soft sweet angelic things.

They get eaten.

My little Choova was born two months later. I hated childbirth. I thought I would be good at it, but I thrashed and stomped and hee-hawed like a male in season. *I will never do this again!* I promised. I didn't think then that the promise would come true.

"Come on, babe, come on, my darling," Leveza said, butting me with her nose as if herding a filly. "It will be over soon, just keep pushing."

Grama had become a friend; I think she saw value in Leveza's mindful way of doing things. "Listen to your family," she told me.

My firstborn finally bedraggled her way out, tawny, knobbly, shivering and thin, pulled by Grama. Leveza scooped my baby up, licked her clean, breathed into her, and then dandled her in front of my face. "This is your beautiful mother." Choova looked at me with intelligent love and grinned.

Grama whinnied the cry that triggers *Happy Birth*! Some of our friends trotted up to see my beautiful babe, stuck their heads through the curtains. They tossed their heads, chortled and nibbled the back of her neck.

"Come on, little one. Stand! Stand!" This is what the ladies had come to see. Leveza propped Choova up on her frail, awkward, heartbreaking legs, and walked her toward me. My baby stumbled forward and collapsed like a pile of sticks, into the sheltering bay of my stomach.

Leveza lowered Kaway in front of Choova's nostrils. "And this is your little groom-brother Kaway."

"Kaway," Choova said.

Our family numbered four.

We did not migrate for one whole year. The colts and fillies would skitter unsteadily across the grass, safe from predators. The old folk sunned themselves on the grass and gossiped. High summer came back with sweeping curtains of rain. Then the days shortened; things cooled and dried.

Water started to come out of the wells muddy; we filtered it. The grass started to go crisp. There was perhaps a month or two of moisture left in the ground. Our children neared the end of their first year, worthy of the name foal.

Except for Leveza's. Kaway lay there like an egg after all these months. He could just about move his eyes. Almost absurdly, Leveza loved him as if he were whole and well.

"You are a miracle," she said to Kaway. People called him the Lump. She would look at him, her face all dim with love, and she would say her fabricated things. She would look at me rapt with wonder.

"What if he knows what the Ancestors knew? We know about cogs and gears and motors and circuits. What if Kaway is born knowing about electricity? About medicine and machines? What he might tell us!"

She told him stories and the stories went like this.

The Ancestors so loved the animals that when the world was dying, they took them into themselves. They made extra seeds for them, hidden away in their own to carry us safely inside themselves, all the animals they most loved.

The sickness came, and the only way for them to escape was to let the seeds grow. And so we flowered out of them; the sickness was strong, and they disappeared.

Leveza looked down at her little ancestral lump. Some of us would have left such a burden out on the plain for the Cats or the Dogs or the scavenging oroobos. But not Leveza. She could carry anything.

I think Leveza loved everyone. Everyone, in this devouring world. And that's why what happened, happened.

The pampas near the camp went bald in patches, where the old and weak had overgrazed it. Without realizing, we began to prepare.

The babysquirrels gathered metal nuts. The bugs in their tummies made them from rust in the ground. The old uncles would smelt them for knives, rifle barrels, and bullets. Leveza asked them to make some rods.

She heated them and bent them backward and Grama looked at them and asked, "What kind of rifle is that going to make, one that shoots backward?"

"It's for Kaway," Leveza replied. She cut off her mane for fabric. I cut mine as well, and to our surprise, so did Grama.

Leveza wove a saddle for her back, so the baby could ride.

Once Grama had always played the superior high-ranker, bossy and full of herself. "Oh, Leveza, how clever. What a good idea." And then, "I'm sorry what I said, earlier." She slipped Leveza's inert mushroom of a boy into the saddle.

Grama had become kind.

Grama being respectful about Leveza and Kaway set a fashion for appreciating who my groom-mate was. Nobody asked me anymore why on Earth I was with her. When the Head Man Fortchee began talking regularly to her about migration defenses, a wave of gossip convulsed the herd. Could Leveza become the Head Mare? Was the Lump really Fortchee's son?

"She's always been so smart, so brave," said Ventoo.

"More like a man," said Lindalfa, with a wrench of a smile.

*

One morning, the Head Man whinnied over and over and trod the air with his forelegs.

Triggered.

Migration.

We took down the pavilions and the windbreaks and stacked the grass-leaf panels in carts. We loaded all our tools and pipes and balls and blankets, and most precious of all, the caked and blackened foundries. The camp's babysquirrels lined up, and chattered goodbye to us, as if they really cared. Everyone nurtured the squirrels, and used them as they use us; even Cats will never eat them.

It started out a fine migration. Oats lined the length of the trail. As we ate, we scattered oat seed behind us, to replace it. Shit, oat seed, and inside the shit, flakes of plastic our bellies made, but there were no squirrels to gather it.

It did not rain, but the watering holes and rivers stayed full. It was sunny but not so hot that flies tormented us.

In bad years your hide never stops twitching because you can't escape the stench of Cat piss left to dry on the ground. That year the ground had been washed and the air was calm and sweet.

We saw no Cats. Dogs, we saw Dogs, but fat and jolly Dogs stuffed to the brim with quail and partridge which Cats don't eat. "Lovely weather!" the Dogs called to us, tongues hanging out, grins wide, and we whinnied back, partly in relief. We can see off Dogs, except when they come in packs.

Leveza walked upright the whole time, gun at the ready, Kaway strapped to her back.

"Leveza," I said, "you'll break your back! Use your palmhoofs!"

She grunted. "Any Cat comes near our babies, and it will be one sorry Cat!"

"What Cats? We've seen none."

"They depend on the migrations. We've missed one. They will be very, very hungry."

Our first attack came the next day. I thought it had started to rain; there was just a hissing in the grass, and I turned and I saw old Alez; I saw her eyes rimmed with white, the terror stare. I didn't even see the four Cats that gripped her legs.

Fortchee brayed a squealing sound of panic. Whoosh, we all took off. I jumped into a gallop, I can tell you, no control or thought; I was away; all I wanted was the rush of grass under my hands.

Then I heard a shot and I turned back and I saw Leveza, all alone, standing up, rifle leveled. A Cat was spinning away from Alez, as if it were a spring-pasture caper. The other Cats stared. Leveza fired again once more and they flickered like fire and were gone. Leveza flung herself flat onto the grass just before a crackling like tindersticks come out of the long grass.

The Cats had guns too.

Running battle.

"Down down!" I shouted to the foals. I galloped toward them. "Just! Get! Flat!" I jumped on top them, ramming them down into the dirt. They wailed in panic and fear. "Get off me! Get off me!" My little Choova started to cry. "I didn't do anything wrong!"

I was all teeth. "What did we tell you about an attack? You run and when the gunfire starts you flatten. What did I say! What did I say?"

Gunsmoke drifted; the dry grass sparkled with shot, our nostrils shivered from the smell of burning.

Cats prefer to pounce first, get one of us down, and have the rest of us gallop away. They know if they fire first, they're more likely to be shot themselves.

The fire from our women was fierce, determined, and constant. We soon realized that the only gunfire we heard was our own and that the Cats had slunk away.

The children still wailed, faces crumpled, tears streaming. Their crying just made us grumpy. Well, we all thought, it's time they learned. "You stupid children. What did you think this was, a game?"

Grama was as hard as any granny. "Do you want to be torn to pieces and me have to watch it happen? Do you think you can say to a Cat very nicely, 'Please don't eat me,' and that will stop them?"

Leveza was helping Alez to stand. Her old groom-mother's legs kept giving way, and she was grinning a wide rictus grin. She looked idiotic.

"Come on, love, that's it." Leveza eased Alez toward Pronto's cart.

"What are you doing?" Pronto said, glaring at her.

"She's in no fit state to walk."

"You mean, I'm supposed to haul her?"

"I know you'd much rather leave her to be eaten, but no thanks, not just this once."

Somehow, more like a goat than a Horse, Alez nipped up into the wagon. Leveza strode back toward us, still on her hind legs.

The children shivered and sobbed. Leveza strode up to us. And then did something new.

"Aw, babies," she said, in a stricken tone I had never heard before. She dropped down on four haunches next to them. "Oh, darlings!" She caressed their backs, laying her jaw on the napes of their necks. "It shouldn't be like this, I know. It is terrible, I know. But we are the only thing they have to eat."

"Mummy shouted at me! She was mean."

"That's because Mummy was so worried and so frightened for you. She was scared because you didn't know what it was and didn't know what to do. Mummy was so frightened that she would lose you."

"The Cats eat us!"

"And the crocodiles in the river. And there are wolves, a kind of Dog. We don't get many here, they are on the edge of the snows in the forests. Here, we get the Cats."

Leveza pulled back their manes and breathed into their nostrils. "It shouldn't be like this."

Should or shouldn't, we thought, that's how it is. Why waste energy wishing it wasn't?

We'd forgotten, you see, that it was a choice, a choice that in the end was ours. Not my Leveza.

The Head Man came up, and his voice was also gentle with the colts and fillies. "Come on, kids. The Cats will be back. We need to move away from here."

He had to whinny to get us moving; he even back-kicked the reluctant Pronto. Alez sat up in the cart looking cross-eyed and beside herself with delight at being carried.

"Store and dry cud," Fortchee told us.

Cudcakes. How I hate cudcakes. You chew them and spit them out on the carts to dry and you always think you'll remember where yours are and you always end up eating someone else's mash of grass and spit.

Leveza walked next to the Head Man, looking at maps, murmuring and tossing her mane toward the east. I saw them make up their minds about something.

I even felt a little tail-flick of jealousy. When she came back, I said a bit sharply, "What was that all about?"

Leveza sounded almost pleased. "Don't tell the others. We're being stalked."

"What?"

"Must be slim pickings. The Cats have left their camp. They've got their cubs with them. They're following us." She sighed, her eyes on the horizon. "It's a nuisance. They think they can herd us. There'll be some kind of trap set ahead, so we've decided to change our route."

We turned directly east. The ground started to rise, toward the hills, where an age-old trail goes through a pass. Rocks began to break through a mat of thick grasses. The slope steepened, and each of the carts needed two big men to haul it up.

The trail followed valleys between high rough humps of ground, dovetailing with small streams cut deeply into the grass. We could hear the water, like thousands of tongues lapping on stone. The most important thing on a migration is to get enough to drink. The water in the streams was delicious, cold and tasting of rocks, not mud.

My name means water, but I think I must taste of mud.

We found ourselves in a new world, looking out on waves of earth, rising and falling and going blue in the distance. On the top of a distant ridge a huge rock stuck out, with a rounded dome like a skull.

Fortchee announced, "We need to make that rock by evening." It was already early afternoon, and everyone groaned.

"Or you face the Cats out here on open ground," he said.

"Come on, you're wasting breath," said Leveza and strode on.

The ground was strange; a deep rich black smelling deliciously of grass and leaves, and it thunked underfoot with a hollow sound like a drum. We grazed as we marched, tearing up the grass, and pulling up with it mouthfuls of soil, good to eat but harsh, hard to digest. It made us fart, pungently, and in each other's faces as we marched. "No need for firelighters!" the old women giggled.

In places the trail had washed away, leaving tumbles of boulders that the carts would creak up and over, dropping down on the other side with a worrying crash. Leveza stomped on, still on two legs, gun ready. She would spring up rocks, heel-hooves clattering and skittering on stone. Sure-footed she wasn't. She did not hop nimbly, but she was relentless.

"They're still here," she muttered to me. All of us wanted our afternoon kip, but Fortchee wouldn't let us. The sun dropped, the shadows lengthened. Everything glowed orange. This triggered fear – low light means you must find safe camping. We snorted, and grew anxious.

Down one hill and up the other: it was sunset, the worst time for us, when we arrived at the skull rock. We don't like stone either.

"We sleep up there," Fortchee said. He had a fight on his hands. We had never heard of such a thing.

"What, climb up that? We'll split our hooves. Or tear our fingers," said Ventoo.

"And leave everything behind in the wagons?" yelped one of the men.

"It'll be windy and cold."

Fortchee tossed his head. "We'll keep each other warm."

"We'll fall off. . . ."

"Don't be a load of squirrels," said Leveza. She went to a cart, picked up a bag of tools, and started to climb.

Fortchee amplified, "Take ammo, all the guns."

"What about the foundries?"

He sighed. "We'll need to leave those."

By some miracle, the dome had a worn hole in the top full of rainwater and we drank. We had our kip, but the Head Man wouldn't let us go down to graze. It got dark and we had another sleep, two hours or more. But you can't sleep all night.

I was woken up by a stench of Cat that seemed to shriek in my nostrils. I heard Leveza sounding annoyed. "Tuh!" she said. "Dear oh dear!" Louder than a danger call – bam! – a gun blast, followed by the yelp of a Cat. Then the other afriradors opened fire. The children whinnied in terror. Peering down into milklight I could see a heaving tide of Cat pulling back from the rock. They even made a sound like water, the scratching of claws on stone.

"What fun," said Leveza.

I heard Grama trying not to giggle. Safety and strength came off Leveza's hide like a scent.

She turned to Fortchee. "Do you think we should go now or wait here?"

"Well, we can't wait until after sunrise, that'll slow us down too much. Now."

Leveza really was acting like Head Mare, and there had not been one of those in a while. She was climbing into the highest status. Not altogether hindered by having, if I may say so, a high-class groom-mate.

The *afriradors* sent out continual shots to drive back the last of the Cats. Then we skittered down the face of the rock back toward the wagons.

At the base of the cliff, a Cat lay in a pool of blood, purring, eyes closed as if asleep. Lindalfa scream-whinnied in horror and clattered backward. The Cat rumbled but did not stir.

Muttering, fearful, we were all pushed back by Cat-stench; we twitched and began to circle just before panic.

Leveza leaned in close to stare.

"Love, come away," I said. I picked my way forward, ready to grab her neck and pull her back if the thing lunged. I saw its face in milklight.

I'd never seen a Cat up close before.

The thing that struck me was that she was handsome. It was a finely formed face, despite the short muzzle, with a divided upper lip which seemed almost to smile, the mouthful of fangs sheathed. The Cat's expression looked simply sad, as if she were asking Life itself one last question.

Leveza sighed and said, "Poor heart."

The beast moaned, a low miserable sound that shook the earth. "You . . . need . . . predators."

"Like cat-shit we do," said Leveza, and stood up and back. "Come on!" she called to the rest of us, as if we were the ones who had been laggard.

The Cats were clever. They had pulled out far ahead of us so we had no idea when they would attack again. Our hooves slipped on the rocks. Leveza went all hearty on us. "Goats do this sort of thing. They have hooves too."

"They're cloven," said one of the bucks.

"Nearly cousins," sniffed Leveza. I think the light, the air, and the view so far above the plain exhilarated her. It depressed me. I wanted to be down there where it was flat and you could run and it was full of grass. The men hauling the wagons never stopped frothing, eyes edged white. They were trapped in yokes and that made them easy prey.

We hated being strung out along the narrow trail, and kept hanging back so we could gather together in clumps. She would stomp on ahead and stomp on back. "Come on, everyone, while it's still dark."

"We're just waiting for the others," quailed Lindalfa.

"No room for the others, love, not on this path."

Lindalfa sounded harassed. "Well, I don't like being exposed like this."

"No, you'd far rather have all your friends around you to be eaten first." It was a terrible thing to say, but absolutely true. Some of us laughed.

Sunrise came, the huge white sky contrasting too much with the silhouetted earth so that we could see nothing. We waited it out in a defensive group, carts around us. As soon as the sun rose high enough, Leveza triggered us to march. Not Fortchee. She urged us on and got us moving, and went ahead to scout. I learned something new about my groom-mate: the most loyal and loving of us was also the one who could most stand being alone.

She stalked on ahead, and I remember seeing the Lump sitting placidly on her back, about as intelligent as a cudcake.

A high wind stroked the grass in waves. Beautiful clouds were piled up overhead, full of wheeling birds, scavengers who were neither hunters nor victims. They knew nothing of ancestors or even speech.

Then we heard over the brow of a hill the snarl of Cats who have gone for the kill and no longer need stealth.

Leveza. Ahead. Alone.

"Gotcha!" they roared in thunder-voices.

We heard gunfire, just a snapping like a twig, and a Cat yelp, and then more gunfire and after that a heartfelt wail that could not have come from a Cat, a long hideous keening, more like that of a bird.

Fortchee broke into a lurching, struggling gallop. He triggered me and I jumped forward into a gallop too, slipping on rocks, heaving my way up the slope. It was like a nightmare where something keeps pulling you back. I heaved myself up onto the summit and saw Leveza, sitting on the ground, Fortchee stretching down to breathe into her ears.

She was staring ahead. Fortchee looked up at me with such sadness.

Before he could speak, Leveza turned her heavy jaws, her great snout, toward the sky and mourned, whinnying now a note for the dead.

"They got the Lump," said the Head Man, and turned and rubbed her shoulders. Her saddle-pack was torn. The baby was gone. Leveza keened, rocking from side to side, her lips forming a circle, the sound coming from far back and down her throat.

"Leveza," said Fortchee, looking forlornly at me.

"Leveza," I agreed, for we knew that she would not forget Kaway soon.

The rest of us, we lose a child, we have another next year; we don't think about it; we can't afford to. We're not strong enough. They die, child after child, and the old beloved aunties, or the wise old men who can no longer leap away. We can hear them being eaten. "Remember me! I love you!" they call to us, heartbroken to be leaving life and leaving us. But we have to forget them.

So we go brittle and shallow, sweet and frightened, smart but dishonest.

Not Leveza. She suddenly snarled, snatched up her rifle, rocked to her feet, and galloped off, after the Cats.

"She can't think that she can get him back!" I said.

"I don't know what she can think," said Fortchee.

The others joined us and we all stood haunches pressed together. None of us went to help, not even me, her beloved groom-mate. You do not chase prides of Cats to rescue anyone. You accept that they have been taken.

We heard distant shots, and the yelping of Cats. We heard hooves.

"She's coming back," whispered Grama and glanced at me. It was as if the hills themselves had stood up to stretch to see if things looked any different. A Horse had been hunting Cats.

Leveza appeared again at the top of the hill and for a moment I thought she had wrought a miracle, for her child dangled from her mouth.

Then I saw the way she swayed when she walked, the dragging of her hooves. She baby-carried a tiny torn head and red bones hanging together by tendons and scraps of skin. Suddenly she just sat on the ground and renewed her wailing. She arched her head round and looked down at herself in despair. Her breasts were seeping milk.

She tried to make the bones drink. She pushed the fragments of child onto her dugs. I cantered to her, lost my footing, and collapsed next to her. "Leveza. Love. Let him be."

She shouted up into my face with unseeing eyes. "What am I supposed to do with him?"

"Oh Leveza," I started to weep for her. "You feel things too much."

"I'm not leaving him!"

You're supposed to walk away. You're supposed to leave them to the birds and then to the sun and then to the rains until they wash back into the earth.

To come again as grass. We eat our grandmothers, in the grass. It shows acceptance, good will toward the world to forget quickly.

Leveza began to tear at the thin pelt of ground that covered the rocks. She gouged at it, skinning her forefingers, broke open the sod, and peeled it back. She laid the scraps on the bare rock, and gently covered what was left of him as if with a blanket. She tucked him in and began to sing a soft milklight song to him.

It simply was not bearable. If a child dies through sickness you take it away from camp, and let the birds and insects get to it. Then later you dance on the bones, to break them up into dust to show scorn for the body and the heart to accept fate.

The Head Man came back, and bumped her with his snout. "Up, Leveza. We must keep moving."

Leveza stroked the ground. "Good night, Kaway. Sleep, Kaway. Grow like a seed. Become beautiful Kaway grass."

We muttered and murmured. We'd all lost people we love like that. Why should she keen and carry on, why should she be different?

"I know it's hard," said Lindalfa. Unspoken was the "but."

Love can't be that special. Love must not cost that much. You'll learn, Leveza, I thought, like all the others. You'll finally learn.

I was looking down at her in some kind of triumph, proved right, when Leveza stood up, and turned everything upside down again.

She shook the tears out of her eyes and then walked away from me, shouldering past Fortchee as if he were an encumbrance. Tamely we trooped after her. She went to a wagon and reloaded her gun. She started to troop back down the hill in the direction of the rock.

"That's the wrong way, isn't it?"

"What's she doing?"

Fortchee called after her, and when she didn't answer, he looked deeply at me and said, "Follow her."

I whinnied for her to wait and started to trot down the hill.

Her determined stomp became a canter, then, explosively a kind of leaping, runaway gallop, thundering slipshod over stones and grass, threatening to break a leg. I chortled the slow-down cry but that checked her only for a moment. At the foot of the Rock she slid to a halt, raising dust.

She levelled her gun at the head of the wounded Cat. A light breeze seemed to blow her words to me up the slope. "Why do we need predators?"

The Cat groaned, her eyes still shut. "The Ancestors destroyed the world."

I reached them. "Leveza, come away," I nickered.

The Cat swallowed heavily. "They killed predators." All her words seemed to start with a growl.

Leveza went very still, I flanked her, and kept saying, leave her, come away. Suddenly she pushed the gun at me. "Shoot her if she moves."

I hated guns. I thought they would explode in my hands, or knock me backward. I knew carrying a gun made you a target. I didn't want the gun; I wanted to get us back to safety. I whinnied in fear.

She pushed on back up the hill, "I'm coming back," she said over her shoulder. I was alone with a Cat.

"Just kill me," said the Cat. The air was black with her blood; everything in me buzzed and went numb. Overhead the scavengers spiralled and I was sure at any moment other Cats would come. Climb the Rock! I told myself, but I couldn't move. I looked up at the trail.

Finally, finally Leveza came back with another gun and a coil of rope.

"Don't you ever do that to me again!" I sobbed.

She looked ferocious, her mane bristling, teeth smiling to bite out flesh. "You want to live, you put up with this," she said. I thought she said it to me.

"What are you fabricating now?" I hated her then, always having to surprise.

She bound the Cat's front paws together, and then the back, and then tied all four limbs to the animal's trunk. Leveza seized the mouth; I squealed and she began to wrap the snout round and round with rope. Blood seeped in woven patterns through the cord. The Cat groaned and rolled her eyes.

Then, oh then, Leveza sat on the ground and rolled the Cat onto her own back. She reached round and turned it so that it was folded sideways over her. Then she turned to me. "I don't suppose there's any chance of you giving me a hand?"

I said nothing. All of this was so unheard of that it triggered nothing, not even fear.

Slowly, forelegs first, Leveza stood up under the weight of the Cat. The Cat growled and dug in those great claws, but that just served to hold her in place. Burdened, Leveza began to climb the hill, her back beginning to streak with blood. I looked up. Everyone was bunched together on the brow of the ridge. I had no words, I forgot all words. I just climbed.

As we drew near, the entire herd, every last one of them including her groom-mother Alez, formed a wall of lowered heads. *Go back, get away.*

I think it was for the Cat, but it felt as if it were for us. Leveza kept coming. Hides started to twitch from the smell of Cat blood carried on the wind. Leveza ignored them and plodded on. The men had also come back with the carts. Old Pronto in harness tried to move sideways in panic and couldn't.

"Think," she told him. "For a change."

He whinnied and danced in place on the verge of bolting with one of our main wagons.

"Oh for heaven's sake!" She plucked out the pin of his yoke with her teeth and he darted away, the yoke still on his shoulders. He trotted to a halt, and then stood there looking sheepish.

Leveza rolled the Cat onto the wagon, tools clanking under the body. Brisk and businesslike, she picked up pliers, and began to pull out, one by one, all of the Cat's claws.

The poor beast groaned, roared, and shivered, rocking her head and trying to bite despite her jaws being tied shut. The Cat flexed her bloodied hands and feet but she no longer had claws. It seemed to take forever as the air whispered about us.

Undirected, all of us just stared.

When it was over, the Cat lay flat, panting. Leveza then took more rope, tied it tight round the predator's neck, lashing the other end to the yoke fittings. She then unwound the rope from her jaws. The Cat roared and rocked in place, her huge green fangs smelling of blood. Leveza took a hammer and chisel, and began to break all the Cat's teeth.

Fortchee stepped forward. "Leveza. Stop. This is cruel."

"But necessary or she'll eat us."

"Why are you doing this? It won't bring Kaway back."

She turned and looked at him, the half wheel of her lower jaw swollen. "To learn from her."

"Learn what?"

"What she knows."

"We have to get moving," said the Head Man.

"Exactly," she said, with flat certainty. "That's why she's in the cart."

"You're taking her with us?" Everything on Fortchee bristled, from his mane to his handsome goatee.

She stood there, and I think I remember her smiling. "You won't be able to stop me."

The entire herd made a noise in unison, a kind of horrified, wondering sigh.

She turned to me with airy unconcern and asked, "Do you think you could get me the yoke?"

Pronto tossed it at her with his head. "Here, have it, demented woman!"

I started to weep. "Leveza, this won't bring him back. Come, love, let it be, leave her alone and let's go."

She looked at me with pity. "Poor Akwa."

*

Leveza pulled the wagon herself. Women are supposed to carry guns; men haul the wagon, two of them together if it is uphill.

I tried to walk with her. No one else could bear to go near the prickling stench of Cat. It made me weep and cough. "I can't stay."

"It's all right, love," she said. "Go to the others, you'll feel safer."

"You'll be alone with that thing."

"She's preoccupied."

Unable to imagine what else to do, I left.

We migrated on. All through that long day, Fortchee did not let us sleep, and we could sometimes hear Leveza behind us, tormenting the poor animal with questions.

"No," we heard her shout. "It's not instinct. You can choose not to eat other people!"

The Cat roared and groaned. "Sometimes there is nothing else to eat! Do you want us to let our children die?"

Leveza roared back. "Why take my baby then? There was no . . ." She whinnied loud in horror, and snorted in fury. "There was no meat on him!"

The Cat groaned. She was talking, but we couldn't hear what she said. Leveza went silent, plodding on alone, listening to the Cat. She fell far behind even the rear guard of *afriradors* who were supposed to protect stragglers. Already it was slightly as though she did not exist.

The light settled low and orange, the shadows grew long. I kept craning behind us but by then I could neither see nor hear Leveza.

"They'll attack her! She'll be taken!" I nickered constantly to Grama.

She laid her head on my neck as we walked. "If anyone can stand alone against Cats, it's her."

We found no outcropping. On top of a hill with a good view all around, Fortchee lifted himself up and trod the air, whinnying. The men in the carts turned left and circled. "Windbreaks!" called the Head Man. We all began to unload windbreak timbers, to slot down the sides of the carts, to make a fortress. I kept looking back for Leveza.

Finally she appeared in the smoky dusk hauling the Cat. Froth had dried on her neck. She looked exhausted; her head dipped as if chastened.

Fortchee stepped in front of her. "You can't come into the circle with that cart."

She halted. Burrs and bracken had got tangled in her mane. She stared at the ground. "She's tied up. She's very weak."

Fortchee snorted in anger and pawed the dirt. "Do you think anybody could sleep with a Cat stinking up the inside of the circle?"

She paused, blinked. "She says the other Cats will kill her."

"Let them!" said Fortchee.

Without answering, Leveza turned and hauled the cart away from the camp. Fortchee froze, looked at her, and then said, "Akwa, see to your groom-mate."

Something in that made Grama snort, and she came with me. As we walked toward the carts, we pressed together the whole length of our bodies from shoulder to haunch for comfort.

Grama said, "She's reliving what happened to Grassa."

"Grassa?"

"Her mother. She saw her eaten, remember?"

"Oh yes, sorry." I did the giggle, the giggle you give to excuse forgetting, the forgetting of the dead out of embarrassment and the need to keep things light "Anyway," I said, "you made things hard enough for her when she was young."

Grama hung her head. "I know." Grama had tried to bully Leveza until she'd head-butted her, though two years younger.

It's not good to remember.

Leveza had already climbed up into the cart, without having watered or grazed. Her eyes flicked back and forth between me and Grama. "Grama, of course, how sensible. Here." She threw something at me and without thinking I caught it in my mouth. It was a bullet, thick with Cat blood and I spat it out.

"Fortchee wouldn't thank you for that. He's always telling us to save metal. Grama, love, do you think you could bring us bark-water, painkillers, thread?"

Grama's hide twitched, but she said, "Yes, of course."

Leveza reached around and tossed her a gun. "Watch yourself. I'll keep my gun ready too."

Grama picked up the bullet, then trotted back through the dusk. I felt undefended but I could not get up into the wagon with that thing. Leveza stood on hindquarters, scanning the camp, her gun leveled. As Grama came back with a pack, Leveza's nostrils moved as if about to speak.

"They're here," she said.

Grama clambered up into the cart. I couldn't see the Cat behind the sideboards, but I could see Grama's eyes flare open, her mane bristle. Even so, she settled on her rear haunches and began to work, dabbing the wounds. I could hear the Cat groan, deep enough to shake the timber of the cart.

Leveza's tail began to flick. I could smell it now: Cat all around us, scent blowing up the hillside like ribbons. The sunset was full of fire, clouds the colour of flowers. Calmly Grama sewed the wound. Leveza eased herself down, eyes still on the pasture, to feel if Grama's gun was loaded.

"Her name's Mai, by the way," said Leveza. Mai meant Mother in both tongues.

The Cat made a noise like *Rergurduh*, Rigadoo. Thanks.

Leveza nickered a gentle safety call to me. I jumped forward, and then stopped. The smell of Cat was a wall.

"Get up into the cart," said Leveza in a slow mothering voice.

It was the Terrible Time, when we can't see. Milklight fills the night, but when the sky blazes and the earth is black, the contrast means we can see nothing. Leveza reached down, bit my neck to help haul me up.

I was only halfway into the cart when out of that darkness a deep rumble formed words. "We will make the Horses eat you first."

Leveza let me go to shriek out the danger call, to tell the others. I tried to kick my way into the cart.

"Then while you cry we will take their delicious legs."

I felt claws rake the back of my calves. I screamed and scrambled. A blast right by my ears deafened me; I pulled myself in; I smelt dust in the air.

Leveza. How could she see? How could she walk upright all day?

She touched a tar lamp, opened its vent, and it gave light. "Aim for eyes," she said.

We saw yellow eyes, narrow and glowing, pure evil, hypnotizing. Ten, fifteen, how many were there, trying to scramble into the wagon?

Grama shot. Leveza shot. I had no gun and yearned to run so stamped my feet and cried for help. Some of the eyes closed and spun away. I looked at Mother Cat. She had folded up, eyes closed, but I was maddened and began to kick her as if she threatened my child. The sun sank.

Finally we heard a battle cry and a thundering of hooves from the circle. Leveza bit my neck and threw me to the floor of the cart. My nostrils were pushed into a pool of Cat juices. I heard shots and metal singing through the air. Our mares were firing wildly at anything. Why couldn't they see?

"Put that lamp out!" shouted Fortchee. Leveza stretched forward and flicked it shut. Then in milklight, our *afriradors* took more careful aim. I felt rather than heard a kind of thumping rustle, bullets in flesh, feet through grass. I peered out over the sides of the wagon and in milklight, I saw the Cats pulling back, slipping up and over rocks, crouching behind them. I lay back down and looked at Mother Cat. She shivered, her eyes screwed shut. A Cat felt fear?

We could still smell them, we could still hear them.

Fortchee said, "All of you, back into the circle. You too, Leveza."

She snuffled from weariness. "Can't!"

I cried, "Leveza! Those are real Cats, they will come back! What you care about her?"

"I did this to her," Leveza said.

Fortchee asked, "Why do other Cats want to kill her?"

A deep voice next to me purred through broken teeth. "Dissh-honour."

Chilled, everyone fell silent.

"Alsho, I talk too much," said Mother Cat. Did she chuckle?

I pleaded. "Choova misses you; she wants her groom-mummy; I miss you; please, Leveza, come back!" Fortchee ordered the men to give her a third gun and some ammo.

Grama looked at me with a question in her eyes I didn't want to see. As far as I was concerned, Fortchee had told us to pull back. I was shaking inside. Grama wasn't the one who had felt claws on her haunches.

All the way back, Grama bit the back of my neck as if carrying me like a mother.

We nestled down under a wagon behind the windbreak walls. Choova worked her way between us. None of us could sleep even the two hours. We paced and pawed. I stood up and looked out, and saw Leveza standing on watch, unfaltering.

At dawnsky when she would have most difficulty seeing, I heard shots, repeated. I fought my way out from under the wagon, and jerked my head over the windbreak between the carts where there are only timbers.

Blank whiteness, blank darkness, and in the middle a lamp glowing like a second sunrise. I could see nothing except swirling smoke and yellow dust and Leveza hunching behind the sides of the wagon, suddenly nipping up to shoot. Someone else glowed orange in that light, firing from the other side.

Leveza had given a gun to the Cat.

I saw leaping arms fanning what looked like knives. Everything spiraled in complete silence. The Cats made no sound at all. I was still rearing up my head over the windbreak to look, when suddenly, in complete silence, a Cat's head launched itself at my face. All I saw was snout, yellow eyes, fangs in a blur jammed up close to me. I leapt back behind the windbreak; the thing roared, a paralyzing sound that froze me. I could feel it make me go numb. The numbness takes away the pain as they eat you.

I couldn't think for a long time after that. I stood there shaking, gradually becoming aware of my pounding heart. Others were up, had begun to work; the sun was high; dawnsky was over. I heard Choova call me, but I couldn't answer. She galloped out to me, crying and weeping. Grama followed, looked concerned, and then began to trot.

It showed in my face. "Did one of them get in here?" she asked.

I couldn't answer, just shook my head, no. Choova cried, frightened for me. "It climbed the wall," I said and realized I'd been holding my breath.

"Leveza's not in the wagon," said Grama. We reared up to look over the wall. The slope was grassy, wide, the day bright. The wagon stood alone, with nothing visible in it. Grama looked at me.

Maybe she'd gone to graze? I scanned the fields, and caught motion from the slopes behind me, turned and my heart shivered with relief. There was Leveza slowly climbing toward us.

"What's she doing down there, that's where the Cats are!"

She held something in her mouth. For a moment I thought she'd gone back again for Kaway. Then I saw feathers. Birds? As she lowered herself, they swayed limply.

"She's been hunting," said Grama.

"She's gone mad," I said.

"I fear so."

We told Choova to stay where she was and Grama and I trotted out to meet her. "Is that what I think it is? Is it?" I shouted at her. I was weepier than I would normally be, shaken.

Leveza reared up and took the dead quail out of her mouth. "She needs to eat something," said Leveza. She was in one of her hearty, blustering moods, cheerful about everything and unstoppable. She strode on two legs. She'd braided her mane and then held it on top of her head with plastic combs, out of her eyes.

Grama sighed. "We don't take life, Leveza. We value it."

She looked merry. She shook the quail. "I value thought. These things can't think."

"That's a horrible thing to say!"

She swept past us. "You'd rather she ate us, I suppose. Or maybe you want her to die. How does that show you value life?"

She trooped on toward the cart.

Grama had an answer. "I'd rather the Cat hunted for herself."

"Good. I'll give her a gun then."

I was furious. "She had a gun last night!"

"Oh. Yes. Well. She was a welcome addition to our resources." Leveza smiled. "Since I was otherwise on my own." She looked at me dead in the eye and her meaning was plain enough.

"If they value life so much, why did they take Kaway then?" I was sorry the instant I said it. I meant that I'd heard her ask the Cat that and I wanted to know the answer too, just like she did.

"Because I broke the bargain," she said, so calmly that I was almost frightened.

I wanted to show her that I was outraged at what they'd done. "What bargain?"

She lost some kind of patience. "Oh come on, Akwa, you're not a child. The bargain! The one where they don't take children so they grow up nice and fat for them to eat later and we let them take our old and sick. They get to eat, and we get rid of people whose only use is that they are experienced and wise, something Horses can't use, because of course we know everything already. So we don't shoot Cats except to scare them off, and they don't shoot us." Her eyes looked like the Cats' reflecting our lamps. "*That* bargain."

"I . . . I'm sorry."

"I shot them when they took the old. They saw I was the leader so I was the target."

Grama and I looked at each other. Grama said, with just a hint of a smile, "You . . . ?"

"Yes me. The Cats can see it even if you can't."

Grama pulled back her lips as if to say, oops, pushed her too far that time. As we followed her Grama butted me gently with her head. *It's just Leveza fabricating.*

Leveza strode ahead of us, as if she didn't need us, and it was uncomfortably like she didn't.

Once at the cart, Leveza took out a knife and began to butcher the quail. I cried and turned away. She pushed the meat toward the Cat, who opened her eyes but did not move. The creature had had to relieve herself in the cart so the stink was worse than ever.

Leveza dropped onto all fours and trotted to the neck of the cart. "Help me into the yoke?"

"You've not asked me about Choova."

"How is she?" She picked up the yoke by herself.

"Terrified and miserable. She saw the empty cart and thought you were dead."

Grama helped settle the yoke, slipping in the pin. At once Leveza started to drag the cart forward

"You're going now?" The camp was not even being dismantled.

"Stragglers get taken. Today I intend to be in front. We start going downhill."

"Let's go!" I said to Grama, furious, but she shook her head and walked on beside the cart. "I've got a gun," she said. "We should guard her."

I should have gone back to take care of Choova, but it felt wrong somehow to leave someone else guarding my groom-mate. I shouted to Choova as we passed the camp. "Groom-mummy is fine, darling; we're just going with her to make sure she's safe."

So all of us walked together, the cart jostling and thunking over rocks.

"So tell them, Mai. Why does the world need predators?"

I looked into the wagon, and saw that the Cat had clenched about herself like fingers curled up inside a hoof. I could sense waves of illness coming off her. I saw the horrible meat. She hadn't touched it. She looked at me with dead eyes.

"Go on, Mai; explain!"

The Cat forced herself to talk, and rolled onto her back, submissively.

"'ere wasssh a ribber ... ," she said, toothlessly. "There was a river and there were many goats and many wolves to eat them." Her voice sounded comic. Everything came out sssh wvuh and boub, like the voices we adopt when we tell jokes. "Verh whuh whvolbss ... there were wolves, and the Ancestors killed all the wolves because they were predators."

It was exactly as though she were telling a funny story. I was triggered. I started to laugh.

"And then the rivers started to die. With nothing to eat them, there were too many goats and they ate all the new trees that held the banks together."

I shook my head to get rid of the laughter. I trembled inside from fear. I wanted to wee.

The Cat groaned. "Issh nop a zhope!" *It's not a joke.*

Leveza craned her neck back, looking as though she was teaching me a lesson, her eyes glinting at me in a strange look of triumph and wonder. "What Memory Sticks do Cats have?"

"We know about the seeds, the seeds inside us."

Grama's ears stood straight up.

Leveza's words kept pace with her heavy feet, as if nothing could ever frighten her or hurry her. "Cats know how Ancestors and beasts mingled. They understand how life is made. We could split us up again, Horse and Ancestor. We could give them something else to eat."

It was all too much for me, as if the Earth were turning in the wind. I was giddy.

Grama marched head bowed, looking thoughtful. "So . . . you know what the other peoples know?"

Leveza actually laughed aloud too. "She does! She does!"

"What do Dogs know?" Grama asked.

The Cat kept telling what sounded like jokes. "Things that are not alive are made of seeds too. Rocks and air and water are all made of tiny things. Dogs know all about those."

"And goats?"

"Ah! Goats know how the universe began."

"And electricity?" Grama actually stepped closer to the Cat. "Everything we know is useless without electricity."

"Bovines," said the Cat. "I've never seen one. But I've heard. You go south and you know you are there because they have lights that glow with electricity!"

"We could make a new kind of herd," Leveza said. "A herd of all the peoples that joins together. We could piece it all together, all that knowledge."

The Cat rolled on her belly and covered her eyes. Grama looked at her and at me, and we thought the same thing. Wounded, no food, no water – I felt nausea, the Cat's sickness in my own belly. Why didn't Leveza?

Grama said, almost as if defending the Cat, "We'd have to all stay together though, all the time. All of us mixed. Or we'd forget it all."

The Cat rumbled. "The Bears have something called writing. It records. But only the big white ones in the south."

"Really!" Leveza said. "If we could do that, we could send knowledge everywhere."

"I've thought that," the Cat said quietly. "Calling all of us together. But my people would eat them all."

It was one of those too-bright days that cloud over, but for now, the sun dazzled.

"The dolphins in the sea," murmured the Cat as if dreaming. "They know how stars are made and stay in the sky. They use them to navigate."

Sun and wind.

"Sea turtles understand all the different elements, how to mix them."

Grama said, "She needs water."

Leveza sniffed. "We've crossed a watershed. We're going downhill; there'll be a stream soon." We marched on, toward cauliflower clouds.

Grama and I took over pulling the wagon for a time. I don't know what hauling it uphill is like, but going downhill, the whole weight of it pushes into your shoulders and your legs go rubbery pushing back to stop it rolling out of control.

It's worrying being yoked: you can't run as fast; you're trapped with the cart. I looked back round and saw Leveza in the cart fast asleep, side by side with a Cat.

I found myself thinking like Leveza, and said to Grama, "I can't aim a gun. You better keep watch."

So I ended up pulling the cart alone, while Grama stood in the wagon with a gun, and I didn't know which one of us was the biggest target.

The slope steepened, and we entered a gully, a dry wash between crags. The wind changed direction constantly, buffeting us with the scent of Cat.

"They're back," I said to Grama.

The scent woke up Leveza. "Thank you," she said. "The two of you should go join the others." She dropped heavily down out of the cart. She searched me with her eyes, some kind of apology in them. "Choova's alone."

Grama's chin tapped me twice. Leveza was right. As we climbed together uphill toward the herd, I said, "Cats don't go out of their territory."

"They're following Leveza. They want Mai, they want her." In other words, Leveza was pulling the Cats with her.

"Don't tell the others," I said.

The wall of faces above us on the hill opened up to admit us, and then closed again behind. We found Choova, who had been having fun with playmates. She'd forgotten Cats, Leveza, everything, and was full of giggles and teasing, pulling my mane. As we walked, the herd gradually caught up with Leveza, and we could hear her and the Cat murmuring to each other.

"What on earth do they find to talk about?" said Raio, my cousin.

"How delicious horseflesh is," said Ventoo.

Choova scowled. "Everybody says that Leveza is bad." I stroked her and tried to explain it and found that I could not. All I could say was, "Leveza wants to learn."

The trail crossed a stream and Fortchee signaled a break. Leveza's cart was already there with Leveza still in harness reaching down to drink. The trickling sound of safe, shallow water triggered a rush. We crowded round the creek, leaning down and thrusting each other's head out of the way. Grama trotted up the hill to make room and found herself the farthest one out, the most exposed. I was about to say, *Grama, get back.*

Three Cats pounced on her. The entire herd pulled back and away from her, swiftly, like smoke blown by wind. Two Cats gripped her hind legs; one was trying to tear out her throat. She was dead, Grama was dead, I was sure of it. I kept leaping forward and back in some kind of impulse to help. Then came a crackle of gunfire. The two Cats on her hindquarters yowled and were thrown back. One spun away and ran; one flipped over backward and was still.

Then one miraculous shot: it sliced through the Cat in front without touching Grama. I looked back in the cart and saw that Leveza had been held down in harness, unable to stand up or reach for her gun.

In the back of the wagon, head and rifle over the sides, was Mother Cat.

Grama shook and shivered, her whole hide twitching independently from the muscles underneath, her eyes ringed round with white. She wasn't even breathing, she was so panicked. I knew exactly how awful that felt. I ronfled the comfort sound over and over as I picked my way to her, touched her. She heaved a huge, painful-sounding breath. I got hold of the back of her neck. "Come on, darling, come on, baby," I said through clenched teeth. I coaxed her back downstream toward the others. Her rattling breath came in sobs.

There were no sympathy nitters. The other Horses actually pulled back from us as if we carried live flame. Grama nodded that she was all right and I let her go. She still shivered, but she stepped gently back and forth to test her torn rear legs. I lifted the healer's pack from her shoulders and took out the bark water to wash her.

I was angry at the others and shouted at them. "It's all right, all of you, leave her be. Just leave her alone. She's nursed you often enough."

Fortchee stepped toward us, breathed in her scent to see how badly hurt she was.

Then he looked over in the direction of the Cat, who still held the gun. He calmly turned and walked toward the cart. Leveza had finally succeeded in slipping out of the yoke and begun to climb the hill back toward him.

I tried to coax Grama back to our wagons, but she firmly shook her head. She wanted to listen to what Fortchee said.

I couldn't quite hear him, but I certainly could hear Leveza. "She has just as much reason to escape them as you do!"

Fortchee's voice went harsher, giving an order.

"No," said Leveza. He said something else, and Leveza replied, "It seems she's done a good job of protecting us."

His voice was loud. "Out, now! You or her or both of you."

"I'm already out. Haven't you noticed?"

She stepped back toward the long neck of the cart and slammed back on the yoke. "I don't need you, and I don't have you!"

She wrenched herself round, almost dragging the cart sideways, turning it down to follow the stream itself. Fortchee shouted for a break. "Afriradors, guard everyone while they drink." To my surprise, Grama began to limp as fast as she could after Leveza's wagon.

I couldn't let her go alone, so I followed, taking Choova with me. As we trooped down the hill, we passed Fortchee trudging up the slope, his head hanging. He ignored us. A Head Man cannot afford to be defied to his face too often.

I caught up to Grama. We hobbled over rocks, or splashed through shallow pools. Choova rubbed her chin against my flank for comfort. Leveza saw us behind her and stopped.

"Hello, darling," Leveza called back to Choova, who clattered forward, glad to see her. They interlaced their heads, breathed each other's breath. I pressed in close, and felt my eyes sting. We were still a family.

Grama stuck her head over the sides of the wagon. "Thank you," she told Mai.

"You nursed me," said the Cat.

"Mai?" said Leveza. "This is my groom-daughter Choova."

"Choova," said the Cat and smiled, and crawled up the wagon to be nearer. "I have a boy, Choova, a little boy." Choova looked uncertain and edged back.

"Is he back . . . with the pride?" Leveza asked.

"Yesh. But he won't want to know me now." Mai slumped back down in the wagon. "Everything with us is the hunt. Nobody thinks about anything else." She shrugged. "He's getting mature now, he would have been driven off soon anyway."

Leveza stopped pulling. "You should drink some water."

As slow as molten metal, the Cat poured herself out of the cart, halting on tender paws. She drank, but not enough, looked weary, and then wove her unsteady way back toward the wagon. She started to laugh. "I can't get back in."

Leveza slipped out of harness and we all helped roll Mai onto Leveza's back. Grama sprang back up into the cart, and helped pull up the Cat.

"Good to be among friends," Mai whispered.

Leveza stroked her head. "Neither one of us can go back home," she said, staring at Mai with a sad smile. Then she looked at me, with an expression that seemed to say, I think she's going to die.

I wanted to say, I'm supposed to care about a Cat?

"Don't you get pushed out too," she said to me, and jerked her head in the direction of the herd. She asked us to bring her lots of lamp fuel, and Grama promised that she would. As we walked toward the others, I couldn't stop myself saying in front of Choova, "She's in love with that bloody Cat!"

That night, Choova, me and Grama slept together again beneath a wagon, behind the windbreak wall.

In the middle of the night, we heard burrowing and saw claws, digging underneath the timbers, trying to get in. We jammed little stakes into the tender places between their toes. I cradled Choova next to me as we heard shots from overhead and Cat cries. We saw flickering light through the boards and smelled smoke. Fortchee stuck his head underneath the wagon. "Leveza's set the hillside on fire! We have to beat it back." He looked wild. "Come on! There's no more Cats but the camp's catching fire!" He head-butted Ventoo. "We need everyone!"

Light on the opposite hillside left dim blue and grey shadows across our eyes. Fire rained slowly down, embers from the grass, drifting sparks. Ash tickled our nostrils; we couldn't quite see. We had fuel and firestarters on the wagons; if those caught alight we'd lose everything.

"That bloody woman!" shouted Ventoo. Blindly, we got out blankets and started to beat back the grass fire, aiming for any blur of light. The men stumbled down the stream with buckets to fill, stepping blindly into dark, wondering if Cats awaited them. The ground sizzled, steamed, and trailed smoke. We slapped wet blankets onto the gnawing red lines in the wood.

It was still milklight, and the fire had not burnt out, when Fortchee called for us to pack up and march. Blearily, we hoisted up the windbreak walls, only too happy to move. The smell of ash was making us ill. I glanced up and saw that Leveza had already gone.

Butt her! I thought. My own milk had given out on the trek, and Choova was hungry. What do you have a groom-mate for if not to help nurse your child? "You'll have to graze, baby," I told her.

We churned up clouds of ash. I wandered though something crisp and tangled and realized I had trodden in the burnt carcass of a Cat. Later in the grass we saw the quail that Leveza had shot, thrown away, the meat gone dark and dry. The Cat still had not eaten.

"I want to see if Mai's all right," said Grama.

In full milklight, we trotted ahead to the wagon to find the Cat asleep and Leveza hauling the wagon on two legs only, keeping watch with the rifle ready. She passed us the gun and settled down onto all fours and started to haul again. Her face and voice were stern. "She says it would be possible to bring Horses back, full-blooded Horses. Can you imagine? They could have something else to eat, all of this could stop!"

"What? How?" said Grama.

"The Ancestors wanted to be able to bring both back. We have the complete information for Horses and Ancestors too. We still carry them inside us!"

"So . . . what do we do?" Grama asked.

"Bee-sh," said a voice from the cart. The Cat sat up, with a clown's expression on her face. She chuckled. "You could carry them forever, and they wouldn't come out. They need something from bees."

For some reason, Leveza chuckled too. She was always so serious and weighty that I could never make her laugh.

"It's called . . ." The Cat paused and then wiggled her eyebrows. "*Ek-die-sshone.*" She paused. "That-ssh a word. I don't know what it mean-sh either. It's just in my head."

That Cat knew her toothless voice was funny. She was playing up to it. I saw then how clever she was, how clever she had been. She knew just what to say to get Leveza on her side.

"Bee-sh make honey, and bee-sh make Horshes."

"So you give the seed something from bees, and we give birth to full-bloods?" Everything about Grama stood up alert and turned toward the Cat.

"Not you too," I moaned.

Finally I made Leveza laugh. "Oh Akwa, you old chestnut!"

"No," said the Cat. "What gets born is much, much closer to Horses. It's a mix of you and a full-blooded Horse, but then we can . . ."

"Breed back!" said Grama. "Just pair off the right ones."

"Yup," said the Cat. "I've alsway-sssh thought I could do it. I jussht needed lotsh of Horshes. My pridemates had sschtrong tendenshee to eat them."

There was something deadly in Leveza's calm. "We could bring back the Ancestors. Imagine what they could tell us! Maybe they have all the Memory Sticks, all together."

The Cat leaned back, her work done. "They knew nothing. They had no memory. Everything they knew, they had to learn. How to walk. How to talk. All over again each time. So they could forget. But they could learn."

Overhead the stars looked like a giant spider's web, all glistening with dew.

"They wanted to travel to the stars. So they thought they would carry the animals and plants inside them. And they were worried that all their knowledge would be lost. 'How,' they asked, 'can we make the information safe?' So they made it like the knowledge every spider has: how to weave a web."

"Kaway," said Lovena, in a mourning voice.

I felt as thought I had gone to sleep on the ground all alone instead of sleeping on my feet to watch. This was madness, just the kind of madness to capture Leveza. I will keep watch now, I promised myself.

"Maybe one day the Ancestors will sail back." Leveza arched her neck and looked up at the stars.

All the next day, as we headed east, they talked their nonsense. Nowadays, I wish that I had listened and could remember it, but all I heard then was that the Cat was subverting my Leveza. I knew it was no good pleading with her to let all of this madness alone, to come home, to be as we were. How I wanted that Cat to die. I've never felt so alone and useless.

"Don't worry, love," said Grama. "It's Leveza's way."

I was too angry to answer.

The stream dipped down through green hills which suddenly fell away. We stopped at the top of a slope, looking out over a turquoise and grey plain. We had made it to the eastern slopes facing the sea. The grass was long and soft and rich, so we grazed as we walked, and I hoped my milk would come back. The foals, Choova included, began to run up and down through the meadows as if already home. We'd made it; we would be fine.

Fortchee kept pushing us, getting us well out of the Cats' range. Still, it was strange; this was flatlands, full of tall grass. Why were there no other Cats? I kept sniffing the wind, we all did, but all we smelled was the pure fresh smell of grazing.

It was not until near sunset that Fortchee brayed for camp. Grama and I went back, and I kicked the grass as I walked. Grama chewed my mane and called me poor love. "She's always loved ideas. The Cat is full of them."

"Yes, she wants us to make new children to feed to her!" I pulled Choova closer to me and nuzzled her.

We camped, grazed, and watered, but I couldn't settle. I paced round and round. I went back to our wagon, slumped down, and tried to feed

Choova again. I couldn't. I wept. I was dry like old grass, and I had no one to help me and felt alone, abandoned. I heard Leveza start to sing! Sing, while sleeping with a Cat. She was blank, unfeeling, something restraining had been left out of her. She didn't love me, she didn't love anything. Just her fabrications. And she'd pulled me and used me up and left me alone.

Choova was restless too. For a while, getting her to sleep occupied me. Finally her breathing fell regular, soft and smelling of hay, sweet and young and trusting, her long slim face resting on my haunches.

I lay there and heard Leveza sing the songs about sunrise, pasture, running through fields, the kinds of songs you sing when you are excited, young.

In love.

Sleep wouldn't come, peace wouldn't come. I turned over and Choova stirred, Grama groaned. I was keeping them awake. Suddenly I was determined to bring all of this to a stop. I was going to go out there and get my groom-mate back. So I rolled quietly out from under the wagon. Everything was still; even birds and insects – no stars, no moon. Yet I thought I heard . . . something.

I reared up to look over the windbreaks and saw light over the horizon, and drifting white smoke. I thought it was the last of the fire, then realized it was in the wrong direction. Did I hear shots? And mewling?

I was about to give the danger call when Fortchee stepped up to me. "*Fuhfuhfoom*," he said, the quiet call. "That's Cat fighting Cat. The ones chasing us have strayed into another pride's territory."

I felt ice on our shoulders. We stood and watched and listened and our focusing ears seemed to pull the sound closer to us.

A battle between Cats.

"We can sleep on a little longer in safety," he said. "I had to tell Leveza to stop singing."

I started to walk. "I need to talk sense to that woman."

"Good luck." He pulled a cart aside, to make a gap for me. "Be careful anyway."

As I walked toward the wagon the sound grew, a growling, roaring, crying, a sound like a creeping wildfire. It was as if all the world had gone mad along with me.

I slipped down the track, silently, rehearsing what I would say to her. I would tell her to come back to Choova and the herd and let the Cat do what she could to survive. I would tell her: You choose. Me or that Cat. I would force her to come back, force her to be sensible.

I got halfway down the track, and clouds moved away from the moon, and I saw.

At first I thought Leveza was just grooming her. That would have been enough to make me sick, the thought of grooming something that smelt of death, of blood.

But it wasn't grooming. The Cat had not eaten for days, was wounded and hungry, and Leveza had leaking tits.

I saw her suckling a Cat.

The Earth spun. I had never known that such perversion existed; I'd never heard of normal groom-mates doing such a thing. But what a fearful confounding was this, of species, of mother, of child? While my Choova starved, that Cat, that monster, was being fed, given horsemilk as if by a loving mother.

I gagged and made a little cry and stumbled and coughed and I think those two in the wagon turned and saw me. I spun around and galloped, hooves pounding, and I was calling over and over, "Foul, foul, foul!"

I wailed and I heard answering shouts from inside the camp. Ventoo and Lindalfa came hobbling out to me.

"Akwa, darling!"

"Akwa, what's wrong?"

They were mean-eyed. "What's *she* done now?" They were yearning for bad news about Leveza

I wept and wailed and tried to pull myself away. "She won't feed Choova but she's feeding that Cat."

"What do you mean, feed?"

I couldn't answer.

"Hunting! Yes we saw! Killing for that thing!"

"Foul, yes, poor Akwa!"

I hauled in a breath that pushed my voice box the wrong way.

"It's not hunting!" I was frothing at the mouth, the spittle and foam splayed over my lips and chin. "Uhhhhh!"

I wished the grass would slash her like a thousand needles. I wanted hot embers poured down her throat, I wanted her consumed, I wanted the Cats to come and make good all their terrible threats. Yes, yes, eat your Cat lover and then be eaten too. Call for me and I will call back to you: *you deserve this!*

Grama was there. "Akwa, calm down. Down, Akwa." She ronfled the soothing noise. I blew out spittle at her, rejecting the trigger from my belly outward. I shriek-whinnied in a mixture of fear, horror, and something like the sickness call.

"She's suckling the Cat!"

Silence.

Someone giggled.

I head-butted the person I thought had laughed. "Suckling. An adult. Cat!"

Grama fell silent. I shouted at her. "Heard of that before, Midwife?" My eyes were round; my teeth were shovels for flesh; I was enraged at everything and everyone.

Grama stepped back. Fortchee stepped forward. "What is all this noise?"

I told him. I told him good, I told him long. Ventoo bit my tail to keep me in place; the others rubbed me with their snouts.

"Poor thing! Her groom-mate."

"Enough," said Fortchee. He turned and started to walk toward their wagon.

"Too true there!" said Ventoo. Old Pronto grabbed a gun.

We all followed, making a sound like a slow small rockslide, down toward the cart.

Leveza stood up in the wagon, waiting. So did the Cat.

"Give us your guns," said Fortchee.

"We can't. . . ."

"I'm not asking, I'm ordering."

Leveza looked at him, as if moonlight still shone on his face. She sighed, and looked up at the stars, and handed him her gun.

"The Cat's too."

Silently Leveza held it out to him.

"Now get down out of that cart and rejoin the herd."

"And Mai?" Such regret, such fondness, such concern for blood-breathed Cat.

The spittle curdled; the heart shriveled; I tasted gall, and I said, "She's taken a Cat for a groom-mate. I don't want her! I don't want her back!"

Her head jerked up at me in wonder.

"All her fabricating!"

I felt myself rear up in the air, and I bucked. I bucked to get away from my own heart, from the things I'd seen, for the way I'd been stretched. I was tired, I was frightened, I wanted her to be as we had been. Our girl-hoods when we galloped beribboned over the hill.

"She'd feed my child to that bloody Cat!"

Reared up, wrenching, I made a noise I had never heard before, never knew could be made.

It was like giving birth through the throat, some ghastly wriggling thing made of sound that needed to be born, and it came out of me, headless and blind. A relentless, howling pushing-back that flecked everything with foam as if I were the sea.

Triggered.

Even Fortchee.

All.

We all moved together, closing like a gate. Our shoulders touched and our haunches. We lowered our heads. We advanced. I saw Leveza look into my eyes and then crumple. She knew what this was, even if I did not, and she knew it had come from me.

We advanced and butted the cart. We pushed all our heads under it and turned the cart over. Leveza and the Cat had to jump out, clumsy, stumbling to find their feet.

The Cat snarled, toothless. Leveza shook her head. "Friends. . . ."

We were deaf. We were upon them. We head-butted them. Leveza slipped backward, onto her knees. Fortchee reared up and clubbed her on the head with his hooves. She stood up, turned. Fortchee, Ventoo, Raio, Pronto, all bared their teeth and bit her buttocks hard. Feet splaying sideways, she began to run.

The Cat bounded, faster in bursts than Leveza was, and leapt up onto her back. Leveza trotted away, carrying her. Her tail waved, defiant. Then milklight closed over them as if they had sunk. We heard light scattering sounds of stones for a while, then even her hoofbeats faded into the whispering sound of spaces between mountains.

Without a word, Grama sprang after them. I saw her go too. There were no Cats on the plain to seize them as the horizon burned.

The herd swung to the left in absolute unison, wheeling around, and then trotted back to the camp. We felt satisfied, strangely nourished, safe and content. I looked back under the cart. Choova raised her head. "What was that, Mummy?"

"Nothing, love, nothing," I said.

Fortchee told us quietly that we should get moving now while the Cats were occupied. We dismantled the windbreaks and packed the tools. Some of the men turned Leveza's cart upright and old Pronto went back to his post in harness. Never did we pack with so little noise, so swiftly, calmly, Nothing was said at all, no mention of it. The horizon burned with someone else's passion.

Choova ran out to graze, her mane bobbing. She never asked about Leveza or Grama, not once, ever. A soft glowing light spread wide across the pampas.

We followed the stream to the sea and then migrated along the sand. It got between our fingers. We did see the turtles. I would have asked them about acids, especially the acids in batteries, but they were laying eggs, and would have been fearful.

Fortchee led us to a wonderful pasture, far to the south, on a lake next to sea, salt and fresh water so close, beside tall sudden cliffs that kept Cats at bay. Oats grew there year round; the rains never left. By digging we found rust shoals, thick layers of it, enough to make metal for several lifetimes. There was no reason to leave. We waited for the trigger to leave, but year in, year out, none came.

Fortchee had us build a stone wall across the small peninsula of land that connected our islet to the mainland, and we were safe from Cats. When he died, we called him our greatest innovator.

On top of a high hill we found the fallen statue of an Ancestor, his face melted, his arms outstretched. As if to welcome Ancestors back from the stars.

No one came to me in the night to comfort me or bite my neck and call me love. I suppose I'd been touched by something strange and so was strange myself. I would have taken a low-rank drifter, only they did not get past the wall. Still, I had my Choova. She brought me her children to bless, and then her grandchildren, though they never really recognized what I was to them. Their children had no idea that I still lived. My loneliness creaked worse than my joints and I yearned for a migration, to sweep me numbly away.

Not once did anyone speak of Leveza, or even once remember her. Our exiled groom-brothers would drift by, to temporarily gladsome cries, and they told us, before moving on, of new wonders on the prairie. But we blanked that too.

Until one dusk, I saw the strangest thing picking its way down toward our lagoon.

It looked like a fine and handsome young girl, beautifully formed though very very long in the trunk. She raised her head from drinking and her mane fell back. The top of her face was missing, from right above the eyes. It was terrible to see, someone so young but so deformed. She whinnied in hope and fear, and I ronfled back comfort to her, and then asked her name. But she couldn't talk.

A horse. I was looking at a full-blooded horse. I felt a chill on my legs and wondered: did they bring the Ancestors back, too?

"Leveza?" I asked it, and it raised and lowered its head, and I thought the creature knew the name. It suddenly took fright, started, and trotted away into the night, as someone else once had.

Then there was a sound like thousands of cards being shuffled, and a score of the creatures emerged from the trees. They bent their long necks down to drink. Their legs worked backward.

A voice said softly, "Is that Akwa?" Against a contrast sky, I saw the silhouette of a monster, two headed, tall. Then I recognized the gun.

She had trained one of the things to carry her, so she would always sit tall and have her hands free. I couldn't speak. Somewhere beyond the trees carts rumbled.

"Hello, my love," she said. I was hemorrhaging memory, a continual stream; and all of it about her – how she spoke, how she smelled, how she always went too far, and how I wished that I'd gone with her too all those years ago.

"We're going south, to find the Bears, get us some of that writing. Want to come?" I still could not speak. "It's perfectly safe. We've bought along something else for them to eat."

I think that word "safe" was the trigger. I did the giggle of embarrassment and fear. I drank sweet water and then followed. We found writing, and here it is.

CITY OF THE DEAD

Paul McAuley

Here's another story by Paul McAuley, whose "Incomers" appears elsewhere in this anthology. In this one he takes us to a distant world that's littered with the ruins of vanished civilizations to unravel an enigmatic – and deadly – biological mystery.

How Marilyn Carter first met Ana Datlovskaya, the Queen of the Hive Rats: late one afternoon she was driving through the endless tracts of alien tombs in the City of the Dead, to the west of the little desert town of Joe's Corner, when she saw a pickup canted on the shoulder of the rough track, its hood up. She pulled over and asked the woman working elbow-deep in the engine of the pickup if she needed any help; the woman said that she believed that she needed a tow truck, this bloody excuse for a pickup she should have sold for scrap long ago had thrown a rod.

"I am Ana Datlovskaya," she added, and stuck out an oily hand.

"Marilyn Carter," Marilyn said, and shook Ana Datlovskaya's hand.

"Our new town constable. That incorrigible gossip Joel Jumonville told me about you," the woman said. She was somewhere in her sixties, short and broadhipped, dressed in a khaki shirt and blue jeans and hiking boots. Her white hair, roughly cropped, stuck up like ruffled feathers; her shrewd gaze didn't seem to miss much. "Although he didn't mention that you have a dog. He is a police dog? I met one once, in Port of Plenty. At the train station. It told me to stand still while its handler searched me for I don't know what."

The black Labrador, Jet, was standing in the loadbed of Marilyn's Bronco, watching them with keen interest.

"He's just a dog," Marilyn said. "He doesn't talk or anything. We can give you a lift into town, if you need one."

"No doubt Joel told you that I am the crazy old woman who lives with hive rats," Ana Datlovskaya said to Marilyn, as they drove off towards Joe's Corner. "It is true I am old, as you can plainly see. And it's true also that I study hive rats. But I am not crazy. In fact, I am the only sane person in this desert. Everyone else hopes to make fortune by finding treasure, or by swindling people looking for treasure. *That* is craziness, if you don't mind me saying so."

"I don't mind in the least, because that's not why I'm here," Marilyn said.

She'd become town constable by accident. She'd stopped for the night in Joe's Corner and had been sitting in its roadhouse, minding her own business, nursing a beer and half-listening to the house band blast out some twentieth-century industrial blues, when a big man a few stools down took exception to something the bartender said and tried to haul him over the counter by his beard. Marilyn intervened and put the big guy on the floor, and the owner of the roadhouse, Joel Jumonville, had given her a steak dinner on the house. Joel was an ex-astronaut who like Marilyn had fought in World War Three. He also owned two of the little town's motels, ran its radio station and its web site, and was, more by default than democracy, its mayor. He and Marilyn got drunk together and told war stories, and by the end of the evening she'd shaken hands on a contract to serve as town constable for one year, replacing a guy who'd quit when a scrap of plastic he'd dug up in one of the tombs had turned out to be a room temperature superconductor.

It wasn't exactly how she'd imagined her life would turn out when she'd won a lottery place on one of the arks.

This was in the heady years immediately after the Jackaroo had arrived in the aftermath of World War Three, and had given the survivors a basic fusion drive and access to a wormhole network linking fifteen M-class red dwarf stars in exchange for rights to the rest of the Solar System; a brief, anarchic age of temporary kingdoms, squabbling emirates, and gloriously foolish attempts at building every kind of Utopia; an age of exploration, heroic ambition, and low farce. Like every other lottery winner, Marilyn had imagined a fresh start, every kind of exotic adventure, but after she'd arrived in Port of Plenty, on the planet of First Foot, short of cash and knowing no one, she'd ended up working for a security firm, which is what she'd been doing before she left Earth. She guarded the mansions and compounds of the city's rich, rode as bodyguard for their wives and children. Some had earned vast fortunes founded on novel principles of physics or mathematics wrested from discarded alien machineries; others were gangsters feeding on the underbelly of Port of Plenty's fast and loose economy. Marilyn's last job had been with an Albanian involved in all kinds of dubious property deals; after he'd been killed by a car bomb, she'd had to get out of Port of Plenty in a hurry because his family suspected that the assassination had been an inside job. She'd drifted west along the coast of First Foot's single continent and ended up in Joe's Corner, but, as she told Ana Datlovskaya, she didn't plan to stay.

"When the year's up I'm moving on. I have a whole new world to explore. And plenty more besides."

"Ha. If I had a euro for every time I'd heard that from people who thought they were passing through but couldn't find a reason to leave," Ana Datlovskaya said, "I'd be riding around the desert in style, instead of nursing that broken-down donkey of a pickup."

Ana was a biologist who'd moved out to the western desert to study hive rats, supporting her research with her savings and the sale of odd little figurines. Like Marilyn, she was originally from London, England, but their sex and nationality were about all they had in common – Marilyn had been born and raised in Streatham, her mother a nurse and her father a driver on the Underground, while Ana's parents had been Russian exiles, poets who'd escaped Stalin's postwar purges and had set up residence in Hampstead. Still, the two women quickly became friends. Ana was a prominent member of Joe's Corner's extensive cast of eccentrics, but she was also an exemplar of the legion of stout-hearted, sensible, and completely fearless women who before World War Three had explored and done every kind of good work in every corner of the globe. Marilyn had met several of these doughty heroines during her service in the army and had admired them all. The evening she gave Ana a lift into town they had a fine time in the roadhouse, swapping war stories and reminiscing about London and how they'd survived World War Three, and on her next free day Marilyn was more than happy to make a fifty kilometre trip beyond the northern edge of the City of the Dead to visit Ana's desert camp.

By then, Joel Jumonville had told Marilyn a fair number of tall tales about the Queen of the Hive Rats. According to him, the old woman had once shot a bandit who'd tried to rob her, and cut up his body and fed it to her hive rats. Also, that the little figurines she sold to support herself, found nowhere else in the City of the Dead, were rumoured to come from the hold of an ancient spaceship she'd uncovered, she kept a tame tigon she'd raised from a kitten, and she'd learned how to enter hive rat gardens without being immediately attacked and killed. Joel was an inveterate gossip and an accomplished fabulist, so Marilyn also took his stories with large pinches of salt, but when she pulled up by Ana's shack, on a bench terrace cut into a stony ridge that overlooked a broad arroyo, she was amazed to see the old woman pottering about the edge of a hive rat garden. The garden stretched away down the arroyo, crowded with the tall yellow blades of century plants. Columns of hardened mud that Marilyn later learned were ventilation chambers stood here and there, hive rat sentries perched on their hind legs at intervals along the perimeter, and there was a big mound with a hole in its flat top that no doubt led to the heart of the nest.

Jet went crazy over the scent of the hive rats. By the time Marilyn had calmed him down, Ana was climbing the path to her shack, cheerfully helloing them. "How nice to see you, my dear. And your lovely dog. Did you by any chance bring any tea? I ran out two days ago."

Sitting on plastic chairs under a canvas awning that cracked and boomed in the hot breeze, they made do with stale instant coffee and flat biscuits, tasting exactly like burnt toast, that Ana had baked using flour ground from cactus tree bark. There wasn't any trick to walking amongst the hive rats, the old woman told Marilyn. She had worked out the system of pheromonal signals that governed much of their cooperative behaviour, and wore a dab of scent that suppressed secretion of alarm and aggression pheromones by sentries and soldiers, so that the hive rats accepted her as one of their own.

Ana talked a long streak about hive rat biology, explaining how their nests were organised in different castes like ants or bees, how they made their gardens. This garden was the largest known, Ana said, and it was unique not only because it was a monoculture of century plants, but because there was an elaborate system of irrigation ditches and dykes scratched across the arroyo floor. She showed Marilyn views from camera feeds she'd installed in the kilometres of tunnels and shafts and chambers of the nest beneath the garden: workers gnawing at the car-sized tuber of a century plant; endless processions of workers toiling up from the deep aquifer, their bellies swollen with water; one of the fungal gardens that processed the hive rats' waste; a chamber in which a hive rat queen, fed and groomed by workers one-tenth her size, extruded blind, squirming pups with machine-like regularity. Unlike other nests, this one housed many queens, Ana said; it had never split into daughter colonies.

"When I know you better, perhaps I'll tell you why. But enough of my work. Tell me about the world."

Marilyn gave Ana the latest local gossip, and ended up promising to do a supply run for the old woman, who said that she would be grateful not to have to bother with dealing with other people: she was far too busy with her research, which was at a very interesting stage. So Marilyn took a dozen little figurines back to Joe's Corner, smoothly knotted shapes fashioned from some kind of resin that when handled induced a pleasant, dreamy sensation that reminded her of her habit, when she'd been eleven or twelve, of standing at the bathroom sink with her hands up to the wrists in warm water, staring into the fogged mirror, wondering what she would become when she grew up. She sold them to the Nigerian assayer in Joe's Corner, bought supplies and picked up several packages from an electronics supplier along with the rest of Ana's mail, and on her next free day took everything out to the old woman's camp.

After a couple of supply runs, Ana gave Marilyn a tiny brown bottle containing a couple of millilitres of oily suppressor scent, telling her that she could use it to check out tombs that happened to be in the middle of hive rat gardens. "Foolish people try to poison or smoke them out. And they usually get bitten badly because the rats are smarter than most people think. They know how to avoid poison, and their nests are extremely well-ventilated. But if you wear just a dab of suppressor, my dear, you can walk right into those tombs, all of them untouched by looters, and pick up any treasures you might find."

Marilyn promised she'd give it a try, but the bottle ended up unopened in the junk-filled glove compartment of her Bronco. For one thing, she wasn't convinced that it would work, and she knew that you could die from infection with flesh-eating bacteria after a single hive rat bite. For another, she didn't really need to supplement her income from sale of scraps looted from tombs. Her salary as town constable was about a quarter of what she'd received for guarding the late unlamented Albanian businessman, but she had a rent-free room in the Westward Ho! motel and ate for free in Joel's roadhouse most nights, and for the first time in her life she was able to put a little money by for a rainy day.

It occurred to her around this time that she was happy. She had a job she liked, and she liked most of the people in Joe's Corner and could tolerate the rest, and she liked the desert, too. When she wasn't visiting Ana Datlovskaya, she spent most of her free time pottering around the tombs of the City of the Dead, exploring the salt-flats and arroyos and low, gullied hills, learning about the patchwork desert ecology, plants and animals native to First Foot and alien species imported from other worlds by previous tenant races. Camping out in the desert at night, she'd lie in her sleeping bag and look up at the rigid pattens of alien constellations, the two swift moons, the luminous milk of the Phoenix nebula sprawled across the eastern horizon. Earth was about two thousand light years beyond the nebula: the wormhole network linked only fifteen stars, but it spanned the Sagittarius arm of the Galaxy. How strange and wonderful that she should be here, so far from Earth. On an alien world twice the size of Earth, where things weighed half as much again, and the day was a shade over twenty hours long. In a desert full of the tombs of a long-vanished alien race . . .

One day, Marilyn was out at the northern edge of the City of the Dead, sitting on a flat boulder on a low ridge and eating her lunch, when Jet raised up and trotted smartly to the edge of the ridge and began to bark. A few moments later, Marilyn heard the noise of a vehicle off in the distance. She finished what was left of her banana in two quick bites, walked over to where her dog stood, and looked out across the dry playa towards distant hills hazed by dusty air and shimmering heat. The hummocks of ancient tombs in ragged lines amongst drifts of sand and rocks; silvery clouds of saltbush and tall clumps of cactus trees; the green oases of hive rat gardens. The nearest garden was only a kilometre away; Marilyn could see the cat-sized, pinkly naked sentries perched upright amongst its piece-work plantings. Beyond it, a thin line of dust boiled up, dragged by a black Range Rover. As it drew nearer, the hive rat sentries started drumming with their feet, a faint pattering that started Jet barking. Soldiers popped up from the mound in the centre of the garden, two or three times the size of the sentries, armoured with scales and armed with recurved claws and strong jaws that could bite through a man's wrist, running towards the Range Rover as it drove straight across the garden. It ploughed through them, leaving some dead and dying and the rest chasing its dusty wake all the way to the garden's boundary, where they tumbled to a halt and stared after it as it headed up a bare apron of rock towards the ridge.

Marilyn walked over to her Bronco and took her pistol from her day bag and stuck it in the waistband of her shorts and walked back to Jet, who was bristling and barking. The Range Rover had stopped at the bottom of the short steep slope. A blond, burly man stood in the angle of the open door on the far side, staring up at Marilyn as a second man climbed out. He had a deep tan and black hair shaved close to his skull, was dressed in black jeans and a white short-sleeved shirt. Black tattoos on his forearms, black sunglasses that heliographed twin discs of sunlight at Marilyn as he said, "How are you doing, Marilyn? It's been a while."

It was one of the men who'd worked for the security firm back in Port of Plenty. Frank something. Frank Parker.

"I'm wondering why you came all the way out here to find me, Frank. I'm also wondering how you found me."

Marilyn was pretty sure that this wasn't anything do with the Albanians, who liked to do their own dirty work, but she was also pretty sure that Frank Parker and his blond bodybuilder friend were some kind of trouble, and a smooth coolness was filling her up inside, something she hadn't felt for a long time.

"I guess you don't feel like coming down here, so I'll come up," Frank Parker said, and began to pick his way up the stony slope, ignoring Marilyn's sharp request to stay where he was, going down on one knee when his black town shoes slipped on the frangible dirt and pushing up and coming on, stopping only when Jet started to bark at him, knuckling sweat from his forehead and saying, "Feisty fellow, ain't he?"

"He's a pretty good judge of people." Marilyn told Jet to sit, said to Frank Parker, "I'm waiting to hear what you want. Maybe you can start by telling me what you're doing out here. It's a long way from Port of Plenty."

"I wouldn't mind a drink of water," Frank Parker said, and took a couple of steps forward. Jet rose up and started barking again and the man held up his hands, palms out, in a gesture of surrender.

"I'm sure you have a bottle or two in that expensive car of yours," Marilyn said. She was watching him and trying to watch his friend down by the Range Rover at the same time. Her Glock was a hard flat weight against the small of her back and she stepped hard on the impulse to show it to Frank Parker. If she did, it would take things up to the next level and there'd be no going back.

"I bring greetings from another old friend," Frank Parker said. "Tom Archibold. He'd like to invite you over for a chat."

"What's Tom doing out here?"

Like Frank Parker, Tom Archibold had been working for the same security firm that had been employing Marilyn when her client had been blown to bloody confetti. She was trying her best to keep the surprise she felt from her face, but Frank Parker must have seen something of it because his smile broadened into a grin. "Tom told me to tell you that he has a little job for you."

"You can thank Tom for me, and tell him that I already have a job."

"He needs your advice on something is all."

"If he wants my advice, he's welcome to visit me when I get back to town tomorrow. My office is right in the middle of our little commercial strip. You can't miss it. It has a sign with "Town Constable" printed on it hung right above the door."

"He kind of needs you on site," Frank Parker said.

"I don't think so."

"We really would like for you to come right away. It's about your friend Ana Datlovskaya," Frank Parker said, and took a step towards Marilyn.

Jet barked and lunged forward, and Frank Parker reached behind himself and jerked a pistol from his belt, Marilyn shouting no!, and shot Jet in the chest. Jet dropped flat and slid down the slope, and Frank Parker turned to Marilyn, his eyes widening behind his sunglasses when she put her Glock on him and told him to put his weapon down.

"Do it right now!" she said, and shot him in the leg when he didn't.

He fell on his ass and dropped his pistol. Marilyn stepped forwards and kicked it away, saw movement at the bottom of the slope, the man behind the Range Rover raising a machine pistol, and threw herself flat as a short burst walked along the edge of the ridge, whining off stones, smacking into dirt, kicking up dust. Marilyn raised up and took aim, and the man ducked out of sight as the round spanged off the window post beside him. She got off two more shots, aiming for the tyres, but the damned things must have been puncture-proof. The Range Rover started with a roar and reversed at speed, its open door flapping. Marilyn braced and took aim and put a shot through the tinted windshield, and the Range Rover spun in a handbrake turn and took off into the playa, leaving only dust in the air.

Frank Parker was holding his thigh with both hands, blood seeping through laced fingers, face pale and tight with pain. "You fucking shot me, you bitch."

"You shot my dog. But don't think that makes us even."

Marilyn picked up his pistol and told him to roll over on his stomach, patted him down and found a gravity knife in an ankle scabbard. She told him to stay absolutely still if he didn't want to get shot again, and crabbed down the slope to where Jet lay, dusty and limp and dead. She carried him up the slope to her Bronco, set him in the well under the shotgun seat. Frank Parker had sat up again and was clutching his thigh and making threats. She told him to shut up and pulled the q-phone from its holster under the dashboard, but although she tried three times she could raise only a faint conversation between two people who seemed to be shouting at each other in a howling gale in a language she didn't recognise. She tried the shortwave radio, too, but every channel was full of static; that wasn't unexpected, as radio reception ran from patchy to non-existent in the City of the Dead, but she'd never before had a problem with the q-phone. A little miracle that fused alien and human technology, it was worth more than the Bronco and shared a bound pair of electrons with the hub station in Joe's Corner, and should have given her an instant connection even if she was standing on other side of the universe.

Well, she didn't know why the damn thing had decided to throw a glitch, but she was a long way from town, and Ana was in trouble. She found her handcuffs in the glove compartment and walked over to Frank Parker and tossed them into his lap and told him to put them on. As he fumbled with them, she asked him why Tom wanted to talk with her, and what it had to do with Ana Datlovskaya.

Frank Parker told her to go fuck herself, closed his eyes when Marilyn cocked her pistol.

"I can knock off plenty of pieces of you before you die," she said. She was angry and out of patience, and anxious too. "Or maybe give you to the hive rats down there. I bet they're still pissed off after you drove straight through their garden."

After a moment, Frank Parker said, "We've taken over Ana Datlovskaya's claim."

"Taken it over? What does that mean? Have you bastards killed her?"

"No. No, no. It's not like that."

"She's alive."

"We think so."

"She is or she isn't."

"We think she's alive," Frank Parker said. "She got out into the damn garden and ducked into a hole. We haven't been able to get near it."

"Because of the hive rats. Did anyone get eaten?"

"One of us got bitten."

"Tom wants me to persuade her to come out."

The man nodded sullenly. "Word is, you're her good friend. Tom thought you could talk some sense into her."

Marilyn thought about this. "How did you know where to find me? This is my day off, I driving around the desert, no one in town knows where I am. Yet you drive straight towards me. Were you following me?"

"You have a q-phone. We have a magic gizmo that tracks them."

"Does this magic gizmo also stop q-phones working?"

"I don't know. Really, I don't," Frank Parker said. "I was told where to find you, and there you were. Look, the old woman is sitting on something valuable. You can have a share of it. All you have to do is talk to her, persuade her to give herself up. Is that so hard?"

"We walk away afterwards, me and Ana."

"Sure. We'll even cut you in for a share. Why not? Help me up, we can drive straight there — "

"What is it you want from her? Those figurines?"

"It's something to do with those rats. Don't ask me what. I wasn't privy to the deal Tom made."

"I bet. Think you can walk over to my pickup?"

"You shot me in the fucking leg. You're going to have to give me a hand."

"Wrong answer," Marilyn said.

Frank Parker flinched and started to raise his cuffed hands, but she was quicker, and rapped him smartly above his ear with the grip of her pistol and laid him flat.

He started to come round when she dumped him in the loadbed of the Bronco, feebly trying to resist as she tied off the nylon cord she'd wrapped around his calves. "You're fucked," he said. "Well and truly fucked."

Marilyn ignored him and went around to the cab and took out the q-phone and tried it again – still no signal – then put it in the plastic box in which she'd packed her lunch, and piled a little cairn of stones over the box. She didn't really believe that Frank Parker had tracked her with some kind of magic gizmo, but better safe than sorry.

Marilyn drove west along the gravel flats of the playa and then north, into a low range of hills. She parked in the shade of a stand of cactus trees and at gunpoint forced her prisoner to climb down and limp inside one of the tombs that stood like a row of bad teeth along the crest of the hill. She told him to stay right where he was, and pulled a shovel from the space behind the Bronco's seats and dug a grave and lined the grave with flat stones and wrapped Jet in plastic sheeting and laid him at the bottom.

She'd found him six months ago, chained to a wrecked car behind a service station on the coast highway, half-starved, sores everywhere under his matted and filthy coat. When the service station owner had tried to stop her taking him, she'd knocked the man on his ass and dragged him back to the wreck and chained him up and left him there. She'd spent two weeks in a motel farther on down the road, nursing Jet back to health. He'd been a good companion ever since, loyal and affectionate and alert, foolishly brave when it came to standing up to dire cats, hydras, and hive rat soldiers. He'd died defending her, and she wasn't ever going to forget that.

Although she'd attended a couple of dozen funerals during her stint in the army, she could remember only a few of the words of the Service for the Dead, so recited the Lord's Prayer instead. "I'll come back and give you a proper headstone later," she said, and filled in the grave, tiled more stones over the mound, and went to see to her prisoner.

Frank Parker was squashed into a corner of the tomb, staring at the eidolons that drifted out of the shadows: monkey-sized semi-transparent stick figures that whispered in clicks and whistles, gesturing in abrupt jerks like overwound clockwork toys. They haunted about one in a hundred of the tombs. Perhaps they were intended to be representations of the dead, or their household gods, or perhaps they were some sort of eternal ceremony of mourning or celebration or remembrance: no one knew. And no one knew how they had been created, either; they were not affected by the removal of every bit of rotten "circuitry" from the tomb they haunted, by scouring its interior clean, or even by destroying it. According to Ana Datlovskaya, they were manifestations of twists in the quantum foam that underpinned space/time, which as far as Marilyn was concerned was like saying that they'd been created by some old wizard out of dragon's blood and dwarfs' teeth.

Marilyn had grown used to the eidolons; they reminded her of old men at bus stops in London before the war, rubbing their hands in the cold, grumbling about the weather and the price of cat meat. Talking to themselves if no one else was about. But they definitely spooked Frank Parker, who watched them closely as they drifted through the dim air like corpses caught in an underwater current, and flinched when Marilyn's shadow fell over him.

"I'm going to fix up your wound," she said. "I don't want you dying on me. Not yet, at least."

She cut off the leg of the man's jeans and salted the wound – a neat through-and-through in the big muscle on the outside of his thigh – with antiseptic powder and fixed a pad of gauze in place with a bandage. Then they had a little talk. Marilyn learned that Tom Archibold had been working for a street banker who'd bought out the gambling debts of a mathematician in Port of Plenty's university. When the mathematician had come up short on his repayments, Tom had had a little talk with him, and had discovered that he'd been corresponding with Ana Datlovskaya about exotic logic systems, and had been helping her write some kind of translation programme.

"This is the bit you're going to have trouble believing," Frank Parker said. "But I swear it's true."

"You'd better spit it out," Marilyn said, "or I'll leave you here without any water."

"Tom believes that the old woman found the wreck of a spaceship," Frank Parker said. "And she's trying to talk to the part of it that's still alive."

Just two hours later, Marilyn Carter was lying on her belly under a patch of the thorny scrub that grew amongst Boxbuilder ruins on top of the ridge that overlooked the arroyo and the giant hive rat garden. Ana Datlovskaya's tarpaper shack was a couple of hundred metres to the left and somewhat below Marilyn's position. Three Range Rovers were parked beside it. A burly man with a shaven head stood close to one of the Range Rovers and the blond bodybuilder Marilyn had chased off was scanning the hive rat garden with binoculars, a hunting rifle slung over his shoulder. Seeing them together now, Marilyn realized that she'd seen them before. In town a couple of weeks ago, sitting at the counter in the diner. She'd paid them little attention then, thinking that they were just a couple of travellers passing through; now she realized that they must have been on a scouting mission.

The blond man fitted the stock of his rifle to his shoulder and took aim. Marilyn tracked his line of fire, saw a sentry standing chest-high in a hole. Then dust kicked up in front of it and it vanished as the sound of the shot whanged back from the bluffs beyond.

Well, she already knew they were mean. She hoped they were dumb, too.

The swollen sun was about an hour away from setting. Ana had once told Marilyn that because it huddled close to its cool red dwarf sun, First Foot should have been tidally locked, always showing one side to its sun, just as the moon always showed one side to Earth. The fact that there were sunrises and sunsets on First Foot was evidence of some stupendous feat of engineering that had otherwise left no trace, Ana had said: some forgotten race must have spun the planet up like a child's top, giving it a rotational period of ten hours that over millennia had slowed to almost twice that.

The old woman loved to talk about the alien tenants – Boxbuilders, Fisher Kings, Ghostkeepers and all the rest – who had once inhabited the planets and moons and reefs of the fifteen stars linked by the wormhole network. Speculating on why they had come here and what they had done, whether they'd simply died out, or had been wiped out by war, or if they had moved on to somewhere else. To other stars, or to other universes. She'd told Marilyn that some people believed that the Jackaroo collected races as people collected pets, and disposed of them when they lost the lustre of novelty; others that the previous tenants had all been absorbed into the Jackaroo, to become part of a collective, symbiotic consciousness. Anything was possible. No one had ever been aboard one of the Jackaroo's floppy ships, and no one knew what the Jackaroo looked like because they visited Earth only in the form of avatars shaped roughly like people. No one had much idea about the physical appearance of any of the previous tenant races of the wormhole network, either. None of them, not even the Ghostkeepers, who had built the City of the Dead and many other necropolises, had left behind any physical remains or sculptures or pictorial representations. Academics argued endlessly over the carved murals in the so-called Vaults of the Fisher Kings, but no one knew what the murals really represented, or even if the patterns and images discerned by human eyes weren't simply optical illusions. All we really know, Ana liked to say, is that we know nothing at all. At least eight alien races lived here before we came, and each one died out or vanished or moved on, and left behind only empty ruins, odd scraps, and a few enigmatic monuments. But if we can find out the answers to those questions, we might be able to begin to understand why the Jackaroo gave us the keys to the wormhole network; we might even be able to take control of our fate.

Ana was full of strange notions, but she was also a tough desert bird who knew how to look after herself. Marilyn had had no trouble believing Frank Parker's story that the old woman had taken off into the garden and climbed down into the nest to escape Tom Archibold and his men, and it certainly looked like they were hunkered down, waiting for her to come out and surrender. They couldn't go after Ana because they'd be taken down by the hive rats, and as far as Marilyn knew the hole on top of the mound was the only way Ana could get in and out. It was a standoff, and Marilyn was going to have to go in and try to save Ana before things escalated. It was her job, for one thing. And then there was the small matter of doing right by poor Jet.

Marilyn crawled backwards on elbows and knees until she was certain that she wouldn't be skylighted when she stood up. The Boxbuilder ruins ran along the top of the ridge like random strings of giant building blocks, their thin walls and roofs spun from polymer and rock dust by a species that had left hundreds of thousands of similar strings and clusters on every planet and reef and moon linked by the wormholes. Marilyn picked her way through the thorny scrub that grew everywhere amongst the ruins, and walked down the reverse side of the ridge to her Bronco, which she'd parked on a stony apron three kilometres south of the arroyo. She checked the shortwave again – still nothing but static – and lifted out her spare can of petrol and took rags from her toolbox and set off to the east.

She twisted strips torn from the rags around catchclaw and cloudbush plants, soaked them in petrol, and set them alight. Fire bloomed quick and bright and the hot wind blew flames flat amongst the dry scrub and it caught with a crackling roar. Marilyn walked along the track towards Ana's shack with huge reefs of white smoke boiling up into the darkening sky behind her. A harsh smell of burning in the air, and flecks and curls of ash fluttering down. There was a stir of movement amongst the Range Rovers, someone shouted a challenge, a spotlight flared. Marilyn raised her hands as three men walked towards her, two circling left and right, the third, Tom Archibold, saying, "I was wondering when you'd turn up."

"Hello, Tom."

"You set a fire as a diversion, and then you walk right in. What are you up to?"

"The fire isn't a diversion, Tom. It's a signal. In about two hours, people from Joe's Corner will be turning up, wondering who set it."

Tom grinned. "You think a bunch of hicks can make any kind of trouble for us? I'm disappointed, Marilyn. You used to be a lot sharper than that."

"Frank Parker said you needed my help. Here I am. Just remember that I came here voluntarily. And remember that you have about two hours. Maybe less."

"Where is Frank?"

"I shot him, not seriously, after he shot my dog. He'll be okay. I'll tell you where to find him when this is over."

"He won't make any kind of hostage, Marilyn. He fucked up, I could care less if he lives or dies, much less about exchanging the old woman for him."

"How about if I help you get whatever it is you came here for?"

Tom Archibold studied her for a few moments. He was a slim man dressed in a brown turtleneck sweater and blue jeans. Black hair swept back from his keen, handsome face, a Bluetooth earpiece plugged into his left ear. At last, he said, "What do you expect in return?"

"To walk away from this with Ana."

"Why not? I might even throw in a few points from the money I'm going to make."

He said it so quickly and casually that Marilyn knew at once he intended to kill her as soon as she was no longer useful to him. She'd guessed it anyhow, but now that she was in his power she felt a strong chill pass through her.

She said, "Is Ana still inside the nest?"

"Yeah. She ran off into the garden – into the hole atop that mound," Tom said, pointing across the dusky arroyo. "We couldn't follow her because of the damn rats. We've been picking off any that show themselves, but there are any number of them, we can't get close."

"You want me to talk her out of there."

"If she's still alive. We kind of winged her."

"You shot her?"

"We shot at her, when she ran. To try to make her stop. One of the shots might have gotten a little too close."

"Where do you think you hit her?"

"The right leg, it looked like. It can't have been serious. It knocked her down, but she managed to crawl into the hole."

"You were supposed to take her prisoner, but she got away, you wounded her . . . It's all gone bad, hasn't it?"

"We have you."

"Only because I wanted to come here. Don't you forget that. I'm curious, by the way. Why involve me at all?"

Tom smiled. "Either you're bluffing, pretending to be ignorant to see if I'll let something slip, or you aren't really the old woman's friend. Let's sit down and talk."

After the blond bodybuilder had quickly and thoroughly patted Marilyn down, she and Tom sat on Ana's plastic chairs and Tom asked her every kind of question about Ana's research. She answered as truthfully as she could, but it quickly became clear that Tom knew a lot more about most of it than she did. He knew that Ana and the mathematician in Port of Plenty had been working up computer models of the hive rats' behaviour, and that they had been developing some kind of artificial intelligence programme. He also knew that Ana had discovered that the behaviour of the hive rats was strongly influenced by pheromones, but he didn't seem to know that Ana had synthesised pheromone analogs.

When he had run out of questions, Marilyn said, "I can help you, but I think I need to talk to your client first."

"What makes you think I have a client?"

"You wouldn't have gone to all this trouble to chase a rumour about a crashed spaceship. It isn't your style, and I doubt that you have the kind of cash to pay for an operation like this. After all, you stumbled on Ana's research when you were working as a debt collector. So you're working for someone. That's the kind of people we are, Tom. We put our lives on the line for other people. I believe that he's sitting in one of those Range Rovers," Marilyn said. "The guy guarding them hasn't budged since I turned up, and you have a Bluetooth connection in your ear. That will only work over a very short range here, and my guess is he'd been using it to listen in to us, and feed you questions. How am I doing?"

Tom didn't answer at once. Marilyn wondered if he was listening to his client, or if she'd pushed him too far, if he was reconsidering his options. At last, he said, "How can you help us?"

"I know the trick Ana used to get inside the nest without being killed and eaten."

Another pause. Tom said, "All right. If you go in there and bring her out, you can speak to my client. Deal?"

"Deal."

"You're in for a surprise," Tom said. "But right now, you had better tell me how you're going to walk in there."

"I need something from Ana's shack."

The hot air inside the shack smelled strongly of Ana Datlovskaya and the smoking oil lamp that was the only illumination. A woman lay on Ana's camp bed. Julie Bell, another of Marilyn's former colleagues. She was unconscious. Her jeans had been cut off at the knees and bandages around her calves were spotted with blood and the flesh above and below the bandages was swollen red and shiny.

"You should get her to a hospital right now," Marilyn told Tom. "Otherwise she's going to die of blood poisoning."

"The sooner we get this done, the sooner we can get out of here. What's that?"

Marilyn had opened the little chemical icebox and taken out a rack of little brown bottles. She explained that they contained artificial pheromones that Ana had synthesised. She held up the largest, the only one with a screw cap, and said that a dab of this would allow her to follow Ana down into the nest.

"I don't think so," Tom said. "If that shit really works, we can do it ourselves."

"It won't work on men. Only women. Something to do with hormones."

"Bullshit," Tom said, but Marilyn could see that he was thinking as he stared at her. Trying to figure out if she was telling the truth or making a move.

"Why don't you try it out?" she said, and handed it to him.

Tom volunteered the blond bodybuilder. The man didn't look very happy as, in the glare of the spotlights on top of two of the Range Rovers, he edged down the path towards the edge of the hive rats' garden. The sun had set now and stars were popping out across the darkening sky, obscured in the east by smoke of the fire Marilyn had set. When the blond man reached the bottom of the path, sentries popped up from holes here and there amongst the tall century plants, and he turned and looked up at his boss and said that he didn't think that this was a good idea.

"Just get on with it," Tom said.

Standing beside him, Marilyn felt a sick eagerness. She knew what was going to happen, and she knew that it was necessary.

The man cocked his pistol and stepped forward, as if onto thin ice. Sentries near and far began to slap their feet, and the ground in front of the bodybuilder collapsed as soldiers heaved out of the gravelly sand, snapping long jaws filled with pointed teeth. The man tried to run, and one of the soldiers sprang forward and seized his ankle. He crashed down full-length and then two more soldiers were on him. He kicked and punched at them, screamed when one bit off his hand. More soldiers were running through the shadows cast by the century plants and Tom pulled his pistol and aimed and shot the bodybuilder in the head, shot at the soldiers as they tore at the body. Dust boiled up around it as it slowly sank.

The surviving goon, the one who'd been guarding the Range Rovers, invoked Jesus Christ, and Tom turned to Marilyn and hit her hard in the face with the back of his hand, knocking her down. She sat looking up at him, not moving, feeling a worm of blood run down her cheek where his signet ring had torn her skin.

"You're going down there," Tom said.

"I need the pheromone first," Marilyn said.

"Right now," Tom said. "Let's see how fast you can run."

Marilyn had rubbed the suppressor scent that Ana had given her over her arms and face before she'd walked up to the shack and surrendered; the stuff she'd told Tom was a pheromone that would guarantee safe passage, but only for women, had been nothing more than the base solution of neutral oil, and gave as much protection from the hive rats' aggression towards trespassers as a sheet of paper against a bullet. She wasn't at all certain that it would keep her safe now that the hive rats had been stirred up, but she reckoned she had a better chance with the rats than with the two men silhouetted above her in the glare of the spotlights as she walked down the path.

The spotlights lit up a wide swathe of the garden like a theatrical set, stark and hyperreal against the darkness of the rest of the arroyo. The blades of century plants that towered above Marilyn, growing in sinuous lines and clumps between irrigation ditches, glowed banana yellow. The churned patch of dirt that had swallowed the blond bodybuilder was directly ahead. Marilyn stepped past it, feeling that her skin was about a size too small, remembering how she'd felt moving from position to position in the ruins of the outskirts of Paris, trying to pinpoint a sniper that had shot three of her squad. A hive rat sentry was watching her from its perch on a flat slab of rock, pink skin glistening, an arc of small black eyes glittering above its tiny undershot mouth. She took a wide detour around it and spotted others standing under the century plants as she made her way towards the mound.

The mound was ten metres high, shaped like a small volcano or the entrance to the lair of monster-movie ants, smooth and unmarked apart from a trail of human footprints. She trod carefully up the slope, aware of the hive rats scattered across the garden and the two men watching her from the bench terrace. At the top, a flat rim circled a hole or vent a couple of metres across. Marilyn stepped up to the lip, saw spikes hammered into the hard crust, a rope ladder dropping into darkness. Hot air blew past her face. It stank of ammonia and a rotten musk. She called Ana's name, and when nothing came back shouted across to Tom Archibold and told him that she was going in.

He shouted back, said that she had thirty minutes. He sounded angry and on edge. The death of his goon had definitely spooked him, and Marilyn hoped that he was beginning to worry that a posse from Joe's Corner might soon turn up.

"I'll take as long as it needs," she said, and with a penlight in her teeth like a pirate's cutlass started to climb down the rope ladder into the hot stinking dark.

The shaft went down a long way, flaring out into a vault whose walls were ribbed with long vertical plates. Marilyn shone the penlight around and saw something jutting out of the wall a few metres below, a wooden platform little bigger than a bed, hung from a web of ropes. Ana Datlovskya sat there with her back to the wall, her face pale in the beam of the penlight and one arm raised straight up, aiming a pistol at Marilyn.

"Tell me you have arrested those fools."

"Not yet," Marilyn said, and explained how she had taken one man prisoner, how another had been badly bitten and a third had been killed by the hive rats after she had tricked him into wearing only the base solvent. "There are only two left. Three, if their client is hiding inside one of those Range Rovers. I managed to convince them that your suppressor only works for women. Can I come down? I feel very vulnerable, hanging here."

Ana told her to be careful, the platform was meant for only one person. When Marilyn reached her, she saw that the old woman had cut away one leg of her jeans and tied a bandage around her thigh. Rusty vines of dry blood wrapped her skinny bare leg. She refused to let Marilyn look at her wound, saying that it was a flesh wound, nothing serious, and she refused the various painkillers Marilyn had brought, too.

"I have a first-aid kit here. I have already treated myself to a Syrette of morphine, and need no more because I must keep a clear head. I climbed down powered by adrenaline, but I don't think I can climb back up."

"Is there any other way out of here?"

"Unless you are very good at digging, no."

Ana sat on a big cushion with her injured leg stretched out straight. Her face was taut with pain and beaded with sweat. There was a laptop beside her – not the notebook she kept in her shack but a cutting-edge q-bit machine that used the same technology as Marilyn's q-phone, phenomenally fast and with a memory so capacious it could swallow the contents of the British Library in a single gulp. Ledges cut into the wall held boxes of canned food and bottled water, a bank of car batteries, a camping stove: a regular little encampment or den.

"I think you had better tell me why Tom Archibold and his client are so interested in you," Marilyn said.

She was planning to climb back out and talk to Tom and his client, stretch things out by pretending to negotiate with them until help arrived. Although she couldn't be sure that anyone in town would have noticed the smoke from the fire before night had fallen, or that they'd link it to the fact that she hadn't returned from her day-trip to the desert, that she might be in trouble . . .

Ana said, "They did not tell you?"

"They told me you found a spaceship."

"And you thought they were lying. Well, it's true. Don't look so surprised. We have spaceships, yes? So did the other tenants. The ones who lived here before us. And one of them crashed here, long, long ago. It was not very big, smaller than a car in fact, and all that's left of it are scraps of hull material, worth nothing. I send a piece to be analysed. Someone has already found something identical on some lonely rock around another star, took a patent out on its composition."

"So it's worthless. That's good. Or it will be, if we can convince the bad guys that you don't have anything worth stealing."

Ana shook her head. "I should not have trusted Zui Lin."

"This is your mathematician friend."

"I needed help to construct the logic of the interface, and the AI programme, but I confided too much to him. You see the goggles, on the shelf? Put them on and take a look below us. They do not like ordinary light, it disrupts their behaviour. But they show up very well in infra red."

Marilyn fitted the goggles over her eyes. The platform creaked as she leaned over the side, holding onto the rope ladder for support. Directly below, grainy white clouds were flowing past each other. Hive rats. Hundreds of them. Thousands. Moving over the floor and lower parts of the wall of the chamber in clusters that merged and broke apart and turned as one like flocks of birds on the wing . . .

Behind her, Ana said, "There was a war. A thousand years ago, ten thousand . . . My friend does not think of time as we do, in days or in seasons, as something with a linear flow. So it is not clear how long ago. But there was a war, and during the war a spaceship crashed here."

"The hive rats were on it? Is that where they came from?"

"No. If there were living things on the spaceship, they died. You remember, we talked about where the former tenants of this shabby little empire went to?"

"They died out. Or they went somewhere else."

"This species, they transformed. They made a very large and very rapid change. At least, some of them did. And those that changed and those that did not change fought . . . The spaceship was a casualty of that war. It was badly damaged and it crashed. What survived was its mind. It was something like a computer, but also something like a kind of bacterial colony. Or a virus culture. I have tried to understand it, but it is hard. It was in any case self-aware. It was damaged and it was dying, so it created a copy of itself and found a platform where the copy could establish itself – a hive rat colony. It infected the hive rats with a logic kernel and a compressed version of the memory files that had survived the crash, and over many years the seed of the logic kernel unpacked and grew as the colony grew. It needs to be very big because it must support many Individuals that do nothing but act as hosts for the ship-mind. The dance you see down there, that is the mind at work."

"There must be hundreds of them," Marilyn said.

It was oddly hypnotic, like watching schools of fish endlessly ribboning back and forth across a reef.

"Many thousands," Ana said. "You can see only part of it from here. Each group processes a number of sub-routines. The members of each group move endless around each other to exchange information, and the different groups merge or flow past each other to share information too. The processing is massively parallel and the mathematics underlying it is fractally compact, but even so, the clock speed is quite slow. Still, I have learnt much."

Marilyn sat back and pulled off the goggles. "Ana, are you trying to say that you can talk to it?"

"At first it tried to talk to me. It made the figurines, but they were not successful. They are supposed to convey information, but only arouse emotions, moods. But they inspired me to work hard on establishing a viable method of communication, and at last, with the help of Zui Lin, I succeeded."

Ana explained that her laptop was connected to a light display set in the heart of the nest. When she typed a question, it was translated into a display that certain groups of rats understood, and other groups formed shapes which a programme written by Zui Lin translated back into English.

"It takes a long time to complete the simplest conversation, but time is what I have, out here. I should have showed you this before. It would make things easier now."

"You didn't trust me. It's all right. I understand."

"I did not think you would believe me. But now you must."

Ana looked about a hundred years old in the beam of the penlight.

"I think you had better give me your gun," Marilyn said. "Maybe I can get the drop on Tom Archibold and his goon. If it comes to it, I'll kill them."

"And his client, too."

"Yes. If it comes to it."

"You may find that hard," Ana said.

"You know who he is, don't you?"

"I have a good idea . . ." Ana took Marilyn's hand. Her grip was feeble and feverish but her gaze was steady. "I also have a way of dealing with those men, and their client. I have everything you need, down here. I would have used it myself if I hadn't been hurt."

"Show me."

After Marilyn had climbed out into the glare of the spotlights, the smell of smoke, and the gentle rain of ash from the fire to the east, she held up the q-bit laptop and said loudly, "This is what you came for."

"Come straight here," Tom Archibold shouted back. "No tricks."

"I've done my part. I expect your client to stick to the agreement. I want him to tell me himself that he'll take this laptop and let me and Ana go free. That you'll all go back to Port of Plenty and you won't ever come after us. Otherwise, I'll sit out here and wait for my friends to come investigate the fire. They can't be far away, now."

There was a long silence. At last, Tom said, "My client says that he has to look at the evidence before he decides what to do."

"Good. He can see that it's exactly as advertised."

Marilyn crabbed down the side of the mound and walked out across the garden. Sentries stood everywhere, making a low drumming sound that raised the hairs on the back of her neck, and crevices were opening all around, full of squirming motion. It occurred to her that Ana's suppressor might not protect her once the entire colony was aroused, but she steeled herself and stopped a dozen metres from the edge of the garden. On the bench terrace above, Tom told her come straight up the path, and she said that he had to be kidding.

"I can talk to your client from here."

"Easier all round if you come up," Tom said. "If I wanted to shoot you, Marilyn, I would have already done it."

"Bullshit," Marilyn said. "You haven't shot me because you know there's no way you could try to retrieve this laptop without being eaten alive."

She had to wait while Tom disappeared from view, presumably to confer directly with his client. Tom's surviving goon stood above, watching her impassively; she stared back at him, trying not to flinch at the stealthy scrabbling noises behind her. And then two figures joined him. One was Tom Archibold; the other was a tall mannequin that moved with stiff little steps.

Tom's client was a Jackaroo avatar.

Marilyn had seen them on TV back on Earth, but had never before faced one. It was two metres tall, dressed in a nondescript black suit, its pale face vaguely male and vaguely handsome. A showroom dummy brought to life; a shell woven from a single molecule of complex plastic doped with metals, linked by a version of q-bit tech to its Jackaroo operator, who could be in orbit around First Foot, or Earth, or a star at the far end of the universe.

In a rich baritone, it questioned Marilyn about the copy of the ship-mind lodged in the hive rat colony, and watched a slide-show of random photographs on the laptop.

"The ship-mind has migrated to that device," it said, at last.

"Ana made a copy of the kernel from which it grew, and found a way of running it in the laptop," Marilyn said. Her arms ached from holding it up.

"There is a copy in the device and a copy in the hive rat colony. Are there any others?"

"Not that I know of," Marilyn said, hoping that neither the Jackaroo nor Tom Archibold would spot the lie.

"You will give us the laptop in exchange for your life."

"My life, and Ana's. You don't have much time," Marilyn said. "People will be here any minute, drawn by the fire. And they'll be wondering why I haven't called in, too."

"How do I know you won't come after me?" Tom said.

"You have my word," Marilyn said.

"You will let the two women live," the avatar told him. "I want only the copy of the ship-mind, and you want only your fee."

Tom didn't look happy about this, but told Marilyn to walk on up the path.

"Tell your man to put up his gun," she said.

Tom gave a brusque order and the goon stepped back. Marilyn pressed the space bar of the laptop and closed it up and started up the path, walking slowly and deliberately, trying to ignore the scratching stir across the garden at her back. Trying to keep count in her head.

When she reached the top of the path, Tom stepped forward and snatched the laptop from her, and the goon grabbed her arms and held her.

"There's a lot more to it than the stuff on the laptop," Marilyn said. "I can tell you what the old woman told me. Everything she told me during our long conversations."

"The ship-mind is all I want," the avatar said.

"They went somewhere else," Marilyn said. She was still counting inside her head. "Is that why you're interested in them? Or are you frightened that we'll learn something you don't want us to know?"

The avatar swung its whole body around so that it could look at her. "Do not presume," it said.

She knew she had hit a nerve and it made her bolder. And the count was almost done. "I was just wondering why you broke your agreement with the UN. This world and the other places – they're where we can make a new start. You aren't ever supposed to come here. You're supposed to leave us alone."

"In ten years or a hundred years or a thousand years it will come to you as it came to the others," the avatar said.

"We'll change," Marilyn said. "We'll become something new."

"From what we have seen so far, it is likely that you will destroy yourselves. As others have done. As others will do, when you are less than a memory. It is inevitable, and it should not be hurried."

Marilyn's countdown reached zero. She said, "Is that why you're here? Are you scared we'll learn something we shouldn't?"

The avatar stiffly turned and looked at the laptop Tom held. "Why is that making a noise?"

"I can't hear anything," Tom said.

"It is at the frequency of twenty-four point two megahertz," the avatar said. "Beyond the range of your auditory system, but not mine."

Tom stepped towards Marilyn, asking her what she'd done, and there was a vast stir of movement in the garden below. In the glare of the spotlights and in the shadows beyond, all around the stalks of the stiff sails of the century plants, the ground was moving.

Ana had once told Marilyn that the hive rat nest contained more than a hundred thousand individuals, a biomass of between two point five and three hundred metric tons. Most of that seemed to be flooding towards the bench terrace: a vast and implacable wave of hive rats clambering over each other, six or seven deep. A flesh-coloured tide that flowed fast and strong between the century plants and smashed into the slope and started to climb. A great hissing high-pitched scream like a vast steam engine about to explode. A wave of ammoniacal stench.

Tom Archibold raised his pistol and aimed it at Marilyn, and the avatar stepped in front of him and in its booming baritone said that it wanted the woman alive, and snatched the laptop from him and wheeled around and began to march towards the Range Rovers. The goon pushed Marilyn forward, but a living carpet of hive rats was already rippling across the ground in front of them and when they stopped and turned there were hive rats behind them too, two waves meeting and climbing over each other and merging in a great stream that chased after the avatar as it stepped stiffly along. The goon let go of Marilyn and ran, and hive rats swarmed up him and he batted at them and went down, screaming. Tom raised his pistol and got off a single round that whooped past Marilyn, and then he was down too, covered in a seething press, jerking and crawling, and then he lay still and the hive rats moved on, chasing after the laptop that the avatar carried.

Ana had released a pheromone into the nest that made the hive rats believe that they were being attacked by another nest, and painted the laptop with a scent that mimicked that of a hive rat queen. This had drawn most of the hive rats in nest to the surface, and they had begun their attack when the laptop had started to play the sound file Marilyn had activated: a recording of a hive rat queen distress call. The nest believed that one of its queens had been captured, and was rushing to her defense.

Marilyn stood still as rats scurried past on either side of her, scared that she'd be bitten if she stepped on one. The avatar wrenched open the door of the nearest Range Rover and bent inside, and a muscular stream of hive rats flowed over it. The avatar was strong and its shell was tough. It managed to start the Range Rover and the big vehicle shot forward, packed with furious movement and pursued by the army of hive rats. It ploughed through the plastic chairs and the awning, swerved snakewise past the shack, and drove straight off the edge of the bench terrace and slammed down nose first into the garden below.

The flood of hive rats washed over it and receded, streaming away, sinking into holes and burrows. Marilyn stepped carefully amongst the hundreds of hive rats that were still moving about the bench terrace, collecting up the injured and dying. Tom Archibold and his goon were messily dead. So was Julie Bell, inside the shack. In the Range Rover, the avatar was half-crushed between the steering wheel and the broken seat. Its suit had been ripped to shreds and its shell had been torn open by the strong teeth and claws of soldier hive rats, and it did not move when Marilyn dared to lean into the Range Rover, searching for and failing to find the laptop – the hive rats must have carried it off to their nest.

The avatar wouldn't or couldn't answer her questions, began to leak acrid white smoke from the broken parts of its shell. Marilyn snatched up a briefcase and beat a hasty retreat when the avatar suddenly burst into flame, burning in a fierce flare that set the Range Rover on fire, too, a funeral pyre that sent hot light and dark smoke beating out across the garden as the last of the hive rats scurried home.

When the posse from Joe's Corner arrived, late and loud and half-drunk, Marilyn was setting up a scaffold tripod over the hole in the top of the mound. She gave Joel Jumonville and the three men he'd brought with him the last of her suppressor, and they reluctantly followed her across the garden and helped her rig up a harness; then she climbed down the rope ladder and helped Ana Datlovskya into the harness and Joel and his men hauled the old woman out by main force. Ana passed out as soon as she reached the top. The men carried her across the garden and drove her off to the clinic in Joe's Corner, and Marilyn drove Joel to the tomb where she had stashed her prisoner, Frank Parker.

Frank Parker lawyered up and parlayed a deal. Marilyn had to agree to drop most of the charges against him in exchange for a lead that pointed the UN police in Port of Plenty to a room in a hotbed motel near the city's docks, where Tom Archibold had stashed Zui Lin. The mathematician had been interrogated by the avatar, and confirmed most of Marilyn's story. The UN provisional authority on First Foot made a formal protest about the avatar's presence, and in due course received apologies from the Jackaroo, who blamed a rogue element and made bland assurances that it would not happen again.

Ana Datlovskaya was in a coma for two weeks, and nearly died from blood loss and infection. Reporters set up camp outside the clinic; Marilyn arrested two who tried to sneak into her room, and deputised townspeople to set up an around-the-clock watch.

When Ana recovered consciousness, she told Marilyn her last little secret. Marilyn and Joel Jumonville drove out to the arroyo and paced off distances from Ana's shack and dug down carefully and retrieved the plastic-wrapped box with Ana's papers and a q-bit hard drive that contained not only a copy of all her work on the hive rats, but also a back-up of the hard drive of the laptop lost somewhere under the hive rat garden.

Marilyn and Joel drank from ice-cold bottles of beer from the cooler they'd brought along, standing side by side at the edge of the bench terrace and looking out at the simmering garden down in the arroyo. It was noon, hot and peaceful. Every blade of century plant stood above its shrunken shadow. Hive rat sentries stood guard on flat stones in front of their pop holes.

"I can almost see why she wants to come back," Joel said.

Ana had told Marilyn that she still had a lot of work to do. "I had only just begun a proper conversation with the ship-mind before I was so rudely interrupted. Now I will have to have to start over again. Things may go more quickly if Zui Lin sticks to his promise and comes out here to help me, but it will be a long time before we know whether or not the Jackaroo avatar told you anything like the truth."

Marilyn warned the old woman that people were already talking about her work with the hive rats and the ship-mind, showed her a fat fan of newspapers that had made it their headline story. "You're famous, Ana. You're going to have to become used to that."

"I will be beleaguered by fools looking for the secret of the universe," the old woman said. She looked frail and shrunken against the clean linen of the clinic bed, but her gaze was still as fierce as a desert owl's.

"The Jackaroo thought that the ship-mind knew something important," Marilyn said. "Something that might help us understand what happened to the other tenant races. What might happen to us."

"As if we can learn from the fate of other species, when we have learnt so little from our own history," Ana said. "Whatever the ship-mind knows, and I do not yet know it knows anything important, we must make our own future."

Marilyn thought about that now, when Joel Jumonville asked her what she was going to do next.

"Why I ask, you're going to be rich," Joel said. "And the last constable, he ran out when he struck it rich with that room-temperature superconductor."

The briefcase Marilyn had pulled out of the avatar's Range Rover had contained a little gizmo that not only tracked and disrupted q-phones, but could also eavesdrop on them – a violation of quantum mechanics that was like catnip to physicists. Marilyn had a patent lawyer, a cousin of the town's assayer, working full time in Port of Plenty to establish her rights to a share of profits from any new technology derived from reverse engineering the gizmo. Marilyn planned to give half of anything she earned to Ana; so far all she had was a bunch of unpaid legal bills.

She took a slug of beer and studied the shimmering hive rat garden, the sentries standing upright and alert beneath the great sails of the century plants. "Oh, I think I'll stick around for a little while," she said. "Someone has to make sure that Ana will be able to get on with her work without being disturbed by tourists and charlatans. And besides, my contract has six months to run."

"And after that?"

"Hell, Joel, who knows what the future holds?"

THE VOYAGE OUT

Gwyneth Jones

One of the most acclaimed British writers of her generation, Gwyneth Jones was a co-winner of the James Tiptree Jr. Memorial Award for work exploring genre issues in science fiction, in her 1991 novel *White Queen*, and has also won the Arthur C. Clarke Award, for her novel *Bold as Love*. She also received two World Fantasy Awards – for her story "The Grass Princess" and for her collection *Seven Tales and a Fable*. Her other books include the novels *North Wind*, *Flowerdust*, *Escape Plans*, *Divine Endurance*, *Phoenix Café*, *Castles Made of Sand*, *Stone Free*, *Midnight Lamp*, *Kairos*, *Life*, *Water in the Air*, *The Influence of Ironwood*, *The Exchange*, *Dear Hill*, *Escape Plans*, *The Hidden Ones*, and *Rainbow Bridge*, as well as more than sixteen young adult novels published under the name Ann Halam. Her too infrequent short fiction has appeared in *Interzone*, *Asimov's Science Fiction*, *Off Limits*, and other magazines and anthologies, and has been collected in *Identifying the Object: A Collection of Short Stories and Seven Tales and a Fable*. She is also the author of the critical study *Deconstructing the Starships: Science Fiction and Reality*. Her most recent book is a new SF novel, *Spirit: The Princess of Bois Dormant*. She has a website at homepage.ntl-world.com/gwynethann/. She lives in Brighton, England, with her husband, her son, and a Burmese cat.

Here she tells the story of a woman who is forced to leave behind everything she knows, and is thrust, quite literally, into the unknown.

I

"DO YOU WANT to dream?"

"No."

The woman in uniform behind the desk looked at her screen and then looked at me, expressionless. I didn't know if she was real and far away; or fake and here.

"Straight to orientation then."

II

I walked. The Kuiper Belt Station – commonly known as the Panhandle – could afford the energy fake gravity requires. It wasn't going anywhere; it was spinning on the moving spot of a minimum-collision orbit, close to six billion kilometres from the sun: a prison isle without a native population. From here I would be transported to my final exile from the United States of Earth, as an algorithm, a string of 0s and 1s. It's illegal to create a code-version of a human being anywhere in the USE, including near-space habitats and planetary colonies. Protected against identity theft, the whole shipload of us, more than a hundred condemned criminals, had been brought to the edge: where we must now be coded individually before we could leave. The number-crunching would take a while, even with the most staggering computation power.

A reprieve, then. A stay of *execution*

In my narrow cabin, or cell, I lay down on the bunk. Walls, floor, fittings: everything was made of the same, grey-green, dingy ceramic fibre. The 'mattress' felt like metal to the touch, but it yielded to the shape and weight of my body. The raised rim made me think of autopsies, crushed viscera. A panel by my head held the room controls: just like a hotel. I could check the status of my vacuum toilet, my dry shower, my air, my pressure, my own emissions, detailed in bright white.

Questions bubbled behind my lips, never to be answered. I was disoriented by weeks of being handled only by automation (sometimes with a human face); never allowed any contact with my fellow prisoners. When did I last speak to a human being? That must have been the orientation on earth, my baggage allowance session. You're given a "weight limit" – actually a code limit – and advised when you've "duplicated". *Gray's Anatomy*, for old sake's sake. A really good set of knives, a really good pair of boots, a field first-aid kit, vegetable and flower seeds. The Beethoven piano sonatas, played by Alfred Brendel; Mozart piano sonatas, likewise. The prison officer told me I couldn't have the first aid. He advised me I must *choose* the data storage device for my minimalist choice of entertainments, and *specify* the lifetime power source. He made me handle the knives, the boots, the miniaturized hardware, even the seeds. What a palaver.

But the locker underneath the bunk was empty.

Do you want to dream?

The transit would happen, effectively, in no time at all. I had no idea how long the coding would take. An hour, a week, a month? I thought of the others, dreaming in fantasy boltholes. Some gorging their appetites, delicate or gross. Some exacting hideous revenge on the forces that brought them here: fathers, mothers, lovers; authority figures, SOCIETY. Some even trying to expiate their crimes in virtual torment; you get all sorts in the prison population. None of that for me. If you want to die have the courage to kill yourself, before you reach a finale like this one. If you don't, then live to the last breath. Face the firing squad without a blindfold.

Scenes from my last trial went through my head. Me, bloody but unbowed of course, still trying to make speeches, thoroughly alienating the courtroom witnesses. My ex-husband making unconscious gestures in a small blank room, as he finally abandoned this faulty domestic appliance to her fate. He was horrified by that Death Row interview: I was not. I had given up on Dirk long ago. Did he *ever* believe in me? Or was he just humouring my unbalanced despair, as he says now – in the years when we were lovers and best friends? Did he really twist his hands around like that, and raise them high, palm outwards, as if he faced a terrorist with a gun?

I thought of the girl who had caught my eye, glimpsed as we sometimes glimpsed each other; waiting to be processed into the Panhandle system. Springy cinnamon braids, sticking out on either side of her head, that made her look like a little girl. Her eyes lobotomized. Who had brushed her hair for her? Why would they waste money sending a lobotomy subject out here? Because it's a numbers game they're playing. The weaklings, casualties of the transit, may ensure in some occult way the survival of a few, who may live long enough to form the foundation stones of a colony, on an earth-like planet of a distant star. Our fate: to be pole-axed and buried in the mud where the bridge of dreams will be built.

I wondered when "orientation" would begin. The cold of deep space penetrated my thin quilt. The steady shift of the clock numerals was oddly comforting, like a heartbeat. I watched them until at some point I fell asleep.

III

The Kuiper Belt Station had been planned as the hub of an international deep space city. Later, after that project had been abandoned and before the Buonarotti Device became practicable for mass exits like this one, it'd been an R&R resort for asteroid miners. They'd dock their little rocket ships and party, escaping from utter solitude to get crazy drunk and murder each other, according to the legends. I thought of those old no-hopers as I followed the guidance lights to my first orientation session; but there was no sign of them, no scars, no graffiti on the drab walls of endless curving corridors. There was only the pervasive hum of the Buonarotti torus, like the engines of a vast majestic passenger liner forging through the abyss. The sound – gentle on the edge of hearing – made me shudder. It was warming up, of course.

In a large bare saloon, prisoners in tan overalls were shuffling past a booth where a figure in medical-looking uniform questioned them and let them by. A circle of chairs, smoothly fixed to the floor or maybe extruded from it, completed the impression of a dayroom in a mental hospital. I joined the line. I didn't speak to anyone and nobody spoke to me, but the girl with the cinnamon braids was there. I noticed her. My turn came. The woman behind the desk, whom I immediately christened Big Nurse, checked off my name and asked me to take the armband that lay on the counter. "It's good to know we have a doctor on the team," she said.

I had qualified as a surgeon but it was years since I'd practised, other than as a volunteer "barefoot" GP in Community Clinics for the under-class. I looked at the armband that said "captain" and wondered how it had got there, untouched by human hand. Waldoes, robot servitors . . . It was disorienting to be reminded of the clunky, mechanical devices around here; the ones I was not allowed to see.

"Where are you in the real world?" I asked, trying to reclaim my dignity. I knew they had ways of dealing with the time-lapse, they could fake almost natural dialogue. "Where is the Panhandle run from these days? Xichang? Or Houston? I'd just like to know what kind of treatment to expect, bad or worse."

"No," said Big Nurse, answering a different question. "I am a bot." She looked me in the eye, with the distant kindness of a stranger to human concerns. "I am in the information system, nowhere else. There is no treatment, no punishment here, Ruth Norman. That's over."

I glanced covertly at my companions, the ones already hovering around the day-room chairs. I'd been in prison before; I'd been in reform camp before. I knew what could happen to a middle-class woman, in jail for the unimpressive "crime" of protesting the loss of our civil liberties. The animal habit of self-preservation won out. I slipped the band over the sleeve of my overalls. Immediately a tablet appeared, in the same place on the counter. It was solid when I picked it up.

I quickly discovered that, of the fourteen people in the circle (there were eighteen names listed on my tablet, the missing four never turned up), less than half had opted to stay awake. I tried to convince the dream-deprived that I had not been responsible for the mix-up. I asked them all to answer to their names. They complied, surprisingly willing to accept my authority – for the moment.

"Hil . . . de . . . " said the girl with the cinnamon braids, struggling with a tongue too thick for her mouth: a sigh and a guttural duh, like the voice of a child's teddy bear, picked up and shaken after long neglect. The braids had not been renewed, fuzzy strands were escaping. Veterans of prison-life glanced at each other uneasily. Nobody commented. There was another woman who didn't speak at all, so lacking in response you wondered how she'd found her way to the dayroom.

We were nine women, four men and one female-identifying male transsexual (to give the Sista her prison-system designation). The details on my tablet were meagre: names, ages, ethnic/national grouping, not much else. Mrs Miqal Rohan was Iranian and wore strict hejabi dress, but spoke perfect, icy English. "Bimbam" was European English, rail thin, and haunted by some addiction that made her chew frantically at the inside of her cheek. The other native Englishwoman, a Caribbean ethnic calling herself Servalan (Angela Morrison, forty-three), looked as if she'd been institutionalized all her life. I had no information about their crimes. But as I entered nicknames, and read the qualifications or professions, I saw a pattern emerging, and I didn't like it. Such useful people! How did you all come to this pass? By what strange accidents did you all earn mandatory death sentences or life-without-parole? Will the serial killers, the drug cartel gangsters, and the re-offending child rapists please identify yourselves?

I kept quiet, and waited to hear what anyone else would say.

The youngest of the men (Koffi, Nigerian; self-declared "business entrepreneur") asked, diffidently, "Does anyone know how long this lasts?"

"There's no way of knowing," said Carpazian, who was apparently Russian, despite the name; a slim and sallow thirty-something, still elegant in the overalls. "The Panhandle is a prison system. It can drug us and deceive us without limit."

The man who'd given his handle as Drummer raised heavy eyes and spoke, sonorous as a prophet, from out of a full black beard. "We will be ordered to the transit chamber as we were ordered to this room; or drugged and carried by robots in our sleep. We will lie down in the Buonarotti capsules, and a code-self, the complex pattern of each human body and soul, will be split into two like a cell dividing. The copies will be sent flying around the torus, at half-light speed. You will collide with yourself and cease utterly to exist at these co-ordinates of space-time. The body and soul in the capsule will be *annihilated*, and know GOD no longer.'

"But then we wake up on another planet?" pleaded Servalan, unexpectedly shy and sweet from that coarsened mask.

"Perhaps."

The prophet resumed staring at the floor.

"Isn't it against your religion to be here, Mr Drummer?"

He made no answer. The speaker was "Gee", a high-flier, corporate, who must have got caught up in something *very* sour. A young and good-looking woman with an impervious air of success, even now. I marked her down as a possible troublemaker, and tried to start a conversation about survival skills. That quickly raised another itchy topic. Is there *really* no starship? Not even a lifepod? Are we *really, truly* meant to pop into existence on the surface of an unknown planet, just as we stand?

"No one knows what happens," said "Flick", another younger woman with impressive quals, and a blank cv. "The ping signal that registers a successful transit travels very, very fast, but it's timebound. They've only been shipping convicts out of here for five years. It'll be another twenty before they know for certain if anyone has reached the First Landfall planet, dead or alive —"

When Big Nurse's amplified voice told us the session was over, and we must return to our cells, my tablet said that two hours had passed. It felt like a lot longer. I was trembling with fatigue. I went over to the booth while the others were filing out.

"Take the armband from me," I muttered.

Annihilation, okay. Six billion kilometres from home, a charade set up around the lethal injection: whatever turns you on, O fascist state authority that ate my country, my world and its freedoms . . . But I refused to accept the role the bastards had dumped on me. I did not stand, I will not serve. I didn't dare to resign, I knew the rest of them wouldn't take that well. The system gives, the system better take away.

"I cannot," said Big Nurse, reasonably. "I am a bot."

"Of course you can. Make this vanish and appoint the next trustie on the list."

Software in human form answered the question that I hadn't asked. "All good government tends towards consensus," she said. "But consensus operates through forms and structures. Leader is your position in this nexus. The system cannot change your relation to the whole."

The girl with the braids was shuffling out, last. She walked as if she was struggling through treacle. Through the veil I saw a young, limber body, full of grace. I could not stop myself imagining the springy crease between her bottom and her thigh, and how it would move. I swallowed hard, and abruptly changed my mind.

Live to the last breath. Play the game, what does it matter?

In my cell, the ration tray that had been waiting for me in the "morning", when I woke, had disappeared. Another prison meal had arrived. I ate it. I had a drinking fountain in a niche in my wall, and the water tasted sweet. My God, what luxuries!

Aside from the four people who never turned up, everyone attended the dayroom, including Drummer and the unresponsive woman. Most of us were playing the game to ward off madness and the abyss. Some of us genuinely got interested in setting up the ground rules for a new world. I couldn't tell the difference; not even in myself.

Carpazian said we would need an established religion.

"Religion," he reasoned, "is not all bad. It contains the incomprehensible in human life. People need deities, doorkeepers between the real and unreal. And the Buonarotti device has made the world stranger than people ever knew before."

I don't think he meant to do it, but he started something. Mike, the fourth man, said he'd heard that the Panhandle was haunted by murdered prospectors. Flick said she'd felt someone in her cell with her, invisible, watching her every move.

"They say the Buonarotti Transit broke something open," offered Koffi. "They say it unleashed monsters. And here we are right next to the torus."

We shouted him down, we rationalists (including Carpazian). We were all feeling vulnerable. It was hard not to get creeped out, with the ever-present hum of that annihilation wheel, Big Nurse our only company, and the knowledge that we had been utterly abandoned. We were little children, frightened in the dark.

I decided to go and see Hilde. We were all quartered on the same corridor, and the doors had nameplates. We were free to make visits, other people were doing it. I didn't know how to make myself known, so I just knocked.

The door slid open. She stared at me, and began to back away.

"Do you mind if I come in?"

She gestured consent, zombie-slow, and embarked on the difficult task of clambering back onto her bunk. There was nowhere else so I sat there too, at the foot of her bed. She fumbled with the room controls, the door closed, we were alone together. It felt perilous, uncertain; but not in a nightmare way.

"I just wanted to say, the sessions are obviously a strain. Is there anything I can do? Nothing's compulsory, you know." Her braids were fuzzed all over, after days without any attention. I wanted to ask if she had a comb.

"I . . . am . . . Not like this . . . willingly . . . Captain."

Beads of sweat stood on her brow, by the end of that momentous effort. Her eyes were dark, her lashes long and curling. Her mouth was very full, almost too much for her narrow face to bear. She would have been pretty, a misfit, awkward prettiness, if there had been any life in her expression.

"Oh no!" I cried, consternated by her struggle. "I'm not the boss, please. The system did that to me, I'm not checking up on you. I meant —"

What did I mean? I could not explain myself.

"Do you have a comb?"

"Ye'uh . . . Ma'am."

She clambered slowly down again, groped inside the dry shower stall and brought out a dingy ceramic fibre comb, Panhandle issue. Her hand flailed piteously as she tried to hand it over; and yet the same thought flashed on me as had come when I first saw her. Somehow she was *untouched*. She was not only the youngest member of my "team", she was nothing like the rest of us: weary criminals, outlaws fallen from high places. She had been cared for, loved and treasured; and become a zombie on Death Row without ever losing that bloom. It was a mystery. What the hell had she done? Was she a psycho? What had made this gentle nineteen-year-old so dangerous?

"Turn around."

I loosened her braids, combed out her wilful mass of hair and set it in order again, as if I were her mother. It was the sweetest thing. I was glad she was turned away, so she couldn't see the tears in my eyes.

"There. That'll do for a while."

She faced me again, another painful, laborious shift. "Th . . . an' . . . *you*."

I had run out of excuses to touch her. "Shall I come again?"

She struggled fiercely. "Yes . . . I like . . . *that*."

IV

The fourth session was a practical. We had been warned on our room screens, but it came as a shock. The dayroom chairs and the booth where Big Nurse sat had gone: as soon as the fourteen of us had arrived the doors closed and we were plunged into a simulation. A grassy plain, scattered trees, and a herd of large animals coming over the horizon . . . Disoriented, bewildered, we co-operated like castaways. The consensus decision was that we should treat these furred, pawed, sabre-toothed bison-things as potential transport. We tried to catch a young one, so we could tame it. My God, it was a disaster, but it was fun. I had to set a broken bone. Koffi, tough guy, got through it without any pain relief; we discussed bottom-up pharmacology and bull-riding.

Sista and Angie (who had announced that she no longer wanted to be called Servalan) started bunking together, and no retribution descended. Gee hustled me for a simulated childbirth drama: thankfully I had no control over what the system chose to throw at us. I found out I'd been wrong about Bimbam the addict. She was not addicted to any recreational drug. She was a former school teacher, amateur mule. Her problem was a little girl of seven, and a little boy of five, from whom she'd been separated for two years. In prison on earth she'd had visiting rights, on screen. Now she would never see them again. She crawled back towards life, carrying the wounds that would never heal. Drummer, too, crawled back to life. He asked us to call him Achmed, his real name. But he would never be easy company: a man who believed himself damned to all eternity, separated from GOD.

Once, I walked along the curving corridor and saw someone oddly familiar, oddly far in the distance, coming to meet me: a trick of perspective. I was mystified by a huge feeling of foreboding, then saw that it was myself. I was walking towards myself. I turned and ran; another figure ran ahead of me, always at vanishing point. I reached my own cabin, my nameplate. I clutched at the glassy surface of the door, sweating.

We all had experiences. They were difficult to dismiss.

I woke in the "night" and heard someone crying out in the corridor. I went to see, hoping that it would be Hilde and I would comfort her. It was the elegant and controlled Carpazian, crouched in a foetal curl, sobbing like a baby.

"Georgiou? What is it?"

"My arm, my arm —"

"What is it? Are you in pain?"

He was nursing his right arm; he pushed up the overall sleeve and showed me the skin. "I cut myself. I have no secret weapon, the ceramic won't cut you; I used my teeth. I was keeping tally of the 'days' and 'nights' in blood, hidden under the rim of my bunk. It's gone. I have asked the woman called Gee, she says I never had a mark on me. I've fucked her but *she isn't real*. This place is haunted, haunted —"

It wasn't like him to use a word like "fucked." There wasn't a scratch on his right arm, or his left. "It's the torus," I said. "It's warming up. That's where the strange phenomena come from, it's affecting our brainchemistry, it's all in our minds. Don't let it get you down."

"Captain Ruth," he whispered, "how long have we been here?"

We stared at each other. "Three days," I said firmly. "No, four."

The Russian shook his head. "'You don't know . . . What if it isn't the torus? What if something got out, what if something is with us, messing with us?"

"Maybe the ghost of one of the old prospectors? I think I'd like that. You're the Patriarch, what should we do, your holiness? Hold a séance; try to make contact with the tough old bird?"

He laughed, shaky but comforted, and went back to his cell. I went back to mine. I wondered if the system itself was telling us something through these spooky hints. That *nothing* is real? That only what Drummer called the soul, subtle distillation of mind and body, exists?

Hilde invited me to her cabin.

Some of us were treating the Panhandle as a Death Row singles bar, and why not? Carpazian was being kept busy, and Koffi and Mike; nobody had dared to approach Drummer aka Achmed. As captain I got to know these things . . . I knew it couldn't be *that*. The girl couldn't possibly be making a sexual approach, but I was unspeakably nervous.

I'd been protecting her with signs of my approval; but being careful not to make her into teacher's pet. I'd had her on my team in the simulation room, things like that. Small, threatened groups are hungry for scapegoats. I knew I wasn't the only one who'd been wondering *why* she'd been kept under such heavy medication.

She was certainly a different person, after five days clear (or was it four?). There was light in her eyes, energy in her movements. It was enough to break your heart, because something told me she had never really been free, never in her life: and now this child would go into the void without ever having walked down a street, bought an ice-cream, skinned her knee, played ball, climbed a tree.

We chatted about the animal-taming. She was going to confess something, I was sure; but I wouldn't rush her.

I wanted to offer to comb her hair again.

"I don't believe it," I said. "This is too much."

"You don't believe that First Landfall exists?"

I shook my head, letting my hand rest on the faintly warm "mattress" where her body had lain. Tastes and smells are the food of the gods; and touch, too.

"No, I can believe they've been identifying habitable planets hundreds of light-years away. I can grasp the science of that idea, and the science that says earth-like planets are bound to exist, though we know for a fact that there's nothing within our material reach except hot and cold rocks; or giant gas-balloons."

She nodded. She had no life experience but she was not ignorant or stupid. She'd proved that in our sessions, as she came out from under the drugs.

"I can even, just about, believe that the torus can send us there, in some weird way that means new bodies will automatically be generated when we make landfall."

The void opened when I said that. None of us really believed we would wake again. The transit was a fairytale, disguising annihilation, annihilation –

I shook my head solemnly, pulling the conversation around. "But I cannot, no, I'm sorry . . . I've tried, but your captain cannot believe in the gruffaloes."

The tawny bison-things, with the clawed paws and sabre teeth, had instantly been named *gruffaloes*. Hilde began to giggle, helplessly. We laughed, leaning close together, white mice trying to understand the experiment. Gallows humour!

"If we wake on that plain," said Hilde, and she stopped smiling. "It will be the first time I've ever been outdoors in my life."

Here it comes, I thought.

"Your hair's a disgrace again," I said. "Do you want me to comb it?"

"I'd love that," she said. She reached for the comb, which was lying on the bunk, moving light and limber, with the grace that I'd seen like a ghost in the shell, when she was drugged to the eyeballs. But she didn't hand it over.

"No . . . Wait, I want to tell you something. I have to look at you while I tell you. I have a termination-level genetic disease."

"Ah." I nodded, shocked and relieved. So this was the secret.

"My parents are . . . I mean they were . . . members of a church that didn't allow pregnancy screening. Their church believed all children should be born, and *then* tested. So, when I was born they found out there was something wrong with me and my parents took me away, to a city; because the elders would have turned us in. When I was old enough to notice that I was different from the children on my tv, my mother and father told me I was allergic to everything, and I would get sick and die if I ever set foot outside my bedroom door. I never wondered why no doctors ever came, if I was so ill. I accepted the world the way it was."

"What happened?"

"I don't know." Her eyes filled with tears. "I don't know, Ruth. I remember my sixteenth birthday, and then it's like a thick blank curtain with holes torn in it. A lot of screaming and crying and slamming doors. A hospital corridor, a horrible jacket that wrapped my arms together, another room where they never let me out . . ." She shook her head. "Just blurred scenes in a nightmare, until I was here."

"What about your parents?"

"I suppose they got found out, I suppose they're in prison."

"Do you remember what they thought was wrong with you? You said 'termination-level'. Who told you that? What gave you that idea?"

She wiped away the tears before they could fall. I saw her struggle, the way she'd struggled to speak the last time I was in here. This time she lost the fight. If she had ever known what was wrong, she didn't know now –

"I can't remember. I think my parents never told me anything, but maybe I heard something in the hospital, or I saw something on the tv." She pressed her fist to her mouth, the knuckles staring white. "I don't know, but I'm scared."

The nail that sticks out will be hammered down. The USE saw certain "traits" as enemies of the state. By no means all of the proscribed genes were life-threatening.

"You don't have to be scared. They don't send just any condemned criminals to the Panhandle, Hilde. We have to be aged between eighteen and forty, and normally fertile. If you'd had a termination-level genetic disease you'd have been sterilized as soon as they spotted you; and you wouldn't be here."

This beautiful girl was a recessive carrier for some kind of cancer they were trying to stamp out, or some other condition that wouldn't harm her until she was fifty and past child-bearing. She'd been condemned like rotten meat by bad science.

I hoped I'd reassured her. Destroyed by longing, I was having trouble keeping my voice level. I was afraid I sounded cold and unsympathetic –

"If we have to be fertile, what about Sista?"

I shook my head. "She's never had a re-assignment, she couldn't afford it. It's all cosmetic. She's classified as a fertile male by the Panhandle system."

I wanted to hold her but I didn't dare to touch her. I despised the crude thrumming in my blood, the shameful heat in my crotch. Thankfully Hilde was too intent on her confession to notice me; still convinced that she was some kind of pariah. Poor kid, hadn't she grasped we were all pariahs together?

"You d-don't have anything about m-my criminal record on your tablet?"

"Not a thing."

This was absolutely true. I had professional profiles, listed qualifications for ten prisoners who were far from ordinary, including myself. Hilde was one of the four non-violent common criminals, all young women, who seemed to have been added to the mix at random: nothing recorded except their names and ages.

"Oh. All right. But, but there's something . . ." She drew a breath, like someone about to dive into deep water, then jumped down and opened her locker.

I'd better go –

I couldn't say that, it betrayed me. I tried to frame a safer exit line. Hilde climbed back into the tray where I'd imagined blood and viscera, in my own cabin, the first "night". Her hands were full of slippery, shining red stuff.

I thought I was hallucinating. Her locker should be *empty*. All our lockers were empty; we had no material baggage.

"*What* —?"

"I found this," she said. "In my locker. There's a green one and a blue one, as well." She was holding up a nightdress, a jewel-bright nightdress, scarlet satin with lace at the bodice and hem. "I know it shouldn't be there, you don't have to tell me, I understand about the transit. Ruth, please help me. What's going on?"

We'd all had strange experiences, but nothing so incongruous, and nothing ever that two people shared. I touched the stuff; I could feel the fabric, slippery and cool. "I don't know," I said. "Strange things happen. Better not think about it."

"My parents used to buy me pretty night clothes. When I was a little girl I imagined I could go to parties in my dreams, like a princess in a fairy-tale." She hugged the satin as if it were a favourite doll, her eyes fixed on mine. "If anyone had asked, when I was drugged, what I most wanted to take with me, I might have said, my nightdresses, like that little girl. *But why can I touch this?*"

"It's the torus. It's messing with our minds."

It flashed on me that the veil was getting thin, orientation was nearly over.

Hilde knelt there with her arms full of satin and lace. "I've never even kissed anyone," she said. "Except my mom and dad. But I've had a life in my mind . . . I know what I want, I know you want it too. There's no time left. Why won't you touch me?"

"I'm thirty-seven, Hilde. You're nineteen. You could be my daughter."

"But I'm not."

So there was no safe exit line, none at all. I kissed her. She kissed me back.

The texture of her hair had been a torment. The touch of her mouth, the pressure of her breasts, drenched me, drowned me. I'd had men as lovers, and they'd satisfied my itch for sex. I'd hardly ever dared to expose myself to another woman, even in outlaw circles where forbidden love was accepted. But nothing compares to the swell of a woman's breast against my own, like to like –

There were laws against homosexuality, and the so-called genetic trait was proscribed. But you could get away with being "metrosexual", as long as it was just a lifestyle choice; as long as you were just fooling around. As long as you were rich, or served the rich, and made ritual submission by lying about it, the USE would ignore most vices. I held her, and I knew she'd guessed my secret, the unforgivable crime behind my catalogue of civil disobedience. I can only love women. Only this love means anything to me, like to like. No "games" of dominance and subordination that are not really games at all. No masters, no slaves, NO to all of that –

My sister, my daughter, put your red dress on. Let me find your breasts, let me suckle through the slippery satin. Undress me, take me with your mouth and with your hands, forget the past, forget who we were, why we are here. We are virgin to each other, virgins together. We can make a new heaven and a new earth, here at the last moment, on this narrow bed –

*

When I went back to my own cabin, I found a note on my room control message board. It was from Carpazian.

> *Dear Captain Ruth,*
> *Something tells me our playtime is nearly over. When we dead awaken, if we awaken, may I respectfully request to be considered for the honour of fathering your first child. Georgiou.*

I laughed until I cried.

V

Hilde's bunk became a paradise, a walled garden of delight. We danced there all the ways two women can dance together, and the jewel-coloured nightdresses figured prominently, absurdly important. I didn't care where they had come from, and I didn't understand what Hilde had been trying to tell me.

Everyone knew, at once: the team must have been keeping watch on whose cabin I visited. I was as absurdly important as those scraps of satin. Mike and Gee came to see me. I thought they wanted to talk about pregnancy. It was a genuine issue, with all this rush of pairing-up. We didn't know if we were still getting our prison-issue contraception, which was traditionally delivered in the drinking water. None of us women had had a period, but that didn't mean much. They wanted to deliver a protest, or a warning. They said "people" felt I ought to be careful about Hilde.

I told them my private life was my own affair

"There's a hex on us," said Mike, darkly. "Who's causing it?"

"You mean the strange phenomena? How could any of us be causing them? It's the torus. Or the Panhandle system, keeping us off balance to keep us docile."

Gee made more sense. "She's not clear of the drugs yet, Captain. I can tell. There's got to be a good reason she was kept under like that."

The hairs rose on the back of my neck; I thought of lynch-mobs.

'Yeah, sure. We're all criminals, you two as well. But it's over now.'

After that deputation. I sent a note to Carpazian, accepting his honourable proposal, should such a time ever come, and made sure I sent it on the public channel. Maybe that was a mistake, but I was feeling a little crazy. If battlelines were drawn, the team better know that Hilde and I had allies, we didn't stand alone.

We had a couple of very dark simulations after that, but we came out of them well. I felt that the system, my secret ally, was telling me that I could trust my girl.

The unresponsive woman woke up, and proved to be an ultra-traditional Japanese (we'd only known that she looked Japanese). She could barely speak English; but she immediately convinced us to surround ourselves with tiny rituals. Whatever we did had to be done *just so*. Sitting down in a chair in the dayroom was a whole tea-ceremony in itself. It was very reassuring.

Angie said to me, strange isn't *wrong*, Ruth.

Miqal, the Iranian, came to my cabin. Most of them had visited me, on the quiet, at one time or another. She confessed that she was terrified of the transit itself. She had heard that when you lay down in the Buonarotti capsule you had terrible, terrible dreams. All your sins returned to you, and all the people you had betrayed. The thrum of those subliminal engines filled my head, everything disappeared. I was walking along the curving corridor again, my doppelganger at vanishing point; but the corridor was suspended in a starry void. The cold was horrific, my lungs were bursting, my body was coming apart. I could see nothing but Miqal's eyes, mirrors of my terror –

The hejabi woman clung to me, and I clung to her.

"Did it happen to you?" we babbled. "Did it happen to you —?"

"Don't tell anyone," I said, when we were brave enough to let go.

Carpazian was right, the stay of execution was over, and any haunting would have been better than this. We lived from moment to moment, under a sword.

$$H_{15750},\ N_{310},\ O_{6500},\ Ca_{2250},\ Ca_{63},\ P_{48},\ K_{15},\ S_{15},\ Na_{10},\ Cl_6,\ Mg_3,\ Fe_1,$$

Trace differences, tiny differences, customising that chemical formula into human lives, secrets and dreams. The Buonarotti process, taking that essence and converting it into some inexplicable algorithm, pure information . . .

"We'll have what we've managed to carry," I said. "And no reason why we shouldn't eat the meat and vegetables, since our bodies will be native to Landfall."

"We could materialize thousands of miles apart," said Hilde.

"Kitty says it doesn't work like that."

Kitty, the woman whose nickname had been "Flick", had come out of a closet of her own. She was, as I had always known but kept it to myself, a highly qualified neurochemist. Take a wild guess at her criminal activities. I'd had to fight a reflex of disgust against her, because I have a horror of what hard drugs can do. She and Achmed knew more than the rest of us put together about the actual Buonarotti process. Achmed had refused to talk about it, after his first pronouncement, but Kitty had told us things, in scraps. She said teams like ours would "land" together, in the same physical area, because we'd become psychically linked.

We were in Hilde's cabin. She was lying on top of me in the narrow bunk, one of the few comfortable arrangements. It was the sixth "night", or maybe the seventh. She stroked my nose, grinning.

"Oh yes, Captain. Very good for morale, Captain. You don't *know*."

"I don't know anything, except it's cold outside and warm in here."

I tipped her off so we were face to face, and made love to her with my eyes closed, in a world of touch and taste. My head was full of coloured stars, the sword was hanging over me, fears I hadn't known I possessed blossomed in the dark. What's wrong with her, what kind of terminal genetic error? Why was she condemned, she still has amnesia, what is it that she doesn't dare to remember? *Oh they will turn you in my arms into a wolf or a snake.* The words of the old song came to me, because I was afraid of her, and my eyes were closed so I didn't know what I was holding —

The texture of her skin changed. I was groping in rough, coarse hair, it was choking me. It changed again; it was scale, slithery and dry. I shot upright, shoving myself away from her. I hit the light. I stared.

My God.

"Am I dreaming?" I gasped. "Am I hallucinating?"

A grotesque, furred and scaly creature shook its head. It shook its head, then slipped and slithered back into the form of a human girl in a red nightdress.

"No," said Hilde. "I became what you were thinking. I lost control —" Hilde; something else, something entirely fluid, like water running.

"I told you I had a genetic disease. This is it."

"Oh my God," I breathed. "And you can read my mind?"

Her mouth took on a hard, tight smile. She was Hilde, but she was someone I'd never met: older, colder, still nineteen but far more bitter.

"*Easily*," she said. "Right now it's no trick."

I fought to speak calmly. "What are you? A . . . a shape-changer? My God, I can hardly say it, a *werewolf*?"

"I don't know," said older, colder Hilde, and I could still see that fluid weirdness in her. "My parents didn't know either. But I've thought about it and I've read about the new science. I've guessed that it's like Koffi said, do you remember? The Buonarotti Transit takes what Carpazian calls the soul apart: and it has unleashed monsters. Only they don't 'happen' near the torus – they get born on earth. The government's trying to stamp them out, and that's what I am. I didn't mean to deceive you, Ruth. I woke up and I was here, knowing nothing and in love with you —"

I wanted to grab my clothes and leave. I had a violent urge to flee.

"You didn't tell me."

"*I didn't know!* I found the nightdresses, I knew that was very strange, I tried to tell you, but even then I didn't know. The memories only just came back."

"Why did they send you out here? Why didn't they *kill* you?"

"I expect they were afraid." Hilde began to laugh, and cry. "They were afraid of what I'd do if they tried to kill me, so they just sent me away, a long, long way away. What does it matter? We are *dead*, Ruth. You are dead, I am dead, the rest is a fairytale. What does it matter if I'm something forbidden? Something that should never have breathed?"

Forbidden, forbidden . . . I held out my arms, I was crying too.

Embrace, close as you can. Everything's falling apart, flesh and bone, the ceramic that yields like soft metal, the slippery touch of satin, all vanishing —

As if they never were.

VI

Straight to orientation, then. There were no guards, only the Panhandle system's bots, but we walked without protest along a drab greenish corridor to the Transit Chamber. We lay down, a hundred of us at least, in the capsules that looked like coffins, our gravegoods no more than neural patterns, speed-burned into our bewildered brains. I was fully conscious. What happened to *orientation*? The sleeve closed over me, and I suddenly realized there was no reprieve, this was it. The end.

I woke and lay perfectly still. I didn't want to try and move because I didn't want to know that I was paralysed, buried alive, conscious but dead. *Oh I could be bounded in a walnut shell and count myself the king of infinite space*. I had not asked for a dream, but a moment since I had been in Hilde's arms. Maybe orientation hasn't begun yet, I thought, cravenly. The surface I was lying on did not yield like the ceramic fibre of the capsule, there was cool air flowing over my face and light on my eyelids. I opened my eyes and saw the grass: something very like blades of bluish, pasture grass, about twenty centimetres high, stirred by a light breeze.

The resurrected sat up, all around me: like little figures in a religious picture from Mediaeval Europe. The team was mainly together, but we were surrounded by a sea of bodies, mostly women, some men. A whole shipload, newly arrived at Botany Bay. The romance of my dream of the crossing was still with me, every detail in my grasp; but already fading, as dreams do. I saw the captain's armband on my sleeve. And Hilde was beside me. I remembered that Kitty had said teams like ours were *linked*. Teams like ours: identified by the system as the leaders in the consensus. I'd known what was going on, while I was in the dream, but I hadn't believed it. I stared at the girl with the cinnamon braids, the shape-changer, the wild card, my lover.

If I'm the captain of this motley crew, I thought, I wonder who *you* are . . .

THE ILLUSTRATED BIOGRAPHY OF LORD GRIMM

Daryl Gregory

New writer Daryl Gregory has made sales to *The Magazine of Fantasy & Science Fiction*, *Asimov's Science Fiction*, *MIT Technology Review*, *Eclipse Two*, *Amazing*, and elsewhere. His stories "Second Person, Present Tense" and "Damascus" were in our nineteenth and twentieth annual collections, respectively. He lives in State College, Pennsylvania.

Here he takes us to an embattled country, where a strange, almost surreal war is being fought – one, however, with very real consequences for the people who live there.

THE 22ND INVASION of Trovenia began with a streak of scarlet against a grey sky fast as the flick of a paintbrush. The red blur zipped across the length of the island, moving west to east, and shot out to sea. The sonic boom a moment later scattered the birds that wheeled above the fish processing plant and sent them squealing and plummeting.

Elena said, "Was that – it was, wasn't it?"

"You've never seen a U-Man, Elena?" Jürgo said.

"Not in person." At nineteen, Elena Pendareva was the youngest of the crew by at least two decades, and the only female. She and the other five members of the heavy plate welding unit were perched 110 meters in the air, taking their lunch upon the great steel shoulder of the Slaybot Prime. The giant robot, latest in a long series of ultimate weapons, was unfinished, its unpainted skin speckled with bird shit, its chest turrets empty, the open dome of its head covered only by a tarp.

It had been Jürgo's idea to ride up the gantry for lunch. They had plenty of time: for the fifth day in a row, steel plate for the Slaybot's skin had failed to arrive from the foundry, and the welding crew had nothing to do but clean their equipment and play cards until the guards let them go home.

It was a good day for a picnic. An unseasonably warm spring wind blew in from the docks, carrying the smell of the sea only slightly tainted by odours of diesel fuel and fish guts. From the giant's shoulder the crew looked down on the entire capital, from the port and industrial sector below them, to the old city in the west and the rows of grey apartment buildings rising up beyond. The only structures higher than their perch were Castle Grimm's black spires, carved out of the sides of Mount Kriegstahl, and the peak of the mountain itself.

"You know what you must do, Elena," Verner said with mock sincerity. He was the oldest in the group, a veteran mechaneer whose body was more metal than flesh. "Your first übermensch, you must make a wish."

Elena said, "Is 'Oh shit,' a wish?"

Verner pivoted on his rubber-tipped stump to follow her gaze. The figure in red had turned about over the eastern sea, and was streaking back toward the island. Sunlight glinted on something long and metallic in its hands.

The UM dove straight toward them,

There was nowhere to hide. The crew sat on a naked shelf of metal between the gantry and the sheer profile of the robot's head. Elena threw herself flat and spread her arms on the metal surface, willing herself to stick.

Nobody else moved. The men were all veterans, former zoomandos and mechaneers and castle guards. They'd seen dozens of U-Men, fought them even. Elena didn't know if they were unafraid or simply too old to care much for their skin.

The UM shot past with a whoosh, making the steel shiver beneath her. She looked up in time to take in a flash of metal, a crimson cape, black boots – and then the figure crashed *through* the wall of Castle Grimm. Masonry and dust exploded into the air.

"Lunch break," Jurgo said in his Estonian accent, "is over."

Toolboxes slammed, paper sacks took to the wind. Elena got to her feet. Jürgo picked up his lunch pail with one clawed foot, spread his patchy, soot-stained wings, and leaned over the side, considering. His arms and neck were skinny as always, but in the past few years he'd grown a beer gut.

Elena said, "Jürgo, can you still fly?"

"Of course," he said. He hooked his pail to his belt and backed away from the edge. "However, I don't believe I'm authorized for this air space."

The rest of the crew had already crowded into the gantry elevator. Elena and Jurgo pressed inside and the cage began to slowly descend, rattling and shrieking.

"What's it about this time, you think?" Verner said, clockwork lungs wheezing. "Old Rivet Head kidnap one of their women?" Only the oldest veterans could get away with insulting Lord Grimm in mixed company. Verner had survived at least four invasions that she knew of. His loyalty to Trovenia was assumed to go beyond patriotism into something like ownership.

Guntis, a grey, pebble-skinned amphibian of Latvian descent, said, "I fought this girlie with a sword once, Energy Lady —"

"*Power Woman*," Elena said in English. She'd read the *Illustrated Biography of Lord Grimm* to her little brother dozens of times before he learned to read it himself. The Lord's most significant adversaries were all listed in the appendix, in multiple languages.

"That's the one, *Par-wer Woh-man*," Guntis said, imitating her. "She had enormous —"

"Abilities," Jürgo said pointedly. Jürgo had been a friend of Elena's father, and often played the protective uncle.

"I think he meant to say 'tits'," Elena said. Several of the men laughed.

"No! Jürgo is right," Guntis said. "They were more than breasts. They had *talents*. I think one of them spoke to me."

The elevator clanged down on the concrete pad and the crew followed Jürgo into the long shed of the 3000 line. The factory floor was emptying. Workers pulled on coats, joking and laughing as if departing on holiday.

Jürgo pulled aside a man and asked him what was going on. "The guards have run away!" the man said happily. "Off to fight the übermensch!"

"So what's it going to be, boss?" Guntis said. "Stay or go?"

Jürgo scratched at the cement floor, thinking. Half-assembled Slaybot 3000's, five-meter-tall cousins to the colossal Prime, dangled from hooks all along the assembly line, wires spilling from their chests, legs missing. The factory was well behind its quota for the month. As well as for the quarter, year, and quinquennium. Circuit boards and batteries were in particularly short supply, but tools and equipment vanished daily. Especially scarce were acetylene tanks, a home-heating accessory for the very cold and the very stupid.

Jürgo finally shook his feathered head and said, "Nothing we can do here. Let's go home and hide under our beds."

"And in our bottles," Verner said.

Elena waved good-bye and walked toward the women's changing rooms to empty her locker.

A block from her apartment she heard Mr Bojars singing out, "Guh-RATE day for sausa-JEZ! Izza GREAT day for SAW-sages!" The mechaneer veteran was parked at his permanent spot at the corner of Glorious Victory Street and Infinite Progress Avenue, in the shadow of the statue of Grimm Triumphant. He saw her crossing the intersection and shouted, "My beautiful Elena! A fat bratwurst to go with that bread, maybe. Perfect for a celebration!"

"No thank you, Mr Bojars." She hoisted the bag of groceries onto her hip and shuffled the welder's helmet to her other arm. "You know we've been invaded, don't you?"

The man laughed heartily. "The trap is sprung! The crab is in the basket!" He wore the same clothes he wore every day, a black nylon ski hat and a green, grease-stained parka decorated at the breast with three medals from his years in the motorized cavalry. The coat hung down to cover where his flesh ended and his motorcycle body began.

"Don't you worry about Lord Grimm," he said. "He can handle any American muscle-head stupid enough to enter his lair. Especially the Red Meteor."

"It was Most Excellent Man," Elena said, using the Trovenian translation of his name. "I saw the Staff of Mightiness in his hand, or whatever he calls it."

"Even better! The man's an idiot. A U-Moron."

"He's defeated Lord Grimm several times," Elena said. "So I hear."

"And Lord Grimm has been declared dead a dozen times! You can't believe the underground newspapers, Elena. You're not reading that trash, are you?"

"You know I'm not political, Mr Bojars."

"Good for you. This Excellent Man, let me tell you something about – yes sir? Great day for a sausage." He turned his attention to the customer and Elena quickly wished him luck and slipped away before he could begin another story.

The small lobby of her apartment building smelled like burnt plastic and cooking grease. She climbed the cement stairs to the third floor. As usual the door to her apartment was wide open, as was the door to Mr Fishman's apartment across the hall. Staticky television laughter and applause carried down the hallway: It sounded like *Mr Sascha's Celebrity Polka Fun-Time*. Not even an invasion could pre-empt Mr Sascha.

She knocked on the frame of his door. "Mr Fishman," she called loudly. He'd never revealed his real name. "Mr Fishman, would you like to come to dinner tonight?"

There was no answer except for the blast of the television. The living room was dark except for the glow of the TV. The little set was propped up on a wooden chair at the edge of a large cast iron bathtub, the light from its screen reflecting off the smooth surface of the water. "Mr Fishman? Did you hear me?" She walked across the room, shoes crinkling on the plastic tarp that covered the floor, and switched off the TV.

The surface of the water shimmied. A lumpy head rose up out of the water, followed by a pair of dark eyes, a flap of nose, and a wide carp mouth.

"I was watching that," the zooman said.

"Some day you're going to pull that thing into the tub and electrocute yourself," Elena said.

He exhaled, making a rude noise through rubbery lips.

"We're having dinner," Elena said. She turned on a lamp. Long ago Mr Fishman had pushed all the furniture to the edge of the room to make room for his easels. She didn't see any new canvasses upon them, but there was an empty liquor bottle on the floor next to the tub. "Would you like to join us?"

He eyed the bag in her arms. "That wouldn't be, umm, fresh catch?"

"It is, as a matter of fact."

"I suppose I could stop by." His head sank below the surface.

In Elena's own apartment, Grandmother Zita smoked and rocked in front of the window, while Mattias, nine years old, sat at the table with his shoe box of coloured pencils and several grey pages crammed with drawings. "Elena, did you hear?" Matti asked. "A U-Man flew over the island! They canceled school!"

"It's nothing to be happy about," Elena said. She rubbed the top of her brother's head. The page showed a robot of Matti's own design marching toward a hyper-muscled man in a red cape. In the background was a huge, lumpy monster with triangle eyes – an escaped MoG, she supposed.

"The last time the U-Men came," Grandmother Zita said, "more than robots lost their heads. This family knows that better than most. When your mother —"

"Let's not talk politics, Grandmother." She kissed the old woman on the cheek, then reached past her to crank open the window – she'd told the woman to let in some air when she smoked in front of Matti, to no avail. Outside, sirens wailed.

Elena had been only eleven years old during the last invasion. She'd slept through most of it, and when she woke to sirens that morning the apartment was cold and the lights didn't work. Her parents were government geneticists – there was no other kind – and often were called away at odd hours. Her mother had left her a note asking her to feed Baby Matti and please stay indoors. Elena made oatmeal, the first of many breakfasts she would make for her little brother. Only after her parents failed to come home did she realize that the note was a kind of battlefield promotion to adulthood: impossible to refuse because there was no one left to accept her refusal.

Mr Fishman, in his blue bathrobe and striped pajama pants, arrived a half hour later, his great webbed feet slapping the floor. He sat at the table and argued with Grandmother Zita about which of the 21 previous invasions was most violent. There was a time in the 1960's and seventies when their little country seemed to be under attack every other month. Matti listened raptly.

Elena had just brought the fried whitefish to the table when the thumping march playing on the radio suddenly cut off. An announcer said, "Please stand by for an important message from His Royal Majesty, the Guardian of our Shores, the Scourge of Fascism, Professor General of the Royal Academy of Sciences, the Savior of Trovenia —"

Mr Fishman pointed at Matti. "Boy, get my television!" Matti dashed out of the room.

After a frantic minute of table-clearing and antenna-fiddling, the screen suddenly cleared to show a large room decorated in Early 1400s: stone floors, flickering torches, and dulled tapestries on the walls. The only piece of furniture was a huge oaken chair reinforced at the joints with iron plates and rivets.

A figure appeared at the far end of the room and strode toward the camera.

"He's still alive then," Grandmother said. Lord Grimm didn't appear on live television more than once or twice a year.

Matti said, "Oh, look at him."

His Majesty wore the traditional black and green cape of Trovenian nobility, which contrasted nicely with the polished suit of armour. His faceplate, hawk-nosed and heavily riveted, suggested simultaneously the prow of a battleship and the beak of the Baltic albatross, their national bird.

Elena had to admit he cut a dramatic figure. She almost felt sorry for people in other countries whose leaders all looked like postal inspectors. You could no more imagine those timid, pinch-faced bureaucrats leading troops into battle than you could imagine Lord Grimm ice skating.

"Sons and daughters of Trovenia," the leader intoned. His deep voice was charged with metallic echoes. "We have been invaded."

"We knew that already," Grandmother said, and Mr Fishman shushed her.

"Once again, an American superpower has violated our sovereignty. With typical, misguided arrogance, a so-called übermensch has trespassed upon our borders, destroyed our property . . ." The litany of crimes went on for some time.

"Look! The U-Man!" Matti said.

On screen, castle guards carried in a red-clad figure and dumped him in the huge chair. His head lolled. Lord Grimm lifted the prisoner's chin to show his bloody face to the camera. One eye was half open, the other swelled shut. "As you can see, he is completely powerless."

Mr Fishman grunted in disappointment.

"What?" Matti asked.

"Again with the captives, and the taunting," Grandmother said.

"Why not? They invaded us!"

Mr Fishman grimaced, and his gills flapped shut.

"If Lord Grimm simply beat up Most Excellent Man and sent him packing, that would be one thing," Grandmother said. "Or even if he just promised to stop doing what he was doing for a couple of months until they forgot about him, then —"

"Then we'd all go back to our business," Mr Fishman said.

Grandmother said, "But no, he's got to keep him captive. Now it's going to be just like 1972."

"And seventy-five," Mr Fishman said. He sawed into his whitefish. "And eighty-three."

Elena snapped off the television. "Matti, go pack your school bag with clothes. Now."

"What? Why?"

"We're spending the night in the basement. You too, Grandmother."

"But I haven't finished my supper!"

"I'll wrap it up for you. Mr Fishman, I can help you down the stairs if you like."

"Pah," he said. "I'm going back to bed. Wake me when the war's over."

A dozen or so residents of the building had also decided to take shelter below. For several hours the group sat on boxes and old furniture in the damp basement under stuttering fluorescent lights, listening to the distant roar of jets, the rumble of mechaneer tanks, and the bass-drum stomps of Slaybot 3000's marching into position.

Grandmother Zita had claimed the best seat in the room, a ripped vinyl armchair. Matti had fallen asleep across her lap, still clutching the *Illustrated Biography of Lord Grimm*. The boy was so comfortable with her. Zita wasn't even a relative, but she'd watched over the boy since he was a toddler and so became his grandmother – another wartime employment opportunity. Elena slipped the book from under Matti's arms and bent to put it into his school bag.

Zita lit another cigarette. "How do you suppose it really started?" she said.

"What, the war?" Elena asked.

"No, the first time." She nodded at Matti's book. "Hating the Americans, okay, no problem. But why the scary mask, the cape?"

Elena pretended to sort out the contents of the bag.

"What possesses a person to do that?" Zita said, undeterred. "Wake up one day and say, 'Today I will put a bucket over my head. Today I declare war on all U-Men. Today I become,' what's the English . . ."

"Grandmother, please," Elena said, keeping her voice low.

"A *super villain*," Zita said.

A couple of the nearest people looked away in embarrassment. Mr Rimkis, an old man from the fourth floor, glared at Grandmother down the length of his gray-bristled snout. He was a veteran with one long tusk and one jagged stump. He claimed to have suffered the injury fighting the U-Men, though others said he'd lost the tusk in combat with vodka and gravity: The Battle of the Pub Stairs.

"*He* is the hero," Mr Rimkis said. "Not these imperialists in long underwear. They invaded his country, attacked his family, maimed him and left him with—"

"Oh please," Grandmother said. "Every villain believes himself to be a hero."

The last few words were nearly drowned out by the sudden wail of an air raid siren. Matti jerked awake and Zita automatically put a hand to his sweat-dampened forehead. The residents stared up at the ceiling. Soon there was a chorus of sirens.

They've come, Elena thought, as everyone knew they would, to rescue their comrade.

From somewhere in the distance came a steady *thump, thump* that vibrated the ground and made the basement's bare cinderblock walls chuff dust into the air. Each explosion seemed louder and closer. Between detonations, slaybot auto-cannons whined and chattered.

Someone said, "Everybody just remain —"

The floor seemed to jump beneath their feet. Elena lost her balance and smacked into the cement on her side. At the same moment she was deafened by a noise louder than her ears could process.

The lights had gone out. Elena rolled over, eyes straining, but she couldn't make out Grandmother or Matti or anyone. She shouted but barely heard her own voice above the ringing in her ears.

Someone behind her switched on an electric torch and flicked it around the room. Most of the basement seemed to have filled with rubble.

Elena crawled toward where she thought Grandmother's chair had been and was stopped by a pile of cement and splintered wood. She called Matti's name and began to push the debris out of the way.

Someone grabbed her foot, and then Matti fell into her, hugged her fiercely. Somehow he'd been thrown behind her, over her. She called for a light, but the torch was aimed now at a pair of men attempting to clear the stairway. Elena took Matti's hand and led him cautiously toward the light. Pebbles fell on them; the building seemed to shift and groan. Somewhere a woman cried out, her voice muffled.

"Grandmother Zita," Matti said.

"I'll come back for Grandmother," she said, though she didn't know for sure if it had been Zita's voice. "First you."

The two men had cleared a passage to the outside. One of them boosted the other to where he could crawl out. The freed man then reached back and Elena lifted Matti to him. The boy's jacket snagged on a length of rebar, and the boy yelped. After what seemed like minutes of tugging and shouting the coat finally ripped free.

"Stay there, Mattias!" Elena called. "Don't move!" She turned to assist the next person in line to climb out, an old woman from the sixth floor. She carried an enormous wicker basket which she refused to relinquish. Elena promised repeatedly that the basket would be the first thing to come out after her. The others in the basement began to shout at the old woman, which only made her grip the handle more fiercely. Elena was considering prying her fingers from it when a yellow flash illuminated the passage. People outside screamed.

Elena scrambled up and out without being conscious of how she managed it. The street lights had gone out but the sky flickered with strange lights. A small crowd of dazed citizens sat or sprawled across the rubble-strewn street, as if a bomb had gone off. The man who'd pulled Matti out of the basement sat on the ground, holding his hands to his face and moaning.

The sky was full of flying men.

Searchlights panned from a dozen points around the city, and clouds pulsed with exotic energies. In that spasmodic light dozens of tiny figures darted: caped invaders, squadrons of Royal Air Dragoons riding pinpricks of fire, winged zoomandos, glowing U-Men leaving iridescent fairy trails. Beams of energy flicked from horizon to horizon; soldiers ignited and dropped like dollops of burning wax.

Elena looked around wildly for her brother. Rubble was everywhere. The front of her apartment building had been sheared off, exposing bedrooms and bathrooms. Protruding girders bent toward the ground like tongues.

Finally she saw the boy. He sat on the ground, staring at the sky. Elena ran to him, calling his name. He looked in her direction. His eyes were wide, unseeing.

She knelt down in front of him.

"I looked straight at him," Matti said. "He flew right over our heads. He was so bright. So bright."

There was something wrong with Matti's face. In the inconstant light she could only tell that his skin was darker than it should have been.

"Take my hand," Elena said. "Can you stand up? Good. Good. How do you feel?"

"My face feels hot," he said. Then, "Is Grandmother out yet?"

Elena didn't answer. She led him around the piles of debris. Once she had to yank him sideways and he yelped. "Something in our way," she said. A half-buried figure lay with one arm and one leg jutting into the street. The body would have been unrecognizable if not for the blue-striped pajamas and the webbed toes.

Matti wrenched his hand from her grip. "Where are we going? You have to tell me where we're going."

She had no idea. She'd thought they'd be safe in the basement. She'd thought it would be like the invasions everyone talked about, a handful of U-Men – a *super team* – storming the castle. No one told her there could be an army of them. The entire city had become the battleground.

"Out of the city," she said. "Into the country."

"But Grandmother —"

"I promise I'll come back for Grandmother Zita," she said.

"And my book," he said. "It's still in the basement."

All along Infinite Progress Avenue, families spilled out of buildings carrying bundles of clothes and plastic jugs, pushing wheelchairs and shopping carts loaded with canned food, TV sets, photo albums. Elena grabbed tight to Matti's arm and joined the exodus north.

After an hour they'd covered only ten blocks. The street had narrowed as they left the residential district, condensing the stream of people into a herd, then a single shuffling animal. Explosions and gunfire continued to sound from behind them and the sky still flashed with parti-coloured lightning. No one glanced back.

The surrounding bodies provided Elena and Matti with some protection against the cold, though frigid channels of night air randomly opened through the crowd. Matti's vision still hadn't returned; he saw nothing but the yellow light of the U-Man. He told her his skin still felt hot, but he trembled as if he were cold. Once he stopped suddenly and threw up into the street. The crowd behind bumped into them, forcing them to keep moving.

One of their fellow refugees gave Matti a blanket. He pulled it onto his shoulders like a cape but it kept slipping as he walked, tripping him up. The boy hadn't cried since they'd started walking, hadn't complained – he'd even stopped asking about Grandmother Zita – but Elena still couldn't stop herself from being annoyed with him. He stumbled again and she yanked the blanket from him. "For God's sake, Mattias," she said. "If you can't hold onto it —" She drew up short. The black-coated women in front of them had suddenly stopped.

Shouts went up from somewhere ahead, and then the crowd surged backward. Elena recognized the escalating whine of an auto-cannon coming up to speed.

Elena pulled Matti up onto her chest and he yelped in surprise or pain. The boy was heavy and awkward; she locked her hands under his buttocks and shoved toward the crowd's edge, aiming for the mouth of an alley. The crowd buffeted her, knocked her off course. She came up hard against the plate glass window of a shop.

A Slaybot 3000 lumbered through the crowd, knocking people aside. Its gun arm, a huge thing like a barrel of steel pipes, jerked from figure to figure, targeting automatically. A uniformed technician sat in the jumpseat on the robot's back, gesturing frantically and shouting, "Out of the way! Out of the way!" It was impossible to tell whether he'd lost control or was deliberately marching through the crowd.

The mass of figures had almost certainly overwhelmed the robot's vision and recognition processors. The 3000 model, like its predecessors, had difficulty telling friend from foe even in the spare environment of the factory QA room.

The gun arm pivoted toward her: six black mouths. Then the carousel began to spin and the barrels blurred, became one vast maw.

Elena felt her gut go cold. She ached to disappear, and would have sunk to the ground, but the mob held her upright, pinned. She twisted to place at least part of her body between the robot and Matti. The glass at her shoulder trembled, began to bow.

For a moment she saw both sides of the glass. Inside the dimly lit shop were two rows of blank white faces, a choir of eyeless women regarding her. And in the window's reflection she saw her own face, and above that, a streak of light like a falling star. The UM flew toward them from the west, moving incredibly fast.

The robot's gun fired even as it flicked upward to acquire the new target.

The glass shattered. The mass of people on the street beside her seemed to disintegrate into blood and cloth tatters. A moment later she registered the sound of the gun, a thunderous *ba-rap*! The crowd pulsed away from her, releasing its pressure, and she collapsed to the ground.

The slaybot broke into a clumsy stomping run, its gun ripping at the air.

Matti had rolled away from her. Elena touched his shoulder, turned him over. His eyes were open, but unmoving, glassy.

The air seemed to freeze. She couldn't breathe, couldn't move her hand from him.

He blinked. Then he began to scream.

Elena got to her knees. Her left hand was bloody and freckled with glass; her fingers glistened. Each movement triggered the prick of a thousand tiny needles. Matti screamed and screamed.

"It's okay, it's okay," she said. "I'm right here."

She talked to him for almost a minute before he calmed down enough to stop screaming.

The window was gone, the shop door blown open. The window case was filled with foam heads on posts, some with wigs askew, others tipped over and bald. She got Matti to take her hand – her good hand – and led him toward the doorway. She was thankful that he could not see the things they stepped over.

Inside, arms and legs of all sizes hung from straps on the walls. Trays of dentures sat out on the countertops. A score of heads sported hairstyles old-fashioned even by Trovenian standards. There were several such shops across the city. Decent business in a land of amputees.

Elena's face had begun to burn. She walked Matti through the dark, kicking aside prosthetic limbs, and found a tiny bathroom at the back of the shop. She pulled on the chain to the fluorescent light and was surprised when it flickered to life.

This was her first good look at Matti's face. The skin was bright red, puffy and raw looking – a second-degree burn at least.

She guided the boy to the sink and helped him drink from the tap. It was the only thing she could think of to do for him. Then she helped him sit on the floor just outside the bathroom door.

She could no longer avoid looking in the mirror.

The shattering glass had turned half of her face into a speckled red mask. She ran her hands under the water, not daring to scrub, and then splashed water on her face. She dabbed at her cheek and jaw with the tail of her shirt but the blood continued to weep through a peppering of cuts. She looked like a cartoon in Matti's Lord Grimm book, the colouring accomplished by tiny dots.

She reached into her jacket and took out the leather work gloves she'd stuffed there when she emptied her locker. She pulled one onto her wounded hand, stifling the urge to shout.

"Hello?" Matti said.

She turned, alarmed. Matti wasn't talking to her. His face was turned toward the hallway.

Elena stepped out. A few feet away were the base of a set of stairs that led up into the back of the building. A man stood on the first landing, pointing an ancient rifle at the boy. His jaw was flesh-toned plastic, held in place by an arrangement of leather straps and mechanical springs. A woman with outrageously golden hair stood higher on the stairs, leaning around the corner to look over the man's shoulder.

The man's jaw clacked and he gestured with the gun. "Go. Get along," he said. The syllables were distorted.

"They're hurt," the wigged woman said.

The man did not quite shake his head. Of course they're hurt, he seemed to say. Everyone's hurt. It's the national condition.

"We didn't mean to break in," Elena said. She held up her hands. "We're going." She glanced back into the showroom. Outside the smashed window, the street was still packed, and no one seemed to be moving.

"The bridge is out," the man said. He meant the Prince's Bridge, the only paved bridge that crossed the river. No wonder then that the crowd was moving so slowly.

"They're taking the wounded to the mill," the woman said. "Then trying to get them out of the city by the foot bridges."

"What mill?" Elena asked.

The wigged woman wouldn't take them herself, but did give directions. "Go out the back," she said.

The millrace had dried out and the mill had been abandoned fifty years ago, but its musty, barn-like interior still smelled of grain. Its rooms were already crowded with injured soldiers and citizens.

Elena found a spot for Matti on a bench inside the building and told him not to move. She went from room to room asking if anyone had aspirin, antibiotic cream, anything to help the boy. She soon stopped asking. There didn't seem to be any doctors or nurses at the mill, only the wounded helping the more severely wounded, and no medicines to be found. This wasn't a medical clinic, or even a triage centre. It was a way station.

She came back to find that Matti had fallen asleep on the grey-furred shoulder of a veteran zoomando. She told the man that if the boy woke up she would be outside helping unload the injured. Every few minutes another farm truck pulled up and bleeding men and women stepped out or were passed down on litters. The emptied trucks rumbled south back into the heart city.

The conversation in the mill traded in rumour and wild speculation. But what report could be disbelieved when it came to the U-Men? Fifty of them were attacking, or a hundred. Lord Grimm was both dead and still fighting on the battlements. The MoGs had escaped from the mines in the confusion.

Like everyone else Elena quickly grew deaf to gunfire, explosions, crackling energy beams. Only when something erupted particularly close – a nearby building bursting into flame, or a terrordactyl careening out of control overhead – did the workers look up or pause in their conversation.

At some point a woman in the red smock of the Gene Corps noticed that Elena's cheek had started bleeding again. "It's a wonder you didn't lose an eye," the scientist said, and gave her a wad of torn-up cloth to press to her face. "You need to get that cleaned up or it will scar."

Elena thanked her curtly and walked outside. The air was cold but felt good on her skin.

She was still dabbing at her face when she heard the sputter of engines. An old mechaneer cavalryman, painted head to wheels in mud, rolled into the north end of the yard, followed by two of his wheeled brethren. Each of them was towing a narrow cart padded with blankets.

The lead mechaneer didn't notice Elena at first, or perhaps noticed her but didn't recognize her. He suddenly said, "My beautiful Elena!" and puttered forward, dragging the squeaking cart after him. He put on a smile but couldn't hold it.

"Not so beautiful, Mr Bojars."

The old man surveyed her face with alarm. "But you are all right?" he asked. "Is Mattias —?"

"I'm fine. Matti is inside. He's sick. I think he . . ." She shook her head. "I see you've lost your sausage oven."

"A temporary substitution only, my dear." The surviving members of his unit had reunited, he told her matter-of-factly, to do what they could. In the hours since the Prince's Bridge had been knocked out they'd been ferrying wounded across the river. A field hospital had been set up at the northern barracks of the city guard. The only ways across the river were the foot bridges and a few muddy low spots in the river. "We have no weapons," Mr Bojars said, "but we can still drive like demons."

Volunteers were already carrying out the people chosen to evacuate next, four men and two women who seemed barely alive. Each cart could carry only two persons at a time, laid head to foot. Elena helped secure them.

"Mr Bojars, does the hospital have anything for radiation poisoning?"

"Radiation?" He looked shocked. "I don't know, I suppose . . ."

One of the mechaneers waved to Mr Bojars, and the two wheeled men began to roll out.

Elena said, "Mr Bojars —"

"Get him," he replied.

Elena ran into the mill, dodging pallets and bodies. She scooped up the sleeping boy, ignoring the pain in her hand, and carried him back outside. She could feel his body trembling in her arms.

"I can't find my book," Matti said. He sounded feverish. "I think I lost it."

"Matti, you're going with Mr Bojars," Elena said. "He's going to take you someplace safe."

He seemed to wake up. He looked around, but it was obvious he still couldn't see. "Elena, no! We have to get Grandmother!"

"Matti, listen to me. You're going across the river to the hospital. They have medicine. In the morning I'll come get you."

"She's still in the basement. She's still there. You promised you would —"

"Yes, I promise!" Elena said. "Now go with Mr Bojars."

"Matti, my boy, we shall have such a ride!" the mechaneer said with forced good humour. He opened his big green parka and held out his arms.

Matti released his grip on Elena. Mr Bojars set the boy on the broad gas tank in front of him, then zipped up the jacket so that only Matti's head was visible. "Now we look like a cybernetic kangaroo, hey Mattias?"

"I'll be there in the morning," Elena said. She kissed Matti's forehead, then kissed the old man's cheek. He smelled of grilled onions and diesel. "I can't thank you enough," she said.

Mr Bojars circled an arm around Matti and revved his engine. "A kiss from you, my dear, is payment enough."

She watched them go. A few minutes later another truck arrived in the yard and she fell in line to help carry in the wounded. When the new arrivals were all inside and the stained litters had all been returned to the truck, Elena stayed out in the yard. The truck drivers, a pair of women in coveralls, leaned against the hood. The truck's two-way radio played ocean noise: whooshing static mixed with high, panicked pleas like the cries of seagulls. The larger of the women took a last drag on her cigarette, tossed it into the yard, and then both of them climbed into the cab. A moment later the vehicle started and began to move.

"Shit," Elena said. She jogged after the truck for a few steps, then broke into a full run. She caught up to it as it reached the road. With her good hand she hauled herself up into the open bed.

The driver slowed and leaned out her window. "We're leaving now!" she shouted. "Going back in!"

"So go!" Elena said.

The driver shook her head. The truck lurched into second gear and rumbled south.

As they rolled into the city proper it was impossible for Elena to tell where they would find the front line of the battle, or if there was a front line at all. Damage seemed to be distributed randomly. The truck would roll through a sleepy side street that was completely untouched, and twenty yards away the buildings would be cracked open, their contents shaken into the street.

The drivers seemed to possess some sixth sense for knowing where the injured were waiting. The truck would slow and men and women would emerge from the dark and hobble toward the headlights of the truck, or call for a litter. Some people stood at street corners and waved them down as if flagging a bus. Elena helped the drivers lift the wounded into the back, and sometimes had to force them to leave their belongings.

"Small boats," the largest driver said over and over. A Trovenian saying: in a storm, all boats are too small.

Eventually she found herself crouched next to a burned dragoon who was half-welded to his jet pack. She held his hand, thinking that might give him something to feel besides the pain, but he only moaned and muttered to himself, oblivious to her presence.

The truck slammed a stop, sending everyone sliding and crashing into each other. Through the slats Elena glimpsed a great slab of blue, some huge, organic shape. A leg. A giant's leg. The U-Man had to be bigger than an apartment building. Gunfire clattered, and a voice like a fog horn shouted something in English.

The truck lurched into reverse, engine whining, and Elena fell forward onto her hands. Someone in the truck bed cried, "Does he see us? Does he see us?"

The truck backed to the intersection and turned hard. The occupants shouted as they collapsed into each other yet again. Half a block more the truck braked to a more gradual stop and the drivers hopped out. "Is everyone okay?" they asked.

The dragoon beside Elena laughed.

She stood up and looked around. They were in the residential district, only a few blocks from her apartment. She made her way to the gate of the truck and hopped down. She said to the driver, "I'm not going back with you."

The woman nodded, not needing or wanting an explanation.

Elena walked slowly between the hulking buildings. The pain in her hand, her face, all seemed to be returning.

She emerged into a large open space. She realized she'd been mistaken about where the truck had stopped – this park was nowhere she recognized. The ground in front of her had been turned to glass.

The sky to the east glowed. For a moment she thought it was another super-powered UM. But no, only the dawn. Below the dark bulk of Mount Kriegstahl stood the familiar silhouette of the Slaybot Prime bolted to its gantry. The air battle had moved there, above the factories and docks. Or maybe no battle at all. There seemed to be only a few flyers in the air now. The planes and TDs had disappeared. Perhaps the only ones left were U-Men.

Power bolts zipped through the air. They were firing at the Prime.

A great metal arm dropped away from its shoulder socket and dangled by thick cables. Another flash of energy severed them. The arm fell away in seeming slow motion, and the sound of the impact reached her a moment later. The übermenschen were carving the damn thing up.

She almost laughed. The Slaybot Prime was as mobile and dangerous as the Statue of Liberty. Were they actually afraid of the thing? Was that why an army of them had shown up for an ordinary hostage rescue?

My God, she thought, the morons had actually believed Lord Grimm's boasting.

She walked west, and the rising sun turned the glazed surface in front of her into a mirror. She knew now that she wasn't lost. The scorched buildings surrounding the open space were too familiar. But she kept walking. After a while she noticed that the ground was strangely warm beneath her feet. Hot even.

She looked back the way she'd come, then decided the distance was shorter ahead. She was too tired to run outright but managed a shuffling trot. Reckoning by rough triangulation from the nearest buildings, she decided she was passing over Mr Bojars' favourite spot, the corner of

Glorious Victory Street and Infinite Progress Avenue. Her own apartment building should have loomed directly in front of her.

After all she'd seen tonight she couldn't doubt that there were beings with the power to melt a city block to slag. But she didn't know what strange ability, or even stranger whim, allowed them to casually trowel it into a quartz skating rink.

She heard another boom behind her. The Slaybot Prime was headless now. The southern gantry peeled away, and then the body itself began to lean. Elena had been inside the thing; the chest assembly alone was as big as a cathedral.

The Slaybot Prime slowly bowed, deeper, deeper, until it tumbled off the pillars of its legs. Dust leaped into the sky where it fell. The tremor moved under Elena, sending cracks snaking across the glass.

The collapse of the Prime seemed to signal the end of the fighting. The sounds of the energy blasts ceased. Figures flew in from all points of the city and coalesced above the industrial sector. In less than a minute there were dozens and dozens of them, small and dark as blackcap geese. Then she realized that the flock of übermenschen was flying toward her.

Elena glanced to her left, then right. She was as exposed as a pea on a plate. The glass plain ended fifty or sixty meters away at a line of rubble. She turned and ran.

She listened to the hiss of breath in her throat and the smack of her heavy boots against the crystalline surface. At every moment she expected to crash through.

Elongated shadows shuddered onto the mirrored ground ahead of her. She ran faster, arms swinging. The glass abruptly ended in a jagged lip. She leaped, landed on broken ground, and stumbled onto hands and knees. Finally she looked up.

Racing toward her with the sun behind them, the U-Men were nothing but silhouettes – shapes that suggested capes and helmets; swords, hammers, and staffs; bows and shields. Even the energy beings, clothed in shimmering auras, seemed strangely desaturated by the morning light.

Without looking away from the sky she found a chunk of masonry on the ground in front of her. Then she stood and climbed onto a tilting slab of concrete.

When the mass of U-Men was directly above her she heaved with all her might.

Useless. At its peak the grey chunk fell laughably short of the nearest figure. It clattered to the ground somewhere out of sight.

Elena screamed, tensed for – longing for – a searing blast of light, a thunderbolt. Nothing came. The U-Men vanished over the roof of the next apartment building, heading out to sea.

Weeks after the invasion, the factory remained closed. Workers began to congregate there anyway. Some mornings they pushed around brooms or cleared debris, but mostly they played cards, exchanged stories of the invasion, and speculated on rumours. Lord Grimm had not been seen since the attack. Everyone agreed that the Saviour of Trovenia had been dead too many times to doubt his eventual resurrection.

When Elena finally returned, eighteen days after the invasion, she found Verner and Guntis playing chess beside the left boot of the Slaybot Prime. The other huge components of the robot's body were scattered across two miles of the industrial sector like the buildings of a new city.

The men greeted her warmly. Verner, the ancient mechaneer, frankly noted the still-red cuts that cross-hatched the side of her face, but didn't ask how she'd acquired them. If Trovenians told the story of every scar there'd be no end to the talking.

Elena asked about Jürgo and both men frowned. Guntis said that the birdman had taken to the air during the fight. As for the other two members of the heavy plate welding unit, no news.

"I was sorry to hear about your brother," Verner said.

"Yes," Elena said. "Well."

She walked back to the women's changing rooms, and when she didn't find what she was looking for, visited the men's. One cinderblock wall had caved in, but the lockers still stood in orderly rows. She found the locker bearing Jürgo's name on a duct tape label. The door was padlocked shut. It took her a half hour to find a cutting rig with oxygen and acetylene cylinders that weren't empty, but only minutes to wheel the rig to the changing rooms and burn off the lock.

She pulled open the door. Jürgo's old-fashioned, rectangle-eyed welding helmet hung from a hook, staring at her. She thought of Grandmother Zita. *What possesses a person to put a bucket on their head?*

The inside of the locker door was decorated with a column of faded photographs. In one of them a young Jürgo, naked from the waist up, stared into the camera with a concerned squint His new wings were unfurled behind him. Elena's mother and father, dressed in their red Gene Corps jackets, stood on either side of him. Elena unpeeled the yellowed tape and put the picture in her breast pocket, then unhooked the helmet and closed the door.

She walked back to the old men, pulling the cart behind her. "Are we working today or what?" she asked.

Guntis looked up from the chess board with amusement in his huge wet eyes. "So you are the boss now, eh, Elena?"

Verner, however, said nothing. He seemed to recognize that she was not quite the person she had been. Damaged components had been stripped away, replaced by cruder, yet sturdier approximations. He was old enough to have seen the process repeated many times.

Elena reached into the pockets of her coat and pulled on her leather work gloves. Then she wheeled the cart over to the toe of the boot and straightened the hoses with a flick of her arm.

"Tell us your orders, Your Highness," Guntis said.

"First we tear apart the weapons," she said. She thumbed the blast trigger and blue flame roared from the nozzle of the cutting torch. "Then we build better ones."

She slid the helmet onto her head, flipped down the mask, and bent to work.

G-MEN

Kristine Kathryn Rusch

Here's a look at an alternate world not really all that different from our own – but my, what a difference that difference makes!

Kristine Kathryn Rusch started out the decade of the 90s as one of the fastest rising and most prolific young authors on the scene, took a few years out mid-decade for a very successful turn as editor of *The Magazine of Fantasy & Science Fiction*, and, since stepping down from that position, has returned to her old standards of production here in the twenty-first century, publishing a slew of novels in four genres, writing fantasy, mystery, and romance novels under various pseudonyms as well as science fiction. She has published more than twenty novels under her own name, including *The White Mists of Power*, *The Disappeared*, *Extremes*, and *Fantasy Life*, the four-volume Fey series, the Black Throne series, *Alien Influences*, and several *Star Wars*, *Star Trek*, and other media tie-in books, both solo and written with husband Dean Wesley Smith and others. Her most recent books (as Rusch, anyway) are the SF novels of the popular Retrieval Artist series, which include *The Disappeared*; *Extreme, Consequences*; *Buried Deep*; *Paloma*; *Recovery Man*; and a collection of Retrieval Artist stories, *The Retrieval Artist and Other Stories*. Her copious short fiction has been collected in *Stained Black: Horror Stories*, *Stories for an Enchanted Afternoon*, *Little Miracles: And Other Tales of Murder*, and *Millennium Babies*. In 1999, she won readers award polls from the readerships of both *Asimov's Science Fiction* and *Ellery Queen's Mystery Magazine*, an unprecedented double honour! As an editor, she was honoured with the Hugo Award for her work on *The Magazine of Fantasy & Science Fiction* and shared the World Fantasy Award with Dean Wesley Smith for her work as editor of the original hardcover anthology version of *Pulphouse*. As a writer, she has won the Herodotus Award for Best Historical Mystery (for *A Dangerous Road*, written as Kris Nelscott) and the *Romantic Times* Reviewer's Choice Award (for *Utterly Charming*, written as Kristine Grayson); as Kristine Kathryn Rusch, she won the John W. Campbell Award, has been a finalist for the Arthur C. Clarke Award, and took home a Hugo Award in 2000 for her story "Millennium Babies," making her one of the few people in genre history to win Hugos for both editing *and* writing. Her most recent book is the novel *Duplicate Effort*.

"There's something addicting about a secret."

– J. Edgar Hoover

THE SQUALID LITTLE alley smelled of piss. Detective Seamus O'Reilly tugged his overcoat closed and wished he'd worn boots. He could feel the chill of his metal flashlight through the worn glove on his right hand.

Two beat cops stood in front of the bodies, and the coroner crouched over them. His assistant was already setting up the gurneys, body bags draped over his arm. The coroner's van had blocked the alley's entrance, only a few yards away.

O'Reilly's partner, Joseph McKinnon, followed him. McKinnon had trained his own flashlight on the fire escapes above, unintentionally alerting any residents to the police presence.

But they probably already knew. Shootings in this part of the city were common. The neighbourhood teetered between swank and corrupt. Far enough from Central Park for degenerates and muggers to use the alleys as corridors, and, conversely, close enough for new money to want to live with a peek of the city's most famous expanse of green.

The coroner, Thomas Brunner, had set up two expensive, battery-operated lights on garbage can lids placed on top of the dirty ice, one at the top of the bodies, the other near the feet. O'Reilly crouched so he wouldn't create any more shadows.

"What've we got?" he asked.

"Dunno yet." Brunner was using his gloved hands to part the hair on the back of the nearest corpse's skull. "It could be one of those nights."

O'Reilly had worked with Brunner for eighteen years now, since they both got back from the war, and he hated it when Brunner said it could be one of those nights. That meant the corpses would stack up, which was usually a summer thing, but almost never happened in the middle of winter.

"Why?" O'Reilly asked. "What else we got?"

"Some coloured limo driver shot two blocks from here." Brunner was still parting the hair. It took O'Reilly a minute to realize it was matted with blood. "And two white guys pulled out of their cars and shot about four blocks from that."

O'Reilly felt a shiver run through him that had nothing to do with the cold. "You think the shootings are related?"

"Dunno," Brunner said. "But I think it's odd, don't you? Five dead in the space of an hour, all in a six-block radius."

O'Reilly closed his eyes for a moment. Two white guys pulled out of their cars, one Negro driver of a limo, and now two white guys in an alley. Maybe they were related, maybe they weren't.

He opened his eyes, then wished he hadn't. Brunner had his finger inside a bullet hole, a quick way to judge calibre.

"Same type of bullet," Brunner said.

"You handled the other shootings?"

"I was on scene with the driver when some fag called this one in."

O'Reilly looked at Brunner. Eighteen years, and he still wasn't used to the man's casual bigotry.

"How did you know the guy was queer?" O'Reilly asked. "You talk to him?"

"Didn't have to." Brunner nodded toward the building in front of them. "Weekly party for degenerates in the penthouse apartment every Thursday night. Thought you knew."

O'Reilly looked up. Now he understood why McKinnon had been shining his flashlight at the upper story windows. McKinnon had worked vice before he got promoted to homicide.

"Why would I know?" O'Reilly said.

McKinnon was the one who answered. "Because of the standing orders."

"I'm not playing twenty questions," O'Reilly said. "I don't know about a party in this building and I don't know about standing orders."

"The standing orders are," McKinnon said as if he were an elementary school teacher, "not to bust it, no matter what kind of lead you got. You see someone go in, you forget about it. You see someone come out, you avert your eyes. You complain, you get moved to a different shift, maybe a different precinct."

"Jesus." O'Reilly was too far below to see if there was any movement against the glass in the penthouse suite. But whoever lived there – whoever partied there – had learned to shut off the lights before the cops arrived.

"Shot in the back of the head," Brunner said before O'Reilly could process all of the information. "That's just damn strange."

O'Reilly looked at the corpses – really looked at them – for the first time. Two men, both rather heavyset. Their faces were gone, probably splattered all over the walls. Gloved hands, nice shoes, one of them wearing a white scarf that caught the light.

Brunner had to search for the wound in the back of the head, which made that the entry point. The exit wounds had destroyed the faces.

O'Reilly looked behind him. No door on that building, but there was one on the building where the party was held. If they'd been exiting the building and were surprised by a queer basher or a mugger, they'd'd've been shot in the front, not the back.

"How many times were they shot?" O'Reilly asked.

"Looks like just the once. Large calibre, close range. I'd say it was a purposeful head shot, designed to do maximum damage." Brunner felt the back of the closest corpse. "There doesn't seem to be anything on the torso."

"They still got their wallets?" McKinnon asked.

"Haven't checked yet." Brunner reached into the back pants pocket of the corpse he'd been searching and clearly found nothing. So he grabbed the front of the overcoat and reached inside.

He removed a long thin wallet – old-fashioned, the kind made for the larger bills of forty years before. Hand-tailored, beautifully made.

These men weren't hurting for money.

Brunner handed the wallet to O'Reilly, who opened it. And stopped when he saw the badge inside. His mouth went dry.

"We got a feebee," he said, his voice sounding strangled.

"What?" McKinnon asked.

"FBI," Brunner said dryly. McKinnon had only moved to homicide the year before. Vice rarely had to deal with FBI. Homicide did only on sensational cases. O'Reilly could count on one hand the number of times he'd spoken to agents in the New York bureau.

"Not just any feebee either," O'Reilly said. "The Associate Director. Clyde A. Tolson."

McKinnon whistled. "Who's the other guy?"

This time, O'Reilly did the search. The other corpse, the heavier of the two, also smelled faintly of perfume. This man had kept his wallet in the inner pocket of his suit coat, just like his companion had.

O'Reilly opened the wallet. Another badge, just like he expected. But he didn't expect the bulldog face glaring at him from the wallet's interior.

Nor had he expected the name.

"Jesus, Mary and Joseph," he said.

"What've we got?" McKinnon asked.

O'Reilly handed him the wallet, opened to the slim paper identification.

"The Director of the FBI," he said, his voice shaking. "Public Hero Number One. J. Edgar Hoover."

Francis Xavier Bryce – Frank to his friends, what few of them he still had left – had just dropped off to sleep when the phone rang. He cursed, caught himself, apologized to Mary, and then remembered she wasn't there.

The phone rang again and he fumbled for the light, knocking over the highball glass he'd used to mix his mom's recipe for sleepless nights, hot milk, butter and honey. It turned out that, at the tender age of 36, hot milk and butter laced with honey wasn't a recipe for sleep; it was a recipe for heartburn.

And for a smelly carpet if he didn't clean the mess up.

He found the phone before he found the light.

"What?" he snapped.

"You live near Central Park, right?" A voice he didn't recognize, but one that was clearly official, asked the question without a hello or an introduction.

"More or less." Bryce rarely talked about his apartment. His parents had left it to him and, as his wife was fond of sniping, it was too fancy for a junior G-Man.

The voice rattled off an address. "How far is that from you?"

"About five minutes." If he didn't clean up the mess on the floor. If he spent thirty seconds pulling on the clothes he'd piled onto the chair beside the bed.

"Get there. Now. We got a situation."

"What about my partner?" Bryce's partner lived in Queens.

"You'll have back-up. You just have to get to the scene. The moment you get there, you shut it down."

"Um." Bryce hated sounding uncertain, but he had no choice. "First, sir, I need to know who I'm talking to. Then I need to know what I'll find."

"You'll find a double homicide. And you're talking to Eugene Hart, the Special Agent in Charge. I shouldn't have to identify myself to you."

Now that he had, Bryce recognized Hart's voice. "Sorry, sir. It's just procedure."

"Fuck procedure. Take over that scene. *Now.*"

"Yes, sir," Bryce said, but he was talking into an empty phone line. He hung up, hands shaking, wishing he had some Bromo-Seltzer.

He'd just come off a long, messy investigation of another agent. Walter Cain had been about to get married when he remembered he had to inform the Bureau of that fact and, as per regulation, get his bride vetted before walking down the aisle.

Bryce had been the one to investigate the future Mrs Cain, and had been the one to find out about her rather seamy past – two Vice convictions under a different name, and one hospitalization after a rather messy back-street abortion. Turned out Cain knew about his future wife's past, but the Bureau hadn't liked it.

And two nights ago, Bryce had to be the one to tell Cain that he couldn't marry his now-reformed, somewhat religious, beloved. The soon-to-be Mrs Cain had taken the news hard. She had gone to Bellevue this afternoon after slashing her wrists.

And Bryce had been the one to tell Cain what his former fiancée had done. Just a few hours ago.

Sometimes Bryce hated this job.

Despite his orders, he went into the bathroom, soaked one of Mary's precious company towels in water, and dropped the thing on the spilled milk. Then he pulled on his clothes, and finger-combed his hair.

He was a mess – certainly not the perfect representative of the Bureau. His white shirt was stained with marinara from that night's take-out, and his tie wouldn't keep a crisp knot. The crease had long since left his trousers and his shoes hadn't been shined in weeks. Still, he grabbed his black overcoat, hoping it would hide everything.

He let himself out of the apartment before he remembered the required and much hated hat, went back inside, grabbed the hat as well as his gun and his identification. Jesus, he was tired. He hadn't slept since Mary walked out. Mary, who had been vetted by the FBI and who had passed with flying colours. Mary, who had turned out to be more of a liability than any former hooker ever could have been.

And now, because of her, he was heading toward something big, and he was one-tenth as sharp as usual.

All he could hope for was that the SAC had overreacted. And he had a hunch – a two in the morning, get-your-ass-over-there-now hunch – that the SAC hadn't overreacted at all.

Attorney General Robert F. Kennedy sat in his favorite chair near the fire in his library. The house was quiet even though his wife and eight children were asleep upstairs. Outside, the rolling landscape was covered in a light dusting of snow – rare for McLean, Virginia, even at this time of year.

He held a book in his left hand, his finger marking the spot. The Greeks had comforted him in the few months since Jack died, but lately Kennedy had discovered Camus.

He had been about to copy a passage into his notebook when the phone rang. At first he sighed, feeling all of the exhaustion that had weighed on him since the assassination. He didn't want to answer the phone. He didn't want to be bothered – not now, not ever again.

But this was the direct line from the White House and if he didn't answer it, someone else in the house would.

He set the Camus book face down on his chair and crossed to the desk before the third ring. He answered with a curt, "Yes?"

"Attorney General Kennedy, sir?" The voice on the other end sounded urgent. The voice sounded familiar to him even though he couldn't place it.

"Yes?"

"This is Special Agent John Haskell. You asked me to contact you, sir, if I heard anything important about Director Hoover, no matter what the time."

Kennedy leaned against the desk. He had made that request back when his brother had been president, back when Kennedy had been the first attorney general since the 1920s who actually demanded accountability from Hoover.

Since Lyndon Johnson had taken over the presidency, accountability had gone by the wayside. These days Hoover rarely returned Kennedy's phone calls.

"Yes, I did tell you that," Kennedy said, resisting the urge to add, *but I don't care about that old man any longer.*

"Sir, there are rumours – credible ones – that Director Hoover has died in New York."

Kennedy froze. For a moment, he flashed back to that unseasonably warm afternoon when he'd sat just outside with the federal attorney for New York City, Robert Morganthau, and the chief of Morganthau's criminal division, Silvio Mollo, talking about prosecuting various organized crime figures.

Kennedy could still remember the glint of the sunlight on the swimming pool, the taste of the tuna fish sandwich Ethel had brought him, the way the men – despite their topic – had seemed lighthearted.

Then the phone rang, and J. Edgar Hoover was on the line. Kennedy almost didn't take the call, but he did and Hoover's cold voice said, *I have news for you. The President's been shot.*

Kennedy had always disliked Hoover, but since that day, that awful day in the bright sunshine, he hated that fat bastard. Not once – not in that call, not in the subsequent calls – did Hoover express condolences or show a shred of human concern.

"Credible rumours?" Kennedy repeated, knowing he probably sounded as cold as Hoover had three months ago, and not caring. He'd chosen Haskell as his liaison precisely because the man didn't like Hoover either. Kennedy had needed someone inside Hoover's hierarchy, unbeknownst to Hoover, which was difficult since Hoover kept his hand in everything. Haskell was one of the few who fit the bill.

"Yes, sir, quite credible."

"Then why haven't I received official contact?"

"I'm not even sure the President knows, sir."

Kennedy leaned against the desk. "Why not, if the rumours are credible?"

"Um, because, sir, um, it seems Associate Director Tolson was also shot, and um, they were, um, in a rather suspect area."

Kennedy closed his eyes. All of Washington knew that Tolson was the closest thing Hoover had to a wife. The two old men had been life-long companions. Even though they didn't live together, they had every meal together. Tolson had been Hoover's hatchet man until the last year or so, when Tolson's health hadn't permitted it.

Then a word Haskell used sank in. "You said shot."

"Yes, sir."

"Is Tolson dead too then?"

"And three other people in the neighbourhood," Haskell said.

"My God." Kennedy ran a hand over his face. "But they think this is personal?"

"Yes, sir."

"Because of the location of the shooting?"

"Yes, sir. It seems there was an exclusive gathering in a nearby building. You know the type, sir."

Kennedy didn't know the type – at least not through personal experience. But he'd heard of places like that, where the rich, famous and deviant could spend time with each other, and do whatever it was they liked to do in something approaching privacy.

"So," he said, "the Bureau's trying to figure out how to cover this up."

"Or at least contain it, sir."

Without Hoover or Tolson. No one in the Bureau was going to know what to do.

Kennedy's hand started to shake. "What about the files?"

"Files, sir?"

"Hoover's confidential files. Has anyone secured them?"

"Not yet, sir. But I'm sure someone has called Miss Gandy."

Helen Gandy was Hoover's longtime secretary. She had been his right hand as long as Tolson had operated that hatchet.

"So procedure's being followed," Kennedy said, then frowned. If procedure were being followed, shouldn't the acting head of the Bureau be calling him?

"No, sir. But the Director put some private instructions in place should he be killed or incapacitated. Private emergency instructions. And those involve letting Miss Gandy know before anyone else."

Even me, Kennedy thought. *Hoover's nominal boss.* "She's not there yet, right?"

"No, sir."

"Do you know where those files are?" Kennedy asked, trying not to let desperation into his voice.

"I've made it my business to know, sir." There was a pause and then Haskell lowered his voice. "They're in Miss Gandy's office, sir."

Not Hoover's like everyone thought. For the first time in months, Kennedy felt a glimmer of hope. "Secure those files."

"Sir?"

"Do whatever it takes. I want them out of there, and I want someone to secure Hoover's house too. I'm acting on the orders of the President. If anyone tells you that they are doing the same, they're mistaken. The President made his wishes clear on this point. He often said if anything happens to that old queer" – and here Kennedy deliberately used LBJ's favourite phrase for Hoover – "then we need those files before they can get into the wrong hands."

"I'm on it, sir."

"I can't stress to you the importance of this," Kennedy said. In fact, he couldn't talk about the importance at all. Those files could ruin his brother's legacy. The secrets in there could bring down Kennedy too, and his entire family.

"And if the rumours about the Director's death are wrong, sir?"

Kennedy felt a shiver of fear. "Are they?"

"I seriously doubt it."

"Then let me worry about that."

And about what LBJ would do when he found out. Because the president upon whose orders Kennedy acted wasn't the current one. Kennedy was following the orders of the only man he believed should be president at the moment.

His brother, Jack.

The scene wasn't hard to find; a coroner's van blocked the entrance to the alley. Bryce walked quickly, already cold, his heartburn worse than it had been when he had gone to bed.

The neighbourhood was in transition. An urban renewal project had knocked down some wonderful turn of the century buildings that had become eyesores. But so far, the buildings that had replaced them were the worst kind of modern – all planes and angles and white with few windows.

In the buildings closest to the park, the lights worked and the streets looked safe. But here, on a side street not far from the construction, the city's shady side showed. The dirty snow was piled against the curb, the streets were dark, and nothing seemed inhabited except that alley with the coroner's van blocking the entrance.

The coroner's van and at least one unmarked car. No press, which surprised him. He shoved his gloved hands in the pockets of his overcoat even though it was against FBI dress code, and slipped between the van and the wall of a grimy brick building.

The alley smelled of old urine and fresh blood. Two beat cops blocked his way until he showed identification. Then, like people usually did, they parted as if he could burn them.

The bodies had fallen side by side in the centre of the alley. They looked posed, with their arms up, their legs in classic P position – one leg bent, the other straight. They looked like they could fit perfectly on the dead body diagrams the FBI used to put out in the 1930s. He wondered if they had fallen like this or if this had been the result of the coroner's tampering.

The coroner had messed with other parts of the crime scene – if, indeed, he had been the one who put the garbage can lids on the ice and set battery-powered lamps on them. The warmth of the lamps was melting the ice and sending runnels of water into a nearby grate.

"I hope to hell someone thought to photograph the scene before you melted it," he said.

The coroner and the two cops who had been crouching beside the bodies stood up guiltily. The coroner looked at the garbage can lids and closed his eyes. Then he took a deep breath, opened them, and snapped his fingers at the assistant who was waiting beside a gurney.

"Camera," he said.

"That's Crime Scene's —" the assistant began, then saw everyone looking at him. He glanced at the van. "Never mind."

He walked behind the bodies, further disturbing the scene. Bryce's mouth thinned in irritation. The cops who stood were in plain clothes.

"Detectives," Bryce said, holding his identification, "Special Agent Frank Bryce of the FBI. I've been told to secure this scene. More of my people will be here shortly."

He hoped that last was true. He had no idea who was coming or when they would arrive.

"Good," said the younger detective, a tall man with broad shoulders and an all-American jaw. "The sooner we get out of here the better."

Bryce had never gotten that reaction from a detective before. Usually the detectives were territorial, always reminding him that this was New York City and that the scene belonged to them.

The other detective, older, face grizzled by time and work, held out his gloved hand. "Forgive my partner's rudeness. I'm Seamus O'Reilly. He's Joseph McAllister and we'll help you in any way we can."

"I appreciate it," Bryce said, taking O'Reilly's hand and shaking it. "I guess the first thing you can do is tell me what we've got."

"A hell of a mess, that's for sure," said McAllister. "You'll understand when . . ."

His voice trailed off as his partner took out two long, old-fashioned wallets and handed them to Bryce.

Bryce took them, feeling confused. Then he opened the first, saw the familiar badge, and felt his breath catch. Two FBI agents, in this alley? Shot side by side? He looked up, saw the darkened windows.

There used to be rumours about this neighbourhood. Some exclusive private sex parties used to be held here, and his old partner had always wanted to visit one just to see if it was a hotbed of Communists like some of the agents had claimed. Bryce had begged off. He was an investigator, not a voyeur.

The two detectives were staring at him, as if they expected more from him. He still had the wallet open in his hand. If the dead men were New York agents, he would know them. He hated solving the deaths of people he knew.

But he steeled himself, looked at the identification, and felt the blood leave his face. His skin grew cold and for a moment he felt lightheaded.

"No," he said.

The detectives still stared at him.

He swallowed. "Have you done a visual i.d.?"

Hoover was recognizable. His picture was on everything. Sometimes Bryce thought Hoover was more famous than the president – any president. He'd certainly been in power longer.

"Faces are gone," O'Reilly said.

"Exit wounds," the coroner added from beside the bodies. His assistant had returned and was taking pictures, the flash showing just how much melt had happened since the coroner arrived.

"Shot in the back of the head?" Bryce blinked. He was tired and his brain was working slowly, but something about the shots didn't match with the body positions.

"If they came out that door," O'Reilly said as he indicated a dark metal door almost hidden in the side of the brick building, "then the shooters had to be waiting beside it."

"Your crime scene people haven't arrived yet, I take it?" Bryce asked.

"No," the coroner said. "They think it's a fag kill. They'll get here when they get here."

Bryce clenched his left fist and had to remind himself to let the fingers loose.

O'Reilly saw the reaction. "Sorry about that," he said, shooting a glare at the coroner. "I'm sure the Director was here on business."

Funny business. But Bryce didn't say that. The rumours about Hoover had been around since Bryce joined the FBI just after the war. Hoover quashed them, like he quashed any criticism, but it seemed like the criticism got made, no matter what.

Bryce opened the other wallet, but he already had a guess as to who was beside Hoover, and his guess turned out to be right.

"You want to tell me why your crime scene people believe this is a homosexual killing?" Bryce asked, trying not to let what Mary called his FBI tone into his voice. If Hoover was still alive and this was some kind of plant, Hoover would want to crush the source of this assumption. Bryce would make sure that the source was worth pursuing before going any further.

"Neighbourhood, mostly," McAllister said. "There're a couple of bars, mostly high-end. You have to know someone to get in. Then there's the party, held every week upstairs. Some of the most important men in the city show up at it, or so they used to say in Vice when they told us to stay away."

Bryce nodded, letting it go at that.

"We need your crime scene people here ASAP, and a lot more cops so that we can protect what's left of this scene, in case these men turn out to be who their identification says they are. You search the bodies to see if this was the only identification on them?"

O'Reilly started. He clearly hadn't thought of that. Probably had been too shocked by the first wallets that he found.

The younger detective had already gone back to the bodies. The coroner put out a hand, and did the searching himself.

"You think this was a plant?" O'Reilly asked.

"I don't know what to think," Bryce said. "I'm not here to think. I'm here to make sure everything goes smoothly."

And to make sure the case goes to the FBI. Those words hung unspoken between the two of them. Not that O'Reilly objected, and now Bryce could understand why. This case would be a political nightmare, and no good detective wanted to be in the middle of it.

"How come there's no press?" Bryce asked O'Reilly. "You manage to get rid of them somehow?"

"Fag kill," the coroner said.

Bryce was getting tired of those words. His fist had clenched again, and he had to work at unclenching it.

"Ignore him," O'Reilly said softly. "He's an asshole and the best coroner in the city."

"I heard that," the coroner said affably. "There's no other identification on either of them."

O'Reilly's shoulders slumped, as if he'd been hoping for a different outcome. Bryce should have been hoping as well, but he hadn't been. He had known that Hoover was in town. The entire New York bureau knew, since Hoover always took it over when he arrived – breezing in, giving instructions, making sure everything was just the way he wanted it.

"Before this gets too complicated," O'Reilly said, "you want to see the other bodies?"

"Other bodies?" Bryce felt numb. He could use some caffeine now, but Hoover had ordered agents not to drink coffee on the job. Getting coffee now felt almost disrespectful.

"We got three more." O'Reilly took a deep breath. "And just before you arrived, I got word that they're agents too."

Special Agent John Haskell had just installed six of his best agents outside the Director's suite of offices when a small woman showed up, key clutched in her gloved right hand. Helen Gandy, the Director's secretary, looked up at Haskell with the coldest stare he'd ever seen outside of the Director's.

"May I go into my office, Agent Haskell?" Her voice was just as cold. She didn't look upset, and if he hadn't known that she never stayed past five unless directed by Hoover himself, Haskell would have thought she was coming back from a prolonged work break.

"I'm sorry, ma'am," he said. "No one is allowed inside. President's orders."

"Really?" God, that voice was chilling. He remembered the first time he'd heard it, when he'd been brought to this suite of offices as a brand-new agent, after getting his "Meet the Boss" training before his introduction to the Director. She'd frightened him more than Hoover had.

"Yes, ma'am. The President says no one can enter."

"Surely he didn't mean me."

Surely he did. But Haskell bit the comment back. "I'm sorry, ma'am."

"I have a few personal items that I'd like to get, if you don't mind. And the Director instructed me that in the case of . . ." and for the first time she paused. Her voice didn't break nor did she clear her throat. But she seemed to need a moment to gather herself. "In case of emergency, I was to remove some of his personal items as well."

"If you could tell me what they are, ma'am, I'll get them."

Her eyes narrowed. "The Director doesn't like others to touch his possessions."

"I'm sorry, ma'am," he said gently. "But I don't think that matters any longer."

Any other woman would have broken down. After all, she had worked for the old man for forty-five years, side by side, every day. Never marrying, not because they had a relationship – Helen Gandy, more than anyone, probably knew the truth behind the Director's relationship with the Associate Director – but because for Helen Gandy, just like for the Director himself, the FBI was her entire life.

"It matters," she said. "Now if you'll excuse me . . ."

She tried to wriggle past him. She was wiry and stronger than he expected. He had to put out an arm to block her.

"Ma'am," he said in the gentlest tone he could summon, "the President's orders supercede the Director's."

How often had he wanted to say that over the years? How often had he wanted to remind everyone in the Bureau that the President led the Free World, not J. Edgar Hoover?

"In this instance," she snapped, "they do not."

"Ma'am, I'd hate to have some agents restrain you." Although he wasn't sure about that. She had never been nice to him or to anyone he knew. She'd always been sharp or rude. "You're distraught."

"I am not." She clipped each word.

"You are because I say you are, ma'am."

She raised her chin. For a moment, he thought she hadn't understood. But she finally did.

The balance of power had shifted. At the moment, it was on his side.

"Do I have to call the President then to get my personal effects?" she asked.

But they both knew she wasn't talking about her personal things. And the President was smart enough to know that as well. As hungry to get those files as the Attorney General had seemed despite his Eastern reserve, the President would be utterly ravenous. He wouldn't let some old skirt, as he'd been known to call Miss Gandy, get in his way.

"Go ahead," Haskell said. "Feel free to use the phone in the office across the hall."

She glared at him, then turned on one foot and marched down the corridor. But she didn't head toward a phone – at least not one he could see.

He wondered who she would call. The President wouldn't listen. The Attorney General had issued the order in the President's name. Maybe she would contact one of Hoover's Assistant Directors, the four or five men that Hoover had in his pocket.

Haskell had been waiting for them. But word still hadn't spread through the Bureau. The only reason he knew was because he'd received a call from the SAC of the New York office. New York hated the Director, mostly because the old man went there so often and harassed them.

Someone had probably figured out that there was a crisis from the moment that Haskell had brought his people in to secure the Director's suite. But no one would know that the Director was dead until Miss Gandy made the calls or until someone in the Bureau started along the chain of command – the one designated in the book Hoover had written all those years ago.

Haskell crossed his arms. Sometimes he wished he hadn't let the A.G. know how he felt about the Director. Sometimes he wished he were still a humble assistant, the man who had joined the FBI because he wanted to be a top cop like his hero J. Edgar Hoover.

A man who, it turned out, never made a real arrest or fired a gun or even understood investigation.

There was a lot to admire about the Director – no matter what you said, he'd built a hell of an agency almost from scratch – but he wasn't the man his press made him out to be.

And that was the source of Haskell's disillusionment. He'd wanted to be a top cop. Instead, he snooped into homes and businesses and sometimes even investigated fairly blameless people, looking for a mistake in their past.

Since he'd been transferred to FBIHQ, he hadn't done any real investigating at all. His arrests had slowed, his cases dwindled.

And he'd found himself investigating his boss, trying to find out where the legend ended and the man began. Once he realized that the old man was just a bureaucrat who had learned where all the bodies were buried and used that to make everyone bow to his bidding, Haskell was ripe for the undercover work the A.G. had asked him to do.

Only now he wasn't undercover any more. Now he was standing in the open before the Director's cache of secrets, on the President's orders, hoping that no one would call his bluff.

As O'Reilly led him to the limousine, Bryce surreptitiously checked his watch. He'd already been on scene for half an hour, and no back-up had arrived. If he was supposed to secure everything and chase off the NYPD, he'd need some manpower.

But for now, he wanted to see the extent of the problem. The night had gotten colder, and this street was even darker than the street he'd walked down. All of the streetlights were out. The only light came from some porch bulbs above a few entrances. He could barely make out the limousine at the end of the block, and then only because he could see the shadowy forms of the two beat cops standing at the scene, their squad cars parking the limo in.

As he got closer, he recognized the shape of the limo. It was thicker than most limos and rode lower to the ground because it was encased in an extra frame, making it bulletproof. Supposedly, the glass would all be bulletproof as well.

"You said the driver was shot inside the limo?" Bryce asked.

"That's what they told me," O'Reilly said. "I wasn't called to this scene. We were brought in because of the two men in the alley. Even then we were called late."

Bryce nodded. He remembered the coroner's bigotry. "Is that standard procedure for cases involving minorities?"

O'Reilly gave him a sideways glance. Bryce couldn't read O'Reilly's expression in the dark.

"We're overtaxed," O'Reilly said after a moment. "Some cases don't get the kind of treatment they deserve."

"Limo drivers," Bryce said.

"If he'd been killed in the parking garage under the Plaza maybe," O'Reilly said. "But not because of who he was. But because of where he was."

Bryce nodded. He knew how the world worked. He didn't like it. He spoke up against it too many times, which was why he was on shaky ground at the Bureau.

Then his already upset stomach clenched. Maybe he wasn't going to get back-up. Maybe they'd put him on his own here to claim he'd botched the investigation, so that they would be able to cover it up.

He couldn't concentrate on that now. What he had to do was take good notes, make the best case he could, and keep a copy of every damn thing – maybe in more than one place.

"You were called in because of the possibility that the men in the alley could be important," Bryce said.

"That's my guess," O'Reilly said.

"What about the others down the block? Has anyone taken those cases?"

"Probably not," O'Reilly said. "Those bars, you know. It's department policy. The coroner checks bodies in the suspect area, and decides, based on . . . um . . . evidence of . . . um . . . activity . . . whether or not to bring in detectives."

Bryce frowned. He almost asked what the coroner was checking for when he figured out that it was evidence on the body itself, evidence not of the crime, but of certain kinds of sex acts. If that evidence was present, apparently no one thought it worthwhile to investigate the crime.

"You'd think the city would revise that," Bryce said. "A lot of people live dual lives – productive and interesting people."

"Yeah," O'Reilly said. "You'd think. Especially after tonight."

Bryce grinned. He was liking this grizzled cop more and more.

O'Reilly spoke to the beat cops, then motioned Bryce to the limo. As Bryce approached, O'Reilly trained his flashlight on the driver's side.

The window wasn't broken like Bryce had expected. It had been rolled down.

"You got here one James Crawford," said one of the beat cops. "He got identification says he's a feebee, but I ain't never heard of no coloured feebee."

"There's only four," Bryce said dryly. And they all worked for Hoover as his personal housekeepers or drivers. "Can I see that identification?"

The beat cop handed him a wallet that matched the ones on Tolson and Hoover. Inside was a badge and identification for James Crawford as well as family photographs. Neither Tolson nor Hoover had had any photographs in their wallets.

Bryce motioned O'Reilly to move a little closer to the body. The head was tilted toward the window. The right side of the skull was gone, the hair glistening with drying blood. With one gloved finger, Bryce pushed the head upright A single entrance wound above the left ear had caused the damage.

"Brunner says the shots are the same calibre," O'Reilly said.

It took Bryce a moment to realize that Brunner was the coroner.

Bryce carefully searched Crawford but didn't find the man's weapon. Nor could he found a holster or any way to carry a weapon.

"It looks like he wasn't carrying a weapon," Bryce said.

"Neither were the two in the alley," O'Reilly said, and Bryce appreciated his caution in not identifying the other two corpses. "You'd think they would have been."

Bryce shook his head. "They were known for not carrying weapons. But you'd think their driver would have one."

"Maybe they had protection," O'Reilly said.

And Bryce's mouth went dry. Of course they did. The office always joked about who would get HooverWatch on each trip. He'd had to do it a few times.

Agents on HooverWatch followed strict rules, like everything else with Hoover. Remain close enough to see the men entering and exiting an area, stop any suspicious characters, and yet somehow remain inconspicuous.

"You said there were two others shot?"

"Yeah. A block or so from here." O'Reilly waved a hand vaguely down the street.

"Pulled out of one car or two?"

"Not my case," O'Reilly said.

"Two," said the beat cop. "Black sedans. Could barely see them on this cruddy street."

HooverWatch. Bryce swallowed hard, that bile back. Of course. He probably knew the men who were shot.

"Let's look," he said. "You two, make sure the coroner's man photographs this scene before he leaves."

"Yessir," said the second beat cop. He hadn't spoken before.

"And don't let anyone near this scene unless I give the o.k.," Bryce said.

"How come this guy's in charge?" the talkative beat cop asked O'Reilly.

O'Reilly grinned. "Because he's a feebee."

"I'm sorry," the beat cop said automatically turning to Bryce. "I didn't know, sir."

Feebee was an insult – or at least some in the Bureau thought so. Bryce didn't mind it. Any more than he minded when some rookie said "Sack" when he meant "Ess-Ay-Cee." Shorthand worked, sometimes better than people wanted it to.

"Point me in the right direction," he said to the talkative cop.

The cop nodded south. "One block down, sir. You can't miss it. We got guys on those scenes too, but we weren't so sure it was important. You know. We coulda missed stuff."

In other words, they hadn't buttoned up the scene immediately. They'd waited for the coroner to make his verdict, and he probably hadn't, not with the three new corpses nearby.

Bryce took one last look at James Crawford. The man had rolled down his window, despite the cold, and in a bad section of town.

He leaned forward. Underneath the faint scent of cordite and mingled with the thicker smell of blood was the smell of a cigar.

He took the flashlight from O'Reilly and trained it on the dirty snow against the curb. It had been trampled by everyone coming to this crime scene.

He crouched, and poked just a little, finding three fairly fresh cigarette butts.

As he stood, he said to the beat cops, "When the scene of the crime guys get here, make sure they take everything from the curb."

O'Reilly was watching him. The beat cops were frowning, but they nodded.

Bryce handed O'Reilly back his flashlight and headed down the street.

"You think he was smoking and tossing the butts out the window?" O'Reilly asked.

"Either that," Bryce said, "or he rolled his window down to talk to someone. And if someone was pointing a gun at him, he wouldn't have done it. This vehicle was armored. He had a better chance starting it up and driving away than he did cooperating."

"If he wasn't smoking," O'Reilly said, "he knew his killer."

"Yeah," Bryce said. And he was pretty sure that was going to make his job a whole hell of a lot harder.

Kennedy took the elevator up to the fifth floor of the Justice Department. He probably should have stayed home, but he simply couldn't. He needed to get into those files and he needed to do so before anyone else.

As he strode into the corridor he shared with the Director of the FBI, he saw Helen Gandy hurry in the other direction. She looked like she had just come from the beauty salon. He had never seen her look anything less than completely put together but he was surprised by her perfect appearance on this night, after the news that her longtime boss was dead.

Kennedy tugged at the overcoat he'd put on over his favorite sweater. He hadn't taken the time to change or even comb his hair. He probably looked as tousled as he had in the days after Jack died.

Although, for the first time in three months, he felt like he had a purpose. He didn't know how long this feeling would last, or how long he wanted it to. But this death had given him an odd kind of hope that control was coming back into his world.

Haskell stood in front of the Director's office suite, arms crossed. The Director's suite was just down the corridor from the Attorney General's offices. It felt odd to go toward Hoover's domain instead of his own.

Haskell looked relieved when he saw Kennedy.

"Was that the dragon lady I just saw?" Kennedy asked.

"She wanted to get some personal effects from her office," Haskell said.

"Did you let her?"

"You said the orders were to secure it, so I have."

"Excellent." Kennedy glanced in both directions and saw no one. "Make sure your staff continues to protect the doors. I'm going inside."

"Sir?" Haskell raised his eyebrows.

"This may not be the right place," Kennedy said. "I'm worried that he moved everything to his house."

The lie came easily. Kennedy would have heard if Hoover had moved files to his own home. But Haskell didn't know that.

Haskell moved away from the door. It was unlocked. Two more agents stood inside, guarding the interior doors.

"Give me a minute, please, gentlemen," Kennedy said.

The men nodded and went outside.

Kennedy stopped and took a deep breath. He had been in Miss Gandy's office countless times, but he had never really looked at it. He'd always been staring at the door to Hoover's inner sanctum, waiting for it to open and the old man to come out.

That office was interesting. In the antechamber, Hoover had memorabilia and photographs from his major cases. He even had the plaster-of-paris death mask of John Dillinger on display. It was a ghastly thing, which made Kennedy think of the way that English kings used to keep severed heads on the entrance to London Bridge to warn traitors of their potential fate.

But this office had always looked like a waiting room to him. Nothing very special. The woman behind the desk was the focal point. Jack had been the one who nicknamed her the dragon lady and had even called her that to her face once, only with his trademark grin, so infectious that she hadn't made a sound or a grimace in protest.

Of course, she hadn't smiled back either.

Her desk was clear except for a blotter, a telephone, and a jar of pens. A typewriter sat on a credenza with paper stacked beside it.

But it wasn't the desk that interested him the most. It was the floor-to-ceiling filing cabinets and storage bins. He walked to them. Instead of the typical system – marked by letters of the alphabet – this one had numbers that were clearly part of a code.

He pulled open the nearest drawer, and found row after row of accordion files, each with its own number, and manila folders with the first number set followed by another. He cursed softly under his breath.

Of course the old dog wouldn't file his confidentials by name. He'd use a secret code. The old man liked nothing more than his secrets.

Still, Kennedy opened half a dozen drawers just to see if the system continued throughout. And it wasn't until he got to a bin near the corner of the desk that he found a file labeled "Obscene."

His hand shook as he pulled it out. Jack, for all his brilliance, had been sexually insatiable. Back when their brother Joe was still alive and no one ever thought Jack would be running for president, Jack had had an affair with a Danish émigré named Inga Arvad. Inga Binga, as Jack used to call her, was married to a man with ties to Hitler. She'd even met and liked Der Führer, and had said so in print.

She'd been the target of FBI surveillance as a possible spy, and during that surveillance who should turn up in her bed but a young naval lieutenant whose father had once been Ambassador to England. The Ambassador, as he preferred to be called even by his sons, found out about the affair, told Jack in no uncertain terms to end it, and then to make sure he did got him assigned to a PT boat in the Pacific, as far from Inga Binga as possible.

Kennedy had always suspected that Hoover had leaked the information to the Ambassador, but he hadn't known for certain until Jack became president when Hoover told them. Hoover had been surveilling all of the Kennedy children at the Ambassador's request. He'd given Kennedy a list of scandalous items as a sample, and hoped that would control the President and his brother.

It might have controlled Jack, but Hoover hadn't known Kennedy very well. Kennedy had told Hoover that if any of this information made it into the press, then other things would appear in print as well, things like the strange FBI budget items for payments covering Hoover's visits to the track or the fact that Hoover made some interesting friends, mobster friends, when he was vacationing in Palm Beach.

It wasn't quite a Mexican stand-off – Jack was really afraid of the old man – but it gave Kennedy more power than any attorney general had had over Hoover since the beginnings of the Roosevelt administration.

But now Kennedy needed those files, and he had a hunch Hoover would label them obscene.

Kennedy opened the file, and was shocked to see Richard Nixon's name on the sheets inside. Kennedy thumbed through quickly, not caring what dirt they'd found on that loser. Nixon couldn't win an election after his defeat in 1960. He'd even told the press after he lost a California race that they wouldn't have him to kick around any more.

Yet Hoover had kept the files, just to be safe.

That old bastard really and truly had known where all the bodies were buried. And it wouldn't be easy to find them.

Kennedy took a deep breath. He stood, shoved his hands in his pockets, and surveyed the walls of files. It would take days to search each folder. He didn't have days. He probably didn't have hours.

But he was Hoover's immediate supervisor, whether the old man had recognized it or not. Hoover answered to him. Which meant that the files belonged to the Justice Department, of which the FBI was only one small part.

He glanced at his watch. No one pounded on the door. He probably had until dawn before someone tried to stop him. If he was really lucky, no one would think of the files until mid-morning.

He went to the door and beckoned Haskell inside.

"We're taking the files to my office," he said.

"All of them, sir?"

"All of them. These first, then whatever is in Hoover's office, and then any other confidential files you can find."

Haskell looked up the wall as if he couldn't believe the command. "That'll take some time, sir."

"Not if you get a lot of people to help."

"Sir, I thought you wanted to keep this secret."

He did. But it wouldn't remain secret for long. So he had to control when the information got out – just like he had to control the information itself.

"Get this done as quickly as possible," he said.

Haskell nodded and turned the doorknob, but Kennedy stopped him before he went out.

"These are filed by code," he said. "Do you know where the key is?"

"I was told that Miss Gandy had the keys to everything from codes to offices," Haskell said.

Kennedy felt a shiver run through him. Knowing Hoover, he would have made sure he had the key to the Attorney General's office as well.

"Do you have any idea where she might have kept the code keys?" Kennedy asked.

"No," Haskell said. "I wasn't part of the need-to-know group. I already knew too much."

Kennedy nodded. He appreciated how much Haskell knew. It had gotten him this far.

"On your way out," Kennedy said, "call building maintenance and have them change all the locks in my office."

"Yes, sir." Haskell kept his hand on the doorknob. "Are you sure you want to do this, sir? Couldn't you just change the locks here? Wouldn't that secure everything for the President?"

"Everyone in Washington wants these files," Kennedy said. "They're going to come to this office suite. They won't think of mine."

"Until they heard that you moved everything."

Kennedy nodded. "And then they'll know how futile their quest really is."

The final crime scene was a mess. The bodies were already gone – probably inside the coroner's van that blocked the alley a few blocks back. It had taken Bryce nearly a half an hour to find someone who knew what the scene had looked like when the police had first arrived.

That someone was Officer Ralph Voight. He was tall and trim, with a pristine uniform despite the fact that he'd been on duty all night.

O'Reilly was the one who convinced him to talk with Bryce. Voight was the first to show the traditional animosity between the NYPD and the FBI, but that was because Voight didn't know who had died only a few blocks away.

Bryce had Voight walk him through the crime scene. The buildings on this street were boarded up, and the lights burned out. Broken glass littered the sidewalk – and it hadn't come from this particular crime. Rusted beer cans, half buried in the ice piles, cluttered each stoop like passed-out drunks.

"Okay," Voight said, using his flashlight as a pointer, "we come up on these two cars first."

The two sedans were parked against the curb, one behind the other. The sedans were too nice for the neighbourhood – new, black, without a dent.

Bryce recognized them as FBI issue – he had access to a sedan like that himself when he needed it.

He patted his pocket, was disgusted to realize he'd left his notebook at the apartment, and turned to O'Reilly. "You got paper? I need those plates."

O'Reilly nodded. He pulled out a notebook and wrote down the plate numbers.

"They just looked wrong," Voight was saying. "So we stopped, figuring maybe someone needed assistance."

He pointed the flashlight across the street. The squad had stopped directly across from the two cars.

"That's when we seen the first body."

He walked them to the middle of the street. This part of the city hadn't been plowed regularly and a layer of ice had built over the pavement. A large pool of blood had melted through that ice, leaving its edges reddish black and revealing the pavement below.

"The guy was face down, hands out like he'd tried to catch himself."

"Face gone?" Bryce asked, thinking maybe it was a head shot like the others.

"No. Turns out he was shot in the back."

Bryce glanced at O'Reilly, whose lips had thinned. This one was different. Because it was the first? Or because it was unrelated?

"We pull our weapons, scan to see if we see anyone else, which we don't. The door's open on the first sedan, but we didn't see anyone in the dome light. And we didn't see anyone obvious on the street, but it's really dark here and the flashlights don't reach far." Voight turned his light toward the block with the parked limousine, but neither the car nor the sidewalk was visible from this distance.

"So we go to the cars, careful now, and find the other body right there."

He flashed his light on the curb beside the door to the first sedan.

"This one's on his back and the door is open. We figure he was getting out when he got plugged. Then the other guy – maybe he was outside his car trying to help this guy with I don't know what, some car trouble or something, then his buddy gets hit, so he runs for cover across the street and gets nailed. End of story."

"Did you check to see if the cars start?" O'Reilly asked. Bryce nodded that was going to be his next question as well.

"I'm not supposed to touch the scene, sir," Voight said with some resentment. "We secured the area, figured everything was okay, then called it in."

"Did you hear the other shots?"

"No," Voight said. "I know we got three more up there, and you'd think I'd've heard the shooting if something happened, but I didn't. And as you can tell, it's damn quiet around here at night."

Bryce could tell. He didn't like the silence in the middle of the city. Neighborhoods that got quiet like this so close to dawn were usually among the worst. The early morning maintenance workers, and the delivery drivers stayed away whenever they could.

He peered in the sedan, then pulled the door open. The interior light went on, and there was blood all over the front seat and steering wheel. There were styrofoam coffee cups on both sides of the little rise between the seats. And the keys were in the ignition. Like all Bureau issue, the car was an automatic.

Carefully, so that he wouldn't disturb anything important in the scene, he turned the key. The sedan purred to life, sounding well-tuned just like it was supposed to.

"Check to see if there are other problems," Bryce said to O'Reilly. "A flat maybe."

Although Bryce knew there wouldn't be one. He shut off the ignition.

"You didn't see the interior light when you pulled up?" he asked Voight.

"Yeah, but it was dim," Voight said. "That's why I figured there was car problems. I figured they left the lights on so they could see."

Bryce nodded. He understood the assumption. He backed out of the sedan, then walked around it, shining his own flashlight at the hole in the ice, and then back at the first sedan.

Directly across.

He walked to the second sedan. Its interior was clean – no styrofoam cups, no wadded up food containers, no notebooks. Not even some tools hastily pulled to help the other drivers in need.

He let out a small sigh. He finally figured out what was bothering him.

"You find weapons on the two men?" he asked Voight.

"Yes, sir."

"Holstered?"

"The guy by the car. The other one had his in his right hand. We figured we just happened on the scene or someone would have taken the weapon."

Or not. People tended to hide for a while after shots were fired, particularly if they had nothing to do with the shootings but might get blamed anyway.

Bryce tried to open the passenger door on the second sedan, but it was locked. He walked around to the driver's door. Locked as well.

"No one looked inside this car?"

"No, sir. We figured Crime Scene would do it."

"But they haven't been here yet?" Bryce asked.

"It's the neighbourhood, sir. Right there" – Voight aimed his flashlight at stairs heading down to a lower level —"is one of those men-only clubs, you know? The kind that you go to when you're . . . you know . . . looking for other men."

Bryce felt a flash of irritation. He'd been running into this all night. "Okay. What I'm hearing in a sideways way from every representative of the NYPD on this scene is that crimes in this neighbourhood don't get investigated."

Voight sputtered. "They get investigated —"

"They get investigated," O'Reilly said, "enough to tell the families they probably want to back off. You heard Brunner. That's what móst in the department call it. The rest of us, we call them lifestyle kills. And we get in trouble if we waste too many resources on them."

"Lovely," Bryce said dryly. His philosophy, which had gotten him in trouble with the Bureau more than once, was that all crimes deserved investigation, no matter how distasteful you found the victims. Which was why he kept getting moved, from Communists to reviewing wire-taps to digging dirt on other agents.

And that was probably why he was here. He was expendable.

"Did you find car keys on either of the victims?" Bryce asked.

"No, sir," Voight said. "And I helped the coroner when he first arrived."

"Then start looking. See if they got dropped in the struggle."

Although Bryce doubted they had.

"I got something to jimmy the lock in my car," O'Reilly said.

Bryce nodded. Then he stood back, surveying the whole thing. He didn't like how he was thinking. It was making his heartburn grow worse.

But it was the only thing that made sense.

Agents worked HooverWatch in pairs. There were two dead agents and two cars. If the second sedan was back-up, there should have been four agents and two cars.

But it didn't look that way. It looked like someone had pulled up behind the HooverWatch vehicle, and got out, carefully locking the door.

Then he went to the door of the HooverWatch car. The driver had got out to talk to him, and the new guy shot him.

At that point, the second HooverWatch agent was an easy target. He scrambled out of the car, grabbed his own weapon, and headed across the street – maybe shooting as he went. The shooter got him, and then casually walked up the street to the limo, which he had to know was there even though he couldn't see it.

As he approached the limo, the limo driver lowered his window. He would have recognized the approaching man, and thought he was going to report on the danger.

Instead, the man shot him, then went to lie in wait for Hoover and Tolson.

Bryce shivered. It would have happened very fast, and long before the beat cops showed up.

The guy in the street had time to bleed out. The limo driver couldn't warn his boss. And the beat cops hadn't heard the shots in the alley, which they would have on such a quiet night.

O'Reilly brought the jimmy, shoved it into the space between the window and the lock, and flipped the lock up with a single movement. Then he opened the door.

No keys in the ignition.

Bryce flipped open the glovebox. Nothing inside but the vehicle registration. Which, as he expected, identified it as an FBI vehicle.

The shooter had planned to come back. He'd planned to drive away in this car. But he got delayed. And by the time he got here, the two beat cops were on scene. He couldn't get his car.

He had to improvise. So he probably walked away or took the subway, hoping the cops would think the extra car belonged to one of the victims.

And that was his mistake.

"How come you guys were here in the middle of the night?" Bryce asked Voight.

Voight swallowed. It was the first sign of nervousness he'd shown. "This is part of our beat."

"But?" Bryce asked.

Voight looked away. "We're supposed to go up Central Park West."

"And you don't."

"Yeah, we do. Just not every time."

"Because?"

"Because I figure, you know, when the bars let out, we could, you know, let our presence be known."

"Prevent a lifestyle kill."

"Yes, sir."

"And you care about this because . . . ?"

"Everyone should," Voight snapped. "Serve and protect, right, sir?"

Voight was touchy. He thought Bryce was accusing him of protecting the lifestyle because he lived it.

"Does your partner like this drive?" Bryce asked.

"He complains, sir, but he lets me do it."

"Have you stopped any crimes?"

"Broken up a few fights," Voight said.

"But not something like this."

"No, sir."

"You don't patrol every night, do you, Voight?"

"No, sir. We get different regions different nights."

"Do you think our killer would have thought that this street was unprotected?"

"It usually is, sir."

O'Reilly was frowning, but not at Voight. At Bryce. "You think this was planned?" O'Reilly asked.

Bryce didn't answer. This was a Bureau matter, and he wasn't sure how the Bureau would handle it.

But he did think the killing was planned. And he had a hunch it would be easy to solve because of the abandoned sedan.

And that abandoned sedan bothered him more than he wanted to admit. Because the presence of that sedan meant only one thing: that the person who had shot all five FBI agents was – almost without a doubt – an FBI agent himself.

*

Kennedy looked at the bins and the filing cabinets stacked around his office and allowed himself one moment to feel overwhelmed. People ribbed him about the office; he had taken the reception area and made it his, rather than use the standard size office in the back.

As a result, his office was as long as a football field, with stunning windows along the walls. The watercolours painted by his children had been covered by the cabinets. His furniture was pushed aside to make room for the bins, and for the first time, this space felt small.

He put his hands on his hips and wondered how to begin.

Since six agents began moving the filing cabinets across the corridor more than an hour ago, Kennedy had received five phone calls from LBJ's chief of staff. Kennedy hadn't taken one of them. The last had been a direct order to come to the Oval Office.

Kennedy ignored it.

He also ignored the ringing telephone – the White House line – and the messages his own assistant (called in after a short night's sleep) had been bringing to him.

Helen Gandy stood in the corridor, arms crossed, her purse hanging off her wrist, and watching with deep disapproval. Haskell was trying to find out if there were remaining files and where they were. But Kennedy had found the one thing he was looking for: the key.

It was in a large, innocuous index file box inside the lowest drawer of Helen Gandy's desk. Kennedy had brought it into his office and was thumbing through it, hoping to understand it before he got interrupted again.

A man from building maintenance had changed the lock on the door leading into the interior offices, and was working on the main doors now that the files were all inside. Kennedy figured he'd have his own office secure by seven am.

Then he heard a rustling in the hallway, a lot of startled, "Mr President, sir!" followed by official, "Make way for the President," and instinctively he turned toward the door. The maintenance man was leaning out of it, the doorknob loose in his hand.

"Where the fuck is that bastard?" Lyndon Baines Johnson's voice echoed from the corridor. "Doesn't anyone in this building have balls enough to tell him that he works for me?"

Even though the question was rhetorical, someone tried to answer. Kennedy heard something about "your orders, sir."

"Horseshit!" Then LBJ stood in the doorway. Two secret service agents flanked him. He motioned with one hand at the maintenance man. "I suggest you get out."

The man didn't have to be told twice. He scurried away, still carrying the doorknob. LBJ came inside alone, pushed the door closed, then grimaced as it popped back open. He grabbed a chair and set it in front of the door, then glared at Kennedy.

The glare was effective in that hang-dog face, despite LBJ's attire. He wore a plaid silk pajama top stuffed into a pair of suitpants, finished with dress shoes and no socks. His hair – what remained of it – hadn't been Brylcreemed down like usual, and stood up on the sides and the back.

"I get a phone call from some weasel underling of that Old Cocksucker, informing me that he's dead, and you're stealing from his tomb. I try to contact you, find out that you are indeed removing files from the Director's office, and that you won't take my calls. Now, I should've sent one of my boys over here, but I figured they're still walking on tip-toe around you because you're in fucking mourning, and this don't require tip-toe. Especially since you got to be wondering about now what the hell you did to deserve all of this."

"Deserve what?" Kennedy had expected LBJ's anger, but he hadn't expected it so soon. He also hadn't expected it here, in his office, instead of in the Oval Office a day or so later.

"Well, there's only two things that tie J. Edgar and your brother. The first is that someone was gunning for them and succeeded. The second is that they went after the mob on your bidding. There's a lot of shit running around here that says your brother's shooting was a mob hit, and I know personally that J. Edgar was doing his best to make it seem like that Oswald character acted alone. But now Edgar is dead and Jack is dead and the only tie they have is the way they kow-towed to your stupid prosecution of the men that got your brother elected."

Kennedy felt lightheaded. He hadn't even thought that the deaths of his brother and J. Edgar were connected. But LBJ had a point. Maybe there was a conspiracy to kill government officials. Maybe the mob was showing its power. He'd had warning.

Hell, he'd had suspicions. He hadn't let himself look at any of the evidence in his brother's assassination, not after he secured the body and prevented a disastrous autopsy in Texas. If those doctors at Parkland had done their job, they would've seen just how advanced Jack's Addison's disease was. The best kept secret of the Kennedy Administration – an administration full of secrets – was how close Jack was to incapacitation and death.

Kennedy clutched the file box. But LBJ knew that. He knew a lot of the secrets – had even promised to keep a few of them. And he wanted the files as badly as Kennedy did.

There had to be a lot in here on LBJ too. Not just the women, which was something he had in common with Jack, but other things, from his days in Congress.

"From what I heard," Kennedy said, making certain his voice was calm even though he wasn't, "all they know is someone shot Hoover. Did you get more details than that? Something that mentions organized crime in particular?"

"I'm sure it'll come out," LBJ said.

"You're sure that saying such things would upset me," Kennedy said. "You're after the files."

"Damn straight," LBJ said. "I'm the head of this government. Those files are mine."

"You're the head of this government for another year. Next January, someone'll take the oath of office and it might not be you. Do you really want to claim these in the name of the presidency? Because you might be handing them over to Goldwater come January."

LBJ blanched.

Someone knocked on the door, and startled both men. Kennedy frowned. He couldn't think of anyone who would have enough nerve to interrupt him when he was getting shouted at by LBJ. But someone had.

LBJ pulled the door open. Helen Gandy stood there.

"You boys can be heard in the hallway," she said, sweeping in as if the leader of the free world wasn't holding the door for her. "And it's embarrassing. It was precisely this kind of thing the Director hoped to avoid."

Then she nodded at LBJ. Kennedy watched her. The dragon lady. Jack, as usual, had been right with his jibes. Only the dragon lady would walk in here as if she were the most important person in the room.

"Mr President," she said, "these files are the Director's personal business. He wanted me to take care of them, and get them out of the office, where they do not belong."

"Personal files, Miss Gandy?" LBJ asked. "These are his secret files."

"If they were secret, Mr President, then you wouldn't be here. Mr Hoover kept his secrets."

Mr Hoover used his secrets, Kennedy thought, but didn't say.

"These are just his confidential files," Miss Gandy was saying. "Let me take care of them and they won't be here to tempt anyone. That's what the Director wanted."

"These are government property," LBJ said with a sly look at Kennedy. For the first time, Kennedy realized his Goldwater argument had gotten through. "They belong here. I do thank you for your time and concern, though, ma'am."

Then he gave her a courtly little bow, put his hand on the small of her back, and propelled her out of the room.

Despite himself Kennedy was impressed. He'd never seen anyone handle the dragon lady that efficiently before.

LBJ grabbed one of the cabinets and slid it in front of the door he had just closed. Kennedy had forgotten how strong the man was. He had invited Kennedy down to his Texas ranch before the election, trying to find out what Kennedy was made of, and instead, Kennedy had realized just what LBJ was made of – strength, not bluster, brains and brawn.

He'd do well to remember that.

"All right," LBJ said as he turned around. "Here's what I'm gonna offer. You can have your family's files. You can watch while we search for them and you can have everything. Just give me the rest."

Kennedy raised his eyebrows. He hadn't felt this alive since November. "No."

"I can fire your ass in five minutes, put someone else in this fancy office, and then you can't do a goddamn thing," LBJ said. "I'm being kind."

"There's historical precedent for a cabinet member barricading himself in his office after he got fired," Kennedy said. "Seems to me it happened to a previous president named Johnson. While I'm barricaded in, I'll just go through the files and find out everything I need to know."

LBJ crossed his arms.

It was a stand-off and neither of them had a good play. They only had a guess as to what was in those files – not just theirs but all of the others as well. They did know that whatever was in those files had given Hoover enough power to last in the office for more than forty years.

The files had brought down presidents. They could bring down congressmen, supreme court justices, and maybe even the current president. In that way, Helen Gandy was right.

The best solution was to destroy everything.

Only Kennedy wouldn't. Just like he knew LBJ wouldn't. There was too much history here, too much knowledge.

And too much power.

"These are our files," Kennedy said after a moment, although the word "our" galled him, "yours and mine. Right now we control them."

LBJ nodded, almost imperceptibly. "What do you want?"

What did he want? To be left alone? To have his family left alone? At midnight, he might have said that. But now, his old self was reasserting itself. He felt like the man who had gone after the corrupt leaders of the Teamsters, not the man who had accidentally gotten his brother murdered.

Besides, there might be things in that file that could head off other problems in the future. Other murders. Other manipulations.

He needed a bullet-proof position. LBJ was right: the Attorney General could be fired. But there was one position, constitutionally, that the President couldn't touch.

"I want to be your Vice President," Kennedy said. "And in 1972, when you can't run again, I want your endorsement. I want you to back me for the nomination."

LBJ swallowed hard. Colour suffused his face and for a moment, Kennedy thought he was going to shout again.

But he didn't.

Instead he said, "And what happens if we don't win?"

"We move these to a location of our choosing. And we do it with trusted associates. We get this stuff out of here."

LBJ glanced at the door. He was clearly thinking of what Helen Gandy had said, how it was better to be rid of all of this than it was to have it corrupting the office, endangering everyone.

But if LBJ and Kennedy controlled the entire cache, they also controlled their own files. LBJ could destroy his and Kennedy could preserve his family's legacy.

If it weren't for the fact that LBJ hated him almost as much as Kennedy hated LBJ, the decision would be easy.

"You'd trust me to a gentleman's agreement?" LBJ asked, not disguising the sarcasm in his tone. He knew Kennedy thought he was too uncouth to ever be considered a gentleman.

"You know where your interests lie. Just like I do," Kennedy said. "If we don't let Miss Gandy have the files, then this is the only choice."

LBJ sighed. "I hoped to be rid of the Kennedys by inauguration day."

"And what if I planned to run against you?" Kennedy asked, even though he knew he wouldn't. Already the party stalwarts had been approaching him about a 1964 presidential bid, and he had put them off. He had been too shaky, too emotionally fragile.

He didn't feel fragile now.

LBJ didn't answer that question. Instead, he said, "You can be an incautious asshole. Why should I trust you?"

"Because I saved Jack's ass more times than you can count," Kennedy said. "I'm saving yours too."

"How do you figure?" LBJ asked.

"Your fear of those files brought you to me, Mr President." Kennedy put an emphasis on the title, which he usually avoided using around LBJ. "If I barricade myself in here, I'll have the keys to the kingdom and no qualms about letting the information free when I go free. If you work with me, your secrets remain just secrets."

"You're a son of bitch, you know that?" LBJ asked.

Kennedy nodded. "The hell of it is you are too or you wouldn't've brought up Jack's death before we knew what really happened to Hoover. So let's control the presidency for the next sixteen years. By then the information in these files will probably be worthless."

LBJ stared at him. It took Kennedy a minute to realize that although he'd won the argument, he wouldn't get an agreement from LBJ, not if Kennedy didn't make the first move.

Kennedy held out his hand. "Deal?"

LBJ stared at Kennedy's extended hand for a long moment before taking it in his own big clammy one.

"You goddamn son of a bitch," LBJ said. "You've got a deal."

It took Bryce only one phone call. The guy who ran the motorpool told him who checked out the sedan without asking why Bryce wanted to know. And Bryce, as he leaned in the cold telephone booth half a block from the first crime scene, instantly understood what had happened and why.

The agent who checked out the sedan was Walter Cain. He should've been on extended leave. Bryce had recommended it after he had told Cain that his ex-fiancée had tried to commit suicide. On getting the news, Cain had just had that look, that blank, my-life-is-over look.

And it had scared Bryce. Scared him enough that he asked Cain be put on indefinite leave. How long ago had that been? Less than twelve hours.

More than enough time to get rid of the morals police – the one man who made all the rules at the FBI. The man who had no morals himself.

J. Edgar Hoover.

Bryce had spent the past week studying Cain's file. Cain had had HooverWatch off and on throughout the past year. Cain knew the procedure, and he knew how to thwart it.

He'd killed five agents.

Because no one would listen to Bryce about that vacant look in Cain's eye.

Bryce let himself out of the phone booth. He walked back to the coroner's van. If he didn't have back-up by now, he'd call for some all over again. They couldn't leave him hanging on this. They had to let him know, if nothing else, what to do with the Director's body.

But he needn't've worried. When he got back to the alley, he saw five more sedans, all FBI issue. And as he stepped into the alley proper, the first person he saw was his boss, crouching over Hoover's corpse.

"I thought I told you to secure the scene," said the SAC for the District of New York, Eugene Hart. "In fact, I ordered you to do it."

"The scene extends over six blocks. I'm just one guy," Bryce said.

Hart walked over to him. He looked tired.

"I need to speak to you," Bryce said. He walked Hart back to the two sedans, explained what he'd learned, and watched Hart's face.

The man flinched, then, to Bryce's surprise, put his hand on Bryce's shoulder. "It's good work."

Bryce didn't thank him. He was worried that Hart hadn't asked any questions. "I'd heard Cain bitch more than once about Hoover setting the moral values for the office. And with what happened this week —"

"I know." Hart squeezed his shoulder. "We'll take care of it."

Bryce turned so quickly that he made Hart lose his grip. "You're going to cover it up."

Hart closed his eyes.

"You weren't hanging me out to dry. You were trying to figure out how to handle this. Son of a bitch. And you're going to let Cain walk."

"He won't walk," Hart said. "He'll just . . . be guilty of something else."

"You can't cover this up. It's too important. So soon after President Kennedy —"

"That's precisely why we're going to handle it," Hart said. "We don't want a panic."

"And you don't want anyone to know where Hoover and Tolson were found. What're you going to say? That they died of natural causes in their beds? Their *separate* beds?"

"It's not your concern," Hart said. "You've done well for us. You'll be rewarded."

"If I keep my mouth shut."

Hart sighed. He didn't seem to have the energy to glare. "I don't honestly care. I'm glad to have the old man gone. But I'm not in charge of this. We've got orders now, and everything'll get taken care of at a much higher level than either you or me. You should be grateful for that."

Bryce supposed he should be. It took the political pressure off him. It also took the personal pressure off.

But he couldn't help feeling if someone had listened to him before, if someone had paid attention, then none of this would have happened.

No one cared that an FBI agent was going to marry a former prostitute. If the Bureau knew – and it did – then not even the KGB could use that as blackmail.

It was all about appearances. It would always be about appearances. Hoover had designed a damn booklet about appearances, and it hadn't stopped him from getting shot in a back alley after a party he would never admit attending.

Hoover had been so worried about people using secrets against each other, he hadn't even realized how his own secrets could be used against him.

Bryce looked at Hart. They were both tired. It had been a long night. And it would be an even longer few weeks for Hart. Bryce would get some don't-tell promotion and he'd stay there for as long as he had to. He had to make sure that Cain got prosecuted for something, that he paid for five deaths.

Then Bryce would resign.

He didn't need the Bureau, any more than he had needed Mary, his own pre-approved wife. Maybe he'd talk to O'Reilly, see if he could put in a good word with the NYPD. At least the NYPD occasionally investigated cases.

If they happened in the right neighbourhood.

To the right people.

Bryce shoved his hands in his pockets and walked back to his apartment. Hart didn't try to stop him. They both knew Bryce's work on this case was done. He wouldn't even have to write a report.

In fact, he didn't dare write a report, didn't dare put any of this on paper where someone else might discover it. The wrong someone. Someone who didn't care about handling and the proper information.

Someone who would use that information to his own benefit.

Like the Director had.

For more than forty-five years.

Bryce shook the thought off. It wasn't his concern. He no longer had concerns. Except getting a good night's sleep.

And somehow he knew that he wouldn't get one of those for a long, long time.

THE ERDMANN NEXUS

Nancy Kress

Nancy Kress began selling her elegant and incisive stories in the mid-1970s, and she has since become a frequent contributor to *Asimov's Science Fiction*, *The Magazine of Fantasy & Science Fiction*, *Omni*, *sci fiction*, and elsewhere. Her books include the novel version of her Hugo- and Nebula-awards-winning story, *Beggars in Spain*, and a sequel, *Beggars and Choosers*, as well as *The Prince of Morning Bells*, *The Golden Grove*, *The White Pipes*, *An Alien Light*, *Brain Rose*, *Oaths & Miracles*, *Stinger*, *Maximum Light*, *Crossfire*, *Nothing Human*, and the space opera trilogy *Probability Moon*, *Probability Sun*, and *Probability Space*. Her short work has been collected in *Trinity and Other Stories*, *The Aliens of Earth*, *Beaker's Dozen*, and *Nano Comes to Clifford Falls and Other Stories*. Her most recent books are the novels *Crucible* and *Dogs*; coming up is a new novel, *Steal Across the Sky*. In addition to the awards for "Beggars in Spain," she has also won Nebula awards for her stories "Out of All Them Bright Stars" and "The Flowers of Aulit Prison."

In the complex and powerful story that follows, she takes us to visit people waiting for death in an old folks' home who discover unexpected new possibilities at the very edge of life.

"Errors, like straws, upon the surface flow,
He who would reach for pearls must dive below."
                                                    – *John Dryden*

THE SHIP, WHICH *would have looked nothing like a ship to Henry Erdmann, moved between the stars, traveling in an orderly pattern of occurrences in the vacuum flux. Over several cubic light-years of space, subatomic particles appeared, existed, and winked out of existence in nanoseconds. Flop transitions tore space and then reconfigured it as the ship moved on. Henry, had he somehow been nearby in the cold of deep space, would have died from the complicated, regular, intense bursts of radiation long before he could have had time to appreciate their shimmering beauty.*

All at once the "ship" stopped moving.

The radiation bursts increased, grew even more complex. Then the ship abruptly changed direction. It accelerated, altering both space and time as it sped on, healing the alterations in its wake. Urgency shot through it. Something, far away, was struggling to be born.

ONE

Henry Erdmann stood in front of the mirror in his tiny bedroom, trying to knot his tie with one hand. The other hand gripped his walker. It was an unsteady business, and the tie ended up crooked. He yanked it out and began again. Carrie would be here soon.

He always wore a tie to the college. Let the students – and graduate students, at that! – come to class in ripped jeans and obscene tee-shirts and hair tangled as if colonized by rats. Even the girls. Students were students, and Henry didn't consider their sloppiness disrespectful, the way so many did at St Sebastian's. Sometimes he was even amused by it, in a sad sort of way. Didn't these intelligent, sometimes driven, would-be physicists know how ephemeral their beauty was? Why did they go to such lengths to look unappealing, when soon enough that would be their only choice?

This time he got the tie knotted. Not perfectly – a difficult operation, one-handed – but close enough for government work. He smiled. When he and his colleagues had been doing government work, only perfection was good enough. Atomic bombs were like that. Henry could still hear Oppie's voice saying the plans for Ivy Mike were "technically sweet." Of course, that was before all the —

A knock on the door and Carries's fresh young voice. "Dr Erdmann? Are you ready?"

She always called him by his title, always treated him with respect. Not like some of the nurses and assistants. "How are we today, Hank?" that overweight blonde asked yesterday. When he answered stiffly, "I don't know about you, madame, but I'm fine, thank you," she'd only laughed. *Old people are so formal – it's so cute!* Henry could just see her saying it to one of her horrible colleagues. He had never been "Hank" in his entire life.

"Coming, Carrie." He put both hands on the walker and inched forward – clunk, clunk, clunk – the walker sounding loud even on the carpeted floor. His class's corrected problem sets lay on the table by the door. He'd given them some really hard problems this week, and only Haldane had succeeded in solving all of them. Haldane had promise. An inventive mind, yet rigorous, too. They could have used him in '52 on Project Ivy, developing the Teller-Ulam staged fusion H-bomb.

Halfway across the living room of his tiny apartment in the Assisted Living Facility, something happened in Henry's mind.

He stopped, astonished. It had felt like a tentative *touch*, a ghostly finger inside his brain. Astonishment was immediately replaced by fear. Was he having a stroke? At ninety, anything was possible. But he felt fine, better in fact than for several days. Not a stroke. So what —

"Dr Erdmann?"

"I'm here." He clunked to the door and opened it. Carrie wore a cherry red sweater, a fallen orange leaf caught on her hat, and sunglasses. Such a pretty girl, all bronze hair and bright skin and vibrant colour. Outside it was drizzling. Henry reached out and gently removed the sunglasses. Carrie's left eye was swollen and discoloured, the iris and pupil invisible under the outraged flesh.

"The bastard," Henry said.

That was Henry and Carrie going down the hall toward the elevator, thought Evelyn Krenchnoted. She waved from her armchair, her door wide open as always, but they were talking and didn't notice. She strained to hear, but just then another plane went overhead from the airport. Those pesky flight paths were too near St Sebastian's! On the other hand, if they weren't, Evelyn couldn't afford to live here. Always look on the bright side!

Since this was Tuesday afternoon, Carrie and Henry were undoubtedly going to the college. So wonderful the way Henry kept busy – you'd never guess his real age, that was for sure. He even had all his hair! Although that jacket was too light for September, and not water-proof. Henry might catch cold. She would speak to Carrie about it. And why was Carrie wearing sunglasses when it was raining?

But if Evelyn didn't start her phone calls, she would be late! People were depending on her! She keyed in the first number, listened to it ring one floor below. "Bob? It's Evelyn. Now, dear, tell me – how's your blood pressure today?"

"Fine," Bob Donovan said.

"Are you sure? You sound a bit grumpy, dear."

"I'm fine, Evelyn. I'm just busy."

"Oh, that's good! With what?"

"Just *busy*."

"Always good to keep busy! Are you coming to Current Affairs tonight?"

"Dunno."

"You should. You really should. Intellectual stimulation is so important for people our age!"

"Gotta go," Bob grunted.

"Certainly, but first, how did your granddaughter do with —"

He'd hung up. Really, very grumpy. Maybe he was having problems with irregularity. Evelyn would recommend a high colonic.

Her next call was more responsive. Gina Martinelli was, as always, thrilled with Evelyn's attention. She informed Gina minutely about the state of her arthritis, her gout, her diabetes, her son's weight problem, her other son's wife's step-daughter's miscarriage, all interspersed with quotations from the Bible ("'Take a little wine for thy stomach' – First Timothy"). She answered all Evelyn's questions and wrote down all her recommendations and —

"Evelyn?" Gina said. "Are you still there?"

"Yes, I —" Evelyn fell silent, an occurrence so shocking that Gina gasped, "Hit your panic button!"

"No, no, I'm fine, I . . . I just remembered something for a moment."

"Remembered something? What?"

But Evelyn didn't know. It hadn't been a memory, exactly, it had been a . . . what? A feeling, a vague but somehow strong sensation of . . . something.

"Evelyn?"

"I'm here!"

"The Lord decides when to call us home, and I guess it's not your time yet. Did you hear about Anna Chernov? That famous ballet dancer on Four? She fell last night and broke her leg and they had to move her to the Infirmary."

"No!"

"Yes, poor thing. They say it's only temporary, until they get her stabilized, but you know what that means."

She did. They all did. First the Infirmary, then up to Seven, where you didn't even have your own little apartment any more, and eventually to Nursing on Eight and Nine. Better to go quick and clean, like Jed Fuller last month. But Evelyn wasn't going to let herself think like that! A positive attitude was so important!

Gina said, "Anna is doing pretty well, I hear. The Lord never sends more than a person can bear."

Evelyn wasn't so sure about that, but it never paid to argue with Gina, who was convinced that she had God on redial. Evelyn said, "I'll visit her before the Stitch 'n Bitch meeting. I'm sure she'll want company. Poor girl – you know, those dancers, they just abuse their health for years and years, so what can you expect?"

"I know!" Gina said, not without satisfaction. "They pay a terrible price for beauty. It's a little vain, actually."

"Did you hear about that necklace she has in the St Sebastian safe?"

"No! What necklace?"

"A fabulous one! Doris Dziwalski told me. It was given to Anna by some famous Russian dancer who was given it by the tsar!"

"What tsar?"

"*The* tsar! You know, of Russia. Doris said it's worth a fortune and that's why it's in the safe. Anna never wears it."

"Vanity," Doris said. "She probably doesn't like the way it looks now against her wrinkly neck."

"Doris said Anna's depressed."

"No, it's vanity. 'Lo, I looked and saw that all was —'"

"I'll recommend acupuncture to her," Evelyn interrupted. "Acupuncture is good for depression." But first she'd call Erin, to tell her the news.

Erin Bass let the phone ring. It was probably that tiresome bore Evelyn Krenchnoted, eager to check on Erin's blood pressure or her cholesterol or her Isles of Langerhans. Oh, Erin should answer the phone, there was no harm in the woman, Erin should be more charitable. But why? Why should one have to be more charitable just because one was old?

She let the phone ring and returned to her book, Graham Greene's *The Heart of the Matter*. Greene's world-weary despair was a silly affectation but he was a wonderful writer, and too much underrated nowadays.

The liner came in on a Saturday evening: from the bedroom window they could see its long grey form steal past the boom, beyond the —

Something was happening.

— steal past the boom, beyond the —

Erin was no longer in St Sebastian's, she was nowhere, she was lifted away from everything, she was beyond the —

Then it was over and she sat again in her tiny apartment, the book sliding unheeded off her lap.

Anna Chernov was dancing. She and Paul stood with two other couples on the stage, under the bright lights. Balanchine himself stood in the second wing, and even though Anna knew he was there to wait for Suzanne's solo, his presence inspired her. The music began. *Promenade en couronne, attitude, arabesque effacé* and into the lift, Paul's arms raising her. She was lifted out of herself and then she was soaring above the stage, over the heads of the corps de ballet, above Suzanne Farrell herself, soaring through the roof of the New York State Theater and into the night sky, spreading her arms in a *porte de bras* wide enough to take in the glittering night sky, soaring in the most perfect jeté in the universe, until . . .

"She's smiling," Bob Donovan said, before he knew he was going to speak at all. He looked down at the sleeping Anna, so beautiful she didn't even look real, except for the leg in its big ugly cast. In one hand, feeling like a fool but what the fuck, he held three yellow roses.

"The painkillers do that sometimes," the Infirmary nurse said. "I'm afraid you can't stay, Mr Donovan."

Bob scowled at her. But it wasn't like he meant it or anything. This nurse wasn't so bad. Not like some. Maybe because she wasn't any spring chicken herself. *A few more years, sister, and you'll be here right with us.*

"Give her these, okay?" He thrust the roses at the nurse.

"I will, yes," she said, and he walked out of the medicine-smelling Infirmary – he hated that smell – back to the elevator. Christ, what a sorry old fart he was. Anna Chernov, that nosy old broad Evelyn Krenchnoted once told him, used to dance at some famous place in New York, Abraham Centre or something. Anna had been famous. But Evelyn could be wrong, and anyway it didn't matter. From the first moment Bob Donovan laid eyes on Anna Chernov, he'd wanted to give her things. Flowers. Jewellery. Anything she wanted. Anything he had. And how stupid and fucked-up was that, at his age? Give me a break!

He took the elevator to the first floor, stalked savagely through the
lobby, and went out the side door to the "remembrance garden". Stupid
name, New Age-y stupid. He wanted to kick something, wanted to bellow
for —

Energy punched through him, from the base of his spine up his back
and into his brain, mild but definite, like a shock from a busted toaster or
something. Then it was gone.

What the fuck was *that*? Was he okay? If he fell, like Anna –

He was okay. He didn't have Anna's thin delicate bones. Whatever it
was, was gone now. Just one of those things.

On a Nursing floor of St Sebastian's, a woman with just a few days to live
muttered in her long, last half-sleep. An IV dripped morphine into her arm,
easing the passage. No one listened to the mutterings; it had been years
since they'd made sense. For a moment she stopped and her eyes, again
bright in the ravaged face that had once been so lovely, grew wide. But for
only a moment. Her eyes closed and the mindless muttering resumed.

In Tijuana, a vigorous old man sitting behind his son's market stall, where
he sold cheap serapes to jabbering *touristos*, suddenly lifted his face to the
sun. His mouth, which still had all its white flashing teeth, made a big O.

In Bombay, a widow dressed in white looked out her window at the teeming streets, her face gone blank as her sari.

In Chengdu, a monk sitting on his cushion on the polished floor of the
meditation room in the ancient Wenshu Monastery shattered the holy
silence with a shocking, startled laugh.

TWO

Carrie Vesey sat in the back of Dr Erdmann's classroom and thought about
murder.

Not that she would ever do it, of course. Murder was wrong. Taking a
life filled her with horror that was only —

   Ground-up castor beans were a deadly poison.

— made worse by her daily witnessing of old people's aching desire to hold
onto life. Also, she —

   *Her step-brother had once shown her how to disable the
brakes on a car.*

— knew she wasn't the kind of person who solved problems that boldly.
And anyway her —

The battered-woman defence almost always earned acquittal from juries.

— lawyer said that a paper trail of restraining orders and ER documentation was by far the best way to —

If a man was passed out from a dozen beers, he'd never feel a bullet from his own service revolver.

— put Jim behind bars legally. That, the lawyer said, "would solve the problem" – as if a black eye and a broken arm and constant threats that left her scared even when Jim wasn't in the same *city* were all just a theoretical "problem," like the ones Dr Erdmann gave his physics students.

He sat on top of a desk in the front of the room, talking about something called the "Bose Einstein condensate." Carrie had no idea what that was, and she didn't care. She just liked being here, sitting unheeded in the back of the room. The physics students, nine boys and two girls, were none of them interested in her presence, her black eye, or her beauty. When Dr Erdmann was around, he commanded all their geeky attention, and that was indescribably restful. Carrie tried – unsuccessfully, she knew – to hide her beauty. Her looks had brought her nothing but trouble: Gary, Eric, Jim. So now she wore baggy sweats and no make-up, and crammed her 24-carat-gold hair under a shapeless hat. Maybe if she was as smart as these students she would have learned to pick a different kind of man, but she wasn't, and she hadn't, and Dr Erdmann's classroom was a place she felt safe. Safer, even, than St Sebastian's, which was where Jim had blackened her eye.

He'd slipped in through the loading dock, she guessed, and caught her alone in the linens supply closet. He was gone after one punch, and when she called her exasperated lawyer and he found out she had no witnesses and St Sebastian's had "security," he'd said there was nothing he could do. It would be her word against Jim's. She had to be able to *prove* that the restraining order had been violated.

Dr Erdmann was talking about "proof," too: some sort of mathematical proof. Carrie had been good at math, in high school. Only Dr Erdmann had said once that what she'd done in high school wasn't "mathematics," only "arithmetic." "Why didn't you go to college, Carrie?" he'd asked.

"No money," she said in a tone that meant: Please don't ask anything else. She just hadn't felt up to explaining about Daddy and the alcoholism and the debts and her abusive step-brothers, and Dr Erdmann hadn't asked. He was sensitive that way.

Looking at his tall, stooped figure sitting on the desk, his walker close to hand, Carrie sometimes let herself dream that Dr Erdmann – Henry – was fifty years younger. Forty to her twenty-eight – that would work. She'd Googled a picture of him at that age, when he'd been working at someplace called the Lawrence Radiation Laboratory. He'd been handsome, dark-haired, smiling into the camera next to his wife, Ida. She hadn't been as pretty as Carrie, but she'd gone to college, so even if Carrie had been born back then, she wouldn't have had a chance with him. Story of her life.

" — have any questions?" Dr Erdmann finished.

The students did – they always did – clamouring to be heard, not raising their hands, interrupting each other. But when Dr Erdmann spoke, immediately they all shut up. Someone leapt up to write equations on the board. Dr Erdmann slowly turned his frail body to look at them. The discussion went on a long time, almost as long as the class. Carrie fell asleep.

When she woke, it was to Dr Erdmann, leaning on his walker, gently jiggling her shoulder. "Carrie?"

"Oh! Oh, I'm sorry!"

"Don't be. We bored you to death, poor child."

"No! I loved it!"

He raised his eyebrows and she felt shamed. He thought she was telling a polite lie, and he had very little tolerance for lies. But the truth is, she always loved being here.

Outside, it was full dark. The autumn rain had stopped and the unseen ground had that mysterious, fertile smell of wet leaves. Carrie helped Dr Erdmann into her battered Toyota and slid behind the wheel. As they started back toward St Sebastian's, she could tell that he was exhausted. Those students asked too much of him! It was enough that he taught one advanced class a week, sharing all that physics, without them also demanding he —

"Dr Erdmann?"

For a long terrible moment she thought he was dead. His head lolled against the seat but he wasn't asleep: His open eyes rolled back into his head. Carrie jerked the wheel to the right and slammed the Toyota alongside the curb. He was still breathing.

"Dr Erdmann? *Henry?*"

Nothing. Carrie dove into her purse, fumbling for her cell phone. Then it occurred to her that his panic button would be faster. She tore open the buttons on his jacket; he wasn't wearing the button. She scrambled again for the purse, starting to sob.

"Carrie?"

He was sitting up now, a shadowy figure. She hit the overhead light. His face, a fissured landscape, looked dazed and pale. His pupils were huge.

"What happened? Tell me." She tried to keep her voice even, to observe everything, because it was important to be able to make as full a report as possible to Dr Jamison. But her hand clutched at his sleeve.

He covered her fingers with his. His voice sounded dazed. "I . . . don't know. I was . . . somewhere else?"

"A stroke?" That was what they were all afraid of. Not death, but to be incapacitated, reduced to partiality. And for Dr Erdmann, with his fine mind . . .

"No." He sounded definite. "Something else. I don't know. Did you call 911 yet?"

The cell phone lay inert in her hand. "No, not yet, there wasn't time for —"

"Then don't. Take me home."

"All right, but you're going to see the doctor as soon as we get there." She was pleased, despite everything, with her firm tone.

"It's seven-thirty. They'll all have gone home."

But they hadn't. As soon as Carrie and Dr Erdmann walked into the lobby, she saw a man in a white coat standing by the elevators. "Wait!" she called, loud enough that several people turned to look, evening visitors and ambulatories and a nurse Carrie didn't know. She didn't know the doctor, either, but she rushed over to him, leaving Dr Erdmann leaning on his walker by the main entrance.

"Are you a doctor? I'm Carrie Vesey and I was bringing Dr Erdmann – a patient, Henry Erdmann, not a medical doctor – home when he had some kind of attack, he seems all right now but someone needs to look at him, he says —"

"I'm not an M.D.," the man said, and Carrie looked at him in dismay. "I'm a neurological researcher."

She rallied. "Well, you're the best we're going to get at this hour so please look at him!" She was amazed at her own audacity.

"All right." He followed her to Dr Erdmann, who scowled because, Carrie knew, he hated this sort of fuss. The non-M.D. seemed to pick up on that right away. He said pleasantly, "Dr Erdmann? I'm Jake DiBella. Will you come this way, sir?" Without waiting for an answer, he turned and led the way down a side corridor. Carrie and Dr Erdmann followed, everybody's walk normal, but still people watched. *Move along, nothing to see here* . . . why were they still staring? Why were people such ghouls?

But they weren't, really. That was just her own fear talking.

You trust too much, Carrie, Dr Erdmann had said just last week.

In a small room on the second floor, he sat heavily on one of the three metal folding chairs. The room held the chairs, a grey filing cabinet, an ugly metal desk, and nothing else. Carrie, a natural nester, pursed her lips, and this Dr DiBella caught that, too.

"I've only been here a few days," he said apologetically. "Haven't had time yet to properly move in. Dr Erdmann, can you tell me what happened?"

"Nothing." He wore his lofty look. "I just fell asleep for a moment and Carrie became alarmed. Really, there's no need for this fuss."

"You fell asleep?"

"Yes."

"All right. Has that happened before?"

Did Dr Erdmann hesitate, ever so briefly? "Yes, occasionally. I *am* ninety, doctor."

DiBella nodded, apparently satisfied, and turned to Carrie. "And what happened to you? Did it occur at the same time that Dr Erdmann fell asleep?"

Her eye. That's why people had stared in the lobby. In her concern for Dr Erdmann, she'd forgotten about her black eye, but now it immediately began to throb again. Carrie felt herself go scarlet.

Dr Erdmann answered. "No, it didn't happen at the same time. There was no car accident, if that's what you're implying. Carrie's eye is unrelated."

"I fell," Carrie said, knew that no one believed her, and lifted her chin.

"Okay," DiBella said amiably. "But as long as you're here, Dr Erdmann, I'd like to enlist your help. Yours, and as many other volunteers as I can enlist at St Sebastian's. I'm here on a Gates Foundation grant in conjunction with Johns Hopkins, to map shifts in brain electrochemistry during cerebral arousal. I'm asking volunteers to donate a few hours of their time to undergo completely painless brain scans while they look at various pictures and videos. Your participation will be an aid to science."

Carrie saw that Dr Erdmann was going to refuse, despite the magic word "science", but then he hesitated. "What kind of brain scans?"

"Asher-Peyton and functional MRI."

"All right. I'll participate."

Carrie blinked. That didn't sound like Dr Erdmann, who considered physics and astronomy the only "true" sciences and the rest merely poor step-children. But this Dr DiBella wasn't about to let his research subject get away. He said quickly, "Excellent! Tomorrow morning at eleven, Lab 6B, at the hospital. Ms Vesey, can you bring him over? Are you a relative?"

"No, I'm an aide here. Call me Carrie. I can bring him." Wednesday wasn't one of her usual days for Dr Erdmann, but she'd get Marie to swap schedules.

"Wonderful. Please call me Jake." He smiled at her, and something turned over in Carrie's chest. It wasn't just that he was so handsome, with his black hair and grey eyes and nice shoulders, but also that he had masculine confidence and an easy way with him and no ring on his left hand . . . *idiot*. There was no particular warmth in his smile; it was completely professional. Was she always going to assess every man she met as a possible boyfriend? Was she really that needy?

Yes. But this one wasn't interested. And anyway, he was an educated scientist and she worked a minimum-wage job. She *was* an idiot.

She got Dr Erdmann up to his apartment and said good-night. He seemed distant, pre-occupied. Going down in the elevator, a mood of desolation came over her. What she really wanted was to stay and watch Henry Erdmann's TV, sleep on his sofa, wake up to fix his coffee and have someone to talk to while she did it. Not go back to her shabby apartment, bolted securely against Jim but never secure enough that she felt really safe. She'd rather stay here, in a home for failing old people, and how perverted and sad was that?

And what *had* happened to Dr Erdmann on the way home from the college?

THREE

Twice now. Henry lay awake, wondering what the hell was going on in his brain. He was accustomed to relying on that organ. His knees had succumbed to arthritis, his hearing aid required constant adjustment, and his prostate housed a slow-growing cancer that, the doctor said, wouldn't kill him until long after something else did – the medical profession's idea of cheerful news. But his brain remained clear, and using it well had always been his greatest pleasure. Greater even than sex, greater than food, greater than marriage to Ida, much as he had loved her.

God, the things that age let you admit.

Which were the best years? No question there: Los Alamos, working on Operation Ivy with Ulam and Teller and Carson Mark and the rest. The excitement and frustration and awe of developing the "Sausage," the first test of staged radiation implosion. The day it was detonated at Eniwetok. Henry, a junior member of the team, hadn't of course been present at the atoll, but he'd waited breathlessly for the results from Bogon. He'd cheered when Teller, picking up the shock waves on a seismometer in California, had sent his three-word telegram to Los Alamos: "It's a boy." Harry Truman himself had requested that bomb —" to see to it that our country is able to defend itself against any possible aggressor" – and Henry was proud of his work on it.

Shock waves. Yes, *that* was what today's two incidents had felt like: shock waves to the brain. A small wave in his apartment, a larger one in Carrie's car. But from what? It could only be some failure of his nervous system, the thing he dreaded most of all, far more than he dreaded death. Granted, teaching physics to graduate students was a long way from Los Alamos or Livermore, and most of the students were dolts – although not Haldane – but Henry enjoyed it. Teaching, plus reading the journals and following the on-line listserves, were his connection with physics. If some neurological "shock wave" disturbed his brain . . .

It was a long time before he could sleep.

"Oh my Lord, dear, what happened to *your* eye?"

Evelyn Krenchnoted sat with her friend Gina Somebody in the tiny waiting room outside Dr O'Kane's office. Henry scowled at her. Just like Evelyn to blurt out like that, embarrassing poor Carrie. The Krenchnoted woman was the most tactless busybody Henry had ever met, and he'd known a lot of physicists, a group not noted for tact. But at least the physicists hadn't been busybodies.

"I'm fine," Carrie said, trying to smile. "I walked into a door."

"Oh, dear, how did that happen? You should tell the doctor. I'm sure he could make a few minutes to see you, even though he must be running behind, I didn't actually have an appointment today but he'd said he'd squeeze me in because something strange happened yesterday that I want to ask him about, but the time he gave me was supposed to start five minutes ago and you must be scheduled after that, he saw Gina already but she —"

Henry sat down and stopped listening. Evelyn's noise, however, went on and on, a grating whine like a dentist drill. He imagined her on Eniwetok, rising into the air on a mushroom cloud, still talking. It was a relief when the doctor's door opened and a woman came out, holding a book.

Henry had seen her before, although he didn't know her name. Unlike most of the old bats at St Sebastian's, she was worth looking at. Not with Carrie's radiant youthful beauty, of course; this woman must be in her seventies, at least. But she stood straight and graceful; her white hair fell in simple waves to her shoulders; her cheekbones and blue eyes were still good. However, Henry didn't care for the way she was dressed. It reminded him of all those stupid childish protestors outside Los Alamos in the 1950s and 60s. The woman wore a white tee-shirt, a long cotton peasant skirt, a necklace of beads and shells, and several elaborate rings.

"Erin!" Evelyn cried. "How was your appointment? Everything okay?"

"Fine. Just a check-up." Erin smiled vaguely and moved away. Henry strained to see the cover of her book: *Tao Te Ching*. Disappointment lanced through him. One of *those*.

"But you weren't scheduled for a check-up, no more than I was. So what happened that —" Erin walked quickly away, her smile fixed. Evelyn said indignantly, "Well, I call that just plain rude! Did you see that, Gina? You try to be friendly to some people and they just —"

"Mrs Krenchnoted?" the nurse said, sticking her head out the office door. "The doctor will see you now."

Evelyn lumbered up and through the door, still talking. In the blessed silence that followed, Henry said to Carrie, "How do you suppose Mr Krenchnoted stood it?"

Carrie giggled and waved her hand toward Mrs Krenchnoted's friend, Gina. But Gina was asleep in her chair, which at least explained how she stood it.

Carrie said, "I'm glad you have this appointment today, Dr Erdmann. You will tell him about what happened in the car yesterday, won't you?"

"Yes."

"You promise?"

"*Yes*." Why were all women, even mild little Carrie, so insistent on regular doctor visits? Yes, doctors were useful for providing pills to keep the machine going, but Henry's view was that you only needed to see a physician if something felt wrong. In fact, he'd forgotten about this regularly scheduled check-up until this morning, when Carrie called to say how convenient it was that his appointment here was just an hour before the one with Dr DiBella at the hospital lab. Ordinarily Henry would have refused to go at all, except that he did intend to ask Dr Jamison about the incident in the car.

Also, it was possible that fool Evelyn Krenchnoted was actually right about something for once. "Carrie, maybe you *should* ask the doctor to look at that eye."

"No. I'm fine."

"Has Jim called or come around again since —"

"No."

Clearly she didn't want to talk about it. Embarrassment, most likely. Henry could respect her reticence. Silently he organized his questions for Jamison.

But after Henry had gone into the office, leaving Carrie in the waiting room, and after he'd endured the tediums of the nurse's measuring his blood pressure, of peeing into a cup, of putting on a ridiculous paper gown, it wasn't Jamison who entered the room but a brusque, impossibly young boy in a white lab coat and officious manner.

"I'm Dr Felton, Henry. How are we today?" He studied Henry's chart, not looking at him.

Henry gritted his teeth. "You would know better than I, I imagine."

"Feeling a bit cranky? Are your bowels moving all right?"

"My bowels are fine. They thank you for your concern."

Felton looked up then, his eyes cold. "I'm going to listen to your lungs now. Cough when I tell you to."

And Henry knew he couldn't do it. If the kid had reprimanded him – "*I don't think sarcasm is appropriate here*" – it would have at least been a response. But this utter dismissal, this treatment as if Henry were a child, or a moron . . . He couldn't tell this insensitive young boor about the incident in the car, about the fear for his brain. It would degrade him to cooperate with Felton. Maybe DiBella would be better, even if he wasn't an M.D.

One doctor down, one to go.

DiBella was better. What he was not was organized.

At Redborn Memorial Hospital he said, "Ah, Dr Erdmann, Carrie. Welcome. I'm afraid there's been a mix-up with Diagnostic Imaging. I thought I had the fMRI booked for you but they seem to have scheduled me out, or something. So we can do the Asher-Peyton scan but not the deep imaging. I'm sorry, I —" He shrugged helplessly and ran his hand through his hair.

Carrie tightened her mouth to a thin line. "Dr Erdmann came all the way over here for your MRI, Dr DiBella."

"'Jake', please. I know. And we do the Asher-Peyton scan back at St Sebastian's. I really am sorry."

Carrie's lips didn't soften. It always surprised Henry how fierce she could be in defence of her "resident-assignees". Why was usually gentle Carrie being so hard on this young man?

"I'll meet you back at St Sebastian's," DiBella said humbly.

Once there, he affixed electrodes on Henry's skull and neck, eased a helmet over his head, and sat at a computer whose screen faced away from Henry. After the room was darkened, a series of pictures projected onto one white wall: a chocolate cake, a broom, a chair, a car, a desk, a glass: four or five dozen images. Henry had to do nothing except sit there, and he grew bored. Eventually the pictures grew more interesting, interspersing a house fire, a war scene, a father hugging a child, Rita Hayworth. Henry chuckled. "I didn't think your generation even knew who Rita Hayworth was."

"Please don't talk, Dr Erdmann."

The session went on for twenty minutes. When it was over, DiBella removed the helmet and said, "Thank you so much. I really appreciate this." He began removing electrodes from Henry's head. Carrie stood, looking straight at Henry.

Now or never.

"Dr DiBella," Henry said, "I'd like to ask you something. Tell you something, actually. An incident that happened yesterday. Twice." Henry liked the word "incident"; it sounded objective and explainable, like a police report.

"Sure. Go ahead."

"The first time I was standing in my apartment, the second time riding in a car with Carrie. The first incident was mild, the second more pronounced. Both times I felt something move through my mind, like a shock wave of sorts, leaving no after-effects except perhaps a slight fatigue. No abilities seem to be impaired. I'm hoping you can tell me what happened."

DiBella paused, an electrode dangling from his hand. Henry could smell the gooey gel on its end. "I'm not an M.D., as I told you yesterday. This sounds like something you should discuss with your doctor at St Sebastian."

Carrie, who had been upset that Henry had not done just that, said, "In the car he sort of lost consciousness and his eyes rolled back in his head."

Henry said, "My doctor wasn't available this morning, and you are. Can you just tell me if that experience sounds like a stroke?"

"Tell me about it again."

Henry did, and DiBella said, "If it had been a TIA – a mini-stroke – you wouldn't have had such a strong reaction, and if it had been a more serious stroke, either ischemic or haemorrhagic, you'd have been left with at least temporary impairment. But you could have experienced a cardiac event of some sort, Dr Erdmann. I think you should have an EKG at once."

Heart, not brain. Well, that was better. Still, fear slid coldly down Henry's spine, and he realized how much he wanted to go on leading his current life, limited though it was. Still, he smiled and said, "All right."

He'd known for at least twenty-five years that growing old wasn't for sissies.

Carrie cancelled her other resident-assignees, checking in with each on her cell, and shepherded Henry through the endless hospital rituals that followed, administrative and diagnostic and that most ubiquitous medical procedure, waiting. By the end of the day, Henry knew that his heart was fine, his brain showed no clots or haemorrhages, there was no reason for him to have fainted. That's what they were calling it now: a faint, possibly due to low blood sugar. He was scheduled for glucose-tolerance tests next week. Fools. It hadn't been any kind of faint. What had happened to him had been something else entirely, *sui generis*.

Then it happened again, the same and yet completely different.

At nearly midnight Henry lay in bed, exhausted. For once, he'd thought, sleep would come easily. It hadn't. Then, all at once, he was lifted out of his weary mind. This time there was no violent wrenching, no eyes rolling back in his head. He just suddenly wasn't in his darkened bedroom any more, not in his body, not in his mind.

He was dancing, soaring with pointed toes high above a polished stage, feeling the muscles in his back and thighs stretch as he sat cross-legged on a deep cushion he had embroidered with ball bearings rolling down a factory assembly line across from soldiers shooting at him as he ducked —

It was gone.

Henry jerked upright, sweating in the dark. He fumbled for the bed lamp, missed, sent the lamp crashing off the nightstand and onto the floor. He had never danced on a stage, embroidered a cushion, worked in a factory, or gone to war. And he'd been awake. Those were memories, not dreams – no, not even memories, they were too vivid for that. They'd been experiences, as vivid and real as if they were all happening now, and all happening simultaneously. *Experiences*. But not his.

The lamp was still glowing. Laboriously he leaned over the side of the bed and plucked it off the floor. As he set it back on the nightstand, it went out. Not, however, before he saw that the plug had been pulled from the wall socket during the fall, well before he bent over to pick it up.

The ship grew more agitated, the rents in space-time and resulting flop transitions larger. Every aspect of the entity strained forward, jumping through the vacuum flux in bursts of radiation that appeared now near one star system, now another, now in the deep black cold where no stars exerted gravity. The ship could move no quicker without destroying either nearby star systems or its own coherence. It raced as rapidly as it could, sent ahead of itself even faster tendrils of quantum-entangled information. Faster, faster . . .

It was not fast enough.

FOUR

Thursday morning, Henry's mind seemed to him as clear as ever. After an early breakfast he sat at his tiny kitchen table, correcting physics papers. The apartments at St Sebastian's each had a small eat-in kitchen, a marginally larger living room, a bedroom and bath. Grab rails, non-skid flooring, overly cheerful colours, and intercoms reminded the residents that they were old – as if, Henry thought scornfully, any of them were likely to forget it. However, Henry didn't really mind the apartment's size or surveillance. After all, he'd flourished at Los Alamos, crowded and ramshackle and paranoid as the place had been. Most of his life went on inside his head.

For each problem set with incomplete answers – which would probably be all of them except Haldane's, although Julia Hernandez had at least come up with a novel and mathematically interesting approach – he tried to follow the student's thinking, to see where it had gone wrong. After an hour of this, he had gone over two papers. A plane screamed overhead, taking off from the airport. Henry gave it up. He couldn't concentrate.

Outside the St Sebastian Infirmary yesterday, the horrible Evelyn Krenchnoted had said that she didn't have a check-up appointment, but that the doctor was "squeezing her in" because "something strange happened yesterday". She'd also mentioned that the aging-hippie beauty, Erin Whatever-Her-Name-Was, hadn't had a scheduled appointment either.

Once, at a mandatory ambulatory-residents' meeting, Henry had seen Evelyn embroidering.

Anna Chernov, St Sebastian's most famous resident, was a ballet dancer. Everyone knew that.

He felt stupid even thinking along these lines. What was he hypothesizing here, some sort of telepathy? No respectable scientific study had ever validated such a hypothesis. Also, during Henry's three years at St Sebastians's – years during which Evelyn and Miss Chernov had also been in residence – he had never felt the slightest connection with, or interest in, either of them.

He tried to go back to correcting problem sets.

The difficulty was, he had two data points, his own "incidents" and the sudden rash of unscheduled doctors' appointments, and no way to either connect or eliminate either one. If he could at least satisfy himself that Evelyn's and Erin's doctor visits concerned something other than mental episodes, he would be down to one data point. One was an anomaly. Two were an indicator of . . . something.

This wasn't one of Henry's days to have Carrie's assistance. He pulled himself up on his walker, inched to the desk, and found the Resident Directory. Evelyn had no listings for either cell phone or email. That surprised him; you'd think such a yenta would want as many ways to bother people as possible. But some St Sebastian residents were still, after all these decades, wary of any technology they hadn't grown up with. *Fools*, thought Henry, who had once driven 400 miles to buy one of the first, primitive, put-it-together-yourself kits for a personal computer. He noted Evelyn's apartment number and hobbled toward the elevators.

"Why, Henry Erdmann! Come in, come in!" Evelyn cried. She looked astonished, as well she might. And – oh, God – behind her sat a circle of women, their chairs jammed in like molecules under hydraulic compression, all sewing on bright pieces of cloth.

"I don't want to intrude on your —"

"Oh, it's just the Christmas Elves!" Evelyn cried. "We're getting an early start on the holiday wall hanging for the lobby. The old one is getting so shabby."

Henry didn't remember a holiday wall hanging in the lobby, unless she was referring to that garish lumpy blanket with Santa Claus handing out babies to guardian angels. The angels had had tight, cotton-wool hair that made them look like Q-tips. He said, "Never mind, it's not important."

"Oh, come on in! We were just talking about – and maybe you have more information on it! – this fabulous necklace that Anna Chernov has in the office safe, the one the tsar gave —"

"No, no, I have no information. I'll —"

"But if you just —"

Henry said desperately, "I'll call you later."

To his horror, Evelyn lowered her eyes and said murmured demurely, "All right, Henry," while the women behind her tittered. He backed away down the hall.

He was pondering how to discover Erin's last name when she emerged from an elevator. "Excuse me!" he called the length of the corridor. "May I speak to you a moment?"

She came toward him, another book in her hand, her face curious but reserved. "Yes?"

"My name is Henry Erdmann. I'd like to ask what will, I know, sound like a very strange question. Please forgive my intrusiveness, and believe that I have a good reason for asking. You had an unscheduled appointment with Dr Felton yesterday?"

Something moved behind her eyes. "Yes."

"Did your reason for seeing him have to do with any sort of . . . of mental experience? A small seizure, or an episode of memory aberration, perhaps?"

Erin's ringed hand tightened on her book. He noted, numbly, that today it seemed to be a novel. She said, "Let's talk."

"I don't believe it," he said. "I'm sorry, Mrs Bass, but it sounds like rubbish to me."

She shrugged, a slow movement of thin shoulders under her peasant blouse. Her long printed skirt, yellow flowers on black, swirled on the floor. Her apartment looked like her: bits of cloth hanging on the walls, a curtain of beads instead of a door to the bedroom, Hindu statues and crystal pyramids and Navaho blankets. Henry disliked the clutter, the childishness of the décor, even as he felt flooded by gratitude toward Erin Bass. She had released him. Her ideas about the "incidents" were so dumb that he could easily dismiss them, along with anything he might have been thinking which resembled them.

"There's an energy in the universe as a whole," she'd said. "When you stop resisting the flow of life and give up the grasping of *trishna*, you awaken to that energy. In popular terms, you have an 'out-of-body experience', activating stored karma from past lives and fusing it into one moment of transcendent insight."

Henry had had no transcendental insight. He knew about energy in the universe – it was called electromagnetic radiation, gravity, the strong and

weak nuclear forces – and none of it had karma. He didn't believe in rein-
carnation, and he hadn't been out of his body. Throughout all three "incidents", he'd felt his body firmly encasing him. He hadn't left; other minds
had somehow seemed to come in. But it was all nonsense, an aberration
of a brain whose synapses and axons, dendrites and vesicles, were simply
growing old.

He grasped his walker and rose. "Thanks anyway, Mrs Bass. Goodbye."

"Again, call me 'Erin'. Are you sure you wouldn't like some green tea
before you go?"

"Quite sure. Take care.."

He was at the door when she said, almost casually, "Oh, Henry? When
I had my own out-of-body Tuesday evening, there were others with me
in the awakened state . . . Were you ever closely connected with – I know
this sounds odd – a light that somehow shone more brightly than many
suns?"

He turned and stared at her.

"This will take about twenty minutes," DiBella said as Henry slid into the
MRI machine. He'd had the procedure before and disliked it just as much
then, the feeling of being enclosed in a tube not much larger than a coffin.
Some people, he knew, couldn't tolerate it at all. But Henry'd be damned if
he let a piece of machinery defeat him, and anyway the tube didn't enclose
him completely; it was open at the bottom. So he pressed his lips together
and closed his eyes and let the machine swallow his strapped-down body.

"You okay in there, Dr Erdmann?"

"I'm fine."

"Good. Excellent. Just relax."

To his own surprise, he did. In the tube, everything seemed very remote.
He actually dozed, waking twenty minutes later when the tube slid him
out again.

"Everything look normal?" he asked DiBella, and held his breath.

"Completely," DiBella said. "Thank you, that's a good baseline for my
study. Your next one, you know, will come immediately after you view a
ten-minute video. I've scheduled that for a week from today."

"Fine." *Normal*. Then his brain was okay, and this weirdness was over.
Relief turned him jaunty. "I'm glad to assist your project, doctor. What is
its focus, again?"

"Cerebral activation patterns in senior citizens. Did you realize, Dr
Erdmann, that the over-sixty-five demographic is the fastest growing one
in the world? And that globally there are now 140 million people over the
age of eighty?"

Henry hadn't realized, nor did he care. The St Sebastian aide came forward to help Henry to his feet. He was a dour young man whose name
Henry hadn't caught. DiBella said, "Where's Carrie today?"

"It's not her day with me."

"Ah." DiBella didn't sound very interested; he was already prepping his screens for the next volunteer. Time on the MRI, he'd told Henry, was tight, having to be scheduled between hospital use.

The dour young man – Darryl? Darrin? Dustin? – drove Henry back to St Sebastian's and left him to make his own way upstairs. In his apartment, Henry lowered himself laboriously to the sofa. Just a few minutes' nap, that's all he needed, even a short excursion tired him so much now – although it would be better if Carrie had been along, she always took such good care of him, such a kind and dear young woman. If he and Ida had ever had children, he'd have wanted them to be like Carrie. If that bastard Jim Peltier ever again tried to —

It shot through him like a bolt of lightning.

Henry screamed. This time the experience *hurt*, searing the inside of his skull and his spinal cord down to his tailbone. No dancing, no embroidering, no meditating – and yet others were there, not as individuals but as a collective sensation, a shared pain, making the pain worse by pooling it. He couldn't stand it, he was going to die, this was the end of —

The pain was gone. It vanished as quickly as it came, leaving him bruised inside, throbbing as if his entire brain had undergone a root canal. His gorge rose, and just in time he twisted his aching body to the side and vomited over the side of the sofa onto the carpet.

His fingers fumbled in the pocket of his trousers for the St Sebastian panic button that Carrie insisted he wear. He found it, pressed the centre, and lost consciousness.

FIVE

Carrie went home early. Thursday afternoons were assigned to Mrs Lopez and her granddaughter had showed up unexpectedly. Carrie suspected that Vicky Lopez wanted money again since that seemed to be the only time she did turn up at St Sebastian's, but that was not Carrie's business. Mrs Lopez said happily that Vicky could just as easily take her shopping instead of Carrie, and Vicky agreed, looking greedy. So Carrie went home.

If she'd been fortunate enough to have a grandmother – to have any relatives besides her no-good step-brothers in California – she would treat that hypothetical grandmother better than did Vicky, she of the designer jeans and cashmere crew necks and massive credit-card debt. Although Carrie wouldn't want her grandmother to be like Mrs Lopez, either, who treated Carrie like not-very-clean hired help.

Well, she *was* hired help, of course. The job as a St Sebastian aide was the first thing she'd seen in the Classifieds the day she finally walked out on Jim. She grabbed the job blindly, like a person going over a cliff who sees a fragile branch growing from crumbly rock. The weird thing was that after the first day, she knew she was going to stay. She liked old people (most of them, anyway). They were interesting and grateful (most of them anyway) – and safe. During that first terrified week at the YMCA, while she searched for a one-room apartment she could actually afford, St Sebastian's was the one place she felt safe.

Jim had changed that, of course. He'd found out the locations of her job and apartment. Cops could find anything.

She unlocked her door after making sure the dingy corridor was empty, slipped inside, shot the deadbolt, and turned on the light. The only window faced an air shaft, and the room was dark even on the brightest day. Carrie had done what she could with bright cushions and Salvation Army lamps and dried flowers, but dark was dark.

"Hello, Carrie," Jim said.

She whirled around, stifling a scream. But the sickening thing was the rest of her reaction. Unbidden and hated – God, how hated! – but still there was the sudden thrill, the flash of excitement that energized every part of her body. "*That's not unusual,*" her counsellor at the Battered Women's Help Centre had said, "*because frequently an abuser and his victim are both fully engaged in the struggle to dominate each other. How triumphant do you feel when he's in the apology-and-wooing phase of the abuse cycle? Why do you think you haven't left before now?*"

It had taken Carrie so long to accept that. And here it was again. Here Jim was again.

"How did you get in?"

"Does it matter?"

"You got Kelsey to let you in, didn't you?" The building super could be bribed to almost anything with a bottle of Scotch. Although maybe Jim hadn't needed that; he had a badge. Not even the charges she'd brought against him, all of which had been dropped, had affected his job. Nobody on the outside ever realized how common domestic violence was in cops' homes.

Jim wasn't in uniform now. He wore jeans, boots, a sports coat she'd always liked. He held a bouquet of flowers. Not supermarket carnations, either: red roses in shining gold paper. "Carrie, I'm sorry I startled you, but I wanted so bad for us to talk. Please, just let me have ten minutes. That's all. Ten minutes isn't much to give me against three years of marriage."

"We're not married. We're legally separated."

"I know. I *know*. And I deserve that you left me. I know that now. But just ten minutes. Please."

"You're not supposed to be here at all! There's a restraining order against you – and you're a cop!"

"I know. I'm risking my career to talk to you for ten minutes. Doesn't that say how much I care? Here, these are for you."

Humbly, eyes beseeching, he held out the roses. Carrie didn't take them.

"You blackened my eye the last time we 'talked', you bastard!"

"I know. If you knew how much I've regretted that . . . If you had any idea how many nights I laid awake hating myself for that. I was out of my mind, Carrie. I really was. But it taught me something. I've changed. I'm going to A.A. now, I've got a sponsor and everything. I'm working my program."

"I've heard this all before!"

"I know. I know you have. But this time is different." He lowered his eyes, and Carrie put her hands on her hips. Then it hit her: she had said all this before, too. She had stood in this scolding, one-up stance. He had stood in his humble stance, as well. This was the apology-and-wooing stage that the counsellor had talked about, just one more scene in their endless script. And she was eating it up as if it had never happened before, was revelling in the glow of righteous indignation fed by his grovelling. Just like the counsellor had said.

She was so sickened at herself that her knees nearly buckled.

"Get out, Jim."

"I will. I *will*. Just tell me that you heard me, that there's some chance for us still, even if it's a chance I don't deserve. Oh, Carrie —"

"Get out!" Her nauseated fury was at herself.

"If you'd just —"

"Out! Out now!"

His face changed. Humility was replaced by astonishment — this wasn't how their script went — and then by rage. He threw the flowers at her. "You won't even *listen* to me? I come here goddamn apologizing and you won't even listen? What makes you so much better than me, you fucking bitch you're nothing but a —"

Carrie whirled around and grabbed for the deadbolt. He was faster. Faster, stronger, and *that* was the old script, too, how could she forget for even a half second he —

Jim threw her to the floor. Did he have his gun? Would he — she caught a glimpse of his face, so twisted with rage that he looked like somebody else, even as she was throwing up her arms to protect her head. He kicked her in the belly. The pain was astonishing. It burned along her body she was burning she couldn't breathe she was going to die . . . His boot drew back to kick her again and Carrie tried to scream. No breath came. This was it then no no *no* —

Jim crumpled to the floor.

Between her sheltering arms, she caught sight of his face as he went down. Astonishment gaped open the mouth, widened the eyes. The image clapped onto her brain. His body fell heavily on top of hers, and didn't move.

When she could breathe again, she crawled out from under him, whimpering with short guttural sounds: *uh uh uh*. Yet a part of her brain worked clearly, coldly. She felt for a pulse, held her fingers over his mouth to find a breath, put her ear to his chest. He was dead.

She staggered to the phone and called 911.

Cops. Carrie didn't know them; this wasn't Jim's precinct. First uniforms and then detectives. An ambulance. A forensic team. Photographs, finger-prints, a search of the one-room apartment, with her consent. You have the right to remain silent. She didn't remain silent, didn't need a lawyer, told what she knew as Jim's body was replaced by a chalked outline and neighbours gathered in the hall. And when it was finally, finally over and she was told that her apartment was a crime scene until the autopsy was performed and where could she go, she said, "St Sebastian's. I work there."

"Maybe you should call in sick for this night's shift, ma'am, it's —"

"I'm going to St Sebastian's!"

She did, her hands shaky on the steering wheel. She went straight to Dr Erdmann's door and knocked hard. His walker inched across the floor, inside. Inside, where it was safe.

"Carrie! What on Earth —"

"Can I come in? Please? The police —"

"Police?" he said sharply. "What police?" Peering around her as if he expected to see blue uniforms filling the hall. "Where's your coat? It's fifty degrees out!"

She had forgotten a coat. Nobody had mentioned a coat. Pack a bag, they said, but nobody had mentioned a coat. Dr Erdmann always knew the temperature and barometer reading, he kept track of such things. Belatedly, and for the first time, she burst into tears.

He drew her in, made her sit on the sofa. Carrie noticed, with the cold clear part of her mind that still seemed to be functioning, that there was a very wet spot on the carpet and a strong odour, as if someone had scrubbed with disinfectant. "Could I . . . could I have a drink?" She hadn't known she was going to say that until the words were out. She seldom drank. Too much like Jim.

Jim . . .

The sherry steadied her. Sherry seemed so civilized, and so did the miniature glass he offered it in. She breathed easier, and told him her story. He listened without saying a word.

"I think I'm a suspect," Carrie said. "Well, of course I am. He just dropped dead when we were fighting . . . but I never so much as laid a hand on him. I was just trying to protect my head and . . . Dr Erdmann, what is it? You're white as snow! I shouldn't have come, I'm sorry, I —"

"Of course you should have come!" he snapped, so harshly that she was startled. A moment later he tried to smile. "Of course you should have come. What are friends for?"

Friends. But she had other friends, younger friends. Joanne and Connie and Jennifer . . . not that she had seen any of them much in the last three months. It had been Dr Erdmann she'd thought of, first and immediately. And now he looked so . . .

"You're not well," she said. "What is it?"

"Nothing. I ate something bad at lunch, in the dining room. Half the building started vomiting a few hours later. Evelyn Krenchnoted and Gina Martinelli and Erin Bass and Bob Donovan and Al Cosmano and Anna Chernov. More."

He watched her carefully as he recited the names, as if she should somehow react. Carrie knew some of those people, but mostly just to say hello.

Only Mr Cosmano was on her resident-assignee list. Dr Erdmann looked stranger than she had ever seen him.

He said, "Carrie, what time did Jim . . . did he drop dead? Can you fix the exact time?"

"Well, let me see . . . I left here at two and I stopped at the bank and the gas station and the convenience store, so maybe three or three-thirty? Why?"

Dr Erdmann didn't answer. He was silent for so long that Carrie grew uneasy. She shouldn't have come, it was a terrible imposition, and anyway there was probably a rule against aides staying in residents' apartments, what was she thinking —

"Let me get blankets and pillow for the sofa," Dr Erdmann finally said, in a voice that still sounded odd to Carrie. "It's fairly comfortable. For a *sofa*."

SIX

Not possible. The most ridiculous coincidence. That was all – coincidence. Simultaneity was not cause-and-effect. Even the dimmest physics undergraduate knew that.

In his mind, Henry heard Richard Feynman say about string theory, "I don't like that they're not calculating anything. I don't like that they don't check their ideas. I don't like that for anything that disagrees with an experiment, they cook up an explanation. . . . The first principle is that you must not fool yourself – and you are the easiest person to fool." Henry hadn't liked Feynman, whom he'd met at conferences at Caltech. A buffoon, with his bongo drums and his practical jokes and his lock-picking. Undignified. But the brilliant buffoon had been right. Henry didn't like string theory, either, and he didn't like ideas that weren't calculated, checked, and verified by experimental data. Besides, the idea that Henry had somehow killed Jim Peltier with his *thoughts* . . . preposterous.

Mere thoughts could not send a bolt of energy through a distant man's body. But the bolt itself wasn't a "cooked-up" idea. It had happened. Henry had felt it.

DiBella had said that Henry's MRI looked completely normal.

Henry lay awake much of Thursday night, which made the second night in a row, while Carrie slept the oblivious deep slumber of the young. In the morning, before she was awake, he dressed quietly, left the apartment with his walker, and made his way to the St Sebastian Infirmary. He expected to find the Infirmary still crammed with people who'd vomited when he had yesterday afternoon. He was wrong.

"Can I help you?" said a stout, middle-aged nurse carrying a breakfast tray. "Are you feeling ill?"

"No, no," Henry said hastily. "I'm here to visit someone. Evelyn Krenchnoted. She was here yesterday."

"Oh, Evelyn's gone back. They've all gone back, the food poisoning was so mild. Our only patients here now are Bill Terry and Anna Chernov."

She said the latter name the way many of the staff did, as if she'd just been waiting for an excuse to speak it aloud. Usually this irritated Henry – what was ballet dancing compared to, say, physics? – but now he seized on it.

"May I see Miss Chernov, then? Is she awake?"

"This is her tray. Follow me."

The nurse led the way to the end of a short corridor. Yellow curtains, bedside table, monitors and IV poles; the room looked like every other hospital room Henry had ever seen, except for the flowers. Masses and masses of flowers, bouquets and live plants and one huge floor pot of brass holding what looked like an entire small tree. A man, almost lost amid all the flowers, sat in the room's one chair.

"Here's breakfast, Miss Chernov," said the nurse reverently. She fussed with setting the tray on the table, positioning it across the bed, removing the dish covers.

"Thank you." Anna Chernov gave her a gracious, practiced smile, and looked inquiringly at Henry. The other man, who had not risen at Henry's entrance, glared at him.

They made an odd pair. The dancer, who looked younger than whatever her actual age happened to be, was more beautiful than Henry had realized, with huge green eyes over perfect cheekbones. She wasn't hooked to any of the machinery on the wall, but a cast on her left leg bulged beneath the yellow bedcover. The man had a head shaped like a garden trowel, aggressively bristly grey crew cut, and small suspicious eyes. He wore an ill-fitting sports coat over a red tee-shirt and jeans. There seemed to be grease under his fingernails – grease, in St Sebastian's? Henry would have taken him for part of the maintenance staff except that he looked too old, although vigorous and walker-free. Henry wished him at the devil. This was going to be difficult enough without an audience.

"Miss Chernov, please forgive the intrusion, especially so early, but I think this is important. My name is Henry Erdmann, and I'm a resident on Three."

"Good morning," she said, with the same practised, detached graciousness she'd shown the nurse. "This is Bob Donovan."

"Hi," Donovan said, not smiling.

"Are you connected in any way with the press, Mr Erdmann? Because I do not give interviews."

"No, I'm not. I'll get right to the point, if I may. Yesterday I had an attack of nausea, just as you did, and you also, Mr Donovan. Evelyn Krenchnoted told me."

Donovan rolled his eyes. Henry would have smiled at that if he hadn't felt so tense.

He continued, "I'm not sure the nausea was food poisoning. In my case, it followed a . . . a sort of attack of a quite different sort. I felt what I can only describe as a bolt of energy burning along my nerves, very powerfully and painfully. I'm here to ask if you felt anything similar."

Donovan said, "You a doctor?"

"Not an M.D. I'm a physicist."

Donovan scowled savagely, as if physics were somehow offensive. Anna Chernov said, "Yes, I did, Dr Erdmann, although I wouldn't describe it as 'painful'. It didn't hurt. But a 'bolt of energy along the nerves' – yes. It felt like —" She stopped abruptly.

"Yes?" Henry said. His heart had started a slow, irregular thump in his chest. Someone else had also felt that energy.

But Anna declined to say what it had felt like. Instead she turned her head to the side. "Bob? Did you feel anything like that?"

"Yeah. So what?"

"I don't know what," Henry said. All at once, leaning on the walker, his knees felt wobbly. Anna noticed at once. "Bob, bring Dr Erdmann the chair, please."

Donovan got up from the chair, dragged it effortlessly over to Henry, and stood sulkily beside a huge bouquet of autumn-coloured chrysanthemums, roses, and dahlias. Henry sank onto the chair. He was at eye level with the card to the flowers, which said FROM THE ABT COMPANY. GET WELL SOON!

Anna said, "I don't understand what you're driving at, Dr Erdmann. Are you saying we all had the same disease and it wasn't food poisoning? It was something with a . . . a surge of energy followed by nausea?"

"Yes, I guess I am." He couldn't tell her about Jim Peltier. Here, in this flower-and-antiseptic atmosphere, under Donovan's pathetic jealousy and Anna's cool courtesy, the whole idea seemed unbelievably wild. Henry Erdmann did not like wild ideas. He was, after all, a *scientist*.

But that same trait made him persist a little longer. "Had you felt anything like that ever before, Miss Chernov?"

"Anna," she said automatically. "Yes, I did. Three times before, in fact. But much more minor, and with no nausea. I think they were just passing moments of dozing off, in fact. I've been laid up with this leg for a few days now, and it's been boring enough that I sleep a lot."

It was said without self-pity, but Henry had a sudden glimpse of what being "laid up" must mean to a woman for whom the body, not the mind, had been the lifelong source of achievement, of pleasure, of occupation, of self. What, in fact, growing old must mean to such a woman. Henry had been more fortunate; his mind was his life source, not his aging body, and his mind still worked fine.

Or did it, if it could hatch that crackpot hypothesis? What would Feynman, Teller, Gell-Mann have said? Embarrassment swamped him. He struggled to rise.

"Thank you, Miss Chernov, I won't take up any more of your —"

"I felt it, too," Donovan said suddenly. "But only two times, like you said. Tuesday and yesterday afternoon. What are you after here, doc? You saying there's something going around? Is it dangerous?"

Henry, holding onto the walker, turned to stare at him. "You felt it, too?"

"I just told you I did! Now you tell me – is this some new catching, dangerous-like disease?"

The man was frightened, and covering fear with belligerence. Did he even understand what a "physicist" was? He seemed to have taken Henry for some sort of specialized physician. What on Earth was Bob Donovan doing with Anna Chernov?

He had his answer in the way she dismissed them both. "No, Bob, there's no dangerous disease. Dr Erdmann isn't in medicine. Now if you don't mind, I'm very tired and I must eat or the nurse will scold me. Perhaps you'd better leave now, and maybe I'll see you both around the building when I'm discharged." She smiled wearily.

Henry saw the look on Donovan's face, a look he associated with under-graduates: hopeless, helpless lovesickness. Amid those wrinkles and sags, the look was ridiculous. And yet completely sincere, poor bastard.

"Thank you again," Henry said, and left as quickly as his walker would allow. How dare she treat him like a princess dismissing a lackey? And yet . . . he'd been the intruder on her world, that feminine arena of flowers and ballet and artificial courtesy. A foreign, somehow repulsive world. Not like the rigorous masculine brawl of physics.

But he'd learned that she'd felt the "energy", too. And so had Donovan, and at the exact same times as Henry. Several more data points for. . . . what?

He paused on his slow way to the elevator and closed his eyes.

When Henry reached his apartment, Carrie was awake. She sat with two strangers, who both rose as Henry entered, at the table where Henry and Ida had eaten dinner for fifty years. The smell of coffee filled the air.

"I made coffee," Carrie said. "I hope you don't mind . . . This is Detective Geraci and Detective Washington. Dr Erdmann, this is his apartment . . ." She trailed off, looking miserable. Her hair hung in uncombed tangles and some sort of black make-up smudged under her eyes. Or maybe just tiredness.

"Hello, Dr Erdmann," the male detective said. He was big, heavily mus-cled, with beard shadow even at this hour – just the sort of thuggish looks that Henry most mistrusted. The Black woman was much younger, small and neat and unsmiling. "We had a few follow-up questions for Ms Vesey about last night."

Henry said, "Does she need a lawyer?"

"That's up to your granddaughter, of course," at the same moment that Carrie said, "I told them I don't want a lawyer," and Henry was adding, "I'll pay for it." In the confusion of sentences, the mistake about "grand-daughter" went uncorrected.

Geraci said, "Were you here when Ms Vesey arrived last night?"

"Yes," Henry said.

"And can you tell us your whereabouts yesterday afternoon, sir?"

Was the man a fool? "Certainly I can, but surely you don't suspect me, sir, of killing Officer Peltier?"

"We don't suspect anyone at this point. We're asking routine questions, Dr Erdmann."

"I was in Redborn Memorial from mid-afternoon until just before Carrie arrived here. The Emergency Room, being checked for a suspected heart attack. Which," he added hastily, seeing Carrie's face, "I did not have. It was merely severe indigestion brought on by the attack of food poisoning St Sebastian suffered yesterday afternoon."

Hah! Take that, Detective Thug!

"Thank you," Geraci said. "Are you a physician, Dr Erdmann?"

"No. A doctor of physics."

He half-expected Geraci to be as ignorant about that as Bob Donovan had been, but Geraci surprised him. "Experimental or theoretical?"

"Theoretical. Not, however, for a long time. Now I teach."

"Good for you." Geraci rose, Officer Washington just a beat behind him. In Henry's hearing the woman had said nothing whatsoever. "Thank you both. We'll be in touch about the autopsy results."

In the elevator, Tara Washington said, "These old-people places give me the creeps."

"One day you and —"

"Spare me the lecture, Vince. I know I have to get old. I don't have to like it."

"You have a lot of time yet," he said, but his mind clearly wasn't on the rote reassurance. "Erdmann knows something."

"Yeah?" She looked at him with interest; Vince Geraci had a reputation in the Department for having a "nose". He was inevitably right about things that smelled hinky. Truth was, she was a little in awe of him. She'd only made detective last month and was fucking lucky to be partnered with Geraci. Still, her natural skepticism led her to say, "That old guy? He sure the hell didn't do the job himself. He couldn't squash a cockroach. You talking about a hit for hire?"

"Don't know." Geraci considered. "No. Something else. Something more esoteric."

Tara didn't know what "esoteric" meant, so she kept quiet. Geraci was smart. Too smart for his own good, some uniforms said, but that was just jealousy talking, or the kind of cops that would rather smash down doors than solve crimes. Tara Washington knew she was no door-smasher. She intended to learn everything she could from Vince Geraci, even if she didn't have his vocabulary. Everything, and then some. She intended to someday be just as good as he was.

Geraci said, "Let's talk to the staff about this epidemic of food poisoning."

But the food poisoning checked out. And halfway through the morning, the autopsy report was called in. Geraci shut his cell and said, "Peltier died of 'a cardiac event'. Massive and instantaneous heart failure."

"Young cop like that? Fit and all?"

"That's what the M.E. says."

"So no foul play. Investigation closed." In a way, she was disappointed. The murder of a cop by a battered wife would have been pretty high-profile. That's why Geraci had been assigned to it.

"Investigation closed," Geraci said. "But just the same, Erdmann knows something. We're just never gonna find out what it is."

SEVEN

Just before noon on Friday, Evelyn lowered her plump body onto a cot ready to slide into the strange-looking medical tube. She had dressed up for the occasion in her best suit, the polyester blue one with all the blue lace, and her good cream pumps. Dr DiBella – such a good-looking young man, too bad she wasn't fifty years younger aha ha ha – said, "Are you comfortable, Mrs Krenchnoted?"

"Call me Evelyn. Yes, I'm fine, I never had one of these – what did you call it?"

"A functional MRI. I'm just going to strap you in, since it's very important you lie completely still for the procedure."

"Oh, yes, I see, you don't want my brain wobbling all over the place while you take a picture of – Gina, you still there? I can't see —"

"I'm here," Gina called. "Don't be scared, Evelyn. 'Though I walk in the valley of —'"

"There's no shadows here and I'm not scared!" Really, sometimes Gina could be Too Much. Still, the MRI tube *was* a bit unsettling. "You just tell me when you're ready to slide me into that thing, doctor, and I'll brace myself. It's tight as a coffin, isn't it? Well, I'm going to be underground a long time but I don't plan on starting now, aha ha ha! But if I can keep talking to you while I go in —"

"Certainly. Just keep talking." He sounded resigned, poor man. Well, no wonder, he must get bored with doing things like this all the live-long day. She cast around for something to cheer him up.

"You're over at St Sebastian's a lot now, aren't you, when you're not here that is, did you hear yet about Anna Chernov's necklace?"

"No, what about it? That's it, just hold your head right here."

"It's fabulous!" Evelyn said, a little desperately. He was putting some sort of vise on her head, she couldn't move it at all. Her heart sped up. "Diamonds and rubies and I don't know what all. The Russian tsar gave it to some famous ballerina who —"

"Really? Which tsar?"

"*The* tsar! Of Russia!" Really, what did the young learn in school these days? "He gave it to some famous ballerina who was Anna Chernov's teacher and she gave it to Anna, who naturally keeps it in the St Sebastian safe because just think if it were stolen, it wouldn't do the Home's reputation any good at all and anyway it's absolutely priceless so – oh!"

"You'll just slide in nice and slow, Evelyn. It'll be fine. Close your eyes if that helps. Now, have you seen this necklace?"

"Oh, no!" Evelyn gasped. Her heart raced as she felt the bed slide beneath her. "I'd love to, of course, but Anna isn't exactly friendly, she's pretty stuck-up, well I suppose that comes with being so famous and all but still – Doctor!"

"Do you want to come out?" he said, and she could tell that he was disappointed, she was sensitive that way, and she did want to come out but she didn't want to disappoint him, so . . . "No! I'm fine! The necklace is something I'd really like to see, though, all those diamonds and rubies and maybe even sapphires too, those are my favourite stones with that blue fire in them, I'd really really like to see it —"

She was babbling, but all at once it seemed she *could* see the necklace in her mind, just the way she'd pictured it. A string of huge glowing diamonds and hanging from them a pendant of rubies and sapphires shining like I-don't-know-what but more beautiful than anything she'd ever seen oh she'd love to touch it just once! If Anna Chernov weren't so stuck-up and selfish then maybe she'd get the necklace from the safe and show it to Evelyn let her touch it *get the necklace from the safe* it would surely be the most wonderful thing Evelyn had ever seen or imagined *get the necklace from the safe* —

Evelyn screamed. Pain spattered through her like hot oil off a stove, burning her nerves and turning her mind to a red cloud . . . So much pain! She was going to die, this was it and she hadn't even bought her cemetery plot yet oh God the pain —

Then the pain was gone and she lay sobbing as the bed slid out of the tube. Dr DiBella was saying something but his voice was far away and growing farther . . . farther . . . farther. . . .

Gone.

Henry sat alone, eating a tuna fish sandwich at his kitchen table. Carrie had gone to work elsewhere in the building. It had been pleasant having her here, even though of course she —

Energy poured through him, like a sudden surge in household current, and all his nerves *glowed*. That was the only word. No pain this time, but something bright grew in his mind, white and red and blue but certainly not a flag, hard as stones . . . yes, stones . . . jewels . . .

It was gone. An immense lassitude took Henry. He could barely hold his head up, keep his eyes open. It took all his energy to push off from the table, stagger into the bedroom, and fall onto the bed, his mind empty as deep space.

Carrie was filling in at a pre-lunch card game in the dining room, making a fourth at euchre with Ed Rosewood, Ralph Galetta, and Al Cosmano. Mr Cosmano was her Friday morning resident-assignee. She'd taken him to buy a birthday gift for his daughter in California, to the Post Office to wrap and mail it, and then to the physical therapist. Mr Cosmano was a complainer. St Sebastian's was too cold, the doctors didn't know nothing, they wouldn't let you smoke, the food was terrible, he missed the old neighbourhood, his daughter insisted on living in California instead of making a home for her old dad, kids these days. . . . Carrie went on smiling. Even Mr Cosmano was better than being home in the apartment where Jim had died. When her lease was up, she was going to find something else, but in the meantime she had signed up for extra hours at St Sebastian's, just to not be home.

"Carrie, hearts led," Ed Rosewood said. He was her partner, a sweet man whose hobby was watching C-Span. He would watch anything at all on C-Span, even hearings of the House Appropriations Committee, for hours and hours. This was good for St Sebastian's because Mr Rosewood didn't want an aide. He had to be pried off the TV even to play cards once a week. Mike O'Kane, their usual fourth, didn't feel well enough to play today, which was why Carrie sat holding five cards as the kitchen staff clattered in the next room, preparing lunch. Outside a plane passed overhead, droned away.

"Oh, yes," Carrie said, "hearts." She had a heart, thank heavens, since she couldn't remember what was trump. She was no good at cards.

"There's the king."

"Garbage from me."

"Your lead, Ed."

"Ace of clubs."

"Clubs going around. . . . Carrie?"

"Oh, yes, I . . ." Who led? Clubs were the only things on the table. She had no clubs, so she threw a spade. Mr Galetta laughed.

Al Cosmano said, with satisfaction, "Carrie, you really shouldn't trump your partner's ace."

"Did I do that? Oh, I'm sorry, Mr Rosewood, I —"

Ed Rosewood slumped in his chair, eyes closed. So did Al Cosmano. Ralph Galetta stared dazedly at Carrie, then carefully laid his head on the table, eyes fixed.

"Mr Cosmano! Help, somebody!"

The kitchen staff came running. But now all three men had their eyes open again, looking confused and sleepy.

"What happened?" demanded a cook.

"I don't know," Carrie said, "they all just got . . . tired."

The cook stared at Carrie as if she'd gone demented. "Tired?"

"Yeah . . . tired," Ed Rosewood said. "I just . . . bye, guys. I'm going to take a nap. Don't want lunch." He rose, unsteady but walking on his own power, and headed out of the dining room. The other two men followed.

"Tired," the cook said, glaring at Carrie.

"All at once! Really, really tired, like a spell of some kind!"

"A simultaneous 'spell,'" the cook said. "Right. You're new here? Well, old people get tired." She walked away.

Carrie wasn't new. The three men hadn't just had normal tiredness. But there was no way to tell this bitch that, no way to even tell *herself* in any terms that made sense. Nothing was right.

Carrie had no appetite for lunch. She fled to the ladies' room, where at least she could be alone.

Vince Geraci's cell rang as he and Tara Washington exited a convenience store on East Elm. They'd been talking to the owner, who may or may not have been involved in an insurance scam. Vince had let Tara do most of the questioning, and she'd felt herself swell like a happy balloon when he said, "Nice job, rookie."

"Geraci," he said into the cell, then listened as they walked. Just before they reached the car, he said, "Okay," and clicked off.

"What do we have?" Tara asked.

"We have a coincidence."

"A coincidence?"

"Yes." The skin on his forehead took on strange topography. "St Sebastian's again. Somebody cracked the safe in the office."

"Anything gone?"

"Let's go find out."

Erin Bass woke on her yoga mat, the TV screen a blue blank except for CHANNEL 3 in the upper corner. She sat up, dazed but coherent. Something had happened.

She sat up carefully, her ringed hands lifting her body slowly off the mat. No broken bones, no pain anywhere. Apparently she had just collapsed onto the mat and then stayed out as the yoga tape played itself to an end. She'd been up to the fish posture, so there had been about twenty minutes left on the tape. And how long since then? The wall clock said 1:20. So about an hour.

Nothing hurt. Erin took a deep breath, rolled her head, stood up. Still no pain. And there hadn't been pain when it happened, but there had been something . . . not the calm place that yoga or meditation sometimes took her, either. That place was pale blue, like a restful vista of valleys seen at dusk from a high, still mountain. This was brightly hued, rushing, more like a river . . . a river of colours, blue and red and white.

She walked into the apartment's tiny kitchen, a slim figure in black leotard and tights. She'd missed lunch but wasn't hungry. From the cabinet she chose a chamomile tea, heated filtered water, and set the tea to steep.

That rushing river of energy was similar to what she'd felt before. Henry Erdmann had asked her about it, so perhaps he had felt it this time, as well. Although Henry hadn't seemed accepting of her explanation of *trishna*, grasping after the material moment, versus awakening. He was a typical scientist, convinced that science was the only route to knowledge, that what he could not test or measure or replicate was therefore not true even if he'd experienced it himself. Erin knew better. But there were a lot of people like Henry in this world, people who couldn't see that while rejecting "religion", they'd made a religion of science.

Sipping her tea, Erin considered what she should do next. She wasn't afraid of what had happened. Very little frightened Erin Bass. This astonished some people and confused the rest. But, really, what was there to be afraid of? Misfortune was just one turn of the wheel, illness another, death merely a transition from one state to another. What was due to come would come, and beneath it all the great flow of cosmic energy would go on, creating the illusion that people thought was the world. She knew that the other residents of St Sebastian's considered her nuts, pathetic, or so insulated from reality as to be both. ("Trust-fund baby, you know. Never worked a day in her life.") It didn't matter. She'd made herself a life here of books and meditation and volunteering on the Nursing floors, and if her past was far different than the other residents imagined, that was their illusion. She herself never thought about the past. It would come again, or not, as *maya* chose.

Still, something should be done about these recent episodes. They had affected not just her but also Henry Erdmann and, surprisingly, Evelyn Krenchnoted. Although on second thought, Erin shouldn't be surprised. Everyone possessed karma, even Evelyn, and Erin had no business assuming she knew anything about what went on under Evelyn's loud, intrusive surface. There were many paths up the mountain. So Erin should talk to Evelyn as well as to Henry. Perhaps there were others, too. Maybe she should —

Her doorbell rang. Leaving her tea on the table, Erin fastened a wrap skirt over her leotard and went to the door. Henry Erdmann stood there, leaning on his walker, his face a rigid mask of repressed emotion. "Mrs Bass, there's something I'd like to discuss with you. May I come in?"

A strange feeling came over Erin. Not the surge of energy from the yoga mat, nor the high blue restfulness of meditation. Something else. She'd had these moments before, in which she recognized that something significant was about to happen. They weren't mystical or deep, these occasions; probably they came from nothing more profound than a subliminal reading of body language. But, always, they presaged something life-changing.

"Of course, Dr Erdmann. Come in."

She held the door open wider, stepping aside to make room for his walker, but he didn't budge. Had he exhausted all his strength? He was ninety, she'd heard, ten years older than Erin, who was in superb shape from a lifetime of yoga and bodily moderation. She had never smoked, drank, over-eaten. All her indulgences had been emotional, and not for a very long time now.

"Do you need help? Can I —"

"No. No." He seemed to gather himself and then inched the walker forward, moving toward her table. Over his shoulder, with a forced afterthought that only emphasized his tension, he said, "Thieves broke into St Sebastian's an hour and a half ago. They opened the safe in the office, the one with Anna Chernov's necklace."

Erin had never heard of Anna Chernov's necklace. But the image of the rushing river of bright colours came back to her with overwhelming force, and she knew that she had been right: something had happened, and nothing was ever going to be the same again.

EIGHT

For perhaps the tenth time, Jake DiBella picked up the fMRI scans, studied them yet again, and put them down. He rubbed his eyes hard with both sets of knuckles. When he took his hands away from his face, his bare little study at St Sebastian's looked blurry but the fMRI scans hadn't changed. *This is your brain on self-destruction*, he thought, except that it wasn't his brain. It was Evelyn Krenchnoted's brain, and after she recovered consciousness, that tiresome and garrulous lady's brain had worked as well as it ever had.

But the scan was extraordinary. As Evelyn lay in the magnetic imaging tube, everything had changed between one moment and the next. First image: a normal pattern of blood flow and oxygenation, and the next —

"Hello?"

Startled, Jake dropped the printouts. He hadn't even heard the door open, or anyone knock. He really was losing it. "Come in, Carrie, I'm sorry, I didn't . . . You don't have to do that."

She had bent to pick up the papers that had skidded across his desk and onto the floor. With her other hand she balanced a cardboard box on one hip. As she straightened, he saw that her face was pink under the loose golden hair, so that she looked like an overdone Victorian figurine. The box held a plant, a picture frame, and various other bits and pieces.

Uh oh. Jake had been down this road before.

She said, "I brought you some things for your office. Because it looks so, well, empty. Cold."

"Thanks. I actually like it this way." Ostentatiously he busied himself with the printouts, which was also pretty cold of him, but better to cut her off now rather than after she embarrassed herself. As she set the box on a folding chair, he still ignored her, expecting her to leave.

Instead she said, "Are those MRI scans of Dr Erdmann? What do they say?"

Jake looked up. She was eyeing the printouts, not him, and her tone was neutral with perhaps just a touch of concern for Dr Erdmann. He remembered how fond of each other she and Henry Erdmann were. Well, didn't that make Jake just the total narcissist? Assuming every woman was interested in *him*. This would teach him some humility.

Out of his own amused embarrassment, he answered her as he would a colleague. "No, these are Evelyn Krenchnoted's. Dr Erdmann's were unremarkable but these are quite the opposite."

"They're remarkable? How?"

All at once he found himself eager to talk, to perhaps explain away his own bafflement. He came around the desk and put the scan in her hand. "See those yellow areas of the brain? They're BOLD signals, blood-oxygen-level dependent contrasts. What that means is that at the moment the MRI image was taken, those parts of the subject's brain were active – in this case, *highly* active. And they shouldn't have been!"

"Why not?"

Carrie was background now, an excuse to put into concrete words what should never have existed concretely at all. "Because it's all wrong. Evelyn was lying still, talking to me, inside the MRI tube. Her eyes were open. She was nervous about being strapped down. The scan should show activity in the optical input area of the brain, in the motor areas connected to moving the mouth and tongue, and in the posterior parietal lobes, indicating a heightened awareness of her bodily boundaries. But instead, there's just the *opposite*. A hugely decreased blood flow in those lobes, and an almost total shut-down of input to the thalamus, which relays information coming into the brain from sight and hearing and touch. Also, an enormous – really enormous – *increase* of activity in the hypothalamus and amygdalae and temporal lobes."

"What does all that increased activity mean?"

"Many possibilities. They're areas concerned with emotion and some kinds of imaginative imagery, and this much activation is characteristic of some psychotic seizures. For another possibility, parts of that profile are characteristic of monks in deep meditation, but it takes experienced meditators hours to build to that level, and even so there are differences in pain areas and – anyway, *Evelyn Krenchnoted*?"

Carrie laughed. "Not a likely monk, no. Do Dr Erdmann's scans show any of that?"

"No. And neither did Evelyn's just before her seizure or just after. I'd say temporal lobe epilepsy except —"

"Epilepsy?" Her voice turned sharp. "Does that 'seizure' mean epilepsy?"

Jake looked at her then, really looked at her. He could recognize fear. He said as gently as he could, "Henry Erdmann experienced something like this, didn't he?"

They stared at each other. Even before she spoke, he knew she was going to lie to him. A golden lioness protecting her cub, except here the lioness was young and the cub a withered old man who was the smartest person Jake DiBella had ever met.

"No," she said, "Dr Erdmann never mentioned a seizure to me."

"Carrie —"

"And you said his MRI looked completely normal."

"It did." Defeated.

"I should be going. I just wanted to bring you these things to brighten up your office."

Carrie left. The box contained a framed landscape he would never hang (a flower-covered cottage, with unicorn), a coffee cup he would never use (JAVA IS JOY IN THE MORNING), a patchwork quilted cushion, a pink African violet, and a pencil cup covered in wallpaper with yellow daisies. Despite himself, Jake smiled. The sheer wrongness of her offerings was almost funny.

Except that nothing was really funny in light of Evelyn Krenchnoted's inexplicable MRI. He needed more information from her, and another MRI. Better yet would be having her hooked to an EEG in a hospital ward for several days, to see if he could catch a definitive diagnosis of temporal-lobe epilepsy. But when he'd phoned Evelyn, she'd refused all further "doctor procedures". Ten minutes of his best persuasion hadn't budged her.

He was left with an anomaly in his study data, a cutesy coffee cup, and no idea what to do next.

"What do we do next?" asked Rodney Caldwell, the chief administrator of St Sebastian's. Tara Washington looked at Geraci, who looked at the floor.

It was covered with papers and small, uniform, taped white boxes with names written neatly on them in block printing: M. MATTISON. H. GERHARDT. C. GARCIA. One box, however, was open, its lid placed neatly beside it, the tissue paper peeled back. On the tissue lay a necklace, a gold Coptic cross set with a single small diamond, on a thin gold chain. The lid said A. CHERNOV.

"I didn't touch anything," Caldwell said, with a touch of pride. In his fifties, he was a tall man with a long, highly coloured face like an animated carrot. "That's what they say on TV, isn't it? Don't touch anything. But isn't it strange that the thief went to all the trouble to 'blow the safe'" – he looked proud of this phrase, too — "and then didn't take anything?"

"Very strange," Geraci said. Finally he looked up from the floor. The safe hadn't been "blown"; the lock was intact. Tara felt intense interest in what Geraci would do next. She was disappointed.

"Let's go over it once more," he said easily. "You were away from your office . . ."

"Yes. I went up to Nursing at eleven-thirty. Beth Malone was on desk. Behind the front desk is the only door to the room that holds both residents' files and the safe, and Beth says she never left her post. She's very reliable. Been with us eighteen years."

Mrs Malone, who was therefore the prime suspect and smart enough to know it, was weeping in another room. A resigned female uniform handed her tissues as she waited to be interrogated. But Tara knew that, after one look, Geraci had dismissed Malone as the perp. One of those conscientious, middle-aged, always-anxious-to-help do-gooders, she would no more have attempted robbery than alchemy. Most likely she had left her post to do something she was as yet too embarrassed to admit, which was when the thief had entered the windowless back room behind the reception desk. Tara entertained herself with the thought that Mrs Malone had crept off to meet a lover in the linen closet. She smiled.

"A thought, Detective Washington?" Geraci said.

Damn, he missed *nothing*. Now she would have to come up with something. The best she could manage was a question. "Does that little necklace belong to the ballerina Anna Chernov?"

"Yes," Caldwell said. "Isn't it lovely?"

To Tara it didn't look like much. But Geraci had raised his head to look at her, and she realized he didn't know that a world-famous dancer had retired to St Sebastian's. Ballet wasn't his style. It was the first time Tara could recall that she'd known something Geraci did not. Emboldened by this, and as a result of being dragged several times a year to Lincoln Center by an eccentric grandmother, Tara continued. "Is there any resident here that might have a special interest in Anna Chernov? A balletomane" – she hoped she was pronouncing the word correctly, she'd only read it in programmes – "or a special friend?"

But Caldwell had stopped listening at "resident". He said stiffly, "None of our residents would have committed this crime, detective. St Sebastian's is a private community and we screen very carefully for any —"

"May I talk to Ms Chernov now?" Geraci asked.

Caldwell seemed flustered. "To Anna? But Beth Malone is waiting for . . . oh, all right, if that's the procedure. Anna Chernov is in the Infirmary right now, with a broken leg. I'll show you up."

Tara hoped that Geraci wasn't going to send her to do the useless questioning of Mrs Malone. He didn't. At the Infirmary door, he said, "Tara, talk to her." Tara would have taken this as a tribute to her knowledge of ballet, except that she had seen Geraci do the same thing before. He liked to observe: the silent listener, the unknown quantity to whoever was being questioned.

As Caldwell explained the situation and made the introductions, Tara tried not to stare at Anna Chernov. She was *beautiful*. Old, yes, seventies maybe, but Tara had never seen anyone old look like that. High cheekbones, huge green eyes, white hair pinned carelessly on top of her head so that curving strands fell over the pale skin that looked not so much wrinkled (though it was) as softened by time. Her hands, long-fingered and slim-wristed, lay quiet on the bedspread, and her shoulders held straight under the white bed jacket. Only the bulging cast on one leg marred the impression of delicacy, of remoteness, and of the deepest sadness that Tara had ever seen. It was sadness for everything, Tara thought confusedly, and couldn't have said what she meant by "everything". Except that the cast was only a small part.

"Please sit down," Anna said.

"Thank you. As Mr Caldwell said, there's been a break-in downstairs, with the office safe. The only box opened had your name on it, with a gold-and-diamond necklace inside. That is yours, isn't it?"

"Yes."

"Is it the one that Tamara Karsavina gave you? That Nicholas II gave her?"

"Yes." Anna looked at Tara more closely, but not less remotely.

"Ms Chernov, is there anyone you can think of who might have a strong interest in that necklace? A member of the press who's been persistent in asking about it, or someone emailing you about it, or a resident?"

"I don't do email, Miss Washington."

It was Detective Washington, but Tara let it go. "Still – anyone?"

"No."

Had the dancer hesitated slightly? Tara couldn't be sure. She went on asking questions, but she could see that she wasn't getting anywhere. Anna

Chernov grew politely impatient. Why wasn't Geraci stopping Tara? She had to continue until he did: "softening them up", he called it. The pointless questioning went on. Finally, just as Tara was running completely out of things to ask, Geraci said almost casually, "Do you know Dr Erdmann, the physicist?"

"We've met once," Anna said.

"Is it your impression that he has a romantic interest in you?"

For the first time, Anna looked amused. "I think Dr Erdmann's only romantic interest is in physics."

"I see. Thank you for your time, Ms Chernov."

In the hall, Geraci said to Tara, "Ballet. Police work sure isn't what it used to be. You did good, Washington."

"Thank you. What now?"

"Now we find out what resident has a romantic interest in Anna Chernov. It's not Erdmann, but it's somebody."

So Anna had hesitated slightly when Tara asked if any resident had a special interest in her! Tara glowed inwardly as she followed Geraci down the hall. Without looking at her, he said, "Just don't let it go to your head."

She said dryly, "Not a chance."

"Good. A cop interested in *ballet* . . . Jesus H. Christ."

The ship grew agitated. Across many cubic light-years between the stars, space-time itself warped in dangerous ways. The new entity was growing in strength – and it was so far away yet!

It was not supposed to occur this way.

If the ship had become aware earlier of this new entity, this could have happened correctly, in accord with the laws of evolution. All things evolved – stars, galaxies, consciousness. If the ship had realized earlier that anywhere in this galactic backwater had existed the potential for a new entity, the ship would have been there to guide, to shape, to ease the transition. But it hadn't realized. There had been none of the usual signs.

They were happening now, however. Images, as yet dim and one-way, were reaching the ship. More critically, power was being drawn from it, power that the birthing entity had no idea how to channel. Faster, the ship must go faster . . .

It could not, not without damaging space-time irretrievably. Space-time could only reconfigure so much, so often. And meanwhile —

The half-formed thing so far away stirred, struggled, howled in fear.

NINE

Henry Erdmann was scared.

He could barely admit his fright to himself, let alone show it to the circle of people jammed into his small apartment on Saturday morning. They sat in a solemn circle, occupying his sofa and armchair and kitchen chairs and other chairs dragged from other apartments. Evelyn Krenchnoted's chair crowded uncomfortably close to Henry's right side, her perfume sickly sweet. She had curled her hair into tiny grey sausages. Stan Dzarkis and Erin Bass, who could still manage it, sat on the floor. The folds of Erin's yellow print skirt seemed to Henry the only colour amid the ashen faces. Twenty people, and maybe there were more in the building who were afflicted. Henry had called the ones he knew of, who had called the ones they knew of. Missing were Anna Chernov, still in the Infirmary, and Al Cosmano, who had refused to attend.

They all looked at him, waiting to begin.

"I think we all know why we're here," Henry said, and immediately a sense of unreality took him. He didn't understand at all why he was here. The words of Michael Faraday, inscribed on the physics building at UCLA, leapt into his mind: "Nothing is too wonderful to be true." The words seemed a mockery. What had been happening to Henry, to all of them, did not feel wonderful and was "true" in no sense he understood, although he was going to do his damnedest to relate it to physics in the only way that hours of pondering had suggested to him. Anything else – anything less – was unthinkable.

He continued, "Things have occurred to all of us, and a good first step is to see if we have indeed had the same experiences." *Collect data.* "So I'll go first. On five separate occasions I have felt some force seize my mind and body, as if a surge of energy was going through me, some sort of neurological shock. On one occasion it was painful, on the others not painful but very tiring. Has anyone else felt that?"

Immediately a clamour, which Henry stilled by raising his arm. "Can we start with a show of hands? Anybody else had that experience? Everybody. Okay, let's go around the circle, introducing yourself as we go, starting on my left. Please be as explicit as possible, but only descriptions at this point. No interpretations."

"Damned teacher," someone muttered, but Henry didn't see who and didn't care. His heart had speeded up, and he felt that his ears had somehow expanded around his hearing aid, so as not to miss even a syllable. He had deliberately not mentioned the times of his "seizures", or outside events concurrent with them, so as not to contaminate whatever information would be offered by the others.

"I'm John Kluge, from 4J." He was a heavy, round-faced man with a completely bald head and a pleasant voice used to making itself heard. High-school teacher, Henry guessed. History or math, plus coaching some sort of sports team. "It's pretty much like Henry here said, except I only felt the 'energy' four times. The first was around seven-thirty on Tuesday night. The second time woke me Wednesday night at eleven-forty-two. I noted the time on my bedside clock. The third time I didn't note the time because I was vomiting after that food poisoning we all got on Thursday, but it was just before the vomiting started, sometime in mid-afternoon. That time the energy surge started near my heart, and I thought it was a heart attack. The last time was yesterday at eleven-forty-five a.m., and in addition to the energy, I had a . . . well, a sort of —" He looked embarrassed.

"Please go on, it's important," Henry said. He could hardly breathe.

"I don't want to say a vision, but colours swirling through my mind, red and blue and white and somehow *hard*."

"Anna Chernov's necklace!" Evelyn shrieked, and the meeting fell apart.

Henry couldn't stop the frantic babble. He would have risen but his walker was in the kitchen; there was no room in the crowded living room. He was grateful when Bob Donovan put two fingers in his mouth and gave a whistle that could have deafened war dogs. "Hey! Shut up or nobody's gonna learn nothing!"

Everyone fell silent and glared resentfully at the stocky man in baggy chinos and cheap acrylic sweater. Donovan scowled and sat back down. Henry leapt into the quiet.

"Mr Donovan is right, we won't learn anything useful this way. Let's resume going around the circle, with no interruptions, please. Mrs Bass?"

Erin Bass described essentially the same events as John Kluge, without the Wednesday night incident but with the addition of the earlier, slight jar Henry had felt as he let Carrie into his apartment Tuesday before class. She described this as a "whisper in my mind". The next sixteen people all repeated the same experiences on Thursday and Friday, although some seemed to not have felt the "energy" on Tuesday, and some not on Tuesday or Wednesday. Henry was the only one to feel all five instances. Throughout these recitations, Evelyn Krenchnoted several times rose slightly in her chair, like a geyser about to burst. Henry did *not* want her to interrupt. He put a restraining hand on her arm, which was a mistake as she immediately covered his hand with her own and squeezed affectionately.

When it was finally Evelyn's turn, she said, "None of you had pain this last time like Henry did on Thursday – except me! I was having a medical MIT at the hospital and I was inside the machine and the pain was horrible! Horrible! And then" – she paused dramatically – "and then I saw Anna Chernov's necklace right at the time it was being stolen! And so did all of you – that was the 'hard colours', John! Sapphires and rubies and diamonds!"

Pandemonium again. Henry, despite his growing fear, groaned inwardly. Why Evelyn Krenchnoted? Of all the unreliable witnesses . . .

"I saw it! I saw it!" Evelyn shrieked. Gina Martinelli had begun to pray in a loud voice. People jabbered to each other or sat silent, their faces gone white. A woman that Henry didn't know reached with a shaking hand into her pocket and pulled out a pill bottle. Bob Donovan raised his fingers to his lips.

Before Donovan's whistle could shatter their eardrums again, Erin Bass rose gracefully, clapped her hands, and cried surprisingly loudly, "Stop! We will get nowhere this way! Evelyn has the floor!"

Slowly the din subsided. Evelyn, who now seemed more excited than frightened by the implication of what she'd just said, launched into a long and incoherent description of her "MIT," until Henry stopped her the only way he could think of, which was to take her hand. She squeezed it again, blushed, and said, "Yes, dear."

Henry managed to get out, "Please. Everyone. There must be an explanation for all this." But before he could begin it, Erin Bass turned from aide to saboteur.

"Yes, and I think we should go around the circle in the same order and offer those explanations. But *briefly*, before too many people get too tired. John?"

Kluge said, "It could be some sort of virus affecting the brain. Contagious. Or some pollutant in the building."

Which causes every person to have the exact same hallucinations and a locked safe to open? Henry thought scornfully. The scorn steadied him. He needed steadying; every person in the room had mentioned feeling the Thursday-afternoon "energy" start in his or her heart, but no one except Henry knew that at that moment Jim Peltier was having an inexplicable heart attack as he battered Carrie.

Erin said, "What we see in this world is just *maya*, the illusion of permanence when in fact, all reality is in constant flux and change. What's happening here is beyond the world of intellectual concepts and distinctions. We're getting glimpses of the mutable nature of reality, the genuine undifferentiated 'suchness' that usually only comes with nirvana. The glimpses are imperfect, but for some reason our collective karma has afforded them to us."

Bob Donovan, next in the circle, said irritably, "That's just crap. We all got some brain virus, like Kluge here said, and some junkie cracked the office safe. The cops are investigating it. We should all see a doctor, except they can't never do anything to cure people anyway. And the people who had pain, Henry and Evelyn, they just got the disease worse."

Most people around the circle echoed the brain-disease theory, some with helpless skepticism, some with evident relief at finding any sort of explanation. A woman said slowly, "It could be the start of Alzheimer's." A man shrugged and said, "As God wills." Another just shook his head, his eyes averted.

Gina Martinelli said, "It is the will of God! These are the End Times, and we're being given signs, if only we would listen! 'Ye shalt have tribulations ten days: be thou faithful unto death, and I will give thee a crown of life.' Also —"

"It might be the will of God, Gina," interrupted Evelyn, unable to restrain herself any longer, "but it's mighty strange anyway! Why, I saw that necklace in my mind plain as day, and at just that moment it was being stolen from the safe! To my mind, that's not God, and not the devil neither or the robbery would have been successful, you see what I mean? The devil knows what he's doing. No, this was a message, all right, but from those who have gone before us. My Uncle Ned could see spirits all the time, they trusted him, I remember one time we all came down to breakfast and the cups had all been turned upside down when nobody was in the room and Uncle Ned, he said —"

Henry stopped listening. Ghosts. God. Eastern mysticism. Viruses. Alzheimer's. Nothing that fit the facts, that adhered even vaguely to the laws of the universe. These people had the reasoning power of termites.

Evelyn went on for a while, but eventually even she noticed that her audience was inattentive, dispirited, or actually asleep. Irene Bromley snored softly in Henry's leather armchair. Erin Bass said, "Henry?"

He looked at them hopelessly. He'd been going to describe the two-slit experiments on photons, to explain that once you added detectors to measure the paths of proton beams, the path became pre-determined, even if you switched on the detector *after* the particle had been fired. He'd planned on detailing how that astonishing series of experiments changed physics forever, putting the observer into basic measurements of reality. Consciousness was woven into the very fabric of the universe itself, and consciousness seemed to him the only way to link these incredibly disparate people and the incredible events that had happened to them.

Even to himself, this "explanation" sounded lame. How Teller or Feynman would have sneered at it! Still, although it was better than anything he'd heard here this morning, he hated to set it out in front of these irrational people, half ignoramuses and the other half nutcases. They would all just reject it, and what would be gained?

But he had called this meeting. And he had nothing else to offer.

Henry stumbled through his explanation, trying to make the physics as clear as possible. Most of the faces showed perfect incomprehension. He finished with, "I'm not saying there's some sort of affecting of reality going on, through group consciousness." But wasn't that exactly what he *was* saying? "I don't believe in telekinesis or any of that garbage. The truth is, I don't know what's happening. But something is."

He felt a complete fool.

Bob Donovan snapped, "None of you know nothing. I been listening to all of you, and you haven't even got the facts right. I *seen* Anna Chernov's necklace. The cops showed it to me yesterday when they was asking me some questions. It don't got no sapphires or rubies, and just one tiny diamond. You're full of it, Evelyn, to think your seizure had anything to do with anything – and how do we know you even felt any pain at the 'very second' the safe was being cracked? All we got's your word."

"Are you saying I'm a liar?" Evelyn cried. "Henry, tell him!"

Tell him what? Startled, Henry just stared at her. John Kluge said harshly, "I don't believe Henry Erdmann is lying about his pain," and Evelyn turned from Donovan to Kluge.

"You mean you think I am? Who the hell do you think you are?"

Kluge started to tell her who he was: among other things, a former notary public. Other people began to argue. Evelyn started to cry, and Gina Martinelli prayed loudly. Erin Bass rose and slipped out the front door. Others followed. Those that remained disputed fiercely, the arguments growing more intense as they were unable to convince their neighbours of their own theories. Somewhere among the anger and contempt, Carrie Vesey appeared by Henry's side, her pretty face creased with bewildered concern, her voice high and strained.

"Henry? What on Earth is going on in here? I could hear the noise all the way down the hall . . . What is this all about?"

"Nothing," he said, which was the stupidest answer possible. Usually the young regarded the old as a separate species, as distant from their own concerns as trilobites. But Carrie had been different. She had always treated Henry as inhabiting the same world as herself, with the same passions and quirks and aims and defeats. This was the first time he had ever seen Carrie look at him as both alien and unsound, and it set the final seal on this disastrous meeting.

"But, Henry —"

"I said it's nothing!" he shouted at her. "Nothing at all! Now just leave me the hell alone!"

TEN

Carrie stood in the ladies' room off the lobby, pulling herself together. She was *not* going to cry. Even if Dr Erdmann had never spoken to her like that before, even if ever since Jim's death she had felt as if she might shatter, even if . . . everything, *she was not going to cry*. It would be ridiculous. She was a professional – well, a professional aide anyway – and Henry Erdmann was an old man. Old people were irritable sometimes. This whole incident meant nothing.

Except that she knew it did. She had stood outside Dr Erdmann's door for a long time as people slipped out, smiling at her vaguely, and Evelyn Krenchnoted babbled on inside. The unprecedented meeting had first piqued her curiosity – Henry Erdmann, hosting a party at ten o'clock on a Saturday morning? Then, as she realized what Evelyn was saying, disbelief took Carrie. Evelyn meant . . . Evelyn thought . . . and even Dr Erdmann believed that "something" had been happening, something weird and unexplainable and supernatural, at the moment that Evelyn was under the MRI . . . *Henry*!

But Jake DiBella had been upset by Evelyn's scans.

The door of the ladies' opened and the first of the Saturday visitors entered, a middle-aged woman and a sulky teenage girl. "Honestly, Hannah," the woman said, "it's only an hour out of your precious day and it won't kill you to sit with your grandmother and concentrate on someone else besides yourself for a change. If you'd just —"

Carrie went to DiBella's office. He was there, working at his desk. No sign of her picture, cushion, coffee cup; she couldn't help her inevitable, stupid pang. He didn't want them. Or her. Another failure.

"Dr DiBella —"

"'Jake.' Remember?" And then, "Carrie, what is it?"

"I just came from Dr Erdmann's apartment. They were having a meeting, about twenty people, all of them who've felt these 'seizures' or whatever they are, all at the same time. Like the one you captured on Evelyn's MRI scan."

He stared at her. "What do you mean, 'at the same time'?"

"Just what I said." She marvelled at her own tone – none of her shakiness showed. "They said that at the exact same time that Evelyn was showing all that weird activity under the MRI, each of them was feeling it, too, only not so strong. And it was the exact same time that Anna Chernov's necklace was being stolen. And they all saw the necklace in their minds." Only – hadn't Mr Donovan said that the necklace looked different from what Evelyn said? Confusion took Carrie.

Jake looked down at whatever he was writing, back at Carrie, down again at his notes. He came around the desk and closed his office door. Taking her arm, he sat her gently in the visitor's chair, unadorned by her cushion. Despite herself, she felt a tingle where his hand touched her.

"Dr Erdmann was involved in this? Tell me again. Slowly, Carrie. Don't leave anything out."

Evelyn Krenchnoted made her way to Gina Martinelli's apartment on Five. Really, Henry had been unbearably rude – to that poor young girl, to everybody at the meeting, and especially to Evelyn herself. He hadn't comforted her when that awful Donovan man called her a liar, he hadn't put his hand on hers again, he'd just yelled and yelled – and just when things between them had been going so well!

Evelyn needed to talk to Gina. Not that Gina had been any help at the meeting, not with all that praying. Gina was really a lot smarter than she looked, she'd been a part-time tax preparer once, but hardly anybody knew it because Gina never opened her mouth except to pray. Not that there was anything wrong with praying, of course! Evelyn certainly believed in God. But you had to help Him along a little if you really wanted something. You couldn't expect the Lord to do everything.

Evelyn had even curled her hair for Henry.

"Gina? Sweetie? Can I come in?"

"You're already in," Gina said. She had to speak loud because she had Frank Sinatra on the record player. Gina loved Frank Sinatra. For once she wasn't reading her Bible, which Evelyn thought was a good sign. She lowered her bulk onto Gina's sofa.

"So what did you think of that meeting?" Evelyn said. She was looking forward to a good two-three hours of rehashing, sympathy, and gossip. It would make her feel a lot better. Less creepy. Less afraid.

But instead, Gina said, "There was a message on the machine when I got back here. Ray is coming next week."

Oh, God, Gina's son. Who was only after her money. Ray hadn't visited in over a year, and now that Gina had told him she was leaving everything to the daughter . . . and there was a lot of everything to leave. Gina's late husband had made major money in construction.

"Oh, sweetie," Evelyn said, a little perfunctorily. Ordinarily she would have adored discussing Gina's anguish; for one thing, it made Evelyn glad she had never had kids. But now, with so much else going on – Henry and the attempted robbery and Evelyn's seizure and the strange comments at the meeting —

Frank Sinatra sang about ants and rubber tree plants. Gina burst into tears.

"Oh, sweetie," Evelyn repeated, got up to put her arms around Gina, and resigned herself to hearing about Ray Martinelli's selfishness.

Bob Donovan sat beside Anna Chernov's bed in the Infirmary. The man simply could not take a hint. She would have to either snub him outright or tell him in so many words to stop visiting her. Even the sight of him, squat and toad-faced and clumsy, made her shudder. Unfair, but there it was.

She had danced with so many beautiful men.

Which had been the best? Frederico, partnering her in *La Valse* – never had she been lifted so effortlessly. Jean, in *Scotch Symphony*, had been equally breathtaking, But the one she always returned to was Bennet. After she'd left the New York City Ballet for American Ballet Theatre and her career had really taken off, they'd always danced together. Bennet, so dazzling as Albrecht in *Giselle*. . . . Guesting at a gala at the Paris Opera, they'd had seventeen curtain calls and —

Her attention was reclaimed by something Bob Donovan said.

"Could you repeat that, please, Bob?"

"What? Old Henry's crackpot theory? Science gibberish!"

"Nonetheless, would you repeat it?" She managed a smile.

He responded to the smile with pathetic eagerness. "Okay, yeah, if you want. Erdmann said, lemme think . . ." He screwed up his already crevassed face in an effort to remember. Although she was being unkind again. He probably wasn't all that bad looking, among his own class. And was she any better? These days she couldn't bear to look in a mirror. And the sight of the ugly cast on her leg filled her with despair.

"Erdmann said there was some experiments in physics, something with two slips, where people's consciences changed the path of some little . . . particles . . . by just thinking about them. Or maybe it was watching them. And that was the link between everybody who had so-called 'energy' at the same time. Group conscience. A new thing."

Consciousness, Anna translated. Group consciousness. Well, was that so strange? She had felt it more than once on stage, when a group of dancers had transcended what they were individually, had become a unity moving to the music in the creation of beauty. Such moments had, for her, taken the place of religion.

Bob was going on now about what other people at the meeting had said, offering up ungrammatical accounts in a desperate bid to please her, but even as she recognized this, Anna had stopped listening. She thought instead about Bennet, with whom she'd had such fantastic chemistry on and off stage, Bennet lifting her in the *grand pas de deux* of Act II, rosin from the raked stage rising around her like an angelic cloud, herself soaring and almost flying . . .

"Tell me again," Jake said.

"Again?" This was the third time! Not that Carrie really minded. She hadn't had his total attention – anybody's total attention – like this since

Jim died. Not that she wanted Jim back . . . She shuddered even as she went through it all again. By the end, she was belligerent.

"Why? Are you saying you believe all this stuff about a group consciousness?"

"No. Of course not. Not without confirmation . . . but Erdmann is a scientist. What other data does he have that he isn't telling you?"

"I don't know what you mean." And she didn't; this conversation was beyond her. Photon detectors, double-slit experiments, observational pre-determination . . . Her memory was good, but she knew she lacked the background to interpret the terms. Her own ignorance made her angry.

"Henry had two other experiences of 'energy' when he was with you, you said. Were there others when he was away from you?"

"How should I know? You better ask him!"

"I will. I'll ask them all."

"It sounds stupid to me." Immediately she was frightened by her own tone. But Jake just looked at her thoughtfully.

"Well, it sounds stupid to me, too. But Henry is right about one thing – *something* is happening. There's hard data in the form of Evelyn's MRI, in the fact that the safe was opened without the lock being either tampered with or moved to the right combination —"

"It *was*?"

"The detective told me, when he was asking questions yesterday. Also, I got the physician here to let me look at the lab results for everybody admitted to the Infirmary Thursday afternoon. Professional courtesy. There was no food poisoning."

"There wasn't?" All at once Carrie felt scared.

"No." DiBella sat thinking a long while. She scarcely dared breathe. Finally he said slowly, as if against his own will or better judgment – and that much she understood, anyway – "Carrie, have you ever heard of the principle of emergent complexity?"

"I did *everything* for that boy," Gina sobbed. "Just everything!"

"Yes, you did," said Evelyn, who thought Gina had done too much for Ray. Always lending him money after he lost each job, always letting him move back home and trash the place. What that kid had needed – and bad – was a good hiding, that's what.

"Angela didn't turn out this way!"

"No." Gina's daughter was a sweetie. Go figure.

"And now I just get it settled in my mind that he's out of my life, I come to grips with it, and he says he's flying back here to see 'his old ma' and he loves me! He'll just stir everything up again like he did when he got home from the Army, and when he divorced Judy, and when I had to find that lawyer for him in New York . . . Evelyn, nobody, but *nobody*, can rip you up inside like your child!"

"I know," said Evelyn, who didn't. She went on making little clucking noises while Gina sobbed. A plane roared overhead, and Frank Sinatra sang about it having been a very good year when he was twenty-one.

Bob Donovan took Anna's hand. Gently she pulled it away. The gentleness was for her, not him – she didn't want a scene. His touch repelled her. But oh, Bennet's touch . . . or Frederico's . . . Still, it was the dancing she missed. And now she would never dance again. She might, the doctors said, not even walk without a limp.

Never dance. Never feel her legs spring into a *balloté* or soar in the exuberance of a *flick jeté*, back arched and arms thrown back, an arrow in ecstatic flight.

"Carrie, have you ever heard of the principle of emergent complexity?"

"No." Jake DiBella was going to make her feel dumb again. But he didn't mean to do that, and as long as she could sit here in his office with him, she would listen. Maybe he needed someone to listen. Maybe he needed her. And maybe he would say something that would help her make it all right with Dr Erdmann.

Jake licked his lips. His face was still paper white. "'Emergent complexity' means that as an evolving organism grows more complex, it develops processes that wouldn't seem implied by the processes it had in simpler form. In other words, the whole becomes greater than the sum of the parts. Somewhere along the line, our primitive human ancestors developed self-awareness. Higher consciousness. That was a new thing in evolution."

Old knowledge stirred in Carrie's mind. "There was a pope – I was raised Catholic – some pope, one of the John Pauls maybe, said there was a point where God infused a soul into an animal heritage. So evolution wasn't really anti-Catholic."

Jake seemed to be looking through her, at something only he could see. "Exactly. God or evolution or some guy named Fred – however it happened, consciousness did emerge. And if, now, the next step in complexity is emerging . . . if that . . ."

Carrie was angered, either by his line of thought or by his ignoring her; she wasn't sure which. She said sharply, "But why now? Why *here*?"

His question brought his gaze back to her. He took a long time to answer, while a plane droned overhead on the flight path out of the airport. Carrie held her breath.

But all he said was, "I don't know."

Gina had worked herself up to such a pitch that she wasn't even praying. Ray, Ray, Ray – This wasn't what Evelyn wanted to talk about. But she had never seen Gina like this. All at once Gina cried passionately, drowning out Sinatra singing "Fly Me to the Moon." "I wish he weren't coming! I wish his plane would just go on to another city or something, just not land here! I don't want him here!"

Never dance again. And the only love available from men like Bob Donovan . . . No. No. Anna would rather be dead.

*

"Well, I don't believe it!" Carrie said. "Emerging complexity – I just don't believe it's happening at St Sebastian's!"

"Neither do I," said Jake. For the first time since she'd entered his office, he smiled at her.

Outside the building, a boom sounded.

Carrie and Jake both looked toward the door. Carrie thought first of terrorism, a car bomb or something, because everybody thought first of terrorism these days. But terrorism at an assisted living facility was ridiculous. It was a gas main exploding, or a bus crash just outside, or . . .

Henry Erdmann appeared in the open doorway to the study. He didn't have his walker with him. He sagged against the doorjamb, his sunken eyes huge and his mouth open. Before Carrie could leap up to help him and just before he slumped to the floor, he croaked, "Call the police. We just brought down a plane."

Anguish ripped through the ship. Not its own agony, but the Other's. No guidance, no leading, it was raging wild and undisciplined. If this went on, it might weaken the ship too much for the ship to ever help it.

If this went on, the Other could damage space-time itself.

The ship could not let that happen.

ELEVEN

When Henry Erdmann collapsed, DiBella moved swiftly to the old man. Carrie stood frozen – stupid! Stupid! "Get the doctor," Jake cried. And then, "Go, Carrie. He's alive."

She ran out of Jake's office, nearly tripping over the walker Henry had left in the hallway. He must have been coming to see Jake when it happened – when what happened? She raced to the lobby and the call phone, her mind so disordered that only as she shoved open the double doors did she realize that of course it would have been faster to hit Henry's panic button – Jake would do that – but Henry seldom wore his panic button, he –

She stopped cold, staring.

The lobby was full of screaming people, mostly visitors. Among them, old people lay fallen to the floor or slumped in wheelchairs. It was Saturday morning and on Saturday morning relatives arrived to take their mothers and grandfathers and great-grandmothers for brunch, for a drive, for a visit home . . . Bundled in sweaters and jackets and shawls, the seniors had all collapsed like so many bundles of dropped laundry. St Sebastian nurses, aides, and even desk volunteers bent ineffectually over the victims.

Fear roiled Carrie's stomach, but it also preternaturally heightened her perceptions.

Mr Aberstein, a St Sebastian resident even though he was only sixty-seven, stood unaffected by the elevators. Mrs Kelly sat alert in her wheelchair, her mouth a wide pink O. She was seventy-one. Mr Schur . . .

"Nurse! Come quick, please, it's Dr Erdmann!" Carrie caught at the sleeve of a passing nurse in purple scrubs, but he shook her off and raced to an old woman lying on the floor. Everyone here was too busy to help Carrie. She ran back to Jake's office.

Henry lay quietly on the floor. Jake had turned him face up and put a cushion – her cushion, Carrie thought numbly, the patchwork one she'd brought Jake – under Henry's feet. Henry wasn't wearing his panic button. She gasped, "No one can come, it's happened to all of them —"

"All who?" Jake said sharply.

She answered without thinking. "All of them over eighty. Is Henry —"

"He's breathing normally. his colour's good, and he's not clammy. I don't think he's in shock. He's just . . . out. *All of them over eighty?*"

"Yes. No. I don't know, I mean, about the age, but all the older ones in the lobby just collapsed and the younger residents seem fine . . . Jake, what *is* it?"

"I don't know. Carrie, do this now: Go to one of the common rooms and turn the TV to the local news channel. See if there's been a . . . a plane crash —"

He stopped. Both of them heard the sirens.

Henry did not wake. All of Redborn Memorial Hospital's ambulances had gone to the crash site. The St Sebastian staff moved afflicted residents to the dining room, which looked like a very peaceful war hospital. The residents didn't wake, moan, or need emergency treatment with the exception of one woman who had broken a hip falling to the floor. She was sent over to Memorial. Monitors couldn't be spared from the Nursing floor, where nearly everyone had fallen into the coma, but a few spare monitors were carried down from the Infirmary. They showed no anomalies in heart rate or blood pressure.

Relatives summoned family doctors, sat by cots, screamed at St Sebastian staff, who kept repeating, "Redborn Memorial is aware of the situation and they'll get the St Sebastian residents over there as soon as they can. *Please*, sir, if you'd just —"

Just be patient. Just believe that we're doing our best. Just be reassured by your mother's peaceful face. Just accept that we don't know any more than you do. Just leave me alone!

Carrie checked on her resident-assignees, one by one. They were all affected, most collapsed in their apartments. They were all moved into the Infirmary. They were all over eighty.

She was hurrying from Al Cosmano's apartment – empty, he must have been elsewhere when it happened – back to the Infirmary when a man caught at her arm. "Hey! Ms Vesey!"

One of the detectives who'd investigated Jim's death. Carrie's belly clenched. "Yes?"

"Where do I find the hospital administrator? Caldwell?"

"He's not here, he went out of town for the weekend, they sent for him – why?"

"I need to see him. Who's in charge? And what the hell happened here?"

So not about Jim's death. Still – a cop. Some part of her mind shuddered – Jim had been a cop – but at the same time, she seized on this. Official authority. Someone who investigated and found answers. Security. There was a reason she'd married Jim in the first place.

She said as calmly as she could manage, "We've had an . . . an epidemic of collapses among the very old. All at the same time. About a half hour ago."

"Disease?"

"No." She heard how positive she sounded. Well, she was positive. "When the plane went down."

He looked baffled, as well he might. She said, "I'll take you to Dr Jamison. He's the St Sebastian's physician."

Jamison wasn't in the dining room. Carrie, leading Detective Geraci, found the doctor in the kitchen, in a shouting match with Jake DiBella. "No, damn it! You're not going to further upset the relatives for some stupid, half-baked theory – No!" Jamison stalked off.

Carrie said, "Dr Jamison, this is —" He pushed past her, heading back to his patients. She expected the detective to follow him, but instead Geraci said to Jake, "Who are you?"

"Who wants to know?"

She had never seen Jake so rude. But he was angry and frustrated and scared – they were all scared.

"Detective Geraci, RPD. You work here?"

Carrie said quickly, before the two men could get really nasty, "This is Dr DiBella. He's doing a medical research project at St Sebastian's, on . . . on brain waves."

Geraci said, "I received an anonymous call. Me, not the Department, on my cell, from the St Sebastian front desk. The caller said there was information here about the plane crash. You know anything about that, doctor?"

Carrie saw that Vince Geraci believed Jake did have information. How did she know that? How did he know that? But it was there in every line of the detective's alert body: He knew that Jake knew something.

Jake didn't answer, just stared at Geraci. Finally Geraci said, "The plane went down half a mile from here. A U.S. Air commuter plane carrying forty-nine passengers, including thirty-one members of the Aces High Senior Citizen Club. They were on a three-day trip to the casinos at Atlantic City. Everyone on board is dead."

Jake said, "I can't talk to you now. I have to take some brain scans while these people are unconscious. After that idiot Jamison realizes what I'm doing and throws me out, we can talk. Carrie, I'll need your help. Go to my office and put all the equipment in the corner onto the dolly, throw a blanket over it, and bring it the back way into the kitchen. Quickly!"

She nodded and hurried off, so fast that she didn't realize Geraci was behind her until they reached Jake's office.

"Let me get that, it's heavy," he said.

"No, it's not." She lugged the console onto its dolly. "Shouldn't you be asking people questions?"

"I am. Does DiBella always order you around like that?"

Did he? She hadn't noticed. "No." She added the helmet and box of peripherals on top of the console, then looked around for a blanket. There wasn't one.

"Do you work for DiBella or for St Sebastian's?"

"St Sebastian's. I have to go to the linen closet."

When she returned with a blanket, Geraci was reading the papers on Jake's desk. Wasn't that illegal? Carrie threw the blanket over the equipment. Geraci grabbed the handle of the dolly before she could.

"You need me," he said. "Anybody stops you, I'll just flash my badge."

"Okay," she said ungraciously. She could have done this, for Jake, by herself.

They brought the equipment into the kitchen. Jake set it up on the counter, ignoring the cook who said helplessly, "So nobody's having lunch, then?" All at once she ripped off her apron, flung it onto the floor, and walked out.

Jake said to Carrie, "Hold the door." He slipped through to the dining room and, a moment later, wheeled in a gurney with an elderly woman lying peacefully on it. "Who is she, Carrie?"

"Ellen Parminter." After a moment she added, "Eighty-three." Jake grunted and began attaching electrodes to Mrs Parminter's unconscious head.

Geraci said, "Come with me, Carrie."

"No." Where did she get the *nerve*? But, somehow, he brought that out in her.

He only smiled. "Yes. This is an official police investigation, as of this minute."

She went, then, following him back to Jake's office. Carrie was shaking, but she didn't want him to see that. He did, though; he seemed to see everything. "Sit down," he said gently. "There, behind the desk – you didn't like me reading DiBella's papers before, did you? It's legal if they're in plain sight. You seem like a really good observer, Carrie. Now, please tell me everything that's been happening here. From the very beginning, and without leaving anything out. Start with why you told DiBella that woman's age. Does her age matter to what he's doing?"

Did it? She didn't know. How could it . . . people aged at such different rates! Absolute years meant very little, except that —

"Carrie?"

All at once it seemed a relief to be able to pour it all out. Yes, he was trained to get people to talk, she knew that, and she didn't really trust his sudden gentleness. It was merely a professional trick. But if she told it all, that might help order her chaotic thoughts. And maybe, somehow, it might help the larger situation, too. All those people dead on the plane —

She said slowly, "You won't believe it."

"Try me anyway."

"*I* don't believe it."

This time he just waited, looking expectant. And it all poured out of her, starting with Henry's "seizure" on the way home from the university. The vomiting epidemic among seven or so patients, that wasn't the food poisoning that St Sebastian's said it was. Evelyn Krenchnoted's functional MRI. Anna Chernov's necklace, what Evelyn thought the necklace looked like and what Bob Donovan said it really was. The secret meeting this morning in Henry's apartment. What Carrie had overheard: Henry's words about photons and how human observation affected the paths of fundamental particles. Jake's lecture on "emergent complexity". Henry's appearance at Jake's office, saying just before he collapsed, "Call the police. We just brought down a plane." The mass collapse of everyone over eighty and of no one younger than that. The brain scans Jake was taking now, undoubtedly to see if they looked normal or like Evelyn's. The more Carrie talked, the more improbable everything sounded.

When she finished, Geraci's face was unreadable.

"That's it," she said miserably. "I have to go see how Henry is."

"Thank you, Carrie." His tone was unreadable. "I'm going to find Dr Jamison now."

He left, but she stayed. It suddenly took too much energy to move. Carrie put her head in her hands. When she straightened again, her gaze fell on Jake's desk.

He'd been writing when she'd burst in with the news of the meeting in Henry's apartment. Writing on paper, not on a computer: thick pale green paper with a faint watermark. The ink was dark blue. "My dearest James, I can't tell you how much I regret the things I said to you on the phone last night, but, love, please remember —"

Carrie gave a short, helpless bark of laughter. *My dearest James . . . God,* she was such a fool!

She shook her head like a dog spraying off water, and went to look for Henry.

The new being was quiet now. That made this a good time to try to reach it. That was always best done through its own culture's symbols. But ship had had so little time to prepare . . . This should have been done slowly, over a long time, a gradual interaction as the new entity was guided, shaped, made ready. And ship was still so far away.

But it tried, extending itself as much as possible, searching for the collective symbols and images that would have eased a normal transition – and roiled in horror.

TWELVE

Evelyn Krenchnoted lay on a cot jammed against the dining room window. She lay dreaming, unaware of the cool air seeping through the glass, or the leaves falling gold and orange in the tiny courtyard beyond. In her dream she walked on a path of light. Her feet made no sound. She moved toward more light, and somewhere in that light was a figure. She couldn't see it or hear it, but she knew it was there. And she knew who it was.

It was someone who really, truly, finally would listen to her.

Al Cosmano squirmed in his sleep. "He's waking," a nurse said.

"No, he's not." Dr Jamison, passing yet again among the rows of cots and gurneys and pallets on the floor, his face weary. "Some of them have been doing that for hours. As soon as the ambulances return, move this row next to the hospital."

"Yes, doctor."

Al heard them and didn't hear them. He was a child again, running along twilight streets toward home. His mother was there, waiting. Home . . .

The stage was so bright! The stage manager must have turned up the lights, turned them up yet again – the whole stage was light. Anna Chernov couldn't see, couldn't find her partner. She had to stop dancing.

Had to stop dancing.

She stood lost on the stage, lost in the light. The audience was out there somewhere in all that brightness, but she couldn't see them any more than she could see Bennet or the corps de ballet. She felt the audience, though. They were there, as bright as the stage, and they were old. Very, very old, as old as she was, and like her, beyond dancing.

She put her hands over her face and sobbed.

Erin Bass saw the path, and it led exactly where she knew it would: deeper into herself. That was where the buddha was, had always been, would always be. Along this path of light, curving and spiraling deeper into her own being, which was all being. All around her were the joyful others, who were her just as she was them —

A jolt, and she woke in an ambulance, her arms and legs and chest strapped down, a young man leaning over her saying, "Ma'am?" The path was gone, the others gone, the heavy world of *maya* back again around her, and a stale taste in her dehydrated mouth.

Lights and tunnels – where the hell was he? An A-test bunker, maybe, except no bunker was ever this brightly lit, and where was Teller or Mark or Oppie? But, no, Oppie hadn't ever worked on this project, Henry was confused, that was it, he was just confused —

And then he wasn't.

He woke all at once, a wrenching transition from sleep-that-wasn't-really sleep to full alertness. In fact, his senses seemed preternaturally sharp. He felt the hard cot underneath his back, the slime of drool on his cheek, the flatness of the dining room fluorescent lights. He heard the roll of rubber gurney wheels on the low-pile carpet and the clatter of cutlery in the kitchen dishwashers. He smelled Carrie's scent, wool and vanilla and young skin, and he could have described every ligament of her body as she sat on the chair next to his cot in the dining room of St Sebastian's, Detective Geraci beside her.

"Henry?" Carrie whispered.

He said, "It's coming. It's almost here."

Ship withdrew all contact. It had never encountered anything like this before. The pre-being did not coalesce.

Its components were not uniform, but scattered among undisciplined and varied matter-specks who were wildly heterozygotic. Unlike the components of every other pre-being that ship had detected, had guided, had become. All the other pre-ships had existed as one on the matter plane, because they were alike in all ways. These, too, were alike, built of the same physical particles and performing the same physical processes, but somewhere something had gone very wrong, and from that uniform matter they had not evolved uniform consciousness. They had no harmony. They used violence against each other.

Possibly they could, if taken in, use that violence against ship.

Yet ship couldn't go away and leave them. Already they were changing space-time in their local vicinity. When their melding had advanced further, the new being could be a dangerous and powerful entity. What might it do?

Ship pondered, and feared, and recoiled from what might be necessary: the destruction of what should have been an integral part of itself.

THIRTEEN

Jake DiBella clutched the printouts so hard that the stiff paper crumpled in his hand. Lying on the sofa, Henry Erdmann frowned at the tiny destruction. Carrie had pulled her chair close enough to hold Henry's hand, while that RPD detective, Geraci, stood at the foot of the couch. What was he doing here, anyway? DiBella didn't know, but he was too agitated to care for more than a fleeting second.

Carrie said to Henry, "I still think you should go to the hospital!"

"I'm not going, so forget it." The old man struggled to sit up. She would have stopped him, but Geraci put a hand on her shoulder and gently restrained her. *Throwing around his authority*, DiBella thought.

Henry said, "Why at St Sebastian's?"

The same question that Carrie had asked. DiBella said, "I have a theory." His voice sounded strange to himself. "It's based on Carrie's observation that nobody under eighty has been . . . affected by this. If it is some sort of uber-consciousness that's . . . that's approaching Earth . . ." He couldn't go on. It was too silly.

It was too real.

Henry Erdmann was apparently not afraid of either silliness or reality – which seemed to have become the same thing. Henry said, "You mean it's coming here because 'uber-consciousness' emerges only among the old, and nowadays there's more old than ever before."

"For the first time in history, you over-eighties exceed one per cent of the population. A 140 million people world-wide."

"But that still doesn't explain why here. Or why us."

"For God's sake, Henry, everything has to start somewhere!"

Geraci said, surprising DiBella, "All bifurcation is local. One lungfish starts to breathe more air than water. One caveman invents an axe. There's always a nexus. Maybe that nexus is you, Dr Erdmann."

Carrie tilted her head to look up at Geraci.

Henry said heavily, "Maybe so. But I'm not the only one. I wasn't the main switch for the energy that brought down that airplane. I was just one of the batteries linked in parallel."

The science analogies comfort Erdmann, DiBella thought. He wished something would comfort him.

Carrie said, "I think Evelyn was the switch to open the safe for Anna Chernov's necklace."

Geraci's face sharpened. But he said, "That doesn't really make sense. I can't go that far."

Henry's sunken eyes grew hard. "You haven't had to travel as far as I have in order to get to this point, young man. Believe me about that. But I *experienced* the . . . the consciousness. That data is anecdotal but real. And those brain scans that Dr DiBella is mangling there aren't even anecdotal. They're hard data."

True enough. The brain scans DiBella had taken of the unconscious oldsters, before that irate idiot Jamison had discovered him at work and thrown him out, were cruder versions of Evelyn Krenchnoted's under the fMRI. An almost total shut-down of the thalamus, the relay station for sensory information flowing into the brain. Ditto for the body-defining posterior parietal lobes. Massive activity in the back of the brain, especially in the temporoparietal regions, amygdalae, and hippocampus. The brain scan of an epileptic mystical state on speed. And as unlike the usual scan for the coma-state as a turtle was to a rocketship to the stars.

DiBella put his hands to his face and pulled at his skin, as if that might rearrange his thoughts. When he'd dropped his hands, he said slowly, "A single neuron isn't smart, isn't even a very impressive entity. All it really does is convert one type of electrical or chemical signal into another. That's it. But neurons connected together in the brain can generate incredibly complex states. You just need enough of them to make consciousness possible."

"Or enough old people for this 'group consciousness'?" Carrie said. "But why only old people?"

"How the hell should I know?" DiBella said. "Maybe the brain needs to have stored enough experience, enough sheer *time*."

Geraci said, "Do you read Dostoyevsky?"

"No," DiBella said. He didn't like Geraci. "Do you?"

"Yes. He said there were moments when he felt a 'frightful' clarity and rapture, and that he would give his whole life for five seconds of that and not feel he was paying too much. Dostoyevsky was an epileptic."

"I know he was an epileptic!" DiBella snapped.

Carrie said, "Henry, can you sense it now? That thing that's coming?"

"No. Not at all. Obviously it's not quantum-entangled in any classical sense."

"Then maybe it's gone away."

Henry tried to smile at her. "Maybe. But I don't think so. I think it's coming for us."

"What do you mean, coming for you?" Geraci said skeptically. "It's not a button man."

"I don't know what I mean," Henry said irritably. "But it's coming, and soon. It can't afford to wait long. Look what we did . . . that plane . . ."

Carrie's hand tightened on Henry's fingers. "What will it do when it gets here?"

"I don't know. How could I know?"

"Henry —" Jake began.

"I'm more worried about what *we* may do before it arrives."

Geraci said, "Turn on CNN."

DiBella said pointedly, "Don't you have someplace you should be, Detective?"

"No. Not if this really is happening."

To which there was no answer.

At 9:43 pm, the power grid went down in a city 200 miles away. "No evident reason," said the talking head on CNN, "given the calm weather and no sign of any —"

"Henry?" Carrie said.

"I . . . I'm all right. But I felt it."

Jake said, "It's happening farther away now. That is, if it was . . . if that was . . ."

"It was," Henry said simply. Still stretched full-length on the sofa, he closed his eyes. Geraci stared at the TV. None of them had wanted any food.

At 9:51, Henry's body jerked violently and he cried out. Carrie whimpered, but in a moment Henry said, "I'm . . . conscious." No one dared comment on his choice of word. Seven minutes later, the CNN anchor announced breaking news: a bridge over the Hudson River had collapsed, plunging an Amtrak train into the dark water.

Over the next few minutes, Henry's face showed a rapid change of expression: fear, rapture, anger, surprise. The expressions were so pronounced, so distorted, that at times Henry Erdmann almost looked like someone else. Jake wondered wildly if he should record this on his cell camera, but he didn't move. Carrie knelt beside the sofa and put both arms around the old man, as if to hold him here with her.

"We . . . can't help it," Henry got out. "If one person thinks strongly enough about – ah, God!"

The lights and TV went off. Alarms sounded, followed by sirens. Then a thin beam of light shone on Henry's face; Geraci had a pocket flashlight. Henry's entire body convulsed in seizure, but he opened his eyes. DiBella could barely hear his whispered words.

"It's a *choice*."

The only way was a choice. Ship didn't understand the necessity – how could any single unit choose other than to become part of its whole? That had never happened before. Birthing entities came happily to join themselves. The direction of evolution was toward greater complexity, always. But choice must be the last possible action here, for this misbegotten and unguided being. If it did not choose to merge –

Destruction. To preserve the essence of consciousness itself, which meant the essence of all.

FOURTEEN

Evelyn, who feared hospitals, had refused to go to Redborn Memorial to be "checked over" after the afternoon's fainting spell. That's all it was, just fainting, nothing to get your blood in a boil about, just a —

She stopped halfway between her microwave and kitchen table. The casserole in her hand fell to the floor and shattered.

The light was back, the one she'd dreamed about in her faint. Only it wasn't a light and this wasn't a dream. It was there in her mind, and it was her mind, and she was it . . . had always been it. How could that be? But the presence filled her and Evelyn knew, beyond any doubt, that if she joined it, she would never, ever be alone again. Why, she didn't need words, had never needed words, all she had to do was choose to go where she belonged anyway . . .

Who knew?

Happily, the former Evelyn Krenchnoted became part of those waiting for her, even as her body dropped to the linguini-spattered floor.

In a shack in the slums of Karachi, a man lay on a pile of clean rags. His toothless gums worked up and down, but he made no sound. All night he had been waiting alone to die, but now it seemed his wait had truly been for something else, something larger than even death, and very old.

Old. It sought the old, and only the old, and the toothless man knew why. Only the old had earned this, had paid for this in the only coin that really mattered: the accumulation of sufficient sorrow.

With relief he slipped away from his pain-wracked body and into the ancient largeness.

*

No. *He wasn't moving*, Bob thought. The presence in his mind terrified him, and terror turned him furious. Let them – whoever – try all their cheap tricks, they were as bad as union negotiators. Offering concessions that would never materialize. Trying to fool him. He wasn't going anywhere, wasn't becoming anything, not until he knew exactly what the deal was, what the bastards wanted.

They weren't going to get him.

But then he felt something else happen. He knew what it was. Sitting in the Redborn Memorial ER, Bob Donovan cried out, "No! Anna – you can't!" even as his mind tightened and resisted until, abruptly, the presence withdrew and he was alone.

In a luxurious townhouse in San José, a man sat up abruptly in bed. For a long moment he sat completely still in the dark, not even noticing that the clock and digital-cable box lights were out. He was too filled with wonder.

Of course – why hadn't he seen this before? He, who had spent long joyful nights debugging computers when they still used vacuum tubes – how could he have missed this? He wasn't the whole program, but rather just one line of code! And it was when you put all the code together, not before, that the program could actually run. He'd been only a fragment, and now the whole was here . . .

He joined it.

Erin Bass experienced *satori*.

Tears filled her eyes. All her adult life she had wanted this, longed for it, practised meditation for hours each day, and had not even come close to the mystical intoxication she felt now. She hadn't known, hadn't dreamed it could be this oneness with all reality. All her previous striving had been wrong. There was no striving, there was no Erin. She had never been created; she was the creation and the cosmos; no individual existed. Her existence was not her own, and when that last illusion vanished so did she, into the all.

Gina Martinelli felt it, the grace that was the glory of God. Only . . . only where was Jesus Christ, the savior and Lord? She couldn't feel him, couldn't find him in the oneness . . .

If Christ was not there, then this wasn't Heaven. It was a trick of the Cunning One, of Satan who knows a million disguises and sends his demons to mislead the faithful. She wasn't going to be tricked!

She folded her arms and began to pray aloud. Gina Martinelli was a faithful Christian. She wasn't going anywhere; she was staying right here, waiting for the one true God.

A tiny woman in Shanghai sat at her window, watching her great-grandchildren play in the courtyard. How fast they were! Ai, once she had been so fast.

She felt it come over her all at once, the gods entering her soul. So it was her time! Almost she felt young again, felt strong . . . that was good. But even if had not been good, when the gods came for you, you went.

One last look at the children, and she was taken to the gods.

Anna Chernov, wide awake in the St Sebastian Infirmary that had become her prison, gave a small gasp. She felt power flow through her, and for a wild moment she thought it was the same force that had powered a life-time of arabesques and jetés, a lifetime ago.

It was not.

This was something outside of herself, separate . . . but it didn't have to be. She could take it in herself, become it, even as it became her. But she held back.

Will there be dancing?

No. Not as she knew it, not the glorious stretch of muscle and thrust of limb and arch of back. Not the creation of beauty through the physical body. No. No dancing.

But there was power here, and she could use that power for another kind of escape, from her useless body and this Infirmary and a life with-out dance. From somewhere distant she head someone cry, "Anna – you can't!" But she could. Anna seized the power, both refusing to join it or to leave it, and bent it onto herself. She was dead before her next breath.

Henry's whole body shuddered. It was here. It was him.

Or not. "It's a choice," he whispered.

On the one hand, everything. All consciousness, woven into the very fabric of space-time itself, just as Wheeler and the rest had glimpsed nearly a hundred years ago. Consciousness at the quantum level, the probability-wave level, the co-evolvee with the universe itself.

On the other hand, the individual Henry Martin Erdmann. If he merged with the uber-consciousness, he would cease to exist as himself, his sepa-rate mind. And his mind was everything to Henry.

He hung suspended for nanoseconds, years, eons. Time itself took on a different character. Half here, half not, Henry knew the power, and what it was, and what humanity was not. He saw the outcome. He had his answer.

"No," he said.

Then he lay again on his sofa with Carrie's arms around him, the other two men illuminated dimly by a thin beam of yellow light, and he was once more mortal and alone.

And himself.

Enough merged. The danger is past. The being is born, and is ship, and is enough.

FIFTEEN

Months to identify all the dead. Years to fully repair all the damage to the world's infrastructure: bridges, buildings, information systems. Decades yet to come, DiBella knew, of speculation about what had actually happened. Not that there weren't theories already. Massive EMP, solar radiation, extrasolar radiation, extrastellar radiation, extraterrestrial attack, global terrorism, Armageddon, tectonic plate activity, genetically engineered viruses. Stupid ideas, all easily disproved, but of course that stopped no one from believing them. The few old people left said almost nothing. Those that did were scarcely believed.

Jake scarcely believed it himself.

He did nothing with the brain scans of Evelyn Krenchnoted and the three others, because there was nothing plausible he could do. They were all dead, anyway. "Only their bodies," Carrie always added. She believed everything Henry Erdmann told her.

Did DiBella believe Henry's ideas? On Tuesdays he did, on Wednesdays not, on Thursdays belief again. There was no replicable proof. It wasn't science. It was . . . something else.

DiBella lived his life. He broke up with James. He visited Henry, long after the study of senior attention patterns was over. He went to dinner with Carrie and Vince Geraci. He was best man at their wedding.

He attended his mother's sixty-fifth birthday party, a lavish shindig organized by his sister in the ballroom of a glitzy downtown hotel. The birthday girl laughed, and kissed the relatives who'd flown in from Chicago, and opened her gifts. As she gyrated on the dance floor with his Uncle Sam, DiBella wondered if she would live long enough to reach eighty.

Wondered how many others in the world would reach eighty.

"It was only because enough of them chose to go that the rest of us lost the emerging power," Henry had said, and DiBella noted that *them* instead of *us*. "If you have only a few atoms of uranium left, you can't reach critical mass."

DiBella would have put it differently: if you have only a few neurons, you don't have a conscious brain. But it came to the same thing in the end.

"If so many hadn't merged, then the consciousness would have had to . . ." Henry didn't finish his sentence, then or ever. But DiBella could guess.

"Come on, boy," Uncle Sam called, "get yourself a partner and dance!"

DiBella shook his head and smiled. He didn't have a partner just now and he didn't want to dance. All the same, old Sam was right. Dancing had a limited shelf life. The sell-by date was already stamped on most human activity. Someday his mother's generation, the largest demographic bulge in history, would turn eighty. And Henry's choice would have to be made yet again.

How would it go next time?

OLD FRIENDS

Garth Nix

New York Times bestselling Australian writer Garth Nix worked as a book publicist, editor, marketing consultant, publicist, and literary agent before launching the bestselling Old Kingdom series, which consists of *Sabriel*, *Lirael: Daughter of the Clayr*, *Abhorsen*, and *The Creature in the Case*. His other books include the Seventh Tower series, consisting of *The Fall, Castle, Aenir, Above the Veil, Into Battle*, and *The Violet Keystone*; the Keys to the Kingdom series, consisting of *Mister Monday, Grim Tuesday, Drowned Wednesday*, and *Sir Thursday*; as well as stand-alone novels such as *The Ragwitch* and *Shade's Children*. His short fiction has been collected in *Across the Wall: Tales of the Old Kingdom and Beyond*. His most recent book is a new novel in the Keys to the Kingdom sequence, *Superior Saturday*. Born in Melbourne, he now lives in Sydney.

In the vivid story that follows, he shows us that old friends can make the most dangerous of enemies.

I'D BEEN LIVING in the city for quite a while, lying low, recovering from an unfortunate jaunt that had turned, in the immortal words of my sometime comrade Hrasvelg, "irredeemably shit-shape".

Though I had almost completely recovered my sight, I still wore a bandage around my eyes. It was made from a rare stuff that I could see through, but it looked like a dense black linen. Similarly, I had regrown my left foot, but I kept up the limp. It gave me an excuse to use the stick, which was, of course, much more than a length of bog oak carved with picaresque scenes of a pedlar's journey.

I had a short lease apartment near the beach, an expensive but necessary accommodation, as I needed both the sunshine that fell into its small living room, and the cool, wet wind from the sea that blew through every open window.

Unfortunately, after the first month, that wind became laden with the smell of rotting weed and as the weeks passed, the stench grew stronger, and the masses of weed that floated just past the breakers began to shift and knit together, despite the efforts of the lifesavers to break up the unsightly, stinking rafts of green.

I knew what was happening, of course. The weed was a manifestation of an old opponent of mine, a slow, cold foe who had finally caught up with me. "Caught" being the operative word, as the weed was just the visible portion of my enemy's activities. A quick examination of almanac and lodestone revealed that all known pathways from this world were denied to me, shut tight by powerful bindings that I could not broach quickly, if at all.

I watched the progress of the weed every morning as I drank my first coffee, usually leaning back in one white plastic chair as I elevated my supposedly injured leg on another. The two chairs were the only furniture in the apartment. I had rigged a hammock above the bath to sleep in.

The day before I adjudged the weed would reach its catalytic potential and spawn servitors, I bought not just my usual black coffee from the café downstairs, but also a triple macchiato that came in a heavy, heat-resistant glass. Because I lived upstairs they always gave me proper cups. The barista who served me, a Japanese guy who worked the espresso machine mornings and surfed all afternoon, put the coffees in a cardboard holder meant for takeaways and said, "Got a visitor today?"

"Not yet," I said. "But I will have shortly. By the way, I wouldn't go surfing here this afternoon . . . or tomorrow."

"Why not?"

"That weed," I replied. "It's toxic. Try another beach."

"How do you know?" he asked as he slid the tray into my waiting fingers. "I mean, you can't . . ."

"I can't see it," I said, as I backed away, turned and started tapping towards the door. "But I can smell it. It's toxic all right. Stay clear."

"OK, thanks. Uh, enjoy the coffee."

I slowly made my way upstairs, and set the coffees down on the floor. My own long black in front of one white chair, and the macchiato at the foot of the other. I wouldn't be resting my leg on the spare chair today.

I had to wait a little while for the breeze to come up, but as it streamed through the room and teased at the hair I should have had cut several weeks before, I spoke.

"Hey, Anax. I bought you a coffee."

The wind swirled around my head, changing direction 270 degrees, blowing out the window it had come in by and in by the window it had been going out. I felt the floor tremble under my feet and experienced a brief dizziness.

Anax, proper name Anaxarte, was one of my oldest friends. We'd grown up together and had served together in two cosmically fucked-up wars, one of which was still slowly bleeding its way to exhaustion in fits and starts, though the original two sides were long out of it.

I hadn't seen Anax for more than thirty years, but we wrote to each other occasionally, and had spoken to each other twice in that time. We talked a lot about meeting up, maybe organizing a fishing expedition with some of the old lads, but it had never come together.

I knew that if he were able to, he would always answer my call. So as the coffee cooled, and the white plastic chair lay vacant, my heart chilled, and I began to grieve. Not for the loss of Anax's help against the enemy, but because another friend had fallen.

I sat in the sunshine for an hour, the warmth a slight comfort against the melancholy that had crept upon me. At the hour's end, the wind shifted again, roiling around me counter-clockwise till it ebbed to a total calm.

Even without the breeze, I could smell the weed. It had a malignant, invasive odour, the kind that creeps through sealed plastic bags and air-tight lids, the smell of decay and corruption.

My options were becoming limited. I took up my stick and went down-stairs once more to the café. The afternoon barista did not know me, though I had seen her often enough through my expansive windows. She did not comment on my order, though I doubt she was often asked for a soy latte with half poured out after it was made, to be topped up again with cold regular milk.

Upstairs, I repeated the summoning, this time with the chill already present, a cold presence of somber expectation lodged somewhere between my heart and ribs.

"Balan," I called softly. "Balan, your luke-warm excuse for a drink is ready."

The wind came up and carried my words away, but as before, there was no reply, no presence in the empty chair. I waited the full hour to be sure, then poured the congealed soy drink down the sink.

I could see the weed clearly in the breakers now. It was almost entirely one huge, long clump that spanned the length of the beach. The lifesavers had given up trying to break it apart with their Jet Skis and Zodiac inflata-bles, and there were two "Beach Closed" signs stuck in the sand, twenty metres apart. Not that anyone was swimming. The beach was almost empty. The reek of the weed had driven away everyone but a sole lifesaver serving out her shift, and a fisherman who was dolefully walking along in search of a weed-free patch of sea.

"Two of my old friends taken," I whispered to the sun, my lips dry, my words heavy. We had never thought much about our futures, not when we were out among the worlds, free. The present was our all, our time the now. None of us knew what lay ahead.

For the third time, I trod my careful way downstairs. There were a dozen people outside the café, a small crowd which parted to allow me pas-sage, with muttered whispers about blindness and letting the sightless man past.

The crowd was watching the weed, while trying not to smell it.

"There, that bit came right out of the water!"

"It kind of looks alive!"

"Must be creating a gas somehow, the decomposition . . ."

". . . check out those huge nodules lifting up . . ."

". . . a gas, methane, maybe. Or hydrogen sulfide . . . nah . . . I'm just guessing. Someone will know . . ."

As I heard the excited comments I knew that I had mistimed my calls for assistance. The weed was very close to catalysis and would very soon spawn its servitors, who would come ashore in search of their target.

I had meant to ask the owner of the café, a short, bearded man who was always called "Mister Jeff" by the staff, if he could give me a glass of brandy, or at a pinch, whisky. A fine Armagnac would be best, but I doubted they'd have any of that. The café had no liquor licence but I knew there was some spirituous alcohol present, purely for Jeff's personal use, since I'd smelled it on his breath often enough.

But as I said, it was too late for that. Palameides might have answered to a double brandy, but I secretly knew that he too must have succumbed. It had been too long since his last missive, and I accounted it one of my failings that I had not been in touch to see where he was, and if all was well with him.

"Someone should do something about that weed," complained a thick-set young man who habitually double-parked his low-slung sports car outside the café around this time. "It really stinks."

"It will be gone by morning," I said. I hadn't meant to use the voice of prophecy, but my words rang out, harsh and bronze, stopping all other conversation.

Everyone looked at me, from inside and outside the café. Even the dog who had been asleep next to one of the outside tables craned his neck to look askance. All was silent, the silence of the embarrassed audience who wished they were elsewhere without knowing why, and were fearful about what was going to come next.

"I am a . . . biologist," I said in my normal tones. "The weed is a known phenomenon. It will disperse overnight."

The silence continued for a few seconds, then normal service resumed, at a lower volume. Even the double-parking guy was more subdued.

I spoke the truth. One way or another, the weed would be gone, and likely enough, I would be gone with it.

As the afternoon progressed, the stench grew much worse. The café was shut, staff and customers retreating to better-smelling climes. Around five o'clock, nearby residents began to leave as well, at the same time the Fire Brigade, the Water Board, the police and several television crews arrived.

An hour after that, only the firefighters remained, and they were wearing breathing apparatus as they went from door to door, checking that everyone had left. Farther afield, way down the northern end of the beach, I could see the television crews interviewing someone who was undoubtedly an expert trying to explain why the noxious odours were so localized, and dissipated so quickly when you got more than three hundred metres from the centre of the beach.

The "DO NOT CROSS" tapes with the biohazard trefoils got rolled out just before dusk, across the street about eighty metres up from my apartment. The firefighters had knocked at my door and called out, gruff voices muffled by masks, but I had not answered. They could probably have seen me from the beach, but no one was heading closer to the smell, however well-protected they were. The sea was bubbling and frothing with noxious vapours, and weedy nodules the size of restaurant refrigerators were bobbing up and down upon the waves. After a while the nodules began to detach from the main mass of weed and the waves carried them in like lost boards, tendrils of weed trailing behind them, reminiscent of Velcro-failed leg-ropes.

I watched the nodules as the sun set behind the city, mentally mapping where they were drifting ashore. When the sun was completely gone, the street lights and the high lamps that usually lit the beach didn't come on, but that didn't matter much to me. Darkness wasn't so much my friend as a close relative. The lack of artificial light caused a commotion among the HAZMAT teams though, particularly when they couldn't get their portable generators and floodlights to work, and the one engine they sent down the street choked and stalled before it had even pulled away from the curb.

I had counted thirteen nodules, but more could be out in the weed mass, or so low in the water I'd missed them. My enemy was not underestimating me, or had presumed I would be able to call upon assistance.

I had presumed I would be able to call upon assistance, a foolish presumption built upon old camaraderie, of long-ago dangers shared, of the maintenance of a continuum. I had not thought that my friends, having survived our two wars, could have had a full stop put to their existence in more mundane environments. For surely they must have been victims of some foe, as the transformations we endured in our training rendered termination by illness or accident extraordinarily unlikely.

"Anax, Balan, Palameides," I whispered. By now there would be three new death-trees laid out in a nice row in the arborial necropolis, with those nameplates at their feet,. There was probably a Nethinim carving my name onto a plaque right now, and readying a sapling. They always knew beforehand, the carriers of water and hewers of wood.

I dismissed this gloomy thought. If my time had come, it had come, but I would not wait in a dark apartment, to acquiesce to my fate like a senescent king grown too tired and toothless to act against his assassins.

I took off the blindfold and tied it around my neck, returning it to its original use as a scarf. It became my only item of apparel, as I shucked white cotton trousers, white T-shirt and underwear.

The stick I gently broke across my knee, sliding the two lengths of wood apart to reveal the sword within. I took the weapon up and made the traditional salute towards my enemies on the beach.

Courtesies complete, I shaded my skin, hair and eyes dark, a green almost heavy enough to match the blackness of the night, and with a moment's concentration grew a defensive layer of young bark, being careful not to over-do it, while overlaying the sheaths in such a way that it would not limit my movement. Novices often made the mistake of armouring up too much, and found themselves extraordinarily tough but essentially sessile. I had not made that mistake since my distant youth.

The wind lifted a little, and the stink of the weed changed, becoming more fragrant. I heard thirteen soft popping noises come from the beach, and knew that the nodules were opening.

There was little point in dragging things out, so I simply walked down the street to the beach, pausing to bid a silent farewell to the café. Their coffee had been quite good.

I paused at the promenade railing, near the block of stone surmounted by the bronze mermaid, and looked across the beach. There was a little starlight, though no moon, and I thought both sea and sand had never looked prettier. The humans should turn the lights off more often, though even then they would not see the way I saw.

The thirteen had emerged from their nodules, or perhaps I should call them pods. Now that I saw them clearly, I knew I had even less chance than I'd thought. I had expected the blocky, bad imitations of human women that looked like Bulgarian weightlifters, armed with slow, two-handed axes that, though devastating when they hit, were fairly unlikely to do so provided I didn't make a mistake.

But my enemy had sent a much superior force, testament I suppose to the number of times I had defeated or evaded previous attempts to curtail my activities. This time they were indeed what long-gone inhabitants of this world had called Valkyries: female human in form, tall, long-limbed and very fast, and the sensing tendrils that splayed back from their heads could easily be mistaken for a wing'd helmet, as their rust-coloured exoskeleton extrusions could look like armour.

They lifted their hatchets – twenty-six of them, as they held one in each hand – when they saw me, and offered the salute. I returned the greeting and waited for the eldest of them (by a matter of seconds, most like) to offer up the obligatory statement, which also served as a disclaimer, thrust all liability for collateral damage upon me and usually offered a chance to surrender.

"Skrymir, renegade, oathbreaker and outcast!"

I inclined my head.

"Called to return eight times; sent for, six times."

Had it been so many? I'd lost count. Too many years, across too many worlds.

"Surrender your sword!"

I shook my head, and the Valkyries attacked before I could even straighten my neck, running full-tilt at the seawall that bordered the promenade. Six stopped short before the wall and six leaped upon their backs to vault the railing, while the last, the senior, stood behind in a position of command.

I lopped two heads as I fell back, the valkyries concerned momentarily confused as their major sensory apparatus went bouncing back down to the sand. As per their imprinting, they stopped still and if it had not been for the others I could have felled them then. But the others were there, attacking me from all sides as I danced and spun back to the road, my sword meeting the helves of their hatchets, nicking at their fibrous flesh, but their weapons in turn carved long splinters from my body.

If they could surround me, I would be done for, so I fought as I had not fought since the wars. I twisted and leaped and slid under parked cars and over them, around rubbish bins and flagpoles, changing sword-hand, kicking, butting, deploying every trick and secret that I knew.

It was not enough. A skilled and vicious blow caught my knee as I took off another head, and in the second I was down a dozen other blows put paid to my legs. I rolled and writhed away, but it was to no avail. The valkyries pinned me down and began to chop away.

The last memory I have from that expression of myself was of the starry sky, the sound of the surf a deeper counterpoint to the thud of axework, and the blessed smell of fresh salt air, the stench of that particular rotten weed gone forever.

I cannot smell anything where I am now, nor see. I can sense light and shade, the movement of air, the welcome sensation of moisture on my extremities, whether above or below the earth.

Neither can I speak, save in a very limited fashion, the conveyance of some slight meaning without words.

But I am not alone. Palameides is here, and Balan, and Anax too. They have grown tall, and overshadow me, but this will not last. I will grow mighty once more, and one day They will have need of us again . . . and then, as we whisper, tapping with our roots, signalling with the rustle of our leaves, then our hearts will bud new travellers, and we shall go forth to do the bidding of our masters, and perhaps, for as long as we can, we four friends shall once again be free.

THE RAY-GUN:
A LOVE STORY

James Alan Gardner

Sometimes your life can turn on the simplest of things, the most seemingly trival of decisions. Such as, do you happen to be looking down as you pass a certain spot? And if you are, and if you see something on the ground, do you pick it up?

James Alan Gardner has made many fiction sales to *The Magazine of Fantasy & Science Fiction*, *Asimov's Science Fiction*, *Amazing*, *Tesseracts*, *On Spec*, *Northern Stars*, and other markets. His books include the SF novels *Expendable*, *Commitment Hour*, *Vigilant*, *Hunted*, *Ascending*, and *Trapped*. His most recent novel is *Radiant*. His short fiction has been collected in *Gravity Wells: Speculative Fiction Stories*.

THIS IS A story about a ray-gun. The ray-gun will not be explained except to say, "It shoots rays."

They are dangerous rays. If they hit you in the arm, it withers. If they hit you in the face, you go blind. If they hit you in the heart, you die. These things must be true, or else it would not be a ray-gun. But it is.

Ray-guns come from space. This one came from the captain of an alien starship passing through our solar system. The ship stopped to scoop up hydrogen from the atmosphere of Jupiter. During this refueling process, the crew mutinied for reasons we cannot comprehend. We will never comprehend aliens. If someone spent a month explaining alien thoughts to us, we'd think we understood but we wouldn't. Our brains only know how to be human.

Although alien thoughts are beyond us, alien actions may be easy to grasp. We can understand the "what" if not the "why". If we saw what happened inside the alien vessel, we would recognize that the crew tried to take the captain's ray-gun and kill him.

There was a fight. The ray-gun went off many times. The starship exploded.

All this happened many centuries ago, before telescopes. The people of Earth still wore animal skins. They only knew Jupiter as a dot in the sky. When the starship exploded, the dot got a tiny bit brighter, then returned to normal. No one on Earth noticed – not even the shamans who thought dots in the sky were important.

The ray-gun survived the explosion. A ray-gun must be resilient, or else it is not a ray-gun. The explosion hurled the ray-gun away from Jupiter and out into open space.

After thousands of years, the ray-gun reached Earth. It fell from the sky like a meteor; it grew hot enough to glow, but it didn't burn up.

The ray-gun fell at night during a blizzard. Travelling thousands of miles an hour, the ray-gun plunged deep into snow-covered woods. The snow melted so quickly that it burst into steam.

The blizzard continued, unaffected. Some things can't be harmed, even by ray-guns.

Unthinking snowflakes drifted down. If they touched the ray-gun's surface they vaporized, stealing heat from the weapon. Heat also radiated outward, melting snow nearby on the ground. Melt-water flowed into the shallow crater made by the ray-gun's impact. Water and snow cooled the weapon until all excess temperature had dissipated. A million more snowflakes heaped over the crater, hiding the ray-gun till spring.

In March, the gun was found by a boy named Jack. He was fourteen years old and walking through the woods after school. He walked slowly, brooding about his lack of popularity. Jack despised popular students and had no interest in anything they did. Even so, he envied them. They didn't appear to be lonely.

Jack wished he had a girlfriend. He wished he were important. He wished he knew what to do with his life. Instead, he walked alone in the woods on the edge of town.

The woods were not wild or isolated. They were crisscrossed with trails made by children playing hide-and-seek. But in spring, the trails were muddy; most people stayed away. Jack soon worried more about how to avoid shoe-sucking mud than about the unfairness of the world. He took wide detours around mucky patches, thrashing through brush that was crisp from winter.

Stalks broke as he passed. Burrs stuck to his jacket. He got farther and farther from the usual paths, hoping he'd find a way out by blundering forward rather than swallowing his pride and retreating.

In this way, Jack reached the spot where the ray-gun had landed. He saw the crater it had made. He found the ray-gun itself.

The gun seized Jack's attention, but he didn't know what it was. Its design was too alien to be recognized as a weapon. Its metal was blackened but not black, as if it had once been another colour but had finished that phase of its existence. Its pistol-butt was bulbous, the size of a tennis ball. Its barrel, as long as Jack's hand, was straight but its surface had dozens of nubs like a briarwood cane. The gun's trigger was a protruding blister you squeezed till it popped. A hard metal cap could slide over the blister to prevent the gun from firing accidentally, but the safety was off; it had been off for centuries, ever since the fight on the starship.

The alien captain who once owned the weapon might have considered it beautiful, but to human eyes, the gun resembled a dirty wet stick with a lump on one end. Jack might have walked by without giving it a second look if it hadn't been lying in a scorched crater. But it was.

The crater was two paces across and barren of plant life. The vegetation had burned in the heat of the ray-gun's fall. Soon enough, new spring growth would sprout, making the crater less obvious. At present though, the ray-gun stood out on the charred earth like a snake in an empty birdbath.

Jack picked up the gun. Though it looked like briarwood, it was cold like metal. It felt solid: not heavy, but substantial. It had the heft of a well-made object. Jack turned the gun in his hands, examining it from every angle. When he looked down the muzzle, he saw a crystal lens cut into hundreds of facets. Jack poked it with his baby-finger, thinking the lens was a piece of glass that someone had jammed inside. He had the idea this might be a toy – perhaps a squirt-gun dropped by a careless child. If so, it had to be the most expensive toy Jack had ever seen. The gun's barrel and its lens were so perfectly machined that no one could mistake the craftsmanship.

Jack continued to poke at the weapon until the inevitable happened: he pressed the trigger blister. The ray-gun went off.

It might have been fatal, but by chance Jack was holding the gun aimed away from himself. A ray shot out of the gun's muzzle and blasted through a maple tree ten paces away. The ray made no sound, and although Jack had seen it clearly, he couldn't say what the ray's colour had been. It had no colour; it was simply a presence, like wind-chill or gravity. Yet Jack was sure he'd seen a force emanate from the muzzle and strike the tree.

Though the ray can't be described, its effect was plain. A circular hole appeared in the maple tree's trunk where bark and wood disintegrated into sizzling plasma. The plasma expanded at high speed and pressure, blowing apart what remained of the surrounding trunk. The ray made no sound, but the explosion did. Shocked chunks of wood and boiling maple sap flew outward, obliterating a cross-section of the tree. The lower part of the trunk and the roots were still there; so were the upper part and branches. In between was a gap, filled with hot escaping gases.

The unsupported part of the maple fell. It toppled ponderously backwards. The maple crashed onto the trees behind, its winter-bare branches snagging theirs. To Jack, it seemed that the forest had stopped the maple's fall, like soldiers catching an injured companion before he hit the ground.

Jack still held the gun. He gazed at it in wonder. His mind couldn't grasp what had happened.

He didn't drop the gun in fear. He didn't try to fire it again. He simply stared.

It was a ray-gun. It would never be anything else.

Jack wondered where the weapon had come from. Had aliens visited these woods? Or was the gun created by a secret government project? Did the gun's owner want it back? Was he, she or it searching the woods right now?

Jack was tempted to put the gun back into the crater, then run before the owner showed up. But was there really an owner nearby? The crater suggested that the gun had fallen from space. Jack had seen photos of meteor impact craters; this wasn't exactly the same, but it had a similar look.

Jack turned his eyes upward. He saw a mundane after-school sky. It had no UFOs. Jack felt embarrassed for even looking.

He examined the crater again. If Jack left the gun here, and the owner never retrieved it, sooner or later the weapon would be found by someone else – probably by children playing in the woods. They might shoot each other by accident. If this were an ordinary gun, Jack would never leave it lying in a place like this. He'd take the gun home, tell his parents, and they'd turn it over to the police.

Should he do the same for *this* gun? No. He didn't want to.

But he didn't know what he wanted to do instead. Questions buzzed through his mind, starting with, "What should I do?" then moving on to, "Am I in danger?" and, "Do aliens really exist?"

After a while, he found himself wondering, "Exactly how much can the gun blow up?" That question made him smile.

Jack decided he wouldn't tell anyone about the gun – not now and maybe not ever. He would take it home and hide it where it wouldn't be found, but where it would be available if trouble came. What kind of trouble? Aliens . . . spies . . . supervillains . . . who knew? If ray-guns were real, was anything impossible?

On the walk back home, Jack was so distracted by "What ifs?" that he nearly got hit by a car. He had reached the road that separated the woods from neighbouring houses. Like most roads in that part of Jack's small town, it didn't get much traffic. Jack stepped out from the trees and suddenly a sports-car whizzed past him, only two steps away. Jack staggered back; the driver leaned on the horn; Jack hit his shoulder on an oak tree; then the incident was over, except for belated adrenaline.

For a full minute afterward, Jack leaned against the oak and felt his heart pound. As close calls go, this one wasn't too bad: Jack hadn't really been near enough to the road to get hit. Still, Jack needed quite a while to calm down. How stupid would it be to die in an accident on the day he'd found something miraculous?

Jack ought to have been watching for trouble. What if the threat had been a bug-eyed monster instead of a car? Jack should have been alert and prepared. In his mind's eye he imagined the incident again, only this time he casually somersaulted to safety rather than stumbling into a tree. That's how you're supposed to cheat death if you're carrying a ray-gun: with cool heroic flair.

But Jack couldn't do somersaults. He said to himself, *I'm Peter Parker, not Spider-Man.*

On the other hand, Jack *had* just acquired great power. And great responsibility. Like Peter Parker, Jack had to keep his power secret, for fear of tragic consequences. In Jack's case, maybe aliens would come for him. Maybe spies or government agents would kidnap him and his family. No matter how farfetched those things seemed, the existence of a ray-gun proved the world wasn't tame.

That night, Jack debated what to do with the gun. He pictured himself shooting terrorists and gang lords. If he rid the world of scum, pretty girls might admire him. But as soon as Jack imagined himself storming into a terrorist stronghold, he realized he'd get killed almost immediately. The ray-gun provided awesome firepower, but no defense at all. Besides if Jack had found an ordinary gun in the forest, he never would have dreamed of running around murdering bad guys. Why should a ray-gun be different?

But it *was* different. Jack couldn't put the difference into words, but it was as real as the weapon's solid weight in his hands. The ray-gun changed everything. A world that contained a ray-gun might also contain flying saucers, beautiful secret agents . . . and heroes.

Heroes who could somersault away from oncoming sports-cars. Heroes who would cope with any danger. Heroes who *deserved* to have a ray-gun.

When he was young, Jack had taken for granted he'd become a hero: brave, skilled and important. Somehow he'd lost that belief. He'd let himself settle for being ordinary. But now he wasn't ordinary: he had a ray-gun.

He had to live up to it. Jack had to be ready for bug-eyed monsters and giant robots. These were no longer childish daydreams; they were real possibilities in a world where ray-guns existed. Jack could picture himself running through town, blasting aliens and saving the planet.

Such thoughts made sense when Jack held the ray-gun in his hands – as if the gun planted fantasies in his mind. The feel of the gun filled Jack with ambition.

All weapons have a sense of purpose.

Jack practised with the gun as often as he could. To avoid being seen, he rode his bike to a tract of land in the country: twenty acres owned by Jack's Great-Uncle Ron. No one went there but Jack. Uncle Ron had once intended to build a house on the property, but that had never happened. Now Ron was in a nursing home. Jack's family intended to sell the land once the old man died, but Ron was healthy for someone in his nineties. Until Uncle Ron's health ran out, Jack had the place to himself.

The tract was undeveloped – raw forest, not a woods where children played. In the middle lay a pond, completely hidden by trees. Jack would float sticks in the pond and shoot them with the gun.

If he missed, the water boiled. If he didn't, the sticks were destroyed. Sometimes they erupted in fire. Sometimes they burst with a bang but no flame. Sometimes they simply vanished. Jack couldn't tell if he was doing something subtly different to get each effect, or if the ray-gun changed modes on its own. Perhaps it had a computer which analysed the target and chose the most lethal attack. Perhaps the attacks were always the same, but differences in the sticks made for different results. Jack didn't know. But as spring led to summer, he became a better shot. By autumn, he'd begun throwing sticks into the air and trying to vaporize them before they reached the ground.

During this time, Jack grew stronger. Long bike rides to the pond helped his legs and his stamina. In addition, he exercised with fitness equipment his parents had bought but never used. If monsters ever came, Jack couldn't afford to be weak – heroes had to climb fences and break down doors. They had to balance on rooftops and hang by their fingers from cliffs. They had to run fast enough to save the girl.

Jack pumped iron and ran every day. As he did so, he imagined dodging bullets and tentacles. When he felt like giving up, he cradled the ray-gun in his hands. It gave him the strength to persevere.

Before the ray-gun, Jack had seen himself as just another teenager; his life didn't make sense. But the gun made Jack a hero who might be needed to save the Earth. It clarified *everything*. Sore muscles didn't matter. Watching TV was a waste. If you let down your guard, that's when the monsters came.

When he wasn't exercising, Jack studied science. That was another part of being a hero. He sometimes dreamed he'd analyse the ray-gun, discovering how it worked and giving humans amazing new technology. At other times, he didn't want to understand the gun at all. He liked its mystery. Besides, there was no guarantee Jack would ever understand how the gun worked. Perhaps human science wouldn't progress far enough in Jack's lifetime. Perhaps Jack himself wouldn't have the brains to figure it out.

But he had enough brains for high school. He did well; he was motivated. He had to hold back to avoid attracting attention. When his gym teacher told him he should go out for track, Jack ran slower and pretended to get out of breath.

Spider-Man had to do the same.

Two years later, in geography class, a girl named Kirsten gave Jack a daisy. She said the daisy was good luck and he should make a wish.

Even a sixteen-year-old boy couldn't misconstrue such a hint. Despite awkwardness and foot-dragging, Jack soon had a girlfriend.

Kirsten was quiet but pretty. She played guitar. She wrote poems. She'd never had a boyfriend but she knew how to kiss. These were all good things. Jack wondered if he should tell her about the ray-gun.

Until Kirsten, Jack's only knowledge of girls came from his big sister, Rachel. Rachel was seventeen and incapable of keeping a secret. She talked with her friends about everything and was too slapdash to hide private things well. Jack didn't snoop through his sister's possessions, but when Rachel left her bedroom door ajar with empty cigarette packs tumbling out of the garbage can, who wouldn't notice? When she gossiped on the phone about sex with her boyfriend, who couldn't overhear? Jack didn't want to listen, but Rachel never lowered her voice. The things Jack heard made him queasy – about his sister, and girls in general.

If he showed Kirsten the ray-gun, would she tell her friends? Jack wanted to believe she wasn't that kind of girl, but he didn't know how many kinds of girl there were. He just knew that the ray-gun was too important for him to take chances. Changing the status quo wasn't worth the risk.

Yet the status quo changed anyway. The more time Jack spent with Kirsten, the less he had for shooting practice and other aspects of hero-dom. He felt guilty for skimping on crisis preparation; but when he went to the pond or spent a night reading science, he felt guilty for skimping on Kirsten. Jack would tell her he couldn't come over to do homework and when she asked why, he'd have to make up excuses. He felt he was treating her like an enemy spy: holding her at arm's length as if she were some femme fatale who was tempting him to betray state secrets. He hated not trusting her.

Despite this wall between them, Kirsten became Jack's lens on the world. If anything interesting happened, Jack didn't experience it directly; some portion of his mind stood back, enjoying the anticipation of having something to tell Kirsten about the next time they met. Whatever he saw, he wanted her to see it too. Whenever Jack heard a joke, even before he started laughing, he pictured himself repeating it to Kirsten.

Inevitably, Jack asked himself what she'd think of his hero-dom. Would she be impressed? Would she throw her arms around him and say he was even more wonderful than she'd thought? Or would she get that look on her face, the one when she heard bad poetry? Would she think he was an immature geek who'd read too many comic books and was pursuing some juvenile fantasy? How could anyone believe hostile aliens might appear in the sky? And if aliens did show up, how delusional was it that a teenage boy might make a difference, even if he owned a ray-gun and could do a hundred push-ups without stopping?

For weeks, Jack agonized: to tell or not to tell. Was Kirsten worthy, or just a copy of Jack's sister? Was Jack himself worthy, or just a foolish boy?

One Saturday in May, Jack and Kirsten went biking. Jack led her to the pond where he practiced with the gun. He hadn't yet decided what he'd do when they got there, but Jack couldn't just *tell* Kirsten about the ray-gun. She'd never believe it was real unless she saw the rays in action. But so much could go wrong. Jack was terrified of giving away his deepest secret. He was afraid that when he saw hero-dom through Kirsten's eyes, he'd realize it was silly.

At the pond, Jack felt so nervous he could hardly speak. He babbled about the warm weather . . . a patch of mushrooms . . . a crow cawing in a tree. He talked about everything except what was on his mind.

Kirsten misinterpreted his anxiety. She thought she knew why Jack had brought her to this secluded spot. After a while, she decided he needed encouragement, so she took off her shirt and her bra.

It was the wrong thing to do. Jack hadn't meant this outing to be a test . . . but it was, and Kirsten had failed.

Jack took off his own shirt and wrapped his arms around her, chest touching breasts for the first time. He discovered it was possible to be excited and disappointed at the same time.

Jack and Kirsten made out on a patch of hard dirt. It was the first time they'd been alone with no risk of interruption. They kept their pants on, but they knew they could go farther: as far as there was. No one in the world would stop them from whatever they chose to do. Jack and Kirsten felt light in their skins – open and dizzy with possibilities.

Yet for Jack, it was all a mistake: one that couldn't be reversed. Now he'd never tell Kirsten about the ray-gun. He'd missed his chance because she'd acted the way Jack's sister would have acted. Kirsten had been thinking like a girl and she'd ruined things forever.

Jack hated the way he felt: all angry and resentful. He really liked Kirsten. He liked making out, and couldn't wait till the next time. He refused to be a guy who dumped a girl as soon as she let him touch her breasts. But he was now shut off from her and he had no idea how to get over that.

In the following months, Jack grew guiltier: he was treating Kirsten as if she were good enough for sex but not good enough to be told about the most important thing in his life. As for Kirsten, every day made her more unhappy: she felt Jack blaming her for something but she didn't know what she'd done. When they got together, they went straight to fondling and more as soon as possible. If they tried to talk, they didn't know what to say.

In August, Kirsten left to spend three weeks with her grandparents on Vancouver Island. Neither she nor Jack missed each other. They didn't even miss the sex. It was a relief to be apart. When Kirsten got back, they went for a walk and a confused conversation. Both produced excuses for why they couldn't stay together. The excuses didn't make sense, but neither Jack nor Kirsten noticed – they were too ashamed to pay attention to what they were saying. They both felt like failures. They'd thought their love would last forever, and now it was ending sordidly.

When the lying was over, Jack went for a run. He ran in a mental blur. His mind didn't clear until he found himself at the pond.

Night was drawing in. He thought of all the things he'd done with Kirsten on the shore and in the water. After that first time, they'd come here a lot; it was private. Because of Kirsten, this wasn't the same pond as when Jack had first begun to practice with the ray-gun. Jack wasn't the same boy. He and the pond now carried histories.

Jack could feel himself balanced on the edge of quitting. He'd turned seventeen. One more year of high school, then he'd go away to university. He realized he no longer believed in the imminent arrival of aliens, nor could he see himself as some great hero saving the world.

Jack knew he wasn't a hero. He'd used a nice girl for sex, then lied to get rid of her.

He felt like crap. But blasting the shit out of sticks made him feel a little better. The ray-gun still had its uses, even if shooting aliens wasn't one of them.

The next day Jack did more blasting. He pumped iron. He got science books out of the library. Without Kirsten at his side several hours a day, he had time to fill, and emptiness. By the first day of the new school year, Jack was back to his full hero-dom program. He no longer deceived himself that he was preparing for battle, but the program gave him something to do: a purpose, a release, and a penance.

So that was Jack's passage into manhood. He was dishonest with the girl he loved.

Manhood means learning who you are.

In his last year of high school, Jack went out with other girls but he was past the all-or-nothingness of First Love. He could have casual fun; he could approach sex with perspective. "Monumental and life-changing" had been tempered to "pleasant and exciting". Jack didn't take his girl-friends for granted, but they were people, not objects of worship. He was never tempted to tell any of them about the gun.

When he left town for university, Jack majored in Engineering Physics. He hadn't decided whether he'd ever analyze the ray-gun's inner workings, but he couldn't imagine taking courses that were irrelevant to the weapon. The ray-gun was the central fact of Jack's life. Even if he wasn't a hero, he was set apart from other people by this evidence that aliens existed.

During freshman year, Jack lived in an on-campus dormitory. Hiding the ray-gun from his roommate would have been impossible. Jack left the weapon at home, hidden near the pond. In sophomore year, Jack rented an apartment off campus. Now he could keep the ray-gun with him. He didn't like leaving it untended.

Jack persuaded a lab assistant to let him borrow a Geiger counter. The ray-gun emitted no radioactivity at all. Objects blasted by the gun showed no significant radioactivity either. Over time, Jack borrowed other equipment, or took blast debris to the lab so he could conduct tests when no one was around. He found nothing that explained how the ray-gun worked.

The winter before Jack graduated, Great-Uncle Ron finally died. In his will, the old man left his twenty acres of forest to Jack. Uncle Ron had found out that Jack liked to visit the pond. "I told him," said big sister Rachel. "Do you think I didn't know where you and Kirsten went?"

Jack had to laugh – uncomfortably. He was embarrassed to discover he couldn't keep secrets any better than his sister.

Jack's father offered to help him sell the land to pay for his education. The offer was polite, not pressing. Uncle Ron had doled out so much cash in his will that Jack's family was now well off. When Jack said he'd rather hold on to the property "until the market improves", no one objected.

After getting his bachelor's degree, Jack continued on to grad school: first his master's, then his Ph.D. In one of his courses, he met Deana, working toward her own doctorate – in Electrical Engineering rather than Engineering Physics.

The two programs shared several seminars, but considered themselves rivals. Engineering Physics students pretended that Electrical Engineers weren't smart enough to understand abstract principles. Electrical Engineers pretended that Engineering Physics students were pie-in-the-sky dreamers whose theories were always wrong until real Engineers fixed them. Choosing to sit side by side, Jack and Deana teased each other every class. Within months, Deana moved into Jack's apartment.

Deana was small but physical. She told Jack she'd been drawn to him because he was the only man in their class who lifted weights. When Deana was young, she'd been a competitive swimmer – "*Very* competitive," she said – but her adolescent growth spurt had never arrived and she was eventually outmatched by girls with longer limbs. Deana had quit the competition circuit, but she hadn't quit swimming nor had she lost the drive to be one up on those around her. She saw most things as contests, including her relationship with Jack. Deana was not beyond cheating if it gave her an edge.

In the apartment they now shared, Jack thought he'd hidden the ray-gun so well that Deana wouldn't find it. He didn't suspect that when he wasn't home she went through his things. She couldn't stand the thought that Jack might have secrets from her.

He returned one day to find the gun on the kitchen table. Deana was poking at it. Jack wanted to yell, "Leave it alone!" but he was so choked with anger he couldn't speak.

Deana's hand was close to the trigger. The safety was off and the muzzle pointed in Jack's direction. He threw himself to the floor.

Nothing happened. Deana was so surprised by Jack's sudden move that she jerked her hand away from the gun. "What the hell are you doing?"

Jack got to his feet. "I could ask you the same question."

"I found this. I wondered what it was."

Jack knew she didn't "find" the gun. It had been buried under old notebooks inside a box at the back of a closet. Jack expected that Deana would invent some excuse for why she'd been digging into Jack's private possessions, but the excuse wouldn't be worth believing.

What infuriated Jack most was that he'd actually been thinking of showing Deana the gun. She was a very very good engineer; Jack had dreamed that together, he and she might discover how the gun worked. Of all the women Jack had known, Deana was the first he'd asked to move in with him. She was strong and she was smart. She might understand the gun. The time had never been right to tell her the truth – Jack was still getting to know her and he needed to be absolutely sure – but Jack had dreamed . . .

And now, like Kirsten at the pond, Deana had ruined everything. Jack felt so violated he could barely stand to look at the woman. He wanted to throw her out of the apartment . . . but that would draw too much attention to the gun. He couldn't let Deana think the gun was important.

She was still staring at him, waiting for an explanation. "That's just something from my Great-Uncle Ron," Jack said. "An African good-luck charm. Or Indonesian. I forget. Uncle Ron travelled a lot." Actually, Ron sold insurance and seldom left the town where he was born. Jack picked up the gun from the table, trying to do so calmly rather than protectively. "I wish you hadn't touched this. It's old and fragile."

"It felt pretty solid to me."

"Solid but still breakable."

"Why did you dive to the floor?"

"Just silly superstition. It's bad luck to have this end point toward you." Jack gestured toward the muzzle. "And it's good luck to be on this end." He gestured toward the butt, then tried to make a joke. "Like there's a Maxwell demon in the middle, batting bad luck one way and good luck the other."

"You believe that crap?" Deana asked. She was an engineer. She went out of her way to disbelieve crap.

"Of course, I don't believe it," Jack said. "But why ask for trouble?"

He took the gun back to the closet. Deana followed. As Jack returned the gun to its box, Deana said she'd been going through Jack's notes in search of anything he had on partial differential equations. Jack nearly let her get away with the lie; he usually let the women in his life get away with almost anything. But he realized he didn't want Deana in his life anymore. Whatever connection she and he had once felt, it was cut off the moment he saw her with the ray-gun.

Jack accused her of invading his privacy. Deana said he was paranoid. The argument grew heated. Out of habit, Jack almost backed down several times, but he stopped himself. He didn't want Deana under the same roof as the ray-gun. His feelings were partly irrational possessiveness, but also justifiable caution. If Deana got the gun and accidentally fired it, the results might be disastrous.

Jack and Deana continued to argue: right there in the closet within inches of the ray-gun. The gun lay in its box, like a child at the feet of parents fighting over custody. The ray-gun did nothing, as if it didn't care who won.

Eventually, unforgivable words were spoken. Deana said she'd move out as soon as possible. She left to stay the night with a friend.

The moment she was gone, Jack moved the gun. Deana still had a key to the apartment – she needed it until she could pack her things – and Jack was certain she'd try to grab the weapon as soon as he was busy elsewhere. The ray-gun was now a prize in a contest, and Deana never backed down.

Jack took the weapon to the university. He worked as an assistant for his Ph.D. supervisor, and he'd been given a locker in the supervisor's lab. The locker wasn't Fort Knox but leaving the gun there was better than leaving it in the apartment. The more Jack thought about Deana, the more he saw her as prying and obsessive, grasping for dominance. He didn't know what he'd ever seen in her.

The next morning, he wondered if he had overreacted. Was he demonizing his ex like a sitcom cliché? If she was so egotistic, why hadn't he noticed before? Jack had no good answer. He decided he didn't need one. Unlike when he broke up with Kirsten, Jack felt no guilt this time. The sooner Deana was gone, the happier he'd be.

In a few days, Deana called to say she'd found a new place to live. She and Jack arranged a time for her to pick up her belongings. Jack didn't want to be there while she moved out; he couldn't stand seeing her in the apartment again. Instead, Jack went back to his home town for a long weekend with his family.

It was lucky he did. Jack left Friday afternoon and didn't get back to the university until Monday night. The police were waiting for him. Deana had disappeared late Saturday.

She'd talked to friends on Saturday afternoon. She'd made arrangements for Sunday brunch but hadn't shown up. No one had seen her since.

As the ex-boyfriend, Jack was a prime suspect. But his alibi was solid: his home town was hundreds of miles from the university, and his family could testify he'd been there the whole time. Jack couldn't possibly have sneaked back to the university, made Deana disappear, and raced back home.

Grudgingly, the police let Jack off the hook. They decided Deana must have been depressed by the break-up of the relationship. She might have run off so she wouldn't have to see Jack around the university. She might even have committed suicide.

Jack suspected otherwise. As soon as the police let him go, he went to his supervisor's lab. His locker had been pried open. The ray-gun lay on a nearby lab bench.

Jack could easily envision what happened. While moving out her things, Deana searched for the ray-gun. She hadn't found it in the apartment. She knew Jack had a locker in the lab and she'd guessed he'd stashed the weapon there. She broke open the locker to get the gun. She'd examined it and perhaps tried to take it apart. The gun went off.

Now Deana was gone. Not even a smudge on the floor. The ray-gun lay on the lab bench as guiltless as a stone. Jack was the only one with a conscience.

He suffered for weeks. Jack wondered how he could feel so bad about a woman who'd made him furious. But he knew the source of his guilt: while he and Deana were arguing in the closet, Jack had imagined vaporizing her with the gun. He was far too decent to shoot her for real, but the thought had crossed his mind. If Deana simply vanished, Jack wouldn't have to worry about what she might do. The ray-gun had made that thought come true, as if it had read Jack's mind.

Jack told himself the notion was ridiculous. The gun wasn't some genie who granted Jack's unspoken wishes. What happened to Deana came purely from her own bad luck and inquisitiveness.

Still, Jack felt like a murderer. After all this time, Jack realized the ray-gun was too dangerous to keep. As long as Jack had it, he'd be forced to live alone: never marrying, never having children, never trusting the gun around other people. And even if Jack became a recluse, accidents could happen. Someone else might die. It would be Jack's fault.

He wondered why he'd never had this thought before. Jack suddenly saw himself as one of those people who own a vicious attack dog. People like that always claimed they could keep the dog under control. How often did they end up on the evening news? How often did children get bitten, maimed or killed?

Some dogs are tragedies waiting to happen. The ray-gun was too. It would keep slipping off its leash until it was destroyed. Twelve years after finding the gun, Jack realized he finally had a heroic mission: to get rid of the weapon that made him a hero in the first place.

I'm not Spider-Man, he thought, *I'm Frodo*.

But how could Jack destroy something that had survived so much? The gun hadn't frozen in the cold of outer space; it hadn't burned up as it plunged through Earth's atmosphere; it hadn't broken when it hit the ground at terminal velocity. If the gun could endure such punishment, extreme measures would be needed to lay it to rest.

Jack imagined putting the gun into a blast furnace. But what if the weapon went off? What if it shot out the side of the furnace? The furnace itself could explode. That would be a disaster. Other means of destruction had similar problems. Crushing the gun in a hydraulic press . . . what if the gun shot a hole in the press, sending pieces of equipment flying in all directions? Immersing the gun in acid . . . what if the gun went off and splashed acid over everything? Slicing into the gun with a laser . . . Jack didn't know what powered the gun, but obviously it contained vast energy. Destabilizing that energy might cause an explosion, a radiation leak, or some even greater catastrophe. Who knew what might happen if you tampered with alien technology?

And what if the gun could protect itself? Over the years, Jack had read every ray-gun story he could find. In some stories, such weapons had built-in computers. They had enough artificial intelligence to assess their situations. If they didn't like what was happening, they took action. What if Jack's gun was similar? What if attempts to destroy the weapon induced it to fight back? What if the ray-gun got mad?

Jack decided the only safe plan was to drop the gun into an ocean – the deeper the better. Even then, Jack feared the gun would somehow make its way back to shore. He hoped that the weapon would take years or even centuries to return, by which time humanity might be scientifically equipped to deal with the ray-gun's power.

Jack's plan had one weakness: both the university and Jack's home town were far from the sea. Jack didn't know anyone with an ocean-going boat suitable for dumping objects into deep water. He'd just have to drive to the coast and see if he could rent something.

But not until summer. Jack was in the final stages of his Ph.D. and didn't have time to leave the university for an extended trip. As a temporary measure, Jack moved the ray-gun back to the pond. He buried the weapon several feet underground, hoping that would keep it safe from animals and anyone else who happened by.

(Jack imagined a new generation of lovesick teenagers discovering the pond. If that happened, he wanted them safe. Like a real hero, Jack cared about people he didn't know.)

Jack no longer practised with the gun, but he maintained his physical regimen. He tried to exhaust himself so he wouldn't have the energy to brood. It didn't work. Lying sleepless in bed, he kept wondering what would have happened if he'd told Deana the truth. She wouldn't have killed herself if she'd been warned to be cautious. But Jack had cared more about his precious secret than Deana's life.

In the dark, Jack muttered, "It was her own damned fault." His words were true, but not true enough.

When Jack wasn't at the gym, he cloistered himself with schoolwork and research. (His doctoral thesis was about common properties of different types of high-energy beams.) Jack didn't socialize. He seldom phoned home. He took days to answer email messages from his sister. Even so, he told himself he was doing an excellent job of acting "normal."

Jack had underestimated his sister's perceptiveness. One weekend, Rachel showed up on his doorstep to see why he'd "gone weird". She spent two days digging under his skin. By the end of the weekend, she could tell that Deana's disappearance had disturbed Jack profoundly. Rachel couldn't guess the full truth, but as a big sister she felt entitled to meddle in Jack's life. She resolved to snap her brother out of his low spirits.

The next weekend Rachel showed up on Jack's doorstep again. This time, she brought Kirsten.

Nine years had passed since Kirsten and Jack had seen each other: the day they both graduated from high school. In the intervening time, when Jack had thought of Kirsten, he always pictured her as a high-school girl. It was strange to see her as a woman. At twenty-seven, she was not greatly changed from eighteen – new glasses and a better haircut – but despite similarities to her teenage self, Kirsten wore her life differently. She'd grown up.

So had Jack. Meeting Kirsten by surprise made Jack feel ambushed, but he soon got over it. Rachel helped by talking loud and fast through the initial awkwardness. She took Jack and Kirsten for coffee, and acted as emcee as they got reacquainted.

Kirsten had followed a path close to Jack's: university and graduate work. She told him, "No one makes a living as a poet. Most of us find jobs as English professors – teaching poetry to others who won't make a living at it either."

Kirsten had earned her doctorate a month earlier. Now she was living back home. She currently had no man in her life – her last relationship had fizzled out months ago, and she'd decided to avoid new involvements until she knew where she would end up teaching. She'd sent her résumé to English departments all over the continent and was optimistic about her chances of success; to Jack's surprise, Kirsten had published dozens of poems in literary magazines. She'd even sold two to *The New Yorker*. Her publishing record would be enough to interest many English departments.

After coffee, Rachel dragged Jack to a mall where she and Kirsten made him buy new clothes. Rachel bullied Jack while Kirsten made apologetic suggestions. Jack did his best to be a good sport; as they left the mall, Jack was surprised to find that he'd actually had a good time.

That evening, there was wine and more conversation. Rachel took Jack's bed, leaving him and Kirsten to make whatever arrangements they chose. The two of them joked about Rachel trying to pair them up again. Eventually Kirsten took the couch in the living room while Jack crawled into a sleeping bag on the kitchen floor . . . but that was only after talking till three in the morning.

Rachel and Kirsten left the next afternoon, but Jack felt cleansed by their visit. He stayed in touch with Kirsten by email. It was casual: not romance, but a knowing friendship.

In the next few months, Kirsten got job interviews with several colleges and universities. She accepted a position on the Oregon coast. She sent Jack pictures of the school. It was directly on the ocean; it even had a beach. Kirsten said she'd always liked the water. She teasingly reminded him of their times at the pond.

But when Jack saw Kirsten's pictures of the Pacific, all he could think of was dumping the ray-gun into the sea. He could drive out to visit her . . . rent a boat . . . sail out to deep water . . .

No. Jack knew nothing about sailing, and he didn't have enough money to rent a boat that could venture far offshore. "How many years have I been preparing?" he asked himself. "Didn't I intend to be ready for any emergency? Now I have an honest-to-god mission, and I'm useless."

Then Kirsten sent him an emailed invitation to go sailing with her.

She had access to a sea-going yacht. It belonged to her grandparents – the ones she'd visited on Vancouver Island just before she and Jack broke up. During her trip to the island, Kirsten had gone boating with her grandparents every day. At the start, she'd done it to take her mind off Jack; then she'd discovered she enjoyed being out on the waves.

She'd spent time with her grandparents every summer since, learning the ins and outs of yachting. She'd taken courses. She'd earned the necessary licences. Now Kirsten was fully qualified for deep-water excursions . . . and as a gift to wish her well on her new job, Kirsten's grandparents were lending her their boat for a month. They intended to sail down to Oregon, spend a few days there, then fly off to tour Australia. When they were done, they'd return and sail back home; but in the meantime, Kirsten would have the use of their yacht. She asked Jack if he'd like to be her crew.

When Jack got this invitation, he couldn't help being disturbed. Kirsten had never mentioned boating before. Because she was living in their home town, most of her email to Jack had been about old high-school friends. Jack had even started to picture her as a teenager again; he'd spent a weekend with the grown-up Kirsten, but all her talk of high-school people and places had muddled Jack's mental image of her. The thought of a bookish teenage girl captaining a yacht was absurd.

But that was a lesser problem compared to the suspicious convenience of her invitation. Jack needed a boat; all of a sudden, Kirsten had one. The coincidence was almost impossible to swallow.

He thought of the unknown aliens who made the ray-gun. Could they be influencing events? If the ray-gun was intelligent, could it be responsible for the coincidence?

Kirsten-had often spent time near the gun. On their first visit to the pond, she and Jack had lain half-naked with the gun in Jack's backpack beside them.

He thought of Kirsten that day. So open. So vulnerable. The gun had been within inches. Had it nurtured Kirsten's interest in yachting . . . her decision to get a job in Oregon . . . even her grandparents' offer of their boat? Had it molded Kirsten's life so she was ready when Jack needed her? And if the gun could do that, what had it done to Jack himself?

This is ridiculous, Jack thought. *The gun is just a gun. It doesn't control people. It just kills them.*

Yet Jack couldn't shake off his sense of eeriness – about Kirsten as well as the ray-gun. All these years, while Jack had been preparing himself to be a hero, Kirsten had somehow done the same. Her self-improvement program had worked better than Jack's. She had a boat; he didn't.

Coincidence or not, Jack couldn't look a gift-horse in the mouth. He told Kirsten he'd be delighted to go sailing with her. Only later did he realize that their time on the yacht would have a sexual subtext. He broke out laughing. "I'm such an idiot. We've done it again." Like that day at the pond, Jack had only been thinking about the gun. Kirsten had been thinking about Jack. Her invitation wasn't a carte-blanche come-on but it had a strong hint of, "Let's get together and see what develops."

Where Kirsten was concerned, Jack had always been slow to catch the signals. He thought, *Obviously, the ray-gun keeps dulling my senses.* This time, Jack meant it as a joke.

Summer came. Jack drove west with the ray-gun in the trunk of his car. The gun's safety was on, but Jack still drove as if he were carrying nuclear waste. He'd taken the gun back and forth between his home town and university many times, but this trip was longer, on unfamiliar roads. It was also the last trip Jack ever intended to make with the gun; if the gun didn't want to be thrown into the sea, perhaps it would cause trouble. But it didn't.

For much of the drive, Jack debated how to tell Kirsten about the gun. He'd considered smuggling it onto the boat and throwing the weapon overboard when she wasn't looking, but Jack felt that he owed her the truth. It was overdue. Besides, this cruise could be the beginning of a new relationship. Jack didn't want to start by sneaking behind Kirsten's back.

So he had to reveal his deepest secret. Every other secret would follow: what happened to Deana; what had really been on Jack's mind that day at the pond; what made First Love go sour. Jack would expose his guilt to the woman who'd suffered from the fallout.

He thought, *She'll probably throw me overboard with the gun.* But he would open up anyway, even if it made Kirsten hate him. When he tossed the ray-gun into the sea, he wanted to unburden himself of everything.

The first day on the boat, Jack said nothing about the ray-gun. Instead, he talked compulsively about trivia. So did Kirsten. It was strange being together, looking so much like they did in high school but being entirely different people.

Fortunately, they had practical matters to fill their time. Jack needed a crash course in seamanship. He learned quickly. Kirsten was a good teacher. Besides, Jack's longstanding program of hero-dom had prepared his mind and muscles. Kirsten was impressed that he knew Morse code and had extensive knowledge of knots. She asked, "Were you a Boy Scout?"

"No. When I was a kid, I wanted to be able to untie myself if I ever got captured by spies."

Kirsten laughed. She thought he was joking.

That first day, they stayed close to shore. They never had to deal with being alone; there were always other yachts in sight, and sailboats, and people on shore. When night came, they put in to harbour. They ate in an ocean-view restaurant. Jack asked, "So where will we go tomorrow?"

"Where would you like? Up the coast, down the coast, or straight out to sea?"

"Why not straight out?" said Jack.

Back on the yacht, he and Kirsten talked long past midnight. There was only one cabin, but two separate fold-away beds. Without discussion, they each chose a bed. Both usually slept in the nude, but for this trip they'd both brought makeshift "pajamas" consisting of a T-shirt and track-pants. They laughed at the clothes, the coincidence, and themselves.

They didn't kiss goodnight. Jack silently wished they had. He hoped Kirsten was wishing the same thing. They talked for an hour after they'd turned out the lights, becoming nothing but voices in the dark.

The next day they sailed due west. Both waited to see if the other would suggest turning back before dark. Neither did. The farther they got from shore, the fewer other boats remained in sight. By sunset, Jack and Kirsten knew they were once more alone with each other. No one in the world would stop them from whatever they chose to do.

Jack asked Kirsten to stay on deck. He went below and got the ray-gun from his luggage. He brought it up into the twilight. Before he could speak, Kirsten said, "I've seen that before."

Jack stared at her in shock. "What? Where?"

"I saw it years ago, in the woods back home. I was out for a walk. I noticed it lying in a little crater, as if it had fallen from the sky."

"Really? You found it too?"

"But I didn't touch it," Kirsten said. "I don't know why. Then I heard someone coming and I ran away. But the memory stayed vivid in my head. A mysterious object in a crater in the woods. I can't tell you how often I've tried to write poems about it, but they never work out." She looked at the gun in Jack's hands. "What is it?"

"A ray-gun," he said. In the fading light, he could see a clump of seaweed floating a short distance from the boat. He raised the gun and fired. The seaweed exploded in a blaze of fire, burning brightly against the dark waves.

"A ray-gun," said Kirsten. "Can I try it?"

Some time later, holding hands, they let the gun fall into the water. It sank without protest.

Long after that, they talked in each other's arms. Jack said the gun had made him who he was. Kirsten said she was the same. "Until I saw the gun, I just wrote poems about myself – overwritten self-absorbed pap, like every teenage girl. But the gun gave me something else to write about. I'd only seen it for a minute, but it was one of those burned-into-your-memory moments. I felt driven to find words to express what I'd seen. I kept refining my poems, trying to make them better. That's what made the difference."

"I felt driven too," Jack said. "Sometimes I've wondered if the gun can affect human minds. Maybe it brainwashed us into becoming who we are."

"Or maybe it's just Stone Soup," Kirsten said. "You know the story? Someone claims he can make soup from a stone, but what he really does is trick people into adding their own food to the pot. Maybe the ray-gun is like that. It did nothing but sit there like a stone. You and I did everything – made ourselves who we are – and the ray-gun is only an excuse."

"Maybe," Jack said. "But so many coincidences brought us here . . ."

"You think the gun manipulated us because it *wanted* to be thrown into the Pacific? Why?"

"Maybe even a ray-gun gets tired of killing." Jack shivered, thinking of Deana. "Maybe the gun feels guilty for the deaths it's caused; it wanted to go someplace where it would never have to kill again."

"Deana's death wasn't your fault," Kirsten said. "Really, Jack. It was awful, but it wasn't your fault." She shivered too, then made her voice brighter. "Maybe the ray-gun orchestrated all this because it's an incurable romantic. It wanted to bring us together: our own personal matchmaker from the stars."

Jack kissed Kirsten on the nose. "If that's true, I don't object."

"Neither do I." She kissed him back.

Not on the nose.

Far below, the ray-gun drifted through the cold black depths. Beneath it, on the bottom of the sea, lay wreckage from the starship that had exploded centuries before. The wreckage had travelled all the way from Jupiter. Because of tiny differences in trajectory, the wreckage had splashed down thousands of miles from where the ray-gun landed.

The ray-gun sank straight toward the wreckage ... but what the wreckage held or why the ray-gun wanted to rejoin it we will never know.

We will never comprehend aliens. If someone spent a month explaining alien thoughts to us, we'd think we understood.

But we wouldn't.

LESTER YOUNG AND THE JUPITER'S MOONS' BLUES

Gord Sellar

New writer Gord Sellar was born in Malawi, grew up in Nova Scotia and Saskatchewan, and currently lives in South Korea, where he teaches at a university. The year 2008 was a big one for him, as he published highly visible stories in *Asimov's Science Fiction, Interzone, Fantasy*, and *Tesseracts Twelve*, one of the splashier debuts in recent years. (He had two previous sales last year, to *Nature* and to *Flurb*, but they went largely unnoticed.) He graduated from Clarion West in 2006. His website is at gordsellar.com.

In addition to writing, Sellar is a jazz buff and plays jazz saxophone, a background he obviously drew upon in writing the clever story that follows, in which a down-and-out jazzman gets a chance to play some literally out-of-this-world music, and hopes that his luck has changed. Which it has, but the question is, which way?

HIS FIRST NIGHT back on Earth after his gig on the Frogships, Bird showed up at Minton's cleaner than a broke-dick dog, with a brand new horn and a head full of crazy-people music. He'd got himself a nice suit somewhere, and a fine new Conn alto. Now, this was back in '48, when everyone – me included – was crazy about Conn and King and only a few younger cats were playing on Selmer horns.

But it wasn't just that big-shouldered suit and the horn; the cat was clean. I mean clean, no more dope, no more liquor, no more fried chicken. Hell, he was always called Bird – short for Yardbird – on account of how much fried chicken he liked to eat. This was like a whole different Charlie Parker. He was living clean as a monk. He was walking straight and talking clear. His eyes weren't all fucked-up and scary anymore, either.

To be honest, I didn't recognize him when he walked into Minton's. It was about three am, and the regular jam session had been going for a long time, and all these cats from Philly had shown up, you know, dressed up like country negroes on Sunday morning and playing all that Philadelphia grandpa-swing they liked used to like to play. Smooth and all, but old-fashioned, especially for 1948. Even in New York City, the hotbed of bebop and the only place where the Frogs were taking jazz musicians on tour, there was still a lotta old guys dressed up in Zoot suits cut for them five years before, trying to play like Coleman Hawkins and Johnny Hodges and Lester Young used to in the old days, before they all disappeared. Bebop was huge, but a lot of ignorant cats, they were trying to resist it, still disrespecting us, calling what we played "Chinese music" and shit.

But Bird, he was clean like I said, but he played some shit like I never heard before, like nobody never heard before. I'm telling you, when he went up on the bandstand and brought that horn up to his mouth, the music that came out of it was . . . well, it made us crazy. Back in those days, we were like mad scientists when it came to sounds. We'd be taking a leak at the same time and one of us would break wind and we all knew what note it was. We'd call it together, turn to one another laughing and shit, and say, "E-flat, Jack, you just farted an E-flat." And that night we'd play every third tune in E-flat.

But them tunes Bird was playing, man, I ain't never heard nobody put notes together like that. The rhythms were so tangled up that even I had to listen close to catch them all. He was playing 37 notes evenly spaced across a four-beat bar in fast swing, crazy licks like that, and he was playing all these halfway tunings, quarter tones and multiphonics and all kinds of craziness. And even so, he was *swinging*.

Everyone went crazy, it was just too much. And Bird just grinned like a goddamn king and said, in that snooty British gentleman accent he used to like to put on sometimes, "Ladies and gents, this music is the wave of the future. It received its *dé-but* off the rings of Saturn, and if you don't like it, you can come right on up here and kiss my royal black ass."

Them old guys, the Zoot suit cats, they didn't like that, but they didn't say nothing. Everyone remembered how Bird never took no shit off nobody back before he went off touring the solar system.

Man, all that scared me a little, but I still wanted to get onto one of them Frogships and hear what kind of music everyone was playing up there. They were hiring cats, everyone knew that, but that was all I knew about it. Now, I hadn't never met Bird before, and I knew he wasn't going to talk to me, but Max Roach, Max was drumming there that night, and I'd met Max one time before there at Minton's, so I figured I could talk to him.

Max, he'd gone up onto the Frogships a year or two back. Well, he looked at me like he knew what I wanted, what I was gonna ask about, but he sat down to talk to me anyway. I told him I wanted onto the ships, wanted to know how to get in.

"You audition, same as for anything else," he said, shrugging. "Who knows what they like? Don't ask me."

"But you been on the ships . . ."

"Uh-huh," Max said, nodded, but didn't say no more.

"What kind of music they hire *you* to play?"

"Oh, man, you just need to play whatever," he said in that quiet, calm voice of his. He was a really cool, soulful cat most of the time. "Some of the time, they take cats who swing the old way, real old-fashioned; like what Duke's band used to play in the old days, or Billy Eckstine's. Hell, sometimes they want New Orleans funeral songs, or some cat who plays like Jelly Roll Morton. Other times they only take cats who play real *hard* bebop, man. You can't never know what they want. But anyway, you don't need to go on up to the ships. It messes a cat up, man." He tapped the tablecloth with his drumsticks, hit my glass of bourbon with one of them. *Ting.*

I know better now, but then I just thought he was stonewalling me. Figured maybe there were only limited spaces, and he was bullshitting me, trying to keep gigs open for cats he knew better.

"What do you mean?" I said. "Look at Bird! Remember when he left? Cat *went up there* looking like death on a soda cracker, and look at him now!" I glanced over and saw him sitting at a table with Diz and Miles and Monk and Art Blakey and Fat Girl Navarro and a couple of them white women who used to hang around at Minton's. They were laughing like a bunch of old women, like someone had just told a joke a second before. Bird, he wasn't fat no more, he was lean, and real clear-headed and healthy-looking, nothing like when they let his ass out of Camarillo. He looked like a cat with a long life ahead of him.

"Bird's been different, *always*, man," Max said. "He's just that kind of cat. Plus, they *fixed* him up. They wanted him bad, so they took him apart and then put him back together out there. A lot of cats, they just . . ." Then he stopped, like he didn't know what to say, and his eyes went a little scary, the way Bird's used to be, and he looked at me like he could see through my skin or something, and said, "Look, cats almost never come back like he did. The things that go on . . . you can't even imagine," he said.

The room went quiet sometime while we were talking, and I could tell Max was relieved. He didn't like talking about the Frogships, didn't want to recommend them to nobody. We both looked around and saw other people were all staring at the back of the club, at the entrance, and what do you know but this big tall-assed Frog had come on in the back and was standing there watching us all.

These days there ain't a lot of cats who remember what the Frogs looked like, really. It's been so long since they moved on, and let me tell you, the pictures don't show not even the half of it. They were like these big frogs who stretched their skin over a real tall man, but they had more eyes and weird-assed hands. No fingers, just some tentacles on the ends of their god-damned arms, man, and they walked on two legs. Now, this Frog, he was fat, and he wore a Zoot suit tailored specially for him, hat and all, which just made him look totally *out*, man, just crazy. He came in with three or four guys, white hipsters, and they sat themselves down at a table in the front of the club that was set out for them in a hurry.

That Frog, he was smoking long, black cigarettes, four or five of them at once, on these long jade cigarette holders. He was looking around, too, with all these eyes on his face, as if to say, *Where's the goddamn music?* I looked at him closely, and noticed that his skin, his face and hands, even his suit, it was all a little blurry, like a badly-shot photograph. He puffed on his cigarettes and looked around.

Nobody said nothing.

But all these cats, especially them sad Philly boys, they all thought it was their big chance. They hurried on up onto the bandstand, and they started to play their jumped-up jive-ass swing. That old Frog just leaned on back in its chair and kept on smoking those slow-burning black cigarettes, sticking its long blue tongue up into the smoke as it puffed it out. There were little black eyes all over its tongue, too, and they swiveled toward the bandstand.

I couldn't tell if it was bored or enjoying the show, but I do know that finally, after they finished a few tunes, Bird had finally had enough. He tapped Thelonious Monk on the shoulder, and Monk nodded, and stood up, and went up to the bandstand. Everyone had heard about what had happened that night at the Three Deuces back in January in 1946; everyone knew how these Frog cats felt about Monk's music.

Man, Thelonious, he just went on up to the piano and sat down, and everyone else on the bandstand just watched him, every one of them quiet and thinking, Oh shit. Monk, he lifted up his hands, all dramatic like he was about to play a Beethoven sonata or whatever, like that, you know what I mean, and when everyone shut up he started playing.

"Straight, No Chaser." That was a fine tune, just a little jagged and twisted up. He played the head real simple, melody with his right hand, old-fashioned blues stride with the left. The alien leaned forward. Everyone knew how much they liked Jelly Roll Morton, Duke Ellington, granddaddy music like that.

But when Monk finished out the head the second time, and started improvising on the changes, man, you could see him sitting with this big-assed grin on his face up there at the piano. He started playing some of his really Monkish shit, all that weird, tangled up melody, banging out tone clusters over and over and plunking out his crooked little comping rhythms.

The Frog, when it heard Monk start up with all that, it stood itself up, dropped its cigarettes on the ground and slapped one hand over its huge front face-eyes and the other behind the back of its head. It was moaning – with three or four voices at once – and this blue stuff starting leaking out of its nose. Then it decided it was time to get the hell out.

It wobbled but finally made it out the door, shaky like a junkie dying to shoot himself up. All them hipster cats it came in with, they all followed it out, making out like they were all nervous and worried. Teddy Hill, who was running Minton's Playhouse back then, he followed them all out with a scared face on, too. Bird, he laughed like a fucking maniac when he saw all that.

"Damn Frogs never could handle Monk," Max said, laughing. "Man, that was beautiful!"

*

A few weeks later, my buddy J.J. came by with this poster he'd found on some lamp-post nearby. He read it out to me while I brushed my teeth one morning.

"Now hiring jazz musicians of all instrumental specialties . . . the intergalactic society of entertainers and artists' guild . . . Colored Americans only please, special preference currently given to aspiring bebop players. No re-hires from previous tours please. One-year (possibly renewable) contracts available. See the solar system! Play blues on the moons of Jupiter! Go someplace where The Man won't be breathing down your neck! Press HERE for more information!"

I spat out the foam from my toothpaste, put down my electrobrush, and asked, "So? Where's the audition?"

He pressed his finger on the word HERE and the sheet went blank for a second. Then a map appeared on it. "Over on West 52nd, at the Onyx."

"*What?*" I was shocked. Going to the Onyx for an audition, man, that was like going on a tour of Mississippi with a busload of negroes, women and children and all. Over at the Onyx, man, it was all what my father used to call ofays – white men – running the joint, every last one of them motherfuckers so goddamned racist it wasn't even funny.

"You heard me. *The Onyx.*"

"Shit. What time?"

"The *Onyx?!*" That was my woman, Francine. She'd been cooking and she'd come up behind J.J. so quiet we hadn't heard her till it was too late. She looked at J.J. and man, it was like, *No bacon for you this morning, motherfucker —*

She pushed past him, put her hands on her hips, and said, "What are you gonna do? Go on up in space, and leave me alone with this baby?" she said, putting her hands under her big belly.

"Francine," I said.

"No, Robbie, don't try to sweet talk me," she said, shaking her head like she was having none of this. "Goddamn! My mama told me I should stay away from you. Said musicians weren't nothing but trouble."

I looked up at J.J. and tilted my head in the direction of the door, and he just nodded and left us alone. She didn't say nothing till the screen door clicked shut.

"Robbie, baby," she said, looking up at me with those sweet brown eyes of hers. "You are *not* going to that audition at the Onyx," she said.

Man, it just about broke my heart, but I knew that I was done, completely done with her. I knew she'd be a good mama, but not to my babies. It was all over right then.

So I looked at her, and I said, "I seen those letters you got all wrapped-up. Up in your sock drawer."

"What letters?" she said, and it was almost believable, except I could see she was pretending. Lying.

"Francine, come on, girl. I wasn't born yesterday. Maybe last week, but not yesterday, baby. I know about you and Thornton. And don't be telling me it's some one-sided thing, because I seen how you wrapped them letters up in a ribbon and hid them and all. And I seen the dates on them, too."

She slumped a little, and said, "Baby, I . . ." and then she stopped. She couldn't lie to me no more, and she knew it. She was tired of lying to me, too, I think. She was a good enough woman, Francine.

"Now listen, baby," she said, and her voice cracked but she tried to sound strong just the same. "It ain't like I never heard about you running around with those other women. I know I ain't the only one of us who been unfaithful."

"Francine, you and I *both* know that baby probably ain't mine, the way you been rationing me around here – which is why I *been* with other women, since you don't give me what I need. Did I complain to you? Have I been nagging your ass? No, that's fine, I understand. But this . . . look, you want that baby to have a daddy, you better go marry the man who done gave it to you."

"This is bullshit," she said. "You can run around as much as you want, but *you* can't never get pregnant. Me, I do it once or twice behind your back, and look what I get."

"I know," I said, and I tried to put my arms around her, but she pushed me away. "Life ain't fair, is it, girl?" I said, and tried again. This time she let me hug her. It was breaking my heart, those brown-sugar eyes all full of tears, her arms shaking a little as she hugged me back. But I wasn't gonna have no other man's baby calling *me* daddy, and I wasn't gonna stay with no woman who been going behind my back with no other cat, so it was probably a mistake, me being so nice to her just then like that.

She started crying, saying, "I'm sorry, baby. I'm sorry." Begging and pleading, and kissing on me. She told me she wouldn't never do it again.

"That's good. You learned your lesson. Like you gonna be a good wife to Teddy Thornton," I said. He was the one who'd written her the letters. Used to play drums around town, though I heard his granddad died and he went into business off the money he inherited.

And I tell you, when I said that, it was like the werewolf in them movies, you know, how he changes shape in a second? That was Francine, man. *Bam.* "What, you mean you ain't staying, now, after all that?" Her eyes were full of a kind of fire only a woman can fill up with.

I shook my head. "I'm gonna get this gig, girl. Damn, Bird, and Hawk, and . . . all those cats who gone up there, they come back richer than Rockefeller. You damn *right* I'm going up there."

"You son of a bitch!" she yelled, tears still running down her cheeks, and she grabbed a lamp from the hallway just outside the bathroom. "You was gonna run off to space no matter what, wasn't you? God-*damn* you!"

Then she threw the lamp at me, but I was quick and jumped sideways, so it hit the floor and broke into a million pieces. Man, *that* pissed me off. It was *my* goddamn lamp, I'd bought it with the money I'd made off gigs, and I knew it'd be good as new in a few hours – it was the new foreign kind that was just coming out then, the kind that could fix itself – but this

shit was still just a pain in the ass. I never did like being disrespected by
no women.

But I just nodded my head. Didn't matter what she broke, long as it
wasn't my horns. I wouldn't need no lamp where I was going.

The Onyx was a nice place, inside. Fancy, I mean. Every cat I knew was
in there, plus a few I wished I knew. Sonny Rollins was in there, Red Dog,
and Art Tatum, and Hot Lips Bell, and some other cats I recognized too.

We were all outside the green room, waiting. *Green room*, that shit was
funny: it'd always been called that, but at the Onyx, during these auditions, it was really the *green* room, with real green Frogs inside. That was
where cats went in to play their auditions, and the Frogs would listen and
decide whether they wanted them on the ships.

I waited my turn. Everyone was real quiet, more than you'd expect, and
through the wall we could hear drums and bass start up every once in a
while after guys went in. The bass sounded like one of those expensive self-
amplified ones, the kind that looked like a regular bass but got real loud all
on its own, except you had to plug it into the wall at night.

Cat after cat went in, played for five or ten minutes, and then left. I sat
there with my buddies, Back Pocket and J.J. and Big Jimmy Hunt, and we
all just cradled our instruments and watched the TV in the corner of the
room, no sound, just colour picture, and waited without talking.

Finally, after a few hours of listening and waiting, it was my turn. The
door opened, and this skinny white hipster came out and called my name:
"Robbie Coolidge?"

"That's me," I said, and I followed him into the room.

There were a couple of Frogs sitting on a couch in there, both of them
smoking bouquets of the same damned cigarettes on long metal cigarette
holders. They were wearing shades and black suits that didn't hide the
bumps they had all over their bodies, and they didn't say nothing to me at
all. On the other side of the room, a couple more of them hipsters sat there
at a small table with piles of old-fashioned paper on it. Nobody bothered
to stand or shake my hand, but one of them hipsters started talking to me.
Didn't introduce himself or nothing, just started talking.

"Tenor player." It wasn't no question.

"Yes sir. I can also play the alto and the flute, a little," I said, just as cool
as I could.

"You got a manager?"

"Uh, no sir. I, uh . . . I manage myself." I wanted to sound cool, but I felt
like a damn country negro right then.

"Well, that's just fine," he said, grinning that white hipster grin of his.
"Why don't you play us a song, then?"

So I called the tune, counted it off, and launched into it. The tune I
played was one of Bird's, "Confirmation", and I guess their machine knew
it, because as soon as I started playing it, bass and drums were piped in
from nowhere. They wanted bebop, so I played my best bebop tune.

"Not bad," the hipster said, and the Frogs were agreeing, nodding. "Can you play anything sweet?" he asked, and I played them a chorus of "Misty" as soulful and pretty as I could.

"That was just fine, Mr Coolidge. Please leave us your phone number and we'll call you soon. Thanks," the boss man hipster said when I handed him my name card, and one of his sidekicks showed me out. After that, I waited around while my buddies all auditioned, and they all said it'd gone pretty much the same.

I wondered whether that was a good sign or a bad one, but a few weeks later, I was on the subway when my pocket phone rang. I fished it out of my pants pocket, and dialed in my access number on the rotary dial to open the connection.

Looking at the face on the little screen for a second, I wondered why this slick, pale-assed young hipster was calling me, until I realized that it was that same hipster from the Onyx.

"Mr Coolidge," he said, "I have some good news for you."

And that was how I ended up touring the solar system with Big C.

The space elevator, that blew me away. It was a fucking gas, man. I only ever rode up it once, and I swear it was smooth as Ingrid Bergman's skin, or Lena Horne's smile, even though it was going faster than anything I'd ever been in before.

J.J. Wilson was the only one of my friends who also got a gig up on the Frogships, and he and I sat there side by side with our seat belts around our waists, looking down through the glass floor – it wasn't really glass but we could see through it – at the Earth and everything we were leaving behind. It seemed so strange to be looking at the whole world like that. I could see South America, the ocean, some of Africa. Clouds, and ice on north pole and south pole. I could see places I've never gone in all the years since then, and probably will never go.

Only a few hours before, J.J.'s wife had driven us up into the Catskills where the Frogs' launchpad had been. She'd cried a little, but soon she was making jokes and small talk. Francine, on the other hand: the first time she called, she was crying, and she pleaded with me on my pocket phone till I hung up on her. Then she called back screaming, and made me listen to her break plates and windows and shit. I'd felt a little lonely on the way up, and a little bad for her, but after that, I was glad she hadn't come along for the ride, and I was sure I'd done the right thing by leaving her.

It was strange, that trip, because I hadn't never seen the Catskills before. Right there by New York, but I never went and saw them till I was leaving to go to outer space. Can you believe it?

We caught us a jet up there, one that flew on up almost into space, but then come down again in some mountains up in north Brazil somewhere. I was hoping we might stop by in the city, so we could try out some Brazilian chicks. I heard good things about them, Brazilian girls, I mean. But we didn't have time for that – it was straight up to the ships for us.

We weren't the only ones strapped down into chairs in the elevator, though. There were all kinds of interesting people in there. There were a couple of skinny Chinese girls with some kind of weird musical instruments, what you might call zithers; and there were a bunch of Mexican and white guys dressed like cowboys with spurs and lassos and all that shit, just like in the Hollywood westerns. There was also this Russian cat in a suit who tried to talk to us through some kind of translator machine, but we couldn't understand him at all. He had a satchel of books with him.

And I swear there were about fifteen French girls in there with us, too. Cute, with fine cheekbones and low asses and long-assed legs, dressed up in their can-can outfits. I caught one of them looking at me a few times, and I just smiled and reminded myself to look her up sometime. French women, you know, sometimes they're less racist than American women. They're *ladies*. But you know, women always bring too much shit along with them when they travel. Those can-can girls each had a big stack of suitcases strapped onto the ground beside them, every last one of them.

Me, I just brought my horns, a couple of extra suits, and my music collection, some on vinyl and some on crystal.

When the elevator got to where it was going, we all unstrapped ourselves, got out of our seats, and stepped out into what looked like an airport. I had pulled on my big old herringbone winter coat, thinking it'd be cold in space, but it wasn't. It was like a train station, and as soon as we were in it, I started hearing a beeping sound. The card they'd given me to hang around my neck was beeping. A glowing red arrow pointed to my left, and same for J.J., too. We went off in that direction, following the can-can girls, full of hope and dreams of long legs.

Turned out we'd all been sent up for the same ship. J.J. and me and the can-can girls arrived together in a small waiting room, and the cowboys came a while later. We figured that once the Russian guy showed up, and the Chinese girlies, maybe someone would come and get us, so we just chatted for a while. Turned out the cowboys were rodeo heroes, you know, the guys who ride bulls and catch cows with lassos and shit like that. They'd been hired as entertainers, just like us, one-year contract. Same pay and everything.

Man, ain't nobody in the world back then who paid a black man and a white man and a Mexican and a woman the same money for the same gig – not before them Frogs done it.

So finally, when the Russian and them Chinese chicks showed up, it was because this big tall-assed Frog in a white suit and tie brought them to the waiting room. Like the Frogs I'd seen on Earth, this one was smoking a few black cigarettes on long cigarette holders, all of them poking out of one side of its mouth. It stuck its tongue out and looked at us slowly, one by one, with all of its gigantic eyes on its face and the little ones on its tongue, as if it was checking us against a memorized list of faces.

"Welcome aboard the space station. This way, please, to the ship that will be your home for the next year." It wasn't the Frog itself speaking; the voice came from a speaker on the collar of the Frog's suit. It waved its three-tentacled hand at the wall of the waiting room, and the wall slid open. There was a hallway on the other side, and at the far end of the hallway was another door, far away, slowly opening in the same way.

We went down the hall in little groups, staying close to the people we'd come with. Walking down that hallway, we all looked like old dogs, walked with our heads down, bracing for some bad shit to come down onto us.

But at the end of that hallway, when we came through the second door, you know what we found? Can you guess?

The whole place was done up like a big-assed hotel or cruise ship or something. There was this huge-assed lobby and ballroom, and main stairs leading up and down. One whole wall of the lobby was transparent, you could see right through it to the stars. Frogs wandered every which way, a few cats and fine skinny women of every colour here and there, all of them dressed bad, *real* hip.

"Welcome on board The *Mmmhumhhunah*!" Ship name sounded something like that, like how people would talk if they had socks in their mouth or something. That was what the Frogs' language sounded like to me, at least at first. He tried to make it sound like we were guests. "Your navigation stubs should guide you to your places of accommodation. Should you have any questions, please feel free to ask any passing staff member, who can be identified by the subordinate rank uniforms they are required to wear, and which have been modeled on uniforms denoting similar positions in your culture. We will begin preparations tomorrow, and the tour will commence a week henceforth."

"What's he talking about, man?" J.J. asked. His eyes were wide, like he'd seen his grandmama's ghost.

"Follow the little arrow thing to your room," I explained. "If you need help with your bass, ask a bellboy. First rehearsal's tomorrow."

"And please give me your instruments," added the Frog. "They need to be treated specially to withstand both repeated decoherence and space travel."

"Deco-*what*?" J.J. was very protective of Big Mama, which was what he liked to call his bass. "Hey, can you put one of them self-amplifiers into her?"

"Yes, of course, that was already planned," the alien said, and its eyes went round in circles. "Everyone else, also, we must collect your instruments. They will be returned to you tomorrow."

"Awright," J.J. said, twisting his head to one aside and the other as he leaned on Big Mama in her carrying case, gave the bass one last hug.

I handed them my tenor sax, but I wasn't happy about it. I didn't know what the hell they was going to do to it, but it was a Conn and had cost me an arm and a leg to get. But I handed it over. I already had the serial numbers written on a piece of paper in my shoe, just in case.

Now, listen up: I know me some drugs. I seen what heroin does to a cat, how it robs him of his soul, turns him into a pathetic junkie. I even tried it once or twice. And I know how spun-around a cat can get on bennies, 'cause I've done lots of them too. I've drunk every goddamn thing a man can drink, a lot of drinks at the same time, even. I've been so fucked up I didn't know what planet I was on. But nothing fucks you up like the drugs they gave us on the ships.

I first tried them at that first rehearsal, day after we arrived on the cruise ship, but before we got our own horns back. Me and J.J. showed up at the same time, and met the cat who was running the music program. He was a fat old brother with a trumpet style nobody ever copied right, nobody ever beat, and his name was Carl Thorton, but everyone called him Big C. He gave us these pills to swallow. Three of them, each one a different colour.

"Yellow one's so you can blur, the way they like. Blue one fixes you up with a better memory, so you can call up everything you ever heard. That one takes a while to kick in. Last one, the green one, that one's for programming memory of all those licks you memorize into your muscles and shit, instant super-chops. That one comes in real quick. You gotta take these sons-a-bitches every day for six months. Don't forget, or you'll turn your own ass so inside-out it ain't even funny. Got it?"

"Uh huh," me and J.J. said, and took the pills with a big glass of water. Water didn't taste quite right, wasn't nice and a little sweet like back in New York.

Big C, he had a bunch of us new guys – enough to play in a big band. He had us all sit down and listen to the old band, outgoing band, who wouldn't be leaving for a couple of days, so we could listen to them and get the hang of things. He told us big bands only went on tour on the Frogships for a year at a time, most times. Man, I didn't know they was looking to make a big band. I hadn't played in one for years, but whatever. I sat and listened. Didn't figure I could back out then, it was too late.

Well, they started to play – some old Basie tune, I think it was, but they were playing it so fast I couldn't tell which one. Badass, these cats – they didn't drop a beat, not a squeak anywhere. They played the head perfectly at what was definitely 300 beats a minute or more.

But when the solo section came, I rubbed my eyes and starting worrying about them drugs Big C had gave us. Big C, I could see him fine and clear, but the lead alto saxman, when he stood up and started playing a solo, he started to blur, and he wasn't playing one solo, it was two solos at once. And then four solos, and five, all of them going in different directions at the same time. He had his horn all the way up, leaning back and screeching altissimo, *and* he was hunched forward and honking at the low end of his horn. All of that at the same time, fast lines and slow lines together. He was like a dozen saxophonists in one.

The drummer was slowly going out of sync with himself, blurring into a smear of sticks and flashing cymbals, and when I looked close, I could see the cymbals moving, and staying still, all at the same time. It was one hell of a sight to see, believe me. I tapped J.J. on the shoulder, told him to check that shit out, and he nodded, so I knew I wasn't crazy. It was like ten drummers all playing at once, almost all the same thing, but a little bit off, each one a little bit different. Different cymbal crashes at different times, the downbeat pushed a little forward and a little back all at the same time. But if you listened, in a way, it all fit together somehow. That blew me away.

The rest of the band started playing backgrounds, but they weren't blurry, so the shout chorus came in together – a few beats quiet, then, in unison, *bop!*, then a few bars, then *ba-doo-BOP!* The alto player was playing three-octave unisons with himself. I swear I could see his right hand on the bottom keys, fingers moving and totally still at the same time.

And then the head of the tune came back, but the whole band was a blur, and everything was craziness, like ten, twenty, a hundred big bands trying to play together and coming close but never lining up the downbeats, pushing them forward and back all at the same time, clashing and smashing – it was something else!

It was a new kind of music, man. Real out. Like hearing bebop again for the first time, but multiplied by all the dope in the world.

"Them pills we took, they gonna let us play like that?"

"I suppose so, J.J."

"Goddamn!" he hollered, and "Sheeeeeeeeeee-it!" and "Check these cats out!" all at once, in three different voices, and he started clapping his hands and not-clapping his hands all at the same time.

"Brother, I been living with these Frog-head bastards a long goddamn time, and trust me, shit ain't right with them. You ever look at one closely?" That was Big C.

"Well, yeah," I answered, looking around his room. "They're blurry. Too many eyes."

"Too many eyes? You ever stop and think that we don't have *enough* eyes?" He squinted at me the way Monk used to do to people. "But that blur . . . ! Now, *that's* what I'm talking about!" he said, waving his hands at me. "They're all blurred up, it's like there's a hundred Frogs inside every one of them cats, walking around, doing things. They can't squash themselves into just one person, the way we all just do naturally."

He wiggled his fingers in front of his face like he was showing me what he meant. "And if they're listening to a band, they need the band to blur too, or they just get bored. That's why they like jazz so much! Best goddamn music in the world. 'Cause we make shit up – we improvise. Can't do that with no goddamn Mozart, now can you? Classical music, that just bores these Frogs to death, everything all written out and the same every time, the same even when you blur it."

I was staring at my hands, watching them blur and unblur. It was kind of like taking a piss, you could control it just by thinking about it. Except I was like a little kid, I didn't know exactly how to control it yet, just that I could kind of make it happen.

"You're getting it, Robbie, just relax into it, man. It'll be like natural soon."

"So how long you been on these ships, Big C?" I asked.

He scratched under his chin, back up where his beard was shaved off, and made a face at me. "What year's it now?"

"Nineteen forty-eight."

"Goddamn," he said. "God-damn!" And he got real quiet, and turned his head away so I wouldn't see him cry.

Our schedule for those first few weeks was crazy, all day practicing and then all night jamming our asses off and hanging out in one another's rooms, horns in our hands, LPs going.

One of the craziest things the drugs did was they let us memorize any kind of music we heard. Hearing it was all it took to program it into our heads, well, except it was more like your fingers would remember the tune.

So we would sit there listening to all kinds of LPs, bebop and swing and ragtime and Bach and Stravinsky and Indian music and whatever, and since we all had good ears, and since we could blur ourselves, each blurred self could listen to a different part of the music – the bass line, harmony lines, and the solo on top of it all – so we could come to the end of a record with the whole thing in our heads.

Now, this wasn't so new: I could listen to a solo a couple of times and hold it in my head, but what was strange was that, after a couple of weeks on them alien drugs, I found I could remember any damn tune I wanted, note-for-note. I could call up any one of Bird's recorded solos on "Anthropology"; I could call up a big band playing Monk's arrangement of "Epistrophy" and play the second trombone line on my sax if I wanted. Every line was right there in my head, and in the muscles of my arms and fingers and lips, and if I blurred out and played back that line even once, I could play it again and again, forever, just by deciding to, without even having to think it through.

In other words, them alien drugs made each and every one of us into one-man jazz record machines.

That was why we spent so much time sitting around listening to everyone else's LPs and crystals, a bunch of us cats blurred out of our minds, laughing and telling ourselves to shut up and soaking that shit up, all of it. There were some bootlegs, too, and man, some of them were amazing: "Bird on Mars," one of them was labelled, and that was some crazy, hip, *bad* music. I could listen to that shit all day long.

But you know, eventually, a cat gets tired of just being around musicians, and he starts wanting himself some jelly. Me, I never had no problem getting me some, women like me and I like them, but it had been a couple of weeks since I'd gotten any, so I decided to go look up them can-can girls and get me some.

I took the elevator down a floor at a time, wandered around till I found them. I saw some crazy-assed sights on the way, too: in one room, there was some kind of Russian circus with these huge blurred-up clowns juggling fire-sticks on the backs of blurry elephants who were dancing to the beat of the some scary Russian music. There were all these bears, too, just as blurred as anything, marching around them all. In another room, I saw those rodeo cowboys again, too, riding on blurred-up horses and swinging lassos in a hundred directions at once. But this one guy I saw, he wasn't just blurred, he split from himselves, ran in ten different directions at once after a bull that blurred and split up in the same damn way. Some of him caught the bull and roped it, and some of him got stomped by it. One of him even got gored in the stomach by its horns, poor bean-eating bastard.

But finally, I got down about ten floors below our floor, which was under the big-assed lobby. All the signs there were in French, so I knew I was in the right place. I went from room to room, saw a bunch of them blurry Frogs in these salons, smoking their cigarettes and talking in their weird voices while skinny East Indian girls in old-fashioned oriental clothing served them dainty little white teacups full of funky tea and whatever else Frogs drank.

But finally, I found the auditorium where the girls danced the can-can. That was the orchestra's night off, so the girls were practicing to these crazy recordings of blurred-up can-can music. When I walked in, they were dancing, those French can-can girls, and they was *fine*, all long strong legs going up and down, arms on each other's shoulders. Ain't nothing in the world turns a cat on like seeing women touch each other, except seeing their legs up in the air.

So I sat there and watched their legs go up and down, down and up, scissoring blurs, and I blurred myself too so I could see them clearly. I scanned up and down the line of them, until I found the one I remembered from the elevator, and let her faces burn into my mind.

After they finished, I went and found my way backstage. There was a bunch of green rooms. It was crazy – every girl had her own little green room on that floor. But I didn't know which one she was in, that fine-built woman I picked out from the can-can lineup, so I blurred myself and went up to all the green rooms I could, knocked on every one of them at once.

The door where she answered, I unblurred myself over to that one, and smiled at her with that innocent-country-boy smile like I always used to use on women. She was wearing some kind of silk kimono, you know, one of them Japanese-type housecoats, and her hair was down, and I could hear jazz wafting out from behind. Heard that jazz and I knew that I was *in*.

"You're the one I 'ave seen in the elevator, *oui*? The one who kept looking at me? But why 'ave you come 'ere?"

"Well, I thought about it, and decided I missed you."

She mumbled something in French, something that sounded a little like I'd be needing to try some other can-can girl next, but then she opened the door wide and smiled at me. "Come in, Monsieur . . ."

"Coolidge," I said, and took off my fedora to bow to her all charming, the way women like when you first meet them. "Robbie Coolidge." I stepped into the room, and could hear the music clearly: it was Nat King Cole, "Stardust." Her can-can outfit was draped over the makeup mirror with the light bulbs all around it, huge peacock feathers sticking up above our heads, and I could smell mentholated smoke in the air.

"I am called Monique," she said. No last name then, just Monique. Then she asked, "You would like some coffee?"

"Mmm, yeah, coffee sounds good."

She excused herself for a minute, and when she came back, she had two cups of coffee in her hands.

"You 'ave cigarette?" she asked.

I nodded. "Got a whole pack," I said, and I fished it out of my coat pocket and set it on the table with a pack of matches on top. They were Mercury Barron's Ultras, the new kind that were supposed to make you live longer if you smoked three a day. "Want one?"

"*Non*," she said, and smiled. "Maybe later."

The coffee was fine, really good French coffee, steaming. Even the god-damn steam smelled good. I held the cup and breathed deep and looked at her sipping from her own cup.

"So where you from?" I asked, and she stared at me for a few minutes. She rubbed an eyelid, and a little of the makeup smudged.

"I don't t'ink you really care, do you?" she asked, and sipped her coffee.

"Sure, girl, I care," I lied, and she leaned forward, and blurred herself, and a million breathy whispers of gay *Pa-ree* tickled in my ear.

That ended up being the night the ship took off for Mars, though Monique and I were too busy to notice. We only found out later, when one of the guys in the band ended up wandering into the lobby and noticing the stars were moving, nice and slow, but still moving.

It was a couple of weeks before Monique was in the habit of coming up and listening to the band play, and some of the guys didn't like it. That was when some of the cats in the band were starting to act all high-and-mighty, turning into what my father used to call "political negroes," and taking it upon themselves to tell everyone else how a black man oughtta live.

What made me real sad was that J.J. had fallen in with that pack of nuts. He used to be real nice, real cool and thoughtful. He'd always been a soulful kind of cat, but when he was with them space-Muslim gum-flappers, talking all that nonsense about how the black man was supposed to colonize the solar system for Allah's glory and to show the devil white man and all that, I couldn't stand to be around him. I hated it when he talked that bullshit.

So this one day, between sets, I'm sitting there at one of the tables with Monique and having a nice time. She's drinking wine and I'm having a cigarette and we're talking, and J.J. comes up with this look on his face. I knew it was trouble, that look, and I stood up before he got close, and said, "J.J., I already got one daddy, and he's in Philly, so I don't need you to . . ."

"Robbie, goddamn it, you *listen* to me," he said, and glanced at Monique as if she might leave if he glanced at her the right way.

"Who is 'e?" she asked, standing up.

"Sit *down*, Monique," I said firmly, and she instantly got that look on her face. You know the look: the one women get when you tell them what to do for their own good.

"Robbie, something's going on round here! We gotta cut out, brother! Them Frogs, they been in my room, man! They put something inside my stomach. Like a worm. No, a woman. Yeah, a *woman worm*! She been crawling inside my stomach, screamin', like, '*J.J.! J.J.! Gimme some ice cream*!' Help me, Robbie! I'm fuckin' dying here, man!" he screamed and blurred before my eyes, all his voices screaming at me at once. Poor cat was scared shitless, and he scared the shit out of me, too.

I pushed Monique off to the side and blurred myself, and each of me reached out to one of them blurs of J.J.

"J.J.," each of me said, all together. "Listen, J.J., you sick or something, man. You need to cool it. Cool it *right now*."

He screamed louder, each of him started to shake, and his blurred selves started moving farther and farther apart. I didn't want him to pull me apart like that too, so I quickly unblurred myself, relaxed back into one, and stepped back from him.

A couple of big old bad-assed Frog bouncers smeared themselves out into an army, and rushed around the room in pairs, grabbing all his blurred selves and hauling them, every last one of J.J.'s selves screaming at the top of its lungs, out one of the exits of the room.

The room went tense and quiet, and many eyes, Frog and human alike, were on me and Monique. Whispering started, and I caught Big C's eye. *Set-break's over*, his look said. *Back on the goddamn bandstand. Now.*

So I tried to kiss Monique on the cheek – she pulled away a little, but I still got her for a second – and hurried back up with my tenor in hand.

"Apologies, everyone!" Big C said into the microphone with a big fake smile on his face. "Show must go on, like they say. Luckily for us, we got a *Mphmnngi* in the house who's proficient at bass." *Mphmnngi*, that was what the Frogs called themselves. Then Big C started saying some bizarre sounds, and I thought he was going crazy too, until some stank old Frog in a tight black suit stood up and bowed his big old froggy head at Big C. Then I realized those weird-assed sounds were this Frog's name.

"Come on up and join us!" Big C said, and the Frog came up on stage, picked up J.J.'s bass with his three-tentacled hands, and strummed the strings to check the tuning.

"Goddamn shame," said Winslow Jackson, the alto player who sat beside me on the bandstand. He and Big C were almost the only guys who had toured before. "Seen too many many guys end up like that."

"How's that?" I asked, wondering if maybe some of outer space had got into the ship, and fucked with J.J.'s head.

"Must've forgot to take his pills," Jackson said, shaking his head. "It's a damn shame."

Not taking your pills for one day would make you go crazy like that? I ain't never heard of no drug like that, and to this day I'm not so sure it was the pills at all. What if I had took my pills every day and ended up the same as him *anyway*? Poor J.J. I didn't know whether I'd ever see him again, but I didn't have any time to worry about that: Big C was talking to the crowd again, and I had to get ready to play.

"Before we dig into the music, I'd like to share some important news with you! We have arrived at Mars orbit!" Big C hollered into the mike, and behind him, a big piece of wall just suddenly went transparent. Everyone turned to look at the red planet out there, except Big C, who kept talking about how exciting it was to be playing at Mars again, how much he enjoyed it every time.

Mars. We were at *Mars*. That shit blew my mind.

"And now, we have another special guest who's going to join us," Big C said into the microphone.

A short, weird-assed looking Frog got up, a long black bassoon under his arm, and started walking toward us. He was wearing a fine brown suit, tight as a motherfucker, and a brown fedora hat that matched his fern-coloured Frog skin. He waved his little tail behind him as he went up to the stage.

"Everyone please welcome Heavy Gills Mmmhmhnngn," Big C said. The names were starting to be more and more pronounceable to me, a fact I didn't exactly appreciate.

Big C turned from the microphone and faced us, snapping his fingers on two and four, and loudly whispered, "Stardust." We all got our horns ready, and he nodded and the rhythm section started us off with a mild blur. We usually played it as a tenor lead tune, meaning it was usually my solo, but of course, when you have a guest feature sitting in, the melody gets played by the guest, so I just improvised harmonies with the other saxes.

The bassoon was awful, like a dog being beat down by a drunk master. It wasn't music. Ain't no other way to say it. He played the whole time blurred up so bad that not a damn thing fit together. The tunes didn't line up right, there was no fugue or harmony or counterpoint that I could find. It was just like a bunch of jumbles laid up on top of one another. I swear, I got dizzy just hearing it. He ended the tune by playing a high E and a high F-natural and a high D-sharp all together, this ugly dissonant sustained cluster that went all through the outro and kept going for two minutes after the rest of the band had stopped playing.

At the end of it, all the Frogs in the audience cheered and groaned and waved their tentacled hands in the air, which was their way of clapping, and I hunkered down for a long night of bullshit.

So J.J., he came back a week later. I saw him drinking coffee in one of the open bars when I came back from window-shopping with Monique in the station dome on Mars. Not that there was anything for me to buy, or that I had any money – that was all waiting for me back on Earth. But there was a lot to see on the station at Mars in those days, and I even picked myself up a real live Mars rock. Still got it, too, at my house.

"Hi," I said to J.J.

He looked up at me and blinked, sniffed the air. "Hello. How are you? I'll see you at rehearsal tomorrow." And then he turned back to his coffee, as if I'd already walked away.

Still, weird as that was, I didn't quite believe it when Big C told me he wasn't J.J. no more. "Might seem like it, might talk like it, but he ain't J.J.," Big C said. "They made some kind of living copy of him, fixed it up all wrong – fixed it up to think more like them than like us – and now he just plain ain't J.J. no more. Just accept it."

Me, I figured that Big C had been on the ships long enough to have lost his mind too. But thinking back on that conversation, I could see that J.J. *was* different. He talked like some kind of white lawyer or something, for one, his voice all stiff and polite. And when time came for the next rehearsal, his playing was dead. There wasn't nothing original in it, no spark. I'd listen along to his bass lines and then go back to my room and listen to my LPs, and I'm telling you, there wasn't a single line he played after he came back that wasn't lifted out of some someone else's playing.

But I really knew it wasn't him because of the time I finally saw how he got himself off. He'd been dropping hints, every once in a while, but I never figured it out until one night, when I went to get back some Mingus LP I'd loaned him. I banged on his door, I knew he was in there, but he didn't answer.

So finally I opened the door myself, and there he was on his bed with two Frogs on top of him, tentacles stuck down his throat and wrapped round his legs, slithering their eyed-tongues all over his balls and shit. I slammed the door and just about threw up.

J.J., he had been always as much of a sex-freak as any other cat in any band I played with, and maybe he was so pent-up with all that celibate living that the space Muslims got him thinking he had to do. Maybe his balls got so blue that he lost his mind. But he'd never, ever talked about screwing no Frogs. That was what convinced me, finally, that J.J. was gone.

I found Monique in the lobby a few days after that, staring out the window at the stars. I hadn't seen her around in a week and a half, hadn't gone down to the French floor, but we were already on our way to Jupiter. It was supposed to take a month or two to get out there, and we'd stay for a week or so, or that was what Big C told us. There was a lot to see and do on all the moons, and some shows not to be missed.

"Where you been, girl?" I asked her.

"Busy," she said. "Very busy."

"Doin' what?" I asked her, as innocently as I could.

"One of our girls, she is sick. She was taken away by *les grenouilles*," she said, and made a face.

"Must've forgot to take her pills," I said, almost to myself.

"*Euh? Quoi?*" Monique said. She surprised me. I looked at her. "*Que dis-tu?*"

"I said, she must have forgotten to take her pills. Like what happened to J.J."

"Non," she said. "One of the alligator . . ."

"Frogs . . ." I corrected her.

"Frog, *oui, les grenouilles*, one of the 'frog,' 'e ask 'er to come to 'is rooms, and she say non, and next day she become very sick." Suddenly I could see J.J. in my head with those tentacles in his mouth and wrapped around his legs. I couldn't stand to think about all that again.

"But baby, you're okay, right?" I took her hand.

She turned and looked at with those eyes of hers, green like Chinese jade. "I want to go 'ome," she said, and squeezed my hand. "I don't know 'ow you can t'ink you are falling in love on a Frog ship. I don't know 'ow anyone can believe in love in a 'orrible place like this."

"Baby, come with me," I said to her.

"*Oui*, I will come with you. But I will not love you, Robbie," she said, and squeezed my hand a little. "And *you* must not love *me*, either," she said.

And then she turned her head and looked out at all them stars for a little while more.

The month we spent travelling out to Jupiter passed so goddamn fast, all blurred awkward sex and blurred awkward music and J.J. all sad and serious up there on his bass, and that dumb, stank-ass Frog Heavy Gills Mmmhmhnngn sitting in on his sad-assed bassoon at least once a week. The band still played like a well-oiled machine, still hit every note exactly right, but there was something going wrong, and I think we all could feel it.

And then one day, right in the middle of our show, Big C does that hamming-up thing that he was always so good at, and the wall went all transparent and I swear, Jupiter – fucking *Jupiter* – was right there in front of us covering the whole window. It looked like a giant bowl of vanilla ice cream and caramel and chocolate sauce all melted together and mixed up, with a big red cherry in the middle of it. It was big, man, biggest thing I ever saw, with these little moons floating around it. I couldn't breathe for a second. I looked out into the audience for Monique, but she wasn't at the table I'd left her at. Too bad, she would have loved to see Jupiter like that, right *there* in front of us.

"Now, as you all know, the orbit of Jupiter is a special place, a place where many people travel and choose to stay because it's so beautiful. While you're here, you should all go down to Io and use this opportunity to see some of the greats of jazz, people like Charlie Parker, Lester Young, Duke Ellington, Dizzy Gillespie, Cab Calloway, Johnny Hodges . . . don't miss them." When I heard that, I couldn't believe my ears. Bird? How could they have Bird up here, when I'd seen him in New York? Had he come back for another tour? I had no idea how that could be. I didn't think it through so good, though, then. My mind went right on back to that *other* name: Lester Young.

"Now," Big C said, "in honour of the jazz mecca that we're at, we're going to play a little tune called 'The Jupiter's Moons' Blues.'"

He counted us in, four, five, four five six seven, and what do you know but that damn Frog's bassoon started up again with the head. By then I swear I would have broken the thing over Heavy Gills Mmmhmhnngn's head if I ever got the chance, I'd heard so much of it.

There was all kinds of cool shit to do on them moons, submarine trips on Europa and Ganymede, volcano jumps on Io; they even let us humans ride along in these special ships that could drop down into the atmosphere of that badass old Jupiter himself and see the critters that the Frogs had transplanted there from some planet near where they came from.

But none of that interested me. Some of the cats in the band, they told me, "Robbie, man, what you doing missing a chance to see all this fine shit?"

"Man, all I wanna see," I told them, "is Lester Young. I'm gonna go see the Prez."

The club on Io was small, quiet. The Frogs didn't get interested in jazz until sometime after they'd checked out everything else that their people had done on Jupiter and the moons, and since ours was the only cruiser to show up for a while, right away was the best time to go in and check out the Prez.

That's what we called Lester Young, "Prez", because he used to be – and according to me up till that day, still was – the President of the Tenor Saxophone. Man, that sound. I'd seen him in New York a few times, and a bunch of times in Philly too, and he always had it, that thing, what Monique always called *je ne sais quoi*, which means *who the fuck knows what*? Man, before the war, Prez always had that up there in his sweet, sweet sound.

So anyway, Monique and me, we ended up in this little club in a bubble floating over Io. There were these big windows all over where you could look out onto the volcanoes spitting fire and smoke and shit. There was even one of them windows in the club, and Monique kept looking out of it.

Prez wasn't playing when we got there, it was too early so some other cats were on the bandstand. Trio of cats, didn't know their names but I was pretty sure I'd met the pianist before. They were alright. Sometimes guys like Prez, man, they did even better with those plain bread-and-butter rhythm sections, playing that kind of old swing style. It was all about *his* beautiful voice, *his* sound. Waiting for Prez, I could hear his tenor sound, man, that touch of vibrato, that strong gentle turn in his melody riding his own beat, just a little off of the bass, you know what I mean.

Monique started to get bored. I could tell. She fiddled with her hair, looked out at the volcanoes.

"Baby, Prez should be on soon," I told her.

She frowned at me, that sexy baby-I'm-pissed-off kind of frown. "I want to go for a walk. See the bubble." We'd passed some nice shop windows and cafes out there, and I guessed she really just wanted to go shopping. But it also felt a little bit like a test, and I never in my life let no woman test me.

"You go on and go shopping if you want, but me, I ain't gonna miss Prez for the world. Not a tune, not a single damn note."

"Fine," she said, and adjusted her purse. "I'll be back later. Maybe," she added with a pout, and turned on her high heel and marched out, adjusting her hair as she went, and wiggling her ass because she knew I was checking it.

I didn't give a shit, man. French can-can girls you can get any old time if you really want one, but there wasn't nowhere to see Lester Young except on Io. This was my last chance to see him in my life, unless he came back to Earth, and he'd been in bad shape the last time I'd seen him.

Well, I ended up sitting there through a half hour of mediocre rhythm section ad lib, sipping my Deep Europa Iced Tea – that's what they called a Long Island Iced Tea in that place, the only drink I could afford – when finally Prez showed up.

Now, seeing Prez that time, hearing him play, it was kind of like the first time you had sex. I don't mean waking up from a dirty dream and finding your bed's all sticky, neither. I mean the first time you're with some girl a year ahead of you in junior high school, and you go on upstairs in her house when her mama's out and maybe you kiss on her a little and then you put it in her, and a minute or two later you're wondering what just happened and is that it and why everyone is always making a big deal about that shit?

It was a shame and a huge fucking letdown, is what I'm trying to say.

Prez, he used to be a *little* fucked-up. Not when he was younger, before the war. Back then, that cat had some kind of magic power, man. People always wanted him to play like Hawk, I mean Coleman Hawkins, but he didn't listen to nobody, he played his own sound, and it was beautiful. He had this way of making melodies just *sing*, so sweet it'd break your heart in half.

But then they sent him to war, and seeing as he was black, they never put him in the army band. *Just who exactly do you think you are, boy? Glenn Miller? Off to the front line with you, nigger*, that's how it was. Folks said it wasn't surprising, him not having his head on straight after all that happened to him: being sent to fight in Europe, and what he saw in Berlin after the Russians dropped that bomb they got from the Frogs onto the city. How he got stuck in a barracks in Paris for all that time after, fighting the local reds, and what happened after we pulled out of Europe, where they court-martialed his ass because his wife was a white woman and didn't take shit off the other soldiers for it. After all that, they said that something inside him was broke, broke in a way that couldn't never be fixed.

Well, you know, I was hoping that maybe the Frogs had somehow fixed him up, like they'd done with Bird. When I seen him, standing tall, cleanest cat you ever seen, with a big old smile and a fine suit and the same old porkpie hat he always wore, I started to think maybe they'd done the world a service, brought back the President of the tenor saxophone.

So anyway, he lifted that horn of his up to his lips, with the neck screwed in a little sideways, so that the body of the horn was lifted up off to the side the way he always used to do, and as he started to blow "Polka Dots and Moonbeams", my heart sank.

It didn't sound like the real Lester Young, not the Prez I knew. It sounded like some kind of King Tut mummy Lester Young sound. Like the outside *shape* of his sound was still there, but that something important inside it had been took out. I'm sure nobody else there could hear it, but I could. I knew it right away.

I could feel my heart splitting in two as I just sat there and watched the Prez, the man who'd been the Prez, drift his way through tune after tune. It was all right, that floating sound of his, the way he always waltzed loose with the rhythm, the sweet tone, the little bursts forward and then the cool, leaning-back thing he'd do after it. But there was something missing.

Then it hit me what was wrong. I knew every last one of the solos he was playing. Not the tunes, I mean, not just the heads and changes. I mean I knew every goddamn note he played. He wasn't improvizing at all. Everything, every lick, was from his old recordings. "My Funny Valentine"; "I Cover the Waterfront"; "Afternoon of a Basieite" . . . Every goddamn note was off one of his old pre-war LPs. He was playing it all exactly the way he'd played it in the studio, at live shows, anywhere he'd been recorded. I knew, because I had all them same recordings up in my head, too, every last one of them.

So I just sat there staring at him with tears in my eyes, and waited for it to be over.

But you know, during the first set break, he came over and sat with me. Of all the people he could have sat with, all the people who'd come to Io just to see him, he came and sat with me, probably the only cat in the place who was disappointed with what he'd heard.

"You're a saxophone player, aren't you, young man?" he said, suave as ever but a bit too cool. He must've seen me eyeing his fingers on the horn.

"Yes sir, I am. I'm from Philadelphia, and my name's Robbie Coolidge."

"Might you happen to be a tenor player by any chance?"

"Yes sir," I said, nodding.

"Mind if I join you here? Seeing as you lost your hat and all," he said, hand on the back of a chair. By "hat," he meant Monique. Everyone knew that was the way Prez talked, funny names for everything. "Hat" was a new one, though. "My 'people' are in need of a little rest, is all," he said, and wiggled his fingers. That was what he called his fingers, his "people".

And of course I told him I didn't mind, and offered to buy him a drink and he laughed and said now that all the drinks were free for him, he didn't want no liquor no more. And then he just started talking to me. Asked me how old I was, asked me if I missed my mama's cooking – I didn't, my mama was a terrible cook, she used food as a kind of weapon when she was mad at me, but I didn't tell him that – and then he told me about his own mama's cooking.

I don't remember exactly what he said, honestly; what I remember was his careful, quiet smile and his bright big eyes lit by some exploding volcano out the big dome window, and how goddamned happy he seemed to be remembering his mama in the kitchen, the smells and the flavours coming back to him across all those years and all those miles from when he'd sat at the kitchen table waiting for dinner.

And don't ask me how I knew, but right then, I realized that they'd done to him whatever they'd done to J.J. and to Bird, and that Lester Young, whoever he was, he was gone from the world, same as J.J. and maybe same as Bird, even. All that was left of the Prez was a shell, filled with something that was supposed to be him but wasn't. That was what I was talking to, and it was all I could do not to cry in his face.

At the end of the set break, when he got up to play again, he told me, "Get off the ships, son. Get yourself on back to the Apple Core," which was what he'd started calling Harlem after the war. "You're way too young for this kind of life."

A little while after he started to play again, Monique came in, and I just took her by the hand and we left.

"Listen, you jive-assed negroes, just listen to me for a minute! This shit they got us playing, man, it ain't jazz! I don't know what the fuck it is, but it ain't human music. Jazz is for *humans*, my brothers!"

Some of them Muslim brothers were nodding their heads as I said this, but I knew one or two of them who wasn't going to go along with this so easy.

"Boy, you all wet. You signed a god-*damned* contract." It was Albert Grubbs, just like I expected. I forget the Muslim name he'd gone and taken for himself, but anyway, I knew him as Albert Grubbs, and sure enough, a few years later, everyone else did too, once he dropped all that religious bullshit. But right then, he was dead against us doing anything to upset relations with the Frogs, because he was still big on the whole space Muslim thing at the time. They figured if we was good enough Uncle Toms, the Frogs might give us some ships of our own, and let us fly around the solar system, so we could brag about beating white people to it. He looked about ready to start quoting the Koran or Mohammed or something like that, so I stood up. I wasn't gonna rehearse no more till we talked it all out.

"Yeah, *I* signed a contract. *You* signed a contract, too. You know who else signed a him a contract? *J.J.* – and look at him now!"

Everyone turned and looked at him. And he was just polishing his bass, oblivious, and he turned and said, "What?"

"Everyone *knows* he ain't the same. Don't matter if you never met him before he got on this ship. He used to be goofy and funny and clean, man, took care of his ass. Now look at him," I said, and cleared my throat. "Hey, J.J.," I called out. "What's your favourite movie? What's your favourite kind of ice cream?"

"Shut up, man," he said. His voice sounded deader than the worst junkie's. "Leave me alone."

Grubbs had a sour look on his face, and he was shaking his head, but some of the other space Muslims, they were nodding and mumbling to one another. Wasn't none of them gonna colonize nothing if they all ended up like J.J.

"See? See that? I'm telling you," I said. "The longer we stay on . . ."

". . . the more of us end up like J.J." It was Big C, nodding his fat bald head. "The kid's got a point. I done something like six tours of the solar system, and one quick trip out to Alpha Centauri, too, and you know, there's always one or two guys who get messed up like that, sometimes more. Lately, it's been more like three or four guys a trip. I've been starting to wonder when my time's gonna come."

This started the guys murmuring, discussing, disagreeing.

Grubbs and this other older guy, another space Muslim I remember was calling himself Yakub El-Hassan, one of the trombone players, they stood up to start preaching. I knew I had to do something quick.

"Hey, Big C," I said. "Tell me, you know anything about what happened to Charlie Parker?" Not even Grubbs had the guts to interrupt Big C.

And that was the story that turned the tide. Bird, man, Bird had been right there on that same ship as we were on, at least that was how Big C told it. He'd gone off dope but was still drinking like a fish, whiskey and wine, still eating fried chicken by the five-pound serving, still smoking three packs of cigarettes a day, all of which, especially the liquor, was killing him.

"They took him away, and some of what they done to him, some of it gave him back what he lost back in Camarillo, that's for sure. But what they did to him was even worse, killed off whatever was left from before Camarillo. Bird, man, he was ruined, all busted up inside. All he could to was play shit off records. Now, he played it crazy and slant. It was beautiful for what it was. But still, that was all he could do anymore. And to tell the truth, I heard they got copies of him. Extras, so they could have him around later. That whatever they took out of him, they kept it for the copies."

The guys were all scared, then, all confused, and I knew finally I could maybe change their minds. Even Grubbs looked like he was starting to have his doubts, starting to feel like maybe we did have to make a stand.

"Man, you gotta think about it this way. They ain't gonna copy nobody who don't play what they like," I said. "I mean, is this any better than slavery? Having your body copied and the most important part of you carried out into space? Your *soul*?" I said, hoping space Muslims believed in souls.

"Okay, so what can we do? Stop playing?" asked Yakub, still defiant, and though even Grubbs finally looked like he was ready to do something, he was nodding as if to say, *Yeah, what can we do?*

"Nuh-uh," I said. "We stop playing, maybe they leave us on Jupiter or something. So we keep the contract. We play, but we play shit they *don't* like. You never know, they might even drop us off at home early. And the only thing I ever promised when I signed up for this was that I'd play *jazz*, man."

"I'm liking the sound of this," Big C said, nodding his head. "Anything in mind?"

"Oh yeah, I got something in mind. Let's go back to my place," I said. "I got some LPs for us listen to, some new tunes to learn."

Big C grinned his big old emcee grin and looked out into the crowd of Frogs. "Welcome, ladies, gentlemen, and whatever else you might happen to be. We're glad to be back on the bandstand after our week off at Jupiter. We've got a whole new repertoire lined up for you, which we've worked hard to get ready, and we just know it's gonna make a big splash. Welcome back, and remember: *we're* the house band for the rest of this tour."

Then he turned and faced the band, snapping his fingers one, two, one two three four, and then Jimmy Roscoe started the tune with a solo on the piano. "Straight, No Chaser," it was, that night, my favourite Monk tune.

The band came in after a couple of bars, and not a goddamned one of us blurred. It wasn't just that we were playing Monk, but we didn't even blur when we played it. That made them crazy. The arrangement was lifted right off a Monk piano performance, the brass clanging out the tone clusters, and the saxes singing out his jagged solo in unison.

I never saw a roomful of Frogs clear out so fast, man. Not at first, of course; most of them waited until we segued into "Trinkle Tinkle" and they couldn't stand it no longer. When aliens got sick off Monk, sometimes they even *puked*. It wasn't pretty. Man, one of the most beautiful things I ever saw in my life was old Heavy Gills slipping on some purple alien puke on the way out, falling right on his bassoon and snapping it in half. I still don't know what it was about Monk that always turned them upside down like that. Even Monk didn't know. Later, after I got back, I told him – Monk – about that night, and it cracked him up. He said some scientist had come and seen him, with some kind of theory, equations and charts and numbers, but he told me he figured the answer was a whole lot simpler than that. "It's just a gift," he said, and he winked.

Anyway, the trip home, man, it was a lot quicker than we expected. We just played a few Monk tunes at the start of every set, and the few Frogs who even bothered to show up left quick and then we had the ballroom to ourselves. For a while, we started playing around with what we could do in music without blurring. We could still make our fingers remember anything, could still remember any music we'd heard since going on board. I'm still that way, all these years later. I got so many goddamn tunes in my head, it's like a music library, even now.

But of course we didn't just work all the time. We jammed, and most of us (except the few who were still trying to be space Muslims) drank all night, and started bringing in the can-can girls – I'd talked Monique into stirring them up, and you know, they were French. They love their revolutions. So they was refusing to blur during their can-can dances, and their auditorium was just as empty as our ballroom, and they had all the time in the world to come drink and hang around with us. All those French girls around, tempting our Muslims from their righteous path and fooling around with the rest of us, it was like heaven for a while.

I think the only people who blurred anymore were the cowboys, because most of them were having the times of their lives chasing those blurred-up cows around all blurred up themselves like that. And some of the animals in the Russian circus, because they didn't know any better. And maybe that Russian guy, too, though him and the Chinese chicks I never did see again.

So anyway, we were supposed to have gone out to Pluto, but a few days off Jupiter, the complaints got so bad that Big C was called up to go see the man – I mean the Frogs running the ship – but when he came back, he said the Frogs agreed we was playing jazz, just like in the contract, and the contract didn't say nothing about no Monk, so there was nothing they could do. I half expected them to start lynching our asses, but they didn't. The ship went ahead and turned around, headed for Earth just as fast as it fucking could. Me and Monique, we had a fine old time partying the nights away, night after night, but we knew this trip wasn't gonna last forever.

"Marry me," I said to her one night when we were lying in bed, both of us smoking. I wasn't sure I meant it, wasn't sure I wanted to marry anyone at all, but it sounded like the thing to say.

"Robbie," she said, "I know you. You are *musicien*. You don't need a wife. You are like a bluebird in the sky."

I puffed on the cigarette. "I guess you're right, baby."

"Let's enjoy the time we 'ave, and when we get 'ome, we don't say good-bye, only 'See you around the later.'"

I laughed a little. "Naw, you mean, 'See you later.' Or 'See you around,' baby. Not . . ."

"Whatever," she said, and yanked the sheets off me.

You know, when we got to Earth, we landed in Africa.

Africa, man, the motherland, the place where all our music started. I was in Africa and the funny thing was, I didn't give a shit. I wanted to get back to New York, to the clubs on West 52nd, to Minton's.

But it took time. We came down an elevator near some city whose name I can't remember, in what was then still Belgian Congo, which was lousy with wealthy Belgian refugees by then, and we rode down into town in jeeps. Monique sat with me, held my hand, but I couldn't see her face through the sunglasses she wore. She had this big sun hat on, too, huge thing I'd never seen before, and she kept looking out across the hillsides.

Finally, when we got into the city, that was it. I lifted her suitcase out of the back of the jeep, and there we were, the guys from the band off to one side, waiting for me so we could all catch a flight back to New York, and all them can-can girls off to the other side waiting for her so they could all go back to Paris.

And there we were in the middle.

"What you gonna do?" I said.

"I am not coming to New York," she said.

"I know. What *are* you gonna do?"

"I am going to go to Paris," she said, but the French way, *Paree*. "I'm going to tell people what I 'ave seen, and ask the everyone to stop co-operating wit' *les grenouilles*." Which was exactly what she did, too, on and on until the Frogs finally just up and left. Not that they left because of her, I don't think, but she never stopped fighting them.

"That sounds good," I said, and I looked at her hands.

"'Ow about you?" she said, a little more softly.

"Me? I'm a musician, Monique. I'm gonna go home and play me some music."

I kissed her, and I wanted that kiss to be magic, like in the stories your folks read you when you're a little kid. When a kiss wakes up a princess or saves the world, that kind of shit. But all that happened was that she kissed me back for a little while, and then she was gone.

It was a hell of a thing, getting back to New York like that. Not just all the new buildings, or them new flying cars zipping around like they owned the place, crashing into one another. The goddamned Frogs, they were pissed at all of us from that tour. Those sons of bitches over at the Onyx, they had already tore up all the contracts, and I didn't ever see more than a few thousand dollars from the whole thing, which was bullshit, really, since I'd signed up for a cool million, and been gone for almost half the time I'd signed up for.

But you know, in the end, I didn't give a shit. Those pills I took, none of them had worn off yet. (Most of them still haven't, even now, and it's been decades.) My mama, she used to say, "Take whatever lemons you get in life, boy, and you go on and make yourself some lemonade." My mama, she couldn't cook to save her life, but she knew something, alright.

So I started making lemonade. I got myself one of those new typewriter-phones that everyone was buying, and sent a phone-letter to my buddies from the band, and on Monday nights, we started meeting down under the 145th Street Bridge.

Man, down under that bridge, with them new flying cars buzzing over-head, we invented a new kind of music. It was all about playing together, at the same time, like in old-fashioned Dixieland music, except that we were swinging it hard, real hard, and half of it was made of chunks of music from the libraries in our heads. Everyone who showed up there, we'd been up on the ships, so we all had libraries in our heads. Our fin-gers were programmed, you know, so we could play anything back that we wanted. You could start with a little Monk, then switch over to Bird, throw in a little Prez, and of course there was room for whatever else you wanted to play up in there, too, and *man* did we play.

All that memory and all those programmable chops that they gave us to make up for the fact that playing blurred was so hard, we used all of that. After a few months, we found none of us could blur anymore even if we wanted to, but we didn't even care. We were doing something new, man, and all the music that's come after, you can hear some of what we did right in there, still!

Time came years later when all of that would start to sound old-fashioned, when people would start talking shit about us for that, criticizing us for ever having gone onto them Frogships and even blaming us for what happened in Russia and Europe, which is just crazy. Man, when we were fighting back, that was the first time ever where anything like that had been done, at least with the Frogs. It was all new. It's easy to disrespect people making mistakes before you were born, way easier than worrying about not making your own mistakes. That's just bullshit, trying to fill us up with regret for what's all long gone now, like the Frogs.

Shit, maybe there *are* things I regret, like leaving Francine the way I did, or how I totally stopped visiting J.J. in the asylum after we got back. But most my regrets are for things that ain't my fault. I regret seeing Prez the way he ended up, for instance, and I regret never seeing Big C again, and Monique for that matter. I used to think about all that a lot, after I first got back. Man, I remember lots of times when I used to stand there under the bridge while everyone was playing back all their favourite lines from old records we all knew, and I'd look up into the sky and find Jupiter. It's easy, you know, just look up. It looks like a star, a bright old star up there. I'd stare on up at Jupiter, back then, and think of Prez, and blow a blues on my horn, the baddest old motherfucker of a blues that anybody anywhere ever heard in the world.

BUTTERFLY, FALLING AT DAWN

Aliette de Bodard

New writer Aliette de Bodard is a software engineer who was born in the United States but grew up in France, where she still lives. Only a couple of years into her career, her short fiction has appeared in *Interzone, Realms of Fantasy, Orson Scott Card's Intergalactic Medicine Show, Writers of the Future, Coyote Wild, Electric Velocipede, Fictitious Force, Shimmer*, and elsewhere.

Here she takes us sideways in time to an alternate world, where the details of history and the fortunes of empires may be very different from those we know, but heartache, loneliness, jealousy, and passion remain very much the same.

E VEN SEEN FROM afar, the Mexica District in Fenliu was distinctive: tall, whitewashed buildings clashing with the glass-and-metal architecture of the other skyscrapers. A banner featuring Huitzilpochtli, protector god of Greater Mexica, flapped in the wind as my aircar passed under the security gates. The god's face was painted as dark as blood.

A familiar sight, even though I'd turned my back on the religion of my forefathers a lifetime ago. I sighed, and tried to focus on the case ahead. Zhu Bao, the magistrate in charge of the district, had talked me into taking on this murder investigation because he thought I would handle the situation better than him, being Mexica-born.

I wasn't quite so sure.

The crime scene was a wide, well-lit dome room on the last floor of 3454 Hummingbird Avenue, with the highest ceiling I had ever seen. The floor was strewn with hologram pedestals, though the holograms were all turned off.

A helical stair led up to a mezzanine dazzlingly high, somewhere near the top of the dome. At the bottom of those stairs, an area had been cordoned off. Within lay the naked body of a woman. She was Mexica, and about thirty years old – she could have been my older sister. Morbidly fascinated, I let my eyes take in everything: the fine dust that covered the body, the yellow make-up she'd spread all over herself, the soft swell of her breasts, the unseeing eyes still staring upwards.

I looked up at the railing high above. I guessed she'd fallen down. Broken neck probably, though I'd have to wait for the lab people to be sure.

A militiaman in silk robes was standing guard near one of the hologram pedestals. "I'm Private Li Fai, ma'am. I was the first man on the scene," he said, saluting as I approached. I couldn't help scrutinising him for signs of contempt. As the only Mexica-born magistrate in the Xuyan administration, I'd had my fair share of racism to deal with. But Li Fai appeared sincere, utterly unconcerned by the colour of my skin.

"I'm Magistrate Hue Ma of Yellow Dragon Falls District," I said, giving him my Xuyan name and title with scarcely a pause. "Magistrate Zhu Bao has transferred the case over to me. When did you get here?"

He shrugged. "We got a call near the Fourth Bi-Hour. A man named Tecolli, who said his lover had fallen to her death."

I almost told him he was pronouncing "Tecolli" wrong, that a Mexica wouldn't have put the accent that way, and then I realized this was pointless. I was there as a Xuyan magistrate, not a Mexica refugee – those days were over, long past. "They told me it was a crime, but this looks like an accident."

Li Fai shook his head. "There are markings on the railing above, ma'am, and her nails are all ragged and bloody. Looks like she struggled, and hard."

"I see." It looked I wasn't going to get out of this so easily.

I wasn't trying to shirk my job. But any contacts with Mexica made me uneasy – reminded me of my childhood in Greater Mexica, cut short by the Civil War. Had Zhu Bao not insisted . . .

No. I was a magistrate. I had a job to do, a murderer to catch.

"Where is this . . . Tecolli?" I asked, finally.

"We're holding him," Li Fai said. "You want to talk to him?"

I shook my head. "Not right now." I pointed to the landing high above. "Have you been there?"

He nodded. "There's a bedroom, and a workshop. She was a hologram designer."

Holograms were the latest craze in Xuya. Like all works of art, they were expensive: one of them, with the artist's electronic signature, would be worth more than my annual stipend. "What was her name?"

"Papalotl," Li Fai said.

Papalotl. Butterfly, in Nahuatl. A graceful name given to beautiful Mexica girls. There had been one of them in my school, back in Tenochtitlán, before the Civil War.

The Civil War . . .

Abruptly, I was twelve again, jammed in the aircar against my brother Cuauhtemoc, hearing the sound of gunfire splitting the window —

No. No. I wasn't a child any more. I'd made my life in Xuya, passed the administrative exams and risen to magistrate, the only Mexica-born to do so in Fenliu.

"Ma'am?" Li Fai asked, staring at me.

"It's all right," I said. "I'll just have a look around, and then we'll see about Tecolli."

I moved towards the nearest hologram pedestal. A plaque showed its title: the journey. It was engraved in Nahuatl, in English and in Xuyan, the three languages of our continent. I turned it on, and watched a cone of white light widen from the pedestal to the ceiling; a young Xuyan coalesced at its centre, wearing the grey silk robes of a eunuch.

"We did not think it would go that far," he said, even as his image faded, replaced by thirteen junks sailing over great waves. "To the East, Si-Jian Ma said as we departed China; to the East, until we struck land —"

I turned the hologram off. Every child on the continent knew what was coming next: the first Chinese explorers landing on the West Coast of the Lands of Dawn, the first tentative contacts with the Mexica Empire, culminating in Hernán Cortés' aborted siege of Tenochtitlán, a siege cut short by Chinese gunpowder and cannon.

I moved to the next hologram, spring among the emerald flowers: a Mexica woman recounting a doomed love story between her and a Xuyan businessman.

The other holograms were much the same: people telling their life's story – or, rather, I suspected, the script Papalotl had written for them.

I headed for the hologram nearest the body. Its plaque read homewards. When turned on, it displayed the image of a swan, the flag-emblem Xuya had chosen after winning its independence from the Chinese motherland two centuries ago. The bird glided, serene, on a lake bordered by weeping willows. After a while, a hummingbird, Greater Mexica's national bird, came and hovered by the swan, its beak opening and closing as if it were speaking.

But there was no sound at all.

I turned it off, and on again, to no avail. I felt around in the pedestal, and confirmed my suspicions: the sound chip was missing. Which was not normal. All holograms came with one – an empty one if necessary, but there was always a sound chip.

I'd have to ask the lab people. Perhaps the missing chip was simply upstairs, in Papalotl's workshop.

I moved around the remaining holograms. Four of the pedestals, those furthest away from the centre, had no chips at all, neither visu nor sound. And yet the plaques all bore titles.

The most probable explanation was that Papalotl had changed the works on display; but given the missing sound chip, there could have been another explanation. Had the murderer touched those holograms – and if so, why?

I sighed, cast a quick glance at the room for anything else. Nothing leapt to my eyes, so I had Li Fai bring me Tecolli, Papalotl's lover.

Tecolli stood watching me without fear – or indeed, without respect. He was a young, handsome Mexica man, but didn't quite have the arrogance or assurance I expected.

"You know why I'm here," I said.

Tecolli smiled. "Because the magistrate thinks I will confide in you."

I shook my head. "I'm the magistrate," I said. "The case has been trans-ferred over to me." I took out a small pad and a pen, ready to take notes during the interview.

Tecolli watched me, no doubt seeing for the first time the unobtrusive jade-coloured belt I wore over my robes. "You are not —" he started, and then changed his posture radically, moving in one fluid gesture from a slouch to a salute. "Apologies, Your Excellency. I was not paying attention."

Something in his stance reminded me, sharply, of my lost childhood in Tenochtitlán, Greater Mexica's capital. "You are a Jaguar Knight?"

He smiled like a delighted boy. "Close," he said, switching from Xuyan to Nahuatl. "I'm an Eagle Knight in the Fifth Black Tezcatlipoca Regiment."

The Fifth Regiment – nicknamed "Black Tez" by the Xuyans – was the one guarding the Mexica embassy. I had not put Tecolli down as a soldier, but I could see now the slight callus under his mouth, where the turquoise lip-plug would usually chafe.

"You weren't born here," Tecolli said. His stance had relaxed. "Xuyan-born can't tell us apart from commoners."

I shook my head, trying to dislodge old, unwelcome memories – my par-ents' frozen faces after I told them I'd become a magistrate in Fenliu, and that I'd changed my name to a Xuyan one. "I wasn't born in Xuya," I said, in Xuyan. "But that's not what we're here to talk about."

"No," Tecolli said, coming back to Xuyan. There was fear in his face now. "You want to know about her." His eyes flicked to the body, and back to me. For all his rigid stance, he looked as though he might be sick.

"Yes," I said. "What can you tell me about this?"

"I came early this morning. Papalotl said we would have a sitting."

"A sitting? I saw no hologram pieces with you."

"It was not done yet," Tecolli snapped, far too quickly for it to be the truth. "Anyway, I came and saw the security system was disengaged. I thought she was waiting for me —"

"Had she ever done this before? Disengaged the security system?"

Tecolli shrugged. "Sometimes. She was not very good at protecting her-self." His voice shook a little, but it didn't sound like grief. Guilt?

Tecolli went on: "I came into the room, and I saw her. As she is now." He paused, choking on his words. "I – I could not think. I checked to see if there was anything I could do . . . but she was dead. So I called the militia."

"Yes, I know. Near the Fourth Bi-Hour. A bit early to be about, isn't it?" In this season, on the West Coast, the sun wouldn't even have risen.

"She wanted me to be early," Tecolli said, but did not elaborate.

"I see," I said. "What can you tell me about the swan?"

Tecolli started. "The swan?"

I pointed to the hologram. "It has no sound chip. And several other pieces have no chips at all."

"Oh, the swan," Tecolli said. He was not looking at me – in fact, he was positively sweating guilt. "It is a commission. By the Fenliu Prefect's Office. They wanted something to symbolize the ties between Greater Mexica and Xuya. I suppose she never had time to complete the audio."

"Don't lie to me." I was annoyed he would play me for a fool. "What's the matter with that swan?"

"I do not see what you are talking about," Tecolli said.

"I think you do," I said, but did not press my point. At least, not yet. Tecolli's mere presence at the scene of the crime gave me the right to bring him back to the tribunal's cells to secure his testimony – and, should I judge it necessary, to ply him with drugs or pain to make him confess. Many Xuyan magistrates would have done that. I found the practice not only abhorrent, but needless. I knew I would not get the truth out of Tecolli that way. "Do you have any idea why she's naked?" I asked.

Tecolli said, slowly, "She liked to work that way. At least with me," he amended. "She said it was liberating. I . . ." He paused, and waited for a reaction. I kept my face perfectly blank.

Tecolli went on, "It turned her on. And we both knew it."

I was surprised at his frankness. "So it isn't surprising." Well, that was one mystery solved – or perhaps not. Tecolli could still be lying to me. "How did you get along with her?"

Tecolli smiled – a smile that came too easily. "As well as lovers do."

"Lovers can kill each other," I said.

Tecolli stared at me, horrified. "Surely you do not think —"

"I'm just trying to determine what your relationship was."

"I loved her," Tecolli snapped. "I would never have harmed her. Are you satisfied?"

I wasn't. He seemed to waver between providing glib answers and avoiding my questions altogether.

"Do you know if she had any enemies?" I asked.

"Papalotl?" Tecolli's voice faltered. He would not look at me. "Some among our people felt she had turned away from the proper customs. She did not have an altar to the gods in her workshop, she seldom prayed or offered blood sacrifices —"

"And they hated her enough to kill?"

"No," Tecolli said. He sounded horrified. "I do not see how anyone could have wanted to —"

"Someone did. Unless you believe it's an accident?" I dangled the question innocently enough, but there was only one possible answer, and he knew it.

"Do not toy with me," Tecolli said. "No one could have fallen over that railing by accident."

"No. Indeed not." I smiled, briefly, watching the fear creep across his face. What could he be hiding from me? If he'd committed the murder, he was a singularly fearful killer – but I had seen those too, those who would weep and profess regrets, but who still had blood on their hands. "Does she have any family?"

"Her parents died in the Civil War," Tecolli said. "I know she came from Greater Mexica twelve years ago with her elder sister, Coaxoch, but I never met her. Papalotl did not talk much about herself."

No. She would not have – not to another Mexica. I knew what one did, when one turned away from Mexica customs, as Papalotl had done, as I had done. One remained silent; one did not speak for fear one would be castigated – or worse, pitied.

"I'll bring her the news," I said. "You'll have to accompany the militiamen to the tribunal, to have your story checked, and some blood samples taken."

"And then?" He was too eager, far too much for an innocent, even an aggrieved one. "I'm free?"

"For the moment – and don't think you can leave Fenliu. I need you at hand, in case I have more questions," I said, darkly. I would catch him soon enough, and tear the truth from him if I had to.

As he turned to leave, he straightened his turtleneck, and I saw a glint of green around his neck. Jade. A necklace of jade, made of small beads – but I knew each of those beads would be worth a month's salary for an ordinary Xuyan worker. "They pay you well, in the army," I said, knowing that they did not.

Startled, Tecolli reached for his neck. "That? It is not what you think. It was an inheritance from a relative."

He said the words quickly, and his eyes flicked back and forth between me and the door.

"I see," I said, sweetly, knowing that he was lying. And that he knew I'd caught him. Good. Let him stew a bit. Perhaps it would make him more co-operative.

After Tecolli had left, I gave orders to Li Fai to trail him, and to report to me through the militia radio channel. Our young lover had looked in a hurry, and I was curious to know why.

Back at the tribunal, I had a brief discussion with Doctor Li: the lab people had examined the body, and they had come up with nothing significant. They confirmed that Papalotl had been thrown over the railing, plummeting from the high-perched mezzanine to her death.

"It's a crime of passion," Doctor Li said, darkly.

"What makes you say that?"

"Whoever did this pushed her over the railing, and she clung to it as she fell – we analysed the marks on the wood. And then the murderer kept on tearing at her until she let go. From the disorderly pattern of wounds on her hands, it's obvious that the perpetrator was not thinking clearly, nor being very efficient."

Passion. A lover's passion, perhaps? A lover who seemed to have rather too much money for his pay – I wondered where Tecolli had earned it, and how.

The lab people had not found the missing audio chip either, which confirmed to me that the swan was important – but I did not know in what way.

"What about fingerprints?" I asked.

"We didn't find any," Doctor Li said. "Not even hers. The railing was obviously wiped clean by the perpetrator."

Damn. The murderer had been thorough.

After that conversation, I made a brief stop by my office. There I lit a stick of incense over my small altar, pausing for a brief, perfunctory prayer to Guan Yin, Goddess of Compassion. Then I turned on my computer. Like almost every computer in the city of Fenliu, it had been manufactured in Greater Mexica, and the screen lit up with a stylised butterfly, symbol of Quetzalcoatl, the Mexica god of knowledge and computers.

This never failed to send a twinge of guilt through me, usually because it reminded me I should call my parents, something I hadn't had the courage to do since becoming a magistrate. This time, though, the image that I could not banish from my mind was of Papalotl, stark naked, falling in slow motion over the railing.

I shook my head. It was not a time for morbid imaginings. I had work to do.

In my mail-box I found the preliminary reports of the militia, who had questioned the neighbours.

I scanned the reports, briefly. Most of the neighbours had not approved of Papalotl's promiscuous attitude. Apparently Tecolli had only been the last in a series of men she'd brought home.

One thing Tecolli had not seen fit to mention to me was that he had quarrelled violently with Papalotl on the previous evening – shouts loud enough to be heard from the other flats. One neighbour had seen Tecolli leave, and Papalotl slam the door behind him.

So she had still been alive at that time.

I'd ask Tecolli about the quarrel. Later, though. I needed more evidence if I wanted to spring a trap, and so far I had little to go on.

In the meantime, I asked one of the clerks at the tribunal to look up the address of Papalotl's sister. I busied myself with administrative matters while he searched in the directory, and soon had my answer.

Papalotl had had only one sister, and no other living relative. Coaxoch lived on 23 Izcopan Square, just a few streets away from her younger sibling, on the edge of the Mexica District – my next destination.

The address turned out to be a Mexica restaurant: The Quetzal's Rest. I parked my aircar a few streets away and walked the rest of the way, mingling with the crowd on the sidewalks – elbowing Mexica businessmen in embroidered cotton suits, and women with yellow makeup and black-painted teeth, who wore knee-length skirts and swayed alluringly as they walked.

The restaurant's facade was painted with a life-sized Mexica woman in a skirt and matching blouse, standing before an electric stove. Over the woman crouched Chantico, Goddess of the Hearth, wearing her crown of maguey cactus thorns and her heavy bracelets of carnelian and amber.

The restaurant itself had two parts: a small shack which churned out food to the aircars of busy men, and a larger room for those who had more time.

I headed for the last of those, wondering where I would find Coaxoch. The room was not unlike a Xuyan restaurant: sitting mats around low circular tables, and on the tables an electric brazier which kept the food warm – in this case maize flatbreads, the staple of Mexica food. The air had that familiar smell of fried oil and spices which always hung in my mother's kitchen.

There were many customers, even though it was barely the Sixth Bi-Hour. Most of them were Mexica, but I caught a glimpse of Xuyans – and even of a paler face under red hair, which could only belong to an Irish American.

I stopped the first waitress I could find, and asked, in Nahuatl, about Coaxoch.

"Our owner? She's upstairs, doing the accounts." The waitress was carrying bowls with various sauces, and it was clear that she had little time to chat with strangers.

"I need to see her," I said.

The waitress looked me up and down, frowning – trying, no doubt, to piece the Mexica face with the Xuyan robes of state. "Not for good news, I'd wager. It's the door on the left."

I found Coaxoch in a small office, entering numbers onto a computer. Next to her, a tall, lugubrious Mexica man with spectacles was checking printed sheets. "Looks like the accounts don't tally, Coaxoch."

"Curses." Coaxoch raised her head. She looked so much like her younger sister that I thought at first they might be twins; but then I saw the small differences: the slightly larger eyes, the fuller lips, and the rounder cheeks.

Coaxoch saw me standing in the doorway, and froze. "What do you want?" she asked.

"I —" Staring at her eyes, I found myself taken aback. "My name is Hue Ma. I'm the magistrate for the Yellow Dragon Falls District. Your sister is dead. I came to inform you, and to ask some questions." I looked at her companion. "Would you mind leaving us alone?"

The man looked at Coaxoch, who had slumped on her desk, her face haggard. "Coaxoch?"

"I'll be all right, Mahuizoh. Can you please go out?"

Mahuizoh threw me a worried glance, and went out, gently closing the door after him.

"So she is dead," Coaxoch said, after a while, staring at her hands. "How?"

"She fell over a railing."

Coaxoch looked up at me, a disturbing shrewdness in her eyes. "Fell? Or was pushed?"

"Was pushed," I admitted, pulling a chair to me, and sitting face-to-face with her.

"And so you have come to find out who pushed her," Coaxoch said.

"Yes. It happened this morning, near the Fourth Bi-Hour. Where were you then?"

Coaxoch shrugged, as if it did not matter that I asked her for an alibi. "Here, sleeping. I have a room on this floor, and the restaurant does not open until the Fifth Bi-Hour. I am afraid there were no witnesses though."

I would check with the staff, but suspected Coaxoch was right and no one could speak for her. I said, carefully, "Do you know of any enemies she might have had?"

Coaxoch looked at her hands again. "I cannot help you."

"She was your sister," I said. "Don't you want to know who killed her?"

"Want to know? Of course," Coaxoch said. "I am not heartless. But I did not know her well enough to know her enemies. Funny, isn't it, how far apart you can move? We came together from Tenochtitlán, each thinking the other's thoughts, and now, twelve years later, I hardly ever saw her."

I thought, uncomfortably, of the last time I'd talked to my parents – of the last time I'd spoken Nahuatl to anyone outside of my job. One, two years ago?

I couldn't. Whenever I visited my parents, I'd see the same thing: the small, dingy flat with the remnants of their lives in Greater Mexica, with photographs of executed friends like so many funeral shrines. I'd smell again the odour of charred flesh in the streets of Tenochtitlán, see my friend Yaotl fall with a bullet in his chest, crying out my name, and I unable to do anything but scream for help that would never come.

Coaxoch was staring at me. I tore myself from my memories and said, "You knew about Papalotl's lovers." I couldn't pin Coaxoch down. One moment she seemed remote, heartless, and the next her voice would crack, and her words come as if with great difficulty.

"She was notorious for them," Coaxoch said. "It was my fault, all of this. I should have seen her more often. I should have asked . . ."

I said nothing. I had not known either of the two sisters, and my advice would have sounded false even to myself. I let Coaxoch's voice trail off, and asked, "When did you last see her?"

"Six days ago," Coaxoch said. "She had lunch with Mahuizoh and me."

Mahuizoh had looked to be about Coaxoch's age, or a little older. "Mahuizoh being . . . ?"

"A friend of the family," Coaxoch said, her face closed.

Something told me I could ask about Mahuizoh, but would receive no true answer. I let the matter slide for the moment, and asked, "And she did not seem upset then?"

Coaxoch shook her head. She opened the drawer of her desk and withdrew a beautiful slender pipe of tortoiseshell, which she filled with shaking hands. As she closed the drawer, I caught a glimpse of an old-fashioned photograph: a young Mexica wearing the cloak of noblemen. It was half-buried beneath papers.

Coaxoch lit her pipe. She inhaled, deeply; the smell of flowers and tobacco filled the small office. "No, she did not seem upset at the time. She was working on a new piece, a commission by the Prefect's Office. She was very proud of it."

"Did you see the commission?"

"No," Coaxoch said. "I knew it was going to be a swan and a humming-bird, the symbols of Xuya and Greater Mexica. But I did not know what text or what music she would choose."

"Does Mahuizoh know?"

"Mahuizoh?" Coaxoch started. "I do not think he would know that, but you can ask him. He was closer to Papalotl than me."

I'd already intended to interview Mahuizoh; I added that to the list of questions I'd have to ask him. "And so she just seemed excited?"

"Yes. But I could be wrong. I had not seen her in a year, almost." Her voice had gone emotionless again.

"Why?" I asked, although I already knew the answer.

Coaxoch shrugged. "We . . . drifted apart after settling in Fenliu, each of us going our own way, I suppose. Papalotl found her refuge in her holograms and in her lovers; I found mine in my restaurant."

"Refuge from what?" I asked.

Coaxoch looked at me. "You know," she said. "You fled the Civil War as well, did you not?"

I said, startled, "You can't know that."

"It is written on your face. And why else would a Mexica become a Xuyan magistrate?"

"There are other reasons," I said, keeping my face stern.

Coaxoch shrugged. "Perhaps. I will tell you what I remember: brother turning on brother, and the streets black with blood; the warriors of the Eagle Regiments fighting one another; snipers on the roof, felling people in the marketplace; priests of Tezcatlipoca entering every house to search for loyalists —"

Every word she spoke conjured confused, dreadful images in my mind, as if the twelve-year-old who had fled over the border was still within me. "Stop," I whispered. "Stop."

Coaxoch smiled, bitterly. "You remember as well."

"I've put it behind me," I said, behind clenched teeth.

Coaxoch's gaze moved up and down, taking in my Xuyan robes and jade-coloured belt. "So I see." Her voice was deeply ironic. But her eyes, brimming with tears, belied her. She was transferring her grief into aggressiveness. "Was there anything else you wanted to know?"

I could have told her that Papalotl had died naked, waiting for her lover. But I saw no point. Either she knew about her sister's eccentric habits and it would come as no surprise, or she did not know everything and I would wound her needlessly.

"No," I said, at last. "There wasn't anything else."

Coaxoch said, carefully, "When will you release the body? I have to make . . . funeral arrangements." And her voice broke then. She buried her face in her hands.

I waited until she looked up again. "We'll let it into your keeping as soon as we can."

"I see. As soon as it is presentable," Coaxoch said with a bitter smile.

There was no answer I could give to that. "Thank you for your time," I said instead.

Coaxoch shrugged, but did not speak again. She turned back to the screen, staring at it with eyes that clearly did not see it. I wondered what memories she could be thinking of, but decided not to intrude any further.

As I exited the room my radio beeped, signalling a private message had been transmitted to my handset. Mahuizoh was waiting outside. "I'd like to have a word with you in a minute," I said, lifting the handset out of my belt.

He nodded. "I'll be with Coaxoch."

In the corridor, I moved to a quiet corner to listen to the message. The frescoes on the walls were of gods: the Protector Huitzilpochtli with his face painted blue and his belt of obsidian knives; Tezcatlipoca, God of War and Fate, standing against a background of burning skyscrapers and stroking the jaguar by his side.

They made me feel uncomfortable, reminding me of what I'd left behind. Clearly Coaxoch had held to the old ways – perhaps clinging too much to them, as she herself had admitted.

The message came from Unit 6 of the militia: after leaving the tribunal, Tecolli had gone to the Black Tez Barracks. The militia, of course, had had to stop there, for the Barracks were Mexica territory. But they had posted a watch on a nearby rooftop, and had seen Tecolli make a long, frantic phone call from the courtyard. He had then gone back to his rooms, and had not emerged.

I called Unit 6, and told them to notify me the moment Tecolli made a move.

Then I went back to Coaxoch's office, to interview Mahuizoh.

When I came in, Mahuizoh was sitting close to Coaxoch, talking in a low voice to her. Behind the spectacles, his eyes shone with an odd kind of fervour. I wondered what he was to Coaxoch, what he had been to Papalotl.

Mahuizoh looked up and saw me. "Your Excellency," he said. His Xuyan was much less accented than Coaxoch's.

"Is there a room where we could have a quiet word?" I asked.

"My office. Next door," Mahuizoh said. Coaxoch was still staring straight ahead, her eyes glassy, her face a blank mask. "Coaxoch —"

She did not answer. One of her hands was playing with the tortoiseshell pipe, twisting and turning it until I feared she would break it.

Mahuizoh's office was much smaller than Coaxoch's, and papered over with huge posters of ballgame players, proudly wearing their knee- and elbow-pads, soaring over the court to put the ball through the vertical steel-hoop.

Mahuizoh did not sit; he leaned against the desk, and crossed his arms over his chest. "What do you want to know?" he said.

"You work here?"

"From time to time," Mahuizoh said. "I'm a computer programmer at Paoli Tech."

"You've known Coaxoch long?"

Mahuizoh shrugged. "I met her and Papalotl when they came here, twelve years ago. My *capulli* clan helped them settle into the district. They were so young, back then," he said, blithely unaware that he wasn't much older than Coaxoch. "So . . . different."

"How so?" I asked.

"Like frightened birds flushed out of the forest," Mahuizoh said.

"The War does that to you," I said, falling back on platitudes. But part of me, the terrified child that had fled Tenochtitlán, knew that those weren't platitudes at all, but the only way to transcribe the unspeakable past into words.

"I suppose," Mahuizoh said. "I was born in Fenliu, so I wouldn't know that."

"They lost both their parents in the War?"

"Their parents were loyal to the old administration – the one that lost the Civil War," Mahuizoh said. "The priests of Tezcatlipoca found them one night, and killed them before Papalotl's eyes. She never recovered from that." His voice shook. "And now —"

I did not say the words he would have me say, all too aware of his grief. "You knew Papalotl well."

Mahuizoh shrugged again. "No more or no less than Coaxoch." I saw the faint flicker of his eyes. Liar.

"She had lovers," I said, carefully probing at a sore space.

"She was always . . . more promiscuous than Coaxoch," Mahuizoh said.

"Who has no fiancé?"

"Coaxoch had a fiancé. Izel was a nobleman in the old administration of Tenochtitlán. He was the one who bargained for Papalotl's and Coaxoch's release from jail, after the priests killed their parents. But he's dead now," Mahuizoh said.

"He's the man whose picture is in her drawer?"

Mahuizoh started. "You've seen that? Yes, that's him. She's never got over him. She still makes funeral offerings even though he's beyond all that nonsense. I hoped that with time she would forget, but she never did."

"How did Izel die?"

"A party of rebel warriors started chasing their aircar a few measures away from the border. Izel told Coaxoch to drive on, and then he leapt out with his gun out. He managed to stop the warriors' aircar, but they caught him. And executed him."

"A hero's death," I said.

Mahuizoh smiled without joy. "And a hero's life. Yes. I can certainly see why Coaxoch wouldn't forget him in a hurry." His voice was bitter, and I thought I knew why: he had hoped to gain a place in Coaxoch's heart, but had always found a dead man standing before him.

"Tell me about Papalotl," I said.

"Papalotl . . . could be difficult," Mahuizoh said. "She was willful, and independent, and she left the clan to focus on her art, abandoning our customs."

"And you disapproved?"

His face twisted. "I didn't see what she saw. I didn't live through a war. I didn't have the right to judge – and neither had the clan."

"So you loved her, in your own way."

Mahuizoh started. "Yes," he said. "You could say that." But there was a deeper meaning to his words, one I could not fathom.

"Do you know Tecolli?"

Mahuizoh's face darkened, and for a moment I saw murder in his eyes. "Yes. He was Papalotl's lover."

"You did not like him?"

"I met him once. I know his kind."

"Know?"

He spat the words. "Tecolli is a parasite. He'll take everything you have to give, and return nothing."

"Not even love?" I asked, seemingly innocently.

"Mark my words," Mahuizoh said, looking up at me, and all of a sudden I was not staring at the face of a frail computer programmer, but into the black-streaked one of a warrior. "He'll suck everything out of you, drink your blood and feast on your pain, and when he leaves there'll be nothing left but a dry husk. He didn't love Papalotl; and I never understood what she saw in him."

And in that last sentence I heard more than hatred for Tecolli.

"You were jealous," I said. "Of both of them."

He recoiled at my words. "No. Never."

"Jealous enough to kill, even."

His face had grown blank, and he said nothing. At last he looked up again, and he had grown smaller, almost penitent. "She didn't understand," he said. "Didn't understand that she was wasting her time. I couldn't make her see."

"Where were you this morning?"

Mahuizoh smiled. "Checking alibis? I have very little to offer you. It was my day off, so I went for a walk near the Blue Crane Pagoda. And then I came here."

"I suppose no one saw you?"

"No one that would recognize me. There were a few passers-by, but I wasn't paying attention to them, and I doubt they were paying attention to me."

"I see," I said, but I could not forget his black rage, could not forget that he might have lost his calm once and for all, finding Papalotl naked in her workshop, waiting for her lover. "Thank you."

"If you don't need me, I'll go back," Mahuizoh said.

I shook my head. "No, I don't need you. I might have further questions."

He looked uncomfortable at that. "I'll do my best to answer them."

I left him, made my way through the crowded restaurant, listening to the hymns blaring out of the loudspeakers, inhaling the smell of maize and *octli* drink. I could not banish Coaxoch's words from my mind: *I will tell you what I remember: brother turning on brother, and the streets black with blood* . . .

It was a nightmare I had left behind, a long time ago. It could neither touch me nor harm me. I was Xuyan, not Mexica. I was safe, ensconced in Xuya's bosom, worshipping the Taoist Immortals and the Buddha, and trusting the protection of the Imperial Family in Dongjing.

Safe.

But the War, it seemed, never truly went away.

I came back to the tribunal in a thoughtful mood, having found no one to confirm either Mahuizoh's or Coaxoch's alibi. Since we were well into the Eighth Bi-Hour, I had a quick, belated lunch at my desk – noodle soup with coriander, and a coconut jelly as a dessert.

I checked my mails. A few reports from the militia were waiting for me. The timestamp dated them earlier than my departure for The Quetzal's Rest, but they had been caught in the network of the bureaucracy and slowed down on their way to the tribunal.

Cursing against weighty administrations, I read them, not expecting much.

How wrong I was.

Unit 7 of the Mexica District Militia had interviewed the left-door neighbour of Papalotl: an old merchant who had insomnia, and who had been awake at the Third Bi-Hour. He had seen Tecolli enter Papalotl's flat a full half-hour before Tecolli actually called the militia.

Damn. There was still a possibility that Tecolli could have found the body earlier, but if so, why hadn't he called the militia at once? Why had he waited so much?

Disposing of evidence, I thought, my heart beating faster and faster.

I should have arrested Tecolli. But instead I had clung to my old ideals, that torture was abhorrent and that a magistrate should find the truth, not wring it out of suspects. I had been weak.

Now . . .

I had him watched. He had been making phone calls. It was only a matter of time before he had to make some kind of move.

I sighed. Once a mistake had been made, you might as well drain the cup to the dregs. I'd wait.

It was a frustrating process. The afternoon passed and deepened into night. I attempted some Buddhist meditations, but I could not focus on my breath properly, and after a while I gave this up as a lost cause.

When the announcement came, I was so coiled up I knocked down the handset trying to pick it up.

"Your Excellency? This is Unit 6 of the militia. Target is on the move. Repeat: target is on the move."

I grabbed my coat and rushed out, shouting for my aircar.

I met up with the aircar of Unit 6 in a fairly seedy neighbourhood of Fenliu: the Gardens of Felicity, once a middle-class area, had sunk back to crowded tenements and derelict buildings, sometimes abandoned halfway through their construction.

I had a brief chat with Li Fai, who was heading the militia: Tecolli had left the Black Tez Barracks and taken the mag-lev train which crisscrossed Fenliu. One of the militiamen had followed Tecolli on the mag-lev, until he alighted at the Gardens of Felicity station, making his way on foot into a small, almost unremarkable shop on Lao Zi Avenue.

Both our aircars were parked at the corner of Lao Zi Avenue, about fifty paces from the shop – and Tecolli had not emerged from there.

I looked at the three militiamen, checking that they had their service weapons, and drew my own Yi Sen semi-automatic. "We're going in," I said, arming the weapon in one swift movement, and hearing the click as the bullet was released into the chamber.

I stood near the closed door of the shop, feeling the reassuring weight of my gun. At this late hour the street was almost deserted, and any stray passers-by gave us a wide berth, not keen on interfering with Xuyan justice.

Li Fai was standing on tiptoe, trying to look through the window. After a while he came down, and raised three fingers. Three people, then. Or more. Li Fai had not seemed very certain.

Armed? I signed, and he shrugged.

Oh well. There came a time when you had to act.

I raised my hand, and gave the signal.

The first of the militiamen kicked open the door, yelling, "Militia!" and rushed inside. I followed, caught between two militiamen, fighting to raise my gun amidst memories of the War, of pressing myself in a doorway as loyalists and rebels shot at each other on Tenochtitlán's marketplace —

No.

Not now.

Inside, everything was dark, save for a dimly-lit door; I caught a glimpse of several figures running through the frame.

I was about to run through the door in pursuit, but someone – Li Fai – laid a hand on my shoulder to restrain me.

I remembered then that I was a District Magistrate, and that they could not take risks with my life. It was frustrating, but I knew I had not been trained for this. I nodded to tell Li Fai I'd understood, and watched the militiamen rush through the door.

Gunshots echoed through the room. The first man who had entered fell, clutching his shoulder. A few more gunshots – I could not see the militiamen; they'd gone beyond the door.

A deathly silence settled over the place. I moved cautiously around the counter, and stepped through the door.

The light I had seen came from several hologram pedestals, which had their visuals on, but not their audios. On the floor were scattered chips – I almost stepped on one.

In the corner of the wood-panelled room was the body of a small, wizened Xuyan woman I did not know. Beside her was the gun she'd used. The militia's bullet had caught her in the chest and thrown her backwards, against the wall.

Tecolli was crouching next to her, in a position of surrender. Two militiamen stood guard over him.

I smiled, grimly. "You're under arrest."

"I've done nothing wrong," Tecolli said, attempting to pull himself upright.

"Sedition will suffice," I said. "Resisting the militia is a serious crime." As I said this, my gaze, roaming the room, caught one of the images on a hologram pedestal, an image that was all too familiar: a Chinese man dressed in the grey silk robes of a eunuch, gradually fading and being replaced by thirteen junks on the ocean.

Papalotl's holograms.

Things that should not have been copied, or sold elsewhere than in Papalotl's workshop.

I remembered the missing chips in Papalotl's pedestals, and suddenly understood where Tecolli's wealth had come from. He had been stealing her chips, copying them and selling the copies on the black market And Papalotl had found out – no doubt the reason for the quarrel.

But for him it was different: he was an Eagle Knight, and subject to harsher laws than commoners. For a crime such as this he would be executed, his family disgraced. He'd had to silence Papalotl, once and for all.

He'll suck everything out of you.

Mahuizoh could not have known the truth behind his words, back when he had spoken them to me. There was no way he could have known.

Tecolli's eyes met mine, and must have seen the loathing I felt for him. All pretence fled from his face. "I did not kill her," he said. "I swear to you I did not kill her." He looked as though he might weep.

I spat, from between clenched teeth, "Take him away. We'll deal with him at the tribunal."

Yi Mei-Lin, one of the clerks, entered my office as I was typing the last of my preliminary report.

"How is he?" I asked.

"Still protesting his innocence. He says he found her already dead, and only used the extra half-hour to wipe off any proof that he might have tampered with the holograms – removing his fingerprints and wiping the pedestals clean." Yi Mei-Lin had a full cardboard box in her hands, with a piece of paper covering it. "These are his things. I thought you might want a look."

I sighed. My eyes ached from looking at the computer. "Yes. I probably should." I already knew that although we'd found the missing chips in the black-market shop, the swan hologram's audio chip had been nowhere to be found. Tecolli denied taking it. Not that I was inclined to trust him currently.

"I'll bring you some jasmine tea," Yi Mei-Lin said, and slipped out the door.

I rifled through Tecolli's things, absentmindedly. The usual: wallet, keys, copper yuans – not even enough to buy tobacco. A metal lip-plug, tarnished from long contact with the skin. A packet of honey-toasted gourd seeds, still wrapped in plastic.

A wad of papers, folded over and over. I reached for it, unwound it, and stared at the letters. It was part of a script – the swan's script, I realized, my heart beating faster. Tecolli had been the voice of the hummingbird, and Papalotl's script was forcefully underlined and annotated in the margins, in preparation for his role.

The swan – Papalotl's voice – merely recited a series of dates: the doomed charge of the Second Red Tezcatlipoca Regiment during Xuya's Independence War with China; the Tripartite War and the triumph of the Mexica-Xuyan alliance over the United States.

And, finally, the Mexica Civil War, twelve years ago: the Xuyan soldiers dispatched to help restore order; the thousands of Mexica fleeing their home cities and settling across the border.

The swan then fell silent, and the hummingbird appeared. It was there that Tecolli's role started.

> *Tonatiuh, the Fifth Sun, has just risen, and outside my cell I hear the priests of Huitzilpochtli chanting their hymns as they prepare the altar for my sacrifice.*
> *I know that you are beyond the border now. The Xuyans will welcome you as they have welcomed so many of our people, and you will make a new life there. I regret only that I will not be there to walk with you —*

Puzzled, I turned the pages. It was a long, poignant monologue, but it did not feel like the other audio chips I'd heard in Papalotl's workshop. It felt . . .

More real, I thought, chilled without knowing why. I scanned the bottom of the second-to-last page.

*They will send this letter on to you, for although they are my
enemies they are honourable men.*

*Weep not for me. I die a warrior's death on the altar, and my
blood will make Tonatiuh strong. But my love is and always
has been yours forever, whether in this world of fading flowers
or in the god's heaven.*

Izel.

Izel.
Coaxoch's fiancé.

It was the Third Bi-Hour when I arrived at The Quetzal's Rest, and the restaurant was deserted, all the patrons since long gone back to their houses.

A light was still on upstairs, in the office. Gently, I pushed the door open,
and saw her standing by the window, her back to me. She wore a robe with
embroidered deer, and a shawl of maguey fibres – the traditional garb of
women in Greater Mexica.

"I was waiting for you," she said, not turning around.

"Where's Mahuizoh?"

"I sent him away." Coaxoch's voice was utterly emotionless. On the
desk stood the faded picture of Izel, and in front of the picture was a
small bowl holding some grass – a funeral offering. "He would not have
understood."

She turned, slowly, to face me. Two streaks of black makeup ran on
either side of her cheeks: the markings put on the dead's faces before they
were cremated.

Surprised, I recoiled, but she made no move towards me. Cautiously, I
extended Tecolli's crumpled paper to her. "Papalotl stole the original letter
from you, didn't she?"

Coaxoch shook her head. "I should have seen her more often, after we
moved here," she said. "I should have seen what she was turning into."
She laid both hands on the desk, as stately as an Empress. "When it
went missing, I didn't think of Papalotl. Mahuizoh thought that maybe
Tecolli —"

"Mahuizoh hates Tecolli," I said.

"It doesn't matter," Coaxoch said. "I went to Papalotl, to ask her
whether she'd seen it. I didn't think." She took a deep breath to steady
herself. Her skin had gone red under the makeup. "When I came in, she
opened the door to me – naked, and she didn't even offer to dress herself.
She left me downstairs and headed for her workshop, to finish something,
she said. I followed her."

Her voice quavered, but she steadied it. "I saw the letter on her table
– she'd taken it. And when I asked her about it, she told me about the
hologram, told me we were going to be famous when she sold this, and the
Prefect's Office would put it where everyone could see it . . ."

I said nothing. I remained where I was, listening to her voice grow more
and more intense, until every word tore at me.

"She was going to . . . sell my pain. To sell my memories just for a piece of fame. She was going —" Coaxoch drew a deep breath. "I told her to stop. I told her it was not right, but she stood on the landing, shaking her head and smiling at me – as if she just had to ask for everything to be made right.

"She didn't understand. She just didn't understand. She'd changed too much." Coaxoch stared at her hands, and then back at the picture of Izel. "I couldn't make her shut up, you understand? I pushed and beat at her, and she wouldn't stop smiling at me, selling my pain —"

She raised her gaze towards me, and I recognised the look in her eyes: it was the look of someone already dead, and who knows it. "I had to make her stop," she said, her voice lower now, almost spent. "But she never did. Even after she fell she was still smiling." There were tears in her eyes now. "Still laughing at me."

I said at last, finding my words with difficulty, "You know how it goes."

Coaxoch shrugged. "Do you think I care, Hue Ma? It ceased to matter a long time ago." She cast a last, longing glance towards Izel's picture, and straightened her shoulders. "It's not right either, what I've done. Do what you have to."

She did not bend, then, as the militia came into the room – did not bend as they closed the handcuffs over her wrists and led her away. I knew she would not bend on the day of her execution either, whatever the manner of it.

As we exited the restaurant, I caught a glimpse of Mahuizoh among the few passers-by who had gathered to watch the militia aircar. His gaze met mine, and held it for a second – and there were such depths of grief behind the spectacles that my breath caught and could not be released.

"I'm sorry," I whispered. "Justice has to be done." But I did not think he could hear me.

Back at the tribunal, I sat at my desk, staring at my computer's screen-saver – one of Quetzalcoatl's butterflies, multiplying until it filled the screen. There was something mindlessly reassuring about it.

I had to deal with Tecolli, had to type a report, had to call Zhu Bao to let him know his trust had not been misplaced and that I had found the culprit. I had to –

I felt hollow, drained of everything. At last I moved, and knelt before my small altar. Slowly, with shaking hands, I lit a stick of incense and placed it upright before the lacquered tablets. Then I sat on my knees, trying to banish the memory of Coaxoch's voice.

I thought of her words to me: *it ceased to matter a long time ago.*

And my own, an eternity ago: *the War does that to you.*

I thought of Papalotl, turning away from Mexica customs to forget her exile and the death of her parents, of what she had made of her life. I saw her letting go of the railing, slowly falling towards the floor; and saw Coaxoch's eyes, those of someone already dead. I thought of my turning away from my inheritance, and thought of Xuya, which had taken me in but not healed me.

Which could never heal me, no matter how far away I ran from my fears.

I closed my eyes for a brief moment, and, before I could change my mind, got up and reached for the phone. My fingers dialled a number I hadn't called for years but still had not forgotten.

The phone rang in the emptiness. I waited, my throat dry.

"Hello? Who is this?"

My stomach felt hollow – but it wasn't fear, it was shame. I said in Nahuatl, every word coming with great difficulty, "Mother? It's me."

I waited for anger, for endless reproaches. But there was nothing of that. Only her voice, on the verge of breaking, speaking the name I'd been given in Tenochtitlán, "Oh, Nenetl, my child. I'm so glad."

And though I hadn't heard that name in years, still it felt right, in a way that nothing else could.

THE TEAR

Ian McDonald

British author Ian McDonald is an ambitious and daring writer with a wide range and an impressive amount of talent. His first story was published in 1982, and since then he has appeared with some frequency in *Interzone, Asimov's Science Fiction,* and elsewhere. In 1989 he won the Locus Best First Novel Award for Desolation Road. He won the Philip K. Dick Award in 1992 for his novel *King of Morning, Queen of Day.* His other books include the novels *Out on Blue Six* and *Hearts, Hands and Voices, Terminal Cafe, Sacrifice of Fools, Evolution's Shore, Kirinya,* a chapbook novella *Tendeleo's Story, Ares Express,* and *Cyberabad,* as well as two collections of his short fiction, *Empire Dreams* and *Speaking in Tongues.* His novel *River of Gods* was a finalist for both the Hugo Award and the Arthur C. Clarke Award in 2005, and a novella drawn from it, *The Little Goddess,* was a finalist for the Hugo and the Nebula. His most recent book is another new novel that's receiving critical raves, *Brasyl.* Coming up is a new collection, *Cyberabad Days.* Born in Manchester, England, in 1960, McDonald has spent most of his life in Northern Ireland, and he now lives and works in Belfast. He has a website at lysator. liu.se/^unicorn/mcdonald/.

The lyrical and dazzling story that follows is filled with enough wild new ideas, evocative milieus, bizarre characters, and twists and turns of plot to fill many another author's four-book trilogy. He takes us to a quiet waterworld to follow a young boy setting out on a voyage of discovery that will take him to many unexpected destinations both across the greater universe and in the hidden depths of his own soul, one that will embroil him in the deadly clash of galactic empires and take him home the long way to find that enemies can be as close and familiar as friends.

PTEY, SAILING

ON THE NIGHT that Ptey voyaged out to have his soul shattered, eight hundred stars set sail across the sky. It was an evening at Great

Winter's ending. The sunlit hours raced toward High Summer, each day lavishly more full of light than the one before. In this latitude, the sun hardly set at all after the spring equinox, rolling along the horizon, fat and idle and pleased with itself. Summer-born Ptey turned his face to the sun as it dipped briefly beneath the horizon, closed his eyes, enjoyed its lingering warmth on his eyelids, in the angle of his cheekbones, on his lips. To the Summer-born, any loss of the light was a reminder of the terrible, sad months of winter and the unbroken, encircling dark.

But we have the stars, his father said, a Winter-born. *We are born looking out into the universe.*

Ptey's father commanded the little machines that ran the catamaran, trimming sail, winding sheets, setting course by the tumble of satellites; but the tiller he held himself. The equinoctial gales had spun away to the west two weeks before and the catboat ran fast and fresh on a sweet wind across the darkening water. Twin hulls cut through the ripple reflections of gas flares from the Temejveri oil platforms. As the sun slipped beneath the huge dark horizon and the warmth fell from the hollows of Ptey's face, so his father turned his face to the sky. Tonight, he wore his Steris Aspect. The ritual selves scared Ptey, so rarely were they unfurled in Ctarisphay: births, namings, betrothals and marriages, divorces and deaths. And of course, the Manifoldings. Familiar faces became distant and formal. Their language changed, their bodies seemed slower, heavier. They became possessed by strange, special knowledges. Only Steris possessed the language for the robots to sail the catamaran and, despite the wheel of positioning satellites around tilted Tay, the latitude and longitude of the Manifold House. The catamaran itself was only run out from its boathouse, to strong songs heavy with clashing harmonies, when a child from Ctarisphay on the edge of adulthood sailed out beyond the outer mole and the fleet of oil platforms to have his or her personality unfolded into eight.

Only two months since, Cjatay had sailed out into the oily black of a late winter afternoon. Ptey was Summer-born, a Solstice boy; Cjatay a late Autumn. It was considered remarkable that they shared enough in common to be able to speak to each other, let alone become the howling boys of the neighbourhood, the source of every broken window and borrowed boat. The best part of three seasons between them, but here was only two moons later, leaving behind the pulsing gas flares and maze of pipe work of the sheltering oil fields, heading into the great, gentle oceanic glow of the plankton blooms, steering by the stars, the occupied, haunted stars. The Manifolding was never a thing of moons and calendars, but of mothers' watchings and grandmothers' knowings and teachers' notings and fathers' murmurings, of subtly shifted razors and untimely lethargies, of deep-swinging voices and stained bedsheets.

On Etjay Quay, where the porcelain houses leaned over the landing, Ptey had thrown his friend's bag down into the boat. Cjatay's father had caught it and frowned. There were observances. Ways. Forms.

"See you," Ptey had said.

"See you." Then the wind caught in the catamaran's tall, curved sails and carried it away from the rain-wet, shiny faces of the houses of Ctarisphay. Ptey had watched the boat until it was lost in the light dapple of the city's lamps on the winter-dark water. See Cjatay he would, after his six months on the Manifold House. But only partially. There would be Cjatays he had never known, never even met. Eight of them, and the Cjatay with whom he had stayed out all the brief Low Summer nights of the prith run on the fishing staithes, skinny as the piers' wooden legs silhouetted against the huge sun kissing the edge of the world, would be but a part, a dream of one of the new names and new personalities. Would he know him when he met him on the great floating university that was the Manifold House?

Would he know himself?

"Are they moving yet?" Steris called from the tiller. Ptey shielded his dark-accustomed eyes against the pervasive glow of the carbon-absorbing plankton blooms and peered into the sky. *Sail of Bright Anticipation* cut two lines of liquid black through the gently undulating sheet of biolight, fraying at the edges into fractal curls of luminescence as the sheets of micro-organisms sought each other.

"Nothing yet."

But it would be soon, and it would be tremendous. Eight hundred stars setting out across the night. Through the changes and domestic rituals of his sudden Manifolding, Ptey had been aware of sky-watch parties being arranged, star-gazing groups setting up telescopes along the quays and in the campaniles, while day on day the story moved closer to the head of the news. Half the world – that half of the world not blinded by its extravagant axial tilt – would be looking to the sky. Watching Steris rig *Sail of Bright Anticipation*, Ptey had felt cheated, like a sick child confined to bed while festival raged across the boats lashed beneath his window. Now, as the swell of the deep dark of his world's girdling ocean lifted the twin prows of *Sail of Bright Anticipation*, on his web of shock-plastic mesh ahead of the mast, Ptey felt his excitement lift with it. A carpet of lights below, a sky of stars above: all his alone.

They were not stars. They were the 826 space habitats of the Anpreen Commonweal, spheres of nano-carbon ice and water five hundred kilometers in diameter that for twice Ptey's lifetime had adorned Bephis, the ringed gas giant, like a necklace of pearls hidden in a velvet bag, far from eye and mind. The negotiations fell into eras. The Panic, when the world of Tay became aware that the gravity waves pulsing through the huge ripple tank that was their ocean-bound planet were the bow-shocks of massive artifacts decelerating from near light-speed. The Denial, when Tay's governments decided it was Best Really to try and hide the fact that their solar system had been immigrated into by eight hundred and some space vehicles, each larger than Tay's petty moons, falling into neat and proper order around Bephis. The Soliciting, when it became obvious that Denial was futile – but on our terms, our terms. A fleet of space probes was dispatched to survey and attempt radio contact with the arrivals – as yet silent as ice. And, when they were not blasted from space or vaporized or collapsed into quantum black holes or any of the plethora of fanciful destructions imagined in the popular media, the Overture. The Sobering, when it was realized that these star-visitors existed primarily as swarms of free-swimming nano-assemblers in the free-fall spherical oceans of their eight hundred and some habitats, one mind with many forms; and, for the Anpreen, the surprise that these archaic hominiforms on this backwater planet were many selves within one body. One thing they shared and understood well. Water. It ran through their histories, it flowed around their ecologies, it mediated their molecules. After one hundred and twelve years of near-light-speed flight, the Anpreen Commonweal was desperately short of water; their spherical oceans shriveled almost into zero gravity teardrops within the immense, nanotech-reinforced ice shells. Then began the era of Negotiation, the most prolonged of the phases of contact, and the most complex. It had taken three years to establish the philosophical foundations: the Anpreen, an ancient species of the great Clade, had long been a colonial mind, arranged in subtle hierarchies of self-knowledge and ability, and did not know who to talk to, whom to ask for a decision, in a political system with as many governments and nations as there were islands and archipelagos scattered across the world ocean of the fourth planet from the sun.

Now the era of Negotiation had become the era of Open Trade. The Anpreen habitats spent their last drops of reaction mass to break orbit around Bephis and move the Commonweal in-system. Their destination was not Tay, but Tejaphay, Tay's sunward neighbour, a huge waterworld of unbroken ocean one hundred kilometers deep, crushing gravity, and endless storms. A billion years before the seed ships probed the remote star system, the gravitational interplay of giant worlds had sent the least of their number spiraling sunwards. Solar wind had stripped away its huge atmosphere and melted its mantle of water ice into a planetary ocean, deep and dark as nightmares. It was that wink of water in the system scale interferometers of the Can-Bet-Merey people, half a million years before, that had inspired them to fill their night sky with solar sails as one hundred thousand slow seed ships rode out on flickering launch lasers toward the new system. An evangelically pro-life people were the Can-Bet-Merey, zealous for the Clade's implicit dogma that intelligence was the only force in the universe capable of defeating the physical death of space-time.

If the tens of thousand of biological packages they had rained into the world-ocean of Tejaphay had germinated life, Tay's probes had yet to discover it. The Can-Bet-Merey did strike roots in the afterthought, that little blue pearl next out from the sun, a tear spun from huge Tejaphay.

One hundred thousand years ago, the Can-Bet-Merey had entered the post-biological phase of intelligence and moved to that level that could no longer communicate with the biological life of Tay, or even the Anpreen.

"Can you see anything yet?" A call from the tiller. *Sail of Bright Anticipation* had left behind the carbon-soaked plankton bloom, the ocean was deep dark and boundless. Sky and sea blurred; stars became confused with the riding lights of ships close on the horizon.

"Is it time?" Ptey called back.

"Five minutes ago."

Ptey found a footing on the webbing, and, one hand wrapped in the sheets, stood up to scan the huge sky. Every child of Tay, crazily tilted at 48 degrees to the ecliptic, grew up conscious that her planet was a ball rolling around the sun and that the stars were far, vast and slow, almost unchanging. But stars could change; Bephis, that soft smudge of light low in the south-east, blurred by the glow of eight hundred moon-sized space habitats, would soon be once again the hard point of light by which his ancestors had steered to their Manifoldings.

"Give it time," Ptey shouted. Time. The Anpreen were already voyaging; had switched on their drives and pulled out of orbit almost an hour before. The slow light of their embarkation had still not reached Tay. He saw the numbers spinning around in his head, accelerations, vectors, space and time all arranged around him like fluttering carnival banners. It had taken Ptey a long time to understand that not everyone could see numbers like him and reach out and make them do what they wanted.

"Well, I'll be watching the football," Cjatay had declared when Teacher Deu had declared a Special Class Project in conjunction with the Noble Observatory of Pteu to celebrate the Anpreen migration. "We're all jumping up and down, Anpreen this, Anpreen that, but when it comes down to it, they aliens and we don't know what they really want, no one does."

"They're not aliens," Ptey had hissed back. "There *are* no aliens, don't you know that? We're all just part of the one big Clade."

Then Teacher Deu had shouted at them quiet you boys and they had straightened themselves at their kneeling-desks, but Cjatay had hissed,

"So if they're our cousins, why don't they give us their star-crosser drive?"

Such was the friendship between Ptey and Cjatay that they would argue over nodes of free-swimming nanotechnology orbiting a gas giant.

"Look! Oh look!"

Slowly, very slowy, Bephis was unraveling into a glowing smudge, like one of the swarms of nuchpas that hung above the waves like smoke on High Summer mornings. The fleet was moving. Eight hundred worlds. The numbers in his skull told Ptey that the Anpreen Commonweal was already at ten per cent of light-speed. He tried to work out the relativistic deformations of space-time but there were too many numbers flocking around him too fast. Instead, he watched Bephis unfurl into a galaxy, that cloud of stars slowly pull away from the bright mote of the gas giant. Crossing the ocean of night. Ptey glanced behind him. In the big dark, his father's face was hard to read, especially as Steris, who was sober and focused, and, Ptey had learned, not particularly bright. He seemed to be smiling.

It is a deep understanding, the realization that you are cleverer than your parents, Ptey thought. Behind that first smirking, satisfied sense of your own smartness comes a more profound understanding; that smart is only smart at some things, in some situations. Clever is conditional: Ptey could calculate the space-time distortion of eight hundred space habitats, plot a course across the dark, steepening sea by the stars in their courses, but he could never harness the winds or whistle the small commands to the machines, all the weather-clevernesses of Steris. That is how our world has shaped our intelligences. A self for every season.

The ravel of stars was unwinding, the Anpreen Migration flowing into a ribbon of sparkles, a scarf of night beyond the veils of the aurora. Tomorrow night, it would adorn Tejaphay, that great blue guide star on the edge of the world, that had become a glowing smudge, a thumbprint of the alien. Tomorrow night, Ptey would look at that blue eye in the sky from the minarets of the Manifold House. He knew that it had minarets; every child knew what the Manifold House and its sister houses all round the world looked like. Great hulks of grey wood gone silvery from salt and sun, built over upon through within alongside until they were floating cities. Cities of children. But the popular imaginations of Teacher Deu's Grade Eight class never painted them bright and loud with voices, they were dark, sooty labyrinths sailing under a perpetual cloud of black diesel smoke that poured from a thousand chimneys, taller even than the masts and towers. The images were sharp in Ptey's mind, but he could never see himself there, in those winding wooden staircases loud with the cries of sea birds, looking out from the high balconies across the glowing sea. Then his breath caught. All his imaginings and failures to imagine were made true as lights disentangled themselves from the skein of stars of the Anpreen migration: red and green stars, the riding lights of the Manifold House. Now he could feel the thrum of its engines and generators through the water and the twin hulls. Ptey set his hand to the carbon nanofiber mast. It sang to deep harmonic. And just as the stars are always farther than you think, so Prey saw that the lights of the Manifold House were closer than he thought, that he was right under them, that *Sail of Bright Anticipation* was slipping through the outer buoys and nets, and that the towers and spires and minarets, rising in his vision, one by one, were obliterating the stars.

NEJBEN, SWIMMING

Beneath a sky of honey, Nejben stood hip deep in water warm as blood, deep as forgetting. This High Summer midnight, the sun was still clear from the horizon, and in its constant heat and light, the wood of the Manifold House's old, warped spires seemed to exhale a spicy musk, the distilled pheromone of centuries of teenage hormones and sexual angsts and identity crises. In cupped hands, Nejben scooped up the waters of the Chalybeate Pool and let them run, gold and thick, through his fingers. He savored the sensuality, observed the flash of sunlight through the falling water, noted the cool, deep plash as the pool received its own. A new Aspect, Nejben; old in observation and knowledge, for the body remained the same though a flock of selves came to roost in it, fresh in interpretation and experience.

When Nejben first emerged, shivering and anoxic, from the Chalybeate Pool, to be wrapped in silvery thermal sheets by the agisters, he had feared himself mad. A voice in his head, that would not go away, that would not be shut up, that seemed to know him, know every part of him.

"It's perfectly normal," said agister Ashbey, a plump, serious woman with the blackest skin Nejben had ever seen. But he remembered that every Ritual Aspect was serious, and in the Manifold House the agisters were never in any other Aspect. None that the novices would ever see. "Perfectly natural. It takes time for your Prior, your childhood Aspect, to find its place and relinquish the control of the higher cognitive levels. Give it time. Talk to him. Reassure him. He will feel very lost, very alone, like he has lost everything that he ever knew. Except you, Nejben."

The time-free, sun-filled days in the sunny, smoggy yards and cloisters of the First Novitiate were full of whisperings; boys and girls like himself whispering goodbye to their childhoods. Nejben learned his Prior's dreads, that the self that had been called Ptey feared that the numbers, the patterns between them, the ability to reduce physical objects to mathematics and see in an instant their relationships and implications, would be utterly lost. He saw also that Nejben in himself scared Ptey: the easy physicality, the unselfconscious interest in his own body, the awareness of the hormones pumping like tidewater through his tubes and cells; the ever-present, ever-tickling nag of sex; everywhere, everywhen, everyone and -thing. Even as a child-self, even as shadow, Ptey knew that the first self to be birthed at the Manifold House was the pubescent self, the sexual self, but he felt this growing, aching youth to be more alien than the disembodied, mathematical Anpreen.

The tiers led down into the palp pool. In its depths, translucencies shifted. Nejben shivered in the warm High Summer midnight.

"Hey! Ptey!"

Names flocked around the Manifold House's towers like sun-gulls. New selves, new identities unfolded every hour of every day and yet old names clung. Agister Ashbey, jokey and astute, taught the social subtleties by which adults knew what Aspect and name to address and which Aspect and name of their own to wear in response. From the shade of the Poljeri Cloister, Puzhay waved. Ptey had found girls frightening, but Nejben liked them, enjoyed their company and the little games of admiring insult and flirting mock-animosity he played with them. He reckoned he understood girls now. Puzhay was small, still boy-figured, her skin Winter-born-pale, a Janni from Bedenderay, where at midwinter the atmosphere froze. She had a barbarous accent and continental manners, but Nejben found himself thinking often about her small, flat boy-breasts with their big, thumbable nipples. He had never thought when he came to the Manifold House that there would be people here from places other than Ctarisphay and its archipelago sisters. People – girls – from the big polar continent. Rude girls who cursed and openly called boys' names.

"Puzhay! What're you doing?"

"Going in."

"For the palps?"

"Nah. Just going in."

Nejben found and enjoyed a sudden, swift swelling of his dick as he watched Puzhay's breasts tauten as she raised her arms above her head and dived, awkward as a Bedenderay land-girl, into the water. Water hid it. Sun dapple kept it secret. Then he felt a shiver run over him and he dived down, deep down. Almost he let the air rush out of him in a gasp as he felt the cool cool water close around his body; then he saw Puzhay in her tight swim-shorts that made her ass look so strong and muscley turn in the water, tiny bubbles leaking from her nose, to grin and wave and beckon him down. Nejben swam down past the descending tiers of steps. Green opened before him, the bottomless emerald beyond the anti-skray nets where the Chalybeate pond was refreshed by the borderless sea. Between her pale red body and the deep green sea was the shimmering curtains of the palps.

They did not make them we did not bring them they were here forever. Ten thousand years of theology, biology, and xenology in that simple kinder-group rhyme. Nejben – all his people – had always known their special place; stranger to this world, spurted into the womb of the world sea as the star-sperm, the seed of sentience. Twenty million drops of life-seed swam ashore and became humanity, the rest swam out to sea and met and smelled and loved the palps, older than forever. Now Nejben turned and twisted like an eel past funny, flirting, heartbreaking Puzhay, turning to show the merest glimpse of his own sperm-eel, down toward the palps. The curtain of living jelly rippled and dissolved into their separate lives. Slick, cold, quivering jelly slid across his sex-warm flesh. Nejben shivered, quivered; repelled yet aroused in a way that was other than sex. The water took on a prickle, a tickle, a tang of salt and fear and ancient ancient lusts, deep as his first stiff dream. Against sense, against reason, against three million years of species wisdom, Nejben employed the tricks of agister Ashbey and opened his mouth. He inhaled. Once he gagged, twice he choked, then he felt the jellied eeling of the palps squirm down his throat: a choke, and into the lungs. He inhaled green salt water. And then, as the palps demurely unravelled their nano-tube outer integuments and infiltrated them into his lungs, his bronchial tubes, his bloodstream, he *became.* Memories stirred, invoked by olfactory summonings, changed as a new voice, a new way of seeing, a new interpretation of those memories and experiences, formed. Nejben swam down, breathing memory-water, stroke by stroke unravelling. There was another down there, far below him, swimming up not through water but through the twelve years of his life. A new self.

Puzhay, against the light of a three o'clock sky. Framed in the arch of a cell window, knees pulled up to her chest. Small budding breasts; strong, boy jawline, fall and arc of hair shadow against lilac. She had laughed, throwing her head back. That first sight of her was cut into Nejben's memory, every line and trace, like the paper silhouettes the limners would cut of friends and families and enemies for Autumn Solstice. That first stirring of sex, that first intimation in the self of Ptey of this then-stranger, now-familiar Nejben.

As soon as he could, he had run. After he had found out where to put his bag, after he had worked out how to use the ancient, gurgling shit-eater, after agister Ashbey had closed the door with a smile and a blessing on the wooden cell – his wooden cell – that still smelled of fresh-cut timber after hundreds of years on the world-ocean of Tay. In the short season in which photosynthesis was possible, Bedenderay's forests grew fast and fierce, putting on meters in a single day. Small wonder the wood still smelled fresh and lively. After the midnight walk along the ceramic lanes and up the wooden staircases and through the damp-smelling cloisters, through the gently undulating quadrangles with the sky-train of the Anpreen migration bright overhead, holding on, as tradition demanded, to the bell-hung by a chain from his agister's waist; after the form filling and the photographings and the registering and the this-is-your-ident-card this is your map I've tattooed onto the back of your hand trust it will guide you and I am your agister and we'll see you in the east Refectory for breakfast; after the climb up the slimy wooden stairs from *Sail of Bright Anticipation* on to the Manifold House's quay, the biolights green around him and the greater lamps of the great college's towers high before him; when he was alone in this alien new world where he would become eight alien new people: he ran.

Agister Ashbey was faithful; the tattoo, a clever print of smart molecules and nanodyes, was meshed into the Manifold House's network and guided him through the labyrinth of dormitories and cloisters and Boy's Pavilions and Girlhearths by the simple, aversive trick of stinging the opposite side his map-hand to the direction in which he was to turn.

Cjatay. Sea-sundered friend. The only other one who knew him, knew him the moment they had met outside the school walls and recognized each other as different from the sailing freaks and fishing fools. Interested in geography, in love with numbers, with the wonder of the world and the worlds, as the city net declared, beyond. Boys who looked up at the sky.

As his burning hand led him left, right, up this spiral staircase under the lightening sky, such was Ptey's impetus that he never thought, would he know Cjatay? Cjatay had been in the Manifold House three months. Cjatay could be – would be – any number of Aspects now. Ptey had grown up with his father's overlapping circles of friends, each specific to a different Aspect, but he had assumed that it was a grown-up thing. That couldn't happen to him and Cjatay! Not them.

The cell was one of four that opened off a narrow oval at the head of a tulip-shaped minaret – the Third Moon of Spring Tower, the legend on the back of Ptey's hand read. Cells were assigned by birth-date and season. Head and heart full of nothing but seeing Cjatay, he pushed open the door – no door in the Manifold House was ever locked.

She was in the arched window, dangerously high above the shingled roofs and porcelain domes of the Vernal Equinox division. Beyond her, only the wandering stars of the Anpreen. Ptey had no name for the sudden rush of feelings that came when he saw Puzhay throw back her head and laugh at some so-serious comment of Cjatay's. Nejben did.

It was only at introductory breakfast in the East Refectory, where he met the other uncertain, awkward boys and girls of his intake, that Ptey saw past the dawn seduction of Puzhay to Cjatay, and saw him unchanged, exactly as he had had been when he had stepped down from Etjay Quay into the catamaran and been taken out across the lagoon to the waste gas flares of Temejveri.

She was waiting crouched on the wooden steps where the water of the Chalybeate Pool lapped, knees pulled to her chest, goose flesh pimpling her forearms and calves in the cool of after-midnight. He knew this girl, knew her name, knew her history, knew the taste of a small, tentative kiss stolen among the crowds of teenagers pushing over 12th Canal Bridge. The memory was sharp and warm, but it was another's.

"Hi there."

He dragged himself out of the water onto the silvery wood, rolled away to hide his nakedness. In the cloister shadow, Ashbey waited with a sea-silk robe.

"Hi there." There was never any easy way to tell someone you were another person from the one they remembered. "I'm Serejen." The name had been there, down among the palps, slipped into him with their mind-altering neurotransmitters.

"Are you?"

"All right. Yes, I'm all right." A tickle in the throat made him cough, the cough amplified into a deep retch. Serejen choked up a lungful of mucus-stained palp-jelly. In the early light, it thinned and ran, flowed down the steps to rejoin its shoal in the Chalybeate Pool. Agister Ashbey took a step forward. Serejen waved her away.

"What time is it?"

"Four thirty."

Almost five hours.

"Serejen." Puzhay looked coyly away. Around the Chalybeate Pool, other soul-swimmers were emerging, coughing up lungfuls of palp, shivering in their thermal robes, growing into new Aspects of themselves. "It's Cjatay. He needs to see you. Dead urgent."

Waiting Ashbey folded new-born Serejen in his own thermal gown, the intelligent plastics releasing their stored heat to his particular body temperature.

"Go to him," his agister said.

"I thought I was supposed to . . ."

"You've got the rest of your life to get to know Serejen. I think you should go."

Cjatay. A memory of fascination with starry skies, counting and numbering and betting games. The name and the face belonged to another Aspect, another life, but that old lust for numbers, for discovering the relationships between things, stirred a deep welling of joy. It was as rich and adult as the swelling of his dick he found in the bright mornings, or when he thought about Puzhay's breasts in his hands and the tattooed triangle of her sex. Different; no less intense.

The shutters were pulled close. The screen was the sole light in the room. Cjatay turned on hearing his lockless door open. He squinted into the gloom of the stair head, then cried excitedly,

"Look at this look at this!"

Pictures from the observation platforms sent to Tejaphay to monitor the doings of the Anpreen. A black-light plane of stars, the blinding blue curve of the waterworld stopped down to prevent screen-burn. The closer habitats showed a disc, otherwise it was moving lights. Patterns of speed and gravity.

"What am I looking at?"

"Look look, they're building a space elevator! I wondered how they were going to get the water from Tejaphay. Simple, duh! They're just going to vacuum it up! They've got some kind of processing unit in stationary orbit chewing up one of those asteroids they brought with them, but they using one of their own habitats to anchor it."

"At twice stationary orbit," Serejen said. "So they're going to have to build down and up at the same time to keep the elevator in tension." He did not know where the words came from. They were on his lips and they were true.

"It must be some kind of nano-carbon compound," Cjatay said, peering at the screen for some hint, some elongation, some erection from the fuzzy blob of the construction asteroid. "Incredible tensile strength, yet very flexible. We have to get that; with all our oil, it could change everything about our technology. It could really make us a proper star-faring people." Then, as if hearing truly for the first time, Cjatay turned from the screen and peered again at the figure in the doorway. "Who are you?" His voice was high and soft and plaintive.

"I'm Serejen."

"You sound like Ptey."

"I was Ptey. I remember him."

Cjatay did a thing with his mouth, a twisting, chewing movement that Serejen recalled from moments of unhappiness and frustration. The time at his sister's nameday party, when all the birth family was gathered and he had shown how it was almost certain that someone in the house on Drunken Chicken Lane had the same nameday as little Sezjma. There had been a long, embarrassed silence as Cjatay had burst into the adult chatter. Then laughter. And again, when Cjatay had worked out how long it would take to walk a light-year and Teacher Deu has asked the class *does anyone understand this?* For a moment, Serejen thought that the boy might cry. That would have been a terrible thing; unseemly, humiliating. Then he saw the bag on the unkempt bed, the ritual white clothes thrust knotted and fighting into it.

"I think what Cjatay wants to say is that he's leaving the Manifold House," agister Ashbey said, in the voice that Serejen understood as the one adults used when they had uncomfortable things to say. In that voice was a hidden word that Ashbey would not, that Serejen and Puzhay could not, and that Cjatay never would speak.

There was one in every town, every district. Kentlay had lived at the bottom of Drunken Chicken Lane, still at fortysomething living with his birth-parents. He had never married, though then-Ptey had heard that some did, and not just others like them. Normals. Multiples. Kentlay had been a figure that drew pity and respect alike; equally blessed and cursed, the Lonely were granted insights and gifts in compensation for their inability to manifold into the Eight Aspects. Kentlay had the touch for skin diseases, warts, and the sicknesses of birds. Ptey had been sent to see him for the charm of a dangling wart on his chin. The wart was gone within a week. Even then, Ptey had wondered if it had been through unnatural gifts or superstitious fear of the alien at the end of the wharf.

Cjatay. Lonely. The words were as impossible together as *green sun* or *bright winter*. It was never to be like this. Though the waters of the Chalybeate Pool would break them into many brilliant shards, though there would be other lives, other friends, even other wives and husbands, there would always be aspects of themselves that remembered trying to draw birds and fishes on the glowing band of the Mid Winter Galaxy that hung in the sky for weeks on end, or trying to calculate the mathematics of the High Summer silverlings that shoaled like silver needles in the Lagoon, how they kept together yet apart, how they were many but moved as one. *Boiling rain. Summer ice. A morning where the sun wouldn't rise. A friend who would always, only be one person.* Impossibilities. Cjatay could not be abnormal. Dark word. A vile word that hung on Cjatay like an oil-stained tarpaulin.

He sealed his bag and slung it over his shoulder.

"I'll give you a call when you get back."

"Yeah. Okay. That would be good." Words and needs and sayings flocked to him, but the end was so fast, so sudden, that all Serejen could do was stare at his feet so that he would not have to see Cjatay walk away. Puzhay was in tears. Cjatay's own agister, a tall, dark-skinned Summer-born, put his arm around Cjatay and took him to the stairs.

"Hey. Did you ever think?" Cjatay threw back the line from the top of the spiral stair. "Why are they here? The Anpreen." Even now, Serejen realized, Cjatay was hiding from the truth that he would be marked as different, as not fully human, for the rest of his life, hiding behind stars and ships and the mystery of the alien. "Why did they come here? They call it the Anpreen migration, but where are they migrating *to*? And what are they migrating *from*? Anyone ever ask that? Ever think about that, eh?"

Then agister Ashbey closed the door on the high tower-top cell.

"We'll talk later."

Gulls screamed. Change in the weather coming. On the screen behind him, stars moved across the face of the great water.

Serejen could not bear to go down to the quay, but watched *Sail of Bright Anticipation* make sail from the cupola of the Bright Glance Netball Hall. The Manifold House was sailing through a plankton bloom and he watched the ritual catamaran's hulls cut two lines of bioglow through the carpet of carbon-absorbing microlife. He stood and followed the sails until they were lost among the hulls of huge ceramic oil tankers pressed low to the orange smog-glow of Ctarisphay down under the horizon. Call each other. They would always forget to do that. They would slip out of each other's lives – Serejen's life now vastly more rich and populous as he moved across the social worlds of his various Aspects. In time, they would slip out of each other's thoughts and memories. So it was that Serejen Nejben ex-Ptey knew that he was not a child any longer. He could let things go.

After morning Shift class, Serejen went down to the Old Great Pool, the ancient flooded piazza that was the historic heart of the Manifold House, and used the techniques he had learned an hour before to effortlessly transfer from Serejen to Nejben. Then he went down into the waters and swam with Puzhay. She was teary and confused, but the summer-warmed water and the physical exercise brightened her. Under a sky lowering with the summer storm that the gulls had promised, they sought out the many secret flooded colonnades and courts where the big groups of friends did not go. There, under the first crackles of lightning and the hiss of rain, he kissed her and she slipped her hand into his swimsuit and cradled the comfortable swell of his cock.

SEREJEN, LOVING

Night, the aurora and sirens. Serejen shivered as police drones came in low over the Conservatorium roof. Through the high, arched windows, fires could still be seen burning on Yaskaray Prospect. The power had not yet been restored, the streets, the towering apartment blocks that lined them, were still dark. A stalled tram sprawled across a set of points, flames flickering in its rear carriage. The noise of the protest had moved off, but occasional shadows moved across the ice beneath the mesmerism of the aurora; student rioters, police security robots. It was easy to tell the robots by the sprays of ice crystals thrown up by their needle-tip, mincing legs.

"Are you still at that window? Come away from there, if they see you they might shoot you. Look, I've tea made."

"Who?"

"What?"

"Who might shoot me? The rioters or the police?"

"Like you'd care if you were dead."

But he came and sat at the table and took the bowl of thin, salty Bedenderay maté.

"But sure I can't be killed."

Her name was Seriantep. She was an Anpreen Prebendary ostensibly attached to the College of Theoretical Physics at the Conservatorium of Jann. She looked like a tall, slim young woman with the dark skin and blue-black hair of a Summer-born Archipelagan, but that was just the form that the swarm of Anpreen nano-processor motes had assumed. She hived. Reris Orhum Fejannen Kekjay Prus Rejmer Serejen Nejben wondered how close you had to get before her perfect skin resolved into a blur of microscopic motes. He had had much opportunity to make this observation. As well as being his notional student – though what a functionally immortal hive-citizen who had crossed one hundred and twenty light-years could learn from a fresh twentysomething meat human was moot – she was his occasional lover.

She drank the tea. Serejen watched the purse of her lips around the delicate porcelain bowl decorated with the ubiquitous Lord of the Fishes motif, even in high, dry continental Jann. The small movement of her throat as she swallowed. He knew a hundred such tiny, intimate movements, but even as she cooed and giggled and gasped to the stimulations of the Five Leaves, Five Fishes ritual, the involuntary actions of her body had seemed like performances. Learned responses. Performances as he made observations. Actor and audience. That was the kind of lover he was as Serejen.

"So what is it really like to fuck a pile of nano-motes?" Puzhay had asked as they rolled around with wine in the cosy warm fleshiness of the Thirteenth Window Coupling Porch at the ancient, academic Ogrun Menholding. "I'd imagine it feels . . . fizzy." And she'd squeezed his cock, holding it hostage, *watch what you say boy*.

"At least nano-motes never get morning breath," he'd said, and she'd given a little shriek of outrage and jerked his dick so that he yelped, and then they both laughed and then rolled over again and buried themselves deep into the winter-defying warmth of the piled quilts.

I should be with her now, he thought. The months-long winter nights beneath the aurora and the stars clouds of the great galaxy were theirs. After the Manifold House, he had gone with her to her Bedenderay and her home city of Jann. The City Conservatorium had the world's best theoretical physics department. It was nothing to do with small, boyish, funny Puzhay. They had formalized a partnering six months later. His parents had complained and shivered through all the celebrations in this cold and dark and barbarous city far from the soft elegance of island life. But ever after winter, even on the coldest mornings when carbon dioxide frost crusted the steps of the Tea Lane Ladyhearth where Puzhay lived, was their season. He should call her, let her know he was still trapped but that at the first sign, the very first sign, he would come back. The cell net was still up. Even an email. He couldn't. Seriantep didn't know. Seriantep wouldn't understand. She had not understood that one time when he tried to explain it in abstracts; that different Aspects could – should – have different relationships with different partners, love separately but equally. *That as Serejen, I love you, Anpreen Prebendary Seriantep, but as Nejben, I love Puzhay*. He could never say that. For an immortal, starcrossing hive of nano motes, Seriantep was very singleminded.

Gunfire cracked in the crystal night, far and flat.

"I think it's dying down," Seriantep said.

"I'd give it a while yet."

So strange, so rude, this sudden flaring of anti-alien violence. In the dreadful dead of winter too, when nothing should rightfully fight and even the trees along Yaskaray Prospect drew down to their heartwood and turned to ice. Despite the joy of Puzhay, Serejen knew that he would always hate the Bedenderay winter. *You watch out now*, his mother had said when he had announced his decision to go to Jann. *They all go dark-mad there.* Accidie and suicide walked the frozen canals of the Winter City. No surprise then that madness should break out against the Anpreen Prebendaries. Likewise inevitable that the popular rage should be turned against the Conservatorium. The university had always been seen as a place apart from the rest of Jann, in summer aloof and lofty above the sweltering streets, like an over-grand daughter; in winter a parasite on this most marginal of economies. Now it was the unofficial alien embassy in the northern hemisphere. There were more Anpreen in its long, small-windowed corridors than anywhere else in the world.

There are no aliens, Serejen thought. *There is only the Clade. We are all family.* Cjatay had insisted that. The ship had sailed over the horizon, they hadn't called, they had drifted from each other's lives. Cjatay's name occasionally impinged on Serejen's awareness through radio interviews and opinion pieces. He had developed a darkly paranoid conspiracy theory around the Anpreen Presence. Serejen, high above the frozen streets of Jann in deeply abstract speculation about the physical reality of mathematics, occasionally mused upon the question of at what point the migration had become a Presence. The Lonely often obsessively took up narrow, focused interests. Now the street was listening, acting. Great Winter always was a dark, paranoid season. *Here's how to understand*, Serejen thought. *There are no aliens after you've had sex with them.*

Helicopter blades rattled from the walls of the College of Theoretical Physics and then retreated across the Central Canal. The silence in the warm, dimly-lit little faculty cell was profound. At last, Serejen said, "I think we could go now."

On the street, cold stabbed even through the quilted layers of Serejen's greatcoat. He fastened the high collar across his throat and still he felt the breath crackle into ice around his lips. Seriantep stepped lightly between the half bricks and bottle shards in nothing more than the tunic and leggings she customarily wore around the college. Her motes gave her full control over her body, including its temperature.

"You should have put something on," Serejen said. "You're a bit obvious."

Past shuttered cafés and closed up stores and the tall brick faces of the student Hearths. The burning tram on the Tunday Avenue junction blazed fitfully, its bitter smoke mingling with the eternal aromatic hydrocarbon smog exhaled by Jann's power plants. The trees that lined the avenue's centre strip were folded down into tight fists, dreaming of summer. Their boot heels rang loud on the street tiles.

A darker shape upon the darkness moved in the narrow slit of an alley between two towering tenement blocks. Serejen froze, his heart jerked. A collar turned down, a face studying his – Obredajay from the Department of Field Physics.

"Safe home."

"Aye. And you."

The higher academics all held apartments within the Conservatorium and were safe within its walls; most of the research staff working late would sit it out until morning. Tea and news reports would see them through. Those out on the fickle streets had reasons to be there. Serejen had heard that Obredajay was head-over-heels infatuated with a new manfriend.

The dangers we court for little love.

On the intersection of Tunday Avenue and Yaskaray Wharf, a police robot stepped out of the impervious dark of the arches beneath General Gatorio Bridge. Piotono hissed it up to its full three meters; green light flicked across Serejen's retinas. Seriantep held up her hand, the motes of her palm displaying her immunity as a Prebendary of the Clade. The machine shrank down, seemingly dejected, if plastic and pumps could display such an emotion.

A solitary tea-shop stood open on the corner of Silver Spider Entry and the Wharf, its windows misty with steam from the simmering urns. Security eyes turned and blinked at the two fleeing academics.

On Tannis Lane, they jumped them. There was no warning. A sudden surge of voices rebounding from the stone staircases and brick arches broke into a wave of figures lumbering around the turn of the alley, bulky and shouldering in their heavy winter quilts. Some held sticks, some held torn placards, some were empty handed. They saw a man in a heavy winter coat, breath frosted on his mouth-shield. They saw a woman almost naked, her breath easy, unclouded. They knew in an instant what she saw. The hubbub in the laneway became a roar.

Serejen and Seriantep were already in flight. Sensing rapid motion, the soles of Serejen's boots extended grips into the rime. As automatically, he felt the heart-numbing panic-rush ebb, felt himself lose his grip on his body and grow pale. Another was taking hold, his flight-or-fight Aspect; his cool, competent emergency service Fejannen.

He seized Seriantep's hand.

"With me. Run!"

Serejen-Fejannen saw the change of Aspect flicker across the tea-shop owner's face like weather as they barged through his door, breathless between his stables. Up to his counter with its looming, steaming urns of hot hot water. This tea-man wanted them out, wanted his livelihood safe.

"We need your help."

The tea-man's eyes and nostrils widened at the charge of rioters that skidded and slipped around the corner into Silver Spider Entry. Then his hand hit the button under the counter and the shutters rolled down. The shop boomed, the shutters bowed to fists striking them. Rocks banged like gunfire from metal. Voices rose and joined together, louder because they were unseen.

"I've called the police," Seriantep said. "They'll be here without delay."

"No, they won't," Fejannen said. He pulled out a chair from the table closest the car and sat down, edgily eying the grey slats of the shutter. "Their job is to restore order and protect property. Providing personal protection to aliens is far down their list of priorities."

Seriantep took the chair opposite. She sat down wary as a settling bird.

"What's going on here? I don't understand. I'm very scared."

The café owner set two glasses of maté down on the table. He frowned, then his eyes opened in understanding. An alien at his table. He returned to the bar and leaned on it, staring at the shutters beyond which the voice of the mob circled.

"I thought you said you couldn't be killed."

"That's not what I'm scared of. I'm scared of you, Serejen."

"I'm not Serejen. I'm Fejannen."

"Who, what's Fejannen?"

"Me, when I'm scared, when I'm angry, when I need to be able to think clearly and coolly when a million things are happening at once, when I'm playing games or hunting or putting a big funding proposal together."

"You sound . . . different."

"I *am* different. How long have you been on our world?"

"You're hard. And cold. Serejen was never hard."

"I'm not Serejen."

A huge crash – the shutter bowed under a massive impact and the window behind it shattered.

"Right, that's it, I don't care what happens, you're going." The tea-man leaped from behind his counter and strode towards Seriantep. Fejannen was there to meet him.

"This woman is a guest in your country and requires your protection."

"That's not a woman. That's a pile of . . . insects. Things. Tiny things."

"Well, they look like mighty scared tiny things."

"I don't think so. Like you said, like they say on the news, they can't really die."

"They can hurt. *She* can hurt."

Eyes locked, then disengaged. The maté-man returned to his towering silos of herbal mash. The noise from the street settled into a stiff, waiting silence. Neither Fejannen nor Seriantep believed that it was true, that the mob had gone, despite the spearing cold out there. The lights flickered once, twice.

Seriantep said suddenly, vehemently, "I could take them."

The tea-man looked up.

"Don't," Fejannen whispered.

"I could. I could get out under the door. It's just a reforming."

The tea-man's eyes were wide. A demon, a winter-grim in his prime location canal-side tea-shop!

"You scare them enough as you are," Fejannen said.

"Why? We're only here to help, to learn from you."

"They think, what have you got to learn from us? They think that you're keeping secrets from us."

"Us?"

"Them. Don't scare them any more. The police will come, eventually, or the Conservatorium proctors. Or they'll just get bored and go home. These things never really last."

"You're right." She slumped back into her seat. "This fucking world . . . Oh, why did I come here?" Seriantep glanced up at the inconstant lumetubes, beyond to the distant diadem of her people's colonies, gravid on decades of water. It was a question, Fejannen knew, that Serejen had asked himself many times. A postgraduate scholar researching space-time topologies and the cosmological constant. A thousand-year-old post-human innocently wearing the body of a twenty-year-old woman, playing the student. She could learn nothing from him. All the knowledge the Anpreen wanderers had gained in their ten thousands year migration was incarnate in her motes. She embodied all truth and she lied with every cell of her body. Anpreen secrets. No basis for a relationship, yet Serejen loved her, as Serejen could love. But was it any more for her than novelty; a tourist, a local boy, a brief summer loving?

Suddenly, vehemently, Seriantep leaned across the table to take Fejannen's face between her hands.

"Come with me."

"Where? Who?"

"Who?" She shook her head in exasperation. "Ahh! Serejen. But it would be you as well, it has to be you. To my place, to the Commonweal. I've wanted to ask you for so long. I'd love you to see my worlds. Hundreds of worlds, like jewels, dazzling in the sun. And inside, under the ice, the worlds within worlds within worlds . . . I made the application for a travel bursary months ago, I just couldn't ask."

"Why? What kept you from asking?" A small but significant traffic of diplomats, scientists, and journalists flowed between Tay and the Anpreen fleet around Tejaphay. The returnees enjoyed global celebrity status, their opinions and experiences sought by think-tanks and talk shows and news-site columns, the details of the faces and lives sought by the press. Serejen had never understood what it was the people expected from the celebrity of others but was not so immured behind the fortress walls of the Collegium, armoured against the long siege of High Winter, that he couldn't appreciate its personal benefits. The lights seemed to brighten, the sense of the special hush outside, that was not true silence but waiting, dimmed as Serejen replaced Fejannen. "Why didn't you ask?"

"Because I thought you might refuse."

"Refuse?" The few, the golden few. "Turn down the chance to work in the Commonweal? Why would anyone do that, why would I do that?"

Seriantep looked long at him, her head cocked slightly, alluringly, to one side, the kind of gesture an alien unused to a human body might devise.

"You're Serejen again, aren't you?"

"I am that Aspect again, yes."

"Because I thought you might refuse because of *her*. That other woman. Puzhay."

Serejen blinked three times. From Seriantep's face, he knew that she expected some admission, some confession, some emotion. He could not understand what.

Seriantep said, "I know about her. We know things at the Anpreen Mission. We check whom we work with. We have to. We know not everyone welcomes us, and that more are suspicious of us. I know who she is and where she lives and what you do with her three times a week when you go to her. I know where you were intending to go tonight, if all this hadn't happened."

Three times again, Serejen blinked. Now he was hot, too hot in his winter quilt in this steamy, fragrant tea-shop.

"But that's a ridiculous question. *I* don't love Puzhay. *Nejben* does."

"Yes, but you *are* Nejben."

"How many times do I have to tell you. . . ." Serejen bit back the anger. There were Aspects hovering on the edge of his consciousness like the hurricane-front angels of the Bazjendi Psalmody; selves inappropriate to Seriantep. Aspects that in their rage and storm might lose him this thing, so finely balanced now in this tea-shop. "It's our way," he said weakly. "It's how we are."

"Yes, but . . ." Seriantep fought for words. "It's *you*, there, that body. You say it's different, you say it's someone else and not you, not Serejen, but how do I know that? How *can* I know that?"

You say that, with your body that in this tea-shop you said could take many forms, any form, Serejen thought. Then Fejannen, shadowed but never more than a thought away in this besieged, surreal environment, heard a shift in the silence outside. The tea-man glanced up. He had heard it too. The difference between *waiting* and *anticipating*.

"Excuse me, I must change Aspects."

A knock on the shutter, glove-muffled. A voice spoke Fejannen's full name. A voice that Fejannen knew from his pervasive fear of the risk his academic Aspect was taking with Seriantep and that Serejen knew from those news reports and articles that broke through his vast visualizations of the topology of the universe and that Nejben knew from a tower top cell and a video screen full of stars.

"Can I come in?"

Fejannen nodded to the tea-man. He ran the shutter up high enough for the bulky figure in the long quilted coat and boots to duck under. Dreadful cold blew around Fejannen.

Cjatay bowed, removed his gloves, banging rime from the knuckles, and made the proper formalities to ascertain which Aspect he was speaking to.

"I have to apologise; I only recently learned that it was you who were caught here."

The voice, the intonations and inflections, the over-precisions and refinements – no time might have passed since Cjatay walked out of the Manifold House. In a sense, no time *had* passed; Cjatay was caught, inviolable, unchangeable by anything other than time and experience. Lonely.

"The police will be here soon," Seriantep said.

"Yes, they will," Cjatay said mildly. He looked Seriantep up and down, as if studying a zoological specimen. "They have us well surrounded now. These things are almost never planned; what we gain in spontaneity of expression we lose in strategy. But when I realized it was you, Fejannen-Nejben, I saw a way that we could all emerge from this intact."

"Safe passage," Fejannen said.

"I will personally escort you out."

"And no harm at all to you, politically."

"I need to distance myself from what has happened tonight."

"But your fundamental fear of the visitors remains unchanged?"

"I don't change. You know that. I see it as a virtue. Some things are solid, some things endure. Not everything changes with the seasons. But fear, you said. That's clever. Do you remember, that last time I saw you, back in the Manifold House. Do you remember what I said?"

"Nejben remembers you asking, where are they migrating to? And what are they migrating from?"

"In all your seminars and tutorials and conferences, in all those questions about the shape of the universe – oh, we have our intelligences too, less broad than the Anpreen's, but subtler, we think – did you ever think to ask that question: why have you come here?" Cjatay's chubby, still childish face was an accusation. "You are fucking her, I presume?"

In a breath, Fejannen had slipped from his seat into the Third Honorable Offense Stance. A hand on his shoulder; the tea-shop owner. No honor in it, not against a Lonely. Fejannen returned to his seat, sick with shuddering rage.

"Tell him," Cjatay said.

"It's very simple," Seriantep said. "We are refugees. The Anpreen Commonweal is the surviving remnant of the effective annihilation of our sub-species of Panhumanity. Our eight hundred habitats are such a minuscule per centage of our original race that, to all statistical purposes, we are extinct. Our habitats once englobed an entire sun. We're all that's left."

"How? Who?"

"Not so much *who*, as *when*," Cjatay said gently. He flexed cold-blued fingers and pulled on his gloves. "They're coming?"

"We fear so," Seriantep said. "We don't know. We were careful to leave no traces, to cover our tracks, so to speak, and we believe we have centuries of a headstart on them. We are only here to refuel our habitats, then we'll go, hide ourselves in some great globular cluster."

"But why, *why* would anyone do this? We're all the same species, that's what you told us. The Clade, Panhumanity."

"Brothers disagree," Cjatay said. "Families fall out, families feud within themselves. No animosity like it."

"Is this true? How can this be true? Who knows about this?" Serejen strove with Fejannen for control and understanding. One of the first lessons the Agisters of the Manifold House had taught was the etiquette of transition between conflicting Aspects. A war in the head, a conflict of selves. He could understand sibling strife on a cosmic scale. But a whole species?

"The governments," Cjatay said. To the tea-man, "Open the shutter again. You be all right with us. I promise." To Serejen, "Politicians, some senior academics, and policy makers. And us. Not you. But we all agree, we don't want to scare anyone. So we question the Anpreen Prebendaries on our world, and question their presence in our system, and maybe sometimes it bubbles into xenophobic violence, but that's fine, that's the price, that's nothing compared to what would happen if we realized that our guests might be drawing the enemies that destroyed them to our homes. Come on. We'll go now."

The tea-man lifted the shutter. Outside, the protestors stood politely aside as Cjatay led the refugees out onto the street. There was not a murmur as Seriantep, in her ridiculous, life-threatening house-clothes, stepped across the cobbles. The great Winter Clock on the tower of Alajnedeng stood at twenty past five. The morning shift would soon be starting, the hot-shops firing their ovens and fry-pots.

A murmur in the crowd as Serejen took Seriantep's hand.

"Is it true?" he whispered.

"Yes," she said. "It is."

He looked up at the sky that would hold stars for another three endless months. The aurora coiled and spasmed over huddling Jann. Those stars were like crystal spearpoints. The universe was vast and cold and inimical to humanity, the greatest of Great Winters. He had never deluded himself it would be otherwise. Power had been restored, yellow street light glinted from the helmets of riot control officers and the carapaces of counterinsurgency drones. Serejen squeezed Seriantep's hand.

"What you asked."

"When?"

"Then. Yes. I will. Yes."

TORBEN, MELTING

The Anpreen shatter-ship blazed star-bright as it turned its face to the sun. A splinter of smart-ice, it was as intricate as a snowflake, stronger than any construct of Taynish engineering. Torben hung in free-fall in the observation dome at the centre of the cross of solar vanes. The Anpreen, being undifferentiated from the motes seeded through the hull, had no need for such architectural fancies. Their senses were open to space; the fractal shell of the ship was one great retina. They had grown the blister – pure and perfectly transparent construction-ice – for the comfort and delight of their human guests.

The sole occupant of the dome, Torben was also the sole passenger on this whole alien, paradoxical ship. Another would have been good. Another could have shared the daily, almost hourly shocks of strange and new and wonder. His other Aspects had felt with Torben the breath-catch of awe, and even greater privilege, when he had looked from the orbital car of the space elevator – the Anpreen's gift to the peoples of Tay – and seen the shatter-ship turn out of occultation in a blaze of silver light as it came in to dock. They had felt his glow of intellectual vindication as he first swam clumsily into the star-dome and discovered, with a shock, that the orbital transfer station was no more than a cluster of navigation lights almost lost in the star fields beyond. No sense of motion. His body had experienced no hint of acceleration. He had been correct. The Anpreen could adjust the topology of space-time. But there was no one but his several selves to tell it to. The Anpreen crew – Torben was not sure whether it was one or many, or if that distinction had any meaning – was remote and alien. On occasion, as he swam down the live-wood panelled corridors, monoflipper and web-mittens pushing thick, humid air, he had glimpsed a swirl of silver motes twisting and knotting like a captive waterspout. Always they had dispersed in his presence. But the ice beyond those wooden walls, pressing in around him, felt alive, crawling, aware.

Seriantep had gone ahead months before him.

"There's work I have to do."

There had been a party; there was always a party at the Anpreen Mission among the ever-green slopes of generous, volcanic Sulanj. Fellow academics, press and PR from Ctarisphay, politicians, family members, and the Anpreen Prebendaries, eerie in their uniform loveliness.

"You can do the research work on *Thirty-Third Tranquil Abode*, that's the idea," Seriantep had said. Beyond the paper lanterns hung in the trees and the glow of the carbon-sink lagoon, the lights of space-elevator cars rose up until they merged with the stars. She would ride that narrow way to orbit within days. Serejen wondered how he would next recognise her.

"You have to go." Puzhay stood in the balcony of the Tea Lane Ladyhearth, recently opened to allow spring warmth into rooms that had sweated and stifled and stunk all winter long. She looked out at the shooting, uncoiling fresh green of the trees along Uskuben Avenue. *Nothing there you have not seen before*, Nejben thought. *Unless it is something that is the absence of me.*

"It's not forever," Nejben said. "I'll be back in a year, maybe two years." *But not here*, he thought. He would not say it, but Puzhay knew it. As a returnee, the world's conservatoriums would be his. Bright cities, sun-warmed campuses far from the terrible cold on this polar continent, the winter that had driven them together.

All the goodbyes, eightfold goodbyes for each of his Aspects. And then he took sail for the ancient hospice of Bleyn, for sail was the only right way

to come to those reefs of ceramic chapels that had clung to the Yesger atoll
for 3,000 hurricane seasons.

"I need . . . another," he whispered in the salt-breezy, chiming cloisters
to Shaper Rejmen. "The curiosity of Serejen is too naive, the suspicion of
Fejannen is too jagged, and the social niceties of Kekjay are too too eager
to be liked."

"We can work this for you," the Shaper said. The next morning, he
went down into the sweet, salt waters of the Othering Pots and let the programmed palps swarm over him, as he did for twenty mornings after. In
the thunder-heavy gloaming of a late spring night storm, he awoke to find
he was Torben. Clever, inquisitive, wary, socially adept and conversation-
ally witty Torben. Extreme need and exceptional circumstances permitted
the creation of Nineths, but only, always, temporarily. Tradition as strong
as an incest taboo demanded that the number of Aspects reflect the eight
phases of Tay's manic seasons.

The Anpreen shatter-ship spun on its vertical axis and Torben Reris
Orhum Fejannen Kekjay Prus Rejmer Serejen Nejben looked on in wonder. Down, up, forward: his orientation shifted with every breath of air in
the observation dome. An eye, a monstrous eye. Superstition chilled him,
childhood stories of the Dejved whose sole eye was the eye of the storm
and whose body was the storm entire. Then he unfolded the metaphor.
An anti-eye. Tejaphay was a shield of heartbreaking blue, streaked and
whorled with perpetual storms. The Anpreen space habitat *Thirty-Third
Tranquil Abode*, hard-docked these two years past to the anchor end of the
space elevator, was a blind white pupil, an anti-pupil, an unseeing opacity.
The shatter-ship was approaching from Tejaphay's axial plane, the mechanisms of the orbital pumping station were visible beyond the habitat's close
horizon. The space elevator was a cobweb next to the habitat's 300-kilo-
metre bulk, less even than a thread compared to enormous Tejaphay, but
as the whole assemblage turned into daylight, it woke sparkling, glittering
as sun reflected from its billions of construction-ice scales. A fresh metaphor came to Torben: the sperm of the divine. *You're swimming the wrong
way!* he laughed to himself, delighted at this infant Aspect's unsuspected
tendency to express in metaphor what Serejen would have spoken in math,
Kekjay in flattery, and Fejannen not at all. *No, it's our whole system it's
fertilizing*, he thought.

The Anpreen ship drew closer, manipulating space-time on the centimetre
scale. Surface details resolved from the ice glare. The hull of *Thirty-Third
Tranquil Abode* was a chaotic mosaic of sensors, docks, manufacturing
hubs, and still less comprehensible technology, all constructed from smart-
ice. A white city. A flight of shatter-ships detached from docking arms like
a flurry of early snow. Were some of those icy mesas defensive systems; did
some of those ice canyons, as precisely cut as a skater's figures, conceal
inconceivable weapons? Had the Anpreen ever paused to consider that to
all cultures of Tay, white was the colour of distrust, the white of snow in
the long season of dark?

Days in free-gee had desensitised Torben sufficiently so that he was aware of the subtle pull of nanogravity in his belly. Against the sudden excitement and the accompanying vague fear of the unknown, he tried to calculate the gravity of *Thirty-Third Tranquil Abode*, changing every hour as it siphoned up water from Tejaphay. While he was still computing the figures, the shatter-ship performed another orientation flip and came in to dock at one of the radial elevator heads, soft as a kiss to a loved face.

On tenth days, they went to the Falls, Korpa and Belej, Sajhay and Hannaj, Yetger and Torben. When he stepped out of the elevator that had taken him down through thirty kilometres of solid ice, Torben had imagined something like the faculty of Jann; wooden-screen cloisters and courts roofed with ancient painted ceilings, thronged with bright, smart, talkative students boiling with ideas and vision. He found Korpa and Belej, Sajhay, Hannaj, and Yetger all together in a huge, windy construct of cells and tunnels and abrupt balconies and netted-in ledges, like a giant wasps' nest suspended from the curved ceiling of the interior hollow.

"Continuum topology is a tad specialized, I'll admit that," Belej said. She was a sting-thin quantum-foam specialist from Yeldes in the southern archipelago of Ninnt, gone even thinner and bonier in the attenuated gravity of *Thirty-Third Tranquil Abode*. "If it's action you're looking for, you should get over to *Twenty-Eighth*. They're sociologists."

Sajhay had taught him how to fly.

"There are a couple of differences from the transfer ship," he said as he showed Torben how to pull up the fish-tail mono-tights and how the plumbing vents worked. "It's lo-gee, but it's not *no*-gee, so you will eventually come down again. And it's easy to build up too much delta-vee. The walls are light but they're strong and you will hurt yourself. And the nets are there for a reason. Whatever you do, don't go through them. If you end up in that sea, it'll take you apart."

That sea haunted Torben's unsettled, nanogee dreams. The world-sea, the 220-kilometre-diameter sphere of water, its slow, huge nanogee waves forever breaking into globes and tears the size of clouds. The seething, dissolving sea into which the Anpreen dissipated, many lives into one immense, diffuse body which whispered to him through the paper tunnels of the Soujourners' house. Not so strange, perhaps. Yet he constantly wondered what it would be like to fall in there, to swim against the tiny but non-negligible gravity and plunge slowly, magnificently, into the boil of water-borne motes. In his imagination, there was never any pain, only the blissful, light-filled losing of self. So good to be free from the unquiet parliament of selves.

Eight is natural, eight is holy, the Bleyn Shaper Yesger had whispered from behind ornate cloister grilles. *Eight arms, eight seasons. Nine must always be unbalanced.*

Conscious of each other's too-close company, the guest scholars worked apart with their pupils. Seriantep met daily with Torben in a bulbous chapter house extruded from the mother nest. Tall hexagon-combed windows opened on the steeply downcurving horizons of *Thirty-Third Tranquil Abode*, stippled with the stalactite towers of those Anpreen who refused the lure of the sea. Seriantep flew daily from such a tower down around the curve of the world to alight on Torben's balcony. She wore the same body he had known so well in the Jann Conservatorium, with the addition of a pair of functional wings in her back. She was a vision, she was a marvel, a spiritual creature from the aeons-lost motherworld of the Clade: an *angel*. She was beauty, but since arriving in *Thirty-Third Tranquil Abode*, Torben had only had sex with her twice. It was not the merman-angel thing, though that was a consideration to metaphor-and-ludicrous-conscious Torben. He didn't love her as Serejen had. She noticed, she commented.

"You're not . . . the same."

Neither are you. What he *said* was, "I know. I couldn't be. Serejen couldn't have lived here. Torben can. Torben is the only one who can." *But for how long, before he splits into his component personalities?*

"Do you remember the way you . . . he . . . used to see numbers?"

"Of course I do. And before that, I remember how Ptey used to see numbers. He could look up into the night sky and tell you without counting, just by *knowing*, how many stars there were. He could see numbers. Serejen could make them do things. For me, Torben; the numbers haven't gone away, I just see them differently. I see them as clearly, as absolutely, but when I see the topospace transformations, I see them as words, as images and stories, as analogies. I can't explain it any better than that."

"I think, no matter how long I try, how long any of us try, we will never understand how your multiple personalities work. To us, you seem a race of partial people, each a genius, a savant, in some strange obsessive way."

Are you deliberately trying to punish me? Torben thought at the flicker-wing angel hovering before the ice-filled windows.

True, he was making colossal intuitive leaps in his twisted, abstruse discipline of space-time geometry. Not so abstruse: the Anpreen space drives, that Taynish physicists said broke the laws of physics, reached into the elevenspace substrate of the universe to locally stretch or compress the expansion of space-time – foreshortening ahead of the vehicle, inflating it behind. Thus the lack of any measurable acceleration, it was the entire continuum within and around the shatter-ship that had moved. Snowflakes and loxodromic curves had danced in Torben's imagination: he had it, he had it. The secret of the Anpreen: relativistic interstellar travel, was now open to the peoples of Tay.

The *other* secret of the Anpreen, that was.

For all his epiphanies above the spherical ocean, Torben knew that seminars had changed. The student had become the teacher, the master the pupil. *What is you want from us?* Torben asked himself. *Truly want, truly need?*

"Don't know, don't care. All I know is, if I can find a commercial way to bubble quantum black holes out of elevenspace and tap the evaporation radiation, I'll have more money than God," said Yetger, a squat, physically uncoordinated Oprann islander who relished his countrymen's reputation for boorishness, though Torben found him an affable conversationalist and a refined thinker. "You coming to the Falls on Tennay?"

So they set off across the sky, a little flotilla of physicists with wine and sweet biscuits to dip in it. Those older and less sure of their bodies used little airscooter units. Torben flew. He enjoyed the exercise. The challenge of a totally alien language of movement intrigued him, the fish-tail flex of the flipper-suit. He liked what it was doing to his ass muscles.

The Soujourners' house's western windows gave distant views of the Falls, but the sense of awe began twenty kilometres out when the thunder and shriek became audible over the constant rumble of sky traffic. The picnic party always flew high, close to the ceiling among the tower roots, so that long vistas would not spoil their pleasure. A dense forest of inverted trees, monster things grown kilometres tall in the nanogee, had been planted around the Falls, green and mist-watered by the spray. The scientists settled onto one of the many platforms sculpted from the boulevard-wide branches. Torben gratefully peeled off his fin-tights, kicked his legs free, and spun to face the Falls.

What you saw, what awed you, depended on how you looked at it. Feet down to the world sea, head up to the roof, it was a true fall, a cylinder of falling water two hundred metres across and forty kilometres long. Feet up, head down, it was even more terrifying, a titanic geyser. The water was pumped through from the receiving station at near supersonic speeds, where it met the ocean-bead the joined waters boiled and leaped kilometres high, broke into high looping curls and crests and globes, like the fantastical flarings of solar prominences. The roar was terrific. But for the noise-abatement properties of the nanoengineered leaves, it would have meant instant deafness. Torben could feel the tree branch, as massive as any buttress wall of Jann fortress-university, shudder beneath him.

Wine was opened and poured. The biscuits, atavistically hand-baked by Hannaj, one of whose Aspects was a master pastry chef, were dipped into it and savoured. Sweet, the light sharpness of the wine and the salt mist of another world's stolen ocean tanged Torben's tongue.

There were rules to Tennays by the Falls. No work. No theory. No relationships. Five researchers made up a big enough group for family jealousy, small enough for cliquishness. Proper topics of conversation looked homeward; partnerships ended, children born, family successes and sicknesses, gossip, politics, and sports results.

"Oh. Here." Yetger sent a message flake spinning lazily through the air. The Soujourners' house exfoliated notes and messages from home onto slips of whisper-thin paper that peeled from the walls like eczema. The mechanism was poetic but inaccurate; intimate messages unfurled from unintended walls to turn and waft in the strange updrafts that ran through the nest's convoluted tunnels. It was the worst of forms to read another's message-scurf.

Torben unfolded the rustle of paper. He read it once, blinked, read it again. Then he folded it precisely in eight and folded it away in his top pocket.

"Bad news?" For a broad beast of a man, Yetger was acute to emotional subtleties. Torben swallowed.

"Nothing strange or startling."

Then he saw where Belej stared. Her gaze drew his, drew that of everyone in the picnic party. The Falls were failing. Moment by moment, they dwindled, from a deluge to a river, from a river to a stream to a jet, a hiding shrieking thread of water. On all the platforms on all the trees, Anpreen were rising into the air, hovering in swarms, as before their eyes the Falls sputtered and ceased. Drops of water, fat as storms, formed around the lip of the suddenly exposed nozzle to break and drift, quivering, down to the spherical sea. The silence was profound. Then the trees seemed to shower blossoms as the Anpreen took to the air in hosts and choirs, flocking and storming.

Numbers and images flashed in Torben's imagination. The fuelling could not be complete, was weeks from being complete. The ocean would fill the entire interior hollow, the stalactite cities transforming into strange reef communities. Fear gripped him and he felt Fejannen struggle to free himself from the binding into Torben. *I need you here, friend,* Torben said to himself, and saw the others had made the same calculations.

They flew back, a ragged flotilla strung across kilometres of airspace, battling through the ghostly aerial legions of Anpreen. The Soujourners' house was filled with fluttering, gusting message slips shed from the walls. Torben snatched one from the air and against all etiquette read it.

> *Sajhay are you all right what's happening? Come home, we are all worried about you. Love Mihenj.*

The sudden voice of Suguntung, the Anpreen liaison, filled every cell of the nest, an order – polite, but an order – to come to the main viewing lounge, where an important announcement would be made. Torben had long suspected that Suguntung never left the Soujourners' house, merely deliquesced from hominiform into airborne motes, a phase transition.

Beyond the balcony nets, the sky seethed, an apocalypse of insect humanity and storm clouds black as squid ink rolling up around the edge of the world ocean.

"I have grave news," Suguntung said. He was a grey, sober creature, light and lithe and androgynous, without any salting of wit or humour. "At 12:18 Taynish Enclave time, we detected gravity waves passing through the system. These are consistent with a large numbers of bodies decelerating from relativistic flight."

Consternation. Voices shouting. Questions questions questions. Suguntung held up a hand and there was quiet.

"On answer to your questions, somewhere in the region of thirty-eight thousand objects. We estimate them at a range of seventy astronomical units beyond the edge of the Kuiper belt, decelerating to ten per cent lightspeed for system transition."

"Ninety-three hours until they reach us," Torben said. The numbers, the coloured numbers, so beautiful, so distant.

"Yes," said Suguntung.

"Who are they?" Belej asked.

"I know," Torben said. "Your enemy."

"We believe so," Suguntung answered. "There are characteristic signatures in the gravity waves and the spectral analysis."

Uproar. By a trick of the motes, Suguntung could raise his voice to a roar that could shout down a crowd of angry physicists.

"The Anpreen Commonweal is making immediate preparations for departure. As a matter of priority, evacuation for all guests and visitors has been arranged and will commence immediately. A transfer ship is already waiting. We are evacuating the system not only for our own protection, but to safeguard you as well. We believe that the Enemy has no quarrel with you."

"Believe?" Yetger spat. "Forgive me if I'm less than completely reassured by that!"

"But you haven't got enough water," Torben said absently, mazed by the numbers and pictures swimming around in his head, as the message leaves of concern and hope and come-home-soon fluttered around. "How many habitats are fully fuelled? Five hundred, five hundred and fifty? You haven't got enough, even this one is at eighty per cent capacity. What's going to happen to them?"

"I don't give a fuck what happens to them!" Hannaj had always been the meekest and least assertive of men, brilliant but forever hamstrung by self-doubt. Now, threatened, naked in space, pieced through and through by the gravity waves of an unknowable power, his anger burned. "I want to know what's going to happen to us."

"We are transferring the intelligences to the interstellar-capable habitats." Suguntung spoke to Torben alone.

"Transferring; you mean copying," Torben said. "And the originals that are left, what happens to them?"

Suguntung made no answer.

Yetger found Torben floating in the exact centre of the viewing lounge, moving his tail just enough to maintain him against the microgee.

"Where's your stuff?"

"In my cell."

"The shatter-ship's leaving in an hour."

"I know."

"Well, maybe you should, you know . . ."

"I'm not going."

"You're what?"

"I'm not going, I'm staying here."

"Are you insane?"

"I've talked to Suguntung and Seriantep. It's fine. There are a couple of others on the other habitats."

"You have to come home, we'll need you when they come . . ."

"Ninety hours and twenty-five minutes to save the world? I don't think so."

"It's home, man."

"It's not. Not since *this*." Torben flicked the folded note of his secret pocket, offered it to Yetger between clenched fingers.

"Oh."

"Yes."

"You're dead. We're all dead, you know that."

"Oh, I know. In the few minutes it takes me to reach wherever the Anpreen migration goes next, you wil have aged and died many times over. I know that, but it's not home. Not now."

Yetger ducked his head in sorrow that did not want to be seen, then in a passion hugged Torben hugely to him, kissed him hard.

"Goodbye. Maybe in the next one."

"No, I don't think so. One is all we get. And that's a good enough reason to go out there where none of our people have ever been before, I think."

"Maybe it is." Yetger laughed, the kind of laughter that is on the edge of tears. Then he spun and kicked off up through the ceiling door, his duffel of small possessions trailing from his ankle.

For an hour now, he had contemplated the sea and thought that he might just be getting the way of it, the fractal patterns of the ripples, the rhythms and the microstorms that blew up in squalls and waves that sent globes of water quivering into the air that, just as quickly, were subsumed back into the greater sea. He understood it as music, deeply harmonised. He wished one of his Aspects had a skill for an instrument. Only choirs, vast ensembles, could capture the music of the water bead.

"It's ready now."

All the while Torben had calculated the music of the sea, Seriantep had worked on the smart-paper substrate of the Soujourners' house. Now the poll was complete, a well in the floor of the lounge. *When I leave, will it revert?* Torben thought, the small, trivial wit that fights fear. *Will it go back to whatever it was before, or was it always only just Suguntung?* The slightest of gestures and Seriantep's wisp-dress fell from her. The floor ate it greedily. Naked and wingless now in this incarnation, she stepped backward into the water, never for an instant taking her eyes from Torben.

"Whenever you're ready," she said. "You won't be hurt."

She lay back into the receiving water. Her hair floated out around her, coiled and tangled as she came apart. There was nothing ghastly about it, no decay into meat and gut and vile bone, no grinning skeleton fizzing apart in the water like sodium. A brightness, a turning to motes of light. The hair was the last to go. The pool seethed with motes. Torben stepped out of his clothes.

I'm moving on. It's for the best. Maybe not for you. For me. You see, I didn't think I'd mind, but I did. You gave it all up

so easily, just like that, off into space. There is someone else.
It's Cjatay. I heard what he was saying, and as time went by,
as I didn't hear from you, it made sense. I know I'm reacting.
I think I owe you that, at least. We're all right together. With
him, you get everything, I find I can live with that. I think I like
it. I'm sorry, Torben, but this is what I want.

The note sifted down through the air like a falling autumn leaf to join
the hundreds of others that lay on the floor. Torben's feet kicked up as
he stepped down into the water. He gasped at the electrical tingle, then
laughed, and, with a great gasp, emptied his lungs and threw himself under
the surface. The motes swarmed and began to take him apart. As the
Thirty-Third Tranquil Abode broke orbit around Tejaphay, the abandoned
space elevator coiling like a severed artery, the bottom of the Soujourners'
house opened, and, like a tear, the mingled waters fell to the sea below.

JEDDEN, RUNNING

Eighty years Jedden had fallen, dead as a stone, silent as light. Every five
years, a few subjective minutes so close to light-speed, he woke up his
senses and sent a slush of photons down his wake to see if the hunter was
still pursuing.

Redshifted to almost indecipherability, the photons told him, *Yes, still
there, still gaining.* Then he shut down his senses, for even that brief wink,
that impact of radiation blueshifted to gamma frequencies on the enemy
engine field, betrayed him. It was decades since he had risked the scalarity
drive. The distortions it left in spacetime advertised his position over most
of a quadrant. Burn quick, burn hot and fast, get to light-speed if it meant
reducing his reaction mass perilously close to the point where he would
not have sufficient ever to brake. Then go dark, run silent and swift, coasting along in high time dilation where years passed in hours.

Between wakings, Jedden dreamed. He dreamed down into the billions
of lives, the dozens of races and civilizations that the Anpreen had encountered in their long migration. The depth of their history had stunned
Jedden, as if he were swimming and, looking down, discovered beneath
him not the green water of the lagoon but the clear blue drop of the continental shelf. Before they englobed their sun with so many habitats that it
became discernible only as a vast infra-red glow, before even the wave of
expansion that had brought them to that system, before even they became
motile, when they wore mere bodies, they had been an extroverted, curious race, eager for the similarities and differences of other sub-species of
Panhumanity. Records of the hundreds of societies they had contacted
were stored in the spin-states of the quantum-ice flake that comprised the
soul of Jedden. Cultures, customs, ways of being human were simulated
in such detail that, if he wished, Jedden could have spent aeons living out
their simulated lives. Even before they had reached the long-reprocessed
moon of their homeworld, the Anpreen had encountered a light-sail probe

of the Ekkad, three hundred years out on a millennium-long survey of potential colony worlds. As they converted their asteroid belts into habitat rings, they had fought a savage war for control of the high country against the Okranda asteroid colonies that had dwelled there, hidden and unsuspected, for twenty thousand years. The doomed Okranda had, as a final, spiteful act, seared the Anpreen homeworld to the bedrock, but not before the Anpreen had absorbed and recorded the beautiful, insanely complex hierarchy of caste, classes, and societies that had evolved in the baroque cavities of the sculpted asteroids. Radio transmission had drawn them out of their Oort cloud across two hundred light-years to encounter the dazzling society of the Jad. From them, the Anpreen had learned the technology that enabled them to pload themselves into free-flying nanomotes and become a true Level Two civilization.

People and beasts, machines and woods, architectures and moralities, and stories beyond counting. Among the paraphernalia and marginalia of a hundred races were the ones who had destroyed the Anpreen, who were now hunting Jedden down over all the long years, closing metre by metre.

So he spent hours and years immersed in the great annual eisteddfod of the Barrant-Hoj, where one of the early generation of seed-ships (early in that it was seed of the seed of the seed of the first flowering of mythical Earth) had been drawn into the embrace of a fat, slow hydrocarbon-rich gas giant and birthed a brilliant, brittle airborne culture, where blimp-cities rode the edge of storms wide enough to drown whole planets and the songs of the contestants – gas-bag-spider creatures huge as reefs, fragile as honeycomb – belled in infrasonic wavefronts kilometers between crests and changed entire climates. It took Barrant-Hoj two hominiform lifetimes to circle its sun – the Anpreen had chanced upon the song-spiel, preserved it, hauled it out of the prison of gas giant's gravity well, and given it to greater Clade.

Jedden blinked back into interstellar flight. He felt – he imagined – tears on his face as the harmonies reverberated within him. Cantos could last days, chorales entire weeks. Lost in music. A moment of revulsion at his body, this sharp, unyielding thing of ice and energies. The hunter's ramscoop fusion engine advertised its presence across a thousand cubic light-years. It was inelegant and initially slow, but, unlike Jedden's scalarity drive, was light and could live off the land. The hunter would be, like Jedden, a ghost of a soul impressed on a Bose-condensate quantum chip, a mote of sentience balanced on top of a giant drive unit. The hunter was closing, but was no closer than Jedden had calculated. Only miscalculation could kill you in interstellar war. The equations were hard but they were fair.

Two hundred and three years to the joke point. It would be close, maybe close enough for the enemy's greed to blind him. Miscalculation and self-deception, these were the killers in space. And luck. Two centuries. Time enough for a few moments rest.

Among all the worlds was one he had never dared visit: the soft blue tear of Tay. There, in the superposed spin states, were all the lives he could have led. The lovers, the children, the friends and joys and mudanities. Puzhay was there, Cjatay too. He could make of them anything he wanted: Puzhay faithful, Cjatay Manifold, no longer Lonely.

Lonely. He understood that now, eighty light-years out and decades to go before he could rest.

Extraordinary, how painless it had been. Even as the cells of Torben's body were invaded by the motes into which Seriantep had dissolved, even as they took him apart and rebuilt him, even as they read and copied his neural mappings, there was never a moment where fleshly Torben blinked out and nanotechnological Torben winked in, there was no pain. Never pain, only a sense of wonder, of potential racing away to infinity on every side, of a new birth – or, it seemed to him, an anti-birth, a return to the primal, salted waters. As the globe of mingled motes dropped slow and quivering and full as a breast toward the world ocean, Torben still thought of himself as Torben, as a man, an individual, as a body. Then they hit and burst and dissolved into the sea of seething motes, and voices and selves and memories and personalities rushed in on him from every side, clamouring, a sea-roar. Every life in every detail. Senses beyond his native five brought him impression upon impression upon impression. Here was intimacy beyond anything he had ever known with Seriantep. As he communed, he was communed with. He knew that the Anpreen government – now he understood the reason for the protracted and ungainly negotiations with Tay: the two representations had almost no points of communication – was unwrapping him to construct a deep map of Tay and its people – rather, the life and Aspects of one under-socialised physics researcher. Music. All was music. As he understood this, Anpreen Commonweal Habitat *Thirty-Third Tranquil Abode*, with its five hundred and eighty-two companions, crossed one hundred and nineteen light-years to the Milius 1183 star system.

One hundred and nineteen light-years, eight months subjective, in which Torben Reris Orhum Fejannen Kekjay Prus Rejmer Serejen Nejben ceased to exist. In the mote-swarm, time, like identity, could be anything you assigned it to be. To the self now known as Jedden, it seemed that he had spent twenty years of re-subjectivized time in which he had grown to be a profound and original thinker in the Commonweal's physics community. Anpreen life had only enhanced his instinctive ability to see and apprehend number. His insights and contributions were startling and creative. Thus it had been a pure formality for him to request a splinter ship to be spun off from *Thirty-Third Tranquil Abode* as the fleet entered the system and dropped from relativistic flight at the edge of the Oort cloud. A big fat splinter ship with lots of fuel to explore space-time topological distortions implicit in the orbital perturbations of inner Kuiper belt cubewanos for a year, a decade, a century, and then come home.

So he missed the annihilation.

Miscalculation kills. Lack of circumspection kills. Blind assumption kills. The Enemy had planned their trap centuries ahead. The assault on the Tay system had been a diversion; the thirty-eight thousand drive signatures mostly decoys; propulsion units and guidance systems and little else scattered among a handful of true battleships dozens of kilometres long. Even as lumbering, barely mobile Anpreen habitats and Enemy attack drones burst across Tay's skies, so bright they even illuminated the sun-glow of high summer, the main fleet was working around Milius 1183. A work of decades, year upon year of slow modifications, staggering energies, careful careful concealment and camouflage, as the Enemy sent their killing hammer out on its long slow loop.

Blind assumption. The Anpreen saw a small red sun at affordable range to the ill-equpped fleet. They saw there was water there, water; worlds of water to re-equip the Commonweal and take it fast and far beyond the reach of the Enemy in the great star clouds that masked the galactic core. In their haste, they failed to note that Milius 1183 was a binary system, a tired red dwarf star and a companion neutron star in photosphere-grazing eight hour orbit. Much less then did they notice that the neutron star was missing.

The trap was perfect and complete. The Enemy had predicted perfectly. Their set-up was flawless. The hunting fleet withdrew to the edges of system, all that remained were the relays and autonomous devices. Blindsided by sunglare, the Anpreen sensoria had only milliseconds of warning before the neutron star impacted Milius 1183 at eight per cent light-speed.

The nova would in time be visible over a light-century radius. Within its spectrum, careful astronomers might note the dark lines of hydrogen, oxygen, and smears of carbon. Habitats blew away in sprays of plasma. The handful of stragglers that survived battled to reconstruct their mobility and life-support systems. Sharkships hidden half a century before in the rubble of asteroid belts and planetary ring systems woke from their long sleeps and went a-hunting.

Alone in his splinter ship in the deep dark, Jedden, his thoughts outwards to the fabric of space-time and at the same time inwards to the beauty of number, the song within him, saw the system suddenly turn white with death light. He heard five hundred billion sentients die. All of them, all at once, all their voices and hearts. He heard Seriantep die, he heard those other Taynish die, those who had turned away from their homeworld in the hope of knowledge and experience beyond anything their world could offer. Every life he had ever touched, that had ever been part of him, that had shared number or song or intimacy beyond fleshly sex. He heard the death of the Anpreen migration. Then he was alone. Jedden went dark for fifty years. He contemplated the annihilation of the last of the Anpreen. He drew up escape plans. He waited. Fifty years was enough. He lit the scalarity drive. Space-time stretched. Behind him, he caught the radiation signature of a fusion drive igniting and the corresponding electromagnetic flicker of a scoopfield going up. Fifty years was not enough.

That would be his last miscalculation.

Twenty years to bend his course away from Tay. Another ten to set up the deception. As you deceived us, *so I will fool you*, Jedden thought as he tacked ever closer to light-speed. *And with the same device, a neutron star.*

*

Jedden awoke from the sleep that was beyond dreams, a whisper away from death, that only disembodied intelligences can attain. The magnetic vortex of the hunter's scoopfield filled half the sky. Less than the diameter of a light-minute separated them. Within the next ten objective years, the Enemy ship would overtake and destroy Jedden. Not with physical weapons or even directed energy, but with information: skullware and dark phages that would dissolve him into nothingness or worse, isolate him from any external sense or contact, trapped in unending silent, nerveless darkness.

The moment, when it came, after ninety light-years, was too fine-grained for hominiformintelligence. Jedden's sub-routines, the autonomous responses that controlled the ship that was his body, opened the scalarity drive and summoned the dark energy. Almost instantly, the Enemy responded to the course change, but that tiny relativistic shift, the failure of simultaneity, was Jedden's escape and life.

Among the memories frozen into the heart of the Bose-Einstein condensate were the star-logs of the Cush Né, a fellow migrant race the Anpreen had encountered – by chance, as all such meets must be – in the big cold between stars. Their star maps charted a rogue star, a neutron dwarf ejected from its stellar system and wandering dark and silent, almost invisible, through deep space. Decades ago, when he felt the enemy ramfield go up and knew that he had not escaped, Jedden had made the choice and the calculations. Now he turned his flight, a prayer short of light-speed, towards the wandering star.

Jedden had long ago abolished fear. Yet he experienced a strange psychosomatic sensation in that part of the splinter ship that corresponded to his testicles. Balls tightening. The angle of insertion was so precise that Jedden had had to calculate the impact of stray hydroxyl radicals on his ablation field. One error would send him at relativistic speed head on into a neutron star. But he did not doubt his ability, he did not fear, and now he understood what the sensation in his phantom testicles was. Excitement.

The neutron star was invisible, would always be invisible, but Jedden could feel its gravity in every part of his body, a quaking, quailing shudder, a music of a hundred harmonies as different parts of the smart-ice hit their resonant frequencies. A chorale in ice and adrenaline, he plunged around the neutron star. He could hope that the hunting ship would not survive the passage, but the Enemy, however voracious, was surely never so stupid as to run a scoop ship through a neutron's star terrifying magnetic terrain with the drive field up. That was not his strategy anyway. Jedden was playing the angles. Whipping tight around the intense gravity well, even a few seconds of slowness would amplify into light-years of distance, decades of lost time. Destruction would have felt like a cheat. Jedden wanted to win by geometry. By calculation, we live.

He allowed himself one tiny flicker of a communication laser. Yes. The Enemy was coming. Coming hard, coming fast, coming wrong. Tides tore at Jedden, every molecule of his smart-ice body croaked and moaned, but his own cry rang louder and he sling-shotted around the neutron. Yes!

Before him was empty space. The splinter ship would never fall of its own accord into another gravity well. He lacked sufficient reaction mass to enter any Clade system. Perhaps the Enemy had calculated this in the moments before he too entered the neutron star's transit. An assumption. In space, assumptions kill. Deep in his quantum memories, Jedden knew what was out there. The slow way home.

FAST MAN, SLOWLY

Kites, banners, pennants, and streamers painted with the scales and heads of ritual snakes flew from the sun rigging on the Festival of Fast Children. At the last minute, the climate people had received budgetary permission to shift the prevailing winds lower. The Clave had argued that the Festival of Fast Children seemed to come round every month and a half, which it did, but the old and slow said, *Not to the children it doesn't.*

Fast Man turned off the dust road onto the farm track. The wooden gate was carved with the pop-eyed, O-mouthed hearth-gods, the chubby, venal guardians of agricultural Yoe Canton. As he slowed to Parent Speed, the nodding heads of the meadow flowers lifted to a steady metronome tick. The wind-rippled grass became a restless choppy sea of current and cross-currents. Above him, the clouds raced down the face of the sun-rod that ran the length of the environment cylinder, and in the wide yard before the frowning eaves of the ancient earthen manor, the children, preparing for the ritual Beating of the Sun-lines, became plumes of dust.

For three days, he had walked up the eternal hill of the cylinder curve, through the tended red forests of Canton Ahaea. Fast Man liked to walk. He walked at Child Speed and they would loop around him on their bicycles and ped-cars and then pull away shouting, "You're not so fast, Fast Man!" He could have caught them, of course, he could have easily outpaced them. They knew that, they knew he could on a wish take the form of a bird, or a cloud, and fly away from them up to the ends of the world. Everyone in the Three Worlds knew Fast Man. He needed neither sleep nor food, but he enjoyed the taste of the highly seasoned, vegetable-based cuisine of the Middle Cantons and their light but fragrant beer, so he would call each night at a hostel or township pub. Then he would drop down into Parent Speed and talk with the locals. Children were fresh and bright and inquiring, but for proper conversation, you needed adults.

The chirping cries of the children rang around the grassy eaves of Toe Yau Manor. The community had gathered, among them the Toe Yau's youngest, a skipping five-year-old. In her own speed, that was. She was months old to her parents; her birth still a fresh and painful memory. The oldest, the one he had come about, was in his early teens. Noha and Jehau greeted Fast Man with water and bread.

"God save all here," Fast Man blessed them. Little Nemaha flickered around him like summer evening bugs. He heard his dual-speech unit translate the greeting into Children-Speech in a chip of sound. This was his talent and his fame; that his mind and words could work in two times at once. He was the generational ambassador to three worlds.

The three great cylinders of the Aeo Taea colony fleet were fifty Adult Years along in their journey to the star Sulpees 2157 in the Anpreen categorisation. A sweet little golden star with a gas giant pressed up tight to it, and, around that gas world, a sun-warmed, tear-blue planet. Their big, slow lathe-sculpted asteroids, two hundred kilometres long, forty across their flats, had appeared as three small contacts at the extreme edge of the Commonweal's sensory array. Too far from their flightpath to the Tay system and, truth be told, too insignificant. The galaxy was festering with little sub-species, many of them grossly ignorant that they were part of an immeasurably more vast and glorious Clade, all furiously engaged on their own grand little projects and empires. Races became significant when they could push light-speed. Ethnologists had noted as a point of curiosity a peculiar time distortion to the signals, as if everything had been slowed to a tenth normal speed. Astrogators had put it down to an unseen gravitational lensing effect and noted course and velocity of the lumbering junk as possible navigation hazards.

That idle curiosity, that moment of fastidiousness of a now-dead, now-vapourized Anpreen who might otherwise have dismissed it, had saved Jedden. There had always been more hope than certainty in the mad plan he had concocted as he watched the Anpreen civilization end in nova light. Hope as he opened up the dark energy that warped space-time in calculations made centuries before that would only bear fruit centuries to come. Hope as he woke up, year upon year in the long flight to the stray neutron star, always attended by doubt. The slightest miscalculation could throw him off by light-years and centuries. He himself could not die, but his reaction mass was all too mortal. Falling forever between stars was worse than any death. He could have abolished that doubt with a thought, but so would the hope have been erased to become mere blind certainty.

Hoping and doubting, he flew out from the slingshot around the neutron star.

Because he could hope, he could weep; smart-ice tears when his long range radars returned three slow-moving images less than five light-hours from the position he had computed. As he turned the last of his reaction mass into dark energy to match his velocity with the Aeo Taea armada, a stray calculation crossed his consciousness. In all his redefinitions and reformations, he had never given up the ability to see numbers, to hear what they whispered to him. He was half a millennium away from the lives he had known on Tay.

For ten days, he broadcast his distress call. *Help, I am a refugee from a star war.* He knew that, in space, there was no rule of the sea, as there had been on Tay's world ocean, no Aspects at once generous, stern, and gallant that had been known as SeaSelves. The Aeo Taea could still kill him with negligence. But he could sweeten them with a bribe.

*

Like many of the country houses of Amoa ark, Toe Yau Manor featured a wooden belvedere, this one situated on a knoll two fields spinward from the old house. Airy and gracious, woven from genetweak willow plaits, it and its country cousins all across Amoa's Cantons had become a place for Adults, where they could mix with ones of their own speed, talk without the need for the hated speech convertors around their necks, gripe and moan and generally gossip, and, through the central roof iris, spy through the telescope on their counterparts on the other side of the world. Telescope parties were the latest excuse for Parents to get together and complain about their children.

But this was their day – though it seemed like a week to them – the Festival of Fast Children, and this day Noha Toe Yau had his telescope trained not on his counterpart beyond the sun, but on the climbing teams fizzing around the sun riggings, tens of kilometres above the ground, running out huge monoweave banners and fighting ferocious kite battles high where the air was thin.

"I tell you something, no child of mine would ever be let do so damn fool a thing," Noha Toe Yau grumbled. "I'll be surprised if any of them make it to the Destination."

Fast Man smiled, for he knew that he had only been called because Yemoa Toe Yau was doing something much more dangerous.

Jehau Toe Yau poured chocolate, thick and cooling and vaguely hallucinogenic.

"As long as he's back before Starship Day," she said. She frowned down at the wide green before the manor where the gathered Fast Children of the neighbourhood in their robes and fancies were now hurtling around the long trestles of festival foods. They seemed to be engaged in a high-velocity food fight. "You know, I'm sure they're speeding the days up. Not much, just a little every day, but definitely speeding them up. Time goes nowhere these days."

Despite a surprisingly sophisticated matter-anti-matter propulsion system, the Aeo Taea fleet was limited to no more than ten per cent of light-speed, far below the threshold where time dilation became perceptible. The crossing to the Destination – Aeo Taea was a language naturally given to Portentous Capitalizations, Fast Man had discovered – could only be made by generation ship. The Aeo Taea had contrived to do it in just one generation. The strangely slow messages the Anpreen had picked up from the fleet were no fluke of space-time distortion. The voyagers' bodies, their brains, their perceptions and metabolisms, had been in-vitro engineered to run at one-tenth hominiform normal. Canned off from the universe, the interior lighting, the gentle spin gravity and the slow, wispy climate easily adjusted to a life lived at a snail's pace. Morning greetings lasted hours, that morning a world-week. Seasons endured for what would have been years in the outside universe, vast languorous autumns. The 350 years of the crossing would pass in the span of an average working career. Amoa was a world of the middle-aged.

Then Fast Man arrived and changed everything.

"Did he give any idea where he was going?" Fast Man asked. It was always the boys. Girls worked it through, girls could see further.

Jehau pointed down. Fast Man sighed. Rebellion was limited in Amoa, where any direction you ran led you swiftly back to your own doorstep. The wires that rigged the long sun could take you high, kilometres above it all in your grand indignation. Everyone would watch you through their telescopes, up there high and huffing, until you got hungry and wet and bored and had to come down again. In Amoa, the young soul rebels went *out*.

Fast Man set down his chocolate glass and began the subtle exercise that reconfigured the motes of his malleable body. To the Toe Yaus, he seemed to effervesce slightly, a sparkle like fine silver talc or the dust from a moth's wings. Jehau's eyes widened. All the three worlds knew of Fast Man, who had brought the end of the Journey suddenly within sight, soothed generational squabbles, and found errant children – and so everyone thought they knew him personally. Truly, he was an alien.

"It would help considerably if they left some idea of where they were going," Fast Man said. "There's a lot of space out there. Oh well. I'd stand back a little, by the way." He stood up, opened his arms in a little piece of theatre, and exploded into a swarm of motes. He towered to a buzzing cylinder that rose from the iris at the centre of the belvedere. *See this through your telescopes on the other side of the world and gossip*. Then, in a thought, he speared into the earth and vanished.

In the end, the Fast Boy was pretty much where Fast Man reckoned he would be. He came speed-walking up through the salt-dead city-scape of the communications gear just above the convex flaring of the drive shield, and there he was, nova-bright in Fast Man's radar sight. A sweet, neat little cranny in the main dish gantry with a fine view over the construction site. Boys and building. His complaining to the Toe Yaus had been part of the curmudgeonly image he liked to project. Boys were predictable things.

"Are you not getting a bit cold up there?" Fast Man said. Yemoa started at the voice crackling in his helmet phones. He looked round, helmet tilting from side to side as he tried to pick the interloper out of the limitless shadow of interstellar space. Fast Man increased his surface radiance. He knew well how he must seem; a glowing man, naked to space, toes firmly planted on the pumice-dusted hull and leaning slightly forward against the spin force. He would have terrified himself at that age, but awe worked for the Fast Children as amiable curmudgeon worked for their slow Parents.

"Go away."

Fast Man's body-shine illuminated the secret roots. Yemoa Toe Yau was spindly even in the tight yellow and green pressure skin. He shuffled around to turn his back; a deadlier insult among the Aeo Taea than among the Aspects of Tay for all their diverse etiquettes. Fast Man tugged at the boy's safety lanyard. The webbing was unfrayed, the carabiner latch operable.

"Leave that alone."

"You don't want to put too much faith in those things. Cosmic rays can weaken the structure of the plastic: put any tension on them, and they snap just like that, just when you need them most. Yes sir, I've seen people just go sailing out there, right away out there."

The helmet, decorated with bright bird motifs, turned toward Fast Man.

"You're just saying that."

Fast Man swung himself up beside the runaway and settled into the little nest. Yemoa wiggled away as far as the cramped space would permit.

"I didn't say you could come up here."

"It's a free ship."

"It's not *your* ship."

"True," said Fast Man. He crossed his legs and dimmed down his self-shine until they could both look out over the floodlit curve of the star drive works. The scalarity drive itself was a small unit – small by Amoa's vistas; merely the size of a well-established country manor. The heavy engineering that overshadowed it, the towering silos and domes and pipeworks, was the transfer system that converted water and anti-water into dark energy. Above all, the lampships hovered in habitat-stationary orbits, five small suns. Fast Man did not doubt that the site hived with desperate energy and activity, but to his Child Speed perceptions, it was as still as a painting, the figures in their bird-bright skinsuits, the heavy engineers in their long-duration work armour, the many robots and vehicles and little jetting skipcraft all frozen in time, moving so slowly that no individual motion was visible, but when you looked back, everything had changed. A long time even for a Parent, Fast Man sat with Yemoa. Beyond the construction lights, the stars arced past. *How must they seem to the adults*, Fast Man thought, and in that thought pushed down into Parent Speed and felt a breathless, deeply internalized gasp of wonder as the stars accelerated into curving streaks. The construction site ramped up into action; the little assembly robots and skippers darting here and there on little puffs of reaction gas.

Ten years, ten grown-up years, since Fast Man had osmsoed through the hull and coalesced out of a column of motes onto the soil of Ga'atu Colony, and still he did not know which world he belonged to, Parent or Fast Children. There had been no Fast Children then, no children at all. That was the contract. When the Destination was reached, that was the time for children, born the old way, the fast way, properly adjusted to their new world. Fast Man had changed all that with the price of his rescue: the promise that the Destination could be reached not in slow years, not even in a slow season, but in hours; real hours. With a proviso; that they detour – a matter of moments to a relativistic fleet – to Fast Man's old homeworld of Tay.

The meetings were concluded, the deal was struck, the Aeo Taea fleet's tight tight energy budget would allow it, just. It would mean biofuels and muscle power for the travellers; all tech resources diverted to assembling the three dark energy scalarity units. But the journey would be over in a single sleep. Then the generous forests and woodlands that carpeted the gently rolling midriffs of the colony cylinders all flowered and released genetweak pollen. Everyone got a cold for three days, everyone got pregnant, and nine Parent months later, the first of the Fast Children was born.

"So where's your clip?"

At the sound of Yemoa's voice, Fast Man geared up into Child Speed. The work on the dazzling plain froze, the stars slowed to a crawl.

"I don't need one, do I?" Fast Man added, "I know exactly how big space is."

"Does it really use dark energy?"

"It does."

Yemoa pulled his knees up to him, stiff from his long vigil in the absolute cold. A splinter of memory pierced Fast Man: the fast-frozen canals of Jann, the months-long dark. He shivered. Whose life was that, whose memory?

"I read about dark energy. It's the force that makes the universe expand faster and faster, and everything in it, you, me, the distance between us. In the end, everything will accelerate away so fast from everything else that the universe will rip itself apart, right down to the quarks."

"That's one theory."

"Every particle will be so far from everything else that it will be in a universe of its own. It will *be* a universe of its own."

"Like I said, it's a theory. Yemoa, your parents . . ."

"You use this as a space drive."

"Your matter/anti-matter system obeys the laws of Thermodynamics, and that's the heat-death of the universe. We're all getter older and colder and more and more distant. Come on, you have to come in. You must be uncomfortable in that suit."

The Aeo Taea skinsuits looked like flimsy dance costumes to don in the empty cold of interstellar space but their hides were clever works of molecular technology, recycling and refreshing and repairing. Still, Fast Man could not contemplate the itch and reek of one after days of wear.

"You can't be here on Starship Day," Fast Man warned. "Particle density is very low out here, but it's still enough to fry you, at light-speed."

"We'll be the Slow ones then," Yemoa said. "A few hours will pass for us, but in the outside universe, it will be fifty years."

"It's all relative," Fast Man said.

"And when we get there," Yemoa continued, "we'll unpack the landers and we'll go down and it'll be the new world, the big Des Tin Ay Shun, but our Moms and Dads, they'll stay up in the Three Worlds. And we'll work, and we'll build that new world, and we'll have our children, and they'll have children, and maybe we'll see another generation after that, but in the end, we'll die, and the Parents up there in the sky, they'll hardly have aged at all."

Fast Man draped his hands over his knees.

"They love you, you know."

"I know. I know that. It's not that at all. Did you think that? If you think that, you're stupid. What does everyone see in you if you think stuff like that? It's just . . . what's the point?"

None, Fast Man thought. *And everything. You are as much point as the universe needs, in your yellow and green skinsuit and mad-bird helmet and fine rage.*

"You know," Fast Man said, "whatever you think about it, it's worse for them. It's worse than anything I think you can imagine. Everyone they love growing old in the wink of an eye, dying, and they can't touch them, they can't help, they're trapped up there. No, I think it's so very much worse for them."

"Yah," said Yemoa. He slapped his gloved hands on his thin knees. "You know, it is freezing up here."

"Come on then." Fast Man stood up and offered a silver hand. Yemoa took it. The stars curved overhead. Together, they climbed down from the aerial and walked back down over the curve of the world, back home.

OGA, TEARING

He stood on the arch of the old Jemejnay bridge over the dead canal. Acid winds blew past him, shrieking on the honed edges of the shattered porcelain houses. The black sky crawled with suppressed lightning. The canal was a desiccated vein, cracked dry, even the centuries of trash wedged in its cracked silts had rusted away, under the bite of the caustic wind, to scabs and scales of slag. The lagoon was a dish of pure salt shimmering with heat haze. In natural light, it would have been blinding but no sun ever challenged the clouds. In Oga's extended vision, the old campanile across the lagoon was a snapped tooth of crumbling masonry.

A flurry of boiling acid rain swept over Oga as he turned away from the burning vista from the dead stone arch on to Ejtay Quay. His motes sensed and changed mode on reflex, but not before a wash of pain burned through him. Feel it. It is punishment. It is good.

The houses were roofless, floorless; rotted snapped teeth of patinated ceramic, had been for eight hundred years. Drunken Chicken Lane. Here Kentlay the Lonely had sat out in the sun and passed the time of day with his neighbours and visitors come for his gift. Here were the Dilmajs and the vile, cruel little son who had caught birds and pulled their feathers so that they could not fly from his needles and knives, street bully and fat boy. Mrs Supris, a sea-widow, a baker of cakes and sweets, a keeper of mournings and ocean-leavings. All dead. Long dead, dead with their city, their world.

This must be a mock Ctarisphay, a stage, a set, a play-city for some moral tale of a prodigal, an abandoner. A traitor. Memories turned to blasted, glowing stumps. A city of ruins. A world in ruins. There was no sea any more. Only endless poisoned salt. This could not be true. Yet this was his house. The acid wind had not yet totally erased the carved squid that stood over the door. Oga reached up to touch. It was hot, biting hot;

everything was hot, baked to an infra-red glow by runaway greenhouse effect. To Oga's carbon-shelled fingertips, it was a small stone prayer, a whisper caught in a shell. If the world had permitted tears, the old, eroded stone squid would have called Oga's. Here was the hall, here the private parlour, curved in on itself like a ceramic musical instrument. The stairs, the upper floors, everything organic had evaporated centuries ago, but he could still read the niches of the sleeping porches cast in the upper walls. How would it have been in the end days, when even the summer sky was black from burning oil? Slow, painful, as year upon year the summer temperatures rose and the plankton blooms, carefully engineered to absorb the carbon from Tay's oil-riches, died and gave up their own sequestered carbon.

The winds keened through the dead city and out across the empty ocean. With a thought, Oga summoned the ship. Ion glow from the re-entry shone through the clouds. Sonic booms rolled across the sterile lagoon and rang from the dead porcelain houses. The ship punched out of the cloud base and unfolded, a sheet of nano motes that, to Oga's vision, called memories of the ancient Bazjendi angels stooping down the burning wind. The ship beats its wings over the shattered campanile, then dropped around Oga like possession. Flesh melted, flesh ran and fused, systems meshed, selves merged. Newly incarnate, Oga kicked off from Ejtay Quay in a pillar of fusion fire. Light broke around the empty houses and plazas, sent shadows racing down the desiccated canals. The salt pan glared white, dwindling to the greater darkness as the light ascended. With a star at his feet, Oga punched up through the boiling acid clouds, up and out until, in his extended shipsight, he could see the infra-glow of the planet's limb curve against space. A tear of blood. Accelerating, Oga broke orbit.

Oga. The name was a festival. Father-of-all-our-Mirths, in subtly inflected Aeo Taea. He was Fast Man no more, no longer a sojourner; he was Parent of a nation. The Clave had ordained three Parent Days of rejoicing as the Aeo Taea colony cylinders dropped out of scalarity drive at the edge of the system. For the children, it had been a month of party. Looking up from the flat end of the cylinder, Oga had felt the light from his native star on his skin, subtle and sensitive in a dozen spectra. He masked out the sun and looked for those sparks of reflected light that were worlds. There Saltpeer, and great Bephis: magnifying his vision, he could see its rings and many moons; there Tejaphay. It too wore a ring now; the shattered icy remnants of the Anpreen Commonweal. And there; there: Tay. Home. Something not right about it. Something missing in its light. Oga had ratcheted up his sight to the highest magnification he could achieve in this form.

There was no water in the spectrum. There was no pale blue dot.

The Clave of Aeo Taea Interstellar Cantons received the message some hours after the surface crews registered the departure of the Anpreen splinter ship in a glare of fusion light: *I have to go home.*

From five A.U.'s out, the story became brutally evident. Tay was a silver ball of unbroken cloud. Those clouds comprised carbon dioxide, carbonic, and sulphuric acid and a memory of water vapour. The surface temperature read at 220 degrees. Oga's ship-self possessed skills and techniques beyond his hominiform self; he could see the perpetual lighting storms cracking cloud to cloud, but never a drop of pure rain. He could see through those clouds, he could peel them away so that the charred, parched surface of the planet lay open to his sight. He could map the outlines of the continents and the continental shelves lifting from the dried ocean. The chains of archipelagos, once jewels around the belly of a beautiful dancer, were ribs, bones, stark mountain chains glowing furiously in the infra-dark.

As he fell sunwards, Oga put the story together. The Enemy had struck Tay casually, almost as an afterthought. A lone warship, little larger than the ritual catamaran on which the boy called Ptey had sailed from this quay so many centuries before, had detached itself from the main fleet action and swept the planet with its particle weapons, a spray of directed fire that set the oil fields burning. Then it looped carelessly back out of the system, leaving a world to suffocate. They had left the space elevator intact. There must be a way out. This was judgment, not murder. Yet two billion people, two thirds of the planet's population, had died.

One third had lived. One third swarmed up the life-rope of the space elevator and looked out at space and wondered where they could go. Where they went, Oga went now. He could hear their voices, a low em-band chitter from the big blue of Tejaphay. His was a long, slow chasing loop. It would be the better part of a year before he arrived in parking orbit above Tejaphay. Time presented its own distractions and seductions. The quantum array that was his heart could as easily recreate Tay as any of scores of cultures it stored. The mid-day aurora would twist and glimmer again above the steep-gabled roofs of Jann. He would fish with Cjatay from the old, weather-silvered fishing stands for the spring run of prith. The Sulanj islands would simmer and bask under the midnight sun and Puzhay would again nuzzle against him and press her body close against the hammering cold outside the Tea Lane Ladyhearth walls. They all could live, they all would believe they lived, *he* could, by selective editing of his consciousness, believe they lived again. He could recreate dead Tay. But it was the game of a god, a god who could take off his omniscience and enter his own delusion, and so Oga chose to press his perception down into a time flow even slower than Parent Time and watch the interplay of gravity wells around the sun.

On the final weeks of approach, Oga returned to world time and opened his full sensory array on the big planet that hung tantalisingly before him. He had come here before, when the Anpreen Commonweal hung around Tejaphay like pearls, but then he had given the world beneath him no thought, being inside a world complete in itself and his curiosity turned outwards to the shape of the universe. Now he beheld Tejaphay and remembered awe. Three times the diameter of Tay, Tejaphay was the true waterworld now. Ocean covered it pole to pole, a hundred kilometres deep. Immense weather systems mottled the planet, white on blue. The surviving spine of the Anpreen space elevator pierced the eye of a perpetual equatorial storm system. Wave trains and swells ran unbroken from equator to pole to smash in stupendous breakers against the polar ice caps. Oga drew near in sea meditation. Deep ocean appalled him in a way that centuries of time and space had not. That was distance. This was hostility. This was elementary fury that knew nothing of humanity.

Yet life clung here. Life survived. From two light-minutes out, Oga had heard a whisper of radio communication, from the orbit station on the space elevator, also from the planet's surface. Scanning sub-Antarctic waters, he caught the unmistakable tang of smart-ice. A closer look: what had on first glance seemed to be bergs revealed a more complex structure. Spires, buttresses, domes, and sprawling terraces. Ice cities, riding the perpetual swell. Tay was not forgotten: these were the ancient Manifold Houses reborn, grown to the scale of vast Tejaphay. Closer again: the berg city under his scrutiny floated at the centre of a much larger boomed circle. Oga's senses teemed with life-signs. This was a complete ecosystem, and ocean farm, and Oga began to appreciate what these refugees had undertaken. No glimpse of life had ever been found on Tejaphay. Waterworlds, thawed from ice-giants sent spiralling sunwards by the gravitational play of their larger planetary rivals, were sterile. At the bottom of the 100-kilometre-deep ocean was pressure ice, 5,000 kilometres of pressure ice down to the iron core. No minerals, no carbon ever percolated up through that deep ice. Traces might arrive by cometary impact, but the waters of Tejaphay were deep and pure. What the Taynish had the Taynish had brought. Even this ice city was grown from the shattered remnants of the Anpreen Commonweal.

A hail from the elevator station, a simple language algorithm. Oga smiled to himself as he compared the vocabulary files to his own memory of his native tongue. Half a millennium had changed the pronunciation and many of the words of Taynish, but not its inner subtleties, the rhythmic and contextual clues as to which Aspect was speaking.

"Attention unidentified ship, this is Tejaphay Orbital Tower approach control. Please identify yourself and your flight plan."

"This is the Oga of the Aeo Taea Interstellar Fleet." He toyed with replying in the archaic speech. Worse than a breach of etiquette, such a conceit might give away information he did not wish known. Yet. "I am a representative with authority to negotiate. We wish to enter into communications with your government regarding fuelling rights in this system."

"Hello, Oga, this is Tejaphay Orbital Tower. By the Aeo Taea Interstellar Fleet, I assume you refer to the these objects." A sub-chatter on the data channel identified the cylinders, coasting in-system. Oga confirmed.

"Hello, Oga, Tejaphay Tower. Do not, repeat, do not approach the tower docking station. Attain this orbit and maintain until you have been contacted by Tower security. Please confirm your acceptance."

It was a reasonable request, and Oga's subtler senses picked up missile foramens unfolding in the shadows of the Orbital Station solar array. He was a runner, not a fighter; Tejaphay's defences might be basic fusion warheads and would need sustained precision hits to split open the Aeo Taea colony cans, but they were more than a match for Oga without the fuel reserves for full scalarity drive.

"I confirm that."

As he looped up to the higher ground, Oga studied more closely the berg cities of Tejaphay, chips of ice in the monstrous ocean. It would be a brutal life down there under two gravities, every aspect of life subject to the melting ice and the enclosing circle of the biosphere boom. Everything beyond that was as lifeless as space. The horizon would be huge and far and empty. City ships might sail for lifetimes without meeting another polis. The Taynish were tough. They were a race of the extremes. Their birthworld and its severe seasonal shifts had called forth a social response that other cultures would regard as mental disease, as socialized schizophrenia. Those multiple Aspects – a self for every need – now served them on the hostile vastnesses of Tejaphay's world ocean. They would survive, they would thrive. Life endured. This was the great lesson of the Clade: that life was hope, the only hope of escaping the death of the universe.

"*Every particle will be so far from everything else that it will be in a universe of its own. It will be a universe of its own,*" a teenage boy in a yellow spacesuit had said up on the hull of mighty Amoa, looking out on the space between the stars. Oga had not answered at that time. It would have scared the boy, and though he had discovered it himself on the long flight from Milius 1183, he did not properly understand to himself, and in that gap of comprehension, he too was afraid. Yes, he would have said. *And in that is our only hope.*

Long range sensors chimed. A ship had emerged around the limb of the planet. Consciousness is too slow a tool for the pitiless mathematics of space. In the split second that the ship's course, design, and drive signature had registered on Oga's higher cognitions, his autonomic systems had plotted course, fuel reserves, and engaged the scalarity drive. At a thousand gees, he pulled away from Tejaphay. Manipulating space-time so close to the planet would send gravity waves rippling through it like a struck gong. Enormous slow tides would circle the globe; the space elevator would flex like a crackled whip. Nothing to be done. It was instinct alone and by instinct he lived, for here came the missiles. Twenty nanotoc warheads on hypergee drives, wiping out his entire rearward vision in a white glare of lightweight MaM engines, but not before he had felt on his skin sensors the unmistakable harmonies of an Enemy deep-space scoopfield going up.

The missiles had the legs, but Oga had the stamina. He had calculated it thus. The numbers still came to him. Looking back at the blue speck into which Tejaphay had dwindled, he saw the engine-sparks of the missiles wink out one after the other. And now he could be sure that the strategy, devised in nanoseconds, would pay off. The warship was chasing him. He would lead it away from the Aeo Taea fleet. But this would be no long stern chase over the light-decades. He did not have the fuel for that, nor the inclination. Without fuel, without weapons, he knew he must end it. For that, he needed space.

It was the same ship. The drive field harmonics, the spectrum of the fusion flame, the timbre of the radar images that he so gently, kiss-soft, bounced off the pursuer's hull, even the configuration he had glimpsed as the ship rounded the planet and launched missiles. This was the same ship that had hunted him down all the years. Deep mysteries here. Time dilation would compress his planned course to subjective minutes and Oga needed time to find an answer.

The ship had known where he would go even as they bucked the stormy cape of the wandering neutron star. It had never even attempted to follow him; instead, it had always known that it must lay in a course that would whip it round to Tay. That meant that even as he escaped the holocaust at Milius 1183, it had known who he was, where he came from, had seen through the frozen layers of smart-ice to the Torben below. The ship had come from around the planet. It was an enemy ship, but not the Enemy. They would have boiled Tejaphay down to its iron heart. Long Oga contemplated these things as he looped out into the wilderness of the Oort cloud. Out there among the lonely ice, he reached a conclusion. He turned the ship over and burned the last of his reaction in a hypergee deceleration burn. The enemy ship responded immediately, but its ramjet drive was less powerful. It would be months, years even, before it could turn around to match orbits with him. He would be ready then. The edge of the field brushed Oga as he decelerated at fifteen hundred gravities and he used his external sensors to modulate a message on the huge web, a million kilometres across: *I surrender.*

Gigayears ago, before the star was born, the two comets had met and entered into their far, cold marriage. Beyond the dramas and attractions of the dust cloud that coalesced into Tay and Tejaphay and Bephis, all the twelve planets of the solar system, they maintained their fixed-grin gazes on each other, locked in orbit around a mutual centre of gravity where a permanent free floating haze of ice crystals hovered, a fraction of a Kelvin above absolute zero. Hidden amongst them, and as cold and seemingly as dead, was the splinter ship. Oga shivered. The cold was more than physical – on the limits of even his malleable form. Within their thermal casing, his motes moved as slowly as Aeo Taea Parents. He felt old as this ice and as weary. He looked up into the gap between ice worlds. The husband-comet floated above his head like a halo. He could have leaped to it in a thought.

Lights against the starlight twinkle of the floating ice storm. A sudden occlusion. The Enemy was here. Oga waited, feeling every targeting sensor trained on him.

No, you won't, will you? Because you have to know.

A shadow detached itself from the black ship, darkest on dark, and looped around the comet. It would be a parliament of self-assembling motes like himself. Oga had worked out decades before that Enemy and Anpreen were one and the same, sprung from the same nanotechnological seed when they attained Class Two status. Theirs was a civil war. *In the Clade, all war was civil war*, Oga thought. Panhumanity was all there was. More like a family feud. Yes, those were the bloodiest fights of all. No quarter and no forgiveness.

The man came walking around the small curve of the comet, kicking up shards of ice crystals from his grip soles. Oga recognized him. He was meant to. He had designed himself so that he would be instantly recognizable, too. He bowed, in the distances of the Oort cloud.

"Torben Reris Orhum Fejannen Kekjay Prus Rejmer Serejen Nejben, sir."

The briefest nod of a head, a gesture of hours in the slow-motion hypercold.

"Torben. I'm not familiar with that name."

"Perhaps we should use the name most familiar to you. That would be Serejen, or perhaps Fejannen, I was in that Aspect when we last met. I would have hoped you still remembered the old etiquette."

"I find I remember too much these days. Forgetting is a choice since I was improved. And a chore. What do they call you now?"

"Oga."

"Oga it shall be, then."

"And what do they call *you* now?"

The man looked up into the icy gap between worldlets. *He has remembered himself well*, Oga thought. *The slight portliness, the child-chubby features, like a boy who never grew up. As he says, forgetting is a chore.*

"The same thing they always have: Cjatay."

"Tell me your story then, Cjatay. This was never your fight, or my fight."

"You left her."

"She left *me*, I recall, and, like you, I forget very little these days. I can see the note still; I could recreate it for you, but it would be a scandalous waste of energy and resources. She went to you."

"It was never me. It was the cause."

"Do you truly believe that?"

Cjatay gave a glacial shrug.

"We made independent contact with them when they came. The Council of governments was divided, all over the place, no coherent approach or strategy. "Leave us alone. We're not part of this." But there's no neutrality in these things. We had let them use our system's water. We had the space elevator they built for us, there was the price, there was the blood money. We knew it would never work – our hope was that we could convince them that some of us had always stood against the Anpreen. They torched Tay anyway, but they gave us a deal. They'd let us survive as a species if some of us joined them on their crusade."

"They *are* the Anpreen."

"*Were* the Anpreen. I know. They took me to pieces. They made us into something else. Better, I think. All of us, there were twenty-four of us.

Twenty-four, that was all the good people of Tay, in their eyes. Everyone who was worth saving."

"And Puzhay?"

"She died. She was caught in the Arphan conflagration. She went there from Jann to be with her parents. It always was an oil town. They melted it to slag."

"But you blame me."

"You are all that's left."

"I don't believe that. I think it was always personal. I think it was always revenge."

"You still exist."

"That's because you don't have all the answers yet."

"We know the kind of creatures we've become; what answers can I not know?"

Oga dipped his head, then looked up to the halo moon, so close he could almost touch it.

"Do you want me to show you what they fear so much?"

There was no need for the lift of the hand, the conjuror's gesture; the pieces of his ship-self Oga had seeded so painstakingly through the wife-comet's structure were part of his extended body. *But I do make magic here*, he thought. He dropped his hand. The star-speckled sky turned white, hard painful white, as if the light of every star were arriving at once. *An Olbers sky*, Oga remembered from his days in the turrets and cloisters of Jann. And as the light grew intolerable, it ended. Blackness, embedding, huge and comforting. The dark of death. Then Oga's eyes grew familiar with the dark, and, though it was the plan and always had been the plan, he felt a plaint of awe as he saw ten thousand galaxies resolve out of the Olbers dazzle. And he knew that Cjatay saw the same.

"Where are we? What have you done?"

"We are somewhere in the region of 230 million light-years outside our local group of galaxies, more precisely, on the periphery of the cosmological galactic supercluster known as the Great Attractor. I made some refinements to the scalarity drive unit to operate in a one dimensional array."

"Faster-than-light travel," Cjatay said, his upturned face silvered with the light of the 10,000 galaxies of the Great Attractor.

"No, you still don't see it," Oga said, and again turned the universe white. Now when he flicked out of hyperscalarity, the sky was dark and starless but for three vast streams of milky light that met in a triskelion hundreds of millions of light-years across.

"We are within the Bootes Supervoid," Oga said. "It is so vast that if our own galaxy were in the centre of it, we would have thought ourselves alone and that our galaxy was the entire universe. Before us are the Lyman alpha-blobs, three conjoined galaxy filaments. These are the largest structures in the universe. On scales larger than this, structure becomes random and grainy. We become grey. These are the last grand vistas, this is the end of greatness."

"Of course, the expansion of space is not limited by light-speed," Cjatay said.

"Still you don't understand." A third time, Oga generated the dark energy from the ice beneath his feet and focused it into a narrow beam between the wife-comet and its unimaginably distant husband. *Two particles in contact will remain in quantum entanglement no matter how far they are removed,* Oga thought. *And is that true also for lives?* He dismissed the scalarity generator and brought them out in blackness. Complete, impenetrable, all-enfolding blackness, without a photon of light.

"Do you understand where I have brought you?"

"You've taken us beyond the visible horizon," Cjatay said. "You've pushed space so far that the light from the rest of the universe has not had time to reach us. We are isolated from every other part of reality. In a philosophical sense, we are a universe in ourselves."

"That was what they feared? You feared?"

"That the scalarity drive had the potential to be turned into a weapon of unimaginable power? Oh yes. The ability to remove any enemy from reach, to banish them beyond the edge of the universe. To exile them from the universe itself, instantly and irrevocably."

"Yes, I can understand that, and that you did what you did altruistically. They were moral genocides. But our intention was never to use it as a weapon – if it had been, wouldn't we have used it on you?"

Silence in the darkness beyond dark.

"Explain then."

"I have one more demonstration."

The mathematics were critical now. The scalarity generator devoured cometary mass voraciously. If there were not enough left to allow him to return them home . . . Trust number, Oga. You always have. Beyond the edge of the universe, all you have is number. There was no sensation, no way of perceiving when he acitivated and deactivated the scalarity field, except by number. For an instant, Oga feared number had failed him, a first and fatal betrayal. Then light blazed down onto the dark ice. A single blinding star shone in the absolute blackness.

"What is that?"

"I pushed a single proton beyond the horizon of this horizon. I pushed it so far that space and time tore."

"So I'm looking at . . ."

"The light of creation. That is an entire universe, new born. A new big bang. A young man once said to me, "Every particle will be so far from everything else that it will be in a universe of its own. It will *be* a universe of its own." An extended object like this comet, or bodies, is too gross, but in a single photon, quantum fluctuations will turn it into an entire universe-in-waiting."

The two men looked up a long time into the nascent light, the surface of the fireball seething with physical laws and forces boiling out. *Now you understand*, Oga thought. *It's not a weapon. It's the way out. The way past the death of the universe. Out there beyond the horizon, we can bud off new universes, and universes from those universes, forever. Intelligence has the last word. We won't die alone in the cold and the dark.* He felt the light of the infant universe on his face, then said, "I think we probably should be getting back. If my calculations are correct – and there is a significant margin of error – this fireball will shortly undergo a phase transition as dark energy separates out and will undergo catastrophic expansion. I don't think that the environs of an early universe would be a very good place for us to be."

He saw portly Cjatay smile.

"Take me home, then. I'm cold and I'm tired of being a god."

"Are we gods?"

Cjatay nodded at the microverse.

"I think so. No, I know I would want to be a man again."

Oga thought of his own selves and lives, his bodies and natures. Flesh indwelled by many personalities, then one personality – one aggregate of experience and memory – in bodies liquid, starship, nanotechnological. And he was tired, so terribly tired beyond the universe, centuries away from all that he had known and loved. All except this one, his enemy.

"Tejaphay is no place for children."

"Agreed. We could rebuild Tay."

"It would be a work of centuries."

"We could use the Aeo Taea Parents. They have plenty of time."

Now Cjatay laughed.

"I have to trust you now, don't I? I could have vapourized you back there, blown this place to atoms with my missiles. And now you create an entire universe . . ."

"And the Enemy? They'll come again."

"You'll be ready for them, like you were ready for me. After all, I am still the enemy."

The surface of the bubble of universe seemed to be in more frenetic motion now. The light was dimming fast.

"Let's go then," Cjatay said.

"Yes," Oga said. "Let's go home."

OGA, RETURNING

HONORABLE MENTIONS

2008

Forrest Aguirre, "The Auctioneer and the Antiquarian, or, 1962," *Asimov's*, June.

Brian W. Aldiss, "Peculiar Bone, Unimaginable Key," *Celebrations*.

Lee Allred, "And Dream Such Dreams," *Otherworldly Maine*.

Erik Amundssen, "Turnipseed," *Fantasy*, March 3.

Charlie Anders, "Love Might Be Too Strong a Word," *Lady Churchill's Rosebud Wristlet*, 22.

_____, "Suicide Drive," *Helix* 7.

Lou Antonelli, "The Witch of Waxahachie," *JBU*, April.

Catherine Asaro, "The Spacetime Pool," *Analog*, January/February.

Neal Asher, "Mason's Rats: Auto Tractor," *Solaris Book of SF II*.

_____, "Mason's Rats: Black Rat," *Solaris Book of SF II*.

_____, "Owner Space," *Galactic Empires*.

_____, "The Rhine World's Incident," *Subterfuge*.

Paolo Bacigalupi, "Pump Six," *F&SF*, September.

Kage Baker, "Caverns of Mystery," *Subterranean: Tales of Dark Fantasy*.

_____, "I Begyn As I Mean to Go On," *Fast Ships, Black Sails*.

_____, "Running the Snake," *Sideways in Crime*.

_____, "Speed, Speed the Cable," *Extraordinary Engines*.

Peter M. Ball, "The Last Great House of Isla Tortuga," *Dreaming Again*.

_____, "On Finding the Photographs of My Former Loves," *Fantasy*, June 2.

Tony Ballantyne, "Undermind," *Subterfuge*.

Jamie Barras, "The Endling," *Interzone*, April.

Neal Barrett Jr., "Radio Station Saint Jack," *Asimov's*, August.

_____, "Slidin'," *Asimov's*, April/May.

Laird Barron, "The Lagerstatte," *Del Rey Book of SF*.

William Barton, "In the Age of the Quiet Sun," *Asimov's*, September.

Lee Battersby, "In from the Snow," *Dreaming Again*.

Stephen Baxter, "Eagle Song," *Postscripts* 15.

_____, "Fate and the Fire-Lance," *Sideways in Crime*.

_____, "The Ice War," *Asimov's*, September.

_____, "The Jubilee Plot," *Celebrations*.

_____, "Repair Kit," *The Starry Rift*.

_____, "The Seer and the Silverman," *Galactic Empires*.

Peter S. Beagle, "King Pelles the Sure," *Strange Roads*.

_____, "The Rabbi's Hobby," *Eclipse Two*.

_____, "The Tale of Junko and Sayur," *OSC'sIGMShow*, July.

_____, "What Tale the Enchantress Plays," *A Book of Wizards*.

Elizabeth Bear, "The Girl Who Sang Rose Madder," Tor.com.

_____, "Shoggoths in Bloom," *Asimov's*, March.

_____, "Sonny Liston Takes the Fall," *Del Rey Book of SF*.

Chris Beckett, "Greenland," *Interzone 218*.

_____, "Poppyfields," *Interzone 218*.

Peter J. Bentley, "Loop," *Cosmos*, February/March.

Beth Bernobich, "Air and Angels," *Subterranean*, Spring.

_____, "The Golden Octopus," *Postscripts 15*.

Deborah Biancotti, "Watertight Lies," *2012*.

Michael Bishop, "Vinegar Peace, or, the Wrong-Way Used-Adult Orphanage," *Asimov's*, July.

Terry Bisson, "Captain Ordinary," *Flurb 5*.

_____, "Catch 'Em in the Act," *Del Rey Book of SF*.

_____, "Private Eye," *F&SF*, October/November.

_____, "The Stamp," *Lone Star Stories*, April.

Jenny Blackford, "Trolls' Night Out," *Dreaming Again*.

Russell Blackford, "Manannan's Children," *Dreaming Again*.

Moal Blaikie, "Offworld Friends Are Best, *GUD*, Spring.

Jayme Lynn Blaschke, "The Whale Below," *Fast Ships, Black Sails*.

Michael Blumlein, "The Big One," *Flurb 6*.

_____, "The Roberts," *F&SF*, July.

Aliette de Bodard, "The Dragon's Tears," *Electric Velocipede*, 15/16.

_____, "Horus Ascending," *OSC'sIGMShow*, April.

Ben Bova, "Moon Race," *JBU*, December.

_____, "Waterbot," *Analog*, June.

Richard Bowes, "AKA St Marks Place," *Del Rey Book of SF*.

_____, "The Cinnamon Cavalier," *Fantasy*, April 21.

_____, "If Angels Fight," *F&SF*, February.

Scott Bradfield, "Dazzle Joins the Screenwriter's Guild," *F&SF*, October/November.

Marie Brennan, "A Heretic by Degrees," *OSCIMS*, December.

_____, "A Mask of Flesh," *Clockwork Phoenix*.

David Brin, "Shoresteading," *JBU*, October.

Keith Brooke, "Hannah," *Extraordinary Engines*.

_____, "The Man Who Built Heaven," *Postscripts 15*.

Corey Brown, "Child of Scorn," *Electric Velocipede*, 15/16.

Eric Brown, "Sunworld," *Solaris Book of SF II*.

John Brown, "From the Clay of His Heart," *OSC'sIGMShow*, April.

Molly Brown, "Living with the Dead," *Celebrations*.

Simon Brown, "The Empire," *Dreaming Again*.

_____, "Oh, Russia," *2012*.

Tobias S. Bucknell, "Manumission," *JBU*, April.

_____, "The People's Machine," *Sideways in Crime*.

_____, "Resistance," *Seeds of Change*.

Mark Budz, "Faceless in Gethsemane," *Seeds of Change*.
Sue Burke, "Spiders," *Asimov's*, March.
Pat Cadigan, "Found in Translation," *Myth-Understandings*.
_____, "Jimmy," *Del Rev Book of SF*.
_____, "The Mudlark," *JBU*, October
_____, "Tales from the Big Dark: Lie of the Land," *Subterfuge*.
_____, "Worlds of Possibilities," *Sideways in Crime*.
James L. Cambias, "The Dinosaur Train," *F&SF*, July.
Alan Campbell, "The Gadgey," *Strange Horizons*, 5/5.
Jeff Carlson, "Long Eyes," *Fast Forward II*.
Paul Carlson, "Shotgun Seat," *Analog*, July/August.
Isobelle Carmody, "Perchance to Dream," *Dreaming Again*.
Von Carr, "The Black-Iron Drum," *Fantasy*, November 17.
Paul Chafe, "The Guardian," *Transhuman*.
A. Bertram Chandler, "Grimes and the Gaijin Daimyo," *Dreaming Again*.
Robert R. Chase, "The Meme Theorist," *Analog*, October.
_____, "Not Even the Past," *Analog*, January/February.
_____, "Soldiers of the Singularity," *Asimov's*, September.
Ted Chiang, "Exhalation," *Eclipse Two*.
Deborah Coates, "How to Hide a Heart," *Strange Horizons*, 1/21.
_____, "The Whale's Lover," *Asimov's*, January.
David B. Coe, "Cassie's Story," *OSC'sIGMShow*, July.
Paul Collins, "Lure," *Dreaming Again*.
Tina Connolly, "The Bitrunners," *Helix 9*.
Brenda Cooper, "Blood Bonds," *Solaris Book of SF II*.
Constance Cooper, "Called Out to Snow Crease Farm," *Strange Horizons*, 7/28.
_____, "The Wily Thing," *Black Gate*, Spring.
Paul Cornell, "Catherine Drewe," *Fast Forward II*.
_____, "Michael Laurtis Is Drowning," *Eclipse Two*.
Gary Couzens, "Jubilee Summer," *Subterfuge*.
Albert E. Cowdrey, "Inside Story," *F&SF*, October/November.
_____, "The Overseer," *F&SF*, March.
_____, "Poison Victory," *F&SF*, July.
_____, "A Skeptical Spirit," *F&SF*, December.
_____, "Thrilling Wonder Stories," *F&SF*, May.
Ian Creasey, "Cut Loose the Bonds of Flesh and Bone," *Asimov's*, September.
Dave Creek, "Stealing Adriana," *Analog*, October.
John Crowley, "Conversation Hearts," *Subterranean Press*.
Julie Czerneda, "The Gossamer Mage," *JBU*, December.
Don D'Ammassa, "The Natural World," *Analog*, January/February.
Tony Daniel, "Ex Cathedra," *Eclipse Two*.
Rowena Cory Daniells, "Purgatory," *Dreaming Again*.
Jack Dann, "Under the Shadow of Jonah," *Postscripts 15*.
Dennis Danvers, "The Angel's Touch," *OSC'sIGMShow*, April.

Cecilia Dart-Thornton, "The Lanes of Camberwell," *Dreaming Again*.
Rjurik Davidson, "Twilight in Caeli-Amur," *Dreaming Again*.
Stephen Dedman, "Lost Arts," *Dreaming Again*.
_____, "Teeth," *Clarkesworld*, March.
Bella De La Rosa, "Nora," *Fantasy*, September 15.
A. M. Dellamonica, "Five Good Things About Meghan Sheedy," *Strange Horizons*, April 21–28.
Paul Di Filippo, "iCity," *Solaris Book of SF II*.
_____, "Murder in Geektopia," *Sideways in Crime*.
_____, "Professor Fluvius's Palace of Many Waters," *Postscripts 15*.
Cory Doctorow, "The Things That Make Me Weak and Strange Get Engineered Away," Tor.com.
Terry Dowling, "The Fooley," *Dreaming Again*.
_____, "Truth Window: A Tale of the Bedlam Rose," *Eclipse Two*.
Debra Doyle and James D. MacDonald, "Philologos, or, Murder in Bistrita," *F&SF*, February.
Brendan DuBois, "Not Enough Stars in the Night," *Cosmos*, 9 May.
_____, "A Souvenir to Remember," *Future Americas*.
Brendan Duffy, "The Green Man," *Postscripts 16*.
Hal Duncan, "The Behold of the Eye," *Lone Star Stories*, August.
Christopher East, "Frame of Mind," *Cosmos Online*, 28 August.
Scott Edleman, "A Very Private Tour of a Very Public Museum," *Postscripts 15*.
Greg Egan, "Lost Continent," *The Starry Rift*.
Carol Emshwiller, "Master of the Road to Nowhere," *Asimov's*, March.
_____, "Wilmer or Wesley," *Asimov's*, August.
Gregory Feeley, "Awskonomuk," *Otherworldly Maine*.
Charles Coleman Finlay, "The Rapeworm," *Noctem Aeternus 1*.
_____ and Rae Carson Finlay, "The Crystal Stair," *Beneath Ceaseless Skies*, 1–3.
Eliot Fintushel, "Uxo, Bomb Dog," *Futurismic*, 3/03.
Jason Fischer, "Undead Camels Ate Their Flesh," *Dreaming Again*.
Karen Fishler, "Africa," *Interzone 217*.
Michael F. Flynn, "Sand and Iron," *Analog*, July/August.
Jeffrey Ford, "After Moreau," *Clarkesworld*, April.
_____, "Daltharee," *Del Rey Book of SF*.
_____, "The Dismantled Invention of Fate," *The Starry Rift*.
_____, "The Dream of Reason," *Extraordinary Engines*.
_____, "The Seventh Expression of the Robot General," *Eclipse Two*.
Eugie Foster, "Daughter of Botu," *Realms of Fantasy*, August.
Ben Francisco and Chris Lynch, "This Is My Blood," *Dreaming Again*.
Stephanie Fray, "Limbo," *OSC'sIGMShow*, April.
Carl Frederick, "The Exoanthropic Principle," *Analog*, July/August.
_____, "Vita Longa," *Analog*, October.
Gregory Frost, "Late in the Day," *Realms of Fantasy*, December.
Neil Gaiman, "Orange," *The Starry Rift*.

Rivka Galchen, "The Region of Unlikeness," The *New Yorker*, March 24.

Stephen Gaskell, "Micro Expressions," *Cosmos Online*, 18 September.

Sara Genge, "Prayers for an Egg," *Asimov's*, October/November.

_____, "The Gong," *Weird Tales*, September/October.

David Gerrold, "Spiderweb," *JBU*, February.

Carolyn Ives Gilman, "Arkfall," *F&SF*, September.

Ari Goelman, "The Annie Oakley Show," *Fantasy*, September 29.

Lisa Goldstein, "Reader's Guide," *F&SF*, July.

Kathleen Ann Goonan, "Memory Dogs," *Asimov's*, April/May.

_____, "Sundiver Day," *The Starry Rift*.

Steven Gould, "Shade," Tor.com.

John Grant, "All the Little Gods We Are," *Clockwork Phoenix*.

_____, "The City in These Pages," PS Publishing.

_____, "Will the Real Veronica Le Barr Please Stand Down?" *Postscripts 16*.

Daryl Gregory, "Glass," *MITTechnology Review*, November/December.

Peni R. Griffin, "The Singers in the Tower," *Realms of Fantasy*, February.

Jon Courtenay Grimwood, "Chicago," *Sideways in Crime*.

_____, "The Crack Angel," *Celebrations*.

Peter F. Hamilton, "The Demon Trap," *Galactic Empires*.

Richard Harland, "A Guided Tour in the Kingdom of the Dead," *Dreaming Again*.

Merrie Haskell, "An Almanac for the Alien Invaders," *Asimov's*, April/May.

Jeff Hass, "Cacophony of the Spheres," *JBU*, June.

Samantha Henderson, "The Mermaid's Tea Party," *Helix 9*.

Howard V. Hendrix, "Knot Your Grandfather's Knot," *Analog*, January/February.

Karen Heuler, "The Difficulties of Evolution," *Weird Tales*, July/August.

Joe Hill, "Gunpowder," PS Publishing.

M. K. Hobson, "The Purple Basil," *Realms of Fantasy*, October.

Sarah A. Hoyt, "Scraps of Fog," *JBU*, April.

_____, "Whom the Gods Love," *Transhuman*.

Matthew Hughes, "The Eye of Vann," *Postscripts 15*.

David Hutchison, "Mellowing Gray," *Celebrations*.

_____, "Multitude," *Subterfuge*.

Guy Immega, "A Little Knowledge," *Postscripts 14*.

Alex Irvine, "Mystery Hill," *F&SF*, January.

_____, "Shad's Mess," *Postscripts 15*.

N. K. Jemison, "Playing Nice with God's Bowling Ball," *JBU*, August.

Way Jeng, "Somebody Desperately Needed to Be Neil Gaiman," *Realms of Fantasy*, August.

Kij Johnson, "26 Monkeys, Also the Abyss," *Asimov's*, July.

Matthew Johnson, "Another Country," *Asimov's*, April/May.

Gwyneth Jones, "Cheats," *The Starry Rift*.

Matthew Jones, "Lagos," *Asimov's*, August.

Theodore Judson, "The Sultan's Emissary," *Sideways in Crime.*

Vylar Kaftan, "Disarm," *Abyss & Apex*, 2nd Quarter.

_____, "Pointing at the Moon," *Cosmos*, December/January.

James Patrick Kelly, "Surprise Party," *Asimov's*, June.

Kay Kenyon, "Cyto Couture," *Fast Forward II.*

_____, "The Space Crawl Blues," *Solaris Book of SF II.*

John Kessel, "Pride and Prometheus," *F&SF*, January.

Caitliln R. Kiernan, "The Steam Dancer," *Subterranean: Tales of Dark Fantasy.*

James Killus, "Plot Device," *Helix 10.*

Stephen King, "The New York Times at Special Bargain Rates," *F&SF*, October/November.

Ted Kosmatka, "The Art of Alchemy," *F&SF*, June.

_____, "Divining Light," *Asimov's*, August.

Mary Robinette Kowal, "Clockwork Chickadee," *Clarkesworld*, June.

_____, "Scenting the Dark," *Apex Magazine*, August 25.

_____, "Waiting for Rain," *Subterranean*, Fall.

Nancy Kress, "Call Back Yesterday," *Asimov's*, June.

_____, "Elevator," *Eclipse Two.*

_____, "First Rites," *JBU*, October.

_____, "The Kindness of Strangers," *Fast Forward II.*

_____, "Sex and Violence," *Asimov's*, February.

Bill Kte'pi, "The End of Tin," *Strange Horizons*, 1/14.

Marc Laidlaw, "Childrun," *F&SF*, August.

Jay Lake, "The Future by Degrees," *Seeds of Change.*

_____, "Last Plane to Heaven: A Love Story," *JBU*, June.

_____, "The Lollygang Save the World on Accident," *Extraordinary Engines.*

_____, "Skinhorse Goes to Mars," *Postscripts 15.*

_____, "Sweet Rocket," *Aeon 14.*

_____, "A Water Matter," Tor.com.

_____ and Ruth Nestvold, "The Rivers of Eden," *Futurismic*, 18/07.

Margo Lanagan, "The Fifth Star in the Southern Cross," *Dreaming Again.*

_____, "An Honest Day's Work," *The Starry Rift.*

_____, "Night of the Firstlings," *Eclipse Two.*

Geoffrey A. Landis, "The Man in the Mirror," *Analog*, January/February.

_____, "Still on the Road," *Asimov's*, December.

Joe R. Lansdale, "Big Man: A Fable," *Subterranean*, Summer.

_____, "Dragon Chili: From the Grand Church Cookbook," *Subterranean*, Winter.

Ann Leckie, "The God of Au," *Helix 8.*

Rand B. Lee, "Bounty," *F&SF*, August.

_____, "Litany," *F&SF*, June.

_____, "Picnic on Pentocost," *F&SF*, September.

Tanith Lee, "The Beautiful and the Damned," *Asimov's*, January.

_____, "The Snake," *Realms of Fantasy*, June.

_____, "Underfog (the Wreckers)," *Subterfuge*.

_____, "The Women," *Clockwork Phoenix*.

Yoon Ha Lee, "Blue Ink," *Clarkesworld*, August.

Tim Lees, "Corner of the Circle," *Interzone 218*.

Rose Lemburg, "Geddarien," *Fantasy*, December 1.

Jonathan Lethem, "Lostronaut," The *New Yorker*, November 15.

David D. Levine, "Firewall," *Transhuman*.

_____, "Sun Magic, Earth Magic," *Beneath Ceaseless Skies, 1*.

Marissa Lingen, "Loki's Net," *JBU*, December.

_____, "Making Alex Frey," *JBU*, June.

_____, "Vainamoinen and the Singing Fish," *Abyss & Apex*, 3rd Quarter.

Kelly Link, "Pretty Monsters," *Pretty Monsters*.

_____, "The Surfer," *The Starry Rift*.

James Lovegrove, "Steampunch," *Extraordinary Engines*.

_____, "Test Subject," *Postscripts 15*.

Richard K. Lyon, "Finalizing History," *Analog*, June.

C. S. MacCath, "Akhila, Divided," *Clockwork Phoenix*.

Ian R. Macleod, "The Camping Wainwrights," *Postscripts 17*.

_____, "Elementals," *Extraordinary Engines*.

_____, "The English Mutiny," *Asimov's*, October/November.

_____, "The Hob Carpet," *Asimov's*, June.

Ken MacLeod, "A Dance Called Armageddon," *Seeds of Change*.

_____, "Wilson at Woking," *Celebrations*.

Elissa Malcohn, "Hermit Crabs," *Electric Velocipede 14*.

Bruce McAllister, "Emilio's Tale," *Journal of Mythic Arts*, Summer.

_____, "Hit," *Aeon 13*.

Paul McAuley, "Adventure," *Fast Forward II*.

_____, "A Brief Guide to Other Histories," *Postscripts 15*.

_____, "Little Lost Robot," *Interzone 217*.

_____, "Searching for Van Gogh at the End of the World," *Postscripts 15*.

_____, "The Thought War," *Postscripts 15*.

_____ and Kim Newman, "Prisoners of the Action," *Del Rey Book of SF*.

Todd McCaffrey, "Tribute," *JBU*, August.

Meghan McCarron, "The Magician's House," *Strange Horizons, 7/14*.

Una McCormack, "The Great Gig in the Sky," *Subterfuge*.

Jack McDevitt, "The Adventure of the South Sea Trunk," *Sideways in Crime*.

_____, "Indomitable," *JBU*, April.

_____, "Molly's Kids," *Fast Forward II*.

Ian McDonald, "The Dust Assassin," *The Starry Rift*.

_____, "[A Ghost Samba]," *Postscripts 15*.

Sandra McDonald, "Recipe for Survival," *Electric Velocipede 14*.

Maureen McHugh, "The Kingdom of the Blind," *Plugged In*.

Will McIntosh, "The Fantasy Jumper," *Black Static*, February.

_____, "Linkworlds," Strange Horizons, March 17–24.

Dean McLaughlin, "Tenbrook of Mars," *Analog*, July/August.

Sean McMullen, "The Constant Past," *Dreaming Again*.

_____, "Oblivion," *2012*.

_____, "The Twilight Year," *F&SF*, January.

John Meaney, "Emptier than Void," *Subterfuge*.

_____, "Via Vortex," *Sideways in Crime*.

Anil Menon, "Into the Night," *Interzone 216*.

Deborah J. Miller, "Dinosaur," *Myth-Understandings*.

Eugene Mirabelli, "Falling Spirit," *F&SF*, December.

David Moles, "Down and Out in the Magic Kingdom," *Eclipse Two*.

Mia Molvray, "Low Life," *Analog*, January/February.

Sarah Monette, "The World Without Sleep," *Postscripts 14*.

Michael Moorcock, "Sumptuous Dress: A Question of Size," *Postscripts 15*.

Silvia Morene-Garcia, "Maquech," *Futurismic, 01/07*.

T. L. Morganfield, "Night Bird Soaring," *GUD*, Fall.

Richard Mueller, "But Wait! There's More," *F&SF*, August.

_____, "Ten Pound Sack of Rice," *F&SF*, March.

Steven Francis Murphy, "The Limb Knitter," *Apex Magazine*, September 08.

Chris Nakashima-Brown, "The Sun Also Explodes," *Fast Forward II*.

David Erik Nelson, "Tucker Teaches the Clockies to Copulate," *Paradox*, Spring.

Ruth Nestvold, "An Act of Conviction," *Helix 9*.

_____, "Mars: A Traveler's Guide," *F&SF*, January.

_____, "Troy and the Aliens," *Abyss & Apex*, 4th Quarter.

R. Neube, "Cascading Violet Hair," *Asimov's*, July.

Garth Nix, "Beyond the Sea Gate of the Scholar-Pirates of Sarsköe," *Fast Ships, Black Sails*.

_____, "Infestation," *The Starry Rift*.

Naomi Novik, "Araminta, or, the Wreck of the Amphidrake," *Fast Ships, Black Sails*.

Nnedi Okorafor-Mbachu, "Spider the Artist," *Seeds of Change*.

Patrick O'Leary, "The Oldest Man on Earth," *Electric Velocipede, 15/16*.

_____, "Skin Deep," *Eclipse Two*.

Paul Park, "The Blood of Peter Francisco," *Sideways in Crime*.

Richard Parks, "On the Banks of the River of Heaven," *Realms of Fantasy*, April.

Norman Partridge, "Apotropaics," *Subterranean*, Fall.

_____, "Road Dogs," *Subterranean*, Spring.

Jennifer Pelland, "Sashenka Redux," *Electric Velocipede 14*.

Lawrence Person, "Gabe's Globster," *Asimov's*, June.

Holly Phillips, "The Small Door," *Fantasy*, May 19.

Tony Pi, "Aesop's Last Fable," *On Spec*, Spring.

Rachel Pollack, "Immortal Snake," *F&SF*, May.

Steven Popkes, "Another Perfect Day," *F&SF*, August.

_____, "Bread and Circus," *F&SF*, February.

Tim Powers, "The Hour of Babel," *Subterranean: Tales of Dark Fantasy*.

Tim Pratt, "The Frozen One," *Lone Star Stories*, February.

_____, "The River Boy," *Clarkesworld*, January.

Christopher Priest, "Fireflies," *Celebrations*.

_____, "The Trace of Him," *Interzone*, February.

Philip Pullman, "Once Upon a Time in the North," *Once Upon a Time in the North*, Knopf.

Tom Purdom, "Madame Pompadour's Blade," *JBU*, June.

_____, "Sepoy Fidelities," *Asimov's*, March.

Philip Raines and Harvey Welles, "Alice and Bob," *Albedo One no. 34.*

Cat Rambo, "Angry Rose's Lament," *Abyss & Apex*, 4th Quarter.

_____, "The Dew Drop Coffee Lounge," *Clockwork Phoenix*.

_____, "Kallakak's Cousins," *Asimov's*, March.

David Reagan, "Solitude Ripples from the Past," *Futurismic*, 1/05.

Robert Reed, "American Cheetah," *Extraordinary Engines*.

_____, "Blackbird," *Postscripts 14.*

_____, "Character Flu," *F&SF*, June.

_____, "Fifty Dinosaurs," *Solaris Book of SF II.*

_____, "The House Left Empty," *Asimov's*, April/May.

_____, "Leave," *F&SF*, December.

_____, "The Man with the Golden Balloon," *Galactic Empires*.

_____, "Leave," *F&SF*, December.

_____, "Old Man Waiting," *Asimov's*, August.

_____, "Reunion," *F&SF*, May.

_____, "Salad for Two," *F&SF*, September.

_____, "Six Foot Easy," *Postscripts 15.*

_____, "Truth," *Asimov's*, October/November.

_____, "The Visionaries," *F&SF*, October/November.

_____, "Weapons of Discretion," *Helix 8.*

Jessica Reisman, "Flowertongue," *Farrago's Wainscot*, April.

_____, "When the Ice Goes Out," *Otherwordly Maine*.

Mike Resnick, "Alastair Baffle's Emporium of Wonders," *Asimov's*, January.

_____, "An Article of Faith," *Postscripts 15.*

_____, "Kilimanjaro: A Fable of Utopia," *Subterranean Press*.

_____ and Pat Cadigan, "Not Quite Alone in the Dream Quarter," *Fast Forward II.*

Alastair Reynolds, "Fury," *Eclipse Two*.

_____, "Soiree," *Celebration*.

_____, "The Star Surgeon's Apprentice," *The Starry Rift*.

Siri Richards, "Orange Is Just Another Color," *Abyss & Apex*, 4th Quarter.

Mercurio D. Rivera, "The Fifth Zhi," *Interzone 219.*

_____, "The Scent of Their Arrival," *Interzone*, February.

_____, "Snatch Me Another," *Abyss & Apex*, 1st Quarter.

Chris Roberson, "Death on the Crosstime Express," *Sideways in Crime*.

_____, "The Line of Dichotomy," *Solaris Book of SF II.*

_____, "Mirror of Fiery Brightness," *Subterranean*, Fall.

_____, "Thy Saffron Wings," *Postscripts 15.*

Adam Roberts, "The Man of the Strong Arm," *Celebrations*.
_____, "Petropunk," *Extraordinary Engines*.
Andy W. Robertson, "Slope," *The West Pier Gazette*.
Justina Robson, "Body of Evidence," *Myth-Understandings*.
_____, "Legolas Does the Dishes," *Postscripts 15*.
Michaela Roessner, "It's a Wonderful Life," *F&SF*, January.
Margaret Ronald, "Knight of Coins," *JBU*, April.
_____, "When the Gentlemen Go By," *Clarkesworld*, July.
Benjamin Rosenbaum and Cory Doctorow, "True Names," *Fast Forward*
　　II.
Mary Rosenblum, "Horse Racing," *Asimov's*, September.
_____, "Sacrifice," *Sideways in Crime*.
Josh Rountree, "No Leaving New Orleans," *Lone Star Stories*, June.
Christopher Rowe, "Gather," *Del Rey Book of SF*.
Rudy Rucker, "The Imitation Game," *Interzone*, April.
_____ and Marc Laidlaw, "The Perfect Wave," *Asimov's*, January.
Kristine Kathryn Rusch, "Dragon's Tooth," *JBU*, August.
_____, "The Observer," *Front Lines*.
_____, "The Power of Human Reason," *Future Americas*.
_____, "The Room of Lost Souls," *Asimov's*, April/May.
_____, "SeniorSource," *Fast Forward II*.
Geoff Ryman, "The Film-Makers of Mars," Tor.com.
_____, "No Bad Thing," *The West Pier Gazette*.
_____, "Talk Is Cheap," *Interzone 216*.
Brandon Sanderson, "Defending Elysium," *Asimov's*, October/November.
Jason Sanford, "The Ships like Clouds, Risen by Their Rain," *Interzone*
　217.
_____, "When Thorns Are the Tips of Trees," *Interzone 219*.
_____, "Where Away You Fall," *Analog*, December.
Erica L. Satifka, "Sea Change," *Ideomancer*, September.
John Scalzi, "After the Coup," Tor.com.
Ken Scholes, "The God-Voices of Settler's Rest," *OSC'sIGMShow*, July.
_____, "Invisible Empire of Ascending Light," *Eclipse Two*.
Karl Schroeder, "Book, Theatre, and Wheel," *Solaris Book of SF II*.
_____ and Tobias S. Bucknell, "Mitigation," *Fast Forward II*.
Ekaterina Sedia, "By the Liter," *Subterranean*, Spring.
_____, "There Is a Monster Under Helen's Bed," *Clockwork Phoenix*.
Gord Sellar, "Country of the Young," *Interzone 219*.
_____, "Dhuluma No More," *Asimov's*, October/November.
_____, "Pahwakhe," *Fantasy*, January 21.
Delia Sherman, "Gift from a Spring," *Realms of Fantasy*, April.
Sharon Shinn, "The Unrhymed Couplets of the Universe,"
　OSC'sIGMShow, January.
William Shunn, "Timesink," *Electric Velocipede*, 15/16.
Steven H. Silver, "Les Lettres de Paston," *Helix 10*.
Janna Silverstein, "After This Life," *OSC'sIGMShow*, January.
Vandana Singh, "Distances," *Aqueduct Press*.

_____, "Oblivion: A Journey," *Clockwork Phoenix*.

Sarah Singleton, "They Left the City at Night," *Subterfuge*.

Amber D. Sistla, "A Place to Call Home," *Cosmos*, April/May.

Jack Skillingstead, "Alone with an Inconvenient Companion," *Fast Forward II*.

_____, "Cat in the Rain," *Asimov's*, October/November.

_____, "What You Are About to See," *Asimov's*, August.

Alan Smale, "Quartet, with Mermaids," *Abyss & Apex*, 1st Quarter.

Jeremy Adam Smith, "The Wreck of the Grampus," *Lone Star Stories*, April.

S. P Somtow, "An Alien Heresy," *Asimov's*, April/May.

Bud Sparhawk, "Pumpkin," *JBU*, December.

_____, "The Super," *JBU*, August.

Cat Sparks, "Palisade," *Clockwork Phoenix*.

Wen Spencer, "Being Human," *Transhuman*.

William Browning Spencer, "Penguins of the Apocalypse," *Subterranean: Tales of Dark Fantasy*.

Kari Sperring, "Seaborne," *Myth-Understandings*.

Jeff Spock, "Everything That Matters," *Interzone 219*.

Nancy Springer, "Rumple What?" *F&SF*, March.

Brian Stableford, "The Best of Both Worlds," *Postscripts 15*.

_____, "Following the Pharmers," *Asimov's*, March.

_____, "The Great Chain of Being," *Future Americas*.

_____, "Next to Godliness," *Celebrations*.

_____, "The Philosopher's Stone," *Asimov's*, July.

Vaughan Stanger, "Stars in Her Eyes," *Postscripts 17*.

Bruce Sterling, "Computer Entertainment Thirty-five Years from Today," *Flurb 6*.

S. M. Stirling, "A Murder in Oddsford," *Sideways in Crime*.

Jason Stoddard, "The Elephant Ironclads," *Del Rey Book of SF*.

_____, "Far Horizons," *Interzone*, February.

_____, "The First Editions," *F&SF*, April

_____, "Willpower," *Futurismic*, 01/12.

Eric James Stone, "Premature Emergence," *JBU*, February.

Dick Strasser, "Conquest," *Dreaming Again*.

Charles Stross, "Down on the Farm," Tor.com.

Tim Sullivan, "Planetesimal Dawn," *F&SF*, October/November.

_____, "Way Down East," *Asimov's*, December.

Tricia Sullivan, "The Dog Hypnotist," *Celebrations*.

_____, "The Ecologist and the Avon Lady," *Myth-Understandings*.

_____, "Post-Ironic Stress Syndrome," *The Starry Rift*.

Lucy Sussex, "Ardant Clouds," *Del Rey Book of SF*.

Michael Swanwick, "The Scarecrow's Boy," *F&SF*, October/November.

_____ and Eileen Gunn, "Shed That Guilt! Double Your Productivity Overnight!" *F&SF*, September.

Rachel Swirsky, "Marrying the Sun," *Fantasy*, June 30.

Melanie Tem and Steve Rasnic Tem, "In Concert," *Asimov's*, December.

Lavie Tidhar, "Hard Rain at the Fortean Café," *Aeon 14.*
_____, "The Secret Protocols of the Elders of Zion," *The West Pier Gazette.*
_____, "Shira," *Del Rey Book of SF.*
_____, "Uganda," *Flurb 5.*
Sarah Totten, "The Stone Man," *Andromedea Spaceways 37.*
George Tucker, "Circle," *F&SF*, May.
Lisa Tuttle, "The Oval Portrait," *Postscripts 16.*
Steven Utley, "All of Creation," *Cosmos Online.*
_____, "The 400-Million-Year Itch," *F&SF*, April.
_____, "Perfect Everything," *Asimov's*, December.
_____, "Sleepless Years," *F&SF*, October/November.
_____, "Slug Hell," *Asimov's*, September
_____, "Variant," *Postscripts 15.*
_____, "The Woman Under the World," *Asimov's*, July.
_____, "The World Within the World," *Asimov's*, March.
Catherynne M. Valente, "A Buyer's Guide to Maps of Antartica,"
    Clarkesworld, May.
Jeff VanderMeer, "Fixing Hanover," *Extraordinary Engines.*
_____, "Island Tales," *Postscripts 14.*
_____, "The Situation," *PS Publishing.*
Mark L. Van Name, "Reunion," *Transhuman.*
James Van Pelt, "Floaters," *Talebones*, Winter.
_____, "Rock House," *Talebones*, Spring.
Carrie Vaughn, "A Letter to Nancy," *Realms of Fantasy*, August.
_____, "The Nymph's Child," *Fast Ships, Black Sails.*
Howard Waldrop, "Avast, Abaft!" *Fast Ships, Black Sails.*
George S. Walker, "The Einstein-Rosen Hunter-Gatherer Society," *Helix 10.*
Peter Watts, "The Eyes of God," *Solaris Book of SF II.*
Janeen Webb, "Paradise Designed," *Dreaming Again.*
Catharine Wells, "Ghost Town," *Asimov's*, April/May.
Scott Westerfeld, "Ass-Hat Magic Spider," *The Starry Rift.*
Leslie What, "Money Is No Object," *Asimov's*, October/November.
Wayne Wightman, "A Foreign Country," *F&SF*, December.
Kate Wilhelm, "The Fountain of Neptune," *F&SF*, April.
_____, "Strangers When We Meet," *Asimov's*, April/May.
Liz Williams, "At Shadow Cope," *Celebrations.*
_____, "Queen of the Sunlit Shore," *Myth-Understandings.*
_____, "Spiderhorse," *Realms of Fantasy*, August.
_____, "Who Pays," *The West Pier Gazette.*
Walter Jon Williams, "Pinochio," *The Starry Rift.*
Chris Willrich, "The Sword of Loving Kindness," *Beneath Ceaseless
    Skies*, 1–2.
Eric Witchery, "Can You See Me Now?" *Clarkesworld 24.*
Nick Wolven, "An Art, like Everything Else," *Asimov's*, April/May.
John C. Wright, "Chosers of the Slain," *Clockwork Phoenix.*
Chelsea Quinn Yarbro, "Endra – from Memory," *Interzone 216.*
Marly Youmans, "Rain Flower Pebbles," *Postscripts 17.*

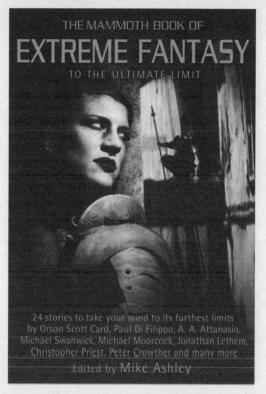

In extreme fantasy *anything* can happen. In Mike Ashley's breathtaking anthology the only rules are those the writer makes – these are stories to liberate the imagination.

Extreme Fantasy is a rediscovery of the wider world of fantasy through bold new ideas or the magical reworking of older arts. Ashley selects 25 stories by the likes of Orson Scott Card, Paul Di Filippo, A.A. Atanassio, Michael Swanwick, Christopher Priest and Peter Crowther.

ISBN: 978-1-84529-806-7
Paperback £7.99

www.constablerobinson.com